Love
Gladys + Carl

Alistair MacLean

SIX COMPLETE NOVELS

ABOUT THE AUTHOR

ALISTAIR MACLEAN was born in Scotland in 1922 and was educated at Glasgow University. During World War II he served in the British Royal Navy, and his first novel, *H.M.S. Ulysses,* was drawn from his naval experiences.

MacLean's wartime experiences were the inspiration for several other suspense novels, most notably *The Guns of Navarone* and *Force 10 from Navarone.* Many of his novels have been made into successful movies, and he is universally considered a top-notch suspense and adventure writer.

In the mid-1960s MacLean took a break from writing and invested in several pubs in the south of England. Though his pubs prospered, he decided, fortunately, to return to writing. Currently, MacLean lives in Great Britain.

Alistair MacLean

SIX COMPLETE NOVELS

The Guns of Navarone

Force 10 from Navarone

Puppet on a Chain

Caravan to Vaccares

Seawitch

Goodbye California

Avenel Books • New York

This Omnibus edition was previously published in separate volumes under the titles:
The Guns of Navarone © MCMLVI by the Curtis Publishing Company
Force 10 from Navarone © MCMLXVIII by Cymbeline Productions Ltd.
Puppet on a Chain © MCMLXIX by Alistair MacLean
Caravan to Vaccares © MCMLXX by Alistair MacLean
Seawitch © MCMLXXVII by Alistair MacLean
Goodbye California © MCMLXXVII by Alistair MacLean
This 1983 edition is published by Avenel Books, distributed by Crown Publishers, Inc.,
by arrangement with Doubleday & Company, Inc.

Manufactured in the United States of America

Library of Congress Cataloging in Publication Data
MacLean, Alistair, 1922–
Six complete novels.
Contents: Guns of Navarone—Force 10 from Navarone—Puppet on a chain—[etc.]
I. Title.
PR6063.A2468A6   1984.   823′.914   83-11728
ISBN 0-517-421739

h g f e d c b a

CONTENTS

The Guns of Navarone

CONTENTS

1
PRELUDE: SUNDAY
0100–0900

THE MATCH scratched noisily across the rusted metal of the corrugated iron shed, fizzled, then burst into a sputtering pool of light, the harsh sound and sudden brilliance alike strangely alien in the stillness of the desert night. Mechanically, Mallory's eyes followed the cupped sweep of the flaring match to the cigarette jutting out beneath the commodore's clipped moustache, saw the light stop inches away from the face, saw too the sudden stillness of that face, the unfocused vacancy of the eyes of a man lost in listening. Then the match was gone, ground into the sand of the airfield perimeter.

"I can hear them," the commodore said softly. "I can hear them coming in. Five minutes, no more. No wind tonight—they'll be coming in on No. 2. Come on, let's meet them in the interrogation room." He paused, looked quizzically at Mallory and seemed to smile. But the darkness deceived, for there was no humour in his voice. "Just curb your impatience, young man—just for a little longer. Things haven't gone too well to-night. You're going to have all your answers, I'm afraid, and have them all too soon." He turned abruptly, strode off towards the squat buildings that loomed vaguely against the pale darkness that topped the level horizon.

Mallory shrugged, then followed on more slowly, step for step with the third member of the group, a broad, stocky figure with a very pronounced roll in his gait. Mallory wondered sourly just how much practice Jensen had required to achieve that sailorly effect. Thirty years at sea, of course—and Jensen had done exactly that—were sufficient warrant for a man to dance a hornpipe as he walked: but that wasn't the point. As the brilliantly successful Chief of Operations of the Subversive Operations Executive in Cairo, intrigue, deception, imitation and disguise were the breath of life to Captain James Jensen, D.S.O., R.N. As a Levantine stevedore agitator, he had won the awed respect of the dock-labourers from Alexandretta to Alexandria: as a cameldriver, he had blasphemously out-camel-driven all available Bedouin competition: and no more pathetic beggar had ever exhibited such realistic sores in the bazaars and market-places of the East. To-night, however, he was just the bluff and simple sailor. He was dressed in white from cap-cover to canvas shoes; the starlight glinted softly on the golden braid on epaulettes and cap peak.

Their footsteps crunched in companionable unison over the hard-packed sand, rang sharply as they moved on to the concrete of the runway. The

5

hurrying figure of the air commodore was already almost lost to sight. Mallory took a deep breath and turned suddenly towards Jensen.

"Look, sir, just what *is* all this? What's all the flap, all the secrecy about? And why am *I* involved in it? Good lord, sir, it was only yesterday that I was pulled out of Crete, relieved at eight hours' notice. A month's leave, I was told. And what happens?"

"Well," Jensen murmured, "what did happen?"

"No leave," Mallory said bitterly. "Not even a night's sleep. Just hours and hours in the S.O.E. Headquarters, answering a lot of silly, damnfool questions about climbing in the Southern Alps. Then hauled out of bed at midnight, told I was to meet you, and then driven for hours across the blasted desert by a mad Scotsman who sang drunken songs and asked hundreds of even more silly, damnfool questions!"

"One of my more effective disguises, I've always thought," Jensen said smugly. "Personally, I found the journey most entertaining!"

"One of your——" Mallory broke off, appalled at the memory of the things he had said to the elderly, bewhiskered Scots captain who had driven the command vehicle. "I—I'm terribly sorry, sir. I never realised——"

"Of course you didn't!" Jensen cut in briskly. "You weren't supposed to. Just wanted to find out if you were the man for the job. I'm sure you are—I was pretty sure you were before I pulled you out of Crete. But where you got the idea about leave I don't know. The sanity of the S.O.E. has often been questioned, but even *we* aren't given to sending a flying-boat for the sole purpose of enabling junior officers to spend a month wasting their substance among the flesh-pots of Cairo," he finished dryly.

"I still don't know——"

"Patience, laddie, patience—as our worthy commodore has just advocated. Time is endless. To wait, and to keep on waiting—that is to be of the East."

"To total four hours' sleep in three days is not," Mallory said feelingly. "And that's all I've had. . . . Here they come!"

Both men screwed up their eyes in automatic reflex as the fierce glare of the landing lights struck at them, the flare path arrowing off into the outer darkness. In less than a minute the first bomber was down, heavily, awkwardly, taxi-ing to a standstill just beside them. The grey camouflage paint of the after fuselage and tail-planes was riddled with bullet and cannon shells, an aileron was shredded and the port outer engine out of commission, saturated in oil. The cabin perspex was shattered and scarred in a dozen places.

For a long time Jensen stared at the holes and scars of the damaged machine, then shook his head and looked away.

"Four hours' sleep, Captain Mallory," he said quietly. "Four hours. I'm beginning to think that you can count yourself damn' lucky to have had even that much."

The interrogation room, harshly lit by two powerful, unshaded lights, was uncomfortable and airless. The furniture consisted of some battered wall-maps and charts, a score or so of equally scuffed chairs and an unvarnished deal table. The commodore, flanked by Jensen and Mallory, was sitting behind this when the door opened abruptly and the first of the flying crews entered, blinking rapidly in the fierceness of the unaccustomed light. They were led by a dark-haired, thick-set pilot, trailing helmet and flying-suit in his left hand. He had an Anzac bush helmet crushed on the back of his head, and the word "Australia" emblazoned in white across each khaki shoulder. Scowling, wordlessly and without permission, he sat down in front of them, produced a pack of cigarettes and rasped a match across the surface of the table. Mallory looked furtively at the commodore. The commodore just looked resigned. He even sounded resigned.

"Gentlemen, this is Squadron Leader Torrance. Squadron Leader Torrance," he added unnecessarily, "is an Australian." Mallory had the impression that the Commodore rather hoped this would explain some things, Squadron Leader Torrance among them. "He led to-night's attack on Navarone. Bill, these gentlemen here—Captain Jensen of the Royal Navy, Captain Mallory of the Long Range Desert Group—have a very special interest in Navarone. How did things go to-night?"

Navarone! So that's why I'm here to-night, Mallory thought. Navarone. He knew it well, rather, knew of it. So did everyone who had served any time at all in the Eastern Mediterranean: a grim, impregnable iron fortress off the coast of Turkey, heavily defended by—it was thought—a mixed garrison of Germans and Italians, one of the few Ægean islands on which the Allies had been unable to establish a mission, far less recapture, at some period of the war. . . . He realised that Torrance was speaking, the slow drawl heavy with controlled anger.

"Bloody awful, sir. A fair cow, it was, a real suicide do." He broke off abruptly, stared moodily with compressed lips through his own drifting tobacco smoke. "But we'd like to go back again," he went on. "Me and the boys here. Just once. We were talking about it on the way home." Mallory caught the deep murmur of voices in the background, a growl of agreement. "We'd like to take with us the joker who thought this one up and shove him out at ten thousand over Navarone, without benefit of parachute."

"As bad as that, Bill?"

"As bad as that, sir. We hadn't a chance. Straight up, we really hadn't. First off, the weather was against us—the jokers in the Met. office were about as right as they usually are."

"They gave you clear weather?"

"Yeah. Clear weather. It was ten-tenths over the target," Torrance said bitterly. "We had to go down to fifteen hundred. Not that it made any difference. We would have to have gone down lower than that anyway—about three thousand feet below sea-level, then fly up the way: that cliff overhang shuts the target clean off. Might as well have dropped a shower of leaflets asking them to spike their own bloody guns. . . . Then they've got every second A.A. gun in the south of Europe concentrated along this narrow 50-degree vector—the only way you can approach the target, or anywhere near the target. Russ and Conroy were belted good and proper on the way in. Didn't even get half-way towards the harbour. . . . They never had a chance."

"I know, I know." The Commodore nodded heavily. "We heard. W/T reception was good. . . . And McIlveen ditched just north of Alex?"

"Yeah. But he'll be all right. The old crate was still awash when we passed over, the big dinghy was out and it was as smooth as a millpond. He'll be all right," Torrance repeated.

The Commodore nodded again, and Jensen touched his sleeve.

"May I have a word with the Squadron Leader?"

"Of course, Captain. You don't have to ask."

"Thanks." Jensen looked across at the burly Australian and smiled faintly.

"Just one little question, Squadron Leader. You don't fancy going back there again?"

"Too bloody right, I don't!" Torrance growled.

"Because?"

"Because I don't believe in suicide. Because I don't believe in sacrificing good blokes for nothing. Because I'm not God and I can't do the impossible." There was a flat finality in Torrance's voice that carried conviction, that brooked no argument.

"It is impossible, you say?" Jensen persisted. "This is terribly important."

"So's my life. So are the lives of all these jokers." Torrance jerked a big thumb over his shoulder. "It's impossible, sir. At least, it's impossible for us." He drew a weary hand down his face. "Maybe a Dornier flying-boat with one of these new-fangled radio-controlled glider-bombs might do it and get off with it. I don't know. But I do know that nothing we've got has a snowball's chance in hell. Not," he added bitterly, "unless you cram a Mosquito full of T.N.T. and order one of us to crash-dive it at four hundred into the mouth of the gun cave. That way there's always a chance."

"Thank you, Squadron Leader—and all of you." Jensen was on his feet. "I know you've done your very best, no one could have done more. And I'm sorry. . . . Commodore?"

"Right with you, gentlemen." He nodded to the bespectacled Intelligence officer who had been sitting behind them to take his place, led the way out through a side door and into his own quarters.

"Well, that is that, I suppose." He broke the seal of a bottle of Talisker, brought out some glasses. "You'll have to accept it as final, Jensen. Bill Torrance's is the senior, most experienced squadron left in Africa to-day. Used to pound the Ploesti oil wells and think it a helluva skylark. If anyone could have done to-night's job it was Bill Torrance, and if he says it's impossible, believe me, Captain Jensen, it can't be done."

"Yes," Jensen looked down sombrely at the golden amber of the glass in his hand. "Yes, I know now. I *almost* knew before, but I couldn't be sure, and I couldn't take the chance of being wrong. . . . A terrible pity that it took the lives of a dozen men to prove me right. . . . There's just the one way left, now."

"There's just the one," the Commodore echoed. He lifted his glass, shook his head. "Here's luck to Kheros!"

"Here's luck to Kheros!" Jensen echoed in turn. His face was grim.

"Look!" Mallory begged. "I'm completely lost. Would somebody please tell me——"

"Kheros," Jensen interrupted. "That was your cue call, young man. All the world's a stage, laddie, etc., and this is where you tread the boards in this particular little comedy." Jensen's smile was quite mirthless. "Sorry you've missed the first two acts, but don't lose any sleep over that. This is no bit part: you're going to be the star, whether you like it or not. This is it. Kheros, Act 3, Scene 1. Enter Captain Keith Mallory."

Neither of them had spoken in the last ten minutes. Jensen drove the big Humber command car with the same sureness, the same relaxed efficiency that hall-marked everything he did: Mallory still sat hunched over the map on his knees, a large-scale Admiralty chart of the Southern Ægean illuminated by the hooded dashboard light, studying an area of the Sporades and Northern Dodecanese heavily squared off in red pencil. Finally he straightened up and shivered. Even in Egypt these late November nights could be far too cold for comfort. He looked across at Jensen.

"I think I've got it now, sir."

"Good!" Jensen gazed straight ahead along the winding grey ribbon of dusty road, along the white glare of the headlights that cleaved through the darkness of the desert. The beams lifted and dipped, constantly, hypnotically, to the cushioning of the springs on the rutted road. "Good!" he repeated. "Now, have another look at it and imagine yourself standing in the town of Navarone—that's on the almost circular bay on the north of the island? Tell me, what would you see from there?"

Mallory smiled.

"I don't have to look again, sir. Four miles or so away to the east I'd see the Turkish coast curving up north and west to a point almost due north of Navarone—a very sharp promontory, that, for the coastline above curves back almost due east. Then, about sixteen miles away, due north beyond this promontory—Cape Demirci, isn't it?—and practically in a line with it I'd see the island of Kheros. Finally, six miles to the west is the island of Maidos, the first of the Lerades group. They stretch away in a north-westerly direction, maybe fifty miles."

"Sixty." Jensen nodded. "You have the eye, my boy. You've got the guts and the experience—a man doesn't survive eighteen months in Crete without both. You've got one or two special qualifications I'll mention by and by." He paused for a moment, shook his head slowly. "I only hope you have the luck—all the luck. God alone knows you're going to need it."

Mallory waited expectantly, but Jensen had sunk into some private reverie. Three minutes passed, perhaps five, and there was only the swish of the tyres, the subdued hum of the powerful engine. Presently Jensen stirred and spoke again, quietly, still without taking his eyes off the road.

"This is Saturday—rather, it's Sunday morning now. There are one thousand two hundred men on the island of Kheros—one thousand two hundred British soldiers—who will be dead, wounded or prisoner by next Saturday. Mostly, they'll be dead." For the first time he looked at Mallory and smiled, a brief smile, a crooked smile, and then it was gone. "How does it feel to hold a thousand lives in your hands, Captain Mallory?"

For long seconds Mallory looked at the impassive face beside him, then looked away again. He stared down at the chart. Twelve hundred men on Kheros, twelve hundred men waiting to die. Kheros and Navarone, Kheros and Navarone. What was that poem again, that little jingle that he'd learnt all these long years ago in that little upland village in the sheeplands outside Queenstown? Chimborazo—that was it. "Chimborazo and Cotopaxi, you have stolen my heart away." Kheros and Navarone—they had the same ring, the same indefinable glamour, the same wonder of romance that took hold of a man and stayed with him. Kheros and—angrily, almost, he shook his head, tried to concentrate. The pieces of the jig-saw were beginning to click into place, but slowly.

Jensen broke the silence.

"Eighteen months ago, you remember, after the fall of Greece, the Germans had taken over nearly all the islands of the Sporades: the Italians, of course, already held most of the Dodecanese. Then, gradually, we began to establish missions on these islands, usually spear-headed by your people, the Long Range Desert Group or the Special Boat Service. By last September we had retaken nearly all the larger islands except Navarone—it was too damned hard a nut, so we just by-passed it—and brought some of the garrisons up to, and beyond, battalion strength." He grinned at Mallory. "You were lurking in your cave somewhere in the White Mountains at the time, but you'll remember how the Germans reacted?"

"Violently?"

Jensen nodded.

"Exactly. Very violently indeed. The political importance of Turkey in this part of the world is impossible to over-estimate—and she's always been a potential partner for either Axis or Allies. Most of these islands are only a few miles off the Turkish coast. The question of prestige, of restoring confidence in Germany, was urgent."

"So?"

"So they flung in everything—paratroopers, airborne troops, crack mountain brigades, hordes of Stukas—I'm told they stripped the Italian front of dive-bombers for these operations. Anyway, they flung everything in—the lot. In a few weeks we'd lost over ten thousand troops and every island we'd ever recaptured—except Kheros."

"And now it's the turn of Kheros?"

"Yes." Jensen shook out a pair of cigarettes, sat silently until Mallory had lit them and sent the match spinning through the window towards the pale gleam of the Mediterranean lying north below the coast road. "Yes, Kheros is for the hammer. Nothing that we can do can save it. The Germans have absolute air superiority in the Ægean. . . ."

"But—but how can you be so sure that it's this week?"

Jensen sighed.

"Laddie, Greece is fairly hotching with Allied agents. We have over two hundred in the Athens-Piraeus area alone and——"

"Two hundred!" Mallory interrupted incredulously. "Did you say——"

"I did." Jensen grinned. "A mere bagatelle, I assure you, compared to the vast hordes of spies that circulate freely among our noble hosts in Cairo and Alexandria." He was suddenly serious again. "Anyway, our information is accurate. An armada of caiques will sail from the Piraeus on Thursday at dawn and island-hop across the Cyclades, holing up in the islands at night." He smiled. "An intriguing situation, don't you think? We daren't move in the Ægean in the daytime or we'd be bombed out of the water. The Germans don't dare move at night. Droves of our destroyers and M.T.B.s and gun-boats move into the Ægean at dusk: the destroyers retire to the South before dawn, the small boats usually lie up in isolated islands creeks. But we can't stop them from getting across. They'll be there Saturday or Sunday—and synchronise their landings with the first of the airborne troops: they've scores of Junkers 52s waiting just outside Athens. Kheros won't last a couple of days." No one could have listened to Jensen's carefully casual voice, his abnormal matter-of-factness and not have believed him.

Mallory believed him. For almost a minute he stared down at the sheen of the sea, at the faery tracery of the stars shimmering across its darkly placid surface. Suddenly he swung around on Jensen.

"But the Navy, sir! Evacuation! Surely the Navy——"

"The Navy," Jensen interrupted heavily, "is not keen. The Navy is sick and tired of the Eastern Med. and the Ægean, sick and tired of sticking out its long-suffering neck and having it regularly chopped off—and all for sweet damn all. We've had two battleships wrecked, eight cruisers out of commission—four of them sunk—and over a dozen destroyers gone. . . . I couldn't even start to count the number of smaller vessels we've lost. And for what? I've told you—for sweet damn all! Just so's our High Command can play round-and-round-the-rugged-rocks and who's the-king-of-the-castle with their opposite numbers in Berlin. Great fun for all concerned—except, of course, for the thousand or so sailors who've been drowned in the course of the game, the ten thousand or so Tommies and Anzacs and Indians who suffered and died on these same islands—and died without knowing why."

Jensen's hands were white-knuckled on the wheel, his mouth tight-drawn and bitter. Mallory was surprised, shocked almost, by the vehemence, the depth of feeling; it was so completely out of character. . . . Or perhaps it was in character, perhaps Jensen knew a very great deal indeed about what went on on the inside. . . .

"Twelve hundred men, you said, sir?" Mallory asked quietly. "You said there were twelve hundred men on Kheros?"

Jensen flickered a glance at him, looked away again.

"Yes. Twelve hundred men." Jensen sighed. "You're right, laddie, of course, you're right. I'm just talking off the top of my head. Of course we can't leave them there. The Navy will do its damnedest. What's two or three more destroyers—sorry, boy, sorry, there I go again. . . . Now listen, and listen carefully.

"Taking 'em off will have to be a night operation. There isn't a ghost of a chance in the daytime—not with two-three hundred Stukas just begging for a glimpse of a Royal Naval destroyer. It'll have to be destroyers—transports and tenders are too slow by half. And they can't possibly go northabout the northern tip of the Lerades—they'd never get back to safety before daylight. It's too long a trip by hours."

"But the Lerades is a pretty long string of islands," Mallory ventured. "Couldn't the destroyers go through——"

"Between a couple of them? Impossible." Jensen shook his head. "Mined to hell and back again. Every single channel. You couldn't take a dinghy through."

"And the Maidos-Navarone channel. Stiff with mines also, I suppose?"

"No, that's a clear channel. Deep water—you can't moor mines in deep water."

"So that's the route you've got to take, isn't it, sir? I mean, they're Turkish territorial waters on the other side and we——"

"We'd go through Turkish territorial waters to-morrow, and in broad daylight, if it would do any good," Jensen said flatly. "The Turks know it and so do the Germans. But all other things being equal, the Western channel is the one we're taking. It's a clearer channel, a shorter route—and it doesn't involve any unnecessary international complications."

"All other things being equal?"

"The guns of Navarone." Jensen paused for a long time, then repeated the words, slowly, expressionlessly, as one would repeat the name of some feared and ancient enemy. "The guns of Navarone. They make everything equal. They cover the northern entrances to both channels. We could take the twelve hundred men off Kheros to-night—if we could silence the guns of Navarone."

Mallory sat silent, said nothing. He's coming to it now, he thought.

"These guns are no ordinary guns," Jensen went on quietly. "Our naval experts say they're about nine-inch rifle barrels. I think myself they're more likely a version of the 210 mm. 'crunch' guns that the Germans are using in Italy—our soldiers up there hate and fear those guns more than anything on earth. A dreadful weapon—shell extremely slow in flight and damnably accurate. Anyway," he went on grimly, "whatever they were they were good enough to dispose of the *Sybaris* in five minutes flat."

Mallory nodded slowly.

"The *Sybaris*? I think I heard——"

"An eight-inch cruiser we sent up there about four months ago to try conclusions with the Hun. Just a formality, a routine exercise, we thought. The *Sybaris* was blasted out of the water. There were seventeen survivors."

"Good God!" Mallory was shocked. "I didn't know——"

"Two months ago we mounted a large-scale amphibious attack on Navarone." Jensen hadn't even heard the interruption. "Commandos, Royal Marine Commandos and Jellicoe's Special Boat Service. Less than an even chance, we knew—Navarone's practically solid cliff all the way round. But then these were very special men, probably the finest assault troops in the world today." Jensen paused for almost a minute, then went on very quietly. "They were cut to ribbons. They were massacred almost to a man.

"Finally, twice in the past ten days—we've seen this attack on Kheros coming for a long time now—we sent in parachute saboteurs: Special Boat Service men." He shrugged his shoulders helplessly. "They just vanished."

"Just like that?"

"Just like that. And then to-night—the last desperate fling of the gambler and what have you." Jensen laughed, briefly and without humour. "That interrogation hut—I kept pretty quiet in there to-night, I tell you. I was the 'joker' that Torrance and his boys wanted to heave out over Navarone. I don't blame them. But I had to do it, I just had to do it. I knew it was hopeless—but it had to be done."

The big Humber was beginning to slow down now, running silently between the tumble-down shacks and hovels that line the Western approach to Alexandria. The sky ahead was already beginning to streak in the first tenuous greys of the false dawn.

"I don't think I'd be much good with a parachute," Mallory said doubtfully. "In fact, quite frankly, I've never even *seen* a parachute."

"Don't worry," Jensen said briefly. "You won't have to use one. You're going into Navarone the hard way."

Mallory waited for more, but Jensen had fallen silent, intent on avoiding the large potholes that were beginning to pock the roadway. After a time Mallory asked:

"Why me, Captain Jensen?"

Jensen's smile was barely visible in the greying darkness. He swerved violently to avoid a gaping hole and straightened up again.

"Scared?"

"Certainly I'm scared. No offence intended, sir, but the way you talk you'd scare anyone. . . . But that wasn't what I meant."

"I know it wasn't. Just my twisted humour. . . . Why you? Special qualifications, laddie, just like I told you. You speak Greek like a Greek. You speak German like a German. Skilled saboteur, first-class organiser and eighteen unscathed months in the White Mountains of Crete—a convincing demonstration of your ability to survive in enemy-held territory." Jensen chuckled. "You'd be surprised to know just how complete a dossier I have on you!"

"No, I wouldn't." Mallory spoke with some feeling. "And," he added, "I know of at least three other officers with the same qualifications."

"There are others," Jensen agreed. "But there are no other Keith Mallorys. Keith Mallory," Jensen repeated rhetorically. "Who hadn't heard of Keith Mallory in the palmy, balmy days before the war? The finest mountaineer, the greatest rock climber New Zealand has ever produced—and by that, of course, New Zealanders mean the world. The human fly, the climber of the unclimbable, the scaler of vertical cliffs and impossible precipices. The entire south coast of Navarone," said Jensen cheerfully, "consists of one vast, impossible precipice. Nary a hand or foot-hold in sight."

"I see," Mallory murmured. "I see indeed. 'Into Navarone the hard way.' That was what you said."

"That was," Jensen acknowledged. "You and your gang—just four others. Mallory's Merry Mountaineers. Hand-picked. Every man a specialist. You'll meet them all tomorrow—this afternoon, rather.''

They travelled in silence for the next ten minutes, turned up right from the dock area, jounced their uncomfortable way over the massive cobbles of the Rue Souers, slewed round into Mohammed Ali square, passed in front of the Bourse and turned right down the Sherif Pasha.

Mallory looked at the man behind the wheel. He could see his face quite clearly now in the gathering light.

"Where to, sir?"

"To see the only man in the Middle East who can give you any help now. Monsieur Eugene Vlachos of Navarone.''

"You are a brave man, Captain Mallory." Nervously Eugene Vlachos twisted the long, pointed ends of his black moustache. "A brave man and a foolish one, I would say—but I suppose we cannot call a man a fool when he only obeys his orders." His eyes left the large drawing lying before him on the table and sought Jensen's impassive face.

"Is there no other way, Captain?" he pleaded.

Jensen shook his head slowly.

"There are. We've tried them all, sir. They all failed. This is the last.''

"He must go, then?"

"There are over a thousand men on Kheros, sir.''

Vlachos bowed his head in silent acceptance, then smiled faintly at Mallory.

"He calls me 'sir.' Me, a poor Greek hotel-keeper and Captain Jensen of the Royal Navy calls me 'sir.' It makes an old man feel good." He stopped, gazed off vacantly into space, the faded eyes and tired, lined face soft with memory. "An old man, Captain Mallory, an old man now, a poor man and a sad one. But I wasn't always, not always. Once I was just middle-aged, and rich and well content. Once I owned a lovely land, a hundred square miles of the most beautiful country God ever sent to delight the eyes of His creatures here below, and how well I loved that land!" He laughed self-consciously and ran a hand through his thick, greying hair. "Ah, well, as you people say, I suppose it's all in the eye of the beholder. 'A lovely land,' I say. 'That blasted rock,' as Captain Jensen has been heard to describe it out of my hearing." He smiled at Jensen's sudden discomfiture. "But we both give it the same name—Navarone.''

Startled, Mallory looked at Jensen. Jensen nodded.

"The Vlachos family has owned Navarone for generations. We had to remove Monsieur Vlachos in a great hurry eighteen months ago. The Germans didn't care overmuch for his kind of collaboration.''

"It was—how do you say—touch and go," Vlachos nodded. "They had reserved three very special places for my two sons and myself in the dungeons in Navarone. . . . But enough of the Vlachos family. I just wanted you to know, young man, that I spent forty years on Navarone and almost four days"—he gestured to the table—"on that map. My information and that map you can trust absolutely. Many things will have changed, of course, but some things never change. The mountains, the bays, the passes, the caves, the roads, the houses and, above all, the fortress itself—these have remained unchanged for centuries, Captain Mallory.''

"I understand, sir." Mallory folded the map carefully, stowed it away in his tunic. "With this, there's always a chance. Thank you very much.''

"It is little enough, God knows." Vlachos's fingers drummed on the table for a moment, then he looked up at Mallory. "Captain Jensen informs me that most of you speak Greek fluently, that you will be dressed as Greek peasants and will carry forged papers. That is well. You will be—what is the word?—self-contained, will operate on your own." He paused, then went on very earnestly.

"Please do not try to enlist the help of the people of Navarone. At all costs you must avoid that. The Germans are ruthless. I know. If a man helps you and is found out, they will destroy not only that man but his entire village—men, women and children. It has happened before. It will happen again."

"It happened in Crete," Mallory agreed quietly. "I've seen it for myself."

"Exactly." Vlanchos nodded. "And the people of Navarone have neither the skill nor the experience for successful guerrilla operations. They have not had the chance—German surveillance has been especially severe in our island."

"I promise you, sir——" Mallory began.

Vlachos held up his hand.

"Just a moment. If your need is desperate, really desperate, there are two men to whom you may turn. Under the first plane tree in the village square of Margaritha—at the mouth of the valley about three miles south of the fortress—you will find a man called Louki. He has been the steward of our family for many years. Louki has been of help to the British before— Captain Jensen will confirm that—and you can trust him with your life. He has a friend, Panayis: he, too, has been useful in the past."

"Thank you, sir. I'll remember. Louki and Panayis and Margaritha—the first plane tree in the square."

"And you will refuse all other aid, Captain?" Vlachos asked anxiously. "Louki and Panayis—only these two," he pleaded.

"You have my word, sir. Besides, the fewer the safer for us as well as your people." Mallory was surprised at the old man's intensity.

"I hope so, I hope so." Vlachos sighed heavily.

Mallory stood up, stretched out his hand to take his leave.

"You're worrying about nothing, sir. They'll never see us," he promised confidently. "Nobody will see us—and we'll see nobody. We're after only one thing—the guns."

"Ay, the guns—those terrible guns." Vlachos shook his head. "But just suppose——"

"Please. It will be all right," Mallory insisted quietly. "We will bring harm to none—and least of all to your islanders."

"God go with you to-night," the old man whispered. "God go with you to-night. I only wish that I could go too."

2

SUNDAY NIGHT

1900–0200

"Coffee, sir?"

Mallory stirred and groaned and fought his way up from the depths of exhausted sleep. Painfully he eased himself back on the metal-framed bucket-seat, wondering peevishly when the Air Force was going to get round to upholstering these fiendish contraptions. Then he was fully awake, tired, heavy eyes automatically focusing on the luminous dial of his wrist-watch. Seven o'clock. Just seven o'clock—he'd been asleep barely a couple of hours. Why hadn't they let him sleep on?

"Coffee, sir?" The young air-gunner was still standing patiently by his side, the inverted lid of an ammunition box serving as a tray for the cups he was carrying.

"Sorry, boy, sorry." Mallory struggled upright in his seat, reached up for a cup of the steaming liquid, sniffed it appreciatively. "Thank you. You know, this smells just like real coffee."

"It is, sir." The young gunner smiled proudly. "We have a percolator in the galley."

"He has a percolator in the galley." Mallory shook his head in disbelief. "Ye gods, the rigours of war in the Royal Air Force!" He leaned back, sipped the coffee luxuriously and sighed in contentment. Next moment he was on his feet, the hot coffee splashing unheeded on his bare knees as he stared out the window beside him. He looked at the gunner, gestured in disbelief at the mountainous landscape unrolling darkly beneath them.

"What the hell goes on here? We're not due till two hours after dark—and it's barely gone sunset! Has the pilot——?"

"That's Cyprus, sir." The gunner grinned. "You can just see Mount Olympus on the horizon. Nearly always, going to Castelrosso, we fly a big dog-leg over Cyprus. It's to escape observation, sir; and it takes us well clear of Rhodes."

"To escape observation, he says!" The heavy trans-atlantic drawl came from the bucket-seat diagonally across the passage: the speaker was lying collapsed—there was no other word for it—in his seat, the bony knees topping the level of the chin by several inches. "My Gawd! To escape observation!" he repeated in awed wonder. "Dog-legs over Cyprus. Twenty miles out from Alex by launch so that nobody ashore can see us takin' off by plane. And then what?" He raised himself painfully in his seat, eased an eyebrow over the bottom of the window, then fell back again, visibly exhausted by the effort. "And then what? Then they pack us into an old crate that's painted the whitest white you ever saw, guaranteed visible to a blind man at a hundred miles—'specially now that it's gettin' dark."

"It keeps the heat out," the young gunner said defensively.

"The heat doesn't worry me, son." The drawl was tireder, more lugubrious than ever. "I like the heat. What I don't like are them nasty cannon shells and bullets that can ventilate a man in all the wrong places." He slid his spine another impossible inch down the seat, closed his eyes wearily and seemed asleep in a moment.

The young gunner shook his head admiringly and smiled at Mallory.

"Worried to hell, isn't he, sir?"

Mallory laughed and watched the boy disappear for'ard into the control cabin. He sipped his coffee slowly, looked again at the sleeping figure across the passage. The blissful unconcern was magnificent: Corporal Dusty Miller of the United States, and more recently of the Long Range Desert Force, would be a good man to have around.

He looked round at the others and nodded to himself in satisfaction. They would all be good men to have around. Eighteen months in Crete had developed in him an unerring sense for assessing a man's capacity for survival in the peculiar kind of irregular warfare in which he himself had

been so long engaged. Offhand he'd have taken long odds on the capacity
of these four to survive. In the matter of picking an outstanding team
Captain Jensen, he reckoned, had done him proud. He didn't know them all
yet—not personally. But he was intimately acquainted with the exhaustive
dossier that Jensen held on each one of them. These were reassuring, to say
the least.

Or was there perhaps a slight question mark against Stevens'. Mallory
wondered, looked across the passage at the fair-haired, boyish figure gazing
out eagerly beneath the gleaming white wing of the Sunderland. Lieutenant
Andy Stevens, R.N.V.R., had been chosen for this assignment for three
reasons. He would navigate the craft that was to take them to Navarone: he
was a first-class Alpinist, with several outstanding climbs to his record: and,
the product of the classical side of a red-brick university, he was an almost
fanatical philhellene, fluent in both Ancient and Modern Greek, and had
spent his last two long vacations before the war as a tourist courier in
Athens. But he was young, absurdly young, Mallory thought as he looked at
him, and youth could be dangerous. Too often, in that island guerilla warfare, it had been fatal. The enthusiasm, the fire, the zeal of youth was not
enough: rather, it was too much, a positive handicap. This was not a war of
bugle calls and roaring engines and magnificent defiance in the clamour of
battle: this was a war of patience and endurance and stability, of cunning
and craft and stealth, and these were not commonly the attributes of youth. . . .
But he looked as if he might learn fast.

Mallory stole another glance at Miller. Dusty Miller, he decided, had
learnt it all a long, long time ago. Dusty Miller on a white charger, the
bugle to his lips—no, his mind just refused to encompass the incongruity
of it. He just didn't look like Sir Launcelot. He just looked as if he had been
around for a long, long time and had no illusions left.

Corporal Miller had, in fact, been around for exactly forty years. By birth
a Californian, by descent three parts Irish and one part Central European,
he had lived and fought and adventured more in the previous quarter of a
century than most men would in a dozen lifetimes. Silver-miner in Nevada,
tunneler in Canada and oil-fire shooter all over the globe, he had been in
Saudi Arabia when Hitler attacked Poland. One of his more remote maternal
ancestors, some time around the turn of the century, had lived in Warsaw,
but that had been affront enough for Miller's Irish blood. He had taken the
first available plane to Britain and lied his way into the Air Force, where, to
his immense disgust, and because of his age, he was relegated to the rear
turret of a Wellington.

His first operational flight had been his last. Within ten minutes of taking
off from the Menidi airfield outside Athens on a January night in 1941,
engine failure had brought them to an ignominious though well-cushioned
end in a paddy field some miles north-west of the city. The rest of the winter
he had spent seething with rage in a cookhouse back in Menidi. At the
beginning of April he resigned from the Air Force without telling anyone
and was making his way north towards the fighting and the Albanian frontier
when he met the Germans coming south. As Miller afterwards told it, he
reached Nauplion two blocks ahead of the nearest panzer division, was
evacuated by the transport *Slamat,* sunk, picked up by the destroyer *Wry-
neck,* sunk, and finally arrived in Alexandria in an ancient Greek caique,
with nothing left him in the world but a fixed determination never again to
venture in the air or on the sea. Some months later he was operating with a
long-range striking force behind the enemy lines in Libya.

He was, Mallory mused, the complete antithesis to Lieutenant Stevens.

Stevens, young, fresh, enthusiastic, correct and immaculately dressed, and Miller, dried-up, lean, stringy, immensely tough and with an almost pathological aversion to spit and polish. How well the nickname "Dusty" suited him: there could hardly have been a greater contrast. Again, unlike Stevens, Miller had never climbed a mountain in his life and the only Greek words he knew were invariably omitted from the dictionaries. And both these facts were of no importance at all. Miller had been picked for one reason only. A genius with explosives, resourceful and cool, precise and deadly in action, he was regarded by Middle East Intelligence in Cairo as the finest saboteur in southern Europe.

Behind Miller sat Casey Brown. Short, dark and compact, Petty Officer Telegraphist Brown was a Clydesider, in peacetime an installation and testing engineer in a famous yacht-builder's yard on the Gareloch. The fact that he was a born and ready-made engine-room artificer had been so blindingly obvious that the Navy had missed it altogether and stuck him in the Communications Branch. Brown's ill luck was Mallory's good fortune. Brown would act as the engineer of the boat taking them to Navarone and would maintain radio contact with base. He had also the further recommendation of being a first-class guerrilla fighter; a veteran of the Special Boat Service, he held the D.C.M. and D.S.M. for his exploits in the Ægean and off the coast of Libya.

The fifth and last member of the party sat directly behind Mallory. Mallory did not have to turn round to look at him. He already knew him, knew him better than he knew anyone else in the world, better even than he knew his own mother. Andrea, who had been his lieutenant for all these eighteen interminable months in Crete, Andrea of the vast bulk, the continual rumbling laughter and tragic past, with whom he had eaten, lived and slept in caves, rock-shelters and abandoned shepherd's huts while constantly harried by German patrols and aircraft—that Andrea had become his *alter ego*, his *doppelganger*: to look at Andrea was to look in a mirror to remind himself what he was like. . . . There was no question as to why Andrea had come along. He wasn't there primarily because he was a Greek himself, with an intimate knowledge of the islanders' language, thought and customs, nor even because of his perfect understanding with Mallory, although all these things helped. He was, instead, there exclusively for the protection and safety he afforded. Endlessly patient, quiet and deadly, tremendously fast in spite of his bulk, and with a feline stealth that exploded into berserker action, Andrea was the complete fighting machine. Andrea was their insurance policy against failure.

Mallory turned back to look out the window again then nodded to himself in imperceptible satisfaction. Jensen probably couldn't have picked a better team if he'd scoured the whole Mediterranean theatre. It suddenly occurred to Mallory that Jensen probably had done just that. Miller and Brown had been recalled to Alexandria almost a month ago. It was almost as long since Stevens's relief had arrived aboard his cruiser in Malta. And if their battery-charging engine hadn't slipped down that ravine in the White Mountains, and if the sorely harassed runner from the nearest listening post hadn't taken a week to cover fifty miles of snowbound, enemy patrolled mountains and another five days to find them, he and Andrea would have been in Alexandria almost a fortnight earlier. Mallory's opinion of Jensen, already high, rose another notch. A far-seeing man who planned accordingly, Jensen must have had all his preparations for this made even before the first of the two abortive parachute landings on Navarone.

*   *   *

It was eight o'clock and almost totally dark inside the plane when Mallory rose and made his way for'ard to the control cabin. The captain, face wreathed in tobacco smoke, was drinking coffee: the co-pilot waved a languid hand at his approach and resumed a bored scanning of the scene ahead.

"Good evening." Mallory smiled. "Mind if I come in?"

"Welcome in my office any time," the pilot assured him. "No need to ask."

"I only thought you might be busy. . . ." Mallory stopped and looked again at the scene of masterly inactivity. "Just who is flying this plane?" he asked.

"George. The automatic pilot." He waved a coffee-cup in the direction of a black, squat box, it's blurred outlines just visible in the near darkness. "An industrious character, and makes a damn' sight fewer mistakes than that idle hound who's supposed to be on watch. . . . Anything on your mind, Captain?"

"Yes. What were your instructions for to-night?"

"Just to set you blokes down in Castelrosso when it was good and dark." The pilot paused, then said frankly, "I don't get it. A ship this size for only five men and a couple of hundred odd pounds of equipment. Especially to Castelrosso. Especially after dark. Last plane that came down here after dark just kept on going down. Underwater obstruction—dunno what it was. Two survivors."

"I know. I heard. I'm sorry, but I'm under orders too. As for the rest, forget it—and I mean forget. Impress on your crew that they mustn't talk. They've never seen us."

The pilot nodded glumly. "We've all been threatened with court-martial already. You'd think there was a ruddy war on."

"There is. . . . We'll be leaving a couple of cases behind. We're going ashore in different clothes. Somebody will be waiting for our old stuff when you get back."

"Roger. And the best of luck, Captain. Official secrets, or no official secrets, I've got a hunch you're going to need it."

"If we are, you can give us a good send-off." Mallory grinned. "Just set us down in one piece, will you?"

"Reassure yourself, brother," said the pilot firmly. "Just set your mind at ease. Don't forget—I'm in this ruddy plane too."

The clamour of the Sunderland's great engines was still echoing in their ears when the stubby little motor-boat chugged softly out of the darkness and nosed alongside the gleaming hull of the flying-boat. There was no time lost, there were no words spoken; within a minute the five men and all their gear had been embarked; within another the little boat was rubbing to a stop against the rough stone Navy jetty of Castelrosso. Two ropes went spinning up into the darkness, were caught and quickly secured by practised hands. Amidships, the rust-scaled iron ladder, recessed deep into the stone, stretched up into the star-dusted darkness above: as Mallory reached the top, a figure stepped forward out of the gloom.

"Captain Mallory?"

"Yes."

"Captain Briggs, Army. Have your men wait here, will you? The Colonel would like to see you." The nasal voice, peremptory in its clipped affectation, was far from cordial. Mallory stirred in slow anger, but said nothing. Briggs sounded like a man who might like his bed or his gin, and maybe their late visitation was keeping him from either or both. War was hell.

They were back in ten minutes, a third figure following behind them. Mallory peered at the three men standing on the edge of the jetty, identified them, then peered around again.

"Where's Miller got to?" he asked.

"Here, boss, here." Miller groaned, eased his back off a big, wooden bollard, climbed wearily to his feet. "Just restin', boss. Recuperatin', as you might say, from the nerve-rackin' rigours of the trip."

"When you're all *quite* ready," Briggs said acidly, "Matthews here will take you to your quarters. You are to remain on call for the Captain, Matthews. Colonel's orders." Briggs's tone left no doubt that he thought the Colonel's orders a piece of arrant nonsense. "And don't forget, Captain— two hours, the Colonel said."

"I know, I know," Mallory said wearily. "I was there when he said it. It was to me he was talking. Remember? All right, boys, if you're ready."

"Our gear, sir?" Stevens ventured.

"Just leave it there. Right, Matthews, lead the way, will you?"

Matthews led the way along the jetty and up interminable flights of steep, worn steps, the others following in Indian file, rubber soles noiseless on the stone. He turned sharply right at the top, went down a narrow, winding alley, into a passage, climbed a flight of creaking, wooden stairs, opened the first door in the corridor above.

"Here you are, sir. I'll just wait in the corridor outside."

"Better wait downstairs," Mallory advised. "No offence, Matthews, but the less you know of this the better."

He followed the others into the room, closing the door behind him. It was a small, bleak room, heavily curtained. A table and half a dozen chairs took up most of the space. Over in the far corner the springs of the single bed creaked as Corporal Miller stretched himself out luxuriously, hands clasped behind his head.

"Gee!" he murmured admiringly. "A hotel room. Just like home. Kinda bare, though." A thought occurred to him. "Where are all you other guys gonna sleep?"

"We aren't," Mallory said briefly. "Neither are you. We're pulling out in less than two hours." Miller groaned. "Come on, soldier," Mallory went on relentlessly. "On your feet."

Miller groaned again, swung his legs over the edge of the bed and looked curiously at Andrea. The big Greek was quartering the room methodically, pulling out lockers, turning pictures, peering behind curtains and under the bed.

"What's he doin'?" Miller asked. "Lookin' for dust?"

"Testing for listening devices," Mallory said curtly. "One of the reasons why Andrea and I have lasted so long." He dug into the inside pocket of his tunic, a dark naval battledress with neither badge nor insignia, pulled out a chart and the map Vlachos had given him, unfolded and spread them out. "Round the table, all of you. I know you've been bursting with curiosity for the past couple of weeks, asking yourselves a hundred questions. Well, here are all the answers. I hope you like them. . . . Let me introduce you to the island of Navarone."

Mallory's watch showed exactly eleven o'clock when he finally sat back, folded away the map and chart. He looked quizzically at the four thoughtful faces round the table.

"Well, gentlemen, there you have it. A lovely set-up, isn't it?" He smiled wryly. "If this was a film, my next line should be, 'Any questions, men?' But we'll dispense with that because I just wouldn't have any of the answers. You all know as much as I do."

"A quarter of a mile of sheer cliff, four hundred feet high, and he calls it the only break in the defences." Miller, his head bent moodily over his tobacco tin, rolled a long, thin cigarette with one expert hand. "This is just crazy, boss. Me, I can't even climb a bloody ladder without falling off." He puffed strong, acrid clouds of smoke into the air. "Suicidal. That's the word I was lookin' for. Suicidal. One buck gets a thousand we never get within five miles of them gawddamned guns!"

"One in a thousand, eh?" Mallory looked at him for a long time without speaking. "Tell me, Miller, what odds are you offering on the boys on Kheros?"

"Yeah." Miller nodded heavily. "Yeah, the boys on Kheros. I'd forgotten about them. I just keep thinkin' about me and that damned cliff." He looked hopefully across the table at the vast bulk of Andrea. "Or maybe Andrea there would carry me up. He's big enough, anyway."

Andrea made no reply. His eyes were half-closed, his thoughts could have been a thousand miles away.

"We'll tie you hand and foot and haul you up on the end of a rope," Stevens said unkindly. "We'll try to pick a fairly sound rope," he added carelessly. The words, the tone, were jocular enough, but the worry on his face belied them. Mallory apart, only Stevens appreciated the almost insuperable technical difficulties of climbing a sheer, unknown cliff in the darkness. He looked at Mallory questioningly. "Going up alone, sir, or——"

"Excuse me, please." Andrea suddenly sat forward, his deep rumble of a voice rapid in the clear, idiomatic English he had learnt during his long association with Mallory. He was scribbling quickly on a piece of paper. "I have a plan for climbing this cliff. Here is a diagram. Does the Captain think this is possible?"

He passed the paper across to Mallory. Mallory looked at it, checked, recovered, all in the one instant. There was no diagram on it. There were only two large, printed words: "Keep talking."

"I see," Mallory said thoughtfully. "Very good indeed, Andrea. This has distinct possibilities." He reversed the paper, held it up before him so that they could all see the words. Andrea had already risen to his feet, was padding cat-footed towards the door. "Ingenious, isn't it, Corporal Miller," he went on conversationally. "Might solve quite a lot of our difficulties."

"Yeah." The expression on Miller's face hadn't altered a fraction, the eyes were still half-closed against the smoke drifting up from the cigarette dangling between his lips. "Reckon that might solve the problem, Andrea— and get me up in one piece, too." He laughed easily, concentrated on screwing a curiously-shaped cylinder on to the barrel of an automatic that had magically appeared in his left hand. "But I don't quite get that funny line and the dot at——"

It was all over in two seconds—literally. With a deceptive ease and nonchalance Andrea opened the door with one hand, reached out with the other, plucked a wildly-struggling figure through the gap, set him on the ground again and closed the door, all in one concerted movement. It had been as soundless as it had been swift. For a second the eavesdropper, a hatchet-faced, swarthy Levantine in badly-fitting white shirt and blue trousers, stood there in shocked immobility, blinking rapidly in the unaccustomed light. Then his hand dived in under his shirt.

"Look out!" Miller's voice was sharp, the automatic lining up as Mallory's hand closed over his.

"Watch!" Mallory said softly.

The men at the table caught only a flicker of blued steel as the knife arm jerked convulsively back and plunged down with vicious speed. And then, incredibly, hand and knife were stopped dead in midair, the gleaming point only two inches from Andrea's chest. There was a sudden scream of agony, the ominous cracking of wrist bones as the giant Greek tightened his grip, and then Andrea had the blade between finger and thumb, had removed the knife with the tender, reproving care of a parent saving a well-loved but irresponsible child from himself. Then the knife was reversed, the point was at the Levantine's throat and Andrea was smiling down pleasantly into the dark and terror-stricken eyes.

Miller let out a long breath, half-sigh, half-whistle.

"Well, now," he murmured, "I guess mebbe Andrea has done that sort of thing before?"

"I guess maybe he has," Mallory mimicked. "Let's have a closer look at exhibit A, Andrea."

Andrea brought his prisoner close up to the table, well within the circle of light. He stood there sullenly before them, a thin, ferret-faced man, black eyes dulled in pain and fear, left hand cradling his crushed wrist.

"How long do you reckon this fellow's been outside, Andrea?" Mallory asked.

Andrea ran a massive hand through his thick, dark, curling hair, heavily streaked with grey above the temples.

"I cannot be sure, Captain. I imagined I heard a noise—a kind of shuffle—about ten minutes ago, but I thought my ears were playing tricks. Then I heard the same sound a minute ago. So I am afraid——"

"Ten minutes, eh?" Mallory nodded thoughtfully, then looked at the prisoner. "What's your name?" he asked sharply. "What are you doing here?"

There was no reply. There were only the sullen eyes, the sullen silence— a silence that gave way to a sudden yelp of pain as Andrea cuffed the side of his head.

"The Captain is asking you a question," Andrea said reproachfully. He cuffed him again, harder this time. "Answer the Captain."

The stranger broke into rapid, excitable speech, gesticulating wildly with both hands. The words were quite unintelligible. Andrea sighed, shut off the torrent by the simple expedient of almost encircling the scrawny throat with his left hand.

Mallory looked questioningly at Andrea. The giant shook his head.

"Kurdistan or Armenian, Captain, I think. But I don't understand it."

"I certainly don't," Mallory admitted. "Do you speak English?" he asked suddenly.

Black, hate-filled eyes glared back at him in silence. Andrea cuffed him again.

"Do you speak English?" Mallory repeated relentlessly.

"Eenglish? Eenglish?" Shoulders and upturned palms lifted in the age-old gesture of incomprehension. "Ka Eenglish!"

"He says he don't speak English," Miller drawled.

"Maybe he doesn't and maybe he does," Mallory said evenly. "All we know is that he *has* been listening and that we can't take any chances. There are far too many lives at stake." His voice suddenly hardened, the eyes were grim and pitiless. "Andrea!"

"Captain?"

"You have the knife. Make it clean and quick. Between the shoulder blades!"

Stevens cried out in horror, sent his chair crashing back as he leapt to his feet.

"Good God, sir, you can't——"

He broke off and stared in amazement at the sight of the prisoner catapulting himself bodily across the room to crash into a distant corner, one arm up-curved in rigid defence, stark, unreasoning panic limned in every feature of his face. Slowly Stevens looked away, saw the triumphant grin on Andrea's face, the dawning comprehension in Brown's and Miller's. Suddenly he felt a complete fool. Characteristically, Miller was the first to speak.

"Waal, waal, whaddya know! Mebbe he *does* speaka da Eenglish after all."

"Maybe he does," Mallory admitted. "A man doesn't spend ten minutes with his ear glued to a keyhole if he doesn't understand a word that's being said. . . . Give Matthews a call, will you, Brown?"

The sentry appeared in the doorway a few seconds later.

"Get Captain Briggs here, will you, Matthews?" he asked. "At once, please."

The soldier hesitated.

"Captain Briggs has gone to bed, sir. He left strict orders that he wasn't to be disturbed."

"My heart bleeds for Captain Briggs and his broken slumbers," Mallory said acidly. "He's had more sleep in a day than I've had in the past week." He glanced at his watch and the heavy brows came down in a straight line over the tired, brown eyes. "We've no time to waste. Get him here at once. Understand? At once!"

Matthews saluted and hurried away. Miller cleared his throat and clucked his tongue sadly.

"These hotels are all the same. The goin's-on—you'd never believe your eyes. Remember once I was at a convention in Cincinnati——"

Mallory shook his head wearily.

"You have a fixation about hotels, Corporal. This is a military establishment and there are army officers' billets."

Miller made to speak but changed his mind. The American was a shrewd judge of people. There were those who could be ribbed and those who could not be ribbed. An almost hopeless mission, Miller was quietly aware, and as vital as it was, in his opinion, suicidal; but he was beginning to understand why they'd picked this tough, sunburnt New Zealander to lead it.

They sat in silence for the next five minutes, then looked up as the door opened. Captain Briggs was hatless and wore a white silk muffler round his throat in place of the usual collar and tie. The white contrasted oddly with the puffed red of the heavy neck and face above. These had been red enough when Mallory had first seen them in the Colonel's office—high blood pressure and even higher living, Mallory had supposed: the extra deeper shades of red and purple now present probably sprung from a misplaced sense of righteous indignation. A glance at the choleric eyes, gleaming light-blue prawns afloat in a sea of vermilion, was quite enough to confirm the obvious.

"I think this is a bit much, Captain Mallory!" The voice was high pitched in anger, more nasal than ever. "I'm not the duty errand-boy, you know. I've had a damned hard day and——"

"Save it for your biography," Mallory said curtly, "and take a gander at this character in the corner."

Briggs's face turned an even deeper hue. He stepped into the room, fists balled in anger, then stopped in his tracks as his eye lit on the crumpled, dishevelled figure still crouched in the corner of the room.

"Good God!" he ejaculated. "Nicolai!"

"You know him." It was a statement, not a question.

"Of course I know him!" Briggs snorted. "Everybody knows him. Nicolai. Our laundry-boy."

"Your laundry-boy! Do his duties entail snooping around the corridors at night, listening at keyholes?"

"What do you mean?"

"What I say." Mallory was very patient. "We caught him listening outside the door."

"Nicolai? I don't believe it!"

"Watch it, mister," Miller growled. "Careful who you call a liar. We all saw him."

Briggs stared in fascination at the black muzzle of the automatic waving negligently in his direction, gulped, looked hastily away.

"Well, what if you did?" He forced a smile. "Nicolai can't speak a word of English."

"Maybe not," Mallory agreed dryly. "But he understands it well enough." He raised his hand. "I've no desire to argue all night and I certainly haven't the time. Will you please have this man placed under arrest, kept in solitary confinement and incommunicado for the next week at least. It's vital. Whether he's a spy or just too damned nosy, he knows far too much. After that, do what you like. My advice is to kick him out of Castelrosso."

"*Your* advice, indeed!" Brigg's colour returned, and with it his courage. "Who the hell are you to give me advice or to give me orders, Captain Mallory?" There was a heavy emphasis on the word "captain."

"Then I'm asking it as a favour," Mallory pleaded wearily. "I can't explain, but it's terribly important. There are hundreds of lives——"

"Hundreds of lives!" Briggs sneered. "Melodramatic stuff and nonsense!" He smiled unpleasantly. "I suggest you keep that for *your* cloak-and-dagger biography, Captain Mallory."

Mallory rose, walked round the table, stopped a foot away from Briggs. The brown eyes were still and very cold.

"I could go and see your Colonel, I suppose. But I'm tired of arguing. You'll do exactly as I say or I'll go straight to Naval H.Q. and get on the radio-telephone to Cairo. And if I do," Mallory went on, "I swear to you that you'll be on the next ship home to England—and on the troop-deck, at that."

His last words seemed to echo in the little room for an interminable time: the stillness was intense. And then, as suddenly as it had arisen, the tension was gone and Brigg's face, and now curiously mottled white and red, was slack and sullen in defeat.

"All right, all right," he said. "No need for all these damned stupid threats—not if it means all that much to you." The attempt to bluster, to patch up the shredded rags of his dignity, was pathetic in its transparency. "Matthews—call out the guard."

The torpedo-boat, great engines throttled back half speed, pitched and lifted, pitched and lifted with monotonous regularity as it thrust its way into the long, gentle swell from the W.N.W. For the hundredth time that night Mallory looked at his watch.

"Running behind time, sir?" Stevens suggested.

Mallory nodded.

"We should have stepped straight into this thing from the Sunderland—there was a hold-up."

Brown grunted. "Engine trouble, for a fiver." The Clyde-side accent was very heavy.

"Yes, that's right." Mallory looked up, surprised. "How did you know?"

"Always the same with these blasted M.T.B. engines," Brown growled. "Temperamental as a film star."

There was silence for a time in the tiny blacked-out cabin, a silence broken only by the occasional clink of a glass. The Navy was living up to its traditional hospitality.

"If we're late," Miller observed at last, "why doesn't the skipper open her up? They tell me these crates can do forty to fifty knots."

"You look green enough already," Stevens said tactlessly. "Obviously, you've never been in an M.T.B. full out in a heavy sea."

Miller fell silent a moment. Clearly, he was trying to take his mind off his internal troubles. "Captain?"

"Yes, what is it?" Mallory answered sleepily. He was stretched full length on a narrow settee, an almost empty glass in his fingers.

"None of my business, I know, boss, but—would you have carried out that threat you made to Captain Briggs?"

Mallory laughed.

"It *is* none of your business, but—well, no, Corporal, I wouldn't. I wouldn't because I couldn't. I haven't all that much authority invested in me—and I didn't even know whether there was a radio-telephone in Castelrosso."

"Yeah. Yeah, do you know, I kinda suspected that." Corporal Miller rubbed a stubbled chin. "If he'd called your bluff, what would you have done, boss?"

"I'd have shot Nicolai," Mallory said quietly. "If the Colonel had failed me, I'd have had no choice left."

"I knew that too. I really believe you would. For the first time I'm beginning to believe we've got a chance. . . . But I kinda wish you *had* shot him—*and* little Lord Fauntleroy. I didn't like the expression on old Briggs' face when you went out that door. Mean wasn't the word. He coulda killed you then. You trampled right over his pride, boss—and to a phoney like that nothin' else in the world matters."

Mallory made no reply. He was already sound asleep, his empty glass fallen from his hand. Not even the banshee clamour of the great engines opening full out as they entered the sheltered calm of the Rhodes channel could plumb his bottomless abyss of sleep.

3

MONDAY

0700–1700

"My dear fellow, you make me feel dreadfully embarrassed." Moodily the officer switched his ivory-handled fly-swat against an immaculately trousered leg, pointed a contemptuous but gleaming toecap at the ancient caique, broad-beamed and two-masted, moored stern on to the even older and more dilapidated wooden pier on which they were standing. "I am positively ashamed. The clients of Rutledge and Company, I assure you, are accustomed only to the best."

Mallory smothered a smile. Major Rutledge of the Buffs, Eton and Sandhurst as to intonation, millimetrically tooth-brushed as to moustache, Savile Row as to the quite dazzling sartorial perfection of his khaki drill, was so magnificently out of place in the wild beauty of the rocky, tree-lined bluffs of that winding creek that his presence there seemed inevitable. Such was the Major's casual assurance, so dominating his majestic unconcern, that it was the creek, if anything, that seemed slightly out of place.

"It *does* look as if it has seen better days," Mallory admitted. "Nevertheless, sir, it's exactly what we want."

"Can't understand it, I really can't understand it." With an irritable but well-timed swipe the Major brought down a harmless passing fly. "I've been providing chaps with everything during the past eight or nine months— caiques, launches, yachts, fishing boats, everything—but no one has ever yet specified the oldest, most dilapidated derelict I could lay hands on. Quite a job laying hands on it, too, I tell you." A pained expression crossed his face. "The chaps know I don't usually deal in this line of stuff."

"What chaps?" Mallory asked curiously.

"Oh, up the islands, you know. Rutledge gestured vaguely to the north and west.

"But—but those are enemy held——"

"So's this one. Chap's got to have his H.Q. somewhere." Rutledge explained patiently. Suddenly his expression brightened. "I say, old boy, I know just the thing for you. A boat to escape observation and investigation—that was what Cairo insisted I get. How about a German E-boat, absolutely perfect condition, one careful owner. Could get ten thou. for her at home. Thirty-six hours. Pal of mine over in Bodrum——"

"Bodrum?" Mallory questioned. "Bodrum? But—but that's in Turkey, isn't it?"

"Turkey? Well, yes, actually, I believe it is," Rutledge admitted. "Chap has to get his supplies from somewhere, you know," he added defensively.

"Thanks all the same"—Mallory smiled—"but this is exactly what we want. We can't wait, anyway."

"On your own heads be it!" Rutledge threw up his hands in admission of defeat. "I'll have a couple of my men shove your stuff aboard."

"I'd rather we did it ourselves, sir. It's—well, it's a very special cargo."

"Right you are," the Major acknowledged. "No questions Rutledge, they call me. Leaving soon?"

Mallory looked at his watch.

"Half an hour, sir."

"Bacon, eggs and coffee in ten minutes?"

"Thanks very much." Mallory grinned. "That's one offer we'll be very glad to accept."

He turned away, walked slowly down to the end of the pier. He breathed deeply, savouring the heady, herb-scented air of an Ægean dawn. The salt tang of the sea, the drowsily sweet perfume of honeysuckle, the more delicate, sharper fragrance of mint all subtly merged into an intoxicating whole, indefinable, unforgettable. On either side, the steep slopes, still brilliantly green with pine and walnut and holly, stretched far up to the moorland pastures above, and from these, faintly borne on the perfumed breeze, came the distant, melodic tinkling of goats' bells, a haunting, a nostalgic music, true symbol of the leisured peace the Ægean no longer knew.

Unconsciously almost, Mallory shook his head and walked more quickly to the end of the pier. The others were still sitting where the torpedo boat had landed them just before dawn. Miller, inevitably, was stretched his full length, hat tilted against the golden, level rays of the rising sun.

"Sorry to disturb you and all that, but we're leaving in half an hour; breakfast in ten minutes. Let's get the stuff aboard." He turned to Brown. "Maybe you'd like to have a look at the engine?" he suggested.

Brown heaved himself to his feet, looked down unenthusiastically at the weather-beaten, paint-peeled caique.

"Right you are, sir. But if the engine is on a par with this bloody wreck. . . ." He shook his head in prophetic gloom and swung nimbly over the side of the pier.

Mallory and Andrea followed him, reaching up for the equipment as the other two passed it down. First they stowed away a sackful of old clothes, then the food, pressure stove and fuel, the heavy boots, spikes, mallets, rock axes and coils of wire-centred rope to be used for climbing, then, more carefully, the combined radio receiver and transmitter and the firing generator fitted with the old-fashioned plunge handle. Next came the guns—two Schmeissers, two Brens, a Mauser and a Colt—then a case containing a weird but carefully selected hodge-podge of torches, mirrors, two sets of identity papers and, incredibly, bottles of Hock, Moselle, *ouzo* and *retsina*.

Finally, and with exaggerated care, they stowed away for'ard in the fore-peak two wooden boxes, one green in colour, medium sized and bound in brass, the other small and black. The green box held high explosive— T.N.T., amatol and a few standard sticks of dynamite, together with grenades, gun-cotton primers and canvas hosing; in one corner of the box was a bag of emery dust, another of ground glass, and a sealed jar of potassium, these last three items having been included against the possibility of Dusty Miller's finding an opportunity to exercise his unique talents as a saboteur. The black box held only detonators, percussion and electrical, detonators with fulminates so unstable that their exposed powder could be triggered off by the impact of a falling feather.

The last box had been stowed away when Casey Brown's head appeared above the engine hatch. Slowly he examined the mainmast reaching up above his head, as slowly turned for'ard to look at the foremast. His face carefully expressionless, he looked at Mallory.

"Have we got sails for these things, sir?"

"I suppose so. Why?"

"Because God only knows we're going to need them!" Brown said bitterly. "Have a look at the engine-room, you said. This isn't an engine-room. It's a bloody scrap-yard. And the biggest, most rusted bit of scrap down there is attached to the propeller shaft. And what do you think it is? An old Kelvin two-cylinder job built more or less on my own doorstep— about thirty years ago." Brown shook his head in despair, his face as stricken as only a Clydeside engineer's can be at the abuse of a beloved machine. "And it's been falling to bits for years, sir. Place is littered with discarded bits and spares. I've seen junk heaps off the Gallowgate that were palaces compared to this."

"Major Rutledge said it was running only yesterday," Mallory said mildly. "Anyway, come on ashore. Breakfast. Remind me we're to pick up a few heavy stones on the way back, will you?"

"Stones!" Miller looked at him in horror. "Aboard that thing?"

Mallory nodded, smiling.

"But that gawddamned ship is sinkin' already!" Miller protested. "What do you want stones for?"

"Wait and see."

Three hours later Miller saw. The caique was chugging steadily north over a glassy, windless sea, less than a mile off the coast of Turkey, when he mournfully finished lashing his blue battledress into a tight ball and heaved it regretfully over the side. Weighted by the heavy stone he had carried aboard, it was gone from sight in a second.

Morosely he surveyed himself in the mirror propped up against the for'ard end of the wheelhouse. Apart from a deep violet sash wrapped round his lean middle and a fancifully embroidered waistcoat with its former glory mercifully faded, he was dressed entirely in black. Black lacing jackboots, black baggy trousers, black shirt and black jacket: even his sandy hair had been dyed to the same colour.

He shuddered and turned away.

"Thank Gawd the boys back home can't see me now!" he said feelingly. He looked critically at the others, dressed, with some minor variations, like himself. "Waal, mebbe I ain't quite so bad after all. . . . Just what is all this quick-change business for, boss?"

"They tell me you've been behind the German lines twice, once as a peasant, once as a mechanic." Mallory heaved his own ballasted uniform over the side. "Well, now you see what the well-dressed Navaronian wears."

"The double change, I meant. Once in the plane, and now."

"Oh, I see. Army khaki and naval whites in Alex., blue battledress in Castelrosso and now Greek clothes? Could have been—almost certainly were—snoopers in Alex. or Castelrosso or Major Rutledge's island. And we've changed from launch to plane to M.T.B. to caique. Covering our tracks, Corporal. We just can't take any chances."

Miller nodded, looked down at the clothes sack at his feet, wrinkled his brows in puzzlement, stooped and dragged out the white clothing that had caught his eye. He held up the long, voluminous clothes for inspection.

"To be used when passing through the local cemeteries, I suppose." He was heavily ironic. "Disguised as ghosts."

"Camouflage," Mallory explained succinctly. "Snow-smocks."

"What!"

"Snow. That white stuff. There are some pretty high mountains in Navarone, and we may have to take to them. So—snow-smocks."

Miller looked stunned. Wordlessly he stretched his length on the deck, pillowed his head and closed his eyes. Mallory grinned at Andrea.

"Picture of a man getting his full quota of sunshine before battling with the Arctic wastes. . . . Not a bad idea. Maybe you should get some sleep, too. I'll keep watch for a couple of hours."

For five hours the caique continued on its course parallel to the Turkish coast, slightly west of north and rarely more than two miles off-shore. Relaxed and warm in the still kindly November sun, Mallory sat wedged between the bulwarks of the blunt bows, his eyes ceaselessly quartering sky and horizon. Amidships, Andrea and Miller lay asleep. Casey Brown still defied all attempts to remove him from the engine-room. Occasionally—very occasionally—he came up for a breath of fresh air, but the intervals between his appearances steadily lengthened as he concentrated more and more on the aged Kelvin engine, regulating the erratic drip-fed lubrication, constantly adjusting the air intake: an engineer to his finger-tips, he was unhappy about that engine: he was drowsy, too, and headachy—the narrow hatchway gave hardly any ventilation at all.

Alone in the wheelhouse—an unusual feature in so tiny a caique—Lieutenant Andy Stevens watched the Turkish coast slide slowly by. Like Mallory's, his eyes moved ceaselessly, but not with the same controlled wandering. They shifted from the coast to the chart: from the chart to the islands up ahead off the port bow, islands whose position and relation to each other changed continually and deceptively, islands gradually lifting from the sea and hardening in definition through the haze of blue refraction: from the islands to the old alcohol compass swinging almost imperceptibly on rusted gimbals, and from the compass back to the coast again. Occasionally, he peered up into the sky, or swung a quick glance through a 180-degree sweep of the horizon. But one thing his eyes avoided all the time. The chipped, fly-blown mirror had been hung up in the wheelhouse again, but it was as if his eyes and the mirror were of opposite magnetic poles: he could not bring himself to look at it.

His forearms ached. He had been spelled at the wheel twice, but still they ached, abominably: his lean, tanned hands were ivory-knuckled on the cracked wheel. Repeatedly, consciously, he tried to relax, to ease the tension that was bunching up the muscles of his arms; but always, as if possessed of independent volition, his hands tightened their grip again. There was a funny taste in his mouth, too, a sour and salty taste in a dry, parched mouth, and no matter how often he swallowed, or drank from the sun-warmed pitcher at his side, the taste and the dryness remained. He could no more exorcise them than he could that twisting, cramping ball that was knotting up his insides, just above the solar plexus, or the queer, uncontrollable tremor that gripped his right leg from time to time.

Lieutenant Andy Stevens was afraid. He had never been in action before, but it wasn't that. This wasn't the first time he had been afraid. He had been afraid all his life, ever since he could remember: and he could remember a long way back, even to his early prep-school days when his famous father, Sir Cedric Stevens, the most celebrated explorer and mountaineer of his time, had thrown him bodily into the swimming pool at home, telling him that this was the only way he could learn to swim. He could remember still how he had fought and spluttered his way to the side of the pool, panic-stricken and desperate, his nose and mouth blocked with water, the pit of his stomach knotted and constricted in that nameless, terrifying ache he was to come to know so well: how his father and two elder brothers, big and jovial and nerveless like Sir Cedric himself, had wiped the tears of mirth from their eyes and pushed him in again. . . .

His father and brothers. . . . It had been like that all through his school-days. Together, the three of them had made his life thoroughly miserable. Tough, hearty, open-air types who worshipped at the shrine of athleticism and physical fitness, they could not understand how anyone could fail to revel in diving from a five-metre springboard or setting a hunter at a five-barred gate or climbing the crags of the Peak district or sailing a boat in a storm. All these things they had made him do and often he had failed in the doing, and neither his father nor his brothers could ever have understood how he had come to dread those violent sports in which they excelled, for they were not cruel men, nor even unkind, but simply stupid. And so to the simple physical fear he sometimes and naturally felt was added the fear of failure, the fear that he was bound to fail in whatever he had to do next, the fear of the inevitable mockery and ridicule: and because he had been a sensitive boy and feared the ridicule above all else, he had come to fear these things that provoked the ridicule. Finally, he had come to fear fear itself, and it was in a desperate attempt to overcome this double fear that he had devoted himself—this in his late teens—to crag and mountain climbing: in this he had ultimately become so proficient, developed such a reputation, that father and brothers had come to treat him with respect and as an equal, and the ridicule had ceased. But the fear had not ceased; rather it had grown by what it fed on, and often, on a particularly difficult climb, he had all but fallen to his death, powerless in the grip of sheer, unreasoning terror. But this terror he had always sought, successfully so far, to conceal. As now. He was trying to overcome, to conceal that fear now. He was afraid of failing—in what he wasn't quite sure—of not measuring up to expectation: he was afraid of being afraid: and he was desperately afraid, above all things, of being seen, of being known to be afraid. . . .

The startling, incredible blue of the Ægean; the soft, hazy silhouette of the Anatolian mountains against the washed-out cerulean of the sky; the heart-catching, magical blending of the blues and violets and purples and indigoes of the sun-soaked islands drifting lazily by, almost on the beam now; the iridescent rippling of the water fanned by the gentle, scent-laden breeze newly sprung from the south-east; the peaceful scene on deck, the reassuring, interminable thump-thump, thump-thump of the old Kelvin engine. . . . All was peace and quiet and contentment and warmth and languor, and it seemed impossible that anyone could be afraid. The world and the war were very far away that afternoon.

Or perhaps, after all, the war wasn't so far away. There were occasional pin-pricks—and constant reminders. Twice a German Arado seaplane had circled curiously overhead, and a Savoia and Fiat, flying in company, had altered course, dipped to have a look at them and flown off, apparently satisfied: Italian planes, these, and probably based on Rhodes, they were almost certainly piloted by Germans who had rounded up their erstwhile Rhodian allies and put them in prison camps after the surrender of the Italian Government. In the morning they had passed within half a mile of a big German caique—it flew the German flag and bristled with mounted machine-guns and a two-pounder far up in the bows; and in the early afternoon a high-speed German launch had roared by so closely that their caique had rolled wickedly in the wash of its passing: Mallory and Andrea had shaken their fists and cursed loudly and fluently at the grinning sailors on deck. But there had been no attempts to molest or detain them: neither British nor German hesitated at any time to violate the neutrality of Turkish territorial waters, but by the strange quixotry of a tacit gentlemen's agreement hostilities between passing vessels and planes were almost unknown. Like the envoys of warring countries in a neutral capital, their behaviour ranged from the impeccably and frigidly polite to a very pointed unawareness of one another's existence.

These, then, were the pin-pricks—the visitations and bygoings, harmless though they were, of the ships and planes of the enemy. The other reminders that this was no peace but an illusion, an ephemeral and a frangible thing, were more permanent. Slowly the minute hands of their watches circled, and every tick took them nearer to that great wall of cliff, barely eight hours away, that had to be climbed somehow: and almost dead ahead now, and less than fifty miles distant, they could see the grim, jagged peaks of Navarone topping the shimmering horizon and reaching up darkly against the sapphired sky, desolate and remote and strangely threatening.

* * *

At half-past two in the afternoon the engine stopped. There had been no warning coughs or splutters or missed strokes. One moment the regular, reassuring thump-thump: the next, sudden, completely unexpected silence, oppressive and foreboding in its absoluteness.

Mallory was the first to reach the engine hatch.

"What's up, Brown?" His voice was sharp with anxiety. "Engine broken down?"

"Not quite, sir." Brown was still bent over the engine, his voice muffled. "I shut it off just now." He straightened his back, hoisted himself wearily through the hatchway, sat on deck with his feet dangling, sucking in great draughts of fresh air. Beneath the heavy tan his face was very pale.

Mallory looked at him closely.

"You look as if you had the fright of your life."

"Not that." Brown shook his head. "For the past two-three hours I've been slowly poisoned down that ruddy hole. Only now I realise it." He passed a hand across his brow and groaned. "Top of my blinkin' head just about lifting off, sir. Carbon monoxide ain't a very healthy thing."

"Exhaust leak?"

"Aye. But it's more than a leak now." He pointed down at the engine. "See that stand-pipe supporting that big iron ball above the engine—the water-cooler? That pipe's as thin as paper, must have been leaking above the bottom flange for hours. Blew out a bloody great hole a minute ago. Sparks, smoke and flames six inches long. Had to shut the damned thing off at once, sir."

Mallory nodded in slow understanding.

"And now what? Can you repair it, Brown?"

"Not a chance, sir." The shake of the head was very definite. "Would have to be brazed or welded. But there's a spare down there among the scrap. Rusted to hell and about as shaky as the one that's on. . . . I'll have a go, sir."

"I'll give him a hand," Miller volunteered.

"Thanks, Corporal. How long, Brown, do you think?"

"Lord only knows, sir. Two hours, maybe four. Most of the nuts and bolts are locked solid with rust: have to shear or saw 'em—and then hunt for others."

Mallory said nothing. He turned away heavily, brought up beside Stevens who had abandoned the wheelhouse and was now bent over the sail locker. He looked up questioningly as Mallory approached.

Mallory nodded. "Just get them out and up. Maybe four hours, Brown says. Andrea and I will do our landlubberly best to help."

Two hours later, with the engine still out of commission, they were well outside territorial waters, closing on a big island some eight miles away to the W.N.W. The wind, warm and oppressive now, had backed to a darkening and thundery east, and with only a lug and a jib—all the sails they had found—bent to the foremast, they could make no way at all into it. Mallory had decided to make for the island—the chances of being observed there were far less than in the open sea. Anxiously he looked at his watch then stared back moodily at the receding safety of the Turkish shore. Then he stiffened, peered closely at the dark line of sea, land and sky that lay to the east.

"Andrea! Do you see——"

"I see it, Captain." Andrea was at his shoulder. "Caique. Three miles.

Coming straight towards us,'' he added softly.

"Coming straight towards us,'' Mallory acquiesced. "Tell Miller and Brown. Have them come here.''

Mallory wasted no time when they were all assembled.

"We're going to be stopped and investigated,'' he said quickly. "Unless I'm much mistaken, it's that big caique that passed us this morning. Heaven only knows how, but they've been tipped off and they're going to be as suspicious as hell. This'll be no kid-glove, hands-in-the-pockets inspection. They'll be armed to the teeth and hunting trouble. There's going to be no half-measures. Let's be quite clear about that. Either they go under or we do: we can't possibly survive an inspection—not with all the gear *we've* got aboard. And,'' he added softly, "we're not going to dump that gear.'' Rapidly he explained his plans. Stevens, leaning out from the wheelhouse window, felt the old sick ache in his stomach, felt the blood leaving his face. He was glad of the protection of the wheelhouse that hid the lower part of his body: that old familiar tremor in his leg was back again. Even his voice was unsteady.

"But, sir—sir——''

"Yes, yes, what is it, Stevens?'' Even in his hurry Mallory paused at the sight of the pale, set face, the bloodless nails clenched over the sill of the window.

"You—you can't do *that,* sir!'' The voice burred harshly under the sharp edge of strain. For a moment his mouth worked soundlessly, then he rushed on. "It's massacre, sir, it's—it's just murder!''

"Shut up, kid!'' Miller growled.

"That'll do, Corporal!'' Mallory said sharply. He looked at the American for a long moment then turned to Stevens, his eyes cold. "Lieutenant, the whole concept of directing a successful war is aimed at placing your enemy at a disadvantage, at *not* giving him an even chance. We kill them or they kill us. They go under or we do—and a thousand men on Kheros. It's just as simple as that, Lieutenant. It's not even a question of conscience.''

For several seconds Stevens stared at Mallory in complete silence. He was vaguely aware that everyone was looking at him. In that instant he hated Mallory, could have killed him. He hated him because—suddenly he was aware that he hated him only for the remorseless logic of what he said. He stared down at his clenched hands. Mallory, the idol of every young mountaineer and cragsman in pre-war England, whose fantastic climbing exploits had made world headlines, in '38 and '39: Mallory, who had twice been baulked by the most atrocious ill-fortune from surprising Rommel in his desert headquarters: Mallory, who had three times refused promotion in order to stay with his beloved Cretans who worshipped him the other side of idolatry. Confusedly these thoughts tumbled through his mind and he looked up slowly, looked at the lean, sunburnt face, the sensitive, chiselled mouth, the heavy, dark eyebrows bar-straight over the lined brown eyes that could be so cold or so compassionate, and suddenly he felt ashamed, knew that Captain Mallory lay beyond both his understanding and his judgment.

"I am very sorry, sir.'' He smiled faintly. "As Corporal Miller would say, I was talking out of turn.'' He looked aft at the caique arrowing up from the south-east. Again he felt the sick fear, but his voice was steady enough as he spoke. "I won't let you down, sir.''

"Good enough. I never thought you would.'' Mallory smiled in turn, looked at Miller and Brown. "Get the stuff ready and lay it out, will you? Casual, easy and keep it hidden. They'll have the glasses on you.''

He turned away, walked for'ard. Andrea followed him.

"You were very hard on the young man." It was neither criticism nor reproach—merely statement of fact.

"I know." Mallory shrugged. "I didn't like it either. . . . I had to do it."

"I think you had," Andrea said slowly. "Yes, I think you had. But it was hard. . . . Do you think they'll use the big gun in the bows to stop us?"

"Might—they haven't turned back after us unless they're pretty sure we're up to something fishy. But the warning shot across the bows—they don't go in for that Captain Teach stuff normally."

Andrea wrinkled his brows.

"Captain Teach?"

"Never mind." Mallory smiled. "Time we were taking up position now. Remember, wait for me. You won't have any trouble in hearing my signal," he finished dryly.

The creaming bow-wave died away to a gentle ripple, the throb of the heavy diesel muted to a distant murmur as the German boat slid alongside, barely six feet away. From where he sat on a fish-box on the port of the fo'c'sle, industriously sewing a button on to the old coat lying on the deck between his legs, Mallory could see six men, all dressed in the uniform of the regular German Navy—one crouched behind a belted Spandau mounted on its tripod just aft of the two-pounder, three others bunched amidships each armed with an automatic machine carbine—Schmeissers, he thought— the captain, a hard, cold-faced young lieutenant with the Iron Cross on his tunic, looking out the open door of the wheelhouse and, finally, a curious head peering over the edge of the engine-room hatch. From where he sat, Mallory couldn't see the poop-deck—the intermittent ballooning of the lug-sail in the uncertain wind blocked his vision; but from the restricted fore-and-aft lateral sweep of the Spandau, hungrily traversing only the for'ard half of their own caique, he was reasonably sure that there was another machine-gunner similarly engaged on the German's poop.

The hard-faced, young lieutenant—a real product of the Hitler Jugend that one, Mallory thought—leaned out of the wheelhouse, cupped his hand to his mouth.

"Lower your sails!" he shouted.

Mallory stiffened, froze to immobility. The needle had jammed hard into the palm of his hand, but he didn't even notice it. The lieutenant had spoken in English! Stevens was so young, so inexperienced. He'll fall for it, Mallory thought with a sudden sick certainty, he's bound to fall for it.

But Stevens didn't fall for it. He opened the door, leaned out, cupped his hand to his ear and gazed vacantly up to the sky, his mouth wide open. It was so perfect an imitation of dull-witted failure to catch or comprehend a shouted message that it was almost a caricature. Mallory could have hugged him. Not in his actions alone, but in his dark, shabby clothes and hair as blackly counterfeit as Miller's, Stevens was the slow, suspicious island fisherman to the life.

"Eh?" he bawled.

"Lower your sails! We are coming aboard!" English again, Mallory noted; a persistent fellow this.

Stevens stared at him blankly, looked round helplessly at Andrea and Mallory: their faces registered a lack of comprehension as convincing as his own. He shrugged his shoulders in despair.

"I am sorry, I do not understand German," he shouted. "Can you not speak my language?" Stevens's Greek was perfect, fluent and idiomatic. It was also the Greek of Attica, not of the islands; but Mallory felt sure that the lieutenant wouldn't know the difference.

He didn't. He shook his head in exasperation, called in slow, halting Greek: "Stop your boat at once. We are coming aboard."

"Stop my boat!" The indignation was so genuine, the accompanying flood of furious oaths so authentic, that even the lieutenant was momentarily taken back. "And why should I stop my boat for you, you—you——"

"You have ten seconds," the lieutenant interrupted. He was on balance again, cold, precise. "Then we will shoot."

Stevens gestured in admission of defeat and turned to Andrea and Mallory.

"Our conquerors have spoken," he said bitterly. "Lower the sails."

Quickly they loosened the sheets from the cleats at the foot of the mast. Mallory pulled the jib down, gathered the sail in his arms and squatted sullenly on the deck—he knew a dozen hostile eyes were watching him—close by the fish box. The sail covering his knees and the old coat, his forearms on his thighs, he sat with head bowed and hands dangling between his knees, the picture of heart-struck dejection. The lug-sail, weighted by the boom at the top, came down with a rush. Andrea stepped over it, walked a couple of uncertain paces aft, then stopped, huge hands hanging emptily by his sides.

A sudden deepening in the muted throbbing of the diesel, a spin of the wheel and the big German caique was rubbing alongside. Quickly, but carefully enough to keep out of the line of fire of the mounted Spandaus—there was a second clearly visible now on the poop—the three men armed with the Schmeissers leapt aboard. Immediately one ran forward, whirled round level with the foremast, his automatic carbine circling gently to cover all of the crew. All except Mallory—and he was leaving Mallory in the safe hands of the Spandau gunner in the bows. Detachedly, Mallory admired the precision, the timing, the clockwork inevitability of an old routine.

He raised his head, look around him with a slow, peasant indifference. Casey Brown was squatting on the deck abreast the engine-room, working on the big ball-silencer on top of the hatch-cover. Dusty Miller, two paces farther for'ard and with his brows furrowed in concentration, was laboriously cutting a section of metal from a little tin box, presumably to help in the engine repairs. He was holding the wire-cutting pliers in his left hand—and Miller, Mallory knew, was right-handed. Neither Stevens nor Andrea had moved. The man beside the foremast still stood there, eyes unwinking. The other two were walking slowly aft, had just passed Andrea, their carriage relaxed and easy, the bearing of men who know they have everything so completely under control that even the idea of trouble is ridiculous.

Carefully, coldly and precisely, at point-blank range and through the folds of both coat and sail, Mallory shot the Spandau machine-gunner through the heart, swung the still chattering Bren round and saw the guard by the mast crumple and die, half his chest torn away by the tearing slugs of the machine-gun. But the dead man was still on his feet, still had not hit the deck, when four things happened simultaneously. Casey Brown had had his hand on Miller's silenced automatic, lying concealed beneath the ball-silencer, for over a minute. Now he squeezed the trigger four times, for he wanted to mak' siccar; the after machine-gunner leaned forward tiredly over his tripod, lifeless fingers locked on the firing-guard. Miller crimped the three-second chemical fuse with the pliers, lobbed the tin box into the enemy engine-room, Stevens spun the armed stick-grenade into the opposite wheelhouse and Andrea, his great arms reaching out with all the speed and precision of striking cobras, swept the Schmeisser gunners' heads together with sickening force. And then all five men had hurled themselves to the deck and the German caique was erupting in a roar of flame and smoke and flying debris: gradually the echoes faded away over the sea and there was left only the whining stammer of the Spandau, emptying itself uselessly skyward; and then the belt jammed and the Ægean was as silent as ever, more silent than it had ever been.

Slowly, painfully, dazed by the sheer physical shock and the ear-shattering proximity of the twin explosions, Mallory pushed himself off the wooden deck and stood shakily on his feet. His first conscious reaction was that of surprise, incredulity almost: the concussive blast of a grenade and a couple of lashed blocks of T.N.T., even at such close range, was far beyond anything he had expected.

The German boat was sinking, sinking fast. Miller's home-made bomb must have torn the bottom out of the engine-room. She was heavily on fire amidships, and for one dismayed instant Mallory had an apprehensive vision of towering black columns of smoke and enemy reconnaissance planes. But only for an instant: timbers and planking, tinder-dry and resinous, were burning furiously with hardly a trace of smoke, and the flaming, crumbling deck was already canted over sharply to port: she would be gone in seconds. His eyes wandered to the shattered skeleton of the wheelhouse, and he caught his breath suddenly when he saw the lieutenant impaled on the splintered wreck of the wheel, a ghastly, mangled caricature of what had once been a human being, decapitated and wholly horrible: vaguely, some part of Mallory's mind registered the harsh sound of retching, violent and convulsive, coming from the wheelhouse, and he knew Stevens must have seen it too. From deep within the sinking caique came the muffled roar of rupturing fuel tanks: a flame-veined gout of oily black smoke erupted from the engine-room and the caique miraculously struggled back on even keel, her gunwales almost awash, and then the hissing waters had overflowed and overcome the decks and the twisting flames, and the caique was gone, her slender masts sliding vertically down and vanishing in a turbulent welter of creaming foam and oil-filmed bubbles. And now the Ægean was calm and peaceful again, as placid as if the caique had never been, and almost as empty: a few charred planks and an inverted helmet drifted lazily on the surface of the shimmering sea.

With a conscious effort of will, Mallory turned slowly to look to his own ship and his own men. Brown and Miller were on their feet, staring down in fascination at where the caique had been, Stevens was standing at the wheelhouse door. He, too, was unhurt, but his face was ashen: during the brief action he had been a man above himself, but the aftermath, the brief glimpse he'd had of the dead lieutenant had hit him badly. Andrea, bleeding from a gash on the cheek, was looking down at the two Schmeisser gunners lying at his feet. His face was expressionless. For a long moment Mallory looked at him, looked in slow understanding.

"Dead?" he asked quietly.

Andrea inclined his head.

"Yes." His voice was heavy. "I hit them too hard."

Mallory turned away. Of all the men he had ever known, Andrea, he thought, had the most call to hate and to kill his enemies. And kill them he did, with a ruthless efficiency appalling in its single-mindedness and thoroughness of execution. But he rarely killed without regret, without the most bitter self-condemnation, for he did not believe that the lives of his fellow-men were his to take. A destroyer of his fellow-man, he loved his fellow-man above all things. A simple man, a good man, a killer with a kindly heart, he was for ever troubled by his conscience, ill at ease with his inner self. But over and above the wonderings and the reproaches, he was informed by an honesty of thought, by a clear-sighted wisdom which sprang from and transcended his innate simplicity. Andrea killed neither for revenge, nor from hate, nor nationalism, nor for the sake of any of the other "isms" which self-seekers and fools and knaves employ as beguilement to the battlefield and justification for the slaughter of millions too young and too unknowing to comprehend the dreadful futility of it all. Andrea killed simply that better men might live.

"Anybody else hurt?" Mallory's voice was deliberately brisk, cheerful. "Nobody? Good! Right, let's get under way as fast as possible. The farther and the faster we leave this place behind, the better for all of us." He looked at his watch. "Almost four o'clock—time for our routine check with Cairo. Just leave that scrapyard of yours for a couple of minutes, Chief. See if you can pick them up." He looked at the sky to the east, a sky now purply livid and threatening, and shook his head. "Could be that the weather forecast might be worth hearing."

It was. Reception was very poor—Brown blamed the violent static on the dark, convoluted thunderheads steadily creeping up astern, now overspreading almost half the sky—but adequate. Adequate enough to hear information they had never expected to hear, information that left them silenced, eyes stilled in troubled speculation. The tiny loudspeaker boomed and faded, boomed and faded, against the scratchy background of static.

"Rhubarb calling Pimpernel! Rhubarb calling Pimpernel!" These were the respective code names for Cairo and Mallory. "Are you receiving me?"

Brown tapped an acknowledgment. The speaker boomed again.

"Rhubarb calling Pimpernel. Now X minus one. Repeat, X minus one." Mallory drew in his breath sharply. X—dawn on Saturday—had been the assumed date for the German attack on Kheros. It must have been advanced by one day—and Jensen was not the man to speak without certain knowledge. Friday, dawn—just over three days.

"Send 'X minus one understood,' " Mallory said quietly.

"Forecast, East Anglia," the impersonal voice went on: the Northern Sporades, Mallory knew. "Severe electrical storms probable this evening, with heavy rainfall. Visibility poor. Temperature falling, continuing to fall next twenty-four hours. Winds east to south-east, force six, locally eight, moderating early tomorrow."

Mallory turned away, ducked under the billowing lug-sail, walked slowly aft. What a set-up, he thought, what a bloody mess. Three days to go, engine u.s. and a first-class storm building up. He thought briefly, hopefully, of Squadron Leader Torrance's low opinion of the backroom boys of the Met. Office, but the hope was never really born. It couldn't be, not unless he was blind. The steep-piled buttresses of the thunderheads towered up darkly terrifying, now almost directly above.

"Looks pretty bad, huh?" The slow nasal drawl came from immediately behind him. There was something oddly reassuring about that measured voice, about the steadiness of the washed-out blue of the eyes enmeshed in a spider's web of fine wrinkles.

"It's not so good," Mallory admitted.

"What's all this force eight business, boss?"

"A wind scale," Mallory explained. "If you're in a boat this size and you're good and tired of life, you can't beat a force eight wind."

Miller nodded dolefully.

"I knew it. I might have known. And me swearing they'd never get me on a gawddamned boat again.'' He brooded a while, sighed, slid his legs over the engine-room hatchway, jerked his thumb in the direction of the nearest island, now less than three miles away. "That doesn't look so hot, either.''

"Not from here,'' Mallory agreed. "But the chart shows a creek with a right-angle bend. It'll break the sea and the wind.''

"Inhabited?''

"Probably.''

"Germans?''

"Probably.''

Miller shook his head in despair and descended to help Brown. Forty minutes later, in the semi-darkness of the overcast evening and in torrential rain, lance-straight and strangely chill, the anchor of the caique rattled down between the green walls of the forest, a dank and dripping forest, hostile in its silent indifference.

4

MONDAY EVENING
1700–2330

"BRILLIANT!'' SAID Mallory bitterly. "Ruddy well brilliant! 'Come into my parlour, said the spider to the fly.' '' He swore in chagrin and exasperated disgust, eased aside the edge of the tarpaulin that covered the for'ard hatchway, peered out through the slackening curtain of rain and took a second and longer look at the rocky bluff that elbowed out into the bend of the creek, shutting them off from the sea. There was no difficulty in seeing now, none at all: the drenching cloudburst had yielded to a gentle drizzle, and grey and white cloud streamers, shredding in the lifting wind, had already pursued the blackly towering cumulonimbus over the far horizon. In a clear band of sky far to the west, the sinking, flame-red sun was balanced on the rim of the sea. From the shadowed waters of the creek it was invisible, but its presence unmistakable from the gold-shot gauze of the falling rain, high above their heads.

The same golden rays highlighted the crumbling old watchtower on the very point of the cliff, a hundred feet above the river. They burnished its fine-grained white Parian marble, mellowed it to a delicate rose: they gleamed on the glittering steel, the evil mouths of the Spandau machine-guns reaching out from the slotted embrasures in the massive walls, illumined the hooked cross of the swastika on the flag that streamed out stiffly from the staff above the parapet. Solid even in its decay, impregnable in its position, commanding in its lofty outlook, the tower completely dominated both waterborne approaches, from the sea and, upriver, down the narrow, winding channel that lay between the moored caique and the foot of the cliff.

Slowly, reluctantly almost, Mallory turned away and gently lowered the tarpaulin. His face was grim as he turned round to Andrea and Stevens, ill-defined shadows in the twilit gloom of the cabin.

"Brilliant!'' he repeated. "Sheer genius. Mastermind Mallory. Probably the only bloody creek within a hundred miles—and in a hundred islands—

with a German guard post on it. And of course I had to go and pick it. Let's have another look at that chart, will you, Stevens?''

Stevens passed it across, watched Mallory study it in the pale light filtering in under the tarpaulin, leaned back against the bulkhead and drew heavily on his cigarette. It tasted foul, stale and acrid, but the tobacco was fresh enough, he knew. The old, sick fear was back again, as strongly as ever. He looked at the great bulk of Andrea across from him, felt an illogical resentment towards him for having spotted the emplacement a few minutes ago. They'll have cannon up there, he thought dully, they're bound to have cannon—couldn't control the creek otherwise. He gripped his thigh fiercely, just above the knee, but the tremor lay too deep to be controlled: he blessed the merciful darkness of the tiny cabin. But his voice was casual enough as he spoke.

''You're wasting your time, sir, looking at that chart and blaming yourself. This is the only possible anchorage within hours of sailing time from here. With that wind there was nowhere else we could have gone.''

''Exactly. That's just it.'' Mallory folded the chart, handed it back. ''There was nowhere else we could have gone. There was nowhere else anyone could have gone. Must be a very popular port in a storm, this—a fact which must have become apparent to the Germans a long, long time ago. That's why I should have known they were almost bound to have a post here. However, spilt milk, as you say.'' He raised his voice. ''Chief!''

''Hallo!'' Brown's muffled voice carried faintly from the depths of the engine-room.

''How's it going?''

''Not too bad, sir. Assembling it now.''

Mallory nodded in relief.

''How long?'' he called. ''An hour?''

''Aye, easy, sir.''

''An hour.'' Again Mallory glanced through the tarpaulin, looked back at Andrea and Stevens. ''Just about right. We'll leave in an hour. Dark enough to give us some protection from our friends up top, but enough light left to navigate our way out of this damned corkscrew of a channel.''

''Do you think they'll try to stop us, sir?'' Stevens voice was just too casual, too matter of fact. He was pretty sure Mallory would notice.

''It's unlikely they'll line the banks and give us three hearty cheers,'' Mallory said dryly. ''How many men do you reckon they'll have up there, Andrea?''

''I've seen two moving around,'' Andrea said thoughtfully. ''Maybe three or four altogether, Captain. A small post. The Germans don't waste men on these.''

''I think you're about right,'' Mallory agreed. ''Most of them'll be in the garrison in the village—about seven miles from here, according to the chart, and due west. It's not likely——''

He broke off sharply, stiffened in rigid attention. Again the call came, louder this time, imperative in its tone. Cursing himself for his negligence in not posting a guard—such carelessness would have cost him his life in Crete—Mallory pulled the tarpaulin aside, clambered slowly on to the deck. He carried no arms, but a half-empty bottle of Moselle dangled from his left hand: as part of a plan prepared before they had left Alexandria, he'd snatched it from a locker at the foot of the tiny companionway.

He lurched convincingly across the deck, grabbed at a stay in time to save himself from falling overboard. Insolently he stared down at the figure on the bank, less than ten yards away—it hadn't mattered about a guard,

Mallory realised, for the soldier carried his automatic carbine slung over his shoulder—insolently he tilted the wine to his mouth and swallowed deeply before condescending to talk to him.

He could see the mounting anger in the lean, tanned face of the young German below him. Mallory ignored it. Slowly, an inherent contempt in the gesture, he dragged the frayed sleeve of his black jacket across his lips, looked the soldier even more slowly up and down in a minutely provocative inspection as disdainful as it was prolonged.

"Well?" he asked truculently in the slow speech of the islands. "What the hell do you want?"

Even in the deepening dusk he could see the knuckles whitening on the stock of the carbine, and for an instant Mallory thought he had gone too far. He knew he was in no danger—all noise in the engine-room had ceased, and Dusty Miller's hand was never far from his silenced automatic—but he didn't want trouble. Not just yet. Not while there were a couple of manned Spandaus in that watch-tower.

With an almost visible effort the young soldier regained his control. It needed little help from the imagination to see the draining anger, the first tentative stirrings of hesitation and bewilderment. It was the reaction Mallory had hoped for. Greeks—even half-drunken Greeks—didn't talk to their overlords like that—not unless they had an overpoweringly good reason.

"What vessel is this?" The Greek was slow and halting but passable. "Where are you bound for?"

Mallory tilted the bottle again, smacked his lips in noisy satisfaction. He held the bottle at arm's length, regarded it with a loving respect.

"One thing about you Germans," he confided loudly. "You do know how to make a fine wine. I'll wager *you* can't lay your hands on this stuff, eh? And the swill they're making up above"—the island term for the mainland—"is so full of resin that it's only good for lighting fires." He thought for a moment. "Of course, if you know the right people in the islands, they *might* let you have some ouzo. But some of us can get ouzo *and* the best Hocks *and* the best Moselles."

The soldier wrinkled his face in disgust. Like almost every fighting man he despised Quislings, even when they were on his side: in Greece they were very few indeed.

"I asked you a question," he said coldly. "What vessel, and where bound?"

"The caique *Aigion*," Mallory replied loftily. "In ballast, for Samos. Under orders," he said significantly.

"Whose orders?" the soldier demanded. Shrewdly Mallory judged the confidence as superficial only. The guard was impressed in spite of himself.

"Herr Commandant in Vathy. General Graebel," Mallory said softly. "You will have heard of the Herr General before, yes?" He was on safe ground here, Mallory knew. The reputation of Graebel, both as a paratroop commander and an iron disciplinarian, had spread far beyond these islands.

Even in the half-light Mallory could have sworn that the guard's complexion turned paler. But he was dogged enough.

"You have papers? Letters of authority?"

Mallory sighed wearily, looked over his shoulder.

"Andrea!" he bawled.

"What do you want?" Andrea's great bulk loomed through the hatchway. He had heard every word that passed, had taken his cue from Mallory: a newly-opened wine bottle was almost engulfed in one vast hand and he was scowling hugely. "Can't you see I'm busy?" he asked surlily. He stopped short at the sight of the German and scowled again, irritably. "And what does this halfling want?"

"Our passes and letters of authority from Herr General. They're down below."

Andrea disappeared, grumbling deep in his throat. A rope was thrown ashore, the stern pulled in against the sluggish current and the papers passed over. The papers—a set different from those to be used if emergency arose in Navarone—proved to be satisfactory, eminently so. Mallory would have been surprised had they been anything else. The preparation of these, even down to the photostatic facsimile of General Graebel's signature, was all in the day's work for Jensen's bureau in Cairo.

The soldier folded the papers, handed them back with a muttered word of thanks. He was only a kid, Mallory could see now—if he was more than nineteen, his looks belied him. A pleasant, open-faced kid—of a different stamp altogether from the young fanatics of the S.S. Panzer Division—and far too thin. Mallory's chief reaction was one of relief: he would have hated to have to kill a boy like this. But he had to find out all he could. He signalled to Stevens to hand him up the almost empty crate of Moselle. Jensen, he mused, had been very thorough indeed: the man had literally thought of everything. . . . Mallory gestured lazily in the direction of the old watch-tower.

"How many of you are up there?" he asked.

The boy was instantly suspicious. His face had tightened up, stilled in hostile surmise.

"Why do you want to know?" he asked stiffly.

Mallory groaned, lifted his hands in despair, turned sadly to Andrea.

"You see what it is to be one of them?" he asked in mournful complaint. "Trust nobody. Think everyone is as twisted as . . ." He broke off hurriedly, turned to the soldier again. "It's just that we don't want to have the same trouble every time we come in here," he explained. "We'll be back in Samos in a couple of days, and we've still another case of Moselle to work through. General Graebel keeps his—ah—special envoys well supplied. . . . It must be thirsty work up there in the sun. Come on, now, a bottle each. How many bottles?"

The reassuring mention that they would be back again, the equally reassuring mention of Graebel's name, plus, probably, the attraction of the offer and his comrades' reaction if he told them he had refused it, tipped the balance, overcame scruples and suspicions.

"There are only three of us," he said grudgingly.

"Three it is," Mallory said cheerfully. "We'll bring you some Hock next time we return." He tilted his own bottle. *"Prosit!"* he said, an islander proud of airing his German, and then, more proudly still, *"Auf Wiedersehen!"*

The boy murmured something in return. He stood hesitating for a moment, slightly shame-faced, then wheeled abruptly, walked off slowly along the river bank, clutching his bottles of Moselle.

"So!" Mallory said thoughtfully. "There are only three of them. That should make things easier——"

"Well done, sir!" It was Stevens who interrupted, his voice warm, his face alive with admiration. "Jolly good show!"

"Jolly good show!" Miller mimicked. He heaved his lanky length over the coaming of the engine hatchway. " 'Good' be damned! I couldn't understand a gawddamned word, but for my money that rates an Oscar. That was terrific, boss!"

"Thank you, one and all," Mallory murmured. "But I'm afraid the congratulations are a bit premature." The sudden chill in his voice struck at them, so that their eyes aligned along his pointing finger even before he went on. "Take a look," he said quietly.

The young soldier had halted suddenly about two hundred yards along the bank, looked into the forest on his left in startled surprise, then dived in among the trees. For a moment the watchers on the boat could see another soldier, talking excitedly to the boy and gesticulating in the direction of their boat, and then both were gone, lost in the gloom of the forest.

"That's torn it!" Mallory said softly. He turned away. "Right, that's enough. Back to where you were. It would look fishy if we ignored that incident altogether, but it would look a damned sight fishier if we paid too much attention to it. Don't let's appear to be holding a conference."

Miller slipped down into the engine-room with Brown, and Stevens went back to the little for'ard cabin. Mallory and Andrea remained on deck, bottles in their hands. The rain had stopped now, completely, but the wind was still rising, climbing the scale with imperceptible steadiness, beginning to bend the tops of the tallest of the pines. Temporarily the bluff was affording them almost complete protection. Mallory deliberately shut his mind to what it must be like outside. They had to put out to sea—Spandaus permitting—and that was that.

"What do you think has happened, sir?" Stevens's voice carried up from the gloom of the cabin.

"Pretty obvious, isn't it?" Mallory asked. He spoke loudly enough for all to hear. "They've been tipped off. Don't ask me how. This is the second time—and their suspicions are going to be considerably reinforced by the absence of a report from the caique that was sent to investigate us. She was carrying a wireless aerial, remember?"

"But why should they get so damned suspicious all of a sudden?" Miller asked. "It doesn't make sense to me, boss."

"Must be in radio contact with their H.Q. Or a telephone—probably a telephone. They've just been given the old tic-tac. Consternation on all sides."

"So mebbe they'll be sending a small army over from their H.Q. to deal with us," Miller said lugubriously.

Mallory shook his head definitely. His mind was working quickly and well, and he felt oddly certain, confident of himself.

"No, not a chance. Seven miles as the crow flies. Ten, maybe twelve miles over rough hill and forest tracks—and in pitch darkness. They wouldn't think of it." He waved his bottle in the direction of the watch-tower. "To-night's their big night."

"So we can expect the Spandaus to open up any minute?" Again the abnormal matter-of-factness of Stevens's voice.

Mallory shook his head a second time.

"They won't. I'm positive of that. No matter how suspicious they may be, how certain they are that we're the big bad wolf, they are going to be shaken to the core when that kid tells them we're carrying papers and letters of authority signed by General Graebel himself. For all they know, curtains for us may be the firing squad for them. Unlikely, but you get the general idea. So they're going to contact H.Q., and the commandant on a small island like this isn't going to take a chance on rubbing out a bunch of characters who may be the special envoys of the Herr General himself. So what? So he codes a message and radios it to Vathy in Samos and bites his nails off to the elbow till a message comes back saying Graebel has never heard of us and why the hell haven't we all been shot dead?'' Mallory looked at the luminous dial of his watch. "I'd say we have at least half an hour.''

"And meantime we all sit around with our little bits of paper and pencil and write out our last wills and testaments.'' Miller scowled. "No percentage in that, boss. We gotta *do* somethin'.''

Mallory grinned.

"Don't worry, Corporal, we are going to do something. We're going to hold a nice little bottle party, right here on the poop.''

The last words of their song—a shockingly corrupted Grecian version of "Lilli Marlene," and their third song in the past few minutes—died away in the evening air. Mallory doubted whether more than faint snatches of the singing would be carried to the watch-tower against the wind, but the rhythmical stamping of feet and waving of bottles were in themselves sufficient evidence of drunken musical hilarity to all but the totally blind and deaf. Mallory grinned to himself as he thought of the complete confusion and uncertainty the Germans in the tower must have been feeling then. This was not the behaviour of enemy spies, especially enemy spies who know that suspicions had been aroused and that their time was running out.

Mallory tilted the bottle to his mouth, held it there for several seconds, then set it down again, the wine untasted. He looked round slowly at the three men squatting there with him on the poop, Miller, Stevens and Brown. Andrea was not there, but he didn't have to turn his head to look for him. Andrea, he knew, was crouched in the shelter of the wheelhouse, a waterproof bag with grenades and a revolver strapped to his back.

"Right!'' Mallory said crisply. "Now's your big chance for *your* Oscar. Let's make this as convincing as we can.'' He bent forward, jabbed his finger into Miller's chest and shouted angrily at him.

Miller shouted back. For a few moments they sat there, gesticulating angrily and, to all appearances, quarrelling furiously with each other. Then Miller was on his feet, swaying in drunken imbalance as he leaned threateningly over Mallory, clenched fists ready to strike. He stood back as Mallory struggled to his feet, and in a moment they were fighting fiercely, raining apparently heavy blows on each other. Then a haymaker from the American sent Mallory reeling back to crash convincingly against the wheelhouse.

"Right, Andrea.'' He spoke quietly, without looking round. "This is it. Five seconds. Good luck.'' He scrambled to his feet, picked up a bottle by the neck and rushed at Miller, upraised arm and bludgeon swinging fiercely down. Miller dodged, swung a vicious foot, and Mallory roared in pain as his shins caught on the edge of the bulwarks. Silhouetted against the pale gleam of the creek, he stood poised for a second, arms flailing wildly, then plunged heavily, with a loud splash, into the waters of the creek.

For the next half-minute—it would take about that time for Andrea to swim under water round the next upstream corner of the creek—everything was a confusion and a bedlam of noise. Mallory trod water as he tried to pull himself aboard: Miller had seized a boathook and was trying to smash it down on his head: and the others, on their feet now, had flung their arms round Miller, trying to restrain him: finally they managed to knock him off his feet, pin him to the deck and help the dripping Mallory aboard. A minute later, after the immemorial fashion of drunken men, the two combatants had shaken hands with one another and were sitting on the engine-room hatch, arms round each other's shoulders and drinking in perfect amity from the same freshly-opened bottle of wine.

"Very nicely done," Mallory said approvingly. "Very nicely indeed. An Oscar, definitely, for Corporal Miller."

Dusty Miller said nothing. Taciturn and depressed, he looked moodily at the bottle in his hand. At last he stirred.

"I don't like it, boss," he muttered unhappily. "I don't like the set-up one little bit. You shoulda let me go with Andrea. It's three to one up there, and they're waiting and ready." He looked accusingly at Mallory. "Dammit to hell, boss, you're always telling us how desperately important this mission is!"

"I know," Mallory said quietly. "That's why I didn't send you with him. That's why none of us has gone with him. We'd only be a liability to him, get in his way." Mallory shook his head. "You don't know Andrea, Dusty." It was the first time Mallory had called him that: Miller was warmed by the unexpected familiarity, secretly pleased. "None of you know him. But I know him." He gestured towards the watch-tower, its square-cut lines in sharp silhouette against the darkening sky. "Just a big, fat, good-natured chap, always laughing and joking." Mallory paused, shook his head again, went on slowly. "He's up there now, padding through that forest like a cat, the biggest and most dangerous cat you'll ever see. Unless they offer no resistance—Andrea never kills unnecessarily—when I send him up there after these three poor bastards I'm executing them just as surely as if they were in the electric chair and I was pulling the switch."

In spite of himself Miller was impressed, profoundly so.

"Known him a long time, boss, huh?" It was half question, half statement.

"A long time. Andrea was in the Albanian war—he was in the regular army. They tell me the Italians went in terror of him—his long-range patrols against the Iulia division, the Wolves of Tuscany, did more to wreck the Italian morale in Albania than any other single factor. I've heard a good many stories about them—not from Andrea—and they're all incredible. And they're all true. But it was afterwards I met him, when we were trying to hold the Servia Pass. I was a very junior liaison lieutenant in the Anzac brigade at the time. Andrea"—he paused deliberately for effect—"Andrea was a lieutenant-colonel in the 19th Greek Motorised Division."

"A what?" Miller demanded in astonishment. Stevens and Brown were equally incredulous.

"You heard me. Lieutenant-colonel. Outranks me by a fairish bit, you might say." He smiled at them quizzically. "Puts Andrea in rather a different light, doesn't it?"

They nodded silently but said nothing. The genial, hail-fellow Andrea—a good-natured, almost simple-minded buffoon—a senior army officer. The idea had come too suddenly, was too incongruous for easy assimilation and immediate comprehension. But, gradually, it began to make sense to them. It explained many things about Andrea to them—his repose, his confidence, the unerring sureness of his lightning reactions, and, above all, the implicit faith Mallory had in him, the respect he showed for Andrea's opinions whenever he consulted him, which was frequently. Without surprise now, Miller slowly recalled that he'd never yet heard Mallory give Andrea a direct order. And Mallory never hesitated to pull his rank when necessary.

"After Servia," Mallory went on, "everything was pretty confused. Andrea had heard that Trikkala—a small country town where his wife and three daughters lived—had been flattened by the Stukas and Heinkels. He reached there all right, but there was nothing he could do. A land-mine had landed in the front garden and there wasn't even rubble left.''

Mallory paused, lit a cigarette. He stared through the drifting smoke at the fading outlines of the tower.

"The only person he found there was his brother-in-law, George. George was with us in Crete—he's still there. From George he heard for the first time of the Bulgarian atrocities in Thrace and Macedonia—and his parents lived there. So they dressed in German uniforms—you can imagine how Andrea got those—commandeered a German army truck and drove to Protosami.'' The cigarette in Mallory's hand snapped suddenly, was sent spinning over the side. Miller was vaguely surprised: emotion, or rather, emotional displays, were so completely foreign to that very tough New Zealander. But Mallory went on quietly enough.

"They arrived in the evening of the infamous Protosami massacre. George has told me how Andrea stood there, clad in his German uniform and laughing as he watched a party of nine or ten Bulgarian soldiers lash couples together and throw them into the river. The first couple in were his father and stepmother, both dead.''

"My Gawd above!'' Even Miller was shocked out of his usual equanimity. "It's just not possible——''

"You know nothing,'' Mallory interrupted impatiently. "Hundreds of Greeks in Macedonia died the same way—but usually alive when they were thrown in. Until you know how the Greeks hate the Bulgarians, you don't even begin to know what hate is. . . . Andrea shared a couple of bottles of wine with the soldiers, found out that they had killed his parents earlier in the afternoon—they had been foolish enough to resist. After dusk he followed them up to an old corrugated-iron shed where they were billeted for the night. All he had was a knife. They left a guard outside. Andrea broke his neck, went inside, locked the door and smashed the oil lamp. George doesn't know what happened except that Andrea went berserk. He was back outside in two minutes, completely sodden, his uniform soaked in blood from head to foot. There wasn't a sound, not even a groan to be heard from the hut when they left, George says.''

He paused again, but this time there was no interruption, nothing said. Stevens shivered, drew his shabby jacket closer round his shoulders: the air seemed to have become suddenly chill. Mallory lit another cigarette, smiled faintly at Miller, nodded towards the watch-tower.

"See what I mean by saying we'd only be a liability to Andrea up there?''

"Yeah. Yeah, I guess I do,'' Miller admitted. "I had no idea, I had no idea. . . . Not all of them, boss! He couldn't have killed——''

"He did,'' Mallory interrupted flatly. "After that he formed his own band, made life hell for the Bulgarian outposts in Thrace. At one time there was almost an entire division chasing him through the Rhodope mountains. Finally he was betrayed and captured, and he, George and four others were shipped to Stavros—they were to go on to Salonika for trial. They overpowered their guards—Andrea got loose among them on deck at night— and sailed the boat to Turkey. The Turks tried to intern him—they might as well have tried to intern an earthquake. Finally he arrived in Palestine, tried to join the Greek Commando Battalion that was being formed in the Middle East—mainly veterans of the Albanian campaign, like himself.'' Mallory laughed mirthlessly. "He was arrested as a deserter. He was released eventually, but there was no place for him in the new Greek Army. But Jensen's bureau heard about him, knew he was a natural for Subversive Operations. . . . And so we went to Crete together.''

Five minutes passed, perhaps ten, but nobody broke the silence. Occasionally, for the benefit of any watchers, they went through the motions of drinking; but even the half-light was fading now and Mallory knew they could only be half-seen blurs, shadowy and indistinct, from the heights of the watch-tower. The caique was beginning to rock in the surge from the open sea round the bluff. The tall, reaching pines, black now as midnight cypress and looming impossibly high against the star-dusted cloud wrack that scudded palely overhead, were closing in on them from either side, sombre, watchful and vaguely threatening, the wind moaning in lost and mournful requiem through their swaying topmost branches. A bad night, an eerie and an ominous night, pregnant with that indefinable foreboding that reaches down and touches the well-springs of the nameless fears, the dim and haunting memories of a million years ago, the ancient racial superstitions of mankind: a night that sloughed off the tissue veneer of civilisation and the shivering man complains that someone is walking over his grave.

Suddenly, incongruously, the spell was shattered and Andrea's cheerful hail from the bank had them all on their feet in a moment. They heard his booming laugh and even the forests seemed to shrink back in defeat. Without waiting for the stern to be pulled in, he plunged into the creek, reached the caique in half a dozen powerful strokes and hoisted himself easily aboard. Grinning down from his great height, he shook himself like some shaggy mastiff and reached out a hand for a convenient wine bottle.

"No need to ask how things went, eh?" Mallory asked smiling.

"None at all. It was just too easy. They were only boys, and they never even saw me." Andrea took another long swig from the bottle and grinned in sheer delight. "And I didn't lay a finger on them," he went on triumphantly. "Well, maybe a couple of little taps. They were all looking down here, staring out over the parapet when I arrived. Held them up, took their guns off them and locked them in a cellar. And then I bent their Spandaus—just a little bit."

This is it, Mallory thought dully, this is the end. This is the finish of everything, the strivings, the hopes, the fears, the loves and laughter of each one of us. This is what it all comes to. This is the end, the end for us, the end for a thousand boys on Kheros. In unconscious futility his hand came up, slowly wiped lips salt from the spray bulleting off the wind-flattened wave-tops, then lifted farther to shade bloodshot eyes that peered out hopelessly into the storm-filled darkness ahead. For a moment the dullness lifted, and an almost intolerable bitterness welled through his mind. All gone, everything—everything except the guns of Navarone. The guns of Navarone. They would live on, they were indestructible. Damn them, damn them, damn them! Dear God, the blind waste, the terrible uselessness of it all!

The caique was dying, coming apart at the seams. She was literally being pounded to death, being shaken apart by the constant battering shocks of wind and sea. Time and time again the poop-deck dipped beneath the foam-streaked cauldron at the stern, the fo'c'sle rearing crazily into the air, dripping forefoot showing clear; then the plummetting drop, the shotgun, shuddering impact as broad-beamed bows crashed vertically down into the cliff-walled trough beyond, an explosive collision that threw so unendurable a strain on the ancient timbers and planks and gradually tore them apart.

It had been bad enough when they'd cleared the creek just as darkness fell, and plunged and wallowed their way through a quartering sea on a northward course for Navarone. Steering the unwieldy old caique had become difficult in the extreme: with the seas fine on the starboard quarter she had yawed wildly and unpredictably through a fifty degree arc, but at least her seams had been tight then; the rolling waves overtaking her in regular formation and the wind settled and steady somewhere east of south. But now all that was gone. With half a dozen planks sprung from the stem-post and working loose from the apron, and leaking heavily through the stuffing-gland of the propeller shaft, she was making water far faster than the ancient, vertical hand-pump could cope with: the wind-truncated seas were heavier, but broken and confused, sweeping down on them now from this quarter, now from that: and the wind itself, redoubled in its shrieking violence, veered and backed insanely from south-west to south-east. Just then it was steady from the south, driving the unmanageable craft blindly on to the closing iron cliffs of Navarone, cliffs that loomed invisibly ahead, somewhere in that all-encompassing darkness.

Momentarily Mallory straightened, tried to ease the agony of the pincers that were clawing into the muscles of the small of his back. For over two hours now he had been bending and straightening, bending and straightening, lifting a thousand buckets that Dusty Miller filled interminably from the well of the hold. God only knew how Miller felt. If anything, he had the harder job of the two and he had been violently and almost continuously seasick for hours on end. He looked ghastly, and he must have been feeling like death itself: the sustained effort, the sheer iron willpower to drive himself on in that condition reached beyond the limits of understanding. Mallory shook his head wonderingly. "My God, but he's tough, that Yank." Unbidden, the words framed themselves in his mind, and he shook his head in anger, vaguely conscious of the complete inadequacy of the words.

Fighting for his breath, he looked aft to see how the others were faring. Casey Brown, of course, he couldn't see. Bent double in the cramped confines of the engine-room, he, too, was constantly sick and suffering a blinding headache from the oil fumes and exhaust gases still filtering from the replacement stand-pipe, neither of which could find any escape in the unventilated engine-room: but, crouched over the engine, he had not once left his post since they had cleared the mouth of the creek, had nursed the straining, ancient Kelvin along with the loving care, the exquisite skill of a man born into a long and proud tradition of engineering. That engine had only to falter once, to break down for the time in which a man might draw a deep breath, and the end would be as immediate as it was violent. Their steerage way, their lives, depended entirely on the continuous thrust of that screw, the laboured thudding of that rusted old two-cylinder. It was the heart of the boat, and when the heart stopped beating the boat died too, slewed broadside on and foundering in the waiting chasms between the waves.

For'ard of the engine-room, straddle-legged and braced against the corner pillar of the splintered skeleton that was all that remained of the wheelhouse, Andrea laboured unceasingly at the pump, never once lifting his head, oblivious of the crazy lurching of the deck of the caique, oblivious, too, of the biting wind and stinging, sleet-cold spray that numbed bare arms and moulded the sodden shirt to the hunched and massive shoulders. Ceaselessly, tirelessly, his arm thrust up and down, up and down, with the metronomic regularity of a piston. He had been there for close on three hours now, and he looked as if he could go on for ever. Mallory, who had yielded him the pump in complete exhaustion after less than twenty minutes' cruel labour, wondered if there was any limit to the man's endurance.

He wondered, too, about Stevens. For four endless hours now Andy

Stevens had fought and overcome a wheel that leapt and struggled in his hands as if possessed of a convulsive life and will of its own—the will to wrench itself out of exhausted hands and turn them into the troughs: he had done a superb job, Mallory thought, had handled the clumsy craft magnificently. He peered at him closely, but the spray lashed viciously across his eyes and blinded him with tears. All he could gather was a vague impression of a tightly-set mouth, sleepless, sunken eyes and little patches of skin unnaturally pale against the mask of blood that covered almost the entire face from hairline to throat. The twisting, towering comber that had stove in the planks of the wheelhouse and driven in the windows with such savage force had been completely unexpected: Stevens hadn't had a chance. The cut above the right temple was particularly bad, ugly and deep: the blood still pulsed over the ragged edge of the wound, dripped monotonously into the water that sloshed and gurgled about the floor of the wheelhouse.

Sick to his heart, Mallory turned away, reached down for another bucket of water. What a crew, he thought to himself, what a really terrific bunch of—of . . . He sought for words to describe them, even to himself, but he knew his mind was far too tired. It didn't matter anyway, for there were no words for men like that, nothing that could do them justice.

He could almost taste the bitterness in his mouth, the bitterness that washed in waves through his exhausted mind. God, how wrong it was, how terribly unfair! Why did such men have to die, he wondered savagely, why did they have to die so uselessly. Or maybe it wasn't necessary to justify dying, even dying ingloriously empty of achievement. Could one not die for intangibles, for the abstract and the ideal? What had the martyrs at the stake achieved? Or what was the old tag—*dulce et decorum est pro patria mori*. If one lives well, what matter how one dies. Unconsciously his lips tightened in quick revulsion and he thought of Jensen's remarks about the High Commands playing who's-the-king-of-the-castle. Well, they were right bang in the middle of their playground now, just a few more pawns sliding into the limbo. Not that it mattered—they had thousands more left to play with.

For the first time Mallory thought of himself. Not with bitterness of self-pity or regret that it was all over. He thought of himself only as the leader of this party, his responsibility for the present situation. It's my fault, he told himself over and over again, it's all my fault. I brought them here, I made them come. Even while one part of his mind was telling him that he'd had no option, that his hand had been forced, that if they had remained in the creek they would have been wiped out long before the dawn, irrationally he still blamed himself the more. Shackleton, of all the men that ever lived, maybe Ernest Shackleton could have helped them now. But not Keith Mallory. There was nothing he could do, no more than the others were doing, and they were just waiting for the end. But he was the leader, he thought dully, he should be planning something, he should be doing something. . . . But there was nothing he could do. There was nothing anyone on God's earth could do. The sense of guilt, of utter inadequacy, settled and deepened with every shudder of the ancient timbers.

He dropped his bucket, grabbed for the security of the mast as a heavy wave swept over the deck, the breaking foam quicksilver in its seething phosphorescence. The waters swirled hungrily round his legs and feet, but he ignored them, stared out into the darkness. The darkness—that was the devil of it. The old caique rolled and pitched and staggered and plunged, but as if disembodied, in a vacuum. They could see nothing—not where the last wave had gone, nor where the next was coming from. A sea invisible and strangely remote, doubly frightening in its palpable immediacy.

Mallory stared down into the hold, was vaguely conscious of the white blur of Miller's face: he had swallowed some seawater and was retching painfully, salt water laced with blood. But Mallory ignored it, involuntarily: all his mind was concentrated elsewhere, trying to reduce some fleeting impression, as vague as it had been evanescent, to a coherent realisation. It seemed desperately urgent that he should do so. Then another and still heavier wave broke over the side and all at once he had it.

The wind! The wind had dropped away, was lessening with every second that passed. Even as he stood there, arms locked round the mast as the second wave fought to carry him away, he remembered how often in the high hills at home he had stood at the foot of a precipice as an onrushing wind, seeking the path of least resistance, had curved and lifted up the sheer face, leaving him standing in a pocket of relative immunity. It was a common enough mountaineering phenomenon. And these two freak waves—the surging backwash! The significance struck at him like a blow. The cliffs! They were on the cliffs of Navarone!

With a hoarse, wordless cry of warning, reckless of his own safety, he flung himself aft, dived full length through the swirling waters for the engine-room hatchway.

"Full astern!" he shouted. The startled white smudge that was Casey Brown's face twisted up to his. "For God's sake, man, full astern! We're heading for the cliffs!"

He scrambled to his feet, reached the wheelhouse in two strides, hand pawing frantically for the flare pocket.

"The cliffs, Stevens! We're almost on them! Andrea—Miller's still down below!"

He flicked a glance at Stevens, caught the slow nod of the set, blood-masked face, followed the line of sight of the expressionless eyes, saw the whitely phosphorescent line ahead, irregular but almost continuous, blooming and fading, blooming and fading, as the pounding seas smashed against and fell back from cliffs still invisible in the darkness. Desperately his hands fumbled with the flare.

And then, abruptly, it was gone, hissing and spluttering along the near-horizontal trajectory of its flight. For a moment, Mallory thought it had gone out, and he clenched his fists in impotent bitterness. Then it smashed against the rock face, fell back on to a ledge about a dozen feet above the water, and lay there smoking and intermittently burning in the driving rain, in the heavy spray that cascaded from the booming breakers.

The light was feeble, but it was enough. The cliffs were barely fifty yards away, black and wetly shining in the fitful radiance of the flare—a flare that illuminated a vertical circle of less than five yards in radius, and left the cliff below the ledge shrouded in the treacherous dark. And straight ahead, twenty, maybe fifteen yards from the shore, stretched the evil length of a reef, gaptoothed and needle-pointed, vanishing at either end into the outer darkness.

"Can you take her through?" he yelled at Stevens.

"God knows! I'll try!" He shouted something else about "steerage way," but Mallory was already half-way to the for'ard cabin. As always in an emergency, his mind was racing ahead with that abnormal sureness and clarity of thought for which he could never afterwards account.

Grasping spikes, mallet and a wire-cored rope, he was back on deck in seconds. He stood stock still, rooted in an almost intolerable tension as he saw the towering, jagged rock bearing down upon them, fine on the starboard bow, a rock that reached halfway up the wheelhouse. It struck the boat with a crash that sent him to his knees, rasped and grated along half the length of the buckled, splintered gunwales: and then the caique had rolled over to port and she was through, Stevens frantically spinning the wheel and shouting for full astern.

Mallory's breath escaped in a long, heavy sigh of relief—he had been quite unaware that he had stopped breathing—and he hurriedly looped the coil of rope round his neck and under his left shoulder and stuck spikes and hammer in his belt. The caique was slewing heavily round now, port side to, plunging and corkscrewing violently as she began to fall broadside into the troughs of the waves, waves shorter and steeper than ever under the double thrust of the wind and the waves and the backwash recoiling from the cliffs: but she was still in the grip of the sea and her own momentum, and the distance was closing with frightening speed. It's a chance I have to take, Mallory repeated to himself over and over again; it's a chance I have to take. But that little ledge, remote and just inaccessible, was fate's last refinement of cruelty, the salt in the wound of extinction, and he knew in his heart of hearts that it wasn't a chance at all, but just a suicidal gesture. And then Andrea had heaved the last of the fenders—worn truck tyres—out board, and was towering above him, grinning down hugely into his face: and suddenly Mallory wasn't so sure any more.

"The ledge?" Andrea's vast, reassuring hand was on his shoulder.

Mallory nodded, knees bent in readiness, feet braced on the plunging, slippery deck.

"Jump for it," Andrea boomed. "Then keep your legs stiff."

There was no time for any more. The caique was swinging in broadside to, teetering on the crest of a wave, as high up the cliff as she would ever be, and Mallory knew it was now or never. His hands swung back behind his body, his knees bent farther, and then, in one convulsive leap he had flung himself upwards, fingers scrabbling on the wet rock of the cliff, then hooking over the rim of the ledge. For an instant he hung there at the length of his arms, unable to move, wincing as he heard the foremast crash against the ledge and snap in two, then his fingers left the ledge without their own volition, and he was almost half-way over, propelled by one gigantic heave from below.

He was not up yet. He was held only by the buckle of his belt, caught on the edge of the rock, a buckle now dragged up to his breastbone by the weight of his body. But he did not paw frantically for a handhold, or wriggle his body or flail his legs in the air—and any of these actions would have sent him crashing down again. At last, and once again, he was a man utterly at home in his own element. The greatest rock climber of his time, men called him, and this was what he had been born for.

Slowly, methodically, he felt the surface of the ledge, and almost at once he discovered a crack running back from the face. It would have been better had it been parallel to the face—and more than the width of a matchstick. But it was enough for Mallory. With infinite care he eased the hammer and a couple of spikes from his belt, worked a spike into the crack to obtain a minimal purchase, slid the other in some inches nearer, hooked his left wrist round the first, held the second spike with the fingers of the same hand and brought up the hammer in his free hand. Fifteen seconds later he was standing on the ledge.

Working quickly and surely, catlike in his balance on the slippery, shelving rock, he hammered a spike into the face of the cliff, securely and at a downward angle, about three feet above the ledge, dropped a clove hitch over the top and kicked the rest of the coil over the ledge. Then, and only then, he turned round and looked below him.

Less than a minute had passed since the caique had struck, but already she was a broken-masted, splintered shambles, sides caving in and visibly disintegrating as he watched. Every seven or eight seconds a giant comber would pick her up and fling her bodily against the cliff, the heavy truck tyres taking up only a fraction of the impact that followed, the sickening, rending crash that reduced the gunwales to matchwood, holed and split the sides and cracked the oaken timbers: and then she would roll clear, port side showing, the hungry sea pouring in through the torn and ruptured planking.

Three men were standing by what was left of the wheelhouse. *Three* men—suddenly, he realised that Casey Brown was missing, realised, too, that the engine was still running, its clamour rising and falling then rising again, at irregular intervals. Brown was edging the caique backwards and forwards along the cliff, keeping her as nearly as humanly possible in the same position, for he knew their lives depended on Mallory—and on himself. "The fool!" Mallory swore. "The crazy fool!"

The caique surged back in a receding trough, steadied, then swept in against the cliff again, heeling over so wildly that the roof of the wheelhouse smashed and telescoped against the wall of the cliff. The impact was so fierce, the shock so sudden, that Stevens lost both hand-grip and footing and was catapulted into the rock face, upflung arms raised for protection. For a moment he hung there, as if pinned against the wall, then fell back into the sea, limbs and head relaxed, lifeless in his limp quiescence. He should have died then, drowned under the hammer-blows of the sea or crushed by the next battering-ram collision of caique and cliff. He should have died and he would have died but for the great arm that hooked down and plucked him out of the water like a limp and sodden rag doll and heaved him inboard a bare second before the next bludgeoning impact of the boat against the rock would have crushed the life out of him.

"Come on, for God's sake!" Mallory shouted desperately. "She'll be gone in a minute! The rope—use the rope!" He saw Andrea and Miller exchange a few quick words, saw them shake and pummel Stevens and stand him on his feet, dazed and retching sea-water, but conscious. Andrea was speaking in his ear, emphasising something and guiding the rope into his hands, and then the caique was swinging in again, Stevens automatically shortening his grip on the rope. A tremendous boost from below by Andrea, Mallory's long arm reaching out and Stevens was on the ledge, sitting with his back to the cliff and hanging on to the spike, dazed still and shaking a muzzy head, but safe.

"You're next, Miller!" Mallory called. "Hurry up, man—jump for it!"

Miller looked at him and Mallory could have sworn that he was grinning. Instead of taking the rope from Andrea, he ran for'ard to the cabin.

"Just a minute, boss!" he bawled. "I've forgotten my toothbrush."

He reappeared in a few seconds, but without the toothbrush. He was carrying the big, green box of explosives, and before Mallory had appreciated what was happening the box, all fifty pounds of it, was curving up into the air, upthrust by the Greek's tireless arms. Automatically Mallory's hands reached for and caught it. He over-balanced, stumbled and toppled forward, still clutching the box, then brought up with a jerk. Stevens, still clutching the spike, was on his feet now, free hand hooked in Mallory's belt: he was shivering violently, with cold and exhaustion and an oddly fear-laced excitement. But, like Mallory, he was a hillman at home again.

Mallory was just straightening up when the waterproofed radio set came soaring up. He caught it, placed it down, looked over the side.

"Leave that bloody stuff alone!" he shouted furiously. "Get up here yourselves—now!"

Two coils of rope landed on the ledge beside him, then the first of the
rucksacks with the food and clothing. He was vaguely aware that Stevens
was trying to stack the equipment in some sort of order.

"Do you hear me?" Mallory roared. "Get up here at once! That's an
order. The boat's sinking, you bloody idiots!"

The caique *was* sinking. She was filling up quickly and Casey Brown had
abandoned the flooded Kelvin. But she was a far steadier platform now,
rolling through a much shorter arc, less violent in her soggy, yielding collisions with the cliff wall. For a moment Mallory thought the sea was dropping away, then he realised that the tons of water in the caique's hold had
drastically lowered her centre of gravity, were acting as a counter-balancing
weight.

Miller cupped a hand to his ear. Even in the near darkness of the sinking
flare his face had an oddly greenish pallor.

"Can't hear a word you say, boss. Besides, she ain't sinkin' yet." Once
again he disappeared into the for'ard cabin.

Within thirty seconds, with all five men working furiously, the remainder
of the equipment was on the ledge. The caique was down by the stern, the
poop-deck covered and water pouring down the engine-room hatchway as
Brown struggled up the rope, the fo'c'sle awash as Miller grabbed the rope
and started after him, and as Andrea reached up and swung in against the
cliff his legs dangled over an empty sea. The caique had foundered, completely gone from sight: no drifting flotsam, not even an air bubble marked
where she had so lately been.

The ledge was narrow, not three feet wide at its broadest, tapering off into
the gloom on either side. Worse still, apart from the few square feet where
Stevens had piled the gear, it shelved sharply outwards, the rock underfoot
treacherous and slippery. Backs to the wall, Andrea and Miller had to stand
on their heels, hands outspread and palms inward against the cliff, pressing
in to it as closely as possible to maintain their balance. But in less than a
minute Mallory had another two spikes hammered in about twenty inches
above the ledge, ten feet apart and joined with a rope, a secure lifeline for
all of them.

Wearily Miller slid down to a sitting position, leaned his chest in heartfelt
thankfulness against the safe barrier of the rope. He fumbled in his breast
pocket, produced a pack of cigarettes and handed them round, oblivious to
the rain that soaked them in an instant. He was soaking wet from the waist
downwards and both his knees had been badly bruised against the cliff wall:
he was bitterly cold, drenched by heavy rain and the sheets of spray that
broke continually over the ledge: the sharp edge of the rock bit cruelly into
the calves of his legs, the tight rope constricted his breathing and he was
still ashen-faced and exhausted from long hours of labour and seasickness:
but when he spoke, it was with a voice of utter sincerity.

"My Gawd!" he said reverently. "Ain't this wonderful!"

5

MONDAY NIGHT
0100–0200

NINETY MINUTES later Mallory wedged himself into a natural rock chimney
on the cliff face, drove in a spike beneath his feet and tried to rest his

aching, exhausted body. Two minutes' rest, he told himself, only two minutes while Andrea comes up: the rope was quivering and he could just hear, above the shrieking of the wind that fought to pluck him off the cliff face, the metallic scraping as Andrea's boots struggled for a foothold on that wicked overhang immediately beneath him, the overhang that had all but defeated him, the obstacle that he had impossibly overcome only at the expense of torn hands and body completely spent, of shoulder muscles afire with agony and breath that rasped in great gulping inhalations into his starving lungs. Deliberately he forced his mind away from the pains that racked his body, from its insistent demands for rest, and listened again to the ringing of steel against rock, louder this time, carrying clearly even in the gale. . . . He would have to tell Andrea to be more careful on the remaining twenty feet or so that separated them from the top.

At least, Mallory thought wryly, no one would have to tell him to be quiet. He couldn't have made any noise with his feet if he'd tried—not with only a pair of torn socks as cover for his bruised and bleeding feet. He'd hardly covered the first twenty feet of the climb when he'd discovered that his climbing boots were quite useless, had robbed his feet of all sensitivity, the ability to locate and engage the tiny toe-holds which afforded the only sources of purchase. He had removed them with great difficulty, tied them to his belt by the laces—and lost them, had them torn off, when forcing his way under a projecting spur of rock.

The climb itself had been a nightmare, a brutal, gasping agony in the wind and the rain and the darkness, an agony that had eventually dulled the danger and masked the suicidal risks in climbing that sheer unknown face, an interminable agony of hanging on by fingertips and toes, of driving in a hundred spikes, of securing ropes then inching on again up into the darkness. It was a climb such as he had not ever made before, such as he knew he would not ever make again, for this was insanity. It was a climb that had extended him to the utmost of his great skill, his courage and his strength, and then far beyond that again, and he had not known that such reserves, such limitless resources, lay within him or any man. Nor did he know the well-spring, the source of that power that had driven him to where he was, within easy climbing reach of the top. The challenge to a mountaineer, personal danger, pride in the fact that he was probably the only man in southern Europe who could have made the climb, even the sure knowledge that time was running out for the men on Kheros—it was none of these things, he knew that: in the last twenty minutes it had taken him to negotiate that overhang beneath his feet his mind had been drained of all thought and all emotion, and he had climbed only as a machine.

Hand over hand up the rope, easily, powerfully, Andrea hauled himself over the smoothly swelling convexity of the overhang, legs dangling in midair. He was festooned with heavy coils of rope, girdled with spikes that protruded from his belt at every angle and lent him the incongruous appearance of a comic-opera Corsican bandit. Quickly he hauled himself up beside Mallory, wedged himself in the chimney and mopped his sweating forehead. As always, he was grinning hugely.

Mallory looked at him, smiled back. Andrea, he reflected, had no right to be there. It was Stevens's place, but Stevens had still been suffering from shock, had lost much blood: besides, it required a first-class climber to bring up the rear, to coil up the ropes as he came and to remove the spikes—there must be no trace left of the ascent: or so Mallory had told him, and Stevens had reluctantly agreed, although the hurt in his face had been easy to see. More than ever now Mallory was glad he had resisted the quiet plea in

Stevens's face: Stevens was undoubtedly a fine climber, but what Mallory had required that night was not another mountaineer but a human ladder. Time and time again during the ascent he had stood on Andrea's back, his shoulders, his upturned palm and once—for at least ten seconds and while he was still wearing his steel-shod boots—on his head. And not once had Andrea protested or stumbled or yielded an inch. The man was indestructible, as tough and enduring as the rock on which he stood. Since dusk had fallen that evening, Andrea had laboured unceasingly, done enough work to kill two ordinary men, and, looking at him then, Mallory realised, almost with despair, that even now he didn't look particularly tired.

Mallory gestured at the rock chimney, then upwards at its shadowy mouth limned in blurred rectangular outline against the pale glimmer of the sky. He leant forward, mouth close to Andrea's ear.

"Twenty feet, Andrea," he said softly. His breath was still coming in painful gasps. "It'll be no bother—it's fissured on my side and the chances are that it goes up to the top."

Andrea looked up the chimney speculatively, nodded in silence.

"Better with your boots off," Mallory went on. "And any spikes we use we'll work in by hand."

"Even on a night like this—high winds and rain, cold and black as a pig's inside—and on a cliff like this?" There was neither doubt nor question in Andrea's voice: rather it was acquiescence, unspoken confirmation of an unspoken thought. They had been so long together, had reached such a depth of understanding that words between them were largely superfluous.

Mallory nodded, waited while Andrea worked home a spike, looped his ropes over it and secured what was left of the long ball of twine that stretched four hundred feet below to the ledge where the others waited. Andrea then removed boots and spikes, fastened them to the ropes, eased the slender, double-edged throwing knife in its leather shoulder scabbard, looked across at Mallory and nodded in turn.

The first ten feet were easy. Palms and back against one side of the chimney and stocking-soled feet against the other, Mallory jack-knifed his way upwards until the widening sheer of the walls defeated him. Legs braced against the far wall, he worked in a spike as far up as he could reach, grasped it with both hands, dropped his legs across and found a toe-hold in the crevice. Two minutes later his hands hooked over the crumbling edge of the precipice.

Noiselessly and with an infinite caution he fingered aside earth and grass and tiny pebbles until his hands were locked on the solid rock itself, bent his knee to seek lodgement for the final toe-hold, then eased a wary head above the cliff-top, a movement imperceptible in its slow-motion, millimetric stealth. He stopped moving altogether as soon as his eyes had cleared the level of the cliff, stared out into the unfamiliar darkness, his whole being, the entire field of consciousness, concentrated into his eyes and his ears. Illogically, and for the first time in all that terrifying ascent, he became acutely aware of his own danger and helplessness, and he cursed himself for his folly in not borrowing Miller's silenced automatic.

The darkness below the high horizon of the lifting hills beyond was just one degree less than absolute: shapes and angles, heights and depressions were resolving themselves in nebulous silhouette, contours and shadowy profiles emerging reluctantly from the darkness, a darkness suddenly no longer vague and unfamiliar but disturbingly reminiscent in what it revealed, clamouring for recognition. And then abruptly, almost with a sense of shock, Mallory had it. The cliff-top before his eyes was exactly as Monsieur Vlachos had drawn and described it—the narrow, bare strip of ground running parallel to the cliff, the jumble of huge boulders behind them and then, beyond these, the steep scree-strewn lower slopes of the mountains. The first break they'd had yet, Mallory thought exultantly—but what a break! The sketchiest navigation but the most incredible luck, right bang on the nose of the target—the highest point of the highest, most precipitous cliffs in Navarone: the one place where the Germans never mounted a guard, because the climb was impossible! Mallory felt the relief, the high elation wash through him in waves. Jubilantly he straightened his leg, hoisted himself half-way over the edge, arms straight, palms down on the top of the cliff. And then he froze into immobility, petrified as the solid rock beneath his hands, his heart thudding painfully in his throat.

One of the boulders had moved. Seven, maybe eight yards away, a shadow had gradually straightened, detached itself stealthily from the surrounding rock, was advancing slowly towards the edge of the cliff. And then the shadow was no longer "it." There could be no mistake now—the long jack-boots, the long greatcoat beneath the waterproof cape, the close-fitting helmet were all too familiar. Damn Vlachos! Damn Jensen! Damn all the know-alls who sat at home, the pundits of Intelligence who gave a man wrong information and sent him out to die. And in the same instant Mallory damned himself for his own carelessness, for he had been expecting this all along.

For the first two or three seconds Mallory had lain rigid and unmoving, temporarily paralysed in mind and body: already the guard had advanced four or five steps, carbine held in readiness before him, head turned sideways as he listened into the high, thin whine of the wind and the deep and distant booming of the surf below, trying to isolate the sound that had aroused his suspicions. But now the first shock was over and Mallory's mind was working again. To go up on to the top of the cliff would be suicidal: ten to one the guard would hear him scrambling over the edge and shoot him out of hand: and if he did get up he had neither the weapons nor, after the exhausting climb, the strength to tackle an armed, fresh man. He would have to go back down. But he would have to slide down slowly, an inch at a time. At night, Mallory knew, side vision is even more acute than direct, and the guard might catch a sudden movement out of the corner of his eye. And then he would only have to turn his head and that would be the end: even in that darkness, Mallory realised, there could be no mistaking the bulk of his silhouette against the sharp line of the edge of the cliff.

Gradually, every movement as smooth and controlled as possible, every soft and soundless breath a silent prayer, Mallory slipped gradually back over the edge of the cliff. Still the guard advanced, making for a point about five yards to Mallory's left, but still he looked away, his ear turned into the wind. And then Mallory was down, only his finger-tips over the top, and Andrea's great bulk was beside him, his mouth to his ear.

"What is it? Somebody there?"

"A sentry," Mallory whispered back. His arms were beginning to ache from the strain. "He's heard something and he's looking for us."

Suddenly he shrank away from Andrea, pressed himself as closely as possible to the face of the cliff, was vaguely aware of Andrea doing the same thing. A beam of light, hurtful and dazzling to eyes so long accustomed to the dark, had suddenly stabbed out at the angle over the edge of the cliff, was moving slowly along towards them. The German had his torch out, was methodically examining the rim of the cliff. From the angle of the beam, Mallory judged that he was walking along about a couple of feet from the edge. On that wild and gusty night he was taking no chances on the crumbly, treacherous top-soil of the cliff: even more likely, he was taking no chances on a pair of sudden hands reaching out for his ankles and jerking him to a mangled death on the rocks and reefs four hundred feet below.

Slowly, inexorably, the beam approached. Even at that slant, it was bound to catch them. With a sudden sick certainty Mallory realised that the German wasn't just suspicious: he *knew* there was someone there, and he wouldn't stop looking until he found them. And there was nothing they could do, just nothing at all. . . . Then Andrea's head was close to his again.

"A stone," Andrea whispered. "Over there, behind him."

Cautiously at first, then frantically, Mallory pawed the cliff-top with his right hand. Earth, only earth, grass roots and tiny pebbles—there was nothing even half the size of a marble. And then Andrea was thrusting something against him and his hand closed over the metallic smoothness of a spike: even in that moment of desperate urgency, with the slender, searching beam only feet away, Mallory was conscious of a sudden, brief anger with himself—he had still a couple of spikes stuck in his belt and had forgotten all about them.

His arm swung back, jerked convulsively forward, sent the spike spinning away into the darkness. One second passed, then another, he knew he had missed, the beam was only inches from Andrea's shoulders, and then the metallic clatter of the spike striking a boulder fell upon his ear like a benison. The beam wavered for a second, stabbed out aimlessly into the darkness and then whipped round, probing into the boulders to the left. And then the sentry was running towards them, slipping and stumbling in his haste, the barrel of the carbine gleaming in the light of the torch held clamped to it. He'd gone less than ten yards when Andrea was over the top of the cliff like a great, black cat, was padding noiselessly across the ground to the shelter of the nearest boulder. Wraith-like, he flitted in behind it and was gone, a shadow long among shadows.

The sentry was about twenty yards away now, the beam of his torch darting fearfully from boulder to boulder when Andrea struck the haft of his knife against a rock, twice. The sentry whirled round, torch shining along the line of the boulders, then started to run clumsily back again, the skirts of the greatcoat fluttering grotesquely in the wind. The torch was swinging wildly now, and Mallory caught a glimpse of a white, straining face, wide-eyed and fearful, incongruously at variance with the gladiatorial strength of the steel helmet above. God only knew, Mallory thought, what wild and panic-stricken thoughts were passing through his confused mind: noises from the cliff-top, metallic sound from either side among the boulders, the long, eerie vigil, afraid and companionless, on a deserted cliff edge on a dark and tempest-filled night in a hostile land—suddenly Mallory felt a deep stab of compassion for this man, a man like himself, someone's well-beloved husband or brother or son who was only doing a dirty and dangerous job as best he could and because he was told to, compassion for his loneliness and his anxieties and his fears, for the sure knowledge that before he had drawn breath another three times he would be dead. . . . Slowly, gauging his time and distance, Mallory raised his head.

"Help!" he shouted. "Help me! I'm falling!"

The soldier checked in mid-stride and spun round, less than five feet from the rock that hid Andrea. For a second the beam of his torch waved wildly around, then settled on Mallory's head. For another moment he stood stock still, then the carbine in his right hand swung up, the left hand reaching down for the barrel. Then he grunted once, a violent and convulsive exhalation of breath, and the thud of the hilt of Andrea's knife striking home against the ribs carried clearly to Mallory's ears, even against the wind. . . .

Mallory stared down at the dead man, at Andrea's impassive face as he wiped the blade of his knife on the greatcoat, rose slowly to his feet, sighed and slid the knife back in its scabbard.

"So, my Keith!" Andrea reserved the punctilious "Captain" for company only. "This is why our young lieutenant eats his heart out down below."

"That is why," Mallory acknowledged. "I knew it—or I almost knew it. So did you. Too many coincidences—the German caique investigating, the trouble at the watch-tower—and now this." Mallory swore, softly and bitterly. "This is the end for our friend Captain Briggs of Castelrosso. He'll be cashiered within the month. Jensen will make certain of that."

Andrea nodded.

"He let Nicolai go?"

"Who else could have known that we were to have landed here, tipped off everyone all along the line?" Mallory paused, dismissed the thought, caught Andrea by the arm. "The Germans are thorough. Even although they must know it's almost an impossibility to land on a night like this, they'll have a dozen sentries scattered along the cliffs." Unconsciously Mallory had lowered his voice. "But they wouldn't depend on one man to cope with five. So——"

"Signals," Andrea finished for him. "They must have some way of letting the others know. Perhaps flares——"

"No, not that," Mallory disagreed. "Give their position away. Telephone. It has to be that. Remember how they were in Crete—miles of field telephone wire all over the shop?"

Andrea nodded, picked up the dead man's torch, hooded it in his huge hand and started searching. He returned in less than a minute.

"Telephone it is," he announced softly. "Over there, under the rocks."

"Nothing we can do about it," Mallory said. "If it does ring, I'll have to answer or they'll come hot-footing along. I only hope to heaven they haven't got a bloody password. It would be just like them."

He turned away, stopped suddenly.

"But someone's got to come sometime—a relief, sergeant of the guard, something like that. Probably he's supposed to make an hourly report. Someone's bound to come—and come soon. My God, Andrea, we'll have to make it fast!"

"And this poor devil?" Andrea gestured to the huddled shadow at his feet.

"Over the side with him." Mallory grimaced in distaste. "Won't make any difference to the poor bastard now, and we can't leave any traces. The odds are they'll think he's gone over the edge—this top soil's as crumbly and treacherous as hell. . . . You might see if he's any papers on him—never know how useful they might be."

"Not half as useful as these boots on his feet." Andrea waved a large hand towards the scree-strewn slopes. "You are not going to walk very far there in your stocking soles."

Five minutes later Mallory tugged three times on the string that stretched down into the darkness below. Three answering tugs came from the ledge, and then the cord vanished rapidly down over the edge of the overhang, drawing with it the long, steel-cored rope that Mallory paid out from the coil on the top of the cliff.

The box of explosives was the first of the gear to come up. The weighted rope plummetted straight down from the point of the overhang, and padded though the box was on every side with lashed rucksacks and sleeping-bags it still crashed terrifyingly against the cliff on the inner arc of every wind-driven swing of the pendulum. But there was no time for finesse, to wait for the diminishing swing of the pendulum after each tug. Securely anchored to a rope that stretched around the base of a great boulder, Andrea leaned far out over the edge of the precipice and reeled in the seventy-pound dead-weight as another man would a trout. In less than three minutes the ammu-nition box lay beside him on the cliff-top: five minutes later the firing generator, guns and pistols, wrapped in a couple of other sleeping-bags and their lightweight, reversible tent—white on one side, brown and green cam-ouflage on the other—lay beside the explosives.

A third time the rope went down into the rain and the darkness, a third time the tireless Andrea hauled it in, hand over hand. Mallory was behind him, coiling in the slack of the rope, when he heard Andrea's sudden exclamation: two quick strides and he was at the edge of the cliff, his hand on the big Greek's arm.

"What's up, Andrea? Why have you stopped——?"

He broke off, peered through the gloom at the rope in Andrea's hand, saw that it was being held between only finger and thumb. Twice Andrea jerked the rope up a foot or two, let it fall again: the weightless rope swayed wildly in the wind.

"Gone?" Mallory asked quietly.

Andrea nodded without speaking.

"Broken?" Mallory was incredulous. "A wire-cored rope?"

"I don't think so." Quickly Andrea reeled in the remaining forty feet. The twine was still attached to the same place, about a fathom from the end. The rope was intact.

"Somebody tied a knot." Just for a moment the giant's voice sounded tired. "They didn't tie it too well."

Mallory made to speak, then flung up an instinctive arm as a great, forked tongue of flame streaked between the cliff-top and unseen clouds above. Their cringing eyes were still screwed tight shut, their nostrils full of the acrid, sulphurous smell of burning, when the first volley of thunder crashed in Titan fury almost directly overhead, a deafening artillery to mock the pitful efforts of embattled man, doubly terrifying in the total darkness that followed that searing flash. Gradually the echoes pealed and faded inland in diminishing reverberation, were lost among the valleys of the hills.

"My God!" Mallory murmured. "That was close. We'd better make it fast, Andrea—this cliff is liable to be lit up like a fairground any minute. . . . What was in that last load you were bringing up?" He didn't really have to ask—he himself had arranged for the breaking up of the equipment into three separate loads before he'd left the ledge. It wasn't even that he sus-pected his tired mind of playing tricks on him; but it was tired enough, too tired, to probe the hidden compulsion, the nameless hope that prompted him to grasp at nameless straws that didn't even exist.

"The food," Andrea said gently. "*All* the food, the stove, the fuel—and the compasses."

For five, perhaps ten seconds, Mallory stood motionless. One half of his mind, conscious of the urgency, the desperate need for haste, was jabbing him mercilessly: the other half held him momentarily in a vast irresolution, an irresolution of coldness and numbness that came not from the lashing wind and sleety rain but from his own mind, from the bleak and comfortless imaginings of lost wanderings on that harsh and hostile island, with neither food nor fire. . . . And then Andrea's great hand was on his shoulder, and he was laughing softly.

"Just so much less to carry, my Keith. Think how grateful our tired friend Corporal Miller is going to be. . . . This is only a little thing."

"Yes," Mallory said. "Yes, of course. A little thing." He turned abruptly, tugged the cord, watched the rope disappear over the edge.

Fifteen minutes later, in drenching, torrential rain, a great, sheeting downpour almost constantly illuminated by the jagged, branching stilettos of the forked lightning, Casey Brown's bedraggled head came into view over the edge of the cliff. The thunder, too, emptily cavernous in that flat and explosive intensity of sound that lies at the heart of a thunderstorm, was almost continuous: but in the brief intervals, Casey's voice, rich in his native Clydeside accent, carried clearly. He was expressing himself fluently in basic Anglo-Saxon, and with cause. He had had the assistance of two ropes on the way up—the one stretched from spike to spike and the one used for raising supplies, which Andrea had kept pulling in as he made the ascent. Casey Brown had secured the end of this round his waist with a bowline, but the bowline had proved to be nothing of the sort but a slip-knot, and Andrea's enthusiastic help had almost cut him in half. He was still sitting on the cliff-top, exhausted head between his knees, the radio still strapped to his back, when two tugs on Andrea's rope announced that Dusty Miller was on his way up.

Another quarter of an hour elapsed, an interminable fifteen minutes when, in the lulls between the thunderclaps, every slightest sound was an approaching enemy patrol, before Miller materialised slowly out of the darkness, half-way down the rock chimney. He was climbing steadily and methodically, then checked abruptly at the cliff-top, groping hands pawing uncertainly on the top-soil of the cliff. Puzzled, Mallory bent down, peered into the lean face: both the eyes were clamped tightly shut.

"Relax, Corporal," Mallory advised kindly. "You have arrived."

Dusty Miller slowly opened his eyes, peered round at the edge of the cliff, shuddered and crawled quickly on hands and knees to the shelter of the nearest boulders. Mallory followed and looked down at him curiously.

"What was the idea of closing your eyes coming over the top?"

"I did not," Miller protested.

Mallory said nothing.

"I closed them at the bottom," Miller explained wearily. "I opened them at the top."

Mallory looked at him incredulously.

"What! All the way?"

"It's like I told you, boss," Miller complained. "Back in Castelrosso. When I cross a street and step up on to the sidewalk I gotta hang on to the nearest lamp-post. More or less." He broke off, looked at Andrea leaning far out over the side of the cliff, and shivered again. "Brother! Oh, brother! Was I scared!"

Fear. Terror. Panic. Do the thing you fear and the death of fear is certain. Do the thing you fear and the death of fear is certain. Once, twice, a hundred times, Andy Stevens repeated the words to himself, over and over again, like a litany. A psychiatrist had told him that once and he'd read it a dozen times since. Do the thing you fear and the death of fear is certain. The mind is a limited thing, they had said. It can only hold one thought at a time, one

impulse to action. Say to yourself, I am brave, I am overcoming this fear,
this stupid, unreasoning panic which has no origin except in my own mind,
and because the mind *can* only hold one thought at a time, and because
thinking and feeling are one, then you *will* be brave, you *will* overcome and
the fear will vanish like a shadow in the night. And so Andy Stevens said
these things to himself, and the shadows only lengthened and deepened,
lengthened and deepened, and the icy claws of fear dug ever more savagely
into his dull exhausted mind, into his twisted, knotted stomach.

His stomach. That knotted ball of jangled, writhing nerve-ends beneath
the solar plexus. No one could ever know how it was, how it felt, except
those whose shredded minds were going, collapsing into complete and final
breakdown. The waves of panic and nausea and faintness that flooded up
through a suffocating throat to a mind dark and spent and sinewless, a mind
fighting with woollen fingers to cling on to the edge of the abyss, a tired
and lacerated mind, only momentarily in control, wildly rejecting the clamorous demands of a nervous system which had already taken far too much
that he should let go, open the torn fingers that were clenched so tightly
round the rope. It was just that easy. "Rest after toil, port after stormy
seas." What was that famous stanza of Spenser's? Sobbing aloud, Stevens
wrenched out another spike, sent it spinning into the waiting sea three
hundred long feet below, pressed himself closely into the face and inched
his way despairingly upwards.

Fear. Fear had been at his elbow all his life, his constant companion, his
alter ego, at his elbow, or in close prospect or immediate recall. He had
become accustomed to that fear, at times almost reconciled, but the sick
agony of this night lay far beyond either tolerance or familiarity. He had
never known anything like this before, and even in his terror and confusion
he was dimly aware that the fear did not spring from the climb itself. True,
the cliff was sheer and almost vertical, and the lightning, the ice-cold rain,
the darkness and the bellowing thunder were a waking nightmare. But the
climb, technically, was simple: the rope stretched all the way to the top and
all he had to do was to follow it and dispose of the spikes as he went. He
was sick and bruised and terribly tired, his head ached abominably and he
had lost a great deal of blood: but then, more often than not, it is in the
darkness of agony and exhaustion that the spirit of man burns most brightly.

Andy Stevens was afraid because his self-respect was gone. Always,
before, that had been his sheet anchor, had tipped the balance against his
ancient enemy—the respect in which other men had held him, the respect
he had had for himself. But now these were gone, for his two greatest fears
had been realised—he was known to be afraid, he had failed his fellow-
man. Both in the fight with the German caique and when anchored above
the watch-tower in the creek, he had known that Mallory and Andrea knew.
He had never met such men before, and he had known all along that he
could never hide his secrets from such men. He should have gone up that
cliff with Mallory, but Mallory had made excuses and taken Andrea instead—Mallory *knew* he was afraid. And twice before, in Castelrosso and
when the German boat had closed in on them, he had almost failed his
friends—and to-night he had failed them terribly. He had not been thought
fit to lead the way with Mallory—and it was he, the sailor of the party, who
had made such a botch of tying that last knot, had lost all the food and the
fuel that had plummetted into the sea a bare ten feet from where he had
stood on the ledge . . . and a thousand men on Kheros were depending on
a failure so abject as himself. Sick and spent, spent in mind and body and
spirit, moaning aloud in his anguish of fear and self-loathing, and not

knowing where one finished and the other began, Andy Stevens climbed blindly on.

The sharp, high-pitched call-up buzz of the telephone cut abruptly through the darkness on the cliff-top. Mallory stiffened and half-turned, hands clenching involuntarily. Again it buzzed, the jarring stridency carrying clearly above the bass rumble of the thunder, fell silent again. And then it buzzed again and kept on buzzing, peremptory in its harsh insistence.

Mallory was half-way towards it when he checked in mid-step, turned slowly round and walked back towards Andrea. The big Greek looked at him curiously.

"You have changed your mind?"

Mallory nodded but said nothing.

"They will keep on ringing until they get an answer," Andrea murmured. "And when they get no answer, they will come. They will come quickly and soon."

"I know, I know." Mallory shrugged. "We have to take that chance—certainty rather. The question is—how long will it be before anyone turns up." Instinctively he looked both ways along the windswept cliff-top: Miller and Brown were posted one on either side about fifty yards away, lost in the darkness. "It's not worth the risk. The more I think of it, the poorer I think my chances would be of getting away with it. In matters of routine the old Hun tends to be an inflexible sort of character. There's probably a set way of answering the phone, or the sentry has to identify himself by name, or there's a password—or maybe my voice would give me away. On the other hand the sentry's gone without trace, all our gear is up and so's everyone except Stevens. In other words, we've practically made it. We've landed—and nobody knows we're here."

"Yes." Andrea nodded slowly. "Yes, you are right—and Stevens should be up in two or three minutes. It would be foolish to throw away everything we've gained." He paused, then went on quietly: "But they are going to come running." The phone stopped ringing as suddenly as it had started. "They are going to come now."

"I know. I hope to hell Stevens . . ." Mallory broke off, spun on his heel, said over his shoulder, "Keep your eye open for him, will you? I'll warn the others we're expecting company."

Mallory moved quickly along the cliff-top, keeping well away from the edge. He hobbled rather than walked—the sentry's boots were too small for him and chafed his toes cruelly. Deliberately he closed his mind to the thought of how his feet would be after a few hours' walking over rough territory in these boots: time enough for the reality, he thought grimly, without the added burden of anticipation. . . . He stopped abruptly as something hard and metallic pushed into the small of his back.

"Surrender or die!" The drawling, nasal voice was positively cheerful: after what he had been through on the caique and the cliff face, just to set foot on solid ground again was heaven enough for Dusty Miller.

"Very funny," Mallory growled. "Very funny indeed." He looked curiously at Miller. The American had removed his oil-skin cape—the rain had ceased as abruptly as it had come—to reveal a jacket and braided waistcoat even more sodden and saturated than his trousers. It didn't make sense. But there was no time for questions.

"Did you hear the phone ringing just now?" he asked.

"Was that what it was? Yeah, I heard it."

"The sentry's phone. His hourly report, or whatever it was, must have been overdue. We didn't answer it. They'll be hotfooting along any minute now, suspicious as hell and looking for trouble. Maybe your side, maybe Brown's. Can't approach any other way unless they break their necks climbing over these boulders." Mallory gestured at the shapeless jumble of rocks behind them. "So keep your eyes skinned."

"I'll do that, boss. No shootin', huh?"

"No shooting. Just get back as quickly and quietly as you can and let us know. Come back in five minutes anyway."

Mallory hurried away, retracing his steps. Andrea was stretched full length on the cliff-top, peering over the edge. He twisted his head round as Mallory approached.

"I can hear him. He's just at the overhang."

"Good." Mallory moved on without breaking step. "Tell him to hurry, please."

Ten yards farther on Mallory checked, peered into the gloom ahead. Somebody was coming along the cliff-top at a dead run, stumbling and slipping on the loose gravelly soil.

"Brown?" Mallory called softly.

"Yes, sir. It's me." Brown was up to him now, breathing heavily, pointing back in the direction he had just come. "Somebody's coming, and coming fast! Torches waving and jumping all over the place—must be running."

"How many?" Mallory asked quickly.

"Four or five at least." Brown was still gasping for breath. "Maybe more—four or five torches, anyway. You can see them for yourself." Again he pointed backwards, then blinked in puzzlement. "That's bloody funny! They're all gone." He turned back swiftly to Mallory. "But I can swear——"

"Don't worry," Mallory said grimly. "You saw them all right. I've been expecting visitors. They're getting close now and taking no chances. . . . How far away?"

"Hundred yards—not more than a hundred and fifty."

"Go and get Miller. Tell him to get back here fast."

Mallory ran back along the cliff edge and knelt beside the huge length of Andrea.

"They're coming, Andrea," he said quickly. "From the left. At least five, probably more. Two minutes at the most. Where's Stevens? Can you see him?"

"I can see him." Andrea was magnificently unperturbed. "He is just past the overhang . . ." The rest of his words were lost, drowned in a sudden, violent thunderclap, but there was no need for more. Mallory could see Stevens now, climbing up the rope, strangely old and enfeebled in action, hand over hand in paralysing slowness, half-way now between the overhang and the foot of the chimney.

"Good God!" Mallory swore. "What's the matter with him? He's going to take all day . . ." He checked himself, cupped his hands to his mouth. "Stevens! Stevens!" But there was no sign that Stevens had heard. He still kept climbing with the same unnatural over-deliberation, a robot in slow motion.

"He is very near the end," Andrea said quietly. "You see he does not even lift his head. When a climber does not lift his head, he is finished." He stirred. "I will go down for him."

"No." Mallory's hand was on his shoulder. "Stay here. I can't risk you both. . . . Yes, what is it." He was aware that Brown was back, bending over him, his breath coming in great heaving gasps.

"Hurry, sir; hurry, for God's sake!" A few brief words but he had to suck in two huge gulps of air to get them out. "They're on top of us!"

"Get back to the rocks with Miller," Mallory said urgently. "Cover us. . . . Stevens! Stevens!" But again the wind swept up the face of the cliff, carried his words away.

"Stevens! For God's sake, man! Stevens!" His voice was low-pitched, desperate, but this time some quality in it must have reached through Stevens' fog of exhaustion and touched his consciousness, for he stopped climbing and lifted his head, hand cupped to his ear.

"Some Germans coming!" Mallory called through funnelled hands, as loudly as he dared. "Get to the foot of the chimney and stay there. Don't make a sound. Understand?"

Stevens lifted his hand, gestured in tired acknowledgment, lowered his head, started to climb up again. He was going even more slowly now, his movements fumbling and clumsy.

"Do you think he understands?" Andrea was troubled.

"I think so. I don't know." Mallory stiffened and caught Andrea's arm. It was beginning to rain again, not heavily yet, and through the drizzle he'd caught sight of a hooded torch beam probing among the rocks thirty yards away to his left. "Over the edge with the rope," he whispered. "The spike at the bottom of the chimney will hold it. Come on—let's get out of here!"

Gradually, meticulous in their care not to dislodge the smallest pebble, Mallory and Andrea inched back from the edge, squirmed round and headed back for the rocks, pulling themselves along on their elbows and knees. The few yards were interminable and without even a gun in his hand Mallory felt defenceless, completely exposed. An illogical feeling, he knew, for the first beam of light to fall on them meant the end not for them but for the man who held the torch. Mallory had complete faith in Brown and Miller. . . . That wasn't important. What mattered was the complete escape from detection. Twice during the last endless few feet a wandering beam reached out towards them, the second a bare arm's length away: both times they pressed their faces into the sodden earth, lest the pale blur of their faces betray them, and lay very still. And then, all at once it seemed, they were among the rocks and safe.

In a moment Miller was beside them, a half-seen shadow against the darker dusk of the rocks around them.

"Plenty of time, plenty of time," he whispered sarcastically. "Why didn't you wait another half-hour?" He gestured to the left, where the flickering of torches, the now clearly audible murmur of guttural voices, were scarcely twenty yards away. "We'd better move farther back. They're looking for him among the rocks."

"For him or for his telephone," Mallory murmured in agreement. "You're right, anyway. Watch your guns on these rocks. Take the gear with you. . . . And if they look over and find Stevens we'll have to take the lot. No time for fancy work and to hell with the noise. Use the automatic carbines."

Andy Stevens had heard, but he had not understood. It was not that he panicked, was too terrified to understand, for he was no longer afraid. Fear is of the mind, but his mind had ceased to function, drugged by the last stages of exhaustion, crushed by the utter, damnable tiredness that held his limbs, his whole body, in leaden thrall. He did not know it, but fifty feet below he had struck his head against a spur of rock, a sharp, wicked projection that had torn his gaping temple wound open to the bone. His strength drained out with the pulsing blood.

He had heard Mallory, had heard something about the chimney he had now reached, but his mind had failed to register the meaning of the words. All that Stevens knew was that he was climbing, and that one always kept on climbing until one reached the top. That was what his father had always impressed upon him, his brothers too. You must reach the top.

He was half-way up the chimney now, resting on the spike that Mallory had driven into the fissure. He hooked his fingers in the crack, bent back his head and stared up towards the mouth of the chimney. Ten feet away, no more. He was conscious of neither surprise nor elation. It was just there: he had to reach it. He could hear voices, carrying clearly from the top. He was vaguely surprised that his friends were making no attempt to help him, that they had thrown away the rope that would have made those last few feet so easy, but he felt no bitterness, no emotion at all: perhaps they were trying to test him. What did it matter anyway—he had to reach the top.

He reached the top. Carefully, as Mallory had done before him, he pushed aside the earth and tiny pebbles, hooked his fingers over the edge, found the same toe-hold as Mallory had and levered himself upwards. He saw the flickering torches, heard the excited voices, and then for an instant the curtain of fog in his mind lifted and a last tidal wave of fear washed over him and he knew that the voices were the voices of the enemy and that they had destroyed his friends. He knew now that he was alone, that he had failed, that this was the end, one way or another, and that it had all been for nothing. And then the fog closed over him again, and there was nothing but the emptiness of it all, the emptiness and the futility, the overwhelming lassitude and despair and his body slowly sinking down the face of the cliff. And then the hooked fingers—they, too, were slipping away, opening gradually, reluctantly as the fingers of a drowning man releasing their final hold on a spar of wood. There was no fear now, only a vast and heedless indifference as his hands slipped away and he fell like a stone, twenty vertical feet into the cradling bottleneck at the foot of the chimney.

He himself made no sound, none at all: the soundless scream of agony never passed his lips, for the blackness came with the pain: but the straining ears of the men crouching in the rocks above caught clearly the dull, sickening crack at his right leg fractured cleanly in two, snapping like a rotten bough.

6

MONDAY NIGHT
0200–0600

THE GERMAN patrol was everything that Mallory had feared—efficient, thorough and very, very painstaking. It even had imagination, in the person of its young and competent sergeant, and that was more dangerous still.

There were only four of them, in high boots, helmets and green, grey and brown mottled capes. First of all they located the telephone and reported to base. Then the young sergeant sent two men to search another hundred yards or so along the cliff, while he and the fourth soldier probed among the rocks that paralleled the cliff. The search was slow and careful, but the two men did not penetrate very far into the rocks. To Mallory, the sergeant's reasoning was obvious and logical. If the sentry had gone to sleep or taken ill, it was unlikely that he would have gone far in among that confused jumble of boulders. Mallory and the others were safely back beyond their reach.

And then came what Mallory had feared—an organised, methodical inspection of the cliff-top itself: worse still, it began with a search along the very edge. Securely held by his three men with interlinked arms—the last with a hand hooked round his belt—the sergeant walked slowly along the rim, probing every inch with the spot-lit beam of a powerful torch. Suddenly he stopped short, exclaimed suddenly and stopped, torch and face only inches from the ground. There was no question as to what he had found— the deep gouge made in the soft, crumbling soil by the climbing rope that had been belayed round the boulder and gone over the edge of the cliff. . . . Softly, silently, Mallory and his three companions straightened to their knees or to their feet, gun barrels lining along the tops of boulders or peering out between cracks in the rocks. There was no doubt in any of their minds that Stevens was lying there helplessly in the crutch of the chimney, seriously injured or dead. It needed only one German carbine to point down that cliff face, however carelessly, and these four men would die. They would have to die.

The sergeant was stretched out his length now, two men holding his legs. His head and shoulders were over the edge of the cliff, the beam from his torch stabbing down the chimney. For ten, perhaps fifteen seconds, there was no sound on the cliff-top, no sound at all, only the high, keening moan of the wind and the swish of the rain in the stunted grass. And then the sergeant had wriggled back and risen to his feet, slowly shaking his head. Mallory gestured to the others to sink down behind the boulders again, but even so the sergeant's soft Bavarian voice carried clearly in the wind.

"It's Ehrich all right, poor fellow." Compassion and anger blended curiously in the voice. "I warned him often enough about his carelessness, about going too near the edge of that cliff. It is very treacherous." Instinctively the sergeant stepped back a couple of feet and looked again at the gouge in the soft earth. "That's where his heel slipped—or maybe the butt of his carbine. Not that it matters now."

"Is he dead, do you think, Sergeant?" The speaker was only a boy, nervous and unhappy.

"It's hard to say. . . . Look for yourself."

Gingerly the youth lay down on the cliff-top, peering cautiously over the lip of the rock. The other soldiers were talking among themselves, in short staccato sentences when Mallory turned to Miller, cupped his hands to his mouth and the American's ear. He could contain his puzzlement no longer.

"Was Stevens wearing his dark suit when you left him?" he whispered.

"Yeah," Miller whispered back. "Yeah, I think he was." A pause. "No, dammit, I'm wrong. We both put on our rubber camouflage capes about the same time."

Mallory nodded. The waterproofs of the Germans were almost identical with thier own: and the sentry's hair, Mallory remembered, had been jet black—the same colour as Stevens's dyed hair. Probably all that was visible from above was a crumpled, cape-shrouded figure and a dark head. The sergeant's mistake in identity was more than understandable: it was inevitable.

The young soldier eased himself back from the edge of the cliff and hoisted himself carefully to his feet.

"You're right, Sergeant. It *is* Ehrich." The boy's voice was unsteady. "He's alive, I think. I saw his cape move, just a little. It wasn't the wind, I'm sure of that."

Mallory felt Andrea's massive hand squeezing his arm, felt the quick surge of relief, then elation, wash through him. So Stevens *was* alive! Thank God for that! They'd save the boy yet. He heard Andrea whispering the news to the others, then grinned wryly to himself, ironic at his own gladness. Jensen definitely would not have approved of this jubilation. Stevens had already done his part, navigated the boat to Navarone and climbed the cliff: and now he was only a crippled liability, would be a drag on the whole party, reduce what pitiful chances of success remained to them. For a High Command who pushed the counters around crippled pawns slowed up the whole game, made the board so damnably untidy. It was most inconsiderate of Stevens not to have killed himself so that they could have disposed of him neatly and without trace in the deep and hungry waters that boomed around the foot of the cliff. . . . Mallory clenched his hands in the darkness and swore to himself that the boy would live, come home again, and to hell with total war and all its inhuman demands. . . . Just a kid, that was all, a scared and broken kid and the bravest of them all.

The young sergeant was issuing a string of orders to his men, his voice quick, crisp and confident. A doctor, splints, rescue stretcher, anchored sheer-legs, ropes, spikes—the trained, well-ordered mind missing nothing. Mallory waited tensely, wondering how many men, if any, would be left on guard, for the guards would have to go and that would inevitably betray them. The question of their quick and silent disposal never entered his mind—a whisper in Andrea's ear and the guards would have no more chance than penned lambs against a marauding wolf. Less chance even than that—the lambs could always run and cry out before the darkness closed over them.

The sergeant solved the problem for them. The assured competence, the tough, unsentimental ruthlessness that made the German N.C.O. the best in the world gave Mallory the chance he never expected to have. He had just finished giving his orders when the young soldier touched him on the arm, then pointed over the edge.

"How about poor Ehrich, Sergeant?" he asked uncertainly. "Shouldn't—don't you think one of us ought to stay with him?"

"And what could you do if you did stay—hold his hand?" the sergeant asked acidly. "If he stirs and falls, then he falls, that's all, and it doesn't matter then if a hundred of us are standing up here watching him. Off you go, and don't forget the mallets and pegs to stay the sheer-legs."

The three men turned and went off quickly to the east without another word. The sergeant walked over to the phone, reported briefly to someone, then set off in the opposite direction—to check the next guard post, Mallory guessed. He was still in sight, a dwindling blur in the darkness, when Mallory whispered to Brown and Miller to post themselves on guard again: and they could still hear the measured crunch of his firm footfalls on a patch of distant gravel as their belayed rope went snaking over the edge of the cliff, Andrea and Mallory sliding swiftly down even before it had stopped quivering.

Stevens, a huddled, twisted heap with a gashed and bleeding cheek lying cruelly along a razor-sharp spur of rock, was still unconscious, breathing stertorously through his open mouth. Below the knee his right leg twisted upwards and outwards against the rock at an impossible angle. As gently as he could, braced against either side of the chimney and supported by Andrea, Mallory lifted and straightened the twisted limb. Twice, from the depths of the dark stupor of his unconsciousness, Stevens moaned in agony, but Mallory had no option but to carry on, his teeth clenched tight until his jaws ached. Then slowly, with infinite care, he rolled up the trouser leg, winced and screwed his eyes shut in momentary horror and nausea as he saw the dim whiteness of the shattered tibia sticking out through the torn and purply swollen flesh.

"Compound fracture, Andrea." Gently his exploring finger slid down the mangled leg, beneath the lip of the jack-boot, stopped suddenly as something gave way beneath his feather touch. "Oh, my God!" he murmured. "Another break, just above the ankle. This boy is in a bad way, Andrea."

"He is indeed," Andrea said gravely. "We can do nothing for him here?"

"Nothing. Just nothing. We'll have to get him up first." Mallory straightened, gazed up bleakly at the perpendicular face of the chimney. "Although how in the name of heaven——"

"I will take him up." There was no suggestion in Andrea's voice either of desperate resolve or consciousness of the almost incredible effort involved. It was simply a statement of intention, the voice of a man who never questioned his ability to do what he said he would. "If you will help me to raise him, to tie him to my back. . . ."

"With his broken leg loose, dangling from a piece of skin and torn muscle?" Mallory protested. "Stevens can't take much more. He'll die if we do this."

"He'll die if we don't," Andrea murmured.

Mallory stared down at Stevens for a long moment, then nodded heavily in the darkness.

"He'll die if we don't," he echoed tiredly. "Yes, we have to do this." He pushed outwards from the rock, slid half a dozen feet down the rope and jammed a foot in the crutch of the chimney just below Stevens's body. He took a couple of turns of rope round his waist and looked up.

"Ready, Andrea?" he called softly.

"Ready." Andrea stooped, hooked his great hands under Stevens's armpits and lifted slowly, powerfully, as Mallory pushed from below. Twice, three times before they had him up, the boy moaned deep down in his tortured throat, the long, quavering "Aahs" of agony setting Mallory's teeth on edge: and then his dangling, twisted leg had passed from Mallory's reach and he was held close and cradled in Andrea's encircling arm, the rain-lashed, bleeding mask of a face lolling grotesquely backwards, forlorn and lifeless with the dead pathos of a broken doll. Seconds later Mallory was up beside them, expertly lashing Stevens's wrists together. He was swearing softly as his numbed hands looped and tightened the rope, softly, bitterly, continuously, but he was quite unaware of this: he was aware only of the broken head that lolled stupidly against his shoulder, of the welling, rain-thinned blood that filmed the unturned face, of the hair above the gashed temple emerging darkly fair as the dye washed slowly out. Inferior bloody boot-blacking, Mallory thought savagely: Jensen shall know of this—it could cost a man's life. And then he became aware of his own thoughts and swore again, still more savagely and at himself this time, for the utter triviality of what he was thinking.

With both hands free—Stevens's bound arms were looped round his neck, his body lashed to his own—Andrea took less than thirty seconds to reach the top: if the dragging, one hundred and sixty pound deadweight on his back made any difference to Andrea's climbing speed and power, Mallory couldn't detect it. The man's endurance was fantastic. Once, just once, as Andrea scrambled over the edge of the cliff, the broken leg caught on the rock, and the crucifying torture of it seared through the merciful shell of insensibility, forced a brief shriek of pain from his lips, a hoarse, bubbling whisper of sound all the more horrible for its muted agony. And then Andrea was standing upright and Mallory was behind him, cutting swiftly at the ropes that bound the two together.

"Straight into the rocks with him, Andrea, will you?" Mallory whispered. "Wait for us at the first open space you come to." Andrea nodded slowly and without raising his head, his hooded eyes bent over the boy in his arms, like a man sunk in thought. Sunk in thought or listening, and all unawares Mallory, too, found himself looking and listening into the thin, lost moaning of the wind, and there was nothing there, only the lifting, drying threnody and the chill of the rain hardening to an ice-cold sleet. He shivered, without knowing why, and listened again; then he shook himself angrily, turned abruptly towards the cliff face and started reeling in the rope. He had it all up, lying around his feet in a limp and rain-sodden tangle when he remembered about the spike still secured to the foot of the chimney, the hundreds of feet of rope suspended from it.

He was too tired and cold and depressed even to feel exasperated with himself. The sight of Stevens and the knowledge of how it was with the boy had affected him more than he knew. Moodily, almost, he kicked the rope over the side again, slid down the chimney, untied the second rope and sent the spike spinning out into the darkness. Less than ten minutes later, the wetly-coiled ropes over his shoulder, he led Miller and Brown into the dark confusion of the rocks.

They found Stevens lying under the lee of a huge boulder, less than a hundred yards inland, in a tiny, cleared space barely the size of a billiard table. An oilskin was spread beneath him on the sodden, gravelly earth, a camouflage cape covered most of his body: it was bitterly cold now, but the rock broke the force of the wind, sheltered the boy from the driving sleet. Andrea looked up as the three men dropped into the hollow and lowered their gear to the ground; already, Mallory could see, Andrea had rolled the trouser up beyond the knee and cut the heavy jackboot away from the mangled leg.

"Sufferin' Christ!" The words, half-oath, half-prayer, were torn involuntarily from Miller: even in the deep gloom the shattered leg looked ghastly. Now he dropped on one knee and stooped low over it. "What a mess!" he murmured slowly. He looked up over his shoulder. "We've gotta do something about that leg, boss, and we've no damned time to lose. This kid's a good candidate for the mortuary."

"I know. We've got to save him, Dusty, we've just *got* to." All at once this had become terribly important to Mallory. He dropped down on his knees. "Let's have a look at him."

Impatiently Miller waved him away.

"Leave this to me, boss." There was a sureness, a sudden authority in his voice that held Mallory silent. "The medicine pack, quick—and undo that tent."

"You sure you can handle this?" God knew, Mallory thought, he didn't really doubt him—he was conscious only of gratitude, of a profound relief, but he felt he had to say something. "How are you going——"

"Look, boss," Miller said quietly. "All my life I've worked with just three things—mines, tunnels and explosives. They're kinda tricky things, boss. I've seen hundreds of busted arms and legs—and fixed most of them myself." He grinned wryly in the darkness. "I was boss myself, then—just one of my privileges, I reckon."

"Good enough!" Mallory clapped him on the shoulder. "He's all yours, Dusty. But the tent!" Involuntarily he looked over his shoulder in the direction of the cliff. "I mean——"

"You got me wrong, boss." Miller's hands, steady and precise with the delicate certainty of a man who has spent a lifetime with high explosives, were busy with a swab and disinfectant. "I wasn't fixin' on settin' up a base hospital. But we need tent-poles—splints for his legs."

"Of course, of course. The poles. Never occurred to me for splints—and I've been thinking of nothing else for——"

"They're not too important, boss." Miller had the medicine pack open now, rapidly selecting the items he wanted with the aid of a hooded torch. "Morphine—that's the first thing, or this kid's goin' to die of shock. And then shelter, warmth, dry clothin'——"

"Warmth! Dry clothing!" Mallory interrupted incredulously. He looked down at the unconscious boy, remembering how Stevens had lost them the stove and all the fuel, and his mouth twisted in bitterness. His own executioner. . . . "Where in God's name are we going to find them?"

"I don't know, boss," Miller said simply. "But we gotta find them. And not just to lessen shock. With a leg like this and soaked to the skin, he's bound to get pneumonia. And then as much sulfa as that bloody great hole in his leg will take—one touch of sepsis in the state this kid's in . . ." His voice trailed away into silence.

Mallory rose to his feet.

"I reckon you're the boss." It was a very creditable imitation of the American's drawl, and Miller looked up quickly, surprise melting into a tired smile, then looked away again. Mallory could hear the chatter of his teeth as he bent over Stevens, and sensed rather than saw that he was shivering violently, continuously, but oblivious to it all in his complete concentration on the job in hand. Miller's clothes, Mallory remembered again, were completely saturated: not for the first time, Mallory wondered how he had managed to get himself into such a state with a waterproof covering him.

"You fix him up. I'll find a place." Mallory wasn't as confident as he felt: still, on the scree-strewn, volcanic slopes of these hills behind, there ought to be a fair chance of finding a rock shelter, if not a cave. Or there would have been in daylight: as it was they would just have to trust to luck to stumble on one. . . . He saw that Casey Brown, grey-faced with exhaustion and illness—the after-effects of carbon monoxide poisoning are slow to disappear—had risen unsteadily to his feet and was making for a gap between the rocks.

"Where are you going, Chief?"

"Back for the rest of the stuff, sir."

"Are you sure you can manage?" Mallory peered at him closely. "You don't look any too fit to me."

"I don't feel it either," Brown said frankly. He looked at Mallory. "But with all respects, sir, I don't think you've seen yourself recently."

"You have a point," Mallory acknowledged. "All right then, come on. I'll go with you."

For the next ten minutes there was silence in the tiny clearing, a silence broken only by the murmurs of Miller and Andrea working over the shattered leg, and the moans of the injured man as he twisted and struggled feebly in his dark abyss of pain: then gradually the morphine took effect and the struggling lessened and died away altogether, and Miller was able to work rapidly, without fear of interruption. Andrea had an oilskin outstretched above them. It served a double purpose—it curtained off the sleet that swept round them from time to time and blanketed the pin-point light of the rubber torch he held in his free hand. And then the leg was set and bandaged and as heavily splinted as possible and Miller was on his feet, straightening his aching back.

"Thank Gawd that's done," he said wearily. He gestured at Stevens. "I feel just the way that kid looks." Suddenly he stiffened, stretched out a warning arm. "I can hear something, Andrea," he whispered.

Andrea laughed. "It's only Brown coming back, my friend. He's been coming this way for over a minute now."

"How do you know it's Brown?" Miller challenged. He felt vaguely annoyed with himself and unobtrusively shoved his ready automatic back into his pocket.

"Brown is a good man among rocks," Andrea said gently; "but he is tired. But Captain Mallory . . ." He shrugged. "People call me 'the big cat' I know, but among the mountains and rocks the captain is more than a cat. He is a ghost, and that was how men called him in Crete. You will know he is here when he touches you on the shoulder."

Miller shivered in a sudden icy gust of sleet.

"I wish you people wouldn't creep around so much," he complained. He looked up as Brown came round the corner of a boulder, slow with the shambling, stumbling gait of an exhausted man. "Hi, there, Casey. How are things goin'?"

"Not too bad." Brown murmured his thanks as Andrea took the box of explosives off his shoulder and lowered it easily to the ground. "This is the last of the gear. Captain sent me back with it. We heard voices some way along the cliff. He's staying behind to see what they say when they find Stevens gone." Wearily he sat down on top of the box. "Maybe he'll get some idea of what they're going to do next, if anything."

"Seems to me he could have left you there and carried that damned box back himself," Miller growled. Disappointment in Mallory made him more outspoken than he'd meant to be. "He's much better off than you are right now, and I think it's a bit bloody much . . ." He broke off and gasped in pain as Andrea's fingers caught his arm like giant steel pincers.

"It is not fair to talk like that, my friend," Andrea said reproachfully. "You forget, perhaps, that Brown here cannot talk or understand a word of German?"

Miller rubbed his bruised arm tenderly, shaking his head in slow self-anger and condemnation.

"Me and my big mouth," he said ruefully. "Always talkin' outa turn Miller, they call me. Your pardon, one and all. . . . And what is next on the agenda, gentlemen?"

"Captain says we're to go straight on into the rocks and up the right shoulder of this hill here." Brown jerked a thumb in the direction of the vague mass, dark and strangely foreboding, that towered above and beyond them. "He'll catch us up within fifteen minutes or so." He grinned tiredly at Miller. "And we're to leave this box and a rucksack for him to carry."

"Spare me," Miller pleaded. "I feel only six inches tall as it is." He looked down at Stevens lying quietly under the darkly gleaming wetness of the oilskins, then up at Andrea. "I'm afraid, Andrea——"

"Of course, of course!" Andrea stooped quickly, wrapped the oilskins round the unconscious boy and rose to his feet, as effortlessly as if the oilskins had been empty.

"I'll lead the way," Miller volunteered. "Mebbe I can pick an easy path for you and young Stevens." He swung generator and rucksacks on to his shoulder, staggering under the sudden weight; he hadn't realised he was so weak. "At first, that is," he amended. "Later on, you'll have to carry us both."

Mallory had badly miscalculated the time it would require to overtake the others; over an hour had elapsed since Brown had left him, and still there were no signs of the others. And with seventy pounds on his back, he wasn't making such good time himself.

It wasn't all his fault. The returning German patrol, after the first shock of discovery, had searched the cliff-top again, methodically and with exasperating slowness. Mallory had waited tensely for someone to suggest descending and examining the chimney—the gouge-marks of the spikes on the rock would have been a dead giveaway—but nobody even mentioned it. With the guard obviously fallen to his death, it would have been a pointless thing to do anyway. After an unrewarding search, they had debated for an unconscionable time as to what they should do next. Finally they had done nothing. A replacement guard was left, and the rest made off along the cliff, carrying their rescue equipment with them.

The three men ahead had made surprisingly good time, although the conditions, admittedly, were now much easier. The heavy fall of boulders at the foot of the slope had petered out after another fifty yards, giving way to broken scree and rain-washed rubble. Possibly he had passed them, but it seemed unlikely: in the intervals between these driving sleet showers—it was more like hail now—he was able to scan the bare shoulder of the hill, and nothing moved. Besides, he knew that Andrea wouldn't stop until he reached what promised at least a bare minimum of shelter, and as yet these exposed, windswept slopes had offered nothing that even remotely approached that.

In the end, Mallory almost literally stumbled upon both men and shelter. He was negotiating a narrow, longitudinal spine of rock, had just crossed its razor-back, when he heard the murmur of voices beneath him and saw a tiny glimmer of light behind the canvas stretching down from the overhang of the far wall of the tiny ravine at his feet.

Miller started violently and swung round as he felt the hand on his shoulder: the automatic was half-way out of his pocket before he saw who it was and sunk back heavily on the rock behind him.

"Come, come, now! Trigger-happy." Thankfully Mallory slid his burden from his aching shoulders and looked across at the softly laughing Andrea. "What's so funny?"

"Our friend here." Andrea grinned again. "I told him that the first thing he would know of your arrival would be when you touched him on the shoulder. I don't think he believed me."

"You might have coughed or somethin'," Miller said defensively. "It's my nerves, boss," he added plaintively. "They're not what they were forty-eight hours ago."

Mallory looked at him disbelievingly, made to speak, then stopped short as he caught sight of the pale blur of a face propped up against a rucksack. Beneath the white swathe of a bandaged forehead the eyes were open, looking steadily at him. Mallory took a step forward, sank down on one knee.

"So you've come round at last!" He smiled into the sunken parchment face and Stevens smiled back, the bloodless lips whiter than the face itself. He looked ghastly. "How do you feel, Andy?"

"Not too bad, sir. Really I'm not." The bloodshot eyes were dark and filled with pain. His gaze fell and he looked down vacantly at his bandaged leg, looked up again, smiled uncertainly at Mallory. "I'm terribly sorry about all this, sir. What a bloody stupid thing to do."

"It wasn't a stupid thing." Mallory spoke with slow, heavy emphasis. "It was criminal folly." He knew everyone was watching them, but knew, also, that Stevens had eyes for him alone. "Criminal, unforgiveable folly," he went on quietly, "——and I'm the man in the dock. I'd suspected you'd lost a lot of blood on the boat, but I didn't know you had these big gashes on your forehead. I should have made it my business to find out." He smiled wryly. "You should have heard what these two insubordinate characters had to say to me about it when they got to the top. . . . And they were right. You should never have been asked to bring up the rear in the state you were in. It was madness." He grinned again. "You should have been hauled up like a sack of coals like the intrepid mountaineering team of Miller and Brown. . . . God knows how you ever made it—I'm sure you'll never know." He leaned forward, touched Stevens's sound knee. "Forgive me, Andy. I honestly didn't realise how far through you were."

Stevens stirred uncomfortably, but the dead pallor of the high-boned cheeks was stained with embarrassed pleasure.

"Please, sir," he pleaded. "Don't talk like that. It was just one of those things." He paused, eyes screwed shut and indrawn breath hissing sharply though his teeth as a wave of pain washed up from his shattered leg. Then he looked at Mallory again. "And there's no credit due to me for the climb," he went on quietly. "I hardly remember a thing about it."

Mallory looked at him without speaking, eyebrows arched in mild interrogation.

"I was scared to death every step of the way up," Stevens said simply. He was conscious of no surprise, no wonder that he was saying the thing he would have died rather than say. "I've never been so scared in all my life."

Mallory shook his head slowly from side to side, stubbled chin rasping in his cupped palm. He seemed genuinely puzzled. Then he looked down at Stevens and smiled quizzically.

"Now I know you *are* new to this game, Andy." He smiled again. "Maybe you think I was laughing and singing all the way up that cliff? Maybe you think *I* wasn't scared?" He lit a cigarette and gazed at Stevens through a cloud of drifting smoke. "Well, I wasn't. 'Scared' isn't the word—I was bloody well terrified. So was Andrea here. We know too much not to be scared."

"Andrea!" Stevens laughed, then cried out as the movement triggered off a crepitant agony in his bone-shattered leg. For a moment Mallory thought he had lost consciousness, but almost at once he spoke again, his voice husky with pain. "Andrea!" he whispered. "Scared! I don't believe it!"

"Andrea *was* afraid." The big Greek's voice was very gentle. "Andrea *is* afraid. Andrea is always afraid. That is why I have lived so long." He stared down at his great hands. "And why so many have died. They were not so afraid as I. They were not afraid of everything a man could be afraid of, there was always something they forgot to fear, to guard against. But Andrea was afraid of everything—and he forgot nothing. It is as simple as that."

He looked across at Stevens and smiled.

"There are no brave men and cowardly men in the world, my son. There

are only brave men. To be born, to live, to die—that takes c⁄
in itself, and more than enough. We are all brave men and we a⁻
and what the world calls a brave man, he, too, is brave and afraiᵈ
the rest of us. Only he is brave for five minutes longer. Or sometimes
minutes, or twenty minutes—or the time it takes a man sick and bleeding
and afraid to climb a cliff.''

Stevens said nothing. His head was sunk on his chest, and his face was
hidden. He had seldom felt so happy, seldom so at peace with himself. He
had known that he could not hide things from men like Andrea and Mallory,
but he had not known that it would not matter. He felt he should say
something, but he could not think what and he was deathly tired. He knew,
deep down, that Andrea was speaking the truth, but not the whole truth; but
he was too tired to care, to try to work things out.

Miller cleared his throat noisily.

"No more talkin', Lieutenant," he said firmly. "You gotta lie down, get
yourself some sleep."

Stevens looked at him, then at Mallory in puzzled inquiry.

"Better do what you're told, Andy," Mallory smiled. "Your surgeon and
medical adviser talking. He fixed your leg."

"Oh! I didn't know. Thanks, Dusty. Was it very—difficult?"

Miller waved a deprecatory hand.

"Not for a man of my experience. Just a simple break," he lied easily.
"Almost let one of the others do it. . . . Give him a hand to lie down, will
you, Andrea?" He jerked his head towards Mallory. "Boss?"

The two men moved outside, turning their backs to the icy wind.

"We gotta get a fire, dry clothing, for that kid," Miller said urgently.
"His pulse is about 140, temperature 103. He's runnin' a fever, and he's
losin' ground all the time."

"I know, I know," Mallory said worriedly. "And there's not a hope of
getting any fuel on this damned mountain. Let's go in and see how much
dried clothing we can muster between us."

He lifted the edge of the canvas and stepped inside. Stevens was still
awake, Brown and Andrea on either side of him. Miller was on his heels.

"We're going to stay here for the night," Mallory announced, "so let's
make things as snug as possible. Mind you," he admitted, "we're a bit too
near the cliff for comfort, but old Jerry hasn't a clue we're on the island,
and we're out of sight of the coast. Might as well make ourselves comfortable."

"Boss . . ." Miller made to speak, then fell silent again. Mallory looked
at him in surprise, saw that he, Brown and Stevens were looking at one
another, uncertainty, then doubt and a dawning, sick comprehension in their
eyes. A sudden anxiety, the sure knowledge that something was far wrong,
struck at Mallory like a blow.

"What's up?" he demanded sharply. "What is it?"

"We have bad news for you, boss," Miller said carefully. "We should
have told you right away. Guess we all thought that one of the others would
have told you. . . . Remember that sentry you and Andrea shoved over the
side?"

Mallory nodded, somberly. He knew what was coming.

"He fell on top of that reef twenty-thirty feet or so from the cliff," Miller
went on. "Wasn't much of him left, I guess, but what was was jammed
between two rocks. He was really stuck good and fast."

"I see," Mallory murmured. "I've been wondering all night how you
managed to get so wet under your rubber cape."

"I tried four times, boss," Miller said quietly. "The others had a rope round me." He shrugged his shoulders. "Not a chance. Them gawddamned waves just flung me back against the cliff every time."

"It will be light in three or four hours," Mallory murmured. "In four hours they will know we are on the island. They will see him as soon as it's dawn and send a boat to investigate."

"Does it really matter, sir," Stevens suggested. "He could still have fallen."

Mallory eased the canvas aside and looked out into the night. It was bitterly cold and the snow was beginning to fall all around them. He dropped the canvas again.

"Five minutes," he said absently. "We will leave in five minutes." He looked at Stevens and smiled faintly. "We are forgetful, too. We should have told you. Andrea stabbed the sentry through the heart."

The hours that followed were hours plucked from the darkest nightmare, endless, numbing hours of stumbling and tripping and falling and getting up again, of racked bodies and aching, tortured muscles, of dropped loads and frantic pawing around in the deepening snow, of hunger and thirst and all-encompassing exhaustion.

They had retraced their steps now, were heading W.N.W. back across the shoulder of the mountain—almost certainly the Germans would think they had gone due north, heading for the centre of the island. Without compass, stars or moon to guide, Mallory had nothing to orientate them but the feel of the slope of the mountain and the memory of the map Vlachos had shown them in Alexandria. But by and by he was reasonably certain that they had rounded the mountan and were pushing up some narrow gorge into the interior.

The snow was the deadly enemy. Heavy, wet and feathery, it swirled all around them in a blanketing curtain of grey, sifted down their necks and jackboots, worked its insidious way under their clothes and up their sleeves, blocked their eyes and ears and mouths, pierced and then anaesthetised exposed faces, and turned gloveless hands into leaden lumps of ice, be-numbed and all but powerless. All suffered, and suffered badly, but Stevens most of all. He had lost consciousness again within minutes of leaving the cave and clad in clinging, sodden clothes as he was, he now lacked even the saving warmth generated by physical activity. Twice Andrea had stopped and felt for the beating of the heart, for he thought that the boy had died: but he could feel nothing for there was no feeling left in his hands, and he could only wonder and stumble on again.

About five in the morning, as they were climbing up the steep valley head above the gorge, a treacherous, slippery slope with only a few stunted carob trees for anchor in the sliding scree, Mallory decided that they must rope up for safety's sake. In single file they scrambled and struggled up the ever-steepening slope for the next twenty minutes: Mallory, in the lead, did not even dare to think how Andrea was getting on behind him. Suddenly the slope eased, flattened out completely, and almost before they realised what was happening they had crossed the high divide, still roped together and in driving, blinding snow with zero visibility, and were sliding down the valley on the other side.

They came to the cave at dawn, just as the first grey stirrings of a bleak and cheerless day struggled palely through the lowering, snow-filled sky to the east. Monsieur Vlachos had told them that the south of Navarone was honey-combed with caves, but this was the first they had seen, and even then it was no cave but a dark, narrow tunnel in a great heap of piled volcanic slabs, huge, twisted layers of rock precariously poised in a gulley that threaded down the slope towards some broad and unknown valley a thousand, two thousand feet, beneath them, a valley still shrouded in the gloom of night.

It was no cave, but it was enough. For frozen, exhausted, sleep-haunted men, it was more than enough, it was more than they had ever hoped for. There was room for them all, the few cracks were quickly blocked against the drifting snow, the entrance curtained off by the boulder-weighted tent. Somehow, impossibly almost in the cramped darkness, they stripped Stevens of his sea- and rain-soaked clothes, eased him into a providentially zipped sleeping-bag, forced some brandy down his throat and cushioned the blood-stained head on some dry clothing. And then the four men, even the tireless Andrea, slumped down to the sodden, snow-chilled floor of the cave and slept like men already dead, oblivious alike of the rocks on the floor, the cold, their hunger and their clammy, saturated clothing, oblivious even of the agony of returning circulation in their frozen hands and faces.

7

TUESDAY
1500–1900

THE SUN, rime-ringed and palely luminous behind the drifting cloud-wrack, was far beyond its zenith and dipping swiftly westwards to the snow-limned shoulder of the mountain when Andrea lifted the edge of the tent, pushed it gently aside and peered out warily down the smooth sweep of the mountainside. For a few moments he remained almost motionless behind the canvas, automatically easing cramped and aching leg muscles, narrowed, roving eyes gradually accustoming themselves to the white glare of the glistening, crystalline snow. And then he had flitted noiselessly out of the mouth of the tunnel and reached far up the bank of the gully in half a dozen steps; stretched full length against the snow, he eased himself smoothly up the slope, lifted a cautious eye over the top.

Far below him stretched the great, curved sweep of an almost perfectly symmetrical valley—a valley born abruptly in the cradling embrace of steep-walled mountains and falling away gently to the north. That towering, buttressed giant on his right that brooded darkly over the head of the valley, its peak hidden in the snow clouds—there could be no doubt about that, Andrea thought. Mt. Kostos, the highest mountain in Navarone: they had crossed its western flank during the darkness of the night. Due east and facing his own at perhaps five miles' distance, the third mountain was barely less high: but its northern flank fell away more quickly, debouching on to the plains that lay in the northeast of Navarone. And about four miles away to the north-northeast, far beneath the snowline and the isolated shepherds' huts, a tiny, flat-roofed township lay in a fold in the hills, along the bank of the little stream that wound its way through the valley. That could only be the village of Margaritha.

Even as he absorbed the topography of the valley, his eyes probing every dip and cranny in the hills for a possible source of danger, Andrea's mind was racing back over the last two minutes of time, trying to isolate, to remember the nature of the alien sound that had cut through the cocoon of sleep and brought him instantly to his feet, alert and completely awake, even before his conscious mind had time to register the memory of the sound. And then he heard it again, three times in as many seconds, the high-pitched, lonely wheep of a whistle, shrill peremptory blasts that echoed briefly and died along the lower slopes of Mt. Kostos: the final echo still hung faintly on the air as Andrea pushed himself backwards and slid down to the floor of the gully.

He was back on the bank within thirty seconds, cheek muscles contracting involuntarily as the ice-chill eyepieces of Mallory's Zeiss-Ikon binoculars screwed into his face. There was no mistaking them now, he thought grimly, his first, fleeting impression had been all too accurate. Twenty-five, perhaps thirty soldiers in all, strung out in a long, irregular line, they were advancing slowly across the flank of Kostos, combing every gully, each jumbled confusion of boulders that lay in their path. Every man was clad in a snow-suit, but even at a distance of two miles they were easy to locate: the arrow-heads of their strapped skis angled up above shoulders and hooded heads: startlingly black against the sheer whiteness of the snow, the skis bobbed and weaved in disembodied drunkenness as the men slipped and stumbled along the scree-strewn slopes of the mountain. From time to time a man near the centre of the line pointed and gestured with an alpenstock, as if co-ordinating the efforts of the search party. The man with the whistle, Andrea guessed.

"Andrea!" The call from the cave mouth was very soft. "Anything wrong?"

Finger to his lips, Andrea twisted round in the snow. Mallory was standing by the canvas screen. Dark-jowled and crumple-clothed, he held up one hand against the glare of the snow while the other rubbed the sleep from his bloodshot eyes. And then he was limping forward in obedience to the crooking of Andrea's finger, wincing in pain at every step he took. His toes were swollen and skinned, gummed together with congealed blood. He had not had his boots off since he had taken them from the feet of the dead German sentry: and now he was almost afraid to remove them, afraid of what he would find. . . . He clambered slowly up the bank of the gully and sank down in the snow beside Andrea.

"Company?"

"The very worst of company," Andrea murmured. "Take a look, my Keith." He handed over the binoculars, pointed down to the lower slopes of Mt. Kostos. "Your friend Jensen never told us that they were here."

Slowly, Mallory quartered the slopes with the binoculars. Suddenly the line of searchers moved into his field of vision. He raised his head, adjusted the focus impatiently, looked briefly once more, then lowered the binoculars with a restrained deliberation of gesture that held a wealth of bitter comment.

"The W.G.B.," he said softly.

"A Jaeger battalion," Andrea conceded. "Alpine Corps—their finest mountain troops. This is most inconvenient, my Keith."

Mallory nodded, rubbed his stubbled chin.

"If anyone can find us, they can. And they'll find us." He lifted the glasses to look again at the line of advancing men. The painstaking thoroughness of the search was disturbing enough: but even more threatening, more frightening, was the snail-like relentlessness, the inevitability of the approach of these tiny figures. "God knows what the Alpenkorps is doing here," Mallory went on. "It's enough that they are here. They must know that we've landed and spent the morning searching the eastern saddle of

Kostos—that was the obvious route for us to break into the interior. They've drawn a blank there, so now they're working their way over to the other saddle. They must be pretty nearly certain that we're carrying a wounded man with us and that we can't have got very far. It's only going to be a matter of time, Andrea."

"A matter of time," Andrea echoed. He glanced up at the sun, a sun all but invisible in a darkening sky. "An hour, an hour and a half at the most. They'll be here before the sun goes down. And we'll still be here." He glanced quizzically at Mallory. "We cannot leave the boy. And we cannot get away if we take the boy—and then he would die anyway."

"We will not be here," Mallory said flatly. "If we stay we all die. Or finish up in one of these nice little dungeons that Monsieur Vlachos told us about."

"The greatest good of the greatest number," Andrea nodded slowly. "That's how it has to be, has it not, my Keith? The greatest number. That is what Captain Jensen would say." Mallory stirred uncomfortably, but his voice was steady enough when he spoke.

"That's how I see it, too, Andrea. Simple proportion—twelve hundred to one. You know it has to be this way." Mallory sounded tired.

"Yes, I know. But you are worrying about nothing." Andrea smiled. "Come, my friend. Let us tell the others the good news."

Miller looked up as the two men came in, letting the canvas screen fall shut behind them. He had unzipped the side of Stevens's sleeping-bag and was working on the mangled leg. A pencil flashlight was propped on a rucksack beside him.

"When are we goin' to do somethin' about this kid, boss?" The voice was abrupt, angry, like his gesture towards the sleep-drugged boy beside him. "This damned waterproof sleeping-bag is soaked right through. So's the kid—and he's about frozen stiff: his leg feels like a side of chilled beef. He's gotta have heat, boss, a warm room and hot drinks—or he's finished. Twenty-four hours." Miller shivered and looked slowly round the broken walls of the rock-shelter. "I reckon he'd have less than an even chance in a first-class general hospital. . . . He's just wastin' his time keepin' on breathin' in this gawddamned icebox."

Miller hardly exaggerated. Water from the melting snow above trickled continuously down the clammy, green-lichened walls of the cave or dripped directly on to the half-frozen gravelly slush on the floor of the cave. With no through ventilation and no escape for the water accumulating at the sides of the shelter, the whole place was dank and airless and terribly chill.

"Maybe he'll be hospitalised sooner than you think," Mallory said dryly. "How's his leg?"

"Worse." Miller was blunt. "A helluva sight worse. I've just chucked in another handful of sulpha and tied things up again. That's all I can do, boss, and it's just a waste of time anyway. . . . What was that crack about a hospital?" he added suspiciously.

"That was no crack," Mallory said soberly, "but one of the more unpleasant facts of life. There's a German search party heading this way. They mean business. They'll find us, all right."

Miller swore. "That's handy, that's just wonderful," he said bitterly. "How far away, boss?"

"An hour, maybe a little more."

"And what are we goin' to do with Junior, here? Leave him? It's his only chance, I reckon."

"Stevens comes with us." There was a flat finality in Mallory's voice.

Miller looked at him for a long time in silence: his face was very cold.

"Stevens comes with us," Miller repeated. "We drag him along with us until he's dead—that won't take long—and then we leave him in the snow. Just like that, huh?"

"Just like that, Dusty." Absently Mallory brushed some snow off his clothes, and looked up again at Miller. "Stevens knows too much. The Germans will have guessed why we're on the island, but they don't know how we propose to get inside the fortress—and they don't know when the Navy's coming through. But Stevens does. They'll make him talk. Scopolamine will make anyone talk."

"Scopolamine! On a dying man?" Miller was openly incredulous.

"Why not? I'd do the same myself. If you were the German commandant and you knew that your big guns and half the men in your fortress were liable to be blown to hell any moment, you'd do the same."

Miller looked at him, grinned wryly, shook his head.

"Me and my——"

"I know. You and your big mouth." Mallory smiled and clapped him on the shoulder. "I don't like it one little bit more than you do, Dusty." He turned away and crossed to the other side of the cave. "How are you feeling, Chief?"

"Not too bad, sir." Casey Brown was only just awake, numbed and shivering in sodden clothes. "Anything wrong?"

"Plenty," Mallory assured him. "Search party moving this way. We'll have to pull out inside half an hour." He looked at his watch. "Just on four o'clock. Do you think you could raise Cairo on the set?"

"Lord only knows," Brown said frankly. He rose stiffly to his feet. "The radio didn't get just the best of treatment yesterday. I'll have a go."

"Thanks, Chief. See that your aerial doesn't stick up above the sides of the gully." Mallory turned to leave the cave, but halted abruptly at the sight of Andrea squatting on a boulder just beside the entrance. His head bent in concentration, the big Greek had just finished screwing telescopic sights on to the barrel of his 7.92 mm. Mauser and was now deftly wrapping a sleeping-bag lining round its barrel and butt until the entire rifle was wrapped in a white cocoon.

Mallory watched him in silence. Andrea glanced up at him, smiled, rose to his feet and reached out for his rucksack. Within thirty seconds he was clad from head to toe in his mountain camouflage suit, was drawing tight the purse-strings of his snowhood and easing his feet into the rucked elastic anklets of his canvas boots. Then he picked up the Mauser and smiled slightly.

"I thought I might be taking a little walk, Captain," he said apologetically. "With your permission, of course."

Mallory nodded his head several times in slow recollection.

"You said I was worrying about nothing," he murmured. "I should have known. You might have told me, Andrea." But the protest was automatic, without significance. Mallory felt neither anger nor even annoyance at this tacit arrogation of his authority. The habit of command died hard in Andrea: on such occasions as he ostensibly sought approval for or consulted about a proposed course of action it was generally as a matter of courtesy and to give information as to his intentions. Instead of resentment, Mallory could feel only an overwhelming relief and gratitude to the smiling giant who towered above him: he had talked casually to Miller about driving Stevens till he died and then abandoning him, talked with an indifference that masked a mind sombre with bitterness at what he must do, but even so he had not known how depressed, how sick at heart this decision had left him until he knew it was no longer necessary.

"I am sorry." Andrea was half-contrite, half-smiling. "I should have told you. I thought you understood. . . . It is the best thing to do, yes?"

"It is the only thing to do," Mallory said frankly: "You're going to draw them off up the saddle?"

"There is no other way. With their skis they would overtake me in minutes if I went down into the valley. I cannot come back, of course, until it is dark. You will be here?"

"Some of us will." Mallory glanced across the shelter where a waking Stevens was trying to sit up, heels of his palms screwing into his exhausted eyes. "We must have food and fuel, Andrea," he said softly. "I am going down into the valley to-night."

"Of course, of course. We must do what we can." Andrea's face was grave, his voice only a murmur. "As long as we can. He is only a boy, a child almost. . . . Perhaps it will not be long." He pulled back the curtain, looked out at the evening sky. "I will be back by seven o'clock."

"Seven o'clock," Mallory repeated. The sky, he could see, was darkening already, darkening with the gloom of coming snow, and the lifting wind was beginning to puff little clouds of air-spun, flossy white into the little gully. Mallory shivered and caught hold of the massive arm. "For God's sake, Andrea," he urged quietly, "look after yourself!"

"Myself?" Andrea smiled gently, no mirth in his eyes, and as gently he disengaged his arm. "Do not think about me." The voice was very quiet, with an utter lack of arrogance. "If you must speak to God, speak to Him about these poor devils who are looking for us." The canvas dropped behind him and he was gone.

For some moments Mallory stood irresolutely at the mouth of the cave, gazing out sightlessly through the gap in the curtain. Then he wheeled abruptly, crossed the floor of the shelter and knelt in front of Stevens. The boy was propped up against Miller's anxious arm, the eyes lack-lustre and expressionless, bloodless cheeks deep-sunken in a grey and parchment face. Mallory smiled at him: he hoped the shock didn't show in his face.

"Well, well, well. The sleeper awakes at last. Better late than never." He opened his waterproof cigarette case, proffered it to Stevens. "How are you feeling now, Andy?"

"Frozen, sir." Stevens shook his head at the case and tried to grin back at Mallory, a feeble travesty of a smile that made Mallory wince.

"And the leg?"

"I think it must be frozen, too." Stevens looked down incuriously at the sheathed whitenss of his shattered leg. "Anyway, I can't feel a thing."

"Frozen!" Miller's sniff was a masterpiece of injured pride. "Frozen, he says! Gawddamned ingratitude. It's the first-class medical care, if I do say so myself!"

Stevens smiled, a fleeting, absent smile that flickered over his face and was gone. For long moments he kept staring down at his leg, then suddenly lifted his head and looked directly at Mallory.

"Look, sir, there's no good kidding ourselves." The voice was soft, quite toneless. "I don't want to seem ungrateful and I hate even the idea of cheap heroics, but—well, I'm just a damned great millstone round your necks and——"

"Leave you, eh?" Mallory interrupted. "Leave you to die of the cold or be captured by the Germans. Forget it, laddie. We can look after you—and these ruddy guns—at the same time."

"But, sir——"

"You insult us, Lootenant." Miller sniffed again. "Our feelings are hurt. Besides, as a professional man I gotta see my case through to convalescence, and if you think I'm goin' to do that in any gawddamned dripping German dungeon, you can——"

"Enough!" Mallory held up his hand. "The subject is closed." He saw the stain high up on the thin cheeks, the glad light that touched the dulled eyes, and felt the self-loathing and the shame well up inside him, shame for the gratitude of a sick man who did not know that their concern stemmed not from solicitude but from fear that he might betray them. . . . Mallory bent forward and began to unlace his high jack-boots. He spoke without looking up.

"Dusty."

"Yeah?"

"When you're finished boasting about your medical prowess, maybe you'd care to use some of it. Come and have a look at these feet of mine, will you? I'm afraid the sentry's boots haven't done them a great deal of good."

Fifteen painful minutes later Miller snipped off the rough edges of the adhesive bandage that bound Mallory's right foot, straightened up stiffly and contemplated his handiwork with pride.

"Beautiful, Miller, beautiful," he murmured complacently. "Not even in John Hopkins in the city of Baltimore . . ." He broke off suddenly, frowned down at the thickly bandaged feet and coughed apologetically. "A small point has just occurred to me, boss."

"I thought it might eventually," Mallory said grimly. "Just how do you propose to get my feet into these damned boots again?" He shivered involuntarily as he pulled on a pair of thick woollen socks, matted and sodden with melted snow, picked up the German sentry's boots, held them at arm's length and examined them in disgust. "Sevens, at the most—and a darned small sevens at that!"

"Nines," Stevens said laconically. He handed over his own jack-boots, one of them slit neatly down the side where Andrea had cut it open. "You can fix that tear easily enough, and they're no damned good to me now. No arguments, sir, please." He began to laugh softly, broke off in a sharply indrawn hiss of pain as the movement jarred the broken bones, took a couple of deep, quivering breaths, then smiled whitely. "My first—and probably my last—contribution to the expedition. What sort of medal do you reckon they'll give me for that, sir?"

Mallory took the boots, looked at Stevens a long moment in silence, then turned as the tarpaulin was pushed aside. Brown stumbled in, lowered the transmitter and telescopic aerial to the floor of the cave and pulled out a tin of cigarettes. They slipped from his frozen fingers, fell into the icy mud at his feet, became brown and sodden on the instant. He swore, briefly, and without enthusiasm, beat his numbed hands across his chest, gave it up and sat down heavily on a convenient boulder. He looked tired and cold and thoroughly miserable.

Mallory lit a cigarette and passed it across to him.

"How did it go, Casey? Manage to raise them at all?"

"They managed to raise me—more or less. Reception was lousy." Brown drew the grateful tobacco smoke deep down into his lungs. "And I couldn't get through at all. Must be that damned great hill to the south there."

"Probably," Mallory nodded. "And what news from our friends in Cairo? Exhorting us to greater efforts? Telling us to get on with the job?"

"No news at all. Too damn' worried about the silence at this end. Said that from now on they were going to come through every four hours, acknowledgment or no. Repeated that about ten times, then signed off."

"That'll be a great help," Miller said acidly. "Nice to know they're on our side. Nothin' like moral support." He jerked his thumb towards the mouth of the cave. "Reckon them bloodhounds would be scared to death if they knew. . . . Did you take a gander at them before you came in?"

"I didn't have to," Brown said morosely. "I could hear them—sounded like the officer in charge shouting directions." Mechanically, almost, he picked up his automatic rifle, eased the clip in the magazine. "Must be less than a mile away now."

The search party, more closely bunched by this time, was less than a mile, was barely half a mile distant from the cave when the Oberleutnant in charge saw that the right wing of his line, on the steeper slopes to the south, was lagging behind once more. Impatiently he lifted his whistle to his mouth for the three sharp, peremptory blasts that would bring his weary men stumbling into line again. Twice the whistle shrilled out its imperative urgency, the piercing notes echoing flatly along the snowbound slopes and dying away in the valley below: but the third *wheep* died at birth, caught up again and tailed off in a wailing, eldritch diminuendo that merged with dreadful harmony into a long, bubbling scream of agony. For two or three seconds the Oberleutnant stood motionless in his tracks, his face shocked and contorted: then he jack-knifed violently forward and pitched down into the crusted snow. The burly sergeant beside him stared down at the fallen officer, looked up in sudden horrified understanding, opened his mouth to shout, sighed and toppled wearily over the body at his feet, the evil, whip-lash crack of the Mauser in his ears as he died.

High up on the western slopes of Mount Kostos, wedged in the V between two great boulders, Andrea gazed down the darkening mountainside over the depressed telescopic sights of his rifle and pumped another three rounds into the wavering, disorganised line of searchers. His face was quite still, as immobile as the eyelids that never flickered to the regular crashing of his Mauser, and drained of all feeling. Even his eyes reflected the face, eyes neither hard nor pitiless, but simply empty and almost frighteningly remote, a remoteness that mirrored his mind, a mind armoured for the moment against all thought and sensation, for Andrea knew that he must not think about this thing. To kill, to take the life of his fellows, that was the supreme evil, for life was a gift that it was not his to take away. Not even in fair fight. And this was murder.

Slowly Andrea lowered the Mauser, peered through the drifting gun-smoke that hung heavily in the frosty evening air. The enemy had vanished, completely, rolled behind scattered boulders or burrowed frantically into the blanketing anonymity of the snow. But they were still there, still potentially as dangerous as ever. Andrea knew that they would recover fast from the death of their officer—there were no finer, no more tenacious fighters in Europe than the ski-troops of the Jaeger mountain battalion—and would come after him, catch and kill him if humanly possible. That was why Andrea's first care had been to kill their officer—he might not have come after him, might have stopped to puzzle out the reason for this unprovoked flank attack.

Andrea ducked low in reflex instinct as a sudden burst of automatic fire whined in murderous ricochet off the boulders before him. He had expected this. It was the old classic infantry attack pattern—advance under covering fire, drop, cover your mate and come again. Swiftly Andrea rammed home another charge into the magazine of his Mauser, dropped flat on his face and inched his way along behind the low line of broken rock that extended fifteen or twenty yards to his right—he had chosen his ambush point with care—and then petered out. At the far end he pulled his snow hood down to the level of his brows and edged a wary eye round the corner of the rock.

Another heavy burst of automatic fire smashed into the boulders he had just left, and half a dozen men—three from either end of the line—broke cover, scurried along the slope in a stumbling, crouching run, then pitched forward into the snow again. *Along* the slope—the two parties had run in opposite directions. Andrea lowered his head and rubbed the back of a massive hand across the stubbled grizzle of his chin. Awkward, damned awkward. No frontal attack for the foxes of the W.G.B. They were extending their lines on either side, the points hooking round in a great, encircling half-moon. Bad enough for himself, but he could have coped with that—a carefully reconnoitred escape gully wound up the slope behind him. But he hadn't foreseen what was obviously going to happen: the curving crescent of line to the west was going to sweep across the rock-shelter where the others lay hidden.

Andrea twisted over on his back and looked up at the evening sky. It was darkening by the moment, darkening with the gloom of coming snow, and daylight was beginning to fail. He twisted again and looked across the great swelling shoulder of Mount Kostos, looked at the few scattered rocks and shallow depressions that barely dimpled the smooth convexity of the slope. He took a second quick look round the rock as the rifles of the W.G.B. opened up once more, saw the same encircling manœuvre being executed again, and waited no longer. Firing blindly downhill, he half-rose to his feet and flung himself out into the open, finger squeezing on the trigger, feet driving desperately into the frozen snow as he launched himself towards the nearest rock-cover, forty yards away if an inch. Thirty-five yards to go, thirty, twenty and still not a shot fired, a slip, a stumble on the sliding scree, a catlike recovery, ten yards, still miraculously immune, and then he had dived into shelter to land on chest and stomach with a sickening impact that struck cruelly into his ribs and emptied his lungs with an explosive gasp.

Fighting for breath, he stuck the magazine cover, rammed home another charge, risked a quick peep over the top of the rock and catapulted himself to his feet again, all inside ten seconds. The Mauser held across his body opened up again, firing downhill at vicious random, for Andrea had eyes only for the smoothly-treacherous ground at his feet, for the scree-lined depression so impossibly far ahead. And then the Mauser was empty, useless in his hand, and every gun far below had opened up, the shells whistling above his head or blinding him with spurting gouts of snow as they rico-chetted off the solid rock. But twilight was touching the hills, Andrea was only a blur, a swiftly-flitting blur against a ghostly background, and uphill accuracy was notoriously difficult at any time. Even so, the massed fire from below was steadying and converging, and Andrea waited no longer. Unseen hands plucking wickedly at the flying tails of his snow-smock, he flung himself almost horizontally forward and slid the last ten feet face down into the waiting depression.

Stretched full length on his back in the hollow, Andrea fished out a steel mirror from his breast pocket and held it gingerly above his head. At first he could see nothing, for the darkness was deeper below and the mirror misted from the warmth of his body. And then the film vanished in the chill mountain air and he could see two, three and then half a dozen men breaking

THE GUNS OF NAVARONE

cover, heading at a clumsy run straight up the face of the hill—and two of them had come from the extreme right of the line. Andrea lowered the mirror and relaxed with a long sigh of relief, eyes crinkling in a smile. He looked up at the sky, blinked as the first feathery flakes of falling snow melted on his eyelids and smiled again. Almost lazily he brought out another charge for the Mauser, fed more shells into the magazine.

"Boss?" Miller's voice was plaintive.

"Yes? What is it?" Mallory brushed some snow off his face and the collar of his smock and peered into the white darkness ahead.

"Boss, when you were in school did you ever read any stories about folks gettin' lost in a snowstorm and wanderin' round and round in circles for days?"

"We had exactly the same book in Queenstown," Mallory conceded.

"Wanderin' round and round until they died?" Miller persisted.

"Oh, for heaven's sake!" Mallory said impatiently. His feet, even in Stevens's roomy boots, hurt abominably. "How can we be wandering in circles if we're going downhill all the time? What do you think we're on—a bloody spiral staircase?"

Miller walked on in hurt silence, Mallory beside him, both men ankle-deep in the wet, clinging snow that had been falling so silently, so persistently, for the past three hours since Andrea had drawn off the Jaeger search party. Even in mid-winter in the White Mountains in Crete Mallory could recall no snowfall so heavy and continuous. So much for the Isles of Greece and the eternal sunshine that gilds them yet, he thought bitterly. He hadn't reckoned on this when he'd planned on going down to Margaritha for food and fuel, but even so it wouldn't have made any difference to his decision. Although in less pain now, Stevens was becoming steadily weaker, and the need was desperate.

With moon and stars blanketed by the heavy snow-clouds—visibility, indeed, was hardly more than ten feet in any direction—the loss of their compasses had assumed a crippling importance. He didn't doubt his ability to find the village—it was simply a matter of walking downhill till they came to the stream that ran through the valley, then following that north till they came to Margaritha—but if the snow didn't let up their chances of locating that tiny cave again in the vast sweep of the hillsides . . .

Mallory smothered an exclamation as Miller's hand closed round his upper arm, dragged him down to his knees in the snow. Even in that moment of unknown danger he could feel a slow stirring of anger against himself, for his attention had been wandering along with his thoughts. . . . He lifted his hand as vizor against the snow, peered out narrowly through the wet, velvety curtain of white that swirled and eddied out of the darkness before him. Suddenly he had it—a dark, squat shape only feet away. They had all but walked straight into it.

"It's the hut," he said softly in Miller's ear. He had seen it early in the afternoon, half-way between their cave and Margaritha, and almost in a line with both. He was conscious of relief, an increase in confidence: they would be in the village in less than half an hour. "Elementary navigation, my dear Corporal," he murmured. "Lost and wandering in circles, my foot! Just put your faith . . ."

He broke off as Miller's fingers dug viciously into his arm, as Miller's head came close to his own.

"I heard voices, boss." The words were a mere breath of sound.

"Are you sure?" Miller's silenced gun, Mallory noticed, was still in his pocket.

Miller hesitated.

"Dammit to hell, boss, I'm sure of nothin'," he whispered irritably. "I've been imaginin' every damn' thing possible in the past hour!" He pulled the snow hood off his head, the better to listen, bent forward for a few seconds then sank back again. "Anyway, I'm sure I *thought* I heard somethin'."

"Come on. Let's take a look-see." Mallory was on his feet again. "I think you're mistaken. Can't be the Jaeger boys—they were half-way back across Mount Kostos when we saw them last. And the shepherds only use these places in the summer months." He slipped the safety catch of his Colt .455, walked slowly, at a half-crouch, towards the nearest wall of the hut, Miller at his shoulder.

They reached the hut, put their ears against the frail, tar-paper walls. Ten seconds passed, twenty, half a minute, then Mallory relaxed.

"Nobody at home. Or if they are, they're keeping mighty quiet. But no chances, Dusty. You go that way. I'll go this. Meet at the door—that'll be on the opposite side, facing into the valley. . . . Walk wide at the corners—never fails to baffle the unwary."

A minute later both men were inside the hut, the door shut behind them. The hooded beam of Mallory's torch probed into every corner of the ramshackle cabin. It was quite empty—an earthen floor, a rough wooden bunk, a dilapidated stove with a rusty lantern standing on it, and that was all. No table, no chair, no chimney, not even a window.

Mallory walked over to the stove, picked up the lamp and sniffed it.

"Hasn't been used for weeks. Still full of kerosene, though. Very useful in that damn' dungeon up there—if we can ever find the place. . . ."

He froze into a sudden listening immobility, eyes unfocused and head cocked slightly to one side. Gently, ever so gently, he set the lamp down, walked leisurely across to Miller.

"Remind me to apologise at some future date," he murmured. "We have company. Give me your gun and keep talking."

"Castelrosso again," Miller complained loudly. He hadn't even raised an eyebrow. "This is downright monotonous. A Chinaman—I'll bet it's a Chinaman this time." But he was already talking to himself.

The silenced automatic balanced at his waist, Mallory walked noiselessly round the hut, four feet out from the walls. He had passed two corners, was just rounding the third when, out of the corner of his eye, he saw a vague figure behind him rising up swiftly from the ground and lunging out with upraised arm. Mallory stepped back quickly under the blow, spun round, swung his balled fist viciously and backwards into the stomach of his attacker. There was a sudden explosive gasp of agony as the man doubled up, moaned and crumpled silently to the ground. Barely in time Mallory arrested the downward clubbing swipe of his reversed automatic.

Gun reversed again, the butt settled securely in his palm, Mallory stared down unblinkingly at the huddled figure, at the primitive wooden baton still clutched in the gloved right hand, at the unmilitary looking knapsack strapped to his back. He kept his gun lined up on the fallen body, waiting: this had been just too easy, too suspicious. Thirty seconds passed and still the figure on the ground hadn't stirred. Mallory took a short step forward and carefully, deliberately and none too gently kicked the man on the outside of the right knee. It was an old trick, and he'd never known it to fail—the pain was brief, but agonising. But there was no movement, no sound at all.

Quickly Mallory stooped, hooked his free hand round the knapsack shoulder straps, straightened and made for the door, half-carrying, half-dragging his captive. The man was no weight at all. With a proportionately much heavier garrison than even in Crete, there would be that much less food for the islanders, Mallory mused compassionately. There would be very little indeed. He wished he hadn't hit him so hard.

Miller met him at the open door, stooped wordlessly, caught the unconscious man by the ankles and helped Mallory dump him unceremoniously on the bunk in the far corner of the hut.

"Nice goin', boss," he complimented. "Never heard a thing. Who's the heavyweight champ?"

"No idea." Mallory shook his head in the darkness. "Just skin and bones, that's all, just skin and bones. Shut the door, Dusty, and let's have a look at what we've got."

8

TUESDAY
1900–0015

A MINUTE passed, two, then the little man stirred, moaned and pushed himself to a sitting position. Mallory held his arm to steady him, while he shook his bent head, eyes screwed tightly shut as he concentrated on clearing the muzziness away. Finally he looked up slowly, glanced from Mallory to Miller and back at Mallory again in the feeble light of the newly-lit, shuttered lantern. Even as the men watched, they could see the colour returning to the swarthy cheeks, the indignant bristling of the heavy, dark moustache, the darkening anger in the eyes. Suddenly the man reached up, tore Mallory's hand away from his arm.

"Who are you?" He spoke in English, clear, precise, with hardly a trace of accent.

"Sorry, but the less you know the better." Mallory smiled, deliberately to rob the words of offence. "I mean that for your own sake. How are you feeling now?"

Tenderly the little man massaged his midriff, flexed his leg with a grimace of pain.

"You hit me very hard."

"I had to." Mallory reached behind him and picked up the cudgel the man had been carrying. "You tried to hit me with this. What did you expect me to do—take my hat off so you could have a better swipe at me?"

"You are very amusing." Again he bent his leg, experimentally, looked up at Mallory in hostile suspicion. "My knee hurts me," he said accusingly.

"First things first. Why the club?"

"I meant to knock you down and have a look at you," he explained impatiently. "It was the only safe way. You might have been one of the W.G.B. . . . Why is my knee——?"

"You had an awkward fall," Mallory said shamelessly. "What are you doing here?"

"Who are you?" the little man countered.

Miller coughed, looked ostentatiously at his watch.

"This is all very entertainin', boss——"

"True for you, Dusty. We haven't all night." Quickly Mallory reached behind him, picked up the man's rucksack, tossed it across to Miller. "See what's in there, will you?" Strangely, the little man made no move to protest.

"Food!" Miller said reverently. "Wonderful, wonderful food. Cooked meat, bread, cheese—and wine." Reluctantly Miller closed the bag and looked curiously at their prisoner. "Helluva funny time for a picnic."

"So! An American, a Yankee." The little man smiled to himself. "Better and better!"

"What do you mean?" Miller asked suspiciously.

"See for yourself," the man said pleasantly. He nodded casually to the far corner of the room. "Look there."

Mallory spun round, realised in a moment that he had been tricked, jerked back again. Carefully he leaned forward and touched Miller's arm.

"Don't look round too quickly, Dusty. And don't touch your gun. It seems our friend was not alone." Mallory tightened his lips, mentally cursed himself for his obtuseness. Voices—Dusty had said there had been voices. Must be even more tired than he had thought. . . .

A tall, lean man blocked the entrance to the doorway. His face was shadowed under an enveloping snow-hood, but there was no mistaking the gun in his hand. A short Lee Enfield rifle, Mallory noted dispassionately.

"Do not shoot!" The little man spoke rapidly in Greek. "I am almost sure that they are those whom we seek, Panayis."

Panayis! Mallory felt the wave of relief wash over him. That was one of the names Eugene Vlachos had given him, back in Alexandria.

"The tables turned, are they not?" The little man smiled at Mallory, the tired eyes crinkling, the heavy black moustache lifting engagingly at one corner. "I ask you again, who are you?"

"S.O.E.," Mallory answered unhesitatingly.

The man nodded in satisfaction. "Captain Jensen sent you?"

Mallory sank back on the bunk and sighed in long relief.

"We are among friends, Dusty." He looked at the little man before him. "You must be Louki—the first plane tree in the square in Margaritha?"

The little man beamed. He bowed, stretched out his hand.

"Louki. At your service, sir."

"And this, of course, is Panayis?"

The tall man in the doorway, dark, saturnine, unsmiling, inclined his head briefly but said nothing.

"You have us right!" The little man was beaming with delight. "Louki and Panayis. They know about us in Alexandria and Cairo, then?" he asked proudly.

"Of course!" Mallory smothered a smile. "They spoke highly of you. You have been of great help to the Allies before."

"And we will again," Louki said briskly. "Come, we are wasting time. The Germans are on the hills. What help can we give you?"

"Food, Louki. We need food—we need it badly."

"We have it!" Proudly, Louki gestured at the rucksacks. "We were on our way up with it."

"You were on your way. . . ." Mallory was astonished. "How did you know where we were—or even that we were on the island?"

Louki waved a deprecating hand.

"It was easy. Since first light German troops have been moving south through Margaritha up into the hills. All morning they combed the east col of Kostos. We knew someone must have landed, and that the Germans were looking for them. We heard, too, that the Germans had blocked the cliff path on the south coast, at both ends. So you must have come over the west col. They would not expect that—you fooled them. So we came to find you."

"But you would never have found us——"

"We would have found you." There was complete certainty in the voice. "Panayis and I—we know every stone, every blade of grass in Navarone." Louki shivered suddenly, stared out bleakly through the swirling snow. "You couldn't have picked worse weather."

"We couldn't have picked better," Mallory said grimly.

"Last night, yes," Louki agreed. "No one would expect you in that wind and rain. No one would hear the aircraft or even dream that you would try to jump——"

"We came by sea," Miller interrupted. He waved a negligent hand. "We climbed the south cliff."

"What? The south cliff!" Louki was frankly disbelieving. "No one could climb the south cliff. It is impossible!"

"That's the way we felt when we were about half-way up," Mallory said candidly. "But Dusty, here, is right. That's how it was."

Louki had taken a step back: his face was expressionless.

"I say it is impossible." he repeated flatly.

"He is telling the truth, Louki," Miller cut in quietly. "Do you never read newspapers?"

"Of course I read newspapers!" Louki bristled with indignation. "Do you think I am—how you say—illiterate?"

"Then think back to just before the war," Miller advised. "Think of mountaineerin'—and the Himalayas. You must have seen his picture in the papers—once, twice, a hundred times." He looked at Mallory consideringly. "Only he was a little prettier in those days. You must remember. This is Mallory, Keith Mallory of New Zealand."

Mallory said nothing. He was watching Louki, the puzzlement, the comical screwing up of the eyes, head cocked to one side: then, all at once, something clicked in the little man's memory and his face lit up in a great, crinkling smile that swamped every last trace of suspicion. He stepped forward, hand outstretched in welcome.

"By heaven, you are right! Mallory! Of course I know Mallory!" He grabbed Mallory's hand, pumped it up and down with great enthusiasm. "It is indeed as the American says. You need a shave. . . . And you look older."

"I feel older," Mallory said gloomily. He nodded at Miller. "This is Corporal Miller, an American citizen."

"Another famous climber?" Louki asked eagerly. "Another tiger of the hills, yes?"

"He climbed the south cliff as it has never been climbed before," Mallory answered truthfully. He glanced at his watch, then looked directly at Louki. "There are others up in the hills. We need help, Louki. We need it badly and we need it at once. You know the danger if you are caught helping us?"

"Danger?" Louki waved a contemptuous hand. "Danger to Louki and Panayis, the foxes of Navarone? Impossible! We are the ghosts of the night." He hitched his pack higher up on his shoulders. "Come. Let us take this food to your friends."

"Just a minute." Mallory's restraining hand was on his arm. "There are two other things. We need heat—a stove and fuel, and we need——"

"Heat! A stove!" Louki was incredulous. "Your friends in the hills—what are they? A band of old women?"

"And we also need bandages and medicine," Mallory went on patiently. "One of our friends has been terribly injured. We are not sure, but we do not think that he will live."

"Panayis!" Louki barked. "Back to the village." Louki was speaking in Greek now. Rapidly he issued his orders, had Mallory describe where the rock-shelter was, made sure that Panayis understood, then stood a moment in indecision, pulling at an end of his moustache. At length he looked up at Mallory.

"Could you find this cave again by yourself?"

"Lord only knows," Mallory said frankly. "I honestly don't think so."

"Then I must come with you. I had hoped—you see, it will be a heavy load for Panayis—I have told him to bring bedding as well—and I don't think——"

"I'll go along with him," Miller volunteered. He thought of his back-breaking labours on the caique, the climb up the cliff, their forced march through the mountains. "The exercise will do me good."

Louki translated his offer to Panayis—taciturn, apparently, only because of his complete lack of English—and was met by what appeared to be a torrent of protest. Miller looked at him in astonishment.

"What's the matter with old sunshine here?" he asked Mallory. "Doesn't seem any too happy to me."

"Says he can manage O.K. and wants to go by himself," Mallory inter-preted. "Thinks you'll slow him up on the hills." He shook his head in mock wonder. "As if any man could slow Dusty Miller up!"

"Exactly!" Louki was bristling with anger. Again he turned to Panayis, fingers stabbing the empty air to emphasise his words. Miller turned, looked apprehensively at Mallory.

"What's he tellin' him now, boss?"

"Only the truth," Mallory said solemnly. "Saying he ought to be hon-oured at being given the opportunity of marching with Monsieur Miller, the world-famous American climber." Mallory grinned. "Panayis will be on his mettle to-night—determined to prove that a Navaronian can climb as well and as fast as any man."

"Oh, my Gawd!" Miller moaned.

"And on the way back, don't forget to give Panayis a hand up the steeper bits."

Miller's reply was luckily lost in a sudden flurry of snowladen wind.

That wind was rising steadily now, a bitter wind that whipped the heavy snow into their bent faces and stung the tears from their blinking eyes. A heavy, wet snow that melted as it touched, and trickled down through every gap and chink in their clothing until they were wet and chilled and thor-oughly miserable. A clammy, sticky snow that built up layer after energy-sapping layer under their leaden-footed boots, until they stumbled along inches above the ground, leg muscles aching from the sheer accumulated weight of snow. There was no visibility worthy of the name, not even of a matter of feet, they were blanketed, swallowed up by an impenetrable co-coon of swirling grey and white, unchanging, featureless: Louki strode on diagonally upwards across the slope with the untroubled certainty of a man walking up his own garden path.

Louki seemed as agile as a mountain goat, and as tireless. Nor was his tongue less nimble, less unwearied than his legs. He talked incessantly, a man overjoyed to be in action again, no matter what action so long as it was against the enemy. He told Mallory of the last three attacks on the island and how they had so bloodily failed—the Germans had been somehow forewarned of the seaborne assault, had been waiting for the Special Boat Service and the Commandos with everything they had and had cut them to pieces, while the two airborne groups had had the most evil luck, been delivered up to the enemy by misjudgment, by a series of unforeseeable coincidences; or how Panayis and himself had on both occasions narrowly escaped with their lives—Panayis had actually been captured the last time, had killed both his guards and escaped unrecognised; of the disposition of the German troops and check-points throughout the island, the location of the road blocks on the only two roads; and, finally, of what little he himself knew of the layout of the fortress of Navarone itself. Panayis, the dark one, could tell him more of that, Louki said: twice Panayis had been inside the fortress, once for an entire night: the guns, the control rooms, the barracks, the officers' quarters, the magazine, the turbo rooms, the sentry points—he knew where each one lay, to the inch.

Mallory whistled softly to himself. This was more than he had ever dared hope for. They had still to escape the net of searchers, still to reach the fortress, still to get inside it. But once inside—and Panayis must know how to get inside. . . . Unconsciously Mallory lengthened his stride, bent his back to the slope.

"Your friend Panayis must be quite something," he said slowly. "Tell me more about him, Louki."

"What can I tell you?" Louki shook his head in a little flurry of snow-flakes. "What do I know of Panayis? What does anyone know of Panayis? That he has the luck of the devil, the courage of a madman and that sooner the lion will lie down with the lamb, the starving wolf spare the flock, than Panayis breathe the same air as the Germans? We all know that, and we know nothing of Panayis. All I know is that I thank God I am no German, with Panayis on the island. He strikes by stealth, by night, by knife and in the back." Louki crossed himself. "His hands are full of blood."

Mallory shivered involuntarily. The dark, sombre figure of Panayis, the memory of the expressionless face, the hooded eyes, were beginning to fascinate him.

"There's more to him than that, surely," Mallory argued. "After all, you are both Navaronians——"

"Yes, yes, that is so."

"This is a small island, you've lived together all your lives——"

"Ah, but that is where the Major is wrong!" Mallory's promotion in rank was entirely Louki's own idea: despite Mallory's protests and explanations he seemed determined to stick to it. "I, Louki, was for many years in foreign lands, helping Monsieur Vlachos. Monsieur Vlachos," Louki said with pride, "is a very important Government official."

"I know," Mallory nodded. "A consul. I've met him. He is a very fine man."

"You have met him! Monsieur Vlachos?" There was no mistaking the gladness, the delight in Louki's voice. "That is good! That is wonderful! Later you must tell me more. He is a great man. Did I ever tell you——"

"We were speaking about Panayis," Mallory reminded him gently.

"Ah, yes, Panayis. As I was saying, I was away for a long time. When I came back, Panayis was gone. His father had died, his mother had married again and Panayis had gone to live with his stepfather and two little stepsisters in Crete. His stepfather, half-fisherman, half-farmer, was killed in fighting the Germans near Candia—this was in the beginning. Panayis took

over the boat of his father, helped many of the Allies to escape until he was
caught by the Germans, strung up by his wrists in the village square—where
his family lived—not far from Casteli. He was flogged till the white of his
ribs, of his backbone, was there for all to see, and left for dead. Then they
burnt the village and Panayis's family—disappeared. You understand, Major?''

"I understand," Mallory said grimly. "But Panayis———"

"He should have died. But he is tough, that one, tougher than a knot in
an old carob tree. Friends cut him down during the night, took him away
into the hills till he was well again. And then he arrived back in Navarone,
God knows how. I think he came from island to island in a small rowing-
boat. He never says why he came back—I think it gives him greater pleasure
to kill on his own native island. I do not know, Major. All I know is that
food and sleep, the sunshine, women and wine—all these are nothing and
less than nothing to the dark one.'' Again Louki crossed himself. "He obeys
me, for I am the steward of the Vlachos family, but even I am afraid of him.
To kill, to keep on killing, then kill again—that is the very breath of his
being." Louki stopped momentarily, sniffed the air like a hound seeking
some fugitive scent, then kicked the snow off his boots and struck off up
the hill at a tangent. The little man's unhesitating sureness of direction was
uncanny.

"How far to go now, Louki?"

"Two hundred yards, Major. No more." Louki blew some snow off his
heavy, dark moustache and swore. "I shall not be sorry to arrive."

"Nor I.'' Mallory thought of the miserable, draughty shelter in the dripping rocks almost with affection. It was becoming steadily colder as they
climbed out of the valley, and the wind was rising, climbing up the register
with a steady, moaning whine: they had to lean into it now, push hard against
it, to make any progress. Suddenly both men stopped, listened, looked at
each other, heads bent against the driving snow. Around them there was
only the white emptiness and the silence: there was no sign of what had
caused the sudden sound.

"You heard something, too?" Mallory murmured.

"It is only I." Mallory spun round as the deep voice boomed out behind
him and the bulky, white-smocked figure loomed out of the snow. "A milk
wagon on a cobbled street is as nothing compared to yourself and your
friend. But the snow muffled your voices and I could not be sure.''

Mallory looked at him curiously. "How come you're here, Andrea?"

"Wood,'' Andrea explained. "I was looking for firewood. I was high up
on Kostos at sunset when the snow lifted for a moment. I could have sworn
I saw an old hut in a gully not far from here—it was dark and square against
the snow. So I left———''

"You are right," Louki interrupted. "The hut of old Leri, the mad one.
Leri was a goatherd. We all warned him, but Leri would listen and speak to
no man, only to his goats. He died in his hut, in a landslide.''

"It is an ill wind . . .'' Andrea murmured. "Old Leri will keep us warm
to-night." He checked abruptly as the gully opened up at his feet, then
dropped quickly to the bottom, surefooted as a mountain sheep. He whistled
twice, a double high-pitched note, listened intently into the snow for the
answering whistle, walked swiftly up the gully. Casey Brown, gun lowered,
met them at the entrance to the cave and held back the canvas screen to let
them pass inside.

The smoking tallow candle, guttering heavily to one side in the icy draught, filled every corner of the cave with dark and flickering shadows from its erratic flame. The candle itself was almost gone, the dripping wick bending over tiredly till it touched the rock, and Louki, snow-suit cast aside, was lighting another stump of candle from the dying flame. For a moment, both candles flared up together, and Mallory saw Louki clearly for the first time— a small, compact figure in a dark-blue jacket black-braided at the seams and flamboyantly frogged at the breast, the jacket tightly bound to his body by the crimson *tsanta* or cummerbund, and, above, the swarthy, smiling face, the magnificent moustache that he flaunted like a banner. A Laughing Cavalier of a man, a miniature d'Artagnan splendidly behung with weapons. And then Mallory's gaze travelled up to the lined, liquid eyes, eyes dark and sad and permanently tired, and his shock, a slow, uncomprehending shock, had barely time to register before the stub of the candle had flared up and died and Louki had sunk back into the shadows.

Stevens was stretched in a sleeping-bag, his breathing harsh and shallow and quick. He had been awake when they had arrived but had refused all food and drink, and turned away and drifted off into an uneasy jerky sleep. He seemed to be suffering no pain at all now: a bad sign, Mallory thought bleakly, the worst possible. He wished Miller would return. . . .

Casey Brown washed down the last few crumbs of bread with a mouthful of wine, rose stiffly to his feet, pulled the screen aside and peered out mournfully at the falling snow. He shuddered, let the canvas fall, lifted up his transmitter and shrugged into the shoulder straps, gathered up a coil of rope, a torch and a groundsheet. Mallory looked at his watch: it was fifteen minutes to midnight. The routine call from Cairo was almost due.

"Going to have another go, Casey? I wouldn't send a dog out on a night like this."

"Neither would I," Brown said morosely. "But I think I'd better, sir. Reception is far better at night and I'm going to climb uphill a bit to get a clearance from that damned mountain there: I'd be spotted right away if I tried to do that in daylight."

"Right you are, Casey. You know best." Mallory looked at him curiously. "What's all the extra gear for?"

"Putting the set under the groundsheet then getting below it myself with the torch," Brown explained. "And I'm pegging the rope here, going to pay it out on my way up. I'd like to be able to get back some time."

"Good enough," Mallory approved. "Just watch it a bit higher up. This gully narrows and deepens into a regular ravine."

"Don't you worry about me, sir." Brown said firmly. "Nothing's going to happen to Casey Brown." A snow-laden gust of wind, the flap of the canvas and Brown was gone.

"Well, if Brown can do it . . . ." Mallory was on his feet now, pulling his snow-smock over his head. "Fuel, gentlemen—old Leri's hut. Who's for a midnight stroll?"

Andrea and Louki were on their feet together, but Mallory shook his head.

"One's enough. I think someone should stay to look after Stevens."

"He's sound asleep," Andrea murmured. "He can come to no harm in the short time we are away."

"I wasn't thinking of that. It's just that we can't take the chance of him falling into German hands. They'd make him talk, one way or another. It would be no fault of his—but they'd make him talk. It's too much of a risk."

"Pouf!" Louki snapped his fingers. "You worry about nothing, Major. There isn't a German within miles of here. You have my word."

Mallory hesitated, then grinned. "You're right. I'm getting the jumps." He bent over Stevens, shook him gently. The boy stirred and moaned, opened his eyes slowly.

"We're going out for some firewood," Mallory said. "Back in a few minutes. You be O.K.?"

"Of course, sir. What can happen? Just leave a gun by my side—and blow out the candle." He smiled. "Be sure to call out before you come in!"

Mallory stooped, blew out the candle. For an instant the flame flared then died and every feature, every person in the cave was swallowed up in the thick darkness of a winter midnight. Abruptly Mallory turned on his heel and pushed out through the canvas into the drifting, wind-blown snow already filling up the floor of the gully, Andrea and Louki close behind.

It took them ten minutes to find the ruined hut of the old goatherd, another five for Andrea to wrench the door off its shattered hinges and smash it up to manageable lengths, along with the wood from the bunk and table, another ten to carry back with them to the rock-shelter as much wood as they could conveniently rope together and carry. The wind, blowing straight north of Kostos, was in their faces now—faces numbed with the chill, wet lash of the driving snow, and blowing almost at gale force: they were not sorry to reach the gully again, drop down gratefully between the sheltering walls.

Mallory called softly at the mouth of the cave. There was no reply, no movement from inside. He called again, listened intently as the silent seconds went by, turned his head and looked briefly at Andrea and Louki. Carefully, he laid his bundle of wood in the snow, pulled out his Colt and torch, eased aside the curtain, lamp switch and Colt safety-catch clicking as one.

The spotlight beam lit up the floor at the mouth of the cave, passed on, settled, wavered, probed into the farthest corner of the shelter, returned again to the middle of the cave and steadied there as if the torch were clamped in a vice. On the floor there was only a crumpled, empty sleeping-bag. Andy Stevens was gone.

9

TUESDAY NIGHT
0015–0200

"So I was wrong," Andrea murmured. "He wasn't asleep."

"He certainly wasn't," Mallory agreed grimly. "He fooled me too—*and* he heard what I said." His mouth twisted. "He knows now why we're so anxious to look after him. He knows now that he was right when he spoke about a mill-stone. I should hate to feel the way he must be feeling right now."

Andrea nodded. "It is not difficult to guess why he has gone."

Mallory looked quickly at his watch, pushed his way out of the cave.

"Twenty minutes—he can't have been gone more than twenty minutes. Probably a bit less to make sure we were well clear. He can only drag himself—fifty yards at the most. We'll find him in four minutes. Use your torches and take the hoods off—nobody will see us in this damn' blizzard. Fan out uphill—I'll take the gully in the middle."

"Uphill?" Louki's hand was on his arm, his voice puzzled. "But his leg——"

"Uphill, I said," Mallory broke in impatiently. "Stevens has brains—and a damn' sight more guts than he thinks we credit him with. He'll figure we'll think he's taken the easy way." Mallory paused a moment then went on sombrely: "Any dying man who drags himself out in this lot is going to do nothing the easy way. Come on!"

They found him in exactly three minutes. He must have suspected that Mallory wouldn't fall for the obvious, or he had heard them stumbling up the slope, for he had managed to burrow his way in behind the overhanging snowdrift that sealed off the space beneath a projecting ledge just above the rim of the gully. An almost perfect place of concealment, but his leg betrayed him: in the probing light of his torch Andrea's sharp eyes caught the tiny trickle of blood seeping darkly through the surface of the snow. He was already unconscious when they uncovered him, from cold or exhaustion or the agony of his shattered leg: probably from all three.

Back in the cave again, Mallory tried to pour some ouzo—the fiery, breath-catching local spirit—down Stevens's throat. He had a vague suspicion that this might be dangerous—or perhaps it was only dangerous in cases of shock, his memory was confused on that point—but it seemed better than nothing. Stevens gagged, spluttered and coughed most of it back up again, but some at least stayed down. With Andrea's help Mallory tightened the loosened splints on the leg, staunched the oozing blood, and spread below and above the boy every dry covering he could find in the cave. Then he sat back tiredly and fished out a cigarette from his waterproof case. There was nothing more he could do until Dusty Miller returned with Panayis from the village. He was pretty sure that there was nothing that Dusty could do for Stevens either. There was nothing anybody could do for him.

Already Louki had a fire burning near the mouth of the cave, the old, tinder-dry wood blazing up in a fierce, crackling blaze with hardly a wisp of smoke. Almost at once its warmth began to spread throughout the cave, and the three men edged gratefully nearer. From half a dozen points in the roof thin, steadily-increasing streams of water from the melting snows above began to splash down on the gravelly floor beneath: with these, and with the heat of the blaze, the ground was soon a quagmire. But, especially to Mallory and Andrea, these discomforts were a small price to pay for the privilege of being warm for the first time in over thirty hours. Mallory felt the glow seep through him like a benison, felt his entire body relax, his eyelids grow heavy and drowsy.

Back propped against the wall, he was just drifting off to sleep, still smoking that first cigarette, when there was a gust of wind, a sudden chilling flurry of snow and Brown was inside the cave, wearily slipping the transmitter straps from his shoulders. Lugubrious as ever, his tired eyes lit up momentarily at the sight of the fire. Blue-faced and shuddering with cold—no joke, Mallory thought grimly, squatting motionless for half an hour on that bleak and frozen hillside—he hunched down silently by the fire, dragged out the inevitable cigarette and gazed moodily into the flames, oblivious alike of the clouds of steam that almost immediately enveloped him, of the acrid smell of his singeing clothes. He looked utterly despondent. Mallory reached for a bottle, poured out some of the heated *retsimo*—mainland wine heavily reinforced with resin—and passed it across to Brown.

"Chuck it straight down the hatch," Mallory advised. "That way you won't taste it." He prodded the transmitter with his foot and looked up at Brown again. "No dice this time either?"

"Raised them no bother, sir." Brown grimaced at the sticky sweetness of the wine. "Reception was first class—both here and in Cairo."

"You got through!" Mallory sat up, leaned forward eagerly. "And were they pleased to hear from their wandering boys to-night?"

"They didn't say. The first thing they told me was to shut up and stay that way." Brown poked moodily at the fire with a steaming boot. "Don't ask me how, sir, but they've been tipped off that enough equipment for two or three small monitoring stations has been sent here in the past fortnight."

Mallory swore.

"Monitoring stations! That's damned handy, that is!" He thought briefly of the fugitive, nomad existence these same monitoring stations had compelled Andrea and himself to lead in the White Mountains of Crete. "Dammit, Casey, on an island like this, the size of a soup plate, they can pinpoint us with their eyes shut!"

"Aye, they can that, sir," Brown nodded heavily.

"Have you heard anything of these stations, Louki?" Mallory asked.

"Nothing, Major; nothing." Louki shrugged. "I am afraid I do not even know what you are talking about."

"I don't suppose so. Not that it matters—it's too late now. Let's have the rest of the good news, Casey."

"That's about it, sir. No sending for me—by order. Restricted to code abbreviations—affirmative, negative, repetitive, wilco and such-like. Continuous sending only in emergency or when concealment's impossible anyway."

"Like from the condemned cell in these ducky little dungeons in Navarone," Mallory murmured. " 'I died with my boots on, ma'.' "

"With all respects, sir, that's not funny," Brown said morosely. "Their invasion fleet—mainly caiques and E-boats—sailed his morning from the Piraeus," he went on. "About four o'clock this morning. Cairo expects they'll be holing up in the Cyclades somewhere to-night."

"That's very clever of Cairo. Where the hell else could they hole up?" Mallory lit a fresh cigarette and looked bleakly into the fire. "Anyway, it's nice to know they're on the way. That the lot, Casey?"

Brown nodded silently.

"Good enough, then. Thanks a lot for going out. Better turn in, catch up with some sleep while you can. . . . Louki reckons we should be down in Margaritha before dawn, hole up there for the day—he's got some sort of abandoned well all lined up for us—and push on to the town of Navarone to-morrow night."

"My God!" Brown moaned. "To-night a leaking cave. To-morrow night an abandoned well—half-full of water, probably. Where are we staying in Navarone, sir? The crypt in the local cemetery?"

"A singularly apt lodging, the way things are going," Mallory said dryly. "We'll hope for the best. We're leaving before five." He watched Brown lie down beside Stevens and transferred his attention to Louki. The little man was seated on a box on the opposite side of the fire, occasionally turning a heavy stone to be wrapped in cloth and put to Stevens's numbed feet, and blissfully hugging the flames. By and by he became aware of Mallory's close scrutiny and looked up.

"You look worried, Major." Louki seemed vexed. "You look—what is the word?—concerned. You do not like my plan, no? I thought we had agreed——"

"I'm not worried about your plan," Mallory said frankly. "I'm not even worried about you. It's that box you're sitting on. Enough H.E. in it to blow up a battleship—and you're only three feet from that fire. It's not just too healthy, Louki.''

Louki shifted uneasily on his seat, tugged at one end of his moustache.

"I have heard that you can throw this T.N.T. into a fire and that it just burns up nicely, like a pine full of sap.''

"True enough," Mallory acquiesced. "You can also bend it, break it, file it, saw it, jump on it and hit it with a sledgehammer, and all you'll get is the benefit of the exercise. But if it starts to sweat in a hot, humid atmosphere—and then the exudation crystallises. Oh, brother! And it's getting far too hot and sticky in this hole.''

"Outside with it!" Louki was on his feet, backing farther into the cave. "Outside with it!" He hesitated. "Unless the snow, the moisture——''

"You can also leave it immersed in salt water for ten years without doing it any harm," Mallory interrupted didactically. "But there are some primers there that might come to grief—not to mention that box of detonators beside Andrea. We'll just stick the lot outside, under a cape.''

"Pouf! Louki has a far better idea!" The little man was already slipping into his cloak. "Old Leri's hut! The very place! Exactly! We can pick it up there whenever we want—and if you have to leave here in a hurry you do not have to worry about it." Before Mallory could protest, Louki had bent over the box, lifted it with an effort, half-walked, half-staggered round the fire, making for the screen. He had hardly taken three steps when Andrea was by his side, had relieved him firmly of the box and tucked it under one arm.

"If you will permit me——''

"No, no!" Louki was affronted. "I can manage easily. It is nothing.''

"I know, I know," Andrea said pacifically. "But these explosives—they must be carried a certain way. I have been trained," he explained.

"So? I did not realise. Of course it must be as you say! I, then, will bring the detonators." Honour satisfied, Louki thankfully gave up the argument, lifted the little box and scuttled out of the cave close on Andrea's heels.

Mallory looked at his watch. One o'clock exactly. Miller and Panayis should be back soon, he thought. The wind had passed its peak and the snow was almost gone: the going would be all that easier, but there would be tracks in the snow. Awkward, these tracks, but not fatal—they themselves would be gone before light, cutting straight downhill for the foot of the valley. The snow wouldn't lie there—and even if there were patches they could take to the stream that wound through the valley, leaving no trace behind.

The fire was sinking and the cold creeping in on them again. Mallory shivered in his still wet clothes, threw some more wood on the fire, watched it blaze up, and flood the cave with light. Brown, huddled on a groundsheet, was already asleep. Stevens, his back to him, was lying motionless, his breathing short and quick. God only knew how long the boy would stay alive: he was dying, Miller said, but "dying" was a very indefinite term: when a man, a terribly injured, dying man, made up his mind not to die he became the toughest, most enduring creature on earth. Mallory had seen it happen before. But maybe Stevens didn't want to live. To live, to overcome these desperate injuries—that would be to prove himself to himself, and to others, and he was young enough, and sensitive enough and had been hurt and had suffered so much in the past that that could easily be the most important thing in the world to him: on the other hand, he knew what an appalling handicap he had become—he had heard Mallory say so; he knew, too, that Mallory's primary concern was not for his welfare but the fear that he would be captured, crack under pressure and tell everything—he had heard Mallory say so; and he knew that he had failed his friends. It was all very difficult, impossible to say how the balance of contending forces would work out eventually. Mallory shook his head, sighed, lit a fresh cigarette and moved closer to the fire.

Andrea and Louki returned less than five minutes later, and Miller and Panayis were almost at their heels. They could hear Miller coming some distance away, slipping, falling and swearing almost continuously as he struggled up the gully under a large and awkward load. He practically fell across the threshold of the cave and collapsed wearily by the fire. He gave the impression of a man who had been through a very great deal indeed. Mallory grinned sympathetically at him.

"Well, Dusty, how did it go? Hope Panayis here didn't slow you up too much."

Miller didn't seem to hear him. He was gazing incredulously at the fire, lantern jaw dropping open as its significance slowly dawned on him.

"Hell's teeth! Would you look at that!" He swore bitterly. "Here I spend half the gawddamned night climbing up a gawddamned mountain with a stove and enough kerosene to bathe a bloody elephant. And what do I find?" He took a deep breath to tell them what he found, then subsided into a strangled, seething silence.

"A man your age should watch his blood pressure," Mallory advised. "How did the rest of it go?"

"Okay, I guess." Miller had a mug of ouzo in his hand and was beginning to brighten up again. "We got the beddin', the medicine kit——"

"If you'll give me the bedding I will get our young friend into it now," Andrea interrupted.

"And food?" Mallory asked.

"Yeah. We got the grub, boss. Stacks of it. This guy Panayis is a wonder. Bread, wine, goat-cheese, garlic sausages, rice—everything."

"Rice?" It was Mallory's turn to be incredulous. "But you can't get the stuff in the islands nowadays, Dusty."

"Panayis can." Miller was enjoying himself hugely now. "He got it from the German commandant's kitchen. Guy by the name of Skoda."

"The German commandant's—you're joking!"

"So help me, boss, that's Gospel truth." Miller drained half the ouzo at a gulp and expelled his breath in a long, gusty sigh of satisfaction. "Little ol' Miller hangs around the back door, knees knockin' like Carmen Miranda's castanets, ready for a smart take off in any direction while Junior here goes in and cracks the joint. Back home in the States he'd make a fortune as a cat-burglar. Comes back in about ten minutes, luggin' that damned suitcase there." Miller indicated it with a casual wave of his hand. "Not only cleans out the commandant's pantry, but also borrows his satchel to carry the stuff in. I tell you, boss, associatin' with this character gives me heart attacks."

"But—but how about guards, about sentries?"

"Taken the night off, I guess, boss. Old Panayis is like a clam—never says a word, and even then I can't understand him. My guess is that everybody's out lookin' for us."

"There and back and you didn't meet a soul." Mallory filled him a mug of wine. "Nice going, Dusty."

"Panayis's doin', not mine. I just tagged along. Besides, we did run into a couple of Panayis's pals—he hunted them up, rather. Musta given him the tip-off about somethin'. He was hoppin' with excitement just afterwards, tried to tell me all about it.'' Miller shrugged his shoulders sadly. ''We weren't operatin' on the same wave-length, boss.''

Mallory nodded across the cave. Louki and Panayis were close together, Louki doing all the listening, while Panayis talked rapidly in a low voice, gesticulating with both hands.

"He's still pretty worked up about something,'' Mallory said thoughtfully. He raised his voice. ''What's the matter, Louki?''

"Matter enough, Major.'' Louki tugged ferociously at the end of his moustache. ''We will have to be leaving soon—Panayis wants to go right away. He has heard that the German garrison is going to make a house-to-house check in our village during the night—about four o'clock, Panayis was told.''

"Not a routine check, I take it?'' Mallory asked.

"This has not happened for many months. They must think that you have slipped their patrols and are hiding in the village.'' Louki chuckled. ''If you ask me, I don't think they know *what* to think. It is nothing to you, of course. You will not be there—and even if you were they would not find you: and it will make it all the safer for you to come to Margaritha afterwards. But Panayis and I—we must not be found out of our beds. Things would go hard with us.''

"Of course, of course. We must take no risks. But there is plenty of time. You will go down in an hour. But first, the fortress.'' He dug into his breast pocket, brought out the map Eugene Vlachos had drawn for him, turned to Panayis and slipped easily into the island Greek. ''Come, Panayis. I hear you know the fortress as Louki here knows his own vegetable patch. I already know much, but I want you to tell me everything about it—the layout, guns, magazines, power rooms, barracks, sentries, guard routine, exits, alarm systems, even where the shadows are deep and the others less deep—just everything. No matter how tiny and insignificant the details may seem to you, nevertheless you must tell me. If a door opens outwards instead of inwards, you must tell me: that could save a thousand lives.''

"And how does the Major mean to get inside?'' Louki asked.

"I don't know yet. I cannot decide until I have seen the fortress.'' Mallory was aware of Andrea looking sharply at him, then looking away. They had made their plans on the M.T.B. for entering the fortress. But it was the keystone upon which everything depended, and Mallory felt that this knowledge should be confined to the fewest number possible.

For almost half an hour Mallory and the three Greeks huddled over the chart in the light of the flames, Mallory checking on what he had been told, meticulously pencilling in all the fresh information that Panayis had to give him—and Panayis had a very great deal to tell. It seemed almost impossible that a man could have assimilated so much in two brief visits to the fortress—and clandestine visits in the darkness, at that. He had an incredible eye and capacity for detail; and it was a burning hatred of the Germans, Mallory felt certain, that had imprinted these details on an all but photographic memory. Mallory could feel his hopes rising with every second that passed.

Casey Brown was awake again. Tired though he was, the babble of voices had cut through an uneasy sleep. He crossed over to where Andy Stevens, half-awake now, lay propped against the wall, talking rationally at times, incoherently at others. There was nothing for him to do there, Brown saw: Miller, cleaning, dusting and rebandaging the wounds had had all the help

he needed—and very efficient help at that—from Andrea. He moved over
to the mouth of the cave, listened blankly to the four men talking in Greek,
moved out past the screen for a breath of the cold, clean night air. With
seven people inside the cave and the fire burning continuously, the lack of
almost all ventilation had made it uncomfortably warm.

He was back in the cave in thirty seconds, drawing the screen tightly shut
behind him.

"Quiet, everybody!" he whispered softly. He gestured behind him. "There's
something moving out there, down the slope a bit. I heard it twice, sir."

Panayis swore softly, twisted to his feet like a wild cat. A foot-long, two-
edged throwing knife gleamed evilly in his hand and he had vanished through
the canvas screen before anyone could speak. Andrea made to follow him,
but Mallory stretched out his hand.

"Stay where you are, Andrea. Our friend Panayis is just that little bit too
precipitate," he said softly. "There may be nothing—or it might be some
diversionary move. . . . Oh, damn!" Stevens had just started babbling to
himself in a loud voice. "He would start talking now. Can't you do something . . ."

But Andrea was already bent over the sick boy, holding his hand in his
own, smoothing the hot forehead and hair with his free hand and talking to
him soothingly, softly, continuously. At first he paid no attention, kept on
talking in a rambling, inconsequential fashion about nothing in particular;
gradually, however, the hypnotic effect of the stroking hand, the gentle
caressing murmur took effect, and the babbling died away to a barely audible
muttering, ceased altogether. Suddenly his eyes opened and he was awake
and quite rational.

"What is it, Andrea? Why are you——?"

"Shh!" Mallory held up his hand. "I can hear someone——"

"It's Panayis, sir." Brown had his eye at a crack in the curtain. "Just
moving up the gully."

Seconds later, Panayis was inside the cave, squatting down by the fire.
He looked thoroughly disgusted.

"There is no one there," he reported. "Some goats I saw, down the hill,
but that was all." Mallory translated to the others.

"Didn't sound like goats to me," Brown said doggedly. "Different kind
of sound altogether."

"I will take a look," Andrea volunteered. "Just to make sure. But I do
not think the dark one would make a mistake." Before Mallory could say
anything he was gone, as quickly and silently as Panayis. He was back in
three minutes, shaking his head. "Panayis is right. There is no one. I did
not even see the goats."

"And that's what it must have been, Casey," Mallory said. "Still, I don't
like it. Snow almost stopped, wind dropping and the valley probably swarming with German patrols—I think it's time you two were away. For God's
sake, be careful. If anyone tries to stop you, shoot to kill. They'll blame it
on us anyway."

"Shoot to kill!" Louki laughed dryly. "Unnecessary advice, Major when
the dark one is with us. He never shoots any other way."

"Right, away you go. Damned sorry you've got yourselves mixed up in
all this—but now that you are, a thousand thanks for all you've done. See
you at half-past six."

"Half-past six," Louki echoed. "The olive grove on the bank of the
stream, south of the village. We will be waiting there."

Two minutes later they were lost to sight and sound and all was still inside the cave again, except for the faint crackling of the embers of the dying fire. Brown had moved out on guard, and Stevens had already fallen into a restless, pain-filled sleep. Miller bent over him for a moment or two, then moved softly across the cave to Mallory. His right hand held a crumpled heap of blood-stained bandages. He held them out towards Mallory.

"Take a sniff at that, boss," he asked quietly. "Easy does it."

Mallory bent forward, drew away sharply, his nose wrinkled in immediate disgust.

"Good lord, Dusty! That's vile!" He paused, paused in sure, sick certainty. He knew the answer before he spoke. "What on earth is it?"

"Gangrene." Miller sat down heavily by his side, threw the bandages into the fire. All at once he sounded tired, defeated. "Gas gangrene. Spreadin' like a forest fire—and he would have died anyway. I'm just wastin' my time."

10

TUESDAY NIGHT

0400–0600

THE GERMANS took them just after four o'clock in the morning, while they were still asleep. Bone-tired and deep-drugged with this sleep as they were, they had no chance, not the slightest hope of offering any resistance. The conception, timing and execution of the coup were immaculate. Surprise was complete.

Andrea was the first awake. Some alien whisper of sound had reached deep down to that part of him that never slept, and he twisted round and elbowed himself off the ground with the same noiseless speed as his hand reached out for his ready-cocked and loaded Mauser. But the white beam of the powerful torch lancing through the blackness of the cave had blinded him, frozen his stretching hand even before the clipped bite of command from the man who held the torch.

"Still! All of you!" Faultless English, with barely a trace of accent, and the voice glacial in its menace. "You move, and you die!" Another torch switched on, a third, and the cave was flooded with light. Wide awake, now, and motionless, Mallory squinted painfully into the dazzling beams: in the back-wash of reflected light, he could just discern the vague, formless shapes crouched in the mouth of the cave, bent over the dulled barrels of automatic rifles.

"Hands clasped above the heads and backs to the wall!" A certainty, an assured competence in the voice that made for instant obedience. "Take a good look at them, Sergeant." Almost conversational now, the tone, but neither torch nor gun barrel had wavered a fraction. "No shadow of expression in their faces, not even a flicker of the eyes. Dangerous men, Sergeant. The English choose their killers well!"

Mallory felt the grey bitterness of defeat wash through him in an almost tangible wave, he could taste the sourness of it in the back of his mouth. For a brief, heart-sickening second he allowed himself to think of what must now inevitably happen and as soon as the thought had come he thrust it savagely away. Everything, every action, every thought, every breath must

be on the present. Hope was gone, but not irrecoverably gone: not so long
as Andrea lived. He wondered if Casey Brown had seen or heard them
coming, and what had happened to him: he made to ask, checked himself
just in time. Maybe he was still at large.

"How did you manage to find us?" Mallory asked quietly.

"Only fools burn juniper wood," the officer said contemptuously. "We
have been on Kostos all day and most of the night. A dead man could have
smelt it."

"On Kostos?" Miller shook his head. "How could——?"

"Enough!" The officer turned to someone behind him. "Tear down that
screen," he ordered in German, "and keep us covered on either side." He
looked back into the cave, gestured almost imperceptibly with his torch.
"All right, you three. Outside—and you had better be careful. Please believe
me that my men are praying for an excuse to shoot you down, you murdering
swine!" The venomous hatred in his voice carried utter conviction.

Slowly, hands still clasped above their heads, the three men stumbled to
their feet. Mallory had taken only one step when the whip-lash of the
German's voice brought him up short.

"Stop!" He stabbed the beam of his torch down at the unconscious
Stevens, gestured abruptly at Andrea. "One side, you! Who is this?"

"You need not fear from him," Mallory said quietly. "He is one of us
but he is terribly injured. He is dying."

"We will see," the officer said tightly. "Move to the back of the cave!"
He waited until the three men had stepped over Stevens, changed his automatic rifle for a pistol, dropped to his knees and advanced slowly, torch in
one hand, gun in the other, well below the line of fire of the two soldiers
who advanced unbidden at his heels. There was an inevitability, a cold
professionalism about it all that made Mallory's heart sink.

Abruptly the officer reached out his gun-hand, tore the covers off the boy.
A shuddering tremor shook the whole body, his head rolled from side to side
as he moaned in unconscious agony. The officer bent quickly over him, the
hard, clean lines of the face, the fair hair beneath the hood high-lit in the
beam of his own torch. A quick look at Stevens's pain-twisted, emaciated
features, a glance at the shattered leg, a brief, distasteful wrinkling of the
nose as he caught the foul stench of the gangrene, and he had hunched back
on his heels, gently replacing the covers over the sick boy.

"You speak the truth," he said softly. "We are not barbarians. I have no
quarrel with a dying man. Leave him there." He rose to his feet, walked
slowly backwards. "The rest of you outside."

The snow had stopped altogether, Mallory saw, and stars were beginning
to twinkle in the clearing sky. The wind, too, had fallen away and was
perceptibly warmer. Most of the snow would be gone by midday, Mallory
guessed.

Carelessly, incuriously, he looked around him. There was no sign of
Casey Brown. Inevitably Mallory's hopes began to rise. Petty Officer Brown's
recommendation for this operation had come from the very top. Two rows
of ribbons to which he was entitled but never wore bespoke his gallantry, he
had a formidable reputation as a guerrilla fighter—and he had had an automatic rifle in his hand. If he were somewhere out there. . . . Almost as if
he had divined his hopes, the German smashed them at a word.

"You wonder where your sentry is, perhaps?" he asked mockingly. "Never
fear, Englishman, he is not far from here, asleep at his post. Very sound
asleep, I'm afraid."

"You've killed him?" Mallory's hands clenched until his palms ached.

The other shrugged his shoulders in vast indifference.

"I really couldn't say. It was all too easy. One of my men lay in the gully and moaned. A masterly performance—really pitiable—he almost had me convinced. Like a fool your man came to investigate. I had another man waiting above, the barrel of his rifle in his hand. A very effective club, I assure you. . . ."

Slowly Mallory unclenched his fists and stared bleakly down the gully. Of course Casey would fall for that, he was bound to after what had happened earlier in the night. He wasn't going to make a fool of himself again, cry "wolf" twice in succession: inevitably, he had gone to check first. Suddenly the thought occurred to Mallory that maybe Casey Brown *had* heard something earlier on, but the thought vanished as soon as it had come. Panayis did not look like the man to make a mistake: and Andrea never made a mistake; Mallory turned back to the officer again.

"Well, where do we go from here?"

"Margaritha, and very shortly. But one thing first." The German, his own height to an inch, stood squarely in front of him, levelled revolver at waist height, switched-off torch dangling loosely from his right hand. "Just a little thing, Englishman. Where are the explosives?" He almost spat the words out.

"Explosives?" Mallory furrowed his brow in perplexity. "What explosives?" he asked blankly, then staggered and fell to the ground as the heavy torch swept round in a vicious half-circle, caught him flush on the side of the face. Dizzily he shook his head and climbed slowly to his feet again.

"The explosives." The torch was balanced in the hand again, the voice silky and gentle. "I asked you where they were."

"I don't know what you are talking about." Mallory spat out a broken tooth, wiped some blood off his smashed lips. "Is this the way the Germans treat their prisoners?" he asked contemptuously.

"Shut up!"

Again the torch lashed out. Mallory was waiting for it, rode the blow as best he could: even so the torch caught him heavily high up on the cheekbone, just below the temple, stunning him with its jarring impact. Seconds passed, then he pushed himself slowly off the snow, the whole side of his face afire with agony, his vision blurred and unfocused.

"We fight a clean war!" The officer was breathing heavily, in barely controlled fury. "We fight by the Geneva Conventions. But these are for soldiers, not for murdering spies——"

"We are no spies!" Mallory interrupted. He felt as if his head was coming apart.

"Then where are your uniforms?" the officer demanded. "Spies, I say—murdering spies who stab in the back and cut men's throats!" The voice was trembling with anger. Mallory was at a loss—nothing spurious about this indignation.

"Cut men's throats?" He shook his head in bewilderment. "What the hell are you talking about?"

"My own batman. A harmless messenger, a boy only—and he wasn't even armed. We found him only an hour ago. Ach, I waste my time!" He broke off as he turned to watch two men coming up the gully. Mallory stood motionless for a moment, cursing the ill luck that had led the dead man across the path of Panayis—it could have been no one else—then turned to see what had caught the officer's attention. He focused his aching eyes with difficulty, looked at the bent figure struggling up the slope, urged on by the ungentle prodding of a bayoneted rifle. Mallory let go a long, silent breath of relief. The left side of Brown's face was caked with blood from a gash above the temple, but he was otherwise unharmed.

"Right! Sit down in the snow, all of you!" He gestured to several of his men. "Bind their hands!"

"You are going to shoot us now, perhaps?" Mallory asked quietly. It was suddenly, desperately urgent that he should know: there was nothing they could do but die, but at least they could die on their feet, fighting; but if they weren't to die just yet, almost any later opportunity for resistance would be less suicidal than this.

"Not yet, unfortunately. My section commander in Margaritha, Hauptmann Skoda, wishes to see you first—maybe it would be better for you if I *did* shoot you now. Then the Herr Kommandant in Navarone—Officer Commanding of the whole island." The German smiled thinly. "But only a postponement, Englishman. You will be kicking your heels before the sun sets. We have a short way with spies in Navarone."

"But, sir! Captain!" Hands raised in appeal, Andrea took a step forward, brought up short as two rifle muzzles ground into his chest.

"Not Captain—Lieutenant," the officer corrected him. "Oberleutnant Turzig, at your service. What is it you want, fat one?" he asked contemptuously.

"Spies! You said spies! I am no spy!" The words rushed and tumbled over one another, as if he could not get them out fast enough. "Before God, I am no spy! I am not one of them." The eyes were wide and staring, the mouth working soundlessly between the gasped-out sentences. "I am only a Greek, a poor Greek. They forced me to come along as an interpreter. I swear it, Lieutenant Turzig, I swear it!"

"You yellow bastard!" Miller ground out viciously, then grunted in agony as a rifle butt drove into the small of his back, just above the kidney. He stumbled, fell forward on his hands and knees, realised even as he fell that Andrea was only playing a part, that Mallory had only to speak half a dozen words in Greek to expose Andrea's lie. Miller twisted on his side in the snow, shook his fist weakly and hoped that the contorted pain on his face might be mistaken for fury. "You two-faced, double-crossing dago! You gawddamned swine, I'll get you . . . ." There was a hollow, sickening thud and Miller collapsed in the snow: the heavy ski-boot had caught him just behind the ear.

Mallory said nothing. He did not even glance at Miller. Fists balled helplessly at his sides and mouth compressed, he glared steadily at Andrea through narrowed slits of eyes. He knew the lieutenant was watching him, felt he must back Andrea up all the way. What Andrea intended he could not even begin to guess—but he would back him to the end of the world.

"So!" Turzig murmured thoughtfully. "Thieves fall out, eh?" Mallory thought he detected the faintest overtones of doubt, of hesitancy, in his voice. But the lieutenant was taking no chances. "No matter, fat one. You have cast your lot with these assassins. What is it the English say? 'You have made your bed, you must lie on it.' " He looked at Andrea's vast bulk dispassionately. "We may need to strengthen a special gallows for you."

"No, no, no!" Andrea's voice rose sharply, fearfully, on the last word. "It is true what I tell you! I am not one of them, Lieutenant Turzig, before God I am not one of them!" He wrung his hands in distress, his great moon-face contorted in anguish. "Why must I die for no fault of my own? I didn't want to come. I am no fighting man, Lieutenant Turzig!"

"I can see that," Turzig said dryly. "A monstrous deal of skin to cover a quivering jelly-bag your size—and every inch of it precious to you." He looked at Mallory, and at Miller, still lying face down in the snow. "I cannot congratulate your friends on their choice of companion."

"I can tell you everything, Lieutenant, I can tell you everything!" Andrea pressed forward excitedly, eager to conolidate his advantage, to reinforce the beginnings of doubt. "I am no friend of the Allies—I will prove it to you—and then perhaps——"

"You damned Judas!" Mallory made to fling himself forward, but two burly soldiers caught him and pointed his arms from behind. He struggled briefly, then relaxed, looked balefully at Andrea. "If you dare to open your mouth, I promise you you'll never live to——"

"Be quiet!" Turzig's voice was very cold. "I have had enough of recriminations, of cheap melodrama. Another word and you join your friend in the snow there." He looked at him a moment in silence, then swung back to Andrea. "I promise nothing. I will hear what you have to say." He made no attempt to disguise the repugnance in his voice.

"You must judge for yourself." A nice mixture of relief, earnestness and the dawn of hope, of returning confidence. Andrea paused a minute and gestured dramatically at Mallory, Miller and Brown. "These are no ordinary soldiers—they are Jellicoe's men, of the Special Boat Service!"

"Tell me something I couldn't have guessed myself," Turzig growled. "The English Earl has been a thorn in our flesh these many months past. If that is all you have to tell me, fat one——"

"Wait!" Andrea held up his hand. "They are still no ordinary men but a specially picked force—an assault unit, they call themselves—flown last Sunday night from Alexandria to Castelrosso. They left that same night from Castelrosso in a motor-boat."

"A torpedo boat," Turzig nodded. "So much we know already. Go on."

"You know already! But how——?"

"Never mind how. Hurry up!"

"Of course, Lieutenant, of course." Not a twitch in his face betrayed Andrea's relief. This had been the only dangerous point in his story. Nicolai, of course, had warned the Germans, but never thought it worth while mentioning the presence of a giant Greek in the party. No reason, of course, why he should have selected him for special mention—but if he had done, it would have been the end.

"The torpedo boat landed them somewhere in the islands, north of Rhodes. I do not know where. There they stole a caique, sailed it up through Turkish waters, met a big German patrol boat—and sunk it." Andrea paused for effect. "I was less than half a mile away at the time in my fishing boat."

Turzig leaned forward. "How did they manage to sink so big a boat?" Strangely, he didn't doubt that it had been sunk.

"They pretended to be harmless fishermen like myself. I had just been stopped, investigated and cleared," Andrea said virtuously. "Anyway, your patrol boat came alongside this old caique. Close alongside. Suddenly there were guns firing on both sides, two boxes went flying through the air—into the engine-room of your boat, I think. Pouf!" Andrea threw up his hands dramatically. "That was the end of that!"

"We wondered . . ." Turzig said softly. "Well, go on."

"You wondered what, Lieutenant?" Turzig's eyes narrowed and Andrea hurried on.

"Their interpreter had been killed in the fight. They tricked me into speaking English—I spent many years in Cyprus—kidnapped me, let my sons sail the boat——"

"Why should they want an interpreter?" Turzig demanded suspiciously. "There are many British officers who speak Greek?"

"I am coming to that," Andrea said impatiently. "How in God's name do you expect me to finish my story if you keep interrupting all the time? Where was I? Ah, yes. They forced me to come along, and their engine broke down. I don't know what happened—I was kept below. I think we were in a creek somewhere, repairing the engine, and then there was a wild bout of drinking—you will not believe this, Lieutenant Turzig, that men on so desperate a mission should get drunk—and then we sailed again.''

"On the contrary, I do believe you." Turzig was nodding his head slowly, as if in secret understanding. "I believe you indeed."

"You do?" Andrea contrived to look disappointed. "Well, we ran into a fearful storm, wrecked the boat on the south cliff of this island and climbed——"

"Stop!" Turzig had drawn back sharply, suspicion flaring in his eyes. "Almost I believed you! I believed you because we know more than you think, and so far you have told the truth. But not now. You are clever, fat one, but not so clever as you think. One thing you have forgotten—or maybe you do not know. We are of the *Wurttembergische Gebirgsbataillion*—we *know* mountains, my friend, better than any troops in the world. I myself am a Prussian, but I have climbed everything worth climbing in the Alps and Transylvania—and I tell you that the south cliff cannot be climbed. It is impossible!"

"Impossible perhaps for you." Andrea shook his head sadly. "These cursed Allies will beat you yet. They are clever, Lieutenant Turzig, damnably clever!"

"Explain yourself," Turzig ordered curtly.

"Just this. They knew men thought the south cliff could not be climbed. So they determined to climb it. You would never dream that this could be done, that an expedition could land on Navarone that way. But the Allies took a gamble, found a man to lead the expedition. He could not speak Greek, but that did not matter, for what they wanted was a man who could climb—and so they picked the greatest rock-climber in the world to-day." Andrea paused for effect, flung out his arm dramatically. "And this is the man they picked, Lieutenant Turzig! You are a mountaineer yourself and you are bound to know him. His name is Mallory—Keith Mallory of New Zealand!"

There was a sharp exclamation, the click of a switch, and Turzig had taken a couple of steps forward, thrust the torch almost into Mallory's eyes. For almost ten seconds he stared into the New Zealander's averted, screwed-up face, then slowly lowered his arm, the harsh spotlight limning a dazzling white circle in the snow at his feet. Once, twice, half a dozen times Turzig nodded his head in slow understanding.

"Of course!" he murmured. "Mallory—Keith Mallory! Of course I know him. There's not a man in my *Abteilung* but has heard of Keith Mallory." He shook his head. "I should have known him, I should have known him at once." He stood for some time with his head bent, aimlessly screwing the toe of his right boot into the soft snow, then looked up abruptly. "Before the war, even during it, I would have been proud to have known you, glad to have met you. But not here, not now. Not any more. I wish to God they had sent someone else." He hesitated, made to carry on, then changed his mind, turned wearily to Andrea. "My apologies, fat one. Indeed you speak the truth. Go on."

"Certainly!" Andrea's round moon face was one vast smirk of satisfaction. "We climbed the cliff, as I said—although the boy in the cave there was badly hurt—and silenced the guard. Mallory killed him," Andrea added unblushingly. "It was fair fight. We spent most of the night crossing the divide and found this cave before dawn. We were almost dead with hunger and cold. We have been here since.''

"And nothing has happened since?''

"On the contrary.'' Andrea seemed to be enjoying himself hugely, revelling in being the focus of attention. "Two people came up to see us. Who they were I do not know—they kept their faces hidden all the time—nor do I know where they came from.''

"It is as well that you admitted that,'' Turzig said grimly. "I knew someone had been here. I recognised the stove—it belongs to Hauptmann Skoda!''

"Indeed?'' Andrea raised his eyebrows in polite surprise. "I did not know. Well, they talked for some time and———''

"Did you manage to overhear anything they were talking about?'' Turzig interrupted. The question came so naturally, so spontaneously, that Mallory held his breath. It was beautifully done. Andrea would walk into it—he couldn't help it. But Andrea was a man inspired that night.

"Overhear them!'' Andrea clamped his lips shut in sorely-tired forbearance, gazed heavenwards in exasperated appeal. "Lieutenant Turzig, how often must I tell you that I am the interpreter? They *could* only talk through me. Of course I know what they were talking about. They are going to blow up the big guns in the harbour.''

"I didn't think they had come here for their health!'' Turzig said acidly.

"Ah, but you don't know that they have the plans of the fortress. You don't know that Kheros is to be invaded on Saturday morning. You don't know that they are in radio contact with Cairo all the time. You don't know that destroyers of the British Navy are coming through the Maidos Straits on Friday night as soon as the big guns have been silenced. You don't know———''

"Enough!'' Turzig clapped his hands together, his face alight with excitement. "The Royal Navy, eh? Wonderful, wonderful! *That* is what we want to hear. But enough! Keep it for Hauptmann Skoda and the Commandant in the fortress. We must be off. But first—one more thing. The explosives—where are they?''

Andrea's shoulders slumped in dejection. He spread out his arms, palms upward.

"Alas, Lieutenant Turzig, I do not know. They took them out and hid them—some talk about the cave being too hot.'' He waved a hand towards the western col, in the diametrically opposite direction to Leri's hut. "That way, I think. But I cannot be sure, for they would not tell me.'' He looked bitterly at Mallory. "These Britishers are all the same. They trust nobody.''

"Heaven only knows that I don't blame them for that!'' Turzig said feelingly. He looked at Andrea in disgust. "More than ever I would like to see you dangling from the highest scaffold in Navarone. But Herr Kommandant in the town is a kindly man and rewards informers. You may yet live to betray some more comrades.''

"Thank you, thank you, thank you! I knew you were fair and just. I promise you, Lieutenant Turzig———''

"Shut up!'' Turzig said contemptuously. He switched into German. "Sergeant, have these men bound. And don't forget the fat one! Later we can untie him, and he can carry the sick man to the post. Leave a man on guard. The rest of you come with me—we must find those explosives.''

"Could we not make one of them tell us, sir?'' the sergeant ventured.

"The only man who would tell us, can't. He's already told us all he knows. As for the rest—well, I was mistaken about them, Sergeant.'' He turned to Mallory, inclined his head briefly, spoke in English. "An error of judgment, Herr Mallory. We are all very tired. I am almost sorry I struck you." He wheeled abruptly, climbed swiftly up the bank. Two minutes later only a solitary soldier was left on guard.

For the tenth time Mallory shifted his position uncomfortably, strained at the cord that bound his hands together behind his back, for the tenth time recognised the futility of both these actions. No matter how he twisted and turned, the wet snow soaked icily though his clothes until he was chilled to the bone and shaking continually with the cold; and the man who had tied these knots had known his job all too well. Mallory wondered irritably if Turzig and his men meant to spend all night searching for the explosives: they had been gone for more than half an hour already.

He relaxed, lay back on his side in the cushioning snow of the gully bank, and looked thoughtfully at Andrea who was sitting upright just in front of him. He had watched Andrea, with bowed head and hunched and lifting shoulders, making one single, titanic effort to free himself seconds after the guard had gestured to them to sit down, had seen the cords bite and gouge until they had almost disappeared in his flesh, the fractional slump of his shoulders as he gave up. Since then the giant Greek had sat quite still and contented himself with scowling at the sentry in the injured fashion of one who has been grievously wronged. That solitary test of the strength of his bonds had been enough. Oberleutnant Turzig had keen eyes, and swollen, chafed and bleeding wrists would have accorded ill with the character Andrea had created for himself.

A masterly creation, Mallory mused, all the more remarkable for its spontaneity, its improvisation. Andrea had told so much of the truth, so much that was verifiable or could be verified, that belief in the rest of his story followed almost automatically. And at the same time he had told Turzig nothing of importance, nothing the Germans could not have found out for themselves—except the proposed evacuation of Kheros by the Navy. Wryly Mallory remembered his dismay, his shocked unbelief when he heard Andrea telling of it—but Andrea had been far ahead of him. There was a fair chance that the Germans might have guessed anyway—they would reason, perhaps, that an assault by the British on the guns of Navarone at the same time as the German assault on Kheros would be just that little bit too coincidental: again, escape for them all quite clearly depended upon how thoroughly Andrea managed to convince his captors that he was all he claimed, and the relative freedom of action that he could thereby gain—and there was no doubt at all that it was the news of the proposed evacuation that had tipped the scales with Turzig: and the fact that Andrea had given Saturday as the invasion date would only carry all the more weight, as that had been Jensen's original date—obviously false information fed to his agents by German counter-Intelligence, who had known it impossible to conceal the invasion preparations themselves; and finally, if Andrea hadn't told Turzig of the destroyers, he might have failed to carry conviction, they might all yet finish on the waiting gallows in the fortress, the guns would remain intact and destroy the naval ships anyway.

It was all very complicated, too complicated for the state his head was in. Mallory sighed and looked away from Andrea towards the other two. Brown and a now conscious Miller were both sitting upright, hands bound behind their backs, staring down into the snow, occasionally shaking muzzy heads from side to side. Mallory could appreciate all too easily how they felt—the whole right-hand side of his face ached cruelly, continuously. Nothing but aching, broken heads everywhere, Mallory thought bitterly. He wondered how Andy Stevens was feeling, glanced idly past the sentry towards the dark mouth of the cave, stiffened in sudden, almost uncomprehending shock.

Slowly, with an infinitely careful carelessness, he let his eyes wander away from the cave, let them light indifferently on the sentry who sat on Brown's transmitter, hunched watchfully over the Schmeisser cradled on his knees, finger crooked on the trigger. Pray God he doesn't turn round, Mallory said to himself over and over again, pray God he doesn't turn round. Let him sit like that just for a little while longer, only a little while longer. . . . In spite of himself, Mallory felt his gaze shifting, being dragged back again towards that cave-mouth.

Andy Stevens was coming out of the cave. Even in the dim starlight every movement was terribly plain as he inched forward agonisingly on chest and belly, dragging his shattered leg behind him. He was placing his hands beneath his shoulders, levering himself upward and forward while his head dropped below his shoulders with pain and the exhaustion of the effort, lowering himself slowly on the soft and sodden snow, then repeating the same heart-sapping process over and over again. Exhausted and pain-filled as the boy might be, Mallory thought, his mind was still working: he had a white sheet over his shoulders and back as camouflage against the snow, and he carried a climbing spike in his right hand. He must have heard at least some of Turzig's conversation: there were two or three guns in the cave, he could easily have shot the guard without coming out at all—but he must have known that the sound of a shot would have brought the Germans running, had them back at the cave long before he could have crawled across the gully, far less cut loose any of his friends.

Five yards Stevens had to go, Mallory estimated, five yards at the most. Deep down in the gully where they were, the south wind passed them by, was no more than a muted whisper in the night; that apart, there was no sound at all, nothing but their own breathing, the occasional stirring as someone stretched a cramped or frozen leg. He's bound to hear him if he comes any closer, Mallory thought desperately, even in that soft snow he's bound to hear him.

Mallory bent his head, began to cough loudly, almost continuously. The sentry looked at him, in surprise first, then in irritation as the coughing continued.

"Be quiet!" the sentry ordered in German. "Stop that coughing at once!"

"*Hüsten? Hüsten?* Coughing, is it? I can't help it," Mallory protested in English. He coughed again, louder, more persistently than before. "It is your Oberleutnant's fault," he gasped. "He has knocked out some of my teeth." Mallory broke into a fresh paroxysm of coughing, recovered himself with an effort. "Is it my fault that I'm choking on my own blood?" he demanded.

Stevens was less than ten feet away now, but his tiny reserves of strength were almost gone. He could no longer raise himself to the full stretch of his arms, was advancing only a few pitiful inches at a time. At length he stopped altogether, lay still for half a minute. Mallory thought he had lost consciousness, but by and by he raised himself up again, to the full stretch this time, had just begun to pivot himself forward when he collapsed, fell heavily in the snow. Mallory began to cough again, but he was too late. The sentry leapt off his box and whirled round all in one movement, the evil mouth of the Schmeisser lined up on the body almost at his feet. Then he relaxed as he realised who it was, lowered the barrel of his gun.

"So!" he said softly. "The fledgling has left its nest. Poor little fledgling!" Mallory winced as he saw the back-swing of the gun ready to smash down on Stevens's defenceless head, but the sentry was a kindly enough man, his reaction had been purely automatic. He arrested the swinging butt inches above the tortured face, bent down and almost gently removed the spike from the feebly threatening hand, sent it spinning over the edge of the gully. Then he lifted Stevens carefully by the shoulders, slid in the bunched-up sheet as pillow for the unconscious head against the bitter cold of the snow, shook his head wonderingly, sadly, went back to his seat on the ammunition box.

Hauptmann Skoda was a small, thin man in his late thirties, neat, dapper, debonair and wholly evil. There was something innately evil about the long, corded neck that stretched up scrawnily above his padded shoulders, something repellent about the incongruously small bullet head perched above. When the thin, bloodless lips parted in a smile, which was often, they revealed a perfect set of teeth: far from lighting his face, the smile only emphasised the sallow skin stretched abnormally taut across the sharp nose and high cheekbones, puckered up the sabre scar that bisected the left cheek from eyebrow to chin: and whether he smiled or not, the pupils of the deep-set eyes remained always the same, still and black and empty. Even at that early hour—it was not yet six o'clock—he was immaculately dressed, freshly shaven, the wetly-gleaming hair—thin, dark, heavily indented above the temples—brushed straight back across his head. Seated behind a flat-topped table, the sole article of furniture in the bench-lined guardroom, only the upper half of his body was visible: even so, one instinctively knew that the crease of the trousers, the polish of the jackboots, would be beyond reproach.

He smiled often, and he was smiling now as Oberleutnant Turzig finished his report. Leaning far back in his chair, elbows on the arm-rests, Skoda steepled his lean fingers under his chin, smiled benignly round the guardroom. The lazy, empty eyes missed nothing—the guard at the door, the two guards behind the bound prisoners, Andrea sitting on the bench where he had just laid Stevens—one lazy sweep of those eyes encompassed them all.

"Excellently done, Oberleutnant Turzig!" he purred. "Most efficient, really most efficient!" He looked speculatively at the three men standing before him, at their bruised and blood-caked faces, switched his glance to Stevens, lying barely conscious on the bench, smiled again and permitted himself a fractional lift of his eyebrows. "A little trouble, perhaps, Turzig? The prisoners were not too—ah—co-operative?"

"They offered no resistance, sir, no resistance at all," Turzig said stiffly. The tone, the manner, were punctilious, correct, but the distaste, the latent hostility were mirrored in his eyes. "My men were maybe a little enthusiastic. We wanted to make no mistake."

"Quite right, Lieutenant, quite right," Skoda murmured approvingly. "These are dangerous men and one cannot take chances with dangerous men." He pushed back his chair, rose easily to his feet, strolled round the table and stopped in front of Andrea. "Except maybe this one, Lieutenant?"

"He is dangerous only to his friends," Turzig said shortly. "It is as I told you, sir. He would betray his mother to save his own skin."

"And claiming friendship with us, eh?" Skoda asked musingly. "One of our gallant allies, Lieutenant." Skoda reached out a gentle hand, brought it viciously down and across Andrea's cheek, the heavy signet ring on his middle finger tearing skin and flesh. Andrea cried out in pain, clapped one hand to his bleeding face and cowered away, his right arm raised above his head in blind defence.

"A notable addition to the armed forces of the Third Reich." Skoda murmured. "You were not mistaken, Lieutenant. A poltroon—the instinctive reaction of a hurt man is an infallible guide. It is curious," he mused, "how often very big men are thus. Part of nature's compensatory process, I suppose. . . . What is your name, my brave friend?"

"Papagos," Andrea muttered sullenly. "Peter Papagos." He took his hand away from his cheek, looked at it with eyes slowly widening with horror, began to rub it across his trouser leg with jerky, hurried movements, the repugnance on his face plain for every man to see. Skoda watched him with amusement.

"You do not like to see blood, Papagos, eh?" he suggested. "Especially your own blood?"

A few seconds passed in silence, then Andrea lifted his head suddenly, his fat face screwed up in misery. He looked as if he were going to cry.

"I am only a poor fisherman, your Honour!" he burst out. "You laugh at me and say I do not like blood, and it is true. Nor do I like suffering and war. I want no part of any of these things!" His great fists were clenched in futile appeal, his face puckered in woe, his voice risen an octave. It was a masterly exhibition of despair, and even Mallory found himself almost believing in it. "Why wasn't I left alone?" he went on pathetically. "God only knows I am no fighting man——"

"A highly inaccurate statement," Skoda interrupted dryly. "That fact must be patently obvious to every person in the room by this time." He tapped his teeth with a jade cigarette-holder, his eyes speculative. "A fisherman you call yourself——"

"He's a damned traitor!" Mallory interrupted. The commandant was becoming just that little bit too interested in Andrea. At once Skoda wheeled round, stood in front of Mallory with his hands clasped behind his back, teetering on heels and toes, and looked him up and down in mocking inspection.

"So!" he said thoughtfully. "The great Keith Mallory! A rather different proposition from our fat and fearful friend on the bench there, eh, Lieutenant?" He did not wait for an answer. "What rank are you, Mallory?"

"Captain," Mallory answered briefly.

"Captain Mallory, eh? Captain Keith Mallory, the greatest mountaineer of our time, the idol of pre-war Europe, the conqueror of the world's most impossible climbs." Skoda shook his head sadly. "And to think that it should all end like this. . . . I doubt whether posterity will rank your last climb as among your greatest: there are only ten steps leading to the gallows in the fortress of Navarone." Skoda smiled. "Hardly a cheerful thought, is it, Captain Mallory?"

"I wasn't even thinking about it," the New Zealander answered pleasantly. "What worries me is your face." He frowned. "Somewhere or other I'm sure I've seen it or something like it before." His voice trailed off into silence.

"Indeed?" Skoda was interested. "In the Bernese Alps, perhaps? Often before the war——"

"I have it now!" Mallory's face cleared. He knew the risk he was taking, but anything that concentrated attention on himself to the exclusion of Andrea was justified. He beamed at Skoda. "Three months ago, it was, in the zoo in Cairo. A plains buzzard that had been captured in the Sudan. A rather old and mangy buzzard, I'm afraid,'' Mallory went on apologetically, "but exactly the same scrawny neck, the same beaky face and bald head———''

Mallory broke off abruptly, swayed back out of reach as Skoda, his face livid and gleaming teeth bared in rage, swung at him with his fist. The blow carried with it all Skoda's wiry strength, but anger blurred his timing and the fist swung harmlessly by: he stumbled, recovered, then fell to the floor with a shout of pain as Mallory's heavy boot caught him flush on the thigh, just above the knee. He had barely touched the floor when he was up like a cat, took a pace forward and collapsed heavily again as his injured leg gave under him.

There was a moment's shocked stillness throughout the room, then Skoda rose painfully, supporting himself on the edge of the heavy table. He was breathing quickly, the thin mouth a hard, white line, the great sabre scar flaming redly in the sallow face drained now of all colour. He looked neither at Mallory nor anyone else, but slowly, deliberately, in an almost frightening silence, began to work his way round to the back of the table, the scuffing of his sliding palms on the leather top rasping edgily across over-tautened nerves.

Mallory stood quite still, watching him with expressionless face, cursing himself for his folly. He had overplayed his hand. There was no doubt in his mind—there could be no doubt in the mind of anyone in that room—that Skoda meant to kill him; and he, Mallory, would not die. Only Skoda and Andrea would die: Skoda from Andrea's throwing knife—Andrea was rubbing blood from his face with the inside of his sleeve, fingertips only inches from the sheath—and Andrea from the guns of the guards, for the knife was all he had. You fool, you fool, you bloody stupid fool, Mallory repeated to himself over and over again. He turned his head slightly and glanced out of the corner of his eye at the sentry nearest him. Nearest him—but still six or seven feet away. The sentry would get him, Mallory knew, the blast of the slugs from that Schmeisser would tear him in half before he could cover the distance. But he would try. He must try. It was the least he owed to Andrea.

Skoda reached the back of the table, opened a drawer and lifted out a gun. An automatic, Mallory noted with detachment—a little, blue-metal, snub-nosed toy—but a murderous toy, the kind of gun he would have expected Skoda to have. Unhurriedly Skoda pressed the release button, checked the magazine, snapped it home with the palm of his hand, flicked off the safety catch and looked up at Mallory. The eyes hadn't altered in the slightest—they were cold, dark and empty as ever. Mallory flicked a glance at Andrea and tensed himself for one convulsive fling backwards. Here it comes, he thought savagely, this is how bloody fools like Keith Mallory die—and then all of a sudden, and unknowingly, he relaxed, for his eyes were still on Andrea and he had seen Andrea doing the same, the huge hand slipping down unconcernedly from the neck, empty of any sign of knife.

There was a scuffle at the table and Mallory was just in time to see Turzig pin Skoda's gun-hand to the table-top.

"Not that, sir!" Turzig begged. "For God's sake, not that way!"

"Take your hands away," Skoda whispered. The staring, empty eyes never left Mallory's face. "Take your hands away, I say—unless you want to go the same way as Captain Mallory."

"You can't kill him, sir!" Turzig persisted doggedly. "You just can't. Herr Kommandant's orders were very clear, Hauptmann Skoda. The leader must be brought to him alive."

"He was shot while trying to escape," Skoda said thickly.

"It's no good." Turzig shook his head. "We can't kill them all—and the other prisoners would talk." He released his grip on Skoda's hands. "Alive, Herr Kommandant said, but he didn't say how much alive." He lowered his voice confidentially. "Perhaps we may have some difficulty in making Captain Mallory talk," he suggested.

"What? What did you say?" Abruptly the death's head smile flashed once more, and Skoda was completely on balance again. "You are over-zealous, Lieutenant. Remind me to speak to you about it some time. You underestimate me: that was exactly what I was trying to do—frighten Mallory into talking. And now you've spoilt it all." The smile was still on his face, the voice light, almost bantering, but Mallory was under no illusions. He owed his life to the young W.G.B. lieutenant—how easily one could respect, form a friendship with a man like Turzig if it weren't for this damned, crazy war. . . . Skoda was standing in front of him again: he had left his gun on the table.

"But enough of this fooling, eh, Captain Mallory?" The German's teeth fairly gleamed in the bright light from the naked lamps overhead. "We haven't all night, have we?"

Mallory looked at him, then turned away in silence. It was warm enough, stuffy almost, in that little guardroom, but he was conscious of a sudden, nameless chill; he knew all at once, without knowing why, but with complete certainty, that this little man before him was utterly evil.

"Well, well, well, we are not quite so talkative now, are we, my friend?" He hummed a little to himself, looked up abruptly, the smile broader than ever. "Where are the explosives, Captain Mallory?"

"Explosives?" Mallory lifted an interrogatory eyebrow. "I don't know what you are talking about."

"You don't remember, eh?"

"I don't know what you are talking about."

"So." Skoda hummed to himself again and walked over in front of Miller. "And what about you, my friend?"

"Sure I remember," Miller said easily. "The captain's got it all wrong."

"A sensible man!" Skoda purred—but Mallory could have sworn to an undertone of disappointment in the voice. "Proceed, my friend."

"Captain Mallory has no eye for detail," Miller drawled. "I was with him that day. He is malignin' a noble bird. It was a vulture, not a buzzard."

Just for a second Skoda's smile slipped, then it was back again, as rigidly fixed and lifeless as if it had been painted on.

"Very, very witty men, don't you think, Turzig? What the British would call music-hall comedians. Let them laugh while they may, until the hangman's noose begins to tighten. . . ." He looked at Casey Brown. "Perhaps you——"

"Why don't you go and take a running jump to yourself?" Brown growled.

"A running jump? The idiom escapes me, but I fear it is hardly complimentary." Skoda selected a cigarette from a thin case, tapped it thoughtfully on a thumb nail. "Hmm. Not just what one might call too co-operative, Lieutenant Turzig."

"You won't get these men to talk, sir." There was a quiet finality in Turzig's voice.

"Possibly not, possibly not." Skoda was quite unruffled. "Nevertheless, I shall have the information I want, and within five minutes." He walked unhurriedly across to his desk, pressed a button, screwed his cigarette into its jade holder, and leaned against the table, an arrogance, a careless contempt in every action, even to the leisurely crossing of the gleaming jackboots.

Suddenly a side door was flung open and two men stumbled into the room, prodded by a rifle barrel. Mallory caught his breath, felt his nails dig savagely into the palms of his hands. Louki and Panayis! Louki and Panayis, bound and bleeding, Louki from a cut above the eye, Panayis from a scalp wound. So they'd got them too, and in spite of his warnings. Both men were shirt-sleeved; Louki, minus his magnificently frogged jacket, scarlet *tsanta* and the small arsenal of weapons that he carried stuck beneath it, looked strangely pathetic and woe-begone—strangely, for he was red-faced with anger, the moustache bristling more ferociously than ever. Mallory looked at him with eyes empty of all recognition, his face expressionless.

"Come now, Captain Mallory," Skoda said reproachfully. "Have you no word of greeting for two old friends? No? Or perhaps you are just over-whelmed?" he suggested smoothly. "You had not expected to see them so soon again, eh, Captain Mallory."

"What cheap trick is this?" Mallory asked contemptuously. "I've never seen these men before in my life." His eyes caught those of Panayis, held there involuntarily: the black hate that stared out of those eyes, the feral malevolence—there was something appalling about it.

"Of course not," Skoda sighed wearily. "Oh, of course not. Human memory is so short, is it not, Captain Mallory." The sigh was pure theatre— Skoda was enjoying himself immensely, the cat playing with the mouse. "However, we will try again." He swung round, crossed over to the bench where Stevens lay, pulled off the blanket and, before anyone could guess his intentions, chopped the outside of his right hand against Stevens's smashed leg, just below the knee. . . . Stevens's entire body leapt in a convulsive spasm, but without even the whisper of a moan: he was still fully conscious, smiling at Skoda, blood trickling down his chin from where his teeth had gashed his lower lip.

"You shouldn't have done that, Hauptmann Skoda," Mallory said. His voice was barely a whisper, but unnaturally loud in the frozen silence of the room. "You are going to die for that, Hauptmann Skoda."

"So? I am going to die, am I?" Again he chopped his hand against the fractured leg, again without reaction. "Then I may as well die twice over— eh, Captain Mallory? This young man is very, very tough—but the British have soft hearts, have they not, my dear Captain?" Gently his hand slid down Stevens's leg, closed round the stockinged ankle. "You have exactly five seconds to tell me the truth, Captain Mallory, and then I fear I will be compelled to rearrange these splints—*Gott in Himmel!* What's the matter with that great oaf?"

Andrea had taken a couple of steps forward, was standing only a yard away, swaying on his feet.

"Outside! Let me outside!" His breath came in short, fast gasps. He bowed his head, one hand to his throat, one over his stomach. "I cannot stand it! Air! Air! I must have air!"

"Ah, no, my dear Papagos, you shall remain here and enjoy—Corporal! Quickly!" He had seen Andrea's eyes roll upwards until only the whites showed. "The fool is going to faint! Take him away before he falls on top of us!"

Mallory had one fleeting glimpse of the two guards hurrying forwards, of the incredulous contempt on Louki's face, then he flicked a glance at Miller and Brown, caught the lazy droop of the American's eyelid in return, the millimetric inclination of Brown's head. Even as the two guards came up behind Andrea and lifted the flaccid arms across their shoulders, Mallory glanced half-left, saw the nearest sentry less than four feet away now, absorbed in the spectacle of the toppling giant. Easy, dead easy—the gun dangling by his side: he could hit him between wind and water before he knew what was happening. . . .

Fascinated, Mallory watched Andrea's forearms slipping nervelessly down the shoulders of the supporting guards till his wrists rested loosely beside their necks, palms facing inwards. And then there was the sudden leap of the great shoulder muscles and Mallory had hurled himself convulsively sidewards and back, his shoulder socketing with vicious force into the guard's stomach, inches below the breast-bone: an explosive *ouf!* of agony, the crash against the wooden walls of the room and Mallory knew the guard would be out of action for some time to come.

Even as he dived, Mallory had heard the sickening thud of heads being swept together. Now, as he twisted round on his side, he had a fleeting glimpse of another guard thrashing feebly on the floor under the combined weights of Miller and Brown, and then of Andrea tearing an automatic rifle from the guard who had been standing at his right shoulder: the Schmeisser was cradled in his great hands, lined up on Skoda's chest even before the unconscious man had hit the floor.

For one second, maybe two, all movement in the room ceased, every sound sheared off by a knife edge: the silence was abrupt, absolute—and infinitely more clamorous than the clamour that had gone before. No one moved, no one spoke, no one even breathed: the shock, the utter unexpectedness of what had happened held them all in thrall.

And then the silence erupted in a staccato crashing of sound, deafening in that confined space. Once, twice, three times, wordlessly, and with great care, Andrea shot Hauptmann Skoda through the heart. The blast of the shells lifted the little man off his feet, smashed him against the wall of the hut, pinned him there for one incredible second, arms outflung as though nailed against the rough planks in spreadeagle crucifixion; and then he collapsed, fell limply to the ground, a grotesque and broken doll that struck its heedless head against the edge of the bench before coming to rest on its back on the floor. The eyes were still wide open, as cold, as dark, as empty in death as they had been in life.

His Schmeisser waving in a gentle arc that covered Turzig and the sergeant, Andrea picked up Skoda's sheath knife, sliced through the ropes that bound Mallory's wrists.

"Can you hold this gun, my Captain?"

Mallory flexed his stiffened hands once or twice, nodded, took the gun in silence. In three steps Andrea was behind the blind side of the door leading to the ante-room, pressed to the wall, waiting, gesturing to Mallory to move as far back as possible out of the line of sight.

Suddenly the door was flung open. Andrea could just see the tip of the rifle barrel projecting beyond it.

"Oberleutnant Turzig! *Was ist los? Wer schoss* . . ." The voice broke off in a coughing grunt of agony as Andrea smashed the sole of his foot against the door. He was round the outside of the door in a moment, caught the man as he fell, pulled him clear of the doorway and peered into the adjacent hut. A brief inspection, then he closed the door, bolted it from the inside.

"Nobody else there, my Captain," Andrea reported. "Just the one gaoler, it seems."

"Fine! Cut the others loose, will you, Andrea?" He wheeled round towards Louki, smiled at the comical expression on the little man's face, the tentative, spreading, finally ear-to-ear grin that cut through the baffled incredulity.

"Where do the men sleep, Louki—the soldiers, I mean?"

"In a hut in the middle of the compound, Major. This is the officers' quarters."

"Compound? You mean——?"

"Barbed wire," Louki said succinctly. "Ten feet high—and all the way round."

"Exits?"

"One and one only. Two guards."

"Good! Andrea—everybody into the side room. No, not you, Lieutenant. You sit down here." He gestured to the chair behind the big desk. "Somebody's bound to come. Tell him you killed one of us—trying to escape. Then send for the guards at the gate."

For a moment Turzig didn't answer. He watched unseeingly as Andrea walked past him, dragging two unconscious soldiers by their collars. Then he smiled. It was a wry sort of smile.

"I am sorry to disappoint you, Captain Mallory. Too much has been lost already through my blind stupidity. I won't do it."

"Andrea!" Mallory called softly.

"Yes?" Andrea stood in the ante-room doorway.

"I think I hear someone coming. Is there a way out of that side room?" Andrea nodded silently.

"Outside! The front door. Take your knife. If the Lieutenant . . ." But he was talking to himself. Andrea was already gone, slipping out through the back door, soundless as a ghost.

"You will do exactly as I say," Mallory said softly. He took position himself in the doorway to the side room, where he could see the front entrance between door and jamb: his automatic rifle was trained on Turzig. "If you don't, Andrea will kill the man at the door. Then we will kill you and the guards inside. Then we will knife the sentries at the gate. Nine dead men—and all for nothing, for we will escape anyway. . . . Here he is now." Mallory's voice was barely a whisper, eyes pitiless in a pitiless face. "Nine dead men, Lieutenant—and just because your pride is hurt." Deliberately, the last sentence was in German, fluent, colloquial, and Mallory's mouth twisted as he saw the almost imperceptible sag of Turzig's shoulders. He knew he had won, that Turzig had been going to take a last gamble on his ignorance of German, that this last hope was gone.

The door burst open and a soldier stood on the threshhold, breathing heavily. He was armed, but clad only in a singlet and trousers, oblivious of the cold.

"Lieutenant! Lieutenant!" he spoke in German. "We heard the shots—"

"It is nothing, Sergeant." Turzig bent his head over an open drawer, pretended to be searching for something to account for his solitary presence in the room. "One of our prisoners tried to escape. . . . We stopped him."

"Perhaps the medical orderly——"

"I'm afraid we stopped him rather permanently." Turzig smiled tiredly. "You can organise a burial detail in the morning. Meantime, you might tell the guards at the gate to come here for a minute. Then get to bed yourself— you'll catch your death of cold!"

"Shall I detail a relief guard——"

"Of course not!" Turzig said impatiently. "It's just for a minute. Besides, the only people to guard against are already in here." His lips tightened for a second as he realised what he had said, the unconscious irony of the words. "Hurry up, man! We haven't got all night!" He waited till the sound of the running footsteps died away, then looked steadily at Mallory. "Satisfied?"

"Perfectly. And my very sincere apologies," Mallory said quietly. "I hate to do a thing like this to a man like you." He looked round the door as Andrea came into the room. "Andrea, ask Louki and Panayis if there's a telephone switchboard in this block of huts. Tell them to smash it up and any receivers they can find." He grinned. "Then hurry back for our visitors from the gate. I'd be lost without you on the reception committee."

Turzig's gaze followed the broad retreating back.

"Captain Skoda was right. I still have much to learn." There was neither bitterness nor rancour in his voice. "He fooled me completely, that big one."

"You're not the first," Mallory reassured him. "He's fooled more people than I'll ever know. . . . You're not the first," he repeated. "But I think you must be just about the luckiest."

"Because I'm still alive?"

"Because you're still alive," Mallory echoed.

Less than ten minutes later the two guards at the gates had joined their comrades in the back room, captured, disarmed, bound and gagged with a speed and noiseless efficiency that excited Turzig's professional admiration, chagrined though he was. Securely tied hand and foot, he lay in a corner of the room, not yet gagged.

"I think I understand now why your High Command chose you for this task, Captain Mallory. If anyone could succeed, you would—but you must fail. The impossible must always remain so. Nevertheless, you have a great team."

"We get by," Mallory said modestly. He took a last look round the room, then grinned down at Stevens.

"Ready to take off on your travels again, young man, or do you find this becoming rather monotonous?"

"Ready when you are, sir." Lying on a stretcher which Louki had miraculously procured, he sighed in bliss. "First-class travel, this time, as befits an officer. Sheer luxury. I don't mind how far we go!"

"Speak for yourself," Miller growled morosely. He had been allocated first stint at the front or heavy end of the stretcher. But the quirk of his eyebrows robbed the words of all offence.

"Right then, we're off. One last thing. Where is the camp radio, Lieutenant Turzig?"

"So you can smash it, I suppose?"

"Precisely."

"I have no idea."

"What if I threaten to blow your head off?"

"You won't." Turzig smiled, though the smile was a trifle lopsided. "Given certain circumstances, you would kill me as you would a fly. But you wouldn't kill a man for refusing such information."

"You haven't as much to learn as your late and unlamented captain thought," Mallory admitted. "It's not all that important. . . . I regret we have to do all this. I trust we do not meet again—not, at least, until the war is over. Who knows, some day we might even go climbing together." He signed to Louki to fix Turzig's gag and walked quickly out of the room. Two minutes later they had cleared the barracks and were safely lost in the darkness and the olive groves that stretched to the south of Margaritha.

When they cleared the groves, a long time later, it was almost dawn. Already the black silhouette of Kostos was softening in the first feathery greyness of the coming day. The wind was from the south, and warm, and the snow was beginning to melt on the hills.

11
WEDNESDAY
1400–1600

ALL DAY long they lay hidden in the carob grove, a thick clump of stunted, gnarled trees that clung grimly to the treacherous, scree-strewn slope abutting what Louki called the "Devil's Playground." A poor shelter and an uncomfortable one, but in every other way all they could wish for: it offered concealment, a first-class defensive position immediately behind, a gentle breeze drawn up from the sea by the sun-baked rocks to the south, shade from the sun that rode from dawn to dusk in a cloudless sky—and an incomparable view of a sun-drenched, shimmering Ægean.

Away to their left, fading through diminishing shades of blue and indigo and violet into faraway nothingness, stretched the islands of the Lerades, the nearest of them, Maidos, so close that they could see isolated fisher cottages sparkling whitely in the sun: through that narrow, intervening gap of water would pass the ships of the Royal Navy in just over a day's time. To the right, and even further away, remote, featureless, back-dropped by the towering Anatolian mountains, the coast of Turkey hooked north and west in a great curving scimitar: to the north itself, the thrusting spear of Cape Demirci, rock-rimmed but dimpled with sandy coves of white, reached far out into the placid blue of the Ægean: and north again beyond the Cape, haze-blurred in the purple distance, the island of Kheros lay dreaming on the surface of the sea.

It was a breath-taking panorama, a heart-catching beauty sweeping majestically through a great semi-circle over the sunlit sea. But Mallory had no eyes for it, had spared it only a passing glance when he had come on guard less than half an hour previously, just after two o'clock. He had dismissed it with one quick glance, settled by the bole of a tree, gazed for endless minutes, gazed until his eyes ached with strain at what he had so long waited to see. Had waited to see and come to destroy—the guns of the fortress of Navarone.

The town of Navarone—a town of from four to five thousand people, Mallory judged—lay sprawled round the deep, volcanic crescent of the harbour, a crescent so deep, so embracing, that it was almost a complete circle with only a narrow bottleneck of an entrance to the north-west, a gateway dominated by searchlights and mortar and machine-gun batteries on either side. Less than three miles distant to the north-east from the carob grove, every detail, every street, every building, every caique and launch in the harbour were clearly visible to Mallory and he studied them over and over again until he knew them by heart: the way the land to the west of the harbour sloped up gently to the olive groves, the dusty streets running down to the water's edge: the way the ground rose more sharply to the south, the streets now running parallel to the water down to the old town: the way the cliffs to the east—cliffs pock-marked by the bombs of Torrance's Liberator Squadron—stretched a hundred and fifty sheer feet above the water, then curved dizzily out over and above the harbour, and the great mound of volcanic rock towering above that again, a mound barricaded off from the town below by the high wall that ended flush with the cliff itself: and, finally, the way the twin rows of A.A. guns, the great radar scanners and the barracks of the fortress, squat, narrow-embrasured, built of big blocks

114

of masonry, dominated everything in sight—including that great, black gash in the rock, below the fantastic overhang of the cliff.

Unconsciously, almost, Mallory nodded to himself in slow understanding. This was the fortress that had defied the Allies for eighteen long months, that had dominated the entire naval strategy in the Sporades since the Germans had reached out from the mainland into the isles, that had blocked all naval activity in that 2,000 square mile triangle between the Lerades and the Turkish coast. And now, when he saw it, it all made sense. Impregnable to land attack—the commanding fortress saw to that: impregnable to air attack—Mallory realised just how suicidal it had been to send out Torrance's squadron against the great guns protected by that jutting cliff, against the great guns protected by that jutting cliff, against those bristling rows of anti-aircraft guns: and impregnable to sea attack—the waiting squadrons of the Luftwaffe on Samos saw to that. Jensen had been right—only a guerrilla sabotage mission stood any chance at all: a remote chance, an all but suicidal chance, but still a chance, and Mallory knew he couldn't ask for more.

Thoughtfully he lowered the binoculars and rubbed the back of his hand across aching eyes. At last he felt he knew exactly what he was up against, was grateful for the knowledge, for the opportunity he'd been given of this long-range reconnaissance, this familiarising of himself with the terrain, the geography of the town. This was probably the one vantage point in the whole island that offered such an opportunity together with concealment and near immunity. No credit to himself, the leader of the mission, he reflected wryly, that they had found such a place: it had been Louki's idea entirely.

And he owed a great deal more than that to the sad-eyed little Greek. It had been Louki's idea that they first move up-valley from Margaritha, to give Andrea time to recover the explosives from old Leri's hut, and to make certain there was no immediate hue and cry and pursuit—they could have fought a rearguard action up through the olive groves, until they had lost themselves in the foothills of Kostos: it was he who had guided them back past Margaritha when they had doubled on their tracks, had halted them opposite the village while he and Panayis had slipped wraith-like through the lifting twilight, picked up outdoor clothes for themselves, and, on the return journey, slipped into the *Abteilung* garage, torn away the coil ignitions of the German command car and truck—the only transport in Margaritha— and smashed their distributors for good measure; it was Louki who had led them by a sunken ditch right up to the road-block guard post at the mouth of the valley—it had been almost ludicrously simple to disarm the sentries, only one of whom had been awake—and, finally, it was Louki who had insisted that they walk down the muddy centre of the valley track till they came to the metalled road, less than two miles from the town itself. A hundred yards down this they had branched off to the left across a long, sloping field of lava that left no trace behind, arrived in the carob copse just on sunrise.

And it had worked. All these carefully engineered pointers, pointers that not even the most sceptical could have ignored and denied, had worked magnificently. Miller and Andrea, who had shared the forenoon watch, had seen the Navarone garrison spending long hours making the most intensive house-to-house search of the town. That should make it doubly, trebly safe for them the following day, Mallory reckoned: it was unlikely that the search would be repeated, still more unlikely that, if it were, it would be carried out with a fraction of the same enthusiasm. Louki had done his work well.

Mallory turned his head to look at him. The little man was still asleep—wedged on the slope behind a couple of tree-trunks, he hadn't stirred for five hours. Still dead tired himself, his legs aching and eyes smarting with sleeplessness, Mallory could not find it in him to grudge Louki a moment of his rest. He'd earned it all—and he'd been awake all though the previous night. So had Panayis, but Panayis was already awakening, Mallory saw, pushing the long, black hair out of his eyes: awake, rather, for his transition from sleep to full awareness was immediate, as fleeting and as complete as a cat's. A dangerous man, Mallory knew, a desperate man, almost, and a bitter enemy, but he knew nothing of Panayis, nothing at all. He doubted if he ever would.

Farther up on the slope, almost in the centre of the grove, Andrea had built a high platform of broken branches and twigs against a couple of carob poles maybe five feet apart, gradually filling up the space between slope and trees until he had a platform four feet in width, as nearly level as he could make it. Andy Stevens lay on this, still on his stretcher, still conscious. As far as Mallory could tell, Stevens hadn't closed his eyes since they had been marched away by Turzig from their cave in the mountains. He seemed to have passed beyond the need for sleep, or had crushed all desire for it. The stench from the gangrenous leg was nauseating, appalling, poisoned all the air around. Mallory and Miller had had a look at the leg shortly after their arrival in the copse, uncovered it, examined it, smiled at one another, tied it up again and assured Stevens that the wound was closing. Below the knee, the leg had turned almost completely black.

Mallory lifted his binoculars to have another look at the town, but lowered them almost at once as someone came sliding down the slope, touched him on the arm. It was Panayis, upset, anxious, almost angry looking. He gesticulated towards the westering sun.

"The time, Captain Mallory?" He spoke in Greek, his voice low, sibilant, urgent—an inevitable voice, Mallory thought, for the lean, dark mysteriousness of the man. "What is the time?" he repeated.

"Half-past two, or thereabouts." Mallory lifted an interrogatory eyebrow. "You are concerned, Panayis. Why?"

"You should have wakened me. You should have wakened me hours ago!" He *was* angry, Mallory decided. "It is my turn to keep watch."

"But you had no sleep last night," Mallory pointed out reasonably. "It just didn't seem fair——"

"It is my turn to keep watch, I tell you!" Panayis insisted stubbornly.

"Very well, then. If you insist." Mallory knew the high fierce pride of the islanders too well to attempt to argue. "Heaven only knows what we would have done without Louki and yourself. . . . I'll stay and keep you company for a while."

"Ah, so that is why you let me sleep on!" There was no disguising the hurt in the eyes, the voice. "You do not trust Panayis——"

"Oh, for heaven's sake!" Mallory began in exasperation, checked himself and smiled. "Of course we trust you. Maybe I should go and get some more sleep anyway; you are kind to give me the chance. You will shake me in two hour's time?"

"Certainly, certainly!" Panayis was almost beaming. "I shall not fail."

Mallory scrambled up to the centre of the grove and stretched out lazily along the ledge he had levelled out for himself. For a few idle moments he watched Panayis pacing restlessly to and fro just inside the perimeter of the grove, lost interest when he saw him climbing swiftly up among the branches of a tree, seeking a high lookout vantage point and decided he might as well follow his own advice and get some sleep while he could.

"Captain Mallory! Captain Mallory!" An urgent, heavy hand was shaking his shoulder. "Wake up! Wake up!"

Mallory stirred, rolled over on his back, sat up quickly, opening his eyes as he did so. Panayis was stooped over him, the dark, saturnine face alive with anxiety. Mallory shook his head to clear away the mists of sleep and was on his feet in one swift, easy movement.

"What's the matter, Panayis?"

"Planes!" he said quickly. "There is a squadron of planes coming our way!"

"Planes? What planes? Whose planes?"

"I do not know, Captain. They are yet far away. But——"

"What direction?" Mallory snapped.

"They come from the north."

Together they ran down to the edge of the grove. Panayis gestured to the north, and Mallory caught sight of them at once, the afternoon sun glinting off the sharp dihedral of the wings. Stukas, all right, he thought grimly. Seven—no, eight of them—less than three miles away, flying in two echelons of four, two thousand, certainly not more than twenty-five hundred feet. . . . He became aware that Panayis was tugging urgently at his arm.

"Come, Captain Mallory!" he said excitedly. "We have no time to lose!" He pulled Mallory round, pointed with outstretched arm at the gaunt, shattered cliffs that rose steeply behind them, cliffs crazily riven by rock-jumbled ravines that wound their aimless way back to the interior—or stopped as abruptly as they had begun. "The Devil's Playground! We must get there at once! At once, Captain Mallory!"

"Why on earth should we?" Mallory looked at him in astonishment. "There's no reason to suppose that they're after us. How can they be? No one knows we're here."

"I do not care!" Panayis was stubborn in his conviction. "I know. Do not ask me how I know, for I do not know that myself. Louki will tell you—Panayis knows these things. I know, Captain Mallory, I *know*!"

Just for a second Mallory stared at him, uncomprehending. There was no questioning the earnestness, the utter sincerity—but it was the machine-gun staccato of the words that tipped the balance of instinct against reason. Almost without realising it, certainly without realising why, Mallory found himself running uphill, slipping and stumbling in the scree. He found the others already on their feet, tense, expectant, shrugging on their packs, the guns already in their hands.

"Get to the edge of the trees up there!" Mallory shouted. "Quickly! Stay there and stay under cover—we're going to have to break for that gap in the rocks." He gestured through the trees at a jagged fissure in the cliff-side, barely forty yards from where he stood, blessed Louki for his foresight in choosing a hideout with so convenient a bolt-hole. "Wait till I give the word. Andrea!" He turned round, then broke off, the words unneeded. Andrea had already scooped up the dying boy in his arms, just as he lay in stretcher and blankets and was weaving his way uphill in and out among the trees.

"What's up, boss?" Miller was by Mallory's side as he plunged up the slope. "I don't see nothin'."

"You can hear something if you'd just stop talking for a moment," Mallory said grimly. "Or just take a look up there."

Miller, flat on his stomach now and less than a dozen feet from the edge of the grove, twisted round and craned his neck upwards. He picked up the planes immediately.

"Stukas!" he said incredulously. "A squadron of gawddamned Stukas! It can't be, boss!"

"It can and it is," Mallory said grimly. "Jensen told me that Jerry has stripped the Italian front of them—over two hundred pulled out in the last few weeks." Mallory squinted up at the squadron, less than half a mile away now. "And he's brought the whole damn' issue down to the Ægean."

"But they're not lookin' for us," Miller protested.

"I'm afraid they are," Mallory said grimly. The two bomber echelons had just dove-tailed into line ahead formation. "I'm afraid Panayis was right."

"But—but they're passin' us by——"

"They aren't," Mallory said flatly. "They're here to stay. Just keep your eyes on that leading plane."

Even as he spoke, the flight-commander tilted his gull-winged Junkers 87 sharply over to port, half-turned, fell straight out of the sky in a screaming power-dive, plummetting straight for the carob grove.

"Leave him alone!" Mallory shouted. "Don't fire!" The Stuka, airbrakes at maximum depression, had steadied on the centre of the grove. Nothing could stop him now—but a chance shot might bring him down directly on top of them: the chances were poor enough as it was. . . . "Keep your hands over your heads—and your heads down!"

He ignored his own advice, his gaze following the bomber every foot of the way down. Five hundred, four hundred, three, the rising crescendo of the heavy engine was beginning to hurt his ears, and the Stuka was pulling sharply out of its plunging fall, its bomb gone.

Bomb! Mallory sat up sharply, screwing up his eyes against the blue of the sky. Not one bomb but dozens of them, clustered so thickly that they appeared to be jostling each other as they arrowed into the centre of the grove, striking the gnarled and stunted trees, breaking off branches and burying themselves to their fins in the soft and shingled slope. Incendiaries! Mallory had barely time to realise that they had been spared the horror of a 500-kilo H.E. bomb when the incendiaries erupted into hissing, guttering life, into an incandescent magnesium whiteness that reached out and completely destroyed the shadowed gloom of the carob grove. Within a matter of seconds the dazzling coruscation had given way to thick, evil-smelling clouds of acrid black smoke, smoke laced with flickering tongues of red, small at first then licking and twisting resinously upwards until entire trees were enveloped in a cocoon of flame. The Stuka was still pulling upwards out of its dive, had not yet levelled off when the heart of the grove, old and dry and tindery, was fiercely ablaze.

Miller twisted up and round, nudging Mallory to catch his attention through the crackling roar of the flames.

"Incendiaries, boss," he announced.

"What did you think they were using?" Mallory asked shortly. "Matches? They're trying to smoke us out, to burn us out, get us in the open. High explosive's not so good among trees. Ninety-nine times out of a hundred this would have worked." He coughed as the acrid smoke bit into his lungs, peered up with watering eyes through the tree-tops. "But not this time. Not if we're lucky. Not if they hold off another half-minute or so. Just look at that smoke!"

Miller looked. Thick, convoluted, shot through with fiery sparks, the rolling cloud was already a third of the way across the gap between grove and cliff, borne uphill by the wandering catspaws from the sea. It was the complete, the perfect smokescreen. Miller nodded.

"Gonna make a break for it, huh, boss?"

"There's no choice—we either go, or we stay and get fried—or blown into very little bits. Probably both." He raised his voice. "Anybody see what's happening up top?"

"Queuing up for another go at us, sir." Brown said lugubriously. "The first bloke's still circling around."

"Waiting to see how we break cover. They won't wait long. This is where we take off." He peered uphill through the rolling smoke, but it was too thick, laced his watering eyes until everything was blurred through a misted sheen of tears. There was no saying how far uphill the smoke-bank had reached, and they couldn't afford to wait until they were sure. Stuka pilots had never been renowned for their patience.

"Right, everybody!" he shouted. "Fifteen yards along the tree-line to that wash, then straight up into the gorge. Don't stop till you're at least a hundred yards inside. Andrea, you lead the way. Off you go!" He peered through the blinding smoke. "Where's Panayis?"

There was no reply.

"Panayis!" Mallory called. "Panayis!"

"Perhaps he went back for somethin'." Miller had stopped half-turned. "Shall I go——"

"Get on your way!" Mallory said savagely. "And if anything happens to young Stevens I'll hold you . . ." But Miller, wisely, was already gone, Andrea stumbling and coughing by his side.

For a couple of seconds Mallory stood irresolute, then plunged back downhill towards the centre of the grove. Maybe Panayis had gone back for something—and he couldn't understand English. Mallory had hardly gone five yards when he was forced to halt and fling his arm up before his face: the heat was searing. Panayis couldn't be down there; no one could have been down there, could have lived for seconds in that furnace. Gasping for air, hair singeing and clothes smouldering with fire, Mallory clawed his way back up the slope, colliding with trees, slipping, falling, then stumbling desperately to his feet again.

He ran along to the east end of the wood. No one there. Back to the other end again, towards the wash, almost completely blind now, the super-heated air searing viciously through throat and lungs till he was suffocating, till his breath was coming in great, whooping, agonised breaths. No sense in waiting longer, nothing he could do, nothing anyone could do except save himself. There was a noise in his ears, the roaring of the flames, the roaring of his own blood—and the screaming, heart-stopping roar of a Stuka in a power-dive. Desperately he flung himself forward over the sliding scree, stumbled and pitched headlong down to the floor of the wash.

Hurt or not, he did not know and he did not care. Sobbing aloud for breath, he rose to his feet, forced his aching legs to drive him somehow up the hill. The air was full of the thunder of engines, he knew the entire squadron was coming in to the attack, and then he had flung himself uncaringly to the ground as the first of the high explosive bombs erupted in its concussive blast of smoke and flame—erupted not forty yards away, to his left and ahead of him. *Ahead* of him! Even as he struggled upright again, lurched forward and upward once more, Mallory cursed himself again and again and again. You mad-man, he thought bitterly, confusedly, you damned crazy mad-man. Sending the others out to be killed. He should have thought of it—oh, God, he should have thought of it, a five-year-old could have thought of it. Of course Jerry wasn't going to bomb the grove: they had seen the obvious, the inevitable, as quickly as he had, were dive-bombing the pall of smoke between the grove and the cliff! A five-year-old—the earth exploded beneath his feet, a giant hand plucked him up and smashed him to the ground and the darkness closed over him.

12

WEDNESDAY
1600–1800

ONCE, TWICE, half a dozen times, Mallory struggled up from the depths of a black, trance-like stupor and momentarily touched the surface of consciousness only to slide back into the darkness again. Desperately, each time, he tried to hang on to these fleeting moments of awareness, but his mind was like the void, dark and sinewless, and even as he knew that his mind was slipping backwards again, loosing its grip on reality, the knowledge was gone, and there was only the void once more. Nightmare, he thought vaguely during one of the longer glimmerings of comprehension, I'm having a nightmare, like when you know you are having a nightmare and that if you could open your eyes it would be gone, but you can't open your eyes. He tried it now, tried to open his eyes, but it was no good, it was still as dark as ever and he was still sunk in this evil dream, for the sun had been shining brightly in the sky. He shook his head in slow despair.

"Aha! Observe! Signs of life at last!" There was no mistaking the slow, nasal drawl. "Ol' Medicine Man Miller triumphs again!" There was a moment's silence, a moment in which Mallory was increasingly aware of the diminishing thunder of aero engines, the acrid, resinous smoke that stung his nostrils and eyes, and then an arm had passed under his shoulders and Miller's persuasive voice was in his ear. "Just try a little of this, boss. Ye olde vintage brandy. Nothin' like it anywhere."

Mallory felt the cold neck of the bottle, tilted his head back, took a long pull. Almost immediately he had jerked himself upright and forward to a sitting position, gagging, spluttering and fighting for breath as the raw, fiery ouzo bit into the mucous membrane of cheeks and throat. He tried to speak but could do no more than croak, gasp for fresh air and stare indignantly at the shadowy figure that knelt by his side. Miller, for his part, looked at him with unconcealed admiration.

"See, boss? Just like I said—nothin' like it." He shook his head admiringly. "Wide awake in an instant, as the literary boys would say. Never saw a shock and concussion victim recover so fast!"

"What the hell are you trying to do?" Mallory demanded. The fire had died down in his throat, and he could breath again. "Poison me?" Angrily he shook his head, fighting off the pounding ache, the fog that still swirled round the fringes of his mind. "Bloody fine physician you are! Shock, you say, yet the first thing you do is administer a dose of spirits——"

"Take your pick," Miller interrupted grimly. "Either that or a damned sight bigger shock in about fifteen minutes or so when brother Jerry gets here."

"But they've gone away. I can't hear the Stukas anymore."

"This lot's comin' up from the town," Miller said morosely. "Louki's just reported them. Half a dozen armoured cars and a couple of trucks with field guns the length of a telegraph pole."

"I see." Mallory twisted round, saw a gleam of light at a bend in the wall. A cave—a tunnel, almost. Little Cyprus, Louki had said some of the older people had called it—the Devil's Playground was riddled with a honeycomb of caves. He grinned wryly at the memory of his momentary panic when he thought his eyes had gone and turned again to Miller. "Trouble again, Dusty, nothing but trouble. Thanks for bringing me round."

"Had to," Miller said briefly. "I guess we couldn't have carried you very far, boss."

Mallory nodded. "Not just the flattest of country hereabouts."

"There's that, too," Miller agreed. "What I really meant is that there's hardly anyone left to carry you. Casey Brown and Panayis have both been hurt, Boss."

"What! Both of them?" Mallory screwed his eyes shut, shook his head in slow anger. "My God, Dusty, I'd forgotten all about the bomb—the bombs." He reached out his hand, caught Miller by the arm. "How—how bad are they?" There was so little time left, so much to do.

"How bad?" Miller shook out a pack of cigarettes and offered one to Mallory. "Not bad at all—if we could get them into hospital. But hellish painful and cripplin' if they gotta start hikin' up and down those gawd-damned ravines hereabouts. First time I've seen canyon floors more nearly vertical than the walls themselves."

"You still haven't told me——"

"Sorry, boss, sorry. Shrapnel wounds, both of them, in exactly the same place—left thigh, just above the knee. No bones gone, no tendons cut. I've just finished tying up Casey's leg—it's a pretty wicked lookin' gash. He's gonna know all about it when he starts walkin'."

"And Panayis?"

"Fixed his own leg," Miller said briefly. "A queer character. Wouldn't even let me look at it, far less bandage it. I reckon he'd have knifed me if I'd tried."

"Better to leave him alone anyway," Mallory advised. "Some of these islanders have strange taboos and superstitions. Just as long as he's alive. Though I still don't see how the hell he managed to get here."

"He was the first to leave," Miller explained. "Along with Casey. You must have missed him in the smoke. They were climbin' together when they got hit."

"And how did I get here?"

"No prizes for the first correct answer." Miller jerked a thumb over his shoulder at the huge form that blocked half the width of the cave. "Junior here did his St. Bernard act once again. I wanted to go with him, but he wasn't keen. Said he reckoned it would be difficult to carry both of us up the hill. My feelin's were hurt considerable." Miller sighed. "I guess I just wasn't born to be a hero, that's all."

Mallory smiled. "Thanks again, Andrea."

"Thanks!" Miller was indignant. "A guy saves your life and all you can say is 'thanks'!"

"After the first dozen times or so you run out of suitable speeches," Mallory said dryly. "How's Stevens?"

"Breathin'."

Mallory nodded forward towards the source of light, wrinkled his nose. "Just round the corner, isn't he?"

"Yeah, it's pretty grim," Miller admitted. "The gangrene's spread up beyond the knee."

Mallory rose groggily to his feet, picked up his gun. "How is he really, Dusty?"

"He's dead, but he just won't die. He'll be gone by sundown. Gawd only knows what's kept him goin' so far."

"It may sound presumptuous," Mallory murmured; "but I think I know too."

"The first-class medical attention?" Miller said hopefully.

"Looks that way, doesn't it?" Mallory smiled down at the still kneeling Miller. "But that wasn't what I meant at all. Come, gentlemen, we have some business to attend to."

"Me, all I'm good for is blowin' up bridges and droppin' a handful of sand in engine bearin's," Miller announced. "Strategy and tactics are far beyond my simple mind. But I still think those characters down there are pickin' a very stupid way of committin' suicide. It would be a damned sight easier for all concerned if they just shot themselves."

"I'm inclined to agree with you." Mallory settled himself more firmly behind the jumbled rocks in the mouth of the ravine that opened on the charred and smoking remains of the carob grove directly below and took another look at the Alpenkorps troops advancing in extended order up the steep, shelterless slope. "They're no children at this game. I bet they don't like it one little bit, either."

"Then why the hell are they doin' it, boss?"

"No option, probably. First off, this place can only be attacked frontally." Mallory smiled down at the little Greek lying between himself and Andrea. "Louki here chose the place well. It would require a long detour to attack from the rear—and it would take them a week to advance through that devil's scrap-heap behind us. Secondly, it'll be sunset in a couple of hours, and they know they haven't a hope of getting us after it's dark. And finally—and I think this is more important than the other two reasons put together—it's a hundred to one that the commandant in the town is being pretty severely prodded by his High Command. There's too much at stake, even in the one in a thousand chance of us getting at the guns. They can't afford to have Kheros evacuated under their noses, to lose——"

"Why not?" Miller interrupted. He gestured largely with his hands. "Just a lot of useless rocks——"

"They can't afford to lose face with the Turks," Mallory went on patiently. "The strategic importance of these islands in the Sporades is negligible, but their political importance is tremendous. Adolph badly needs another ally in these parts. So he flies in Alpenkorps troops by the thousand and Stukas by the hundred, the best he has—and he needs them desperately on the Italian front. But you've got to convince your potential ally that you're a pretty safe bet before you can persuade him to give up his nice, safe seat on the fence and jump down on your side."

"Very interestin'," Miller observed. "So?"

"So the Germans are going to have no compunction about thirty or forty of their best troops being cut into little pieces. It's no trouble at all when you're sitting behind a desk a thousand miles away. . . . Let 'em come another hundred yards or so closer. Louki and I will start from the middle and work out: you and Andrea start from the outside."

"I don't like it, boss," Miller complained.

"Don't think that I do either," Mallory said quietly. "Slaughtering men forced to do a suicidal job like this is not my idea of fun—or even of war. But if we don't get them, they get us." He broke off and pointed across the burnished sea to where Kheros lay peacefully on the hazed horizon, striking golden glints off the westering sun. "What do you think they would have us do, Dusty?"

"I know, I know, boss." Miller stirred uncomfortably. "Don't rub it in."
He pulled his woollen cap low over his forehead and stared bleakly down
the slope. "How soon do the mass executions begin?"

"Another hundred yards, I said." Mallory looked down the slope again
towards the coast road and grinned suddenly, glad to change the topic.
"Never saw telegraph poles shrink so suddenly before, Dusty."

Miller studied the guns drawn up on the road behind the two trucks and
cleared his throat.

"I was only sayin' what Louki told me," he said defensively.

"What Louki told you!" The little Greek was indignant. "Before God,
Major, the Americano is full of lies!"

"Ah, well, mebbe I was mistaken," Miller said magnanimously. He
squinted again at the guns, forehead lined in puzzlement. "That first one's
a mortar, I reckon. But what in the universe that other weird looking contraption can be——"

"Also a mortar," Mallory explained. "A five-barrelled job, and very
nasty. The *Nebelwerfer* or Moanin' Minnie. Howls like all the lost souls in
hell. Guaranteed to turn the knees to jelly, especially after nightfall—but
it's still the other one you have to watch. A six-inch mortar, almost certainly
using fragmentation bombs—you use a brush and shovel for clearing up
afterwards."

"That's right," Miller growled. "Cheer us all up." But he was grateful
to the New Zealander for trying to take their minds off what they had to do.
"Why don't they use them?"

"They will," Mallory assured him. "Just as soon as we fire and they find
out where we are."

"Gawd help us," Miller muttered. "Fragmentation bombs, you said!"
He lapsed into gloomy silence.

"Any second now," Mallory said softly. "I only hope that our friend
Turzig isn't among this lot." He reached out for his field-glasses but stopped
in surprise as Andrea leaned across Louki and caught him by the wrist
before he could lift the binoculars. "What's the matter, Andrea?"

"I would not be using these, my Captain. They have betrayed us once
already. I have been thinking, and it can be nothing else. The sunlight
reflecting from the lenses . . ."

Mallory stared at him, slowly released his grip on the glasses, nodded
several times in succession.

"Of course, of course! I had been wondering. . . . Someone has been
careless. There was no other way, there *could* have been no other way. It
would only require a single flash to tip them off." He paused, remembering,
then grinned wryly. "It could have been myself. All this started just after I
had been on watch—and Panayis didn't have the glasses." He shook his
head in mortification. "It *must* have been me, Andrea."

"I do not believe it," Andrea said flatly. "You couldn't make a mistake
like that, my Captain."

"Not only could, but did, I'm afraid. But we'll worry about that afterwards." The middle of the ragged line of advancing soldiers, slipping and
stumbling on the treacherous scree, had almost reached the lower limits of
the blackened, stunted remains of the copse. "They've come far enough.
I'll take the white helmet in the middle, Louki." Even as he spoke he could
hear the soft scrape as the three others slid their automatic barrels across and
between the protective rocks in front of them, could feel the wave of revulsion that washed through his mind. But his voice was steady enough as he
spoke, relaxed and almost casual. "Right. Let them have it now!"

His last words were caught up and drowned in the tearing, rapid-fire crash

of the automatic carbines. With four machine-guns in their hands—two
Brens and two 9 mm. Schmeissers—it was no war, as he had said, but
sheer, pitiful massacre, with the defenceless figures on the slope below,
figures still stunned and uncomprehending, jerking, spinning round and
collapsing like marionettes in the hands of a mad puppeteer, some to lie
where they fell, others to roll down the steep slope, legs and arms flailing
in the grotesque disjointedness of death. Only a couple stood still where
they had been hit, vacant surprise mirrored in their lifeless faces, then
slipped down tiredly to the stony ground at their feet. Almost three seconds
had passed before the handful of those who still lived—about a quarter of
the way in from either end of the line where converging streams of fire had
not yet met—realised what was happening and flung themselves desperately
to the ground in search of the cover that didn't exist.

The frenetic stammering of the machine-guns stopped abruptly and in
unison, the sound sheared off as by a guillotine. The sudden silence was
curiously oppressive, louder, more obtrusive than the clamour that had gone
before. The gravelly earth beneath his elbows grated harshly as Mallory
shifted his weight slightly, looked at the two men to his right, Andrea with
his impassive face empty of all expression, Louki with the sheen of tears in
his eyes. Then he became aware of the low murmuring to his left, shifted
round again. Bitter-mouthed, savage, the American was swearing softly and
continuously, oblivious to the pain as he pounded his fist time and again into
the sharp-edged gravel before him.

"Just one more, Gawd." The quiet voice was almost a prayer. "That's
all I ask. Just one more."

Mallory touched his arm. "What is it, Dusty?"

Miller looked round at him, eyes cold and still and empty of all recognition, then he blinked several times and grinned, a cut and bruised hand
automatically reaching for his cigarettes.

"Jus' daydreamin', boss" he said easily. "Jus' daydreamin'." He shook
out his pack of cigarettes. "Have one?"

"That inhuman bastard that sent these poor devils up that hill," Mallory
said quietly. "Make a wonderful picture seen over the sights of your rifle,
wouldn't he?"

Abruptly Miller's smile vanished and he nodded.

"It would be all of that." He risked a quick peep round one of the
boulders, eased himself back again. "Eight, mebbe ten of them still down
there, boss," he reported. "The poor bastards are like ostriches—trying to
take cover behind stones the size of an orange. . . . We leave them be?"

"We leave them be!" Mallory echoed emphatically. The thought of any
more slaughter made him feel almost physically sick. "They won't try
again." He broke off suddenly, flattened himself in reflex instinct as a burst
of machine-gun bullets struck the steep-walled rock above their heads and
whined up the gorge in vicious ricochet.

"Won't try again, huh?" Miller was already sliding his gun around the
rock in front of him when Mallory caught his arm and pulled him back.

"Not them? Listen!" Another burst of fire, then another, and now they
could hear the savage chatter of the machine-gun, a chatter rhythmically
interrupted by a weird, half-human sighing as its belt passed through the
breech. Mallory could feel the prickling of the hairs on the nape of his neck.

"A Spandau. Once you've heard a Spandau you can never forget it. Leave
it alone—it's probably fixed on the back of one of the trucks and can't do
us any harm. . . . I'm more worried about these damned mortars down
there."

"I'm not," Miller said promptly. "They're not firing at us."

"That's why I'm worried. . . . What do you think, Andrea?"

"The same as you, my Captain. They are waiting. This Devil's Playground, as Louki calls it, is a madman's maze, and they can only fire as blind men——"

"They won't be waiting much longer," Mallory interrupted grimly. He pointed to the north. "Here come their eyes."

At first only specks above the promontory of Cape Demirci, the planes were soon recognisable for what they were, droning in slowly over the Ægean at about fifteen hundred feet. Mallory looked at them in astonishment, then turned to Andrea.

"Am I seeing things, Andrea?" He gestured at the first of the two planes, a high-winged little monoplane fighter. "That can't be a PZL?"

"It can be and it is," Andrea murmured. "An old Polish plane we had before the war," he explained to Miller. "And the other is an old Belgian plane—Breguets, we called them." Andrea shaded his eyes to look again at the two planes, now almost directly overhead. "I thought they had all been lost during the invasion."

"Me too," Mallory said. "Must have patched up some bits and pieces. Ah, they've seen us—beginning to circle. But why on earth they use these obsolete death traps——"

"I don't know and I don't care," Miller said rapidly. He had just taken a quick look round the boulder in front of him. "These damned guns down there are just linin' up on us, and muzzle-on they look a considerable sight bigger than telegraph poles. Fragmentation bombs, you said! Come on, boss, let's get the hell outa here!"

Thus the pattern was set for the remainder of that brief November afternoon, for the grim game of tip-and-run, hide-and-seek among the ravines and shattered rocks of the Devil's Playground. The planes held the key to the game, cruised high overhead observing every move of the hunted group below, relaying the information to the guns on the coast road and the company of Alpenkorps that had moved up through the ravine above the carob grove soon after the planes reported that the positions there had been abandoned. The two ancient planes were soon replaced by a couple of modern Henschels—Andrea said that the PZL couldn't remain airborne for more than an hour anyway.

Mallory was between the devil and the deep sea. Inaccurate though the mortars were, some of the deadly fragmentation bombs found their way into the deep ravines where they took temporary shelter, the blast of metal lethal in the confined space between the sheering walls. Occasionally they came so close that Mallory was forced to take refuge in some of the deep caves that honeycombed the walls of the canyons. In these they were safe enough, but the safety was an illusion that could lead only to ultimate defeat and capture; in the lulls, the Alpenkorps, whom they had fought off in a series of brief, skirmishing rearguard actions during the afternoon, could approach closely enough to trap them inside. Time and time again Mallory and his men were forced to move on to widen the gap between themselves and their pursuers, following the indomitable Louki wherever he chose to lead them, and taking their chance, often a very slender and desperate chance, with the mortar bombs. One bomb arced into a ravine that led into the interior, burying itself in the gravelly ground not twenty yards ahead of them, by far the nearest anything had come during the afternoon. By one chance in a thousand, it didn't explode. They gave it as wide a berth as possible, almost holding their breaths until they were safely beyond.

About half an hour before sunset they struggled up the last few boulder-strewn yards of a steeply-shelving ravine floor, halted just beyond the shelter of the projecting wall where the ravine dipped again and turned sharply to the right and the north. There had been no more mortar bombs since the one that had failed to explode. The six-inch and the weirdly-howling *Nebelwerfer* had only a limited range, Mallory knew, and though the planes still cruised overhead, they cruised uselessly: the sun was dipping towards the horizon and the floors of the ravines were already deep-sunk in shadowed gloom, invisible from above. But the Alpenkorps, tough, dogged, skilful soldiers, soldiers living only for the revenge of their massacred comrades, were very close behind. And they were highly-trained mountain troops, fresh, resilient, the reservoir of their energies barely tapped: whereas his own tiny band, worn out from continuous days and sleepless nights of labour and action. . . .

Mallory sank to the ground near the angled turn of the ravine where he could keep lookout, glanced at the others with a deceptive casualness that masked his cheerless assessment of what he saw. As a fighting unit they were in a pretty bad way. Both Panayis and Brown were badly crippled, the latter's face grey with pain. For the first time since leaving Alexandria, Casey Brown was apathetic, listless and quite indiffereent to everything: this Mallory took as a very bad sign. Nor was Brown helped by the heavy transmitter still strapped to his back—with point-blank truculence he had ignored Mallory's categorical order to abandon it. Louki was tired, and looked it: his physique, Mallory realised now, was no match for his spirit, for the infectious smile that never left his face, for the panache of that magnificently upswept moustache that contrasted so oddly with the sad, tired eyes above. Miller, like himself, was tired, but, like himself, could keep on being tired for a long time yet. And Stevens was still conscious, but even in the twilit gloom of the canyon floor his face looked curiously transparent, while the nails, lips and eyelids were drained of blood. And Andrea, who had carried him up and down all these killing canyon tracks—where there had been tracks—for almost two interminable hours, looked as he always did: immutable, indestructible.

Mallory shook his head, fished out a cigarette, made to strike a light, remembered the planes still cruising overhead and threw the match away. Idly his gaze travelled north along the canyon and he slowly stiffened, the unlit cigarette crumpling and shredding between his fingers. This ravine bore no resemblance to any of the others through which they had so far passed—it was broader, dead straight, at least three times as long—and, as far as he could see in the twilight, the far end was blocked off by an almost vertical wall.

"Louki!" Mallory was on his feet now, all weariness forgotten. "Do you know where you are. Do you know this place?"

"But certainly, Major!" Louki was hurt. "Have I not told you that Panayis and I, in the days of our youth——"

"But this is a cul-de-sac, a dead-end!" Mallory protested. "We're boxed in, man, we're trapped!"

Louki grinned impudently and twirled a corner of his moustache. The little man was enjoying himself.

"So? The Major does not trust Louki, is that it?" He grinned again, relented, patted the wall by his side. "Panayis and I, we have been working this way all afternoon. Along this wall there are many caves. One of them leads through to another valley that leads down to the coast road.''

"I see, I see." Relief washing through his mind, Mallory sank down on the ground again. "And where does this other valley come out?''

"Just across the strait from Maidos.''

"How far from the town?''

"About five miles, Major, maybe six. Not more.''

"Fine, fine! And you're sure you can find this cave?''

"A hundred years from now and my head in a goatskin bag!'' Louki boasted.

"Fair enough!'' Even as he spoke, Mallory catapulted himself violently to one side, twisted in midair to avoid falling across Stevens and crashed heavily into the wall between Andrea and Miller. In a moment of unthinking carelessness he had exposed himself to view from the ravine they had just climbed: the burst of machine-gun fire from its lower end—a hundred and fifty yards away at the most—had almost blown his head off. Even as it was, the left shoulder of his jacket had been torn away, the shell just grazing his shoulder. Miller was already kneeling by his side, fingering the gash, running a gently exploratory hand across his back.

"Careless, damn careless,'' Mallory murmured. "But I didn't think they were so close.'' He didn't feel as calm as he sounded. If the mouth of that Schmeisser had been another sixteenth of an inch to the right, he'd have had no head left now.

"Are you all right, boss?'' Miller was puzzled. "Did they——''

"Terrible shots,'' Mallory assured him cheerfully. "Couldn't hit a barn.'' He twisted round to look at his shoulder. "I hate to sound heroic, but this really is just a scratch. . . .'' He rose easily to his feet, and picked up his gun. "Sorry and all that, gentlemen, but it's time we were on our way again. How far along is this cave, Louki?''

Louki rubbed his bristly chin, the smile suddenly gone. He looked quickly at Mallory, then away again.

"Louki!''

"Yes, yes, Major. The cave.'' Louki rubbed his chin again.

"Well, it is a good way along. In fact, it is at the end,'' he finished uncomfortably.

"The *very* end?'' asked Mallory quietly.

Louki nodded miserably, stared down at the ground at his feet. Even the ends of his moustache seemed to droop.

"That's handy,'' Mallory said heavily. "Oh, that's very handy!'' He sank down to the ground again. "Help us no end, that does.''

He bowed his head in thought and didn't even lift it as Andrea poked a Bren round the angle of the rock, and fired a short downhill burst more in token of discouragement than in any hope of hitting anything. Another ten seconds passed, then Louki spoke again, his voice barely audible.

"I am very, very sorry. This is a terrible thing. Before God, Major, I would not have done it but that I thought they were still far behind.''

"It's not your fault, Louki.'' Mallory was touched by the little man's obvious distress. He touched his ripped shoulder jacket. "I thought the same thing.''

"Please!'' Stevens put his hand on Mallory's arm. "What's wrong? I don't understand.''

"Everybody else does, I'm afraid, Andy. It's very, very simple. We have half a mile to go along this valley here—and not a shred of cover. The Alpenkorps have less than two hundred yards to come up that ravine we've just left.'' He paused while Andrea fired another retaliatory short burst, then continued. "They'll do what they're doing now—keep probing to see if we're still here. The minute they judge we're gone, they'll be up here in a flash. They'll nail us before we're halfway, quarter way to the cave—you know we can't travel fast. And they're carrying a couple of Spandaus—they'll cut us to ribbons."

"I see," Stevens murmured. "You put it all so nicely, sir."

"Sorry, Andy, but that's how it is."

"But could you not leave two men as a rearguard, while the rest——"

"And what happens to the rearguard?" Mallory interrupted dryly.

"I see what you mean," he said in a low voice. "I hadn't thought of that."

"No, but the rearguard would. Quite a problem, isn't it?"

"There is no problem at all," Louki announced. "The Major is kind, but this is all my fault. I will——"

"You'll do damn all of the kind!" Miller said savagely. He tore Louki's Bren from his hand and laid it on the ground. "You heard what the boss said—it wasn't your fault." For a moment Louki stared at him in anger, then turned dejectedly away. He looked as if he were going to cry. Mallory, too, stared at the American, astonished at the sudden vehemence, so completely out of character. Now that he came to think of it, Dusty had been strangely taciturn and thoughtful during the past hour or so—Mallory couldn't recall his saying a word during all that time. But time enough to worry about that later on. . . .

Casey Brown eased his injured leg, looking hopefully at Mallory. "Couldn't we stay here till it's dark—real dark—then make our way——"

"No good. The moon's almost full to-night—and not a cloud in the sky. They'd get us. Even more important, we have to get into the town between sunset and curfew to-night. Our last chance. Sorry, Casey, but it's no go."

Fifteen seconds, half a minute passed, and passed in silence, then they all started abruptly as Andy Stevens spoke.

"Louki *was* right, you know," he said pleasantly. The voice was weak, but filled with a calm certainty that jerked every eye towards him. He was propped up on one elbow, Louki's Bren cradled in his hands. It was a measure of their concentration on the problem on hand that no one had heard or seen him reach out for the machine-gun. "It's all very simple," Stevens went on quietly. "Just let's use our heads, that's all. . . . The gangrene's right up past the knee, isn't it, sir?"

Mallory said nothing: he didn't know what to say, the complete unexpectedness had knocked him off balance. He was vaguely aware that Miller was looking at him, his eyes begging him to say "No."

"Is it or isn't it?" There was patience, a curious understanding in the voice, and all of a sudden Mallory knew what to say.

"Yes," he nodded. "It is." Miller was looking at him in horror.

"Thank you, sir." Stevens was smiling in satisfaction. "Thank you very much indeed. There's no need to point out all the advantages of my staying here." There was an assurance in his voice no one had ever heard before, the unthinking authority of a man completely in charge of a situation. "Time I did something for my living anyway. No fond farewells, please. Just leave me a couple of boxes of ammo, two or three thirty-six grenades and away you go."

"I'll be damned if we will!" Miller was on his feet, making for the boy, then brought up abruptly as the Bren centered on his chest.

"One step nearer and I'll shoot you," Stevens said calmly. Miller looked at him in long silence, sank slowly back to the ground.

"I would, you know," Stevens assured him. "Well, good-bye, gentlemen. Thank you for all you've done for me."

Twenty seconds, thirty, a whole minute passed in a queer, trance-like silence, then Miller heaved himself to his feet again, a tall, rangy figure with tattered clothes and a face curiously haggard in the gathering gloom.

"So long kid. I guess—waal, mebbe I'm not so smart after all." He took Stevens's hand, looked down at the wasted face for a long moment, made to say something else, then changed his mind. "Be seein' you," he said abruptly, turned and walked off heavily down the valley. One by one the others followed him, wordlessly, except for Andrea who stopped and whispered in the boy's ear, a whisper that brought a smile and a nod of complete understanding, and then there was only Mallory left. Stevens grinned up at him.

"Thank you, sir. Thanks for not letting me down. You and Andrea—you understand. You always did understand."

"You'll—you'll be all right, Andy?" God, Mallory thought, what a stupid, what an inane thing, to say.

"Honest, sir, I'm O.K." Stevens smiled contentedly. "No pain left—I can't feel a thing. It's wonderful!"

"Andy, I don't——"

"It's time you were gone, sir. The others will be waiting. Now if you'll just light me a gasper and fire a few random shots down that ravine . . ."

Within five minutes Mallory had overtaken the others, and inside fifteen they had all reached the cave that led to the coast. For a moment they stood in the entrance, listening to the intermittent firing from the other end of the valley, then turned wordlessly and plunged into the cave. Back where they had left him, Andy Stevens was lying on his stomach, peering down into the now almost dark ravine. There was no pain left in his body, none at all. He drew deeply on a cupped cigarette, smiled as he pushed another clip home into the magazine of the Bren. For the first time in his life Andy Stevens was happy and content beyond his understanding, a man at last at peace with himself. He was no longer afraid.

13

WEDNESDAY EVENING

1800–1915

EXACTLY FORTY minutes later they were safely in the heart of the town of Navarone, within fifty yards of the great gates of the fortress itself.

Mallory, gazing out at the gates and the still more massive arch of stone that encased them, shook his head for the tenth time and tried to fight off the feeling of disbelief and wonder that they should have reached their goal at last—or as nearly as made no difference. They had been due a break some time, he thought, the law of averages has been overwhelmingly against the continuation of the evil fortune that had dogged them so incessantly since they had arrived on the island. It was only right, he kept telling himself, it was only just that this should be so: but even so, the transition from that dark valley where they had left Andy Stevens to die to this tumbledown old house on the east side of the town square of Navarone had been so quick, so easy, that it still lay beyond immediate understanding or unthinking acceptance.

Not that it had been too easy in the first fifteen minutes or so, he remembered. Panayis's wounded leg had given out on him immediately after they had entered the cave, and he had collapsed; he must have been in agony, Mallory had thought, with his torn, roughly-bandaged leg, but the failing light and the dark, bitter, impassive face had masked the pain. He had begged Mallory to be allowed to remain where he was, to hold off the Alpenkorps when they had overcome Stevens and reached the end of the valley, but Mallory had roughly refused him permission. Brutally he had told Panayis that he was far too valuable to be left there—and that the chances of the Alpenkorps picking that cave out of a score of others were pretty remote. Mallory had hated having to talk to him like that, but there had been no time for gentle blandishments, and Panayis must have seen his point for he had made neither protest nor struggle when Miller and Andrea picked him up and helped him to limp through the cave. The limp, Mallory had noticed, had been much less noticeable then, perhaps because of the assistance, perhaps because now that he had been baulked of the chance of killing a few more Germans it had been pointless to exaggerate his hurt.

They had barely cleared the mouth of the cave on the other side and were making their way down the tree-tufted, sloping valley side towards the sea, the dark sheen of the Ægean clearly visible in the gloom, when Louki, hearing something, had gestured them all to silence. Almost immediately Mallory, too, heard it, a soft guttural voice occasionally lost in the crunch of approaching feet on gravel, had seen that they were providentially screened by some stunted trees, given the order to stop and sworn in quick anger as he had heard the soft thud and barely muffled cry behind them. He had gone back to investigate and found Panayis stretched on the ground unconscious. Miller, who had been helping him along, had explained that Mallory had halted them so suddenly that he'd bumped into Panayis, that the Greek's bad leg had given beneath him, throwing him heavily, his head striking a stone as he had fallen. Mallory had stooped down in instantly renewed suspicion—Panayis was a throw-back, a natural-born killer, and he was quite capable of faking an accident if he thought he could turn it to his advantage, line a few more of the enemy up on the sights of his rifle . . . but there had been no fake about that: the bruised and bloodied gash above the temple was all too real.

The German patrol, having had no inkling of their presence, moved noisily up the valley till they had finally gone out of earshot. Louki had thought that the commandant in Navarone was becoming desperate, trying to seal off every available exit from the Devil's Playground. Mallory had thought it unlikely, but had not stayed to argue the point. Five minutes later they had cleared the mouth of the valley, and in another five had not only reached the coast road but silenced and bound two sentries—the drivers, probably—who had been guarding a truck and command car parked by the roadside, stripped them of denims and helmets and bundled them out of sight behind some bushes.

The trip into Navarone had been ridiculously simple, but the entire lack of opposition was easily understandable, because of the complete unexpectedness of it all. Seated beside Mallory on the front seat, clad, like Mallory, in captured clothes, Louki had driven the big car, and driven it magnificently, an accomplishment so unusual to find in a remote Ægean island that Mallory had been completely mystified until Louki had reminded him that he had been Eugene Vlachos's Consulate chauffeur for many years. The drive into town had taken less then twelve minutes—not only did the little man handle the car superbly, but he knew the road so well that he got the utmost possible out of the big machine, most of the time without benefit of any lights at all.

Not only a simple journey, but quite uneventful. They had passed several parked trucks at intervals along the road, and less than two miles from the town itself had met a group of about twenty soldiers marching in the opposite direction in column of twos. Louki had slowed down—it would have been highly suspicious had he accelerated, endangering the lives of the marching men—but had switched on the powerful headlights, blinding them, and blown raucously on the horn, while Mallory had leaned out of the right-hand window, sworn at them in perfect German and told them to get out of his damned way. This they had done, while the junior officer in charge had come smartly to attention, throwing up his hand in punctilious salute.

Immediately afterwards they had run through an area of high-walled, terraced market gardens, passed between a decaying Byzantine church and a whitewashed orthodox monastery that faced each other incongruously across the same dusty road, then almost at once were running through the lower part of the old town. Mallory had had a vague impression of narrow, winding, dim-lit streets only inches wider than the car itself, hugely cobbled and with almost knee-high pavements, then Louki was making his way up an arched lane, the car climbing steeply all the time. He had stopped abruptly, and Mallory had followed his quick survey of the darkened lane: completely deserted though over an hour yet to curfew. Beside them had been a flight of white stone steps innocent of any hand-rail, running up parallel to the wall of a house, with a highly ornamented lattice-work grill protecting the outside landing at the top. A still groggy Panayis had led them up these stairs, through a house—he had known exactly where he was—across a shallow roof, down some more steps, through a dark court-yard and into this ancient house where they were now. Louki had driven the car away even before they had reached the top of the stairs; it was only now that Mallory remembered that Louki hadn't thought it worth while to say what he intended to do with the car.

Still gazing out the windowless hole in the wall at the fortress gate, Mallory found himself hoping intensely that nothing would happen to the sad-eyed little Greek, and not only because in his infinite resource and local knowledge he had been invaluable to them and was likely to prove so again; all these considerations apart, Mallory had formed the deepest affection for him, for his unvarying cheerfulness, his enthusiasm, his eagerness to help and to please, above all for his complete disregard of self. A thoroughly lovable little man, and Mallory's heart warmed to him. More than he could say for Panayis, he thought sourly, and then immediately regretted the thought: it was no fault of Panayis's that he was what he was, and in his own dark and bitter way he had done as much for them as Louki. But the fact remained that he was sadly lacking in Louki's warm humanity.

He lacked also Louki's quick intelligence, the calculated opportunism that amounted almost to genius. It had been a brilliant idea on Louki's part, Mallory mused, that they should take over this abandoned house: not that there had been any difficulty in finding an empty house—since the Germans had taken over the old castle the inhabitants of the town had left in their scores for Margaritha and other outlying villages, none more quickly than those who had lived in the town square itself; the nearness of the fortress wall that formed the north side of the square had been more than many of them could stomach, with the constant coming and going of their conquerors through the fortress gates, the sentries marching to and fro, the never-ceasing reminders that their freedom was a vanished thing. So many had gone that more than half the houses on the west side of the square—those nearest the fortress—were now occupied by German officers. But this same enforced close observation of the fortress's activities had been exactly what Mallory had wanted. When the time came to strike they had only yards to go. And although any competent garrison commander would always be prepared against the unexpected, Mallory considered it unlikely indeed that any reasonable man could conceive of a sabotage group so suicidally minded as to spend an entire day within a literal stone's throw of the fortress wall.

Not that the house as such had much to recommend it. As a home, a dwelling place, it was just about as uncomfortable as possible, as dilapidated as it could be without actually falling down. The west side of the square—the side perched precariously on the cliff-top—and the south side were made up of fairly modern buildings of whitewashed stone and Parian granite, huddled together in the invariable fashion of houses in these island towns, flat-roofed to catch as much as possible of the winter rains. But the east side of the square, where they were, was made up of antiquated timber and turf houses, of the kind much more often found in remote mountain villages.

The beaten earth floor beneath his feet was hummocky, uneven, and the previous occupants had used one corner of it—obviously—for a variety of purposes, not least as a refuse dump. The ceiling was of rough-hewn, blackened beams, more or less covered with planks, these in turn being covered with a thick layer of trodden earth: from previous experience of such houses in the White Mountains, Mallory knew that the roof would leak like a sieve whenever the rain came on. Across one end of the room was a solid ledge some thirty inches high, a ledge that served, after the fashion of similar structures in Eskimo igloos, as bed, table or settee as the occasion demanded. The room was completely bare of furniture.

Mallory started as someone touched him on the shoulder and turned round. Miller was behind him, munching away steadily, the remains of a bottle of wine in his hand.

"Better get some chow, boss," he advised. "I'll take a gander through this hole from time to time."

"Right you are, Dusty. Thanks." Mallory moved gingerly towards the back of the room—it was almost pitch dark inside and they dared not risk a light—and felt his way till he brought up against the ledge. The tireless Andrea had gone through their provisions and prepared a meal of sorts—dried figs, honey, cheese, garlic sausages and pounded roast chestnuts. A horrible mixture, Mallory thought, but the best Andrea could do; besides he was too hungry, ravenously so, to worry about such niceties as the pleasing of his palate. And by the time he had washed it down with some of the local wine that Louki and Panayis had provided the previous day, the sweetly-resinous rawness of the drink had obliterated every other taste.

Carefully, shielding the match with his hand, Mallory lit a cigarette and began to explain for the first time his plan for entering the fortress. He did not have to bother lowering his voice—a couple of looms in the next house, one of the few occupied ones left on that side of the square, clacked incessantly throughout the evening. Mallory had a shrewd suspicion that this was more of Louki's doing, although it was difficult to see how he could have got word through to any of his friends. But Mallory was content to accept the situation as it was, to concentrate on making sure that the others understood his instructions.

Apparently they did, for there were no questions. For a few minutes the talk became general, the usually taciturn Casey Brown having the most to say, complaining bitterly about the food, the drink, his injured leg and the hardness of the bench where he wouldn't be able to sleep a wink all night long. Mallory grinned to himself but said nothing; Casey Brown was definitely on the mend.

"I reckon we've talked enough, gentlemen." Mallory slid off the bench and stretched himself. God, he was tired! "Our first and last chance to get a decent night's sleep. Two hour watches—I'll take the first."

"By yourself?" It was Miller calling softly from the other end of the room. "Don't you think we should share watches, boss? One for the front, one for the back. Besides, you know we're all pretty well done up. One man by himself might fall asleep." He sounded so anxious that Mallory laughed.

"Not a chance, Dusty. Each man will keep watch by the window there and if he falls asleep he'll damn' soon wake up when he hits the floor. And it's because we're so darned bushed that we can't afford to have anyone lose sleep unnecessarily. Myself first, then you, then Panayis, then Casey, then Andrea."

"Yeah, I suppose that'll be O.K.," Miller conceded grudgingly.

He put something hard and cold into his hand. Mallory recognised it at once—it was Miller's most cherished possession, his silenced automatic.

"Just so's you can fill any nosy customers full of little holes without wakin' the whole town." He ambled off to the back of the room, lit a cigarette, smoked it quietly for a few moments, then swung his legs up on the bench. Within five minutes everyone except the silently watchful man at the window was sound asleep.

Two or three minutes later Mallory jerked to unmoving attention as he heard a stealthy sound outside—from the back of the house, he thought. The clacking of the looms next door had stopped, and the house was very still. Again there came the noise, unmistakable this time, a gentle tapping at the door at the end of the passage that led from the back of the room.

"Remain there, my Captain." It was Andrea's soft murmur, and Mallory marvelled for the hundredth time at Andrea's ability to rouse himself from the deepest of sleeps at the slightest alien sound: the violence of a thunderstorm would have left him undisturbed. "I will see to it. It must be Louki."

It was Louki. The little man was panting, near exhaustion, but extraordinarily pleased with himself. Gratefully he drank the cup of wine that Andrea poured for him.

"Damned glad to see you back again!" Mallory said sincerely. "How did it go? Someone after you?"

Mallory could almost see him drawing himself up to his full height in the darkness.

"As if any of these clumsy fools could see Louki, even on a moonlit night, far less catch him," he said indignantly. He paused to draw some deep breaths. "No, no, Major, I knew you would be worried about me so I ran back all the way. Well, nearly all the way," he amended. "I am not so young as I was, Major Mallory."

"All the way from where," Mallory asked. He was glad of the darkness that hid his smile.

"From Vygos. It is an old castle that the Franks built there many generations ago, about two miles from here along the coast road to the east." He paused to drink another mouthful of wine. "More than two miles, I would say—and I only walked twice, a minute at a time, on the way back." Mallory had the impression that Louki already regretted his momentary weakness in admitting that he was no longer a young man.

"And what did you do there?" Mallory asked.

"I was thinking, after I left you," Louki answered indirectly. "Me, I am always thinking," he explained. "It is a habit of mine. I was thinking that when the soldiers who are looking for us out in the Devil's Playground find out that the car is gone, they will know that we are no longer in that accursed place."

"Yes," Mallory agreed carefully. "Yes, they will know that."

"Then they will say to themselves, 'Ha, those *verdammt Englanders* have little time left.' They will know that we will know that they have little hope of catching us in the island—Panayis and I, we know every rock and tree and path and cave. So all they can do is to make sure that we do not get into the town—they will block every road leading in, and to-night is our last chance to get in. You follow me?" he asked anxiously.

"I'm trying very hard."

"But first——" [Louki spread his hands dramatically] "but first they will make sure we are not in the town. They would be fools to block the roads if we were already in the town. They *must* make sure we are not in the town. And so—the search. The very great search. With—how do you say?—the teeth-comb!"

Mallory nodded his head in slow understanding.

"I'm afraid he's right, Andrea."

"I, too, fear so," Andrea said unhappily. "We should have thought of this. But perhaps we could hide—the roof-tops or——"

"With a teeth-comb, I said!" Louki interrupted impatiently. "But all is well. I, Louki have thought it all out. I can smell rain. There will be clouds over the moon before long, and it will be safe to move. . . . You do not want to know what I have done with the car, Major Mallory?" Louki was enjoying himself immensely.

"Forgotten all about it," Mallory confessed. "What *did* you do with the car?"

"I left it in the courtyard of Vygos castle. Then I emptied all the petrol from the tank and poured it over the car. Then I struck a match."

"You did *what*?" Mallory was incredulous.

"I struck a match. I think I was standing too near the car, for I do not seem to have any eyebrows left." Louki sighed. "A pity—it was such a splendid machine." Then he brightened. "But before God, Major, it burned magnificently."

Mallory stared at him.

"Why on earth——?"

"It is simple," Louki explained patiently. "By this time the men out in the Devil's Playground must know that their car has been stolen. They see the fire. They hurry back to—how do you say?"

"Investigate?"

"So. Investigate. They wait till the fire dies down. They investigate again. No bodies, no bones in the car, so they search the castle. And what do they find?"

There was silence in the room.

"Nothing!" Louki said impatiently. "They find nothing. And then they search the countryside for half a mile around. And what do they find? Again nothing. So then they know that they have been fooled, and that we are in the town, and will come to search the town."

"With the teeth-comb," Mallory murmured.

"With the teeth-comb. And what do they find?" Louki paused, then hurried on before anyone could steal his thunder. "Once again, they will find nothing,'' he said triumphantly. ''And why? For by then the rain will have come, the moon will have vanished, the explosives will be hidden—and we will be gone!''

''Gone where?'' Mallory felt dazed.

''Where but to Vygos castle, Major Mallory. Never while night follows day will they think to look for us there!''

Mallory looked at him in silence for long seconds without speaking, then turned to Andrea.

''Captain Jensen's only made one mistake so far,'' he murmured. ''He picked the wrong man to lead this expedition. Not that it matters anyway. With Louki here on our side, how can we lose?''

Mallory lowered his rucksack gently to the earthen roof, straightened and peered up into the darkness, both hands shielding his eyes from the first drizzle of rain. Even from where they stood—on the crumbling roof of the house nearest the fortress on the east side of the square—the wall stretched fifteen, perhaps twenty feet above their heads; the wickedly out- and down-curving spikes that topped the wall were all but lost in the darkness.

''There she is, Dusty,'' Mallory murmured. ''Nothing to it.''

''Nothin' to it!'' Miller was horrified. I've—I've gotta get over *that*?''

''You'd have a ruddy hard time going through it,'' Mallory answered briefly. He grinned, clapped Miller on the back and prodded the rucksack at his feet. ''We chuck this rope up, the hook catches, you shin smartly up——''

''And bleed to death on those six strands of barbed wire,'' Miller interrupted. ''Louki says they're the biggest barbs he's ever seen.''

''We'll use the tent for padding,'' Mallory said soothingly.

''I have a very delicate skin, boss,'' Miller complained. ''Nothin' short of a spring mattress——''

''We'll you've only an hour to find one,'' Mallory said indifferently. Louki had estimated that it would be at least an hour before the search party would clear the northern part of the town, give himself and Andrea a chance to begin a diversion. ''Come on, let's cache this stuff and get out of here. We'll shove the rucksacks in this corner and cover 'em with earth. Take the rope out first, though; we'll have no time to start undoing packs when we get back here.''

Miller dropped to his knees, hands fumbling with straps, then exclaimed in sudden annoyance.

''This can't be the pack,'' he muttered in disgust. Abruptly his voice changed. ''Here, wait a minute, though.''

''What's up, Dusty?''

Miller didn't answer immediately. For a few seconds his hands explored the contents of the pack, then he straightened.

''The slow-burnin' fuse, boss.'' His voice was blurred with anger, with a vicious anger that astonished Mallory. ''It's gone!''

''What!'' Mallory stooped, began to search through the pack. ''It can't be, Dusty, it just *can't*! Dammit to hell, man, you packed the stuff yourself!''

''Sure I did, boss,'' Miller grated. ''And then some crawlin' bastard comes along behind my back and unpacks it again.''

''Impossible!'' Mallory protested. ''It's just downright impossible, Dusty. *You* closed that rucksack—I saw you do it in the grove this morning—and Louki has had it all the time since then. And I'd trust Louki with my life.''

''So would I, boss.''

"Maybe we're both wrong," Mallory went on quietly. "Maybe you did miss it out. We're both helluva tired, Dusty."

Miller looked at him queerly, said nothing for a moment, then began to swear again. "It's my own fault, boss, my own gawddamned fault."

"What do you mean, your own fault? Heavens above, man, I was there when . . ." Mallory broke off, rose quickly to his feet and stared through the darkness at the south side of the square. A single shot had rung out there, the whiplash crack of a carbine followed the thin, high whine of a ricochet, and then silence.

Mallory stood quite still, hands clenched by his sides. Over ten minutes has passed since he and Miller had left Panayis to guide Andrea and Brown to the Castle Vygos—they should have been well away from the square by this time. And almost certainly Louki wouldn't be down there. Mallory's instructions to him had been explicit—to hide the remainder of the T.N.T. blocks in the roof and then wait there to lead himself and Miller to the keep. But something could have gone wrong, something could always go wrong. Or a trap, maybe, a ruse. But what kind of trap?

The sudden, off-beat stammering of a heavy machine-gun stilled his thoughts, and for a moment or two he was all eyes and straining ears. And then another and lighter machine-gun cut in, just for a few seconds: as abruptly as they had started, both guns died away, together. Mallory waited no longer.

"Get the stuff together again," he whispered urgently. "We're taking it with us. Something's gone wrong." Within thirty seconds they had ropes and explosives back in their knapsacks, had strapped them on their backs and were on their way.

Bent almost double, careful to make no noise whatsoever, they ran across the roof-tops towards the old house where they had hidden earlier in the evening, where they were now to rendezvous with Louki. Still running, they were only feet away from the house when they saw his shadowy figure rise up, only it wasn't Louki, Mallory realised at once, it was far too tall for Louki and without breaking step he catapulted the horizontal driving weight of his 180 pounds at the unknown figure in a homicidal tackle, his shoulder catching the man just below the breast-bone, emptying every last particle of air from the man's lungs with an explosive, agonised *whoosh*. A second later both of Miller's sinewy hands were clamped round the man's neck, slowly choking him to death.

And he would have choked to death, neither of the two men were in any mind for half-measures, had not Mallory, prompted by some fugitive intuition, stooped low over the contorted face, the staring, protruding eyes, choked back a cry of sudden horror.

"Dusty!" he whispered hoarsely. "For God's sake, stop! Let him go! It's Panayis!"

Miller didn't hear him. In the gloom his face was like stone, his head sunk farther and farther between hunching shoulders as he tightened his grip, strangling the Greek in a weird and savage silence.

"It's Panayis, you bloody fool, Panayis!" Mallory's mouth was at the American's ear, his hands clamped round the other's wrists as he tried to drag him off Panayis's throat. He could hear the muffled drumming of Panayis's heels on the turf of the roof, tore at Miller's wrists with all his strength: twice before he had heard that sound as a man had died under Andrea's great hands, and he knew with sudden certainty that Panayis would go the same way, and soon, if he didn't make Miller understand. But all at once Miller understood, relaxed heavily, straightened up, still kneeling, hands hanging limply by his sides. Breathing deeply he stared down in silence at the man at his feet.

"What the hell's the matter with you?" Mallory demanded softly. "Deaf or blind or both?"

"Just one of these things, I guess." Miller rubbed the back of a hand across his forehead, his face empty of expression. "Sorry, boss, sorry."

Why the hell apologise to me?" Mallory looked away from him, looked down at Panayis: the Greek was sitting up now, hands massaging his bruised throat, sucking in long draughts of air in great, whooping gasps. "But maybe Panayis here might appreciate——"

"Apologies can wait," Miller interrupted brusquely. "Ask him what's happened to Louki."

Mallory looked at him for a moment, made to reply, changed his mind, translated the question. He listened to Panayis's halting answer—it obviously hurt him even to try to speak—and his mouth tightened in a hard, bitter line. Miller watched the fractional slump of the New Zealander's shoulders, felt he could wait no longer.

"Well, what is it, boss? Somethin's happened to Louki, is that it?"

"Yes," Mallory said tonelessly. "They'd only got as far as the lane at the back when they found a small German patrol blocking their way. Louki tried to draw them off and the machine-gunner got him through the chest. Andrea got the machine-gunner and took Louki away. Panayis says he'll die for sure."

14

WEDNESDAY NIGHT

1915–2000

THE THREE men cleared the town without any difficulty, striking out directly across country for the Castle Vygos and avoiding the main road. It was beginning to rain now, heavily, persistently, and the ground was mired and sodden, the few ploughed fields they crossed almost impassable. They had just struggled their way through one of these and could just see the dim outline of the keep—less than a cross-country mile from the town instead of Louki's exaggerated estimate—when they passed by an abandoned earthen house and Miller spoke for the first time since they had left the town square of Navarone.

"I'm bushed, boss." His head was sunk on his chest, and his breathing was laboured. "Ol' man Miller's on the downward path, I reckon, and the legs are gone. Couldn't we squat inside here for a couple of minutes, boss, and have a smoke?"

Mallory looked at him in surprise, thought how desperately weary his own legs felt and nodded in reluctant agreement. Miller wasn't the man to complain unless he was near exhaustion.

"Okay, Dusty, I don't suppose a minute or two will harm." He translated quickly into Greek and led the way inside, Miller at his heels complaining at length about his advancing age. Once inside, Mallory felt his way across to the inevitable wooden bunk, sat down gratefully, lit a cigarette then looked up in puzzlement. Miller was still on his feet, walking slowly round the hut, tapping the walls as he went.

"Why don't you sit down?" Mallory asked irritably. "That was why you came in here in the first place, wasn't it?"

"No boss, not really." The drawl was very pronounced. "Just a low-down trick to get us inside. Two-three very special things I want to show you."

"Very special. What the devil are you trying to tell me?"

"Bear with me, Captain Mallory," Miller requested formally. "Bear with me just a few minutes. I'm not wastin' your time. You have my word, Captain Mallory."

"Very well." Mallory was mystified, but his confidence in Miller remained unshaken. "As you wish. Only don't be too long about it."

"Thanks, boss." The strain of formality was too much for Miller. "It won't take long. There'll be a lamp or candles in here—you said the islanders never leave an abandoned house without 'em?"

"And a very useful superstition it's been to us, too." Mallory reached under the bunk with his torch, straightened his back. "Two or three candles here."

"I want a light, boss. No windows—I checked. O.K.?"

"Light one and I'll go outside to see if there's anything showing." Mallory was completely in the dark about the American's intentions. He felt Miller didn't want him to say anything, and there was a calm surety about him that precluded questioning. Mallory was back in less than a minute. "Not a chink to be seen from the outside," he reported.

"Fair enough. Thanks, boss." Miller lit a second candle, then slipped the rucksack straps from his shoulders, laid the pack on the bunk and stood in silence for a moment.

Mallory looked at his watch, looked back at Miller.

"You were going to show me something," he prompted.

"Yeah, that's right. Three things, I said." He dug into the pack, brought out a little black box hardly bigger than a match-box. "Exhibit A, boss."

Mallory looked at it curiously. "What's that?"

"Clockwork fuse." Miller began to unscrew the back panel. "Hate the damned things. Always make me feel like one of those bolshevik characters with a dark cloak, a moustache like Louki's and carryin' one of those black cannon-ball things with a sputterin' fuse stickin' outa it. But it works." He had the back off the box now, examining the mechanism in the light of his torch. "But this one doesn't, not any more," he added softly. "Clock's O.K., but the contact arm's been bent right back. This thing could tick till Kingdom Come and it couldn't even set off a firework."

"But how on earth——?"

"Exhibit B." Miller didn't seem to hear him. He opened the detonator box, gingerly lifted a fuse from its felt and cotton-wool bed and examined it closely under his torch. Then he looked at Mallory again. "Fulminate of mercury, boss. Only seventy-seven grains, but enough to blow your fingers off. Unstable as hell, too—the littlest tap will set it off." He let it fall to the ground, and Mallory winced and drew back involuntarily as the American smashed a heavy heel down on top of it. But there was no explosion, nothing at all.

"Ain't workin' so good either, is it, boss? A hundred to one the rest are all empty, too." He fished out a pack of cigarettes, lit one, and watched the smoke eddy and swirl above the heat of the candles. He slid the cigarettes into his pocket.

"There was a third thing you were going to show me," Mallory said quietly.

"Yeah, I was goin' to show you somethin' else." The voice was very gentle, and Mallory felt suddenly cold. "I was goin' to show you a spy, a traitor, the most vicious, twistin', murderin', double-crossin' bastard I've ever known." The American had his hand out of his pocket now, the silenced automatic sitting snugly against his palm, the muzzle trained over Panayis's heart. He went on, more gently than ever. "Judas Iscariot had nothin' on the boy-friend, here, boss. . . . Take your coat off, Panayis."

"What the devil are you doing! Are you crazy?" Mallory started forward, half-angry, half-amazed, but brought up sharply against Miller's extended arm, rigid as a bar of iron. "What bloody nonsense is this? He doesn't understand English!"

"Don't he, though? Then why was he out of the cave like a flash when Casey reported hearin' sounds outside . . . and why was he the first to leave the carob grove this afternoon if he didn't understand your order? Take your coat off, Judas, or I'll shoot you through the arm. I'll give you two seconds."

Mallory made to throw his arms round Miller and bring him to the ground, but halted in mid-step as he caught the look on Panayis's face—teeth bared, murder glaring out from the coal-black eyes. Never before had Mallory seen such malignity in a human face, a malignity that yielded abruptly to shocked pain and disbelief as the .32 bullet smashed into his upper arm, just below the shoulder.

"Two seconds and then the other arm," Miller said woodenly. But Panayis was already tearing off his jacket, the dark, bestial eyes never leaving Miller's face. Mallory looked at him, shivered involuntarily, looked at Miller. Indifference, he thought, that was the only word to describe the look on the American's face. Indifference. Unaccountably, Mallory felt colder than ever.

"Turn round!" The automatic never wavered.

Slowly Panayis turned round. Miller stepped forward, caught the black shirt by the collar, ripped it off his back with one convulsive jerk.

"Waal, waal, now, whoever woulda thought it?" Miller drawled. "Surprise, surprise, surprise! Remember, boss, this was the character that was publicly flogged by the Germans in Crete, flogged until the white of his ribs showed through. His back's in a helluva state, isn't it?"

Mallory looked but said nothing. Completely off balance, his mind was in a kaleidoscopic whirl, his thoughts struggling to adjust themselves to a new set of circumstances, a complete reversal of all his previous thinking. Not a scar, not a single blemish, marked the dark smoothness of that skin.

"Just a natural quick healer," Miller murmured. "Only a nasty, twisted mind like mine would think that he had been a German agent in Crete, became known to the Allies as a fifth columnist, lost his usefulness to the Germans and was shipped back to Navarone by fast motor-launch under cover of night. Floggin'! Island-hoppin' his way back here in a rowboat! Just a lot of bloody eyewash!" Miller paused, and his mouth twisted. "I wonder how many pieces of silver he made in Crete before they got wise to him?"

"But heavens above, man, you're not going to condemn someone just for shooting a line!" Mallory protested. Strangely, he didn't feel nearly as vehement as he sounded. "How many survivors would there be among the Allies if——"

"Not convinced yet, huh?" Miller waved his automatic negligently at Panayis. "Roll up the left trouser leg, Iscariot. Two seconds again."

Panayis did as he was told. The black, venomous eyes never looked away from Miller's. He rolled the dark cloth up to the knee.

"Farther yet? That's my little boy," Miller encouraged him. "And now take that bandage off—right off." A few seconds passed, then Miller shook his head sadly. "A ghastly wound, boss, a ghastly wound!"

"I'm beginning to see your point," Mallory said thoughtfully. The dark sinewy leg wasn't even scratched. "But why on earth——"

"Simple. Four reasons at least. Junior here is a treacherous, slimy bastard—no self-respectin' rattlesnake would come within a mile of him—but he's a clever bastard. He faked his leg so he could stay in the cave in the Devil's Playground when the four of us went back to stop the Alpenkorps from comin' up the slope below the carob grove."

"Why? Frightened he'd stop something?"

Miller shook his head impatiently.

"Junior here's scared o' nothin'. He stayed behind to write a note. Later on he used his leg to drop behind us some place, and leave the note where it could be seen. Early on, this must have been. Note probably said that we would come out at such and such a place, and would they kindly send a welcomin' committee to meet us there. They sent it, remember: it was their car we swiped to get to town. . . . That was the first time I got real suspicious of the boy-friend: after he'd dropped behind he made up on us again real quick—too damn' quick for a man with a game leg. But it wasn't till I opened that rucksack in the square this evenin' that I really knew."

"You only mentioned two reasons," Mallory prompted.

"Comin' to the others. Number three—he could fall behind when the welcomin' committee opened up in front—Iscariot here wasn't goin' to get himself knocked off before he collected his salary. And number four— remember that real touchin' scene when he begged you to let him stay at the far end of the cave that led into the valley we came out? Goin' to do his Horatio-on-the-bridge act?"

"Going to show them the right cave to pick, you mean."

"Check. After that he was gettin' pretty desperate. I still wasn't sure, but I was awful suspicious, boss. Didn't know what he might try next. So I clouted him good and hard when that last patrol came up the valley."

"I see," Mallory said quietly. "I see indeed." He looked sharply at Miller. "You should have told me. You had no right——"

"I was goin' to, boss. But I hadn't a chance—Junior here was around all the time. I was just startin' to tell you half an hour back, when the guns started up."

Mallory nodded in understanding. "How did you happen on all this in the first place, Dusty?"

"Juniper," Miller said succinctly. "Remember that's how Turzig said he came to find us? He smelt the juniper."

"That's right. We *were* burning juniper."

"Sure we were. But he said he smelt it on Kostos—and the wind was blowin' off Kostos all day long."

"My God!" Mallory whispered. "Of course, of course! And I missed it completely."

"But Jerry knew we were there. How? Waal, he ain't got second sight no more than I have. So he was tipped off—he was tipped off by the boy-friend here. Remember I said he'd talked to some of his pals in Margaritha when we went down there for the supplies?" Miller spat in disgust. "Fooled me all along the line. Pals? I didn't know how right I was. Sure they were his pals—his German pals! And that food he said he got from the commandant's kitchen—he got it from the kitchen all right. Almost certainly he goes in and asks for it—and old Skoda hands him his own suitcase to stow it in."

"But the German he killed on the way back to the village? Surely to God——"

"Panayis killed him." There was a tired certainty in Miller's voice. "What's another corpse to Sunshine here. Probably stumbled on the poor bastard in the dark and had to kill him. Local colour. Louki was there, remember, and he couldn't have Louki gettin' suspicious. He would have blamed it on Louki anyway. The guy ain't human. . . . And remember when he was flung into Skoda's room in Margaritha along with Louki, blood pourin' from a wound in his head?"

Mallory nodded.

"High-grade ketchup. Probably also from the commandant's kitchen," Miller said bitterly. "If Skoda had failed by every other means, there would still have been the boy-friend here as a stool-pigeon. Why he never asked Louki where the explosives were I don't know."

"Obviously he didn't know Louki knew."

"Mebbe. But one thing the bastard did know—how to use a mirror. Musta heliographed the garrison from the carob grove and given our position. No other way, boss. Then sometime this morning he must have got hold of my rucksack, whipped out all the slow fuse and fixed the clock fuse and detonators. He should have had his hands blown off tamperin' with them fulminates. Lord only knows where he learnt to handle the damn' things."

"Crete," Mallory said positively. "The Germans would see to that. A spy who can't also double as a saboteur is no good to them."

"And he was very good to them," Miller said softly. "Very, very good. They're gonna miss their little pal. Iscariot here was a very smart baby indeed."

"He was. Except to-night. He should have been smart enough to know that at least one of us would be suspicious——"

"He probably was," Miller interrupted. "But he was misinformed. I think Louki's unhurt. I think Junior here talked Louki into letting him stay in his place—Louki was always a bit scared of him—then he strolled across to his pals at the gate, told 'em to send a strong-arm squad out to Vygos to pick up the others, asked them to fire a few shots—he was very strong on local colour, was our loyal little pal—then strolls back across the square, hoists himself up on the roof and waits to tip off his pals as soon as we came in the back door. But Louki forgot to tell him just one thing—that we were goin' to rendezvous on the roof of the house, not inside. So the boy-friend here lurks away for all he's worth up top, waiting to signal his friends. Ten to one that he's got a torch in his pocket."

Mallory picked up Panayis's coat and examined it briefly. "He has."

"That's it, then." Miller lit another cigarette, watched the match burn down slowly to his fingers, then looked up at Panayis. "How does it feel to know that you're goin' to die, Panayis, to feel like all them poor bastards who've felt just as you're feeling now, just before they died—all the men in Crete, all the guys in the sea-borne and air landings on Navarone who died because they thought you were on their side? How does it feel, Panayis?"

Panayis said nothing. His left hand clutching his torn right arm, trying to stem the blood, he stood there motionless, the dark, evil face masked in hate, the lips still drawn back in that less than human snarl. There was no fear in him, none at all, and Mallory tensed himself for the last, despairing attempt for life that Panayis must surely make, and then he had looked at

Miller and knew there would be no attempt, because there was a strange sureness and inevitability about the American, an utter immobility of hand and eye that somehow precluded even the thought, far less the possibility of escape.

"The prisoner has nothin' to say." Miller sounded very tired. "I suppose I should say somethin'. I suppose I should give out with a long spiel about me bein' the judge, the jury and the executioner, but I don't think I'll bother myself. Dead men make poor witnesses. . . . Mebbe it's not your fault, Panayis, mebbe there's an awful good reason why you came to be what you are. Gawd only knows. I don't, and I don't much care. There are too many dead men. I'm goin' to kill you, Panayis, and I'm goin' to kill you now." Miller dropped his cigarette, ground it into the floor of the hut. "Nothin' at all to say?"

And he had nothing at all to say, the hate, the malignity of the black eyes said it all for him and Miller nodded, just once, as if in secret understanding. Carefully, accurately, he shot Panayis through the heart, twice, blew out the candles, turned his back and was half-way towards the door before the man had crashed to the ground.

"I am afraid I cannot do it, Andrea." Louki sat back wearily, shook his head in despair. "I am very sorry, Andrea. The knots are too tight."

"No matter." Andrea rolled over from his side to a sitting position, tried to ease his tightly-bound legs and wrists. "They are cunning, these Germans, and wet cords can only be cut." Characteristically, he made no mention of the fact that only a couple of minutes previously he had twisted round to reach the cords on Louki's wrist and undone them with half a dozen tugs of his steel-trap fingers. "We will think of something else."

He looked away from Louki, glanced across the room in the faint light of the smoking oil-lamp that stood by the grille door, a light so yellow, so dim that Casey Brown, trussed like a barnyard fowl and loosely secured, like himself, by a length of rope to the iron hooks suspended from the roof, was no more than a shapeless blur in the opposite corner of the stone-flagged room. Andrea smiled to himself, without mirth. Taken prisoner again, and for the second time that day—and with the same ease and surprise that gave no chance at all of resistance: completely unsuspecting, they had been captured in an upper room, seconds after Casey had finished talking to Cairo. The patrol had known exactly where to find them—and with their leader's assurance that it was all over, with his gloating explanation of the part Panayis had played, the unexpectedness, the success of the coup was all too easy to understand. And it was difficult not to believe his assurance that neither Mallory nor Miller had a chance. But the thought of ultimate defeat never occurred to Andrea.

His gaze left Casey Brown, wandered round the room, took in what he could see of the stone walls and floor, the hooks the ventilation ducts, the heavy grille door. A dungeon, a torture dungeon, one would have thought, but Andrea had seen such places before. A castle, they called this place, but it was really only an old keep, no more than a manor house built round the crenellated towers. And the long-dead Frankish nobles who had built these keeps had lived well. No dungeon this, Andrea knew, but simply the larder where they had hung their meat and game, and done without windows and light for the sake of . . .

The light! Andrea twisted round, looked at the smoking oil lamp, his eyes narrowing.

"Louki!" he called softly. The little Greek turned round to look at him. "Can you reach the lamp?"

"I think so. . . . Yes, I can."

"Take the glass off," Andrea whispered. "Use a cloth—it will be hot. Then wrap it in the cloth, hit it on the floor—gently. The glass is thick— you can cut me loose in a minute or two."

Louki stared at him for an uncomprehending moment, then nodded in understanding. He shuffled across the floor—his legs were still bound— reached out, then halted his hand abruptly, only inches from the glass. The peremptory, metallic clang had been only feet away, and he raised his head slowly to see what had caused it.

He could have stretched out his and, touched the barrel of the Mauser that protruded threateningly through the bars of the grille door. Again the guard rattled the rifle angrily between the bars, shouted something he didn't understand.

"Leave it alone, Louki," Andrea said quietly. His voice was tranquil, unshadowed by disappointment. "Come back here. Our friend outside is not too pleased." Obediently Louki moved back, heard the guttural voice again, rapid and alarmed this time, the rattle as the guard withdrew his rifle quickly from the bars of the door, the urgent pounding of his feet on the flagstones outside as he raced up the passage.

"What's the matter with our little friend?" Casey Brown was as lugubrious, as weary as ever. "He seems upset."

"He is upset." Andrea smiled. "He's just realised that Louki's hands are untied."

"Well, why doesn't he tie them up again?"

"Slow in the head he may be, but he is no fool," Andrea explained. "This could be a trap and he's gone for his friends."

Almost at once they heard a thud, like the closing of a distant door, the sound of more than one pair of feet running down the passage, the tinny rattling of keys on a ring, the rasp of a key against the lock, a sharp click, the squeal of rusty hinges and then two soldiers were in the room, dark and menacing with their jackboots and ready guns. Two or three seconds elapsed while they looked around them, accustoming their eyes to the gloom, then the man nearest the door spoke.

"A terrible thing, boss, nothin' short of deplorable! Leave 'em alone for a couple of minutes and see what happens? The whole damn' bunch tied up like Houdini on an off night!"

There was a brief, incredulous silence, then all three were sitting upright, staring at them. Brown recovered first.

"High time, too," he complained. "Thought you were never going to get here."

"What he means is that he thought we were never going to see you again," Andrea said quietly. "Neither did I. But here you are, safe and sound."

"Yes," Mallory nodded. "Thanks to Dusty and his nasty suspicious mind that cottoned on to Panayis while all the rest of us were asleep."

"Where is he?" Louki asked.

"Panayis?" Miller waved a negligent hand. "We left him behind—he met with a sorta accident." He was across at the other side of the room now, carefully cutting the cords that pinioned Brown's injured leg, whistling tunelessly as he sawed away with his sheath knife. Mallory, too, was busy, slicing through Andrea's bonds, explaining rapidly what had happened, listening to the big Greek's equally concise account of what had befallen the others in the keep. And then Andrea was on his feet, massaging his numbed hands, looking across at Miller.

"That whistling, my Captain. It sounds terrible and, what is worse, it is very loud. The guards——"

"No worry there," Mallory said grimly. "They never expected to see Dusty and myself again. . . . They kept a poor watch." He turned round to look at Brown, now hobbling across the floor.

"How's the leg, Casey?"

"Fine, sir." Brown brushed it aside as of no importance. "I got through to Cairo, to-night, sir. The report——"

"It'll have to wait, Casey. We must get out as fast as we can. You all right, Louki?"

"I am heart-broken, Major Mallory. That a countryman of mine, a trusted friend——"

"That, too, will have to wait, Come on!"

"You are in a great hurry," Andrea protested mildly. They were already out in the passage, stepping over the cell guard lying in a crumpled heap on the floor. "Surely if they're all like our friend here——"

"No danger from this quarter," Mallory interrupted impatiently. "The soldiers in the town—they're bound to know by now that we've either missed Panayis or disposed of him. In either case they'll know that we're certain to come hot-footing out here. Work it out for yourself. They're probably half-way here already, and if they do come . . ." He broke off, stared at the smashed generator and the ruins of Casey Brown's transmitter set lying in one corner of the entrance hall. "Done a pretty good job on these, haven't they?" he said bitterly.

"Thank the Lord," Miller said piously. "All the less to tote around, is what I say. If you could only see the state of my back with that damned generator——"

"Sir!" Brown had caught Mallory's arm, an action so foreign to the usually punctilious petty officer that Mallory halted in surprise. "Sir, it's terribly important—the report, I mean. You *must* listen, sir!"

The action, the deadly earnestness, caught and held Mallory's full attention. He turned to face Brown with a smile.

"O.K., Casey, let's have it," he said quietly. "Things can't possibly be any worse than they are now."

"They can, sir." There was something tired, defeated about Casey Brown, and the great, stone hall seemed strangely chill. "I'm afraid they can, sir. I got through to-night. First-class reception. Captain Jensen himself, and he was hopping mad. Been waiting all day for us to come on the air. Asked how things were, and I told him that you were outside the fortress just then, and hoped to be inside the magazine in an hour or so."

"Go on."

"He said that was the best news he'd ever had. He said his information had been wrong, he'd been fooled, that the invasion fleet didn't hole up overnight in the Cyclades, that they had come straight through under the heaviest air and E-boat escort ever seen in the Med., and are due to hit the beaches on Kheros some time before dawn to-morrow. He said our destroyers had been waiting to the south all day, moved up at dusk and were waiting word from him to see whether they would attempt the passage of the Maidos Straits. I told him maybe something could go wrong, but he said not with Captain Mallory and Miller inside and besides he wasn't—he couldn't risk the lives of twelve hundred men on Kheros just on the off chance that he might be wrong." Brown broke off suddenly and looked down miserably at his feet. No one else in the hall moved or made any sound at all.

"Go on?" Mallory repeated in a whisper. His face was very pale.

"That's all, sir. That's all there is. The destroyers are coming through the Straits at midnight." Brown looked down at his luminous watch. "Midnight. Four hours to go."

"Oh, God! Midnight!" Mallory was stricken, his eyes for the moment unseeing, ivory-knuckled hands clenched in futility and despair. "They're coming through at midnight! God help them! God help them all now!"

15

WEDNESDAY NIGHT
2000–2115

EIGHT-THIRTY, his watch said. Eight-thirty. Exactly half an hour to curfew. Mallory flattened himself on the roof, pressed himself as closely as possible against the low retaining wall that almost touched the great, sheering sides of the fortress, swore softly to himself. It only required one man with a torch in his hand to look over the top of the fortress wall—a catwalk ran the whole length of the inside of the wall, four feet from the top—and it would be the end of them all. The wandering beam of a torch and they were bound to be seen, it was impossible not to be seen: he and Dusty Miller—the American was stretched out behind him and clutching the big truck battery in his arms—were wide open to the view of anyone who happened to glance down that way. Perhaps they should have stayed with the others a couple of roofs away, with Casey and Louki, the one busy tying spaced knots in a rope, the other busy splicing a bent wire hook on to a long bamboo they had torn from a bamboo hedge just outside the town, where they had hurriedly taken shelter as a convoy of three trucks had roared past them heading for the castle Vygos.

Eight thirty-two. What the devil was Andrea doing down there, Mallory wondered irritably and at once regretted his irritation. Andrea wouldn't waste an unnecessary second. Speed was vital, haste fatal. It seemed unlikely that there would be any officers inside—from what they had seen, practically half the garrison were combing either the town or the countryside out in the direction of Vygos—but if there were and even one gave a cry it would be the end.

Mallory stared down at the burn on the back of his hand, thought of the truck they had set on fire and grinned wryly to himself. Setting the truck on fire had been his only contribution to the night's performance so far. All the other credit went to either Andrea or Miller. It was Andrea who had seen in this house on the west side of the square—one of several adjoining houses used as officers' billets—the only possible answer to their problem. It was Miller, now lacking all time-fuses, clockwork, generator and every other source of electric power who had suddenly stated that he must have a battery, and again it was Andrea, hearing the distant approach of a truck, who had blocked the entrance to the long driveway to the keep with heavy stones from the flanking pillars, forcing the soldiers to abandon their truck at the gates and run up the drive towards their house. To overcome the driver and his mate and bundle them senseless into a ditch had taken seconds only,

scarcely more time than it had taken Miller to unscrew the terminals of the
heavy battery, find the inevitable jerrican below the tailboard and pour the
contents over engine, cab and body. The truck had gone up in a roar and
whoosh of flames: as Louki had said earlier in the night, setting petrol-
soaked vehicles on fire was not without its dangers—the charred patch on
his hand stung painfully—but, again as Louki had said, it had burned
magnificently. A pity, in a way—it had attracted attention to their escape
sooner than was necessary—but it had been vital to destroy the evidence,
the fact that a battery was missing. Mallory had too much experience of and
respect for the Germans ever to underrate them: they could put two and two
together better than most.

He felt Miller tug at his ankle, started, twisted round quickly. The American was pointing beyond him, and he turned again and saw Andrea signalling to him from the raised trap in the far corner: he had been so engrossed
in his thinking, the giant Greek so catlike in his silence, that he had completely failed to notice his arrival. Mallory shook his head, momentarily
angered at his own abstraction, took the battery from Miller, whispered to
him to get the others, then edged slowly across the roof, as noiselessly as
possible. The sheer deadweight of the battery was astonishing, it felt as if it
weighed a ton, but Andrea plucked it from his hands, lifted it over the trap
coaming, tucked it under one arm and nimbly descended the stairs to the
tiny hall-way as if it weighed nothing at all.

Andrea moved out through the open doorway to the covered balcony that
overlooked the darkened harbour, almost a hundred vertical feet beneath.
Mallory, following close behind, touched him on the shoulder as he lowered
the battery gently to the ground.

"Any trouble?" he asked softly.

"None at all, my Keith." Andrea straightened. "The house is empty. I
was so surprised that I went over it all, twice, just to make sure."

"Fine! Wonderful! I suppose the whole bunch of them are out scouring
the country for us—interesting to know what they would say if they were
told we were sitting in their front parlour?"

"They would never believe it," Andrea said without hesitation. "This is
the last place they would ever think to look for us."

"I've never hoped so much that you're right!" Mallory murmured fervently. He moved across to the latticed railing that enclosed the balcony,
gazed down into the blackness beneath his feet and shivered. A long, long
drop and it was very cold; that sluicing, vertical rain chilled one to the
bone. . . . He stepped back, shook the railing.

"This thing strong enough, do you think?" he whispered.

"I don't know, my Keith, I don't know at all." Andrea shrugged. "I
hope so."

"I hope so," Mallory echoed. "It doesn't really matter. This is how it
has to be." Again he leaned far out over the railing, twisted his head to the
right and upwards. In the rain-filled gloom of the night he could just faintly
make out the still darker gloom of the mouth of the cave housing the two
great guns, perhaps forty feet away from where he stood, at least thirty feet
higher—and all vertical cliff-face between. As far as accessibility went, the
cave mouth could have been on the moon.

He drew back, turned round as he heard Brown limping on to the balcony.

"Go to the front of the house and stay there, Casey, will you? Stay by the
window. Leave the front door unlocked. If we have any visitors, let them
in."

"Club 'em, knife 'em, no guns," Brown murmured. "Is that it, sir?"

"That's it, Casey."

"Just leave this little thing to me," Brown said grimly. He hobbled away through the doorway.

Mallory turned to Andrea. "I make it twenty-three minutes."

"I, too. Twenty-three minutes to nine."

"Good luck," Mallory murmured. He grinned at Miller. "Come on, Dusty. Opening time."

Five minutes later, Mallory and Miller were seated in a *taverna* just off the south side of the town square. Despite the garish blue paint with which the *tavernaris* had covered everything in sight—walls, tables, chairs, shelves all in the same execrably vivid colour (blue and red for the wine shops, green for the sweetmeats shops was the almost invariable rule throughout the islands)—it was a gloomy, ill-lit place, as gloomy almost as the stern, righteous, magnificently-moustached heroes of the Wars of Independence whose dark, burning eyes glared down at them from a dozen faded prints scattered at eye-level along the walls. Between each pair of portraits was a brightly-coloured wall advertisement for Fix's beer: the effect of the décor, taken as a whole, was indescribable, and Mallory shuddered to think what it would have been like had the *tavernaris* had at his disposal any illumination more powerful than the two smoking oil lamps placed on the counter before him.

As it was, the gloom suited him well. Their dark clothes, braided jackets, *tsantas* and jackboots looked genuine enough, Mallory knew, and the black-fringed turbans Louki had mysteriously obtained for them looked as they ought to look in a tavern where every islander there—about eight of them—wore nothing else on their heads. Their clothes had been good enough to pass muster with the *tavernaris*—but then even the keeper of a wine shop could hardly be expected to know every man in a town of five thousand, and a patriotic Greek, as Louki had declared this man to be, wasn't going to lift even a faintly suspicious eyebrow as long as there were German soldiers present. And there were Germans present—four of them, sitting round a table near the counter. Which was why Mallory had been glad of the semi-darkness. Not, he was certain, that he and Dusty Miller had any reason to be physically afraid of these men. Louki had dismissed them contemptuously as a bunch of old women—headquarters clerks, Mallory guessed—who came to this tavern every night of the week. But there was no point in sticking out their necks unnecessarily.

Miller lit one of the pungent, evil-smelling local cigarettes, wrinkling his nose in distaste.

"Damn' funny smell in this joint, boss."

"Put your cigarette out," Mallory suggested.

"You wouldn't believe it, but the smell I'm smelling is a damn' sight worse than that."

"Hashish," Mallory said briefly. "The curse of these island ports." He nodded over towards a dark corner. "The lads of the village over there will be at it every night in life. It's all they live for."

"Do they have to make that gawddamned awful racket when they're at it?" Miller asked peevishly. "Toscanini should see this lot!"

Mallory looked at the small group in the corner, clustered round the young man playing a *bouzouko*—a long-necked mandolin—and singing the haunting, nostalgic *rembetika* songs of the hashish smokers of the Piraeus. He supposed the music did have a certain melancholy, lotus-land attraction, but right then it jarred on him. One had to be in a certain twilit, untroubled mood to appreciate that sort of thing; and he had never felt less untroubled in his life.

"I suppose it *is* a bit grim," he admitted. "But at least it lets us talk together, which we couldn't do if they all packed up and went home."

"I wish to hell they would," Miller said morosely. "I'd gladly keep my mouth shut." He picked distastefully at the *meze*—a mixture of chopped olives, liver, cheese and apples—on the plate before him; as a good American and a bourbon drinker of long standing he disapproved strongly of the invariable Greek custom of eating when drinking. Suddenly he looked up and crushed his cigarette against the table top. "For Gawd's sake, boss, how much longer?"

Mallory looked at him, then looked away. He knew exactly how Dusty Miller felt, for he felt that way himself—tense, keyed-up, every nerve strung to the tautest pitch of efficiency. So much depended on the next few minutes; whether all their labour and their suffering had been necessary, whether the men on Kheros would live or die, whether Andy Stevens had lived and died in vain. Mallory looked at Miller again, saw the nervous hands, the deepened wrinkles round the eyes, the tightly compressed mouth, white at the outer corners, saw all these signs of strain, noted them and discounted them. Excepting Andrea alone, of all the men he had ever known he would have picked the lean, morose American to be his companion that night. Or maybe even including Andrea. "The finest saboteur in southern Europe" Captain Jensen had called him back in Alexandria. Miller had come a long way from Alexandria, and he had come for this alone. To-night was Miller's night.

Mallory looked at his watch.

"Curfew in fifteen minutes," he said quietly. "The balloon goes up in twelve minutes. For us, another four minutes to go."

Miller nodded, but said nothing. He filled his glass again from the beaker in the middle of the table, lit a cigarette. Mallory could see a nerve twitching high up in his temple and wondered dryly how many twitching nerves Miller could see in his own face. He wondered, too, how the crippled Casey Brown was getting on in the house they had just left. In many ways he had the most responsible job of all—and at the critical moment he would have to leave the door unguarded, move back to the balcony. One slip up there. . . . He saw Miller look strangely at him and grinned crookedly. This had to come off, it just had to: he thought of what must surely happen if he failed, then shied away from the thought. It wasn't good to think of these things, not now, not at this time.

He wondered if the other two were at their posts, unmolested; they should be, the search party had long passed through the upper part of the town; but you never knew what could go wrong, there was so much that could go wrong, and so easily. Mallory looked at his watch again: he had never seen a second hand move so slowly. He lit a last cigarette, poured a final glass of wine, listened without really hearing to the weird, keening threnody of the *rembetika* song in the corner. And then the song of the hashish singers died plaintively away, the glasses were empty and Mallory was on his feet.

"Time bringeth all things," he murmured. "Here we go again."

He sauntered easily towards the door, calling good night to the *tavernaris*. Just at the doorway he paused, began to search impatiently through his pockets as if he had lost something: it was a windless night, and it was raining, he saw, raining heavily, the lances of rain bouncing inches off the cobbled street—and the street itself was deserted as far as he could see in either direction. Satisfied, Mallory swung round with a curse, forehead furrowed in exasperation, started to walk back towards the table he had just left, right hand now delving into the capacious inner pocket of his jacket. He saw without seeming to that Dusty Miller was pushing his chair back, rising to his feet. And then Mallory had halted, his face clearing and his hands no longer searching. He was exactly three feet from the table where the four Germans were sitting.

"Keep quite still!" He spoke in German, his voice low but as steady, as menacing, as the Navy Colt .455 balanced in his right hand. "We are desperate men. If you move we will kill you."

For a full three seconds the soldiers sat immobile, expressionless except for the shocked widening of their eyes. And then there was a quick flicker of the eyelids from the man sitting nearest the counter, a twitching of the shoulder and then a grunt of agony as the .32 bullet smashed into his upper arm. The soft thud of Miller's silenced automatic couldn't have been heard beyond the doorway.

"Sorry, boss," Miller apologised. "Mebbe he's only sufferin' from St. Vitus' Dance." He looked with interest at the pain-twisted face, the blood welling darkly between the fingers clasped tightly over the wound. "But he looks kinda cured to me."

"He is cured," Mallory said grimly. He turned to the innkeeper, a tall, melancholy man with a thin face and mandarin moustache that drooped forlornly over either corner of his mouth, spoke to him in the quick, collo-quial speech of the islands. "Do these men speak Greek?"

The *tavernaris* shook his head. Completely unruffled and unimpressed, he seemed to regard armed hold-ups in his tavern as the rule rather than the exception.

"Not them!" he said contemptuously. "English a little, I think—I am sure. But not our language. That I do know."

"Good. I am a British Intelligence officer. Have you a place where I can hide these men?"

"You shouldn't have done this," the *tavernaris* protested mildly. "I will surely die for this."

"Oh, no, you won't." Mallory had slid across the counter, his pistol boring into the man's midriff. No one could doubt that the man was being threatened—and violently threatened—no one, that is, who couldn't see the broad wink that Mallory had given the inn-keeper. "I'm going to tie you up with them. All right?"

"All right. There is a trap-door at the end of the counter here. Steps lead down to the cellar."

"Good enough. I'll find it by accident." Mallory gave him a vicious and all too convincing shove that sent the man staggering, vaulted back across the counter walked over to the *rembetika* singers at the far corner of the room."

"Go home," he said quickly. "It is almost curfew time anyway. Go out the back way, and remember—you have seen nothing, no one. You under-stand?"

"We understand." It was the young *bouzouko* player who spoke. He jerked his thumb at his companions and grinned. "Bad men—but good Greeks. Can we help you?"

"No!" Mallory was emphatic. "Think of your families—these soldiers have recognised you. They must know you well—you and they are here most nights, is that not so?"

The young man nodded.

"Off you go, then. Thank you all the same."

A minute later, in the dim, candle-lit cellar, Miller prodded the soldier nearest him—the one most like himself in height and build. "Take your clothes off!" he ordered.

"English pig!" the German snarled.

"Not *English,*" Miller protested. "I'll give you thirty seconds to get your coat and pants off."

The man swore at him, viciously, but made no move to obey. Miller sighed. The German had guts, but time was running out. He took a careful bead on the soldier's hand and pulled the trigger. Again the soft *plop* and the man was staring down stupidly at the hole torn in the heel of his left hand.

"Mustn't spoil the nice uniforms, must we?" Miller asked conversationally. He lifted the automatic until the soldier was staring down the barrel of the gun. "The next goes between the eyes." The casual drawl carried complete conviction. "It won't take me long to undress you, I guess." But the man had already started to tear his uniform off, sobbing with anger and the pain of his wounded hand.

Less than another five minutes had passed when Mallory, clad like Miller in German uniform, unlocked the front door of the tavern and peered cautiously out. The rain, if anything, was heavier than ever—and there wasn't a soul in sight. Mallory beckoned Miller to follow and locked the door behind him. Together the two men walked up the middle of the street, making no attempt to seek either shelter or shadows. Fifty yards took them into the town square, where they turned right along the south side of the square, then left along the east side, not breaking step as they passed the old house where they had hidden earlier in the evening, not even as Louki's hand appeared mysteriously behind the partly opened door, a hand weighted down with two German Army rucksacks—rucksacks packed with rope, fuses, wire and high explosive. A few yards farther on they stopped suddenly, crouched down behind a couple of huge wine barrels outside a barber's shop, gazed at the two armed guards in the arched gateway, less than a hundred feet away, as they shrugged into their packs and waited for their cue.

They had only moments to wait—the timing had been split-second throughout. Mallory was just tightening the waist-belt of his rucksack when a series of explosions shook the centre of the town, not three hundred yards away, explosions followed by the vicious rattle of a machine-gun, then by further explosions. Andrea was doing his stuff magnificently with his grenades and home-made bombs.

Both men suddenly shrank back as a broad, white beam of light stabbed out from a platform high above the gateway, a beam that paralleled the top of the wall to the east, showed up every hooked spike and strand of barbed wire as clearly as sunlight. Mallory and Miller looked at each other for a fleeting moment, their faces grim. Panayis hadn't missed a thing: they would have been pinned on these strands like flies on flypaper and cut to ribbons by machine-guns.

Mallory waited another half-minute, touched Miller's arm, rose to his feet and started running madly across the square, the long hooked bamboo pressed close to his side, the American pounding behind him. In a few seconds they had reached the gates of the fortress, the startled guards running the last few feet to meet them.

"Every man to the Street of Steps!" Mallory shouted. "Those damned English saboteurs are trapped in a house down there! We've got to have some mortars. Hurry, man, hurry, in the name of God!"

"But the gate!" one of the two guards protested. "We cannot leave the gate!" The man had no suspicions, none at all: in the circumstances—the near darkness, the pouring rain, the German-clad soldier speaking perfect German, the obvious truth that there was a gun-battle being fought near-hand—it would have been remarkable had he shown any signs of doubt.

"Idiot!" Mallory screamed at him. "*Dummkopf!* What is there to guard against here? The English swine are in the Street of Steps. They must be destroyed! For God's sake, hurry!" he shouted desperately. "If they escape again it'll be the Russian Front for all of us!"

Mallory had his hand on the man's shoulder now, ready to push him on his way, but his hand fell to his side unneeded. The two men were already gone, running pell-mell across the square, had vanished into the rain and the darkness already. Seconds later Mallory and Miller were deep inside the fortress of Navarone.

Everywhere there was complete confusion—a bustling purposeful confusion as one would expect with the seasoned troops of the Alpenkorps, but confusion nevertheless, with much shouting of orders, blowing of whistles, starting of truck engines, sergeants running to and fro chivvying their men into marching order or into the waiting transports. Mallory and Miller ran too, once or twice through groups of men milling round the tailboard of a truck. Not that they were in any desperate hurry for themselves, but nothing could have been more conspicuous—and suspicious—than the sight of a couple of men walking calmly along in the middle of all that urgent activity. And so they ran, heads down or averted whenever they passed through a pool of light, Miller cursing feelingly and often at the unaccustomed exercise.

They skirted two barrack blocks on their right, then the powerhouse on their left, then an ordnance depot on their right and then the *Abteilung* garage on their left. They were climbing, now, almost in darkness, but Mallory knew where he was to the inch: he had so thoroughly memorised the closely tallying descriptions given him by Vlachos and Panayis that he would have been confident of finding his way with complete accuracy even if the darkness had been absolute.

"What's that, boss?" Miller had caught Mallory by the arm, was pointing to a large, uncompromisingly rectangular building that loomed gauntly against the horizon. "The local hoosegow?"

"Water storage tank," Mallory said briefly. "Panayis estimates there's half a million gallons in there—magazine flooding in an emergency. The magazines are directly below." He pointed to a squat, box-like, concrete structure a little farther on. "The only entrance to the magazine. Locked and guarded."

They were approaching the senior officers' quarters now—the commandant had his own flat on the second story, directly overlooking the massive, reinforced ferro-concrete control tower that controlled the two great guns below. Mallory suddenly stopped, picked up a handful of dirt, rubbed it on his face and told Miller to do the same.

"Disguise," he explained. "The experts would consider it a bit on the elementary side, but it'll have to do. The lighting's apt to be a bit brighter inside this place."

He went up the steps to the officers' quarters at a dead run, crashed through the swing doors with a force that almost took them off their hinges. The sentry at the keyboard looked at him in astonishment, the barrel of his sub-machine-gun lining up on the New Zealander's chest.

"Put that thing down, you damned idiot!" Mallory snapped furiously. "Where's the commandant? Quickly, you oaf! It's life or death!"

"Herr—Herr Kommandant?" the sentry stuttered. "He's left—they are all gone, just a minute ago."

"What? All gone?" Mallory was staring at him with narrowed, dangerous eyes. "Did you say 'all gone'?" he asked softly.

"Yes. I—I'm sure they're . . ." He broke off abruptly as Mallory's eyes shifted to a point behind his shoulder.

"Then who the hell is that?" Mallory demanded savagely.

The sentry would have been less than human not to fall for it. Even as he was swinging round to look, the vicious judo cut took him just below the ear. Mallory had smashed open the glass of the keyboard before the unfortunate guard had hit the floor, swept all the keys—about a dozen in all—off their rings and into his pocket. It took them another twenty seconds to tape the man's mouth and hands and lock him in a convenient cupboard; then they were on their way again, still running.

One more obstacle to overcome, Mallory thought as they pounded along in the darkness, the last of the triple defences. He did not know how many men would be guarding the locked door to the magazine, and in that moment of fierce exaltation he didn't particularly care. Neither, he felt sure, did Miller. There were no worries now, no taut-nerved tensions or nameless anxieties. Mallory would have been that last man in the world to admit it, or even believe it, but this was what men like Miller and himself had been born for.

They had their hand-torches out now, the powerful beams swinging in the wild arcs as they plunged along, skirting the massed batteries of A.A. guns. To anyone observing their approach from the front, there could have been nothing more calculated to disarm suspicion than the sight and sound of the two men running towards them without any attempt at concealment, one of them shouting to the other in German, both with lit torches whose beams lifted and fell, lifted and fell as the men's arms windmilled by their sides. But these same torches were deeply hooded, and only a very alert observer indeed would have noticed that the downward arc of the lights never passed backwards beyond the runners' feet.

Suddenly Mallory saw two shadows detaching themselves from the darker shadow of the magazine entrance, steadied his torch for a brief second to check. He slackened speed.

"Right!" he said softly. "Here they come—only two of them. One each—get as close as possible first. Quick and quiet—a shout, a shot, and we're finished. And for God's sake don't start clubbing 'em with your torch. There'll be no lights on in that magazine and I'm not going to start crawling around there with a box of bloody matches in my hand!" He transferred his torch to his left hand, pulled out his Navy Colt, reversed it, caught it by the barrel, brought it up sharply only inches away from the guards now running to meet them.

"Are you all right?" Mallory gasped. "Anyone been here? Quickly, man, *quickly!*"

"Yes, yes, we're all right." The man was off guard, apprehensive. "What in the name of God is all that noise——"

"Those damned English saboteurs!" Mallory swore viciously. "They've killed the guards and they're inside! Are you sure no one's been here? Come, let me see."

He pushed his way past the guard, probed his torch at the massive padlock, then straightened his back.

"Thank heaven for that anyway!" He turned round, let the dazzling beam of his torch catch the man square in the eyes, muttered an apology and switched off the light, the sound of the sharp click lost in the hollow, soggy thud of the heel of his Colt catching the man behind the ear, just below the helmet. The sentry was still on his feet, just beginning to crumple, when Mallory staggered as the second guard reeled into him, staggered, recovered, clouted him with the Colt for good measure, then stiffened in sudden dismay as he heard the vicious, hissing *plop* of Miller's automatic, twice in rapid succession.

"What the hell——"

"Wily birds, boss," Miller murmured. "Very wily indeed. There was a third character in the shadows at the side. Only way to stop him." Automatic cocked in his ready hand, he stooped over the man for a moment, then straightened. "Afraid he's been stopped kinda permanent, boss." There was no expression in his voice.

"Tie up the others." Mallory had only half-heard him; he was already busy at the magazine door, trying a succession of keys in the lock. The third key fitted, the lock opened and the heavy steel door gave easily to his touch. He took a last swift look round, but there was no one in sight, no sound but the revving engine of the last of the trucks clearing the fortress gates, the distant rattle of machine-gun fire. Andrea was doing a magnificent job—if only he didn't overdo it, leave his withdrawal till it was too late. . . . Mallory turned quickly, switched on his torch, stepped inside the door. Miller would follow when he was ready.

A vertical steel ladder fixed to the rock led down to the floor of the cave. On either side of the ladder were hollow lift-shafts, unprotected even by a cage, oiled wire ropes glistening in the middle, a polished metal runner at each side of the square to guide and steady the spring-loaded side-wheels of the lift itself. Spartan in their simplicity but wholly adequate, there was no mistaking these for anything but what they were—the shell hoist shafts going down to the magazine.

Mallory reached the solid floor of the cave and swept his torch round through a 180-degree arc. This was the very end of that great cave that opened out beneath the towering overhang of rock that dominated the entire harbour. Not the natural end, he saw after a moment's inspection, but a man-made addition: the volcanic rock around him and been drilled and blasted out. There was nothing here but the two shafts descending into the pitchy darkness and another steel ladder, also leading to the magazine. But the magazine could wait: to check that there were no more guards down here and to ensure an emergency escape route—these were the two vital needs of the moment.

Quickly Mallory ran along the tunnel, flipping his torch on and off. The Germans were past-masters of booby traps—explosive booby traps—for the protection of important installations, but the chances were that they had none in that tunnel—not with several hundred tons of high explosive stored only feet away.

The tunnel itself, dripping-damp and duckboard floored, was about seven feet high and even wider, but the central passage was very narrow—most of the space was taken up by the roller conveyors, one on either side, for the great cartridges and shells. Suddenly the conveyors curved away sharply to left and right, the sharply-sheering tunnel roof climbed steeply up into the near-darkness of the vaulted dome above, and, almost at his feet, their burnished steel caught in the beam from his torch, twin sets of parallel rails, imbedded in the solid stone and twenty feet apart, stretched forward into the lightened gloom ahead, the great, gaping mouth of the cave. And just before he switched off the torch—searchers returning from the Devil's Playground might easily catch the pin-point of light in the darkness—Mallory had a brief glimpse of the turn-tables that crowned the far end of these shining rails and, crouched massively above, like some nightmare monsters from an ancient and other world, the evil, the sinister silhouettes of the two great guns of Navarone.

Torch and revolver dangling loosely in his hands, only dimly aware of the curious tingling in the tips of his fingers, Mallory walked slowly forward. Slowly, but not with the stealthy slowness, the razor-drawn expectancy of a man momentarily anticipating trouble—there was no guard in the cave, Mallory was quite sure of that now—but with that strange, dream-like slowness, the half-belief of a man who has accomplished something he had known all along he could never accomplish, with the slowness of a man at last face to face with a feared but long-sought enemy. I'm here at last, Mallory said to himself over and over again, I'm here at last, I've made it, and these are the guns of Navarone: these are the guns I came to destroy, the guns of Navarone, and I have come at last. But somehow he couldn't quite believe it. . . .

Slowly still Mallory approached the guns, walked half-way round the perimeter of the turn-table of the gun of the left, examined it as well as he could in the gloom. He was staggered by the sheer size of it, the tremendous girth and reach of the barrel that stretched far out into the night. He told himself that the experts thought it was only a nine-inch crunch gun, that the crowding confines of the cave were bound to exaggerate its size. He told himself these things, discounted them: twelve-inch bore if an inch, that gun was the biggest thing he had ever seen. Big? Heavens above, it was gigantic! The fools, the blind, crazy fools who had sent the *Sybaris* out against these . . .

The train of thought was lost, abruptly. Mallory stood quite still, one hand resting against the massive gun carriage, and tried to recall the sound that had jerked him back to the present. Immobile, he listened for it again, eyes closed the better to hear, but the sound did not come again, and suddenly he knew that it was no sound at all but the absence of sound that had cut through his thoughts, triggered off some unconscious warning bell. The night was suddenly very silent, very still: down in the heart of the town the guns had stopped firing.

Mallory swore softly to himself. He had already spent far too much time daydreaming, and time was running short. It *must* be running short—Andrea had withdrawn, it was only a matter of time until the Germans discovered that they had been duped. And then they would come running—and there was no doubt where they would come. Swiftly Mallory shrugged out of his rucksack, pulled out the hundred-foot wire-cored rope coiled inside. Their emergency escape route—whatever else he did he must make sure of that.

The rope looped around his arm, he moved forward cautiously, seeking a belay but had only taken three steps when his right knee-cap struck something hard and unyielding. He checked the exclamation of pain, investigated the obstacle with his free hand, realised immediately what it was—an iron railing stretched waist-high across the mouth of the cave. Of course! There had been bound to be something like this, some barrier to prevent people from falling over the edge, especially in the darkness of the night. He hadn't been able to pick it up with the binoculars from the carob grove that afternoon—close though it was to the entrance, it had been concealed in the gloom of the cave. But he should have thought of it.

Quickly Mallory felt his way along to the left, to the very end of the railing, crossed it, tied the rope securely to the base of the vertical stanchion next to the wall, paid out the rope as he moved gingerly to the lip of the cave mouth. And then, almost at once, he was there and there was nothing below his probing foot but a hundred and twenty feet of sheer drop to the land-locked harbour of Navarone.

Away to his right was a dark, formless blur lying on the water, a blur that might have been Cape Demirci: straight ahead, across the darkly velvet sheen of the Maidos Straits, he could see the twinkle of far-away lights—it was a measure of the enemy's confidence that they permitted these lights at all, or, more likely, these fisher cottages were useful as a bearing marker for the guns at night: and to the left, surprisingly near, barely thirty feet away in a horizontal plane, but far below the level where he was standing, he could see the jutting end of the outside wall of the fortress where it abutted on the cliff, the roofs of the houses on the west side of the square beyond that, and, beyond that again, the town itself curving sharply downwards and outwards, to the south first, then to the west, close-girdling and matching the curve of the crescent harbour. Above—but there was nothing to be seen above, that fantastic overhang above blotted out more than half the sky; and below, the darkness was equally impenetrable, the surface of the harbour inky and black as night. There were vessels down there, he knew, Grecian caiques and German launches, but they might have been a thousand miles away for any sign he could see of them.

The brief, all encompassing glance had taken barely ten seconds, but Mallory waited no longer. Swiftly he bent down, tied a double bowline in the end of the rope and left it lying on the edge. In an emergency they could kick it out into the darkness. It would be thirty feet short of the water, he estimated—enough to clear any launch or masted caique that might be moving about the harbour. They could drop the rest of the way, maybe a bone-breaking fall on to the deck of a ship, but they would have to risk it. Mallory took one last look down into the Stygian blackness and shivered; he hoped to God that he and Miller wouldn't have to take that way out.

Dusty Miller was kneeling on the duckboards by the top of the ladder leading down to the magazine as Mallory came running back up the tunnel, his hands busy with wires, fuses, detonators and explosives. He straightened up as Mallory approached.

"I reckon this stuff should keep 'em happy, boss." He set the hands of the clockwork fuse, listened appreciatively to the barely audible hum, then eased himself down the ladder. "In here among the top two rows of cartridges, I thought."

"Wherever you say," Mallory acquiesced. "Only don't make it too obvious—or too difficult to find. Sure there's no chance of them suspecting that we knew the clock and fuses were dud?"

"None in the world," Miller said confidently. "When they find this here contraption they'll knock holes in each others' backs congratulatin' themselves—and they'll never look any further."

"Fair enough." Mallory was satisfied. "Lock the door up top?"

"Certainly I locked the door!" Miller looked at him reproachfully. "Boss, sometimes I think . . ."

But Mallory never heard what he thought. A metallic, reverberating clangour echoed cavernously through the cave and magazine, blotting out Miller's words, then died away over the harbour. Again the sound came, while

the two men stared bleakly at one another, then again and again, then
escaped for a moment of time.

"Company," Mallory murmured. "Complete with sledge-hammers. Dear
God, I only hope that door holds." He was already running along the
passage towards the guns, Miller close behind him.

"Company!" Miller was shaking his head as he ran. "How in the hell
did they get here so soon?"

"Our late lamented little pal," Mallory said savagely. He vaulted over the
railing, edged back to the mouth of the cave. "And we were suckers enough
to believe he told the whole truth. But he never told us that opening that
door up top triggered off an alarm bell in the guardroom."

16

WEDNESDAY NIGHT

2115–2345

SMOOTHLY, SKILLFULLY, Miller paid out the wire-cored rope—double-turned
round the top rail—as Mallory sank out of sight into the darkness. Fifty feet
had gone, he estimated, fifty-five, sixty, then there came the awaited sharp
double tug on the signal cord looped round his wrist and he at once checked
the rope, stooped and tied it securely to the foot of the stanchion.

And then he had straightened again, belayed himself to the rail with the
rope's end, leaned far out over the edge, caught hold of the rope with both
hands as far down as he could reach and began, slowly, almost imperceptibly
at first, then with gradually increasing momentum, to swing man and rope
from side to side, pendulum-wise. As the swings of the pendulum grew
wider, the rope started to twist and jump in his hands, and Miller knew that
Mallory must be striking outcrops of rock, spinning uncontrollably as he
bounced off them. But Miller knew that he couldn't stop now, the clanging
of the sledges behind him was almost continuous: he only stooped the lower
over the rope, flung all the strength of his sinewy arms and shoulders into
the effort of bringing Mallory nearer and still nearer to the rope that Brown
would by now have thrown down from the balcony of the house where they
had left him.

Far below, half-way between the cave mouth and the invisible waters of
the harbour, Mallory swung in a great arc through the rain-filled darkness
of the sky, forty rushing, bone-bruising feet between the extremities of the
swings. Earlier he had struck his head heavily on an outcrop of rock, all but
losing consciousness and his grip on the rope. But he knew where to expect
that projection now and pushed himself clear each time as he approached it,
even although this made him spin in a complete circle every time. It was as
well, he thought, that it was dark, that he was independent of sight anyway:
the blow had reopened an old wound Turzig had given him, his whole upper
face was masked with blood, both eyes completely gummed.

But he wasn't worried about the wound, about the blood in his eyes. The
rope—that was all that mattered. Was the rope there? Had anything happened to Casey Brown? Had he been jumped before he could get the rope
over the side? If he had, then all hope was gone and there was nothing they

could do, no other way they could span the forty sheer feet between house and cave. It just *had* to be there. But if it were there, why couldn't he find it? Three times now, at the right extremity of a swing, he had reached out with his bamboo pole, heard the hook scrape emptily, frustratingly, against the bare rock.

And then, the fourth time, stretched out to the straining limit of both arms, he felt the hook catch on! Immediately, he jerked the pole in, caught the rope before he dropped back on the downward swing, jerked the signal cord urgently, checked himself gradually as he fell back. Two minutes later, near exhaustion from the sixty-foot climb up the wet, slippery rope, he crawled blindly over the lip of the cave and flung himself to the ground, sobbing for breath.

Swiftly, without speaking, Miller bent down, slipped the twin loops of the double bowline from Mallory's legs, undid the knot, tied it to Brown's rope, gave the latter a tug and watched the joined ropes disappear into the darkness. Within two minutes the heavy battery was across, underslung from the two ropes, lowered so far by Casey Brown then hauled up by Mallory and Miller. Within another two minutes, but with infinitely more caution, this time, the canvas bag with the nitro, primers and detonators, had been pulled across, lay on the stone floor beside the battery.

All noise had ceased, the hammering of the sledges against the steel door had stopped completely. There was something threatening, foreboding about the stillness, the silence was more menacing than all the clamour that had gone before. Was the door down, the lock smashed, the Germans waiting for them in the gloom of the tunnel, waiting with cradled machine-carbines that would tear the life out of them? But there was not time to wonder, no time to wait, no time now to stop to weigh the chances. The time for caution was past, and whether they lived or died was of no account any more.

The heavy Colt .455 balanced at his waist, Mallory climbed over the safety barrier, padded silently past the great guns and through the passage, his torch clicking on half-way down its length. The place was deserted, the door above still intact. He climbed swiftly up the ladder, listened at the top. A subdued murmur of voices, he thought he heard, and a faint hissing sound on the other side of the heavy steel door, but he couldn't be sure. He leaned forward to hear better, the palm of his hand against the door, drew back with a muffled exclamation of pain. Just above the lock, the door was almost red-hot. Mallory dropped down to the floor of the tunnel just as Miller came staggering up with the battery.

"That door's hot as blazes. They must be burning——"

"Did you hear anything?" Miller interrupted.

"There was a kind of hissing——"

"Oxy-acetylene torch," Miller said briefly. "They'll be burnin' out the lock. It'll take time—that door's made of armoured steel."

"Why don't they blow it in—gelignite or whatever you use for that job?"

"Perish the thought," Miller said hastily. "Don't even *talk* about it, boss. Sympathetic detonation's a funny thing—there's an even chance that the whole damned lot would go up. Give me a hand with this thing, boss, will you?"

Within seconds Dusty Miller was again a man absorbed in his own element, the danger outside, the return trip he had yet to make across the face of the cliff, completely forgotten for the moment. The task took him four minutes from beginning to end. While Mallory was sliding the battery below the floored well of the lift, Miller squeezed in between the shining steel runners of the lift shaft itself, stooped to examine the rear one with his torch and establish, by the abrupt transition from polished to dull metal, exactly where the spring-loaded wheel of the shell-hoist came to rest. Satisfied, he pulled out a roll of sticky black tape, wound it a dozen times round the shaft, stepped back to look at it: it was quite invisible.

Quickly he taped the ends of two rubber-covered wires on the insulated strip, one at either side, taped these down also until nothing was visible but the bared steel cores at the tips, joined these to two four-inch strips of bared wire, taped these also, top and bottom, to the insulated shaft, vertically and less than half an inch apart. From the canvas bag he removed the T.N.T., the primer and the detonator—a bridge mercury detonator lugged and screwed to his own specification—fitted them together and connected one of the wires from the steel shaft to a lug on the detonator, screwing it firmly home. The other wire from the shaft he led to the positive terminal on the battery, and a third wire from the negative terminal to the detonator. It only required the ammunition hoist to sink down into the magazine—as it would do as soon as they began firing—and the spring-loaded wheel would short out the bare wires, completing the circuit and triggering off the detonator. A last check on the position of the bared vertical wires and he sat back satisfied. Mallory had just descended the ladder from the tunnel. Miller tapped him on the leg to draw his attention, negligently waving the steel blade of his knife within an inch of the exposed wires.

"Are you aware, boss," he said conversationally, "that if I touched this here blade across those terminals, the whole gawd-damned place would go up in smithereens." He shook his head musingly. "Just one little slip of the hand, just one teeny little touch and Mallory and Miller are among the angels."

"For God's sake put that thing away!" Mallory snapped nervously. "And let's get the hell out of here. They've got a complete half-circle cut through that door already!"

Five minutes later Miller was safe—it had been a simple matter of sliding down a 45-degree tautened rope to where Brown waited. Mallory took a last look back into the cave, and his mouth twisted. He wondered how many soldiers manned the guns and magazine during action stations. One thing, he thought, they'll never know anything about it, the poor bastards. And then he thought, for the hundredth time, of all the men on Kheros and the destroyers, and his lips tightened and he looked away. Without another backward glance he slipped over the edge, dropped down into the night. He was half-way there, at the very lowest point of the curve and about to start climbing again, when he heard the vicious, staccato rattle of machine-gun fire directly overhead.

It was Miller who helped him over the balcony rail, an apprehensive-looking Miller who glanced often over his shoulder in the direction of the gun-fire—and the heaviest concentration of fire, Mallory realised with sudden dismay, was coming from their own, the west side of the square, only three or four houses away. Their escape route was cut off.

"Come on, boss!" Miller said urgently. "Let's get away from this joint. Gettin' downright unhealthy round these parts."

Mallory jerked his head in the direction of the fire. "Who's down there?" he asked quickly.

"A German patrol."

"Then how in the hell can we get away?" Mallory demanded. "And where's Andrea?"

"Across the other side of the square, boss. That's who those birds along there are firing at."

"The other side of the square!" He glanced at his watch. "Heavens above, man, what's he doing there?" He was moving through the house now, speaking over his shoulder. "Why did you let him go?"

"I didn't let him go, boss," Miller said carefully. "He was gone when I came. Seems that Brown here saw a big patrol start a house to house search of the square. Started on the other side and were doin' two or three houses at a time. Andrea—he'd come back by this time—thought it a sure bet that they'd work right round the square and get here in two or three minutes, so he took off like a bat across the roofs."

"Going to draw them off?" Mallory was at Louki's side staring out of the window. "The crazy fool! He'll get himself killed this time—get himself killed for sure! There are soldiers everywhere. Besides, they won't fall for it again. He tricked them once up in the hills, and the Germans——".

"I'm not so sure, sir," Brown interrupted excitedly. "Andrea's just shot out the searchlight on his side. They'll think for certain that we're going to break out over the wall and—look, sir, look! There they go!" Brown was almost dancing with excitement, the pain of his injured leg forgotten. "He's done it, sir, he's done it!"

Sure enough, Mallory saw, the patrol had broken away from their shelter in the house to their right and were running across the square in extended formation, their heavy boots clattering on the cobbles, stumbling, falling, recovering again as they lost footing on the slippery wetness of the uneven stones. At the same time Mallory could see torches flickering on the roofs of the houses opposite, the vague forms of men crouching low to escape observation and making swiftly for the spot where Andrea had been when he had shot out the great Cyclops eye of the searchlight.

"They'll be on him from every side." Mallory spoke quietly enough, but his fists clenched until the nails cut into the palms of his hands. He stood stock-still for some seconds, stooped quickly and gathered a Schmeisser up from the floor. "He hasn't a chance. I'm going after him." He turned abruptly, brought up with equal suddenness: Miller was blocking his way to the door.

"Andrea left word that we were to leave him be, that he'd find his own way out." Miller was very calm, very respectful. "Said that no one was to help him, not on any account."

"Don't try to stop me, Dusty." Mallory spoke evenly, mechanically almost. He was hardly aware that Dusty Miller was there. He only knew that he must get out at once, get to Andrea's side, give him what help he could. They had been together too long, he owed too much to the smiling giant to let him go so easily. He couldn't remember how often Andrea had come after *him,* more than once when he had thought hope was gone. . . . He put his hand against Miller's chest.

"You'll only be in his way, boss," Miller said urgently. "That's what you said . . ."

Mallory pushed him aside, strode for the door, brought up his fist to strike as hands closed round his upper arm. He stopped just in time, looked down into Louki's worried face.

"The American is right," Louki said insistently. "You must not go. Andrea said you were to take us down to the harbour."

"Go down yourselves," Mallory said brusquely. "You know the way, you know the plans."

"You would let us all go, let us all——"

"I'd let the whole damn' world go if I could help him." There was an utter sincerity in the New Zealander's voice. "Andrea would never let me down."

"But you would let him down," Louki said quietly. "Is that it, Major Mallory?"

"What the devil do you mean?"

"By not doing as he wishes. He may be hurt, killed even, and if you go after him and are killed too, that makes it all useless. He would die for nothing. Is it thus you would repay your friend?"

"All right, all right, you win," Mallory said irritably.

"That is how Andrea would want it," Louki murmured. "Any other way you would be——"

"Stop preaching at me! Right, gentlemen, let's be on our way." He was back on balance again, easy, relaxed, the primeval urge to go out and kill well under control. "We'll take the high road—over the roofs. Dig into that kitchen stove there, rub the ashes all over your hands and faces. See that there's nothing white on you anywhere. And no talking!"

The five-minute journey down to the harbour wall—a journey made in soft-footed silence with Mallory hushing even the beginnings of a whisper—was quite uneventful. Not only did they see no soldiers, they saw no one at all. The inhabitants of Navarone were wisely observing the curfew, and the streets were completely deserted. Andrea had drawn off pursuit with a vengeance. Mallory began to fear that the Germans had taken him, but just as they reached the water's edge he heard the gunfire again, a good deal farther away this time, in the very north-east corner of the town, round the back of the fortress.

Mallory stood on the low wall above the harbour, looked at his companions, gazed out over the dark oiliness of the water. Through the heavy rain he could just distinguish, to his right and left, the vague blurs of caiques moored stern on to the wall. Beyond that he could see nothing.

"Well, I don't suppose we can get much wetter than we are right now," he observed. He turned to Louki, checked something the little man was trying to say about Andrea. "You sure you can find it all right in the darkness?" "It" was the commandant's personal launch, a thirty-six-foot ten-tonner always kept moored to a buoy a hundred feet off shore. The engineer, who doubled as guard, slept aboard, Louki had said.

"I am already there," Louki boasted. "Blindfold me as you will and I——"

"All right, all right," Mallory said hastily. "I'll take your word for it. Lend me your hat, will you, Casey?" He jammed the automatic into the crown of the hat, pulled it firmly on to his head, slid gently into the water and struck out by Louki's side.

"The engineer," Louki said softly. "I think he will be awake, Major."

"I think so, too," Mallory said grimly. Again there came the chatter of machine-carbines, the deeper whiplash of a Mauser. "So will everyone else in Navarone, unless they're deaf or dead. Drop behind as soon as we see the boat. Come when I call."

Ten seconds, fifteen passed, then Louki touched Mallory on the arm.

"I see it," Mallory whispered. The blurred silhouette was less than fifteen yards away. He approached silently, neither legs nor arms breaking water, until he saw the vague shape of a man standing on the poop, just aft of the engine-room hatchway. He was immobile, staring out in the direction of the fortress and the upper town: Mallory slowly circled round the stern of the boat and came up behind him, on the other side. Carefully he removed his hat, took out the gun, caught the low gunwale with his left hand. At the range of seven feet he knew he couldn't possibly miss, but he couldn't shoot the man, not then. The guard-rails were token affairs only, eighteen inches high at the most, and the splash of the man falling into the water would almost certainly alert the guards at the harbour mouth emplacements.

"If you move I will kill you!" Mallory said softly in German. The man stiffened. He had a carbine in his hand, Mallory saw.

"Put the gun down. Don't turn round." Again the man obeyed, and Mallory was out of the water and on to the deck, in seconds, neither eye nor automatic straying from the man's back. He stepped softly forward, reversed the automatic, struck, caught the man before he could fall overboard and lowered him quietly to the deck. Three minutes later all the others were safely aboard.

Mallory followed the limping Brown down to the engine-room, watched him as he switched on his hooded torch, looked around with a professional eye, looked at the big, gleaming, six-cylinder in line Diesel engine.

"This," said Brown reverently, "is an engine. What a beauty! Operates on any number of cylinders you like. I know the type, sir."

"I never doubted but you would. Can you start her up, Casey?"

"Just a minute till I have a look round, sir." Brown had all the unhurried patience of the born engineer. Slowly, methodically, he played the spotlight round the immaculate interior of the engine-room, switched on the fuel and turned to Mallory. "A dual control job, sir. We can take her from up top."

He carried out the same painstaking inspection in the wheelhouse, while Mallory waited impatiently. The rain was easing off now, not much, but sufficiently to let him see the vague outlines of the harbour entrance. He wondered for the tenth time if the guards there had been alerted against the possibility of an attempted escape by boat. It seemed unlikely—from the racket Andrea was making, the Germans would think that escape was the last thing in their minds. . . . He leaned forward, touched Brown on the shoulder.

"Twenty past eleven, Casey," he murmured. "If these destroyers came through early we're apt to have a thousand tons of rock falling on our heads."

"Ready now, sir," Brown announced. He gestured at the crowded dash-board beneath the screen. "Nothing to it really."

"I'm glad you think so," Mallory murmured fervently. "Start her moving, will you? Just keep it slow and easy."

Brown coughed apologetically. "We're still moored to the buoy. And it might be a good thing, sir, if we checked on the fixed guns, searchlights, signalling lamps, life-jackets and buoys. It's useful to know where these things are," he finished deprecatorily.

Mallory laughed softly, clapped him on the shoulder.

"You'd make a great diplomat, Chief. We'll do that." A landsman first and last, Mallory was none the less aware of the gulf that stretched between him and a man like Brown, made no bones about acknowledging it to himself. "Will you take her out, Casey?"

"Right, sir. Would you ask Louki to come here—I think it's steep to both sides, but there may be snags or reefs. You never know."

Three minutes later the launch was half-way to the harbour mouth, purring along softly on two cylinders, Mallory and Miller, still clad in German uniform, standing on the deck for'ard of the wheelhouse, Louki crouched low inside the wheelhouse itself. Suddenly, about sixty yards away, a signal lamp began to flash at them, its urgent clacking quite audible in the stillness of the night.

"Dan'l Boone Miller will now show how it's done," Miller muttered. He edged closer to the machine-gun on the starboard bow. "With my little gun I shall . . ."

He broke off sharply, his voice lost in the sudden clacking from the wheelhouse behind him, the staccato off-beat chattering of a signal shutter triggered by professional fingers. Brown had handed the wheel over to Louki, was morsing back to the harbour entrance, the cold rain lancing palely through the flickering beams of the lamp. The enemy lamp had stopped but now began flashing again.

"My, they got a lot to say to each other," Miller said admiringly. "How long do the exchange of courtesies last, boss?"

"I should say they are just about finished." Mallory moved back quickly to the wheelhouse. They were less than a hundred feet from the harbour entrance. Brown had confused the enemy, gained precious seconds, more time than Mallory had ever thought they could gain. But it couldn't last. He touched Brown on the arm.

"Give her everything you've got when the balloon goes up." Two seconds later he was back in position in the bows, Schmeisser ready in his hands. "Your big chance, Dan'l Boone. Don't give the searchlights a chance to line up—they'll blind you."

Even as he spoke, the light from the signal lamp at the harbour mouth cut off abruptly and two dazzling white beams, one from either side of the harbour entrance, stabbed blindingly through the darkness, bathing the whole harbour in their savage glare—a glare that lasted for only a fleeting second of time, yielded to a contrastingly stygian darkness as two brief bursts of machine-gun fire smashed them into uselessness. From such short range it had been almost impossible to miss.

"Get down, everyone!" Mallory shouted. "Flat on the deck!"

The echoes of the gunfire were dying away, the reverberations fading along the great sea wall of the fortress when Casey Brown cut in all six cylinders of the engine and opened the throttle wide, the surging roar of the big Diesel blotting out all other sounds in the night. Five seconds, ten seconds, they were passing through the entrance, fifteen, twenty, still not a shot fired, half a minute and they were well clear, bows lifting high out of the water, the deep-dipped stern trailing its long, seething ribbon of phosphorescent white as the engine crescendoed to its clamorous maximum power and Brown pulled the heeling craft sharply round to starboard, seeking the protection of the steep-walled cliffs.

"A desperate battle, boss, but the better men won." Miller was on his feet now, clinging to a mounted gun for support as the deck canted away beneath his feet. "My grandchildren shall hear of this."

"Guards probably all up searching the town. Or maybe there *were* some poor blokes behind these searchlights. Or maybe we just took 'em all by surprise." Mallory shook his head. "Anyway you take it, we're just plain damn' lucky."

He moved aft, into the wheelhouse. Brown was at the wheel, Louki almost crowing with delight.

"That was magnificent, Casey," Mallory said sincerely. "A first-class job of work. Cut the engine when we come to the end of the cliffs. Our job's done. I'm going ashore."

"You don't have to, Major."

Mallory turned. "What's that?"

"You don't have to. I tried to tell you on the way down, but you kept telling me to be quiet." Louki sounded injured, turned to Casey. "Slow down, please. The last thing Andrea told me, Major, was that we were to come this way. Why do you think he let himself be trapped against the cliffs to the north instead of going out into the country, where he could have hidden easily."

"Is this true, Casey?" Mallory asked.

"Don't ask me, sir. Those two—they always talk in Greek."

"Of course, of course." Mallory looked at the low cliffs close of the starboard beam, barely moving now with the engine shut right down, looked back at Louki. "Are you quite sure . . ."

He stopped in mid-sentence, jumped out through the wheelhouse door. The splash—there had been no mistaking the noise—had come from almost directly ahead. Mallory, Miller by his side, peered into the darkness, saw a dark head surfacing above the water less than twenty feet away, leaned far over with outstretched arm as the launch slid slowly by. Five seconds later Andrea stood on the deck, dripping mightily and beaming all over his great moon face. Mallory led him straight into the wheelhouse, switched on the soft light of the shaded chartlamp.

"By all that's wonderful, Andrea, I never thought to see you again. How did it go?"

"I will soon tell you," Andrea laughed. "Just after——"

"You've been wounded!" Miller interrupted. "Your shoulder's kinda perforated." He pointed to the red stain spreading down the sea-soaked jacket.

"Well, now, I believe I have." Andrea affected vast surprise. "Just a scratch, my friend."

"Oh, sure, sure, just a scratch! It would be the same if your arm had been blown off. Come on down to the cabin—this is just a kindergarten exercise for a man of my medical skill."

"But the Captain——"

"Will have to wait. And your story. Ol' Medicine Man Miller permits no interference with his patients. Come on!"

"Very well, very well," Andrea said docilely. He shook his head in mock resignation, followed Miller out of the wheelhouse.

Brown opened up to full throttle again, took the launch north almost to Cape Demirci to avoid any hundred to one chance the harbour batteries might take, turned due east for a few miles then headed south into the Maidos Straits. Mallory stood by his side in the wheelhouse, gazing out over the dark, still waters. Suddenly he caught a gleam of white in the distance, touched Brown's arm and pointed for'ard.

"Breakers ahead, Casey, I think. Reefs, perhaps?"

Casey looked in long silence, finally shook his head.

"Bow-wave," he said unemotionally. "It's the destroyers coming through."

17

WEDNESDAY NIGHT

Midnight

COMMANDER VINCENT Ryan, R.N., Captain (Destroyers) and Commanding officer of His Majesty's latest S-class destroyer *Sirdar,* looked round the cramped chart-room and tugged thoughtfully at his magnificent Captain Kettle beard. A scruffier, a more villainous, a more cut and battered-looking bunch of hard cases he had never seen, he reflected, with the possible exception of a Bias Bay pirate crew he had helped round up when a very junior officer on the China Station. He looked at them more closely, tugged his beard again, thought there was more to it than mere scruffiness. He wouldn't care to be given the task of rounding this lot up. Dangerous, highly dangerous, he mused, but impossible to say why, there was only this quietness, this relaxed watchfulness that made him feel vaguely uncomfortable. His "hatchet-men," Jensen had called them: Captain Jensen picked his killers well.

"Any of you gentlemen care to go below," he suggested. "Plenty of hot water, dry clothes—and warm bunks. We won't be using them to-night."

"Thank you very much, sir." Mallory hesitated. "But we'd like to see this through."

"Right, then, the bridge it is," Ryan said cheerfully. The *Sirdar* was beginning to pick up speed again, the deck throbbing beneath their feet. "It is at your own risk, of course."

"We lead charmed lives," Miller drawled. "Nothin' ever happens to us."

The rain had stopped and they could see the cold twinkling of stars through broadening rifts in the clouds. Mallory looked around him, could see Maidos broad off the port bow and the great bulk of Navarone slipping by to starboard. Aft, about a cable length away, he could just distinguish two other ships, high-curving bow-waves piled whitely against tenebrious silhouettes. Mallory turned to the captain.

"No transports, sir?"

"No transports." Ryan felt a vague mixture of pleasure and embarrassment that this man should called him "sir." "Destroyers only. This is going to be a smash-and-grab job. No time for dawdlers to-night—and we're behind schedule already."

"How long to clear the beaches?"

"Half an hour."

"What! Twelve hundred men?" Mallory was incredulous.

"More." Ryan sighed. "Half the ruddy inhabitants want to come with us, too. We could still do it in half an hour, but we'll probably take a bit longer. We'll embark all the mobile equipment we can."

Mallory nodded, let his eye travel along the slender outlines of the *Sirdar*. "Where are you going to put 'em all, sir?"

"A fair question," Ryan admitted. "5 p.m. on the London Underground will be nothing compared to this little lot. But we'll pack them in somehow."

Mallory nodded again and looked across the dark waters at Navarone. Two minutes, now, three at the most, and the fortress would open behind that headland. He felt a hand touch his arm, half-turned and smiled down at the sad-eyed little Greek by his side.

"Not long now, Louki," he said quietly.

"The people, Major," he murmured. "The people in the town. Will they be all right?"

"They'll be all right. Dusty says the roof of the cave will go straight up. Most of the stuff will fall into the harbour."

"Yes, but the boats——?"

"Will you stop worrying! There's nobody aboard them—you know they have to leave at curfew time." He looked round as someone touched his arm.

"Captain Mallory, this is Lieutenant Beeston, my gunnery officer." There was a slight coolness in Ryan's voice that made Mallory think that he wasn't overfond of his gunnery officer. "Lieutenant Beeston is worried."

"I *am* worried!" The tone was cold, aloof, with an indefinable hint of condescension. "I understand that you have advised the captain not to offer any resistance?"

"You sound like a B.B.C. communiqué," Mallory said shortly. "But you're right. I did say that. You couldn't locate the guns except by search-light and that would be fatal. Similarly with gunfire."

"I'm afraid I don't understand." One could almost see the lift of the eyebrows in the darkness.

"You'd give away your position," Mallory said patiently "They'd nail you first time. Give 'em two minutes and they'd nail you anyway. I have good reason to believe that the accuracy of their gunners is quite fantastic."

"So has the Navy," Ryan interjected quietly. "Their third shell got the *Sybaris's* B magazine."

"Have you got any idea why this should be, Captain Mallory?" Beeston was quite unconvinced.

"Radar-controlled guns," Mallory said briefly. "They have two huge scanners atop the fortress."

"The *Sirdar* had radar installed last month," Beeston said stiffly. "I imagine we could register some hits ourselves if——"

"You could hardly miss." Miller drawled out the words, the tone dry and provocative. "It's a helluva big island, Mac."

"Who—who are you?" Beeston was rattled. "What the devil do you mean?"

"Corporal Miller." The American was unperturbed. "Must be a very selective instrument, Lootenant, that can pick out a cave in a hundred square miles of rock."

There was a moment's silence, then Beeston muttered something and turned away.

"You've hurt the Guns's feelings, Corporal," Ryan murmured. "He's very keen to have a go—but we'll hold our fire. . . . How long till we clear that point, Captain?"

"I'm not sure." He turned. "What do you say, Casey?"

"A minute, sir. No more."

Ryan nodded, said nothing. There was a silence on the bridge, a silence only intensified by the sibilant rushing of the waters, the weird, lonesome pinging of the Asdic. Above, the sky was steadily clearing, and the moon, palely luminous, was struggling to appear through a patch of thinning cloud. Nobody spoke, nobody moved. Mallory was conscious of the great bulk of Andrea beside him, of Miller, Brown and Louki behind. Born in the heart of the country, brought up on the foothills of the Southern Alps, Mallory knew himself as a landsman first and last, an alien to the sea and ships: but he had never felt so much at home in his life, never really known till now what it was to belong. He was more than happy, Mallory thought vaguely to himself, he was content. Andrea and his new friends and the impossible well done—how could a man be but content? They weren't all going home, Andy Stevens wasn't coming with them, but strangely he could feel no sorrow, only a gentle melancholy. . . . Almost as if he had divined what Mallory was thinking, Andrea leaned towards him, towering over him in the darkness.

"He should be here," he murmured. "Andy Stevens should be here. That is what you are thinking, is it not?"

Mallory nodded and smiled, and said nothing.

"It doesn't really matter, does it, my Keith?" No anxiety, no questioning, just a statement of fact. "It doesn't really matter."

"It doesn't matter at all."

Even as he spoke, he looked up quickly. A light, a bright orange flame had lanced out from the sheering wall of the fortress; they had rounded the headland and he hadn't even noticed it. There was a whistling roar—Mallory thought incongruously of an express train emerging from a tunnel—directly overhead, and the great shell had crashed into the sea just beyond them. Mallory compressed his lips, unconsciously tightened his clenched fists. It was easy now to see how the *Sybaris* had died.

He could hear the gunnery officer saying something to the captain, but the words failed to register. They were looking at him and he at them and he did not see them. His mind was strangely detached. Another shell, would that be next? Or would the roar of the gunfire of that first shell come echoing across the sea? Or perhaps . . . Once again, he was back in that dark magazine entombed in the rocks, only now he could see men down there, doomed, unknowing men, could see the overhead pulleys swinging the great shells and cartridges towards the well of the lift, could see the shell hoist descending slowly, the bared, waiting wires less than half an inch apart, the shining, spring-loaded wheel running smoothly down the gleaming rail, the gentle bump as the hoist . . .

A white pillar of flame streaked up hundreds of feet into the night sky as the tremendous detonation tore the heart out of the great fortress of Navarone. No after-fire of any kind, no dark, billowing clouds of smoke, only that one blinding white column that lit up the entire town for a single instant of time, reached up incredibly till it touched the clouds, vanished as if it had never been. And then, by and by, came the shock waves, the solitary thunderclap of the explosion, staggering even at that distance, and finally the deep-throated rumbling as thousands of tons of rock toppled majestically into the harbour—thousands of tons of rock and the two great guns of Navarone.

The rumbling was still in their ears, the echoes fading away far out across the Ægean, when the clouds parted and the moon broke through, a full moon silvering the darkly-rippling waters to starboard, shining iridescently through the spun phosphorescence of the *Sirdar's* boiling wake. And dead ahead, bathed in the white moonlight, mysterious, remote, the island of Kheros lay sleeping on the surface of the sea.

Force 10 from Navarone

CONTENTS

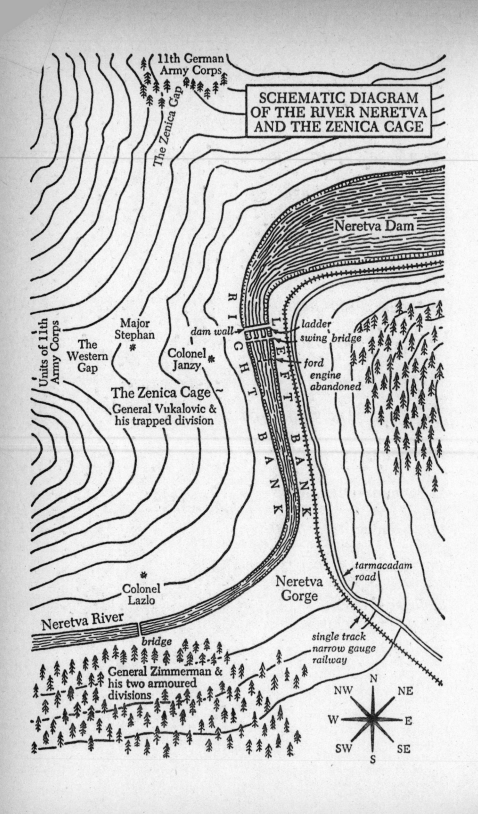

SCHEMATIC DIAGRAM
OF THE RIVER NERETVA
AND THE ZENICA CAGE

11th German
Army Corps

The Zenica Gap

Neretva Dam

Units of 11th Army Corps

The
Western
Gap

Major
Stephan

Colonel
Janzy

RIGHT BANK

dam wall

LEFT BANK

ladder
swing bridge

ford
engine
abandoned

The Zenica Cage ~
General Vukalovic &
his trapped division

Colonel
Lazlo

Neretva
Gorge

tarmacadam
road

Neretva River

bridge

General Zimmerman &
his two armoured
divisions

single track
narrow gauge
railway

N
NW   NE
W   E
SW   SE
S

1

PRELUDE—THURSDAY
0001–0600

COMMANDER VINCENT Ryan, R.N., Captain (Destroyers) and commanding officer of His Majesty's latest S-class destroyer *Sirdar,* leaned his elbows comfortably on the coaming of his bridge, brought up his night glasses and gazed out thoughtfully over the calm and silvered water of the moonlit Ægean.

He looked first of all due north, straight out over the huge and smoothly sculpted and whitely phosphorescent bow wave thrown up by the knife-edged forefoot of his racing destroyer: four miles away, no more, framed in its backdrop of indigo sky and diamantine stars, lay the brooding mass of a darkly cliff-girt island: the island of Kheros, for months the remote and beleaguered outpost of two thousand British troops who had expected to die that night and who would now not die.

Ryan swung his glasses through 180° and nodded approvingly. This was what he liked to see. The four destroyers to the south were in such perfect line astern that the hull of the leading vessel, a gleaming bone in its teeth, completely obscured the hulls of the three ships behind. Ryan turned his binoculars to the east.

It was odd, he thought inconsequentially, how unimpressive, even how disappointing, the aftermath of either natural or man-made disaster could be. Were it not for that dull red glow and wisping smoke that emanated from the upper part of the cliff and lent the scene a vaguely Dantean aura of primeval menace and foreboding, the precipitous far wall of the harbour looked as it might have done in the times of Homer. That great ledge of rock, that looked from that distance so smooth and regular and somehow inevitable, could have been carved out by the wind and weather of a hundred million years: it could equally well have been cut away fifty centuries ago by the masons of Ancient Greece seeking marble for the building of their Ionian temples: what was almost inconceivable, what almost passed rational comprehension, was the fact that ten minutes ago that ledge had not been there at all, that there had been in its place tens of thousands of tons of rock, the most impregnable German fortress in the Ægean and, above all, the two great guns of Navarone, now all buried forever three hundred feet under the sea. With a slow shake of his head Commander Ryan lowered his binoculars and turned to look at the men responsible for achieving more in five minutes than nature could have done in five million years.

Captain Mallory and Corporal Miller. That was all he knew of them, that

171

and the fact that they had been sent on this mission by an old friend of his, a naval captain by the name of Jensen who, he had learnt only twenty-four hours previously—and that to his total astonishment—was the Chief of Allied Intelligence in the Mediterranean. But that was all he knew of them and maybe he didn't even know that. Maybe their names weren't Mallory and Miller. Maybe they weren't even a captain and a corporal. They didn't look like any captain or corporal he'd ever seen. Come to that, they didn't look like any soldiers he'd ever seen. Clad in salt-water and bloodstained German uniforms, filthy, unshaven, quiet and watchful and remote, they belonged to no category of men he'd ever encountered: all he could be certain of as he gazed at the blurred and bloodshot sunken eyes, the gaunt and trenched and stubbled-grey faces of two men no longer young, was that he had never before seen human beings so far gone in total exhaustion.

"Well, that seems to be about it," Ryan said. "The troops on Kheros waiting to be taken off, our flotilla going north to take them off and the guns of Navarone no longer in any position to do anything about our flotilla. Satisfied, Captain Mallory?"

"That was the object of the exercise," Mallory agreed.

Ryan lifted his glasses again. This time, almost at the range of night vision, he focussed on a rubber dinghy closing in on the rocky shoreline to the west of Navarone harbour. The two figures seated in the dinghy were just discernible, no more. Ryan lowered his glasses and said thoughtfully:

"Your big friend—and the lady with him—don't believe in hanging about. You didn't—ah—introduce me to them, Captain Mallory."

"I didn't get the chance to. Maria and Andrea. Andrea's a colonel in the Greek Army, 19th Motorised Division."

"Andrea *was* a colonel in the Greek Army," Miller said. "I think he's just retired."

"I rather think he has. They were in a hurry, Commander, because they're both patriotic Greeks, they're both islanders and there is much for both to do in Navarone. Besides, I understand they have some urgent and very personal matters to attend to."

"I see." Ryan didn't press the matter, instead looked out again over the smoking remains of the shattered fortress. "Well, that seems to be that. Finished for the evening, gentlemen?"

Mallory smiled faintly. "I think so."

"Then I would suggest some sleep."

"What a wonderful word that is." Miller pushed himself wearily off the side of the bridge and stood there swaying as he drew an exhausted forearm overe bloodshot aching eyes. "Wake me up in Alexandria."

"Alexandria?" Ryan looked at him in amusement. "We won't be there for thirty hours yet."

"That's what I meant," Miller said.

Miller didn't get his thirty hours. He had, in fact, been asleep for just over thirty minutes when he was wakened by the slow realisation that something was hurting his eyes: after he had moaned and feebly protested for some time he managed to get one eye open and saw that that something was a bright overhead light let into the deckhead of the cabin that had been provided for Mallory and himself. Miller propped himself up on a groggy elbow, managed to get his second eye into commission and looked without enthusiasm at the other two occupants of the cabin: Mallory was seated by a table, apparently transcribing some kind of message, while Commander Ryan stood in the open doorway.

"This is outrageous," Miller said bitterly. "I haven't closed an eye all night."

"You've been asleep for thirty-five minutes," Ryan said. "Sorry. But Cairo said this message for Captain Mallory was of the greatest urgency."

"It is, is it?" Miller said suspiciously. He brightened. "It's probably about promotions and medals and leave and so forth." He looked hopefully at Mallory who had just straightened after decoding the message. "Is it?"

"Well, no. It starts off promisingly enough, mind you, warmest congratulations and what-have-you, but after that the tone of the message deteriorates a bit."

Mallory reread the message: SIGNAL RECEIVED. WARMEST CONGRATULATIONS. MAGNIFICENT ACHIEVEMENT. YOU BLOODY FOOLS. WHY YOU LET ANDREA GET AWAY? ESSENTIAL CONTACT HIM IMMEDIATELY. WILL EVACUATE BEFORE DAWN. UNDER DIVERSIONARY AIR ATTACK. AIR STRIP ONE MILE SOUTHEAST MANDRAKOS. SEND CE VIA SIRDAR. URGENT 3 REPEAT URGENT 3. BEST LUCK. JENSEN.

Miller took the message from Mallory's outstretched hand, moved the paper to and fro until he had brought his bleary eyes into focus, read the message in horrified silence, handed it back to Mallory and stretched out his full length on his bunk. He said: "Oh, my God!" and relapsed into what appeared to be a state of shock.

"That about sums it up," Mallory agreed. He shook his head wearily and turned to Ryan. "I'm sorry, sir, but we must trouble you for three things. A rubber dinghy, a portable radio transmitter and an immediate return to Navarone. Please arrange to have the radio lined up on a pre-set frequency to be constantly monitored by your W.T. room. When you receive a CE signal, transmit it to Cairo."

"CE?" Ryan asked.

"Uh-huh. Just that."

"And that's all?"

"We could do with a bottle of brandy," Miller said. "Something—anything—to see us through the rigours of the long night that lies ahead."

Ryan lifted an eyebrow. "A bottle of five-star, no doubt, Corporal?"

"Would you," Miller asked morosely, "give a bottle of three star to a man going to his death?"

As it happened, Miller's gloomy expectations of an early demise turned out to be baseless—for that night, at least. Even the expected fearful rigours of the long night ahead proved to be no more than minor physical inconveniences.

By the time the *Sirdar* had brought them back to Navarone and as close in to the rocky shores as was prudent, the sky had become darkly overcast, rain was falling and a swell was beginning to blow up from the southwest so that it was little wonder to either Mallory or Miller that, by the time they had paddled their dinghy within striking distance of the shore, they were in a very damp and miserable condition indeed: and it was even less wonder that, by the time they had reached the boulder-strewn beach itself, they were soaked to the skin for a breaking wave flung their dinghy against a sloping shelf of rock, overturning their rubber craft and precipitating them both into the sea. But this was of little enough account in itself: their Schmeisser machine pistols, their radio, their torches were securely wrapped in waterproof bags and all of those were safely salvaged. All in all, Mallory reflected, an almost perfect three-point landing compared to the last time they had come to Navarone   boat, when their Greek caique, caught in the teeth of a giant storm, had been battered to pieces against the jaggedly vertical—and supposedly unclimbable—south cliff of Navarone.

Slipping, stumbling and with suitably sulphuric comments, they made their way over the wet shingles and massively rounded boulders until their way was barred by a steeply angled slope that soared up into the near-darkness above. Mallory unwrapped a pencil torch and began to quarter the face of the slope with its narrow, concentrated beam. Miller touched him on the arm.

"Taking a bit of a chance, aren't we? With that thing, I mean?"

"No chance," Mallory said. "There won't be a soldier left on guard on the coasts tonight. They'll all be fighting the fires in the town. Besides, who is left for them to guard against? We are the birds and the birds, duty done, have flown. Only a madman would come back to the island again."

"I know what we are," Miller said with feeling. "You don't have to tell me."

Mallory smiled to himself in the darkness and continued his search. Within a minute he had located what he had been hoping to find—an angled gully in the slope. He and Miller scrambled up the shale- and rock-strewn bed of the gully as fast as the treacherous footing and their encumbrances would permit: within fifteen minutes they had reached the plateau above and paused to take their breath. Miller reached inside the depths of his tunic, a discreet movement that was at once followed by a discreet gurgling.

"What are you doing?" Mallory enquired.

"I thought I heard my teeth chattering. What's all this 'urgent 3 repeat urgent 3' business in the message, then?"

"I've never seen it before. But I know what it means. Some people, somewhere, are about to die."

"I'll tell you two for a start. And what if Andrea won't come? He's not a member of our armed forces. He doesn't have to come. *And* he said he was getting married right away."

Mallory said with certainty: "He'll come."

"What makes you so sure?"

"Because Andrea is the one completely responsible man I've ever met. He has two great responsibilities—one to others, one to himself. That's why he came back to Navarone—because he knew the people needed him. And that's why he'll leave Navarone when he sees this 'urgent 3' signal, because he'll know that someone, in some other place, needs him even more."

Miller secured the brandy bottle from Mallory and thrust it securely inside his tunic again. "Well, I can tell you this. The future Mrs. Andrea Stavros isn't going to be very happy about it."

"Neither is Andrea Stavros and I'm not looking forward to telling him," Mallory said candidly. He peered at his luminous watch and swung to his feet. "Mandrakos in half an hour."

In precisely thirty minutes, their Schmeissers removed from their water-proof bags and now shoulder-slung at hip level, Mallory and Miller moved swiftly but very quietly from shadow to shadow through the plantations of carob trees on the outskirts of the village of Mandrakos. Suddenly, from directly ahead, they heard the unmistakable clink of glasses and bottlenecks.

For the two men a potentially dangerous situation such as this was so routine as not even to warrant a glance at each other. They dropped silently to their hands and knees and crawled forward, Miller sniffing the air appreciatively as they advanced: the Greek resinous spirit *ouzo* has an extraordinary ability of permeating the atmosphere for a considerable distance around it. Mallory and Miller reached the edge of a clump of bushes, sank prone and looked ahead.

From their richly befrogged waistcoats, cummerbunds and fancy head-gear, the two characters propped against the bolt of a plane tree in the clearing ahead were obviously men of the island: from the rifles across their knees, their role appeared to be that of guards of some kind: from the almost vertical angle at which they had to tip the *ouzo* bottle to get at what little was left of its contents, it was equally apparent that they weren't taking their duties too seriously, nor had been for some considerable time past.

Mallory and Miller withdrew somewhat less stealthily than they had advanced, rose and glanced at each other. Suitable comment seemed lacking. Mallory shrugged and moved on, circling around to his right. Twice more, as they moved swiftly into the centre of Mandrakos, flitting from the shadow of carob grove to carob grove, from the shadow of plane tree to plane tree, from the shadow of house to house, they came upon but easily avoided other ostensible sentries all busy interpreting their duties in a very liberal fashion. Miller pushed Mallory into a doorway.

"Our friends back there," he said. "What were they celebrating?"

"Wouldn't you? Celebrate, I mean. Navarone is useless to the Germans now. A week from now and they'll all be gone."

"All right. So why are they keeping a watch?" Miller nodded to a small, whitewashed Greek Orthodox church standing in the centre of the village square. From inside came a far from subdued murmur of voices. Also from inside came a great deal of light escaping through very imperfectly blacked-out windows. "Could it be anything to do with that?"

Mallory said: "Well, there's one sure way to find out."

They moved quietly on, taking advantage of all available cover and shadow until they came to a still deeper shadow caused by two flying buttresses supporting the wall of the ancient church. Between the buttresses were one of the few more successfully blacked-out windows with only a tiny chink of light showing along the bottom edge of one of the windows. Both men stooped and peered through the narrow aperture.

The church appeared even more ancient inside than on the outside. The high unpainted wooden benches, adze-cut oak from centuries long gone, had been blackened and smoothed by untold generations of churchgoers, the wood itself cracked and splintered by the ravages of time: the whitewashed walls looked as if they required buttresses within as well as without, crumbling to an extinction that could not now be long delayed: the roof appeared to be in imminent danger of falling in at any moment.

The now even louder hum of sound came from islanders of almost every age and sex, many in ceremonial dress, who occupied nearly every available seat in the church: the light came from literally hundreds of guttering candles, many of them ancient and twisted and ornamented and evidently called out for this special occasion, that lined the walls, the central aisle and the altar: by the altar itself, a priest, a bearded patriarch in Greek Orthodox robes, waited impassively.

Mallory and Miller looked interrogatively at each other and were on the point of standing upright when a very deep and very quiet voice spoke behind them.

"Hands behind the necks," it said pleasantly. "And straighten very slowly. I have a Schmeisser machine pistol in my hands."

Slowly and carefully, just as the voice asked, Mallory and Miller did as they were told.

"Turn round. Carefully, now."

So they turned round, carefully. Miller looked at the massive dark figure who indeed had, as he'd claimed, a machine pistol in his hands, and said irritably: "Do you mind? Point that damned thing somewhere else."

The dark figure gave a startled exclamation, lowered the gun to his side and bent forward, the dark craggy lined face expressing no more than a passing flicker of surprise. Andrea Stavros didn't go in much for registering unnecessary emotional displays and the recovery of his habitual composure was instantaneous.

"The German uniforms," he explained apologetically. "They had me fooled."

"You could have fooled me, too," Miller said. He looked incredulously at Andrea's clothes, at the unbelievably baggy black trousers, the black jackboots, the intricately ornamented black waistcoat and violently purple cummerbund, shuddered and closed his eyes in pain. "Been visiting the Mandrakos pawnshop?"

"The ceremonial dress of my ancestors," Andrea said mildly. "You two fall overboard?"

"Not intentionally," Mallory said. "We came back to see you."

"You could have chosen a more convenient time." He hesitated, glanced at a small lighted building across the street and took their arms. "We can talk in here."

He ushered them in and closed the door behind him. The room was obviously, from its benches and Spartan furnishings, some sort of communal meeting place, a village hall: illumination came from three rather smoky oil lamps the light from which was most hospitably reflected by the scores of bottles of spirit and wine and beer and glasses that took up almost every available inch of two long trestle tables. The haphazardly unaesthetic layout of the refreshments bespoke a very impromptu and hastily improvised preparation for a celebration: the serried rows of bottles heralded the intention of compensating for lack of quality by an excess of quantity.

Andrea crossed to the nearest table, picked up three glasses and a bottle of *ouzo,* and began to pour drinks. Miller fished out his brandy and offered it, but Andrea was too preoccupied to notice. He handed them the *ouzo* glasses.

"Health." Andrea drained his glass and went on thoughtfully: "You did not return without a good reason, my Keith."

Silently, Mallory removed the Cairo radio message from its waterproof oilskin wallet and handed it to Andrea, who took it half-unwillingly, then read it, scowling blackly.

He said: "Urgent 3 means what I think it means?"

Again Mallory remained silent, merely nodding as he watched Andrea unwinkingly.

"This is most inconvenient for me." The scowl deepened. "*Most* inconvenient. There are many things for me to do in Navarone. The people will miss me."

"It's also inconvenient for me," Miller said. "There are many things *I* could profitably be doing in the West End of London. They miss me, too. Ask any barmaid. But that's hardly the point."

Andrea regarded him for an impassive moment, then looked at Mallory. "*You* are saying nothing."

"I've nothing to say."

The scowl slowly left Andrea's face, though the brooding frown remained. He hesitated, then reached again for the bottle of *ouzo*. Miller shuddered delicately.

"Please." He indicated the bottle of brandy.

Andrea smiled, briefly and for the first time, poured some of Miller's five-star into their glasses, reread the message and handed it back to Mallory. "I must think it over. I have some business to attend to first."

Mallory looked at him thoughtfully. "Business?"

"I have to attend a wedding."

"A wedding?" Miller said politely.

"Must you two repeat everything I say. A wedding."

"But who do *you* know?" Miller asked. "And at this hour of night."

"For some people in Navarone," Andrea said drily, "the night is the only safe time." He turned abruptly, walked away, opened the door and hesitated.

Mallory said curiously: "Who's getting married?"

Andrea made no reply. Instead he walked back to the nearest table, poured and drained a half tumbler of the brandy, ran a hand through his thick dark hair, straightened his cummerbund, squared his shoulders and walked purposefully towards the door. Mallory and Miller stared after him, then at the door that closed behind him: then they stared at each other.

Some fifteen minutes later they were still staring at each other, this time with expressions which alternated between the merely bemused and slightly stunned.

They were seated in the back seat of the Greek Orthodox church—the only part of any pew in the entire church not now occupied by islanders. From where they sat, the altar was at least sixty feet away but as they were both tall men and sitting by the central aisle, they had a pretty fair view of what was going on up there.

There was, to be accurate, nothing going on up there any more. The ceremony was over. Gravely, the Orthodox priest bestowed his blessing and Andrea and Maria, the girl who had shown them the way into the fortress of Navarone, turned with the slow dignity becoming the occasion, and walked down the aisle. Andrea bent over, tenderness and solicitousness both in expression and manner, and whispered something in her ear, but his words, it would have seemed, bore little relation to the way in which they were expressed for halfway down the aisle a furious altercation broke out between them. Between, perhaps, is not the right word: it was less an altercation than a very one-sided monologue. Maria, her face flushed and dark eyes flashing, gesticulating and clearly mad through, was addressing Andrea in far from low tones of not even barely controlled fury: Andrea, for his part, was deprecatory, placatory, trying to hush her up with about the same amount of success as Canute held back the tide and looking apprehensively around. The reaction of the seated guests varied from disbelief through open-mouthed astonishment and bafflement to down-right horror: clearly all regarded the spectacle as a highly unusual aftermath to a wedding ceremony.

As the couple approached the end of the aisle opposite the pew where Mallory and Miller were seated, the argument, if such it could be called, raged more furiously than ever. As they passed by the end pew, Andrea, hand over his mouth, leaned over towards Mallory.

"This," he said, *sotto voce,* "is our first married quarrel."

He was given time to say no more. An imperative hand seized his arm and almost literally dragged him through the church doorway. Even after they had disappeared from sight, Maria's voice, loud and clear, could still be heard by everyone within the church. Miller turned from surveying the empty doorway and looked thoughtfully at Mallory.

"Very high-spirited girl, that. I wish I understood Greek. What was she saying there?"

Mallory kept his face carefully expressionless. "What about my honeymoon?"

"Ah!" Miller's face was equally dead-pan. "Don't you think we'd better follow them?"

"Why?"

"Andrea can take care of most people." It was the usual masterly Miller understatement. "But he's stepped out of his class this time."

Mallory smiled, rose and went to the door, followed by Miller who was in turn followed by an eager press of guests understandably anxious to see the second act of this unscheduled entertainment: but the village square was empty of life.

Mallory did not hesitate. With the instinct born from the experience of long association with Andrea, he headed across the square to the communal hall where Andrea had made the earlier of his two dramatic gestures. His instincts hadn't betrayed him. Andrea, with a large glass of brandy in his hand and moodily fingering a spreading patch of red on his cheek, looked up as Mallory and Miller entered.

He said moodily: "She's gone home to her mother."

Miller glanced at his watch. "One minute and twenty-five seconds," he said admiringly. "A world record."

Andrea glowered at him and Mallory moved in hastily.

"You're coming, then."

"Of course I'm coming," Andrea said irritably. He surveyed without enthusiasm the guests now swarming into the hall and brushing unceremoniously by as they headed, like the camel for the oasis, towards the bottle-laden tables. "Somebody's got to look after you two."

Mallory looked at his watch. "Three and a half hours yet before that plane is due. We're dead on our feet, Andrea. Where can we sleep—a safe place to sleep. Your perimeter guards are drunk."

"They've been that way ever since the fortress blew up," Andrea said. "Come, I'll show you."

Miller looked around the islanders, who, amid a loud babel of cheerful voices, were already quite exceptionally busy with bottles and glasses. "How about your guests?"

"How about them, then?" Andrea surveyed his compatriots morosely. "Just look at that lot. Ever know a wedding reception yet where anybody paid any attention to the bride and groom? Come."

They made their way southwards through the outskirts of Mandrakos to the open countryside beyond. Twice they were challenged by guards, twice a scowl and growl from Andrea sent them back hurriedly to their *ouzo* bottles. It was still raining heavily, but Mallory's and Miller's clothes were already so saturated that a little more rain could hardly make any appreciable difference to the way they felt, while Andrea, if anything, seemed even more oblivious of it. Andrea had the air of a man who had other things on his mind.

After a fifteen minute walk, Andrea stopped before the swing doors of a small, dilapidated and obviously deserted roadside barn.

"There's hay inside," he said. "We'll be safe here."

Mallory said: "Fine. A radio message to the *Sirdar* to send her CE message to Cairo and——"

"CE?" Andrea asked. "What's that?"

"To let Cairo know we've contacted you and are ready for pickup. . . . And after that, three lovely long hours' sleep."

Andrea nodded. "Three hours it is."

"Three *long* hours," Mallory said meditatively.

A smile slowly broke on Andrea's craggy face as he clapped Mallory on the shoulder.

"In three long hours," he said, "a man like myself can accomplish a great deal."

He turned and hurried off through the rain-filled night. Mallory and Miller looked after him with expressionless faces, looked at each other, still with the same expressionless faces, then pushed open the swing doors of the barn.

The Mandrakos airfield would not have received a license from any Civil Air Board anywhere in the world. It was just over half a mile long, with hills rising steeply at both ends of the alleged runway, not more than forty yards wide and liberally besprinkled with a variety of bumps and potholes virtually guaranteed to wreck any undercarriage in the aviation business. But the R.A.F. had used it before so it was not impossible that they might be able to use it at least once again.

To the south, the airstrip was lined with groves of carob trees. Under the pitiful shelter afforded by one of those, Mallory, Miller and Andrea sat waiting. At least Mallory and Miller did, hunched, miserable and shivering violently in their still sodden clothes. Andrea, however, was stretched out luxuriously with his hands behind his head, oblivious of the heavy drips of rain that fell on his upturned face. There was about him an air of satisfaction, of complacency almost, as he gazed at the first greyish tinges appearing in the sky to the east over the black-walled massif of the Turkish coast.

Andrea said: "They're coming now."

Mallory and Miller listened for a few moments, then they too heard it— the distant, muted roar of heavy aircraft, approaching. All three rose and moved out to the perimeter of the airstrip. Within a minute, descending rapidly after their climb over the mountains to the south and at a height of less than a thousand feet, a squadron of eighteen Wellingtons, as much heard as seen in the light of early dawn, passed directly over the airstrip, heading for the town of Navarone. Two minutes later, the three watchers both heard the detonations and saw the brilliant orange mushrooming of light as the Wellingtons unloaded their bombs over the shattered fortress to the north. Sporadic lines of upward flying tracer, obviously exclusively small-arm, attested to the ineffectuality, the weakness of the ground defences. When the fortress had blown up, so had all the antiaircraft batteries in the town. The attack was short and sharp: less than two minutes after the bomardment had started it ceased as abruptly as it had begun and then there was only the fading dying sound of desynchronised engines as the Wellingtons pulled away, first to the north and then the west, across the still-dark waters of the Ægean.

For perhaps a minute the three watchers stood silent on the perimeter of the Mandrakos airstrip, then Miller said wonderingly: "What makes us so important?"

"I don't know," Mallory said. "But I don't think you're going to enjoy finding out."

"And that won't be long now." Andrea turned round and looked towards the mountains to the south. "Hear it?"

Neither of the others heard it, but they did not doubt that, in fact, there was something to hear. Andrea's hearing was on a par with his phenomenal eyesight. Then, suddenly, they could hear it, too. A solitary bomber—also a Wellington—came sinking in from the south, circled the perimeter area once as Mallory blinked his torch upward in rapidly successive flashes, lined up its approach, landed heavily at the far end of the airstrip and came taxiing towards them, bumping heavily across the atrocious surface of the airfield. It halted less than a hundred yards from where they stood: then a light started winking from the flight deck.

Andrea said: "Now, don't forget. I've promised to be back in a week."

"Never make promises," Miller said severely. "What if we aren't back in a week? What if they're sending us to the Pacific?"

"Then when we get back I'll send you in first to explain."

Miller shook his head. "I don't really think I'd like that."

"We'll talk about your cowardice later on," Mallory said. "Come on. Hurry up."

The three men broke into a run towards the waiting Wellington.

The Wellington was half an hour on the way to its destination, wherever its destination was, and Andrea and Miller, coffee mugs in hand, were trying, unsuccessfully, to attain a degree of comfort on the lumpy palliasses on the fuselage floor, when Mallory returned from the flight deck. Miller looked up at him in weary resignation, his expression characterised by an entire lack of enthusiasm and the spirit of adventure.

"Well, what did you find out?" His tone of voice made it abundantly clear that what he had expected Mallory to find out was nothing short of the very worst. "Where to, now? Rhodes? Beirut? The fleshpots of Cairo?"

"Termoli, the man says."

"Termoli, is it. Place I've always wanted to see." Miller paused. "Where the hell's Termoli?"

"Italy, so I believe. Somewhere on the South Adriatic coast."

"Oh, no!" Miller turned on his side and pulled a blanket over his head. "I *hate* spaghetti."

2
THURSDAY
1400–2330

The landing on Termoli airfield, on the Adriatic coast of southern Italy, was every bit as bumpy as the harrowing take-off from the Mandrakos airstrip had been. The Termoli fighter air base was officially and optimistically listed as newly constructed but in point of fact was no more than half-finished and felt that way for every yard of the excruciating touchdown and the jack rabbit run-up to the prefabricated control tower at the eastern end of the field. When Mallory and Andrea swung down to terra firma neither of them looked particularly happy: Miller, who came a very shaky last, and who was widely known to have an almost pathological loathing and detestation of all conceivable forms of transport, looked very ill indeed.

Miller was given time neither to seek nor receive commiseration. A camouflaged British Fifth Army jeep pulled up alongside the plane, and the sergeant at the wheel, having briefly established their identity, waved them inside in silence, a silence which he stonily maintained on their drive through the shambles of the war-torn streets of Termoli. Mallory was unperturbed by the apparent unfriendliness. The driver was obviously under the strictest instructions not to talk to them, a situation which Mallory had encountered all too often in the past. There were not, Mallory reflected, very many groups of untouchables, but his, he knew, was one of them: no one, with two or three rare exceptions, was ever permitted to talk to them. The process, Mallory knew, was perfectly understandable and justifiable, but it was an attitude that did tend to become increasingly wearing with the passing of the years. It tended to make for a certain lack of contact with one's fellow man.

After twenty minutes, the jeep stopped below the broad-flagged steps of a house on the outskirts of the town. The jeep driver gestured briefly to an armed sentry on the top of the steps who responded with a similarly perfunctory greeting. Mallory took this as a sign that they had arrived at their destination and, not wishing to violate the young sergeant's vow of silence, got out without being told. The others followed and the jeep at once drove off.

The house—it looked more like a modest palace—was a rather splendid example of late Renaissance architecture, all colonnades and columns and everything in veined marble, but Mallory was more interested in what was inside the house than what it was made of on the outside. At the head of the steps their path was barred by the young corporal sentry armed with a Lee-Enfield .303. He looked like a refugee from high school.

"Names, please."

"Captain Mallory."

"Identity papers? Pay books?"

"Oh, my God," Miller moaned. "And me feeling so sick, too."

"We have none," Mallory said gently. "Take us inside, please."

"My instructions are——"

"I know, I know," Andrea said soothingly. He leaned across, effortlessly removed the rifle from the corporal's desperate grasp, ejected and pocketed the magazine and returned the rifle. "Please, now."

Red-faced and furious, the youngster hesitated briefly, looked at the three men more carefully, turned, opened the door behind him and gestured for the three to follow him.

Before them stretched a long, marble-flagged corridor, tall leaded windows on one side, heavy oil paintings and the occasional set of double-leather doors on the other. Halfway down the passage Andrea tapped the corporal on the shoulder and handed the magazine back without a word. The corporal took it, smiling uncertainly, and inserted it into his rifle without a word. Another twenty paces and he stopped before the last pair of leather doors, knocked, heard a muffled acknowledgement and pushed open one of the doors, standing aside to let the three men pass him. Then he moved out again, closing the door behind him.

It was, obviously, the main drawing room of the house—or palace— furnished in an almost medieval opulence, all dark oak, heavily brocaded silk curtains, leather upholstery, leather-bound books, what were undoubtedly a set of old masters on the walls and a flowing sea of dull bronze carpeting from wall to wall. Taken all in all, even a member of the old prewar Italian nobility wouldn't have turned up his nose at it.

The room was pleasantly redolent with the smell of burning pine, the source of which wasn't difficult to locate: one could have roasted a very

large ox indeed in the vast and crackling hearth place at the far end of the
room. Close by this hearth place stood three young men who bore no
resemblance whatsoever to the rather ineffectual youngster who had so
recently tried to prevent their entry. They were, to begin with, a good few
years older, though still young men. They were heavily built, broad-shouldered characters and had about them a look of tough and hard-bitten competence. They were dressed in the uniform of that elite of combat troops,
the Marine Commandos, and they looked perfectly at home in those uniforms.

But what caught and held the unwavering attention of Mallory and his
two companions was neither the rather splendidly effete decadence of the
room and its furnishings nor the wholly unexpected presence of the three
commandos: it was the fourth figure in the room, a tall, heavily built and
commanding figure who leaned negligently against a table in the centre of
the room. The deeply trenched face, the authoritative expression, the splendid grey beard and the piercing blue eyes made him a prototype for the
classic British naval captain, which, as the immaculate white uniform he
wore indicated, was precisely what he was. With a collective sinking of
their hearts, Mallory, Andrea and Miller gazed again, and with a marked
lack of enthusiasm, upon the splendidly piratical figure of Captain Jensen,
R.N., Chief of Allied Intelligence, Mediterranean, and the man who had so
recently sent them on their suicidal mission to the island of Navarone. All
three looked at one another and shook their heads in slow despair.

Captain Jensen straightened, smiled his magnificent sabre-toothed tiger's
smile and strode forward to greet them, his hand outstretched.

"Mallory! Andrea! Miller!" There was a dramatic five-second pause
between the words. "I don't know what to say! I just don't know what to
say! A magnificent job, a magnificent——" He broke off and regarded
them thoughtfully. "You—um—don't seem all that surprised to see me,
Captain Mallory?"

"I'm not. With respects, sir, whenever and wherever there's dirty work
afoot, one looks to find——"

"Yes, yes, yes. Quite, quite. And how are you all?"

"Tired," Miller said firmly. "Terribly tired. We need a rest. At least, I
do."

Jensen said earnestly: "And that's exactly what you're going to have, my
boy. A rest. A long one. A very *long* one."

"A *very* long one?" Miller looked at him in frank incredulity.

"You have my word." Jensen stroked his beard in momentary diffidence.
"Just as soon, that is, as you get back from Yugoslavia."

"Yugoslavia!" Miller stared at him.

"Tonight."

"Tonight!"

"By parachute."

"By *parachute!*"

Jensen said with forbearance: "I am aware, Corporal Miller, that you
have had a classical education and are, moreover, just returned from the
Isles of Greece. But we'll do without the Ancient Greek Chorus bit, if you
don't mind."

Miller looked moodily at Andrea. "Bang goes your honeymoon."

"What was that?" Jensen asked sharply.

"Just a private joke, sir."

Mallory said in mild protest: "You're forgetting sir, that none of us has
ever made a parachute jump."

"I'm forgetting nothing. There's a first time for everything. What do you gentlemen know about the war in Yugoslavia?"

"What war?" Andrea said wearily.

"Precisely." There was satisfaction in Jensen's voice.

"I heard about it," Miller volunteered. "There's a bunch of what-do-you-call-'em—Partisans, isn't it—offering some kind of underground resistance to the German occupation troops."

"It is probably as well for you," Jensen said heavily, "that the Partisans cannot hear you. They're not underground, they're very much over ground and at the latest count there were 350,000 of them tying down twenty-eight German and Bulgarian divisions in Yugoslavia." He paused briefly. "More, in fact, than the combined Allied armies are tying down here in Italy."

"Somebody should have told me," Miller complained. He brightened. "If there are 350,000 of them around, what would they want us for?"

Jensen said acidly: "You must learn to curb your enthusiasm, Corporal. The fighting part of it you may leave to the Partisans—and they're fighting the cruellest, hardest, most brutal war in Europe today. A ruthless, vicious war with no quarter and no surrender on either side. Arms, munitions, food, clothes—the Partisans are desperately short of all of those. But they have those twenty-eight divisions pinned down."

"I don't want any part of that," Miller muttered.

Mallory said hastily: "What do you want us to do, sir?"

"This." Jensen removed his glacial stare from Miller. "Nobody appreciates it yet, but the Yugoslavs are our most important Allies in southern Europe. Their war is our war. And they're fighting a war they can never hope to win. Unless——"

Mallory nodded. "The tools to finish the job."

"Hardly original, but true. The tools to finish the job. We are the *only* people who are at present supplying them with rifles, machine guns, ammunition, clothing and medical supplies. And those are not getting through." He broke off, picked up a cane, walked almost angrily across the room to a large wall map hanging between a couple of old masters and rapped the tip of the bamboo against it. "Bosnia-Herzegovina, gentlemen. West-central Yugoslavia. We've sent in four British Military Missions in the past two months to liaise with the Yugoslavs—the Partisan Yugoslavs. The leaders of all four missions have disappeared without trace. Ninety percent of our recent air-lift supplies have fallen into German hands. They have broken all our radio codes and have established a network of agents in southern Italy here with whom they are apparently able to communicate as and when they wish. Perplexing questions, gentlemen. Vital questions. I want the answers. Force 10 will get me the answers."

"Force 10?" Mallory said politely.

"The code name for your operation."

"Why that particular name?" Andrea asked.

"Why not? Ever heard of *any* code name that had *any* bearing on the operation on hand. It's the whole essence of it, man."

"It wouldn't, of course," Mallory said woodenly, "have anything to do with a frontal attack on something, a storming of some vital place." He observed Jensen's total lack of reaction and went on in the same tone: "On the Beaufort scale, Force 10 means a storm."

"A storm!" It is very difficult to combine an exclamation and a moan of anguish in the same word, but Miller managed it without any difficulty. "Oh, my God, and all I want is a flat calm, and that for the rest of my life."

"There are limits to my patience, Corporal Miller," Jensen said. "I may—I say *may*—have to change my mind about a recommendation I made on your behalf this morning.''

''On my behalf?'' Miller said guardedly.

''For the Distinguished Conduct Medal.''

''*That* should look nice on the lid of my coffin,'' Miller muttered.

''What was that?''

''Corporal Miller was just expressing his appreciation.'' Mallory moved closer to the wall map and studied it briefly. ''Bosnia-Herzegovina—well, it's a fair-sized area, sir.''

''Agreed. But we càn pinpoint the spot—the approximate location of the disappearances—to within twenty miles.''

Mallory turned from the map and said slowly: ''There's been a lot of homework on this one. That raid this morning on Navarone. The Wellington standing by to take us here. All preparations—I infer this from what you've said—laid on for tonight. Not to mention——''

''We've been working on this for almost two months. You three were supposed to have come here some days ago. But—ah—well, you know.''

''We know.'' The threatened withholding of his D.C.M. had left Miller unmoved. ''Something else came up. Look, sir, why us? We're saboteurs, explosive experts, combat troops—this is a job for undercover espionage agents who speak Serbo-Croat or whatever.''

''You must allow me to be the best judge of that.'' Jensen gave them another flash of his sabre-toothed smile. ''Besides, you're lucky.''

''Luck deserts tired men,'' Andrea said. ''And we are very tired.''

''Tired or not, I can't find another team in southern Europe to match you for resource, experience and skill.'' Jensen smiled again. ''And luck. I have to be ruthless, Andrea. I don't like it, but I have to. But I take the point about your exhaustion. That's why I have decided to send a back-up team with you.''

Mallory looked at the three young soldiers standing by the hearth, then back to Jensen, who nodded.

''They're young, fresh and just raring to go. Marine Commandos, the most highly trained combat troops we have today. Remarkable variety of skills, I assure you. Take Reynolds, here.'' Jensen nodded to a very tall, dark sergeant in his late twenties, a man with a deeply tanned aquiline face. ''He can do anything from underwater demolition to flying a plane. And he will be flying a plane tonight. And, as you can see, he'll come in handy for carrying any heavy cases you have.''

Mallory said mildly: ''I've always found that Andrea makes a pretty fair porter, sir.''

Jensen turned to Reynolds. ''They have their doubts. Show them you can be of some use.''

''Reynolds hesitated, then stooped, picked up a heavy brass poker and proceeded to bend it between his hands. Obviously, it wasn't an easy poker to bend. His face turned red, the veins stood out on his forehead and the tendons in his neck, his arms quivered with the strain, but slowly, inexorably, the poker was bent into a figure ''U.'' Smiling almost apologetically, Reynolds handed the poker over to Andrea. Andrea took it reluctantly. He hunched his shoulders, his knuckles gleamed white but the poker remained in its ''U'' shape. Andrea looked up at Reynolds, his expression thoughtful, then quietly laid the poker down.

''See what I mean?'' Jensen said. ''Tired. Or Sergeant Groves here. Hot-foot from London, via the Middle East. Ex-Air Navigator, with all the latest in sabotage, explosives and electrics. For booby traps, time bombs and concealed microphones, a human mine detector. And Sergeant Saunders here—a top-flight radio operator."

Miller said morosely to Mallory: "You're a toothless old lion and you're over the hill."

"Don't talk rubbish, Corporal!" Jensen's voice was sharp. "Six is the ideal number. You'll be duplicated in every department, and those men are *good*. They'll be invaluable. If it's any salve to your pride, they weren't originally picked to go with you: they were picked as a reserve team in case you—un—well——"

"I see." The lack of conviction in Miller's voice was total.

"All clear, then?"

"Not quite," Mallory said. "Who's in charge?"

Jensen said in genuine surprise: "You are, of course."

"So." Mallory spoke quietly and pleasantly. "I understand the training emphasis today—especially in the Marine Commandos—is on initiative, self-reliance, independence in thought and action. Fine—if they happen to be caught out on their own." He smiled, almost deprecating. "Otherwise I shall expect immediate, unquestioning and total compliance with orders. My orders. Instant and total."

"And if not?" Reynolds asked.

"A superfluous question, sergeant. You know the wartime penalty for disobeying an officer in the field."

"Does that apply to your friends, too?"

"No."

Reynolds turned to Jensen. "I don't think I like that, sir."

Mallory sank wearily into a chair, lit a cigarette, nodded at Reynolds, and said, "Replace him."

"What!" Jensen was incredulous.

"Replace him, I said. We haven't even left and already he's questioning my judgment. What's it going to be like in action? He's dangerous. I'd rather carry a ticking time bomb with me."

"Now, look here, Mallory——"

"Replace him or replace me."

"And me," Andrea said quietly.

"And me," Miller added.

There was a brief and far from companionable silence in the room, then Reynolds approached Mallory's chair.

"Sir."

Mallory looked at him without encouragement.

"I'm sorry," Reynolds went on. "I stepped out of line. I will never make the same mistake twice. I *want* to go on this trip, sir."

Mallory glanced at Andrea and Miller. Miller's face registered only his shock at Reynolds' incredibly foolhardy enthusiasm for action. Andrea, impassive as ever, nodded almost imperceptibly. Mallory smiled and said: "As Captain Jensen said, I'm sure you'll be a great asset."

"Well, that's it, then." Jensen affected not to notice the almost palpable relaxation of tension in the room. "Sleep's the thing now. But first I'd like a few minutes' report on Navarone, you know." He looked at the three sergeants. "Confidential, I'm afraid."

"Yes, sir," Reynolds said. "Shall we go down to the field, check flight plans, weather, parachutes and supplies."

Jensen nodded. As the three sergeants closed the double doors behind them, Jensen crossed to a side door, opened it and said: "Come in, General."

The man who entered was very tall, very gaunt. He was probably about thirty-five, but looked a great deal older. The care, the exhaustion, the endless privations inseparable from too many years' ceaseless struggle for survival had heavily silvered the once black hair and deeply etched into the swarthy sunburnt face the lines of physical and mental suffering. The eyes were dark and glowing and intense, the hypnotic eyes of a man inspired by a fanatical dedication to some as yet unrealised ideal. He was dressed in a British Army officer's uniform, bereft of insignia and badges.

Jensen said: "Gentlemen, General Vukalovic. The general is second-in-command of the Partisan forces in Bosnia-Herzegovina. The R.A.F. flew him out yesterday. He is here as a Partisan doctor seeking medical supplies. His true identity is known only to us. General, those are your men."

Vukalovic looked them over severely and steadily, his face expressionless. He said: "Those are tired men, Captain Jensen. So much depends . . . too tired to do what has to be done."

"He's right, you know," Miller said earnestly.

"There's maybe a little mileage left in them yet," Jensen said mildly. "It's a long haul from Navarone. Now, then——"

"Navarone?" Vukalovic interrupted. "These—these are the men——"

"An unlikely looking lot, I agree."

"Perhaps I was wrong about them."

"No, you weren't, General," Miller said. "We're exhausted. We're completely——"

"Do you mind?" Jensen said acidly. "Captain Mallory. With two exceptions the general will be the only person in Bosnia who knows who you are and what you are doing. Whether the general reveals the identity of the others is entirely up to him. General Vukalovic will be accompanying you to Yugoslavia, but not in the same planes."

"Why not?" Mallory asked.

"Because his plane will be returning. Yours won't."

"Ah!" Mallory said. There was a brief silence while he, Andrea and Miller absorbed the significance behind Jensen's words. Abstractedly, Andrea threw some more wood on the sinking fire and looked around for a poker: but the only poker was the one that Reynolds had already bent into a "U"-shape. Andrea picked it up. Absentmindedly, effortlessly, Andrea straightened it out, poked the fire into a blaze and laid the poker down, a performance Vukalovic watched with a very thoughtful expression on his face.

Jensen went on: "Your plane, Captain Mallory, will not be returning because your plane is expendable in the interests of authenticity."

"Us, too?" Miller asked.

"You won't be able to accomplish very much, Corporal Miller, without actually putting your feet on the ground. Where you're going, no plane can possibly land: so you jump—and the plane crashes."

"That sounds very authentic," Miller muttered.

Jensen ignored him. "The realities of total war are harsh beyond belief. Which is why I sent those three youngsters on their way—I don't want to dampen their enthusiasm."

"Mine's waterlogged," Miller said dolefully.

"Oh, do be quiet. Now, it would be fine if, by way of a bonus, you could discover why 80 percent of our air-drops fall into the German hands, fine if you could locate and rescue our captured mission leaders. But not important. Those supplies, those agents are militarily expendable. What are not expendable are the 7000 men under the command of General Vukalovic here, 7000 men trapped in an area called the Zenica Cage, 7000 starving men with almost no ammunition left, 7000 men with no future.''

"*We* can help them?" Andrea asked heavily. "Six men?"

Jensen said candidly: "I don't know."

"But you have a plan?"

"Not yet. Not as such. The glimmerings of an idea. No more." Jensen rubbed his forehead wearily. "I myself arrived from Alexandria only six hours ago." He hesitated, then shrugged. "By tonight, who knows? A few hours' sleep this afternoon might transform us all. But, first, the report on Navarone. It would be pointless for you other three gentlemen to wait—there are sleeping quarters down the hall. I daresay Captain Mallory can tell me all I want to know."

Mallory waited till the door closed behind Andrea, Miller and Vukalovic, and said: "Where shall I begin my report, sir?"

"What report?"

"Navarone, of course."

"The hell with Navarone. That's over and done with." He picked up his cane, crossed to the wall, pulled down two more maps. "Now, then."

"You—you *have* a plan," Mallory said carefully.

"Of course I have a plan," Jensen said coldly. He rapped the map in front of him. "Ten miles north of here. The Gustav line. Right across Italy along the line of the Sangro and Liri rivers. Here the Germans have the most impregnable defensive positions in the history of modern warfare. Monte Cassino here—our finest Allied divisions have broken on it, some forever. And here—the Anzio beachhead. Fifty thousand Americans fighting for their lives. For five solid months now we've been battering our heads against the Gustav line and the Anzio perimeter. Our losses in men and machines—incalculable. Our gains—not one solitary inch."

Mallory said diffidently: "You mentioned something about Yugoslavia, sir."

"I'm coming to that," Jensen said with restraint. "Now, our only hope of breaching the Gustav line is by weakening the German defensive forces and the only way we can do *that* is by persuading them to withdraw some of their frontline divisions. So we practice the Allenby technique."

"I see."

"You don't see at all. General Allenby, Palestine, 1918. He had an east-west line from the Jordan to the Mediterranean. He planned to attack from the west—so he convinced the Turks the attack was coming from the east. He did this by building up in the east a huge city of army tents occupied by only a few hundred men who came out and dashed around like beavers whenever enemy planes came over on reconnaissance. He did this by letting the same planes see large army truck convoys pouring to the east all day long—what the Turks didn't know was that the same convoys poured back to the west all night long. He even had fifteen thousand canvas dummies of horses built. Well, we're doing the same."

"Fifteen thousand canvas horses?"

"Very, very amusing." Jensen rapped the map again. "Every airfield between here and Bari is jammed with dummy bombers and gliders. Outside Foggia, is the biggest military encampment in Italy—occupied by two hundred men. The harbours of Bari and Taranto are crowded with assault landing craft, the whole lot made of plywood. All day long columns of trucks and tanks converge on the Adriatic coast. If you, Mallory, were in the German High Command, what would you make of this?"

"I'd suspect an airborne and sea invasion of Yugoslavia. But I wouldn't be sure."

"The German reaction exactly," Jensen said with some satisfaction. "They're badly worried, worried to the extent that they have already transferred two divisions from Italy to Yugoslavia to meet the threat."

"But they're not certain?"

"Not quite. But almost." Jensen cleared his throat. "You see, our four captured mission leaders were all carrying unmistakable evidence pointing to an invasion of central Yugoslavia in early May."

"They carried evidence———" Mallory broke off, looked at Jensen for a long and speculative moment, then went on quietly: "And how *did* the Germans manage to capture them all?"

"We told them they were coming."

"You did what!"

"Volunteers all, volunteers all," Jensen said quickly. There were, apparently, some of the harsher realities of total war that even he didn't care to dwell on too long. "And it will be your job, my boy, to turn near-conviction into absolute certainty." Seemingly oblivious of the fact that Mallory was regarding him with a marked lack of enthusiasm, he wheeled round dramatically and stabbed his cane at a large-scale map of central Yugoslavia.

"The valley of the Neretva," Jensen said. "The vital sector of the main north-south route through Yugoslavia, and whoever controls this valley controls Yugoslavia—and no one knows this better than the Germans. If the blow falls, they know, it must fall here. They are fully aware that an invasion of Yugoslavia is on the cards, they are terrified of a link-up between the Allies and the Russians advancing from the East and they *know* that any such link-up must be along this valley. They already have two armoured divisions along the Neretva, two divisions that, in the event of invasion, could be wiped out in a night. From the north—here—they are trying to force their way south to the Neretva with a whole Army Corps—but the only way is through the Zenica Cage here. And Vukalovic and his 7000 men block the way."

"Vukalovic knows about this?" Mallory asked. "About what you really have in mind, I mean?"

"Yes. And the Partisan command. They know the risks, the odds against them. They accept them."

"Photographs?" Mallory asked.

"Here." Jensen pulled some photographs from a desk drawer, selected one and smoothed it out on the table. "This is the Zenica Cage. Wellnamed: a perfect cage, a perfect trap. To the North and West, impassable mountains. To the East, the Neretva Dam and the Neretva Gorge. To the South, the Neretva River. To the North of the cage here, at the Zenica Gap, the German 11th Army Corps are trying to break through. To the West here—they call it the West Gap—more units of the 11th trying to do the same. And to the South here, over the river and hidden in the trees, two armoured divisions under a General Zimmerman."

"And this?" Mallory pointed to a thin black line spanning the river just north of the two armoured divisions.

"That," Jensen said thoughtfully, "is the bridge at Neretva."

Close-up, the bridge at Neretva looked vastly more impressive than it had done in the large-scale photograph: it was a massively cantilevered structure in solid steel, with a black asphalt roadway laid on top. Below the bridge rushed the swiftly flowing Neretva, greenish-white in colour and swollen with melting snow. To the south there was a narrow strip of green meadowland bordering the river and, to the south of this again, a dark and towering pine forest began. In the safe concealment of the forest's gloomy depths, General Zimmerman's two armoured divisions crouched, waiting.

Parked close to the edge of the wood was the divisional command radio truck, a bulky and very long vehicle so beautifully camouflaged as to be invisible at more than twenty paces.

General Zimmerman and his A.D.C., Captain Warburg, were at that moment inside the truck. Their mood appeared to match the permanent twilight of the woods. Zimmerman had one of those high-foreheaded, lean and aquiline and intelligent faces which so rarely betray any emotion, but there was no lack of emotion now, no lack of anxiety and impatience as he removed his cap and ran his hand through his thinning grey hair. He said to the radio operator seated behind the big transceiver:

"No word yet? Nothing?"

"Nothing, sir."

"You are in constant touch with Captain Neufeld's camp?"

"Every minute, sir."

"And his operator is keeping a continuous radio watch?"

"All the time, sir. Nothing. Just nothing."

Zimmerman turned and descended the steps, followed by Warburg. He walked, head down, until he was out of earshot of the truck, then said: "Damn it! Damn it! God damn it all!"

"You're as sure as that, sir." Warburg was tall, good-looking, flaxen-haired and thirty, and his face at the moment reflected a nice balance of apprehension and unhappiness. "That they're coming?"

"It's in my bones, boy. One way or another it's coming, coming for all of us."

"You can't be *sure* sir," Warburg protested.

"True enough." Zimmerman sighed. "I can't be sure. But I'm sure of this. If they do come, if the 11th Army Corps can't break through from the North, if we can't wipe out those damned Partisans in the Zenica Cage——"

Warburg waited for him to continue, but Zimmerman seemed lost in reverie. Apparently apropos of nothing, Warburg said: "I'd like to see Germany again, sir. Just once more."

"Wouldn't we all, my boy, wouldn't we all." Zimmerman walked slowly to the edge of the wood and stopped. For a long time he gazed out over the bridge at Neretva. Then he shook his head, turned and was almost at once lost to sight in the dark depths of the forest.

The pine fire in the great hearth place in the drawing room in Termoli was burning low. Jensen threw on some more logs, straightened, poured two drinks, and handed one to Mallory.

Jensen said: "Well?"

"That's the plan?" No hint of his incredulity, of his near-despair, showed in Mallory's impassive face. "That's *all* of the plan?"

"Yes."

"Your health." Mallory paused. "And mine." After an even longer pause he said reflectively: "It should be interesting to watch Dusty Miller's reaction when he hears about this little lot this evening."

As Mallory had said, Miller's reactions were interesting, even if wholly predictable. Some six hours later, clad now, like Mallory and Andrea, in British Army uniform, Miller listened in visibly growing horror as Jensen outlined what he regarded should be their proposed course of action in the next twenty-four hours or so. When he had finished, Jensen looked directly at Miller and said: "Well? Feasible?"

"Feasible?" Miller was aghast. "It's suicidal!"

"Andrea?"

Andrea shrugged, lifted his hands palms upward and said nothing.

Jensen nodded and said: "I'm sorry, but I'm fresh out of options. We'd better go. The others are waiting at the airstrip."

Andrea and Miller left the room, began to walk down the long passage-way. Mallory hesitated in the doorway, momentarily blocking it, then turned to face Jensen who was watching him with a surprised lift of the eyebrows.

Mallory said in a low voice: "Let me tell Andrea, at least."

Jensen looked at him for a considering moment or two, shook his head briefly and brushed by into the corridor.

Twenty minutes later, without a further word being spoken, the four men arrived at the Termoli airstrip to find Vukalovic and two sergeants waiting for them: the third, Reynolds, was already at the controls of the Wellington, one of two standing at the end of the airstrip, propellers already turning. Ten minutes later both planes were airborne, Vukalovic in one, Mallory, Miller, Andrea, and the three sergeants in the other, each plane bound for its separate destination.

Jensen, alone on the tarmac, watched both planes climbing, his straining eyes following them until they disappeared into the overcast darkness of the moonless sky above. Then, just as General Zimmerman had done that afternoon, he shook his head in slow finality, turned and walked heavily away.

3

FRIDAY

0030–0200

SERGEANT REYNOLDS, Mallory reflected, certainly knew how to handle a plane, especially this one. Although his eyes showed him to be always watchful and alert, he was precise, competent, calm and relaxed in every-thing he did. No less competent was Groves: the poor light and cramped confines of his tiny plotting table clearly didn't worry him at all and as an air navigator he was quite clearly as experienced as he was proficient. Mallory peered forward through the windscreen, saw the white-capped wa-ters of the Adriatic rushing by less than a hundred feet beneath their fuse-lage, and turned to Groves.

"The flight plan calls for us to fly as low as this?"

"Yes. The Germans have radar installations on some of the outlying islands off the Yugoslav coast. We start climbing when we reach Dalmatia."

Mallory nodded his thanks, turned to watch Reynolds again. He said, curiously: "Captain Jensen was right about you. As a pilot. How on earth does a Marine Commando come to learn to drive one of those things?"

"I've had plenty of practice," Reynolds said. "Three years in the R.A.F., two of them as sergeant-pilot in a Wellington bomber squadron. One day in Egypt I took a Lysander up without permission. People did it all the time— but the crate I'd picked had a defective fuel gauge."

"You were grounded?"

"With great speed." He grinned. "There were no objections when I applied for a service transfer. I think they felt I wasn't somehow quite right for the R.A.F."

Mallory looked at Groves. "And you?"

Groves smiled broadly. "I was his navigator in that old crate. We were fired on the same day."

Mallory said consideringly: "Well, I should think that might be rather useful."

"What's useful?" Reynolds asked.

"The fact that you're used to this feeling of disgrace. It'll enable you to act your part all the better when the time comes. If the times comes."

Reynolds said carefully: "I'm not quite sure——"

"Before we jump, I want you—all of you—to remove every distinguishing badge or emblem of rank on your clothes." He gestured to Andrea and Miller at the rear of the flight deck to indicate that they were included as well, then looked at Reynolds again. "Sergeant's stripes, regimental flashes, medal ribbons—the lot."

"Why the hell should I?" Reynolds, Mallory thought, had the lowest boiling point he'd come across in quite some time. "I *earned* those stripes, those ribbons, that flash. I don't see——"

Mallory smiled. "Disobeying an officer on active service?"

"Don't be so damned touchy," Reynolds said.

"Don't be so damned touchy, *sir*."

"Don't be so damned touchy, *sir*." Reynolds suddenly grinned. "O.K., so who's got the scissors?"

"You see," Mallory explained, "the last thing we want to happen is to fall into enemy hands."

"Amen," Miller intoned.

"But if we're to get the information we want we're going to have to operate close to or even inside their lines. We might get caught. So we have our cover story."

Groves said quietly: "Are we permitted to know just what that cover story is, sir?"

"Of course, you are," Mallory said in exasperation. He went on earnestly: "Don't you realise that, on a mission like this, survival depends on one thing and one thing only—complete and mutual trust? As soon as we start having secrets from each other—we're finished."

In the deep gloom at the rear of the flight deck, Andrea and Miller glanced at each other and exchanged their wearily cynical smiles.

As Mallory left the flight deck for the fuselage, his right hand brushed Miller's shoulder. After about two minutes Miller yawned, stretched and made his way aft. Mallory was waiting towards the rear of the fuselage. He had two pieces of folded paper in his hand, one of which he opened and showed to Miller, snapping on a flashlight at the same time. Miller stared at it for some moments, then lifted an eyebrow.

"And what is this supposed to be?"

"It's the triggering mechanism for a 750 pound submersible mine. Learn it by heart."

Miller looked at it without expression, then glanced at the other paper Mallory held.

"And what have you there?"

Mallory showed him. It was a large scale map, the central feature of which appeared to be a winding lake with a very long eastern arm which bent abruptly at right angles into a very short southern arm, which in turn ended abruptly at what appeared to be a dam wall. Beneath the dam, a river flowed away through a winding gorge.

Mallory said: "What does it look like to you? Show them both to Andrea and tell him to destroy them."

Mallory left Miller engrossed in his homework and moved forward again to the flight deck. He bent over Groves' chart table.

"Still on course?"

"Yes, sir. We're just clearing the southern tip of the island of Hvar. You can see a few lights on the mainland ahead." Mallory followed the pointing hand, located a few clusters of lights, then reached out a hand to steady himself as the Wellington started to climb sharply. He glanced at Reynolds.

"Climbing now, sir. There's some pretty lofty stuff ahead. We should pick up the Partisan landing lights in about half an hour."

"Thirty-three minutes," Groves said. "One-twenty near enough."

For almost half an hour Mallory remained on a jump seat in the flight deck, just looking ahead. After a few minutes Andrea disappeared and did not reappear. Miller did not return. Groves navigated, Reynolds flew, Saunders listened in to his portable transceiver and nobody talked at all. At one fifteen Mallory rose, touched Saunders on the shoulder, told him to pack up his gear and headed aft. He found Andrea and a thoroughly miserable-looking Miller with their parachute snap catches already clipped on to the jumping wire. Andrea had the door pulled back and was throwing out tiny pieces of shredded paper which swirled away in the slipstream. Mallory shivered in the suddenly intense cold. Andrea grinned, beckoned him to the open doorway and pointed downward. He yelled in Mallory's ear: "There's a lot of snow down there."

There was indeed a lot of snow down there. Mallory understood now Jensen's insistence on not landing a plane in those parts. The terrain below was rugged in the extreme, consisting almost entirely of a succession of deep and winding valleys and steep-sided mountains. Maybe half of the landscape below was covered in dense forests of pine trees: all of it was covered in what appeared to be a very heavy blanket of snow. Mallory drew back into the comparative shelter of the Wellington's fuselage and glanced at his watch.

"One sixteen." Like Andrea he had to shout.

"Your watch is a little fast, maybe?" Miller bawled unhappily. Mallory shook his head, Miller shook his. A bell rang and Mallory made his way to the flight deck, passing Saunders going the other way. As Mallory entered, Reynolds looked briefly over his shoulder then pointed directly ahead. Mallory bent over his shoulder and peered forward and downward. He nodded.

The three lights, in the form of an elongated V, were still some miles ahead, but quite unmistakable. Mallory turned, touched Groves on the shoulder and pointed aft. Groves rose and left. Mallory said to Reynolds: "Where are the red and green jumping lights?"

Reynolds indicated them.

"Press the red light. How long?"

"Thirty seconds. About."

Mallory looked ahead again. The lights were less than half as distant as they had been when first he'd looked. He said to Reynolds: "Automatic pilot. Close the fuel switches."

"Close the—for all the petrol that's left——"

"Shut off the bloody tanks! And get aft. Five seconds."

Reynolds did as he was told. Mallory waited, briefly made a last check of the landing lights ahead, rose and made his way swiftly aft. By the time he reached the jump door, even Reynolds, the last of the first five, was gone. Mallory clipped on his snap catch, braced his hands round the edge of the doorway and launched himself out into the bitter Bosnian night.

The sudden jarring impact from the parachute harness made him look quickly upward: the concave circle of a fully open parachute was a reassuring spectacle. He glanced downwards and saw the equally reassuring spectacle of another five open parachutes, two of which were swaying quite wildly across the sky—just as was his own. There were some things, he reflected, about which he, Andrea and Miller had a great deal to learn. Controlling parachute descents was one of those things.

He looked up and to the east to see if he could locate the Wellington, but it was no longer visible. Suddenly, as he looked and listened, both engines, almost in perfect unison, cut out. Long seconds passed when the only sound was the rush of the wind in his ears, then there came an explosively metallic sound as the bomber crashed either into the ground or into some unseen mountainside ahead. There was no fire or none that he could see; just the crash, then silence. For the first time that night, the moon broke through.

Andrea landed heavily on an uneven piece of ground, rolled over twice, rose rather experimentally to his feet, discovered he was still intact, pressed the quick release button of his parachute, then automatically, instinctively—Andrea had a built-in computer for assuring survival—swung through a complete 360° circle. But no immediate danger threatened, or none that he could see. Andrea made a more leisurely survey of their landing spot.

They had, he thought grimly, been most damnably lucky. Another hundred yards to the south and they'd have spent the rest of the night, and for all he knew, the rest of the war, clinging to the tops of the most impossibly tall pine trees he had ever seen. As it was, luck had been with them and they had landed in a narrow clearing which abutted closely on the rocky scarp of a mountainside.

Or rather, all but one. Perhaps fifty yards from where Andrea had landed, an apex of the forest elbowed its way into the clearing. The outermost tree in this apex had come between one of the parachutists and terra firma. Andrea's eyebrows lifted in quizzical astonishment, then he broke into an ambling run.

The parachutist who had come to grief was dangling from the lowermost bow of the pine. He had his hands twisted in the shrouds, his legs bent, knees and ankles close together in the classic landing position, his feet perhaps thirty inches from the ground. His eyes were screwed tightly shut. Corporal Miller seemed acutely unhappy.

Andrea came up and touched him on the shoulder, gently. Miller opened his eyes and glanced at Andrea, who pointed downward. Miller followed his glance and lowered his legs, which were then four inches from the ground. Andrea produced a knife, sliced through the shreds and Miller completed the remainder of his journey. He straightened his jacket, his face splendidly impassive, and lifted an enquiring elbow. Andrea, his face equally impassive, pointed down the clearing. Three of the other four parachutists had already landed safely: the fourth, Mallory, was just touching down.

Two minutes later, just as all six were coming together some little distance away from the most easterly landing flare, a shout announced the appearance of a young soldier running towards them from the edge of the forest. The parachutists' guns came up and were almost immediately lowered again: this was no occasion for guns. The soldier was trailing his by the barrel, excitedly waving his free hand in greeting. He was dressed in a faded and tattered near-uniform that had been pillaged from a variety of armies, had long flowing hair, a cast to his right eye and a straggling ginger beard. That he was welcoming them, was beyond doubt. Repeating some incomprehensible greeting over and over again, he shook hands all round and then a second time, the huge grin on his face reflecting his delight.

Within thirty seconds he'd been joined by at least a dozen others, all bearded, all dressed in the same nondescript uniforms, no two of which were alike, all in the same almost festive mood. Then, as at a signal almost, they fell silent and drew slightly apart as the man who was obviously their leader appeared from the edge of the forest. He bore little resemblance to his men. He differed in that he was completely shaven and wore a uniform, a British battle dress, which appeared to be all of one piece. He differed in that he was not smiling: he had about him the air of one who was seldom if ever given to smiling. He also differed from the others in that he was a hawk-faced giant of a man, at least six feet four inches in height, carrying no fewer than four wicked-looking Bowie-type knives in his belt—an excess of armament that on another man might have looked incongruous or even comical but which on this man provoked no mirth at all. His face was dark and sombre and when he spoke it was in English, slow and stilted, but precise.

"Good evening." He looked round questioningly. "I am Captain Droshny."

Mallory took a step forward. "Captain Mallory."

"Welcome to Yugoslavia, Captain Mallory—Partisan Yugoslavia." Droshny nodded towards the dying flare, his face twitched in what may have been an attempt at a smile; but he made no move to shake hands. "As you can see, we were expecting you."

"Your lights were a great help," Mallory acknowledged.

"Thank you." Droshny stared away to the east, then back to Mallory, shaking his head. "A pity about the plane."

"All war is a pity."

Droshny nodded. "Come. Our headquarters is close by."

No more was said. Droshny, leading, moved at once into the shelter of the forest. Mallory, behind him, was intrigued by the footprints, clearly visible in the now bright moonlight, left by Droshny in the deep snow. They were, thought Mallory, most peculiar. Each sole left three V-shaped marks, the heel one: the right-hand side of the leading V on the right sole had a clearly defined break in it. Unconsciously, Mallory filed away this little oddity in his mind. There was no reason why he should have done so other than that the Mallorys of this world always observe and record the unusual. It helps them to stay alive.

The slope steepened, the snow deepened and the pale moonlight filtered thinly down through the spreading, snow-laden branches of the pines. The light wind was from the East: the cold was intense. For almost ten minutes no voice was heard, then Droshny's came, softly but clearly and imperative in its staccato urgency.

"Be still." He pointed dramatically upward. "Be still! Listen!"

They stopped, looked upward and listened intently. At least, Mallory and his men looked upward and listened intently, but the Yugoslavs had other things on their minds: swiftly, efficiently and simultaneously, without either spoken or gestured command being given, they rammed the muzzles of their machine guns and rifles into the sides and backs of the six parachutists with a force and uncompromising authority that rendered any accompanying orders quite superfluous.

The six men reacted as might have been expected. Reynolds, Groves and Saunders, who were rather less accustomed to the vicissitudes of fate than their three older companions, registered a very similar combination of startled anger and open-mouthed astonishment. Mallory looked thoughtful. Miller lifted a quizzical eyebrow. Andrea, predictably, registered nothing at all: he was too busy exhibiting his usual reaction to physical violence.

His right hand, which he had instantly lifted halfway to his shoulder in an apparent token of surrender, clamped down on the barrel of the rifle of the guard to his left, forcing it away from him, while his left elbow jabbed viciously into the solar plexus of the guard to his left, who gasped in pain and staggered back a couple of paces. Andrea, with both hands now on the rifle of the other guard, wrenched it effortlessly free, lifted it high and brought the barrel down in one continuous blur of movement. The guard collapsed as if a bridge had fallen on him. The winded guard to the left, still bent and whooping in agony, was trying to line up his rifle when the butt of Andrea's rifle struck him in the face: he made a brief coughing sound and fell senseless to the forest floor.

It took all of the three seconds that this action had lasted for the Yugoslavs to release themselves from their momentary thrall of incredulity. Half-a-dozen soldiers flung themselves on Andrea, bearing him to the ground. In the furious, rolling struggle that followed, Andrea laid about him in his usual willing fashion but when one of the Yugoslavs started pounding him on the head with the barrel of a pistol, Andrea elected for discretion and lay still. With two guns in his back and four hands on either arm Andrea was dragged to his feet: two of his captors already looked very much the worse for wear.

Droshny, his eyes bleak and bitter, came up to Andrea, unsheathed one of his knives and thrust its point against Andrea's throat with a force savage enough to break the skin and draw blood that trickled on to the gleaming blade. For a moment it seemed that Droshny would push the knife home to the hilt, then his eyes moved sideways and downwards to look at the two huddled men lying in the snow. He nodded to the nearest man.

"How are they?"

A young Yugoslav dropped to his knees, looked first at the man who had been struck by the rifle barrel, touched his head briefly, examined the second man, then stood up. In the filtered moonlight, his face was unnaturally pale.

"Josef is dead. I think his neck is broken. And his brother—he's breathing—but his jaw seems to be——" The voice trailed away uncertainly.

Droshny transferred his gaze back to Andrea. His lips drew back, he smiled the way a wolf smiles and leaned a little harder on the knife.

"I *should* kill you now. I *will* kill you later." He sheathed his knife, held up his clawed hands in front of Andrea's face, and shouted: "Personally. With those hands."

"With those hands." Slowly, meaningfully, Andrea examined the four pairs of hands pinioning his arms, then looked contemptuously at Droshny. He said: "Your courage terrifies me."

There was a brief and unbelieving silence. The three young sergeants stared at the tableau before them with faces reflecting various degrees of consternation and incredulity. Mallory and Miller looked on impassively. For a moment or two, Droshny looked as if he hadn't heard aright, then his face twisted in savage anger as he struck Andrea backhanded across the face. Immediately a trickle of blood appeared at the right-hand corner of Andrea's mouth but Andrea himself remained unmoving, his face without expression.

Droshny's eyes narrowed. Andrea smiled again, briefly. Droshny struck again, this time with the back of the other hand. The effect was as before, with the exception that this time the trickle of blood came from the left-hand corner of the mouth. Andrea smiled again but to look into his eyes was to look into an open grave. Droshny wheeled and walked away, then halted as he approached Mallory.

"You *are* the leader of those men, Captain Mallory?"

"I am."

"You're a very—*silent* leader, Captain?"

"What am I to say to a man who turns his guns on his friends and allies." Mallory looked at him dispassionately. "I'll talk to your commanding officer, not to a madman."

Droshny's face darkened. He stepped forward, his arm lifted to strike. Very quickly, but so smoothly and calmly that the movement seemed unhurried, and totally ignoring the two rifle muzzles pressing into his side, Mallory lifted his Luger and pointed it at Droshny's face. The click of the Luger safety catch being released came like a hammer blow in the suddenly unnatural intensity of silence.

And unnatural intensity of silence there was. Except for one little movement, so slow as to be almost imperceptible, both Partisans and parachutists had frozen into a tableau that would have done credit to the frieze on an Ionic temple. The three sergeants, like most of the Partisans, registered astonished incredulity. The two men guarding Mallory looked at Droshny with questioning eyes. Droshny looked at Mallory as if he were mad. Andrea wasn't looking at anyone, while Miller wore that look of world-weary detachment which only he could achieve. But it was Miller who made that one little movement, a movement that now came to an end with his thumb resting on his Schmeisser's safety release. After a moment or two he removed his thumb: there would come a time for Schmeissers, but this wasn't it.

Droshny lowered his hand in a curious slow-motion gesture and took two paces backward. His face was still dark with anger, the dark eyes cruel and unforgiving, but he had himself well in hand. He said: "Don't you know we have to take precautions? Till we are satisfied with your identity?"

"How should I know that?" Mallory nodded at Andrea. "Next time you tell your men to take precautions with my friend here, you might warn them to stand a little farther back. He reacted the only way he knows how. And I know why."

"You can explain later. Hand over your guns."

"No." Mallory returned the Luger to its holster.

"Are you mad? I can take them from you."

"That's so," Mallory said reasonably. "But you'd have to kill us first, wouldn't you? I don't think you'd remain a captain very long, my friend."

Speculation replaced anger in Droshny's eyes. He gave a sharp order in Serbo-Croat and again his soldiers levelled their guns on Mallory and his five companions. But they made no attempt to remove the prisoners' guns. Droshny turned, gestured, and started moving up the steeply sloping forest floor again. Droshny wasn't, Mallory reflected, a man likely to be given to taking too many chances.

For twenty minutes they scrambled awkwardly up the slippery hillside. A voice called out from the darkness ahead and Droshny answered without breaking step. They passed by two sentires armed with machine carbines and, within a minute, were in Droshny's HQ.

It was a moderately sized military encampment—if a wide circle of rough-hewn adze-cut cabins could be called an encampment—set in one of those very deep hollows in the forest floor that Mallory was to find so characteristic of the Bosnian area. From the base of this hollow grew two concentric rings of pines far taller and more massive than anything to be found in western Europe, massive pines whose massive branches interlocked eighty to a hundred feet above the ground, forming a snow-shrouded canopy of such impenetrable density that there wasn't even a dusting of snow on the hard-packed earth of the camp compound: by the same token, the same canopy also effectively prevented any upward escape of light: there was no attempt at any blackout in several illuminated cabin windows and there were even some oil lamps suspended on outside hooks to illuminate the compound itself. Droshny stopped and said to Mallory:

"You come with me. The rest of you stay here."

He led Mallory towards the door of the largest hut in the compound. Andrea, unbidden, slipped off his pack and sat on it, and the others, after various degrees of hesitation, did the same. Their guards looked them over uncertainly, then withdrew to form a ragged but watchful semicircle. Reynolds turned to Andrea, the expression on his face registering a complete absence of admiration and good will.

"You're crazy." Reynolds voice came in a low furious whisper. "Crazy as a loon. You could have got yourself killed. You could have got all of us killed. What are you, shell-shocked or something?"

Andrea did not reply. He lit one of his obnoxious cigars and regarded Reynolds with mild speculation or as near an approach to mildness as it was possible for him to achieve.

"Crazy isn't half the word for it." Groves, if anything, was even more heated than Reynolds. "Or didn't you *know* that was a Partisan you killed? Don't you *know* what that means? Don't you *know* people like that must always take precautions?"

Whether he knew or not, Andrea wasn't saying. He puffed at his cigar and transferred his peaceable gaze from Reynolds to Groves.

Miller said soothingly: "Now, now. Don't be like that. Maybe Andrea *was* a mite hasty but——"

"God help us all," Reynolds said fervently. He looked at his fellow sergeants in despair. "A thousand miles from home and help and saddled with a trigger-happy bunch of has-beens." He turned back to Miller and mimicked: " 'Don't be like that.' "

Miller assumed his wounded expression and looked away.

The room was large and bare and comfortless. The only concession to comfort was a pine fire crackling in a rough hearth place. The only furniture consisted of a cracked deal table, two chairs and a bench.

Those things Mallory noted only subconsciously. He didn't even register when he heard Droshny say: "Captain Mallory. This is my commanding officer." He seemed to be too busy staring at the man seated behind the table.

The man was short, stocky and in his mid-thirties. The deep lines around eyes and mouth could have been caused by weather or humour or both: just at that moment he was smiling slightly. He was dressed in the uniform of a captain in the German Army and wore an Iron Cross at his throat.

4

FRIDAY

0200–0330

THE GERMAN captain leaned back in his chair and steepled his fingers. He had the air about him of a man enjoying the passing moment.

"Hauptmann Neufeld, Captain Mallory." He looked at the places on Mallory's uniform where the missing insignia should have been. "Or so I assume. You are surprised to see me?"

"I am *delighted* to meet you, Hauptmann Neufeld." Mallory's astonishment had given way to the beginnings of a long slow smile and now he sighed in deep relief. "You just can't imagine *how* delighted." Still smiling, he turned to Droshny, and at once the smile gave way to an expression of consternation. "But who *are* you? Who is this man, Hauptmann Neufeld? Who in the name of God are those men out there? They must be—they must be——"

Droshny interrupted heavily: "One of his men killed one of my men tonight."

"What!" Neufeld, the smile now in turn vanished from his fact, stood abruptly: the backs of his legs sent his chair crashing to the floor. Mallory ignored him, looked again at Droshny.

"*Who are you?* For God's sake, tell me!"

Droshny said slowly: "They call us Cetniks."

"Cetniks? Cetniks? What on earth are Cetniks?"

"You will forgive me, Captain, if I smile in weary disbelief." Neufeld was back on balance again, and his face had assumed a curiously wary impassivity, an expression in which only the eyes were live: things, Mallory reflected, unpleasant things could happen to people misguided enough to underrate Hauptmann Neufeld. "You? The leader of a special mission to this country and you haven't been well enough briefed to know that the Cetniks are our Yugoslav allies?"

"Allies? Ah!" Mallory's face cleared in understanding. "Traitors? Yugoslav Quislings? Is that it?"

A subterranean rumble came from Droshny's throat and he moved towards Mallory, his right hand closing round the shaft of a knife. Neufeld halted him with a sharp word of command and a brief downward-chopping motion of his hand.

"And what do you mean by a special mission?" Mallory demanded. He looked at each man in turn and smiled in wry understanding. "Oh, we're special mission all right, but not in the way you think. At least, not in the way I think you think."

"No?" Neufeld's eyebrow-raising technique, Mallory reflected, was almost on a par with Miller's. "Then why do you think we were expecting you?"

"God only knows," Mallory said frankly. "We thought the Partisans were. That's why Droshny's man was killed, I'm afraid."

"That's why Droshny's man——" Neufeld regarded Mallory with his warily impassive eyes, picked up his chair and sat down thoughtfully. "I think perhaps, you had better explain yourself."

As befitted a man who had adventured far and wide in the West End of

London, Miller was in the habit of using a napkin when at meals, he was using one now, tucked into the top of his tunic, as he sat on his rucksack in the compound of Neufeld's camp and fastidiously consumed some indeterminate goulash from a mess tin. The three sergeants, seated nearby, briefly observed this spectacle with open disbelief, then resumed a low-voiced conversation. Andrea, puffing the inevitable nostril-wrinkling cigar and totally ignoring half-a-dozen watchful and understandably apprehensive guards, strolled unconcernedly about the compound, poisoning the air wherever he went. Clearly through the frozen night air came the distant sound of someone singing a low-voiced accompaniment to what appeared to be guitar music. As Andrea completed his circuit of the compound, Miller looked up and nodded in the direction of the music.

"Who's the soloist?"

Andrea shrugged. "Radio, maybe."

"They want to buy a new radio. My trained ear——"

"Listen." Reynolds' interrupting whisper was tense and urgent. "We've been talking."

Miller performed some fancy work with his napkin and said kindly: "Don't. Think of the grieving mothers and sweethearts you'd leave behind you."

"What do you mean?"

"About making a break for it is what I mean," Miller said. "Some other time, perhaps?"

"Why not now?" Groves was belligerent. "They're off guard——"

"Are they now." Miller sighed. "So young, so young. Take another look. You don't think Andrea *likes* exercise, do you?"

The three sergeants took another look, furtively, surreptitiously, then glanced interrogatively at Andrea.

"Five dark windows," Andrea said. "Behind them, five dark men. With five dark machine guns."

Reynolds nodded and looked away.

"Well, now." Neufeld, Mallory noted, had a great propensity for steepling his fingers: Mallory had once known a hanging judge with exactly the same propensity. "This *is* a most remarkably odd story you have to tell us, my dear Captain Mallory."

"It is," Mallory agreed. "It would have to be, wouldn't it, to account for the remarkably odd position in which we find ourselves at this moment."

"A point, a point." Slowly, deliberately, Neufeld ticked off other points on his fingers. "You have for some months, you claim, been running a penicillin and drug-running ring in the south of Italy. As an Allied liaison officer you found no difficulty in obtaining supplies from American Army and Air Force bases."

"We found a little difficulty towards the end," Mallory admitted.

"I'm coming to that. Those supplies, you also claim, were funnelled through to the Wehrmacht."

"I wish you wouldn't keep using the word 'claim' in that tone of voice," Mallory said irritably. "Check with Field-Marshal Kesselring's Chief of Military Intelligence in Padua."

"With pleasure." Neufeld picked up a phone, spoke briefly in German and replaced the receiver.

Mallory said in surprise: "You have a direct line to the outside world? From *this* place?"

"I have a direct line to a hut fifty yards away where we have a very powerful radio transmitter. So. You further claim that you were caught, court-martialled and were awaiting the confirmation of your death sentence. Right?''

"If your espionage system in Italy is all we hear it is, you'll know about it tomorrow," Mallory said drily.

"Quite, quite. You then broke free, killed your guards and overheard agents in the briefing room being briefed on a mission to Bosnia." He did some more finger-steepling. "You may be telling the truth at that. What did you say their mission was?''

"I didn't say. I didn't really pay attention. It had something to do with locating missing British mission leaders and trying to break your espionage set-up. I'm not sure. We had more important things to think about.''

"I'm sure you had," Neufeld said distastefully. "Such as your skins. What happened to your epaulettes, Captain? The medal ribbons? The buttons?''

"You've obviously never attended a British court-martial, Hauptmann Neufeld.''

Neufeld said mildly: "You could have ripped them off yourself.''

"And then, I suppose, emptied three-quarters of the fuel from the tanks before we stole the plane?''

"Your tanks were only a quarter full?" Mallory nodded. "And your plane crashed without catching fire?''

"We didn't mean to crash," Mallory said in weary patience. "We meant to land. But we were out of fuel, and, as we know now, at the wrong place.''

Neufeld said absently: "Whenever the Partisans put up landing flares we try a few ourselves—*and* we knew that you—or someone—were coming. No petrol, eh?" Again Neufeld spoke briefly on the telephone, then turned back to Mallory. "All very satisfactory—if true. There just remains to explain the death of Captain Droshny's man here.''

"I'm sorry about that. It was ghastly blunder. But surely you can understand. The last thing we wanted was to land among you, to make direct contact with you. We've heard what happens to British parachutists dropping over German territory.''

Neufeld steepled his fingers again. "There is a state of war. Proceed.''

"Our intention was to land in Partisan territory, slip across the lines and give ourselves up. When Droshny turned his guns on us we thought the Partisans were on to us, that they had been notified that we'd stolen the plane. And that could mean only one thing for us.''

"Wait outside. Captain Droshny and I will join you in a moment.''

Mallory left. Andrea, Miller and the three sergeants were sitting patiently on their rucksacks. From the distance there still came the sound of distant music. For a moment Mallory cocked his head to listen to it, then walked across to join the others. Miller patted his lips delicately with his napkin and looked up at Mallory.

"Had a cosy chat?''

"I spun him a yarn. The one we talked about in the plane." He looked at the three sergeants. "Any of you speak German?''

All three shook their heads.

"Fine. Forget you speak English too. If you're questioned you know nothing.''

"If I'm not questioned," Reynolds said bitterly, "I still don't know anything.''

"All the better," Mallory said encouragingly. "Then you can never tell anything, can you?''

He broke off and turned round as Neufeld and Droshny appeared in the doorway. Neufeld advanced and said: "While we're waiting for some confirmation, a little food and wine, perhaps." As Mallory had done, he cocked his head and listened to the singing. "But, first of all, you must meet our minstrel boy."

"We'll settle for just the food and wine," Andrea said.

"Your priorities are wrong. You'll see. Come."

The dining hall, if it could be dignified by such a name, was about forty yards away. Neufeld opened the door to reveal a crude and makeshift hut with two rickety trestle tables and four benches set on the earthen floor. At the far end of the room the inevitable pine fire burnt in the inevitable stone hearth place. Close to the fire, at the end of the farther table, three men—obviously, from their high-collared coats and guns propped by their sides, some kind of temporarily off-duty guards—were drinking coffee and listening to the quiet singing coming from a figure seated on the ground by the fire.

The singer was dressed in a tattered anorak-type jacket, an even more incredibly tattered pair of trousers and a pair of knee boots that gaped open at almost every possible seam. There was little to be seen of his face other than a mass of dark hair and a large pair of rimmed dark spectacles.

Beside him, apparently asleep with her head on his shoulder, sat a girl. She was clad in a high-collared British Army greatcoat in an advanced state of dilapidation, so long that it completely covered her tucked-in-legs. The uncombed platinum hair spread over her shoulders would have done justice to any Scandinavian, but the broad cheekbones, dark eyebrows and long dark lashes lowered over very pale cheeks were unmistakably Slavonic.

Neufeld advanced across the room and stopped by the fireside. He bent over the singer and said: "Petar, I want you to meet some friends."

Petar lowered his guitar, looked up, then turned and touched the girl on the arm. Instantly, the girl's head lifted and her eyes, great dark sooty eyes, opened wide. She had the look, almost, of a hunted animal. She glanced around her, almost wildly, then jumped quickly to her feet, dwarfed by the greatcoat which reached almost to her ankles, then reached down to help the guitarist to his feet. As he did so, he stumbled: he was obviously blind.

"This is Maria," Neufeld said. "Maria, this is Captain Mallory."

"Captain Mallory." Her voice was soft and a little husky: she spoke in almost accentless English. "You are English, Captain Mallory?"

It was hardly, Mallory thought, the time or the place for proclaiming his New Zealand ancestry. He smiled. "Well, sort of."

Maria smiled in turn. "I've always wanted to meet an Englishman." She stepped forward towards Mallory's out-stretched hand, brushed it aside and struck him, open-handed and with all her strength, across the face.

"Maria!" Neufeld stared at her. "He's on our side."

"An Englishman *and* a traitor!" She lifted her hand again but the swinging arm was suddenly arrested in Andrea's grip. She struggled briefly, futilely, then subsided, dark eyes glowing in an angry face. Andrea lifted his free hand and rubbed his own cheek in fond recollection.

He said admiringly: "By heavens, she reminds me of my own Maria," then grinned at Mallory. "Very handy with their hands, those Yugoslavs."

Mallory rubbed his cheek ruefully with his hand and turned to Neufeld. "Perhaps Petar—that's his name——"

"No." Neufeld shook his head definitely. "Later. Let's eat now." He led the way across to the table at the far end of the room, gestured the others to seats, sat down himself and went on: "I'm sorry. That was my fault. I should have known better."

Miller said delicately: "Is she, um, all right?"

"A wild animal, you think?"

"She'd make a rather dangerous pet, wouldn't you say?"

"She's a graduate of the University of Belgrade. Languages. With honours, I'm told. Sometime after graduation she returned to her home in the Bosnian mountains. She found her parents and two small brothers butchered. She—well, she's been like this ever since."

Mallory shifted in his seat and look at the girl. Her eyes, dark and unmoving and unwinking, were fixed on him and their expression was less than encouraging. Mallory turned back to Neufeld.

"Who did it? To her parents, I mean."

"The Partisans," Droshny said savagely. "Damn their black souls, the Partisans. Maria's people were our people. Cetniks."

"And the singer?" Mallory asked.

"Her elder brother." Neufeld shook his head. "Blind from birth. Wherever they go, she leads him by the hand. She is his eyes: she is his life."

They sat in silence until food and wine were brought in. If any army marched on its stomach, Mallory thought, this one wasn't going to get very far: he had heard that the food situation with the Partisans was close to deperate, but if this were a representative sample, the Cetniks and Germans appeared to be in little better case. Unenthusiastically, he spooned—it would have been impossible to use a fork—a little of the greyish stew, a stew in which little oddments of indefinable meat floated forlornly in a mushy gravy of obscure origin, glanced across at Andrea and marvelled at the gastronomic fortitude that lay behind the already almost empty plate. Miller averted his eyes from the plate before him and delicately sipped the rough red wine. The three sergeants, so far, hadn't even looked at their food: they were too occupied in looking at the girl by the fireside. Neufeld saw their interest, and smiled.

"I do agree, gentlemen, that I've never seen a more beautiful girl and heaven knows what she'd look like if she had a wash. But she's not for you, gentlemen. She's not for any man. She's wed already." He looked at the questioning faces and shook his head. "Not to any man. To an ideal—if you can call death an ideal. The death of the Partisans."

"Charming," Miller murmured. There was no other comment, for there was none to make. They ate in a silence broken only by the soft singing from the fireside, the voice was melodious enough, but the guitar sounded sadly out of tune. Andrea pushed away his empty plate, looked irritably at the blind musician and turned to Neufeld.

"What's that he's singing?"

"An old Bosnian love song, I've been told. Very old and very sad. In English you have it too." He snapped his fingers, "Yes, that's it. 'The Girl I Left Behind Me.' "

"Tell him to sing something else," Andrea muttered. Neufeld looked at him, puzzled, then looked away as a German sergeant entered and bent to whisper in his ear. Neufeld nodded and the sergeant left.

"So." Neufeld was thoughtful. "A radio report from the patrol that found you plane. The tanks *were* empty. I hardly think we need await confirmation from Padua, do you, Captain Mallory?"

"I don't understand."

"No matter. Tell me, have you ever heard of a General Vukalovic?"

"General which?"

"Vukalovic."

"He's not on our side," Miller said positively. "Not with a name like that."

"You must be the only people in Yugoslavia who *don't* know him. Every-body else does. Partisans, Cetniks, Germans, Bulgarians, everyone. He is one of their national heroes."

"Pass the wine," Andrea said.

"You'd do better to listen." Neufeld's tone was sharp. "Vukalovic com-mands almost a division of Partisan infantry who have been trapped in a loop of the Neretva River for almost three months. Like the men he leads, Vukalovic is insane. They have no shelter, none. They are short of weapons, have almost no ammunition left and are close to starvation. Their army is dressed in rags. They are finished."

"Then why don't they escape?" Mallory asked.

"Escape is impossible. The precipices of the Neretva cut them off to the East. To the North and West are impenetrable mountains. The only conceiv-able way out is to the South, over the bridge at Neretva. And we have two armoured divisions waiting there."

"No gorges?" Mallory asked. "No passes through the mountains?"

"Two. Blocked by our best combat troops."

"Then why don't they give up?" Miller asked reasonably. "Has no one told them the rules of war?"

"They're insane, I tell you," Neufeld said. "Quite insane."

At that precise moment in time, Vukalovic and his Partisans were proving to some other Germans just how extraordinary their degree of insanity was.

The Western Gap was a narrow, tortuous, boulder-strewn and precipi-tiously walled gorge that afforded the only passage through the impassable mountains that shut off the Zenica Cage to the East. For three months now German infantry units—units which had recently included an increasing number of highly skilled Alpine troops—had been trying to force the pass: for three months they had been bloodily repulsed. But the Germans never gave up trying and on this intensely cold night of fitful moonlight and gently, intermittently, falling snow, they were trying again.

The Germans carried out their attack with the coldly professional skill and economy of movement born of long and harsh experience. They ad-vanced up the gorge in three fairly even and judiciously spaced lines: the combination of white snowsuits, of the utilisation of every scrap of cover and of confining their brief forward rushes to those moments when the moon was temporarily obscured made it almost impossible to see them. There was, however, no difficulty in locating them: they had obviously ammunition and to spare for machine pistols and rifles alike and the fire-flashes from those muzzles were almost continuous. Almost as continuous, but some distance behind them, the sharp flat cracks of fixed mountain pieces pin-pointed the source of the creeping artillery barrage that preceded the Ger-mans up the boulder-strewn slope of that narrow defile.

The Yugoslav Partisans waited at the head of the gorge, entrenched behind a redoubt of boulders, hastily piled stones and splintered tree trunks that had been shattered by German artillery fire. Although the snow was deep and the east wind full of little knives, few of the Partisans wore greatcoats. They were clad in an extraordinary variety of uniforms, uniforms that had belonged in the past to members of British, German, Italian, Bulgarian and Yugoslav armies: the one identifying feature that all had in common was a red star sewn on to the right-hand side of their forage caps. The uniforms, for the most part, were thin and tattered, offering little protection against the piercing cold so that the men shivered almost continuously. An astonish-ing proportion of them appeared to be wounded: there were splinted legs, arms in slings and bandaged heads everywhere. But the most common characteristic among this ragtag collection of defenders was their pinched and emaciated faces, faces where the deeply etched lines of starvation were matched only by the calm and absolute determination of men who have no longer anything to lose.

Near the centre of the group of defenders, two men stood in the shelter of the thick bole of one of the few pines still left standing. The silvered black hair, the deeply trenched—and now even more exhausted—face of General Vukalovic was unmistakable. But the dark eyes glowed as brightly as ever as he bent forward to accept a cigarette and light from the officer sharing his shelter, a swarthy, hook-nosed man with at least half of his black hair concealed under a bloodstained bandage. Vukalovic smiled.

"Of course, I'm insane, my dear Stephan. You're insane—or you would have abandoned this position weeks ago. We're all insane. Didn't you know?"

"I know this." Major Stephan rubbed the back of his hand across a week-old growth of beard. "Your parachute landing, an hour ago. That was insane. Why, you——" He broke off as a rifle fired only feet away, moved across to where a thin youngster, not more than seventeen years of age, was peering down into the white gloom of the gorge over the sights of a Lee-Enfield. "Did you get him?"

The boy twisted and looked up. A child, Vukalovic thought despairingly, no more than a child: he should still have been at school. The boy said: "I'm not sure, sir."

"How many shells have you left? Count them."

"I don't have to. Seven."

"Don't fire till you are sure." Stephan turned back to Vukalovic. "God above, General, you were almost blown into German hands."

"I'd have been worse off without the parachute," Vukalovic said mildly.

"There's so little time." Stephan struck a clenched fist against a palm. "So little time left. You were crazy to come back. They need you far more——" He stopped abruptly, listened for a fraction of a second, threw himself at Vukalovic and brought them both crashing heavily to the ground as a whining mortar shell buried itself among loose rocks a few feet away, exploding on impact. Close by, a man screamed in agony. A second mortar shell landed, then a third and a fourth, all within thirty feet of one another.

"They've got the range now, damn them." Stephan rose quickly to his feet and peered down the gorge. For long seconds he could see nothing, for a band of dark cloud had crossed the face of the moon: then the moon broke through and he could see the enemy all too clearly. Because of some almost certainly prearranged signal, they were no longer making any attempt to seek cover: they were pounding straight up the slope with all the speed they could muster, machine carbines and rifles at the ready in their hands and as soon as the moon broke through they squeezed the triggers of those guns. Stephan threw himself behind the shelter of a boulder.

"Now!" he shouted. "Now!"

The first ragged Partisan fusillade lasted for only a few seconds, then a black shadow fell over the valley. The firing ceased.

"Keep firing," Vukalovic shouted. "Don't stop now. They're closing in." He loosed off a burst from his own machine pistol and said to Stephan, "They know what they are about, our friends down there."

"They should." Stephan armed a stick grenade and spun it down the hill. "Look at all the practice we've given them."

The moon broke through again. The leading German infantry were no more than twenty-five yards away. Both sides exchanged hand grenades, fired at point blank range. Some German soldiers fell, but many more came on, flinging themselves on the redoubt. Matters became temporarily confused. Here and there bitter hand-to-hand fighting developed. Men shouted at each other, cursed each other, killed each other. But the redoubt remained unbroken. Suddenly, dark heavy clouds again rolled over the moon, darkness flooded the gorge and everything slowly fell quiet. In the distance the thunder of artillery and mortar fire fell away to a muted rumble then finally died.

"A trap?" Vukalovic said softly to Stephan. "You think they will come again?"

"Not tonight." Stephan was positive. "They're brave men, but——"

"But not insane?"

"But not insane."

Blood poured down over Stephan's face from a reopened wound in his face, but he was smiling. He rose to his feet and turned as a burly sergeant came up and delivered a sketchy salute.

"They've gone, Major. We lost seven of ours, this time, and fourteen wounded."

"Set pickets two hundred metres down," Stephan said. He turned to Vukalovic. "You heard, sir? Seven dead. Fourteen hurt."

"Leaving how many?"

"Two hundred. Perhaps two hundred and five."

"Out of four hundred." Vukalovic's mouth twisted. "Dear God, out of four hundred."

"And sixty of those are wounded."

"At least you can get them down to the hospital now."

"There is no hospital," Stephan said heavily. "I didn't have time to tell you. It was bombed this morning. Both doctors killed. All our medical supplies—poof! Like that."

"Gone? All gone?" Vukalovic paused for a long moment. "I'll have some sent up from HQ. The walking wounded can make their own way to HQ."

"The wounded won't leave, sir. Not any more."

Vukalovic nodded in understanding and went on: "How much ammunition?"

"Two days. Three, if we're careful."

"Sixty wounded." Vukalovic shook his head in slow disbelief. "No medical help whatsoever for them. Ammunition almost gone. No food. No shelter. And they won't leave. Are they insane, too?"

"Yes, sir."

"I'm going down to the river," Vukalovic said. "To see Colonel Lazlo at HQ."

"Yes, sir." Stephan smiled faintly. "I doubt if you'll find his mental equilibrium any better than mine."

"I don't suppose I will," Vukalovic said.

Stephan saluted and turned away, mopping blood from his face, walked a few short swaying steps then knelt down to comfort a badly wounded man. Vukalovic looked after him expressionlessly, shaking his head: then he, too turned and left.

Mallory finished his meal and lit a cigarette. He said: "So what's going to happen to the Partisans in the Zenica Cage, as you call it?"

"They're going to break out," Neufeld said. "At least, they're going to try to."

"But you've said yourself that's impossible."

"Nothing is too impossible for those mad Partisans to try. I wish to heaven," Neufeld said bitterly, "that we were fighting a normal war against normal people, like the Britsh or Americans. Anyway, we've had information—reliable information—that an attempted break-out is imminent. Trouble is, there are those two passes—they might even try to force the bridge at Neretva—and we don't know where the break-out is coming."

"This is very interesting." Andrea looked sourly at the blind musician who was still giving his rendering of the same old Bosnian love song. "Can we get some sleep, now?"

"Not tonight, I'm afraid." Neufeld exchanged a smile with Droshny. "*You* are going to find out for us where this breakout is coming."

"We are?" Miller drained his glass and reached for the bottle. "Infectious stuff, this insanity."

Neufeld might not have heard him. "Partisan HQ is about ten kilometers from here. You are going to report there as the bona-fide British mission that has lost its way. Then, when you've found out their plans, you tell them that you are going to their main HQ at Drvar, which, of course, you don't. You come back here instead. What could be simpler?"

"Miller's right," Mallory said with conviction. "You *are* mad."

"I'm beginning to think there's altogether too much talk of this madness." Neufeld smiled. "You would prefer, perhaps, that Captain Droshny here turned you over to his men. I assure you, they are most unhappy about their—ah—late comrade."

"You can't ask us to do this?" Mallory was hard-faced in anger. "The Partisans are bound to get a radio message about us. Sooner or later. And then—well, you know what then. You just can't ask this of us."

"I can and I will." Neufeld looked at Mallory and his five companions without enthusiasm. "It so happens that I don't care for dope-peddlers and drug-runners."

"I don't think your opinion will carry much weight in certain circles," Mallory said.

"And that means?"

"Kesselring's Director of Military Intelligence isn't going to like this at all."

"If you don't come back, they'll never know. If you do"—Neufeld smiled and touched the Iron Cross at his throat—"they'll probably give me an oak leaf to this."

"Likeable type, isn't he?" Miller said to no one in particular.

"Come then." Neufeld rose from the table. "Petar?"

The blind singer nodded, slung his guitar over his shoulder and rose to his feet, his sister rising with him.

"What's this, then," Mallory asked.

"Guides."

"*Those* two?"

"Well," Neufeld said reasonably, "you can't very well find your own way there, can you? Petar and his sister—well, his sister—know Bosnia better than the foxes."

"But won't the Partisans——" Mallory began, but Neufeld interrupted.

"You do not know your Bosnia. These two wander wherever they like and no one will turn them from their door. The Bosnians believe, and God knows with sufficient reason, that they are accursed and have the evil eye on them. This is a land of superstition, Captain Mallory."

"But—but how will they know where to take us?"

"They'll know." Neufeld nodded to Droshny, who talked rapidly to Maria in Serbo-Croat: she in turn spoke to Petar, who made some strange noises in his throat.

"That's an odd language," Miller observed.

"He's got a speech impediment," Neufeld said shortly. "He was born with it. He can sing, but not talk—it's not unknown. Do you wonder people think they are cursed?" He turned to Mallory. "Wait outside with your men."

Mallory nodded, gestured to the others to precede him. Neufeld, he noted, was immediately engaged in a short, low-voiced discussion with Droshny, who nodded, summoned one of his Cetniks and dispatched him on some errand. Once outside, Mallory moved with Andrea slightly apart from the others and murmured something in his ear, inaudible to all but Andrea, whose nodded acquiescence was almost imperceptible.

Neufeld and Droshny emerged from the hut, followed by Maria who was leading Petar by the hand. As they approached Mallory's group, Andrea walked casually towards them, smoking the inevitable noxious cigar. He planted himself in front of a puzzled Neufeld and arrogantly blew smoke into his face.

"I don't think I care for you every much, Hauptmann Neufeld," Andrea announced. He looked at Droshny. "Nor for the cutlery salesman here."

Neufeld's face immediately darkened, became tight in anger. But he brought himself quickly under control and said with restraint: "Your opinion of me is of no concern to me." He nodded to Droshny. "But do not cross Captain Droshny's path, my friend. He is a Bosnian and a proud one—and the best man in the Balkans with a knife."

"The best man——" Andrea broke off with a roar of laughter, and blew smoke into Droshny's face. "A knife-grinder in a comic opera."

Droshny's disbelief was total but of brief duration. He bared his teeth in a fashion that would have done justice to any Bosnian wolf, swept a wickedly curved knife from his belt and threw himself on Andrea, the gleaming blade hooking viciously upward, but Andrea, whose prudence was exceeded only by the extraordinary speed with which he could move his vast bulk, was no longer there when the knife arrived. But his hand was. It caught Droshny's knife wrist as it flashed upward and almost at once the two big men crashed heavily to the ground, rolling over and over in the snow while they fought for possession of the knife.

So unexpected, so wholly incredible the speed with which the fight had developed from nowhere that, for a few seconds, no one moved. The three young sergeants, Neufeld and the Cetniks registered nothing but utter astonishment. Mallory, who was standing close beside the wide-eyed girl, rubbed his chin thoughtfully while Miller, delicately tapping the ash off the end of his cigarette, regarded the scene with a sort of weary interest.

Almost at the same instant, Reynolds, Groves and two Cetniks flung themselves upon the struggling pair on the ground and tried to pull them apart. Not until Groves and Neufeld lent a hand did they succeed. Droshny and Andrea were pulled to their feet, the former with contorted face and hatred in his eyes, Andrea calmly resuming the smoking of the cigar which he'd somehow picked up after they had been separated.

"You madman!" Reynolds said savagely to Andrea. "You crazy maniac. You—you're a bloody psychopath. You'll get us all killed."

"That wouldn't surprise me at all," Neufeld said thoughtfully. "Come. Let us have no more of this foolishness."

He led the way from the compound, and as he did so they were joined by a group of half-a-dozen Cetniks, whose apparent leader was the youth with the straggling ginger beard and cast to his eye, the first of the Cetniks to greet them when they had landed.

"Who are they and what are they for?" Mallory demanded of Neufeld. "They're not coming with us."

"Escort," Neufeld explained. "For the first seven kilometers only."

"Escorts? What would we want with escorts? We're in no danger from you, nor, according to what you say, will we be from the Yugoslav Partisans."

"We're not worried about you," Neufeld said drily. "We're worried about the vehicle that is going to take you most of the way there. Vehicles are very few and very precious in this part of Bosnia—and there are many Partisan patrols about."

Twenty minutes later, in a now moonless night and with snow falling, they reached a road, a road which was little more than a winding track, running through a forested valley floor. Waiting for them there was one of the strangest four-wheeled contraptions Mallory or his companions had even seen, an incredibly ancient and battered truck which at first sight, from the vast clouds of smoke emanating from it, appeared to be on fire. It was, in fact, a very much prewar wood-burning truck, of a type at one time common in the Balkans. Miller regarded the smoke-shrouded truck in astonishment and turned to Neufeld.

"You call this a vehicle?"

"You call it what you like. Unless you'd rather walk."

"Ten kilometres? I'll take my chance on asphyxiation." Miller climbed in, followed by the others, till only Neufeld and Droshny remained outside.

Neufeld said: "I shall expect you back before noon."

"If we ever come back," Mallory said. "If a radio message has come through——"

"You can't make an omelette without breaking eggs," Neufeld said indifferently.

With a great rattling and shaking and emission of smoke and steam, all accompanied by much red-eyed coughing from the canvas-covered rear, the truck jerked uncertainly into motion and moved off slowly along the valley floor, Neufeld and Droshny gazing after it. Neufeld shook his head. "Such clever little men."

"Such *very* clever little men," Droshny agreed. "But I want the big one, Captain."

Neufeld clapped him on the shoulder. "You shall have him, my friend. Well, they're out of sight. Time for you to go."

Droshny nodded and whistled shrilly between his fingers. There came the distant whirr of an engine starter, and soon an elderly Fiat emerged from behind a clump of pines and approached along the hard-packed snow of the road, its chains clanking violently, and stopped beside the two men. Droshny climbed into the front passenger seat and the Fiat moved off in the wake of the truck.

5

FRIDAY

0330–0500

FOR THE fourteen people jammed on the narrow side benches under the canvas-hooped roof, the journey could hardly be called pleasurable. There were no cushions on the seats, just as there appeared to be a total absence of springs on the vehicle, and the torn and badly fitting hood admitted large quantities of icy night air and eye-smarting smoke in about equal proportions. At least, Mallory thought, it all helped considerably to keep them awake.

Andrea was sitting directly opposite him, seemingly oblivious of the thick choking atmosphere inside the truck, a fact hardly surprising considering that the penetrating power and the pungency of the smoke from the truck was of a lower order altogether than that emanating from the black cheroot clamped between Andrea's teeth. Andrea glanced idly across and caught Mallory's eye. Mallory nodded once, a millimetric motion of the head that would have gone unremarked by even the most suspicious. Andrea dropped his eyes until his gaze rested on Mallory's right hand, lying loosely on his knee. Mallory sat back and sighed, and as he did his right hand slipped until his thumb was pointing directly at the floor. Andrea puffed out another Vesuvian cloud of acrid smoke and looked away indifferently.

For some kilometres the smoke-enshrouded truck clattered and screeched its way along the valley floor, then swung off to the left, on to an even narrower track, and began to climb. Less than two minutes later, with Droshny sitting impassively in the front passenger seat, the pursuing Fiat made a similar turn off.

The slope was now so steep and the spinning driving wheels losing so much traction on the frozen surface of the track that the ancient wood-burning truck was reduced to little more than a walking pace. Inside the truck, Andrea and Mallory were as watchful as ever, but Miller and the three sergeants seemed to be dozing off, whether through exhaustion or incipient asphyxiation it was difficult to say. Maria and Petar, hand in hand, appeared to be asleep. The Cetniks, on the other hand, could hardly have been more wide awake, and were making it clear for the first time that the rents and holes in the canvas cover had not been caused by accident: Droshny's six men were now kneeling on the benches with the muzzles of their machine pistols thrust through the apertures in the canvas. It was clear that the truck was now moving into Partisan territory or, at least, what passed for no-man's-land in that wild and rugged territory.

The Cetnik farthest forward in the truck suddenly withdrew his face from a gap in the canvas and rapped the butt of his gun against the driver's cab. The truck wheezed to a grateful halt, the ginger-bearded Cetnik jumped down, checked swiftly for any signs of ambush, then gestured the others to disembark, the repeatedly urgent movements of his hand making it clear that he was less than enamoured of the idea of hanging around that place for a moment longer than necessity demanded. One by one Mallory and his companions jumped down on to the frozen snow. Reynolds guided the blind singer down to the ground then reached up a hand to help Maria as she clambered over the tailboard. Wordlessly, she struck his hand aside and leapt nimbly to the ground: Reynolds stared at her in hurt astonishment.

The truck, Mallory observed, had stopped opposite a small clearing in the forest. Backing and filling and issuing denser clouds of smoke than ever, it used this space to turn around in a remarkably short space of time and clanked its way off down the forest path at a considerably higher speed than it had made the ascent. The Cetniks gazed impassively from the back of the departing truck, made no gesture of farewell.

Maria took Petar's hand, looked coldly at Mallory, jerked her head and set off up a tiny footpath leading at right angles from the track. Mallory shrugged, and set off, followed by the three sergeants. For a moment or two Andrea and Miller remained where they were, gazing thoughtfully at the corner round which the truck had just disappeared. Then they, too, set off, talking in low tones to each other.

The ancient wood-burning truck did not maintain its initial impetus for any lengthy period of time. Less than four hundred yards after rounding the corner which blocked it from the view of Mallory and his companions it braked to a halt. Two Cetniks, the ginger-bearded leader of the escort and another black-bearded man jumped over the tailboard and moved at once into the protective covering of the forest. The truck rattled off once more, its belching smoke hanging heavily in the freezing night air.

A kilometre farther down the track, an almost identical scene was taking place. The Fiat slid to a halt, Droshny scrambled from the passenger's seat and vanished among the pines. The Fiat reversed quickly and moved off down the track.

The track up through the heavily wooded slope was very narrow, very winding: the snow was no longer hard-packed, but soft and deep and making for very hard going. The moon was quite gone now, the snow, gusted into their faces by the east wind, was becoming steadily heavier and the cold was intense. The path frequently arrived at a V-shaped branch but Maria, in the lead with her brother, never hesitated: she knew, or appeared to know, exactly where she was going. Several times she slipped in the deep snow, on the last occasion so heavily that she brought her brother down with her. When it happened yet again, Reynolds moved forward and took the girl by the arm to help her. She struck out savagely and drew her arm away. Reynolds stared at her in astonishment, then turned to Mallory.

"What the devil's the matter with—I mean, I was only trying to help——"

"Leave her alone," Mallory said. "You're one of them."

"I'm one of——"

"You're wearing a British uniform. That's all the poor kid understands. Leave her be."

Reynolds shook his head uncomprehendingly. He hitched his pack more securely on his shoulders, glanced back down the trail, made to move on, then glanced backward again. He caught Mallory by the arm and pointed.

Andrea had already fallen thirty yards behind. Weighed down by his rucksack and Schmeisser and weight of years, he was very obviously making heavy weather of the climb and was falling steadily behind by the second. At a gesture and word from Mallory the rest of the party halted and peered back down through the driving snow, waiting for Andrea to make up on them. By this time Andrea was beginning to stumble almost drunkenly and clutched at his right side as if in pain. Reynolds looked at Groves: they both looked at Saunders: all three slowly shook their heads. Andrea came up with them and a spasm of pain flickered across his face:

"I'm sorry." The voice was gasping and hoarse. "I'll be all right in a moment."

Saunders hesitated, then advanced towards Andrea. He smiled apologetically, then reached out a hand to indicate the rucksack and Schmeisser.

"Come on, Dad. Hand them over."

For the minutest fraction of a second a flicker of menace, more imagined than seen, touched Andrea's face, then he shrugged off his rucksack and wearily handed it over. Saunders accepted it and tentatively indicated the Schmeisser.

"Thanks." Andrea smiled wanly. "But I'd feel lost without it."

Uncertainly, they resumed their climb, looking back frequently to check on Andrea's progress. Their doubts were well-founded. Within thirty seconds Andrea had stopped, his eyes screwed up and bent almost double in pain. He said, gaspingly: "I must rest. Go on. I'll catch up with you."

Miller said solicitously: "I'll stay with you."

"I don't need anybody to stay with me," Andrea said surlily. "I can look after myself."

Miller said nothing. He looked at Mallory and jerked his head in an uphill direction. Mallory nodded, once, and gestured to the girl. Reluctantly, they moved off, leaving Andrea and Miller behind. Twice, Reynolds looked back over his shoulder, his expression an odd mixture of worry and exasperation: then he shrugged his shoulders and bent his back to the hill.

Andrea, scowling blackly and still clutching his ribs, remained bent double until the last of the party had rounded the nearest uphill corner, then straightened effortlessly, tested the wind with a wetted forefinger, established that it was moving uptrail, produced a cigar, lit it and puffed in deep and obvious contentment. His recovery was quite astonishing, but it didn't appear to astonish Miller, who grinned and nodded downhill. Andrea grinned in return, made a courteous gesture of precedence.

Thirty yards downtrail, at a position which gave them an uninterrupted view of almost a hundred yards of the track below them, they moved into the cover of the bole of a giant pine. For about two minutes they stood there, staring downhill and listening intently, then suddenly Andrea nodded, stooped and carefully laid his cigar in a sheltered dried patch of ground behind the bole of the pine.

They exchanged no words: there was need of none. Miller crawled round to the downhill-facing front of the pine and carefully arranged himself in a spread-eagled position in the deep snow, both arms outflung, his apparently sightless face turned up to the falling snow. Behind the pine, Andrea reversed his grip on his Schmeisser, holding it by the barrel, produced a knife from the recesses of his clothing and stuck it in his belt. Both men remained as motionless as if they had died there and frozen solid over the long and bitter Yugoslav winter.

Probably because his spread-eagled form was sunk so deeply in the soft snow as to conceal most of his body, Miller saw the two Cetniks coming quite some time before they saw him. At first they were no more than two shapeless and vaguely ghostlike forms gradually materialising from the falling snow: as they drew nearer, he identified them as the Cetnik escort leader and one of his men.

They were less than thirty yards away before they saw Miller. They stopped, stared, remained motionless for at least five seconds, looked at each other, unslung their machine pistols and broke into a stumbling uphill run. Miller closed his eyes. He didn't require them any more, his ears gave him all the information he wanted, the closing sound of crunching footsteps in the snow, the abrupt cessation of those, the heavy breathing as a man bent over him.

Miller waited until he could actually feel the man's breath in his face, then opened his eyes. Not twelve inches from his own were the eyes of the ginger-bearded Cetnik. Miller's outflung arms curved upward and inward, his sinewy fingers hooked deeply into the throat of the startled man above him.

Andrea's Schmeisser had already reached the limit of its back-swing as he stepped soundlessly round the bole of the pine. The black-bearded Cetnik was just beginning to move to help his friend when he caught sight of Andrea from the corner of one eye, and flung up both arms to protect himself. A pair of straws would have served him as well. Andrea grimaced at the sheer physical shock of the impact; dropped the Schmeisser, pulled out his knife and fell upon the other Cetnik still struggling desperately in Miller's stranglehold.

Miller rose to his feet and he and Andrea stared down at the two dead men. Miller looked in puzzlement at the ginger-bearded man then suddenly stooped, caught the beard and tugged. It came away in his hand revealing beneath it a clean-shaven face and a scar which ran from the corner of a lip to the chin.

Andrea and Miller exchanged speculative glances, but neither made comment. They dragged the dead men some little way off the path into the concealment of some undergrowth. Andrea picked up a dead branch and swept away the drag-marks in the snow and, by the base of the pine, all traces of the encounter: inside the hour, he knew, the brushmarks he had made would have vanished under a fresh covering of snow. He picked up his cigar and threw the branch deep into the woods. Without a backward glance, the two men began to walk briskly up the hill.

Had they given this backward glance, it was barely possible that they might have caught a glimpse of a face peering round the trunk of a tree farther downhill. Droshny had arrived at the bend in the track just in time to see Andrea complete his brushing operations and throw the branch away: what the meaning of this might be he couldn't guess.

He waited until Andrea and Miller had disappeared from his sight, waited another two minutes for good measure and safety, then hurried up the track, the expression on his swarthy brigand's face nicely balanced between puzzlement and suspicion. He reached the pine where the two Cetniks had been ambushed, briefly quartered the area then followed the line of brush-marks leading into the woods, the puzzlement on his face giving way first to pure suspicion, then the suspicion to complete certainty.

He parted the bushes and peered down at the two Cetniks lying half-buried in a snow-filled gully with that curiously huddled shapelessness that only the dead can achieve. After a few moments he straightened, turned and looked uphill in the direction in which Andrea and Miller had vanished: his face was not pleasant to look upon.

Andrea and Miller made good time up the hill. As they approached one of the innumerable bends in the trail they heard up ahead the sound of a softly played guitar, curiously muffled and softened in tone by the falling snow. Andrea slowed up, threw away his cigar, bent forward and clutched his ribs. Solicitously, Miller took his arm.

The main party, they saw, was less than thirty yards ahead. They, too, were making slow time: the depth of snow and the increasing slope of the

track made any quicker movement impossible. Reynolds glanced back—
Reynolds was spending a great deal of his time in looking over his shoulder,
he appeared to be in a highly apprehensive state—caught sight of Andrea
and Miller and called out to Mallory who halted the party and waited for
Andrea and Miller to make up with them. Mallory looked worriedly at
Andrea.

"Getting worse?"

"How far to go?" Andrea asked hoarsely.

"Must be less than a mile."

Andrea said nothing, he just stood there breathing heavily and wearing
the stricken look of a sick man contemplating the prospect of another upward mile through deep snow. Saunders, already carrying two rucksacks,
approached Andrea diffidently, tentatively. He said: "It would help,
you know, if——"

"I know." Andrea smiled painfully, unslung his Schmeisser and handed
it to Saunders. "Thanks, son."

Petar was still softly plucking the strings of his guitar, an indescribably
eerie sound in those dark and ghostly pine woods. Miller looked at him and
said to Mallory: "What's the music while we march for?"

"Petar's password, I should imagine."

"Like Neufeld said? Nobody touches our singing Cetnik?"

"Something like that."

They moved on up the trail. Mallory let the others pass by until he and
Andrea were bringing up the rear. Mallory glanced incuriously at Andrea,
his face registering no more than a mild concern for the condition of his
friend. Andrea caught his glance and nodded fractionally: Mallory looked
away.

Fifteen minutes later they were halted, at gun-point by three men, all
armed with machine pistols, who simply appeared to have materialised from
nowhere, a surprise so complete that not even Andrea could have done
anything about it—even if he had had his gun. Reynolds looked urgently at
Mallory, who smiled and shook his head.

"It's all right. Partisans—look at the red star on their forage caps. Just
outposts guarding one of the main trails."

And so it proved. Maria talked briefly to one of the soldiers, who listened,
nodded and set off up the path, gesturing to the party to follow him. The
other two Partisans remained behind, both men crossing themselves as Petar
again strummed gently on his guitar. Neufeld, Mallory reflected, hadn't
exaggerated about the degree of awed respect and fear in which the blind
singer and his sister were held.

They came to Partisan HQ inside another ten minutes, an HQ curiously
similar in appearance and choice of location to Hauptmann Neufeld's camp,
and the same rough circle of crude huts set deep in the same *jamba* (depression) with similar massive pines towering high above. The guide spoke to
Maria and she turned coldly to Mallory, the disdain in her face making it
very plain how much against the grain it went for her to speak to him at all.

"We are to go to the guest hut. You are to report to the commandant.
This soldier will show you."

The guide beckoned in confirmation. Mallory followed him across the
compound to a fairly large, fairly well-lit hut. The guide knocked, opened
the door and waved Mallory inside, he himself following.

The commandant was a tall lean dark man with that aquiline, aristocratic
face so common among the Bosnian mountain men. He advanced towards
Mallory with outstretched hand and smiled.

"Major Broznik, and at your service. Late, late hours, but as you see we are still up and around. Although I must say I did expect you before this."

"I don't know what you're talking about."

"You don't know—you *are* Captain Mallory, are you not?"

"I've never heard of him." Mallory gazed steadily at Broznik, glanced briefly sideways at the guide, then looked back to Broznik again. Broznik frowned for a moment, then his face cleared. He spoke to the guide, who turned and left. Mallory put out his hand.

"Captain Mallory, at your service. I'm sorry about that, Major Broznik, but I insist we must talk alone."

"You trust no one? Not even in *my* camp."

"No one."

"Not even your own men?"

"I don't trust them not to make mistakes. I don't trust myself not to make mistakes. I don't trust *you* not to make mistakes."

"Please." Broznik's voice was as cold as his eyes.

"Did you ever have two of your men disappear, one with ginger hair, the other with black, the ginger-haired man with a cast to his eye and a scar running from mouth to chin?"

Broznik came closer. "What do you know about those men?"

"Did you? Know them, I mean?"

Broznik nodded and said slowly: "They were lost in action. Last month."

"You found their bodies?"

"No."

"There were no bodies to be found. They had deserted—gone over to the Cetniks."

"But they *were* Cetniks—converted to our cause."

"They'd been reconverted. They followed us tonight. On the orders of Captain Droshny. I had them killed."

"You—had—them—killed?"

"Think, man," Mallory said wearily. "If they had arrived here—which they no doubt intended to do a discreet interval after our arrival—we wouldn't have recognised them and you'd have welcomed them back as escaped prisoners. They'd have had reported our every movement. Even if we had recognised them after they had arrived here and done something about it, you may have *other* Cetniks here who would have reported back to their masters that we had done away with their watch dogs. So we disposed of them very quietly, no fuss, in a very remote place then hid them."

"There are no Cetniks in my command, Captain Mallory."

Mallory said drily: "It takes a very clever farmer, Major, to see two bad apples on the top of the barrel and be quite certain that there are none lower down. No chances. None. Ever." Mallory smiled to remove any offence from his words and went on briskly: "Now, Major, there's some information that Hauptmann Neufeld wants."

To say that the guest hut hardly deserved so hospitable a title would have been a very considerable understatement. As a shelter for some of the less-regarded domesticated animals it might have been barely acceptable: as an overnight accommodation for human beings it was conspicuously lacking in what our modern effete European societies regard as the minimum essentials for civilized living. Even the Spartans of ancient Greece would have considered it as too much of a good thing. One rickety trestle table, one bench, a dying fire and lots of hard-packed earthen floor. It fell short of being a home from home.

There were six people in the hut, three standing, one sitting, two stretched out on the lumpy floor. Petar, for once without his sister, sat on the floor, silent guitar clasped in his hands, gazing sightlessly into the fading embers. Andrea, stretched in apparently luxurious ease in a sleeping bag, peacefully puffed at what, judging from the frequent suffering glances cast in his direction, appeared to be a more than normally obnoxious cigar. Miller, similarly reclining, was reading what appeared to be a slender volume of poetry. Reynolds and Groves, unable to sleep, stood idly by the solitary window, gazing out abstractedly into the dimly-lit compound: they turned as Saunders removed his radio transmitter from its casing and made for the door.

With some bitterness Saunders said: "Sleep well."

"Sleep well?" Reynolds raised an eyebrow. "And where are you going?"

"Radio hut across there. Message to Termoli. Mustn't spoil your beauty sleep when I'm transmitting."

Saunders left. Groves went and sat by the table, cradling a weary head in his hands. Reynolds remained by the window, watched Saunders cross the compound and enter a darkened hut on the far side. Soon a light appeared in the window as Saunders lit a lamp.

Reynold's eyes moved in response to the sudden appearance of an oblong of light across the compound. The door to Major Broznik's hut had opened and Mallory stood momentarily framed there, carrying what appeared to be a sheet of paper in his hand. Then the door closed and Mallory moved off in the direction of the radio hut.

Reynolds suddenly became very watchful, very still. Mallory had taken less than a dozen steps when a dark figure detached itself from the even darker shadow of a hut and confronted him. Quite automatically, Reynolds' hand reached for the Luger at his belt, then slowly withdrew. Whatever this confrontation signified for Mallory it certainly wasn't danger, for Maria, Reynolds knew, did not carry a gun. And, unquestionably, it was Maria who was now in such apparent close conversation with Mallory.

Bewildered now, Reynolds pressed his face close against the glass. For almost two minutes he stared at this astonishing spectacle of the girl who had slapped Mallory with such venom, who had lost no opportunity of displaying an animosity bordering on hatred, now talking to him not only animatedly, but also clearly very amicably. So total was Reynolds' baffled incomprehension at this inexplicable turn of events that his mind moved into a trancelike state, a spell that was abruptly snapped when he saw Mallory put a reassuring arm around her shoulder and pat her in a way that might have been comforting or affectionate or both but which in any event clearly evoked no resentment on the part of the girl. This was still inexplicable: but the only interpretation that could be put upon it was an uncompromisingly sinister one. Reynolds whirled round and silently and urgently beckoned Groves to the window. Groves rose quickly, moved to the window and looked out, but by the time he had done so there was no longer any sign of Maria: Mallory was alone, walking across the compound towards the radio hut, the paper still in his hand. Groves glanced questioningly at Reynolds.

"They were together," Reynolds whispered. "Mallory and Maria. I saw them! They were talking."

"What? You sure?"

"God's my witness. I *saw* them, man. He even had his arm around— Get away from this window—Maria's coming."

Without haste, so as to arouse no comment from Andrea or Miller, they turned and walked unconcernedly towards the table and sat down. Seconds later, Maria entered and, without looking at or speaking to anyone, crossed to the fire, sat by Peter and took his hand. A minute or so later Mallory entered, and sat on a palliasse beside Andrea, who removed his cigar and glanced at him in mild enquiry. Mallory casually checked to see that he wasn't under observation, then nodded. Andrea returned to the contemplation of his cigar.

Reynolds looked uncertainly at Groves then said to Mallory: "Shouldn't we be setting a guard, sir?"

"A guard?" Mallory was amused. "Whatever for? This is a Partisan camp, Sergeant. Friends, you know. And, as you've seen, they have their own excellent guard system."

"You never know——"

"*I* know. Get some sleep."

Reynolds went on doggedly: "Saunders is alone over there. I don't like——"

"He's coding and sending a short message for me. A few minutes, that's all."

"But——"

"Shut up," Andrea said. "You heard the captain?"

Reynolds was by now thoroughly unhappy and uneasy, an unease which showed through in his instantly antagonistic irritation.

"Shut up? Why should I shut up? I don't take orders from you. And while we're telling each other what to do, you might put out that damned stinking cigar."

Miller wearily lowered his book of verse.

"I quite agree about the damned cigar, young fellow. But do bear in mind that you are talking to a ranking colonel in the army."

Miller reverted to his book. For a few moments Reynolds and Groves stared open-mouthed at each other, then Reynolds stood up and looked at Andrea.

"I'm extremely sorry, sir. I—I didn't realise——"

Andrea waved him to silence with a magnanimous hand and resumed his communion with his cigar. The minutes passed in silence. Maria, before the fire, had her head on Petar's shoulder, but otherwise had not moved: she appeared to be asleep. Miller shook his head in rapt admiration of what appeared to be one of the more esoteric manifestations of the poetic muse, closed his book reluctantly and slid down into his sleeping bag. Andrea ground out his cigar and did the same. Mallory seemed to be already asleep. Groves lay down and Reynolds, leaning over the table, rested his forehead on his arms. For five minutes, perhaps longer, Reynolds remained like this, uneasily dozing off, then he lifted his head, sat up with a jerk, glanced at his watch, crossed to Mallory and shook him by the shoulder. Mallory stirred.

"Twenty minutes," Reynolds said urgently. "Twenty minutes and Saunders isn't back yet."

"All right, so it's twenty minutes," Mallory said patiently. "He could take that long to make contact, far less transmit the message."

"Yes, sir. Permission to check, sir?"

Mallory nodded wearily and closed his eyes. Reynolds picked up his Schmeisser, left the hut and closed the door softly behind him. He released the safety catch on his gun and ran across the compound.

The light still burned in the radio hut. Reynolds tried to peer through the window but the frost of that bitter night had made it completely opaque. Reynolds moved around to the door. It was slightly ajar. He set his finger to the trigger and opened the door in the fashion in which all Commandos were trained to open doors—with a violent kick of his right foot.

There was no one in the radio hut, no one, that is, who could bring him to any harm. Slowly, Reynolds lowered his gun and walked in in a hesitant, almost dreamlike fashion, his face masked in shock.

Saunders was leaning tiredly over the transmitting table, his head resting on it at an unnatural angle, both arms dangling limply towards the ground. The hilt of a knife protruded between his shoulder blades: Reynolds noted, almost subconsciously, that there was no trace of blood: death had been instantaneous. The transmitter itself lay on the floor, a twisted and mangled mass of metal that was obviously smashed beyond repair. Tentatively, not knowing why he did so, he reached out and touched the dead man on the shoulder: Saunders seemed to stir, his cheek slid along the table and he toppled to one side, falling heavily across the battered remains of the transmitter. Reynolds stooped low over him. Grey parchment, now, where a bronzed tan had been; sightless, faded eyes uselessly guarding a mind now flown. Reynolds swore briefly, bitterly, straightened and ran from the hut.

Everyone in the guest hut was asleep, or appeared to be. Reynolds crossed to where Mallory lay, dropped to one knee and shook him roughly by the shoulder. Mallory stirred, opened weary eyes and propped himself up on one elbow. He gave Reynolds a look of unenthusiastic enquiry.

"Among friends, you said!" Reynolds' voice was low, vicious, almost a hissing sound. "Safe, you said. Saunders will be all right, you said. You *knew,* you said. You bloody well knew."

Mallory said nothing. He sat up abruptly on his palliasse, and the sleep was gone from his eyes. He said: "Saunders?"

Reynolds said: "I think you'd better come with me."

In silence the two men left the hut, in silence they crossed the deserted compound and in silence they entered the radio hut. Mallory went no farther than the doorway. For what was probably no more than ten seconds but for what seemed to Reynolds to be an unconscionably long time, Mallory stared at the dead man and the smashed transmitter, his eyes bleak, his face registering no emotional reaction. Reynolds mistook the expression, or lack of it, for something else, and could suddenly no longer contain his pent-up fury.

"Well, aren't you bloody well going to do something about it instead of standing there all night?"

"Every dog's entitled to his one bite," Mallory said mildly. "But don't talk to me like that again. Do what, for instance?"

"Do what?" Reynolds visibly struggled for his self-control. "Find the nice gentleman who did this."

"Finding him will be very difficult." Mallory considered. "Impossible I should say. If the killer came from the camp here, then he'll have gone to earth in the camp here. If he came from outside, he'll be a mile away by this time and putting more distance between himself and us every second. Go and wake Andrea and Miller and Groves and tell them to come here. Then go and tell Major Broznik what's happened."

"I'll tell them what's happened," Reynolds said bitterly. "And I'll also tell them it never *would* have happened if you'd listened to me. But oh, no, you wouldn't listen, would you?"

"So you were right and I was wrong. Now do as I ask you."

Reynolds hesitated, a man obviously on the brink of outright revolt. Suspicion and defiance alternated in the angry face. Then some strange quality in the expression in Mallory's face tipped the balance for sanity and compliance and he nodded in sullen antagonism, turned and walked away.

Mallory waited until he had rounded the corner of the hut, brought out his torch and started, not very hopefully, to quarter the hard-packed snow outside the door of the radio hut. But almost at once he stopped, stooped and brought the head of the torch close to the surface of the ground.

It was a very small portion of footprint indeed, only the front half of the sole of a right foot. The pattern showed two V-shaped marks, the leading V with a cleanly cut break in it. Mallory, moving more quickly now, followed the direction indicated by the pointed toe print and came across two more similar indentations, faint but unmistakable, before the frozen snow gave way to the frozen earth of the compound, ground so hard as to be incapable of registering any footprints at all. Mallory retraced his steps, carefully erasing all three prints with the toe of his boot and reached the radio hut only seconds before he was joined by Reynolds, Andrea, Miller and Groves. Major Broznik and several of his men joined them soon after.

They searched the interior of the radio hut for clues as to the killer's identity, but clues there were none. Inch by inch they searched the hard-packed snow surrounding the hut, with the same completely negative results. Reinforced, by this time, by perhaps sixty or seventy sleepy-eyed Partisan soldiers, they carried out a simultaneous search of all the buildings and of the woods surrounding the encampment: but neither the encampment nor the surrounding woods had any secrets to yield.

"We may as well call it off," Mallory said finally. "He's got clear away."

"It looks that way," Major Broznik agreed. He was deeply troubled and bitterly angry that such a thing should have happened in his encampment. "We'd better double the guards for the rest of the night."

"There's no need for that," Mallory said. "Our friend won't be back."

" 'There's no need for that,' " Reynolds mimicked savagely. "There was no need for that for poor Saunders, you said. And where's Saunders now? Sleeping comfortably in his bed? Is he hell! No need——"

Andrea muttered warningly and took a step nearer Reynolds, but Mallory made a brief conciliatory movement of his right hand. He said: "It's entirely up to you, of course, Major. I'm sorry that we have been responsible for giving you and your men so sleepless a night. See you in the morning." He smiled wryly. "Not that that's so far away." He turned to go, found his way blocked by Sergeant Groves, a Groves whose normally cheerful countenance now mirrored the tight hostility of Reynolds'.

"So he's got clear away, has he? Away to hell and gone. And that's the end of it, eh?"

Mallory looked at him consideringly. "Well, no. I wouldn't quite say that. A little time. We'll find him."

"A little time? Maybe even before he dies of old age?"

Andrea looked at Mallory. "Twenty-four hours?"

"Less."

Andrea nodded and he and Mallory turned and walked away towards the guest hut. Reynolds and Groves, with Miller slightly behind them, watched the two men as they went, then looked at each other, their faces still bleak and bitter.

"Aren't they a nice warmhearted couple now? Completely broken up about old Saunders." Groves shook his head. "They don't care. They just don't care."

"Oh, I wouldn't say that," Miller said diffidently. "It's just that they don't *seem* to care. Not at all the same thing."

"Faces like wooden Indians," Reynolds muttered. "They never even said they were *sorry* that Saunders was killed."

"Well," Miller said patiently, "it's a cliché, but different people react in different ways. Okay, so grief and anger is that natural reaction to this sort of thing, but if Mallory and Andrea spent their time in reacting in that fashion to all the things that have happened to *them* in their lifetimes, they'd have come apart at the seams years ago. So they don't react that way any more. They *do* things. Like they're going to do things to your friend's killer. Maybe you didn't get it, but you just heard a death sentence being passed."

"How do *you* know?" Reynolds said uncertainly. He nodded in the direction of Mallory and Andrea who were just entering the guest hut. "And how did *they* know? Without talking, I mean?"

"Telepathy."

"What do you mean 'telepathy'?"

"It would take too long," Miller said wearily. "Ask me in the morning."

· 6

FRIDAY

0800–1000

CROWNING THE tops of the towering pines, the dense, interlocking snow-laden branches formed an almost impenetrable canopy that effectively screened Major Broznik's camp, huddled at the foot of the *jamba,* from all but the most fleeting glimpses of the sky above. Even at high noon on a summer's day, it was never more than a twilit dusk down below: on a morning such as this, an hour after dawn with snow falling gently from an overcast sky, the quality of light was such as to be hardly distinguishable from a starlit midnight. The interior of the dining hut, where Mallory and his company were at breakfast with Major Broznik, was gloomy in the extreme, the darkness emphasised rather than alleviated by the two smoking oil lamps which formed the only primitive means of illumination.

The atmosphere of gloom was significantly deepened by the behaviour and expressions of those seated round the breakfast table. They ate in a moody silence, heads lowered, for the most part not looking at one another: the events of the previous night had clearly affected them all deeply but none so deeply as Reynolds and Groves in whose faces was still unmistakably reflected the shock caused by Saunders' murder. They left their food untouched.

To complete the atmosphere of quiet desperation, it was clear that the reservations held about the standard of the Partisan early morning cuisine were of a profound and lasting nature. Served by two young *partisankas* (women members of Marshal Tito's army), it consisted of *polenta,* a highly unappetising dish made from ground corn, and *raki,* a Yugoslav spirit of unparalleled fierceness. Miller spooned his breakfast with a marked lack of enthusiasm.

"Well," he said to no one in particular, "it makes a change, I'll say that."

"It's all we have," Broznik said apologetically. He laid down his spoon and pushed his plate away from him. "And even that I can't eat. Not this morning. Every entrance to the *jamba* is guarded, yet there was a killer loose in my camp last night. But maybe he *didn't* come in past the guards, maybe he was already inside. Think of it—a traitor in my own camp. And if there is, I can't even find him. I can't even believe it!''

Comment was superfluous, nothing could be said that hadn't been said already, nobody as much as looked in Brozsnik's direction: his acute discomfort, embarrassment and anger was apparent to everyone in his tone of voice. Andrea, who had already emptied his plate with apparent relish, looked at the two untouched plates in front of Reynolds and Groves and then enquiringly at the two sergeants themselves, who shook their heads. Andrea reached out, brought their plates before him and set to with every sign of undiminished appetite. Reynolds and Groves looked at him in shocked disbelief, possibly awed by the catholicity of Andrea's tastes, more probably astonished by the insensitivity of a man who could eat so heartily only a few hours after the death of one of his comrades. Miller, for his part, looked at Andrea in near-horror, tried another tiny portion of his *polenta* and wrinkled his nose in delicate distaste. He laid down his spoon and looked morosely at Petar who, guitar slung over his shoulder, was awkwardly feeding himself.

Miller said irritably: "Does he *always* wear that damned guitar?"

"Our lost one," Broznik said softly. "That's what we call him. Our poor blind lost one. Always he carries it or has it by his side. Always. Even when he sleeps—didn't you notice last night? That guitar means as much to him as life itself. Some weeks ago, one of our men, by way of a joke, tried to take it from him: Petar, blind though he is, almost killed him.''

"He must be stone tone deaf," Miller said wonderingly. "It's the most god-awful guitar I ever heard.''

Broznik smiled faintly. "Agreed. But don't you understand? He can feel it. He can touch it. It's his own. It's the only thing left to him in the world, a dark and lonely and empty world. Our poor lost one.''

"He could at least tune it," Miller muttered.

"You are a good man, my friend. You try to take our minds off what lies ahead this day. But no man can do that." He turned to Mallory. "Any more than you can hope to carry out your crazy scheme of rescuing your captured agents and breaking up the German counterespionage network here. It is insanity. Insanity!''

Mallory waved a vague hand. "Here you are. No food. No artillery. No transport. Hardly any guns—and practically no ammunition for those guns. No medical supplies. No tanks. No planes. No hope—and you keep on fighting. That makes you sane?''

"*Touché.*" Broznik smiled, pushed across the bottle of *raki,* waited until Mallory had filled his glass. "To the madmen of this world.''

"I've just been talking to Major Stephan up at the Western Gap," General Vukalovic said. "He thinks we're all mad. Would you agree, Colonel Lazlo?''

The man lying prone beside Vukalovic lowered his binoculars. He was a burly, sun-tanned, thick-set, middle-aged man with a magnificent black moustache that had every appearance of being waxed. After a moment's consideration, he said: "Without a doubt, sir.''

"Even you?" Vukalovic said protestingly. "With a Czech father?''

"He came from the High Tatra," Lazlo explained. "They're all mad there.''

Vukalovic smiled, settled himself more comfortably on his elbows, peered downhill through the gap between two rocks, raised his binoculars and scanned the scene to the south of him, slowly raising his glasses as he did so.

Immediately in front of where he lay was a bare, rocky hillside, dropping gently downhill for a distance of about two hundred feet. Beyond its base it merged gradually into a long flat grassy plateau, no more than two hundred yards wide at its maximum, but stretching almost as far as the eye could see on both sides, on the right-hand side stretching away to the west, on the left curving away to the east, northeast and finally north.

Beyond the edge of the plateau, the land dropped abruptly to form the bank of a wide and swiftly flowing river, a river of that peculiarly Alpine greenish-white colour, green from the melting ice-water of spring, white from where it foamed over jagged rocks and over falls in the bed of the river. Directly to the south of where Vukalovic and Lazlo lay, the river was spanned by a green and white painted and very solidly constructed cantilevered steel bridge. Beyond the river, the grassy bank on the far side rose in a very easy slope for a distance of about a hundred yards to the very regularly defined limit of a forest of giant pines which stretched away into the southern distance. Scattered through the very outermost of the pines were a few dully metallic objects, unmistakably tanks. In the farthest distance, beyond the river and beyond the pines, towering, jagged mountains dazzled in their brilliant covering of snow and above that again, but more to the southeast, an equally white and dazzling sun shone from an incongruously blue patch in an otherwise snow-cloud covered sky.

Vukalovic lowered his binoculars and sighed.

"No idea at all how many tanks are across in the woods there?"

"I wish to heaven I knew." Lazlo lifted his arms in a small, helpless gesture. "Could be ten. Could be two hundred. We've no idea. We've sent scouts, of course, but they never came back. Maybe they were swept away trying to cross the Neretva." He looked at Vukalovic, speculation in his eyes. "Through the Zenica Gap, through the Western Gap or across that bridge there—you don't know where the attack is coming from, do you, sir?"

Vukalovic shook his head.

"But you expect it soon?"

"Very soon." Vukalovic struck the rocky ground with a clenched fist. "Is there *no* way of destroying that damned bridge?"

"There have been five R.A.F. attacks," Lazlo said heavily. "To date, twenty-seven planes lost—there are two hundred AA guns along the Neretva and the nearest Messerschmitt station only ten minutes flying time away. The German radar picks up the British bombers crossing our coast—and the Messerschmitts are here, waiting, by the time they arrive. And don't forget that the bridge is set in rock on either side."

"A direct hit or nothing?"

"A direct hit on a target seven metres wide from three thousand metres. It is impossible. And a target so camouflaged that you can hardly see it five hundred metres away on land. Doubly impossible."

"And impossible for us," Vukalovic said bleakly.

"Impossible for us. We made our last attempt two nights ago."

"You made—I told you not to."

"You *asked* us not to. But, of course, I, Colonel Lazlo, knew better. They started firing star shells when our troops were halfway across the plateau. God knows how they knew they were coming. Then the searchlights——"

"Then the shrapnel shells," Vukalovic finished. "And the Oerlikons. Casualties?"

"We lost half a battalion."

"Half a battalion! And tell me, my dear Lazlo, what would have happened in the unlikely event of your men reaching the bridge?"

"They had some amatol blocks, some hand grenades——"

"No fireworks?" Vukalovic asked in heavy sarcasm. "That might have helped. That bridge is built of steel set in reinforced concrete, man! You were mad even to try."

"Yes, sir," Lazlo looked away. "Perhaps you ought to relieve me."

"I think I should." Vukalovic looked closely at the exhausted face. "In fact I would. But for one thing."

"One thing?"

"All my other regimental commanders are as mad as you are. And if the Germans do attack—maybe even tonight?"

"We stand here. We are Yugoslavs and we have no place to go. What else can we do?"

"What else?" Two thousand men with pop guns, most of them weak and starving and lacking ammunition, against what may perhaps be two first-line German armoured divisions. And you stand here. You could always surrender, you know."

Lazlo smiled. "With respects, General, this is no time for facetiousness."

Vukalovic clapped his shoulder. "I didn't think it funny either. I'm going up to the dam, to the northeastern redoubt. I'll see if Colonel Janzy is as mad as you are. And Colonel?"

"Sir?"

"If the attack comes, I may give the order to retreat."

"Retreat?"

"Not surrender. Retreat. Retreat to what, one hopes, may be victory."

"I am sure the general knows what he is talking about."

"The general isn't." Oblivious to possible sniper fire from across the Neretva, Vukalovic stood up in readiness to go. "Ever heard of a man called Captain Mallory. Keith Mallory, a New Zealander?"

"No," Lazlo said promptly. He paused, then went on: "Wait a minute though. Fellow who used to climb mountains?"

"That's the one. But he has also, I'm given to understand, other accomplishments." Vukalovic rubbed a stubbly chin. "If all I hear about him is true, I think you could quite fairly call him a rather gifted individual."

"And what about this gifted individual?" Lazlo asked curiously.

"Just this." Vukalovic was suddenly very serious, even sombre. "When all things are lost and there is no hope left, there is always, somewhere in the world, one man you can turn to. There may be only that one man. More often than not there *is* only that one man. But that one man is always there." He paused reflectively. "Or so they say."

"Yes, sir," Lazlo said politely. "But about this Keith Mallory——"

"Before you sleep tonight, pray for him. I will."

"Yes, sir. And about us? Shall I pray for us, too?"

"That," said Vukalovic, "wouldn't be at all a bad idea."

The sides of the *jamba* leading upward from Major Broznik's camp were very steep and very slippery and the ascending cavalcade of men and ponies were making very heavy going of it. Or most of them were. The escort of dark stocky Bosnian Partisans, to whom such terrain was part and parcel of existence, appeared quite unaffected by the climb: and it in no way appeared to interfere with Andrea's rhythmic puffing of his usual vile-smelling cigar. Reynolds noticed this, a fact which fed fresh fuel to the already dark doubts and torments in his mind.

He said sourly: "You seem to have made a remarkable recovery from the nighttime. Colonel Stavros, sir."

"Andrea." The cigar was removed. "I have a heart condition. It comes and it goes." The cigar was replaced.

"I'm sure it does," Reynolds muttered. He glanced suspiciously and for the twentieth time, over his shoulder. "Where the hell is Mallory?"

"Where the hell is *Captain* Mallory," Andrea chided.

"Well, where?"

"The leader of an expedition has many responsibilities," Andrea said. "Many things to attend to. Captain Mallory is probably attending to something at this very moment."

"You can say that again," Reynolds muttered.

"What was that?"

"Nothing."

Captain Mallory was, as Andrea had so correctly guessed, attending to something at that precise moment. Back in Broznik's office, he and Broznik were bent over a map spread out on the trestle table. Broznik pointed to a spot near the northern limit of the map.

"I agree. This *is* the nearest possible landing strip for a plane. But it is very high up. At this time of year there will still be almost a metre of snow up there. There are other places, better places."

"I don't doubt that for a moment," Mallory said. "Faraway fields are always greener, maybe even faraway airfields. But I haven't the time to go to them." He stabbed his forefinger on the map. "I want a landing strip here and only here by nightfall. I'd be most grateful if you'd send a rider to Konjic within the hour and have my request radioed immediately to your Partisan HQ at Drvar."

Broznik said drily: "You are accustomed to asking for instant miracles, Captain Mallory?"

"This doesn't call for miracles. Just a thousand men. The feet of a thousand men. A small price for seven thousand lives?" He handed Broznik a slip of paper. "Wavelength and code. Have Konjic transmit it as soon as possible." Mallory glanced at his watch. "They have twenty minutes on me already. I'd better hurry."

"I suppose you'd better," Broznik said hurriedly. He hesitated, at a momentary loss for words, then went on awkwardly: "Captain Mallory, I—I——"

"I know. Don't worry. The Mallorys of this world never make old bones anyway. We're too stupid."

"Aren't we all, aren't we all?" Broznik gripped Mallory's hand. "Tonight, I make a prayer for you."

Mallory remained silent for a moment, then paused and nodded.

"Make it a long one."

The Bosnian scouts, now, like the remainder of the party, mounted on ponies, led the winding way down through the gentle slopes of the thickly forested valley, followed by Andrea and Miller riding abreast, then by Petar, whose pony's bridle was in the hand of his sister. Reynolds and Groves, whether by accident or design, had fallen some little way behind and were talking in soft tones.

Groves said speculatively: "I wonder what Mallory and the major are talking about back there?"

Reynolds' mouth twisted in bitterness. "It's perhaps as well we don't know."

"You may be right at that. I just don't know." Groves paused, went on almost pleadingly: "Broznik is on the up-and-up. I'm sure of it. Being what he is, he *must* be."

"That's as may be. Mallory too, eh?"

"*He* must be, too."

"Must?" Reynolds was savage. "God alive, man, I tell you I saw him with my own eyes." He nodded towards Maria, some twenty yards ahead, and his face was cruel and hard. "That girl hit him—and *how* she hit him—back in Neufeld's camp and the next thing I see is the two of them having a cosy little lovey-dovey chat outside Broznik's hut. Odd, isn't it? Soon after, Saunders was murdered. Coincidence, isn't it? I tell you, Groves, Mallory could have done it himself. The girl *could* have had time to do it before she met Mallory—except that it would have been physically impossible for her to drive a six-inch knife home to the hilt. But Mallory could have done it all right. He'd time enough—and opportunity enough—when he handed that damned message into the radio hut."

Groves said protestingly: "Why in God's name should he do that?"

"Because Broznik had given him some urgent information. Mallory *had* to make a show of passing this information back to Italy. But maybe sending that message was the last thing he wanted. Maybe he stopped it in the only way he knew how—and smashed the transmitter to make sure no one else could send a message. Maybe that's why he stopped me from mounting a guard or going to see Saunders—to prevent me from discovering the fact that Saunders was already dead—in which case, of course, because of the time factor, suspicion would have automatically fallen on him."

"You're imagining things." Despite his discomfort, Groves was reluctantly impressed by Reynolds' reasoning.

"You think so? That knife in Saunders' back—did I imagine that too?"

Within half-an-hour, Mallory had rejoined the party. He jogged past Reynolds and Groves, who studiously ignored him, past Maria and Petar, who did the same and took up position behind Andrea and Miller.

It was in this order, for almost an hour, that they passed through the heavily wooded Bosnian valleys. Occasionally, they came to clearings in the pines, clearings that had once been the site of human habitation, small villages or hamlets. But now there were no humans, no habitations, for the villages had ceased to exist. The clearings were all the same, chillingly and depressingly the same. Where the hardworking but happy Bosnians had once lived in their simple but sturdy homes, there was now only the charred and blackened remains of what had once been thriving communities, the air still heavy with the acrid smell of ancient smoke, the sweet-sour stench of corruption and death, mute testimony to the no-quarter viciousness and total ruthlessness of the war between the Germans and the Partisan Yugoslavs. Occasionally, here and there, still stood a few small, stone-built houses which had not been worth the expenditure of bombs or shells or mortars or petrol: but few of the larger buildings had escaped complete destruction. Churches and schools appeared to have been the primary targets: on one occasion, as evidenced by some charred steel equipment that could have come from only an operating theatre, they passed by a small cottage hospital that had been so razed to the ground that no part of the resulting ruins was more than three feet high. Mallory wondered what would have happened to the patients occupying the hospital at the time: but he no longer wondered at the hundreds of thousands of Yugoslavs—350,000 had been the figure quoted by Captain Jensen, but, taking women and children into account, the number must have been at least a million—who had rallied under the banner of Marshal Tito. Patriotism apart, the burning desire for liberation and revenge apart, there was no place else left for them to go. They were a people, Mallory realised, with literally nothing left, with nothing to lose but their lives which they apparently held of small account, but with everything to gain by the destruction of the enemy: were he a German soldier, Mallory reflected, he would not have felt particularly happy about the prospect of a posting to Yugoslavia. It was a war which the Wehrmacht could never win, which the soldiers of no Western European country could ever have won, for the peoples of the high mountains are virtually indestructible.

The Bosnian scouts, Mallory observed, looked neither to left nor right as they passed through the lifeless shattered villages of their countrymen, most of whom were now almost certainly dead. They didn't *have* to look, he realised: they had their memories, and even their memories would be too much for them. If it were possible to feel pity for an enemy, then Mallory at that moment felt pity for the Germans.

By and by they emerged from the narrow winding mountain track on to a narrow, but comparatively wider road, wide enough, at least, for single-file vehicular traffic. The Bosnian scout in the lead threw up his hand and halted his pony.

"Unofficial no-man's-land, it would seem," Mallory said.

"I think this is where they turfed us off the truck this morning."

Mallory's guess appeared to be correct. The Partisans wheeled their horses, smiled widely, waved, shouted some unintelligible words of farewell and urged their horses back the way they had come.

With Mallory and Andrea in the lead and the two sergeants bringing up the rear, the seven remaining members of the party moved off down the track. The snow had stopped now, the clouds above had cleared away and the sunlight was filtering down between the now thinning pines. Suddenly Andrea, who had been peering to his left, reached out and touched Mallory on the arm. Mallory followed the direction of Andrea's pointing hand. Downhill, the pines petered out less than a hundred yards away and through the trees could be glimpsed some distant object, a startling green in colour. Mallory swung round in his saddle.

"Down there. I want to take a look. *Don't* move below the tree line."

The ponies picked their delicate sure-footed way down the steep and slippery slope. About ten yards from the tree line and at a signal from Mallory, the riders dismounted and advanced cautiously on foot, moving from the cover of one pine to the next. The last few feet they covered on hands and knees, then finally stretched out flat in the partial concealment of the boles of the lowermost pines. Mallory brought out his binoculars, cleared the cold-clouded lenses and brought it to his eyes.

The snow line, he saw, petered out some three or four hundred yards below them. Below that again was a mixture of fissured and eroded rock faces and brown earth and beyond that again a belt of sparse and discouraged-looking grass. Along the lower reaches of this belt of grass ran a tarmacadam road, a road which struck Mallory as being, for that area, in remarkably good condition: the road was more or less exactly paralleled, at a distance of about a hundred yards, by a single-track and extremely narrow-gauge railway: a grass-grown and rusted line that looked as if it hadn't been used for many years. Just beyond the line the land dropped in a precipitous cliff to a narrow winding lake, the farther margin of which was marked by far more towering precipices leading up without break and with hardly any variation in angle to rugged snow-capped mountains.

From where he lay Mallory was directly overlooking a right-angled bend in the lake, a lake which was almost incredibly beautiful. In the bright clear sparkling sunlight of that spring morning it glittered and gleamed like the purest of emeralds. The smooth surface was occasionally ruffled by errant cat's paws of wind, cat's paws which had the effect of deepening the emerald colour to an almost translucent aquamarine. The lake itself was nowhere much more than a quarter of a mile in width, but obviously miles in length: the long right-hand arm, twisting and turning between the mountains, stretched to the east almost as far as the eye could see: to the left, the short southern arm hemmed in by increasingly vertical walls which finally appeared almost to meet overhead, ended against the concrete ramparts of a dam. But what caught and held the attention of the watchers was the incredible mirrored gleam of the far mountains in that equally incredible emerald mirror.

"Well, now," Miller murmured, "that *is* nice." Andrea gave him a long expressionless look, then turned his attention to the lake again.

Groves' interest momentarily overcame his animosity.

"What lake is that, sir?"

Mallory lowered the binoculars. "Haven't the faintest idea. Maria?" She made no answer. "Maria! What—lake—is—that?"

"That's the Neretva Dam," she said sullenly. "The biggest in Yugoslavia."

"It's important, then?"

"It is important. Whoever controls that controls central Yugoslavia."

"And the Germns control it, I suppose?"

"They control it. *We* control it." There was more than a hint of triumph in her smile. "We—the Germans—have got it completely sealed off. Cliffs on both sides. To the east there—the upper end—they have a boom across a gorge only ten yards wide. And that boom is patrolled night and day. So is the dam wall itself. the only way in is by a set of steps—ladders, rather— fixed to the cliff face just below the dam."

Mallory said drily: "Very interesting information—for a parachute brigade. But we've other and more urgent fish to fry. Come on." He glanced at Miller, who nodded and began to ease his way back up the slope, followed by the two sergeants, Maria and Petar. Mallory and Andrea lingered for a few moments longer.

"I wonder what it's like," Mallory murmured.

"What's what like?" Andrea asked.

"The other side of the dam."

"And the ladder let into the cliff?"

"And the ladder let into the cliff."

From where General Vukalovic lay, high on a clifftop on the right-hand or western side of the Neretva Gorge, he had an excellent view of the ladder let into the cliff: he had, in fact, an excellent view of the entire outer face of the dam wall and of the gorge which began at the foot of the wall and extended southwards for almost a mile before vanishing from sight round an abrupt right-hand corner.

The dam wall itself was quite narrow, not much more than thirty yards in width, but very deep, stretching down in a slightly Veed formation from between overhanging cliff faces to the greenish-white torrent of water foaming from the outlet pipes at the base. On top of the dam, at the eastern end and on a slight eminence, was the control station and two small huts one of which, judging from the clearly visible soldiers patrolling the top of the wall, was almost certainly a guard room. Above those buildings the walls of the gorge rose quite vertically for about thirty feet then jutted out in a terrifying overhang.

From the control room, a zigzag, green-painted iron ladder, secured by brackets to the rock face, led down to the floor of the gorge. From the base of the ladder a narrow path extended down the gorge for a distance of about a hundred yards, ending abruptly at a spot where some ancient landslide had gouged a huge scar into the side of the gorge. From here a bridge spanned the river to another path on the right-hand bank.

As bridges go, it wasn't much, an obviously very elderly and rickety wooden swing bridge which looked as if its own weight would be enough to carry it into the torrent at any moment: what was even worse, it seemed, at first glance, as if its site had been deliberately picked by someone with an unhinged mind, for it lay directly below an enormous boulder some forty feet up the landslide, a boulder so clearly in a highly precarious state of balance that none but the most foolhardy would have lingered in the crossing of the bridge. In point of fact, no other site would have been possible.

From the western edge of the bridge, the narrow, boulder-strewn path followed the line of the river, passing by what looked like an extremely hazardous ford, and finally curving away from sight with the river.

General Vukalovic lowered his binoculars, turned to the man at his side and smiled.

"All quiet on the eastern front, eh, Colonel Janzy?"

"All quiet on the eastern front," Janzy agreed. He was small puckish humorous-looking character with a youthful face and incongruous white hair. He twisted round and gazed to the North. "But not so quiet on the northern front, I'm afraid."

The smile faded from Vukalovic's face as he turned, lifted his binoculars again and gazed to the North. Less than three miles away and clearly visible in the morning sunlight, lay the heavily wooded Zenica Gap, for weeks a hotly contested strip of territory between Vukalovic's northern defensive forces, under the command of Colonel Janzy, and units of the investing German 11th Army Corps. At that moment frequent puffs of smoke could be seen, to the left a thick column of smoke spiralled up to form a dark pall against the now cloudless blue of the sky while the distant rattle of small-arms fire, punctuated by the occasional heavier boom of artillery, was almost incessant. Vukalovic lowered his glasses and looked thoughtfully at Janzy.

"The softening up before the main attack?"

"What else? The final assault."

"How many tanks?"

"It's difficult to be sure. Collating reports, my staff estimates a hundred and fifty."

"One hundred and fifty!"

"That's what they make it—and at least fifty of those are Tiger tanks."

"Let's hope to heaven your staff can't count." Vukalovic rubbed a weary hand across his bloodshot eyes: he'd had no sleep during the night just gone, no sleep during the night previous to that. "Let's go and see how many *we* can count."

Maria and Petar led the way now, with Reynolds and Groves, clearly in no mood for other company, bringing up the rear almost fifty yards behind. Mallory, Andrea and Miller rode abreast along the narrow road. Andrea looked at Mallory, his eyes speculative.

"Saunders' death? Any idea?"

Mallory shook his head. "Ask me something else."

"The message you'd given him to send. What was it?"

"A report of our safe arrival in Broznik's camp. Nothing more."

"A psycho," Miller announced. "The handy man with the knife, I mean. Only a psycho would kill for that reason."

"Maybe he didn't kill for that reason," Mallory said mildly. "Maybe he thought it was some other kind of message."

"Some other kind of message?" Miller lifted an eyebrow in the way that only he knew how. "Now what kind——" He caught Andrea's eye, broke off and changed his mind about saying anything more. Both he and Andrea gazed curiously at Mallory who seemed to have fallen into a mood of intense introspection.

Whatever its reason, the period of deep preoccupation did not last for long. With the air of a man who has just arrived at a conclusion about something, Mallory lifted his head and called to Maria to stop, at the same time reining in his own pony. Together they waited until Reynolds and Groves had made up on them.

"There are a good number of options open to us," Mallory said, "but for better or worse this is what I have decided to do." He smiled faintly. "For better, I think, if for no other reason than that this is the course of action that will get us out of here fastest. I've talked to Major Broznik and found out what I wanted. He tells me——"

"Got your information for Neufeld, then, have you?" If Reynolds was attempting to mask the contempt in his voice he made a singularly poor job of it.

"The hell with Neufeld," Mallory said without heat. "Partisan spies have discovered where the four captured Allied agents are being held."

"They have?" Reynolds said. "Then why don't the Partisans do something about it?"

"For a good enough reason. The agents are held deep in German territory. In an impregnable blockhouse high up in the mountains."

"And what are *we* going to do about the allied agents held in this impregnable blockhouse?"

"Simple." Mallory corrected himself. "Well, in theory it's simple. We take them out of there and make our break tonight."

Reynolds and Groves stared at Mallory, then at each other, in frank disbelief and consternation. Andrea and Miller carefully avoided looking at each other or at anyone else.

"You're mad!" Reynolds spoke with total conviction.

"You're mad, *sir,*" Andrea said reprovingly.

Reynolds looked uncomprehendingly at Andrea, then turned back to Mallory again.

"You must be!" he insisted. "Break? Break for where, in heaven's name?"

"For home. For Italy."

"Italy!" It took Reynolds all of ten seconds to digest this startling piece of information, then he went on sarcastically: "We're going to fly there, I suppose?"

"Well, it's a long swim across the Adriatic, even for a fit youngster like you. How else?"

"Flying?" Groves seemed slightly dazed.

"Flying. Not ten kilometres from here is a high—a very high mountain plateau, mostly in Partisan hands. There'll be a plane there at nine o'clock tonight."

In the fashion of people who have failed to grasp something they have just heard, Groves repeated the statement in the form of a question. "There'll be a plane there at nine o'clock tonight?"

"You've just arranged this?"

"How could I? We've no radio."

Reynolds' distrustful face splendidly complemented the scepticism in his voice. "But *how* can you be sure—well, at nine o'clock?"

"Because starting at six o'clock this evening there'll be a Wellington bomber over the airstrip every three hours for the next week if necessary."

Mallory kneed his pony and the party moved on, Reynolds and Groves taking up their usual position well to the rear of the others. For some time Reynolds, his expression alternating between hostility and speculation, stared fixedly at Mallory's back: then he turned to Groves.

"Well, well, well. Isn't that very convenient indeed. We just *happen* to be sent to Broznik's camp. He just *happens* to know where the four agents are held. It just *happens* that an airplane will be over a certain airfield at a certain time—and it also so happens that I know for an absolute certainty that there are no airfields up in the high plateaus. Still think everything clean and above board?"

It was quite obvious from the unhappy expression on Groves' face that he thought nothing of the kind. He said: "What in God's name are we going to do?"

"Watch our backs."

Fifty yards ahead of them Miller cleared his throat and said delicately to Mallory: "Reynolds seems to have lost some of his—um—earlier confidence in you, sir."

Mallory said drily: "It's not surprising. He thinks I stuck that knife in Saunders' back."

This time Andrea and Miller did exchange glances, their faces registering expressions as close to pure consternation as either of those poker-faced individuals were capable of achieving.

7

FRIDAY

1000–1200

HALF A mile from Neufeld's camp they were met by Captain Droshny and some half-dozen of his Cetniks. Droshny's welcome was noticeably lacking in cordiality but at least he managed, at what unknown cost, to maintain some semblance of inoffensive neutrality.

"So you came back?"

"As you can see," Mallory agreed.

Droshny looked at the ponies. "And travelling in comfort."

"A present from our good friend Major Broznik." Mallory grinned. "He thinks we're heading for Konjic on them."

Droshny didn't appear to care very much what Major Broznik had thought.

He jerked his head, wheeled his horse and set off at a fast trot for Neufeld's camp.

When they had dismounted inside the compound, Droshny immediately led Mallory into Neufeld's hut. Neufeld's welcome, like Droshny's, was something less than ecstatic, but at least he succeeded in imparting a shade more benevolence to his neutrality. His face held, also, just a hint of surprise, a reaction which he explained at once.

"Candidly, Captain, I did not expect to see you again. There were so many—ah—imponderables. However, I am delighted to see you—you would not have returned without the information I wanted. Now then, Captain Mallory, to business."

Mallory eyed Neufeld without enthusiasm. "You're not a very business-like partner, I'm afraid."

"I'm not?" Neufeld said politely. "In what way?"

"Business partners don't tell lies to each other. Sure you said Vukalovic's troops are massing. So they are indeed. But not, as you said, to break out. Instead, they're massing to defend themselves against the final German attack, the assault that is to crush them once and for all, and this assault they believe to be imminent."

"Well, now, you surely didn't expect me to give away our military se-crets—which you might, I say just might, have relayed to the enemy—before you had proved yourselves," Neufeld said reasonably. "You're not that naïve. About this proposed attack. Who gave you the information?"

"Major Broznik." Mallory smiled in recollection. "He was very expan-sive."

Neufeld leaned forward, his tension reflected in the sudden stillness of his face, in the way his unblinking eyes held Mallory's. "And did they say where they expected this attack to come?"

"I only know the name. The bridge at Neretva."

Neufeld sank back into his chair, exhaled a long soundless sigh of relief and smiled to rob his next words of any offence. "My friend, if you weren't British, a deserter, a renegade and a dope-peddler, you'd get the Iron Cross for this. By the way," he went on, as if by casual afterthought, "you've been cleared from Padua. The bridge at Neretva? You're sure of this?"

Mallory said irritably: "If you doubt my word——"

"Of course not, of course not. Just a manner of speaking." Neufeld paused for a few moments, then said softly: "The bridge at Neretva." The way he spoke them, the words sounded almost like a litany.

Droshny said softly: "This fits in with all we suspected."

"Never mind what you suspected," Mallory said rudely. "To *my* business now, if you don't mind. We have done well, you would say? We have fulfilled your request, got the precise information you wanted?" Neufeld nodded. "Then get us the hell out of here. Fly us deep into some German-held territory. Into Austria or Germany itself, if you like—the farther away from here the better. You know what will happen to us if we ever again fall into British or Yugoslav hands?"

"It's not hard to guess," Neufeld said almost cheerfully. "But you mis-judge us, my friend. Your departure to a place of safety has already been arranged. A certain Chief of Military Intelligence in northern Italy would very much like to make your personal acquaintance. He has reason to believe that you can be of great help to him."

Mallory nodded his understanding.

General Vukalovic trained his binoculars on the Zenica Gap, a narrow and heavily wooded valley floor lying between the bases of two high and steep-shouldered mountains, mountains almost identical in both shape and height.

The German 11th Army Corps tanks among the pines were not difficult to locate, for the Germans had made no attempt either to camouflage or conceal them, measure enough, Vukalovic thought grimly, of the Germans' total confidence in themselves and in the outcome of the battle that lay ahead. He could clearly see soldiers working on some stationary vehicles: other tanks were backing and filling and manoeuvring into position as if making ready to take up battle formation for the actual attack: the deep rumbling roar of the heavy engines of Tiger tanks was almost incessant.

Vukalovic lowered his glasses, jotted down a few more pencil marks on a sheet of paper already almost covered with similar pencil marks, performed a few exercises in addition, laid paper and pencil aside with a sigh and turned to Colonel Janzy, who was similarly engaged.

Vukalovic said wryly: "My apologies to your staff, Colonel. They can count just as well as I can."

For once, Captain Jensen's piratical swagger and flashing, confident smile were not very much in evidence: at that moment, in fact, they were totally absent. It would have been impossible for a face of Jensen's generous proportions ever to assume an actually haggard appearance, but the set, grim face displayed unmistakable signs of strain and anxiety and sleeplessness as he paced up and down the Fifth Army Operations Headquarters in Termoli in Italy.

He did not pace alone. Beside him, matching him step for step, a burly grey-haired officer in the uniform of a Lieutenant-General in the British Army accompanied him backward and forward, the expression on his face an exact replica of that on Jensen's. As they came to the farther end of the room, the general stopped and glanced interrogatively at a headphone-wearing sergeant seated in front of a large RCA transceiver. The sergeant slowly shook his head. The two men resumed their pacing.

The general said abruptly: "Time is running out. You do appreciate, Jensen, that once you launch a major offensive you can't possibly stop it?"

"I appreciate it," Jensen said heavily. "What are the latest reconnaissance reports, sir?"

"There is no shortage of reports, but God alone knows what to make of them all." The general sounded bitter. "There's intense activity all along the Gustav line, involving—as far as we can make out—two Panzer divisions, one German infantry division, one Austrian infantry division and two Jeger battalions—their crack Alpine troops. They're not mounting an offensive, that's for sure—in the first place, there's no possibility of their making an offensive from the area in which they are manoeuvring and in the second place if they *were* contemplating an offensive they'd take damn good care to keep all their preparations secret."

"All this activity, then? If they're not planning an attack."

The general sighed. "Informed opinion has it that they're making all preparations for a lightning pull-out. Informed opinion! All that concerns me is that those blasted divisions are still in the Gustav line. Jensen, *what has gone wrong?*"

Jensen lifted his shoulders in a gesture of helplessness. "It was arranged for a radio rendezvous every two hours from 4 A.M.——"

"There have been no contacts whatsoever."

Jensen said nothing.

The general looked at him, almost speculatively. "The best in southern Europe, you said."

"Yes, I did say that."

The general's unspoken doubts as to the quality of the agents Jensen had selected for operation Force 10 would have been considerably heightened if he had been at that moment present with those agents in the guest hut in Hauptmann Neufeld's camp in Bosnia. They were exhibiting none of the harmony, understanding and implicit mutual trust which one would have expected to find among a team of agents rated as the best in the business. There was, instead, tension and anger in the air, an air of suspicion and mistrust so heavy as to be almost palpable. Reynolds, confronting Mallory, had his anger barely under control.

"I want to know now!" Reynolds almost shouted the words.

"Keep your voice down," Andrea said sharply.

"I want to know now," Reynolds repeated. This time his voice was little more than a whisper, but nonetheless demanding and insistent for that.

"You'll be told when the time comes." As always, Mallory's voice was calm and neutral and devoid of heat. "Not till then. What you don't know, you can't tell."

Reynolds clenched his fists and advanced a step. "Are you damn well insinuating that——"

Mallory said with restraint: "I'm insinuating nothing. I was right, back in Termoli, Sergeant. You're no better than a ticking time bomb."

"Maybe." Reynolds' fury was out of control now. "But at least there's something honest about a bomb."

"Repeat that remark," Andrea said quietly.

"What?"

"Repeat it."

"Look, Andrea——"

"Colonel Stavros, sonny."

"Sir."

"Repeat it and I'll guarantee you a minimum of five years for insubordination in the field."

"Yes, sir." Reynolds' physical effort to bring himself under control was apparent to everyone. "But *why* should he *not* tell us his plans for this afternoon and at the same time let us all know that we'll be leaving from this Ivenici place tonight?"

"Because our plans are something the Germans can do something about," Andrea said patiently. "If they find out. If one of us talked under duress. But they can't do anything about Ivenici—that's in Partisan hands."

Miller pacifically changed the subject. He said to Mallory: "Seven thousand feet up, you say. The snow must be thigh deep up there. How in God's name does anyone hope to clear all that lot away?"

"I don't know," Mallory said vaguely. "I suspect somebody will think of something."

And, seven thousand feet up on the Ivenici plateau, somebody had indeed thought of something.

The Ivenici plateau was a wilderness in white, a bleak and desolate and, for many months of the year, a bitterly cold and howling and hostile wilderness, totally inimicable to human life, totally intolerant of human presence. The plateau was bounded to the west by a five hundred foot high cliff face, quite vertical in some parts, fractured and fissured in others. Scattered along its length were numerous frozen waterfalls and occasional lines of pine trees, impossibly growing on impossibly narrow ledges, their frozen branches drooped and laden with the frozen snow of six long months gone by. To the east the plateau was bounded by nothing but an abrupt and sharply defined line marking the top of another cliff face which dropped away perpendicularly into the valleys below.

The plateau itself consisted of a smooth, absolutely level unbroken expanse of snow, snow which at that height of 2000 metres and in the brilliant sunshine gave off a glare and dazzling reflection which was positively hurtful to the eyes. In length, it was perhaps half a mile: in width, nowhere more than a hundred yards. At its southern end, the plateau rose sharply to merge with the cliff face which here tailed off and ran into the ground.

On this prominence stood two tents, both white, one small, the other a large marquee. Outside the small tent stood two men, talking. The taller and older man, wearing a heavy greatcoat and a pair of smoked glasses, was Colonel Vis, the commandant of a Sarajevo-based brigade of Partisans: the younger, slighter figure was his adjutant, a Captain Vlanovich. Both men were gazing out over the length of the plateau.

Captain Vlanovich said unhappily: "There must be easier ways of doing this, sir."

"You name it, Boris, my boy, and I'll do it." Both in appearance and voice Colonel Vis gave the impression of immense calm and competence. "Bulldozers, I agree, would help. So would snowploughs. But you will agree that to drive either of them up vertical cliff faces in order to reach here would call for considerable skill on the part of the drivers. Besides, what's an army for, if not for marching?"

"Yes, sir," Vlanovich said, dutifully and doubtfully.

Both men gazed out over the length of the plateau to the North.

To the North, and beyond, for all around a score of encircling mountain peaks, some dark and jagged and sombre, others rounded and snow-capped and rose-coloured, soared up into the cloudless washed-out pale blue of the sky. It was an immensely impressive sight.

Even more impressive was the spectacle taking place on the plateau itself. A solid phalanx of a thousand uniformed soldiers, perhaps half in the buff grey of the Yugoslav Army, the rest in a motley array of other countries' uniforms, were moving, at a snail-like pace, across the virgin snow.

The phalanx was fifty people wide but only twenty deep, each line of fifty linked arm-in-arm, heads and shoulders bowed forward as they laboriously trudged at a painfully slow pace through the snow. That the pace was so slow was no matter for wonder, the leading line of men were ploughing their way through waist-deep snow, and already the signs of strain and exhaustion were showing in their faces. It was killingly hard work, work which, at that altitude, doubled the pulse rate, made a man fight for every gasping breath, turned a man's legs into leaden and agonised limbs where only the pain could convince a man that they were still only part of him.

And not only men. After the first five lines of soldiers, there were almost as many women and girls in the remainder of the phalanx as there were men although everyone was so muffled against the freezing cold and biting winds of those high altitudes that it was impossible almost to tell man from woman. The last two lines of the phalanx were composed entirely of *partisankas* and it was significantly ominous of the murderous labour still to come that even they were sinking knee-deep in the snow.

It was a fantastic sight, but a sight that was far from unique in wartime Yugoslavia. The airfields of the lowlands, completely dominated by the armoured divisions of the Wehrmacht, were permanently barred to the Yugoslavs and it was thus that the Partisans constructed many of their airstrips in the mountains. In snow of this depth and in areas completely inaccessible to powered mechanical aids, there was no other way open to them.

Colonel Vis looked away and turned to Captain Vukalovic.

"Well, Boris, my boy, do you think you're up here for the winter sports? Get the food and soup kitchens organised. We'll use up a whole week's rations of hot food and hot soup in this one day."

"Yes, sir." Vlanovich cocked his head, then removed his ear-flapped fur cap the better to listen to the newly begun sound of distant explosions to the north. "What on earth is that?"

Vis said musingly: "Sound does carry far in our pure Yugoslavian mountain air, does it not?"

"Sir? Please?"

"That, my boy," Vis said with considerable satisfaction, "is the Messerschmitt fighter base at Novo Derventa getting the biggest plastering of its lifetime."

"Sir?"

Vis sighed in long-suffering patience. "I'll make a soldier of you some day. Messerschmitts, Boris, are fighters, carrying all sorts of nasty cannon and machine guns. What, at this moment, is the finest fighter target in Yugoslavia?"

"What is——" Vlanovich broke off and looked again at the trudging phalanx. "Oh!"

" 'Oh,' indeed. The British Air Force have diverted six of their best Lancaster heavy bomber squadrons from the Italian front just to attend to our friends at Novo Derventa." He in turn removed his cap, the better to listen. "Hard at work, aren't they? By the time they're finished there won't be a Messerschmitt able to take off from that field for a week. If, that is to say, there are any left to take off."

"If I might venture a remark, sir?"

"You may so venture, Captain Vlanovich."

"There are other fighter bases."

"True." Vis pointed upward. "See anything?"

Vis craned his neck, shielded his eyes against the brilliant sun, gazed into the empty blue sky and shook his head.

"Neither do I," Vis agreed. "But at seven thousand metres—and with their crews even colder than we are—squadrons of Beau fighters will be keeping relief patrol up there until dark."

"Who—who *is* he, sir? Who can ask for all our soldiers down here, for squadrons of bombers and fighters?"

"Fellow called Captain Mallory, I believe."

"A *captain?* Like me?"

"A captain. I doubt, Boris," Vis went on kindly, "whether he's quite like you. But it's not the rank that counts. It's the name. Mallory."

"Never heard of him."

"You will, my boy, you will."

"But—but this man Mallory. What does he want all this *for?*"

"Ask him when you see him tonight."

"When I—he's coming here tonight?"

"Tonight. If," Vis added sombrely, "he lives that long."

Neufeld, followed by Droshny, walked briskly and confidently into his radio hut, a bleak, ramshackle lean-to furnished with a table, two chairs, a large portable transceiver and nothing else. The German corporal seated before the radio looked up enquiringly at their entrance.

"The Seventh Armoured Corp HQ at the Neretva bridge," Neufeld ordered. He seemed in excellent spirits. "I wish to speak to General Zimmerman personally."

The corporal nodded acknowledgement, put through the call-sign and was answered within seconds. He listened briefly, looked up at Neufeld. "The general is coming now, sir."

Neufeld reached out a hand for the earphones, took them and nodded towards the door. The corporal rose and left the hut while Neufeld took the vacated seat and adjusted the headphones to his satisfaction. After a few seconds he automatically straightened in his seat as a voice came crackling over the earphones.

"Hauptmann Neufeld here, Herr General. The Englishmen have returned. Their information is that the Partisan division in the Zenica Cage is expecting a full-scale attack from the south across the Neretva bridge."

"Are they now?" General Zimmerman, comfortably seated in a swivel chair in the back of the radio truck parked on the tree line due south of the Neretva bridge, made no attempt to conceal the satisfaction in his voice. The canvas hood of the truck was rolled back and he removed his peaked cap the better to enjoy the pale spring sunshine. "Interesting, very interesting. Anything else?"

"Yes," Neufeld's voice crackled metallically over the loudspeaker. "They've asked to be flown to sanctuary. Deep behind our lines, even to Germany. They feel—ah—unsafe here."

"Well, well, well. Is that how they feel?" Zimmerman paused, considered, then continued. "You are fully informed of the situation, Hauptmann Neufeld? You are aware of the delicate balance of—um—niceties involved?"

"Yes, Herr General."

"This calls for a moment's thought. Wait."

Zimmerman swung idly to and fro in his swivel chair as he pondered his decision. He gazed thoughtfully but almost unseeingly to the north, across the meadows bordering the south bank of the Neretva, the river spanned by the iron bridge, then the meadows on the far side rising steeply to the rocky redoubt which served as the first line of defense for Colonel Lazlo's Partisan defenders. To the east, as he turned, he could look up the green-white rushing waters of the Neretva, the meadows on either side of it narrowing until, curving north, they disappeared suddenly at the mouth of the cliff-sided gorge from which the Neretva emerged. Another quarter turn and he was gazing into the pine forest to the south, a pine forest which at first seemed innocuous enough and empty of life—until, that was, one's eyes became accustomed to the gloom and scores of large rectangular shapes, effectively screened from both observation from the air and from the northern bank of the Neretva by camouflage canvas, camouflage nets and huge piles of dead branches. The sight of those camouflaged spearheads of his two Panzer divisions somehow helped Zimmerman to make up his mind. He picked up the microphone.

"Hauptmann Neufeld? I have decided on a course of action and you will please carry out the following instructions precisely . . . ."

Droshny removed the duplicate pair of earphones that he had been wearing and said doubtfully to Neufeld: "Isn't the general asking rather a lot of us?"

Neufeld shook his head reassuringly. "General Zimmerman *always* knows what he is doing. His psychological assessment of the Captain Mallorys of this world is invariably a hundred percent right.''

"I hope so." Droshny was unconvinced. "For our sakes, I hope so."

They left the hut. Neufeld said to the radio operator: "Captain Mallory in my office, please. And Sergeant Baer."

Mallory arrived in the office to find Neufeld, Droshny and Baer already there. Neufeld was brief and businesslike.

"We've decided on a ski plane to fly you out—they're the only planes that can land in those damned mountains. You'll have time for a few hours sleep—we don't leave till four. Any questions?"

"Where's the landing strip?"

"A clearing. A kilometre from here. Anything else?"

"Nothing. Just get us out of here, that's all."

"You need have no worry on that score," Neufeld said emphatically. "My one ambition is to see you safely on your way. Frankly, Mallory, you're just an embarrassment to me and the sooner you're on your way the better."

Mallory nodded and left. Neufeld turned to Baer and said: "I have a little task for you, Sergeant Baer. Little but very important. Listen carefully."

Mallory left Neufeld's hut, his face pensive, and walked slowly across the compound. As he approached the guest hut, Andrea emerged and passed wordlessly by, wreathed in cigar smoke and scowling. Mallory entered the hut where Petar was again playing the Yugoslavian version of "The Girl I Left Behind Me." It seemed to be his favourite song. Mallory glanced at Maria, Reynolds and Groves, all sitting silently by, then at Miller who was reclining in his sleeping bag with his volume of poetry.

Mallory nodded towards the doorway. "Something's upset our friend."

Miller grinned and nodded in turn towards Petar. "He's playing Andrea's tune again."

Mallory smiled briefly and turned to Maria. "Tell him to stop playing. We're pulling out late this afternoon and we all need all the sleep we can get."

"We can sleep in the plane," Reynolds said sullenly. "We can sleep when we arrive at our destination—wherever that may be."

"No, sleep now."

"Why now?"

"Why now?" Mallory's unfocussed eyes gazed into the far distance. He said in a quiet voice: "For now is all the time there may be."

Reynolds looked at him strangely. For the first time that day his face was empty of hostility and suspicion. There was puzzled speculation in his eyes, and wonder and the first faint beginnings of understanding.

On the Ivenici plateau, the phalanx moved on, but they moved no more like human beings. They stumbled along now in the advanced stages of exhaustion, automatons, no more, zombies resurrected from the dead, their faces twisted from pain and unimaginable fatigue, their limbs on fire and their minds benumbed. Every few seconds someone stumbled and fell and could not get up again and had to be carried to join scores of others already lying in an almost comatose condition by the side of the primitive runway, where *partisankas* did their best to revive their frozen and exhausted bodies with mugs of hot soup and liberal doses of *raki*.

Captain Vlanovich turned to Colonel Vis. His face was distressed, his voice low and deeply earnest.

"This is madness, Colonel, madness! It's—it's impossible, you can see it's impossible. We'll never—look, sir, two hundred and fifty dropped out in the first two hours. The altitude, the cold, sheer physical exhaustion. It's madness."

"All war is madness," Vis said calmly. "Get on the radio. We require five hundred more men."

8

FRIDAY

1500–2115

Now IT had come, Mallory knew. He looked at Andrea and Miller and Reynolds and Groves and knew that they knew it too. In their faces he could see very clearly reflected what lay at the very surface of his own mind, the explosive tension, the hair-trigger alertness straining to be translated into equally explosive action. Always it came, this moment of truth that stripped men bare and showed them for what they were. He wondered how Reynolds and Groves would be: he suspected they might acquit themselves well. It never occurred to him to wonder about Miller and Andrea, for he knew them too well: Miller, when all seemed lost, was a man above himself while the normally easygoing, almost lethargic Andrea was transformed into an unrecognisable human being, an impossible combination of an icily calculating mind and berserker fighting machine entirely without the remotest parallel in Mallory's knowledge or experience. When Mallory spoke his voice was as calmly impersonal as ever.

"We're due to leave at four. It's now three. With any luck we'll catch them napping. Is everything clear?"

Reynolds said wonderingly, almost unbelievingly: "You mean if anything goes wrong we're to shoot our way out?"

"You're to shoot and shoot to kill. That, Sergeant, is an order."

"Honest to God," Reynolds said, "I just don't know what's going on." The expression on his face clearly indicated that he had given up all attempts to understand what was going on.

Mallory and Andrea left the hut and walked casually across the compound towards Neufeld's hut. Mallory said: "They're on to us, you know."

"I know. Where are Petar and Maria?"

"Asleep, perhaps? They left the hut a couple of hours ago. We'll collect them later."

"Later may be too late. They are in great peril, my Keith."

"What can a man do, Andrea. I've thought of nothing else in the past ten hours. It's a crucifying risk to have to take, but I have to take it. They are expendable, Andrea. You know what it would mean if I showed my hand now."

"I know what it would mean," Andrea said heavily. "The end of everything."

They entered Neufeld's hut without benefit of knocking. Neufeld, sitting behind his desk with Droshny by his side, looked up in irritated surprise and glanced at his watch.

He said curtly: "Four o'clock, I said, not three."

"Our mistake," Mallory apologised. He closed the door. "Please do not be foolish."

Neufeld and Droshny were not foolish, few people would have been while staring down the muzzles of two Lugers with perforated silencers screwed to the end: they just sat there, immobile, the shock slowly draining from their faces. There was a long pause, then Neufeld spoke, the words coming almost haltingly.

"I have been seriously guilty of underestimating——"

"Be quiet. Broznik's spies have discovered the whereabouts of the four captured Allied agents. We know roughly where they are. You know precisely where they are. You will take us there. Now."

"You're mad," Neufeld said with conviction.

"We don't require you to tell us that." Andrea walked round behind Neufeld and Droshny, removed their pistols from their holsters, ejected the shells and replaced the pistols. He then crossed to a corner of the hut, picked up two Schmeisser machine pistols, walked back round to the front of the table and placed the Schmeissers on its top, one in front of Neufeld, one in front of Droshny.

"There you are, gentlemen," Andrea said affably. "Armed to the teeth."

Droshny said viciously: "Suppose we decide not to come with you?"

Andrea's affability vanished. He walked unhurriedly round the table and rammed the Luger's silencer with such force against Droshny's teeth that he gasped in pain. "Please"—Andrea's voice was almost beseeching—"*please* don't tempt me."

Droshny didn't tempt him. Mallory moved to the window and peered out over the compound. There were, he saw, at least a dozen Cetniks within thirty feet of Neufeld's hut, all of them armed. Across the other side of the compound he could see that the door to the stables was open indicating that Miller and the two sergeants were in position.

"You will walk across the compound to the stables," Mallory said. "You will talk to nobody, warn nobody, make no signals. We will follow about ten yards behind."

"Ten yards behind. What's to prevent us making a break for it. You wouldn't dare hold a gun on us out there."

"That's so," Mallory agreed. "From the moment you open this door you'll be covered by three Schmeissers from the stables. If you try any-thing—*anything*—you'll be cut to pieces. That's why we're keeping well behind you—we don't want to be cut to pieces too."

At a gesture from Andrea, Neufeld and Droshny slung their empty Schmeissers in angry silence. Mallory looked at them consideringly and said: "I think you'd better do something about your expressions. They're a dead giveaway that something is wrong. If you open that door with faces like that, Miller will cut you down before you reach the bottom step. Please try to believe me."

They believed him and by the time Mallory opened the door had managed to arrange their features into a near enough imitation of normality. They went down the steps and set off across the compound to the stables. When they had reached halfway Andrea and Mallory left Neufeld's hut and fol-lowed them. One or two glances of idle curiosity came their way, but clearly no one suspected that anything was amiss. The crossing to the stables was completely uneventful.

So, also, two minutes later, was their departure from the camp. Neufeld and Droshny, as would have been proper and expected, rode together in the lead, Droshny in particular looking very warlike with his Schmeisser, pistol and the wickedly curved knives at his waist. Behind them rode Andrea, who appeared to be having some trouble with the action of his Schmeisser, for he had it in his hands and was examining it closely: he certainly wasn't looking at either Droshny or Neufeld and the fact that the gun barrel, which Andrea had sensibly pointed towards the ground, had only to be lifted a foot and the trigger pressed to riddle the two men ahead was a preposterous idea that would not have occurred to even the most suspicious. Behind Andrea, Mallory and Miller rode abreast: like Andrea, they appeared unconcerned, even slightly bored. Reynolds and Groves brought up the rear, almost but not quite attaining the degree of nonchalance of the other three: their still faces and restlessly darting eyes betrayed the strain they were under. But their anxiety was needless for all seven passed from the camp not only unmolested but without as much as even an enquiring glance being cast in their direction.

They rode for over two and a half hours, climbing nearly all the time, and a blood-red sun was setting among the thinning pines to the west when they came across a clearing set on, for once, a level stretch of ground. Neufeld and Droshny halted their ponies and waited until the others came up with them. Mallory reined in and gazed at the building in the middle of the clearing, a low, squat, immensely strong-looking blockhouse, with narrow, heavily barred windows and two chimneys, from one of which smoke was coming.

"This the place?" Mallory asked.

"Hardly a necessary question." Neufeld's voice was dry, but the under-lying resentment and anger unmistakable. "You think I spent all this time leading you to the wrong place?"

"I wouldn't put it past you," Mallory said. He examined the building more closely. "A hospitable-looking place."

"Yugoslav Army ammunition dumps were never intended as first-class hotels."

"I daresay not," Mallory agreed. At a signal from him they urged their ponies forward into the clearing, and as they did so two metal strips in the facing wall of the blockhouse slid back to reveal a pair of embrasures with machine pistols protruding. Exposed as they were, the seven mounted men were completely at the mercy of those menacing muzzles.

"Your men keep a good watch," Mallory acknowledged to Neufeld. "You wouldn't require many men to guard and hold a place like this. How many are there?"

"Six," Neufeld said reluctantly.

"Seven and you're a dead man," Andrea warned.

"Six."

As they approached, the guns, almost certainly because the men behind them had identified Neufeld and Droshny, were withdrawn, the embrasures closed and the heavy metal front door opened. A sergeant appeared in the doorway and saluted respectfully, his face registering a certain surprise.

"An unexpected pleasure, Hauptmann Neufeld," the sergeant said. "We had no radio message informing us of your arrival."

"It's out of action for the moment." Neufeld waved them inside but Andrea gallantly insisted on the German officer taking precedence, reinforcing his courtesy with a threatening hitch to his Schmeisser. Neufeld entered, followed by Droshny and the other five men.

The windows were so narrow that the burning oil lamps were obviously a necessity, the illumination they afforded being almost doubled by a large log fire blazing in the hearth. Nothing could ever overcome the bleakness created by four rough-cut stone walls, but the room itself was surprisingly well furnished with a table, chairs, two armchairs and a sofa: there were even some pieces of carpet. Three doors led off from the room, one heavily barred. Including the sergeant who had welcomed them, there were three armed soldiers in the room. Mallory glanced at Neufeld who nodded, his face tight in suppressed anger.

Neufeld said to one of the guards: "Bring out the prisoners." The guard nodded, lifted a heavy key from the wall and headed for the barred door. The sergeant and the other guard were sliding the metal screens back across the embrasures. Andrea walked casually towards the nearest guard, then suddenly and violently shoved him against the sergeant. Both men cannoned into the guard who had just inserted the key into the door. The third man fell heavily to the ground: the other two, though staggering wildly, managed to retain a semblance of balance or at least remain on their feet. All three twisted round to stare at Andrea, anger and startled incomprehension in their faces, and all three remained very still, and wisely so. Faced with a Schmeisser machine pistol at three paces, the wise man always remains still.

Mallory said to the sergeant: "There are three other men. Where are they?"

There was no reply: the guard glared at him in defiance. Mallory repeated the question, this time in fluent German: the guard ignored him and looked questioningly at Neufeld, whose lips were tight-shut in a face a mask of stone.

"Are you mad?" Neufeld demanded of the sergeant. "Can't you see those men are killers? Tell him."

"The night guards. They're asleep." The sergeant pointed to a door. "That one."

"Open it. Tell them to walk out. Backward and with their hands clasped behind their necks."

"Do exactly as you're told," Neufeld ordered.

The sergeant did exactly what he was told and so did the three guards who had been resting in the inner room, who walked out as they had been instructed, with obviously no thought of any resistance in their minds. Mallory turned to the guard with the key who had by this time picked himself up somewhat shakily from the floor, and nodded to the barred door.

"Open it."

The guard opened it and pushed the door wide. Four British officers moved out slowly and uncertainly into the outer room. Long confinement indoors had made them very pale, but apart from this prison pallor and the fact that they were rather thin, they were obviously unharmed. The man in the lead, with a major's insignia and a Sandhurst moustache—and, when he spoke, a Sandhurst accent—stopped abruptly and stared in disbelief at Mallory and his men.

"Good God above! What on earth are you chaps——"

"Please." Mallory cut him short. "I'm sorry, but later. Collect your coats, whatever warm gear you have, and wait outside."

"But—but where are you taking us?"

"Home. Italy. Tonight. Please hurry!"

"Italy. You're talking——"

"Hurry!" Mallory glanced in some exasperation at his watch. "We're late already."

As quickly as their dazed condition would allow, the officers collected what warm clothing they had and filed outside. Mallory turned to the sergeant again. "You must have ponies here, a stable."

"Round the back of the blockhouse," the sergeant said promptly. He had obviously made a rapid readjustment to the new facts of life.

"Good lad," Mallory said approvingly. He looked at Groves and Reynolds. "We'll need two more ponies. Saddle them up, will you?"

The two sergeants left. Under the watchful guns of Mallory and Miller, Andrea searched each of the six guards in turn, found nothing, and ushered them all into the cell, turning the heavy key and hanging it up on the wall. Then, just as carefully, Andrea searched Neufeld and Droshny: Droshny's face, as Andrea carelessly flung his knives into a corner of the room, was thunderous.

Mallory looked at the two men and said: "I'd shoot you if necessary. It's not. You won't be missed before morning."

"They might not be missed for a good few mornings," Miller pointed out.

"So they're overweight anyway," Mallory said indifferently. He smiled. "I can't resist leaving you with a last little pleasant thought, Hauptmann Neufeld. Something to think about until someone comes and finds you." He looked consideringly at Neufeld, who said nothing, then went on: "About that information I gave you this morning, I mean."

Neufeld looked at him guardedly. "What about the information you gave me this morning?"

"Just this. It wasn't, I'm afraid, quite accurate. Vukalovic expects the attack from the *north,* through the Zenica Gap, *not* across the bridge at Neretva from the south. There are, we know, close on two hundred of your tanks massed in the woods just to the north of the Zenica Gap—but there won't be at 2 A.M. this morning when your attack is due to start. Not after I've got through to our Lancaster squadrons in Italy. Think of it, think of the target. Two hundred tanks bunched in a tiny trap a hundred and fifty yards wide and not more than three hundred long. The R.A.F. will be there at 1:30. By two this morning there won't be a single tank left in commission."

Neufeld looked at him for a long moment, his face very still, then said, slowly and softly: "Damn you! Damn you! Damn you!"

"Damning is all you'll have for it," Mallory said agreeably. "By the time you are released—hopefully assuming that you will be released—it will be all over. See you after the war."

Andrea locked the two men in a side room and hung the key up by the one to the cell. Then they went outside, locked the outer door, hung the key on a nail by the door, mounted their ponies—Groves and Reynolds had already two additional ones saddled—and started climbing once again, Mallory, map in hand, studying in the fading light of dusk the route they had to take.

Their route took them up alongside the perimeter of a pine forest. Not more than half a mile after leaving the blockhouse, Andrea reined in his pony, dismounted, lifted the pony's right foreleg and examined it carefully. He looked up at the others who had also reined in their ponies.

"There's a stone wedged under the hoof," he announced. "Looks bad— but not too bad. I'll have to cut it out. Don't wait for me—I'll catch you up in a few minutes."

Mallory nodded, gave the signal to move on. Andrea produced a knife, lifted the hoof and made a great play of excavating the wedged stone. After a minute or so, he glanced up and saw that the rest of the party had vanished

round a corner of the pine wood. Andrea put away his knife and led the
pony, which quite obviously had no limp whatsoever, into the shelter of the
wood and tethered it there, then moved on foot some way down the hill
towards the blockhouse. He sat down behind the bole of a convenient pine
and removed his binoculars from its case.

He hadn't long to wait. The head and shoulders of a figure appeared in
the clearing below, peering out cautiously from behind the trunk of a tree.
Andrea, flat in the snow now and with the icy rims of the binoculars
clamped hard against his eyes, had no difficulty at all in making an immediate identification: Sergeant Baer, moon-faced, rotund and about seventy
pounds overweight for his unimpressive height, had an unmistakable physical presence which only the mentally incapacitated could easily forget.

Baer withdrew into the woods, then reappeared shortly afterward leading
a string of ponies, one of which carried a bulky covered object strapped to
a pannier bag. Two of the following ponies had riders, both of whom had
their hands tied to the pommels of their saddles. Petar and Maria, without a
doubt. Behind them appeared four mounted soldiers. Sergeant Baer beckoned them to follow him across the clearing and within moments all had
disappeared from sight behind the blockhouse. Andrea regarded the now
empty clearing thoughtfully, lit a fresh cigar and made his way uphill towards his tethered pony.

Sergeant Baer dismounted, produced a key from his pocket, caught sight
of the key suspended from the nail beside the door, replaced his own, took
down the other, opened the door with it and passed inside. He glanced
around, took down one of the keys hanging on the wall and opened a side
door with it. Hauptmann Neufeld emerged, glanced at his watch and smiled.

"You have been very punctual, Sergeant Baer. You have the radio?"

"I have the radio. It's outside."

"Good, good, good." Neufeld looked at Droshny and smiled again. "I
think it's time for us to make our rendezvous with the Ivenici plateau."

Sergeant Baer said respectfully: "How can you be so sure that it is the
Ivenici plateau, Hauptmann Neufeld?"

"How can I be so sure? Simple, my dear Baer. Because Maria—you have
her with you?"

"But of course, Hauptmann Neufeld."

"Because Maria told me. The Ivenici plateau it is."

Night had fallen on the Ivenici plateau, but still the phalanx of exhausted
soldiers were trudging out the landing strip for the plane. The work was not
by this time so cruelly and physically exacting, for the snow was now almost
trampled and beaten hard and flat: but, even allowing for the rejuvenation
given by the influx of another five hundred fresh soldiers, the over-all level
of utter weariness was such that the phalanx was in no better condition than
its original members who had trudged out the first outline of the airstrip in
the virgin snow.

The phalanx, too, had changed its shape. Instead of being fifty wide by
twenty deep it was now twenty wide by fifty deep: having achieved a safe
clearance for the wings of the aircraft, they were now trudging out what was
to be as close as possible an iron-hard surface for the landing wheels.

A three-quarters moon, intensely white and luminous, rode low in the
sky, with scattered bands of cloud coming drifting down slowly from the
North. As the successive bands moved across the face of the moon,
the black shadows swept lazily across the surface of the plateau: the pha-

lanx, at one moment bathed in silvery moonlight, was at the next almost
lost to sight in the darkness. It was a fantastic scene with a remarkably
faerylike quality of eeriness and foreboding about it. In fact it was, as
Colonel Vis had just unromantically mentioned to Captain Vlanovich, like
something out of Dante's *Inferno,* only a hundred degrees colder. At least a
hundred degrees, Vis had amended: he wasn't sure how hot it was in hell.

It was this scene which, at twenty minutes to nine in the evening, confronted Mallory and his men when they topped the brow of a hill and reined
in their ponies just short of the edge of the precipice which abutted on the
western edge of the Ivenici plateau. For at least two minutes they sat there
on their ponies, not moving, not speaking, mesmerised by the other-world
quality of a thousand men with bowed heads and bowed shoulders, shuffling
exhaustedly across the level floor of the plain beneath, mesmerised because
they all knew they were gazing at an unique spectacle which none of them
had ever seen before and would never see again. Mallory finally broke free
from the trancelike condition, looked at Miller and Andrea, and slowly
shook his head in an expression of profound wonder conveying his disbelief,
his refusal to accept the reality of what his own eyes told him was real and
actual beyond dispute. Miller and Andrea returned his look with almost
identical negative motions of their own heads. Mallory wheeled his pony to
the right and led the way along the cliff face to the point where the cliff ran
into the rising ground below.

Ten minutes later they were being greeted by Colonel Vis.

"I did not expect to see you, Captain Mallory." Vis pumped his hand
enthusiastically. "Before God, I did not expect to see you. You—and your
men—must have a remarkable capacity for survival."

"Say that in a few hours," Mallory said drily, "and I would be very
happy indeed to hear it."

"But it's all over now. We expect the plane"—Vis glanced at his watch—
"in exactly eight minutes. We have a bearing surface for it and there should
be no difficulty in landing and taking off provided it doesn't hang around
too long. You have done all that you came to do and achieved it magnificently. Luck has been on your side."

"Say that in a few hours," Mallory repeated.

"I'm sorry." Vis could not conceal his puzzlement. "You expect something to happen to the plane?"

"I don't expect anything to happen to the plane. But what's gone, what's
past, is—was, rather—only the prologue."

"The—the prologue?"

"Let me explain."

Neufeld, Droshny and Sergeant Baer left their ponies tethered inside the
woodline and walked up the slight eminence before them, Sergeant Baer
making heavy weather of their uphill struggle through the snow because of
the weight of the large portable transceiver strapped to his back. Near the
summit they dropped to their hands and knees and crawled forward till they
were within a few feet of the edge of the cliff overlooking the Ivenici
plateau. Neufeld unslung his binoculars and then replaced them: the moon
had just moved from behind a dark barred cloud, high-lighting every aspect
of the scene below: the intensely sharp contrast afforded by black shadow
and snow so deeply and gleamingly white as to be almost phosphorescent
made the use of binoculars superfluous.

Clearly visible and to the right were Vis' command tents and, nearby, some hastily erected soup kitchens. Outside the smallest of the tents could be seen a group of perhaps a dozen people, obviously, even at that distance, engaged in close conversation. Directly beneath where they lay, the three men could see the phalanx turning round at one end of the runway and beginning to trudge back slowly, so terribly slowly, so terribly tiredly, along the wide path already tramped out. As Mallory and his men had been, Neufeld, Droshny and Baer were momentarily caught and held by the weird and other-worldly dark grandeur of the spectacle below. Only by a conscious act of will could Neufeld bring himself to look away and return to the world of normality and reality.

"How very kind," he murmured, "of our Yugoslav friends to go to such lengths on our behalf." He turned to Baer and indicated the transceiver. "Get through to the general, will you?"

Baer unslung his transceiver, settled it firmly in the snow, extended the telescopic aerial, preset the frequency and cranked the handle. He made contact almost at once, talked briefly then handed the microphone and headpiece to Neufeld, who fitted on the phones and gazed down, still half mesmerised, at the thousand men and women moving ant-like across the plain below. The headphones suddenly crackled in his ears and the spell was broken.

"Herr General?"

"Ah. Hauptmann Neufeld." In the earphones the general's voice was faint but very clear, completely free from distortion or static. "Now then. About my psychological assessment of the English mind?"

"You have mistaken your profession, Herr General. Everything has happened exactly as you forecast. You will be interested to know, sir, that the Royal Air Force is launching a saturation bombing attack on the Zenica Gap at precisely 1:30 A.M. this morning."

"Well, well, well," Zimmerman said thoughtfully. "That is interesting. But hardly surprising."

"No, sir." Neufeld looked up as Droshny touched him on the shoulder and pointed to the North. "One moment, sir."

Neufeld removed the earphones and cocked his head in the direction of Droshny's pointing arm. He lifted his binoculars but there was nothing to be seen. But unquestionably there was something to be heard—the distant clamour of aircraft engines, closing. Neufeld readjusted the earphones.

"We have to give the English full marks for punctuality, sir. The plane is coming in now."

"Excellent, excellent. Keep me informed."

Neufeld eased off one earphone and gazed to the North. Still nothing to be seen, the moon was now temporarily behind a cloud, but the sound of the aircraft engines was unmistakably closer. Suddenly, somewhere down on the plateau, came three sharp shrill blasts on a whistle. Immediately, the marching phalanx broke up, men and women stumbling off the runway into the deep snow on the eastern side of the plateau, leaving behind them, obviously by prearrangement, about eighty men who spaced themselves out on either side of the runway.

"They're organised, I'll say that for them," Neufeld said admiringly.

Droshny smiled his wolf's smile. "All the better for us, eh?"

"Everybody seems to be doing their best to help us tonight," Neufeld agreed.

Overhead, the dark and obscuring band of cloud drifted away to the south and the white light of the moon raced across the plateau. Neufeld could immediately see the plane, less than half a mile away, its camouflaged shape sharply etched in the brilliant moonlight as it sunk down towards the end of the runway. Another sharp blast of the whistle and at once the men lining both sides of the runway switched on handlamps—a superfluity, really, in those almost bright as day perfect landing conditions, but essential had the moon been hidden behind cloud.

"Touching down now," Neufeld said into the microphone. "It's a Wellington bomber."

"Let's hope it makes a safe landing," Zimmerman said.

"Let's hope so indeed, sir."

The Wellington made a safe landing, a perfect landing considering the extremely difficult conditions. It slowed down quickly then steadied its speed as it headed towards the end of the runway.

Neufeld said into the microphone: "Safely down, Herr General, and rolling to rest."

"Why doesn't it stop?" Droshny wondered.

"You can't accelerate a plane over snow as you can over a concrete runway," Neufeld said. "They'll require every yard of the runway for the take-off."

Quite obviously, the pilot of the Wellington was of the same opinion. He was about fifty yards from the end of the runway when two groups of people broke from the hundreds lining the edge of the runway, one group heading for the already opened door in the side of the bomber, the other heading for the tail of the plane. Both groups reached the plane just as it rolled to a stop at the very end of the runway, a dozen men at once flinging themselves upon the tail unit and beginning to turn the Wellington through 180°.

Droshny was impressed. "By heavens, they're not wasting much time, are they?"

"They can't afford to. If the plane stays there any time at all it'll start sinking in the snow." Neufeld lifted his binoculars and spoke into the microphone.

"They're boarding now, Herr General. One, two, three . . . seven, eight, nine. Nine it is." Neufeld sighed in relief and at the release of tension. "My warmest congratulations, Herr General. Nine it is, indeed."

The plane was already facing the way it had come. The pilot stood on the brakes, revved the engines up to a crescendo, then, twenty seconds after it had come to a halt, the Wellington was on its way again, accelerating down the runway. The pilot took no chances, he waited till the very far end of the airstrip before lifting the Wellington off, but when he did it rose cleanly and easily and climbed steadily into the night sky.

"Airborne, Herr General," Neufeld reported. "Everything perfectly according to plan." He covered the microphone, looked after the disappearing plane, then smiled at Droshny. "I think we should wish them *bon voyage*, don't you?"

Mallory, one of the hundreds lining the perimeter of the airstrip, lowered his binoculars. "And a very pleasant journey to them all."

Colonel Vis shook his head sadly. "All this work just to send five of my men on a holiday to Italy."

"I daresay they needed a break," Mallory said.

"The hell with them. How about us?" Reynolds demanded. In spite of the words, his face showed no anger, just a dazed and total bafflement. "*We* should have been aboard that damned plane."

"Ah. Well. I changed my mind."

"Like hell you changed your mind," Reynolds said bitterly.

Inside the fuselage of the Wellington, the moustached major surveyed his

three fellow escapees and the five Partisan soldiers, shook his head in disbelief and turned to the captain by his side.

"A rum do, what?"

"Very rum indeed, sir," said the captain. He looked curiously at the
papers the major held in his hand. "What have you there?"

"A map and papers that I'm to give to some bearded naval type when we
land back in Italy. Odd fellow, that Mallory, what?"

"Very odd indeed, sir," the captain agreed.

Mallory and his men, together with Vis and Vlanovich, had detached
themselves from the crowd and were now standing outside Vis' command
tent.

Mallory said to Vis: "You have arranged for the ropes? We must leave at
once."

"What's all the desperate hurry, sir?" Groves asked. Like Reynolds,
much of his resentment seemed to have gone to be replaced by a helpless
bewilderment. "All of a sudden, like, I mean?"

"Petar and Maria," Mallory said grimly. "They're the hurry."

"What about Petar and Maria?" Reynolds asked suspiciously. "Where
do they come into this?"

"They're being held captive in the ammunition blockhouse. And when
Neufeld and Droshny get back there——"

"Get back there," Groves said dazedly. "What do you mean, get back
there. We—we left them locked up. And how in God's name do you know
that Petar and Maria are being held in the blockhouse. How can they be? I
mean, they weren't there when we left there—and that wasn't so long ago."

"When Andrea's pony had a stone in its hoof on the way up here from
the blockhouse, it didn't have a stone in its hoof. Andrea was keeping
watch."

"You see," Miller explained, "Andrea doesn't trust anyone."

"He saw Sergeant Baer taking Petar and Maria there," Mallory went on.
"Bound. Baer released Neufeld and Droshny and you can bet your last cent
our precious pair were up on the cliff side there checking that we really did
fly out."

"You don't tell us very much, do you, sir?" Reynolds said bitterly.

"I'll tell you this much," Mallory said with certainty. "If we don't get
there soon, Maria and Petar are for the high jump. Neufeld and Droshny
don't *know* yet, but by this time they must be pretty convinced that it was
Maria who told me where those four agents were being kept. They've always
known who we really were—Maria told them. Now they know who Maria
is. Just before Droshny killed Saunders——"

"Droshny?" Reynolds' expression was that of a man who has almost
given up all attempt to understand. "Maria?"

"I made a miscalculation." Mallory sounded tired. "We all make mis-
calculations, but this was a bad one." He smiled, but the smile didn't touch
his eyes. "You will recall that you had a few harsh words to say about
Andrea here when he picked that fight with Droshny outside the dining hut
in Neufeld's camp?"

"Sure I remember. It was one of the craziest——"

"You can apologise to Andrea at a later and more convenient time,"
Mallory interrupted. "Andrea provoked Droshny because I asked him to. I
knew that Neufeld and Droshny were up to no good in the dining hut after
we had left and I wanted a moment to ask Maria what they had been

discussing. She told me that they intended to send a couple of Cetniks after us into Broznik's camp—suitably disguised, of course—to report on us. They were two of the men acting as our escort in that wood-burning truck. Andrea and Miller killed them.''

"Now you tell us," Groves said almost mechanically. "Andrea and Miller killed them."

"What I didn't know was that Droshny was also following us. He saw Maria and myself together." He looked at Reynolds. "Just as you did. I didn't know at the time that he'd seen us, but I've known for some hours now. Maria has been as soon as under sentence of death since this morning. But there was nothing I could do about it. Not until now. If I'd shown my hand, we'd have been finished."

Reynolds shook his head. "But you've just said that Maria betrayed us——"

"Maria," Mallory said, "is a top-flight British espionage agent. English father, Yugoslav mother. She was in this country even before the Germans came. As a student in Belgrade. She joined the Partisans, who trained her as a radio operator then arranged for her defection to the Cetniks. The Cetniks had captured a radio operator from one of the first British missions. They—the Germans, rather—trained her to imitate this operator's hand— every radio operator has his own unmistakable style—until their styles were quite undistinguishable. And her English, of course, was perfect. So then she was in direct contact with Allied Intelligence in both North Africa and Italy. The Germans thought they had us completely fooled: it was, in fact, the other way round."

Miller said complainingly: "You didn't tell me any of this, either."

"I've so much on my mind. Anyway, she was notified direct of the arrival of the last four agents to be parachuted in. She, of course, told the Germans. And all those agents carried information reinforcing the German belief that a second front—a full-scale invasion—of Yugoslavia was imminent."

Reynolds said slowly: "They *knew* we were coming too?"

"Of course. They knew everything about us all along, what we really were. What they didn't know, of course, is that we knew they knew and though what they knew of us was true it was only part of the truth."

Reynolds digested this. He said, hesitating: "Sir?"

"Yes?"

"I since have been wrong about you, sir."

"It happens," Mallory agreed. "From time to time, it happens. You were wrong, Sergeant, of course you were, but you were wrong from the very best motives. The fault is mine. Mine alone. But my hands were tied." Mallory touched him on the shoulder. "One of these days you might get round to forgiving me."

"Petar?" Groves asked. "He's not her brother?"

"Petar is Petar. No more. A front."

"There's still an awful lot——" Reynolds began, but Mallory interrupted him.

"It'll have to wait. Colonel Vis, a map please." Captain Vlanovich brought one from the tent and Mallory shone a torch on it. "Look. Here. The Neretva Dam and the Zenica Cage. I told Neufeld that Broznik had told me that the Partisans believe that the attack is coming across the Neretva bridge from the south. But, as I've just said, Neufeld knew—he knew even before we had arrived—who and what we *really* were. So he was convinced I was lying. He was convinced that I was convinced that the attack was coming through the Zenica Gap to the north here. Good reason for believing that, mind you: there are two hundred German tanks up there."

Vis stared at him. "Two hundred!"

"One hundred and ninety of them are made of plywood. So the only way Neufeld—and, no doubt, the German High Command—could ensure that this useful information got through to Italy was to allow us to stage this rescue bid. Which, of course, they very gladly did, assisting us in every possible way even to the extent of gladly collaborating with us in permitting themselves to be captured. They *knew*, of course, that we had no option left but to capture them and force them to lead us to the blockhouse—an arrangement they had ensured by previously seizing and hiding away the only other person who could have helped us in this—Maria. And, of course, knowing this in advance, they had arranged for Sergeant Baer to come and free them."

"I see." It was plain to everyone that Colonel Vis did not see at all. "You mentioned an R.A.F. saturation attack on the Zenica Gap. This, of course, will now be switched to the bridges?"

"No." You wouldn't have us break our word to the Wehrmacht, would you? As promised, the attack comes on the Zenica Gap. As a diversion. To convince them, in case they have any last doubts left in their minds, that we have been fooled. Besides, you know as well as I do that that bridge is immune to high level air attack. It will have to be destroyed in some other way."

"In what way?"

"We'll think of something. The night is young. Two last things, Colonel Vis. There'll be another Wellington in at midnight and a second at 3 A.M. Let them both go. The next in, at 6 A.M., hold it against our arrival. Well, our possible arrival. With any luck we'll be flying out before dawn."

"With any luck," Vis said sombrely.

"And radio General Vukalovic, will you? Tell him what I've told you, the exact situation. And tell him to begin intensive small-arms fire at one o'clock in the morning."

"What are they supposed to fire at?"

"They can fire at the moon for all I care." Mallory swung aboard his pony. "Come on, let's be off."

"The moon," General Vukalovic agreed, "is a fair-sized target, though rather a long way off. However, if that's what our friend wants, that's what he shall have." Vukalovic paused for a moment, looked at Colonel Janzy who was sitting beside him on a fallen log in the woods to the south of the Zenica Gap, then spoke again into the radio mouthpiece.

"Anyway, many thanks, Colonel Vis. So the Neretva bridge it is. And you think it will be unhealthy for us to remain in the immediate vicinity of this area after 1 A.M. Don't worry, we won't be here." Vukalovic removed the headphones and turned to Janzy. "We pull out, quietly, at midnight. We have a few men to make a lot of noise."

"The ones who are going to fire at the moon?"

"The ones who are going to fire at the moon. Radio Colonel Lazlo at Neretva, will you? Tell him we'll be with him before the attack. Then radio Major Stephan. Tell him to leave just a holding force, pull out of the Western Gap and make his way to Colonel Lazlo's HQ." Vukalovic paused for a thoughtful moment. "We should be in for a few very interesting hours, don't you think?"

"Is there any chance in the world for this man Mallory?" Janzy's tone carried with it its own answer.

"Well, look at it this way," Vukalovic said reasonably. "Of course there's a chance. There has to be a chance. It is, after all, my dear Janzy, a question of options—and there are no other options left open to us."

Janzy made no reply but nodded several times in slow succession as if Vukalovic had just said something profound.

9

FRIDAY
2115–SATURDAY: 0040

THE PONYBACK ride downhill through the thickly wooded forests from the Ivenici plateau to the blockhouse took Mallory and his men barely a quarter of the time it had taken them to make the ascent. In the deep snow the going underfoot was treacherous to a degree, collision with the bole of a pine was always an imminent possibility and none of the five riders made any pretence towards being an experienced horseman, with the inevitable result that slips, stumbles and heavy falls were as frequent as they were painful. Not one of them escaped the indignity of involuntarily leaving his saddle and being thrown headlong into the deep snow, but it was the providential cushioning effect of that snow that was the saving of them, that, and, more often, the sure-footed agility of their mountain ponies: whatever the reason or combination of reasons, bruises and winded falls there were in plenty, but broken bones, miraculously, there were none.

The blockhouse came in sight. Mallory raised a warning hand, slowing them down until they were about two hundred yards distant from their objective, where he reined in, dismounted and led his pony into a thick cluster of pines, followed by the others. Mallory tethered his horse and indicated to the others to do the same.

Miller said complainingly: "I'm sick of this damned pony but I'm sicker still of walking through deep snow. Why don't we just ride on down there?"

"Because they'll have ponies tethered down there. They'll start whinnying if they hear or see or smell other ponies approaching."

"They might start whinnying anyway."

"And there'll be guards on watch," Andrea pointed out. "I don't think, Corporal Miller, that we could make a very stealthy and unobtrusive approach on ponyback."

"Guards. Guarding against what? As far as Neufeld and company are concerned, we're halfway over the Adriatic at this time."

"Andrea's right," Mallory said. "Whatever else you may think about Neufeld, he's a first-class officer who takes no chances. There'll be guards." He glanced up at the night sky where a narrow bar of cloud was just approaching the face of the moon. "See that?"

"I see it," Miller said miserably.

"Thirty seconds, I'd say. We make a run for the far gable end of the blockhouse—there are no embrasures there. And, for God's sake, once we get there, keep dead quiet. If they hear anything, if they as much as suspect that we're outside, they'll bar the doors and use Petar and Maria as hostages. Then we'll just have to leave them."

"You'd do that, sir?" Reynolds asked.

"I'd do that. I'd rather cut a hand off, but I'd do that. I've no choice, Sergeant."

"Yes, sir. I understand."

The dark bar of cloud passed over the moon. The five men broke from the concealment of the pines and pounded downhill through the deep clogging snow, heading for the further gable wall of the blockhouse. Thirty yards away, at a signal from Mallory, they slowed down lest the sound of their crunching running footsteps be heard by any watchers who might be keeping guard by the embrasures and completed the remaining distant by walking as quickly and quietly as possible in single file, each man using the footprints left by the man in front of him.

They reached the blank gable end undetected, with the moon still behind the cloud. Mallory did not pause to congratulate either himself or any of the others. He at once dropped to his hands and knees and crawled round the corner of the blockhouse, pressing close in to the stone wall.

Four feet from the corner came the first of the embrasures. Mallory did not bother to lower himself any deeper into the snow—the embrasures were so deeply recessed in the massive stone walls that it would have been quite impossible for any watcher to see anything at a lesser distance than six feet from the embrasure. He concentrated, instead, on achieving as minimal a degree of sound as was possible, and did so with success, for he safely passed the embrasure without any alarm being raised. The other four were equally successful even though the moon broke from behind the cloud as the last of them, Groves, was directly under the embrasure. But he, too, remained undetected.

Mallory reached the door. He gestured to Miller, Reynolds and Groves to remain prone where they were: he and Andrea rose silently to their feet and pressed their ears close against the door.

Immediately they heard Droshny's voice, thick with menace, heavy with hatred.

"A traitress! That's what she is. A traitress to our cause. Kill her now!"

"Why did you do it, Maria?" Neufeld's voice, in contrast to Droshny's, was measured, calm, almost gentle.

"Why did she do it?" Droshny snarled. "Money. That's why she did it. What else?"

"Why?" Neufeld was quietly persistent. "Did Captain Mallory threaten to kill your brother?"

"Worse than that." They had to strain to catch Maria's low voice. "He threatened to kill me. Who would have looked after my blind brother then?"

"We waste time," Droshny said impatiently. "Let me take them both outside."

"No." Neufeld's voice, still calm, admitted of no argument. "A blind boy? A terrified girl? What are you, man?"

"A Cetnik!"

"And I'm an officer of the Wehrmacht."

Andrea whispered in Mallory's ear: "Any minute now and someone's going to notice our foottracks in the snow."

Mallory nodded, stood aside and made a small gesturing motion of his hand. Mallory was under no illusions as to their respective capabilities when it came to bursting open doors leading into rooms filled with armed men. Andrea was the best in the business—and proceeded to prove it in his usual violent and lethal fashion.

A twist of the door handle, a violent kick with the sole of the right foot and Andrea stood framed in the doorway. The wildly swinging door had still not reached the full limit of travel on its hinges when the room echoed to the flat staccato chatter of Andrea's Schmeisser: Mallory, peering over Andrea's shoulder through the swirling cordite smoke, saw two German soldiers, lethally cursed with overfast reactions, slumping wearily to the floor. His own machine pistol levelled, Mallory followed Andrea into the room.

There was no longer any call for Schmeissers. None of the other soldiers in the room was carrying any weapon at all while Neufeld and Droshny, their faces frozen into expressions of total incredulity, were clearly, even if only momentarily, incapable of any movement at all, far less being capable of the idea of offering any suicidal resistance.

Mallory said to Neufeld: "You've just bought yourself your life." He turned to Maria, nodded towards the door, waited until she had led her brother outside, then looked again at Neufeld and Droshny and said curtly: "Your guns."

Neufeld managed to speak, although his lips moved in a strangely mechanical fashion. "What in the name of God——"

Mallory was in no mind for small talk. He lifted his Schmeisser. "Your guns."

Neufeld and Droshny, like men in a dream, removed their pistols and dropped them to the floor.

"The keys." Droshny and Neufeld looked at him in almost uncomprehending silence. "The keys," Mallory repeated. "Now. Or the keys won't be necessary."

For several seconds the room was completely silent, then Neufeld stirred, turned to Droshny and nodded. Droshny scowled—as well as any man can scowl when his face is still overspread with an expression of baffled astonishment and homicidal fury—reached into his pocket and produced the keys. Miller took them, unlocked and opened wide the cell door, wordlessly and with a motion of his machine pistol invited Neufeld, Droshny, Baer and the other soldiers to enter, waited until they had done so, swung shut the door, locked it and pocketed the key. The room echoed again as Andrea squeezed the trigger of his machine pistol and destroyed the radio beyond any hope of repair. Five seconds later they were all outside, Mallory, the last man to leave, locking the door and sending the key spinning to fall yards away, buried from sight in the deep snow.

Suddenly he caught sight of the number of ponies tethered outside the blockhouse. Seven. Exactly the right number. He ran across to the embrasure outside the cell window and shouted: "Our ponies are tethered two hundred yards uphill just inside the pines. Don't forget." Then he ran quickly back and ordered the other six to mount. Reynolds looked at him in astonishment.

"You think of this, sir? At such a time?"

"I'd think of this at any time." Mallory turned to Petar, who had just awkwardly mounted his horse, then turned to Maria. "Tell him to take off his glasses."

Maria looked at him in surprise, nodded in apparent understanding and spoke to her brother, who looked at her uncomprehendingly, then ducked his head obediently, removed his dark glasses and thrust them deep inside his tunic. Reynolds looked on in astonishment, then turned to Mallory.

"I don't understand, sir."

Mallory wheeled his pony and said curtly: "It's not necessary that you do."

"I'm sorry, sir."

Mallory turned his pony again and said, almost wearily: "It's already eleven o'clock, boy, and almost already too late for what we have to do."

"Sir." Reynolds was deeply if obscurely pleased that Mallory should call him boy. "I don't really want to know, sir."

"You've asked. We'll have to go as quickly as our ponies can take us. A blind man can't see obstructions, can't balance himself according to the level of the terrain, can't anticipate in advance how he should brace himself for an unexpectedly sharp drop, can't lean in the saddle for a corner his pony knows is coming. A blind man, in short, is a hundred times more liable to fall off in a downhill gallop than we are. It's enough that a blind man should be blind for life. It's too much that we should expose him to the risk of a heavy fall with his glasses on, to expose him to the risk of not only being blind but of having his eyes gouged out and being in agony for life."

"I hadn't thought—I mean—I'm sorry, sir."

"Stop apologising, boy. It's really my turn, you know—to apologise to you. Keep an eye on him, will you?"

Colonel Lazlo, binoculars to his eyes, gazed down over the moonlit rocky slope below him towards the bridge at Neretva. On the southern bank of the river, in the meadows between the south bank and the beginning of the pine forest beyond, and, as far as Lazlo could ascertain, in the fringes of the pine forest itself, there was a disconcertingly ominous lack of movement, of any sign of life at all. Lazlo was pondering the disturbingly sinister significance of this unnatural peacefulness when a hand touched his shoulder. He twisted, looked up and recognised the figure of Major Stephan, commander of the Western Gap.

"Welcome, welcome. The general has advised me of your arrival. Your battalion with you?"

"What's left of it." Stephan smiled without really smiling. "Every man who could walk. And all those who couldn't."

"God knows we don't need them all tonight. The general has spoken to you of this man Mallory?" Major Stephan nodded, and Lazlo went on: "If he fails? If the Germans cross the Neretva tonight——"

"So?" Stephan shrugged. "We were all due to die tonight anyway."

"A well-taken point," Lazlo said approvingly. He lifted his binoculars and returned to his contemplation of the bridge at Neretva.

So far, and almost incredibly, neither Mallory nor any of the six galloping behind him had parted company with their ponies. Not even Petar. True, the incline of the slope was not nearly so steep as it had been from the Ivenici plateau down to the blockhouse, but Reynolds suspected it was because Mallory had imperceptibly succeeded in slowing down the pace of their earlier headlong gallop. Perhaps, Reynolds thought vaguely, it was because Mallory was subconsciously trying to protect the blind singer, who was riding almost abreast with him, guitar firmly strapped over his shoulder, reins abandoned and both hands clasped desperately to the pommel of his saddle. Unbidden, almost, Reynolds' thoughts strayed back to that scene inside the blockhouse. Moments later, he was urging his pony forward until he had drawn alongside Mallory.

"Sir?"

"What is it?" Mallory sounded irritable.

"A word, sir. It's urgent. Really it is."

Mallory threw up a hand and brought the company to a halt. He said curtly: "Be quick."

"Neufeld and Droshny, sir." Reynolds paused in a moment's brief uncertainty, then continued. "Do you reckon they know where you're going?"

"What's that to do with anything?"

"Please."

"Yes, they do. Unless they're complete morons. And they're not."

"It's a pity, sir." Reynolds said reflectively, "that you hadn't shot them after all."

"Get to the point," Mallory said impatiently.

"Yes, sir. You reckoned Sergeant Baer released them earlier on?"

"Of course." Mallory was exercising all his restraint. "Andrea saw them arrive. I've explained all this. They—Neufeld and Droshny—had to go up to the Ivenici plateau to check that we'd really gone."

"I understand that, sir. So you knew that Baer was following us. How did he get into the blockhouse?"

Mallory's restraint vanished. He said in exasperation: "Because I left both keys hanging outside."

"Yes, sir. You were expecting him. But Sergeant Baer didn't know you were expecting him—and even if he did he wouldn't be expecting to find keys so conveniently to hand."

"Good God in heaven! Duplicates!" In bitter chagrin, Mallory smacked the fist of one hand into the palm of the other. "Imbecile! Imbecile! Of *course* he would have his own keys!"

"And Droshny," Miller said thoughtfully, "may know a short-cut."

"That's not all of it." Mallory was completely back on balance again, outwardly composed, the relaxed calmness of the face the complete antithesis of his racing mind. "Worse still, he may make straight for his camp radio and warn Zimmerman to pull his armoured divisions back from the Neretva. You've earned your passage tonight, Reynolds. Thanks, boy. How far to Neufeld's camp, do you think, Andrea?"

"A mile." The words came over Andrea's shoulder, for Andrea, as always in situations which he knew called for the exercise of his highly specialised talents, was already on his way.

Five minutes later they were crouched at the edge of the forest less than twenty yards from the perimeter of Neufeld's camp. Quite a number of the huts had illuminated windows, music could be heard coming from the dining hut and several Cetnik soldiers were moving about the compound.

Reynolds whispered to Mallory: "How do we go about it, sir?"

"We don't do anything at all. We just leave it to Andrea."

Groves spoke, his voice low. "One man? Andrea? We leave it to one man?"

Mallory sighed. "Tell them, Corporal Miller."

"I'd rather not. Well, if I have to. The fact is," Miller went on kindly, "Andrea is rather good at this sort of thing."

"So are we," Reynolds said. "We're Commandos. We've been trained for this sort of thing."

"And very highly trained, no doubt," Miller said approvingly. "Another half a dozen years' experience and half a dozen of you might be just about able to cope with him. Although I doubt it very much. Before the night is out, you'll learn—I don't mean to be insulting, Sergeants—that you are little lambs to Andrea's wolf." Miller paused and went on sombrely: "Like whoever happens to be inside that radio hut at this moment."

"Like whoever happens——" Groves twisted round and looked behind him. "Andrea? He's gone. I didn't see him go."

"No one ever does," Miller said. "And those poor devils won't ever see him come." He looked at Mallory. "Time's-a-wasting."

Mallory glanced at the luminous hands of his watch. "Eleven thirty. Time *is* a-wasting."

For almost a minute there was a silence broken only by the restless movements of the ponies tethered deep in the woods behind them, then Groves gave a muffled exclamation as Andrea materialised beside him. Mallory looked up and said: "How many?"

Andrea held up two fingers and moved silently into the woods towards his pony. The others rose and followed him, Groves and Reynolds exchanging glances which indicated more clearly than any words could possibly have done that they could have been even more wrong about Andrea than they had ever been about Mallory.

At precisely the moment that Mallory and his companions were remounting their ponies in the woods fringing Neufeld's camp, a Wellington bomber came sinking down towards a well-lit airfield—the same airfield from which Mallory and his men had taken off less than twenty-four hours previously. Termoli, Italy. It made a perfect touchdown and as it taxied along the runway an army radio truck curved in on an interception course, turning to parallel the last hundred yards of the Wellington's run down. In the left-hand front seat and in the right hand back seat of the truck sat two immediately recognisable figures: in the front, the piratical splendidly bearded figure of Captain Jensen, in the back the British Lieutenant-General with whom Jensen had recently spent so much time in pacing the Termoli Operations Room.

Plane and truck came to a halt at the same moment. Jensen, displaying a surprising agility for one of his very considerable bulk, hopped nimbly to the ground and strode briskly across the tarmac and arrived at the Wellington just as its door opened and the first of the passengers, the moustached major, swung to the ground.

Jensen nodded to the papers clutched in the major's hand and said without preamble: "Those for me?" The major blinked uncertainly, then nodded stiffly in return, clearly irked by this abrupt welcome for a man just returned from durance vile. Jensen took the papers without a further word, went back to his seat in the jeep, brought out a flashlight and studied the papers briefly. He twisted in his seat and said to the radio operator seated beside the general: "Flight plan as stated. Target as indicated. Now." The radio operator began to crank a handle.

Some fifty miles to the southeast, in the Foggia area, the buildings and runways of the R.A.F. heavy bomber base echoed and reverberated to the thunder of scores of aircraft engines: at the dispersal area at the west end of the main runway several squadrons of Lancaster heavy bombers were lined up ready for take-off, obviously awaiting the signal to go. The signal was not long in coming.

Halfway down the airfield, but well to one side of the main runway was parked a jeep identical to the one in which Jensen was sitting in Termoli. In the back seat a radio operator was crouched over a radio, earphones to his head. He listened intently, then looked up and said matter-of-factly: "Instructions as stated. Now. Now. Now."

"Instructions as stated," a captain in the front seat repeated. "Now. Now. Now." He reached for a wooden box, produced three Very pistols, aimed directly across the runway and fired each in turn. The brilliantly arcing flares burst into incandescent life, green, red and green again, before curving slowly back to earth. The thunder at the far end of the airfield mounted to a rumbling crescendo and the first of the Lancasters began to move. Within a few minutes the last of them had taken off and was lifting into the darkly hostile night skies of the Adriatic.

"I did say, I believe," Jensen remarked conversationally and comfortably to the general in the back seat, "that they are the best in the business. Our friends from Foggia are on their way."

"The best in the business. Maybe. I don't know. What I do know is that those damned German and Austrian divisions are still in positive in the Gustav line. Zero hour for the assault on the Gustav line is"—he glanced at his watch—"in exactly thirty hours."

"Time enough," Jensen said confidently.

"I wish I shared this blissful confidence."

Jensen smiled cheerfully at him as the jeep moved off, then faced forward in his seat again. As he did, the smile vanished completely from his face and his fingers beat a drum tattoo on the seat beside him.

The moon had broken through again as Neufeld, Droshny and their men came galloping into camp and reined in ponies so covered with steam from their heaving flanks and distressed breathing as to have a weirdly insubstantial appearance in the pale moonlight. Neufeld swung from his pony and turned to Sergeant Baer.

"How many ponies left in the stables?"

"Twenty. About that."

"Quickly. And as many men as there are ponies. Saddle up."

Neufeld gestured to Droshny and together they ran towards the radio hut. The door, ominously enough on that icy night, was standing wide open. They were still ten feet short of the door when Neufeld shouted: "The Neretva bridge at once. Tell General Zimmerman——"

He halted abruptly in the doorway, Droshny by his shoulder. For the second time that evening the faces of both men reflected their stunned disbelief, their total uncomprehending shock.

Only one small lamp burned in the radio hut, but that one small lamp was enough. Two men lay on the floor in grotesquely huddled positions, the one lying partially across the other: both were quite unmistakably dead. Beside them, with its face-plate ripped off and interior smashed, lay the mangled remains of what had once been a transmitter. Neufeld gazed at the scene for some time before shaking his head violently as if to break the shocked spell and turned to Droshny.

"The big one," he said quietly. "The big one did this."

"The big one," Droshny agreed. He was almost smiling. "You will remember what you promised, Hauptmann Neufeld? The big one. He's for me."

"You shall have him. Come. They can be only minutes ahead." Both men turned and ran back to the compound where Sergeant Baer and a group of soliders were already saddling up the ponies.

"Machine pistols only," Neufeld shouted. "No rifles. It will be close quarter work tonight. And Sergeant Baer?"

"Hauptmann Neufeld?"

"Inform the men that we will not be taking prisoners."

As those of Neufeld and his men had been, the ponies of Mallory and his six companions were almost invisible in the dense clouds of steam rising from their sweat-soaked bodies: their lurching staggering gait which could not now even be called a trot, was token enough of the obvious fact that they had reached the limits of exhaustion. Mallory glanced at Andrea, who nodded and said: "I agree. We'd make faster time on foot now."

"I must be getting old," Mallory said, and for a moment he sounded that way. "I'm not thinking very well tonight, am I?"

"I do not understand."

"Ponies. Neufeld and his men will have fresh ponies from the stables. We should have killed them—or at least driven them away."

"Age is not the same thing as lack of sleep. It never occurred to me either. A man cannot think of everything, my Keith." Andrea reined in his pony and was about to swing down when something in the slope below caught his attention. He pointed ahead.

A minute later they drew up alongside a very narrow gauge railway line, of a type still common in central Yugoslavia. At this level the snow had petered out and the track, they could see, was overgrown and rusty but, for all that, apparently in fair enough mechanical condition: undoubtedly, it was the same track that had caught their eye when they had paused to examine the green waters of the Neretva Dam on the way back from Major Broznik's camp that morning. But what simultaneously caught and held the attention of both Mallory and Miller was not the track itself, but a little siding leading on to the track—and a diminutive wood-burning locomotive that stood on the siding. The locomotive was practically a solid block of rust and looked as if it hadn't moved from its present position since the beginning of the war: in all probability, it hadn't.

Mallory produced a large-scale map from his tunic and flashed a torch on it. He said: "No doubt of it, this is the track we saw this morning. It goes down along the Neretva for at least five miles before bearing off to the South." He paused and went on thoughtfully: "I wonder if we could get that thing moving."

"What?" Miller looked at him in horror. "It'll fall to pieces if you touch it—it's only the rust that's holding the damn thing together. And that gradient there!" He peered in dismay down the slope. "What do you think our terminal velocity is going to be when we hit one of those monster pine trees a few miles down the track?"

"The ponies are finished," Mallory said mildly, "and you know how much you love walking."

Miller looked at the locomotive with loathing. "There must be some other way."

"Shh!" Andrea cocked his head. "They're coming. I can hear them coming."

"Get the chocks away from those front wheels," Miller shouted. He ran forward and after several violent and well-directed kicks which clearly took into no account the future state of his toes, succeeded in freeing the triangular block which was attached to the front of the locomotive by a chain: Reynolds, no less energetically, did the same for the other chock.

All of them, even Maria and Petar helping, flung all their weight against the rear of the locomotive. The locomotive remained where it was. They tried again, despairingly: the wheels refused to budge even a fraction of an inch. Groves said, with an odd mixture of urgency and diffidence: "Sir, on a gradient like this, it would have been left with its brakes on."

"Oh! my God!" Mallory said in chagrin. "Andrea. Quickly. Release the brake lever."

Andrea swung himself on to the foot plate. He said complainingly: "There are a dozen damned levers up here."

"Well, open the dozen damned levers then." Mallory glanced anxiously back up the track. Maybe Andrea had heard something, maybe not: there was certainly no one in sight yet. But he knew that Neufeld and Droshny, who must have been released from the blockhouse only minutes after they had left there themselves and who knew those woods and paths better than they did, must be very close indeed by this time.

There was a considerable amount of metallic screeching and swearing coming from the cab and after perhaps half a minute Andrea said: "That's the lot."

"Shove," Mallory ordered.

They shoved, heels jammed in the sleepers and backs to the locomotive, and this time the locomotive moved off so easily, albeit with a tortured squealing of rusted wheels, that most of those pushing were caught wholly by surprise and fell on their backs on the track. Moments later they were on their feet and running after the locomotive which was already perceptibly beginning to increase speed. Andrea reached down from the cab, swung Maria and Petar aboard in turn, then lent a helping hand to the others. The last, Groves, was reaching for the foot plate when he suddenly braked, swung round, ran back to the ponies, unhitched the climbing ropes, flung them over his shoulder and chased after the locomotive again. Mallory reached down and helped him on to the foot plate.

"It's not my day," Mallory said sadly. "Evening rather. First, I forget about Baer's duplicate keys. Then about the ponies. Then the brakes. Now the ropes. I wonder what I'll forget about next?"

"Perhaps about Neufeld and Droshny." Reynolds' voice was carefully without expression.

"What about Neufeld and Droshny?"

Reynolds pointed back up the railway track with the barrel of his Schmeisser. "Permission to fire, sir."

Mallory swung round. Neufeld, Droshny and an indeterminate number of other pony-mounted soldiers had just appeared around a bend in the track and were hardly more than a hundred yards away.

"Permission to fire," Mallory agreed. "The rest of you get down." He unslung and brought up his own Schmeisser just as Reynolds squeezed the trigger of his. For perhaps five seconds the closed metallic confines of the tiny cabin reverberated deafeningly to the crash of the two machine pistols, then, at a nudge from Mallory, the two men stopped firing. There was no target left to fire at. Neufeld and his men had loosed off a few preliminary shots but immediately realised that the wildly swaying saddles of their ponies made an impossibly unsteady firing position as compared to the cab of the locomotive and had pulled their ponies off into the woods on either side of the track. But not all of them had pulled off in time: two men lay motionless and face down in the snow while their ponies still galloped down the track in the wake of the locomotive.

Miller rose, glanced wordlessly at the scene behind, then tapped Mallory

on the arm. "A small point occurs to me, sir. How do we stop this thing."
He gazed apprehensively through the cab window. "Must be doing sixty
already."

"Well, we're doing at least twenty," Mallory said agreeably. "But fast
enough to outdistance those ponies. Ask Andrea. He released the brake."

"He released a dozen levers," Miller corrected. "Any one could have
been the brake."

"Well, you're not going to sit around doing nothing, are you?" Mallory
asked reasonably. "Find out how to stop the damn thing."

Miller looked at him coldly and set about trying to find out how to stop
the damn thing. Mallory turned as Reynolds touched him on the arm.
"Well?"

Reynolds had an arm round Maria to steady her on the now swaying
platform. He whispered: "They're going to get us, sir. They're going to get
us for sure. Why don't we stop and leave those two, sir? Give them a chance
to escape into the woods?"

"Thanks for the thought. But don't be mad. With us they have a chance—
a small one to be sure, but a chance. Stay behind and they'll be butchered."

The locomotive was no longer doing the twenty miles per hour Mallory
had mentioned and if it hadn't approached the figure that Miller had so
fearfully mentioned it was certainly going quickly enough to make it rattle
and sway to what appeared to be the very limits of its stability. By this time
the last of the trees to the right of the track had petered out, the darkened
waters of the Neretva Dam were clearly visible to the west and the railway
track was now running very close indeed to the edge of what appeared to be
a dangerously steep precipice. Mallory looked back into the cab. With the
exception of Andrea, everyone now wore expressions of considerable apprehension on their faces. Mallory said: "Found out how to stop this damn
thing yet?"

"Easy." Andrea indicated a lever. "This handle here."

"Okay, brakeman. I want to have a look."

To the evident relief of most of the passengers in the cab, Andrea leaned
back on the brake lever. There was an eldritch screeching that set teeth on
edge, clouds of sparks flew up past the sides of the cab as some wheels or
other locked solid in the lines, then the locomotive eased slowly to a halt,
both the intensity of sound from the squealing brakes and the number of
sparks diminishing as it did so. Andrea, duty done, leaned out the side of
the cab with all the bored aplomb of the crack loco engineer: one had the
feeling that all he really wanted in life at that moment was a piece of oily
waste and a whistle cord to pull.

Mallory and Miller climbed down and ran to the edge of the cliff, less
than twenty yards away. At least Mallory did. Miller made a much more
cautious approach, inching forward the last few feet on hands and knees.
He hitched one cautious eye over the edge of the precipice, screwed both
eyes shut, looked away and just as cautiously inched his way back from the
edge of the cliff: Miller claimed that he couldn't even stand on the bottom
step of a ladder without succumbing to the overwhelming compulsion to
throw himself into the abyss.

Mallory gazed down thoughtfully into the depths. They were, he saw,
directly over the top of the dam wall, which, in the strangely shadowed half-
light cast by the moon, seemed almost impossibly far below in the dizzying
depths. The broad top of the dam wall was brightly lit by floodlights and
patrolled by at least half a dozen German soliders, jackbooted and helmeted.
Beyond the dam, on the lower side, the ladder Maria had spoken of was

invisible, but the frail-looking swing bridge, still menaced by the massive bulk of the boulder on the scree on the left bank, and, further down, the white water indicating what might or might not have been a possible—or passable—ford were plainly in sight. Mallory, momentarily abstracted in thought, gazed at the scene below for several moments, recalled that the pursuit must be again coming uncomfortably close and hurriedly made his way back to the locomotive. He said to Andrea: "About a mile and a half, I should think. No more." He turned to Maria. "You know there's a ford—or what seems to be a ford—some way below the dam. Is there a way down?"

"For a mountain goat."

"Don't insult him," Miller said reprovingly.

"I don't understand."

"Ignore him," Mallory said. "Just tell us when we get there."

Some five or six miles below the Neretva Dam General Zimmerman paced up and down the fringe of the pine forest bordering the meadow to the south of the bridge at Neretva. Beside him paced a colonel, one of his divisional commanders. To the south of them could just dimly be discerned the shapes of hundreds of men and scores of tanks and other vehicles, vehicles with all their protective camouflage now removed, each tank and vehicle surrounded by its coterie of attendants making last-minute and probably wholly unnecessary adjustments. The time for hiding was over. The waiting was coming to an end. Zimmerman glanced at his watch.

"Twelve-thirty. The first infantry battalions start moving across at fifteen minutes, and spread out along the north bank. The tanks at two o'clock."

"Yes, sir." The details had been arranged many hours ago, but somehow one always found it necessary to repeat the instructions and the acknowledgements. The colonel gazed to the North. "I sometimes wonder if there's *anybody* at all across there."

"It's not the North I'm worrying about," Zimmerman said sombrely. "It's the West."

"The Allies? You—you think their air armadas will come soon? It's still in your bones, Herr General?"

"Still in my bones. It's coming soon. For me, for you, for all of us." He shivered, then forced a smile. "Some ill-mannered lout has just walked over my grave."

10

SATURDAY

0040–0120

"WE'RE COMING up to it now," Maria said. Blond hair streaming in the passing wind, she peered out again through the cab window of the clanking, swaying locomotive, withdrew her head and turned to Mallory. "About three hundred metres."

Mallory glanced at Andrea. "You heard, brakeman?"

"I heard." Andrea leaned hard on the brake lever. The result was as before, a banshee shrieking of locked wheels on the rusty lines and a pyro-technical display of sparks. The locomotive came to a juddering halt as Andrea looked out his cab window and observed a V-shaped gap in the edge of the cliff directly opposite where they had come to a stop. "Within the yard, I should say?"

"Within the yard," Mallory agreed. "If you're unemployed after the war, there should always be a place for you in a shunter's yard." He swung down to the side of the track, lent a helping hand to Maria and Petar, waited until Miller, Reynolds and Groves had jumped down, then said impatiently to Andrea: "Well, hurry up, then."

"Coming." Andrea said peaceably. He pushed the handbrake all the way off, jumped down and gave the locomotive a shove: the ancient vehicle at once moved off, gathering speed as it went. "You never know," Andrea said wistfully. "It might hit somebody somewhere."

They ran towards the cut in the edge of the cliff, a cut which obviously represented the beginning of some prehistoric landslide down to the bed of the Neretva, a maelstrom of white water far below, the boiling rapids result-ing from scores of huge boulders which had slipped from this landslide in that distant aeon. By some exercise of the imagination, that scar in the side of the cliff face might just perhaps have been called a gully, but it was in fact an almost perpendicular drop of scree and shale and small boulders, all of it treacherous and unstable to a frightening degree, the whole dangerous sweep broken only by a small ledge of jutting rock about halfway down. Miller took one brief glance at this terrifying prospect, stepped hurriedly back from the edge of the cliff and looked at Mallory in a silently dismayed incredulity.

"I'm afraid so," Mallory said.

"But this is terrible. Even when I climbed the south cliff in Nava-rone——"

"You didn't climb the south cliff in Navarone," Mallory said unkindly. "Andrea and I pulled you up at the end of a rope."

"Did you? I forget. But this—this is a climber's nightmare."

"So we don't have to climb it. Just lower ourselves down. You'll be all right—as long as you don't start rolling."

"I'll be all right as long as I don't start rolling," Miller repeated mechan-ically. He watched Mallory join two ropes together and pass them around the bole of a stunted pine. "How about Petar and Maria?"

"Petar doesn't have to see to make this descent. All he has to do is to lower himself on this rope—and Petar is as strong as a horse. Somebody will be down there before him to guide his feet on to the ledge. Andrea will look after the young lady here. Now, hurry. Neufeld and his men will be up with us any minute here—and if they catch us on this cliff face, well that's that. Andrea, off you go with Maria."

Immediately, Andrea and the girl swung over the edge of the gully and began to lower themselves swiftly down the rope. Groves watched them, hesitated, then moved towards Mallory.

"I'll go last, sir, and take the rope with me."

Miller took his arm and led him some feet away. He said, kindly: "Gen-erous, son, generous, but it's just not on. Not as long as Dusty Miller's life depends on it. In a situation like this, I must explain, all our lives depend upon the anchor man. The captain, I am informed, is the best anchor man in the world."

"He's what?"

"It's one of the non-coincidences why he was chosen to lead this mission.

Bosnia is known to have rocks and cliffs and mountains all over it. Mallory was climbing the Himalayas, laddie, before you were climbing out of your cot. Even you are not too young to have heard of him.''

"*Keith* Mallory? The New Zealander?"

"Indeed. Used to chase sheep around, I gather. Come on, your turn."

The first five made it safely. Even the last but one, Miller, made the descent to the ledge without incident, principally by employing his favourite mountain-climbing technique of keeping his eyes closed all the time. Then Mallory came last, coiling the rope with him as he came, moving quickly and surely and hardly ever seeming to look where he put his feet but at the same time not as much as disturbing the slightest pebble or piece of shale. Groves observed the descent with a look of almost awed disbelief in his eyes.

Mallory peered over the edge of the ledge. Because of a slight bend in the gorge above, there was a sharp cut-off in the moonlight just below where they stood so that while the phosphorescent whiteness of the rapids was in clear moonlight, the lower part of the slope beneath their feet was in deep shadow. Even as he watched, the moon was obscured by a shadow, and all the dimly seen detail in the slope below vanished. Mallory knew that they could never afford to wait until the moon reappeared for Neufeld and his men could well have arrived by then. Mallory belayed a rope round an outcrop of rock and said to Andrea and Maria: "This one's really dangerous. Watch for loose boulders.''

Andrea and Maria took well over a minute to make their invisible descent, a double tug on the rope announcing their safe arrival at the bottom. On the way down they had started several small avalanches, but Mallory had no fears that the next man down would trigger off a fall of rock that would injure or even kill Andrea and Maria: Andrea had lived too long and too dangerously to die in so useless and so foolish a fashion—and he would undoubtedly warn the next man down of the same danger. For the tenth time Mallory glanced up towards the top of the slope they had just descended but if Neufeld, Droshny and his men had just arrived they were keeping very quiet about it and being most circumspect indeed: it was not a difficult conclusion to arrive at that, after the events of the past few hours, circumspection would be the last thing in their minds.

The moon broke through again as Mallory finally made his descent. He cursed the exposure it might offer if any of the enemy suddenly appeared on the clifftop, even though he knew that Andrea would be guarding against precisely that danger: on the other hand it afforded him the opportunity of descending at twice the speed he could have made in the earlier darkness. The watchers below watched tensely as Mallory, without any benefit of rope, made his perilous descent: but he never even looked like making one mistake. He descended safely to the boulder-strewn shore and gazed out over the rapids.

He said to no one in particular: "You know what's going to happen if they arrive at the top and find us halfway across here and the moon shining down on us?" The ensuing silence left no doubt but that they all knew what was going to happen. "Now is all the time. Reynolds, you think you can make it?" Reynolds nodded. "Then leave your gun."

Mallory knotted a bowline round Reynolds' waist, taking the strain, if one were to arise, with Andrea and Groves. Reynolds launched himself bodily into the rapids, heading for the first of the rounded boulders which offered so treacherous a hold in that seething foam. Twice he was knocked off his feet, twice he regained them, reached the rock, but immediately beyond it was washed away off balance and swept downriver. The men on the bank hauled him ashore again, coughing and spluttering and fighting mad. Without a word to or look at anybody Reynolds again hurled himself into the rapids and this time so determined was the fury of his assault that he succeeded in reaching the far bank without once being knocked off his feet.

He dragged himself on to the stony beach, lay there for some moments recovering from his exhaustion, then rose, crossed to a stunted pine at the base of the cliff rising on the other side, undid the rope round his waist and belayed it securely round the bolt of the tree. Mallory, on his side, took two turns round a large rock and gestured to Andrea and the girl.

Mallory glanced upward again to the top of the gully. There were still no signs of the enemy. Even so, Mallory felt that they could afford to wait no longer, that they had already pushed their luck too far. Andrea and Maria were barely halfway across when he told Groves to give Petar a hand across the rapids. He hoped to God the rope would hold, but hold it did for Andrea and Maria made it safely to the far bank. No sooner had they grounded than Mallory sent Miller on his way, carrying a pile of automatic arms over his left shoulder.

Groves and Petar also made the crossing without incident. Mallory himself had to wait until Miller reached the far bank for he knew the chances of his being carried away were high and if he were then Miller too would be precipitated into the water and their guns rendered useless.

Mallory waited until he saw Andrea give Miller a hand into the shallow water on the far bank and waited no longer. He unwound the rope from the rock he had been using as a belay, fastened a bowline round his own waist and plunged into the water. He was swept away at exactly the same point where Reynolds had been on his first attempt and was finally dragged ashore by his friends on the far bank with a fair amount of the waters of the Neretva in his stomach but otherwise unharmed.

"Any injuries, any cracked bones or skulls?" Mallory asked. He himself felt as if he had been over the Niagara in a barrel. "No? Fine." He looked at Miller. "You stay here with me. Andrea, take the others up round the first corner there and wait for us."

"Me?" Andrea objected mildly. He nodded towards the gully. "We've got friends that might be coming down there at any moment."

Mallory took him some little way aside. "We also have friends," he said quietly, "who might just possibly be coming downriver from the dam garrison." He nodded at the two sergeants, Petar and Maria. "What would happen to them if they ran into an Alpenkorps patrol, do you think?"

"I'll wait for you round the corner."

Andrea and the four others made their slow way upriver, slipping and stumbling over the wetly-slimy rocks and boulders. Mallory and Miller withdrew into the protection and concealment of two large boulders and stared upward.

Several minutes passed. The moon still shone and the top of the gully was still innocent of any sign of the enemy. Miller said uneasily: "What do you think has gone wrong? They're taking a damned long time about turning up."

"No, I think that it's just that they are taking a damned long time in turning back."

"Turning back?"

"They don't *know* where we've gone." Mallory pulled out his map, examined it with a carefully hooded pencil torch. "About three-quarters of a mile down the railway track, there's a sharp turn to the left. In all probability the locomotive would have left the track there. Last time Neufeld and Droshny saw us we were aboard that locomotive and the logical thing for them to have done would have been to follow the track till they came to where we had abandoned the locomotive, expecting to find us somewhere in the vicinity. When they found the crashed engine, they would know at once what would have happened—but that would have given them another mile and a half to ride—and half of that uphill on tired ponies.''

"That must be it. I wish to God," Miller went on grumblingly, "that they'd hurry up."

"What is this?" Mallory queried. "Dusty Miller yearning for action?''

"No, I'm not," Miller said definitely. He glanced at his watch. "But time is getting very short.''

"Time," Mallory agreed soberly, "is getting terribly short.''

And then they came. Miller, glancing upward, saw a faint metallic glint in the moonlight as a head peered cautiously over the edge of the gully. He touched Mallory on the arm.

"I see him," Mallory murmured. Together both men reached inside their tunics, pulled out their Lugers and removed their waterproof coverings. The helmeted head gradually resolved itself into a figure standing fully silhouetted in the moonlight against the sharply etched skyline. He began what was obviously meant to be a cautious descent, then suddenly flung up both arms and fell backward and outward. If he cried out, from where Mallory and Miller were the cry could not have been heard above the rushing of the waters. He struck the ledge halfway down, bounced off and outward for a quite incredible distance then landed spread-eagled on the stony river bank below, pulling down a small avalanche behind him.

Miller was grimly philosophical. "Well, you said it was dangerous.''

Another figure appeared over the lip of the precipice to make the second attempt at a descent, and was followed in short order by several more men. Then, for the space of a few minutes, the moon went behind a cloud, while Mallory and Miller stared across the river until their eyes ached, anxiously and vainly trying to pierce the impenetrable darkness that shrouded the slope on the far side.

The leading climber, when the moon did break through, was just below the ledge, cautiously negotiating the lower slope. Mallory took careful aim with his Luger, the climber stiffened convulsively, toppled backward and fell to his death. The following figure, clearly oblivious of the fate of his companion, began the descent of the lower slope. Both Mallory and Miller sighted their Lugers but just then the moon was suddenly obscured again and they had to lower their guns. When the moon again reappeared, four men had already reached the safety of the opposite bank, two of whom, linked together by a rope, were just beginning to venture the crossing of the ford.

Mallory and Miller waited until they had safely completed two-thirds of the crossing of the ford. They formed a close and easy target and at that range it was impossible that Mallory and Miller should miss, nor did they. There was a momentary reddening of the white waters of the rapids, as much imagined as seen, then, still lashed together, they were swept away down the gorge. So furiously were their bodies tumbled over and over by the rushing waters, so often did cartwheeling arms and legs break surface, that they might well have given the appearance of men who though without hope were still desperately struggling for their lives. In any event, the two men left standing on the far bank clearly did not regard the accident as being

significant of anything amiss in any sinister way. They stood and watched
the vanishing bodies of their companions in perplexity, still unaware of what
was happening. A matter of two or three seconds later and they would never
have been aware of anything else again but once more a wisp of errant dark
cloud covered the moon and they still had a little time, a very little time, to
live. Mallory and Miller lowered their guns.

Mallory glanced at his watch and said irritably: "Why the hell don't they
start firing? It's five past one."

"What don't who start firing?" Miller asked cautiously.

"You heard. You were there. I asked Vis to ask Vukalovic to give us
sound cover at one. Up by the Zenica Gap there, less than a mile away.
Well, we can't wait any longer. It'll take——" He broke off and listened to
the sudden outburst of rifle fire, startlingly loud even at that comparatively
close distance, and smiled. "Well, what's five minutes here or there. Come
on. I have the feeling that Andrea must be getting a little anxious about us."

Andrea was. He emerged silently from the shadows as they rounded the
first bend in the river. He said reproachfully: "Where have you two been?
You had me worried stiff."

"I'll explain in an hour's time—if we're all still around in an hour's
time," Mallory amended grimly. "Our friends the bandits are two minutes
behind. I think they'll be coming in force—although they've lost four already—six including the two Reynolds got from the locomotive. You stop
at the next bend upriver and hold them off. You'll have to do it by yourself.
Think you can manage?"

"This is no time for joking," Andrea said with dignity. "And then?"

"Groves and Reynolds and Petar and his sister come with us upriver,
Reynolds and Groves as nearly as possible to the dam, Petar and Maria
wherever they can find some suitable shelter, possibly in the vicinity of the
swing bridge—as long as they're well clear of that damned great boulder
perched above it."

"Swing bridge, sir?" Reynolds asked. "A boulder?"

"I saw it when we got off the locomotive to reconnoitre."

"*You* saw it. Andrea didn't."

"I mentioned it to him," Mallory went on impatiently. He ignored the
disbelief in the sergeant's face and turned to Andrea. "Dusty and I can't
wait any longer. Use your Schmeisser to stop them." He pointed northwest-
wards towards the Zenica Gap, where the rattle of musketry was now almost
continuous. "With all that racket going on, they'll never know the difference."

Andrea nodded, settled himself comfortably behind a pair of large boulders and slid the barrel of his Schmeisser into the V between them. The
remainder of the party moved upstream, scrambling awkwardly around and
over the slippery boulders and rocks that covered the right-hand bank of the
Neretva, until they came to a rudimentary path that had been cleared among
the stones. This they followed for perhaps a hundred yards, till they came
to a slight bend in the gorge. By mutual consent and without any order being
given, all six stopped and gazed upward.

The towering breath-taking ramparts of the Neretva Dam wall had suddenly come into full view. Above the dam on either side precipitous walls
of rock soared up into the night sky, at first quite vertical then both leaning
out in an immense overhang which seemed to make them almost touch at
the top although this, Mallory knew from the observation he had made from
above, was an optical illusion. On top of the dam wall itself the guardhouses
and radio huts were clearly visible as were the pygmy shapes of several
patrolling German soldiers. From the top of the eastern side of the dam,

where the huts were situated, an iron ladder—Mallory knew it was painted green, but in the half-shadow cast by the dam wall it looked black—fastened by iron supports to the bare rock-face, zigzagged downward to the foot of the gorge, close by where foaming white jets of water boiled from the outlet pipes at the base of the dam wall. Mallory tried to estimate how many steps there would be in that ladder. Two hundred, perhaps two hundred and fifty, and once you started to climb or descend you just had to keep on going, for nowhere was there any platform or back-rest to afford even the means for a temporary respite. Nor did the ladder at any point afford the slightest scrap of cover from watchers on the bridge. As an assault route, Mallory mused, it was scarcely the one he would have chosen: he could not conceive of a more hazardous one.

About halfway between where they stood and the foot of the ladder on the other side, a swing bridge spanned the boiling waters of the gorge. There was little about its ancient, rickety and warped appearance to inspire any confidence: and what little confidence that might have been left could hardly have been able to survive the presence of an enormous boulder, directly above the eastern edge of the bridge, which seemed in imminent danger of breaking loose from its obviously insecure footing in the deep scar in the cliffside.

Reynolds assimilated all of the scene before him, then turned to Mallory. He said quietly: "We've been very patient, sir."

"You've been very patient, Sergeant—and I'm grateful. You know, of course, that there is a Yugoslav division trapped in the Zenica Cage—that's just behind the mountains to our left, here. You know, too, that the Germans are going to launch two armoured divisions across the Neretva bridge at 2 A.M. this morning and that if once they do get across—and normally there would be nothing to stop them—the Yugoslavs armed with only their pop guns and with hardly any ammunition left, would be cut to pieces. You know the only way to stop them is to destroy the Neretva bridge? You know that this counterespionage and rescue mission was only a cover for the real thing?"

Reynolds said bitterly: "I know that—now." He pointed down the gorge. "And I also know that the bridge lies that way."

"And so it does. I also know that even if we could approach it—which would be quite impossible—we couldn't blow that bridge up with a truck-load of explosives: steel bridges anchored in reinforced concrete take a great deal of destroying." He turned and looked at the dam. "So we do it another way. See that dam wall there—there's thirty million tons of water behind it—enough to carry away the Sydney bridge, far less the one over the Neretva."

Groves said in a low voice: "You're crazy," and then, as an afterthought, "sir."

"Don't we know it? But we're going to blow up that dam all the same. Dusty and I."

"But—but all the explosives we have is a few hand grenades," Reynolds said, almost desperately. "And in that dam wall there must be ten to twenty feet thicknesses of reinforced concrete. Blow it up? How?"

Mallory shood his head. "Sorry."

"Why, you close-mouthed——"

"Be quiet! Dammit, man, will you never, *never* learn. Even up to the very last minute you could be caught and made to tell—and then what would happen to Vukalovic's division trapped in the Zenica Cage? What you don't know, you can't tell."

"But you know." Reynolds' voice was thick with resentment. "You and

Dusty and Andrea—Colonel Stavros—*you* know. Groves and I knew all along that you knew. And *you* could be made to talk."

Mallory said with considerable restraint: "Get Andrea to talk? Perhaps you might—if you threatened to take away his cigars. Sure, Dusty and I could talk—but *someone* had to know."

Groves said in the tone of a man reluctantly accepting the inevitable: "How do you get behind the dam wall—you can't blow it up from the front, can you?"

"Not with the means at present available to us," Mallory agreed. "We get behind it. We climb up there." Mallory pointed to the precipitous gorge wall on the other side.

"We climb up there, eh?" Miller asked conversationally. He looked stunned.

"Up that ladder. But not all the way. Three-quarters of the way up the ladder we leave it and climb vertically up the cliff face till we're about forty feet above the top of the dam wall, just where the cliff begins to overhang there. From there, there's a ledge—well, more of a crack, really——"

"A crack!" Miller said hoarsely. He was horror-stricken.

"A crack. It stretches about a hundred and fifty feet clear across the top of the dam wall at an ascending angle of maybe twenty degrees. We go that way."

Reynolds looked at Mallory in an almost dazed incredulity. "It's madness!"

"Madness!" Miller echoed.

"I wouldn't do it from choice," Mallory admitted. "Nevertheless, it's the only way in."

"But you're bound to be seen," Reynolds protested.

"Not bound to be." Mallory dug into his rucksack and produced from it a black rubber frogman's suit, while Miller reluctantly did the same from his. As both men started to pull their suits on, Mallory continued: "We'll be like black flies against a black wall."

"He hopes," Miller muttered.

"Then with any luck we expect them to be looking the other way when the R.A.F. start in with the fireworks. And if we do seem in any danger of discovery—well, that's where you and Groves come in. Captain Jensen was right—as things have turned out we couldn't have done this without you."

"Compliments?" Groves said to Reynolds. "Compliments from the captain? I've a feeling there's something nasty on the way."

"There is," Mallory admitted. He had his suit and hood in position now and was fixing into his belt some pitons and a hammer he had extracted from his rucksack. "If we're in trouble, you two create a diversion."

"What kind of diversion?" Reynolds asked suspiciously.

"From somewhere near the foot of the dam you start firing up at the guards atop the dam wall."

"But—but we'll be completely exposed." Groves gazed across at the rocky scree which composed the left bank at the base of the dam and at the foot of the ladder. "There's not an ounce of cover. What kind of chance will we have?"

Mallory secured his rucksack and hitched a long coil of rope over his shoulder. "A very poor one, I'm afraid." He looked at his luminous watch. "But then, for the next forty-five minutes, you and Groves are expendable. Dusty and I are not."

"Just like that?" Reynolds said flatly. "Expendable."

"Just like that."

"Want to change places?" Miller said hopefully. There was no reply for Mallory was already on his way. Miller, with a last apprehensive look at the towering rampart of rock above, gave a last hitch to his rucksack and followed. Reynolds made to move off, but Groves caught him by the arm and signed to Maria to go ahead with Petar. He said to her: "We'll wait a bit and bring up the rear. Just to be sure."

"What is it?" Reynolds asked in a low voice.

"This. Our Captain Mallory admitted that he has already made four mistakes tonight. I think he's making a fifth now."

"I'm not with you."

"He's putting all our eggs in one basket and he's overlooked certain things. For instance, asking the two of us to stand by at the base of the dam wall. If we have to start a diversion, one burst of machine gun fire from the top of the dam wall will get us both in seconds. One man can create as successful a diversion as two—and where's the point in the two of us getting killed? Besides, with one of us left alive, there's always the chance that something can be done to protect Maria and her brother. I'll go to the foot of the dam while you——"

"Why should you be the one to go? Why not——"

"Wait, I haven't finished yet. I also think Mallory's very optimistic if he thinks that Andrea can hold off that lot coming up the gorge. There must be at least twenty of them and they're not out for an evening's fun and games. They're out to kill us. So what happens if they do overwhelm Andrea and come up to the swing bridge and find Maria and Petar there while we are busy being sitting targets at the base of the dam wall. They'll knock them both off before you can bat an eyelid."

"Or maybe not knock them off," Reynolds muttered. "What if Neufeld were to be killed before they reached the swing bridge? What if Droshny were the man in charge—Maria and Petar might take some time in dying."

"So you'll stay near the bridge and keep our backs covered? With Maria and Petar in shelter somewhere near?"

"You're right, I'm sure you're right. But I don't like it," Reynolds said uneasily. "He gave us his orders and he's not a man who likes having his orders disobeyed."

"He'll never know—even if he ever comes back, which I very much doubt, he'll never know. *And* he's started to make mistakes."

"Not this kind of mistake." Reynolds was still more than vaguely uneasy.

"Am I right or not?" Groves demanded.

"I don't think it's going to matter a great deal at the end of the day," Reynolds said wearily. "Okay, let's do it your way."

The two sergeants hurried off after Maria and Petar.

Andrea listened to the scraping of heavy boots on stones, the very occasional metallic chink of a gun striking against a rock, and waited, stretched out flat on his stomach, the barrel of his Schmeisser rock-steady in the cleft between the boulders. The sounds heralding the stealthy approach up the river bank were not more than forty yards away when Andrea rasied himself slightly, squinted down the barrel and squeezed the trigger.

The reply was immediate. At once three or four guns, all of them, Andrea realised, machine pistols, opened up. Andrea stopped firing, ignored the bullets whistling above his head and ricochetting from the boulders on either side of him, carefully lined up on one of the flashes issuing from a machine pistol and fired a one-second burst. The man behind the machine pistol straightened convulsively, his upflung right arm sending his gun spinning, then slowly toppled sideways into the Neretva and was carried away in the whitely swirling waters. Andrea fired again and a second man twisted round and fell heavily among the rocks. There came a suddenly barked order and the firing downriver ceased.

There were eight men in the downriver group and now one of them detached himself from the shelter of a boulder and crawled towards the second man who had been hit: as he moved, Droshny's face revealed his usual wolfish grin, but it was clear that he was feeling very far from smiling. He bent over the huddled figure in the stones, and turned him on his back: it was Neufeld, with blood streaming down from a gash in the side of the head. Droshny straightened, his face vicious in anger, and turned round as one of his Cetniks touched his arm.

"Is he dead?"

"Not quite. Concussed and badly. He'll be unconscious for hours, maybe days. I don't know, only a doctor can tell." Droshny beckoned to two other men. "You three—get him across the ford and up to safety. Two stay with him, the other come back. And for God's sake tell the others to hurry up and get here."

His face still contorted with anger and for the moment oblivious of all danger, Droshny leapt to his feet and fired a long continuous burst upstream, a burst which apparently left Andrea completely unmoved, for he remained motionless where he was, resting peacefully with his back to his protective boulder, watching with mild interest but apparent unconcern as ricochets and splintered fragments of rock flew off in all directions.

The sound of the firing carried clearly to the ears of the guards patrolling the top of the dam. Such was the bedlam of small arms fire all around and such were the tricks played on the ears by the baffling variety of echoes that reverberated up and down the gorge and over the surface of the dam itself, that it was quite impossible precisely to locate the source of the recent bursts of machine pistol fire: what was significant, however, was that it *had* been machine gun fire and up to that moment the sounds of musketry had consisted exlusively of rifle fire. And it *had* seemed to emanate from the south, from the gorge below the dam. One of the guards on the dam went worriedly to the captain in charge, spoke briefly then walked quickly across to one of the small huts on the raised concrete platform at the eastern end of the dam wall. The hut, which had no front, only a rolled-up canvas protection, held a large radio transceiver manned by a corporal.

"Captain's orders," the sergeant said. "Get through to the bridge at Neretva. Pass a message to General Zimmerman that we—the captain, that is—is worried. Tell him that there's a great deal of small arms fire all around us and that some of it seems to be coming from downriver."

The sergeant waited impatiently while the operator put the call through and even more impatiently as the earphones crackled two minutes later and the operator started writing down the message. He took the completed message from the operator and handed it to the captain, who read it out aloud.

"General Zimmerman says there is no cause at all for anxiety, the noise is being made by our Yugoslav friends up by the Zenica Gap, who are whistling in the dark because they are momentarily expecting an all-out assault by units of the 11th Army Corps. And it will be a great deal noisier later on when the R.A.F. starts dropping bombs in all the wrong places. But they won't be dropping them near you, so don't worry.' " The captain lowered the paper. "That's good enough for me. If the general says we are not to worry, then that's good enough for me. You know the general's reputation, Sergeant?''

"I know his reputation, sir." Some distance away and from some unidentifiable direction, came several more bursts of machine pistol fire. The sergeant stirred unhappily.

"You are still troubled by something?" the captain asked.

"Yes, sir. I know the general's reputation, of course, and trust him implicitly." He paused, then went on worriedly: "I could have *sworn* that that last burst of machine pistol fire came from down the gorge there."

"You're becoming just an old woman, Sergeant," the captain said kindly, "and you must report to our divisional surgeon soon. Your ears need examining."

The sergeant, in fact, was not becoming an old woman and his hearing in fact, was in considerably better shape than that of the officer who had reproached him. The current burst of machine pistol firing was, as he'd thought, coming from the gorge, where Droshny and his men, now redoubled in numbers, were moving forward, singly or in pairs, but never more than two at a time, in a series of sharp but very short rushes, firing as they went. Their firing, necessarily wildly inaccurate as they stumbled and slipped on the treacherous going underfoot, elicited no response from Andrea, possibly because he felt himself in no great danger, probably because he was conserving his ammunition. The latter supposition seemed the more likely as Andrea had slung his Schmeisser and was now examining with interest a stick-grenade which he had just withdrawn from his belt.

Farther upriver, Sergeant Reynolds, standing at the eastern edge of the rickety wooden bridge which spanned the narrowest part of the gorge where the turbulent, racing, foaming waters beneath would have offered no hope of life at all to any person so unfortunate as to fall in there, looked unhappily down the gorge towards the source of the machine pistol firing and wondered for the tenth time whether he should take a chance, recross the bridge and go to Andrea's aid: even in the light of his vastly revised estimate of Andrea, it seemed impossible, as Groves had said, that one man could for long hold off twenty others bent on vengeance. On the other hand, he had promised Groves to remain there to look after Petar and Maria. There came another burst of firing from downriver. Reynolds made his mind up. He would offer his gun to Maria to afford herself and Petar what protection it might, and leave them for as little time as it might be necessary to Andrea what hope he required.

He turned to speak to her, but Maria and Petar were no longer there. Reynolds looked wildly around, his first reaction was that they had both fallen into the rapids, a reaction that he at once dismissed as ridiculous. Instinctively he gazed up the bank towards the base of the dam and, even though the moon was then obscured by a large bank of cloud, he saw them at once, making their way towards the foot of the iron ladder, where Groves was standing. For a brief moment he puzzled why they should have moved upstream without permission, then remembered that neither he nor Groves had, in fact, remembered to give them instructions to remain by the bridge. Not to worry, he thought, Groves will soon send them back down to the bridge again and when they arrived he would tell them of his decision to return to Andrea's aid. He felt vaguely relieved at the prospect, not because he entertained fears of what might possibly happen to him when he rejoined Andrea and faced up to Droshny and his men but because it postponed, if even only briefly, the necessity of implementing a decision which could be only marginally justifiable in the first place.

Groves, who had been gazing up the seemingly endless series of zigzags of that green iron ladder so precariously, it seemed, attached to that vertical cliff face, swung round at the soft grate of approaching footsteps on the shale and stared at Maria and Petar, walking, as always, hand in hand. He said angrily: "What in God's name are you people doing here? You've no right to be here—can't you see, the guards have only to look down and you'll be killed? Go on. Go back and rejoin Sergeant Reynolds at the bridge. Now!"

Maria said softly: "You are kind to worry, Sergeant Groves. But we don't want to go. We want to stay here."

"And what in hell's name good can you do by staying here?" Groves asked roughly. He paused, then went on, almost kindly: "I know who you are now, Maria. I know what you've done, how good you are at your own job. But this is not your job. Please."

"No." She shook her head. "And I *can* fire a gun."

"You haven't got one to fire. And Petar here, what right have you to speak for him. Does he know where he is?"

Maria spoke rapidly to her brother in incomprehensible Serbo-Croat: he responded by making his customary odd sounds in his throat. When he had finished, Maria turned to Groves.

"He says he knows he is going to die tonight. He has what you people call the second sight and he says there is no future beyond tonight. He says he is tired of running. He says he will wait here till the time comes."

"Of all the stubborn, thick-headed——"

"Please, Sergeant Groves." The voice, though still low, was touched by a new note of asperity. "His mind is made up, and you can never change it."

Groves nodded in acceptance. He said: "Perhaps I can chance yours."

"I do not understand."

"Petar cannot help us anyway, no blind man could. But you can. If you would."

"Tell me."

"Andrea is holding off a mixed force of at least twenty Cetniks and German troops." Groves smiled wryly. "I have recent reason to believe that Andrea probably has no equal anywhere as a guerrilla fighter, but one man cannot hold off twenty for ever. When he goes, then there is only Reynolds left to guard the bridge—and if he goes then Droshny and his men will be through in time to warn the guards, almost certainly in time to save the dam, certainly in time to send a radio message through to General Zimmerman to pull his tanks back on to high ground. I think, Maria, that Reynolds may require your help. Certainly, you can be of no help here—but if you stand by Reynolds you *could* make all the difference between success and failure. And you did say you can fire a gun."

"And as *you* pointed out, I haven't got a gun."

"That was then. You have now." Groves unslung his Schmeisser and handed it to her along with some spare ammunition.

"But——" Maria accepted gun and ammunition reluctantly. "But now *you* haven't a gun."

"Oh, yes I have." Groves produced his silenced Luger from his tunic. "This is all I want tonight. *I* can't afford to make any noise tonight, not so close to the dam as this."

"But I *can't* leave my brother."

"Oh, I think you can. In fact, your going to. No one on earth can help your brother any more. Not now. Please hurry."

"Very well." She moved off a few reluctant paces, stopped, turned and said: "I suppose you think you're very clever, Sergeant Groves?"

"I don't know what you're talking about," Groves said woodenly. She looked at him steadily for a few moments, then turned and made her way downriver. Groves smiled to himself in the near-darkness.

The smile vanished in the instant of time that it took for the gorge to be suddenly flooded with bright moonlight as a black, sharply edged cloud moved away from the face of the moon. Groves called softly, urgently to Maria: "Face down on the rocks and keep still," saw her at once do what he ordered, then looked up the green ladder, his face registering the strain and anxiety in his mind.

About three-quarters of the way up the ladder, Mallory and Miller, bathed in the brilliant moonlight, clung to the top of one of the angled sections as immobile as if they had been carved from the rock itself. Their unmoving eyes, set in equally unmoving faces, were obviously fixed—or transfixed by—the same point in space.

That point was a scant fifty feet away, above and to their left, where two obviously very jumpy guards were leaning anxiously over the parapet at the top of the dam: they were gazing into the middle distance, down the gorge, toward the location of what seemed to be the sound of firing. They had only to move their eyes downward and discovery for Groves and Maria was certain: they had only to shift their gaze to the left and discovery for Mallory and Miller would have been equally certain. And death for all inevitable.

11

SATURDAY

0120–0135

LIKE MALLORY and Miller, Groves, too, had caught sight of the two German sentries leaning out over the parapet at the top of the dam and staring anxiously down the gorge. As a situation for conveying a feeling of complete nakedness, exposure and vulnerability it would, Groves felt, take a lot of beating. And if he felt like that, how must Mallory and Miller, clinging to the ladder and less than a stone's throw from the guards, be feeling? Both men, Groves knew, carried silenced Lugers, but their Lugers were inside their tunics and their tunics encased in their zipped-up frogmen's suits, making them quite inaccessible. At least, making them quite inaccessible without, clinging as they were to that ladder, performing a variety of contortionist movements to get at that—and it was certain that the least untoward movement would have been immediately spotted by the two guards. How it was that they hadn't already been seen, even without movement, was incomprehensible to Groves: in that bright moonlight, which cast as much light on the dam and in the gorge as one would have expected on any reasonably dull afternoon, any normally peripheral vision should have picked them all up immediately. And it was unlikely that any front line troops of the Wehrmacht had less than standard peripheral vision. Groves could only conclude that the intentness of the guards' gaze did not necessarily mean that they were looking intently: it could have been that all their being was at that moment concentrated on their hearing, straining to locate the source of the desultory machine pistol fire down the gorge. With infinite caution Groves eased his Luger from his tunic and lined it up. At that distance, even allowing for the high muzzle velocity of the gun, he reckoned his chances of getting either of the guards to be so remote as to be hardly worth considering: but, at least, as a gesture it was better than nothing.

Groves was right on two counts. The two sentries on the parapet, far from being reassured by General Wasserman's encouraging reassurance, were, in fact, concentrating all their beings on listening to the downriver bursts of machine pistol fire, which were becoming all the more noticeable not only because they seemed—as they were—to be coming closer, but also because the ammunition of the Partisan defenders of the Zenica Gap was running low and their fire was becoming more sporadic. Groves had been right, too, about the fact that neither Mallory nor Miller had made any attempt to get at their Lugers. For the first few seconds, Mallory, like Groves, had felt sure that any such move would be bound to attract immediate attention, but, almost at once and long before the idea had occurred to Groves, Mallory had realised that the men were in such a trancelike state of listening that a hand could almost have been passed before their faces without their being aware of it. And now, Mallory was certain, there would be no need to do anything at all because, from his elevation, he could see something that was quite invisible to Groves from his position at the foot of the dam: another dark band of cloud was almost about to pass across the face of the moon.

Within seconds, a black shadow flitting across the waters of the Neretva Dam turned the colour from dark green to the deepest indigo, moved rapidly across the top of the dam wall, blotted out the ladder and the two men clinging to it, then engulfed the gorge in darkness. Groves sighed in soundless relief and lowered his Luger. Maria rose and made her way downriver towards the bridge. Petar moved his unseeing gaze around in the sightless manner of the blind. And, up above, Mallory and Miller at once began to climb again.

Mallory now abandoned the ladder at the top of one of its zigs and struck vertically up the cliff face. The rock face, providentially, was not completely smooth, but such hand and foot holds it afforded were few and small and awkwardly situated, making for a climb that was as arduous as it was technically difficult: normally, had he been using the hammer and pitons that were stuck in his belt, Mallory would have regarded it as a climb of no more than moderate difficulty: but the use of pitons was quite out of the question. Mallory was directly opposite the top of the dam wall and no more than 35 feet from the nearest guard: one tiny chink of hammer on metal could not fail to register on the hearing of the most inattentive listener: and, as Mallory had just observed, inattentive listening was the last accusation that could have been levelled against the sentries on the dam. So Mallory had to content himself with the use of his natural talents and the vast experience gathered over many years of rock climbing and continue the climb as he was doing, sweating profusely inside the hermetic rubber suit, while Miller, now some forty feet below, peered upward with such tense anxiety on his face that he was momentarily oblivious of his own precarious perch on top of one of the slanted ladders, a predicament which would normally have sent him into a case of mild hysterics.

Andrea, too, was at that moment peering at something about fifty feet away, but it would have required a hyperactive imagination to detect any signs of anxiety in that dark and rugged face. Andrea, as the guards on the dam had so recently been doing, was listening rather than looking. From his point of view all he could see was a dark and shapeless jumble of softly glistening boulders with the Neretva rushing whitely alongside. There was no sign of life down there, but that only meant that Droshny, Neufeld and his men having learnt their lessons the hard way—for Andrea could not know at this time that Neufeld had been wounded—were inching their way forward on elbows and knees, not once moving out from one safe cover until they had located another.

A minute passed, then Andrea heard the inevitable: a barely discernible "click," as two tiny pieces of stone knocked together. It came, Andrea estimated, from about thirty feet away. He nodded as if in satisfaction, armed the grenade, waited two seconds then gently lobbed it downstream, dropping flat behind his protective boulder as he did so. There was the typically flat crack of a grenade explosion, accompanied by a briefly white flash of light in which two soldiers could be seen being flung bodily sideways.

The sound of the explosion came clearly to Mallory's ear. He remained still, allowing only his head to turn slowly till he was looking down on top of the dam wall, now almost twenty feet beneath him. The same two guards who had been previously listening so intently stopped their patrol a second time, gazed down the gorge again, looked at each other uneasily, shrugged uncertainly, then resumed their patrol. Mallory resumed his climb.

He was making better time now. The former negligible finger and toe holds had given way, occasionally, to small fissures in the rock into which he was able to insert the odd piton to give him a great deal more leverage than would have been otherwise possible. When next he stopped climbing and looked upward he was no more than six feet below the longitudinal crack he had been looking for—and, as he had said to Miller earlier, it *was* no more than a crack. Mallory made to begin again, then paused, his head cocked towards the sky.

Just barely audible at first above the roaring of the waters of the Neretva and the sporadic small-arms fire from the direction of the Zenica Gap, but swelling power with the passing of every second, could be heard a low and distant thunder, a sound unmistakable to all who had ever heard it during the war, a sound that heralded the approach of squadrons, of a fleet of heavy bombers. Mallory listened to the rapidly approaching clamour of scores of aero engines and smiled to himself.

Many men smiled to themselves that night when they heard the approach from the west of those squadrons of Lancasters. Miller, still perched on his ladder and still exercising all his available will power not to look down, managed to smile to himself, as did Groves at the foot of the ladder and Reynolds by the bridge. On the right bank of the Neretva, Andrea smiled to himself, reckoned that the roar of those fast-approaching engines would make an excellent cover for any untoward sound and picked another grenade from his belt. Outside a soup tent high up in the biting cold of the Ivenici plateau, Colonel Vis and Captain Vlanovich smiled their delight at each other and solemnly shook hands. Behind the southern redoubts of the Zenica Cage, General Vukalovic and his three senior officers, Colonel Janzy, Colonel Lazlo and Major Stephan, for once removed the glasses through which they had been so long peering at the Neretva bridge and the menacing woods beyond, and smiled their incredulous relief at one another. And, most strangely of all, already seated in his command truck just inside the woods to the south of the Neretva bridge, General Zimmerman smiled perhaps the most broadly of all.

Mallory resumed his climb, moving even more quickly now, reached the longitudinal crack, worked his way up above it, pressed a piton into a

convenient crack in the rock, withdrew his hammer from his belt and prepared to wait. Even now, he was not much more than forty feet above the
dam wall, and the piton that Mallory now wanted to anchor would require
not one blow but a dozen of them, and powerful ones at that: the idea that,
even above the approaching thunder of the Lancasters' engines, the metallic
hammering would go unremarked was preposterous. The sound of the heavy
aero engines was now deepening by the moment.

Mallory glanced down directly beneath him. Miller was gazing upward,
tapping his wrist watch as best a man can when he has both arms wrapped
round the same rung of a ladder, and making urgent gestures. Mallory, in
turn, shook his head and made a downward restraining motion with his free
hand. Miller shook his own head in resignation.

The Lancasters were on top of them now. The leader arrowed in diagonally across the dam, lifted slightly as it came to the high mountains on the
other side and then the earth shook and ripples of dark waters shivered their
erratic way across the surface of the Neretva Dam before the first explosion
reached their ears, as the first of a stick of 1000-pound bombs crashed
squarely into the Zenica Gap. From then on the sound of the explosions of
the bombs raining down on the Gap were so close together as to be almost
continuous: what little time lapse there was between some of the explosions
was bridged by the constantly rumbling echoes that rumbled through the
mountains and valleys of central Bosnia.

Mallory had no longer any need to worry about sound any more, he
doubted he could even have heard himself speak, for most of those bombs
were landing in a concentrated area less than a mile from where he clung to
the side of the cliff, their explosions making an almost constant white glare
that showed clearly above the mountains to the west. He hammered home
his piton, belayed a rope around it, and dropped the rope to Miller, who
immediately seized it and began to climb: he looked, Mallory thought,
uncommonly like one of the early Christian martyrs. Miller was no mountaineer, but, no mistake, he knew how to climb a rope: in a remarkably short
time he was up beside Mallory, feet firmly wedged into the longitudinal
crack, both hands gripping tightly to the piton.

"Think you can hang on that piton?" Mallory asked. He almost had to
shout to make himself heard above the still undiminished thunder of the
falling bombs.

"Just try to prise me away."

"I won't." Mallory grinned.

He coiled up the rope which Miller had used for his ascent, hitched it
over his shoulder and started to move quickly along the longitudinal crack.
"I'll take this across the top of the dam, belay it to another piton. Then you
can join me. Right?"

Miller looked down into the depths and shuddered. "If you think I'm
going to stay here, you must be mad."

Mallory grinned again and moved away.

To the south of the Neretva bridge, General Zimmerman, with an aide by
his side, was still listening to the sounds of the aerial assault on the Zenica
Gap. He glanced at his watch.

"Now," he said. "First line assault troops into position."

At once heavily armed infantry, bent almost double to keep themselves
below parapet level, began to move quickly across the Neretva bridge: once
on the other side, they spread out east and west along the northern bank of

the river, concealed from the Partisans by the ridge of high ground abutting on the river bank. Or they thought they were concealed: in point of fact a Partisan scout, equipped with night glasses and field telephone, lay prone in a suicidally positioned slit trench less than a hundred yards from the bridge itself, sending back a constant series of reports to Vukalovic.

Zimmerman glanced up at the sky and said to his aide: "Hold them. The moon's coming through again." Again he looked at his watch. "Start the tank engines in twenty minutes."

"They've stopped coming across the bridge, then?" Vukalovic said.

"Yes, sir." It was the voice of his advance scout. "I think it's because the moon is about to break through in a minute or two."

"I think so too," Vukalovic said. He added grimly: "And I suggest you start working your way back before it does break through or it will be the last chance you'll ever have."

Andrea, too, was regarding the night sky with interest. His gradual retreat had now taken him into a particularly unsatisfactory defensive position, practically bereft of all cover: a very unhealthy situation to be caught in, he reflected, when the moon came out from behind the clouds. He paused for a thoughtful moment, then armed another grenade and lobbed it in the direction of a cluster of dimly seen boulders about fifty feet away. He did not wait to see what effect it had, he was already scrambling his way up-river before the grenade exploded. The one certain effect it did have was to galvanise Droshny and his men into immediate and furious retaliation, at least half a dozen machine pistols loosing off almost simultaneous bursts at the position Andrea had so recently and prudently vacated. One bullet plucked at the sleeve of his tunic, but that was as near as anything came. He reached another cluster of boulders without incident and took up a fresh defensive position behind them: when the moon did break through it would be Droshny and his men who would be faced with the unpalatable prospect of crossing that open stretch of ground.

Reynolds, crouched by the swing bridge with Maria now by his side, heard the flat crack of the exploding grenade and guessed that Andrea was now no more than a hundred yards downstream on the far bank. And like so many people at that precise instant, Reynolds, too, was gazing up at what could be seen of the sky through the narrow north-south gap between the precipitous walls of the gorge.

Reynolds had intended going to Andrea's aid as soon as Groves had sent Petar and Maria back to him, but three factors had inhibited him from taking immediate action. In the first place, Groves had been unsuccessful in sending back Petar: secondly, the frequent bursts of machine pistol firing down the gorge, coming steadily closer, was indication enough that Andrea was making a very orderly retreat and was still in fine fighting fettle: and thirdly, even if Droshny and his men did get Andrea, Reynolds knew that by taking up position behind the boulder directly above the bridge, he could deny Droshny and his men the crossing of the bridge for an indefinite period.

But the sight of the large expanse of starlit sky coming up behind the dark clouds over the moon made Reynolds forget the tactically sound and cold-blooded reasons for remaining where he was. It was not in Reynolds' nature to regard any other man as an expendable pawn and he suspected strongly that when he was presented with a sufficiently long period of moonlight Droshny would use it to make the final rush that would overwhelm Andrea. He touched Maria on the shoulder.

"Even the Colonel Stavroses of this world need a hand at times. Stay here. We shouldn't be long.'' He turned and ran across the swaying swing bridge.

Damn it, Mallory thought bitterly, damn it, damn it and damn it all. Why couldn't there have been heavy dark cloud covering the entire sky? Why couldn't it have been raining? Or snowing? Why hadn't they chosen a moonless night for this operation? But he wasn't, he knew, only kicking against the pricks. No one had had any choice, for tonight was the only time there was. But still, that damnable moon!

Mallory looked to the North, where the northern wind, driving banded cloud across the moon, was leaving behind it a large expanse of starlit sky. Soon the entire dam and gorge would be bathed in moonlight for a considerable period: Mallory thought wryly that he could have wished himself to be in a happier position for that period.

By this time, he had traversed about half the length of the longitudinal crack. He glanced to his left and reckoned he had still between thirty and forty feet to go before he was well clear of the dam wall and above the waters of the dam itself. He glanced to his right and saw, not to his surprise, that Miller was still where he had left him, clinging to the piton with both hands as if it were his dearest friend on earth, which at that moment it probably was. He glanced downward: he was directly above the dam wall now, some fifty feet above it, forty feet above the roof of the guardhouse. He looked at the sky again: a minute, no more, and the moon would be clear. What was it that he had said to Reynolds that afternoon? Yes, that was it. For now is all the time there may be. He was beginning to wish he hadn't said that. He was a New Zealander, but only a second generation New Zealander: all his forebears were Scots and everyone knew how the Scots indulged in those heathenish practices of second sight and peering into the future. Mallory briefly indulged in the mental equivalent of the second sight and continued on his traverse.

At the foot of the iron ladder, Groves, to whom Mallory was now no more than a half-seen, half-imagined dark shape against a black cliff face, realised that Mallory was soon going to move out of his line of sight altogether, and when that happened he would be in no position to give Mallory any covering fire at all. He touched Petar on the shoulder and with the pressure of his hand indicated that he should sit down at the foot of the ladder. Petar looked at him sightlessly, uncomprehendingly, then suddenly appeared to gather what was expected of him, for he nodded obediently and sat down. Groves thrust his silenced Luger deep inside his tunic and began to climb.

A mile to the West, the Lancasters were still pounding the Zenica Gap. Bomb after bomb crashed down with surprising accuracy into that tiny target area, blasting down trees, throwing great eruptions of earth and stones into the air, starting all over the area scores of small fires which had already incinerated nearly all of the German plywood tanks. Seven miles to the South, Zimmerman still listened with interest and still with satisfaction to the continuing bombardment to the North. He turned to the aide seated beside him in the command car.

"You will have to admit that we must give the Royal Air Force full marks for industry, if for nothing else. I hope our troops are well clear of the area?''

"There's not a German soldier within two miles of the Zenica Gap, Herr General.''

"Excellent, excellent." Zimmerman appeared to have forgotten about his earlier forebodings. "Well, fifteen minutes. The moon will soon be through, so we'll hold our infantry. The next wave of troops can go across with the tanks."

Reynolds, making his way down the right bank of the Neretva towards the sound of firing, now very close indeed, suddenly became very still indeed. Most men react the same way when they feel the barrel of a gun grinding into the side of their necks. Very cautiously, so as not to excite any nervous trigger fingers, Reynolds turned both eyes and head slightly to the right and realised with a profound sense of relief that this was one instance where he need have no concern about jittery nerves.

"You had your orders," Andrea said mildly. "What are you doing here?"

"I—I thought you might need some help." Reynolds rubbed the side of his neck. "Mind you, I could have been wrong."

"Come on. It's time we got back and crossed the bridge." For good measure and in very quick succession, Andrea spun another couple of grenades downriver, then made off quickly up the river bank, closely followed by Reynolds.

The moon broke through. For the second time that night, Mallory became absolutely still, his toes jammed into the longitudinal crack, his hands round the piton which he had thirty seconds earlier driven into the rock and to which he had secured the rope. Less than ten feet from him Miller, who, with the aid of the rope, had already safely made the first part of the traverse, froze into similar immobility. Both men stared down on to the top of the dam wall.

There were six guards visible, two at the farther or western end, two at the middle and the remaining two almost directly below Mallory and Miller. How many more there might have been inside the guardhouse neither Mallory nor Miller had any means of knowing. All they could know for certain was that their exposed vulnerability was complete, their position desperate.

Three quarters of the way up the iron ladder, Groves, too, became very still. From where he was, he could see Mallory, Miller and the two guards very clearly indeed. He knew with a sudden conviction that this time there would be no escape, they could never be so lucky again. Mallory, Miller, Petar or himself—who would be the first to be spotted. On balance, he thought he himself was the most likely candidate. Slowly, he wrapped his left arm round the ladder, pushed his right hand inside his tunic, withdrew his Luger and laid the barrel along his left forearm.

The two guards on the eastern end of the dam wall were restless, apprehensive, full of namely fears. As before, they both leaned out over the parapet and stared down the valley. They can't help but see me, Groves thought, they're *bound* to see me, good God, I'm almost directly in their line of sight. Discovery must be immediate.

It was, but not for Groves. Some strange instinct made one of the guards glance upward and to his left and his mouth fell open at the astonishing spectacle of two men in rubber suits clinging like limpets to the sheer face of the cliff. It took him several interminable seconds before he could recover himself sufficiently to reach out blindly and grab his companion by the arm. His companion followed the other guard's line of sight then his jaw, too, dropped in an almost comical fashion. Then, at precisely the same moment, both men broke free from their thrall-like spell and swung their guns, one a Schmeisser, the other a pistol, upward to line up on the two men pinned helplessly to the cliff face.

Groves steadied his Luger against both his left arm and the side of the ladder, sighted unhurriedly along the barrel and squeezed the trigger. The guard with the Schmeisser dropped the weapon, swayed briefly on his feet and started to fall outward. Almost three seconds passed before the other guard, startled and momentarily quite uncomprehending, reached out to grab his companion, but he was far too late, he never even succeeded in touching him. The dead man, moving in an almost grotesquely slow-motion fashion, toppled wearily over the edge of the parapet and tumbled head over heels into the depths of the gorge beneath.

The guard with the pistol leaned far out over the parapet, staring in horror after his falling comrade. It was quite obvious that he was momentarily at a total loss to understand what had happened, for he had heard no sound of a shot. But realisation came within the second as a piece of concrete chipped away inches from his left elbow and a spent bullet ricochetted its whistling way into the night sky. The guard's eyes lifted and widened in shock, but this time the shock had no inhibiting effect on the speed of his reactions. More in blind hope than in any real expectation of success, he loosed off two quick snap-shots and bared his teeth in satisfaction as he heard Groves cry out and saw the right hand, the forefinger still holding the Luger by the trigger guard, reach up to clutch the shattered left shoulder.

Groves' face was dazed and twisted with pain, the eyes already clouded by the agony of the wound, but those responsible for making Groves a Commando sergeant had not picked him out with a pin, and Groves was not quite finished yet. He brought his Luger down again. There was something terribly wrong with his vision now, he dimly realised, he thought he had a vague impression that the guard on the parapet was leaning far out, pistol held in both hands to make sure of his killing shot, but he couldn't be sure. Twice Groves squeezed the trigger of his Luger and then he closed his eyes, for the pain was gone and he suddenly felt very sleepy.

The guard by the parapet pitched forward. He reached out desperately to grab the coaming of the parapet but to pull himself back to safety he had to swing his legs up to retain his balance and he found he could no longer control his legs, which slid helplessly over the edge of the parapet. His body followed his legs almost of its own volition, for the last vestiges of strength remain for only a few seconds with a man through whose lungs two Luger bullets have just passed. For a moment of time his clawed hands hooked despairingly on to the edge of the parapet and then his fingers opened.

Groves seemed unconscious now, his head lolling on his chest, the left hand sleeve and the left hand side of his uniform already saturated with blood from the terrible wound in his shoulder. Were it not for the fact that his right arm was jammed between a rung of the ladder and the cliff face behind it, he must certainly have fallen. Slowly, the fingers of his right hand opened and the Luger fell from his hand.

Seated at the foot of the ladder, Petar stared as the Luger struck the shale less than a foot from where he was sitting. He looked up instinctively, then rose, made sure that the inevitable guitar was firmly secured across his back, reached out for the ladder and started climbing.

Mallory and Miller stared down, watching the blind singer climb up toward the wounded and obviously unconscious Groves. After a few moments, as if by telepathic signal, Mallory glanced across at Miller who caught his eye almost at once. Miller's face was strained, almost haggard. He freed one hand momentarily from the rope and made an almost desperate gesture in the direction of the wounded sergeant. Mallory shook his head.

Miller said hoarsely: "Expendable, huh?"

"Expendable."

Both men looked down again, Petar was now not more then ten feet below Groves, and Groves, though Mallory and Miller could not see this, had his eyes closed and his right arm was beginning to slip through the gap between the rung and the rock. Gradually, his right arm began to slip more quickly, until his elbow was free, and then his arm came free altogether and slowly, so very slowly, he began to topple outward from the wall. But Petar got to him first, standing on the step beneath Groves and reaching out an arm to encircle him and press him back against the ladder. Petar had him and for the moment Petar could hold him. But that was all he could do.

The moon passed behind a cloud.

Miller covered the last ten feet separating him from Mallory. He looked at Mallory and said: "They're both going to go, you know that?"

"I know that." Mallory sounded even more tired than he looked. "Come on. Another thirty feet and we should be in position." Mallory, leaving Miller where he was, continued his traverse along the crack. He was moving very quickly now, taking risks that no sane cragsman would ever have contemplated, but he had no option now, for time was running out. Within a minute he had reached a spot where he judged that he had gone far enough, hammered home a piton and securely belayed the rope to it.

He signalled to Miller to come and join him. Miller began the last stage of the traverse, and as he was on his way across, Mallory unhitched another rope from his shoulders, a sixty foot length of climbers' rope, knotted at fifteen inch intervals. One end of this he fastened to the same piton as held the rope that Miller was using for making his traverse: the other end he let fall down the cliffside. Miller came up and Mallory touched him on the shoulder and pointed downward.

The dark waters of the Neretva Dam were directly beneath them.

12

SATURDAY

0135–0200

ANDREA AND Reynolds lay crouched among the boulders at the western end of the elderly swing bridge over the gorge. Andrea looked across the length of the bridge, his gaze travelling up the steep gully behind it till it came to rest on the huge boulder perched precariously at the angle where the steep slope met the vertical cliff face behind it. Andrea rubbed a bristly chin, nodded thoughtfully and turned to Reynolds.

"You cross first. I'll give you covering fire. You do the same for me when you get to the other side. Don't stop, don't look round. Now."

Reynolds made for the bridge in a crouching run, his footsteps seeming to him abnormally loud as he reached the rotting planking of the bridge itself. The palms of his hands gliding lightly over the hand ropes on either side he continued without check or dimunition of speed, obeying Andrea's instructions not to risk a quick backward glance, and feeling a very strange sensation between his shoulder blades. To his mild astonishment he reached the far bank without a shot being fired, headed for the concealment and shelter offered by a large boulder a little way up the bank, was startled momentarily to see Maria hiding behind the same boulder, then whirled round and unslung his Schmeisser.

On the far bank there was no sign of Andrea. For a brief moment Reynolds experienced a quick stab of anger, thinking that Andrea had used this ruse merely to get rid of him, then smiled to himself as he heard two flat explosive sounds some little way down the river on the far bank. Andrea, Reynolds remembered, had still had two grenades left and Andrea was not the man to let such handy things rust from disuse. Besides, Reynolds realised, it would provide Andrea with extra valuable seconds to make good his escape, which indeed it did, for Andrea appeared on the far bank almost immediately and, like Reynolds, effected the crossing of the bridge entirely without incident. Reynolds called softly and Andrea joined them in the shelter of the boulder.

Reynolds said in a low voice: "What's next?"

"First things first." Andrea produced a cigar from a waterproof box, a match from another waterproof box, struck the match in his huge cupped hands and puffed in immense satisfaction. When he removed the cigar, Reynolds noticed that he held it with the glowing end safely concealed in the curved palm of his hand. "What's next? I tell you what's next. Company coming to join us across the bridge, and coming very soon, too. They've taken crazy risks to try to get me—and paid for them—which shows they are pretty desperate. Crazy men don't hang about for long. You and Maria here move fifty or sixty yards nearer the dam and take cover there—and keep your guns on the far side of the bridge."

"You staying here?" Reynolds asked.

Andrea blew out a noxious cloud of cigar smoke. "For the moment, yes."

"Then I'm staying, too."

"If you want to get killed, it's all right by me," Andrea said mildly. "But this beautiful young lady here wouldn't look that way any more with the top of her head blown off."

Reynolds was startled by the crudeness of the words. He said angrily: "What the devil do you mean?"

"I mean this." Andrea's voice was no longer mild. "This boulder gives you perfect concealment from the bridge. But Droshny and his men can move another thirty or forty yards farther up the bank on their side. What concealment will you have then?"

"I never thought of that," Reynolds said.

"There'll come a day when you say that once too often," Andrea said sombrely, "and then it will be too late to think of anything again."

A minute later they were in position. Reynolds was hidden behind a huge boulder which afforded perfect concealment both from the far side of the bridge and from the bank on the far side up to the point where it petered out: it did not offer concealment from the dam. Reynolds looked to his left where Maria was crouched farther in behind the rock. She smiled at him, and Reynolds knew he had never seen a braver girl for the hands that held the Schmeisser were trembling. He moved out a little and peered downriver, but there appeared to be no signs of life whatsoever at the western edge of the bridge. The only signs of life at all, indeed, were to be seen behind the huge boulder up in the gully, where Andrea, completely screened from anyone at or near the far side of the bridge, was industriously loosening the foundations of rubble and earth round the base of the boulder.

Appearances, as always, were deceptive. Reynolds had judged there to be no life at the western end of the bridge but there was, in fact, life and quite a lot of it although, admittedly, there was no action. Concealed in the massive boulders about twenty feet back from the bridge, Droshny, a Cetnik sergeant and perhaps a dozen German soldiers and Cetniks lay in deep concealment among the rocks.

Droshny had binoculars to his eyes. He examined the ground in the neighbourhood of the far side of the swing bridge, then traversed to his left up beyond the boulder where Reynolds and Maria lay hidden until he reached the dam wall. He lifted the glasses, following the dimly seen zigzag outline of the iron ladder, checked, adjusted the focus as finely as possible, then stared again. There could be no doubt: there were two men clinging to the ladder, about three-quarters of the way up towards the top of the dam.

"Good God in heaven!" Droshny lowered the binoculars, the gaunt craggy features registering an almost incredulous horror, and turned to the Cetnik sergeant by his side. "Do you know what they mean to do?"

"The dam!" The thought had not occurred to the sergeant until that instant but the stricken expression on Droshny's face made the realisation as immediate as it was inevitable. "They're going to blow up the dam!" It did not occur to either man to wonder *how* Mallory could possibly blow up the dam: as other men had done before them, both Droshny and the sergeant were beginning to discover in Mallory and his modus operandi an extraordinary quality of inevitability that transformed remote possibilities into very likely probabilities.

"General Zimmerman!" Droshny's gravelly voice had become positively hoarse. "He must be warned! If that dam bursts while his tanks and troops are crossing——"

"Warn him? Warn him? How in God's name can we warn him?"

"There's a radio up on the dam."

The sergeant stared at him. He said: "It might as well be on the moon. There'll be a rear-guard, they're bound to have left a rear-guard. Some of us are going to get killed crossing that bridge, Captain."

"You think so?" Droshny glanced up sombrely at the dam. "And just what do you think is going to happen to us all down here if *that* goes?"

Slowly, soundlessly and almost invisibly, Mallory and Miller swam northwards through the dark waters of the Neretva Dam, away from the direction of the dam wall. Suddenly Miller, who was slightly in the lead, gave a low exclamation and stopped swimming.

"What's up?" Mallory asked.

"This is up." With an effort Miller lifted a section of what appeared to be a heavy wire cable just clear of the water. "Nobody mentioned this little lot."

"Nobody did," Mallory agreed. He reached under the water. "And there's a steel mesh below."

"An anti-torpedo net?"

"Just that."

"Why?" Miller gestured to the North where, at a distance of less than two hundred yards, the dam made an abrupt right-angled turn between the towering cliff faces. "It's impossible for any torpedo bomber—any bomber— to get a run-in on the dam wall."

"Someone should have told the Germans. They take no chances—and it makes things a damned sight more difficult for us." He peered at his watch. "We'd better start hurrying. We're late."

They eased themselves over the wire and started swimming again, more quickly this time. Several minutes later, just after they had rounded the corner of the dam and lost sight of the dam wall, Mallory touched Miller on the shoulder. Both men trod water, turned and looked back in the direction from which they had come. To the South, not much more than two miles away, the night sky had suddenly blossomed into an incandescent and multicoloured beauty as scores of parachute flares, red and green and white and orange, drifted slowly down towards the Neretva River.

"Very pretty, indeed," Miller conceded. "And what's all this in aid of?"

"It's in aid of us. Two reasons. First of all, it will take any person who looks at that—and *everyone* will look at it—at least ten minutes to recover his night sight, which means that any odd goings-on in this part of the dam are all that less likely to be observed: and if everyone is going to be busy looking that way, then they can't be busy looking this way at the same time."

"Very logical," Miller approved. "Our friend Captain Jensen doesn't miss out on very much, does he?"

"He has, as the saying goes, all his marbles about him." Mallory turned again and gazed to the East, his head cocked the better to listen. He said: "You have to hand it to them. Dead on target, dead on schedule. I hear him coming now.

The Lancaster, no more than five hundred feet above the surface of the dam, came in from the East, its engines throttled back almost to stalling speed. It was still two hundred yards short of where Mallory and Miller were treading water when suddenly huge black silk parachutes bloomed beneath it: almost simultaneously, engine power was increased to maximum revolutions and the big bomber went into a steeply banking climbing turn to avoid smashing into the mountains on the far side of the dam.

Miller gazed at the slowly descending black parachutes, turned, and looked at the brilliantly burning flares to the south. "The skies," he announced, "are full of things tonight."

He and Mallory began to swim in the direction of the falling parachutes.

Petar was near to exhaustion. For long minutes now he had been holding Groves' dead weight pinned against the iron ladder and his aching arms were beginning to quiver with the strain. His teeth were clenched hard, his face, down which rivulets of sweat poured, was twisted with the effort and the agony of it all. Plainly, Petar could not hold out much longer.

It was by the light of those flares that Reynolds, still crouched with Maria in hiding behind the big boulder, first saw the predicament of Petar and Groves. He turned to glance at Maria: one look at the stricken face was enough to tell Reynolds that she had seen it, too.

Reynolds said hoarsely: "Stay here. I must go and help them."

"No!" She caught his arm, clearly exerting all her will to keep herself under control: her eyes, as they had been when Reynolds had first seen her, had the look of a hunted animal about them. "Please, Sergeant, no. You must stay here."

Reynolds said desperately: "Your brother——"

"There are more important things——"

"Not for you, there aren't." Reynolds made to rise, but she clung to his arm with surprising strength, so that he couldn't release himself without hurting her. He said, almost gently: "Come on, lass, let me go."

"No! If Droshny and his men get across——" She broke off as the last of the flares finally fizzled to extinction, casting the entire gorge into what was, by momentary contrast, an almost total darkness. Maria went on simply: "You'll have to stay now, won't you?"

"I'll have to stay now." Reynolds moved out from the shelter of the boulder and put his night glasses to his eyes. The swing bridge and, as far as he could tell, the far bank seemed innocent of any sign of life. He traversed up the gully and could just make out the form of Andrea, his excavations finished, resting peacefully behind the big boulder. Again, with a feeling of deep unease, Reynolds trained his glasses on the bridge. He suddenly became very still. He removed the glasses, wiped the lenses very carefully, rubbed his eyes and lifted the glasses again.

His night sight, momentarily destroyed by the flares, was now almost back to normal and there could be no doubt or any imagination about what he was seeing—seven or eight men, Droshny in the lead, and flat on their stomachs, were inching their way on elbows, hands and knees across the wooden slats of the swing bridge.

Reynolds lowered the glasses, stood upright, armed a grenade and threw it as far as he could towards the bridge. It exploded just as it landed, at least forty yards short of the bridge. That it achieved nothing but a flat explosive bang and the harmless scattering of some shale was of no account, for it had never been intended to reach the bridge: it had been intended as a signal for Andrea, and Andrea wasted no time.

He placed the soles of both feet against the boulder, braced his back against the cliff face and heaved. The boulder moved the merest fraction of an inch. Andrea momentarily relaxed, allowing the boulder to roll back, then repeated the process: this time the forward motion of the boulder was quite perceptible. Andrea relaxed again, then pushed for the third time.

Down below on the bridge, Droshny and his men, uncertain as to the exact significance of the exploding grenade, had frozen into complete immobility. Only their eyes moved, darting almost desperately from side to side to locate the source of a danger that lay so heavily in the air as to be almost palpable.

The boulder was distinctly rocking now. With every additional heave it received from Andrea, it was rocking an additional inch farther forward, an additional inch farther backward. Andrea had slipped farther and farther down until now he was almost horizontal on his back. He was gasping for breath and sweat was streaming down his face. The boulder rolled back almost as if it were going to fall upon him and crush him. Andrea took a deep breath then convulsively straightened back and legs in one last titanic heave. For a moment the boulder teetered on the point of imbalance, reached the point of no return and fell away.

Droshny could most certainly have heard nothing and, in that near darkness, it was as certain as could be that he had seen nothing. It could only have been an instinctive awareness of impending death that made him glance upward in sudden conviction that this was where the danger lay. The huge boulder, just rolling gently when Droshny's horror-stricken eyes first caught sight of it, almost at once began to bound in ever-increasing leaps, hurtling down the slope directly towards them, trailing a small avalanche behind it. Droshny screamed a warning. He and his men scrambled desperately to their feet, an instinctive reaction that was no more than a useless and token gesture in the face of death, because, for most of them, it was already far too late and they had no place to go.

With one last great leap the hurtling boulder smashed straight into the centre of the bridge, shattering the flimsy woodwork and slicing the bridge in half. Two men who had been directly in the path of the boulder died instantaneously: five others were catapulted into the torrent below and swept away to almost equally immediate death. The two broken sections of the

bridge, still secured to either bank by the suspension ropes, hung down into
the rushing waters, their lowermost parts banging furiously against the
boulder-strewn banks.

There must have been at least a dozen parachutes attached to the three
dark cylindrical objects that now lay floating, though more than half submerged, in the equally dark waters of the Neretva Dam. Mallory and Miller
sliced those away with their knives then joined the three cylinders in line
astern, using short wire strops that had been provided for that precise purpose. Mallory examined the leading cylinder and gently eased back a lever
set in the top. There was a subdued roar as compressed air violently aerated
the water astern of the leading cylinder and sent it surging forward, tugging
the other two cylinders behind it. Mallory closed the lever and nodded to
the other two cylinders.

"These levers on the right hand side control the flooding valves. Open
that one till you just have negative buoyancy and no more. I'll do the same
on this one."

Miller cautiously turned a valve and nodded at the leading cylinder. "What's
that for?"

"Do *you* fancy towing a ton and a half of amatol as far as the dam wall?
Propulsion unit of some kind. Looks like a sawn-off section of a 21 inch
torpedo tube to me. Compressed air, maybe at a pressure of 5000 pounds a
square inch, passing through reduction gear. Should do the job all right."

"Just so long as Miller doesn't have to do it." Miller closed the valve on
the cylinder. "About that?"

"About that." All three cylinders were now just barely submerged. Again
Mallory eased back the compressed air lever on the leading cylinder. There
was a throaty burble of sound, a sudden flurry of bubbles streaming out
astern and then all three cylinders were under way, heading down towards
the angled neck of the dam, both men clinging to and guiding the leading
cylinder.

When the swing bridge had disintegrated under the impact of the boulder,
seven men had died: but two still lived.

Droshny and his sergeant, furiously buffeted and badly bruised by the
torrent of water, clung desperately to the broken end of the bridge. At first,
they could do no more than hold on but gradually, and after a most exhausting struggle, they managed to haul themselves clear of the rapids and hang
there, arms and legs hooked round broken sections of what remained of the
bridge, fighting for breath. Droshny made a signal to some unseen person
or persons across the rapids, then pointed upward in the direction from
which the boulder had come.

Crouched among the boulders on the far side of the river, three Cetniks—
the fortunate three who had not yet moved on to the bridge when the boulder
had fallen—saw the signal and understood. About seventy feet above where
Droshny—completely concealed from sight on that side by the high bank of
the river—was still clinging grimly to what was left of the bridge, Andrea,
now bereft of cover, had begun to make a precarious descent from his
previous hiding place. On the other side of the river, one of the three Cetniks
took aim and fired.

Fortunately for Andrea, firing uphill in semidarkness is a tricky business
at the best of times. Bullets smashed into the cliff face inches from Andrea's
left shoulder, the whining ricochets leaving him almost miraculously un-

scathed. There would be a correction factor for the next burst, Andrea knew: he flung himself to one side, lost his balance and what little precarious purchase he had and slid and tumbled helplessly down the boulder-strewn slope. Bullets, many bullets, struck close by him on his way down, for the three Cetniks on the right bank, convinced now that Andrea was the only person left for them to deal with, had risen, advanced to the edge of the river and were concentrating all their fire on Andrea.

Again fortunately for Andrea, this period of concentration lasted for only a matter of a few seconds. Maria emerged from cover and ran down the bank, stopping momentarily to fire at the Cetniks across the river who at once forgot all about Andrea to meet this new and unexpected threat. Just as they did so, Andrea, in the midst of a small avalanche, still fighting furiously but hopelessly to arrest his fall, struck the bank of the river with appalling force, struck the side of his head against a large stone and collapsed, his head and shoulders hanging out over the wild torrent below.

Reynolds flung himself flat on the shale of the river bank, forced himself to ignore the bullets striking to left and right of him and whining above him and took a slow and careful aim. He fired a long burst, a very long one, until the magazine of his Schmeisser was empty. All three Cetniks crumpled and died.

Reynolds rose. He was vaguely surprised to notice that his hands were shaking. He looked at Andrea, lying unconscious and dangerously near the side of the bank, took a couple of paces in his direction then checked and turned as he heard a low moan behind him. Reynolds broke into a run.

Maria was half-sitting, half-lying on the stony bank. Both hands cradled her leg just above the right knee and the blood was welling between her fingers. Her face, normally pale enough, was ashen and drawn with shock and pain. Reynolds cursed bitterly but soundlessly, produced his knife and began to cut away the cloth around the wound. Gently, he pulled away the material covering the wound and smiled reassuringly at the girl: her lower lip was caught tightly between her teeth and she watched him steadily with eyes dimmed by pain and tears.

It was a nasty enough looking flesh wound, but, Reynolds knew, not dangerous. He reached for his medical pack, gave her a reassuring smile and then forgot all about his medical pack. The expression in Maria's eyes had given way to one of shock and fear and she was no longer looking at him.

Reynolds twisted round. Droshny had just hauled himself over the edge of the river bank, had risen to his feet and was now heading purposefully towards Andrea's prostrate body, with the very obvious intention of heaving the unconscious man into the gorge.

Reynolds picked up his Schmeisser and pulled the trigger. There was an empty click—he'd forgotten the magazine had been emptied. He glanced around almost wildly in an attempt to locate Maria's gun, but there was no sign of it. He could wait no longer. Droshny was only a matter of feet from where Andrea lay. Reynolds picked up his knife and rushed along the bank. Droshny saw him coming and he saw too that Reynolds was armed with only a knife. He smiled as a wolf would smile, took one of his wickedly curved knives from his belt and waited.

The two men approached closely and circled warily. Reynolds had never wielded a knife in anger in his life and so had no illusions at all as to his chances: Hadn't Neufeld said that Droshny was the best man in the Balkans with a knife? He certainly looked it, Reynolds thought. His mouth felt very dry.

Thirty yards away Maria, dizzy and weak with pain and dragging her wounded leg, crawled towards the spot where she thought her gun had fallen when she had been hit. After what seemed a very long time, but what was probably no more than ten seconds, she found it half-hidden among rocks. Nauseated and faint from the pain of her wounded leg, she forced herself to sit upward and brought the gun to her shoulder. Then she lowered it again.

In her present condition, she realised vaguely, it would have been impossible for her to hit Droshny without almost certainly hitting Reynolds at the same time: in fact, she might well have killed Reynolds while missing Droshny entirely. For both men were now locked chest to chest, each man's knife hand—the right—clamped in the grip of the other's left.

The girl's dark eyes, which had so recently reflected pain and shock and fear, now held only one expression—despair. Like Reynolds, Maria knew of Droshny's reputation—but, unlike Reynolds, she had seen Droshny kill with that knife and knew too well how lethal a combination that man and that knife were. A wolf and a lamb, she thought, a wolf and a lamb. After he kills Reynolds—her mind was dulled now, her thoughts almost incoherent—after he kills Reynolds I shall kill him. But first, Reynolds would have to die, for there could be no help for it. And then the despair left the dark eyes to be replaced by an almost unthinkable hope for she knew with an intuitive certainty that with Andrea by one's side hope need never be abandoned.

Not that Andrea was as yet by anyone's side. He had forced himself up to his hands and knees and was gazing down uncomprehendingly at the rushing white waters below, shaking his leonine head from side to side in an attempt to clear it. And then, still shaking his head, he levered himself painfully to his feet and he wasn't shaking his head any more. In spite of her pain, Maria smiled.

Slowly, inexorably, the Cetnik giant twisted Reynolds' knife hand away from himself while at the same time bringing the lancet point of his own knife nearer to Reynolds' throat. Reynolds' sweat-sheened face reflected his desperation, his total awareness of impending defeat and death. He cried out with pain as Droshny twisted his right wrist almost to the breaking point, forcing him to open his fingers and drop his knife. Droshny kneed him viciously at the same time freeing his left hand to give Reynolds a violent shove that sent him staggering to crash on his back against the stones and lie there winded and gasping in agony.

Droshny smiled his smile of wolfish satisfaction. Even though he must have known that the need for haste was paramount he yet had to take time off to carry out the execution in a properly leisurely fashion, to savour to the full every moment of it, to prolong the exquisite joy he always felt at moments like these. Reluctantly, almost, he changed to a throwing grip on his knife and slowly raised it high. The smile was broader than ever, a smile that vanished in an instant of time as he felt a knife being plucked from his own belt. He whirled round. Andrea's face was a mask of stone.

Droshny smiled again. "The Gods have been kind to me." His voice was low, almost reverent, his tone a caressing whisper. "I have dreamed of this. It is better that you should die this way. This will teach you, my friend—"

Droshny, hoping to catch Andrea unprepared, broke off in mid-sentence and lunged forward with catlike speed. The smile vanished again as he looked in almost comical disbelief at his right wrist locked in the vicelike grip of Andrea's left hand.

Within seconds, the tableau was as it had been in the beginning of the earlier struggle, both knife wrists locked in the opponents' left hands. The two men appeared to be absolutely immobile, Andrea with his face totally impassive, Droshny with his white teeth bared, but no longer in a smile. It was, instead, a vicious snarl compounded of hate and fury and baffled anger—for this time Droshny, to his evident consternation and disbelief, could make no impression whatsoever on his opponent. The impression this time was being made on him.

Maria, the pain in her leg in temporary abeyance, and a slowly recovering Reynolds, stared in fascination as Andrea's left hand, in almost millimetric slow-motion, gradually twisted Droshny's right wrist so that the blade moved slowly away and the Cetnik's fingers began, almost imperceptibly at first, to open. Droshny, his face darkening in colour and the veins standing out on forehead and neck, summoned every last reserve of power to his right hand: Andrea, rightly sensing that all of Droshny's power and will and concentration were centered exclusively upon breaking his crushing grip suddenly tore his own right hand free and brought his knife scything round and under and upward with tremendous power: the knife went in under the breastbone, burying itself to the hilt. For a moment or two the giant stood there, lips drawn far back over bared teeth smiling mindlessly in the rictus of death, then, as Andrea stepped away, leaving the kinfe still imbedded, Droshny toppled slowly over the edge of the ravine. The Cetnik sergeant, still clinging to the shattered remains of the bridge, stared in uncomprehending horror as Droshny, the hilt of the knife easily distinguishable, fell head-first into the boiling rapids and was immediately lost to sight.

Reynolds rose painfully and shakily to his feet and smiled at Andrea. He said: "Maybe I've been wrong about you all along. Thank you, Colonel Stavros."

Andrea shrugged. "Just returning a favour, my boy. Maybe I've been wrong about you, too." He glanced at his watch. "Two o'clock! *Two* o'clock! Where are the others?"

"God, I'd almost forgotten. Maria there is hurt. Groves and Petar are on the ladder. I'm not sure, but I think Groves is in a pretty bad way."

"They may need help. Get to them quickly. I'll look after the girl."

At the southern end of Neretva bridge, General Zimmerman stood in his command car and watched the sweep-second hand of his watch come up to the top.

"Two o'clock," Zimmerman said, his tone almost conversational. He brought his right hand down in a cutting gesture. A whistle shrilled and at once tank engines roared and treads clattered as the spearhead of Zimmerman's first armoured division began to cross the bridge at Neretva.

13

SATURDAY

0200–0215

"MAURER AND Schmidt! Maurer and Schmidt!" The captain in charge of the guard on the top of the Neretva Dam wall came running from the guardhouse, looked around almost wildly and grabbed his sergeant by the arm. "For God's sake, where are Maurer and Schmidt? No one seen them? No one? Get the searchlight."

Petar, still holding the unconscious Groves pinned against the ladder, heard the sound of the words but did not understand them. Petar, with both arms around Groves, now had his forearms locked at an almost impossible angle between the stanchions and the rock face behind. In this position, as long as his wrists or forearms didn't break, he could hold Groves almost indefinitely. But Petar's grey and sweatcovered face, the racked and twisted face, were mute testimony enough to the almost unendurable agony he was suffering.

Mallory and Miller also heard the urgently shouted commands, but, like Petar, were unable to understand what it was that was being shouted. It would be something, Mallory thought vaguely, that would bode no good for them, then put the thought from his mind: he had other and more urgently immediate matters to occupy his attention. They had reached the barrier of the torpedo net and he had the supporting cable in one hand, a knife in the other when Miller exclaimed and caught his arm.

"For God's sake, no!" The urgency in Miller's voice had Mallory looking at him in astonishment. "Jesus, what do I use for brains. That's not a wire."

"It's not——"

"It's an insulated power cable. Can't you see?"

Mallory peered closely. "Now I can."

"Two thousand volts, I'll bet." Miller still sounded shaken. "Electric chair power. We'd have been frizzled alive. *And* it would have triggered off an alarm bell."

"Over the top with them," Mallory said.

Struggling and pushing, heaving and pulling, for there was only a foot of clear water between the wire and the surface of the water, they managed to ease the compressed air cylinder over and had just succeeded in lifting the nose of the first of the amatol cylinders on to the wire when, less than a hundred yards away, a six-inch searchlight came to life on the top of the dam wall, its beam momentarily horizontal, then dipping sharply to begin a traverse of the water close in to the side of the dam wall.

"That's all we bloody well need," Mallory said bitterly. He pushed the nose of the amatol block back off the wire, but the wire strop securing it to the compressed air cylinder held it in such a position that it remained with its nose nine inches clear of the water. "Leave it. Get under. Hang on to the net."

Both men sank under the water as the sergeant atop the dam wall continued his traverse with the searchlight. The beam passed over the nose of the first of the amatol cylinders, but a black-painted cylinder in dark waters makes a poor subject for identification and the sergeant failed to see it. The light moved on, finished its traverse of the water alongside the dam, then went out.

Mallory and Miller surfaced cautiously and looked swiftly around. For the moment, there was no other sign of immediate danger. Mallory studied the luminous hands of his watch. He said: "Hurry! For God's sake, hurry! We're almost three minutes behind schedule."

They hurried. Desperate now, they had the two amatol cylinders over the wire inside twenty seconds, opened the compressed air valve on the leading cylinder and were alongside the massive wall of the dam inside another twenty. At that moment, the clouds parted and the moon broke through again, silvering the dark waters of the dam. Mallory and Miller were now in a helplessly exposed position but there was nothing they could do about it and they knew it. Their time had run out and they had no option other than to secure and arm the amatol cylinders as quickly as ever possible. Whether they were discovered or not could still be all-important: but there was nothing they could do to prevent that discovery.

Miller said softly: "Forty feet apart and forty feet down, the experts say. We'll be too late."

"No. Not yet too late. The idea is to let the tanks across first then destroy the bridge before the petrol bowsers and the main infantry battalions cross."

Atop the dam wall, the sergeant with the searchlight returned from the western end of the dam and reported to the captain.

"Nothing, sir. No sign of anyone."

"Very good." The captain nodded towards the gorge. "Try that side. You may find something there."

So the sergeant tried the other side and he did find something there, and almost immediately. Ten seconds after he had begun his traverse with the searchlight he picked up the figures of the unconscious Groves and the exhausted Petar and, only feet below them and climbing steadily, Sergeant Reynolds. All three were hopelessly trapped, quite powerless to do anything to defend themselves: Reynolds had no longer even his gun.

On the dam wall, a Wehrmacht soldier, levelling his machine pistol along the beam of the searchlight, glanced up in astonishment as the captain struck down the barrel of his gun.

"Fool!" The captain sounded savage. "I want them alive. You two, fetch ropes, get them up here for questioning. We *must* find out what they have been up to."

His words carried clearly to the two men in the water for, just then, the last of the bombing ceased and the sound of the small-arms fire died away. The contrast was almost too much to be borne, the suddenly hushed silence strangely ominous, deathly, almost, in its sinister foreboding.

"You heard?" Miller whispered.

"I heard." More cloud, Mallory could see, thinner cloud but still cloud, was about to pass across the face of the moon. "Fix these float suckers to the wall. I'll do the other charge." He turned and swam slowly away, towing the second amatol cylinder behind him.

When the beam of the searchlight had reached down from the top of the dam wall, Andrea had been prepared for almost instant discovery but the prior discovery of Groves, Reynolds and Petar had saved Maria and himself, for the Germans seemed to think that they had caught all there were to be caught and, instead of traversing the rest of the gorge with the searchlights, had concentrated, instead, on bringing up to the top of the wall the three men they had found trapped on the ladder. One man, obviously unconscious—that would be Groves, Andrea thought—was hauled up at the end of a rope: the other two, with one man lending assistance to the other, had completed the journey up the ladder by themselves. All this Andrea had seen while he was bandaging Maria's injured leg, but he had said nothing of it to her.

Andrea secured the bandage and smiled at her. "Better?"

"Better." She tried to smile her thanks but the smile wouldn't come.

"Fine. Time we were gone." Andrea consulted his watch. "If we stay here any longer I have the feeling that we're going to get very very wet."

He straightened to his feet and it was this sudden movement that saved his life. The knife that had been intended for his back passed cleanly through his upper left arm. For a moment, almost as if uncomprehending, Andrea stared down at the tip of the narrow blade emerging from his arm then, apparently oblivious of the agony it must have cost him, turned slowly round, the movement wrenching the hilt of the knife from the hand of the man who held it.

The Cetnik sergeant, the only other man to have survived with Droshny the destruction of the swing bridge, stared at Andrea as if he were petrified, possibly because he couldn't understand why he had failed to kill Andrea, more probably because he couldn't understand how a man could suffer such a wound in silence and, in silence, still be able to tear the knife from his grasp. Andrea had now no weapon left him nor did he require one. In what seemed an almost grotesque slow motion, Andrea lifted his right hand: but there was nothing slow-motion about the dreadful edge-handed chopping blow which caught the Cetnik sergeant on the base of the neck. The man was probably dead before he struck the ground.

Reynolds and Petar sat with their backs to the guard hut at the eastern end of the dam. Beside them lay the still unconscious Groves, his breathing now stertorous, his face ashen and of a peculiar waxed texture. From overhead, fixed to the roof of the guardhouse, a bright light shone down on them, while nearby was a watchful guard with his carbine trained on them. The Wehrmacht captain of the guard stood above them, an almost awestruck expression on his face.

He said incredulously: ''You hoped to blow up a dam this size with a few little sticks of dynamite? You must be mad!''

''No one told us the dam was as big as this,'' Reynolds said sullenly.

''No one told you—God in heaven, talk of mad dogs and Englishmen! And where is this dynamite?''

''The wooden bridge broke.'' Reynolds' shoulders were slumped in abject defeat. ''We lost all the dynamite—and all our other friends.''

''I wouldn't have believed it, I just wouldn't have believed it.'' The captain shook his head and turned away, then checked as Reynolds called him. ''What is it?''

''My friend here.'' Reynolds indicated Groves. ''He is very ill, you can see that. He needs medical attention.''

''Later.'' The captain turned to the soldier in the open transceiver cabin. ''What news from the South?''

''They have just started to cross the Neretva bridge, sir.''

The words carried clearly to Mallory, at that moment some distance apart from Miller. He had just finished securing his float to the wall and was on the point of rejoining Miller when he caught a flash of light out of the corner of his eye. Mallory remained still and glanced upward and to his right.

There was a guard on the dam wall above, leaning over the parapet as he moved along, flashing a torch downward. Discovery, Mallory at once realised, was certain. One or both of the supporting floats were bound to be seen. Unhurriedly, and steadying himself against his float, Mallory unzipped the top of his rubber suit, reached under his tunic, brought out his Luger, unwrapped it from its waterproof cover and eased off the safety catch.

The pool of light from the torch passed over the water, close in to the side of the dam wall. Suddenly, the beam of the torch remained still. Clearly to be seen in the centre of the light was a small, torpedo-shaped object fastened to the dam wall by suckers and, just beside it, a rubber-suited man with a gun in his hand. And the gun—it had, the sentry automatically noticed, a silencer screwed to the end of the barrel—was pointed directly at him. The sentry opened his mouth to shout a warning but the warning never came for a red flower bloomed in the centre of his forehead, and he leaned forward tiredly, the upper half of his body over the edge of the parapet, his arms dangling downward. The torch slipped from his lifeless hand and tumbled down into the water.

The impact of the torch on the water made a flat, almost cracking sound. In the now deep silence it was bound to be heard by those above, Mallory thought. He waited tensely, the Luger ready in his hand, but after twenty seconds had passed and nothing happened Mallory decided he could wait no longer. He glanced at Miller, who had clearly heard the sound, for he was staring at Mallory, and at the gun in Mallory's hand with a puzzled frown on his face. Mallory pointed up towards the dead guard hanging over the parapet. Miller's face cleared and he nodded his understanding. The moon went behind a cloud.

Andrea, the sleeve of his left arm soaked in blood, more than half carried the hobbling Maria across the shale and through the rocks: she could hardly put her right foot beneath her. Arrived at the foot of the ladder, both of them stared upward at the forbidding climb, at the seemingly endless zigzags of the iron ladder reaching up into the night. With a crippled girl and his own damaged arm, Andrea thought, the prospects were poor indeed. And God only knew when the wall of the dam was due to go. He looked at his watch. If everything was on schedule, it was due to go now: Andrea hoped to God that Mallory, with his passion for punctuality, had for once fallen behind schedule. The girl looked at him and understood.

"Leave me," she said. "Please leave me."

"Out of the question," Andrea said firmly. "Maria would never forgive me."

"Maria?"

"Not you." Andrea lifted her on to this back and wound her arms round his neck: "My wife. I think I'm going to be terrified of her." He reached out for the ladder and started to climb.

The better to see how the final preparations for the attack were developing, General Zimmerman had ordered his command car out on to the Neretva bridge itself and now had it parked exactly in the middle, pulled close in to the right hand side. Within feet of him clanked and clattered and roared a seemingly endless column of tanks and self-propelled guns and trucks laden with assault troops: as soon as they reached the northern end of the bridge, tanks and guns and trucks fanned out east and west along the banks of the river, to take temporary cover behind the steep escarpment ahead before launching the final concerted attack.

From time to time, Zimmerman raised his binoculars and scanned the skies to the west. A dozen times he imagined he heard the distant thunder of approaching air armadas, a dozen times he deceived himself. Time and again he told himself he was a fool, a prey to useless and fearful imaginings wholly unbecoming to a general in the Wehrmacht: but still this deep feeling of unease persisted, still he kept examining the skies to the West. It never once occurred to him, for there was no reason why it should, that he was looking in the wrong direction.

Less than half a mile to the North, General Vukalovic lowered his binoculars and turned to Colonel Janzy.

"That's it, then." Vukalovic sounded weary and inexpressibly sad. "They're across—or almost all across. Five more minutes. Then we counterattack."

"Then we counterattack," Janzy said tonelessly. "We'll lose a thousand men in fifteen minutes."

"We asked for the impossible," Vukalovic said. "We pay for our mistakes."

Mallory, a long trailing lanyard in his hand, rejoined Miller. He said: "Fixed?"

"Fixed." Miller had a lanyard in his own hand. "We pull those leads to the hydrostatic chemical fuses and take off?"

"Three minutes. You know what happens to us if we're still in this water after three minutes?"

"Don't even talk about it," Miller begged. He suddenly cocked his head and glanced quickly at Mallory. Mallory, too, had heard it, the sound of running footsteps up above. He nodded at Miller. Both men sank beneath the surface of the water.

The captain of the guard, because of inclination, a certain rotundity of figure and very proper ideas as to how an officer of the Wehrmacht should conduct himself, was not normally given to running. He had, in fact, been walking, quickly and nervously, along the top of the dam wall when he caught sight of one of his guards leaning over the parapet in what he could only consider an unsoldierly and slovenly fashion. It then occurred to him that a man leaning over a parapet would normally use his hands and arms to brace himself and he could not see the guard's hands and arms. He remembered the missing Maurer and Schmidt and broke into a run.

The guard did not seem to hear him coming. The captain caught him roughly by the shoulder then stood back aghast as the dead man slid back off the parapet and collapsed at his feet, face upward: the place where his forehead had been was not a pretty sight. Seized by a momentary paralysis, the captain stared for long seconds at the dead man then, by a conscious effort of will, drew out both his torch and pistol, snapped on the beam of the one and released the safety catch of the other and risked a very quick glance over the dam parapet.

There was nothing to be seen. Rather, there was nobody to be seen, no sign of the enemy who must have killed his guard within the past minute or so. But there *was* something to be seen, additional evidence, as if he ever needed such evidence, that the enemy had been there: a torpedo-shaped object—no, *two* torpedo shaped objects—clamped to the wall of the dam just at water level. Uncomprehendingly, at first, the captain stared at those, then the significance of their presence there struck him with the violence, almost, of a physical blow. He straightened and started running towards the eastern end of the dam, shouting "Radio! Radio!" at the top of his voice.

Mallory and Miller surfaced. The shouts—they were almost screams—of the running captain of the guard—carried clear over the now silent waters of the dam. Mallory swore.

"Damn and damn and damn again!" His voice was almost vicious in his chagrin and frustration. "He can give Zimmerman seven, maybe eight minutes' warning. Time to pull the bulk of his tanks on to the high ground."

"So now?"

"So now we pull those lanyards and get the hell out of here."

The captain, racing along the wall, was now less than thirty yards from the radio hut and where Petar and Reynolds sat with their backs to the guardhouse.

"General Zimmerman!" he shouted. "Get through. Tell him to pull his tanks to the high ground. Those damned English have mined the dam!"

Petar took off his dark glasses and rubbed his eyes.

"Ah, well." Petar's voice was almost a sigh. "All good things come to an end."

Reynolds stared at him, his face masked in astonishment. Automatically, involuntarily, his hand reached out to take the dark glasses Petar was passing him, automatically his eyes followed Petar's hand moving away again and then, in a state of almost hypnotic trance, he watched the thumb of that hand press a catch in the side of the guitar. The back of the instrument fell open to reveal inside the trigger, magazine and gleamingly oiled mechanism of a submachine gun.

Petar's forefinger closed over the trigger. The submachine gun, its first shell shattering the end of the guitar, stuttered and leapt in Petar's hands. The dark eyes were narrowed, watchful and cool. And Petar had his priorities right.

The soldier guarding the three prisoners doubled over and died, almost cut in half by the first blast of shells. Two seconds later the corporal of the guard, by the radio hut, while still desperately trying to unsling his Schmeisser, went the same way. The captain of the guard, still running, fired his pistol repeatedly at Petar, but Petar still had his priorities right. He ignored the captain, ignored a bullet which struck his right shoulder and emptied the remainder of the magazine into the radio transceiver then toppled sideways to the ground, the smashed guitar falling from his nerveless hands, blood pouring from his shoulder and a wound on his head.

The captain replaced his still smoking revolver in his pocket and stared down at the unconscious Petar. There was no anger in the captain's face now, just a peculiar sadness, the dull acceptance of ultimate defeat. His eye moved and caught Reynolds': in a moment of rare understanding both men shook their heads in a strange and mutual wonder.

Mallory and Miller, climbing the knotted rope, were almost opposite the top of the dam wall when the last echoes of the firing drifted away across the waters of the dam. Mallory glanced down at Miller, who shrugged as best a man can shrug when hanging on to a rope and shook his head wordlessly. Both men resumed their climb, moving even more quickly than before.

Andrea, too, had heard the shots, but had no idea what their significance might be. At that moment, he did not particularly care. His left upper arm felt as if it were burning in a fierce bright flame, his sweat-covered face reflected his pain and near-exhaustion. He was not yet, he knew, halfway up the ladder. He paused briefly, aware that the girl's grip around his neck was slipping, eased her carefully in toward the ladder, wrapped his left arm round her waist and continued his painfully slow and dogged climb. He wasn't seeing very well now and he thought vaguely that it must be because of the loss of blood. Oddly enough, his left arm was beginning to become numb and the pain was centreing more and more on his right shoulder which all the time took the strain of their combined weights.

"Leave me!" Maria said again. "For God's sake leave me. You can save yourself."

Andrea gave her a smile or what he thought was a smile and said kindly: "You don't know what you're saying. Besides, Maria would murder me."

"Leave me! Leave me!" She struggled and exclaimed in pain as Andrea tightened his grip. "You're hurting me."

"Then stop struggling," Andrea said equably. He continued his pain-racked slow-motion climb.

Mallory and Miller reached the longitudinal crack running across the top of the dam wall and edged swiftly along crack and rope until they were directly above the arc lights on the eaves of the guardhouse some fifty feet below: the brilliant illumination from those lights made it very clear indeed just what had happened. The unconscious Groves and Petar, the two dead German guards, the smashed radio transceiver and, above all, the subma- chine gun still lying in the shattered casing of the guitar told a tale that could not be misread. Mallory moved another ten feet along the crack and peered down again: Andrea, with the girl doing her best to help by pulling on the rungs of the ladder, was now almost two-thirds of the way up, but making dreadfully slow progress of it: they'll never make it in time, Mallory thought, it is impossible that they will ever make it in time. It comes to us all, he thought tiredly, some day it's bound to come to us all: but that it should come to the indestructible Andrea pushed fatalistic acceptance be- yond its limits. Such a thing was inconceivable: and the inconceivable was about to happen now.

Mallory rejoined Miller. Quickly he unhitched a rope—the knotted rope he and Andrea had used to descend to the Neretva Dam—secured it to the rope running above the longitudinal crack and lowered it until it touched softly on the roof of the guardhouse. He took the Luger in his hand and was about to start sliding down when the dam blew up.

The twin explosions occurred within two seconds of each other: the detonation of 1500 pounds of high explosive should normally have produced a titanic outburst of sound, but because of the depth at which they took place, the explosions were curiously muffled, felt, almost, rather than heard. Two great columns of water soared up high above the top of the dam wall, but for what seemed an eternity of time but certainly was not more than four or five seconds, nothing appeared to happen. Then, very very slowly, reluc- tantly, almost, the entire central section of the dam wall, at least eighty feet in width and right down to its base, toppled outward into the gorge: the entire section seemed to be all still in one piece.

Andrea stopped climbing. He had heard no sound, but he felt the shud- dering vibration of the ladder and he knew what had happened, what was coming. He wrapped both arms around Maria and the stanchions, pressed her close to the ladder and looked over her head. Two vertical cracks made their slow appearance on the outside of the dam wall, then the entire wall fell slowly towards them, almost as if it were hinged on its base, and then was abruptly lost to sight as countless millions of gallons of greenish-dark water came boiling through the shattered dam wall. The sound of the crash of a thousand tons of masonry falling into the gorge below should have been heard miles away: but Andrea could hear nothing above the roaring of the escaping waters. He had time only to notice that the dam wall had vanished and now there was only this mighty green torrent, curiously smooth and calm in its initial stages then pouring down to strike the gorge beneath in a seething white maelstrom of foam before the awesome torrent was upon them. In a second of time Andrea released one hand, turned the girl's terrified face and buried it against his chest for he knew that if she should impossibly live that that battering ram of water, carrying with it sand and pebbles and God only knew what else, would tear the delicate skin from her face and leave her forever scarred. He ducked his own head against the fury of the coming onslaught and locked his hands together behind the ladder.

The impact of the waters drove the breath from his gasping body. Buried in this great falling crushing wall of green, Andrea fought for his life and that of the girl. The strain upon him, battered and already bruising badly from the hammer blows of this hurtling cascade of water which seemed so venomously bent upon his instant destruction, was, even without the cruel handicap of his badly injured arm, quite fantastic. His arms, it felt, were momentarily about to be torn from their sockets, it would have been the easiest thing in the world, the wisest thing in the world to unclasp his hands and let kindly oblivion take the place of the agony that seemed to be tearing limbs and muscles asunder. But Andrea did not let go and Andrea did not break. Other things broke. Several of the ladder supports were torn away from the wall and it seemed that both ladder and climbers must be inevitably swept away. The ladder twisted, buckled and leaned far out from the wall so that Andrea was now as much lying beneath the ladder as hanging on to it: but still Andrea did not let go, still some remaining supports held. Then very gradually, after what seemed to the dazed Andrea as an interminable period of time, the dam level dropped, the force of the water weakened, not much but just perceptibly, and Andrea started to climb again. Half a dozen times, as he changed hands on the rungs, his grip loosened and he was almost torn away: half a dozen times his teeth bared in the agony of effort, the great hands clamped tight and he impossibly retained his grip. After almost a minute of this titanic struggle he finally won clear of the worst of the waters and could breathe again. He looked at the girl in his arms. The blond hair was plastered over her ashen cheeks, the incongruously dark eyelashes closed. The ravine seemed almost full to the top of its precipitously sided walls with this whitely boiling torrent of water sweeping everything before it, its roar, as it thundered down the gorge with a speed faster than that of an express train, a continuous series of explosions, an insane and banshee shrieking of sound.

Almost thirty seconds elapsed from the time of the blowing up of the dam until Mallory could bring himself to move again. He did not know why he should have been held in thrall for so long. He told himself, rationalising, that it was because of the hypnotic spectacle of the dramatic fall in the level of the dam coupled with the sight of that great gorge filled almost to the top with those whitely seething waters: but, without admitting it to himself, he knew it was more than that, he knew he could not accept the realisation that Andrea and Maria had been swept to their deaths, for Mallory did not know that at that instant Andrea, completely spent and no longer knowing what he was doing, was vainly trying to negotiate the last few steps of the ladder to the top of the dam. Mallory seized the rope and slid down recklessly, ignoring or not feeling the burning of the skin in the palms of his hands, his mind irrationally filled with murder—irrationally, because it was he who had triggered the explosion that had taken Andrea to his death.

And then, as his feet touched the roof of the guardhouse, he saw the ghost—the ghosts, rather—as the heads of Andrea and a clearly unconscious Maria appeared at the top of the ladder. Andrea, Mallory noticed, did not seem to be able to go any further. He had a hand on the top rung, and was making convulsive, jerking movements, but making no progress at all. Andrea, Mallory knew, was finished.

Mallory was not the only one who had seen Andrea and the girl. The captain of the guard and one of his men were staring out in stupefaction over the awesome scene of destruction, but a second guard had whirled round, caught sight of Andrea's head and brought up his machine pistol. Mallory, still clinging to the rope, had no time to bring his Luger to bear and release the safety catch and Andrea should have assuredly died then: but Reynolds had already catapulted himself forward in a desperate dive and brought down the gun in the precise instant that the guard opened fire. Reynolds died instantaneously. The guard died two seconds later. Mallory lined up the still smoking barrel of his Luger on the captain and the guard.

"Drop those guns," he said.

They dropped their guns. Mallory and Miller swung down from the guardhouse roof and, while Miller covered the Germans with his gun, Mallory ran quickly across to the ladder, reached down a hand and helped the unconscious girl and the swaying Andrea to safety. He looked at Andrea's exhausted, blood-flecked face, at the flayed skin on his hands, at the left sleeve saturated in blood and said severely: "And where the hell have you been?"

"Where have I been?" Andrea asked vaguely. "I don't know." He stood rocking on his feet, barely conscious, rubbed a hand across his eyes and tried to smile. "I think I must have stopped to admire the view."

General Zimmerman was still in his command car and his car was still parked in the right centre of the bridge at Neretva. Zimmerman had again his binoculars to his eyes, but for the first time he was gazing neither to the West nor to the North. He was gazing instead to the East, upriver toward the mouth of the Neretva Gorge. After a little time he turned to his aide, his face at first uneasy, then the uneasiness giving way to apprehension, then the apprehension to something very like fear.

"You hear it?" he asked.

"I hear it, Herr General."

"And feel it?"

"And I feel it."

"What in the name of God almighty can it be?" Zimmerman demanded. He listened as a great and steadily increasing roar filled all the air around them. "That's not thunder. It's far too loud for thunder. And too continuous. And that wind—that wind coming out of the gorge there." He could now hardly hear himself speak above the almost deafening roar of sound coming from the East. "It's the dam! The dam at Neretva! They've blown the dam! Get out of here!" he screamed at the driver. "For God's sake get out of here."

The command car jerked and moved forward, but it was too late for General Zimmerman, just as it was too late for his massed echelons of tanks and thousands of assault troops concealed on the banks of the Neretva by the low escarpment to the north of them and waiting to launch the devastating attack that was to annihilate the seven thousand fanatically stubborn defenders of the Zenica Gap. A mightly wall of white water, eighty feet high, carrying with it the irresistible pressure of millions of tons of water and sweeping before it a gigantic battering ram of boulders and trees, burst out of the mouth of the gorge.

Mercifully, for most of the men in Zimmerman's armoured corps, the realisation of impending death and death itself were only moments apart. The Neretva bridge, and all the vehicles on it, including Zimmerman's command car, were swept away to instant destruction. The giant torrent overspread both banks of the river to a depth of almost twenty feet, sweeping before its all-consuming path tanks, guns, armoured vehicles, thousands of troops and all that stood in its way: when the great flood finally subsided, there was not one blade of grass left growing along the banks of the Neretva. Perhaps a hundred or two of combat troops on both sides of the river succeeded in climbing in terror to higher ground and the most temporary of safety for they too would not have long to live, but for ninety-five percent of Zimmerman's two armoured divisions destruction was as appallingly sudden as it was terrifyingly complete. In sixty seconds, no more, it was all over. The German armoured corps was totally destroyed. But still the mighty wall of water continued to boil forth from the mouth of the gorge.

"I pray God that I shall never see the like again." General Vukalovic lowered his glasses and turned to Colonet Janzy, his face registering neither jubilation nor satisfaction, only an awe-struck wonder mingled with a deep compassion. "Men should not die like that, even our enemies should not die like that." He was silent for a few moments, then stirred. "I think a hundred or two of their infantry escaped to safety on this side, Colonel. You will take care of them?"

"I'll take care of them," Janzy said sombrely. "This is a night for prisoners, not killing, for there won't be any fight. It's as well, General. For the first time in my life I'm not looking forward to a fight."

"I'll leave you then." Vukalovic clapped Janzy's shoulder and smiled, a very tired smile. "I have an appointment. At the Neretva Dam—or what's left of it."

"With a certain Captain Mallory?"

"With Captain Mallory. We leave for Italy to-night. You know, Colonel, we could have been wrong about that man."

"I never doubted him," Janzy said firmly.

Vukalovic smiled and turned away.

Captain Neufeld, his head swathed in a bloodstained bandage and supported by two of his men, stood shakily at the top of the gully leading down to the ford in the Neretva and stared down, his face masked in shocked horror and an almost total disbelief, at the whitely boiling maelstrom, its seething surface no more than twenty feet below where he stood, of what had once been the Neretva Gorge. He shook his head very very slowly in unspeakable weariness and final acceptance of defeat, then turned to the soldier on his left, a youngster who looked as stupified as he, Neufeld, felt.

"Take the two best ponies," Neufeld said. "Ride to the nearest Wehrmacht command post north of the Zenica Gap. Tell them that General Zimmerman's armoured divisions have been wiped out—we don't *know*, but they must have been. Tell them the valley of Neretva is a valley of death and that there is no one left to defend it. Tell them the Allies can send in their airborne divisions tomorrow and that there won't be a single shot fired. Tell them to notify Berlin immediately. You understand, Lindemann?"

"I understand, sir." From the expression on Lindemann's face, Neufeld thought that Lindemann had understood very little of what he had said to him: but Neufeld felt infinitely tired and he did not feel like repeating his instructions. Lindemann mounted a pony, snatched the reins of another and spurred his pony up alongside the railway track.

Neufeld said, almost to himself: "There's not all that hurry, boy."

"Herr Capitan?" The other soldier was looking at him strangely.

"It's too late now," Neufeld said.

Mallory gazed down the still foaming gorge, turned and gazed at the Neretva Dam whose level had already dropped by at least fifty feet, then turned to look at the men and the girl behind him. He felt inexpressibly weary.

Andrea, battered and bruised and bleeding, his left arm now roughly bandaged, was demonstrating once again his quite remarkable powers of recuperation: to look at him it would have been impossible to guess that, only ten minutes ago, he had been swaying on the edge of total collapse. He held Maria cradled in his arms: she was coming to, but very very slowly. Miller finished dressing the head wound of a now sitting Petar who, though wounded in shoulder and head, seemed more than likely to survive, crossed to Groves and stooped over him. After a moment or two he straightened and stared down at the young sergeant.

"Dead?" Mallory asked.

"Dead."

"Dead." Andrea smiled, a smile full of sorrow. "Dead—and you and I are alive. Because this young lad is dead."

"He was expendable," Miller said.

"And young Reynolds." Andrea was inexpressibly tired. "He was expendable too. What was it you said to him this afternoon, my Keith—for now is all the time there may be? And that was all the time there was. For young Reynolds. He saved my life tonight—twice. He saved Maria's. He saved Petar's. But he wasn't clever enough to save his own. *We* are the clever ones, the old ones, the wise ones, the knowing ones. And the old ones are alive and the young ones are dead. And so it always is. We mocked them, laughed at them, distrusted them, marvelled at their youth and stupidity and ignorance." In a curiously tender gesture he smoothed Maria's wet blond hair back from her face and she smiled at him. "And in the end they were better men than we were. . . ."

"Maybe they were at that," Mallory said. He looked at Petar and shook his head in sad wonder. "And to think that all three of them are dead and not one of them ever knew that you were the head of British espionage in the Balkans."

"Ignorant to the end." Miller drew the back of his sleeve angrily across his eyes. "Some people never learn. Some people just never learn."

EPILOGUE

Once again Captain Jensen and the British Lieutenant-General were back in the Operations Room in Termoli, but now they were no longer pacing up and down. The days for pacing were over. True, they still looked very tired, their faces probably fractionally more deeply lined than they had been a few days previously: but the faces were no longer haggard, the eyes no longer clouded with anxiety, and, had they been walking instead of sitting deep in comfortable armchairs, it was just conceivable that they might have had a new spring to their steps. Both men had glasses in their hands, large glasses.

Jensen sipped his whisky and said, smiling: "I thought a general's place was at the head of his troops?"

"Not in these days, Captain," the general said firmly. "In 1944 the wise general leads from behind his troops—about twenty miles behind. Besides, the armoured divisions are going so quickly I couldn't possibly hope to catch up with them."

"They're moving as fast as that?"

"Not quite as fast as the German and Austrian divisions that pulled out of the Gustav line last night and are now racing for the Yugoslav border. But they're coming along pretty well." The general permitted himself a large gulp of his drink and a smile of considerable satisfaction. "Deception complete, breakthrough complete. On the whole, your men have done a pretty fair job."

Both men turned in their chairs as a respectful rat-a-tat of knuckles preceded the opening of the heavy leather doors. Mallory entered, followed by Vukalovic, Andrea and Miller. All four were unshaven, all of them looked as if they hadn't slept for a week. Andrea carried his arm in a sling.

Jensen rose, drained his glass, set it on a table, looked at Mallory dispassionately and said: "Cut it a bit bloody fine, didn't you?"

Mallory, Andrea and Miller exchanged expressionless looks. There was a fairly long silence then Mallory said: "Some things take longer than others."

Petar and Maria were lying side by side, hands clasped, in two regulation army beds in the Termoli military hospital, when Jensen entered, followed by Mallory, Miller and Andrea.

"Excellent reports about both of you, I'm glad to hear," Jensen said briskly. "Just brought some—ah—friends to say goodbye."

"What sort of hospital is this, then?" Miller asked severely. "How about the high army moral tone, hey? Don't they have separate quarters for men and women?"

"They've been married for almost two years," Mallory said mildly. "Did I forget to tell you?"

"Of course you didn't forget," Miller said disgustedly. "It just slipped your mind."

"Speaking of marriage——" Andrea cleared his throat and tried another tack. "Captain Jensen may recall that back in Navarone——"

"Yes, yes." Jensen held up a hand. "Quite so. Quite. Quite. But I thought perhaps—well, the fact of the matter is—well, it so happens that another little job, just a tiny little job really, has just come up and I thought that seeing you were here anyway . . ."

Andrea stared at Jensen. His face was horror-stricken.

Puppet on a Chain

1

"WE SHALL be arriving in Schiphol airport, Amsterdam, in just a few minutes." Mellifluous, accentless, the Dutch stewardess' voice could have been precisely duplicated on any of a dozen European airlines. "Please fasten your seat belts and extinguish your cigarettes. We hope you have enjoyed your flight; we are sure you will enjoy your stay in Amsterdam."

I'd spoken briefly to the stewardess on the way across. A charming girl, but given to a certain unwarranted optimism in her outlook on life in general and I had to take issue with her on two points: I hadn't enjoyed the flight and I didn't expect to enjoy my stay in Amsterdam. I hadn't enjoyed the flight because I hadn't enjoyed any flight since that day two years ago when the engines of a DC-8 had failed only seconds after take-off and led to the discovery of two things: that an unpowered jet has the gliding characteristics of a block of concrete and that plastic surgery can be very long, very painful, very expensive and occasionally not very successful. Nor did I expect to enjoy Amsterdam, even although it is probably the most beautiful city in the world with the friendliest inhabitants you'll find anywhere: it's just that the nature of my business trips abroad automatically precludes the enjoyment of anything.

As the big KLM DC-8—I'm not superstitious, any plane can fall out of the sky—sank down, I glanced round its crowded interior. The bulk of the passengers, I observed, appeared to share my belief in the inherent madness of flying: those who weren't using their fingernails to dig holes in KLM's upholstery were either leaning back with excessive nonchalance or chattering with the bright, gay animation of those brave spirits who go to their impending doom with a quip on their smiling lips, the type who would have waved cheerfully to the admiring throngs as their tumbril drew up beside the guillotine. In short, a pretty fair cross section of humanity. Distinctly law-abiding. Definitely non-villainous. Ordinary; even nondescript.

Or perhaps that's unfair—the nondescript bit, I mean. To qualify for that rather denigrating description there must exist comparative terms of reference to justify its use; unfortunately for the remainder of the passengers there were two others aboard that plane that would have made anyone look nondescript.

I looked at them three seats behind me on the other side of the aisle. This was hardly a move on my part liable to attract any attention as most of the men within eyeing distance of them had done little else but look at them since leaving Heathrow airport: not to have looked at them at all would have been an almost guaranteed method of attracting attention.

Just a couple of girls sitting together. You can find a couple of girls sitting together almost anywhere but you'd have to give up the best years of your life to the search of finding a couple like those. One with hair as dark as a raven's wing, the other a shining platinum blonde, both clad, albeit marginally, in mini-dresses, the dark one in an all-white silk affair, the blonde all in black, and both of them possessed as far as one could see—and one could see a great deal—of figures that demonstrated clearly the immense strides forward made by a select few of womankind since the days of Venus de Milo. Above all, they were strikingly beautiful, but not with that vapid and empty brand of unformed good looks which wins the Miss World contest: curiously alike, they had the delicately formed bone structure, the cleanly cut features, and the unmistakable quality of intelligence which would keep them still beautiful twenty years after the faded Miss Worlds of yesterday had long since given up the unequal competition.

The blonde girl smiled at me, a smile at once pert and provocative but friendly. I gave her my impassive look, and, as the trainee plastic surgeon who had worked his will on me hadn't quite succeeded in matching up the two sides of my face, my impassive expression is noticeably lacking in encouragement, but still she smiled at me. The dark girl nudged her companion, who looked away from me, saw the reproving frown, made a face and stopped smiling. I looked away.

We were less than two hundred yards from the end of the runway now and to take my mind off the near-certainty of the undercarriage crumpling as soon as it touched the tarmac, I leaned back, closed my eyes and thought about the two girls. Whatever else I lacked, I reflected, no one could claim that I picked my assistants without regard to some of the more aesthetic aspects of life. Maggie, the dark girl, was twenty-seven and had been with me for over five years now; she was clever to just short of the point of being brilliant, she was methodical, painstaking, discreet, reliable and almost never made a mistake—in our business there is no such thing as a person who never makes mistakes. More important, Maggie and I were fond of each other and had been for years, an almost essential qualification where a momentary loss of mutual faith and interdependence could have consequences of an unpleasant and permanent nature; but we weren't, so far as I knew, too fond of each other for that could have been equally disastrous.

Belinda, blonde, twenty-two, Parisian, half French, half English, on her first operational assignment, was an almost totally unknown quantity to me. Not an enigma, just unknown as a person: when the Sûreté lend you one of their agents, as they had lent Belinda to me, the accompanying dossier on that agent is so overwhelmingly comprehensive that no relevant fact in that person's background or past is left unmentioned. On a personal basis all I had been able to gather so far was that she was markedly lacking in that respect—if no unstinted admiration—that the young should accord to their elders and professional superiors, which in this case was myself. But she had about her that air of quietly resourceful competence which more than outweighed any reservations she might hold about her employer.

Neither girl had ever been to Holland before which was one of the main reasons why they were accompanying me there; apart from which, lovely young girls in our unlovely profession are rarer than fur coats in the Congo and hence all the more unlikely to attract the attention of the suspicious and the ungodly.

The DC-8 touched down, the undercarriage remained in one piece, so I opened my eyes and began to think of matters of more immediate urgency. Duclos. Jimmy Duclos was waiting to meet me at Schiphol airport and Jimmy Duclos had something of importance and urgency to convey to me. Too important to send, even although coded, through normal channels of communication; too urgent to wait even for the services of a diplomatic courier, from our embassy in The Hague. The probable content of the message I did not concern myself with: I'd know it in five minutes. And I knew it would be what I wanted. Duclos' sources of information were impeccable, the information itself always precise and one hundred percent accurate. Jimmy Duclos never made mistakes—not, at least, of this nature.

The DC-8 was slowing down and I could already see the crocodile disembarkation tube angling out from the side of the main building ready to line up with the plane's exit when it came to a halt. I unfastened my seat belt, rose, glanced at Maggie and Belinda without expression or recognition and headed for the exit while the plane was still moving, a manoeuvre frowned upon by the airline authorities and certainly, in this case, by the other passengers in the plane whose expressions clearly indicated that they were in the presence of a big-headed and churlish boor who couldn't wait to take his turn along with the rest of long-suffering and queueing mankind. I ignored them. I had long ago resigned myself to the realisation that popularity was never to be my lot.

The stewardess smiled at me, though, but this was no tribute to either my appearance or personality. People smile at other people when they are impressed or apprehensive or both. Whenever I travel aboard a plane except when on holiday—which is about once every five years—I hand the stewardess a small sealed envelope for transmission to the plane's captain and the captain, usually as anxious as the next man to impress a pretty girl, generally divulges the contents to her, which is a lot of fol-de-rol about complete priority under all circumstances and invariably wholly unnecessary except that it ensures one of impeccable and immediate lunch, dinner and bar service. Wholly necessary, though, was another privilege that several of my colleagues and I enjoyed—diplomatic-type immunity to Customs search, which was just as well as my luggage usually contained a couple of efficient pistols, a small but cunningly designed kit of burglar's tools and some few other nefarious devices generally frowned upon by the immigration authorities of the more advanced countries. I never wore a gun aboard a plane, for apart from the fact that a sleeping man can inadvertently display a shoulder-holstered gun to a seat companion, thereby causing a whole lot of unnecessary consternation, only a madman would fire a gun within the pressurised cabin of a modern plane. Which accounts for the astonishing success of the skyjackers: the results of implosion tend to be very permanent indeed.

The exit door opened and I stepped out into the corrugated disembarkation tube. Two or three airport employees politely stood to one side while I passed by and headed for the far end of the tube which debouched onto the terminal floor and the two contra-moving platforms which brought passengers to and from the immigration area.

There was a man standing at the end of the outward bound moving platform with his back to it. He was of middle height, lean and a great deal less than prepossessing. He had dark hair, a deeply trenched swarthy face, black cold eyes and a thin slit where his mouth should have been: not exactly the kind of character I would have encouraged to come calling on my daughter. But he was respectably enough dressed in a black suit and black overcoat and—although this was no criterion of respectability—was carrying a large and obviously brand-new airline bag.

But non-existent suitors for non-existent daughters were no concern of mine. I'd moved far enough now to look up the outward bound moving platform, the one that led to the terminal floor where I stood. There were four people on the platform and the first of them, a tall, thin, grey-suited

man with a hairline moustache and all the outward indications of a successful accountant, I recognised at once. Jimmy Duclos. My first thought was
that he must have considered his information to be of a vital and urgent
nature indeed to come this length to meet me. My second thought was that
he must have forged a police pass to get this far into the terminal and that
made sense for he was a master forger. My third thought was that it would
be courteous and friendly to give him a wave and a smile and so I did. He
waved and smiled back.

The smile lasted for all of a second then jelled almost instantly into an
expression of pure shock. It was then that I observed, almost subconsciously, that the direction of his line of sight had shifted fractionally.

I turned round quickly. The swarthy man in the dark suit and coat no
longer had his back to the travelator. He had come through 180° and was
facing it now, his airline bag no longer dangling from his hand but held
curiously high under his arm.

Still not knowing what was wrong, I reacted instinctively and jumped at
the man in the black coat. At least, I started to jump. But it had taken me a
whole long second to react and the man immediately—and I mean immediately—proceeded to demonstrate to both his and my total conviction that
a second was what he regarded as being ample time to carry out any violent
manoeuvre he wished. He'd been prepared, I hadn't, and he proved to be
very violent indeed. I'd hardly started to move when he swung round in a
viciously convulsive quarter circle and struck me in the solar plexus with
the edge of his airline bag.

Airline bags are usually soft and squashy. This one wasn't. I've never
been struck by a pile driver nor have any desire to be, but I can make a fair
guess now as to what the feeling is likely to be. The physical effort was
about the same. I collapsed to the floor as if some giant hand had swept my
feet from beneath me, and lay there motionless. I was quite conscious. I
could see, I could hear, I could to some extent appreciate what was going
on around me. But I couldn't even writhe, which was all I felt like doing at
the moment. I'd heard of numbing mental shocks; this was the first time I'd
ever experienced a totally numbing physical shock.

Everything appeared to happen in the most ridiculous slow motion. Duclos looked almost wildly around him but there was no way he could get off
that travelator. To move backwards was impossible, for three men were
crowded close behind him, three men who were apparently quite oblivious
of what was going on—it wasn't until later, much later, that I realised that
they must be accomplices of the man in the dark suit, put there to ensure
that Duclos had no option other than to go forward with that moving platform and to his death. In retrospect, it was the most diabolically cold-
blooded execution I'd heard of in a lifetime of listening to stories about
people who had not met their end in the way their Maker had intended.

I could move my eyes, so I moved them. I looked at the airline bag and
at one end, from under the flap, there protruded the colander-holed cylinder
of a silencer. This was the pile driver that had brought about my momentary
paralysis—I hoped it was momentary—and with the force with which he
had struck me I wondered he hadn't bent it into a U-shape. I looked up at
the man who was holding the gun, his right hand concealed under the flap
of the bag. There was neither pleasure nor anticipation in that swarthy face,
just the calm certainty of a professional who knew how good he was at his
job. Somewhere a disembodied voice announced the arrival of flight KL 132
from London—the plane we had arrived on. I thought vaguely and inconsequentially that I would never forget that flight number, but then it would

have been the same no matter what flight I'd used for Duclos had been condemned to die before he could ever see me.

I looked at Jimmy Duclos and he had the face of a man condemned to die. His expression was desperate but it was a calm and controlled desperation as he reached deep inside the hampering folds of his coat. The three men behind him dropped to the moving platform and again it was not until much later that the significance of this came upon me. Duclos' gun came clear of his coat and as it did there was a muted thudding noise and the hole appeared halfway down the left lapel of his coat. He jerked convulsively, then pitched forward and fell on his face; the travelator carried him on to the terminal area and his dead body rolled against mine.

I won't ever be certain whether my total inaction in the few seconds prior to Duclos' death was due to a genuine physical paralysis or whether I had been held in thrall by the inevitability of the way in which he died. It is not a thought that will haunt me for I had no gun and there was nothing I could have done. I'm just slightly curious, for there is no question that the touch of his dead body had an immediately revivifying effect upon me.

There was no miraculous recovery. Waves of nausea engulfed me and now that the initial shock of the blow was wearing off my stomach really started to hurt. My forehead ached, and far from dully, from where I must have struck my head on the floor as I had fallen. But a fair degree of muscular control had returned and I rose cautiously to my feet, cautiously; because of the nausea and dizziness I was quite prepared to make another voluntary return to the floor at any moment. The entire terminal area was swaying around in the most alarming fashion and I found that I couldn't see very well and concluded that the blow to my head must have damaged my eyesight which was very odd as it had appeared to work quite effectively while I was lying on the floor. Then I realised that my eyelids were gumming together and an exploratory hand revealed the reason for this: blood, what briefly but wrongly appeared to me to be a lot of blood, was seeping down from a gash just on the hairline of the forehead. Welcome to Amsterdam, I thought, and pulled out a handkerchief; two dabs and my vision was twenty-twenty again.

From beginning to end the whole thing could have taken no more than ten seconds but already there was a crowd of anxious people milling around as always happened in cases like this: sudden death, violent death, is to man what the opened honeypot is to bees—the immediate realisation of the existence of either calls them forth in spectacular numbers from areas which, seconds previously, appeared to be devoid of all life.

I ignored them, as I ignored Duclos. There was nothing I could do for him now nor he for me, for a search of his clothes would have revealed nothing: like all good agents Duclos never committed anything of value to paper or tape but just filed it away in a highly trained memory.

The dark and deadly man with the deadly gun would have made good his escape by this time: it was purely the routine and now ingrained instinct of checking even the uncheckable that made me glance towards the immigration area to confirm that he had indeed disappeared.

The dark man had not yet made good his escape. He was about two thirds the way along towards the immigration area, ambling unconcernedly along the inbound moving platform, casually swinging his airline bag and seemingly unaware of the commotion behind him. For a moment I stared at him, not comprehending, but only for a moment: this was the way the professional made good his escape. The professional pickpocket at Ascot who has just relieved the grey top-hatted gentleman by his side of his wallet doesn't

plunge away madly through the crowd to the accompaniment of cries of
"Stop thief" and the certainty of rapid apprehension: he is more likely to
ask his victim his tip for the next race. A casual unconcern, a total normality, that was how the honours graduates in crime did it. And so it was with
the dark man. As far as he was concerned I was the only witness to his
action for it was now that I belatedly realised for the first time the part the
other three men had played in Duclos' death—they were still in the cluster
of people round the dead man but there was nothing I or anybody else could
ever prove against them. And, as far as the dark man knew, he'd left me in
a state in which I'd be unable to provide him with any trouble for some
considerable time to come.

I went after him.

My pursuit didn't even begin to verge on the spectacular. I was weak,
giddy and my midriff ached so wickedly that I found it impossible to straighten
up properly so that the combination of my weaving staggering run along that
moving platform with my forward inclination of about thirty degrees must
have made me look like nothing as much as a nonagenarian with lumbago
in pursuit of God knows what.

I was halfway along the travelator, with the dark man almost at its end
when instinct or the sound of my running feet made him whirl round with
the same catlike speed he'd shown in crippling me seconds before. It was
immediately clear that he had no difficulty in distinguishing me from any
nonagenarians he might have known for his left hand immediately jerked up
his airline bag while the right hand slid under the flap. I could see that what
had happened to Duclos was going to happen to me—the travelator would
discharge me or what was left of me on to the floor at the end of its track;
an ignominious way to die.

I briefly wondered what folly had prompted me, an unarmed man, to
come in pursuit of a proven killer with a silenced pistol and was on the point
of throwing myself flat on the platform when I saw the silencer waver and
the dark man's unwinking gaze switch slightly to the left. Ignoring the
probability of being shot in the back of the head, I swung round to follow
his line of sight.

The group of people surrounding Duclos had temporarily abandoned their
interest in him and transferred it to us: in view of what they must have
regarded as my unhinged performance on the travelator it would have been
odd if they hadn't. From the brief glance I had of their faces, their expressions ranged from astonishment to bafflement; there were no traces of
understanding. Not in that particular knot of people. But there was understanding in plenty and a chilling purposefulness in the faces of the three
men who had followed Duclos to his death: they were now walking briskly
up the inbound travelator behind me, no doubt bent on following me to my
death.

I heard a muffled exclamation behind me and turned again. The travelator
had reached the end of its track, obviously catching the dark man off guard,
for he was now staggering to retain his balance. As I would have expected
of him by then he regained it very quickly, turned his back on me and began
to run: killing a man in front of a dozen witnesses was a different matter
entirely from killing a man in front of one unsupported witness although I
felt obscurely certain that he would have done so had he deemed it essential
and the hell with the witnesses. I left the wondering why to later. I started
to run again, this time with a deal more purpose, more like a lively septuagenarian.

The dark man, steadily gaining on me, ran headlong through the immigration hall to the obvious confusion and consternation of the immigration officials, for people are not supposed to rush through immigration halls, they are supposed to stop, show their passports and give a brief account of themselves, which is what immigration halls are for. By the time it came to my turn to run the gamut, the dark man's hurried departure combined with my weaving staggering run and blood-streaked face had clearly alerted them to the fact that there was something amiss, for two of the immigration officials tried to detain me but I brushed by them—"brushed" was not the word they used in their later complaints—and passed through the exit door the dark man had just used.

At least, I tried to pass through it, but the damned door was blocked by a person trying to enter. A girl, that was all I'd the time or the inclination to register, just any girl. I dodged to the right and she dodged to the left, I dodged to my left, she dodged to her right. Check. You can see the same performance take place practically any minute on an city pavement when two overpolite people, each bent on giving the right of way to the other, side-step with such maladroit effectiveness that they succeed only in blocking each other's way; given the right circumstances where two really super-sensitive souls encounter each other the whole embarrassing fandango can continue almost indefinitely.

I'm as quick an admirer of a well-executed *pas de deux* as the next man but I was in no mood to be detained indefinitely and after another bout of abortive side-stepping I shouted "Get out of my damned way" and ensured that she did so by catching her by the shoulder and shoving her violently to one side. I thought I heard a bump and exclamation of pain, but I ignored it: I'd come back and apologise later.

I was back sooner than I expected. The girl had cost me not more than a few seconds, but those few seconds had been more than enough for the dark man. When I reached the concourse, the inevitably crowded concourse, there was no sign whatsoever of him, it would have been difficult to identify a Red Indian chief in full regalia among those hundreds of apparently aimlessly milling people. And it would be pointless to alert the airport security police, by the time I'd established my bona fides he'd be halfway to Amsterdam: even had I been able to get immediate action, their chances of apprehending the dark man would have been remote: highly skilled professionals were at work here, and such men always had the options on their escape routes wide open. I retraced my steps, this time at a leaden trudge, which was by now all I could muster. My head ached viciously but compared to the condition of my stomach I felt it would have been wrong to complain about my head. I felt awful and a glimpse of my pale and blood-smeared face in a mirror did nothing to make me feel any better.

I returned to the scene of my ballet performance where two large uniformed men, with holstered pistols, seized me purposefully by the arms.

"You've got the wrong man," I said wearily, "so kindly take your damned hands off me and give me room to breathe." They hesitated, looked at each other, released me and moved away: they moved away nearly all of two inches. I looked at the girl who was being talked to gently by someone who must have been a very important airport official for he wasn't wearing a uniform. I looked at the girl again because my eyes ached as well as my head and it was easier looking at her than at the man by her side.

She was dressed in a dark dress and dark coat with the white roll of a polo-necked jumper showing at the throat. She would have been about in her mid-twenties, and her dark hair, brown eyes, almost Grecian features and the olive blush to her complexion made it clear she was no native of those parts. Put her alongside Maggie and Belinda and you'd have to spend not only the best years of your life but also most of the declining ones to find a trio like them, although, admittedly, this girl was hardly looking at her best at that moment: her face was ashen and she was dabbing with a large white handkerchief, probably borrowed from the man at her side, at the blood oozing from an already swelling bruise on her left temple.

"Good God!" I said. I sounded contrite and I felt it for no more than the next man am I given to the wanton damaging of works of art. "Did *I* do that?"

"Of course not." Her voice was low and husky but maybe that was only since I'd knocked her down. "I cut myself shaving this morning."

"I'm terribly sorry. I was chasing a man who's just killed someone and you got in my way. I'm afraid he escaped."

"My name is Schroeder. I work here." The man by the girl's side, a tough and shrewd-looking character in perhaps his mid-fifties, apparently suffered from the odd self-depreciation which unaccountably afflicts so many men who have reached positions of considerable responsibility. "We have been informed of the killing. Regrettable, most regrettable. That this should happen in Schiphol airport!"

"Your fair reputation," I agreed. "I hope the dead man is feeling thoroughly ashamed of himself."

"Such talk doesn't help." Schroeder said sharply. "Did you know the dead man?"

"How the hell should I? I've just stepped off the plane. Ask the stewardess, ask the captain, ask a dozen people who were aboard the plane. KL 132 from London, arrival time fifteen fifty-five." I looked at my watch. "Good God! Only six minutes ago."

"You haven't answered my question." Schroeder not only looked shrewd, he was shrewd.

"I wouldn't know him even if I saw him now."

"Mm. Has it eever occurred to you, Mr.—ah——"

"Sherman."

"Has it ever occurred to you, Mr. Sherman, that normal members of the public don't set off in pursuit of an armed killer?"

"Maybe I'm subnormal."

"Or perhaps you carry a gun, too?"

I unbuttoned my jacket and held the sides wide.

"Did you—by any chance—recognize the killer?"

"No." But I'd never forget him, though. I turned to the girl. "May I ask you a question, Miss——"

"Miss Lemay," Schroeder said shortly.

"Did you recognize the killer? You must have had a good look at him. Running men invariably attract attention."

"Why should I know him?"

I didn't try to be shrewd as Schroeder had been. I said: "Would you like to have a look at the dead man? Maybe you might recognize *him?*"

She shuddered and shook her head.

Still not being clever I said: "Meeting someone?"

"I don't understand."

"You're standing at the immigration exit."

She shook her head again. If a beautiful girl can look ghastly, then she looked ghastly.

"Then why be here? To see the sights? I should have thought the immigration hall in Schiphol was the most unsightly place in Amsterdam."

"That'll do." Schroeder was brusque. "Your questions are without point and the young lady is clearly distressed." He gave me a hard look to remind me that I was responsible for her distress. "Interrogation is for police officers."

"I am a police officer." I handed over my passport and warrant card and as I did Maggie and Belinda emerged from the exit. They glanced in my direction, broke step and stared at me with a mixture of concern and consternation as well they might considering the way I felt and undoubtedly looked, but I just scowled at them, as a self-conscious and injured man will scowl at anyone who stares at him, so they hurriedly put their faces straight again and moved on their way. I returned my attention to Schroeder who was now regarding me with a quite different expression on his face.

"Major Paul Sherman, London Bureau of Interpol. This makes a considerable difference, I must say. It also explains why you behaved like a policeman and interrogate like a policeman. But I shall have to check your credentials, of course."

"Check whatever you like with whoever you like," I said, assuming that Mr. Schroeder's English grammar wouldn't be up to picking faults in my syntax. "I suggest you start with Colonel van de Graaf at the Central HQ."

"You know the Colonel?"

"It's just a name I picked out of my head. You'll find me in the bar." I made to move off, then checked as the two big policemen made to follow me. I looked at Schroeder. "I've no intention of buying drinks for them."

"It's all right," Schroder said to the two men, "Major Sherman will not run away."

"Not as long as you have my passport and warrant card," I agreed. I looked at the girl. "I am sorry, Miss Lemay. This must have been a great shock to you and it's all my fault. Will *you* come and have a drink with me? You look as if you need one."

She dabbed her cheek some more and looked at me in a manner that demolished all thoughts of instant friendship.

"I wouldn't even cross the road with you," she said tonelessly. The way she said it indicated that she would willingly have gone halfway across a busy street with me and then abandoned me there. If I had been a blind man.

"Welcome to Amsterdam," I said drearily and trudged off in the direction of the nearest bar.

2

I DON'T normally stay at five-star hotels for the excellent reason that I can't afford to but when I'm abroad I have a practically unlimited expense account about which questions are seldom asked and never answered and as those foreign trips tend to be exhausting affairs I saw no reason to deny myself a few moments of peace and relaxation in the most comfortable and luxurious hotels possible.

The Hotel Excelsior was undoubtedly one such. It was rather a magnificent if somewhat ornate edifice perched on a corner of one of the innermost ring canals of the old city; its splendidly carved balconies actually overhung the canal itself so that any careless sleepwalker could at least be reassured that he wouldn't break his neck if he toppled over the edge of his balcony—

not, that is, unless he had the misfortune to land on top of one of the glass-sided canal touring boats which passed by at very frequent intervals; a superb eye-level view of those same boats could be had from the ground-floor restaurant which claimed, with some justification, to be the best in Holland.

My yellow Mercedes cab drew up at the front door and while I was waiting for the doorman to pay the cab and get my bag my attention was caught by the sound of "The Skaters' Waltz" being played in the most excruciatingly off-key, tinny and toneless fashion I'd ever heard. The sound emanated from a very large, high, ornately painted and obviously very ancient mechanical barrel organ parked across the road in a choice position to obstruct the maximum amount of traffic in that narrow street. Beneath the canopy of the barrel organ, a canopy which appeared to have been assembled from the remnants of an unknown number of faded beach umbrellas, a row of puppets, beautifully made and, to my uncritical eye, exquisitely gowned in a variety of Dutch traditional costumes, jiggled up and down on the ends of rubber-covered springs; the motive power for the jiggling appeared to derive purely from the vibration inherent in the operation of this museum piece itself.

The owner, or operator, of this torture machine was a very old and very stooped man with a few straggling grey locks plastered to his head. He looked old enough to have built the organ himself when he was in his prime, but not, obviously, when he was in his prime as a musician. He held in his hand a long stick to which was attached a round tin can which he rattled continuously and was as continuously ignored by the passers-by he solicited so I thought of my elastic expense account, crossed the street and dropped a couple of coins in his box. I can't very well say that he flashed me an acknowledging smile but he did give me a toothless grin and, as token of gratitude, changed into high gear and started in on the unfortunate "Merry Widow." I retreated in haste, followed the porter and my bag up the vestibule steps, turned on the top step and saw that the ancient was giving me a very old-fashioned look indeed; not to be outdone in courtesy I gave him the same look right back and passed inside the hotel.

The assistant manager behind the reception desk was tall, dark, thin-moustached, impeccably tail-coated and his broad smile held all the warmth and geniality of that of a hungry crocodile, the kind of smile you knew would vanish instantly the moment your back was half-turned to him but which would be immediately in position, and more genuinely than ever, no matter how quickly you turned to face him again.

"Welcome to Amsterdam, Mr. Sherman," he said. "We hope you will enjoy your stay."

There didn't seem any ready reply to this piece of fatuous optimism so I just kept silent and concentrated on filling in the registration card. He took it from me as if I were handing him the Cullinan diamond and beckoned to a bellboy who came trotting up with my case, leaning over sideways at an angle of about twenty degrees.

"Boy! Room 616 for Mr. Sherman."

I reached across and took the case from the hand of the far from reluctant "boy." He could have been—barely—the younger brother of the organ-grinder outside.

"Thank you." I gave the bellboy a coin. "But I think I can manage."

"But that case looks very heavy, Mr. Sherman." The assistant manager's protesting solicitude was even more sincere than his welcoming warmth. The case was, in fact, very heavy, all those guns and ammunition and metal tools for opening up a variety of things did tot up to a noticeable poundage but I didn't want any clever character with clever ideas and even cleverer keys opening up and inspecting the contents of my bag when I wasn't around. Once inside an hotel suite there are quite a few places where small objects can be hidden with remote risk of discovery and the search is seldom assiduously pursued if the case is left securely locked in the first place. . . .

I thanked the assistant manager for his concern, entered the nearby lift and pressed the sixth-floor button. Just as the lift moved off I glanced through one of the small circular peephole windows inset in the door. The assistant manager, his smile now under wraps, was talking earnestly into a telephone.

I got out at the sixth floor. Inset in a small alcove directly opposite the lift gates was a small table with a telephone on it, and, behind the table, a chair with a young man with gold-embroidered livery in it. He was an unprepossessing young man, with about him that vague air of indolence and insolence which is impossible to pin down and about which complaint only makes one feel slightly ridiculous: such youths are usually highly specialized practitioners in the art of injured innocence.

"Six-one-six?" I asked.

He crooked a predictably languid thumb. "Second door along." No "sir," no attempt to get to his feet. I passed up the temptation to clobber him with his own table and instead promised myself the tiny, if exquisite pleasure of dealing with him before I left the hotel.

I asked: "You the floor waiter?"

He said, "Yes, sir," and got to his feet. I felt a twinge of disappointment. "Get me some coffee."

I'd no complaints with 616. It wasn't a room, but a rather sumptuous suite. It consisted of a hall, a tiny but serviceable kitchen, a sitting room, bedroom and bathroom. Both sitting room and bedroom had doors leading onto the same balcony. I made my way out there.

With the exception of an excruciating, enormous and neon-lit monstrosity of a sky-high advertisement for an otherwise perfectly innocuous cigarette, the blaze of coloured lights coming up over the darkening streets and skyline of Amsterdam belonged to something out of a fairy tale, but my employers did not pay me—and give me that splendid expenses allowance—just for the privilege of mooning over any city skyline, no matter how beautiful. The world I lived in was as remote from the world of fairy tales as the most far-flung galaxy on the observable rim of the universe. I turned my attention to more immediate matters.

I looked down towards the source of the far from muted traffic roar that filled all the air around. The broad highway directly beneath me—and about seventy feet beneath me—appeared to be inextricably jammed with clanging tram cars, hooting vehicles and hundreds upon hundreds of motor-scooters and bicycles all of whose riders appeared to be bent on instant suicide. It appeared inconceivable that any of those two-wheeled gladiators could reasonably expect any insurance policy covering a life expectancy of more than five minutes, but they appeared to regard their imminent demise with an insouciant bravado which never fails to astonish the newcomer to Amsterdam. As an afterthought, I hoped that if anyone was going to fall or be pushed from this balcony it wasn't going to be me.

I looked up. Mine was obviously—as I had specified—the top storey of the hotel. Above the brick wall separating my balcony from that of the suite next door, there was some sort of stone-carved baroque griffin supported on a stone pier. Above that again—perhaps thirty inches above—ran the concrete coaming of the roof. I went inside.

I took from the inside of the case all the things I'd have found acutely embarrassing to be discovered by other hands. I fitted on a felt-upholstered underarm pistol which hardly shows at all if you patronise the right tailor, which I did, and tucked a spare magazine in a back trouser pocket. I'd never had to fire more than one shot from that gun far less had to fall back on the spare magazine, but you never know, things were getting worse all the time. I then unrolled the canvas-wrapped array of burglarious instruments—this belt again, and with the help of an understanding tailor again, is invisible when worn round the waist—and from this sophisticated plethora extracted a humble but essential screwdriver. With this I removed the back of the small portable fridge in the kitchen—it's surprising how much empty space there is behind even a small fridge—and there cached all I thought it advisable to cache. Then I opened the door to the corridor. The floor waiter was still at his post.

"Where's my coffee?" I asked. It wasn't exactly an angry shout but it came pretty close to it.

This time I had him on his feet first time out.

"It come by dumb-waiter. Then I bring."

"You better bring fast." I shut the door. Some people never learn the virtues of simplicity, the dangers of over-elaboration. His phoney attempts at laboured English were as unimpressive as they were pointless.

I took a bunch of rather oddly shaped keys from my pocket and tried them, in succession, on the outer door. The third fitted—I'd have been astonished if none had. I pocketed the keys, went to the bathroom and had just turned the shower up to maximum when the outer door bell rang followed by the sound of the door opening. I turned off the shower, called to the floor waiter to put the coffee on the table and turned the shower on again. I hoped that the combination of the coffee and the shower might induce whoever required to be induced that here was a respectable guest unhurriedly preparing for the leisurely evening that lay ahead but I wouldn't have bet pennies on it. Still, one can but try.

I heard the outer door close but left the shower running in case the waiter was leaning his ear against the door—he had the look about him of a man who would spend much of his time leaning against doors or peering through keyholes. I went to the front door and stooped. He wasn't peering through this particular keyhole. I opened the door fractionally, taking my hand away, but no one fell into the hallway, which meant that either no one had any reservations about me or that someone had so many that he wasn't going to run any risks of being found out: a great help either way. I closed and locked the door, pocketed the bulky hotel key, poured the coffee down the kitchen sink, turned off the shower and left via the balcony door: I had to leave it wide open, held back in position by a heavy chair: for obvious reasons, few hotel balcony doors have a handle on the outside.

I glanced briefly down to the street, across at the windows of the building opposite, then leaned over the concrete balustrade and peered to left and right to check whether the occupants of the adjoining suites were peering in my direction. They weren't. I climbed onto the balustrade, reached for the ornamental griffin, a griffin so grotesquely carved that it presented a number of excellent handholds, then reached for the concrete coaming of the roof and hauled myself up top. I don't say I liked doing it but I didn't see what else I could do.

The flat glass-grown roof was, as far as could be seen, deserted. I rose and crossed to the other side, skirting TV aerials, ventilation outlets and those curious miniature greenhouses which in Amsterdam serve as skylights, reached the other side and peered cautiously down. Below was a very narrow and very dark alley for the moment, at least, devoid of life. A few yards to my left I located the fire escape and descended to the second floor. The escape door was locked, as nearly all such doors are from the inside, and the lock itself was of the double action type but no match for the sophisticated load of ironmongery I carried about with me.

The corridor was deserted. I descended to the ground floor by the main stairs because it is difficult to make a cautious exit from a lift which opens on to the middle of the reception area. I needn't have bothered. There was no sign of the assistant manager, the bellboy or the doorman and, moreover, the hall was crowded with a new batch of plane arrivals besieging the reception desk. I joined the crowd at the desk, politely tapped a couple of shoulders, reached an arm through, deposited my room key on the desk, walked unhurriedly to the bar, passed as unhurriedly through it and went out by the side entrance.

Heavy rain had fallen during the afternoon and the streets were still wet, but there was no need to wear the coat I had with me so I carried it slung over my arm and strolled along hatless, looking this way and that, stopping and starting again as the mood took me, letting the wind blow me where it listeth every inch, I hoped, the tourist sallying forth for the first time to savour the sights and sounds of nighttime Amsterdam.

It was while I was ambling along the Herengracht, dutifully admiring the facades of the houses of the merchant princes of the 17th century, when I first became sure of this odd tingling feeling in the back of the neck. No amount of training or experience will ever develop this feeling. Maybe it has something to do with ESP. Maybe not. Either you're born with it or you aren't. I'd been born with it.

I was being followed.

The Amsterdamers, so remarkably hospitable in every other way, are strangely neglectful when it comes to providing benches for their weary visitors—or their weary citizens, if it comes to that—along the banks of their canals. If you want to peer out soulfully and restfully over the darkly gleaming waters of their nighttime canals the best thing to do is to lean against a tree so I leaned against a convenient tree and lit a cigarette.

I stood there for several minutes, communing, so I hoped it would seem, with myself, lifting the cigarette occasionally, but otherwise immobile. Nobody fired silenced pistols at me, nobody approached me with a sandbag preparatory to lowering me reverently into the canal. I'd given him every chance but he'd taken no advantage of it. And the dark man in Schiphol had had me in his sights but hadn't pulled the trigger. Nobody wanted to do away with me. Correction. Nobody wanted to do away with me yet. It was a crumb of comfort, at least.

I straightened, stretched and yawned, glancing idly about me, a man awakening from a romantic reverie. He was there all right, not leaning as I was with my back to the tree but with his shoulder to it so that the tree stood between him and myself but it was a very thin tree and I could clearly distinguish his front and rear elevations.

I moved on and turned right into the Leidsestraat and dawdled along this doing some inconsequential window shopping as I went. At one point I stepped into a shop doorway and gazed at some pictorial exhibits of so highly intrinsic an artistic nature that, back in England, they'd have had the shop owner behind bars in nothing flat. Even more interestingly, the window formed a near-perfect mirror. He was about twenty yards away now peering earnestly into the shuttered window of what might have been a fruit shop. He wore a grey suit and a grey sweater and that was all that could be said about him: a grey nondescript anonymity of a man.

At the next corner I turned right again, past the flower market on the banks of the Singel canal. Halfway along I stopped at a stall, inspected the contents and bought a carnation; thirty yards away the grey man was similarly inspecting a stall but either he was mean-souled or hadn't an expense account like mine for he bought nothing, just stood and looked.

I had thirty yards on him and when I turned right again into the Vijzelstraat I strode along very briskly indeed until I came to the entrance of an Indonesian restaurant. I turned in, closing the door behind me. The doorman, obviously a pensioner, greeted me civilly enough but made no attempt to rise from his stool.

I looked through the door and within just a few seconds the grey man came by. I could see now that he was more elderly than I had thought, easily in his sixties, and I must admit that for a man of his years he was putting up a remarkable turn of speed. He looked unhappy.

I put on my coat and mumbled an apology to the doorman. He smiled and said "Good night" as civilly as he had said "Good evening." They were probably full up anyway. I went outside, stood in the doorway, took a folded trilby from one pocket and a pair of wire spectacles from the other and put them both on. Sherman, I hoped, transformed.

He was about thirty yards distant now, proceeding with a curious scuttling action, stopping every now and again to peer into a doorway. I took life and limb in hand, launched myself across the street and arrived at the other side intact but unpopular. Keeping a little way behind, I paralleled the grey man for about another hundred yards when he stopped. He hesitated, then abruptly began to retrace his steps, almost running now, but this time stopping to go inside every place that was open to him. He went into the restaurant I'd so briefly visited and came out in ten seconds. He went in the side entrance of the Hotel Carlton and emerged from the front entrance, a detour that could not have made him very popular as the Hotel Carlton does not care overmuch for shabby old men with roll-neck sweaters using their foyer as a shortcut. He went into another Indonesian restaurant at the end of the block and reappeared wearing the chastened expression of a man who has been thrown out. He dived into a telephone box and when he emerged he looked more chastened than ever. From there he took up his stance on the central reservation tram stop on the Muntplein. I joined the queue.

The first tram along, a three-coach affair, bore the number "16" and the destination board "Centraal Station." The grey man boarded the first coach. I entered the second and moved to the front seat where I could keep a watchful eye on him at the same time positioning myself so as to present as little as possible of myself to his view should he begin to interest himself in his fellow passengers. But I needn't have worried, his lack of interest in his fellow passengers was absolute. From the continual shift and play of expressions, all unhappy, on his face and the clasping and unclasping of his hands, here clearly was a man with other and more important things on his mind, not least of which was the degree of sympathetic understanding he could expect from his employers.

The man in grey got off at the Dam. The Dam, the main square in Amsterdam, is full of historical landmarks such as the Royal Palace and the New Church which is so old that they have to keep shoring it up to prevent it from collapsing entirely, but neither received as much as a glance from the grey man that night. He scuttled down a side street by the Hotel Krasnapolsky, turned left, in the direction of the docks, along the Oudezijds Voorburgwal canal, then turned right again and dipped into a maze of side streets that obviously penetrated more and more deeply into the warehouse area of the town, one of the few areas not listed among the tourist attractions of

Amsterdam. He was the easiest man to follow I'd ever come across. He looked neither to left or right, far less behind him, I could have been riding an elephant ten paces behind him and he'd never have noticed.

I stopped at a corner and watched him make his way along a narrow, ill-lit and singularly unlovely street, lined exclusively by warehouses on both sides, tall five-storey buildings whose gable roofs leaned out towards those on the other side of the street, lending an air of claustrophobic menace, of dark foreboding and brooding watchfulness which I didn't much care for at all.

From the fact that the grey man had now broken into a shambling run I concluded that this excessive demonstration of zeal could only mean that he was near journey's end, and I was right. Halfway along the street he ran up a set of handrailed steps, produced a key, opened a door and disappeared inside a warehouse. I followed at my leisure, but not too slowly and glanced incuriously at the nameplate above the door of the warehouse. "Morgenstern & Muggenthaler" the legend read. I'd never heard of the firm, but it was a name I'd be unlikely to forget. I passed on without breaking a step.

It wasn't much of an hotel room, I had to admit, but then it wasn't much of an hotel to begin with. Just as the outside of the hotel was small and drab and paint-peeling and unprepossessing, so was the interior of this room. The few articles of furniture the room contained, which included a single bed and a sofa which obviously converted into a bed, had been sadly over-taken by the years since the long-dead days of their prime, if they'd ever had a prime. The carpet was threadbare, but nowhere near as threadbare as the curtains and bed coverlet; the tiny bathroom leading off the room had the floor space of a telephone box. But the room was saved from complete disaster by a pair of redeeming features that would have lent a certain aura of desirability to even the bleakest of prison cells. Maggie and Belinda, perched side by side on the edge of the bed, looked at me without enthusiasm as I lowered myself wearily on to the couch.

"Tweedledum and Tweedledee," I said. "All alone in wicked Amster-dam. Everything all right?"

"No." There was a positive note in Belinda's voice.

"No?" I let my surprise show.

She gestured to indicate the room. "Well, I mean, look at it."

I looked at it. "So?"

"Would *you* live here?"

"Well, frankly, no. But then five-star hotels are for managerial types like myself. For a couple of struggling typists these quarters are perfectly ade-quate. For a couple of young girls who are not the struggling typists they appear to be this provides about as complete a degree of anonymity of background as you can hope to achieve." I paused. "At least, I hope. I *assume* you're both in the clear. Anyone on the plane you recognised?"

"No." They spoke in unison with an identical shake of the head.

"Anyone in Schiphol you recognised?"

"No."

"Anyone take any particular interest in you at Schiphol?"

"No."

"This room bugged?"

"No."

"Been out?"

"Yes."

"Been followed?"

"No."

"Room searched in your absence?"

"No."

"You look amused, Belinda," I said. She wasn't exactly giggling but she was having a little difficulty with her facial muscles. "Do tell. I need cheering up."

"Well." She was suddenly thoughtful, perhaps recalling that she hardly knew me at all. "Nothing. I'm sorry."

"Sorry about what, Belinda?" An avuncular and encouraging tone which had the odd effect of making her wriggle uncomfortably.

"Well, all those cloak-and-dagger precautions for a couple of girls like us. I don't see the need——"

"Do be quiet, Belinda!" That was my Maggie, quicksilver as ever in the old man's defence though God knew why, I'd had my professional successes that, considered by themselves, toted up to a pretty impressive list but a list that, compared to the quota of failures, paled into a best-forgotten insignificance. "Major Sherman," Maggie went on severely, "always knows what he is doing."

"Major Sherman," I said frankly, "would give his back teeth to believe in that." I looked at him speculatively. "I'm not changing the subject, but how about some of the old commiseration for the wounded master?"

"We know our place," Maggie said primly. She rose, peered at my forehead and sat down again. "Mind you, it does seem a very small piece of sticking plaster for what seemed such a lot of blood."

"The managerial classes bleed easily, something to do with sensitive skins, I understand. You heard what happened?"

Maggie nodded. "This dreadful shooting, we heard you tried——"

"To intervene. Tried, as you so rightly said." I looked at Belinda. "You must have found it terribly impressive, first time out with your new boss and he gets clobbered the moment he sets foot in a foreign country."

She glanced involuntarily at Maggie, blushed—platinum blondes of the right sort blush very easily—and said defensively: "Well, he was too quick for you."

"He was all of that," I agreed. "He was also too quick for Jimmy Duclos."

"Jimmy Duclos?" They had a gift for speaking in unison.

"The dead man. One of our very best agents and a friend of mine for many years. He had urgent and, I assume, vital information that he wished to deliver to me in person in Schiphol. I was the only person in England who knew he would be here. But someone in this city knew. My rendezvous with Duclos was arranged through two completely unconnected channels, but someone not only knew I was coming but also knew the precise flight and time so was conveniently on hand to get to Duclos before he could get to me. You will agree, Belinda, that I wasn't changing the subject? You will agree that if they knew that much about me and one of my associates, they may be equally well informed about some other of my associates."

They looked at each other for a few moments then Belinda said in a low voice: "Duclos was one of us?"

"Are you deaf?" I said irritably.

"And that we—Maggie and myself, that is——"

"Precisely."

They seemed to take the implied threats to their lives fairly calmly, but then they'd been trained to do a job and were here to do a job and not fall about in maidenly swoons. Maggie said: "I'm sorry about your friend."

I nodded.

"And I'm sorry if I was silly," Belinda said. She meant it too, all contrition, but it wouldn't last. She wasn't the type. She looked at me, extraordinary green eyes under dark eyebrows, and said slowly: "They're on to you, aren't they?"

"That's my girl," I said approvingly. "Worrying about her boss. On to me? Well, if they're not they have half the staff at the Hotel Excelsior keeping tabs on the wrong man. Even the side entrances are watched: I was tailed when I left tonight."

"He didn't follow you far." Maggie's loyalty could be positively embarrassing.

"He was incompetent and obvious. So are the others there. People operating on the fringes of junky-land frequently are. On the other hand they may be deliberately trying to provoke a reaction. If that's their intention, they're going to be wildly successful."

"Provocation?" Maggie sounded sad and resigned. Maggie knew me.

"Endless. Walk, run or stumble into everything. With both eyes tightly shut."

"This doesn't seem a very clever or scientific way of investigation to me," Belinda said doubtfully. Her contrition was waning fast.

"Jimmy Duclos was clever. The cleverest we had. And scientific. He's in the city mortuary."

Belinda looked at me oddly. "You will put your neck under the block?"

"On the block, dear," Maggie said absently. "And don't go on telling your new boss what he can and can't do." But her heart wasn't in her words for the worry was in her eyes.

"It's suicide," Belinda persisted.

"So? Crossing the streets in Amsterdam is suicide—or looks like it. Tens of thousands of people do it every day." I didn't tell them that I had reason to believe that my early demise did not head the list of the ungodly's priorities, not because I wished to improve my heroic image, but because it would only lead to the making of more explanations which I did not at the moment wish to make.

"You didn't bring us here for nothing," Maggie said.

"That's so. But any toe-tramping is my job. You keep out of sight. Tonight, you're free. Also tomorrow, except that I want Belinda to take a walk with me tomorrow evening. After that, if you're both good girls, I'll take you to a naughty night club."

"I come all the way from Paris to go to a naughty night club?" Belinda was back at being amused again. "Why?"

"I'll tell you why. I'll tell you some things about night clubs you don't know. I'll tell you why we're here. In fact," I said expansively, "I'll tell you everything." By "everything" I meant everything I thought they needed to know, not everything there was to tell: the differences were considerable. Belinda looked at me with anticipation, Maggie with a wearily affectionate scepticism, but then Maggie knew me. "But first, some Scotch."

"We have no Scotch, Major." Maggie had a very puritanical side to her at times.

"Not even *au fait* with the basic principles of intelligence. You must learn to read the right books." I nodded to Belinda. "The phone. Get some. Even the managerial classes must relax occasionally."

Belinda stood up, smoothing down her dark dress and looking at me with a sort of puzzled disfavour. She said slowly: "When you spoke about your friend in the mortuary I watched and you showed nothing. He's still there and now you are—what is the word—flippant. Relaxing, you say. How can you do this?''

"Practice. And a syphon of soda.''

3

IT WAS classical night that night at the Hotel Excelsior with the barrel organ giving forth with a rendition of an excerpt from Beethoven's Fifth that would have had the old composer down on his knees giving eternal thanks for his almost total deafness. Even at fifty yards, the distance from which I was prudently observing through the now gently drizzling rain, the effect was appalling: it was an extraordinary tribute to the tolerance of the people of Amsterdam, city of music lovers and home of the world-famous Concertgebouw, that they didn't lure the elderly operator into a convenient tavern and, in his absence, trundle his organ into the nearest canal. The ancient was still rattling his can at the end of his stick, a purely reflex action for there was no one about that night, not even the doorman, who had either been driven inside by the rain or was a music lover.

I turned down the side street by the bar entrance. There was no figure lurking about adjacent doorways or in the entrance to the bar itself, nor had I expected to find any. I made my way round to the alley and the fire escape, climbed up to the roof, crossed it and located the stretch or coaming that directly overhung my own balcony.

I peered over the edge. I could see nothing, but I could smell something. Cigarette smoke, but not emanating from a cigarette made by one of the more reputable tobacco companies, who don't include reefers among their marketable products. I leaned farther out to almost the point of imbalance and then I could see things, not much, but enough: two pointed toe-caps and, for a moment, the arcing glowing tip of a cigarette, obviously on the downswing of an arm.

I withdrew in caution and with silence, rose, recrossed to the fire escape, descended to the sixth floor, let myself through the fire escape door, locked it again, walked quietly along to the door of Room 616 and listened. Nothing. I opened the door quietly with the skeleton I'd tried earlier and went inside, closing the door as quickly as I could: otherwise indetectable draughts can eddy cigarette smoke in the way to attract the attention of the alert smoker. Not that junkies are renowned for their alertness.

This one was no exception. Predictably enough, it was the floor waiter. He was sitting comfortably in an armchair, feet propped up on the balcony sill, smoking a cigarette in his left hand; his right lay loosely on his knee and cradled a gun.

Normally, it is very difficult to approach anyone, no matter how soundlessly, from behind without some form of sixth sense giving them warning of your approach; but many drugs have a depressive influence on this instinct and what the floor waiter was smoking was one of them.

I was behind him with my gun at his right ear and he still didn't know I was there. I touched him on the right shoulder. He swung round with a convulsive jerk of his body and cried out in pain as his movement gouged the barrel of my gun into his right eye. He lifted both hands to his momentarily injured eye and I took the gun from him without resistance, pocketed it, reached for his shoulder and jerked hard. The waiter catapulted over backwards, completing a somersault, and landing very heavily on his back and the back of his head. For maybe ten seconds he lay there, quite dazed, then propped himself up on one arm. He was making a curious hissing sound, his bloodless lips had vanished to reveal tobacco-stained teeth set in a vulpine snarl and his eyes were dark with hate. I didn't see much chance of our having a friendly get-together.

"We do play rough, don't we?" he whispered. Junkies are great patronisers of the violent cinema and their dialogue is faultless.

"Rough?" I was surprised. "Oh, dear me, no. Later we play rough. If you don't talk." Maybe I went to the same cinema as he did. I picked up the cigarette that lay smouldering on the carpet, sniffed at it in disgust and squashed it out in an ash tray. The waiter rose unsteadily, still shaken and unsteady on his feet, and I didn't believe any of it. When he spoke again, the snarl had gone from his face and voice. He had decided to play it cool, the calm before the storm, an old and worn-out script, maybe we should both start attending the opera instead.

"What would you like to talk about?" he asked.

"About what you're doing in my room for a start. And who sent you here."

He smiled wearily. "The law has already made me try to tell things. I know the law. You can't make me talk. I've got my rights. The law says so."

"The law stops right outside my front door here. This side of that door we're beyond the law. You know that. In one of the great civilised cities of the world you and I are living in our own jungle. But there's a law there too. Kill or be killed."

Maybe it was my own fault for putting ideas in his head. He dived hard and low to get under my gun but not low enough for his chin to get under my knee. It hurt my knee quite badly and by that token should have laid him out, but he was tough, grabbed at the only leg I had left in contact with the ground and brought us both down. My gun went spinning and we rolled about on the floor for a bit, belabouring each other enthusiastically. He was a strong boy, too, as strong as he was tough, but he laboured under two disadvantages: a strict training on marijuana had blunted the honed edge of his physical fitness and though he had a highly developed instinct for dirty fighting he'd never really been trained to it. By and by we were on our feet again with my left hand pushing his right wrist somewhere up between his shoulder blades.

I pushed his wrist higher and he screamed as if in agony, which he might well have been as his shoulder was making a peculiar cracking noise but I couldn't be sure so I pushed a bit higher and removed all doubt, then thrust him out onto the balcony in front of me and forced him over the balustrade until his feet were clear of the ground and he was hanging on to the balustrade with his free left hand as if his life depended on it, which indeed it did.

"You an addict or a pusher?" I enquired.

He mouthed an obscenity in Dutch, but I know Dutch, including all the words I shouldn't. I put my right hand over his mouth for the sort of sound he was about to make could be heard even above the roar of the traffic, and I didn't want to alarm the citizens of Amsterdam unnecessarily. I eased the pressure and removed my hand.

"Well?"

"A pusher." His voice was a sobbing croak. "I sell them."

"Who sent you?"

"No! No! No!"

"Your decision. When they pick what's left of you from the pavement there they'll think you're just another cannabis smoker who got too high and took a trip into the wild blue yonder."

"That's murder!" He was still sobbing, but his voice was only a husky whisper now, maybe the view was making him dizzy. "You wouldn't——"

"Wouldn't I? Your people killed a friend of mine this afternoon. Exterminating vermin can be a pleasure. Seventy feet's a long drop—and not a mark of violence. Except that every bone in your body will be broken. Seventy feet. Look!"

I heaved him a bit farther over the balustrade so that he could have a better look and had to use both hands to haul him back again.

"Talk?"

He made a hoarse sound in his throat, so I hauled him off the balustrade and pushed him inside to the center of the room. I said: "Who sent you?"

I've said he was tough, but he was great deal tougher than I had ever imagined. He should have been fear-stricken and in agony, and I have no doubt that he was both, but that didn't stop him from whirling round convulsively to his right in a full circle and breaking free from my grip. The sheer unexpectedness of it had caught me off guard. He came at me again, a knife that had suddenly appeared in his left hand curving upwards in a wicked arc and aimed for a point just below the breastbone. Normally, he would probably have done a nice job of carving but the circumstances were abnormal: his timing and reactions were gone. I caught and clamped his knife wrist in both my hands, threw myself backwards, straightened a leg under him as I jerked his arm down and sent him catapulting over me. The thud of his landing shook the room and probably quite a few adjacent rooms at that.

I twisted and got to my feet in one motion but the need for haste was gone. He was on the floor on the far side of the room, his head resting on the balcony sill. I lifted him by his lapels and his head lolled back till it almost touched his shoulder blades. I lowered him to the floor again. I was sorry he was dead, because he'd probably had information that could have been invaluable to me, but that was the only reason I was sorry.

I went through his pockets which held a good number of interesting articles but only two that were of interest to me: a case half full of handmade reefers and a couple of scraps of paper. One paper bore the typed letters and figures MOO 144, the other two numbers—910020 and 2797. Neither meant a thing to me but on the reasonable assumption that the floor waiter wouldn't have been carrying them on his person unless they had some significance for him I put them away in a safe place that had been provided for me by my accommodating tailor, a small pocket that had been let into the inside of the right trouser leg about six inches above the ankle.

I tidied up what few signs of struggle there had been, took the dead man's gun, went out on the balcony, leaned out over the balustrade and spun the gun upwards and to the left. It cleared the coaming and landed soundlessly on the roof about twenty feet away. I went back inside, flushed the reefer end down the toilet, washed the ash tray and opened every door and window to let the sickly smell evaporate as soon as possible. Then I dragged the waiter across to the tiny hall and opened the door on to the passage.

The hallway was deserted. I listened intently, but could hear nothing, no sound of approaching footfalls. I crossed to the lift, pressed the button, waited for the lift to appear, opened the door a crack, inserted a matchbox between jamb and door so that the latter couldn't close and complete the electrical circuit then hurried back to my suite. I dragged the waiter across to the lift, opened the door, dumped him without ceremony on the lift floor, withdrew the matchbox and let the door swing to. The lift remained where it was: obviously, no one was pressing the button of that particular lift at that particular moment.

I locked the outside door to my suite with the skeleton and made my way back to the fire escape, by now an old and trusted friend. I reached street level unobserved and made my way round to the main entrance. The ancient at the barrel organ was playing Verdi now and Verdi was losing by a mile. The operator had his back to me as I dropped a guilder into his tin can. He turned to thank me, his lips parted in a toothless smile, then he saw who it was and his jaw momentarily dropped open. He was at the very bottom of the heap and no one had bothered to inform him that Sherman was abroad. I gave him a kindly smile and passed into the foyer.

There were a couple of uniformed staff behind the desk, together with the manager, whose back was at the moment towards me. I said loudly: "Six-one-six, please."

The manager turned round sharply, his eyebrows raised high but not high enough. Then he gave me his warm-hearted crocodile smile.

"Mr. Sherman. I didn't know you were out."

"Oh yes, indeed. Pre-dinner constitutional. Old English custom, you know."

"Of course, of course." He smiled at me archly as if there was something vaguely reprehensible about this old English custom, then allowed a slightly puzzled look to replace the smile. He was as phoney as they come. "I don't remember seeing you go out."

"Well now," I said reasonably, "you can't be expected to attend to all of your guests all of the time, can you?" I gave him his own phoney smile back again, took the key and walked towards the bank of lifts. I was less than half-way there when I brought up short as a piercing scream cut through the foyer and brought instant silence, which lasted only long enough for the woman who had screamed to draw a deep breath and start in again. The source of this racket was a middle-aged, flamboyantly dressed female, a caricature of the American tourist abroad, who was standing in front of a lift, her mouth opened in a rounded "O," her eyes like saucers. Beside her a portly character in a seersucker suit was trying to calm her, but he didn't look any too happy himself and gave the impression that he wouldn't have minded doing a little screaming himself.

The assistant manager rushed past me and I followed more leisurely. By the time I reached the lift the assistant manager was on his knees, bent over the sprawled-out form of the dead waiter.

"My goodness," I said. "Is he ill, do you think?"

"Ill? Ill?" The assistant manager glared at me. "Look at the way his neck is. The man's dead."

"Good God, I do believe you're right." I stooped and peered more closely at the waiter. "Haven't I seen this man somewhere before?"

"He was your floor waiter," the assistant manager said, which is not an easy remark to make with your teeth clamped together.

"I thought he looked familiar. In the midst of life——" I shook my head sadly. "Where's the restaurant?"

"Where's the—where's the——"

"Never mind," I said soothingly, "I can see you're upset. I'll find it myself."

The restaurant of the Hotel Excelsior may not be, as the owners claim, the best in Holland, but I wouldn't care to take them to court on a charge of misrepresentation. From the caviar to the fresh out-of-season strawberries— I wondered idly whether to charge this in the expense account as entertainment or bribes—the food was superb. I thought briefly, but not guiltily, about Maggie and Belinda, but such things had to be. The red plush sofa on which I was sitting was the ultimate in dining comfort, so I leaned back in it, lifted my brandy glass and said "Amsterdam!"

"Amsterdam!" said Colonel van de Graaf. The Colonel, deputy head of the city's police, had joined me, without invitation, only five minutes previously. He was sitting in a large chair which seemed too small for him. A very broad man of only medium height, he had iron-grey hair, a deeply trenched, tanned face, the unmistakable cast of authority and an air about him of almost dismaying competence. He went on dryly: "I'm glad to see you enjoying yourself, Major Sherman, after such an eventful day."

"Gather ye rosebuds while you may, Colonel—life is all too short. What events?"

"We have been unable to discover very much about this man, James Duclos, who was shot and killed at the airport today." A patient man and not one to be easily drawn, was Colonel de Graaf. "We know only that he arrived from England three weeks ago, that he checked into the Hotel Schiller for one night and then disappeared. He seems, Major Sherman, to have been meeting your plane. Was this, one asks, just a coincidence?"

"He was meeting me." De Graaf was bound to find out sooner or later. "One of my men. I think he must have got hold of a forged police pass from somewhere—to get past immigration, I mean."

"You surprise me." He sighed heavily and didn't seem in the least surprised. "My friend, it makes it very difficult for us if we don't know those things. I should have been told about Duclos. As we have instructions from Interpol in Paris to give you every possible assistance, don't you think it would be better if we can work together? We can help you—you can help us." He sipped some brandy. His grey eyes were very direct. "One would assume that this man of yours had information—and now we have lost it."

"Perhaps. Well, let's start by you helping me. Can you see if you have a Miss Astrid Lemay on your files? Works in a night club but she doesn't sound Dutch and she doesn't look Dutch so you may have something on her."

"The girl you knocked down at the airport? How do you know she works in a night club?"

"She told me," I said unblushingly.

He frowned. "The airport officials made no mention of any such remark to me."

"The airport officials are a bunch of old women."

"Ah!" It could have meant anything. "This information I can obtain. Nothing more?"

"Nothing more."

"One other little event we have not referred to?"

"Tell me."

"The sixth-floor waiter—an unsavoury fellow about whom we know a little—was *not* one of your men?"

"Colonel!"

"I didn't for a moment think he was. Did you know that he died of a broken neck?"

"He must have had a very heavy fall," I said sympathetically.

De Graaf drained his brandy and stood up.

"We are not acquainted with you, Major Sherman, but you have been too long in Interpol and gained too much of a European reputation for us not to be acquainted with your methods. May I remind you that what goes in Istanbul and Marseilles and Palermo—to name but a few places—does not go in Amsterdam?"

"My word," I said. "You *are* well informed."

"Here, in Amsterdam, we are all subject to the law." He might not have heard me. "Myself included. You are no exception."

"Nor would I expect to be," I said virtuously. "Well, then, cooperation. The purpose of my visit. When can I talk to you?"

"My office, ten o'clock." He looked around the restaurant without enthusiasm. "Here is hardly the time and place."

I raised an eyebrow.

"The Hotel Excelsior," said de Graaf heavily, "is a listening post of international renown."

"You astonish me," I said.

De Graaf left. I wondered why the hell he thought I'd chosen to stay in the Hotel Excelsior.

Colonel de Graaf's office wasn't in the least bit like the Hotel Excelsior. It was a large enough room but bleak and bare and functional, furnished mainly with steel-grey filing cabinets, a steel-grey table and steel-grey seats which were as hard as steel. But at least the decor had the effect of making you concentrate on the matter on hand: there was nothing to distract the mind or eye. De Graaf and I, after ten minutes of preliminary discussion, were concentrating although I think it came more easily to de Graaf than it did to me. I had lain awake to a late hour the previous night and am never at my best at 10 A.M. on a cold and blustery morning.

"All drugs," de Graaf agreed. "Of course we're concerned with all drugs—opium, cannabis, amphetamine, LSD, STP, cocaine, amyl acetate—you name it, Major Sherman, and we're concerned in it. They all destroy or lead on to destruction. But in this instance we are confining ourselves to the really evil one—heroin. Agreed?"

"Agreed." The deep incisive voice came from the doorway. I turned round and looked at the man who stood there, a tall man in a well-cut dark business suit, cool penetrating grey eyes, a pleasant face that could stop being pleasant very quickly, very professional-looking. There was no mistaking his profession. Here was a cop and not one to be taken lightly either.

He closed the door and walked across to me with the light springy step of a man much younger than one in his middle forties, which he was at least. He put out his hand and said: "Van Gelder. I've heard a lot about you, Major Sherman."

I thought this one over, briefly but carefully, decided to refrain from comment. I smiled and shook his hand.

"Inspector van Gelder," de Graaf said. "Head of our narcotics bureau. He will be working with you, Sherman. He will offer you the best cooperation possible."

"I sincerely hope we can work well together." Van Gelder smiled and sat down. "Tell me, what progress your end? Do you think you can break the supply ring in England?"

"I think we could. It's a highly organised distributive pipeline, very highly integrated with almost no cutoffs—and it's because of that that we have been able to identify dozens of their pushers and the half-dozen or so main distributors."

"You could break the ring but you won't. You're leaving it strictly alone?"

"What else, Inspector? We break them up and the next distribution ring will be driven so far underground that we'll never find it. As it is, we can pick them up when and if we want to. The thing we really want to find out is how the damned stuff gets in—and who's supplying it."

"And you think—obviously, or you wouldn't be here—that the supplies come from here? Or hereabouts?"

"Not hereabouts. Here. And I don't think, I know. Eighty percent of those under surveillance—and I refer to the distributors and their intermediates—have links with this country. To be precise, with Amsterdam— nearly all of them. They have relatives here, or they have friends. They have business contacts here or personally conduct business here or they come here on holiday. We've spent five years on building up this dossier."

De Graaf smiled. "On this place called 'here.' "

"On Amsterdam, yes."

Van Gelder asked: "There are copies of this dossier?"

"One."

"With you?"

"Yes."

"On you?"

"In the only safe place." I tapped my head.

"As safe a place as any," de Graaf approved, then added thoughtfully: "As long, of course, as you don't meet up with people who might be inclined to treat you the way you treat them."

"I don't understand, Colonel."

"I speak in riddles," de Graaf said affably. "All right, I agree. At the moment the finger points at the Netherlands. Not to put too fine a point on it, as you don't put too fine a point on it, at Amsterdam. We, too, know our unfortunate reputation. We wish it was untrue, but it isn't. We *know* the stuff comes in in bulk. We *know* it goes out again all broken up—but from where or how we have no idea."

"It's your bailiwick," I said mildly.

"It's what?"

"It's your province. It's in Amsterdam. You run the law in Amsterdam."

"Do you make many friends in the course of a year?" van Gelder enquired politely.

"I'm not in this business to make friends."

"You're in this business to destroy people who destroy people," de Graaf said pacifically. "We know about you. We have a splendid dossier on you. Would you like to see it?"

"Ancient history bores me."

"Predictably." De Graaf sighed. "Look, Sherman, the best police force in the world can come up against a concrete wall. That's what we have done—not that I claim we're the best. All we require is *one* lead—one single solitary lead. . . . Perhaps you have some idea, some plan?"

"I arrived only yesterday." I fished inside the inside of my lower right trouser leg and gave the Colonel the two scraps of paper I'd found in the dead floor waiter's pockets. "Those figures. Those numbers. They mean anything to you?"

De Graaf gave them a cursory glance, held them up before a bright desk lamp, laid them down on the desk. "No."

"Can you find out? If they have any meaning?"

"I have a very able staff. By the way, where did you get these?"

"A man gave them to me."

"You mean you got them from a man."

"There's a difference?"

"There could be a very great difference." De Graaf leaned forward, face and voice very earnest. "Look, Major Sherman, we know about your technique of getting people off balance and keeping them there. We know about your propensity for stepping outside the law——"

"Colonel de Graaf!"

"A well-taken point. You're probably never inside it to start with. We know about this deliberate policy—admittedly as effective as it is suicidal—of endless provocation, waiting for something, for somebody to break. But please, Major Sherman, *please* do not try to provoke too many people in Amsterdam. We have too many canals."

"I won't provoke anyone," I said. "I'll be very careful."

"I'm sure you will." De Graaf sighed. "And now, I believe, van Gelder has a few things to show you."

Van Gelder had. He drove me in his own black Opel from the police HQ in the Marnixstraat to the city mortuary and by the time I left there I was wishing he hadn't.

The city mortuary lacked the old-world charm, the romance and nostalgic beauty of old Amsterdam. It was like the city mortuary in any big town, cold—very cold—and clinical and inhuman and repelling. The central block had down its centre two rows of white slabs of what appeared to be marble and almost certainly weren't, while the sides of the room were lined with very large metal doors. The principal attendant here, resplendent in an immaculately starched white coat, was a cheerful rubicund genial character, who appeared to be in perpetual danger of breaking out into gales of laughter, a very odd characteristic indeed, one would have thought, to find in a mortuary attendant until one recalled that more than a handful of England's hangmen in the past were reckoned to be the most rollicking tavern companions one could ever hope to have.

At a word from van Gelder, he led us to one of the big metal doors, opened it and pulled out a wheeled metal rack that ran smoothly on steel runners. A white-sheeted form lay on this rack.

"The canal he was found in is called the Qroquius Kad," van Gelder said. He seemed quite unemotional about it. "Not what you might call the Park Lane of Amsterdam—it's down by the docks. Hans Gerber. Nineteen. I won't show you his face—he's been too long in the water. The fire brigade found him when they were fishing out a car. He could have been there another year—or two. Someone had twisted a few old lead pipes about his middle."

He lifted a corner of the sheet to expose a flaccid emaciated arm. It looked for all the world as if someone had trod all over it with spiked climbing boots. Curious purple lines joined many of those punctures and the whole arm was badly discoloured. Van Gelder covered it up without a word and turned away. The attendant wheeled the rack inside again, closed the door, led us to another door and repeated the performance of wheeling out another corpse, smiling hugely the while like a bankrupt English duke showing the public round his historic castle.

"I won't show you this one's face either," van Gelder said. "It is not nice to look on a boy of twenty-three who has the face of a man of seventy."

He turned to the attendant. "Where was this one found?"

"The Oosterhook," the attendant beamed. "On a coal barge."

Van Gelder nodded. "That's right. With a bottle—an empty bottle—of gin beside him. The gin was all inside him. You know what a splendid combination gin and heroin is." He pulled back the sheet to reveal an arm similar to the one I'd just seen. "Suicide—or murder."

"It all depends."

"On?"

"Whether he bought the gin himself. That would make it suicide—or accidental death. Someone could have put the full bottle in his hand. That would make it murder. We had a case, just like it, last month, in the Port of London. We'll never know."

At a nod from van Gelder, the attendant led us happily to a slab in the middle of the room. This time van Gelder pulled back the sheet from the top. The girl was very young and very lovely and had golden hair.

"Beautiful, isn't she?" van Gelder asked. "Not a mark on her face. Julia Rosemeyer from East Germany. All we know of her, all we will ever know of her. Sixteen, the doctors guess."

"What happened to her?"

"Fell six stories to a concrete pavement."

I thought briefly of the ex-floor waiter and how much better he would have looked on this slab, then asked: "Pushed?"

"Fell. Witnesses. They were all high. She'd been talking all night about flying to England. She had some obsession about meeting the Queen. Suddenly she scrambled on to the parapet of the balcony, said she was flying to see the Queen—and, well, she flew. Fortunately, there was no one passing beneath at the time. Like to see more?"

"I'd like to have a drink at the nearest pub, if you don't mind."

"No." He smiled but there wasn't anything humorous about it. "Van Gelder's fireside. It's not far. I have my reasons."

"Your reasons?"

"You'll see."

We said goodbye and thanks to the happily smiling attendant who looked as if he would have liked to say "Haste ye back" but didn't. The sky had darkened since early morning and big heavy scattered drops of rain were beginning to fall. To the east the horizon was livid and purple, more than vaguely threatening and foreboding. It was seldom that a sky reflected my mood as accurately as this.

Van Gelder's fireside could have given points to most English pubs I knew: an oasis of bright cheerfulness compared to the sheeting rain outside, to the rippled waves of water running down the windows, it was warm and cosy and comfortable and homely, furnished in rather heavy Dutch furniture with overstuffed armchairs, but I have a strong partiality for overstuffed armchairs: they don't mark you so much as the understuffed variety. There was a russet carpet on the floor and the walls were painted in different shades of warm pastel colours. The fire was all a fire ever should be and van Gelder, I was happy to observe was thoughtfully studying a very well-stocked glass liquor cupboard.

"Well," I said, "you took me to that damned mortuary to make your point. I'm sure you made it. What was it?"

"Points, not point. The first one was to convince you that we here are up against an even more vicious problem than you have at home. There's another half-dozen drug addicts in the mortuary there and how many of them died a natural death is anyone's guess. It's not always as bad as this, those deaths seem to come in waves, but it still represents an intolerable loss of life and mainly young life at that; and for every one there, how many hundred hopeless addicts are there in the streets?''

"Your point being that you have even more incentive than I to seek out and destroy those people—and that we are attacking a common enemy, a central source of supply?''

"Every country has only one king.''

"And the other point?''

"To reinforce Colonel de Graaf's warning. Those people are totally ruthless. Provoke them too much, get too close to them—well, there's still a few slabs left in the mortuary.''

"How about that drink?'' I said.

A telephone bell rang in the hallway outside. Van Gelder murmured an apology and went to answer it. Just as the door closed behind him a second door leading to the room opened and a girl entered. She was tall and slender and in her early twenties and was dressed in a dragon-emblazoned multihued housecoat that reached almost to her ankles. She was quite beautiful, with flaxen hair, an oval face and huge violet eyes that appeared to be at once humorous and perceptive, so striking in overall appearance that it was quite some time before I remembered what passed for my manners and struggled to my feet, no easy feat from the depths of that cavernous armchair.

"Hullo,'' I said. "Paul Sherman.'' It didn't sound much but I couldn't think of anything else to say.

Almost as if embarrassed, the girl momentarily sucked the tip of her thumb, then smiled to reveal perfect teeth.

"I am Trudi. I do not speak good English.'' She didn't either, but she'd the nicest voice for speaking bad English I'd come across in a long time. I advanced with my hand out, but she made no move to take it: instead she put her hand to her mouth and giggled shyly. I am not accustomed to have fully grown girls giggle shyly at me and was more than a little relieved to hear the sound of the receiver being replaced and van Gelder's voice as he entered from the hall.

"Just a routine report on the airport business. Nothing to go on yet——''

Van Gelder saw the girl, broke off, smiled and advanced to put his arm round her shoulders.

"I see you two have met each other.''

"Well,'' I said, "not quite——'' then broke off in turn as Trudi reached up and whispered in his ear glancing at me out of the corner of her eye. Van Gelder smiled and nodded and Trudi went quickly from the room. The puzzlement must have shown in my face, for van Gelder smiled again and it didn't seem a very happy smile to me.

"She'll be right back, Major. She's shy at first, with strangers. Just at first.''

As van Gelder had promised, Trudi was back almost immediately. She was carrying with her a very large puppet, so wonderfully made that at first glance it could have been mistaken for a real child. It was almost three feet in length with a white wimple hat covering flaxen curls of the same shade as Trudi's own and was wearing an ankle-length billowy striped silk dress and a most beautifully embroidered bodice. Trudi clasped this puppet as tightly as if it had been a real child. Van Gelder again put his arm round her shoulders.

"This is my daughter, Trudi. A friend of mine, Trudi. Major Sherman, from England."

This time she advanced without any hesitation, put her hand out, made a small bobbing motion like the beginnings of a curtsey, and smiled.

"How do you do, Major Sherman?"

Not to be outdone in courtesy I smiled and bowed slightly. "Miss van Gelder. My pleasure."

"My pleasure." She turned and looked enquiringly at van Gelder.

"English is not one of Trudi's strong points," van Gelder said apologetically. "Sit down, Major, sit down."

He took a bottle of Scotch from the sideboard, poured drinks for myself and himself, handed me mine and sank into his chair with a sigh. Then he looked up at his daughter, who was gazing steadily at me in a way that made me feel more than vaguely uncomfortable.

"Won't you sit down, my dear?"

She turned to van Gelder, smiled brightly, nodded and handed him the huge puppet to him. He accepted it so readily that he was obviously used to this sort of thing.

"Yes, Papa," she said, then without warning but at the same time as unaffectedly as if it were the most natural thing in the world, she sat down on my knee, put an arm around my neck and smiled at me. I smiled right back though, for just that instant, it was a Herculean effort.

Trudi regarded me solemnly and said: "I like you."

"And I like you too, Trudi." I squeezed her shoulder to show her how much I liked her. She smiled at me, put her head on my shoulder and closed her eyes. I looked at the top of the blonde head for a moment then glanced in mild enquiry at van Gelder. He smiled, a smile full of sorrow.

"If I do not wound you, Major Sherman, Trudi loves everyone."

"All girls of a certain age do."

"You are a man of quite extraordinary perception."

I didn't think it called for any great perception at all to make the remark I had just made, so I didn't answer, just smiled and turned again to Trudi. I said, very gently: "Trudi?"

She said nothing. She just stirred and smiled again, a curiously contented smile that for some obscure reason made me feel more than a little of a fraud, closed her eyes even more tightly and snuggled close to me.

I tried again. "Trudi. I'm sure you must have beautiful eyes. Can I see them?"

She thought this over for a bit, smiled again, sat up, held herself at straight arms' length with her hands on my shoulders, then opened her eyes very wide as a child would do on such a request.

The huge violet eyes were beautiful, no doubt about that. But they were something else also. They were glazed and vacant and did not seem to reflect the light; they sparkled, a sparkle that would have deceptively high-lit any still photograph taken of her, for the sparkle was superficial only: behind lay a strange quality of opacity.

Still gently, I took her right hand from my shoulder and pushed the sleeve up as far as the elbow. If the rest of her were anything to go by it should have been a beautiful forearm but it wasn't: it was shockingly mutilated by the punctures left by a countless number of hypodermic needles. Trudi, her lips trembling, looked at me in dismay as if fearful of reproach, snatched down the sleeve of her dress, flung her arms about me, buried her face in my neck and started to cry. She cried as if her heart was breaking. I patted her as soothingly as one can pat anyone who seems bent on choking you and looked over at van Gelder.

"Now I know your reasons," I said. "For insisting I come here."

"I'm sorry. Now you know."

"You make a third point?"

"I make a third point. God alone knows I wish I didn't have to. But you will understand that in all fairness to my colleagues I must let them know these things."

"De Graaf knows?"

"Every senior police officer in Amsterdam knows," van Gelder said simply. "Trudi!"

Trudi's only reaction was to cling even more tightly. I was beginning to suffer from anoxia.

"Trudi!" Van Gelder was more insistent this time. "Your afternoon's sleep. You know what the doctor says. Bed!"

"No," she sobbed. "No bed."

Van Gelder sighed and raised his voice: "Herta!"

Almost as if she had been waiting for her cue—which she probably had been, listening outside the door—a most outlandish creature entered the room. As far as health farms were concerned, she was the challenge to end all challenges. She was a huge and enormously fat waddling woman—to describe her method of locomotion as walking would have been a gross inaccuracy—dressed in exactly the same type of clothes as Trudi's puppet was wearing. Long blonde pigtails tied with bright blue ribbon hung down her massive front. Her face was old—she had to be at least over seventy—deeply trenched and had the texture and appearance of cracked brown leather. The contrast between the gaily hued clothes and the blonde pigtails on the one hand and the enormous old hag that wore them on the other, was bizarre, horrible, so grotesque as to be almost obscene, but the contrast appeared to evoke no such responses in either van Gelder or Trudi.

The old woman crossed the room—for all her bulk and waddling gait she made ground quite quickly—nodded a curt acknowledgment to me and, without saying a word, laid a kindly but firm hand on Trudi's shoulder. Trudi looked up at once, her tears gone as quickly as they had come, smiled, nodded docilely, disengaged her arms from my neck and rose. She crossed to van Gelder's chair, recovered her puppet, kissed him, crossed to where I was sitting, kissed me as unaffectedly as a child saying good night, and almost skipped from the room, the waddling Herta close behind. I exhaled a long sigh and just managed to refrain from mopping my brow.

"You might have warned me," I complained. "About Trudi *and* Herta. Who is she anyway—Herta, I mean? A nurse?"

"An ancient retainer, you'd say in English." Van Gelder took a large gulp of his whisky as if he needed it and I did the same for I needed it even more: after all he was used to this sort of thing. "My parents' old housekeeper—from the island of Huyler in the Zuider Zee. As you may have noticed they are a little—what do you say—conservative in their dress. She's been with us for only a few months—but, well, you can see how she is with Trudi."

"And Trudi?"

"Trudi is eight years old. She has been eight years old for the past fifteen years, she always will be eight years old. Not my daughter, as you may have guessed—but I could never love a daughter more. My brother's adopted daughter. He and I worked in Curaçao until last year—I was in narcotics, he was the security officer for a Dutch oil company. His wife died some years ago—and then he and *my* wife were killed in a car crash last year. Someone had to take Trudi. I did. I didn't want her—and now I couldn't live without her. She will never grow up, Mr. Sherman.''

And all the time his subordinates probably thought that he was just their lucky superior with no other thought or concern in his mind other than to put as many malefactors behind bars as possible. Sympathetic comment and commiseration were never my forte, so I said: "This addiction—when did it start?''

"God knows. Years ago. Years before my brother found out.''

"Some of those hypo punctures are recent.''

"She's on withdrawal treatment. Too many injections, you would say?''

"I would say.''

"Herta watches her like a hawk. Every morning she takes her to the Vondel Park—she loves to feed the birds. In the afternoon Trudi sleeps. But sometimes in the evening Herta gets tired—and I am often from home in the evening.''

"You've had her watched?''

"A score of times. I don't know how it's done.''

"They get at her to get at you?''

"To bring pressure to bear on me. What else? She has no money to pay for fixes. They are fools and do not realise that I must see her die slowly before my eyes before I can compromise myself. So they keep trying.''

"You could have a twenty-four-hour guard placed on her.''

"And then that would make it official. Such an official request is brought to the automatic notice of the health authorities. And then?''

"An institution,'' I nodded. "For the mentally retarded. And she'd never come out again.''

"She'd never come out again.''

I didn't know what to say except goodbye, so I did that and left.

4

I SPENT the afternoon in my hotel room going over the carefully documented and cross-indexed files and case histories which Colonel de Graaf's office had given me. They covered every known case of drug-taking and drug prosecutions, successful or not, in Amsterdam in the past two years. They made very interesting reading if, that is, your interest lay in death and degradation and suicide and broken homes and ruined careers. But there was nothing in it for me. I spent a helpless hour trying to rearrange and reassemble the various cross indexes but no significant pattern even began to emerge. I gave up. Highly trained minds like de Graaf's and van Gelder's would have spent many many hours in the same fruitless pastime and if they had failed to establish any form or pattern there was no hope for me.

In the early evening I went down to the foyer and handed in my key. The smile of the assistant manager behind the desk lacked a little of the sabre-toothed quality of old, it was deferential, even apologetic: he'd obviously been told to try a new tack with me.

"Good evening, good evening, Mr. Sherman.'' An affable ingratiation that I cared for even less than his normal approach. "I'm afraid I must have sounded a little abrupt last evening, but you see——''

"Don't mention it, my dear fellow, don't mention it.'' I wasn't going to

let any old hotel manager outdo me in affability. "It was perfectly understandable in the circumstances. Must have come as a very great shock to
you." I glanced through the foyer doors at the falling rain. "The guidebooks
didn't mention this."

He smiled widely as if he hadn't heard the same inane remark a thousand
times before then said cunningly: "Hardly the night for your English constitutional, Mr. Sherman."

"No chance anyway. It's Zaandam for me tonight."

"Zaandam." He made a face. "My commiserations, Mr. Sherman." He
evidently knew a great deal more about Zaandam than I did which was
hardly surprising as I'd just picked the name from a map.

I went outside. Rain or no rain the barrel organ was still grinding and
screeching away at the top of its form. It was Puccini who was on the air
tonight and he was taking a terrible beating. I crossed to the organ and stood
there for some time, not so much listening to the music, for there was none
to speak of, but looking without seeming to look at a handful of emaciated
and ill-dressed teenagers—a rare sight indeed in Amsterdam where they
don't go in for emaciation very much—who leaned their elbows on the
barrel organ and seemed lost in rapture. My thoughts were interrupted by a
gravelly voice behind me.

"Mynheer likes music?" I turned. The ancient was smiling at me in a
tentative sort of fashion.

"I love music."

"So do I, so do I." I peered at him closely for in the nature of things his
time must be close and there could be no forgiveness for that remark. I
smiled at him, one music lover to the other.

"I shall think of you tonight. I'm going to the opera."

"Mynheer is kind."

I dropped two coins in the tin can that had mysteriously appeared under
my nose.

"Mynheer is too kind."

Having the suspicions I did about him, I thought the same myself, but I
smiled charitably and, recrossing the street, nodded to the doorman; with
the masonic legerdemain known only to doormen, he materialised a taxi out
of nowhere. I told him "Schiphol airport" and got inside.

We moved off. We did not move off alone. At the first traffic lights,
twenty yards from the hotel, I glanced through the tinted rear window. A
yellow-striped Mercedes taxi was two cars behind us, a taxi I recognised as
one that habitually frequented the rank not far from the hotel. But it could
have been coincidence. The lights turned to green and we made our way
into the Vijzelstraat. So did the yellow-striped Mercedes.

I tapped the driver on the shoulder. "Stop here, please. I want to buy
some cigarettes." I got out. The Mercedes was right behind us, stopped.
No one got in, no one got out. I went into an hotel foyer, bought some
cigarettes I didn't need and came out again. The Mercedes was still there.
We moved off and after a few moments I said to the driver: "Turn right
along the Prinsengracht."

He protested. "That is not the way to Schiphol."

"It's the way I want to go. Turn right."

He did and so did the Mercedes.

"Stop." He stopped. The Mercedes stopped. Coincidence was coincidence but this was ridiculous. I got out, walked back to the Mercedes and
opened the door. The driver was a small fat man with a shiny blue suit and
a disreputable air. "Good evening. Are you for hire?"

"No." He looked me up and down trying out first that air of easy insou-
ciance, then that of insolent indifference, but he wasn't right for either part.

"Then why are you stopped?"

"Any law against a man stopping for a smoke?"

"None. Only you're not smoking. You know the Police HQ in the Marnixstraat?" The sudden lack of enthusiasm in his expression made it quite
clear that he knew it all too well. "I suggest you go there and ask for either
Colonel de Graaf or Inspector van Gelder and tell them that you have a
complaint to lodge about Paul Sherman, Room 616, Hotel Excelsior."

"Complaint?" he said warily. "What complaint?"

"Tell them that he took the car keys from your ignition and threw them
into the canal." I took the car keys from the ignition and threw them into
the canal and a very satisfactory plop they made too as they vanished forever
into the depths of the Prinsengracht. "Don't follow me around," I said and
closed the door in a manner befitting the end of our brief interview but
Mercedes are well-made cars and the door didn't fall off.

Back in my own taxi I waited till we were back on the main road again
then stopped the taxi. "I've decided to walk," I said and paid what was
owing.

"What! to Schiphol?"

I gave him the sort of tolerant smile one might expect to receive from a
long-distance walker whose prowess has been called in question, waited till
he had moved from sight, hopped on a 16 tram and got off at the Dam.
Belinda, dressed in a dark coat and with a dark scarf over her blonde hair,
was waiting for me in the tram shelter. She looked damp and cold.

"You're late," she said accusingly.

"Never criticise your boss, even by implication. The managerial classes
always have things to attend to."

We crossed the square, retracing the steps the grey man and I had taken
the previous night, down the alley by the Krasnapolsky and along the tree-
lined Oudezijds Voorburgwal, an area that is one of the cultural highlights
of Amsterdam, but Belinda seemed in no mood for culture. A mercurial
girl, she seemd withdrawn and remote that night, and the silence was hardly
companionable. Belinda had something on her mind and if I were beginning
to become any judge of Belinda my guess was that she would let me know
about it sooner rather than later. I was right.

She said abruptly: "We don't really exist for you, do we?"

"Who doesn't exist?"

"Me, Maggie, all the people who work for you. We're just cyphers."

"Well, you know how it is," I said pacifically. "Ship's captain never
mingles socially with the crew."

"That's what I mean. That's what I say—we don't really exist for you.
We're just puppets to be manipulated so that the master puppeteer can
achieve certain ends. And other puppets would do as well."

I said mildly: "We're here to do a very nasty and unpleasant job and
achieving that end is all that matters. Personalities don't enter into it. You
forget that I am your boss, Belinda! I really don't think that you should be
talking to me like that."

"I'll talk to you any way I like." Not only mercurial but a girl of spirit,
Maggie would never have dreamed of talking to me like that. She considered
her last remark, then said more quietly: "I'm sorry. I shouldn't have spoken
like that. But do you have to treat us in this—this detached and remote
fashion and never make contact with us? We *are* people, you know—but
not for you. You'd pass me in the street tomorrow and not recognise me.
You don't *notice* us."

"Oh, I notice all right. Take yourself, for instance." I carefully refrained from looking at her as we walked along although I knew she was observing me pretty closely. "New girl to Narcotics. Limited experience Deuxième Bureau, Paris. Dressed in navy coat, navy scarf spotted with little white edelweiss, knitted white knee stockings, sensible flat-heeled navy shoes, buckled, five feet four, a figure, to quote a famous American writer, to make a bishop kick a hole through a stained glass window, a quite beautiful face, platinum blonde hair that looks like spun silk when the sun shines through it, black eyebrows, green eyes, perceptive and, best of all, beginning to worry about her boss, especially his lack of humanity. Oh, I forgot. Cracked fingernail polish, third finger, left hand and a devastating smile enhanced— if, that is to say, that's possible—by a slightly crooked left upper eyetooth."

"Wow!" She was at a momentary loss for words, which I was beginning to guess was not at all in character. She glanced at the fingernail in question and the polish was cracked, then turned to me with a smile that was just as devastating as I'd said it was. "Maybe you do at that."

"Do at what?"

"Care about us."

"Of course I care." She was beginning to confuse me with Sir Galahad and that could be a bad thing. "All my operatives, Category Grade 1, young, female, good-looking, are like daughters to me."

There was a long pause, then she murmured something, very *sotto voce* indeed, but it sounded to me very like "Yes, Papa."

"What was that?" I asked suspiciously.

"Nothing. Nothing at all."

We turned into the street which housed the premises of Morgenstern and Muggenthaler. This, my second visit to the place, more than confirmed the impression I had formed the previous night. It seemed darker than ever, bleaker and more menacing, cobbles and pavement more cracked than before, the gutters more choked with litter. Even the gabled houses leaned closer towards one another: this time tomorrow and they would be touching.

Belinda stopped abruptly and clutched my right arm. I glanced at her. She was staring upwards, her eyes wide, and I followed her gaze where the gabled warehouses marched away into the diminishing distance, their hoisting beams clearly silhouetted against the night sky. I knew she felt there was evil abroad: I felt it myself.

"This must be the place," she whispered. "I *know* it must be."

"This is the place," I said matter-of-factly. "What's wrong?"

She snatched her hand away as if I had just said something wounding, but I regained it, tucked her arm under mine and held on firmly to her hand. She made no attempt to remove it.

"It—it's so *creepy*. What are those horrible things sticking out under the gables?"

"Hoisting beams. In the old days the houses here were rated on the width of the frontage, so the thrifty Dutch made their houses uncommonly narrow. Unfortunately, this made their staircases even narrower still. So, the hoisting beams for the bulky stuff—grand pianos up, coffins down, that sort of thing."

"Stop it!" She lifted her shoulders and shuddered involuntarily. "This is a horrible place. Those beams—they're like the gallows they hang people from. This is a place where people come to die."

"Nonsense, my dear girl," I said heatedly. I could feel stiletto-tipped fingers of ice play Chopin's "Death March" up and down my spine and was suddenly filled with longing for that dear old nostalgic music from the barrel organ outside the Excelsior; I was probably as glad to hang on to Belinda's hand as she was to mine. "You mustn't fall prey to those Gallic imaginings of yours."

"I'm not imagining things," she said sombrely, then shivered again. "Did we have to come to this awful place?" She was shivering violently now, violently and continuously, and though it was cold it wasn't as cold as all that.

"Can you remember the way we came?" I asked. She nodded, puzzled and I went on: "You make your way back to the hotel and I'll join you later."

"Back to the hotel?" She was still puzzled.

"I'll be all right. Now, off you go."

She tore her hand free from mine and before I could realise what was happening she was gripping both my lapels in her hands and giving me a look that was clearly designed to shrivel me on the spot. If she was shaking now it was with anger; I'd never realised that so beautiful a girl could look so furious. "Mercurial" was no word for Belinda, just a pale and innocuous substitute for the one I really wanted. I looked down at the fists gripping my lapels. The knuckles were white. She was actually trying to shake me.

"Don't ever say anything like that to me again!" She was furious, no doubt about it.

There was a brief but spirited conflict between my ingrained instinct for discipline and the desire to put my arms round her; discipline won, but it was a close-run thing. I said humbly: "I'll never say anything like that to you again."

"All right." She released my sadly crushed lapels and grabbed my hand instead. "Well, come on then." Pride would never let me say that she dragged me along but to the detached onlooker it must have seemed uncommonly like it.

Fifty paces farther along and I stopped. "Here we are."

Belinda read the nameplate. "Morgenstern and Muggenthaler."

"Topping the bill at this week's Palladium." I climbed the steps and got to work on the lock. "Watch the street."

"And then what do I do?"

"Watch my back."

A determined wolf cub with a bent hairpin would have found that lock no deterrent. We went inside and I closed the door behind us. The torch I had was small but powerful; it didn't have much to show us on that first floor. It was piled almost ceiling high with empty wooden boxes, paper, cardboard, bales of strawing and baling and binding machinery. A packing station, nothing else.

We climbed up the narrow winding wooden steps to the next floor. Halfway up I glanced round and saw that Belinda, too, was glancing apprehensively behind her, her torch swivelling and darting in a dozen different directions.

The next floor was given over entirely to vast quantities of Dutch pewter, windmills, clogs, pipes and a dozen other articles associated solely with the tourist souvenir trade. There were tens of thousands of those articles, on shelves along the walls or on parallel racks across the warehouse, and although I couldn't possibly examine them all they all looked perfectly innocuous to me. What didn't look quite so innocuous, however, was a fifteen by twenty room that projected from one corner of the warehouse, or, more precisely, the door that led into that room although obviously it wasn't going to lead into that room tonight. I called Belinda over and shone my torch on the door. She stared at it then stared at me and I could see the puzzlement in the reflected wash of light.

"A time lock," she said. "Why would anyone want a time lock on a simple office door?"

"It's not a simple office door," I pointed out. "It's made of steel. By the same token you can bet those simple wooden walls are lined with steel and that the simple old rustic window overlooking the street is covered with close-meshed bars set in concrete. In a diamond warehouse, yes, you could understand it. But here? Why, they've nothing to hide here."

"It looks as if we may have come to the right place," Belinda said.

"Did you ever doubt me?"

"No, sir." Very demure. "What *is* this place, anyway?"

"It's obvious, isn't it—a wholesaler in the souvenir trade. The factories or the cottage industries or whatever send their goods in bulk for storage here and the warehouse supplies the shops on demand. Simple, isn't it? Harmless, isn't it?"

"But not very hygienic."

"How's that again?"

"It smells horrible."

"Cannabis does to some people."

"Cannabis!"

"You and your sheltered life. Come on."

I led the way up to the third floor, waited for Belinda to join me. "Still guarding the master's back?" I enquired.

"Still guarding the master's back," she said mechanically. True to form, the fire-breathing Belinda of a few minutes ago had disappeared. I didn't blame her. There was something inexplicably sinister and malevolent about this old building. The sickly smell of cannabis was even stronger now but there appeared to be nothing on this floor even remotely connected with it. Three sides of the entire floor, together with a number of transverse racks, were given over entirely to pendulum clocks, all of them, fortunately, stopped. They covered the whole gamut of shape, design and size and varied in quality from small, cheap, garishly painted models for the tourist trade, nearly all made from yellow pine, to very large, beautifully made and exquisitely designed metal clocks that were obviously very old and expensive, or modern replicas of those which couldn't have been all that cheaper.

The fourth side of the floor came, to say the least, as a considerable surprise. It was given up to, of all things, row upon row of Bibles. I wondered briefly what on earth Bibles were doing in a souvenir warehouse, but only briefly: there were too many things I didn't understand.

I picked one of them up and examined it. Embossed in gold on the lower half of the leather cover were the words "THE GABRIEL BIBLE . . ." I opened it and on the flyleaf was the printed inscription "WITH THE COMPLIMENTS OF THE FIRST REFORMED CHURCH OF THE AMERICAN HUGUENOT SOCIETY."

"There's one of those in our hotel room," Belinda said.

"I shouldn't be surprised if there's one of those in most of the hotel rooms in the city. Question is, what are they doing here? Why not in a publisher's or stationer's warehouse, where you would expect to find them. Queer, isn't it?"

She shivered. "Everything here is queer."

I clapped her on the back. "You've got a cold coming on, that's what it is. I've warned you before about these mini-skirts. Next floor."

The next floor was given over entirely to the most astonishing collection of puppets imaginable. Altogether, their number must have run into thousands. They ranged in size from tiny miniatures to models even bigger than the one Trudi had been carrying; all, without exception, were exquisitely modelled, all beautifully dressed in a variety of traditional Dutch costumes. The bigger puppets were either freestanding or supported by a metal stay; the smaller ones dangled by strings from overhead rails. The beam of my torch finally focussed on a group of dolls all dressed in the same particular costume.

Belinda had forgotten about the importance of minding my back: she resumed her arm-clutching again.

"It's—it's so eerie. They're so alive, so watchful." She looked at the dolls spot-lit by the beam of my torch. "Something special about those?"

"There's no need to whisper. They may be looking at you but I assure you they can't hear you. Those puppets there. Nothing special really, just that they come from the island of Huyler out in the Zuider Zee. Van Gelder's housekeeper, a charming old beldam who's lost her broomstick, dresses like that."

"Like that?"

"It's hard to imagine," I admitted. "And Trudi has a big puppet dressed in exactly the same way."

"The sick girl?"

"The sick girl."

"There's something terribly sick about this place." She let go of my arm and got back to the business of minding my back again. Seconds later I heard the sound of her sharply indrawn breath and turned round. She had her back to me, not more than four feet away, and as I watched she started to walk slowly and silently backwards, her eyes evidently lined up on something caught in the beam of her torch, her free hand reaching out gropingly behind her. I took it and she came close to me, still not turning her head.

She spoke in an urgent whisper.

"There's somebody there. Somebody watching."

I glanced briefly along the beam of her torch but could see nothing, but then hers wasn't a very powerful torch compared to the one I carried. I looked away, squeezed her hand to attract her attention, and when she turned round I looked questioningly at her.

"There *is* someone there." Still the same insistent whisper, the green eyes wide. "I saw them. I *saw* them."

"Them?"

"Eyes. I saw them!"

I never doubted her. Imaginative girl she might be but she'd been trained and highly trained not to be imaginative in the matter of observation. I brought up my own torch, not as carefully as I might have done, for the beam struck her eyes in passing, momentarily blinding her and as she raised a reflex hand to her eyes I settled the beam on the area she had just indicated. I couldn't see any eyes, but what I did see was two adjacent puppets swinging so gently that their motion was almost imperceptible. Almost, but not quite—and there wasn't a draught, a breath of air stirring in that fourth floor of the warehouse.

I squeezed her hand again and smiled at her. "Now, Belinda——"

"Don't you 'now Belinda' me!" Whether this was meant to be a hiss or a whisper with a tremor in it I couldn't be sure. "I *saw* them. Horrible staring eyes. I swear I saw them. I swear it."

"Yes, yes, of course, Belinda——"

She moved to face me, frustration in the intent eyes as if she suspected me of sounding as if I were trying to humour her, which I was. I said, "I believe you, Belinda. Of *course* I believe you." I hadn't changed my tone.

"Then why don't you do something about it?"

"Just what I'm going to do. I'm going to get the hell out of here." I made a last unhurried inspection with my torch, as if nothing had happened, then turned and took her arm in a protective fashion. "Nothing for us here—and we've both been too long in here. A drink, I think, for what's left of our nerves."

She stared at me, her face reflecting a changing pattern of anger and frustration and incredulity and, I suspected, more than a little relief. But the anger was dominant now: most people become angry when they feel they are being disbelieved and humoured at the same time.

"But I tell you——"

"Ah—ah!" I touched my lips with my forefinger. "You don't tell me anything. The boss, remember, always knows best. . . ."

She was too young to go all puce and apoplectic, but the precipitating emotions were there all the same. She glared at me, apparently decided that there were no words to meet the situation, and started off down the stairs, outrage in every stiff line of her back. I followed and my back wasn't quite normal either, it had a curious tingling feeling to it that didn't go away until I had the front door to the warehouse safely locked behind me.

We walked quickly up the street, keeping about three feet apart; it was Belinda who maintained the distance, her attitude clearly proclaiming that the hand-holding and the arm-clutching was over for the night and more likely for keeps. I cleared my throat.

"He who fights and runs away, lives to fight another day."

She was so seething with anger that she didn't get it.

"Please don't talk to me," she snapped so I didn't, not, at least, till I came to the first tavern in the sailors' quarter, an unsalubrious dive rejoicing in the name of The Cat o' Nine Tails. The British Navy must have stopped by here once. I took Belinda's arm and guided her inside. She wasn't keen, but she didn't fight about it.

It was a smoky airless drinking den and that was about all you could say about it. Several sailors, resentful of this intrusion by a couple of trippers of what they probably rightly regarded as their own personal property, scowled at me when I came in, but I was in a much better scowling mood than they were and after the first disparaging reception they left us strictly alone. I led Belinda to a small table, a genuine antique wooden table whose original surface hadn't been touched by soap or water since time immemorial.

"I'm having Scotch," I said. "You?"

"Scotch," she said huffily.

"But you don't drink Scotch."

"I do tonight."

She was half right. She knocked back half of her glass of neat Scotch in a defiant swig and then started sputtering, coughing and choking so violently that I saw I could have been wrong about her developing symptoms of apoplexy. I patted her helpfully on the back.

"Take your hand away," she wheezed.

I took my hand away.

"I don't think I can work with you any more, Major Sherman," she said after she'd got her larynx in working order again.

"I'm sorry to hear that."

"I can't work with people who don't trust me, who don't believe me. You not only treat us like puppets, you treat us like children."

"I don't regard you as a child," I said pacifically. I didn't either.

" 'I believe you, Belinda,' " she mimicked bitterly. " 'Of course I believe you, Belinda.' You don't believe Belinda at all."

"I *do* believe Belinda," I said. "I do believe I care for Belinda after all. That's why I took Belinda out of there."

She stared at me. "You believe—then why——"

"There *was* someone there, hidden behind that rack of puppets. I saw two of the puppets sway slightly. Someone was behind that rack, watching, wanting to see, I'm certain, what if anything we found out. He'd no murderous intent or he'd have shot us in the back when we were going down the stairs. But if I'd reacted as you wanted me to, then I'd have been forced to go look for him and he'd have gunned me down from his place of concealment before I'd even set eyes on him. And then he'd have gunned you down, for he couldn't have any witnesses, and you're really far too young to die yet. Or maybe I could have played hide and seek with him and stood an even chance of getting him—if you weren't there. But you were, you haven't a gun, you've no experience at all in the nasty kind of games we play and you were as good as a hostage to him. So I took Belinda out of there. There now, wasn't that a nice speech?"

"I don't know about the speech." Mercurial as ever, there were tears in her eyes. "I only know it's the nicest thing anybody ever said about me."

"Fiddlesticks!" I drained my Scotch, finished hers off for her and took her back to her hotel. We stood in the foyer entrance a moment, sheltering from the now heavily falling rain and she said: "I'm sorry. I was such a fool. And I'm sorry for you too."

"For me?"

"I can see now why you'd rather have puppets than people working for you. One doesn't cry inside when a puppet dies."

I said nothing. I was beginning to lose my grip on this girl, the old master-pupil relationship wasn't quite what it used to be.

"Another thing," she said. She spoke almost happily. I braced myself. "I won't ever be afraid of you any more."

"You were afraid? Of me?"

"Yes, I was. Really. But it's like the man said——"

"What man?"

"Shylock, wasn't it? You know, cut me and I bleed——"

"Oh, do be quiet!"

She kept quiet. She just gave me that devastating smile again, kissed me without any great haste, gave me some more of the same smile and went inside. I watched the glass swing doors until they came to a rest. Much more of this, I thought gloomily, and discipline would be gone to hell and back again.

5

I WALKED two or three hundred yards till I was well clear of the girls' hotel, picked up a taxi and was driven back to the Excelsior. I stood for a moment under the foyer canopy, looking at the barrel organ across the road. The ancient was not only indefatigable but apparently also impermeable, rain meant nothing to him, nothing except an earthquake would have stopped him from giving his evening performance. Like the old trouper who feels that the show must go on he perhaps felt he had a duty to his public, and a public he incredibly had, half a dozen youths whose threadbare clothes gave every indication of being completely sodden, a group of acolytes lost in the mystic contemplation of the death agonies of Strauss, whose turn it was to be stretched on the rack tonight. I went inside.

The assistant manager caught sight of me as I turned from hanging up my coat. His surprise appeared to be genuine.

"Back so soon? From Zaandam?"

"Fast taxi," I explained and passed through to the bar, where I ordered a jonge Genever and a Pils and drank both slowly while I considered the relationship between fast men with fast guns and pushers and sick girls and hidden eyes behind puppets and people and taxis who followed me everywhere I went and policemen being blackmailed and venal managers and doorkeepers and tinny barrel organs. It all added up to nothing. I wasn't, I felt sure, being provocative enough and was coming to the reluctant conclusion that there was nothing else for it but a visit to the warehouse again later that night—without, of course, ever letting Belinda know about it—when I happened to look up for the first time at the mirror in front of me. I wasn't prompted by instinct or anything of the kind, it was just that my nostrils had been almost unconsciously titillated for some time past by a perfume that I'd just identified as sandalwood and as I am rather partial to it I just wanted to see who was wearing it. Sheer old-fashioned noseyness.

The girl was sitting at a table directly behind me, a drink on the table before her, a paper in her hand. I could have thought that I imagined that her eyes dropped to the paper as soon as I had glanced up to the mirror, but I wasn't given to imagining things like that. She had been looking at me. She seemed young, was wearing a green coat and had a blonde mop of hair that, in the modern fashion, had every appearance of having been trimmed by a lunatic hedge-cutter. Amsterdam seemed to be full of blondes that were forced on my attention in one way or another.

I said "The same again" to the bartender, placed the drinks on a table close to the bar, left them there and walked slowly towards the foyer, passed the girl like one lost deep in thought, not even looking at her, went through the front door and out into the street. Strauss had succumbed but not the ancient who to demonstrate his catholicity of taste was now giving a ghoulish rendering of "The bonnie, bonnie banks of Loch Lomond." If he tried that lot on in Sauchihall Street in Glasgow both he and his barrel organ would be but a faded memory inside fifteen minutes. The youthful acolytes had vanished, which could have meant that they were either very anti-Scottish or very pro-Scottish indeed. In point of fact their absence, as I was to discover later, meant something else entirely: the evidence was all there before me and I missed it and because I missed it, too many people were going to die.

The ancient saw me and registered his surprise.

"Mynheer said that he——"

"He was going to the opera. And so I did." I shook my head sadly. "Prima donna reaching for a high E. Heart attack." I clapped him on the shoulder. "No panic. I'm only going as far as the phone box there."

I dialled the girls' hotel. I got through to the desk immediately and then, after a long wait, to the girls' room. Belinda sounded peevish.

"Hullo. Who is it?"

"Sherman. I want you over here at once."

"Now?" Her voice was a wail. "But I'm in the middle of a bath."

"Regrettably, I can't be in two places at once. You're clean enough for the dirty work I have in hand. And Maggie."

"But Maggie's asleep."

"Then you'd better wake her up, hadn't you? Unless you want to carry her." Injured silence. "Be here at my hotel in ten minutes. Hang about outside, about twenty yards away."

"But it's bucketing rain!" She was still at the wailing.

"Ladies of the street don't mind how damp they get. Soon there'll be a girl leaving here. Your height, your age, your figure, your hair——"

"There must be ten thousand girls in Amsterdam who——"

"Ah—But this one is beautiful. Not as beautiful as you are, of course, but beautiful. She's also wearing a green coat—to go with her green umbrella—sandalwood perfume and, on her left temple, a fairly well camouflaged bruise that I gave her yesterday afternoon."

"A fairly well—you didn't tell us anything about assaulting girls."

"I can't remember every irrelevant detail. Follow her. When she gets to her destination, one of you stay put, the other report back to me. No, you can't come here, you know that. I'll be at the Old Bell at the far corner of the Rembrandtsplein."

"What will you be doing there?"

"It's a pub. What do you think I'll be doing?"

The girl in the green coat was still sitting there at the same table when I returned. I went to the reception desk first, asked for and got some notepaper and took it across to the table where I'd left my drinks. The girl in green was no more than six feet away, at right angles and so should have had an excellent view of what I was doing while herself remaining comparatively free from observation.

I took out my wallet, extracted my previous night's dinner bill, smoothed it out on the table before me and started to make notes on a piece of paper. After a few moments I threw my pen down in disgust, screwed up the paper and flung it into a convenient wastebasket. I started on another sheet of paper and appeared to reach the same unsatisfactory conclusion. I did this several times more, then screwed my eyes shut and rested my head on my hands for almost five minutes, a man, it must have seemed, lost in the deepest concentration. The fact was, that I wasn't in too much of a hurry. Ten minutes, I'd said to Belinda, but if she managed to get out of a bath, get dressed and be across here with Maggie in time I knew even less than I thought I did about women.

For a time I resumed the scribbling, the crumpling and the throwing away and by that time twenty minutes had elapsed. I finished the last of my drink, rose, said good night to the barman and went away. I went as far as the plush wine curtains that screened the bar from the foyer and waited, peering cautiously round the edge of the curtain. The girl in green rose to her feet, crossed to the bar, ordered herself another drink and then casually sat down in the chair I had just vacated, her back to me. She looked around, also casually, to make sure that she was unobserved then just as casually reached down into the wastebasket and picked up the top sheet of crumpled paper. She smoothed it out on the table before her and I moved soundlessly up to her chair. I could see the side of her face now and I could see that it had gone very still. I could even read the message she had smoothed out on the table. It read: ONLY NOSEY YOUNG GIRLS LOOK IN WASTEPAPER BASKETS.

"All the other papers have the same secret message," I said. "Good evening, Miss Lemay."

She twisted round and looked up at me. She'd camouflaged herself pretty well to conceal the natural olive blush of her complexion, but all the paint and powder in the world was useless to conceal the blush that spread from her neck all the way up to the forehead.

"My word," I said. "What a charming shade of pink."

"I am sorry. I do not speak English."

I very gently touched the bruise and said kindly: "Concussive amnesia. It'll pass. How's the head, Miss Lemay?"

"I'm sorry, I——"

"Do not speak English. You said that. But you understand it well enough, don't you? Especially the written word. My word, for an ageing character like myself it's refreshing to see that the young girls of today can blush so prettily. You *do* blush prettily, you know."

She rose in confusion, twisting and crushing the papers in her hand. On the side of the ungodly she might be—and who but those on the side of the ungodly would have tried, as no question she had tried, to block my pursuit in the airport—but I couldn't hold back a twinge of pity. There was something forlorn and defenceless about her. She could have been a consummate actress but then consummate actresses would have been earning a fortune on the stage or screen. Then, unaccountably, I thought of Belinda. Two in the one day were two too many. I was going soft in the head. I nodded at the papers.

"You may retain those, if you wish," I said nastily.

"Those." She looked at the papers. "I don't want to——"

"Ha! The amnesia is wearing off."

"Please, I——"

"Your wig's slipped, Miss Lemay."

Automatically her hands reached and touched her hair, then she slowly lowered them to her sides and bit her lip in chagrin. There was something close to desperation in the brown eyes. Again I had the unpleasant sensation of not feeling very proud of myself.

"Please leave me," she said, so I stepped to one side to let her pass. For a moment she looked at me and I could have sworn there was a beseeching look in her eyes and her face was puckering slightly almost as if she were about to cry, then she shook her head and hurried away. I followed more slowly, watched her run down the steps and turn in the direction of the canal. Twenty seconds later Maggie and Belinda passed by in the same direction. Despite the umbrellas they had, they looked very wet indeed and most unhappy. Maybe they'd got there in ten minutes after all.

I went back to the bar which I'd had no intention of leaving in the first place although I'd had to convince the girl that I was. The bartender, a friendly soul, beamed. "Good evening again, sir. I thought you had gone to bed."

"I wanted to go to bed. But my taste buds said, 'No, another jonge Genever.' "

"One should always listen to one's taste buds, sir," the bartender said gravely. He handed over the little glass. "Prost, sir!" I lifted my glass and got back to my thinking. I thought about naïveté and how unpleasant it was to be led up garden paths and whether young girls could blush to order. I thought I'd heard of certain actresses that could but wasn't sure, so I called for another Genever to jog my memory.

The next glass I lifted in my hand was of a different order altogether, a great deal heavier and containing a great deal darker liquid. It was, in fact, a pint pot of Guinness which might seem to be a very odd thing to find in a continental tavern, as indeed it was. But not in this one, not in the Old Bell, a horse-brass-behung hostelry more English than most English hostelries could ever hope to be. It specialised in English beers—and, as my glass testified, Irish stout.

The pub was well patronised but I had managed to get a table to myself facing the door, not because I have any Wild West aversion to sitting with my back to the door but because I wanted to spot Maggie or Belinda, whichever it was, when she came in. In the event it was Maggie. She crossed to my table and sat down. She was a very bedraggled Maggie and despite scarf and umbrella her raven hair was plastered to her cheeks.

"You all right?" I asked solicitously.

"If you call all right being soaked to the skin, then yes." It wasn't at all like my Maggie to be as waspish as this: she must be very wet indeed.

"And Belinda?"

"She'll survive too. But I think she worries too much about you." She waited pointedly until I'd finished taking a long satisfying swig at the Guinness. "She hopes you aren't overdoing things."

"Belinda is a very thoughtful girl." Belinda knew damn well what I was doing.

"Belinda's young," Maggie said.

"Yes, Maggie."

"And vulnerable."

"Yes, Maggie."

"I don't want her hurt, Paul." This made me sit up, mentally, anyway. She never called me "Paul" unless we were alone, and even then only when she was sufficiently lost in thought or emotion to forget about what she regarded as the proprieties. I didn't know what to make of her remark and wondered what the hell the two of them might have been talking about. I was beginning to wish I'd left the two of them at home and brought along a couple of Doberman Pinschers instead. At least a Doberman would have made short work of our lurking friend in Morgenstern and Muggenthaler.

"I said——" Maggie began.

"I heard what you said." I drank some more stout. "You're a very dear girl, Maggie."

She nodded, not to indicate any agreement with what I said, just to show that for some obscure reason she found this a satisfactory answer and sipped some of the sherry I'd got for her. I skated swiftly back onto thick ice.

"Now. Where is our other lady friend that you've been following?"

"She's in church."

"What!" I spluttered into my tankard.

"Singing hymns."

"Good God! And Belinda?"

"She's in church too."

"Is *she* singing hymns?"

"I don't know. I didn't go inside."

"Maybe Belinda shouldn't have gone in either."

"What safer place than a church?"

"True. True." I tried to relax but felt uneasy.

"One of us had to stay."

"Of course."

"Belinda said you might like to know the *name* of the church."

"Why should I——" I stared at Maggie. "The First Reformed Church of the American Huguenot Society." Maggie nodded. I pushed back my chair and rose. "Now you tell me. Come on."

"What? And leave all that lovely Guinness that is so good for you?"

"It's Belinda's health I'm thinking of, not mine."

We left, and as we left it suddenly occurred to me that the name of the church had meant nothing to Maggie. It had meant nothing to Maggie because Belinda hadn't told her when she got back to the hotel and she hadn't told her because Maggie had been asleep. And I'd wondered what the hell the two of them might have been talking about. They hadn't been talking about anything. Either this was very curious or I wasn't very clever. Or both.

As usual it was raining and as we passed along the Rembrandtsplein by the Hotel Schiller, Maggie gave a well-timed shiver.

"Look," she said. "There's a taxi. In fact, lots of taxis."

"I wouldn't say that there's not a taxi in Amsterdam that's not in the pay of the ungodly," I said with feeling. "But I wouldn't bet a nickel on it. It's not far."

Nor was it—by taxi. By foot it was a very considerable way indeed. But I had no intention of covering the distance on foot. I led Maggie down the Thorbeckeplein, turned left, right and left again till we came out on the Amstel. Maggie said: "You do seem to know your way around, don't you, Major Sherman?"

"I've been here before."

"When?"

"I forget. Last year, sometime."

"When last year?" Maggie knew or thought she knew all my movements over the past five years and Maggie could be easily piqued. She didn't like what she called irregularities.

"In the spring, I think it was."

"Two months, maybe?"

"About that."

"You spent two months in Miami last spring," she said accusingly. "That's what the records say."

"You know how I get my dates mixed up."

"No, I don't." She paused. "I thought you'd never seen Colonel de Graaf and van Gelder before?"

"I hadn't."

"But——"

"I didn't want to bother them." I stopped by a phone box. "A couple of calls to make. Wait here."

"I will not!" A very heady atmosphere, was Amsterdam's. She was getting as bad as Belinda. But she had a point—the slanting rain was sheeting down very heavily now. I opened the door and let her precede me into the booth. I called a nearby cab company whose number I knew, started to dial another number.

"I didn't know you spoke Dutch," Maggie said.

"Neither do our friends. That's why we must get an honest taxi driver."

"You really don't trust anyone, do you?" Maggie said admiringly.

"I trust you, Maggie."

"No, you don't. You just don't want to burden my beautiful head with unnecessary problems."

"That's my line," I complained. De Graaf came on the phone. After the usual courtesies I said: "Those scraps of paper? No luck yet? Thank you, Colonel de Graaf. I'll call back later." I hung up.

"What scraps of paper?" Maggie asked.

"Scraps of paper I gave him."

"Where did you get them from?"

"A chap gave them to me last night."

Maggie gave me her old-fashioned resigned look but said nothing. After a couple of minutes a taxi came along. I gave him an address in the old city and when we got there walked with Maggie down a narrow street to one of the canals in the dock area. I stopped at the corner.

"This is it?"

"This is it," said Maggie.

"This" was a little grey church about fifty yards away along the canal bank. It was an ancient sway-backed crumbling edifice that appeared to be maintained in the near-vertical by faith alone for to my untrained eye it looked to be in imminent danger of toppling into the canal. It had a short square stone tower, at least five degrees off the perpendicular, topped by a tiny steeple that leaned dangerously in the other direction. The time was ripe for the First Reformed Church of the American Huguenot Society to launch a major fund-raising drive.

That some of the adjacent buildings had been in even greater danger of collapse was evidenced by the fact that a large area of building on the canal side beyond the church had already been demolished; a giant crane with the most enormous boom I had ever seen almost lost in the darkness above stood in the middle of this cleared lot where rebuilding had already reached the stage of the completion of the reinforced foundations.

We walked slowly along the canal side towards the church. Clearly audible now were the sound of organ music and of women singing. It sounded very pleasant and safe and homely and nostalgic, the music drifting out over the darkened waters of the canal.

"The service seems to be still in progress," I said. "You go in there——"

I broke off and did a double take at a blonde girl in a belted white raincoat who was just walking by.

"Hey!" I said.

The blonde girl had it all buttoned up about what to do when accosted by strange men in a lonely street. She took one look at me and started to run. She didn't get very far. She slipped on the wet cobbles, recovered, but only made another two or three paces before I caught up with her. She struggled briefly to escape, then relaxed and flung her arms about my neck. Maggie joined us, that old puritanical look on her face again.

"A very old friend, Major Sherman?"

"Since this morning. This is Trudi. Trudi van Gelder."

"Oh." Maggie laid a reassuring hand on Trudi's arm but Trudi ignored her, tightened her grip around my neck and gazed admiringly into my face from a distance of about four inches.

"I like you," Trudi announced. "You're nice."

"Yes, I know, you told me. Oh hell!"

"What to do?" Maggie asked.

"What to do. I've got to get her home. I've got to *take* her home. Put her in a taxi and she'd skip at the first traffic lights. A hundred to one the old battle-axe who's supposed to be guarding her has dozed off and by this time her father's probably scouring the town. He'd find it cheaper to use a ball and chain."

I unlocked Trudy's arms, not without some difficulty, and pushed up the sleeve of her left arm. I looked first of all at her arm then at Maggie whose eyes widened and then lips pursed as she saw the unlovely pattern left by the hypodermic needles. I pulled down the sleeve—instead of breaking into tears as she had done last time Trudi just stood there and giggled as if it were all great fun—and examined the other forearm. I pulled that sleeve down too.

"Nothing fresh," I said.

"You mean there's nothing fresh that you can see," Maggie said.

"What do you expect me to do? Make her stand here in this icy rain and do a strip tease on the banks of the canal to the organ music? Wait a moment."

"Why?"

"I want to think," I said patiently.

So I thought, while Maggie stood there with an expression of dutiful expectation on her face while Trudi clutched my arm in a proprietorial fashion and gazed adoringly up at me. Finally, I said:

"You haven't been seen by anybody in there?"

"Not as far as I know."

"But Belinda has, of course."

"Of course. But not so she would be recognised again. All the people in there have their heads covered. Belinda's wearing a scarf *and* the hood of her coat *and* she's sitting in shadow—I saw that from the doorway."

"Get her out. Wait till the service is over, then follow Astrid. And try to memorise the faces of as many as possible of those who are attending the service."

Maggie looked doubtful. "I'm afraid that's going to be difficult."

"Why?"

"Well, they all look alike."

"They all—what are they, Chinese or something?"

"Most of them are nuns, carrying Bibles and those beads at their waists, and you can't see their hair, and they have those long black clothes and those white——"

"Maggie." I restrained myself with difficulty. "I know what nuns look like."

"Yes, but there's something else. They're nearly all young and good-looking—some *very* good-looking——"

"You don't have to have a face like a bus smash to be a nun. Phone your hotel and leave the number of whereever you happen to finish up. Come on, Trudi. Home."

She went with me docilely enough, by foot first and then by taxi, where she held my hand all the time and talked a lot of bright nonsense in a very vivacious way, like a young child being taken out on an unexpected treat. At van Gelder's house I asked the taxi to wait.

Trudi was duly scolded by both van Gelder and Herta with that vehemence and severity that always cloaks profound relief then was led off, presumably, to bed. Van Gelder poured a couple of drinks with the speed of a man who feels he requires one and asked me to sit down. I declined.

"I've a taxi outside. Where can I find Colonel de Graaf at this time of night? I want to borrow a car from him, preferably a fast one."

Van Gelder smiled. "No questions from me, my friend. You'll find the Colonel at his office—I know he's working late tonight." He raised his glass. "A thousand thanks. I was a very, very worried man."

"You had a police alert out for her."

"An unofficial police alert." Van Gelder smiled again, but wryly. "You know why. A few trusted friends—but there are nine hundred thousand people in Amsterdam."

"Any idea why she was so far from home?"

"At least there's no mystery about that. Herta takes her there often—to

the church, I mean. All the Huyler people in Amsterdam go there. It's a
Huguenot church—there's one in Huyler as well, not so much a church,
some sort of business premises they use on Sundays as a place of worship.
Herta takes her there too—the two of them go out to the island often. The
churches and the Vondel Park—those are the only outings the child has.''

Herta waddled into the room and van Gelder looked at her anxiously.
Herta, with what might conceivably have passed for an expression of satisfaction on her leathery features, shook her head and waddled out again.

''Well, thank God for that.'' Van Gelder drained his glass. ''No injections.''

''Not this time.'' I drained my glass in turn, said goodbye and left.

I paid off the taxi in the Marnixstraat. Van Gelder had phoned ahead to
say I was coming and Colonel de Graaf was waiting for me. If he was busy,
he showed no signs of it. He was engaged in his usual occupation of
overflowing the chair he was sitting in, the desk in front of him was bare,
his fingers were steepled under his chin and as I entered he brought his eyes
down a leisured contemplation of infinity.

''One assumes you make progress?'' he greeted me.

''One assumes wrongly, I'm afraid.''

''What? No vistas of broad highways leading to the final solution?''

''Cul-de-sacs only.''

''Something about a car, I understand from the Inspector.''

''Please.''

''May one enquire why you wish this vehicle?''

''To drive up the cul-de-sacs. But that's not really what I came to ask you
about.''

''I hardly thought it was.''

''I'd like a search warrant.''

''What for?''

''To make a search,'' I said patiently. ''Accompanied by a senior officer
or officers, of course, to make it legal.''

''Who? Where?''

''Morgenstern and Muggenthaler. Souvenir warehouse. Down by the
docks—I don't know the address.''

''I've heard of them,'' de Graaf nodded. ''I know nothing against them.
Do you?''

''No.''

''So what makes you so curious about them?''

''I honest to God don't know. I want to find out why I *am* so curious. I
was in their place tonight——''

''They're closed at nighttime, surely.''

I dangled a set of skeleton keys in front of his eyes.

''You know it's a felony to be in possession of such instruments,'' de
Graaf said severely.

I put the keys back in my pockets. ''What instruments?''

''A passing hallucination,'' de Graaf said agreeably.

''I'm curious about why they have a time lock on the steel door leading
to their office. I'm curious about the large stocks of Bibles carried on their
premises.'' I didn't mention the smell of cannabis or the lad lurking behind
the puppets. ''But what I'm really interested in getting hold of is their list
of suppliers.''

''A search warrant we can arrange on any pretext,'' de Graaf said. ''I'll
accompany you myself. Doubtless you'll explain your interest in greater
detail in the morning. Now about this car. Van Gelder has an excellent
suggestion. A specially engined police car, complete with everything from

two-way radio to handcuffs, but to all appearances a taxi, will be here in two minutes. Driving a taxi, you understand, poses certain problems.''

"I'll try not to make too much on the side. Have you anything else for me?''

"Also in two minutes. Your car is bringing some information from the Records Office.''

Two minutes it was and a folder was delivered to de Graaf's desk. He looked through some papers.

"Astrid Lemay. Her real name, perhaps oddly enough. Dutch father, Grecian mother. He was a vice-consul in Athens, now deceased. Whereabouts of mother unknown. Twenty-four. Nothing known against her—nothing much known for her, either. Must say the background is a bit vague. Works as a hostess in the Balinova night club, lives in a small flat nearby. Has one known relative, brother George, aged twenty. Ah! This may interest you. George, apparently, has spent six months as Her Majesty's guest.''

"Drugs?''

"Assault and attempted robbery, very amateurish effort, it seems. He made the mistake of assaulting a plainclothes detective. Suspected of being an addict—probably trying to get money to buy more. All we have.'' He turned to another paper. "This MOO 144 number you gave me is the radio call-sign for a Belgian coaster, the *Marianne,* due in from Bordeaux tomorrow. I have a pretty efficient staff, no?''

"Yes.''

"When does it arrive?''

"Noon. We search it?''

"You wouldn't find anything. But please don't go near it. Any ideas on the other two numbers?''

"Nothing, I'm afraid, on 910020. Or on 2797.'' He paused reflectively. "Or could that be 797 twice—you know, 797797.''

"Could be anything.''

De Graaf took a telephone directory from a drawer, put it away again, picked up a phone. "A telephone number,'' he said, "797797. Find out who's listed under that number. At once, please.''

We sat in silence till the phone rang. De Graaf listened briefly, replaced the receiver.

"The Balinova night club,'' he said.

"The efficient staff has a clairvoyant boss.''

"And where does this clairvoyance lead you to?''

"The Balinova night club.'' I stood up. "I have a rather readily identifiable face, wouldn't you say, Colonel?''

"It's not a face people forget. And those white scars. I don't think your plastic surgeon was really trying.''

"He was trying all right. To conceal his almost total ignorance of plastic surgery. Have you any brown stain in this HQ?''

"Brown stain?'' He blinked at me, then smiled widely, "Oh no, Major Sherman! Disguise! In this day and age? Sherlock Holmes has been dead these may years.''

"If I'd half the brains Sherlock had,'' I said heavily, "I wouldn't be needing any disguise.''

6

THE YELLOW and red taxi they'd given me appeared, from the outside, to be a perfectly normal Opel, but they seemed to have managed to put an extra engine into it. They'd put a lot of extra work into it too. It had a pop-up siren, a pop-up police light and a panel at the back which fell down to illuminate a "Stop" sign. Under the front passenger seats were ropes and first-aid kits and tear-gas canisters; in the door pockets were handcuffs with keys attached. God alone knew what they had in the boot. Nor did I care. All I wanted was a fast car, and I had one.

I pulled up in a prohibited parking area outside the Balinova night club, right opposite where a uniformed and beholstered policeman was standing. He nodded almost imperceptibly and walked away with measured stride. He knew a police taxi when he saw one and had no wish to explain to the indignant populace why a taxi could get away with an offence that would have automatically got them a ticket.

I got out, locked the door and crossed the pavement to the entrance of the night club which had above it the flickering neon sign "Balinova" and the outlined neon figures of two hula-hula dancers, although I failed to grasp the connection between Hawaii and Indonesia. Perhaps they were meant to be Balinese dancers, but if that were so they had the wrong kind of clothes on—or off. Two large windows were set one on either side of the entrance, and these were given up to an art exhibition of sorts which gave more than a delicate indication of the nature of the cultural delights and more esoteric scholarly pursuits that were to be found within. The occasional young lady depicted as wearing earrings and bangles and nothing else seemed almost indecently overdressed. Of even greater interest, however, was the coffee-coloured countenance that looked back at me from the reflection in the glass: if I hadn't known who I was, I wouldn't have recognised myself. I went inside.

The Balinova, in the best time-honoured tradition, was small, stuffy, smoky and full of some indescribable incense, the main ingredient of which seemed to be burnt rubber, which was probably designed to induce in the customers the right frame of mind for the maximum enjoyment of the entertainment being presented to them but which had, in fact, the effect of producing olfactory paralysis in the space of a few seconds. Even without the assistance of the drifting clouds of smoke the place was deliberately ill-lit except for the garish spotlight on the stage which, as was again fairly standard, was no stage at all but merely a tiny circular dance floor in the centre of the room.

The audience was almost exclusively male, running the gamut of ages from goggle-eyed teen-agers to sprightly and beady-eyed octogenarians whose visual acuity appeared to have remained undimmed with the passing of the years. Almost all of them were well dressed, for the better-class Amsterdam night clubs—those which still manage to cater devotedly to the refined palates of the jaded connoisseurs of certain of the plastic arts—are not for those who are on relief. They are, in a word, not cheap and the Balinova was very very expensive, one of the extremely few clip joints in the city. There were a few women present, but only a few. To my complete lack of surprise, Maggie and Belinda were seated at a table near the door, with some sickly coloured drinks before them. Both of them wore aloof expressions, although Maggie's was unquestionably the more aloof of the two.

My disguise, at the moment, seemed completely superfluous. Nobody looked at me as I entered and it was quite clear that nobody even wanted to look at me, which was understandable, perhaps, in the circumstances, as the audience were almost splitting their pebble glasses in their eagerness to miss none of the aesthetic nuances or symbolic significances of the original and thought-compelling ballet performance taking place before their enraptured eyes, in which a shapely young harridan in a bubble bath, to the accompaniment of the discordant thumpings and asthmatic wheezings of an excruciating band that would not otherwise have been tolerated in a boiler factory, endeavoured to stretch out for a bath towel that had been craftily placed about a yard beyond her reach. The air was electric with tension as the audience tried to figure out the very limited number of alternatives that were open to the unfortunate girl. I sat down at the table beside Belinda and gave her what, in the light of my new complexion, must have been a pretty dazzling smile. Belinda moved a rapid six inches away from me, lifting her nose a couple of inches higher in the air.

"Hoity-toity," I said. Both girls turned to stare at me and I nodded towards the stage. "Why doesn't one of you go and help her?"

There was a long pause then Maggie said with great restraint: "What on earth has happened to you?"

"I am in disguise. Keep your voice down."

"But—but I phoned the hotel only two or three minutes ago," Belinda said.

"And don't whisper either. Colonel de Graaf put me on to this place. She came straight back here?"

They nodded.

"And hasn't gone out again?"

"Not by the front door," Maggie said.

"You tried to memorise the faces of the nuns as they came out? As I told you to?"

"We tried," Maggie said.

"Notice anything odd, peculiar, out of the ordinary about any of them?"

"No, nothing. Except," Belinda added brightly, "that they seem to have very good-looking nuns in Amsterdam."

"So Maggie has already told me. And that's all?"

They looked at each other, hesitating, then Maggie said: "There was something funny. We seemed to see a lot more people going into that church than came out."

"There *were* a lot more people in that church than came out," Belinda said. "I was there, you know."

"I know," I said patiently. "What do you mean by 'a lot'?"

"Well," Belinda said defensively, "a good few."

"Ha! So now we're down to a good few. You both checked, of course, that the church was empty?"

It was Maggie's turn to be defensive. "You told us to follow Astrid Lemay. We couldn't wait."

"Has it occurred that some may have remained behind for private devotions? Or that maybe you're not very good counters?"

Belinda's mouth tightened angrily but Maggie put a hand on hers.

"That's not fair, Major Sherman." And this was Maggie talking. "We may make mistakes, but that's not fair." When Maggie talked like that, I listened.

"I'm sorry, Maggie. I'm sorry, Belinda. When cowards like me get worried they take it out on people who can't hit back." They both at once gave me that sweetly sympathetic smile that would normally have had me climbing the walls, but which I found curiously affecting at that moment, maybe that brown stain had done something to my nervous system. "God only knows I make more mistakes than you do." I did, and I was making one of my biggest then: I should have listened more closely to what the girls were saying.

"And now?" Maggie asked.

"Yes, what do we do now?" Belinda said.

I was clearly forgiven. "Circulate around the night clubs hereabouts. Heaven knows there's no shortage of them. See if you can recognise anyone there—performer, staff, maybe even a member of the audience—who looks like anyone you saw in the church tonight."

Belinda stared at me in disbelief. "Nuns in a night club?"

"Why not? Bishops go to garden parties, don't they?"

"It's not the same thing."

"Entertainment is entertainment the world over," I said pontifically. "Especially check for those who are wearing full long-sleeve dresses or those fancy elbow-length gloves."

"Why those?" Belinda asked.

"Use your head. See—if you do find anyone—if you can find out where they live. Be back in your hotel by one o'clock. I'll see you there."

"And what are you going to do?" Maggie asked.

I looked leisurely around the club. "I've got a lot of research to do here yet."

"I'll bet you have," Belinda said.

Maggie opened her mouth to speak but Belinda was saved the inevitable lecture by the reverential "oohs" and "aahs" and gasps of unstinted admiration, freely given, that suddenly echoed round the club. The audience were almost put off their seats. The distressed artiste had resolved her dreadful dilemma by the simple but ingenious and highly effective expedient of tipping the tin bath over and using it, tortoise-shell fashion, to conceal her maidenly blushes as she covered the negligible distance towards the salvation of the towel. She stood up, swathed in her towel, Venus arising from the depths, and bowed with regal graciousness towards the audience, Madame Melba taking her final farewell of Covent Garden. The ecstatic audience whistled and called for more, none more so than the octogenarians, but in vain: her repertoire exhausted she shook her head prettily and minced off the stage, trailing clouds of soap bubbles behind her.

"Well, I never!" I said admiringly. "I'll bet neither of you two would have thought of that."

"Come, Belinda," Maggie said. "This is no place for us."

They rose and left. As Belinda passed she gave me a twitch of her eyebrows which looked suspiciously like a wink, smiled sweetly, said "I rather like you like that" and left me pondering suspiciously as to the meaning of her remark. I followed their progress to the exit to see if anyone followed them, and followed they were, first of all by a very fat, very heavily built character with enormous jowls and an air of benevolence, but this was hardly of any significance as he was immediately followed by several dozen others. The highlight of the evening was over, great moments like those came but seldom and the summits were to be rarely scaled again—except three times a night, seven nights a week—and they were off now to greener pastures where hooch could be purchased at a quarter of the price.

The club was half empty now, the pall of smoke thinning and the visibility correspondingly improving. I looked around but in this momentary lull in the proceedings saw nothing of interest. Waiters circulated. I ordered a Scotch and was given a drink that rigorous chemical analysis might have found to contain a trace element of whisky. An old man mopped the tiny dance floor with the deliberate and stylised movements of a priest performing sacred rites. The band, mercifully silent, enthusiastically quaffed beer presented them by some tone-deaf customer. And then I saw the person I'd come to see only it looked as if I wouldn't be seeing her for very long.

Astrid Lemay was standing in an inner doorway at the back end of a room, pulling a wrap around her shoulders while another girl whispered in her ear: from their tense expressions and hurried movements it appeared to be a message of some urgency. Astrid nodded several times then almost ran across the tiny floor and passed through the front entrance. Somewhat more leisurely, I followed her.

I closed up on her and was only a few feet behind as she turned into the Rembrandtsplein. She stopped. I stopped, looked at what she was looking at and listened to what she was listening to.

The barrel organ was parked in the street outside a roofed-in, overhead-heated but windowless sidewalk café. Even at that time of night the café was almost full and the suffering customers had about them the look of people about to pay someone large sums of money to move elsewhere. This organ appeared to be a replica of the one outside the Excelsior, with the same garish colour scheme, multicoloured canopy and identically dressed puppets dancing at the end of their elasticised strings, although this machine was clearly inferior, mechanically and musically, to the Excelsior one. This machine, too, was manned by an ancient but this one sported a foot-long flowing grey beard that had been neither washed nor combed since he'd stopped shaving and wore a stetson hat and a British army greatcoat which fitted snugly around his ankles. Amidst the clankings, groanings and wheezings emitted by the organ I thought I detected an excerpt from *La Boheme* although heaven knew that Puccini never made the dying Mimi suffer the way she would have suffered had she been in the Rembrandtsplein that night.

The ancient had a close and apparently attentive audience of one. I recognised him as being one of the group I had seen by the organ outside the Excelsior. His clothes were threadbare but neatly kept, his lanky black hair tumbled down to his painfully thin shoulders, the blades of which protruded through his jacket like sticks. Even at that distance of about twenty feet I could see that his degree of emaciation was advanced. I could see only part of the side of his face but that little showed a cadaverously sunken cheek with skin the colour of old parchment.

He was leaning on the end of the barrel organ, but not from any love of Mimi. He was leaning on the barrel organ because if he hadn't leant on something he would surely have fallen down. He was obviously a very sick young man indeed with total collapse only one unpremeditated move away. Occasionally his whole body was convulsed by uncontrollable spasms of shaking; less frequently he made harsh sobbing or guttural noises in his throat. Clearly the old man in the greatcoat did not regard him as being very good for business for he kept hovering around him indecisively, making reproachful clucking noises and ineffectual movements of his arms, very much like a rather demented hen. He also kept glancing over his shoulder and apprehensively round the square as if he were afraid of something or someone.

Astrid walked quickly towards the barrel organ with myself close behind. She smiled apologetically at the bearded ancient, put her arm around the young man and pulled him away from the organ. Momentarily he tried to straighten up and I could see that he was a pretty tall youngster, at least six inches taller than the girl; his height served only to accentuate his skeleton frame. His eyes were staring and glazed and his face the face of a man dying from starvation, his cheeks so incredibly hollowed that one would have sworn that he could have no teeth. Astrid tried to half lead, half carry him away, but though his emaciation had reached a degree where he could scarcely be any heavier than the girl, if at all, his uncontrollable lurching made her stagger across the pavement.

I approached them without a word, put my arm around him—it was like putting my arm around a skeleton—and took his weight off Astrid. She looked at me and the brown eyes were sick with anxiety and fear. I don't suppose my sepia complexion gave her much confidence either.

"Please!" Her voice was beseeching. "Please leave me. I can manage."

"You can't. He's a very sick boy, Miss Lemay."

She stared at me. "Mr. Sherman!"

"I'm not sure if I like that," I said reflectively. "An hour or two ago you'd never seen me, never even knew my name. But now that I've gone all suntanned and attractive— Oops!"

George, whose rubbery legs had suddenly turned to jelly, had almost slipped from my grip. I could see that the two of us weren't going to get very far waltzing like this along the Rembrandtsplein, so I stooped down to hoist him over my shoulder in a fireman's lift. She caught my arm in panic.

"No! Don't do that! Don't do that!"

"Why ever not?" I said reasonably. "It's easier this way."

"No, no! If the police see you they will take him away."

I straightened, put my arm around him again and tried to maintain him as nearly to the vertical as was possible. "The hunter and the hunted," I said. "You and van Gelder both."

"Please?"

"And, of course, brother George is——"

"How do you know his name?" she whispered.

"It's my business to know things," I said loftily. "As I was saying, brother George is under the further disadvantage of not being exactly unknown to the police. Having an ex-convict for a brother can be a distinct social disadvantage."

She made no reply. I doubt if I've ever seen anyone who looked so completely miserable and defeated.

"Where does he live?" I asked.

"With me, of course." The question seemed to surprise her. "It's not far."

It wasn't either, not more than fifty yards down a side street—if so narrow and gloomy a lane could be called a street—past the Balinova. The stairs up to Astrid's flat were the narrowest and most twisted I had ever come across and even with George slung over my shoulder I had difficulty in negotiating them. Astrid unlocked the door to her flat which proved to be hardly larger than a rabbit hutch, consisting, as far as I could see, of a tiny sitting room with an equally tiny bedroom leading off it. I went through to the bedroom, laid George on the narrow bed, straightened and mopped my brow.

"I've climbed better ladders than those damned stairs of yours," I said feelingly.

"I'm sorry. The girls' hostel is cheaper, but with George— They don't pay very highly at the Balinova."

It was obvious from the two tiny rooms, neat but threadbare like George's clothes, that they paid very little. I said: "People in your position are lucky to get anything."

"Please?"

"Not so much of the 'please' stuff. You know damned well what I mean. Don't you, Miss Lemay—or may I call you Astrid?"

"How do you know my name?" Offhand I couldn't ever recall having seen a girl wring her hands but that's what she was doing now. "How—how do you know things about me?"

"Come off it," I said roughly. "Give some credit to your boy friend."

"Boy friend? I haven't got a boy friend."

"Ex-boy friend, then. Or does 'late boy friend' suit you better?"

"Jimmy?" she whispered.

"Jimmy Duclos," I nodded. "He may have fallen for you—fatally fallen for you—but he'd already told me something about you. I even have a picture of you."

She seemed confused. "But—but at the airport——"

"What *did* you expect me to do—embrace you? Jimmy was killed at the airport because he was on to something. What was that something?"

"I'm sorry. I can't help you."

"Can't? Or won't?"

She made no reply.

"Did you love him, Astrid? Jimmy?"

She looked at me dumbly, her eyes glistening. She nodded slowly.

"And you won't tell me?" Silence. I sighed and tried another tack. "Did Jimmy Duclos tell you what he was?"

She shook her head.

"But you guessed?"

She nodded.

"And told someone what you guessed."

This got her. "No! No! I told nobody. Before God, I told nobody!" She'd loved him, all right, and she wasn't lying.

"Did he ever mention me?"

"No."

"But you know who I am?"

She just looked at me, two big tears trickling slowly down her cheeks.

"You know damn well that I run Interpol's narcotics bureau in London."

More silence. I caught her shoulders and shook her angrily. "Well, don't you?"

She nodded. A great girl for silences.

"Then if Jimmy didn't tell you, who did?"

"Oh God! Please leave me alone!" A whole lot of other tears were chasing the first two down her cheeks now. It was her day for crying and mine for sighing, so I sighed and changed my tack again and looked through the door at the boy on the bed.

"I take it," I said, "that George is not the breadwinner of the family?"

"George cannot work." She said it as if she were stating a simple law of nature. "He hasn't worked for over a year. But what has George to do with this?"

"George has everything to do with it." I went and bent over him, looked at him closely, lifted an eyelid and dropped it again. "What do you do for him when he's like this?"

"There is nothing one can do."

I pushed the sleeve up George's skeletonlike arm. Punctured, mottled and discoloured from innumerable injections, it was a revolting sight; Trudi's had been nothing compared to this. I said: "There's nothing anyone will ever be able to do for him. You know that, don't you?"

"I know that." She caught my speculative look, stopped dabbing her face with a lace handkerchief about the size of a postage stamp and smiled bitterly. "You want me to roll up *my* sleeve."

"I don't insult nice girls. What I want to do is to ask you some simple questions that you can answer. How long has George been like this?"

"Three years."

"How long have you been in the Balinova?"

"Three years."

"Like it there?"

"Like it!" This girl gave herself away every time she opened her mouth. "Do you know what it *is* to work in a night club—a night club like that? Horrible, nasty lonely old men leering at you——"

"Jimmy Duclos wasn't horrible or nasty or old."

She was taken aback. "No. No, of course not. Jimmy——"

"Jimmy Duclos is dead, Astrid. Jimmy is dead because he fell for a night club hostess who's being blackmailed."

"Nobody's blackmailing me."

"No? Then who's putting the pressure on you to keep silent, to work at a job you obviously loathe? And why are they putting pressure on you? Is it because of George here? What has he done or what do they say he has done? I know he's been in prison, so it can't be that. What is it, Astrid, that made you spy on me? What do you know of Jimmy Duclos' death? I know *how* he died. But who killed him and why?"

"I didn't know he'd been killed!" She sat down on the bed-sofa, her hands covering her face, her shoulders heaving. "I didn't *know* he would be killed."

"All right, Astrid." I gave up because I was achieving nothing except a mounting dislike for myself, she'd probably loved Duclos, he was only a day dead and here was I lacerating bleeding wounds. "I've known too many people who walk in the fear of death to even try to make you talk. But think about it, Astrid, for God's sake and your own sake, think about it. It's your life, and that's all that's left for you to worry about now. George has no life left."

"There's nothing I can do, nothing I can say." Her face was still in her hands. "Please go."

I didn't think there was anything more I could do or say either, so I did as she asked and left.

Clad only in trousers and singlet I looked at myself in the tiny mirror in the tiny bathroom. All traces of the stain seemed to have been removed from my face, neck and hands, which was more than I could say for the large and once white towel I held in my hands. It was sodden and stained beyond recovery to a deep chocolate colour.

I went through the door into the bedroom that was hardly big enough to take the bed and the bed-settee it contained. The bed was occupied by Maggie and Belinda, both sitting upright, both looking very fetching in very attractive nightdresses which appeared to consist mainly of holes. But I'd more urgent problems on my mind at the moment than the way in which some nightwear manufacturers skimped on their material.

"You've ruined our towel," Belinda complained.

"Tell them you were removing your make-up." I reached for my shirt, which was a deep russet colour all round the inside of the neckband, but there was nothing I could do about that. "So most of the night club girls live in this Hostel Paris?"

Maggie nodded. "So Mary said."

"So Mary said."

"Mary?"

"This nice English girl working in the Trianon."

"There are no nice English girls working in the Trianon, only naughty English girls. Was she one of the girls in church?" Maggie shook her head. "Well, that at least bears out what Astrid said."

"Astrid?" Belinda said. "You spoke to her?"

"I passed the time of day with her. Not very profitably, I'm afraid. She wasn't communicative." I told them briefly how uncommunicative she'd been then went on: "Well, it's time you two started doing a little work instead of hanging about night clubs." They looked at each other then coldly at me. "Maggie, take a stroll in the Vondel Park tomorrow. See if Trudi is there—you know her. Don't let her see you—she knows you. See what she does, if she meets anyone, talks to anyone: it's a big park but you should have little difficulty in locating her if she's there—she'll be accompanied by an old dear who's about five feet round the middle. Belinda, keep tabs on that hostel tomorrow evening. If you recognise any girl who was in the church, follow her and see what she's up to." I shrugged into my very damp jacket. "Good night."

"That was all? You're off?" Maggie seemed faintly surprised.

"My, you are in a hurry," Belinda said.

"Tomorrow night," I promised, "I'll tuck you both in and tell you all about Goldilocks and the three bears. Tonight I have things to attend to."

7

I PARKED the police car on top of a "No Parking" sign painted on the road and walked the last hundred yards to the hotel. The barrel organ had gone to wherever barrel organs go in the watches of the night, and the foyer was deserted except for the assistant manager who was sitting dozing in a chair behind the desk. I reached over, quietly unhooked the key and walked up the first two flights of stairs before taking the lift in case I waked the assistant manager from what appeared to be a sound—and no doubt well-deserved—sleep.

I took off my wet clothes—which meant all of them—showered, put on a dry outfit, went down by lift and banged my room key noisily on the desk. The assistant manager blinked himself awake, looked at me, his watch and the key in that order.

"Mr. Sherman. I—I didn't hear you come in."

"Hours ago. You were asleep. This quality of childlike innocence——"

He wasn't listening to me. For a second time he peered fuzzily at his watch.

"What are you doing, Mr. Sherman?"

"I am sleepwalking."

"It's half past two in the morning!"

"I don't sleepwalk during the day," I said reasonably. I turned and peered through the vestibule. "What? No doorman, no porter, no taxi man, no organ-grinder, not a tail or shadow in sight. Lax. Remiss. You will be held to account for this negligence."

"Please?"

"Eternal vigilance is the price of admiralty."

"I do not understand."

"I'm not sure I do either. Are there any barbers open at this time of night?"

"Are there any—did you say——"

"Never mind. I'm sure I'll find one somewhere."

I left. Twenty yards from the hotel I stepped into a doorway, cheerfully prepared to clobber anyone who seemed bent on following me but after two or three minutes it became clear that no one was. I retrieved my car and drove down towards the docks area, parking it some distance and two streets away from the First Reformed Church of the American Huguenot Society. I walked down to the canal.

The canal, lined with the inevitable elm and lime trees, was dark and brown and still and reflected no light at all from the dimly lit narrow streets on either side. Not one building on either side of the canal showed a light. The church looked more dilapidated and unsafe than ever and had about it that strange quality of stillness and remoteness and watchfulness that many churches seem to possess at night. The huge crane with its massive boom was silhouetted menacingly against the night sky. The absence of any indication of life was total. All that was lacking was a cemetery.

I crossed the street, mounted the steps and tried the church door. It was unlocked. There was no reason why it should have been locked but I found it vaguely surprising that it wasn't. The hinges must have been well oiled for the door opened and closed soundlessly.

I switched on the torch and made a quick 360° traverse. I was alone. I made a more methodical inspection. The interior was small, even smaller than one would have guessed from outside, blackened and ancient, so ancient that I could see that the oaken pews had originally been fashioned by adzes. I lifted the beam of the torch but there was no balcony, just half a dozen small dusty stained glass windows that even on a sunny day could have admitted only a minimal quality of light. The entrance door was the only external door to the church. The only other door was in a corner at the top end of the church, halfway between the pulpit and an antique bellows-operated organ.

I made for this door, laid my hand on the knob and switched off the torch. This door creaked, but not loudly. I stepped forward cautiously and softly and it was as well that I did for what I stepped on was not another floor beyond but the first step in a flight of descending stairs. I followed these steps down, eighteen of them in a complete circle, and moved forward gingerly, my hand extended in front of me to locate the door which I felt must be in front of me. But there was no door in front of me. I switched on my torch.

The room I found myself in was about half the size of the church above. I made another quick circuit with the torch. There were no windows here, just two naked overhead lights. I located the switch and switched it on. The room was even more blackened than the church proper. The rough wooden floor was filthy with the trampled dirt of countless years. There were some tables and chairs in the centre of the room and the two side walls were lined with half-booths, very narrow and very high. The place looked like a medieval café.

I felt my nostrils twitch involuntarily at a well-remembered and unloved smell. It could have come from anywhere but I fancied it came from the row of booths on my right. I put my torch away, took my pistol from its felt underarm holster, dug in a pocket for a silencer and screwed it on. I walked catfooted across the room and my nose told me that I was heading in the right direction. The first booth was empty. So was the second. Then I heard the sound of breathing. I moved forward with millimetric stealth and my left eye and the barrel of the pistol went round the corner of the third booth at the same instant.

My precautions were unnecessary. No danger offered here. Two things rested on the narrow deal table, an ash tray with a cigarette end burnt away to the butt, and the arms and head of a man who was slumped forward, sound asleep, his face turned away from me. I didn't have to see his face, George's gaunt frame and threadbare clothes were unmistakable. Last time I'd seen him I'd have sworn he would have been unable to stir from his bed for the next twenty-four hours—or I would have sworn, had he been a normal person. But junkies in an advanced state of addiction are as far from normal as any person can ever become and are capable of astonishing if very brief feats of recovery. I left him where he was. For the moment, he presented no problem.

There was a door at the end of this room between the two rows of booths. I opened it, with rather less care than previously, went inside, located a switch and pressed it.

This was a wide but very narrow room, running the full width of the church but no more than ten feet across. Both sides of the room were lined with shelves and those shelves were stacked high with Bibles. It came as no surprise to discover that they were replicas of those I had examined in the warehouse of Morgenstern and Muggenthaler, the ones that the First Reformed Church handed out with such liberality to the Amsterdam hotels. There didn't seem to be anything to be gained by having another look at them so I stuck my gun in my belt and went ahead and looked at them anyway. I picked several at random from the front row on a shelf and flicked through them; they were as innocuous as Bibles can be, which is as innocuous as you can get. I reached into the second row and the same cursory examination yielded up the same result. I pushed part of the second row to one side and picked up a Bible from the third row.

This copy may or may not have been innocuous, depending upon your interpretation of the reason for its savagely mutilated state, but as a Bible as such it was a complete failure because the hole that had been smoothly scooped out from its centre extended almost the entire width of the book; the hole itself was about the size and shape of a large fig. I examined several more Bibles from the same row: all had the same hollowed-out centre, obviously machine-made. Keeping one of the mutilated copies to one side I replaced the other Bibles as I had found them and moved towards the door opposite the one by which I'd entered the narrow room. I opened it and pressed the light switch.

The First Reformed Church, I had to admit, had certainly done their level and eminently successful best to comply with the exhortations of the avant-garde clergy of today that it was the church's duty to keep abreast with and participate in the technological age in which we live. Conceivably, they might have expected to be taken a degree less literally, but then unspecified exhortation, when translated into practice, is always liable to a certain amount of executive misdirection, which appeared to be what had happened in this case: this room, which took up nearly half the basement area of the church, was, in fact, a superbly equipped machine shop.

To my untrained eye, it had everything—lathes, milling machines, presses, crucibles, moulds, a furnace, a large stamping machine and benches to which were bolted a number of smaller machines whose prupose was a mystery to me. One end of the floor was covered with what appeared to be brass and copper shaving, for the main part lying in tightly twisted coils. In a bin in one corner lay a large and untidy heap of lead pipes, all evidently old, and some rolls of used lead roof sheathing. Altogether, a highly functional place and one clearly devoted to manufacture; what the end products were was anyone's guess for certainly no examples of them were lying around.

I was halfway along the room, walking slowly, when I as much imagined as heard the very faintest sensation of sound from about the area of the doorway I'd just passed through: and I could feel again that uncomfortable tingling sensation in the back of my neck: someone was examining it, and with no friendly intent, from a distance of only a very few yards.

I walked on unconcernedly, which is no easy thing to do when the chances are good that the next step you take may be anticipated by a .38 bullet or something equally lethal in the base of the skull, but walk I did for to turn round armed with nothing but a hollowed-out Bible in my left hand—my gun was still in my belt—seemed a sure way of precipitating that involuntary pressure of the nervous trigger finger. I had behaved like a moron, with a blundering idiocy for which I would have bawled out anyone else, and it looked very much as if I might pay the moron's price. The unlocked main door, the unlocked door leading to the basement, the access free and open to anyone who might care to investigate bespoke only one thing: the presence of a quiet man with a gun whose job it was not to prevent entry but to prevent departure in the most permanent way. I wondered where he had been hiding, perhaps in the pulpit, perhaps in some side door leading off the stairs, the existence or otherwise of which I'd been too careless to investigate.

I reached the end of the room, glanced slightly to my left behind the end lathe in the room, made a slight murmur of surprise and stooped low behind the lathe. I didn't stay in that position for more than two seconds for there seemed little point in postponing what I knew must be inevitable; when I lifted the top of my head quickly above the lathe, the barrel of my silenced gun was already lined up with my right eye.

He was no more than fifteen feet away, advancing on soundless rubber mocassins, a wizened, rodent-faced figure of a man, with a paper-white face and glowing dark-coal eyes. What he was pointing in the general direction of the lathe in front of me was far worse than any .38 pistol, it was a blood-chilling whippet, a double-barrelled twelve-bore shotgun sawn off at both barrels and stock, probably the most lethally effective short-range weapon ever devised.

I saw him and squeezed the trigger of my gun in the same moment for if anything was certain it was that I would never be given a second moment.

A red rose bloomed in the centre of the wizened man's forehead. He took one step back, the reflex step of a man already dead, and crumpled to the floor almost as soundlessly as he had been advancing towards me, the whippet still clutched in his hand. I switched my eyes towards the door but if there were any reinforcements to hand they were prudently concealing the fact. I straightened and went quickly across the room to where the Bibles were stored, but there was no one there nor was there in any of the booths in the next room where George was still lying unconscious across his table.

I hauled George none too gently from his seat, got him over my shoulder, carried him upstairs to the church proper and dumped him unceremoniously behind the pulpit where he would be out of sight of anyone who might glance in casually from the main door although why anyone should take it into his head to glance in at that time of night I couldn't imagine. I opened the main door and glanced out, although far from casually, but the canal street was deserted in both directions.

Three minutes later I had the taxi parked not far from the church. I went inside, retrieved George, dragged him down the steps and across the road and bundled him into the back seat of the taxi. He promptly fell off the seat onto the floor and as he was probably safer in that position I left him there, quickly checked again that no one was taking any interest in what I was doing and went back inside the church again.

The dead man's pockets yielded nothing except a few homemade cigarettes which accorded well enough with the fact that he had obviously been hopped to the eyes when he had come after me with the whippet. I took the whippet in my left hand, seized the dead man by the collar of his coat—any other method of conveying him from there would have resulted in a bloodstained suit and this was the only serviceable suit I'd left—and dragged him across the basement and up the stairs, closing doors and putting out lights as I went.

Again the cautious reconnaissance at the church main door, again the deserted street. I dragged the man across the street into what little cover was offered by the taxi and lowered him into the canal as soundlessly as he would doubtless have lowered me if he'd been a bit handier with the whippet, which I now lowered into the canal after him. I went back to the taxi and was about to open the driver's door when a door of the house next to the church swung wide and a man appeared, who looked around uncertainly and then made his way across to where I was standing.

He was a big, burly character dressed in what appeared to be some kind of voluminous nightgown with a bathing wrap over it. He had rather an impressive head, with a splendid mane of white hair, a white moustache, a pink-cheeked healthy complexion and, at that moment, an air of slightly bemused benevolence.

"Can I be of help?" He had the deep resonant modulated voice of one obviously accustomed to hearing quite a lot of it. "Is there anything wrong?"

"What should be wrong?"

"I thought I heard a noise coming from the church."

"The church?" It was my turn to look bemused.

"Yes. My church. There." He pointed to it in case I couldn't recognise a church when I saw one. "I'm the pastor. Goodbody. Dr. Thaddeus Goodbody. I thought some intruder was perhaps moving around——"

"Not me, Reverend. I haven't been inside a church for years."

He nodded as if he weren't at all surprised. "We live in a godless age. A strange hour to be abroad, young man."

"Not for a taxi driver on the night shift."

He looked at me with an unconvinced expression and peered into the back of the taxi. "Merciful heavens. There's a body on the floor."

"There isn't a body on the floor. There's a drunken sailor on the floor and I'm taking him back to his ship. He just fell to the floor a few seconds ago so I stopped to get him back on his seat again. I thought," I added virtuously, "that it would be the Christian thing to do. With a corpse, I wouldn't bother."

My professional appeal availed nothing. He said, in the tone which he presumably kept for reproaching the more backsliding of his flock: "I insist on seeing for myself."

He pressed firmly forward and I pressed him firmly back again. I said: "Don't make my lose my licence. Please."

"I knew it! I knew it! Something is far amiss. So I can make you lose your licence?"

"Yes. If I throw you into the canal then I'll lose my licence. If, that is," I added consideringly, "you manage to climb back out again."

"What! The canal! Me? A man of God? Are you threatening me with violence, sir?"

"Yes."

Dr. Goodbody backed off several rapid paces.

"I have your licence, sir. I shall report you———"

The night was wearing on and I wanted some sleep before the morning, so I climbed into the car and drove off. He was shaking his fist at me in a fashion that didn't say much for his concept of brotherly love and appeared to be delivering himself of some vehement harangue but I couldn't hear any of it. I wondered if he would lodge a complaint with the police and thought that the odds were against it.

I was getting tired of carrying George upstairs. True, he weighed hardly anything at all, but what with the lack of sleep and dinner I was a good way below par and, moreover, I'd had my bellyful of junkies. I found the door to Astrid's tiny flat unlocked which was what I would have expected to find if George had been the last person to use it. I opened it, switched on the light, walked past the sleeping girl and deposited George none too gently on his own bed. I think it must have been the noise the mattress made and not the bright overhead light in her room that wakened Astrid; in any event, she was sitting up in her bed-settee and rubbing eyes still bemused from sleep as I returned to her room. I looked down at her in what I hoped was a speculative fashion and said nothing.

"He was asleep, then I went to sleep," she said defensively. "He must have got up and gone out again." When I treated this masterpiece of deduction with the silence it deserved she went on almost desperately: "I didn't hear him go out. I didn't. Where did you find him?"

"You'd never guess, I'm sure. In a garage, over a barrel organ, trying to get the cover off. He wasn't making much progress."

As she had done earlier that night, she buried her face in her hands; this time she wasn't crying although I supposed drearily that would be only a matter of time.

"What's so upsetting about that?" I asked. "He's very interested in barrel organs, isn't he, Astrid? I wonder why. It is curious. He's musical, perhaps?"

"No. Yes. Ever since he was a little boy———"

"Oh, be quiet. If he was musical he'd rather listen to a pneumatic drill. There's a very simple reason why he dotes on those organs. Very simple— and both you and I know what it is."

She stared at me, not in surprise: her eyes were sick with fear. Wearily, I sank down on the edge of the bed and took both her hands in mine.

"Astrid?"

"Yes?"

"You're almost as accomplished a liar as I am. You didn't go looking for George because you knew damn well where George was and you know damn well where I found him, in a place where he was safe and sound, in a place where the police would never find him because they would never think to look for anyone there." I sighed. "A smoke is not the needle, but I suppose it's better than nothing."

She looked at me with a stricken face then got back to burying her face in her hands. Her shoulders shook as I knew they would. How obscure or what my motives were I didn't know, I just couldn't sit there without holding out at least a tentatively comforting hand and when I did she looked up at me numbly through tear-filled eyes, reached up her hands and sobbed bitterly on my shoulder. I was becoming accustomed to this treatment in Amsterdam but still far from reconciled to it, so I tried to ease her arms gently away but she only tightened them the more. It had, I knew, nothing whatsoever to do with me; for the moment she needed something to cling to and I happened to be there. Gradually the sobs eased and she lay there, her tear-stained face defenceless and full of despair.

I said: "It's not too late, Astrid."

"That's not true. You know as well as I know, it was too late from the beginning."

"For George, yes, it is. But don't you see I'm trying to help you?"

"How can you help me?"

"By destroying the people who have destroyed your brother. By destroying the people who are destroying you. But I need help. In the end, we all need help—you, me, everyone. Help me—and I'll help you. I promise you, Astrid."

I wouldn't say that the despair in her face was replaced by some other expression but at least it seemed to become a degree less total as she nodded once or twice, smiled shakily and said: "You seem very good at destroying people."

"You may have to be, too," I said and I gave her a very small gun, a Lilliput, the effectiveness of which belies its tiny .21 bore.

I left ten minutes later. As I came out into the street I saw two shabbily dressed men sitting on a step in a doorway almost opposite, arguing heatedly but not loudly, so I transferred my gun to my pocket and walked across to where they were. Ten feet away I sheered off for the pungent odour of rum in the air was so overwhelming as to give rise to the thought that they hadn't so much been drinking the stuff but were newly arisen from immersion in a vat of the best Demerara. I was beginning to see spooks in every flickering shadow and what I needed was sleep, so I collected the taxi, drove back to the hotel and went to sleep.

8

REMARKABLY, THE sun was shining when my portable alarm went off the following morning—or the same morning. I showered, shaved, dressed, went downstairs and breakfasted in the restaurant with such restoring effect that I was able to smile at and say a civil good morning to the assistant manager, the doorman and the barrel organ attendant in that order. I stood for a minute or two outside the hotel looking keenly around me with the air of a man waiting for his shadow to turn up but it seemed that discouragement had set in and I was able to make my unaccompanied way to where I'd left the police taxi the previous night. Even though, in broad daylight, I'd stopped starting at shadows I opened the hood all the same but no one had fixed any lethal explosive device during the night so I drove off and arrived at the Marnixstraat HQ at precisely ten o'clock, the promised time.

Colonel de Graaf, complete with search warrant, was waiting for me in the street. So was Inspector van Gelder. Both men greeted me with the courteous restraint of those who think their time is being wasted but are too courteous to say so and led me to a chauffer-driven police car which was a great deal more luxurious than the one they'd given me.

"You still think our visit to Morgenstern and Muggenthaler is desirable?" de Graaf asked. "And necessary?"

"More so than ever."

"Something has happened? To make you feel that way?"

"No," I lied. I touched my head. "I'm fey at times."

De Graaf and van Gelder looked briefly at each other. "Fey?" de Graaf said carefully.

"I get premonitions."

There was another brief interchange of glances to indicate their mutual opinion of police officers who operated on this scientific basis, then de Graaf said, circumspectly changing the topic: "We have eight plain-clothes officers standing by down there in a plain van. But you say you don't really want the place searched?"

"I want it searched, all right—rather, I want to give the appearance of a search. What I really want are the invoices giving a list of all the suppliers of souvenir items to the warehouse."

"I hope you know what you are doing," van Gelder said. He sounded grave.

"*You* hope," I said. "How do you think *I* feel?"

Neither of them said how they thought I felt and as it seemed that the line of conversation was taking an unprofitable turn we all kept quiet until we arrived at our destination. We drew up outside the warehouse behind a nondescript grey van and got out and as we did a man in a dark suit climbed down from the front of the grey van and approached us. His civilian suit didn't do much for him as disguises went: I could have picked him out as a cop at fifty yards.

He said to de Graaf: "We're ready, sir."

"Bring your men."

"Yes, sir." The policeman pointed upwards. "What do you make of that, sir?"

We followed the direction of his arm. There was a wind blowing gustily that morning, nothing much but enough to give a slow if rather erratic pendulum swing to a gaily coloured object suspended from the hoisting beam at the top of the warehouse; it swung through an arc of about four feet and was, in its setting, one of the most gruesome things I had ever encountered.

Unmistakably, it was a puppet, and a very large puppet at that, well over three feet tall and dressed, inevitably, in the usual immaculate and beautifully tailored traditional Dutch costume, the long striped skirt billowing coquettishly in the wind. Normally, wires or ropes are used to pass through the pulleys of hoisting beams but in this instance someone had elected to use a chain instead; the puppet was secured to the chain by what could be seen, even at that elevation, to be a wicked-looking hook, a hook that was fractionally too small for the neck it passed round, so small that it had obviously had to be forced into position for the neck had been crushed at one side so that the head leaned over at a grotesque angle, almost touching the right shoulder. It was, after all, no more than a mutilated doll: but the effect was horrifying to the point of obscenity. And obviously I wasn't the only one that felt that way.

"What a macabre sight." De Graaf sounded shocked and he looked it too. "What in the name of God is that for? What—what's the point of it, what's the purpose behind it? What kind of sick mind could perpetrate an—an obscenity like that?"

Van Gelder shook his head. "Sick minds are everywhere and Amsterdam has its fair share. A jilted sweetheart, a hated mother-in-law——''

"Yes, yes, those are legion. But this—this is abnormality to the point of insanity. To express your feelings in this terrible way.'' He looked at me oddly, as if he were having second thoughts about the purposelessness of this visit. "Major Sherman, doesn't it strike you as very strange——''

"It strikes me the way it strikes you. The character responsible has a cast-iron claim to the first vacancy in a psychotic ward. But that isn't why I came here.''

"Of course not, of course not.'' De Graaf had a last long look at the dangling puppet, as if he could hardly force himself to look away, then gestured abruptly with his head and led the way up the steps towards the warehouse. A porter of sorts took us to the second floor and then to the office in the corner which, unlike the last time I had seen it, now had its time-locked door hospitably open.

The office, in sharp contrast to the warehouse itself, was spacious and uncluttered and modern and comfortable, beautifully carpeted and draped in different shades of lime and equipped with very expensive up-to-the-minute Scandinavian furniture more appropriate to a luxurious lounge than to a dockside office. Two men seated in deep armchairs behind separate large and leather-covered desks rose courteously to their feet and ushered de Graaf, van Gelder and myself into other and equally restful armchairs while they themselves remained standing. I was glad they did for this way I could have a better look at them and they were both, in their way very similar, well worth looking at. But I didn't wait more than a few seconds to luxuriate in the warmth of their beaming reception.

I said to de Graaf: "I have just forgotten something very important. It is imperative I make a call on a friend immediately.'' It was too; I don't often get this chilled and leaden feeling in the stomach but when I do I'm anxious to take remedial action without the least delay.

De Graaf looked his surprise. "A matter so important, it could have slipped your mind?''

"I have other things on my mind. This just came into it.'' Which was the truth.

"A phone call, perhaps——''

"No, no. Must be personal.''

"You couldn't tell me the nature——''

"Colonel de Graaf!'' He nodded in quick understanding, appreciating the fact that I wouldn't be likely to divulge state secrets in the presence of the proprietors of a warehouse about which I obviously held serious reservations. "If I could borrow your car and driver——''

"Certainly,'' he said unenthusiastically.

"And if you could wait till I come back before——''

"You ask a great deal, Mr. Sherman.''

"I know. But I'll only be minutes.''

I was only minutes. I had the driver stop at the first café we came to, went inside and used their public telephone. I heard the dialling tone and could feel my shoulders sag with relief as the receiver at the other end, after relay through an hotel desk, was picked up almost immediately. I said: "Maggie?''

"Good morning, Major Sherman.'' Always polite and punctilious was Maggie and I was never more glad to hear her so.

"I'm glad I caught you. I was afraid that you and Belinda might already have left—she hasn't left, has she?'' I was much more afraid of several other things but this wasn't the time to tell her.

"She's still here," Maggie said placidly.

"I want you both to leave your hotel at once. When I say at once, I mean within ten minutes. Five if possible."

"Leave? you mean——"

"I mean pack up, check out and don't ever go near it again. Go to another hotel. Any hotel. . . . No, you blithering idiot, not mine. A suitable hotel. Take as many taxis as you like, make sure you're not followed. Telephone the number to the office of Colonel de Graaf in the Marnixstraat. Reverse the number."

"Reverse it?" Maggie sounded shocked. "You mean you don't trust the police either?"

"I don't know what you mean by 'either' but I don't trust anyone, period. Once you've booked in go look for Astrid Lemay. She'll be home—you have the address—or in the Balinova. Tell her she's to come to stay at your hotel till I tell her it's safe to move."

"But her brother——"

"George can stay where he is. He's in no danger." I couldn't remember later whether that statement was the sixth or seventh major mistake I'd made in Amsterdam. "She is. If she objects, tell her you're going, on my authority, to the police about George."

"But why should we go to the police——"

"No reason. But she's not to know that. She's so terrified that at the very mention of the word 'police'——"

"That's downright cruel," Maggie interrupted severely.

"Fiddlesticks!" I shouted and banged the phone back on its rest.

One minute later I was back in the warehouse and this time I had leisure to have a longer and closer look at the two proprietors. Both of them were almost caricatures of the foreigner's conception of the typical Amsterdamer. They were both very big, very fat, rubicund and heavily jowled men who, in the first brief introduction I had had to them, had had their faces deeply creased in lines of good will and joviality, an expression that was now conspicuously lacking in both. Evidently, de Graaf had become impatient even with my very brief absence and had started the proceedings without me. I didn't reproach him and, in return, he had the tact not to enquire how things had gone with me. Both Muggenthaler and Morgenstern were still standing in almost the identical positions in which I'd left them, gazing at each other in consternation and dismay and complete lack of understanding. Muggenthaler, who was holding a paper in his hand, let it fall to his side with a gesture of total disbelief.

"A search warrant." The overtones of pathos and heartbreak and tragedy would have moved a statue to tears, had he been half his size he'd have been a natural for Hamlet. "A search warrant for Morgenstern and Muggenthaler! For a hundred and fifty years our two families have been respected, no, honoured tradesmen in the city of Amsterdam. And now this!" He groped behind him and sank into a chair in what appeared to be some kind of stupor, the paper falling from his hand "A search warrant!"

"A search warrant," Morgenstern intoned. He, too, had found it necessary to seek an armchair. "A search warrant, Ernst. A black day for Morgenstern and Muggenthaler! My God! The shame of it! The ignominy of it! A search warrant!"

Muggenthaler waved a despairingly listless hand. "Go on, search all you want."

"Don't you want to know what we're searching for?" de Graaf asked politely.

"Why should I want to know?" Muggenthaler tried to raise himself to a momentary state of indignation, but he was too stricken. "In one hundred and fifty years——"

"Now, now, gentlemen," de Graaf said soothingly, "don't take it so hard. I appreciate the shock you must feel and in my own view we're on a wild goose chase. But an official request has been made and we must go through the official motions. We have information that you have illicitly obtained diamonds——"

"Diamonds!" Muggenthaler stared in disbelief at his partner. "You hear that, Jan? Diamonds?" He shook his head and said to de Graaf: "If you find some, give me a few, will you?"

De Graaf was unaffected by the morose sarcasm. "And, much more important, diamond cutting machinery."

"We're crammed from floor to ceiling with diamond cutting machinery," Morgenstern said heavily. "Look for yourselves."

"And the invoice books?"

"Anything, anything," Muggenthaler said wearily.

"Thank you for your cooperation." De Graaf nodded to van Gelder who rose and left the room. De Graaf went on confidentially: "I apologise, in advance, for what is, I'm sure, a complete waste of time. Candidly, I'm more interested in that horrible thing dangling by a chain from your hoisting beam. A puppet."

"A what?" Muggenthaler demanded.

"A puppet. A big one."

"A puppet on a chain." Muggenthaler looked both flabbergasted and horrified, which is not an easy thing to achieve. "In front of *our* warehouse? Jan——!"

It wouldn't quite be accurate to say that we raced up the stairs, for Morgenstern and Muggenthaler weren't built along the right lines, but we made pretty good time for all that. On the third floor we found van Gelder and his men at work and at a word from de Graaf van Gelder joined us. I hoped his men didn't wear themselves out looking, for I knew they'd never find anything. They'd never even come across the smell of cannabis which had hung so heavily on that floor the previous night although I felt that the sickly sweet smell of some powerful flower-based air freshener that had taken its place could scarely be described as an improvement. But it hardly seemed the time to mention it to anyone.

The puppet, its back to us and the dark head resting on its right shoulder, was still swaying gently in the breeze. Muggenthaler, supported by Morgenstern and obviously feeling none too happy in his precarious position, reached out gingerly, caught the chain just above the hook and hauled it in sufficiently for him, not without considerable difficulty, to unhook the puppet from the chain. He held it in his arms and stared down at it for long moments, then shook his head and looked up at Morgenstern.

"Jan, he who did this wicked thing, this sick sick joke—he leaves our employment this very day."

"This very hour," Morgenstern corrected. His face twisted in repugnance, not at the puppet, but at what had been done to it. "And such a beautiful puppet!"

Morgenstern was in no way exaggerating. It was indeed a beautiful puppet and not only or indeed primarily because of the wonderfully cut and fitted bodice and gown. Despite the fact that the neck had been broken and cruelly gouged by the hook, the face itself was arrestingly beautiful, a work of great artistic skill in which the colours of the dark hair, the brown eyes

and the complexion blended so subtly and in which the delicate features had
been so exquisitely shaped that it was hard to believe that this was the face
of a puppet and not that of a human being with an existence and distinctive
personality of her own. Nor was I the only person who felt that way.

De Graaf took the puppet from Muggenthaler and gazed at it. "Beautiful," he murmured. "How beautiful. And how real, how living. This lives."
He glanced at Muggenthaler. "Would you have any idea who made this
puppet?"

"I've never seen one like it before. It's not one of ours, I'm sure, but the
floor foreman is the man to ask. But I know it's not ours."

"And this exquisite colouring," de Graaf mused. "It's so right for the
face, so inevitable. No man could have created this from his own mind.
Surely, surely, he must have worked from a living model, from someone he
knew. Wouldn't you say so, Inspector?"

"It couldn't have been done otherwise," van Gelder said flatly.

"I've the feeling, almost, that I've seen this face before," de Graaf
continued. "Any of you gentlemen ever seen a girl like this?"

We all shook our heads slowly and none more slowly than I did. The old
leaden feeling was back in my stomach again but this time the lead was
coated with a thick layer of ice. It wasn't just that the puppet bore a
frighteningly accurate resemblance to Astrid Lemay; it was so lifelike, it
was Astrid Lemay.

Fifteen minutes later, after the thorough search carried out in the warehouse had produced its predictably total negative result, de Graaf took his
farewell of Muggenthaler and Morgenstern on the steps of the warehouse,
while van Gelder and I stood by. Muggenthaler was back at his beaming
while Morgenstern stood by his side, smiling with patronising satisfaction.
De Graaf shook hands warmly with both in turn.

"Again, a thousand apologies." De Graaf was being almost effusive.
"Our information was about as accurate as it usually is. All records of this
visit will be struck from the books." He smiled broadly. "The invoices will
be returned to you as soon as certain interested parties have failed to find
all the different illicit diamond suppliers they expected to find there. Good
morning, gentlemen."

Van Gelder and I said our farewells in turn and I shook hands especially
warmly with Morgenstern and reflected that it was just as well that he lacked
the obvious ability to read thoughts and had unluckily come into this world
without my inborn ability to sense when death and danger stood very close
at hand: for Morgenstern it was who had been at the Balinova night club last
night and had been the first to leave after Maggie and Belinda had passed
out into the street.

We made the journey back to the Marnixstraat in partial silence, by which
I mean that de Graaf and van Gelder talked freely but I didn't. They appeared to be much more interested in the curious incident of the broken
puppet than they were in the ostensible reason for our visit to the warehouse,
which probably demonstrated quite clearly what they thought of the ostensible reason, and as I hardly liked to intrude to tell them that they had their
priorities right, I kept silent.

Back in his office, de Graaf said: "Coffee? We have a girl here who
makes the best coffee in Amsterdam."

"A pleasure to be postponed. Too much of a hurry, I'm afraid."

"You have plans? A course of action, perhaps?"

"Neither. I want to lie on my bed and think."

"Then why——"

"Why come up here in the first place? Two small requests. Find out, please, if any telephone message has come through for me."

"Message?"

"From this person I had to go to see when we were down in the warehouse." I was getting so that I could hardly tell myself whether I was telling the truth or lying.

De Graaf nodded, picked up a phone, talked briefly wrote down a long screed of letters and figures and handed the paper to me. The letters were meaningless; the figures, reversed, would be the girls' new telephone number. I put the paper in my pocket.

"Thank you. I'll have to decode this."

"And the second small request?"

"Could you lend me a pair of binoculars?"

"Binoculars?"

"I want to do some bird-watching," I explained.

"Of course," van Gelder said heavily. "You will recall, Major Sherman, that we are supposed to be cooperating closely?"

"Well?"

"You are not, if I may say so, being very communicative."

"I'll communicate with you when I've something worthwhile communicating. Don't forget that you've been working on this for over a year. I haven't been here for two days yet. Like I say, I have to go and lie down and think."

I didn't go and lie down and think. I drove to a telephone box which I judged to be a circumspect distance from the police headquarters and dialled the number de Graaf had given me.

The voice at the other end of the line said: "Hotel Touring."

I knew it but had never been inside it: it wasn't the sort of hotel that appealed to my expense account, but it was the sort of hotel I would have chosen for the two girls.

I said: "My name is Sherman. Paul Sherman. I believe two young ladies registered with you this morning. Could I speak to them, please?"

"I'm sorry, they are out at present." There was no worry there, if they weren't out locating or trying to locate Astrid Lemay they would be carrying out the assignments I'd given them in the early hours of the morning. The voice at the other end anticipated my next question. "They left a message for you, Mr. Sherman. I am to say that they failed to locate your mutual friend and are now looking for some other friends. I'm afraid it's a bit vague, sir."

I thanked him and hung up. "Help me," I'd said to Astrid, "and I'll help you." It was beginning to look as if I were helping her all right, helping her into the nearest canal or coffin. I jumped into the police taxi and made a lot of enemies in the brief journey to the rather unambitious area that bordered on the Rembrandtsplein.

The door to Astrid's flat was locked but I still had my belt of illegal ironmongery around my waist. Inside, the flat was as I'd first seen it, neat and tidy and threadbare. There were no signs of violence, no signs of any hurried departure. I looked in the few drawers and closets there were and it seemed to me that they were very bare of clothes indeed. But then, as Astrid had pointed out, they were very poor indeed, so that probably meant nothing. I looked everywhere in the tiny flat where a message of some sorts could have been left, but if any had been, I couldn't find it: I didn't believe any had been. I locked the front door and drove to the Balinova night club.

For a night club those were still the unearthly early hours of the morning and the doors, predictably, were locked. They were strong doors and remained unaffected by the hammering and the kicking that I subjected them to which, luckily, was more than could be said for one of the people inside whose slumber I must have so irritatingly disturbed, for a key turned and the door opened a crack. I put my foot in the crack and widened it a little, enough to see the head and shoulders of a faded blonde who was modestly clutching a wrap high at her throat; considering that the last time I had seen her she had been clad in a thin layer of transparent soap bubbles I thought that this was overdoing it a little.

"I wish to see the manager, please."

"We don't open till six o'clock."

"I don't want a reservation. I don't want a job. I want to see the manager. Now."

"He's not here."

"So. I hope your next job is as good as this one."

"I don't understand." No wonder they had the lights so low last night in the Balinova, in daylight that raddled face would have emptied the place like a report that one of the customers had bubonic plague. "What do you mean, my job?"

I lowered my voice, which you have to do when you speak with solemn gravity. "Just that you won't have any if the manager finds that I called on a matter of the greatest urgency and you refused to let me see him."

She looked at me uncertainly then said: "Wait here." She tried to close the door but I was a lot stronger than she was and after a moment she gave up and went away. She came back inside thirty seconds accompanied by a man still dressed in evening clothes.

I didn't take to him at all. Like most people I don't like snakes and this was what this man irresistibly reminded me of. He was very tall and very thin and moved with a sinuous grace. He was effeminately elegant and dandified and had the unhealthy pallor of a creature of the night. His face was of alabaster, his features smooth, his lips non-existent; the dark hair, parted in the middle, was plastered flat against his skull. His dress suit was elegantly cut but he hadn't as good a tailor as I had: the bulge under the left armpit was quite perceptible. He held a jade cigarette holder in a thin, white, beautifully manicured hand; his face held an expression, which was probably permanent, of quietly contemptuous amusement. Just to have him look at you was a good enough excuse to hit him. He blew a thin steam of cigarette smoke into the air.

"What's all this, my dear fellow?" He looked French or Italian, but he wasn't: he was English. "We're not open, you know."

"You are now," I pointed out. "You the manager?"

"I'm the manager's representative. If you care to call back later"—he puffed some more of his obnoxious smoke into the air—"much later, then we'll see——"

"I'm a lawyer from England and on urgent business." I handed him a card saying I was a lawyer from England. "It is essential that I see the manager at once. A great deal of money is involved."

If such an expression as he wore could be said to soften, then his did, though you had to have a keen eye to notice the difference. "I promise nothing, Mr. Harrison." That was the name on the card. "Mr. Durrell may be persuaded to see you."

He moved away like a ballet dancer on his day off and was back in moments. He nodded to me and stood to one side to let me precede him down a large and dimly lit passage, an arrangement which I didn't like but had to put up with. At the end of the passage with a door opening on a brightly lit room and as it seemed to be intended that I should enter without knocking I did just that. I noted in the passing that the door was of the type that the vaults manager—if there is such a person—of the Bank of England would have rejected as being excessive to his requirements.

The interior of the room looked more than a little like a vault itself. Two large safes, tall enough for a man to walk into, were let into one wall. Another wall was given over to a battery of lockable metal cabinets of the rental left-luggage kind commonly found in railway stations. The other two walls may well have been windowless but it was impossible to be sure: they were completely covered with crimson and violet drapes.

The man sitting behind the large mahogany desk didn't look a bit like a bank manager, at any rate like a British banker, who typically has a healthy outdoor appearance about him owing to his penchant for golf and the short hours he spends behind his desk. This man was sallow, about eighty pounds overweight, with greasy black hair, a greasy complexion and permanently bloodshot yellowed eyes. He wore a well-cut blue alpaca suit, a large variety of rings on both hands and a welcoming smile that didn't become him at all.

"Mr. Harrison?" He didn't try to rise, probably experience had convinced him that the effort wasn't worth it. "Pleased to meet you. My name is Durrell."

Maybe it was, but it wasn't the name he had been born with: I thought him Armenian, but couldn't be sure. But I greeted him as civilly as if his name had been Durrell.

"You have some business to discuss with me?" he beamed. Mr. Durrell was cunning and knew that lawyers didn't come all the way from England without matters of weighty import, invariably of a financial nature, to discuss.

"Well, not actually with you. With one of your employees."

The welcoming smile went into cold storage. "With one of my employees?"

"Yes."

"Then why bother me?"

"Because I couldn't find her at her home address. I am told she works here."

"She?"

"Her name is Astrid Lemay."

"Well now." He was suddenly more reasonable, as if he wanted to help. "Astrid Lemay? Working here." He frowned thoughtfully. "We have many girls, of course—but that name?" He shook his head.

"But friends of hers told me," I protested.

"Some mistake. Marcel?"

The snakelike man smiled his contemptuous smile. "No one of that name here."

"Or ever worked here?"

Marcel shrugged, walked across to a filing cabinet, produced a folder and laid it on the desk, beckoning to me. "All the girls who work here or have done in the past year. Look for yourself."

I didn't bother looking. I said: "I've been misinformed. My apologies for disturbing you."

"I suggest you try some of the other night clubs." Durrell, in the standard tycoon fashion, was already busy making notes on a sheet of paper to indicate that the interview was over. "Good day, Mr. Harrison."

Marcel had already moved to the doorway. I followed, and as I passed through, turned and smiled apologetically. "I'm really sorry——"

"Good day." He didn't even bother to lift his head. I did some more uncertain smiling, then courteously pulled the door to behind me. It looked a good solid soundproof door.

Marcel, standing just inside the passageway, gave me his warm smile again and, not even condescending to speak, contemptuously indicated that I should precede him down the passageway. I nodded and as I walked past him I hit him in the middle with considerable satisfaction and a great deal of force and although I thought that was enough I hit him again, this time on the side of the neck. I took out my gun, screwed on the silencer, took the recumbent Marcel by the collar of his jacket and dragged him towards the office door which I opened with my gun hand.

Durrell looked up from his desk. His eyes widened as much as eyes can widen when they're almost buried in folds of fat. Then his face became very still as faces become when the owners want to conceal their thoughts or intentions.

"Don't do it," I said. "Don't do any of the standard clever things. Don't reach for a button, don't press any switches on the floor and don't, please, be so naïve as to reach for the gun which you probably have in the top right-hand drawer, you being a right-handed man."

He didn't do any of the standard clever things.

"Push your chair back two feet."

He pushed his chair back two feet. I dropped Marcel to the floor, reached behind me, closed the door, turned the very fancy key in the lock then pocketed the key. I said: "Get up."

Durrell got up. He stood scarcely more than five feet high. In build, he closely resembled a bullfrog. I nodded to the nearer of the two large safes.

"Open it."

"So that's it." He was good with his face but not so good with his voice. He wasn't able to keep that tiny trace of relief out of his voice. "Robbery, Mr. Harrison."

"Come here," I said. He came. "Do you know who I am?"

"Know who you are?" A look of puzzlement. "You just told me——"

"That my name is Harrison. Who am I?"

"I don't understand."

He screeched with pain and fingered the already bleeding welt left by the silencer of my gun.

"Who am I?"

"Sherman." Hate was in the eyes and the thick voice. "Interpol."

"Open that door.'

"Impossible. I have only half the combination Marcel here has——"

The second screech was louder, the weal on the other cheek comparably bigger.

"Open that door."

He twiddled with the combination and pulled the door open. The safe was about thirty inches square, of a size to hold a great deal of guilders, but, then, if all the tales about the Balinova were true, tales that whispered darkly of gaming rooms and much more interesting shows in the basement and the brisk retail of items not commonly found in ordinary retail shops, the size was probably barely adequate.

I nodded to Marcel. "Junior here. Shove him inside."

"In there?" He looked horrified.

"I don't want him coming to and interrupting our discussion."

"Discussion?"

"Open up."

"He'll suffocate. Ten minutes and——"

"The next time I have to ask it will be after I put a bullet through your kneecap so that you'll never walk without a stick again. Believe me?"

He believed me. Unless you're a complete fool, and Durrell wasn't, you can always tell when a man means something. He dragged Marcel inside, which was probably the hardest work he'd done in years because he had to do quite a bit of bending and pushing to get Marcel to fit on the tiny floor of the safe in such a way that the door could be closed. The door was closed.

I searched Durrell. He'd no offensive weapon on him. The right-hand drawer of his desk predictably yielded up a large automatic of a type unknown to me, which was not unusual as I'm not very good with guns except when aiming and firing them.

"Astrid Lemay," I said. "She works here."

"She works here."

"Where is she?"

"I don't know. Before God, I don't know." The last was almost in a scream as I'd lifted the gun again.

"You could find out?"

"How could I find out?"

"Your ignorance and reticence do you credit," I said. "But they are based on fear. Fear of someone, fear of something. But you'll become all knowledgeable and forthcoming when you learn to fear something else more. Open that safe."

He opened the safe. Marcel was still unconscious.

"Get inside."

"No." The single word came out like a hoarse scream. "I tell you, it's airtight, hermetically sealed. Two of us in there—we'll be dead in minutes if I go in there."

"You'll be dead in seconds if you don't."

He went inside. He was shaking now. Whoever this was, he wasn't one of the kingpins: whoever masterminded the drug racket was a man—or men—possessed of a toughness and ruthlessness that were absolute and this man was possessed of neither.

I spent the next five minutes without profit in going through every drawer and file available to me. Everything I examined appeared to be related in one way or another to legitimate business dealing which made sense, for Durrell would be unlikely to keep documents of a more incriminating nature where the office cleaner could get her hands on them. After five minutes I opened the safe door.

Durrell had been wrong about the amount of breathable air available inside that safe. He'd overestimated. He was semicollapsed with his knees resting on Marcel's back which made it fortunate for Marcel that he was still unconscious. At least, I thought he was unconscious. I didn't bother to check. I caught Durrell by the shoulder and pulled. It was like pulling a bull moose out of a swamp, but he came eventually and rolled out onto the floor. He lay there for a bit then pushed himself groggily to his knees. I waited patiently until the laboured stertorous whooping sound dropped to a mere gasping wheeze and his complexion ran through the spectrum from a bluish-violet colour to what would have been a becomingly healthy pink had I not known that his normal complexion more resembled the colour of old newspaper. I prodded him and indicated that he should get to his feet and he managed this after a few tries.

"Astrid Lemay?" I said.

"She was here this morning." His voice came as a hoarse whisper but audible enough all the same. "She said that very urgent family matters had come up. She had to leave the country."

"Alone?"

"No, with her brother."

"He was here?"

"No."

"Where did she say she was going?"

"Athens. She belonged there."

"She came here just to tell you this?"

"She had two months' back pay due. She needed it for the fare."

I told him to get back inside the safe. I had a little trouble with him, but he finally decided that it offered a better chance than a bullet, so he went. I didn't want to terrify him any more, I just didn't want him to hear what I was about to say.

I got through to Schiphol on a direct line, and was finally connected with the person I wanted.

"Inspector van Gelder, Police HQ, here," I said. "An Athens flight this morning. Probably KLM. I want to check if two people, names Astrid Lemay and George Lemay, were on board. Their descriptions are as follows—what was that?"

The voice at the other end told me that they had been aboard. There had been some difficulty, apparently, about George being allowed on the flight as his condition was such that both medical and police authorities at the airport had questioned the wisdom of it but the girl's pleading had prevailed. I thanked my informant and hung up.

I opened the door of the safe. It hadn't been shut more than a couple of minutes this time and I didn't expect to find them in such bad shape and they weren't. Durrell's complexion was no more than puce, and Marcel had not only recovered consciousness but recovered it to the extent of trying to lug out his underarm gun, which I had carelessly forgotten to remove. As I took the gun from him before he could damage himself with it, I reflected that Marcel must have the most remarkable powers of recuperation. I was to remember this with bitter chagrin on an occasion that was to be a day or so later and very much more inauspicious for me.

I left them both sitting on the floor and as there didn't seem to be anything worthwhile to say none of the three of us said it. I unlocked the door, opened it, closed and locked it behind me, smiled pleasantly at the faded blonde and dropped the key through a street grille outside the Balinova. Even if there wasn't a spare key available, there were telephones and alarm bells still operating from inside that room and it shouldn't take an oxyacetylene torch more than two or three hours to open it. There should be enough air inside the room to last that time. But it didn't seem very important one way or another.

I drove back to Astrid's flat and did what I should have done in the first place—asked some of her immediate neighbors if they had seen her that morning. Two had, and their stories checked. Astrid and George with two or three cases had left two hours previously in a taxi.

Astrid had skipped and I felt a bit sad and empty about it not because she had said she would help me and hadn't but because I felt she had closed the last escape door open to her.

Her masters hadn't killed her for two reasons. They knew I could have tied them up with her death and that would be coming too close to home. And they didn't have to because she was gone and no longer a danger to them: fear, if it is sufficiently great, can seal lips as effectively as death.

I'd liked her and would have liked to see her happy again. I couldn't blame her. For her, all the doors had been closed.

9

THE VIEW from the top of the towering Havengebouw, the skyscraper in the harbour, is unquestionably the best in Amsterdam. But I wasn't interested in the view that morning, only in the facilities this vantage point had to offer. The sun was shining, but it was breezy and cool at that altitude and even at sea level the wind was strong enough to ruffle the blue-grey waters into irregular wavy patterns of white horses.

The observation platform was crowded with tourists, for the most part with wind-blown hair, binoculars and cameras, and although I didn't carry any camera I didn't think I looked different from any other tourist. Only my purpose in being up there was.

I leaned on my elbows and gazed out to sea. De Graaf had certainly done me proud with those binoculars, they were as good as any I had ever come across and with the near-perfect visibility that day the degree of definition was all that I could ever have wished for.

The glasses were steadied on a coastal steamer of about a thousand tons that was curving into harbour. Even when I first picked it up I could detect the large rust-streaked patches on the hull and see that she was flying the Belgian flag. And the time, shortly before noon, was right. I followed her progress and it seemed to me that she was taking a wider sweep than one or two vessels that had preceded her and was going very close indeed to the buoys that marked the channel: but maybe that was where the deepest water lay.

I followed her progress till she closed on the harbour and then I could distinguish the rather scarred name on the rusty bows. *Marianne* the name read. The captain was certainly a stickler for punctuality but whether he was such a stickler for abiding by the law was another question.

I went down to the Havenrestaurant and had lunch. I wasn't hungry but mealtimes in Amsterdam, as my experience had been since coming there, tended to be irregular and infrequent. The food in the Havenrestaurant is well spoken of and I've no doubt it merits its reputation: but I don't remember what I had for lunch that day.

I arrived at the Hotel Touring at one-thirty. I didn't really expect to find that Maggie and Belinda had returned yet and they hadn't. I told the man behind the desk that I'd wait in the lounge, but I don't much fancy lounges, especially when I had to study papers like the papers I had to study from the folder we'd taken from Morgenstern and Muggenthaler's, so I waited till the desk was momentarily unmanned, took the lift to the fourth floor and let myself into the girls' room. It was a fractionally better room than the previous one they'd had, and the couch, which I immediately tested, was fractionally softer, but there wasn't enough in it to make Maggie and Belinda turn cartwheels for joy, apart from the fact that the first cartwheel in any direction would have brought them up against a solid wall.

I lay on that couch for over an hour, going through all the warehouse's invoices and a very unexciting and innocuous list of invoices they turned out to be. But there was one name among all the others that turned up with surprising frequency and as its products marched with the line of my developing suspicions, I made a note of its name and map location.

A key turned in the lock and Maggie and Belinda entered. Their first reaction on seeing me seemed to be one of relief, which was quickly followed by an unmistakable air of annoyance. I said mildly: "Is there something up, then?"

"You had us worried," Maggie said coldly. "The man at the desk said you were waiting for us in the lounge and you weren't there."

"We waited half an hour." Belinda was almost bitter about it. "We thought you had gone."

"I was tired. I had to lie down. Now that I've apologised, how did your morning go?"

"Well." Maggie didn't seem very mollified. "We had no luck with Astrid———"

"I know. The man at the desk gave me your message. We can quit worrying about Astrid. She's gone."

"Gone?" they said.

"Skipped the country."

"Skipped the country?"

"Athens."

"Athens?"

"Look," I said. "Let's keep the vaudeville act for later. She and George left Schiphol this morning."

"Why?" Belinda asked.

"Scared. The bad men were leaning on her from one side and the good guy—me—on the other. So she lit out."

"How do you *know* she's gone?" Maggie enquired.

"A man at the Balinova told me." I didn't elaborate, if they'd any illusions left about the nice boss they had I wanted them to keep them. "And I checked with the airport."

"Mm." Maggie was unimpressed by my morning's work, she seemed to have the feeling that it was all my fault that Astrid had gone and as usual she was right. "Well, Belinda or me first?"

"This first." I handed her the paper with the figures 910020 written on it. "What does it mean?"

Maggie looked at it, turned it upside down and looked at the back. "Nothing," she said.

"Let me see it," Belinda said brightly. "I'm good at anagrams and crosswords." She was too. Almost at once she said: "Reverse it. 020019. Two A.M. on the nineteenth, which is tomorrow morning."

"Not bad at all," I said indulgently. It had taken me half an hour to work it out.

"What happens then?" Maggie asked suspiciously.

"Whoever wrote these figures forgot to explain that," I said evasively for I was getting tired of telling outright lies. "Well, Maggie, you."

"Well." She sat down and smoothed out a lime-green cotton dress which looked as if it had shrunk an awful lot with repeated washing. "I put on this new dress to the park because Trudi hadn't seen it before and the wind was blowing so I had a scarf over my head and———"

"And you were wearing dark glasses."

"Right." Maggie wasn't an easy girl to throw off stride. "I wandered around for half an hour, dodging pensioners and prams most of the time. Then I saw her—rather I saw this enormous fat old—old——"

"Beldam?"

"Beldam. Dressed like you said she would be. Then I saw Trudi. Long-sleeved white cotton dress, couldn't keep still, skipped about like a lamb." Maggie paused and said reflectively: "She really is a rather beautiful girl."

"You have a generous soul, Maggie."

Maggie took the hint. "By and by they sat down on a bench. I sat on another about thirty yards away, just looking over the top of a magazine. A Dutch magazine."

"A nice touch," I approved.

"Then Trudi started plaiting the hair of this puppet——"

"What puppet?"

"The puppet she was carrying," Maggie said patiently. "If you keep on interrupting I find it difficult to remember all the details. While she was doing this a man came up and sat beside them. A big man in a dark suit with a priest's collar, white moustache, marvellous white hair. He seemed a very nice man."

"I'm sure he was," I said mechanically. I could well imagine the Reverend Thaddeus Goodbody as a man of instant charm except, perhaps, at half past three in the morning.

"Trudi seemed very fond of him. After a minute or two, she reached an arm around his neck and whispered something in his ear. He made a great play of being shocked but you could see he wasn't really for he reached a hand into his pocket and pressed something into her hand. Money, I suppose." I was on the point of asking if she was sure it wasn't a hypodermic syringe, but Maggie was far too nice for that. "Then she rose, still clutching this puppet, and skipped across to an ice-cream van. She bought an ice-cream cornet—and then she started walking straight towards me."

"You left?"

"I held the magazine higher," Maggie said with dignity. "I needn't have bothered. She headed past me towards another open van about twenty feet away."

"To admire the puppets?"

"How did you know?" Maggie sounded disappointed.

"Every second van in Amsterdam seems to sell puppets."

"That's what she did. Fingered them, stroked them. The old man in charge tried to look angry but who could be angry with a girl like that? She went right round the van then went back to the bench. She kept on offering the cornet to the puppet."

"And didn't seem upset when the puppet didn't want any. What were the old girl and the pastor doing the while?"

"Talking. They seemed to have a lot to talk about. Then Trudi got back and they all talked some more, then the pastor patted Trudi on the back, they all rose, he took his hat off to the old girl, as you call her, and they all went away."

"An idyllic scene. They went away together?"

"No. The pastor went by himself."

"Try to follow any of them?"

"No."

"Good girl. Were you followed?"

"I don't think so."

"You don't think so?"

"There was a whole crowd of people leaving at the same time as I did. Fifty, sixty, I don't know. It would be silly for me to say that I was sure nobody had an eye on me. But nobody followed me back here."

"Belinda?"

"There's a coffee shop almost opposite the Hostel Paris. Lots of girls came and went from the hostel but I was on my fourth cup before I recognised one who'd been in the church last night. A tall girl with auburn hair, striking, I suppose you would call her——"

"How do you know what I'd call her? She was dressed like a nun last night?"

"Yes."

"Then you couldn't have seen that she had auburn hair."

"She had a mole high up on her left cheekbone."

"And black eyebrows?" Maggie put in.

"That's her," Belinda agreed. I gave up. I believed them. When one good-looking girl examines another good-looking girl her eyes are turned into long-range telescopes. "I followed her to the Kalverstrat," Belinda continued. "She went into a big store. She seemed to walk haphazardly through the ground floor but she wasn't being haphazard really for she fetched up pretty quickly at a counter marked 'SOUVENIRS: EXPORT ONLY.' The girl examined the souvenirs casually but I knew she was far more interested in the puppets than anything else."

"Well, well, well," I said. "Puppets again. How did you know she was interested?"

"I just knew," Belinda said in the tone of one trying to describe various colours to a person who has been blind from birth. "Then after a while she started to examine a particular group of puppets very closely. After shilly-shallying for a while she made her choice but I knew she wasn't shilly-shallying." I kept prudent silence. "She spoke to the assistant who wrote something down on a piece of paper."

"The time it would——"

"The time it would take to write the average address." She'd carried on blandly as if she hadn't heard me. "Then the girl passed over money and left."

"You followed her?"

"No. Am I a good girl too?"

"Yes."

"And I wasn't followed."

"Or watched? In the store, I mean. By, for instance, any big fat middle-aged man."

Belinda giggled. "Lots of big——"

"All right, all right, so lots of big fat middle-aged men spend a lot of time watching you. And lots of young thin ones, too, I shouldn't wonder." I paused consideringly. "Tweedledum and Tweedledee, I love you both."

They exchanged glances. "Well," Belinda said, "that is nice."

"Professionally speaking, dear girls, professionally speaking. Excellent reports from both, I must say. Belinda, you saw the puppet the girl chose?"

"I'm *paid* to see things," she said primly.

"I eyed her speculatively, but let it go. "Quite. It was a Huyler-costumed puppet. Like the one we saw in the warehouse."

"How on earth did you know?"

"I could say I'm psychic. I could say 'genius.' The fact of the matter is that I have access to certain information that you two don't."

"Well then, share it with us." Belinda, of course.

"No."

"Why not?"

"Because there are men in Amsterdam who could take you and put you in a quiet dark room and make you talk."

There was a long pause, then Belinda said: "And you wouldn't?"

"I might at that," I admitted. "But they wouldn't find it so easy to get me into that quiet dark room in the first place." I picked up a batch of the invoices. "Either of you ever heard of the Kasteel Linden? No? Neither had I. It seems, however, that they supply our friends Morgenstern and Muggenthaler with a large proportion of pendulum clocks."

"Why pendulum clocks?" Maggie asked.

"I don't know," I lied frankly. "There may be a connection. I'd asked Astrid to try to trace the source of a certain type of clock—she had, you understand, a lot of underworld connections that she didn't want. But she's gone now. I'll look into it tomorrow."

"We'll do it today," Belinda said. "We could go to this Kasteel place and——"

"You do that and you're on the next plane back to England. Alternatively, I don't want to waste time dragging you up from the bottom of the moat that surrounds this castle. Clear?"

"Yes, sir," they said meekly and in unison. It was becoming distressingly and increasingly plain that they didn't regard my bite as being anywhere nearly as bad as my bark.

I gathered the papers and rose. "The rest of the day is yours. I'll see you tomorrow morning."

Oddly, they didn't seem too happy about getting the rest of the day to themselves. Maggie said: "And you?"

"A car trip to the country. To clear my head. Then sleep, then maybe a boat trip tonight."

"One of those romantic night cruises on the canals?" Belinda tried to speak lightly but it didn't come off. She and Maggie appeared to be onto something I'd missed. "You'll need someone to watch your back, won't you? I'll come."

"Another time. But *don't* you two go out on the canals. *Don't* go near the canals. *Don't* go near the night clubs. And, above all, *don't* go near the docks or that warehouse."

And *don't* you go out tonight either." I stared at Maggie. Never in five years had she spoken so vehemently, so fiercely even; and she's certainly never told me what to do. She caught my arm, another unheard-of thing. "Please."

"Maggie."

"Do you have to take that boat trip tonight?"

"Now, Maggie——"

"At two o'clock in the morning?"

"What's wrong, Maggie? It's not like you to——"

"I don't know. Yes, I *do* know. Somebody seems to be walking over my grave with hobnailed boots."

"Tell him to mind how he goes."

Belinda took a step towards me. "Maggie's right. You mustn't go tonight." Her face was tight with concern.

"You too, Belinda?"

"Please."

There was a curious tension in the room which I couldn't even begin to comprehend. Their faces were pleading, a curious near-desperation in their eyes, much as if I'd just announced that I was going to jump off a cliff.

Belinda said: "What Maggie means is, don't leave us."

Maggie nodded. "Don't go out tonight. Stay with us."

"Oh hell!" I said. "Next time I need help abroad I'm going to bring a couple of big girls with me." I made to move past them towards the door, but Maggie barred the way, reached up and kissed me. Only seconds later Belinda did the same.

"This is very bad for discipline," I said. Sherman out of his depth. "Very bad indeed."

I opened the door and turned to see if they agreed with me. But they said nothing, just stood there looking curiously forlorn. I shook my head in irritation and left.

On the way back to the Excelsior I bought brown paper and string. In the hotel room I used this to wrap up a complete kit of clothes that were now more or less recovered from the previous night's soaking, printed a fictitious name and address on it and took it down to the desk. The assistant manager was in position.

"Where's the nearest post office?" I asked.

"My dear Mr. Sherman." The punctiliously friendly greeting was automatic but he'd stopped smiling by this time. "We can attend to that for you."

"Thank you, but I wish to register it personally."

"Ah, I understand." He didn't understand at all, which was that I didn't want brows raised or foreheads creased over the sight of Sherman leaving with a large brown parcel over his arm. He gave me the address I didn't want.

I put the parcel in the boot of the police car and drove through the city and the suburbs until I was out in the country, heading north. By and by I knew I was running alongside the waters of the Zuider Zee but I couldn't see them because of the high retaining dyke to the right of the road. There wasn't much to see to the left-hand side either: the Dutch countryside is not designed to send the tourist into raptures.

Presently I came to a signpost reading "HUYLER 5 km." and a few hundred yards farther on turned left off the road and stopped the car soon after in the tiny square of a tiny picture postcard village. The square had its post office and outside the post office was a public telephone box. I locked the boot and doors of the car and left it there.

I made my way back to the main road, crossed it and climbed up the sloping grass-covered dyke until I could look out over the Zuider Zee. A fresh breeze sparkled the waters blue and white under the late afternoon sun, but scenically, one couldn't say much more for that stretch of water for the encompassing land was so low that it appeared, when it appeared at all, as no more than a flat dark bar on the horizon. The only distinctive feature anywhere to be seen was an island to the northeast, about a mile offshore.

This was the island of Huyler and it wasn't even an island. It had been but some engineers had built a causeway out to it from the mainland to expose them more fully to the benefits of civilization and the tourist trade. Along the top of this causeway a tarmac highway had been laid.

Nor did the island itself even deserve the description of distinctive. It was so low-lying and flat that it seemed that a wave of any size must wash straight over it, but its flatness was relieved by scattered farmhouses, several big Dutch barns and, on the western shore of the island, facing towards the mainland, a village nestling round a tiny harbour. And, of course, it had its canals. That was all there was to be seen so I left, regained the road, walked along till I came to a bus stop and caught the first bus back to Amsterdam.

I elected for an early dinner, for I did not expect to have much opportunity to eat later that night and I had the suspicion that whatever the fates had in store for me that night had better not be encountered on a full stomach. And then I went to bed, for I didn't anticipate having any sleep later that night either.

The travel alarm awoke me at half past midnight. I didn't feel particularly rested. I dressed carefully in a dark suit, navy roll-neck jersey, dark rubber-soled canvas shoes and a dark canvas jacket. The gun I wrapped in a zipped oilskin bag and jammed into the shoulder holster. Two spare magazines went into a similar pouch and I secured those in a zipped pocket of the canvas jacket. I looked longingly at the bottle of Scotch on the sideboard and decided against it. I left.

I left, as was by now second nature to me, by the fire escape. The street below, as usual, was deserted and I knew that nobody followed me as I left the hotel. It wasn't necessary for anyone to follow me for those who wished me ill knew where I was going and where they could expect to find me. I knew they knew. What I hoped was that no one knew that I knew.

I elected to walk because I didn't have the car any more and because I had become allergic to the taxis of Amsterdam. The streets were empty, at least the streets I chose were. It seemed a very quiet and peaceful city.

I reached the docks area, located myself, and moved on till I stood in the dark shadow of a storage shed. The luminous dial of my watch told me that it was twenty minutes to two. The wind had increased in strength and the air turned much colder, but there was no rain about although there was rain in the air. I could smell it over the strong nostalgic odours of sea and tar and ropes and all the other things that make dockside areas smell the same the world over. Tattered dark clouds scudded across the only fractionally less dark sky, occasionally revealing a glimpse of a pale high half-moon, more often obscuring it; but even when the moon was hidden the darkness was never absolute for above there were always rapidly changing patches of starlit sky.

In the brighter intervals I looked out across the harbour that stretched away into first dimness and then nothingness. There were literally hundreds of barges to be seen in this, one of the great barge harbours of the world, ranging in size from tiny twenty-footers to the massive Rhine barges, all jammed in a seemingly inextricable confusion. The confusion, I knew, was more apparent than real. Close-packed the barges undoubtedly were but although it would call for the most intricate manoeuvring each barge had, in fact, access to a narrow sea lane, which might intersect with two or three progressively larger lanes before reaching the open water beyond. The barges were connected to land by a series of long side-floating gangways, which in turn had other and narrower gangways attached at right angles to them.

The moon went behind a cloud. I moved out of the shadows onto one of the main central gangways, my rubber shoes quite soundless on the wet wood and even had I been clumping along in hobnailed boots I question whether anyone—other than those who were ill-intentioned to me—would have paid any heed, because although all the barges were almost certainly inhabited by their crews and in many cases their crews and families there were only one or two scattered cabin lights to be seen among all the hundreds of craft lying there; and apart from the faint threnody of the wind and the soft creaking and rubbing as the wind made the barges work gently at their moorings, the silence was total. The barge harbour was a city in itself and the city was asleep.

I'd traversed about a third of the length of the main gangway when the moon broke through. I stopped and looked around.

About fifty yards behind me two men were walking purposefully and silently towards me. They were but shadows, silhouettes, but I could see that the silhouettes of their right arms were longer than those of their left arms. They were carrying something in their right hands. I wasn't surprised to see those objects in their hands just as I hadn't been surprised to see the men themselves.

I glanced briefly to my right. Two more men were advancing steadily from land on the adjacent paralleling gangway to the right. They were abreast with the two on my own gangway.

I glanced to the left. Two more of them, two more moving dark silhouettes. I admired their coordination.

I turned and kept on walking towards the harbour. As I went, I extracted the gun from its holster, removed the waterproof covering, zipped up the covering again and replaced it in a zipped pocket. The moon went behind a cloud. I began to run, and as I did so I glanced over my shoulder. The three pairs of men had also broken into a run. I made another five yards and glanced over my shoulder again. The two men on my gangway had stopped and were lining up their guns on me or seemed to be because it was difficult to see in the starlight, but a moment later I was convinced they had for narrow red flames licked out in the darkness although there was no sound of shots which was perfectly understandable for no man in his right senses was going to upset hundreds of tough Dutch, German and Belgian bargees if he could possibly help it. They appeared, however, to have no objection to upsetting me. The moon came out again and I started to run a second time.

The bullet that hit me did more damage to my clothes than it did to me although the swift burning pain on the outside of my upper right arm made me reach up involuntarily to clasp it. Enough was enough. I swerved off the main gangway, jumped onto the bows of a barge that was moored by a small gangway at right angles and ran silently along the deck till I got in the shelter of the wheelhouse aft. Once in shelter I edged a cautious eye round the corner.

The two men on the central gangway had stopped and were making urgent sweeping motions to their friends on the right, indicating that I should be outflanked and, more likely than not, shot in the back. They had, I thought, very limited ideas about what constituted fair play and sportsmanship; but there was no questioning their efficiency. Quite plainly if they were going to get me at all, and I rated their chances as good, it was going to be by this encircling or outflanking method and it would obviously be a very good thing for me if I could disabuse them of this idea as soon as I could so I temporarily ignored the two men on the central gangway assuming, and correctly, I hoped, that they would remain where they were and wait for the outflankers to catch me unawares, and turned round to face the left gangway.

Five seconds and they were in view, not running, but walking deliberately and peering into the moon shadows cast by the wheelhouses and cabins of the barges, which was a very foolhardy or just simply foolish thing to do because I was in the deepest shadow I could find while they, by contrast, were almost brutally exposed by the light of the half-moon and I saw them long before they ever saw me. I doubt whether they ever saw me. One of them, for a certainty, did not, for he never saw anything again: he must have been dead before he struck the gangway and slid with a curious absence of noise, no more than a sibilant splash, into the harbour. I lined up for a second shot, but the other man had reacted very quickly indeed and flung himself backwards out of my line of sight before I could squeeze the trigger again. It occurred to me, for no reason at all, that my sportsmanship was on an even lower par than theirs but I was in the mood for sitting ducks that night.

I turned and moved for'ard again and peered round the edge of the wheelhouse. The two men on the central gangway hadn't moved. Perhaps they didn't know what had happened. They were a very long way away for an accurate pistol shot by night but I took a long steady careful aim and tried anyway. But this duck was too far away I heard a man give an exclamation and clutch his leg but from the alacrity with which he followed his companion and jumped from the gangway into the shelter of a barge he couldn't have been badly hurt. The moon went behind a cloud again, a very small cloud, but the only cloud for the next minute or so and they had me pin-pointed. I scrambled along the barge, regained the main gangway and started to run farther out into the harbour.

I hadn't got ten yards when that damned moon made its presence felt again. I flung myself flat, landing so that I faced inshore. To my left the gangway was empty which was hardly surprising as the confidence of the remaining man there must have been badly shaken. I glanced to my right. The two men there were much closer than the two who had just so prudently vacated the central gangway and from the fact that they were still walking forward in a purposeful and confident manner it was apparent that they did not yet know that one of their number was at the bottom of the harbour, but they were as quick to learn the virtue of prudence as the other three had been for they disappeared from the gangway very quickly when I loosed off two quick and speculative shots at them, both of which clearly missed. The two men who had been on the central gangway were making a cautious attempt to regain it, but they were too far away to worry me or I them.

For another five minutes this deadly game of hide and seek went on, running, taking cover, loosing off a shot, then running again, while all the time they closed in inexorably on me. They were being very circumspect now, taking the minimum of chances and using their superior numbers cleverly to advantage, one or two engaging my attention while the others scuttled forward from the shelter of one barge to the next. I was soberly and coldly aware that if I didn't do something different and do it very soon, there could be only one end to this game, and that it must come soon.

Of all the inappropriate times to do so I chose several of the brief occasions I spent sheltering behind cabins and wheelhouse to think about Belinda and Maggie. Was this, I wondered, why they had behaved so queerly the last time I had seen them? Had they guessed, or known by some peculiarly feminine intuitive progress, that something like this was going to happen to me and known what the end would be and had been afraid to tell me? It was as well, I thought, that they couldn't see me now, for not only would they have known they had been right but their faith in the infallibility of their boss would have been sadly shaken. I felt desperate and I supposed I must have looked pretty much the same way; I'd expected to find a man with a quick gun or a quicker knife lying in wait for me and I think I could have coped with that, with luck even with two of them: but I had not expected this. What had I said to Belinda outside the warehouse? "He who fights and runs away lives to fight another day." But now I had no place to run to for I was only twenty yards short of the end of the main gangway. It was a macabre feeling to be hunted to death like a wild animal or a dog with rabies while hundreds of people were sleeping within a hundred yards of me and all I had to do to save myself was to unscrew my silencer and fire two shots in the air and within seconds the entire barge habour would have been in life-saving uproar. But I couldn't bring myself to do this for what I had to do had to be done tonight and I knew this was the last chance I would ever have. My life in Amsterdam after tonight wouldn't be worth a crooked farthing. I couldn't bring myself to do it if there was left to me even the slenderest chance imaginable. I didn't think there was, not what a sane man would call a chance. I don't think I was quite sane then.

I looked at my watch. Six minutes to two. In yet another way, time had almost run out. I looked at the sky. A small cloud was drifting towards the moon and this would be the minute they would choose for the next and almost certainly last assault: it would have to be the moment I chose for my next and almost certainly last attempt to escape. I looked at the deck of the barge: its cargo was scrap and I picked up a length of metal. I again gauged the direction of that dark little cloud, which seemed to have grown even littler. Its centre wasn't going to pass directly across the moon but it would have to do.

I'd five shots left in my second magazine and I fired them off in quick succession at where I knew or guessed my pursuers had taken cover. I hoped this might hold them for a few seconds but I don't think I really believed it. Quickly I shoved the gun back in its waterproof covering, zipped it up and for extra security stowed it not in its holster but in a zipped pocket of my canvas coat, ran along the barge for a few steps, stepped on the gunwale and threw myself onto the main gangway. I scrambled desperately to my feet and as I did I realised that that damned cloud had missed the moon altogether.

I suddenly felt very calm because there were no options left open to me now. I ran, because there was nothing else in the world I could do, weaving madly from side to side to throw my would-be executioners off aim. Half a dozen times in three seconds I heard soft thudding sounds—they were as close to me as that now—and twice felt hands that I could not see tugging fiercely at my clothes. Suddenly I threw my head back, flung both arms high in the air and sent the piece of metal spinning into the water and had crashed heavily to the gangway even before I heard the splash. I struggled drunkenly and briefly to my feet clutched my throat, and toppled over backwards into the canal. I took as deep a breath as possible and held it against the impact.

The water was cold, but not icily so, opaque and not very deep. My feet touched mud and I kept them touching mud. I began to exhale, very slowly, very carefully, husbanding my air reserves which probably weren't very much as I didn't go in for this sort of thing very often. Unless I had miscalculated the eagerness of my pursuers to do away with me—and I hadn't—the two men on the central gangway would have been peering hopefully down at the spot where I had disappeared within five seconds of my disappearance. I hoped that they drew all the wrong conclusions from the slow stream of bubbles drifting to the top of the water and I hoped they drew them soon for I couldn't keep up this kind of performance very much longer.

After what seemed about five minutes but was probably not more than thirty seconds I stopped exhaling and sending bubbles to the surface for the excellent reason that I had no more air left in my lungs to exhale. My lungs were beginning to hurt a little now, I could almost hear my heart—I could certainly feel it—thudding away in an empty chest, and my ears ached. I pushed clear of the mud and swam to my right and hoped to God I'd got myself orientated right. I had. My hand came in contact with the keel of a barge and I used the purchase obtained to pass quickly under then swam up to the surface.

I don't think I could have stayed below for even a few seconds longer without swallowing water. As it was, when I broke surface it took considerable restraint and will power to prevent me from drawing in a great lungful of air with a whoop that could have been heard halfway across the harbour but in certain circumstances, such as when your life depends on it, one can exercise a very considerable amount of will power indeed and I made do with several large but silent gulps of air.

At first I could see nothing at all but this was just because of the oily film on the surface of the water that had momentarily glued my eyelids together. I cleared this but still there wasn't much to see, just the dark hull of the barge I was hiding behind, the main gangway in front of me and another parallel barge about ten feet distant. I could hear voices, a soft murmuring of voices. I swam silently to the stern of the barge, steadied myself by the rudder and peered cautiously round the stern. Two men, one with a torch, were standing on the gangway peering down at the spot where I had so recently disappeared: the waters were satisfactorily dark and still.

The two men straightened. One of them shrugged and made a gesture with the palms of both hands held upwards; the second man nodded agreement and rubbed his leg tenderly. The first man lifted his arms and crossed them above his head twice, first to his left, then to his right. Just as he did so there was a staccato and spluttering coughing sound as a marine diesel, somewhere very close indeed, started up. It was obvious that neither of the two men cared very much for this new development for the man who had made the signal at once grabbed the arm of the other and led him away, hobbling badly, at the best speed he could muster.

I hauled myself aboard the barge, which sounds a very simple exercise indeed but when a sheer-sided hull is four feet clear of the water this simple exercise can turn out to be a near-impossibility and so it turned out for me. But I made it eventually with the aid of the stern rope, flopped over the gunwale and lay there for a full half minute, gasping away like a stranded whale, before a combination of the beginnings of recovery from a complete exhaustion and a mounting sense of urgency had me on my feet again and heading towards the barge's bows and the main gangway.

The two men who had been so lately bent on my destruction and were now no doubt full of that righteous glow which comes from the satisfaction of a worthwhile job well done, were now no more than two vaguely discerned shadows disappearing into the even deeper shadows of the storage sheds on shore. I pulled myself onto the gangway and crouched there for a moment until I had located the source of the diesel then stooped, ran quickly along the gangway till I came to the place where the barge was secured to a side gangway, first dropping to my hands and knees, then inching along on knees and elbows before peering over the edge of the gangway.

The barge was at least seventy feet in length, broad in proportion and as totally lacking in grace of design as it was possible to be. The for'ard three quarters of the barge was given up entirely to battened holds, then after that came the wheelhouse and, right aft and joined to the wheelhouse, the crew accommodation. Yellow lights shone through the curtained windows. A large man in a dark peaked cap was leaning out of a wheelhouse window

talking to a crew member who was about to clamber onto the side gangway
to cast off.

The stern of the barge was hard against the main gangway on which I
was lying. I waited till the crew member had climbed onto the side gangway
and was walking away to cast off for'ard then slithered down soundlessly
onto the stern of the barge and crouched low behind the cabin until I heard
the sound of ropes being thrown aboard and the hollow thump of feet on
wood as the man jumped down from the side gangway. I moved silently
for'ard until I came to an iron ladder fitted to the fore end of the cabin,
climbed up this and edged for'ard in a prone position till I was stretched flat
on the stepped wheelhouse roof. The navigation lights came on but this was
no worry: they were so positioned on either side of the wheelhouse roof that
they had the comforting effect of throwing the position in which I lay into
comparatively deeper shadow.

The engine note deepened and the side gangway slowly dropped astern. I
wondered bleakly if I had stepped from the frying pan into the fire.

10

I HAD been pretty certain that I would be putting out to sea that night and
anyone who did that under the conditions I expected to experience should
also have catered for the possibility of becoming very wet indeed and if I
had used even a modicum of forethought in that respect I should have come
along fully fitted out with a waterproof scuba suit; but the thought of a
waterproof scuba suit had never even crossed my mind and I had no alternative now but to lie where I was and pay the price for my negligence.

I felt as if I were rapidly freezing to death. The night wind out in the
Zuider Zee was bitter enough to have chilled even a warmly clad man who
was forced to lie motionless and I wasn't warmly clad. I was soaked to the
skin with sea water and that chilling wind had the effect of making me feel
that I had turned into a block of ice with the difference that a block of ice is
inert while I shivered continuously like a man with blackwater fever. The
only consolation was that I didn't give a damn if it rained: I couldn't possibly
become any wetter than I was already.

With numbed and frozen fingers that wouldn't stay steady I unzipped my
jacket pockets, took both the gun and the remaining magazine from their
waterproof coverings, loaded the gun and stuck it inside my canvas coat. I
wondered idly what would happen if, in an emergency, I found that my
trigger finger had frozen solid so I pushed my right hand inside my sodden
jacket. The only effect this had was to make my hand feel colder than ever
so I took it out again.

The lights of Amsterdam were dropping far behind now and we were well
out into the Zuider Zee. The barge, I noticed, seemed to be following the
same widely curving course as the *Marianne* had done when she had come
into harbour at noon on the previous day. It passed very close indeed to a
couple of buoys and, looking over the bow, it seemed to me as if it was on
a collision course with a third buoy about four hundred yards ahead. But I
didn't doubt for a minute that the barge skipper knew just exactly what he
was doing.

The engine note dropped as the revolutions dropped and two men emerged
on deck from the cabin—the first crew to appear outside since we'd cleared

the barge harbour. I tried to press myself even closer to the wheelhouse roof but they didn't come my way, they headed towards the stern. I twisted round the better to observe them.

One of the men carried a metal bar to which was attached a rope at either end. The two men, one on either side of the poop, paid out a little of their lines until the bar must have been very close to water level. I twisted and looked ahead. The barge, moving very slowly now, was no more than twenty yards distant from the flashing buoy and on a course that would take it within twenty feet of it. I heard a sharp word of command from the wheelhouse, looked aft again and saw that the two men were beginning to let the lines slip through their fingers, one man counting as he did so. The reason for the counting was easy to guess. Although I couldn't see any in the gloom, the ropes must have been knotted at regular intervals to enable the two men who were paying them out to keep the iron bar at right angles to the barge's passage through the water.

The barge was exactly abreast the buoy when one of the men called out softly and at once, slowly but steadily, they began to haul their lines inboard. I knew now what was going to happen but I watched pretty closely all the same. As the two men continued to pull, a two-foot cylindrical buoy bobbed clear of the water. This was followed by a four-bladed grapnel, one of the flukes of which was hooked round the metal bar. Attached to this grapnel was a rope. The buoy, grapnel and metal bar were hauled aboard, then the two men began to pull on the grapnel rope, until eventually an object came clear of the water and was brought inboard. The object was a grey, metal-banded metal box, about eighteen inches square and twelve deep. It was taken immediately inside the cabin but even before this was done the barge was under full power again and the buoy beginning to drop rapidly astern. The entire operation had been performed with the ease and surety which bespoke a considerable familiarity with the technique just employed.

Time passed, and a very cold, shivering and miserable time it was too. I thought it was impossible for me to become any colder and wetter than I was but I was wrong for about four in the morning the sky darkened and it began to rain and I had never felt rain so cold. By this time what little was left of my body heat had managed partially to dry off some of the inner layers of clothing, but from the waist down—the canvas jacket provided reasonable protection—it just proved to have been a waste of time. I hoped that when the time came I had to move and take to the water again I wouldn't have reached that state of numbed paralysis where all I could do was sink.

The first light of the false dawn was in the sky now and I could vaguely distinguish the blurred outlines of land to the south and east. Then it became darker again and for a time I could see nothing and then the true dawn began to spread palely from the east and I could see land once more and gradually came to the conclusion that we were fairly close in to the north shore of Huyler and about to curve away to the southwest and then south towards the island's little harbour.

I had never appreciated that those damned barges moved so slowly. As far as the coastline of Huyler was concerned, the barge seemed to be standing still in the water. The last thing I wished to happen was to approach the Huyler shore in broad daylight and give rise to comment on the part of the inevitable ship-watchers as to why a crew member should be so eccentric as to prefer the cold roof of the wheelhouse to the warmth inside. I thought of the warmth inside and put the thought out of my mind.

The sun appeared over the far shore of the Zuider Zee but it was no good to me, it was one of those peculiar suns that were no good at drying out clothes and after a little I was glad to see that it was one of those early morning suns that promised only to deceive, for it was quickly overspread by a pall of dark cloud and soon that slanting freezing rain was hard at work again stopping what little circulation I had left. I was glad because the cloud had the effect of darkening the atmosphere again and the rain might persuade the harbour rubberneckers to stay at home.

We were coming towards journey's end. The rain, now mercifully, had strengthened to the extent where it was beginning to hurt my exposed face and hands and was hissing whitely into the sea; visibility was down to only a couple of hundred yards and although I could see the end of the row of navigation marks towards which the barge was now curving I couldn't see the harbour beyond.

I wrapped the gun up in its waterproof cover and jammed it in its holster. It would have been safer, as I'd done previously, to have put it in the zipped pocket of my canvas jacket, but I wasn't going to take the canvas jacket with me. At least, not far: I was so numbed and weakened by the long night's experience that the cramping and confining effects of that cumbersome jacket could have made all the difference between my reaching shore or not: another thing I'd carelessly forgotten to take with me was an inflatable life jacket or belt.

I wriggled out of the canvas jacket and balled it up under my arm. The wind suddenly felt a good deal icier than ever but the time for worrying about that was gone. I slithered along the wheelhouse roof, slid silently down the ladder, crawled below the level of the now uncurtained cabin windows, glanced quickly forward—an unnecessary precaution, no one in his right mind would have been out on deck at that moment unless he had to—dropped the canvas jacket overboard, swung across the stern-quarter, lowered myself to the full length of my arms, checked that the screw was well clear of my vicinity and let go.

It was warmer in the sea than it had been on the wheelhouse roof which was as well for me as I felt myself to be almost frighteningly weak. It had been my intention to tread water until the barge had entered harbour or at least, under those prevailing conditions, it had disappeared into the murk of the rain, but if ever there was a time for dispensing with refinements this was it. My primary concern, my only concern at the moment, was survival. I ploughed on after the fast receding stern of the barge with the best speed I could muster.

It was a swim, not more than ten minutes in duration, that any six-year-old in good training could have accomplished with ease but I was way below that standard that morning and though I can't claim it was a matter of touch and go I couldn't possibly have done it a second time. When I could clearly see the harbour wall I sheered off from the navigation marks, leaving them to my left, and finally made shore.

I sloshed my way up the beach and, as if by a signal, the rain suddenly stopped. Cautiously, I made my way up the slight eminence of earth before me, the top of which was level with the top of the harbour wall, stretched myself flat on the soaking ground and cautiously lifted my head.

Immediately to the right of me were the two tiny rectangular harbours of Huyler, the outer leading by a narrow passage to the inner. Beyond the inner harbour lay the pretty picture postcard village of Huyler itself, which, with the exception of the one long and two very short straight streets lining the inner harbour itself, was a charming maze of twisting roads and a crazy conglomeration of, mainly, green and white painted houses mounted on stilts as a precaution against floodwater. The stilts themselves were walled in for use as cellars, the entrance to the houses being by outside wooden stairs to the first floor.

I returned my attention to the outer harbour. The barge was berthed alongside its inner wall and the unloading of the cargo was already busily under way. Two small shore derricks lifted a succession of crates and sacks from the unbattened holds but I had no interest in those crates and sacks which were certainly perfectly legitimate cargo, but in the small metal box that had been picked up from the sea and which I was equally certain was the most illegitimate cargo imaginable. So I let the legitimate cargo look after itself and concentrated my attention on the cabin of the barge. I hoped to God I wasn't already too late, although I could hardly see how I could have been.

I wasn't, but it had been a near-thing. Less than thirty seconds after I had begun my surveillance of the cabin, two men emerged, one carrying a sack over his shoulder. Although the sack's contents had clearly been heavily padded there was an unmistakable angularity to it that left me in little doubt that this was the case that interested me.

The two men went ashore. I watched them for a few moments to get a general idea of the direction they were taking, slid back down the muddy bank—another item on my expense account, my suit had taken a terrible beating that night—and set off to follow the two men.

They were easy to follow. Not only had they plainly no suspicion that they were being followed, those narrow and crazily winding lanes made Huyler a shadow's paradise. Eventually the two men brought up at a long, low building on the northern outskirts of the village. The ground floor—or cellar as it would be in this village—was made of concrete. The upper storey, reached by a set of wooden steps similar to another concealing set of steps from which I was watching at a safe distance of forty yards, had tall and narrow windows with bars so closely set that a cat would have had difficulty in penetrating; the heavy door had two metal bars across it and was secured by two large padlocks. Both men mounted the stairs, the unburdened man unlocking the two padlocks and opening the door, then both passed inside. They reappeared again within twenty seconds, locked the door behind them and left. Both men were now unburdened.

I felt a momentary pang of regret that the weight of my burglar's belt had compelled me to leave it behind that night but one does not go swimming with considerable amounts of metal belted around one's waist. But the regret was only momentary. Apart from the fact that fifty different windows overlooked the entrance to this heavily barred building and the fact that a total stranger would almost certainly be instantly recognisable to any of the villagers in Huyler, it was too soon yet to show my hand: minnows might make fair enough eating but it was the whales I was after and I needed the bait in that box to catch them.

I didn't need a street guide to find my way out of Huyler. The harbour lay to the west so the terminus of the causeway must lie to the east. I made my way along a few narrow winding lanes in no mood to be affected by the quaint old-world charm that drew so many tens of thousands of tourists to the village each summer and came to a small arched bridge that spanned a narrow canal. The first three people I'd seen in the village so far, three Huyler matrons dressed in their traditional flowing costumes, passed me by as I crossed the bridge. They glanced at me incuriously then as indifferently looked away again as if it were the most natural thing in the world to meet in the streets of Huyler in the early morning a man who had obviously been recently immersed in the sea.

A few yards beyond the canal lay a surprisingly large car park—at the moment it held only a couple of cars and half a dozen bicycles, none of which had padlock or chain or any other securing device. Theft, apparently, was no problem on the island of Huyler, a face which I found hardly surprising: when the honest citizens of Huyler went in for crime they went in for it in an altogether bigger way. The car park was deserted of human life nor had I expected to find an attendant at that hour. Feeling guiltier about it than about any other action I had performed since arriving at Schiphol airport, I selected the most roadworthy of the bicycles, trundled it up to the locked gate, lifted it over, followed myself and pedalled on my way. There were no cries of "Stop thief!" or anything of the kind.

It was years since I'd been on a bicycle and although I was in no fit state to recapture that first fine careless rapture I got the hang of it again quickly enough and while I hardly enjoyed the trip it was at least better than walking and had the effect of getting some of my red corpuscles on the move again.

I parked the bicycle in the tiny village square where I'd left the police taxi—it was still there—and looked thoughtfully first at the telephone box then at my watch: I decided it was still too early, so I unlocked the car and drove off.

Half a mile along the Amsterdam road I came to an old Dutch barn standing well apart from its farmhouse. I stopped the car on the road in such a position that the barn came between it and anyone who might chance to look out from the farmhouse. I unlocked the boot, took out the brown paper parcel, made for the barn, found it unlocked, went inside and changed into a completely dry set of clothing. It didn't have the effect of transforming me into a new man. I still found it impossible to stop shivering, but at least I wasn't sunk in the depths of that clammily ice-cold misery that I'd been in for hours past.

I went on my way again. After only another half mile I came to a roadside building about the size of a small bungalow whose sign defiantly claimed that it was a motel. Motel or not, it was open, and I wanted no more. The plump proprietrix asked if I wanted breakfast but I indicated that I had other and more urgent needs. They have in Holland the charming practice of filling your glass of jonge Genever right to the very brim and the proprietrix watched in astonishment and considerable apprehension as my shaking hands tried to convey the liquid to my mouth. I didn't lose more than half of it in spillage but I could see she was considering calling either police or medical aid to cope with an alocholic with the DT's or a drug addict who had lost his hypodermic, whichever the case might be, but she was a brave woman and supplied me with my second jonge Genever on demand. This time I didn't lose more than a quarter of it and third time round not only did I spill hardly a drop but I could distinctly feel the rest of my layabout red corpuscles picking up their legs and giving themselves a brisk workout. With the fourth jonge Genever my hand was steady as a rock.

I borrowed an electric razor then had a gargantuan breakfast of eggs and meat and ham and cheeses, about four different kinds of bread and a half a gallon, as near as dammit, of coffee. The food was superb. Fledgling motel it might have been, but it was going places. I asked to use the phone.

I got through to the Hotel Touring in seconds which was a great deal less time than it took for the desk to get any reply from Maggie and Belinda's room. Finally a very sleepy-voiced Maggie said: "Hullo. Who is it?" I could just see her standing there, stretching and yawning.

"Out on the tiles last night again, eh?" I said severely.

"What?" She still wasn't with me.

"Sound asleep in the middle of the day." It was coming up for 8 A.M. "Nothing but a couple of mini-skirted layabouts."

"Is it—is it *you?*"

"Who else but the lord and master?" The jonge Genevers were beginning to make their delayed effect felt.

"Belinda! He's back!" A pause. "Lord and master, he says."

"I'm so glad!" Belinda's voice. "I'm so glad. We——"

"You're not half as glad as I am. You can get back to your bed. Try to beat the milkman to it tomorrow morning."

"We didn't leave our room." She sounded very subdued. "We talked and worried and hardly slept a wink and we thought——"

"I'm sorry. Maggie? Get dressed. Forget about the foam baths and breakfast. Get——"

"No breakfast? I'll bet you had breakfast." Belinda was having a bad influence on this girl.

"I had."

"And stayed the night in a luxury hotel?"

"Rank hath its privileges. Get a taxi, drop it on the outskirts of the town, phone for a local taxi and come out towards Huyler."

"Where they make the puppets?"

"That's it. You'll meet me coming south in a yellow and red taxi." I gave her the registration number. "Have your driver stop. Be as fast as you can."

I hung up, paid up, and went on my way. I was glad I was alive. Glad to be alive. It had been the sort of night that didn't look like having any morning, but here I was and I was glad. The girls were glad. I was warm and dry and fed, the jonge Genever was happily chasing the red corpuscles in a game of merry-go-round, all the coloured threads were weaving themselves into a beautiful pattern and by day's end it would all be over. I had never felt so good before.

I was never to feel so good again.

Nearing the suburbs I was flagged down by a yellow taxi. I stopped and crossed the road just as Maggie got out. She was dressed in a navy skirt and jacket and white blouse and if she'd spent a sleepless night she certainly showed no signs of it. She looked beautiful, but then she always looked that way: there was something special about her that morning.

"Well, well, well," she said. "What a healthy-looking ghost. May I kiss you?"

"Certainly not," I said with dignity. "Relationships between employer and employed are——"

"Do be quiet, Paul." She kissed me without permission. "What do you want me to do?"

"Go out to Huyler. Plenty of places down by the harbour where you can get breakfast. There's a place I want you to keep under fairly close but not constant surveillance." I described the window-barred building and its location. "Just try to see who goes in and out of that building and what goes on there. And remember, you're a tourist. Stay in company or as close as you can to company all the time. Belinda's still in her room?"

"Yes." Maggie smiled. "Belinda took a phone call while I was dressing. Good news, I think."

"Who does Belinda know in Amsterdam?" I said sharply. "Who called?"

"Astrid Lemay."

"What in God's name are you talking about? Astrid's skipped the country. I've got proof."

"Sure she skipped it." Maggie was enjoying herself. "She skipped it because you'd given her a very important job to do and she couldn't do it because she was being followed everywhere she went. So she skipped out, got off at Paris, got a refund on her Athens ticket and skipped straight back in again. She and George are staying in a place outside Amsterdam with friends she can trust. She says to tell you she followed that lead you gave her. She says to tell you she's been out to the Kasteel Linden and that———"

"Oh my God!" I said. "Oh my God!" I looked at Maggie standing there, the smile slowly dying on her lips and for one brief moment I felt like turning savagely on her, for her ignorance, for her stupidity, for her smiling face, for her empty talk of good news, and then I felt more ashamed of myself than I had ever done in my life, for the fault was mine, not Maggie's, and I would have cut off my hand sooner than hurt her so instead I put my arm round her shoulders and said: "Maggie, I must love you."

She smiled at me uncertainly. "I'm sorry. I don't understand."

"Maggie?"

"Yes, Paul?"

"How do you think Astrid Lemay found out the telephone number of your new hotel?"

"Oh, dear God!" she said, for now she understood.

I ran across to my car without looking back, started up and accelerated through the gears like a man possessed, which I suppose I really was. I operated the switch that popped up the blue flashing police light and turned on the siren, then clamped the earphones over my head and started fiddling desperately with the radio control knobs. Nobody had ever shown me how to work it and this was hardly the time to learn. The car was full of noise, the high-pitched howling of the overstressed engine, the clamour of the siren, the static and crackle of the earphones and, what seemed loudest of all to me, the sound of my harsh and bitter and futile swearing as I tried to get that damned radio to work. Then suddenly the crackling ceased and I heard a calm assured voice.

"Police headquarters," I shouted. "Colonel de Graaf. Never mind who the hell I am. Hurry, man, hurry!" There was a long and infuriating silence as I weaved through the morning rush-hour traffic and then a voice on the earphones said: "Colonel de Graaf is not in his office yet."

"Then get him at home!" I shouted. Eventually they got him at home. "Colonel de Graaf? Yes, yes, yes. Never mind that. That puppet we saw yesterday. I *have* seen a girl like that before. Astrid Lemay." De Graaf started to ask questions but I cut him short. "God's sake, never mind that. The warehouse——I think she's in desperate danger. We're dealing with a criminal maniac. For God's sake, hurry."

I threw the earphones down and concentrated on driving and cursing myself. If you want a candidate for easy outwitting, I thought savagely, Sherman's your man. But at the same time I was conscious that I was being at least a degree unfair to myself: I was up against a brilliantly directed criminal organisation, that was for sure, but an organisation that contained within it an unpredictable psychopathic element that made normal prediction almost impossible. Sure, Astrid had sold Jimmy Duclos down the river but it had been Duclos or George, and George was a brother. They'd sent her to get to work on me, for she herself could have had no means of knowing that I was staying at the Excelsior, but instead of enlisting my aid and sympathy she'd chickened out at the last moment and I'd had her traced and that was when the trouble had begun, that was when she had begun to become a liability instead of an asset. She had begun seeing me—or I her—without their ostensible knowledge. I could have been seen taking George away from that barrel organ in the Rembrandtsplein or at the church or by those two drunks outside her flat who weren't drunks at all.

They'd eventually decided that it was better to have her out of the way, but not in such a fashion that would make me think that harm had come to her because they probably thought, and rightly, that if I thought she'd been taken prisoner and was otherwise in danger I'd have abandoned all hope of achieving my ultimate objective and done what they knew now was the very last thing I wanted to do—to go to the police and lay before them all I knew, which they probably suspected was a great deal. This, too, was the last thing they wanted me to do because although by going to the police I would have defeated my own ultimate ends I could at least have so severely damaged their organisation that it might have taken months, perhaps years, to build it up again. And so Durrell and Marcel had played their part yesterday morning in the Balinova while I had overplayed mine to the hilt and had convinced me beyond doubt that Astrid and George had left for Athens. Sure they had. They'd left all right, been forced off the plane at Paris and forced to return to Amsterdam. When she'd spoken to Belinda, she'd done so with a gun at her head.

And now, of course, Astrid was no longer of any use to them. Astrid had gone over to the enemy and there was only one thing to do with people like that. And now, of course, they need no longer fear any reaction from me, for I had died at two o'clock that morning down in the barge harbour. I had the key to it all now because I knew why they had been waiting. But I knew the key was too late to save Astrid.

I hit nothing and killed no one driving through Amsterdam but that was only because its citizens have very quick reactions. I was in the old town now, nearing the warehouse and travelling at high speed down the narrow one-way street leading to it when I saw the police barricade, a police car across the street with an armed policeman at either end of it. I skidded to a halt. I jumped out of the car and a policeman approached me.

"Police," he said, in case I thought he was an insurance salesman or something. "Please turn back."

"Don't you recognise one of your own cars?" I snarled. "Get out of my damned way."

"No one is allowed into this street."

"It's all right." De Graaf appeared round the corner and if I hadn't known from the police car the expression on his face would have told me. "It's not a very pleasant sight, Major Sherman."

I walked past him without speaking, rounded the corner and looked upwards. From this distance the puppetlike figure swinging lazily from the hoisting beam at the top of Morgenstern and Muggenthaler's warehouse looked hardly larger than the puppet I had seen yesterday morning, but then I had seen that one from directly underneath, so this one had to be bigger, much bigger. It was dressed in the same traditional costume as had been the puppet that had swayed to and fro there only so short a time ago; I didn't have to get any closer to know that the puppet's face of yesterday would be a perfect replica of the face that was there now. I turned away and walked round the corner, de Graaf with me.

"Why don't you take her down?" I asked. I could hear my own voice coming as if from a distance, abnormally, icily calm and quite toneless.

"It's a job for a doctor. He's gone up there now."

"Of course." I paused and said: "She can't have been there long. She

was alive less than an hour ago. Surely the warehouse was open long before———"

"This is Saturday. They don't work on Saturdays."

"Of course," I repeated mechanically. Another thought had come into
my head, a thought that struck an even deeper fear and chill into me. Astrid,
with a gun at her head, had phoned the Touring. But she had phoned with a
message for me, and that message had been meaningless and could or
should have achieved nothing, for I was lying at the bottom of the harbour.
It could only have had a purpose if the message had been relayed to me. It
would only have been made if they knew I was still alive. How could they
have known I was still alive? Who could have conveyed the information that
I was still alive? Nobody had seen me—except the three matrons on Huyler.
And why should they concern themselves———

There was more. Why should they make her telephone me and then put
themselves and their plans in jeopardy by killing Astrid after having been at
such pains to convince me that she was alive and well. Suddenly, certainly,
I knew the answer. They had forgotten something, I'd forgotten something.
They'd forgotten what Maggie had forgotten, that Astrid did not know the
telephone number of their new hotel; and I'd forgotten that neither Maggie
nor Belinda had ever met Astrid or heard her speak. I walked back round
the corner. Below the gable of the warehouse the chain and hook still stirred
slightly; but the burden was gone.

I said to de Graaf: "Get the doctor." He appeared in two minutes, a
youngster, I should have thought, fresh out of medical school and looking
paler, I suspected, than he normally did.

I said harshly: "She's been dead for hours, hasn't she?"

He nodded. "Four, five, I can't be sure."

"Thank you." I walked away back round the corner, de Graaf accompanying me. His face held a score of unasked questions, but I didn't feel like
answering any of them.

"I killed her," I said. "I think I may have killed someone else, too."

"I don't understand," de Graaf said.

"I think I have sent Maggie to die."

"Maggie?"

"I'm sorry. I didn't tell you. I had two girls with me, both from Interpol.
Maggie was one of them. The other is at the Hotel Touring." I gave him
Belinda's name and telephone number. "Contact her for me, will you please?
Tell her to lock her door and stay there till she hears from me and that she
is to ignore any phone or written message that does not contain the word
'Birmingham.' Will you do it personally please?"

"Of course."

I nodded at de Graaf's car. "Can you get through on the radio telephone
to Huyler?"

He shook his head.

"Then police headquarters please." As de Graaf spoke to his driver, a
grim-faced van Gelder came round the corner. He had a handbag with him.

"Astrid Lemay's?" I asked. He nodded. "Give it to me please."

He shook his head firmly. "I can't do that. In case of murder———"

"Give it to him," de Graaf said.

"Thank you." I said to de Graaf: "Five feet four, long black hair, blue
eyes, very good looking, navy skirt and jacket, white blouse and white
handbag. She'll be in the area———"

"One moment." De Graaf leaned towards his driver, then said: "The
lines to Huyler appear to be dead. Death does seem to follow you around,
Major Sherman."

"I'll call you later this morning," I said, and turned for my car.

"I'll come with you," van Gelder said.

"You have your hands full here. Where I'm going I don't want any policeman."

Van Gelder nodded. "Which means you are going to step outside the law."

"I'm already outside the law. Astrid Lemay is dead. Jimmy Duclos is dead. Maggie may be dead. I want to talk to people who make other people dead."

"I think you should give us your gun," van Gelder said soberly.

"What do you expect me to have in my hands when I talk to them. A Bible? To pray for their souls? First you kill me, van Gelder, then you take away the gun."

De Graaf said: "You have information and you are witholding it from us?"

"Yes."

"This is not courteous, wise or legal."

I got into my car. "As for the wisdom, you can judge later. Courtesy and legality no longer concern me."

I started the engine and as I did van Gelder made a move towards me and I heard de Graaf saying: "Leave him be, Inspector, leave him be."

11

I DIDN'T make many friends on the way back out to Huyler but then I wasn't in the mood for making friends. Under normal circumstances, driving in the crazy and wholly irresponsible way I did, I should have been involved in at least half a dozen accidents, all of them serious, but I found that the flashing police light and siren had a near-magical effect in clearing the way in front of me. At distances up to half a mile approaching vehicles or vehicles going in the same direction as I was would slow down or stop, pulling very closely in to the side of the road. I was briefly pursued by a police car that should have known better but the police driver lacked my urgency of motivation and he was clearly and sensibly of the opinion that there was no point in killing himself just to earn his weekly wage. There would be, I knew, an immediate radio alert, but I had no fear of road blocks or any such form of molestation: once the license plate number was received at HQ I'd be left alone.

I would have preferred to complete the journey in another car or by bus, for one quality in which a yellow and red taxi is conspicuously lacking is unobtrusiveness, but haste was more important than discretion. I compromised by driving along the final stretch of the causeway at a comparatively sedate pace: the spectacle of a yellow and red taxi approaching the village at a speed of something in the region of a hundred miles an hour would have given rise to some speculation even among the renownedly incurious Dutch.

I parked the car in the already rapidly filling car park, removed my jacket, shoulder holster and tie, upended my collar, rolled up my sleeves and emerged from the car with my jacket hung carelessly over my left arm: under the jacket I carried my gun with the silencer in place.

The notoriously fickle Dutch weather had changed dramatically for the better. Even as I had left Amsterdam the skies had been clearing and now there were only drifting cotton-wool puffs in an otherwise cloudless sky and the already hot sun was drawing up steam from the houses and adjoining fields. I walked leisurely but not too leisurely towards the building I'd asked Maggie to keep under observation. The door stood wide open now and at intervals I could see people, all women in their traditional costumes, moving around the interior; occasionally one emerged and went into the village, occasionally a man came out with a carton which he would place on a wheelbarrow and trundle into the village. This was the home of a cottage industry of some sort: what kind of industry was impossible to judge from the outside. That it appeared to be an entirely innocuous industry was evidenced by the fact that tourists who occasionally happened by were smilingly invited to come inside and look around. All the ones I saw go inside came out again, so clearly it was the least sinister of places. North of the building stretched an almost unbroken expanse of hayfields and in the distance I could see a group of traditionally dressed matrons tossing hay in the air to dry it off in the morning sun. The men of Huyler, I reflected, seemed to have it made: none of them appeared to do any work at all.

There was no sign of Maggie. I wandered back into the village, bought a pair of tinted spectacles—heavy dark spectacles instead of acting as an aid to concealment tend to attract attention, which is probably why so many people wear them—and a floppy straw hat that I wouldn't have been seen dead in outside Huyler. It was hardly what one could call a perfect disguise, for nothing short of stain could ever conceal the white scars on my face, but at least it helped to provide me with a certain degree of anonymity and I didn't think I looked all that different from scores of other tourists wandering about the village.

Huyler was a small village but when you start looking for someone concerning whose whereabouts you have no idea at all and when that someone may be wandering around at the same time as you are then even the smallest village can become embarrassingly large. As briskly as I could without attracting attention I covered every lane in Huyler and saw no trace of Maggie.

I was in a pretty fair way towards quiet desperation now, ignoring the voice in my mind that told me with numbing certainty that I was too late, and feeling all the more frustrated by the fact that I had to conduct my search with at least a modicum of leisure. I now started on a tour of all the shops and cafés although, if Maggie were still alive and well, I hardly expected to find her in any of those in view of the assignment I had given her. But I couldn't afford to ignore any possibility.

The shops and cafés round the inner harbour yielded nothing—and I covered every one of them. I then moved out in a series of expanding concentric circles, as far as one can assign so geometrical a term to the maze of haphazard lanes that was Huyler. And it was on the outermost of those circles that I found Maggie, finding her alive, well and totally unscathed; my relief was hardly greater than my sense of foolishness.

I found her where I should have thought to find her right away if I had been using my head as she had been. I'd told her to keep the building under surveillance but at the same time to keep in company and she was doing just that. She was inside a large crowded souvenir shop, fingering some of the articles for sale, but not really looking at them: she was looking fixedly, instead, at the large building less than thirty yards away, so fixedly, that she quite failed to notice me. I took a step to go inside the door to speak to her when I suddenly saw something that held me quite still and made me look as fixedly as Maggie was, although not in the same direction.

Trudi and Herta were coming down the street. Trudi, dressed in a sleeveless pink frock and wearing long white cotton gloves, skipped along in her customary childish fashion, her blonde hair swinging, a smile on her face; Herta, clad in her usual outlandish dress, waddled gravely alongside, carrying a large leather bag in her hand.

I didn't stand on the order of my going. I stepped quickly inside the shop; but not in Maggie's direction, whatever else happened I didn't want those two to see me talking to her. Instead I took up a strategic position behind a tall revolving stand of picture postcards and waited for Herta and Trudi to pass by.

They didn't pass by. They passed by the front door, sure enough, but that was as far as they got, for Trudi suddenly stopped, peered through the window where Maggie was standing and caught Herta by the arm. Seconds later she coaxed the plainly reluctant Herta inside the shop, took her arm away from Herta who remained hovering there broodingly like a volcano about to erupt, stepped forward and caught Maggie by the arm.

"I know you," Trudi said delightedly. "I know you!"

Maggie turned and smiled. "I know you too. Hullo, Trudi."

"And this is Herta." Trudi turned to Herta who clearly approved of nothing that was taking place. "Herta, this is my friend Maggie."

Herta scowled in acknowledgment.

Trudi said: "Major Sherman is my friend."

"I know that," Maggie smiled.

"Are you my friend, Maggie?"

"Of course I am, Trudi."

Trudi seemed delighted. "I have lots of other friends. Would you like to see them?" She almost dragged Maggie to the door and pointed. She was pointing to the north and I knew it could be only at the haymakers at the far end of the field. "Look. There they are."

"I'm sure they're very nice friends," Maggie said politely.

A picture postcard hunter edged close to me, as much as to indicate that I should move over and let him have a look; I'm not quite sure what kind of look I gave him but it certainly was sufficient to make him move away very hurriedly.

"They are *lovely* friends," Trudi was saying. She nodded at Herta and indicated the bag she was carrying. "When Herta and I come here we always take them out food and coffee in the morning." She said impulsively: "Come and see them, Maggie," and when Maggie hesitated said anxiously: "You *are* my friend, aren't you?"

"Of course, but——"

"They are such *nice* friends," Trudi said pleadingly. "They are so happy. They make music. If we are very good, they may do the hay dance for us."

"The hay dance?"

"Yes, Maggie. The hay dance. Please, Maggie. You are all my friends. Please come. Just for me, Maggie?"

"Oh very well." Maggie was laughingly reluctant. "Just for you, Trudi. But I can't stay long."

"I *do* like you, Maggie." Trudi squeezed Maggie's arm. "I do like you."

The three of them left. I waited a discreet period of time then moved cautiously out of the shop. They were already fifty yards away, past the building I'd asked Maggie to watch and out into the hayfield. The haymakers were at least six hundred yards away, building their first haystack of the day close in to what looked even at that distance, to be a pretty ancient and decrepit Dutch barn. I could hear the chatter of voices as the three of them moved out over the stubbled hay and all the chatter appeared to come from

Trudi who was back at her usual gambit of gambolling like a spring lamb.
Trudi never walked: she always skipped.

I followed, but not skipping. A hedgerow ran alongside the edge of the
field and I prudently kept this between myself and Herta and the two girls,
trailing thirty or forty yards behind. I've no doubt that my method of locomotion looked almost as peculiar as that of Trudi's because the hedgerow
was less than five feet in height and I spent most of the six hundred yards
bent forward at the hips like a septuagenarian suffering from a bout of
lumbago.

By and by the three of them reached the old barn and sat down on the
west side, in the shadow from the steadily strengthening sun. I got the barn
between them and the haymakers on the one hand and myself on the other,
ran quickly across the intervening space and let myself in by a side door.

I hadn't been wrong about the barn. It must have been at least a century
old and appeared to be in a very dilapidated condition indeed. The floor-
boards sagged, the wooden walls bulged at just about every point where
they could bulge and some of the original air-filtering cracks between the
horizontal planks had warped and widened to the extent that one could
almost put one's head through them.

There was a loft to the barn, the floor of which appeared to be in imminent
danger of collapse: it was rotted and splintered and riddled with woodworm,
even an English house agent would have had difficulty in disposing of the
place on the basis of its antiquity. It didn't look as if it could support an
averagely built mouse far less my weight, but the lower part of the barn was
of little use for observation and, besides, I didn't want to peer out of one of
those cracks in the wall and find someone else peering in about two inches
away, so I reluctantly took the crumbling flight of wooden steps that led up
to the loft.

The loft, the east side of which was still half full of last year's hay, was
every bit as dangerous as it looked but I picked my steps with caution and
approached the west side of the barn. This part of the barn had an even
better selection of gaps between the planks and I eventually located the ideal
one, at least six inches in width and affording an excellent view. I could see
the heads of Maggie, Trudi and Herta directly beneath; I could see the
matrons, about a dozen in all, assiduously and expertly building a haystack,
the tines of their long-handled hayforks gleaming in the sun; I could even
see part of the village itself, including most of the car park. I had a feeling
of unease and could not understand the reason for this: the haymaking scene
taking place out on the field there was as idyllic as even the most bucolic-
minded could have wished to see. I think the odd sense of apprehension
sprang from the least unlikely source, the actual haymakers themselves, for
not even here, in their native setting, did those flowing striped robes, those
exquisitely embroidered dresses and snowy wimple hats appear quite natural. There was a more than faintly theatrical quality about them, an aura of
unreality. I had the feeling, almost, that I was witnessing a play being staged
for my benefit.

About half an hour passed during which the matrons worked away steadily
and the three sitting beneath me engaged in only desultory conversation; it
was that kind of day, warm and still and peaceful, the only sounds being
the swish of the hayforks and the distant murmuring of bees that seems to
make conversation of any kind unnecessary. I wondered if I dared risk a
cigarette and decided I dared; I fumbled in the pocket of my jacket for
matches and cigarettes, laid my coat on the floor with the silenced gun on
top of it and lit the cigarette, careful not to let any of the smoke escape
through the gaps in the planks.

By and by Herta consulted a wrist watch about the size of a kitchen alarm clock and said something to Trudi, who rose, reached down a hand and pulled Maggie to her feet. Together they walked towards the haymakers, presumably to summon them to their morning break, for Herta was spreading a chequered cloth on the ground and laying out cups and unwrapping food from folded napkins.

A voice behind me said: "Don't try to reach for your gun. If you do, you'll never live to touch it."

I believed the voice. I didn't try to reach for my gun.

"Turn round very slowly."

I turned round very slowly. It was that kind of voice.

"Move three paces away from the gun. To your left."

I couldn't see anyone. But I heard him all right. I moved three paces away. To the left.

There was a stirring in the hay on the other side of the loft and two figures emerged: the Reverend Thaddeus Goodbody and Marcel, the snakelike dandy I'd clobbered and shoved in the safe in the Balinova. Goodbody didn't have a gun in his hand but, then, he didn't need one: the blunderbuss Marcel carried in his was as big as two ordinary guns and, to judge from the gleam in the flat black unwinking eyes he was busily searching for the remotest thread of an excuse to use it. Nor was I encouraged by the fact that his gun had a silencer to it: this meant that they didn't care how often they shot me, nobody would hear a thing.

"Most damnably hot in there," Goodbody said complainingly. "And ticklish." He smiled in that fashion that made little children want to take him by the hand. "Your calling leads you into the most unexpected places, I must say, my dear Sherman."

"My calling?"

"Last time I met you, you were, if I remember correctly, purporting to be a taxi driver."

"Ah, that time. I'll bet you didn't report me to the police after all."

"I did have second thoughts about it," Goodbody conceded generously. He walked across to where my gun lay and picked it up distastefully before throwing it into the hay. "Crude, unpleasant weapons."

"Yes, indeed," I agreed. "You now prefer to introduce an element of refinement into your killings."

"As I am shortly about to demonstrate." Goodbody wasn't bothering to lower his voice but he didn't have to, the Huyler matrons were at their morning coffee now and even with their mouths full they all appeared capable of talking at once. Goodbody walked across to the hay, unearthed a canvas bag and produced a length of rope. "Be on the alert, my dear Marcel. If Mr. Sherman makes the slightest move, however harmless it may seem, shoot him. Not to kill. Through the thigh."

Marcel licked his lips. I hoped he wouldn't consider the movement of my shirt, caused by the accelerated pumping of my heart, as one that could be suspiciously interpreted. Goodbody approached circumspectly from the rear, tied the rope firmly round my right wrist, passed it over a rafter and then, after what seemed an unnecessarily lengthy period for adjustment, secured it round my left wrist. My hands were held at the level of my ears. Goodbody brought out another length of rope.

"From my friend Marcel here," Goodbody said conversationally, "I have learned that you have a certain expertise with your hands. It occurs that you might be similarly gifted with your feet." He stooped and fastened my ankles together with an enthusiasm that boded ill for the circulation of my feet. "It further occurs that you might have comment to make on the scene you are about to witness. We would prefer to do without the comment.'' He stuffed a far from clean handkerchief into my mouth and bound it in position with another one. ''Satisfactory, Marcel, you would say?''

Marcel's eyes gleamed. ''I have a message to deliver to Sherman from Mr. Durrell.''

''Now, now, my dear fellow, not so precipitate. Later, later. For the moment, we want our friend to be in full possession of his faculties, eyesight undimmed, hearing unimpaired, the mind at its keenest to appreciate all the artistic nuances of the entertainment we have arranged for his benefit.''

''Of course, Mr. Goodbody,'' Marcel said obediently. He was back at his revolting lip-licking. ''But afterwards——''

''Afterwards,'' Goodbody said generously, ''you may deliver as many messages as you like. But remember—I want him still alive when the barn burns down tonight. It is a pity that we shall be unable to witness it from close quarters.'' He looked genuinely sad. ''You and that charming young lady out there—when they find your charred remains among the embers— well, I'm sure they'll draw their own conclusions above love's careless young dream. Smoking in barns, as you have just done, is a most unwise practice. Most unwise. Goodbye, Mr. Sherman, and I do not mean au revoir. I think I must observe the hay dance from closer range. *Such* a charming old custom, I think you will agree.''

He left, leaving Marcel to his lip-licking. I didn't much fancy being left alone with Marcel, but that was hardly of any importance in my mind at that moment. I twisted and looked through the gap in the planking.

The matrons had finished their coffee and were lumbering to their feet. Trudi and Maggie were directly beneath where I was standing.

''Were the cakes not nice, Maggie?'' Trudi asked. ''And the coffee?''

''Lovely, Trudi, lovely. But I have been too long away. I have shopping to do. I must go now.'' Maggie paused and looked up. ''What's that?''

Two piano accordions had begun to play, softly, gently. I could see neither of the musicians: the sound appeared to come from the far side of the haystack the matrons had just finished building.

Trudi jumped to her feet, clapping her hands excitedly. She reached down and pulled Maggie to hers.

''It's the hay dance!'' Trudi cried, a child having her birthday treat. ''The hay dance! They are going to do the hay dance! They must like you, too, Maggie. They do it for you! You are their friend now.''

The matrons, all of them middle-aged or older, with faces curiously, almost frighteningly lacking in expression began to move with a sort of ponderous precision. Shouldering their hayforks like rifles, they formed a straight line and began to clump heavily to and fro, their beribboned pigtails swinging as the music from the accordions swelled in volume. They pirouetted gravely, then resumed their rhythmic marching to and fro. The straight line, I saw, was now gradually curving into the shape of a half-moon.

''I've never seen a dance like this before.'' Maggie's voice was puzzled. I'd never seen a dance like it either and I knew with a sick and chilling certainty that I would never want to see one again—not, it seemed now, that I would ever have the chance to see one again.

Trudi echoed my thoughts, but their sinister implication escaped Maggie.

''And you will never see a dance like this again, Maggie,'' she said. ''They are only starting. Oh, Maggie, they must like you—see, they want you!''

''Me?''

''Yes, Maggie. They like you. Sometimes they ask me. Today, you.''

"I must go, Trudi."

"Please, Maggie. For a moment. You don't do anything. You just stand facing them. *Please,* Maggie. They will be hurt if you don't do this."

Maggie laughed protestingly resignedly. "Oh, very well."

Seconds later a reluctant and very embarrassed Maggie was standing at the focal point as a semicircle of hayfork-bearing matrons advanced and retreated towards and from her. Gradually the pattern and the tempo of the dance changed and quickened as the dancers now formed a complete circle about Maggie. The circle contracted and expanded, contracted and expanded, the women bowing gravely as they approached most closely to Maggie, then flinging their heads and pigtails back as they stamped away again.

Goodbody came into my line of view, his smile gently amused and kindly as he participated vicariously in the pleasure of the charming old dance taking place before him. He stood beside Trudi, and put a hand on her shoulder; she smiled delightedly up at him.

I felt I was going to be sick. I wanted to look away, but to look away would have been an abandonment of Maggie and I could never abandon Maggie; but God only knew that I could never help her now. There was embarrassment in her face, now, and puzzlement, and more than a hint of uneasiness. She looked anxiously at Trudi through a gap between two of the matrons; Trudi smiled widely and waved in gay encouragement.

Suddenly the accordion music changed. What had been a gently lilting dance tune, albeit with a military beat to it, increased rapidly in volume as it changed into something of a different nature altogether, something that went beyond the merely martial, something that was harsh and primitive and savage and violent. The matrons, having reached their fully expanded circle, were beginning to close in again. From my elevation I could still see Maggie, her eyes wide now and fear showing in her face; she leaned to one side to look almost desperately for Trudi. But there was no salvation in Trudi: her smile had gone now, her cotton-clad hands were clasped tightly together and she was licking her lips slowly, obscenely. I turned to look at Marcel, who was busy doing the same thing; but he still had his gun on me, and watched me as closely as he watched the scene outside. There was nothing I could do.

The matrons were now stamping their way inwards. Their moonlike faces had lost their expressionless quality and were now pitiless, implacable, and the deepening fear in Maggie's eyes gave way to terror, her eyes staring as the music became more powerful, more discordant still. Then abruptly, with military precision, the shoulder-borne pitchforks were brought sweeping down until they were pointed directly at Maggie. She screamed and screamed again but the sound she made was barely audible above the almost insanely discordant crescendo of the accordions. And then Maggie was down and, mercifully, all I could see was the back view of the matrons as their forks time and again jerked high and stabbed down convulsively at something that now lay motionless on the ground. For the space of a few moments I could look no longer. I had to look away, and there was Trudi, her hands opening and closing, her mesmerised entranced face with a hideous animal-like quality to it; and beside her the Reverend Goodbody, his face as benign and gently benevolent as ever, an expression that belied his staring eyes. Evil minds, sick minds that had long since left the borders of sanity far behind.

I forced myself to look back again as the music slowly subsided, losing its primeval atavistic quality. The frenzied activities of the matrons had subsided, the stabbing had ceased and as I watched one of the matrons

turned aside and picked up a forkful of hay. I had a momentary glimpse of
a crumpled figure with a white blouse no longer white lying on the stubble,
then a forkful of hay covered her from sight. Then came another forkful and
another and another, and as the two accordions, soft and gentle and muted
now, spoke nostalgically of old Vienna, they built a haystack over Maggie.
Dr. Goodbody and Trudi, she again smiling and chattering gaily, walked off
arm in arm towards the village.

Marcel turned away from the gap in the planks and sighed. "Dr. Goodbody manages those things so well, don't you think? The flair, the sensitivity, the time, the place, the atmosphere—exquisitely done, exquisitely done."
The beautifully modulated Oxbridge accent emanating from that snake's
head was no less repellent than the context in which the words were used:
he was like the rest of them, quite mad.

He approached me circumspectly from the back, undid the handkerchief
which had been tied round my head and plucked out the filthy lump of cotton
that had been shoved into my mouth. I didn't think that he was being
motivated by any humanitarian considerations, and he wasn't. He said off-
handedly: "When you scream, I want to hear it. I don't think the ladies out
there will pay too much attention."

I was sure they wouldn't. I said: "I'm surprised Dr. Goodbody could
drag himself away." My voice didn't sound like any voice I'd ever used
before: it was hoarse and thick and I'd difficulty in forming the words as if
I'd damaged my larynx.

Marcel smiled. "Dr. Goodbody has urgent things to attend to in Amsterdam. Important things."

"And important things to transport from here to Amsterdam."

"Doubtless." He smiled again and I could almost see his hood distend-
ing. "Classically, my dear Sherman, when a person is in your position and
has lost out and is about to die, it is customary for a person in my position
to explain in loving detail, just where the victim went wrong. But apart from
the fact that your list of blunders is so long as to be tedious to enumerate, I
simply can't be bothered. So let's get on with it, shall we?"

"Get on with what?" Here it comes now, I thought, but I didn't much
care: it didn't seem to matter much any more.

"The message from Mr. Durrell, of course." Pain sliced like a butcher's
cleaver through my head and the side of my face as he slashed the barrel of
his gun across it. I thought my left cheekbone must be broken, but couldn't
be sure; but my tongue told me that two at least of my teeth had been
loosened beyond repair.

"Mr. Durrell," Marcel said happily, "told me to tell you that he doesn't
like being pistol-whipped." He went for the right side of my face this time,
and although I saw and knew it was coming and tried to jerk my head back
I couldn't get out of the way. This one didn't hurt so badly, but I knew I
was badly hurt from the temporary loss of vision that followed the brilliant
white light that seemed to explode just in front of my eyes. My face was on
fire, my head was coming apart, but my mind was strangely clear. Very little
more of this systematic clubbing, I knew, and even a plastic surgeon would
shake his head regretfully; but what really mattered was that with very little
more of this treatment I would lose consciousness, perhaps for hours. There
seemed to be only one hope: to make his clubbing unsystematic.

I spat out a tooth and said: "Pansy."

For some reason this got him. The veneer of civilized urbanity couldn't
have been thicker than an onionskin to begin with and it just didn't slough
off, it vanished in an instant of time and what was left was a mindless

berserker savage who attacked me with the wanton, unreasoning and insensate fury of the mentally unhinged, which he almost certainly was. Blows rained from all directions on my head and shoulders, blows from his gun and blows from his fists, and when I tried to protect myself as best I could with my forearms he switched his insane assault to my body. I moaned, my eyes turned up, my legs turned to jelly and I would have collapsed had I been in a position to; as it was, I just hung limply from the rope securing my wrists.

Two or three more agony-filled seconds elapsed before he recovered himself sufficiently to realise that he was wasting his time: from Marcel's point of view there could be little point in inflicting punishment on a person who was beyond feeling the effects of it. He made a strange noise in his throat which probably indicated disappointment more than anything else, then just stood there breathing heavily. What he was contemplating doing next I couldn't guess for I didn't dare open my eyes.

I heard him move away a little and risked a quick glance from the corner of my eye. The momentary madness was over and Marcel, who was obviously as opportunistic as he was sadistic, had picked up my jacket and was going through it hopefully but unsuccessfully, for wallets carried in the inner breast pocket of a jacket invariably fall out when that jacket is carried over the arm and I'd prudently transferred my wallet with its money, passport and driving licence to my hip pocket. Marcel wasn't long in arriving at the right conclusion for almost immediately I heard his footsteps and felt the wallet being removed from my hip pocket.

He was standing by my side now. I couldn't see him, but I was aware of this. I moaned and swung helplessly at the end of the rope that secured me to the rafter. My legs were trailed out behind me, the upper parts of the toes of my shoes resting on the floor. I opened my eyes, just a fraction.

I could see his feet, not more than a yard from where I was. I glanced up, for the fleeting part of a second. Marcel, with an air of concentration and pleased surprise, was engrossed in the task of translating the very considerable sums of money I carried in my wallet to his own pocket. He held the wallet in his left hand while his gun dangled by the trigger guard, from the crooked middle finger of the same hand. He was so absorbed that he didn't see my hands reach up to get a better purchase on the securing ropes.

I jackknifed my body convulsively forward and upwards with all the hate and the fury and the pain that was in me and I do not think that Marcel ever saw my scything feet coming. He made no sound at all, just jackknifed forward in turn as convulsively as I had done, fell against me and slithered slowly to the floor. He lay there and his head rolled from side to side, whether in unconscious reflex or in the conscious reflex of a body otherwise numbed in a paroxysm of agony, I could not say and was in no way disposed to take chances. I stood upright, took a long step back as far as my bonds would permit and came at him again. I was vaguely surprised that his head still stayed on his shoulders: it wasn't pretty but then I wasn't dealing with pretty people.

The gun was still hooked round the middle finger of his left hand. I pulled it off with the toes of my shoes. I tried to get a purchase on the gun between my shoes but the friction coefficient between the metal and the leather was too low and the gun kept sliding free. I removed my shoes by dragging the heels against the floor and then, a much longer process, my socks by using the same technique. I abraded a fair amount of skin and collected my quota of wooden splinters in so doing, but was conscious of no real sensation of hurt: the pain in my face made other minor irritation insignificant to the point of non-existence.

My bare feet gave me an excellent purchase on the gun. Keeping them tightly clamped together I brought both ends of the rope together and hauled myself up till I reached the rafter. This gave me four feet of slack rope to play with, more than enough. I hung by my left hand, reached down with my right while I doubled up my legs. And then I had the gun in my hand.

I lowered myself to the floor, held the rope pinioning my left wrist taut and placed the muzzle of the gun against it. The first shot severed it as neatly as any knife could have done. I untied all the knots securing me, ripped off the front of Marcel's snow-white shirt to wipe my bloodied face and mouth, retrieved my wallet and money and left. I didn't know whether Marcel was alive or dead, he looked very dead to me but I wasn't interested enough to investigate.

12

IT WAS early afternoon when I got back to Amsterdam and the sun that had looked down on Maggie's death that morning had symbolically gone into hiding. Heavy dark clouds had rolled in from the Zuider Zee. I could have reached the city an hour earlier than I did, but the doctor in the outpatients department of the suburban hospital where I'd stopped by to have my face fixed had been full of questions and annoyed at my insistence that sticking plaster—a large amount of it, admittedly—was all I required at the moment and that the stitching and the swathes of white bandaging could wait until later. What with the plaster and assorted bruises and a half-closed left eye I must have looked like the sole survivor from an express train crash but at least I wasn't bad enough to send young children screaming for their mothers.

I parked the police taxi not far from a hire garage where I managed to persuade the owner to let me have a small black Opel. He wasn't very keen as my face was enough to give rise in anyone's mind to doubts about my past driving record but he let me have it in the end. The first drops of rain were beginning to fall as I drove off, stopped by the police car, picked up Astrid's handbag and two pairs of handcuffs for luck and went on my way.

I parked the car in what was by now becoming a rather familiar side street to me and walked down towards the canal. I poked my head around the corner and as hastily withdrew it again; next time I looked I merely edged an eye round.

A black Mercedes was parked by the door of the church of the American Huguenot Society. Its capacious boot was open and two men were lifting an obviously very heavy box inside; there were already two or three similar boxes deeper inside the boot. One of the men was instantly identifiable as the Reverend Goodbody; the other man, thin, of medium height, clad in a dark suit and with dark hair and a very swarthy face, was as instantly recognisable: the dark and violent man who had gunned down Jimmy Duclos in Schiphol airport. For a moment or two I forgot about the pain in my face. I wasn't positively happy at seeing this man again but I was far from dejected as he had seldom been very far from my thoughts. The wheel, I felt, was coming full circle.

They staggered out from the church with one more box, stowed it away and closed the boot. I headed back for my Opel and by the time I'd brought it down to the canal Goodbody and the dark man were already a hundred yards away in the Mercedes. I followed at a discreet distance.

The rain was falling in earnest now as the black Mercedes headed west and south across the city. Though not yet midafternoon, the sky was as thunderously overcast as if dusk, still some hours away, was falling. I didn't mind, it made for the easiest of shadowing: in Holland it is required that you switch your lights on in heavy rain, and in those conditions one car looked very like the dark shapeless mass of the next.

We cleared the last of the suburbs and headed out into the country. There was no wild element of pursuit or chase about our progress. Goodbody, though driving a powerful car, was proceeding at a very sedate pace indeed, hardly surprising, perhaps, in view of the very considerable weight he was carrying in the boot. I was watching road signs closely and soon I was in no doubt as to where we were heading: I never really had been.

I thought it wiser to arrive at our mutual destination before Goodbody and the dark man did, so I closed up till I was less than twenty yards behind the Mercedes. I had no worry about being recognised by Goodbody in his driving mirror for he was throwing up so dense a cloud of spray that all he could possibly have seen following him was a pair of dipped headlamps. I waited till I could see ahead what seemed to be a straight stretch of road, pulled out and accelerated past the Mercedes. As I drew level Goodbody glanced briefly and incuriously at the car that was overtaking him, then looked as incuriously away again. His face had been no more than a pale blur to me and the rain was so heavy and the spray thrown up by both cars so blinding that I knew it was impossible that he should have recognised me. I pulled ahead and got into the right-hand lane again, not slackening speed.

Three kilometers farther on I came to a right-hand fork which read "KASTEEL LINDEN 1 km." I turned down this and in a minute passed an imposing stone archway with the words "KASTEEL LINDEN " engraved in gilt above it. I carried on for perhaps another two hundred yards, then turned off the road and parked the Opel in a deep thicket.

I was going to get very wet again but I didn't seem to have much in the way of options. I left the car and ran across some thinly wooded grassland till I came to a thick belt of pines that obviously served as some kind of windbreak for a habitation. I made my way through the pines, very circumspectly, and there was the habitation all right: the Kasteel Linden. Oblivious of the rain beating down on my unprotected back I stretched out in the concealment of long grass and some bushes and studied the place.

Immediately before me stretched a circular gravelled driveway which led off to my right to the archway I'd just passed. Beyond the gravel lay the Kasteel Linden itself, a rectangular four-storey building, windowed on the first two stories, embrasured above, with the top turreted and crenellated in the best medieval fashion. Encircling the castle was a continuous moat fifteen feet in width and, according to the guidebook, almost as deep. All that was lacking was a drawbridge, although the chain pulleys for it were still to be seen firmly embedded in the thick masonry of the walls; instead, a flight of about twenty wide and shallow stone steps spanned the moat and led to a pair of massive closed doors, which seemed to be made of oak. To my left, about thirty yards distant from the castle, was a rectangular, one-storeyed building in brick and obviously of fairly recent construction.

The black Mercedes appeared through the gateway, crunched its way onto the gravel and pulled up close to the rectangular building. While Goodbody remained inside the car, the dark man got out and made a complete circuit of the castle; Goodbody never had struck me as the kind of man to take chances. Goodbody got out and together the two men carried the contents of the boot into the building; the door had been locked but obviously Goodbody had the right key for it and not a skeleton either. As they carried the last of the boxes inside the door closed behind them.

I rose cautiously to my feet and moved around behind the bushes until I came to the side of the building. Just as cautiously I approached the Mercedes and looked inside. But there was nothing worthy of remark there—not what I was looking for anyway. With an even greater degree of caution I tiptoed up to a side window of the building and peered inside.

The interior was clearly a combination of workshop, store and display shop. The walls were behung with old-fashioned—or replicas of old-fashioned—pendulum clocks of every conceivable shape, size and design. Other clocks and a very large assortment of parts of other clocks lay on four large worktables, in the process of manufacture or reassembly or reconstruction. At the far end of the room lay several wooden boxes similar to the ones that Goodbody and the dark man had just carried inside; these boxes appeared to be packed with straw. Shelves above these boxes held a variety of other clocks each having lying beside it its own pendulum, chain and weights.

Goodbody and the dark man were working beside these shelves. As I watched, they delved into one of the open boxes and proceeded to bring out a series of pendulum weights. Goodbody paused, produced a paper and proceeded to study it intently. After some time Goodbody pointed at some item on this paper and said something to the dark man who nodded and went on with his work; Goodbody, still studying the paper as he went, passed through a side door and disappeared from sight. The dark man studied another paper and began arranging pairs of identical weights beside each other.

I was beginning to wonder where Goodbody had got to when I found out. His voice came from directly behind me.

"I *am* glad you haven't disappointed me, Mr. Sherman."

I turned round slowly. Predictably, he was smiling his saintly smile and, equally predictably, he had a large gun in his hand.

"No one is indestructible, of course," he beamed, "but you do have a certain quality of resilience, I must confess. It is difficult to underestimate policemen, but I may have been rather negligent in your case. Twice in this one day I had thought I had got rid of your presence, which I must admit, was becoming something of an embarrassment to me. However, I'm sure the third time, for me, will prove lucky. You should have killed Marcel, you know."

"I didn't?"

"Come, come, you must learn to mask your feelings and not let your disappointment show through. He recovered for a brief moment but long enough to attract the attention of the good ladies in the field. But I fear he has a fractured skull and some brain hemorrhaging. He may not survive." He looked at me thoughtfully. "But he appears to have given a good account of himself."

"A fight to the death," I agreed. "Must we stand in the rain?"

"Indeed not." He ushered me into the building at the point of his gun. The dark man looked around with no great surprise: I wondered how long had elapsed since they had the warning message from Huyler.

"Jacques," Goodbody said. "This is Mr. Sherman—*Major* Sherman. I believe he is connected with Interpol or some other such futile organisation."

"We've met," Jacques grinned.

"Of course. How forgetful of me." Goodbody pointed his gun at me while Jacques took mine away.

"Just the one," he reported. He raked the sights across my cheek tearing some of the plaster away and grinned again. "I'll bet that hurts, eh?"

"Restrain yourself, Jacques, restrain yourself," Goodbody admonished. He had his kindly side to him, if he'd been a cannibal he'd probably have knocked you over the head before boiling you alive. "Point his gun at him, will you?" He put his own away. "I must say I never did care for those weapons. Crude, noisy, lacking a certain delicacy——"

"Like hanging a girl from a hook?" I asked. "Or stabbing one to death with pitchforks?"

"Come, come, let us not distress ourselves." He sighed. "Even the best of you people are so clumsy, so obvious. I had, I must confess, expected rather more from you. You, my dear fellow, have a reputation which you've totally failed to live up to. You blunder around. You upset people, fondly imagining you are provoking reactions in the process. You let yourself be seen in all the wrong places. Twice you go to Miss Lemay's flat without taking precautions. You rifle pockets of pieces of paper that were put there for you to discover and there was no need," he added reproachfully, "to kill the waiter in the process. You walk through Huyler in broad daylight—every person on Huyler, my dear Sherman, is a member of my flock. You even left your calling card in the basement of my church night before last—blood. Not that I bear you any ill will for that, my dear fellow—I was in fact contemplating getting rid of Henri who had become rather a liability to me and you solved the problem rather neatly. And what do you think of our unique arrangements here—those are all reproductions for sale——"

"My God," I said. "No wonder the churches are empty."

"Ah! But one *must* savour those moments, don't you think? Those weights there. We measure and weigh them and return at suitable times with replacement weights—like those we brought tonight. Not that our weights are *quite* the same. They have something inside them. Then they're boxed, Customs-inspected, sealed and sent off with official government approval to certain—friends—abroad. One of my better schemes, I always maintain."

Jacques cleared his throat deferentially. "You said you were in a hurry, Mr. Goodbody."

"Ever the pragmatist, Jacques, ever the pragmatist. But you're right, of course. First we attend to our—ah—ace investigator, then to business. See if the coast is clear."

Goodbody distastefully produced his pistol again while Jacques made a quiet reconnaissance. He returned in a few moments, nodding, and they made me precede them out the door, across the gravel and up the steps over the moat to the massive oaken door. Goodbody produced a key of the right size to open the door and we passed inside. We went up a flight of stairs, along a passage and into a room.

It was a very big room indeed, almost literally festooned with hundreds of clocks. I'd never seen so many clocks in one place and certainly, I knew, never so valuable a collection of clocks. All, without exception, were pendulum clocks, some of a very great size, all of great age. Only a very few of them appeared to be working, but, even so, their collective noise was barely below the level of toleration. I couldn't have worked in that room for ten minutes.

"One of the finest collections in the world," Goodbody said proudly as if it belonged to him, "if not the finest. And as you shall see—or hear—they *all* work."

I heard his words but they didn't register. I was staring at the floor, at the man lying there with the long black hair reaching down to the nape of his neck, at the thin shoulder blades protruding through the threadbare jacket. Lying beside him were some pieces of single-core rubber-insulated electrical cable. Close to his head lay a pair of sorbo-rubber-covered earphones.

I didn't have to be a doctor to know that George Lemay was dead.

"An accident," Goodbody said regretfully, "a genuine accident. We did not mean it to happen like this. I fear the poor fellow's system must have been greatly weakened by the privations he has suffered over the years."

"You killed him," I said.

"Technically, in a manner of speaking, yes."

"Why?"

"Because his high-principled sister—who has erroneously believed for years that we have evidence leading to the proof of her brother's guilt as a murderer—finally prevailed upon him to go to the police. So we had to remove them from the Amsterdam scene temporarily—but not, of course, in such a way as to upset you. I'm afraid, Mr. Sherman, that you must hold yourself partly to blame for the poor lad's death. And for that of his sister. And for that of your lovely assistant—Maggie, I think her name was." He broke off and retreated hastily, holding his pistol at arm's length. "Do not throw yourself on my gun. I take it you did not enjoy the entertainment? Neither, I'm sure, did Maggie. And neither, I'm afraid, will your other friend Belinda, who must die this evening. Ah! That strikes deep, I see. You would like to kill me, Mr. Sherman." He was smiling still but the flat staring eyes were the eyes of a madman.

"Yes," I said tonelessly. "I'd like to kill you."

"We have sent her a little note." Goodbody was enjoying himself immensely. "Code word 'Birmingham' I believe. . . . She is to meet you at the warehouse of our good friends Morgenstern and Muggenthaler, who will now be above suspicion forever. Who but the insane would ever contemplate perpetrating *two* such hideous crimes on their own premises? So fitting, don't you think? Another puppet on a chain. Like all the thousands of other puppets throughout the world—hooked and dancing to our tune."

I said: "You know, of course, that you are quite mad?"

"Tie him up," Goodbody said harshly. His urbanity had cracked at last. The truth must have hurt him.

Jacques bound my wrists with the thick rubber-covered flex. He did the same for my ankles, pushed me to one side of the room and attached my wrists by another length of rubber cable to an eyebolt on the wall.

"Start the clocks!" Goodbody ordered. Obediently, Jacques set off around the room starting the pendulums to swing; significantly, he didn't bother about the smaller clocks.

"They all work and they all chime, some most loudly," Goodbody said with satisfaction. He was back on balance again, urbane and unctuous as ever. "These earphones will amplify the sound about ten times. There is the amplifier there and the microphone there, both, as you can see, well beyond your reach. The earphones are unbreakable. In fifteen minutes you will be insane, in thirty minutes unconscious. The resulting coma lasts from eight to ten hours. You will wake up still insane. But you won't wake up. Already beginning to tick and chime quite loudly, aren't they?"

"This is how George died, of course. And you will watch it all happen. Through the top of that glass door, of course. Where it won't be so noisy."

"Regrettably, not all. Jacques and I have some business matters to attend to. But we'll be back for the most interesting part, won't we, Jacques?"

"Yes, Mr. Goodbody," said Jacques, still industriously swinging pendulums.

"If I disappear——"

"Ah, but you won't. I had intended to have you disappear last night in the harbour but that was crude, a panic measure lacking the hallmark of my professionalism. I have come up with a much better idea, haven't I, Jacques?"

"Yes indeed, Mr. Goodbody." Jacques had now almost to shout to make himself heard.

"The point is you're not going to disappear, Mr. Sherman. Oh, dear me, no. You'll be found, instead, only a few minutes after you've drowned."

"Drowned?"

"Precisely. Ah, you think, then the authorities will immediately suspect foul play. An autopsy. And the first thing they see are forearms riddled with injection punctures—I have a system that can make two-hour-old punctures look two months old. They will proceed further and find you full of dope—as you will be. Injected when you are unconscious about two hours before we push you, in your car, into a canal, then call the police. This they will not believe. Sherman, the intrepid Interpol narcotics investigator? Then they go through your luggage. Hypodermics, needles, heroin in your pockets, traces of cannabis. Sad, sad. Who would have thought it? Just another of those who hunted with the hounds and ran with the hare."

"I'll say this much for you," I said, "you're a clever madman."

He smiled which probably meant he couldn't hear me above the increasing clamour of the clocks. He clamped the sorbo-rubber earphones to my head and secured them immovably in position with literally yards of Scotch tape. Momentarily the room became almost hushed—the earphones were acting as temporary sound insulators. Goodbody crossed the room towards the amplifier, smiled at me again and pulled a switch.

I felt as if I had been subjected to some violent physical blow or a severe electrical shock. My whole body arched and twisted in convulsive jerks and I knew what little could be seen of my face under the plaster and Scotch tape must be convulsed in agony. For I was in agony, an agony a dozen times more piercing and unbearable than the best—or the worst—that Marcel had been able to inflict upon me. My ears, my entire head, were filled with this insanely shrieking banshee cacophony of sound. It sliced through my head like white-hot skewers, it seemed to be tearing my brain apart, I couldn't understand why my eardrums didn't shatter, I had always heard and believed that a loud enough explosion of sound, set off close enough to your ears, can deafen you immediately and for life; but it wasn't working in my case. As it obviously hadn't worked in George's case. In my torment I vaguely remembered Goodbody attributing George's death to his weakened physical condition.

I rolled from side to side, an instinctive animal reaction to escape from what is hurting you, but I couldn't roll far, Jacques had used a fairly short length of rubber cable to secure me to the eyebolt and I could roll no more than a couple of feet in either direction. At the end of one roll I managed to focus my eyes long enough to see Goodbody and Jacques, now both outside the room peering at me with interest through the glass-topped door; after a few seconds Jacques raised his left wrist and tapped his watch. Goodbody nodded in reluctant agreement and both men hurried away. I supposed in my blinding sea of pain that they were in a hurry to come back to witness the grand finale.

Thirty minutes before I was unconscious, Goodbody had said. I didn't believe a word of it, nobody could stand up to this for two or three minutes without being broken both mentally and physically. I twisted violently from side to side, tried to smash the earphones on the floor or to tear them free. But Goodbody had been right, the earphones *were* unbreakable and the Scotch tape had been so skilfully and tightly applied that my efforts to tear the phones free resulted only in reopening the wounds on my face.

The pendulums swung, the clocks ticked, the chimes rang out almost continuously. There was no relief, no letup, not even the most momentary respite from this murderous assault on the nervous system that triggered off those uncontrollable epileptic convulsions. It was one continuous electric shock at just below the lethal level and I could now all too easily give credence to tales I had heard of patients undergoing electric shock therapy who had eventually ended up on the operation table for the repair of limbs fractured through involuntary muscular contraction.

I could feel my mind going and, for a brief period, I tried to help the feeling along. Oblivion, anything for oblivion, I'd failed, I'd failed along the line, everything I'd touched had turned to destruction and death. Maggie was dead, Duclos was dead, Astrid was dead and her brother George. Only Belinda was left and she was going to die that night. A grand slam.

And then I knew. I knew I couldn't let Belinda die. That was what saved me, I knew I could not let her die. Pride no longer concerned me, my failure no longer concerned me, the total victory of Goodbody and his evil associates was of no concern to me. They could flood the world with their damned narcotics for all I cared. But I couldn't let Belinda die.

Somehow I pushed myself up till my back was against the wall. Apart from the frequent convulsions, I was vibrating in every limb in my body, not just shaking like a man with the ague, that would have been easily tolerated, but vibrating as a man would have been had he been tied to a giant pneumatic drill. I could no longer focus for more than a second or two, but I did my best to look fuzzily, desperately around to see if there was anything that offered any hope of salvation. There was nothing. Then without warning, the sound in my head abruptly rose to a shattering crescendo—it was probably a big clock near the microphone striking the hour—and I fell sideways as if I'd been hit on the temple by a two-by-four. As my head struck the floor it also struck some projection low down on the skirting board.

My focussing powers were now entirely gone but I could vaguely distinguish objects less than a few inches away and this one was no more than three. It says much for my now almost completely incapacitated mind that it took me several seconds to realise what it was, but when I did I forced myself into a sitting position again. The object was an electrical wall socket.

My hands were bound behind my back and it took me forever to locate and take hold of the two free ends of the electrical cable that held me prisoner. I touched their ends with my fingertips: the wire core was exposed in both cases. Desperately, I tried to force the ends into the sockets—it never occurred to me that it might have been a shuttered plug, although it would have been unlikely in so old a house as this—but my hands shook so much that I couldn't locate them. I could feel consciousness slipping away. I could feel the damned plug, I could feel the sockets with my fingertips but I couldn't match the ends of the wire with the holes. I couldn't see any more, I had hardly any feeling left in my fingers, the pain was beyond human tolerance and I think I was screaming soundlessly in my agony when suddenly there was a brilliant bluish-white flash and I fell sideways to the floor.

How long I lay there unconscious I could not later tell: it must have been at least a matter of minutes. The first thing I was aware of was the incredible glorious silence, not a total silence, for I could still hear the chiming of clocks, but a muffled chiming only for I had blown the right power fuse and the earphones were again acting as insulators. I sat up till I was in a half-reclining position. I could feel blood trickling down my chin and was to find later that I'd bitten through my lower lip; my face was bathed in sweat, my entire body felt as if it had been on the rack. I didn't mind any of it, I was conscious of only one thing: the utter blissfulness of silence. Those lads in the Noise Abatement Society knew what they were about.

The effects of this savage punishment passed off more swiftly than I would have expected, but far from completely: that pain in my head and eardrums and the overall soreness of my body would be with me for quite a long time to come, that I knew. But the effects weren't wearing off quite as quickly as I thought because it took me over a minute to realise that if Goodbody and Jacques came back that moment and found me sitting against the wall with what was unquestionably an idiotic expression of bliss on my face, they wouldn't be indulging in any half measures next time round. I glanced quickly up at the glass-topped door but there were no raised eyebrows in sight yet.

I stretched out on the floor again and resumed my rolling to and fro. I was hardly more than ten seconds too soon, for on my third or fourth roll towards the door I saw Goodbody and Jacques thrust their heads into view. I stepped up my performance, rolled about more violently than ever, arched my body and flung myself so convulsively to and fro that I was suffering almost as much as I had been when I was undergoing the real thing. Every time I rolled towards the door I let them see my contorted face, my eyes either staring wide or screwed tightly shut in agony and I think that my sweat-sheened face and the blood welling from my lip and from one or two of the reopened gashes that Marcel had given must have added up to a fairly convincing spectacle. Goodbody and Jacques were both smiling broadly, although Jacques' expression came nowhere near Goodbody's benign saintliness.

I gave one particularly impressive leap that carried my entire body clear of the ground and as I nearly dislocated my shoulder as I landed I decided that enough was enough—I doubt if even Goodbody really knew the par for the course—and allowed my strugglings and writhings to become feebler and feebler until eventually, after one last convulsive jerk, I lay still.

Goodbody and Jacques entered. Goodbody strode across to switch off the amplifier, smiled beatifically and switched it on again: he had forgotten that his intention was not only to render me unconscious but insane. Jacques, however, said something to him, and Goodbody nodded reluctantly and switched off the amplifier again—perhaps Jacques, activated not by compassion but the thought that it might make it difficult for them if I were to die before they injected the drugs, had pointed this out—while Jacques went around stopping the pendulums of the biggest clocks. Then both came across to examine me. Jacques kicked me experimentally in the ribs but I'd been through too much to react to that.

"Now, now, my dear fellow." I could faintly hear Goodbody's reproachful voice. "I approve your sentiments but no marks, no marks. The police wouldn't like it."

"But look at his face," Jacques protested.

"That's so," Goodbody agreed amicably. "Anyway cut his wrists free—wouldn't do to have gouge marks showing on them when the fire brigade fish him out of the canal; and remove those earphones and hide them." Jacques did both in the space of ten seconds; when he removed the earphones it felt as if my face was coming with it: Jacques had a very cavalier attitude towards Scotch tape.

"As for him"—Goodbody nodded at George Lemay—"dispose of him. You know how. I'll send Maier out to help you bring Sherman in." There was silence for a few moments. I knew he was looking down at me, then he sighed. "Ah, me. Ah, me. Life is but a walking shadow."

With that, Goodbody took himself off. He was humming as he went, and as far as one can hum soulfully, Goodbody was giving as soulful a rendition of "Abide with Me" as ever I had heard. He had a sense of occasion, had the Reverend Goodbody.

Jacques went to a box in the corner of the room, produced half a dozen large pendulum weights and proceeded to thread a piece of rubber cable through their eyelets and attach the cable to George's waist: Jacques was leaving little doubt as to what he had in mind. He dragged George from the room out into the corridor and I could hear the sound of the dead man's heels rubbing along the floor as Jacques dragged him to the front of the castle. I rose, flexed my hands experimentally and followed.

As I neared the doorway I could hear the sound of the Mercedes starting up and getting under way. I looked round the corner. Jacques, with George lying on the floor beside him, had the window open and was giving a sketchy salute: it could only have been to the departing Goodbody.

Jacques turned from the window to attend to George's last rites. Instead he stood there motionless, his face frozen in total shock. I was only five feet from him and I could tell even from his stunned lack of expression that he could tell from mine that he had reached the end of his murderous road. Frantically, he scrabbled for the gun under his arm but for what may well have been the first and was certainly the last time in his life Jacques was too slow, for that moment of paralysed incredulity had been his undoing. I hit him just beneath the ribs as his gun came clear and when he doubled forward wrested the gun from his almost unresisting hand and struck him savagely with it across the temple. Jacques, unconscious on his feet, took one involuntary step back, the window sill caught him behind the legs and he began to topple outwards and backwards in oddly slow motion. I just stood there and watched him go and when I heard the splash and only then, I went to the window and looked out. The roiled waters of the moat were rippling against the bank and the castle walls and from the middle of the moat a stream of bubbles ascended. I looked to the left and could see Goodbody's Mercedes rounding the entrance arch to the castle. By this time, I thought, he should have been well into the fourth verse of "Abide with Me."

I withdrew from the window and walked downstairs. I went out, leaving the door open behind me. I paused briefly on the steps over the moat and looked down and as I did the bubbles from the bottom of the moat gradually became fewer and smaller and finally ceased altogether.

13

I SAT in the Opel, looked at my gun which I'd recovered from Jacques, and pondered. If there was one thing that I had discovered about that gun it was that people seemed to be able to take it from me whenever they felt so inclined. It was a chastening thought but one that carried with it the inescapable conclusion that what I needed was another gun, a second gun, so I brought up Astrid's handbag from under the seat and took out the little Lilliput I had given her. I lifted my left trouser leg a few inches, thrust the little gun barrel downwards, inside my sock and the inside top of my shoe, pulled the sock up and the trouser leg down. I was about to close the bag when I caught sight of the two pairs of handcuffs. I hesitated, for on the form to date the likelihood was that, if I took them with me, they'd end up on my own wrists, but as it seemed too late in the day now to stop taking the chances that I'd been taking all along ever since I'd arrived in Amsterdam I put both pairs in my left-hand jacket pocket and the duplicate keys in my right.

When I arrived back in the old quarter of Amsterdam, having left my usual quota of fist-shaking and police-telephoning motorists behind me, the first shades of early darkness were beginning to fall. The rain had eased, but the wind was steadily gaining in strength, ruffling and eddying the waters of the canals.

I turned into the street where the warehouse was. It was deserted, neither cars nor pedestrians in sight. That is to say, at street level it was deserted: on the third floor of Morgenstern and Muggenthaler's premises, a burly shirt-sleeved character was leaning with his elbows on the sill of an open window and from the way in which his head moved constantly from side to side it was apparent that the savouring of Amsterdam's chilly evening air was not his primary purpose for being there. I drove past the warehouse and made my way up to the vicinity of the dam where I called de Graaf from a public phone box.

"Where have you been?" de Graaf demanded. "What have you been doing?"

"Nothing that would interest you." It must have been the most unlikely statement I'd ever made. "I'm ready to talk now."

"Talk."

"Not here. Not now. Not over the telephone. Can you and van Gelder come to Morgenstern and Muggenthaler's place now?"

"You'll talk there?"

"I promise you."

"We are on our way," de Graaf said grimly.

"One moment. Come in a plain van and park farther along the street. They have a guard posted at one of the windows."

"They?"

"That's what I'm going to talk to you about."

"And the guard?"

"I'll distract him. I'll think up a diversion of some kind."

"I see." De Graaf paused and went on heavily: "On your form to date I shudder to think what form the diversion will take." He hung up.

I went into a local ironmongery store and bought a ball of twine and the biggest Stillson wrench they had on their shelves. Four minutes later I had the Opel parked less than a hundred yards from the warehouse, but not in the same street.

I made my way up the very narrow and extremely ill-lit service alley between the street in which the warehouse stood and the one running parallel to it. The first warehouse I came to on my left had a rickety wooden fire escape that would have been the first thing to burn down in a fire, but that was the first and last. I went at least fifty yards past the building I reckoned to be Morgenstern and Muggenthaler's, and nary another fire escape did I come to: knotted sheets must have been at a premium in that part of Amsterdam.

I went back to the one and only fire escape and made my way up to the roof. I took an instant dislike to this roof as I did to all the other roofs I had to cross to arrive at the one I wanted. All the ridgepoles ran at right angles to the street, the roofs themselves were steeply pitched and treacherously slippery from the rain and, to compound the difficulties, the architects of yesteryear, with what they had mistakenly regarded as the laudable intent of creating a diversity of skyline styles, had craftily arranged matters so that no two roofs were of precisely the same design or height. At first I proceeded cautiously, but caution got me nowhere and I soon developed the only practical method of getting from one ridgepole to the next—running down one steeply pitched roofside and letting the momentum carry me as far as possible up the other side before falling flat and scrabbling the last few feet up on hands and knees. At last I came to what I thought would be the roof I wanted, edged out to street level, leaned out over the gable and peered down.

I was right first time, which made a change for me. The shirt-sleeved sentry, almost twenty feet directly below me, was still maintaining his vigil. I attached one end of the ball of twine securely to the hole in the handle of the Stillson, lay flat so that my arm and the cord would clear the hoisting beam and lowered the Stillson about fifteen feet before starting to swing it in a gentle pendulum arc, which increased with every movement of my hand. I increased it as rapidly as possible for only feet beneath me a bright light shone through the crack between the two loading doors in the top storey and I had no means of knowing how long those doors would remain unopened.

The Stillson, which must have weighed at least four pounds, was now swinging through an arc of almost 90°. I lowered it three more feet and wondered how long it would be before the guard would become puzzled by the soft swish of sound that it must inevitably be making in its passage through the air, but at that moment his attention was fortunately distracted. A blue van had just entered the street and its arrival helped me in two ways: the watcher leaned farther out to investigate this machine and at the same time the sound of its engine covered any intimation of danger from the swinging Stillson above.

The van stopped thirty yards away and the engine died. The Stillson was at the outer limit of its swing. As it started to descend I let the cord slip another couple of feet through my fingers. The guard, suddenly but far too late aware that something was amiss, twisted his head round just in time to catch the full weight of the Stillson on the forehead. He collapsed as if a bridge had fallen on him and slowly toppled backwards out of sight.

The door of the van opened and de Graaf got out. He waved to me. I made two beckoning gestures with my right arm, checked to see that the small gun was still firmly anchored inside my sock and shoe, lowered myself till my stomach was resting on the hoisting beam, then transferred my position till I was suspended by my hands. I took my gun from its shoulder holster, held it in my teeth, swung back, just once, then forward, my left foot reaching for the loading sill, and my right foot kicking the doors open as I reached out my hands to get purchase on the door jambs. I took the gun in my right hand.

There were four of them there, Belinda, Goodbody and the two partners. Belinda, white-faced, struggling, but making no sound, was already clad in a flowing Huyler costume and embroidered bodice, her arms held by the rubicund, jovially good-natured Morgenstern and Muggenthaler whose beamingly avuncular smiles now began to congeal in almost grotesque slow motion: Goodbody, who had had his back to me and had been adjusting Belinda's wimpled headgear to his aesthetic satisfaction, turned round very slowly. His mouth fell slowly open, his eyes widened and the blood drained from his face until it was almost the colour of his snowy hair.

I took two steps into the loft and reached an arm for Belinda. She stared at me for unbelieving seconds then shook off the nerveless hands of Morgenstern and Muggenthaler and came running to me. Her heart was racing like a captive bird's but she seemed otherwise not much the worse for what could have only been the most ghastly experience.

I looked at the three men and smiled as much as I could without hurting my face too much. I said: "Now *you* know what death looks like."

They knew all right. Their faces frozen, they stretched their hands upwards as far as they could. I kept them like that, not speaking, until de Graaf and van Gelder came pounding up the stairs and into the loft. During that time nothing happened. I will swear none of them as much as blinked. Belinda had begun to shake uncontrollably from the reaction, but she managed to smile wanly at me and I knew she would be all right: Paris Interpol hadn't just picked her out of a hat.

De Graaf and van Gelder, both with guns in their hands, looked at the tableau. De Graaf said: "What in God's name do you think you are about, Sherman? Why are those three men——"

"Suppose I explain?" I interrupted reasonably.

"It will require some explanation," van Gelder said heavily. "Three well-known and respected citizens of Amsterdam——"

"Please don't make me laugh," I said. "It hurts my face."

"That too," de Graaf said. "How on earth——"

"I cut myself shaving." That was Astrid's line, really, but I wasn't at my inventive best. "Can I tell it?"

De Graaf sighed and nodded.

"In my way?"

He nodded again.

I said to Belinda: "You know Maggie's dead?"

"I know she's dead." Her voice was a shaking whisper, she wasn't as recovered as I'd thought. "He's just told me. He told me and he smiled."

"It's his Christian compassion shining through. He can't help it. Well," I said to the policemen, "take a good look, gentlemen. At Goodbody. The most sadistically psychopathic killer I've ever met—or heard of, for that matter. The man who hung Astrid Lemay on a hook. The man who had Maggie pitchforked to death in a hayfield in Huyler. The man——"

"You said pitchforked?" de Graaf asked. You could see his mind couldn't accept it.

"Later. The man who drove George Lemay so mad that he killed him. The man who tried to kill me the same way: the man who tried to kill me three times today. The man who puts bottles of gin in the hands of dying junkies. The man who drops people into canals with lead piping wrapped round their waists after God knows what suffering and tortures. Apart from being the man who brings degradation and dementia and death to thousands of crazed human beings throughout the world. By his own admission, the master puppeteer who dangles a thousand hooked puppets from the end of his chains and makes them all dance to his tune. The dance of death."

"It's not possible," van Gelder said. He seemed dazed. "It can't be. Dr. Goodbody? The pastor of——"

"His name is Ignatius Catanelli and he's on our files. An ex-member of an eastern seaboard *Cosa Nostra*. But even the Mafiosi couldn't stomach

him. By their lights they never kill wantonly, only for sound business reasons. But Catanelli killed because he's in love with death. When he was a
little boy he probably pulled the wings off flies. But when he grew up, flies
weren't enough for him. He had to leave the States, for the Mafia offered
only one alternative."

"This—this is fantastic." Fantastic or not the colour still wasn't back in
Goodbody's cheeks. "This is outrageous. This is——"

"Be quiet," I said. "We have your prints and cephalic index. I must say
that he has, in the American idiom, a sweet setup going for him here.
Incoming coasters drop heroin in a sealed and weighted container at a
certain offshore buoy. This is dragged up by barge and taken to Huyler,
where it finds its way to a cottage factory there. This cottage factory makes
puppets, which are then transferred to the warehouse here. What more
natural—except that the very occasional and specially marked puppet contains heroin."

Goodbody said: "Preposterous, preposterous. You can't prove any of
this."

"As I intend to kill you in a minute or two I don't have to prove anything.
Ah yes, he had his organisation, had friend Catanelli. He had everybody
from barrel organ players to strip-tease dancers working for him—a combination of blackmail, money, addiction and the final threat of death made
them all keep the silence of the grave."

"Working for him?" De Graaf was still a league behind me. "In what
way?"

"Pushing and forwarding. Some of the heroin—a relatively small amount—
left here in puppets: some went to the shops, some to the puppet van in the
Vondel Park—and other vans, for all I know. Goodbody's girls went to the
shops and purchased those puppets—which were secretly marked—in perfectly legitimate stores and had them sent to minor heroin suppliers, or
addicts, abroad. The ones in the Vondel Park were sold cheap to the barrel
organ men—they were the connections for the down and outs who were in
so advanced a condition that they couldn't be allowed to appear in respectable places—if, that is to say, you call sleazy dives like the Balinova a
respectable place."

"Then how in God's name did *we* never catch on to any of this?" de
Graaf demanded.

"I'll tell you in a moment. Still about the distribution. An even larger
proportion of the stuff went from here in crates of Bibles—the ones which
our saintly friend here so kindly distributed gratis all over Amsterdam.
Some of the Bibles had hollow centres. The sweet young things that Goodbody here, in the ineffable goodness of his Christian heart, was trying to
rehabilitate and save from a fate worse than death, would turn up at his
services with Bibles clutched in their sweet little hands—some of them,
God help us, fetchingly dressed as nuns—then go away with different Bibles
clutched in their sweet little hands and then peddle the damned stuff in the
night clubs. The rest of the stuff—the *bulk* of the stuff—went to the Kasteel
Linden. Or have I missed something, Goodbody?"

From the expression on his face, it was pretty evident that I hadn't missed
much of importance, but he didn't answer me. I lifted my gun slightly and
said: "Now, I think, Goodbody."

"No one's taking the law into his own hands here!" de Graaf said sharply.

"You can see he's trying to escape," I said reasonably. Goodbody was
standing motionless: he couldn't possibly have reached his fingers up another millimetre.

Then, for the second time that day, a voice behind me said: "Drop that gun, Mr. Sherman."

I turned slowly and dropped my gun. Anybody could take my gun from me. This time it was Trudi, emerging from shadows and only five feet away with a Luger held remarkably steadily in her right hand.

"Trudi!" De Graaf stared at the young happily smiling blonde girl in shocked incomprehension. "What in God's name——" He broke off his words and cried out in pain instead as the barrel of van Gelder's gun smashed down on his wrist. De Graaf's gun clattered to the floor and as he turned to look at the man who struck him de Graaf's eyes held only stupefaction. Goodbody, Morgenstern and Muggenthaler lowered their hands, the last two producing guns of their own from under their jackets: so vastly voluminous was the yardage of cloth required to cover their enormous frames that they, unlike myself, did not require the ingenuity of specialised tailors to conceal the outline of their weapons.

Goodbody produced a handkerchief, mopped a brow which stood in urgent need of mopping and said querulously to Trudi: "You took your time about coming forward, didn't you?"

"Oh, *I enjoyed* it!" She giggled, a happy and carefree sound that would have chilled the blood of a frozen flounder. "I enjoyed every moment of it!"

"A touching pair, aren't they?" I said to de Graaf. "Herself and her saintly pal here. This quality of trusting childlike innocence——"

"Shut up," van Gelder said coldly. He approached, ran his hand over me for weapons, found none. "Sit on the floor. Keep your hands where I can see them. You too, de Graaf."

We did as we were told. I sat cross-legged, my forearms on my thighs, my dangling hands close to my ankles. De Graaf stared at me, his face a mirror for his absolute lack of understanding.

"I was coming to this bit," I said apologetically. "I was just on the point of telling you *why* you've made so little progress yourselves in tracing the source of those drugs. Your trusted lieutenant, Inspector van Gelder, made good and sure that no progress was made."

"Van Gelder." De Graaf, even with all the physical evidence to the contrary before him, still couldn't conceive of a senior police officer's treachery. "How can this be? It *can't* be."

"That's not a lollipop he's pointing at you," I said mildly. "Van Gelder's the boss, van Gelder's the brain. He's the Frankenstein, all right; Goodbody's just the monster that's run out of control. Right, van Gelder?"

"Right!" The baleful glance van Gelder directed at Goodbody didn't augur too well for Goodbody's future, although I didn't believe he had one anyway.

I looked at Trudi without affection. "And as for Little Red Ridinghood, van Gelder, this sweet little mistress of yours——"

"Mistress?" De Graaf was so badly off balance that he no longer even looked stunned.

"You heard. But I think van Gelder has rather fallen out of love with her, haven't you, van Gelder? She has, shall we say, become too much of a psychopathic soulmate for the Reverend here." I turned to de Graaf. "Our little rosebud is no addict. Goodbody knows how to make those marks on her arms look real. He told me so. Her mental age is not eight, it's older than sin itself. And twice as evil."

"I don't know." De Graaf sounded tired. "I don't understand——"

"She served three useful purposes," I said. "With van Gelder having a daughter like that, who would ever doubt that he was a dedicated enemy of drugs and all the evil men who profit by them? She was the perfect go-between for van Gelder and Goodbody—they never made contact, not even on the phone. And, most important, she was the vital link in the drug supply line. She took her puppet out to Huyler, switched it there for one loaded with heroin, took it back to the puppet van in the Vondel Park and switched it again. The van, of course, brought it here when it returned for more supplies. She is a very endearing child, is our Trudi. But she shouldn't have used belladonna to give her eyes that glazed addict look. I didn't catch on at the time, but give me time and clobber me over the head with a two-by-four and eventually I'll catch on to anything. It wasn't the right look, I've talked to too many junkies who had the right look. And then I knew.''

Trudi giggled again and licked her lips. ''Can I shoot him now? In the leg? High up?''

''You're a charming little morsel,'' I said, ''but you should get your priorities right. Why don't you look around you?''

She looked around her. Everybody looked around him. I didn't, I just looked straight at Belinda then nodded almost imperceptibly at Trudi, who was standing between her and the open loading doors. Belinda, in turn, glanced briefly at Trudi and I knew she understood.

''You fools!'' I said contemptuously. ''How do you think I got all my information? I was given it! I was given it by two people who got scared to death and sold you down the river for a free pardon! Morgenstern and Muggenthaler!''

There were some pretty inhuman characters among those present, no doubt about that, but they were all human in their reactions. They all stared in consternation at Morgenstern and Muggenthaler, who stood there with unbelieving eyes and mouths agape and it was with mouths agape that they died, for they were both carrying guns and the gun I now had in my hand was very small and I couldn't afford just to wound them. In the same moment of time Belinda flung herself back against an off-guard Trudi, who staggered backwards, teetered on the edge of the loading sill then fell from sight.

Her thin wailing scream had not yet ended when de Graaf reached up desperately for van Gelder's gun hand, but I'd no time to see how de Graaf made out, for I'd pushed myself to my toes, still in a crouching position, and launched myself in a low dive for Goodbody who was struggling to get his gun out. Goodbody pitched backwards with a crash that spoke well for the basic soundness of the warehouse floors which remained where they were and a second later I'd twisted round behind his back and had him making strange croaking noises in his throat, because I'd my arm hooked around his neck as if I were trying to make the front and back ends meet.

De Graaf was lying on the floor, blood streaming from a cut on his forehead. He was moaning a little. Van Gelder held a struggling Belinda in front of him, using her as a shield, just as I was using Goodbody as a shield. Van Gelder was smiling. Both our guns were pointing at each other.

''I know the Shermans of this world.'' Van Gelder's tone was calm, conversational. ''They'd never risk hurting an innocent person—especially a girl so lovely as this. As for Goodbody there, I don't care if he's shot as full of holes as a colander. I make a point?''

I looked at the right side of Goodbody's face, which was the only part of it I could see. It's colour varied between purple and mauve and whether this was because he was being slowly strangled by me or because of his reaction to his erstwhile partner's ready and callous abandonment of him was difficult to say. Why I looked at him I don't know, the last thought in my mind was to weigh up the respective values of Belinda and Goodbody as hostages: as long as van Gelder had Belinda as a hostage he was safe as a man in a church. Well, any church, that was, except the Reverend Goodbody's.

"You make a point," I said.

"I make another point," van Gelder went on. "You have a popgun there. I have a police Colt." I nodded. "So, my safe-conduct." He began to move towards the head of the stairs, keeping Belinda between us. "There's a blue police van at the foot of the street. My van. I'm taking that. On the way there I'm going to smash the office telephones. If, when I reach the van, I do not see you at the loading door there then I shall no longer require her. You understand?"

"I understand. And if you kill her wantonly, you will never be able to sleep easy again. You know that."

He said "I know that" and disappeared walking backwards down the stairs, dragging Belinda behind him. I paid no attention to his going. I saw de Graaf sitting up and taking a handkerchief to his bleeding forehead, so apparently he was still able to fend for himself. I released my throttling grip on Goodbody's neck, reached over and took his gun away, then, still seated behind him, brought out the handcuffs and secured both his wrists, one to the wrist of the dead Morgenstern, the other to the wrist of the dead Muggenthaler. I then rose, walked round to the front of Goodbody and helped a very shaky de Graaf to a chair. I looked back at Goodbody who was staring at me with a face carved in a rictus of terror. When he spoke his normally deep, pontifical voice almost an insane scream.

"You're not going to leave me like this!"

I surveyed the two massive merchants to whom he was chained.

"You can always tuck one under either arm and make good your escape."

"In God's name, Sherman——"

"You put Astrid on a hook. I told her I would help her and you put her on a hook. You had Maggie pitchforked to death. My Maggie. You were going to hang Belinda on a hook. My Belinda. You're the man who loves death. Try it at close quarters for a change." I moved towards the loading door, checked and looked at him again. "And if I don't find Belinda alive, I'm not coming back."

Goodbody moaned like some stricken animal and gazed with a horrified and shuddering revulsion at the two dead men who made him prisoner. I walked to the loading doors and glanced down.

Trudi was lying spread-eagled on the pavement below. I didn't spare her a second glance. Across the street van Gelder was leading Belinda towards the police van. At the door of the van he turned, looked up, saw me, nodded and opened the door.

I turned away from the loading doors, crossed to the still groggy de Graaf, helped him to his feet and towards the head of the stairs. There, I turned and looked back at Goodbody. His eyes were staring in a fear-crazed face and he was making strange hoarse noises deep in his throat. He looked like a man lost forever in a dark and endless nightmare, a man pursued by fiends and knowing he can never escape.

14

DARKNESS HAD almost fallen on the streets of Amsterdam. The drizzle was only light, but penetratingly cold as it was driven along by the high and gusting wind. In the gaps between the wind-torn clouds the first stars winked palely: the moon was not yet up.

I sat waiting behind the driving wheel of the Opel, parked close to a telephone box. By and by the box door opened and de Graaf, dabbing with his handkerchief at the blood still oozing from the gash on his forehead, came out and entered the car. I glanced up at him interrogatively.

"The area will be completely cordoned within ten minutes. And when I say cordoned, I mean escape-proof. Guaranteed." He mopped some more blood. "But how can you be so sure——"

"He'll be there." I started the engine and drove off. "In the first place, van Gelder will figure it's the last place in Amsterdam we'd ever think of looking for him. In the second place Goodbody, only this morning, removed the latest supply of heroin from Huyler. In one of those big puppets, for a certainty. The puppet wasn't in his car out at the castle, so it *must* have been left in the church. He'd no time to take it anywhere else. Besides, there's probably another fortune of the stuff lying about the church. Van Gelder's not like Goodbody and Trudi. He's not in the game for the kicks. He's in it for the money—and he's not going to pass up all that lively lolly."

"Lolly?"

"Sorry. Money. Maybe millions of dollars worth of the stuff."

"Van Gelder." De Graaf shook his head very slowly. "I can't believe it. A man like that! With a magnificent police record."

"Save your sympathy for his victims," I said harshly. I hadn't meant to speak like that to a sick man but I was still a sick man myself: I doubted whether the condition of my head was even fractionally better than that of de Graaf's. "Van Gelder's worse than any of them. You can at least say for Goodbody and Trudi that their minds were so sick and warped and diseased that they were no longer responsible for their actions. But van Gelder isn't sick that way. He does it all cold-bloodedly for money. He knows the score. He knew what was going on, how his psychopathic pal Goodbody was behaving. And he tolerated it. If he could have kept the racket going on forever, he'd have tolerated Goodbody's lethal aberrations forever." I looked at de Graaf speculatively. "You know that his brother-in-law and wife were killed in a car smash in Curaçao?"

De Graaf paused before replying. "It was not a tragic accident?"

"It was not a tragic accident. We'll never prove it but I'd wager my pension that it was caused by a combination of his brother-in-law, who was a trained security officer, finding out too much about him and van Gelder's desire to be rid of a wife who was coming between him and Trudi—in the days before Trudi's more lovable qualities came to the surface. My point is that the man's an ice-cold calculator, quite ruthless and totally devoid of what we'd regard as normal human feelings."

"You'll never live to collect your pension," de Graaf said sombrely.

"Maybe not. But I was right about one thing." We'd turned into the canal street of Goodbody's church and there, directly ahead, was the plain blue police van. We didn't stop, but drove past it, parked at the door of the church and got out. A uniformed sergeant came down the steps to greet us and any reactions he had caused by the sight of the two crocks in front of him he hid very well.

"Empty, sir," he said. "We've even been up the belfry."

De Graaf turned away and looked at the blue van.

"If Sergeant Gropius says there's no one there, then there's no one there." He paused, then said slowly: "Van Gelder's a brilliant man. We know that now. He's not in the church. He's not in Goodbody's house. My men have both sides of the canal and the street sealed off. So, he's not here. He's elsewhere.''

"He's elsewhere, but he's here," I said. "If we don't find him, how long will you keep the cordon in position?''

"Till we've searched and then doubled-checked every house in the street. Two hours, maybe three.''

"And then he could walk away?''

"He could. If he was here.''

"He's here," I said with certainty. "It's Saturday evening. Do the building workers turn out on Sundays?''

"No.''

"So that gives him thirty-six hours. Tonight, even tomorrow night, he comes down and walks away.''

"My head." Again de Graaf dabbed at his wound. "Van Gelder's gun butt was very hard. I'm afraid——''

"He's not down here," I said patiently. "Searching the houses is a waste of time. And I'm damned certain he's not at the bottom of the canal holding his breath all this time. So where can he be?''

I looked speculatively up into the dark and wind-torn sky. De Graaf followed my line of sight. The shadowy outline of the towering crane seemed to reach up almost to the clouds, the tip of its massive horizontal boom lost in the surrounding darkness. The great crane had always struck me as having a weirdly menacing atmosphere about it; tonight—probably because of what I had in mind—it looked awesome and forbidding and sinister to a degree.

"Of course," de Graaf whispered. "Of course.''

I said: "Well then, I'd better be going.''

"Madness! Madness! Look at you, look at your face. You're not well.''

"I'm well enough.''

"Then I'm coming with you," de Graaf said determinedly.

"No.''

"I have young, fit police officers——''

"You haven't the moral right to ask any of your men, young and fit or not, to do this. Don't argue. I refuse. Besides, this is no case for a frontal assault. Secrecy, stealth—or nothing.''

"He's bound to see you." Unwillingly or not, de Graaf was coming round to my point of view.

"Not bound to. From his point of view everything below must be in darkness.''

"We can wait," he urged. "He's bound to come down. Sometime before Monday morning he's bound to come down.''

"Van Gelder takes no delight in death. That we know. But he's totally indifferent to death. That we know also. Lives—other people's lives—mean nothing to him.''

"So?''

"Van Gelder is not down here. But neither is Belinda. So she's up there with him—and when he does come down he'll bring his living shield with him. I won't be long.''

He made no further effort to restrain me. I left him by the church door, crossed into the building lot, reached the body of the crane and began to climb the endless series of diagonally placed ladders located within the lattice framework of the crane. It was a long climb and one that, in my present physical condition, I could well have done without, but there was nothing particularly exhausting or dangerous about it. Just a long and very tiring climb; the dangerous bit still lay ahead. About three quarters of the way up I paused to catch my breath and looked down.

There was no particular impression of height for the darkness was too complete, the faint street lamps along the canal were only pin points of light and the canal itself but a dully gleaming ribbon. It all seemed so remote, so unreal. I couldn't make out the shape of any of the individual houses: all I could discern was the weathercock on the tip of the church steeple and even that was a hundred feet beneath me.

I looked up. The control cabin of the crane was still fifty feet above me, a vaguely seen rectangular darkness against a sky almost as dark. I started to climb again.

Ten feet only separated me from the trap door inset in the floor of the cabin when a gap appeared in the clouds and a low moon shone through, a half-moon only, but the contrasting brightness bathed the yellow-painted crane and its massive boom in an oddly garish flood of light that high-lit every girder and cross member of the structure. It also high-lit me and had the peculiar effect of making me feel, as aircraft pilots feel when being caught in a searchlight, of being pinned to a wall. I looked up again and could see every rivet head in the trap door and the thought occurred to me that if I could see so well upwards anyone inside could see just as well downwards and as the more time spent in that exposed position increased the chances of discovery I took my gun from its holster and crept silently up the last few steps of the ladder. I was less than four feet away when the trap door lifted a little and a long and very ugly-looking gun barrel protruded through the crack. I should, I know, have felt the chagrin and sickness which comes with the despair of the knowledge of ultimate defeat but I'd been through too much that day, I'd used up all my emotions, and I accepted the inevitable with a fatalism that surprised even myself. It wasn't any question of willing submission, give me half a chance and I'd have shot it out with him. But I had no chance at all and I just accepted that.

"This is a twenty-four-shot riot gun," van Gelder said. His voice had a metallically cavernous ring to it with sepulchral overtones that didn't seem at all out of place. "You know what that means?"

"I know what that means."

"Let me have your gun, butt first."

I handed over my gun with the good grace and expertise that came from long experience of handing over guns.

"Now that little gun in your sock."

I handed over the little gun in my sock. The trap door opened and I could see van Gelder quite clearly in the moonlight shining through the cabin windows.

"Come in," he said. "There's plenty of room."

I clambered up into the cabin. As van Gelder had said, there was plenty of room, the cabin could have accommodated a dozen people at a pinch. Van Gelder, his usual calm and unruffled self, carried a shoulder-slung and very unpleasant-looking automatic gun. Belinda sat on the floor in a corner, pale-faced and exhausted with a large Huyler puppet lying beside her. Belinda tried to smile at me but her heart wasn't in it: she had that defenceless and forlorn air about her that nearly had me at van Gelder's throat, gun or no gun, but sanity and a swift estimate of the distance involved made me settle for lowering the trap door gently and straightening up in an equally circumspect manner. I looked at the gun.

"I suppose you got that from the police car?" I said.

"You suppose right."

"I should have checked on that."

"You should." Van Gelder sighed. "I knew you would come, but you've come a long way for nothing. Turn round."

I turned round. The blow that struck the back of my head was delivered with nothing like the vigour and the pride in his handiwork that Marcel had displayed, but it was still enough to stun me for a moment and bring me to my knees. I was vaguely conscious of something cold and metallic encircling my left wrist and when I began to take an active interest in what was going on around me again I found that I was sitting almost shoulder to shoulder with Belinda, handcuffed to her right wrist and with the chain passing through the metal handgrip above the trap door. I rubbed the back of my head tenderly: what with the combined efforts of Marcel and Goodbody and now van Gelder, it had had a rough passage that day and ached abominably just about wherever a head could ache.

"Sorry about the head," van Gelder said. "But I'd as soon have put handcuffs on a conscious tiger. Well, the moon's almost obscured. One minute and I'll be gone. Three minutes and I'll be on terra firma."

I stared at him in disbelief. "You're going down?"

"What else? But not quite in the way you imagine. I've seen the police cordon getting in position—but no one seems to have caught on to the fact that the tip of the crane extends over the canal and at least sixty feet beyond the cordon. I have already lowered the hood to ground level."

My head hurt too much for me to come up with a suitable comment; in the circumstances, there probably was none. Van Gelder slung his gun crosswise over one shoulder and secured the puppet with cord over his other shoulder. Then he said softly: "Ah, the moon is gone."

It was. Van Gelder was only a vaguely seen shadow as he crossed to the door let into the front of the cabin near the control panel, opened it and stepped outside.

"Goodbye, van Gelder," I said. He said nothing. The door closed and we were alone. She caught my handcuffed hand.

"I knew you would come," she whispered, then, with a flash of the old Belinda: "But you did take your time about it, didn't you?"

"It's like I told you—the managerial classes always have things to attend to."

"And did you—did you have to say goodbye to a man like that?"

"I thought I'd better—I'll never see him again. Not alive." I fumbled in my right-hand jacket pocket. "Who would have thought it? Van Gelder, his own executioner."

"Please?"

"It was his idea to lend me a police taxi—so that I would be instantly recognisable and easily tailed wherever I went. I had handcuffs—I used them to secure Goodbody. And keys for the handcuffs. These."

I unlocked the handcuffs, rose and crossed to the front of the cabin. The moon was behind a cloud, true enough, but van Gelder had overestimated the density of the cloud: admittedly, there was no more than a pale wash of light in the sky but enough to let me see van Gelder, about forty feet out now, the tails of his jacket and the gown of the puppet being tugged by the high wind, as he scuttled like a giant crab across the lattice framework of the boom.

My pencil flash was one of the few things that hadn't been taken from me that day. I used it to locate an overhead breaker and pulled the lever down. Lights glowed in the control panel and I studied it briefly. I was aware that Belinda was now standing by my side.

"What are you going to do?" She was back at her whispering again.

"Do I have to explain?"

"No! No! You can't!" I don't think she knew exactly what I intended to do but from what must have been some element of irrevocable finality in my voice she clearly guessed that the results of whatever action I took would be of a very permanent nature. I looked again at van Gelder, who was by now three quarters of the way out towards the tip of the boom, then turned to Belinda and put my hands on her shoulders.

"Look. Don't you know that we can never prove anything against van Gelder? Don't you know he may have destroyed a thousand lives? And don't you know he's carrying enough heroin with him to destroy another thousand?"

"You could turn the boom! So that he comes down inside the police cordon."

"They'll never take van Gelder alive. I know that, you know that, we all know that. And he has a riot gun with him. How many good men do you want to die, Belinda?"

She said nothing and turned away. I looked out again. Van Gelder had reached the tip of the boom and was wasting no time for immediately he swung out and down, wrapped his legs and hands around the cable and started to slide, moving with an almost precipitate haste for which there was ample justification: the cloud band was thinning rapidly and the intensity of light in the sky increasing by the moment.

I looked down and for the first time could see the streets of Amsterdam, but it was no longer Amsterdam, just a toy town with tiny streets and canals and houses, very much like those scaled-down railroad models that one sees in big stores at Christmas time.

I looked behind me. Belinda was sitting on the floor again, her face in her hands: she was making doubly certain that she couldn't see what was going to happen. I looked towards the cable again, and this time I had no difficulty at all in seeing van Gelder clearly, for the moon had come from behind the cloud.

He was about halfway down now, beginning to sway from side to side as the high wind caught at him increasing the arc of his pendulum with the passing of every moment. I reached for a wheel and turned it to the left.

The cable started to ascend, van Gelder ascending with it: astonishment must have momentarily frozen him to the cable. Then he clearly realised what was happening and he started sliding downwards at a much accelerated speed, at least three times that at which the cable was ascending.

I could see the giant hook at the end of the cable now, not forty feet below van Gelder. I centred the wheel again and again van Gelder clung motionless to the cable. I knew I had to do what I had to do but I wanted it over and done as quickly as was humanly possible. I turned the wheel to the right, the cable started to descend at full speed, then abruptly centred the wheel again. I could feel the shuddering jerk as the cable brought up to an abrupt standstill. Van Gelder's grip broke and in that moment I closed my eyes. I opened them, expecting to find an empty cable and van Gelder vanished from sight, but he was still there, no longer clinging to the cable: he was lying, face down, impaled on the giant hook, swaying to and fro in ponderous arcs, fifty feet above the houses of Amsterdam. I turned away, crossed to where Belinda sat, knelt and took her hands from her face. She looked up at me, I had expected to find revulsion in her face, but there was none, only sadness and weariness and that little girl lost expression on her face again.

"It's all over?" she whispered.

"It's all over."

"And Maggie's dead." I said nothing. "Why should Maggie be dead and not me?"

"I don't know, Belinda."

"Maggie was good at her job, wasn't she?"

"Maggie was good."

"And me?" I said nothing. "You don't have to tell me," she said dully. "I should have pushed van Gelder down the stairs in the warehouse, or crashed his van, or pushed him in the canal, or knocked him off the steps on the crane or—or——" She said wonderingly: "He didn't have his gun on me at any time."

"He didn't have to, Belinda."

"You knew?"

"Yes."

"Category Grade 1, Female operative," she said bitterly. "First job in Narcotics——"

"Last job in Narcotics."

"I know." She smiled wanly. "I'm fired."

"That's my girl," I said approvingly. I pulled her to her feet. "At least you know the regulations, or the one that concerns you anyway." She stared at me for a long moment, then the slow smile came for the first time that night. "That's the one," I said. "Married women are not permitted to remain in the service." She buried her face in my shoulder which at least spared her the punishment of having to look at my sadly battered face.

I looked past the blonde head at the world beyond and below. The great hook with its grisly load was swaying wildly now and at the extremity of one of the swings both gun and puppet slipped from van Gelder's shoulders and fell away. They landed on the cobbles on the far side of the deserted canal street, the riot gun and the beautiful puppet from Huyler, over which the shadow, like a giant pendulum of a giant clock, of the cable, the hook and its burden swung in ever increasing arcs across the night skies of Amsterdam.

Caravan to Vaccares

PROLOGUE

THEY HAD come a long way, those gypsies encamped for their evening meal on the dusty greensward by the winding mountain road in Provence. From Transylvania they had come, from the *pustas* of Hungary, from the High Tatra of Czechoslovakia, from the Iron Gate, even from as far away as the gleaming Romanian beaches washed by the waters of the Black Sea. A long journey, hot and stifling and endlessly, monotonously repetitive across the already baking plains of Central Europe or slow and difficult and exasperating and occasionally dangerous in the traversing of the great ranges of mountains that had lain in their way. Above all, one would have thought, even for those nomadic travellers *par excellence,* a tiring journey.

No traces of any such tiredness could be seen in the faces of the gypsies, men, women and children all dressed in their traditional finery, who sat or squatted in a rough semicircle round two glowing coke braziers, listening in quietly absorbed melancholy to the hauntingly soft and nostalgic *tsigane* music of the Hungarian steppes. For this apparent lack of any trace of exhaustion there could have been a number of reasons: as the very large, modern, immaculately finished and luxuriously equipped caravans indicated, the gypsies of today travel in a degree of comfort unknown to their forebears who roamed Europe in the horse-drawn, garishly painted and fiendishly uncomfortable covered-wagon caravans of yesteryear: they were looking forward that night to the certainty of replenishing coffers sadly depleted by their long haul across Europe—in anticipation of this they had already changed from their customary drab travelling clothes: only three days remained until the end of their pilgrimage, for pilgrimage this was: or perhaps they just had remarkable powers of recuperation. Whatever the reason, their faces reflected no signs of weariness, only gentle pleasure and bittersweet memories of faraway homes and days gone by.

But one man there was among them whose expression—or lack of it— would have indicated to even the most obtusely unobservant that, for the moment at least, his lack of musical appreciation was total and his thoughts and intentions strictly confined to the present. His name was Czerda and he was sitting on top of the steps of his caravan, apart from and behind the others, a half-seen shadow on the edge of darkness. Leader of the gypsies and hailing from some unpronounceable village in the delta of the Danube, Czerda was of middle years, lean, tall and powerfully built, with about him that curiously relaxed but instantly identifiable stillness of one who can immediately transform apparent inertia into explosive action. He was dressed all in black and had black hair, black eyes, black moustache and the face of a hawk. One hand, resting limply on his knee, held a long thin smouldering black cigar, the smoke wisping up to his eyes, but Czerda did not seem to notice or care.

429

His eyes were never still. Occasionally he glanced at his fellow gypsies, but only briefly, casually, dismissively. Now and again he looked at the range of the Alpilles, their gaunt forbidding limestone crags sleeping palely in the brilliant moonlight under a star-dusted sky, but for the most part he glanced alternately left and right along the line of parked caravans. Then his eyes stopped roving, although no expression came to replace the habitual stillness of that face. Without haste he rose, descended the steps, ground his cigar into the earth and walked soundlessly to the end of the row of caravans.

The man who stood waiting in the shadows was a youthful scaled-down replica of Czerda himself. Not quite so broad, not quite so tall, his swarthily aquiline features were cast in a mold so unmistakably similar to that of the older man that it was unthinkable that he could be anything other than his son. Czerda, clearly a man not much given to superfluous motion or speech, raised a questioning eyebrow: his son nodded, led him out onto the dusty roadway, pointed and made a downward slicing, chopping motion with his hand.

From where they stood and less than fifty yards away soared an almost vertical massive outcrop of white limestone rock, but an outcrop which has no parallel anywhere in the world, for its base was honeycombed with enormous rectangular entrances, cut by the hand of man, for no feat of nature could possibly have reproduced the sharply geometrical linearity of those apertures in the cliff face: one of those entrances was quite huge, being at least sixty feet in height and no less in width.

Czerda nodded, just once, turned and looked down the road to his right. A vague shape detached itself from shadow and lifted an arm. Czerda returned the salute and pointed towards the limestone bluff. There was no acknowledgment and clearly none was necessary, for the man at once disappeared, apparently into the rock face. Czerda turned to his left, located yet another man in the shadows, made a similar gesture, accepted a torch handed him by his son and began to walk quickly and quietly towards the giant entrance in the cliff face. As they went, moonlight glinted on the knives both men held in their hands, very slender knives, long-bladed and curved slightly at the ends. As they passed through the entrance of the cave they could still distinctly hear the violinists change both mood and tempo and break into the lilting cadences of a gypsy dance.

Just beyond the entrance the interior widened out and heightened until it was like the inside of a great cathedral or a giant tomb of antiquity. Both Czerda and his son switched on their torches, the powerful beams of which failed to penetrate the farthest reaches of this awesome man-made cave, and man-made it unquestionably was, for clearly visible on the towering side walls were the thousands of vertical and horizontal scores where long-dead generations of Provençals had sawn huge blocks of the limestone for building purposes.

The floor of this entrance cavern—for, vast though it was, it was no more than that—was pitted with rectangular holes, some of them large enough to hold a motorcar, others wide and deep enough to bury a house. Scattered in a few odd corners were mounds of rounded limestone rock but, for the most part, the floor looked as if it had been swept only that day. To the right and left of the entrance cavern led off two other huge openings, the darkness lying beyond them total, impenetrable. A doom-laden place, implacable in its hostility, foreboding, menacing, redolent of death. But Czerda and his son seemed unaware of any of this, quite unmoved: they turned and walked confidently towards the entrance to the right-hand chamber.

*   *   *

Deep inside the heart of this vast limestone warren, a slight figure, a barely distinguishable blur in the pale wash of moonlight filtering down through a crack in the cavern roof, stood with his back to a limestone wall, fingers splayed and pressed hard against the clammy rock behind him in the classically frozen position of the fugitive at bay. A youth, no more than twenty, he was clad in dark trousers and a white shirt. Around his neck he wore a silver crucifix on a slender silver chain. The crucifix rose and fell, rose and fell with metronomic regularity as the air rasped in and out of his throat and his heaving lungs tried vainly to satisfy the demands of a body that couldn't obtain oxygen quickly enough. White teeth showed in what could have been a smile but was no smile, although frozen lips drawn back in the rictus of terror can look like one. The nostrils were distended, the dark eyes wide and staring, his face was masked in sweat as if it had been smeared with glycerine. It was the face of a boy with two demons riding on his shoulders: almost at the end of his physical resources, the knowledge of the inevitability of death had triggered off the unreasoning and irrecoverable panic that pushes a man over the edge of the abyss into the mindless depths of madness.

Momentarily, the fugitive's breathing stopped entirely as he caught sight of two dancing pools of light on the floor of the cavern. The wavering beams, steadily strengthening, came from the left-hand entrance. For a moment the young gypsy stood as one petrified, but if reason had deserted him the instinct for survival was still operating independently, for with a harsh sobbing sound he pushed himself off the wall and ran towards the right-hand entrance to the cavern, canvas-soled shoes silent on the rocky floor. He rounded the corner, then slowed down suddenly, reached out groping hands in front of him as he waited for his eyes to become accustomed to the deeper darkness, then moved on slowly into the next cavern, his painfully gasping breathing echoing back in eerie whispers from the unseen walls around him.

Czerda and his son, their torch beams, as they advanced, ceaselessly probing through an arc of 180°, strode confidently through the archway linking the entrance cavern to the one just vacated by the fugitive. At a gesture from Czerda, both men stopped and deliberately searched out the farthermost recesses of the cavern: it was quite empty. Czerda nodded, almost as if in satisfaction, and gave a peculiar, low-pitched two-tone whistle.

In his hiding place, which was no hiding place at all, the gypsy appeared to shrink. His terrified eyes stared in the direction of his imagined source of the whistle. Almost at once, he heard an identical whistle, but one which emanated from another part of this subterranean labyrinth. Automatically, his eyes lined up to search out the source of this fresh menace, then he twisted his head to the right as he heard a third whistle, exactly the same in timbre and volume as the previous two. His staring eyes tried desperately to locate this third danger, but there was nothing to be seen but the all-encompassing darkness and no sound at all to break the brooding silence except the far-off keening of the gypsy violins, a far-off reminder of another safer and saner world that served only to intensify the sinister stillness inside that vaulted place of horror.

For a few moments he stood, fear-crazed now and wholly irresolute, then, within the space of as many seconds, the three double whistles came again, but this time they were all closer, much closer, and when he again saw the faint wash of light emanating from the two torches he had seen earlier, he turned and ran blindly in the only direction which seemed to afford a momentary respite, careless or oblivious of the fact that he might run into a limestone wall at any moment. Reason should have told him this but he was now bereft of reason: it was but instinct again, the age-old one that told him that a man does not die before he has to.

He had taken no more than half a-dozen steps when a powerful torch snapped on less than ten yards ahead of him. The fugitive stopped abruptly, staggering but not falling, lowered the forearm that he had flung up in automatic reflex to protect his eyes and stared for the first time, with narrowed eyes, in a barely conscious attempt to identify the extent and immediacy of this fresh danger confronting him, but all his shrinking eyes could make out was the vaguely discernible bulk of the shapeless figure of the man behind the torch. Then slowly, very slowly, the man's other hand came forward until it was brightly lit by the beam of the torch: the hand held an evilly curved knife that glittered brilliantly in the torchlight. Knife and torch began to move slowly forward.

The fugitive whirled around, took two steps, then stopped as abruptly as he had before. Two other torches, knives again showing in their powerful beams, were scarcely farther away than the man behind him. What was so terrifying, so nerve-destroying, about the measured advances of all three was the unhurriedly remorseless certainty.

"Come now, Alexandre," Czerda said pleasantly. "We're all old friends, aren't we? Don't you want to see us any more?"

Alexandre sobbed and flung himself to his right in the direction where the light from the three torches showed the entrance to yet another cavern. Panting as a deer does just before the hounds drag it down, he half-stumbled, half-ran through the entrance. None of his three pursuers made any attempt to cut him off or run after him: they merely followed, again walking with that same purposeful lack of haste.

Inside this third cavern, Alexandre stopped and looked wildly around. A small cavern this time, small enough to let him see that all the walls here were solid, hostilely and uncompromisingly solid, without as much as the tiniest aperture to offer any hope of further flight. The only exit was by the way he had come in and this was the end of the road.

Then the realization gradually penetrated his mind, numbed though it was, that there was something different about this particular cavern. His pursuers with their torches were not yet in sight, so how was it that he could see so well? Not clearly, there wasn't enough light for that, but well enough in contrast with the Stygian darkness of the cavern he had just left behind.

Almost at his feet lay a huge pile of rock and rubble, clearly the result of some massive fall or cave-in in the past. Instinctively, Alexandre glanced upwards. The rubble, piled at an angle of about 40° from the horizontal, didn't seem to have a summit. It just stretched on and on and Alexandre's gradually lifting eyes could see that it stretched upwards for a vertical height of at least sixty feet before it ended. And where it ended it had to end—for there, at the very top, was a circular patch of star-studded sky. That was where the light came from, he dimly realized, from some roof collapse of long ago.

His body was already beyond exhaustion but now some primeval drive had taken over and the body was no longer its own master, in much the same way as his mind had lost control of it. Without a glance to see whether his pursuers were in sight or not, Alexandre flung himself at the great rock pile and began to claw his way upwards.

The rock pile was unstable and dangerous to a degree, a secure footing impossible to obtain, he slid a foot backwards for every eighteen inches of upward progress made, but for all that the momentum induced by this frenzied desperation overcame the laws of gravity and friction co-efficients and he made steady if erratic progress up that impossibly crumbling slope that no man in his normal senses would ever have attempted.

About one-third of the way up, conscious of an increase in the amount of illumination beneath him, he paused briefly and looked downwards. There were three men standing at the foot of the rubble now, lit torches still in their hands. They were gazing up towards him but making no attempt to follow. Oddly enough, their torch beams were not pointing up towards him but were directed towards the floor at their feet. Even had his confused mind been able to register this oddity Alexandre had no time to consider it, for he felt his precarious hand- and footholds giving way beneath him and started scrabbling his way upwards again.

His knees ached abominably, his shins were flayed, his fingernails broken, the palms of his bleeding hands open almost to the bone. But still Alexandre climbed on.

About two-thirds of the way up he was forced to pause a second time not because he chose to but because, for the moment, his bleeding limbs and spent muscles could take him no farther. He glanced downwards and the three men at the foot of the rockfall were as they had been before, immobile, their torches still pointed at their feet, all three gazing upwards. There was an intensity in their stillness, a curious aura of expectancy. Vaguely, some-where deep in the deep befogged recesses of what little was left of his mind, Alexandre wondered why. He turned his head and looked up to the starry sky above and then he understood.

A man, highlit under the bright moon, was seated on the rim of the rockfall. His face was partly in shadow but Alexandre had little difficulty in making out the bushy moustache, the gleam of white teeth. He looked as if he was smiling. Maybe he was smiling. The knife in his left hand was as easily visible as the torch in his right. The man pressed the button of his torch as he came sliding over the rim.

Alexandre's face showed no reaction for he had nothing left to react with. For a few moments he remained immobile as the man with the moustache came sliding down towards him, triggering off a small avalanche of boulders as he came, then tried to fling himself despairingly to one side to avoid the impact and the knife of his pursuer, but because of his frantic haste and the fact that he was now being severely buffeted about the body by the bounding limestone rocks he lost his footing and began to slide helplessly downwards, rolling over and over quite uncontrollably with no hope in the world of stopping himself. So treacherously loose had the surface of the rockfall become that even his pursuer was able to preserve his balance only by taking huge bounding leaps down the rockfall and the volume of the torrent of stones now crashing on to the floor of the cavern was indicated clearly enough by the alacrity with which the three men at the foot of the rockfall moved back at least ten paces. As they did so they were joined by a fourth man who had just come through the cavern entrance, then immediately afterwards by Alexandre's pursuer, whose great leaping steps had taken him past the still tumbling boy.

Alexandre landed heavily on the floor, arms instinctively clutched over his head to protect it from the cascading stones that continued to strike his body for a period of several seconds until the rain of rocks ceased. For as long again he remained dazed, uncomprehending, then he propped himself to his hands and knees before rising shakily to his feet. He looked at the semicircle of five men, each with a knife in hand, closing in inexorably on him and now his mind was no longer uncomprehending. But now he no longer had the look of a hunted animal, for he had already been through all the terrors of death and he was now beyond that. Now, unafraid; for there was nothing left of which to be afraid, he could look into the face of death. He stood there quietly and waited for it to come to him.

Czerda stooped, laid a final limestone rock on top of the mound that had now grown at the foot of the rockfall, straightened, looked at the handiwork of his men and himself, nodded in apparent satisfaction and gestured towards the others to leave the cavern. They left. Czerda took one last look at the oblong mound of stones, nodded again, and followed.

Once outside the entrance cave and into what now appeared to be the intolerably harsh glare of bright moonlight that bathed the Alpilles, Czerda beckoned to his son who slowed his pace and let the others precede them.

Czerda asked quietly: "Any more would-be informers amongst us, do you think, Ferenc?"

"I don't know." Ferenc shrugged his doubt. "Josef and Pauli I do not trust. But who can be sure?"

"But you will watch them, Ferenc, won't you? As you watched poor Alexandre." Czerda crossed himself. "God rest his soul."

"I will watch them, Father." Ferenc dismissed the answer to the question as being too obvious for further elaboration. "We'll be at the hotel inside the hour. Do you think we shall make much money tonight?"

"Who cares what pennies the idle and foolish rich throw our way? Our paymaster is not in that damned hotel, but that damned hotel we have visited for a generation and must keep on visiting." Czerda sighed heavily. "Appearances are all, Ferenc, my son, appearances are all. That you must never forget."

"Yes, Father," Ferenc said dutifully. He hastily stuck his knife out of sight.

Unobtrusively, unseen, the five gypsies made their way back to the encampment and sat down, at a discreet distance from one another, just outside the perimeter of an audience still lost in the sadly happy rapture of nostalgia as the volume and pace of the violin music mounted to a crescendo. The braziers were burning low now, a faint red glow barely visible in the bright moonlight. Then, abruptly and with a splendid flourish, the music ceased, the violinists bowed low and the audience called out their appreciation and clapped enthusiastically, none more so than Czerda who buffeted his palms together as if he had just heard Heifetz giving of his best in Carnegie Hall. But even as he clapped, his eyes wandered, away from the violinists, away from the audience and the gypsy camp, until he was gazing again at the honeycombed face of the limestone cliffs where a cave had so lately become a tomb.

1

THE CLIFF *battlements of Les Baux, cleft and rent as by a giant axe, and the shattered, gaunt and terrible remnants of the ancient fortress itself are the most awesomely desolate of all ruins in Europe. Or so the local guide-*

book said. It went on: *Centuries after its death Les Baux is still an open tomb, a dreadful and dreadfully fitting memorial to a mediaeval city that lived most violently and perished in agony: to look upon Les Baux is to look upon the face of death imperishably carved in stone.*

Well, it was pitching it a bit high, perhaps, guidebooks do tend towards the hyperbolic, but the average uncertified reader of the guide would take the point and turn no somersaults if some wealthy uncle had left him the place in his will. It was indisputably the most inhospitable, barren and altogether uninviting collection of fractured and misshapen masonry in western Europe, a total and awesome destruction that was the work of seventeenth-century demolition squads who had taken a month and heaven alone knew how many tons of gunpowder to reduce Les Baux to its present state of utter devastation: one would have been equally prepared to believe that the same effect had been achieved in a couple of seconds that afternoon with the aid of an atom bomb: an annihilation of the old fortress was as total as that. But people still lived up there, lived and worked and died.

At the foot of the western vertical cliff face of Les Baux lay a very fittingly complementary feature of the landscape which was sombrely and justifiably called the Valley of Hell, partly because of the barren desolation of its setting between the battlements of Les Baux to the east and a spur of the Alpilles to the west, partly because in summertime this deeply sunk gorge, which opened only to the south, could become almost unbearably hot.

But there was one area, right at the northern extremity of this grim cul-de-sac, that was in complete and unbelievably startling contrast to the bleakly forlorn wastes that surrounded it, a green and lovely and luxurious oasis that, in the context, could have been taken straight out of the pages of a fairy tale.

It was, in brief, an hotel, an hotel with gratefully tree-lined precincts, exotically designed gardens and a gleamingly blue swimming pool. The gardens lay to the south, the immaculate pool was in the centre, beyond that a large tree-shaded patio and finally the hotel itself with its architectural ancestry apparently stemming from a cross between a Trappist monastery and a Spanish hacienda. It was, in point of fact, one of the best and—almost by definition—one of the most exclusive and expensive hotel-restaurants in southern Europe.

To the right of the patio, approached by a flight of steps, was a very large forecourt and leading off from this to the south, through an archway in a magnificently sculptured hedge, was a large and rectangular parking area, all the parking places being more than adequately shaded from the hot summer sun by closely interwoven wickerwork roofing.

The patio was discreetly illuminated by all but invisible lights hung in the two large trees which dominated most of the area, overhanging the fifteen tables scattered in expensively sophisticated separation across the stone flags. Even the tables were something to behold. The cutlery gleamed. The crockery shone. The crystal glittered. And one did not have to be told that the food was superb, that the Châteauneuf had ambrosia whacked to the wide: the absorbed silence that had fallen upon the entranced diners could be matched only by the reverential hush one finds in the great cathedrals of the world. But even in this gastronomical paradise there existed a discordant note.

This discordant note weighed about 220 pounds and he talked all the time, whether his mouth was full or not. Clearly, he was distracting all the other guests, he'd have distracted them even if they had been falling en

masse down the north face of the Eiger. To begin with, his voice was
uncommonly loud, but not in the artificial fashion of the *nouveau riche* or
the more impoverished members of the lesser aristocracy who feel it incumbent upon them to call to the attention of the lesser orders the existence of
another and superior strain of Homo sapiens. Here was the genuine article:
he didn't give a damn whether people heard him or not. He was a big man,
tall, broad and heavily built: the buttons anchoring the straining folds of his
double-breasted dinner jacket must have been sewn on with piano wire. He
had black hair, a black moustache, a neatly trimmed goatee beard and a
black-beribboned monocle through which he was peering closely at the large
menu card in his hand. His table companion was a girl in her mid-twenties,
clad in a blue minidress and quite extravagantly beautiful in a rather lan-
guorous fashion. At that moment she was gazing in mild astonishment at
her bearded escort who was clapping his hands imperiously, an action which
resulted in the almost instantaneous appearance of a dark-jacketed restaurant
manager, a white-tied headwaiter and a black-tied assistant waiter.

"*Encore*," said the man with the beard. In retrospect, his gesture of
summoning the waiting staff seemed quite superfluous: they could have
heard him in the kitchen without any trouble.

"Of course." The restaurant manager bowed. "Another *entrecôte* for the
Duc de Croytor. Immediately." The headwaiter and his assistant bowed in
unison, turned and broke into a discreet trot while still less than twelve feet
distant. The blond girl stared at the Duc de Croytor with a bemused expression on her face.

"But, Monsieur le Duc———"

"Charles to you," the Duc de Croytor interrupted firmly. "Titles do not
impress me even although hereabouts I'm referred to as Le Grand Duc, no
doubt because of my impressive girth, my impressive appetite and my vice-
regal manner of dealing with the lower orders. But Charles to you, Lila, my
dear."

The girl, clearly embarrassed, said something in a low voice which apparently her companion couldn't hear for he lost no time in letting his ducal
impatience show through.

"Speak up, speak up! Bit deaf in this ear, you know."

She spoke up. "I mean—you've just *had* an *enormous entrecôte* steak."

"One never knows when the years of famine will strike," Le Grand Duc
said gravely. "Think of Egypt. Ah!"

An impressively escorted headwaiter placed a huge steak before him with
all the ritual solemnity of the presentation of crown jewels except that, quite
clearly, both the waiter and Le Grand Duc obviously regarded the *entrecôte*
as having the edge on such empty baubles any time. An assistant waiter set
down a large ashet of creamed potatoes and another of vegetables while yet
another waiter reverently placed an ice bucket containing two bottles of rosé
on a serving table close by.

"Bread for Monsieur le Duc?" the restaurant manager enquired.

"You know very well I'm on a diet." He spoke as if he meant it, too,
then, clearly as an afterthought, turned to the blond girl. "Perhaps Made-
moiselle Delafont———"

"I couldn't possibly." As the waiters left she gazed in fascination at his
plate. "In twenty seconds———"

"They know my little ways," Le Grand Duc mumbled. "It is difficult to
speak clearly when one's mouth is full of *entrecôte*."

"And I don't." Lila Delafont looked at him speculatively. "I don't know,
for instance, why you should invite me———"

"Apart from the fact that no one ever denies Le Grand Duc anything, four reasons." When you're a Duke you can interrupt without apology. He drained about half a pint of wine and his enunciation improved noticeably. "As I say, one never knows when the years of famine will strike." He eyed her appreciatively so that she shouldn't miss his point. "I knew—I know—your father, the Count Delafont well—my credentials are impeccable. You are the most beautiful girl in sight. And you are alone."

Lila, clearly embarrassed, lowered her voice, but it was no good. By this time the other diners clearly regarded it as *lèse-majesté* to indulge in any conversation themselves while the Duc de Croytor was holding the floor, and the silence was pretty impressive.

"I'm not alone. Nor the most beautiful girl in sight. Neither." She smiled apologetically, as if afraid she had been overheard, and nodded in the direction of a nearby table. "Not while my friend Cecile Dubois is here."

"The girl you were with earlier this evening?"

"Yes."

"My ancestors and I have always preferred blondes." His tone left little room for doubt that brunettes were for the plebs only. Reluctantly, he laid down his knife and fork and peered sideways. "Passable, passable I must say." He lowered his voice to a conspiratorial whisper that couldn't have been heard more than twenty feet away. "Your friend, you say. Then who's that dissipated-looking layabout with her?"

Seated at a table about ten feet away and clearly well within earshot of Le Grand Duc, a man removed his horn-rimmed glasses and folded them with an air of finality: he was conservatively and expensively dressed in grey gabardine, was tall, broad-shouldered, black-haired and just escaped being handsome because of the slightly battered irregularity of his deeply tanned face. The girl opposite him, tall, dark, smiling and with amusement in her green eyes, put a restraining hand on his wrist.

"Please, Mr. Bowman. It's not worth it, is it? Really?"

Bowman looked into the smiling face and subsided. "I am strongly tempted, Miss Dubois, strongly tempted." He reached for his wine but his hand stopped halfway. He heard Lila's voice, disapproving, defensive.

"He looks more like a heavyweight boxer to me."

Bowman smiled at Cecile Dubois and raised his glass.

"Indeed." Le Grand Duc quaffed another half goblet of rosé. "One about twenty years past his prime."

Wine spilled on the table as Bowman set down his glass with a force that should have shattered the delicate crystal. He rose abruptly to his feet, only to find that Cecile, in addition to all her other obviously fine points, was possessed of a set of excellent reflexes. She was on her feet as quickly as he was, had insinuated herself between Bowman and Le Grand Duc's table, took his arm and urged him gently but firmly in the direction of the swimming pool: they looked for all the world like a couple who had just finished dinner and decided to go for a stroll for the digestion's sake. Bowman, though with obvious reluctance, went along with this. He had about him the air of a man for whom the creation of a disturbance with Le Grand Duc would have been a positive pleasure but who drew the line at having street brawls with young ladies.

"I'm sorry." She squeezed his arm. "But Lila *is* my friend. I didn't want her embarrassed."

"Ha! You didn't want *her* embarrassed. Doesn't matter, I suppose, how embarrassed *I* am?"

"Oh, come on. Just sticks and stones, you know. You really don't look the least little bit dissipated to me.'' Bowman stared at her suspiciously, but there was no malicious amusement in her eyes: she was pursing her lips in mock but friendly seriousness. "Mind you, I can see that not everyone would like to be called a layabout. By the way, what *do* you do? Just in case I have to defend you to the Duke—verbally, that is.''

"Hell with the Duke.''

"That's not an answer to my question.''

"And a very good question it is too.'' Bowman paused reflectively, took off his glasses and polished them. "Fact is, I don't do anything.''

They were now at the farther end of the pool. Cecile took her hand away from his arm and looked at him without any marked enthusiasm.

"Do you mean to tell me, Mr. Bowman——''

"Call me Neil. All my friends do.''

"You make friends very easily, don't you?'' she asked with inconsequential illogic.

"I'm like that,'' Bowman said simply.

She wasn't listening or, if she was, she ignored him.

"Do you mean to tell me you never work? You never do anything?''

"Never.''

"You've no job? You've been trained for nothing? You can't do *anything?*''

"Why should I spin and toil?'' Bowman said reasonably. "My old man's made millions. Still making them, come to that. Every other generation should take it easy, don't you think—a sort of recharging of the family batteries. Besides, I don't *need* a job. Far be it from me,'' he finished piously, "to deprive some poor fellow who really needs it.''

"Of all the specious arguments . . . How could I have misjudged a man like that?''

"People are always misjudging me,'' Bowman said sadly.

"Not you. The Duke. His perception.'' She shook her head, but in a way that looked curiously more like an exasperated affection than cold condemnation. "You really are an idle layabout, Mr. Bowman.''

"Neil.''

"Oh, you're incorrigible.'' For the first time, irritation.

"And envious.'' Bowman took her arm as they approached the patio again and because he wasn't smiling she made no attempt to remove it. "Envious of you. Your spirit, I mean. Your year-long economy and thrift. For you two English girls to be able to struggle by here at £200 a week each on your typists' salaries or whatever—''

"Lila Delafont and I are down here to gather material for a book.'' She tried to be stiff but it didn't become her.

"On what?'' Bowman asked politely. "Provençal cookery? Publishers don't pay that kind of speculative advance money. So who picks up the tab? UNESCO? The British Council?'' Bowman peered at her closely through his horn-rimmed glasses but clearly she wasn't the lip-biting kind. "Let's all pay a silent truce to good old Daddy, shall we? A truce, my dear. This is too good to spoil. Beautiful night, beautiful food, beautiful girl.'' Bowman adjusted his spectacles and surveyed the patio. "Your girl friend's not bad either. Who's the slim Jim with her?''

She didn't answer at once, probably because she was momentarily hypnotized by the spectacle of Le Grand Duc holding an enormous balloon glass of rosé in one hand while with the other he directed the activities of a waiter who appeared to be transferring the contents of the dessert trolley onto the plate before him. Lila Delafont's mouth had fallen slightly open.

"I don't know. He says he's a friend of her father." She looked away with some difficulty, saw and beckoned the passing restaurant manager. "Who's the gentlemen with my friend?"

"The Duc de Croytor, madam. A very famous wine-grower."

"A very famous wine-drinker, more like." Bowman ignored Cecile's disapproving look. "Does he come here often?"

"For the past three years at this time."

"The food is especially good at this time?"

"The food, sir, is superb here at any time." The manager wasn't amused. "Monsieur le Duc comes for the annual gypsy festival at Saintes-Maries."

Bowman peered at the Duc de Croyter again. He was spooning down his dessert with a relish matched only by his speed of operation.

"You can see why he has to have an ice bucket," Bowman observed. "To cool down his cutlery. Don't see any signs of gypsy blood there."

"Monsieur le Duc is one of the foremost folklorists in Europe," the manager said severely, adding with a suave sideswipe: "The study of ancient customs, Mr. Bowman. For centuries, now, the gypsies have come from all over Europe, at the end of May, to worship and venerate the relics of Sara, their patron saint. Monsieur le Duc is writing a book about it."

"This place," Bowman said, "is hotching with the most unlikely authors you ever saw."

"I do not understand, sir."

"I understand all right." The green eyes, Bowman observed, could also be very cool. "There's no need—what on earth is that?"

The at first faint then gradually swelling sound of many engines in low gear sounded like a tank regiment on the move. They glanced down towards the forecourt as the first of many gypsy caravans came grinding up the steeply winding slope towards the hotel. Once in the forecourt the leading caravans began arranging themselves in neat rows round the forecourt while others passed through the archway in the hedge towards the parking lot beyond. The racket, and the stench of diesel and petrol fumes, while not exactly indescribable or unsupportable, were in marked contrast to the peaceful luxury of the hotel and disconcerting to a degree, this borne out by the fact that Le Grand Duc had momentarily stopped eating. Bowman looked at the restaurant manager, who was gazing up at the stars and obviously communing with himself.

"Monsieur le Duc's raw material?" Bowman asked.

"Indeed, sir."

"And now? Entertainment? Gypsy violin music? Street roulette? Shooting galleries? Candy stalls? Palm reading?"

"I'm afraid so, sir."

"My God!"

Cecile said distinctly: "Snob!"

"I fear, madam," the restaurant manager said distantly, "that my sympathies lie with Mr. Bowman. But it's an ancient custom and we have no wish to offend either the gypsies or the local people." He looked down at the forecourt again and frowned. "Excuse me, please."

He hurried down the steps and made his way across the forecourt to where a group of gypsies appeared to be arguing heatedly. The main protagonists appeared to be a powerfully built hawk-faced gypsy in his middle forties and a clearly distraught and very voluble gypsy woman of the same age who seemed to be very close to tears.

"Coming?" Bowman asked Cecile.

"What? Down there?"

"Snob!"

"But you said——"

"Idle layabout I may be but I'm a profound student of human nature."

"You mean you're nosy?"

"Yes."

Bowman took her reluctant arm and made to move off, then stepped courteously to one side to permit the passage of a bustling Le Grand Duc, if a man of his build could be said to bustle, followed by a plainly reluctant Lila. He carried a notebook and had what looked to be a folklorist's gleam in his eye. But bent though he was on the pursuit of knowledge he hadn't forgotten to fortify himself with a large red apple at which he was munching away steadily. Le Grand Duc looked like the sort of man who would always get his priorities right.

Bowman, a hesitant Cecile beside him, followed rather more leisurely. When they were halfway down the steps a jeep was detached from the leading caravan, three men piled aboard and the jeep took off down the hill at speed. As Bowman and the girl approached the knot of people where the gypsy was vainly trying to calm the now sobbing woman, the restaurant manager broke away from them and hurried towards the steps. Bowman barred his way.

"What's up?"

"Woman says her son has disappeared. They've sent a search party back along the road."

"Oh?" Bowman removed his glasses. "But people don't disappear just like that."

"That's what I say. That's why I'm calling the police."

He hurried on his way. Cecile, who had followed Bowman without any great show of enthusiasm, said: "What's all the fuss? Why is that woman crying?"

"Her son's disappeared."

"And?"

"That's all."

"You mean that nothing's happened to him?"

"Not that anyone seems to know."

"There could be a dozen reasons. Surely she doesn't have to carry on like that."

"Gypsies," Bowman said by way of explanation. "Very emotional. Very attached to their offspring. Do you have any children?"

She wasn't as calmly composed as she looked. Even in the lamplight it wasn't difficult to see the red touching her cheeks. She said: "That wasn't fair."

Bowman blinked, looked at her and said: "No, it wasn't. Forgive me. I didn't mean it that way. If you had kids and one was missing, would you react like that?"

"I don't know."

"I said I was sorry."

"I'd be worried, of course." She wasn't a person who could maintain anger or resentment for more than a fleeting moment of time. "Maybe I'd be worried stiff. But I wouldn't be so—so violently grief-stricken, so hysterical, well not unless——"

"Unless what?"

"Oh, I don't know. I mean, if I'd reason to believe that—that——"

"Yes?"

"You know perfectly well what I mean?"

"I'll never know what women mean," Bowman said sadly, "but this time I can guess."

They moved on and literally bumped into Le Grand Duc and Lila. The girls spoke and introductions, Bowman saw, were inevitable and in order. Le Grand Duc shook his hand and said, "Charmed, charmed," but it was plain to see that he wasn't in the least bit charmed, it was just that the aristocracy knew how to behave. He hadn't, Bowman noted, the soft flabby hand one might have expected: the hand was hard and the grip that of a strong man carefully not exerting too much pressure.

"Fascinating," he announced. He addressed himself exclusively to the two girls. "Do you know that *all* those gypsies have come from the far side of the Iron Curtain? Hungarian or Romanian, most of them. Their leader, fellow called Czerda—met him last year, that's him with that woman there—has come all the way from the Black Sea."

"But how about frontiers?" Bowman asked. "Especially between East and West."

"Eh? What? Ah?" He finally became aware of Bowman's presence. "They travel without let or hindrance, most of all when people know that they are on their annual pilgrimage. Everyone fears them, thinks that they have the evil eye, that they put spells and curses on those who offend them: the Communists believe it as much as anyone, more, for all I know. Nonsense, of course, sheer balderdash. But it's what people believe that matters. Come, Lila, come. I have the feeling that they are going to prove in a most co-operative mood tonight."

They moved off. After a few paces the Duke stopped and glanced round. He looked in their direction for some time, then turned away, shaking his head. "A pity," he said to Lila in what he probably imagined to be *sotto voce,* "about the colour of her hair." They moved on.

"Never mind," Bowman said kindly. "I like you as you are." She compressed her lips, then laughed. Grudges were not for Cecile Dubois.

"He's right, you know." She took his arm, all was forgiven, and when Bowman was about to point out that the Duke's convictions about the intrinsic superiority of blond hair did not carry with it the stamp of divine infallibility, she went on, gesturing around her: "It really is quite fascinating."

"If you like the atmosphere of circuses and fairgrounds," Bowman said fastidiously, "both of which I will go a long way to avoid, I suppose it is. But I admire experts."

And that the gypsies were unquestionably experts at the particular task on hand was undeniable. The speed and co-ordinated skill with which they assembled their various stalls and other media of entertainment were remarkable. Within minutes and ready for operation they had assembled roulette stands, a shooting gallery, no fewer than four fortunetellers' booths, a food stall, a candy stall, two clothing stalls selling brilliantly hued gypsy clothes and, oddly enough, a large cage of mynah birds clearly possessed of that species' usual homicidal outlook on life. A group of four gypsies, perched on the steps of a caravan, began to play soulful mid-European music on their violins. Already the areas of the forecourt and car park were almost uncomfortably full of scores of people circulating slowly around, guests from the hotel, guests, he supposed, from other hotels, villagers from Les Baux, a good number of gypsies themselves. As variegated a cross-section of humanity as one could hope to find, they shared, for the moment, what appeared to be a marked unanimity of outlook—all, from Le Grand Duc downwards, were clearly enjoying themselves with the notable exception of the restaurant manager who stood on the top of the forecourt steps surveying the scene with the brokenhearted despair and martyred resignation of a Bing watching the Metropolitan being taken over by a hippie festival.

A policeman appeared at the entrance to the forecourt. He was large and red and perspiring freely and clearly regarded the pushing of ancient bicycles up precipitous roads as a poor way of spending a peacefully warm May evening. He propped his bicycle against a wall just as the sobbing gypsy woman put her hands to her face, turned and ran towards a green-and-white-painted caravan.

Bowman nudged Cecile. "Let's just saunter over there and join them, shall we?"

"I will not. It's rude. Besides, gypsies don't like people who pry."

"Prying? Since when is concern about a missing man prying? But suit yourself."

As Bowman moved off the jeep returned, skidding to an unnecessary if highly dramatic stop on the gravel of the court. The young gypsy at the wheel jumped out and ran towards Czerda and the policeman. Bowman wasn't far behind, halting a discreet number of feet away.

"No luck, Ferenc?" Czerda asked.

"No sign anywhere, Father. We searched all the area."

The policeman had a black notebook out. "Where was he last seen?"

"Less than two kilometres back, according to his mother," Czerda said. "We stopped for our evening meal not far from the caves."

The policeman asked Ferenc: "You searched in there?"

Ferenc crossed himself and remained silent. Czerda said: "That's no question to ask and you know it. No gypsy would ever enter those caves. They have an evil reputation. Alexandre—that's the name of the missing boy—would never have gone in there."

The policeman put his book away. "I wouldn't go in there myself. Not at this time of night. The local people believe it's cursed and haunted and—well—I was born here. Tomorrow, when it's daylight——"

"He'll have turned up long before then," Czerda said confidently. "Just a lot of fuss about nothing."

"Then that woman who just left—she is his mother——"

"Yes."

"Then why is she so upset?"

"He's only a boy and you know what mothers are." Czerda half-shrugged in resignation. "I suppose I'd better go and tell her."

He left. So did the policeman. So did Ferenc. Bowman didn't hesitate. He could see where Czerda was going, he could guess where the policeman was heading for—the nearest *estaminet*—so was momentarily interested in the movements of neither. But in Ferenc he was interested, for there was something in the alacrity and purposefulness with which he walked quickly through the archway into the parking lot that bespoke some fixed intent. Bowman followed more leisurely and stopped in the archway.

On the right-hand side of the lot was a row of four fortunetellers' booths, got up in the usual garishly coloured canvas. The first in the row was occupied, a notice said, by a certain Madame Marie-Antoinette who offered a money back if not satisfied guarantee. Bowman went inside immediately, not because of any particular predilection for royalty or parsimony or both, but because just as Ferenc was entering the most distant booth he paused and looked round directly at Bowman and Ferenc's face was stamped with the unmistakably unpleasant characteristics of one whose suspicions could be instantly aroused. Bowman passed inside.

Marie-Antoinette was a white-haired old crone with eyes of polished mahogany and a gin trap for a mouth. She gazed into a cloudy crystal ball that was cloudy principally because it hadn't been cleaned for months, spoke to Bowman encouragingly about the longevity, health, fame and happiness that could not fail to be his, took four francs from him and appeared to go into a coma, a sign Bowman took to indicate that the interview was over. He left. Cecile was standing just outside, swinging her handbag in what could have been regarded as an unnecessarily provocative fashion and looking at him with a degree of speculative amusement perhaps uncalled for in the circumstances.

"Still studying human nature?" she asked sweetly.

"I should never have gone in there." Bowman took off his glasses and peered myopically around. The character running the shooting gallery across the parking lot, a short thick-set lad with the face of a boxer who had had a highly unspectacular career brought to an abrupt end, was regarding him with a degree of interest that verged on the impolite. Bowman put his spectacles back on and looked at Cecile.

"Your fortune?" she enquired solicitously. "Bad news?"

"The worst. Marie-Antoinette says I will be married in two months. She must be wrong."

"And you not the marrying kind," she said sympathetically. She nodded at the next booth, which bore a legend above the entrance. "I think you should ask Madame What's-her-name for a second opinion."

Bowman studied Madame Zetterling's come-on, then looked again across the car park. The gallery attendant appeared to be finding him as fascinating as ever. Bowman followed Cecile's advice and went inside.

Madame Zetterling looked like Marie-Antoinette's elder sister. Her technique was different inasmuch as the tools of her trade consisted of a pack of very greasy playing cards which she shuffled and dealt with a speed and dexterity that would have had her automatically black-balled in any casino in Europe, but the forecast for his future was exactly the same. So was the price.

Cecile was still waiting outside, still smiling. Ferenc was standing now by the archway in the hedge and had clearly taken over the eye-riveting stint from the shooting-stall attendant. Bowman polished his glasses some more.

"God help us," Bowman said. "This is nothing but a matrimonial agency. Extraordinary. Uncanny." He replaced his glasses. Lot's wife had nothing on Ferenc. "Quite incredible, in fact."

"What is?"

"Your resemblance," Bowman said solemnly, "to the person I'm supposed to marry."

"My, my!" She laughed pleasantly and with genuine amusement. "You *do* have an original mind, Mr. Bowman."

"Neil," Bowman said, and without waiting for further advice entered the next booth. In the comparative obscurity of the entrance he looked round in time to see Ferenc shrug his shoulders and move off into the forecourt.

The third fortuneteller made up the cast for the three witches of *Macbeth*. She used tarot cards and ended up by telling Bowman that he would shortly be journeying across the seas where he would meet and marry a raven-haired beauty and when he said he was getting married to a blonde the following month she just smiled sadly and took his money.

Cecile, who now clearly regarded him as the best source of light entertainment around, had a look of frankly malicious amusement on her face.

"What shattering revelations this time?"

Bowman took his glasses off again and shook his head in perplexity: as

far as he could see he was no longer the object of anyone's attention. "I
don't understand. She said: 'Her father was a great seaman, as was his, as
was his.' Doesn't make any kind of sense to me."

It did to Cecile. She touched a switch somewhere and the smile went out.
She stared at Bowman, green eyes full of perplexed uncertainty.

"My father is an admiral," she said slowly. "So was my grandfather.
And great-grandfather. You—you could have found this out."

"Sure, sure. I carry a complete dossier on every girl I'm about to meet
for the first time. Come up to my room and I'll show you my filing cabinets—I carry them about in a pantechnicon. And wait, there's more. I
quote again: 'She has a rose-shaped strawberry birthmark in a place where
it can't be seen'."

"Good God!"

"I couldn't have put it better myself. Hang on. There may be worse yet
to come." Bowman made no excuse and gave no reason for entering the
fourth booth, the only one that held any interest for him, nor was it necessary: the girl was so shaken by what she'd just been told that the oddity of
Bowman's behaviour must have suddenly become of very secondary importance.

The booth was dimly lit, the illumination coming from an anglepoise
lamp with a very low wattage bulb that cast a pool of light on a green baize
table and a pair of hands that lay lightly clasped on the table. Little of the
person to whom the hands belonged could be seen as she sat in shadow with
her head bent but enough to realize that she would never make it as one of
the three witches of *Macbeth* or even as Lady Macbeth herself. This one
was young, with flowing titian hair reaching below her shoulders and gave
the vague impression, although her features were almost indistinguishable,
that she must be quite beautiful: her hands certainly were.

Bowman sat on the chair opposite her and looked at the card on the table
which bore the legend: *Countess Marie le Hobenaut*.

"You really a countess, ma'am?" Bowman asked politely.

"You wish to have your hand read?" Her voice was low, gentle and soft.
No Lady Macbeth: here was Cordelia.

"Of course."

She took his hand in both of hers and bent over it, her head so low that
the titian hair brushed the table. Bowman kept still—it wasn't easy but he
kept still—as two warm tears fell on his hands. With his left hand he twisted
the anglepoise and she put a forearm up to protect her eyes but not before
he had time to see that her face *was* beautiful and that the big brown eyes
were sheened with tears.

"Why is Countess Marie crying?"

"You have a long lifeline——"

"Why are you crying?"

"Please."

"All right. Why are you crying, please?"

"I'm sorry. I—I'm upset."

"You mean I've only got to walk into a place——"

"My young brother is missing."

"Your brother? I know someone's missing. Everyone knows. Alexandre.
But your brother. They haven't found him?"

She shook her head, the titian hair brushing across the table.

"And that's your mother in the big green-and-white caravan?"

A nod this time. She didn't look up.

"But why all the tears? He's only been missing for a little while. He'll
turn up, you'll see."

Again she said nothing. She put her forearms on the table and her head on her forearms and cried silently, her shoulders shaking uncontrollably. Bowman, his face bitter, touched the young gypsy's shoulder, rose and left the booth. But when he emerged the expression on his face was one of dazed bewilderment. Cecile glanced at him in some trepidation.

"Four kids," Bowman said quietly. He took her unresisting arm and led her through the archway towards the forecourt. Le Grand Duc, the blond girl still with him, was talking to an impressively scar-faced and heavily built gypsy dressed in dark trousers and frilled off-white shirt. Bowman ignored Cecile's disapproving frown and halted a few convenient feet away.

"A thousand thanks, Mr. Koscis, a thousand thanks," Le Grand Duc was saying in his most gracious lord-of-the-manor voice. "Immensely interesting, immensely. Come, Lila, my dear, enough is enough. I think we have earned ourselves a drink and a little bite to eat." Bowman watched them make their way towards the steps leading to the patio, then turned and looked consideringly at the green-and-white caravan.

Cecile said: "Don't."

Bowman looked at her in surprise.

"And what's wrong with wanting to help a sorrowing mother? Maybe I can comfort her, help in some way, perhaps even go looking for her missing boy. If more people would be more forthcoming in times of trouble, be more willing to risk a snub——"

"You really are a fearful hypocrite," she said admiringly.

"Besides, there's a technique to this sort of thing. If Le Grand Duc can do it, I can. Still your apprehensions."

Bowman left her there nibbling the tip of a thumb in what did appear to be a very apprehensive manner indeed and mounted the caravan steps.

At first sight the interior appeared to be deserted: then his eyes became accustomed to the gloom and he realized he was standing in an unlighted vestibule leading to the main living quarters beyond, identifiable by a crack of light from an imperfectly constructed doorway and the sound of voices, women's voices.

Bowman took a step through the outer doorway. A shadow detached itself from a wall, a shadow possessed of the most astonishing powers of acceleration and the most painful solidity. It struck Bowman on the breastbone with the top of a head that had the unforgiving consistency of a cement bollard: Bowman made it all the way to the ground without the benefit of even one of the caravan steps. Out of the corner of an eye he was dimly aware of Cecile stepping hurriedly and advisedly to one side, then he landed on his back with a momentarily numbing impact that took care of any little air that the bullethead had left in his lungs in the first place. His glasses went flying off into the middle distance and as he lay there whooping and gasping for the oxygen that wouldn't come the shadow came marching purposefully down the steps. He was short, thickset, unfriendly, had a speech to make and was clearly determined on making it. He stooped, grabbed Bowman by the lapels and hauled him to his feet with an ease that boded ill for things to come.

"You will remember me, my friend." His voice had the pleasant timbre of gravel being decanted from a metal hopper. "You will remember that Hoval does not like trespassers. You will remember that next time Hovel will not use his fists."

From this Bowman gathered that on this occasion Hoval did intend to use his fists and he did. Only one, but it was more than enough. Hoval hit him in the same place and, as far as Bowman could judge from the symptoms transmitted by a now nearly paralyzed midriff, with approximately the same

amount of force. He took half-a-dozen involuntary backward steps and then
came heavily to earth again, this time in a seated position with his hands
splayed out behind him. Hoval dusted off his hands in an unpleasant fashion
and marched back up into the caravan again. Cecile looked around till she
located Bowman's glasses, then came and offered him a helping hand which
he wasn't too proud to accept.

"I think Le Grand Duc must use a different technique," she said gravely.

"There's a lot of ingratitude in this world," Bowman wheezed.

"Isn't there just! Through with studying human nature for the night?"
Bowman nodded, it was easier than speaking. "Then for goodness' sake
let's get out of here. After that, I need a drink."

"What do you think *I* require?" Bowman croaked.

She looked at him consideringly. "Frankly, I think a nanny would be in
order." She took his arm and led him up the steps to the patio. Le Grand
Duc, with a large bowl of fruit before him and Lila by his side, stopped
munching a banana and regarded Bowman with a smile so studiously impersonal as to be positively insulting.

"That was a rousing set-to you had down there," he observed.

"He hit me when I wasn't looking," Bowman explained.

"Ah!" Le Grand Duc said non-committally, then added in a penetrating
whisper when they'd moved on less than half-a-dozen feet: "As I said, long
past his prime." Cecile squeezed Bowman's arm warningly but unnecessarily: he gave her the wan smile of one whose cup is overful and led her to
their table. A waiter brought drinks.

Bowman fortified himself and said: "Well, now. Where shall we live?
England or France?"

"What?"

"You heard what the fortuneteller said."

"Oh, my God!"

Bowman lifted his glass. "To David."

"David?"

"Our eldest. I've chosen his name."

The green eyes regarding Bowman so steadily over the rim of a glass
were neither amused nor exasperated, just very thoughtful. Bowman became very thoughtful himself. It could be that Cecile Dubois was, in that
well-turned phrase, rather more than just a pretty face.

2

CERTAINLY, TWO hours later, no one could have referred to Bowman's as a
pretty face. It could be said in fairness that, owing to various troubles it had
encountered from time to time, it didn't have very much going for it in the
first place but the black stocking mask he'd pulled up almost to the level of
his eyes gave it an even more discouraging look than it normally possessed.

He'd changed his grey gabardine suit for a dark one and his white shirt
for a navy roll-neck pullover. Now he put the spectacles he had worn for
disguise away in his suitcase, switched off the overhead light and stepped
out onto the terrace.

All the bedrooms on that floor opened on to the same terrace. Lights
came from two of them. In the first, the curtains were drawn. Bowman
moved to the door and its handle gave fractionally under his hand. Cecile's

room, he knew: a trusting soul. He moved on to the next lit window, this one uncurtained, and peered stealthily round the edge. A commendable precaution, but superfluous: had he done an Apache war dance outside that window it was doubtful whether either of the two occupants would have noticed or, if they had, would have cared very much. Le Grand Duc and Lila, his black and her blond head very close together, were seated side by side in front of a narrow table: Le Grand Duc, a tray of canapés beside him, appeared to be teaching the girl the rudiments of chess. One would have thought that the customary vis-à-vis position would have been more conducive to rapid learning: but then, Le Grand Duc had about him the look of a man who would always adopt his own strongly original attitude to all that he approached. Bowman moved on.

The moon still rode high but a heavy bar of black cloud was approaching from the far battlements of Les Baux. Bowman descended to the main terrace by the swimming pool but did not cross. The management, it seemed, kept the patio lights burning all night and anyone trying to cross the patio and descend the steps to the forecourt would have been bound to be seen by any gypsy still awake: and that there were gypsies who were just that Bowman did not doubt for a moment.

He took a side path to the left, circled the hotel to the rear and approached the forecourt uphill from the west. He moved very slowly and very quietly on rubber soles and kept to deep shadow. There was, of course, no positive reason why the gypsies should have any watcher posted: but as far as this particular lot were concerned, Bowman felt, there was no positive reason why they shouldn't. He waited till a cloud drifted over the moon and moved into the forecourt.

All but three of the caravans were in darkness. The nearest and biggest of the lit caravans was Czerda's: bright light came from both the half-opened door and a closed but uncurtained side window. Bowman went up to that window like a cat stalking a bird across a sunlit lawn and hitched an eye over the sill.

There were three gypsies seated round a table and Bowman recognized all three: Czerda, his son Ferenc and Koscis, the man whom Le Grand Duc had so effusively thanked for information received. They had a map spread on the table and Czerda, pencil in hand, was indicating something on it and clearly making an explanation of some kind. But the map was on so small a scale that Bowman was unable to make out what it was intended to represent, far less what Czerda was pointing out on it, nor, because of the muffling effect of the closed window, could he distinguish what Czerda was saying. The only reasonable assumption he could make from the scene before him was that whatever it was Czerda was planning it wouldn't be for the benefit of his fellow man. Bowman moved away as soundlessly as he had arrived.

The side window of the second illuminated caravan was open and the curtains only partially drawn. Closing in on this window Bowman could at first see no one in the central portion of the caravan. He moved close, bent forward and risked a quick glance to his right and there, at a small table near the door, two men were sitting playing cards. One of the men was unknown to Bowman but the other he immediately and feelingly recognized as Hoval, the gypsy who had so unceremoniously ejected him from the green-and-white caravan earlier in the night. Bowman wondered briefly why Hoval had transferred himself to the present one and what purpose he had been serving in the green-and-white caravan. From the ache Bowman could still feel in his midriff the answer to that one seemed fairly clear. But why?

Bowman glanced to his left. A small compartment lay beyond an open doorway in a transverse partition. From Bowman's angle of sight nothing was visible in the compartment. He moved along to the next window. The curtains on this one were drawn, but the window itself was partly open from the top, no doubt for ventilation. Bowman moved the curtains very very gently and applied his eye to the crack he had made. The level of illumination inside was very low, the only light coming from the rear of the caravan. But there was enough light to see, at the very front of the compartment, a three-tiered bunk and here lay three men, apparently asleep. Two of them were lying with their faces turned towards Bowman but it was impossible to distinguish their features: their faces were no more than pale blurs in the gloom. Bowman eased the curtains again and headed for the caravan that really intrigued him—the green-and-white one.

The rear door at the top of the caravan steps was open but it was dark inside. By this time Bowman had developed a thing about the unlit vestibules of caravans and gave this one a wide berth. In any event it was the illuminated window halfway down the side of the caravan that held the more interest for him. The window was half-open, the curtains half-drawn. It seemed ideal for some more peeking.

The caravan's interior was brightly lit and comfortably furnished. There were four women there, two on a settee and two on chairs by a table. Bowman recognized the titian-haired Countess Marie with, beside her, the grey-haired woman who had been involved in the altercation with Czerda— Marie's mother and the mother of the missing Alexandre. The two other young women at the table, one auburn-haired and about thirty, the other a slight dark girl with most ungypsy-like cropped hair and scarcely out of her teens, Bowman had not seen before. Although it must have been long past their normal bedtimes, they showed no signs of making any preparations for retiring. All four looked sad and forlorn to a degree: the mother and the dark young girl were in tears. The dark girl buried her face in her hands.

"Oh, God!" She sobbed so bitterly it was difficult to make the words out. "When is it all going to end? *Where* is it all going to end?"

"We must hope, Tina," Countess Marie said. Her voice was dull and totally devoid of hope. "There is nothing else we can do."

"There *is* no hope." The dark girl shook her head despairingly. "You know there's no hope. Oh, God, why did Alexandre have to do it?" She turned to the auburn-haired girl. "Oh, Sara, Sara, your husband warned him only today——"

"He did, he did." This was from the girl called Sara and she sounded no happier than the others. She put her arm round Tina. "I'm so terribly sorry, my dear, so terribly sorry." She paused. "But Marie's right, you know. Where there's life there's hope."

There was silence in the caravan. Bowman hoped, and fervently, that they would break it and break it soon. He had come for information but had so far come across nothing other than the mildly astonishing fact of four gypsies talking in German and not in Romany. But he wanted to learn more and learn it quickly for the prospect of hanging around that brightly illuminated window indefinitely lacked appeal of any kind: there was something in the brooding atmosphere of tragedy inside that caravan and menace outside calculated to instill a degree of something less than confidence in the bystander.

"There is no hope," the grey-haired woman said heavily. She dabbed at her eyes with a handkerchief. "A mother knows."

Marie said: "But, Mother——"

"There's no hope because there's no life," her mother interrupted wearily. "You'll never see your brother again, nor you your fiancé, Tina. I know my son is dead."

There was silence again which was just as well for Bowman for it was then that he heard the all but imperceptible sound of a fractionally disturbed piece of gravel, a sound which probably saved his life.

Bowman whirled round. He'd been right about one thing, anyway: there was menace abroad that night. Koscis and Hoval were frozen in a crouched position less than five feet away. Both men were smiling. Both held long curving knives in their hands and the lamplight gleamed dully off them in a very unpleasant fashion.

They'd been waiting for him, Bowman realized, or someone like him, they'd been keeping tabs on him ever since he'd entered the forecourt or maybe even long before that, they'd just wanted to give him enough rope to hang himself, to prove that he was up to what they would regard as no good—no good for themselves—and, when satisfied, eliminate the source of irritation: their actions, in turn, certainly proved to him that there was something sadly amiss with this caravan heading for Saintes-Maries.

The realization of what had happened was instantaneous and Bowman wasted no time on self-recriminations. There would be a time for those but the time was assuredly not when Koscis and Hoval were standing there taking very little trouble to conceal the immediacy of their homicidal intentions. Bowman lunged swiftly and completely unexpectedly—for a man with a knife does not usually anticipate that one without a knife will indulge in such suicidal practices—towards Koscis, who instinctively drew back, lifting his knife high in self-defence. Prudently enough, Bowman didn't complete his movement, but threw himself to his right and ran across the few intervening yards of forecourt leading to the patio steps.

He heard Koscis and Hoval pounding across the gravel in pursuit. They were saying things, to Bowman unintelligible things, but even in Romany the burden of their remarks was clear. Bowman reached the fourth step on his first bound, checked so abruptly that he almost but didn't quite lose his balance, wheeled round and swung his right foot all in one movement. Koscis it was who had the misfortune to be in the lead: he grunted in agony, the knife flying back from his hand, as he fell backwards on to the forecourt.

Hoval came up the steps as Koscis went down them, his right arm, knife pointing upwards, hooking viciously. Bowman felt the tip of the knife burning along his left forearm and then he'd hit Hoval with a great deal more force than Hoval had earlier hit him, which was understandable enough, for when Hoval had hit him he'd been concerned only with his personal satisfaction: Bowman was concerned with his life. Hoval, too, fell backwards, but he was luckier than Koscis: he fell on top of him.

Bowman pushed up his left sleeve. The wound on the forearm was about eight inches long but, although bleeding quite heavily, was little more than a superficial cut and would close up soon. In the meantime, he hoped it wouldn't incapacitate him too much.

He forgot about that trouble when he saw a new one approaching. Ferenc was running across the forecourt in the direction of the patio steps. Bowman turned, hurried across the patio to the steps leading to the upper terrace and stopped briefly to look back. Ferenc had both Koscis and Hoval on their feet and it was clear that it was only a matter of seconds before all three were on their way.

Three to one and the three with knives. Bowman carried no weapon of any kind and the immediate prospect was uninviting. Three determined men

with knives will always hunt down an unarmed man, especially three men
who appeared to regard the use of knives as second nature. A light still
showed from Le Grand Duc's room. Bowman pulled down his black face
mask and burst through the doorway: he felt he didn't have time to knock.
Le Grand Duc and Lila were still playing chess but Bowman again felt that
he didn't have time to worry about mildly surprising matters of that nature.

"For God's sake, help me hide!" The gasping, he thought, might have
been slightly overdone but in the circumstances it came easily. "They're
after me!"

Le Grand Duc looked in no way perturbed, far less startled. He merely
frowned in ducal annoyance and completed a move.

"Can't you see we're busy?" He turned to Lila who was staring at
Bowman with parted lips and very large rounded eyes. "Careful, my dear,
careful. Your bishop is in great danger." He spared Bowman a cursory
glance, viewing him with distaste. "Who are after you?"

"The gypsies, that's who. Look!" Bowman rolled up his left sleeve.
"They've knifed me!"

The expression of distaste deepened.

"You must have given them some cause for offence."

"Well, I was down there——"

"Enough!" He held up a magisterial hand. "Peeping Toms can expect
no sympathy from me. Leave at once."

"Leave at once? But they'll get me——"

"My dear." Bowman didn't think Le Grand Duc was addressing him and
he wasn't. He patted Lila's knee in a proprietorial fashion. "Excuse me
while I call the management. No cause for alarm, I assure you."

Bowman ran out through the doorway, checked briefly to see if the terrace
was still deserted. Le Grand Duc called: "You might close that door after
you."

"But, Charles——" That was Lila.

"Checkmate," said Le Grand Duc firmly, "in two moves."

There was the sound of footsteps, running footsteps, coming across the
patio to the base of the terrace steps. Bowman moved quickly to the nearest
port in the storm.

Cecile wasn't asleep either. She was sitting up in bed holding a magazine
and attired in some fetching negligee that, in happier circumstances, might
well have occasioned admiring comment. She opened her mouth, whether
in astonishment or the beginning of a shout for help, then closed it again
and listened with surprising calmness as Bowman stood there with his back
to the closed door and told her his story.

"You're making all this up," she said.

Bowman hoisted his left sleeve again, an action which by now he didn't
much like doing as the coagulating blood was beginning to stick wound and
material together.

"Including this?" Bowman asked.

She made a face. "It *is* nasty. But why should they——"

"Ssh!" Bowman had caught the sound of voices outside, voices which
rapidly became very loud. An altercation was taking place and Bowman had
little doubt that it concerned him. He turned the handle of the door and
peered out through a crack not much more than an inch in width.

Le Grand Duc, with Lila watching from the open doorway, was standing
with arms outspread like an overweight traffic policeman, barring the way
of Ferenc, Koscis and Hoval. That they weren't immediately recognizable
as those three was due to the fact that they'd obviously considered it prudent

to take time out to wrap some dirty handkerchiefs or other pieces of cloth about their faces in primitive but effective forms of masks, which explained why Bowman had been given the very brief breathing space he had been.

"This is private property for guests only," Le Grand Duc said sternly.

"Stand aside!" Ferenc ordered.

"Stand aside? I am the Duc de Croytor——"

"You'll be the dead Duc de——"

"How dare you, sir!" Le Grand Duc stepped forward with a speed and co-ordination surprising in a man of his bulk and caught the astonished and completely unprepared Ferenc with a roundhouse right to the chin. Ferenc staggered back into the arms of his companions who had momentarily to support him to prevent his collapse. There was some moments' hesitation then they turned and ran from the terrace, Koscis and Hoval still having to support a very wobbly Ferenc.

"Charles." Lila had her hands clasped in what is alleged to be the classic feminine gesture of admiration. "How brave of you!"

"A bagatelle. Aristocracy versus ruffians—class always tells." He gestured towards his doorway. "Come, we have yet to finish both the chess and the canapés."

"But—but how can you be so calm? I mean, aren't you going to phone? The management? Or the police?"

"What point? They were masked and will be far away by this time. After you."

They went inside and closed their door. Bowman closed his.

"You heard?" She nodded. "Good old Duke. That's taken the heat off for the moment." He reached for the door handle. "Well, thanks for the sanctuary."

"Where are you going?" She seemed troubled or disappointed or both.

"Over the hills and far away."

"In your car?"

"I haven't got one."

"You can take mine. Ours, I mean."

"You mean that?"

"Of course, silly."

"You're going to make me a very happy man one day. But for the car, some other time. Good night."

Bowman closed her door behind him and was almost at his own room when he stopped. Three figures had emerged from the shadows.

"First you, my friend." Ferenc's voice was no more than a whisper, maybe the idea of disturbing the Duke again didn't appeal to him. "Then we attend to the little lady."

Bowman was three paces from his own door and he had taken the first even before Ferenc had stopped talking—people generally assume that you will courteously hear them out—and had taken the third before they had moved, probably because the other two were waiting for the lead from Ferenc and Ferenc's reactions were temporarily out of kilter since his brief encounter with Le Grand Duc. In any event, Bowman had the door shut behind him before Ferenc's shoulder hit it and had the key turned before Ferenc could twist the door handle from his grip.

He spent no time on brow-mopping and self-congratulation but ran to the back of the apartment, opened the window and looked out. The branches of a sufficiently stout tree were less than six feet away. Bowman withdrew his head and listened. Someone was giving the door handle a good going over, then abruptly the sound ceased to be replaced by that of running footsteps.

Bowman waited no longer: if there was one thing that had been learnt from dealing with those men it was that procrastination was uninsurable.

As a piece of arboreal trapeze work there was little to it. He just stood on the sill, half-leaned and half-fell outwards, caught a thick branch, swung into the bole of the tree and slid to the ground. He scrambled up the steep bank leading to the road that encircled the hotel from the rear. At the top he heard a low and excited call behind him and twisted round. The moon was out again and he could clearly see the three of them starting to climb up the bank: it was equally clear that the knives they held in their hands weren't impeding their progress at all.

Before Bowman lay the choice of running downhill or up. Downhill lay open country, uphill lay Les Baux with its winding streets and back alleys and labyrinth of shattered ruins. Bowman didn't hesitate. As one famous heavyweight boxer said of his opponents—this was after he had lured the unfortunates into the ring—"They can run but they can't hide." In Les Baux Bowman could both run and hide. He turned uphill.

He ran up the winding road towards the old village as quickly as the steepness, his wind and the state of his legs would permit. He hadn't indulged in this sort of thing in years. He spared a glance over his shoulder. Neither, apparently, had the three gypsies. They hadn't gained any that Bowman could see: but they hadn't lost any either. Maybe they were just pacing themselves for what they might consider to be a long run that lay ahead: if that were the case, Bowman thought, he might as well stop running now.

The straight stretch of road leading to the entrance to the village was lined with car parks on both sides but there were no cars there and so no place to hide. He passed on through the entrance.

After about another hundred yards of what had already become this gasping lung-heaving run Bowman came to a fork in the road. The fork on the right curved down to the battlemented walls of the village and had every appearance of leading to a cul-de-sac. The one to the left, narrow and winding and very steep, curved upwards out of sight and while he dreaded the prospect of any more of that uphill marathon it seemed to offer the better chance of safety so he took it. He looked behind again and saw that his momentary indecision had enabled his pursuers to make up quite a bit of ground on him. Still running in this same unnerving silence, the knives in their hands glinting rhythmically as their arms pumped to and fro, they were now less than thirty yards distant.

At the best speed he could, Bowman continued up this narrow winding road. He slowed down occasionally to peer briefly and rather desperately into various attractive dark openings on both sides, but mainly to the right, but he knew it was his labouring lungs and leaden legs that told him that those entrances were inviting, his reason told him that those attractions were almost certainly fatal illusions, leading to cul-de-sacs or some other form of trap from which there could be no escape.

And now, for the first time, Bowman could hear behind him the hoarse and gasping breathing of the gypsies. They were clearly in as bad shape as he was himself but when he glanced over his shoulder he realized this was hardly cause for any wild rejoicing, he was hearing them now simply because they were that much closer than they had been: their mouths were open in gasping exertion, their faces contorted by effort and sheened in sweat and they stumbled occasionally as their weakening legs betrayed them on the unsure footing of the cobblestones. But now they were only fifteen yards away, the price Bowman had paid for his frequent examinations of possible places of refuge. But at least their nearness made one decision inevitable for him: there was no point in wasting any further time in searching for hiding places on either side for wherever he went they were bound to see him go and follow. For him the only hope of life lay among the shattered ruins of the ancient fortress of Les Baux itself.

Still pounding uphill he came to a set of iron railings that apparently completely blocked what had now turned from a narrow road into no more than a winding metalled path. I'll have to turn and fight, he thought, I'll have to turn and then it will be all over in five seconds, but he didn't have to turn for there was a narrow gap between the right-hand side of the railing and a desk in an inlet recess in the wall which was clearly the pay box where you handed over your money to inspect the ruins. Even in that moment of overwhelming relief at spotting this gap, two thoughts occurred to Bowman: the first the incongruous one that that was a bloody stupid setup for a pay box where the more parsimoniously minded could slip through at will, the second that this was the place to stand and fight, for they could only squeeze through that narrow entrance one at a time and would have to turn sideways to do so, a circumstance which might well place a swinging foot on a par with a constricted knife arm: or it did seem like a good idea to him until it fortunately occurred that while he was busy trying to kick the knife from the hand of one man the other two would be busy throwing their knives at him through or over the bars of the railing and at a distance of two or three feet it didn't seem very likely that they would miss. And so he ran on, if the plodding, lumbering, stumbling progress that was now all he could raise could be called running.

A small cemetery lay to his right. Bowman thought of the macabre prospect of playing a lethal hide-and-seek among the tombstones and hastily put all thought of the cemetery out of his mind. He ran on another fifty yards, saw before him the open plateau of the Les Baux massif, where there was no place to hide and from which escape could be obtained only by jumping down the vertical precipices which completely enclosed the massif, turned sharply to his left, ran up a narrow path alongside what looked like a crumbling chapel and was soon among the craggy ruins of the Les Baux fortress itself. He looked downhill and saw that his pursuers had fallen back to a distance of about forty yards which was hardly surprising as his life was at stake and their lives weren't. He looked up, saw the moon riding high and serene in a now cloudless sky and swore bitterly to himself in a fashion that would have given great offence to uncounted poets both alive and dead. On a moonless night he could have eluded his pursuers with ease amidst that great pile of awesome ruins.

And that they were awesome was beyond dispute. The contemplation of large masses of collapsed masonry did not rank among Bowman's favourite pastimes but as he climbed, fell, scrambled and twisted among that particular mass of masonry and in circumstances markedly unconducive to any form of aesthetic appreciation there was inexorably borne in upon him a sense of the awful grandeur of the place. It was inconceivable that any ruins anywhere could match those in their wild, rugged yet somehow terrifyingly beautiful desolation. There were mounds of shattered building stones fifty feet high: there were great ruined pillars reaching a hundred feet into the night sky, pillars overlooking vertical cliff faces of which the pillars appeared to be a natural continuation and in some cases were: there were natural stairways in the shattered rock face, natural chimneys in the remnants of those man-made cliffs, there were hundreds of apertures in the rock, some just large enough for a man to squeeze through, others large enough to accommodate a double-decker. There were strange paths let into the natural rock, some man-made, some not, some precipitous, some almost horizontal, some wide enough to bowl along in a coach and four, others narrow and winding enough to have daunted the most mentally retarded of mountain goats. And there were broken, ruined blocks of masonry everywhere, some big as a child's hand, others as large as a suburban house. And it was all white, eerie and dead and white: in that brilliantly cold pale moonlight it was the most chillingly awe-inspiring sight Bowman had ever encountered and not, he reflected, a place that he would willingly have called home. But, here, tonight, he had to live or die.

Or they had to live or die, Ferenc and Koscis and Hoval. When it came to the consideration of this alternative there was no doubt at all in Bowman's mind as to what the proper choice must be and the choice was not based primarily on the instinct of self-preservation although Bowman would have been the last to deny that it was an important factor: those were evil men and they had but one immediate and all-consuming ambition in life and that was to kill him but that was not what ultimately mattered. There was no question of morality or legality involved just the simple factor of logic. If they killed him now they would, he knew, go on to commit more and more heinous crimes: if he killed them, then they wouldn't. It was as simple as that. Some men deserve to die and the law cannot deal with them until it is too late and the law is not an ass in this respect, it's just because of inbuilt safeguards in every legal constitution designed to protect the rights of the individual that it is unable to cope in advance with those whose ultimate evil or murderous intent is beyond rational dispute but beyond legal proof. It was the old old story of the greatest good of the greatest number and it was merely fortuitous, Bowman reflected wryly, that he happened to be one of the greatest number. If he had been scared he was no longer scared now, his mind was quite cold and detached. He had to get high. If he got to a certain height where they couldn't reach him it would be stalemate: if he went higher and they still tried to follow him the danger to the greatest good of the greatest number was going to be effectively reduced. He looked up at the towering shattered crags and neolithic ruins bathed in the white moonlight and started to climb.

Bowman had never had any pretensions towards being a climber but he climbed well that night. With the devil himself behind him he would normally have made good speed: with three of them he made excellent time. Looking back from time to time, he could see that he was steadily outdistancing them but not to the extent that they ever lost sight of him for more than a few seconds at a time. And now they were clearly recognizable for whom they were for now they had completely removed their homemade masks. They had probably arrived, and rightly, at the safe conclusion that up in the wild desolation of those ruins in the middle of the night they no longer required them and even if they were seen on the way back it wouldn't matter, for the *corpus delicti* would have vanished forever and no charge could be laid against them other than that of entering the fortress without paying the required admission fee of a franc per head which they would probably have regarded as a reasonable exchange for a night's work well done.

Bowman stopped climbing. Through no fault of his own, because he was totally unfamiliar with the terrain, he had made a mistake. He had been aware that the walls of the narrow gully up which he was scrambling had been rapidly steepening on both sides, which hadn't worried him unduly because it had happened twice before, but now as he rounded a corner he found himself faced with a vertical wall of solid rock. It was a perfect cul-de-sac from which there was no escape except by climbing, and the vertical walls were wholly unclimbable. The blank wall facing Bowman was riddled by cracks and apertures but a quick glance at the only three or four that were accessible to him showed no moonlight at the far end, only uncompromising darkness.

He ran back to the corner, convinced he was wasting his time. He was. The three men had been in no doubt as to the direction in which he had disappeared. They were forty yards away, no more. They saw Bowman, stopped and came on again. But not so hurriedly now. The very fact that Bowman had turned back to check on their whereabouts would be indication enough that he was in serious trouble.

A man does not die before he has to. He ran back into the cul-de-sac and looked desperately at the apertures in the rock. Only two were large enough to allow a man to enter. If he could get inside one and turn around the darkness behind him would at least counterbalance the advantages of a man with a knife—and, of course, only one man could come at a time. For no reason at all he chose the right-hand aperture, scrambled up and wriggled inside.

The limestone tunnel started narrowing almost immediately. But he had to go on, he was not yet in total concealment. By the time he estimated that he was hidden the tunnel was no more than two feet wide and scarcely as high. It would be impossible for him to turn, all he could do was lie there and be hacked piecemeal at someone's leisure. And even that, he realized now, would not be necessary: all they would have to do would be to wall up the entrance and go home for a good night's sleep. Bowman inched ahead on hands and knees.

He saw a pale glow of light ahead. He was imagining it, he thought, he knew he must be imagining it, but when he suddenly realized that what lay ahead was a corner in the tunnel, he knew he wasn't. He reached the corner and wriggled round with difficulty. Before him he saw a patch of star-studded sky.

The tunnel had suddenly become a cave. A small cave, to be sure, a good deal less than head-high and its lip ending in nothingness less than six feet away: but a cave. He crawled to the lip and looked down. He at once wished he hadn't: the plain lay hundreds of sheerly vertical feet below, the rows of dusty olive trees so impossibly distant that they couldn't even be fairly described as toy bushes.

He leaned out another few vertiginous inches and twisted his head to look upwards. The top of the cliff lay no more than twenty feet above—twenty smoothly vertical feet with neither finger- nor toehold in sight.

He looked to the right and that was it. That was the path that even the moronic mountain goat would have baulked at, a narrow broken ledge extending down at not too acute an angle to a point that passed, as he now saw, some four feet below the lip of the cave. The path, for want of a better word, went right to the top.

But even the moronic goat, which Bowman was not, will refuse suicidal chances acceptable to the sacrificial goat, which Bowman undoubtedly was, for death and suicide come to the same thing anyway. He didn't hesitate, for he knew with certainty that if he did he would elect to remain and fight it out in that tiny cave sooner than face that dreadful path. He swung out gingerly over the rim, lowered himself till he had located the ledge with his feet and started to edge his way upwards.

He shuffled along with his face to the wall, arms wide outstretched, palms in constant contact with the rock face, but not because of any purchase that could be gained, for there was none, but because he was no mountaineer, had no particular head for heights and knew very well that if he looked down he'd inevitably just lean out and go tumbling head over heels to the olive groves below. A crack Alpinist, it was possible, would have regarded the climb as just a light Sunday afternoon workout but for Bowman it was the most terrifying experience of his life. Twice his foot slipped on loose stone, twice chunks of limestone disappeared into the abyss, but after a lifetime that was all of two minutes long he made it and hauled himself over the brink and into safety, sweating like a man in a Turkish bath and trembling like a withered leaf in the last gale of autumn. He'd thought he wouldn't be scared again and he had been wrong: but now he was back on terra firma and it was on terra firma that he operated best.

He ventured a quick glance over the edge. There was no one in sight. He wondered briefly what had delayed them, maybe they'd thought he was lurking in the shadow in the cul-de-sac, maybe they'd picked the wrong aperture to start with, maybe anything. He'd no time to waste wondering, he had to find out, and immediately, whether there was any escape from the pinnacle he was perched on. He had to find out for three very good and urgent reasons. If there was no other escape route he knew in his heart that no power on earth would ever make him face that descent to the cave and that he'd just have to stay there till the buzzards bleached his bones—he doubted whether there were any buzzards in those parts but the principle of the thing was pretty well fixed in his mind. If there was an escape route, then he'd have to guard against the possibility of being cut off by the gypsies. Thirdly, if there was such a route and they regarded it as unassailable, they might just elect to leave him there and go off to deal with Cecile Dubois whom they clearly, if erroneously, suspected of being a party to his irritatingly interfering behaviour.

He crossed no more than ten yards of the flat limestone summit, lowered himself flat and peered over the edge. His circumspection was needless. There *was* an escape route, a very steep scree-laden slope that debouched gradually into an area of massive limestone boulders which in turn gave on to Les Baux plateau massif itself. Uninviting but feasible.

He made his way back to the cliffside and heard voices, at first indistinctly, then clearly.

"This is madness!" It was Hoval speaking and for the first time Bowman shared a point of view with him.

"For you, Hoval, for a mountaineer from the High Tatra?" Ferenc's voice. "If he went this way, we can too. You know that if we do not kill this man everything will be lost."

Bowman looked down. He could see Hoval quite clearly and the heads of Ferenc and Koscis.

Koscis, apparently trying to postpone a decision, said: "I do not like killing, Ferenc."

Ferenc said: "Too late to be queasy now. My father's orders are that we do not return until this man lies dead."

Hoval nodded reluctantly, reached down his feet, found the ledge and started to edge his way along. Bowman rose, looked around, located a limestone boulder that must have weighed at least fifty pounds, lifted it chest high and returned to the brink of the precipice.

Hoval was obviously a great deal more experienced than Bowman for he was making about twice the best speed that Bowman had been able to manage. Ferenc and Koscis, heads and shoulders clearly visible now, were glancing anxiously sideways, watching Hoval's progress and almost certainly far from relishing the prospect of having to emulate him. Bowman waited till Hoval was directly beneath him. Hoval had once already tried to murder and now was coming to try to murder again. Bowman felt no pity and opened his hands.

The boulder, with a curious absence of sound, struck head and shoulders: the whole brief sequence, indeed, was characterized by an eerie silence. Hoval made no sound at all on the long way down and may well have been dead before he started to fall: and no sound of what must have been an appalling impact came from either Hoval or the boulder that had killed him as they plunged into the olive groves far away. They just disappeared soundlessly from sight, vanished in the darkness below.

Bowman looked at Ferenc and Koscis. For several seconds they crouched there, their faces stunned, for catastrophe rarely registers instantaneously, then Ferenc's face became savagely transformed. He reached inside his jacket, snatched out a gun, pointed it upwards and fired. He knew Bowman was up there but he could have had no idea where he was. It was no more than the uncontrollable expression of an access of blind fury but Bowman took a couple of rapid backward steps all the same.

The gun introduced a new dimension. Clearly, because of their predilection for knives, they had intended to dispose of Bowman as quietly and unobtrusively as possible, but Ferenc, Bowman felt sure, did not carry a gun unless he intended to use it in the last resort and that was plainly at hand: they were going to get him at no matter what risk to themselves. Bowman reflected briefly that whatever he had so nearly stumbled across must literally be a matter of life and death, then he turned and ran. Ferenc and Koscis would already be heading back through the tunnel on the assumption that there might be an escape route open to Bowman: in any event it would be pointless for them to remain where they were as any action they might try to take there would result only in their untimely end. Untimely, that is, from their point of view.

He ran down the steep slope of scree because he had no alternative but to run, taking increasingly huge bounding steps to maintain what was left of his balance. Three-quarters of the way down to the waiting jumble of limestone boulders his loss of balance passed the point of no return and he fell, rolling diagonally downhill, trying frantically and with a total lack of success to brake himself. The braking was done for him, violently and painfully, by the first of the boulders with which he came into contact and it was his right knee that took the major brunt of the impact.

He was sure he had smashed the right kneecap for when he tried to rise his leg just gave under him and he sat down again. A second time he tried it and this time with a little more success: the third time he made it and he knew the kneecap had just been momentarily paralyzed. Now it felt merely numb although he knew it must hurt badly later and would be severely bruised. He hobbled on his way through the thinning scattering of boulders at about half the best speed he could normally have made for the knee kept collapsing under him as if it had a will of its own.

A puff of white smoke flew off from a boulder just in front of him and the sound of the shot was almost simultaneous. Ferenc had anticipated too well. Bowman didn't try to take cover because Ferenc would just have walked down to the place of concealment and put the pistol to his head to make quite sure that he didn't miss. Bowman made off down the slope, twisting and doubling among the rocks to throw Ferenc off aim, not even trying to locate where his pursuers were, for the knowledge would have been useless to him anyway. Several shots came close, one kicking up a small cloud of soil at his right foot, but the combination of his swerving run and the fact that Ferenc had himself to dodge in and out among the rocks must have made him an almost impossible target. Besides, to shoot accurately downhill is notoriously difficult at the best of times. In between the shots Bowman could hear the sound of their pounding footsteps and he knew they were gaining on him: but still he didn't look round for if he were going to be shot through the back of the head he felt he'd just as soon not know about it in advance.

He was clear of the rocks now and running straight over the hard-packed earth towards the railed entrance to the village. Ferenc, closing up and also running straight, should have had his chance then but the firing had stopped and Bowman could only assume that he had run out of ammunition. He might well, Bowman realized, carry a spare magazine but even if he did he would have been hard put to it to reload on the dead run.

Bowman's knee was hurting now but, contradictorily, it was bearing up much better. He glanced behind. His pursuers were still gaining, but less slowly. Bowman passed through the railed upper entrance to the village and ran down the fork where he had hesitated on the way up. The two gypsies were not yet in sight but the sound of their running feet was clear. They would expect him, Bowman hoped, to continue out through the lower entrance to the village, so he turned left down the short road that led to the old battlements of the town. The road debouched into a small square, a cul-de-sac, but he was past caring about that. He registered the fact, without knowing why, that an ancient wrought-iron cross stood in the centre of the square. To the left was an equally ancient church, facing it was a low wall with apparently nothing beyond it and, between church and wall, a high face of vertical rock with deep man-made apertures cut into it, for reasons that couldn't be guessed at.

He ran across to the low rock and peered over it. It was certainly no low rock on the other side: it dropped almost two hundred vertical feet to what looked like scrub trees at the foot.

Ferenc had been cleverer than Bowman thought he would have been. He was still peering over the wall when he heard the sound of running feet approaching the square, one set of feet: they'd split up to investigate both avenues of escape. Bowman straightened and hurried on soundlessly across the square and hid in the shadows of one of the deep recesses cut in the natural rock.

Koscis it was. He slowed down on entering the square, his stertorous breathing carrying clearly in the night air, walked past the iron cross, glanced at the open doorway of the church, then, as if guided by some natural instinct, came heading straight towards the particular niche where Bowman stood as deeply pressed back in the shadow as he possibly could. There was a peculiar inevitability about the hesitating manner of his approach. He held his knife, thumb on top of the handle, in what appeared to be his favourite waist-high level.

Bowman waited until the gypsy was fractionally away from the point which would make discovery certain, then hurled himself from the dark niche, managing to grab his knife wrist more by good luck than good judgment. Both men fell heavily to the ground fighting for possession of the knife. Bowman tried to twist Koscis' right wrist but it seemed to be made of overlaid strands of wire hawser and Bowman could feel the wrist slowly breaking free from his grasp. He anticipated the inevitable by suddenly letting go and falling over twice, rising to his feet at the same instant as

Koscis did. For a moment they looked at each other, immobile, then Bowman backed away slowly until his hands touched the low wall behind him. He had no place to run to any more and no place to hide.

Koscis advanced. His face, at first implacable, broke into a smile that was notably lacking in warmth. Koscis, the expert with a knife, was savouring the passing moment.

Bowman threw himself forward, then to the right but Koscis had seen this one before. He flung himself forward to intercept the second stage of the movement, his knife arcing up from knee level, but what Koscis had forgotten was that Bowman knew he had seen this one before. Bowman checked with all the strength of his right leg, dropped to his left knee and as the knife hooked by inches over his head, his right shoulder and upper arm hit the gypsy's thighs. Bowman straightened up with a convulsive jerk and this, combined with the speed and accelerating momentum of Koscis' onrush, lifted the gypsy high into the air and sent him, useless knife still in hand, sailing helplessly over the low wall into the darkness below. Bowman twisted round and watched him as he fell, a diminishing manikin tumbling over and over in almost incredibly slow motion, his passing marked only by a fading scream in the night. And then Bowman couldn't see him any more and the screaming stopped.

For a few seconds Bowman stood there, a man held in thrall, but only for a few seconds. If Ferenc hadn't been afflicted with a sudden and total deafness he was bound to have heard that eldritch fear-crazed scream and to come to investigate and immediately.

Bowman ran from the square towards the main street: halfway up the narrow connecting lane he slid into a darkened alleyway for he'd heard Ferenc coming and for a brief moment saw him as he passed the end of the alleyway, pistol in one hand, knife in the other. Whether the pistol had been reloaded or not or whether Ferenc had baulked at firing it so near the village was impossible to say. Even in what must have been that moment of intolerable stress Ferenc was still possessed of a sufficient instinct of self-preservation to keep exactly to the middle of the road where he couldn't be ambushed by an unarmed man. His lips were drawn back in an unconscious snarl compounded of rage and hate and fear and his face was the face of a madman.

3

IT ISN'T every woman who, wakened in the middle of the night, can sit bolt upright in bed, sheets hauled up to the neck, hair dishevelled and eyes blurred with sleep and still look as attractive as if she were setting out for a ball, but Cecile Dubois must have been one of the few. She blinked, perhaps, rather more than a would-be dancer would have done, then gave Bowman what appeared to be a rather penetrating and critical look, possibly because as a result of all that climbing in the ruins and falling down scree-covered slopes Bowman's dark broadcloth had lost some of its showroom sheen: in fact, now that he could clearly see it for the first time, it was filthily dirty, stained and ripped beyond repair. He waited for her reaction, sarcastic, cynical or perhaps just plain annoyed, but she wasn't an obvious sort of girl.

She said: "I thought you'd be in the next county by this time."

"I was almost in another land altogether." He took his hand from the

light switch and eased the door until it was almost but not quite closed.
"But I came back. For the car. And for you."

"For me?"

"Especially for you. Hurry up and get dressed. Your life's not worth a
tinker's cuss if you stay here."

"My life? But why should I——"

"Up, dress and pack. Now." He crossed to the bed and looked at her,
and although his appearance wasn't very encouraging it must have been
convincing for she compressed her lips slightly, then nodded. Bowman
returned to the door and looked out through the crack he had left. Very
fetching though the dark-haired Miss Dubois might be, he reflected, it did
not mean that she had to conform to the beautiful brunette pattern: she made
decisions, quickly accepted what she regarded as being inevitable and the
"if you think I'm going to get dressed while you're standing there" routine
apparently hadn't even crossed her mind. Not that he would have seriously
objected but, for the moment, the imminent return of Ferenc held prior
claim to his attentions. He wondered briefly what was holding Ferenc up,
he should have posted by hotfoot by that time to report to his old man that
they had encountered some unexpected difficulties in the execution of their
assignment. It could have been, of course, that even then Ferenc was prowl-
ing hopefully and stealthily through the back alleys of Les Baux with a gun
in one hand, a knife in the other and murder in his heart.

"I'm ready," Cecile said.

Bowman looked round in mild astonishment. She was, too, even to the
extent of having combed her hair. A strapped suitcase lay on her bed. "And
packed?" Bowman asked.

"Last night." She hesitated. "Look, I can't just walk off without——"

"Lila? Leave her a note. Say you'll contact her Poste Restante, Saintes-
Maries. Hurry back in a minute—I have to collect my stuff."

He left her there, went quickly to his own room and paused briefly at the
door. The south wind sighed through the trees and he could hear the splash
of the fountain in the swimming pool but that was all he could hear. He
went into his room, crammed clothes anyhow into a suitcase and was back
in Cecile's room within the promised minute. She was still scribbling away
industriously.

"Poste Restante, Saintes-Maries, that's all you've got to write," Bowman said nastily. "Your life story she probably knows about."

She glanced up at him, briefly and expressionlessly over the rims of a
pair of glasses that he was only mildly surprised to see that she was wearing,
reduced him to the status of an insect on the wall then got back to her
writing. After another twenty seconds she signed her name with what seemed
to Bowman to be a wholly unnecessary flourish considering the urgency of
the moment, snapped the spectacles in the case and nodded to indicate that
she was ready. He picked up her suitcase and they left, switching off the
light and closing the door behind them. Bowman picked up his own suitcase, waited until the girl had slid the folded note under Lila's door, then
both walked quickly and quietly along the terrace, then up the path to the
road that skirted the back of the hotel. The girl followed closely and in
silence behind Bowman and he was just beginning to congratulate himself
on how quickly and well she was responding to his training methods when
she caught his left arm firmly and hauled him to a stop. Bowman looked at
her and frowned but it didn't seem to have any effect. Shortsighted, he
thought charitably.

"We're safe here?" she asked.

"For the moment, yes."

"Put those cases down."

He put the cases down. He'd have to revise his training methods.

"So far and no farther," she said matter-of-factly. "I've been a good little girl and I've done what you asked because I thought there was possibly one chance in a hundred that you weren't mad. The other ninety-nine per cent of my way of thinking makes me want an explanation. Now."

Her mother hadn't done much about training her either, Bowman thought. Not, at least, in the niceties of drawing-room conversation. But someone had done a very good job in other directions, for if she were upset or scared in any way it certainly didn't show.

"You're in trouble," Bowman said. "I got you into it. Now it's my responsibility to get you out of it."

"I'm in trouble?"

"Both of us. Three characters from the gypsy caravan down there told me that they were going to do me in. Then you. But first me. So they chased me up to Les Baux and then through the village and the ruins."

She looked at him speculatively, not at all worried or concerned as she ought to have been. "But if they chased you——"

"I shook them off. The gypsy leader's son, a lovable little lad by the name of Ferenc, is possibly still up there looking for me. He has a gun in one hand, a knife in the other. When he doesn't find me he'll come back and tell Dad and then a few of them will troop up to our rooms. Yours and mine."

"What on earth have I done?" she demanded.

"You've been seen with me all evening and you've been seen to give me refuge, that's what you've done."

"But—but this is ridiculous. I mean, taking to our heels like this." She shook her head. "I was wrong about that possible one per cent. You *are* mad."

"Probably." It was, Bowman thought, a justifiable point of view.

"I mean, you've only got to pick up the phone."

"And?"

"The police, silly."

"No police—because I'm not silly, Cecile. I'd be arrested for murder."

She looked at him and slowly shook her head in disbelief or incomprehension or both.

"It wasn't so easy to shake them off tonight," Bowman went on. "There was an accident. Two accidents."

"Fantasy." She shook her head again as she whispered the word again. "Fantasy."

"Of course." He reached out and took her hand. "Come, I'll show you the bodies." He knew he could never locate Hoval in the darkness but Koscis' whereabouts would present no problem and as far as proving his case was concerned one corpse would be as good as two any time. And then he knew he didn't have to prove anything, not any more. In her face, very pale now but quite composed, something had changed. He didn't know what it was, he just registered the change. And then she came close to him and took his free hand in hers. She didn't start having the shakes, she didn't shrink away in horrified revulsion from a self-confessed killer, she just came close and took his other hand.

"Where do you want to go?" Her voice was low but there were no shakes in it either. "Riviera? Switzerland?"

He could have hugged her but decided to wait for a more propitious moment. He said: "Saintes-Maries."

"Saintes-Maries!"

"That's where all the gypsies are going. So that's where I want to go."

There was a silence, then she said without any particular inflection in her voice: "To die in Saintes-Maries."

"To live in Saintes-Maries, Cecile. To justify living, if you like. We idle layabouts have to, you know." She looked at him steadily, but kept silent: he would have expected this by now, she was a person who would always know when to be silent. In the pale wash of moonlight the lovely face was grave to the point of sadness. "I want to find out why a young gypsy is missing," Bowman went on. "I want to find out why a gypsy mother and three gypsy girls are terrified out of their lives. I want to find out why three other gypsies tried their damnedest to kill me tonight. And I want to find out why they're even prepared to go to the extraordinary lengths of killing you. Wouldn't you like to find those things out too, Cecile?"

She nodded and took her hands away. He picked up the suitcases and they walked down circumspectly past the main entrance to the hotel. There was no one around, no sound of any person moving around, no hue and cry, nothing but the soft quiet and peacefulness of the Elysian Fields or, perhaps, of any well-run cemetery or morgue. They carried on down the steeply winding road to where it joined the transverse road running north and south through the Valley of Hell and there they turned sharply right—a 90° turn. Another thirty yards and Bowman gratefully set the cases down on the grassy verge.

"Where's your car parked?" he asked.

"At the inner end of the parking area."

"That *is* handy. Means it has to be driven out through the parking lot and the forecourt. What make?"

"Peugeot 504. Blue."

He held out his hand. "The keys."

"Why? Think I'm not capable of driving my own car out of——"

"Not out of, *chérie*. Over. Over anyone who tries to get in your way. Because they will."

"But they'll be asleep——"

"Innocence, innocence. They'll be sitting around drinking slivovitz and waiting happily for the good news of my death. The keys."

She gave him a very old-fashioned look, one compounded of an odd mixture of irritation and speculative amusement, dug into her handbag and brought out the keys. He took them and, as he moved off, she made to follow. He shook his head.

"Next time," he said.

"I see." She made a face. "I don't think you and I are going to get along too well."

"We'd better," he said. "For your sake, for my sake, we'd better. And it would be nice to get you to that altar unscarred. Stay here."

Two minutes later, pressed deeply into shadow, he stood at the side of the entrance to the forecourt. Three caravans, the three he had examined earlier, still had their lights burning, but only one of them—Czerda's—showed any sign of human activity. It came as no surprise to him to discover that his guess as to what Czerda and his henchmen would be doing had proved to be so remarkably accurate, except that he had no means of checking whether the alcohol they were putting away in such copious quantities was slivovitz or not. It was certainly alcohol. The two men sitting with Czerda on the caravan steps were cast in the same mould as Czerda himself, swarthy, lean, powerfully built, unmistakably Central European and unprepossessing to a degree. Bowman had never seen either before nor, looking at them, did he care very much whether he ever saw either of them again. From the desultory conversation, he gathered they were called Maca and Masaine: whatever their names it was clear that fate had not cast them on the side of the angels.

Almost directly between them and Bowman's place of concealment stood Czerda's jeep, parked so that it faced the entrance of the forecourt—the only vehicle there so positioned: in an emergency, clearly, it would be the first vehicle that would be pressed into service and it seemed to Bowman prudent to do something about that. Crouched low, moving slowly and silently across the forecourt and at all times keeping the jeep directly between him and the caravan steps, he arrived at the front end of the jeep, edged cautiously towards the near front tyre, unscrewed the valve cap and inserted the end of a match into the valve using a balled-up handkerchief to muffle the hiss of the escaping air. By and by the rim of the wheel settled down until it was biting into the inner carcass of the tread. Bowman hoped, fervently if belatedly, that Czerda and his friends weren't regarding the front near wing in any way closely for they could not have failed to be more than mildly astonished by the fact that it had sunk a clear three inches closer to the ground. But Czerda and his friends had, providentially, other and more immediate concerns to occupy their attention.

"Something is wrong," Czerda said positively. "Very far wrong. You know that I can always tell about those things."

"Ferenc and Koscis and Hoval can look after themselves." It was the man whose name Bowman thought to be Maca and he spoke confidently. "If this Bowman ran, he could have run a very long way."

"No." Bowman risked a quick glance round the wing of the jeep and Czerda was now on his feet. "They've been gone too long, far too long. Come. We must look for them."

The other two gypsies rose reluctantly to their feet but remained there, as Czerda did, their heads cocked and slowly turning. Bowman had heard the sound as soon as they had, the sound of pounding feet from the patio by the pool. Ferenc appeared at the top of the steps, came down three at a time and ran across the forecourt to Czerda's caravan. It was the lurching stumbling run of a man very close to exhaustion and from his distressed breathing, sweating face and the fact that he made no attempt to conceal the gun in his hand it was clear that Ferenc was in a state of considerable agitation.

"They're dead, Father!" Ferenc's voice was a hoarse gasping wheeze. "Hoval and Koscis. They're dead!"

"God's name, what are you saying?" Czerda demanded!

"Dead! Dead, I tell you! I found Koscis. His neck is broken. I think every bone in his body is broken. God knows where Hoval is."

Czerda seized his son by the lapels and shook him violently. "Talk sense! Killed?" His voice was almost a shout.

"This man Bowman. He killed them."

"He killed—he killed—and Bowman?"

"Escaped."

"Escaped! Escaped! You young fool, if this man escapes Gaiuse Strome will kill us all. Quickly! Bowman's room!"

"And the girl's." Ferenc's wheezing had eased fractionally. "And the girl's."

"The girl?" Czerda asked. "The dark one?"

Ferenc nodded violently. "She gave him shelter."

"And the girl's," Czerda agreed viciously. "Hurry."

The four men ran off towards the patio steps. Bowman moved to the offside front tyre and because this time he didn't have to bother about muffling the escaping hiss of air he merely unscrewed the valve and threw it away. He rose and, still stooping, ran across the forecourt and through the sculptured arch in the hedge to the parking space beyond.

Here he ran into an unexpected difficulty. A blue Peugeot, Cecile had said. Fine. A blue Peugeot he could recognize any time—in broad daylight. But this wasn't daytime, it was nighttime, and even although the moon was shining the thickly woven wickerwork roofing cast an almost impenetrable shadow on the cars parked beneath it. Just as by night all cats are grey so by night all cars look infuriatingly the same. Easy enough, perhaps, to differentiate between a Rolls and a Mini, but in this age of mindless conformity the vast majority of cars are disturbingly alike in size and profile. Or so, dismayingly, Bowman found that night. He moved quickly from one car to the next, having to peer closely in each case for an infuriating length of time, only to discover that it was not the car he was seeking.

He heard the sound of low voices, but voices angry and anxious, and moved quickly to the archway. Close by Czerda's caravan, the four gypsies, who had clearly discovered that their birds had flown, were gesticulating and arguing heatedly, holding their council of war and obviously wondering what in the hell to do next, a decision Bowman didn't envy their having to make, for in their position he wouldn't have had the faintest idea himself.

Abruptly, the centre of his attention altered. Out of the corner of an eye he had caught sight of something which, even in that pale moonlight, definitely constituted a splash of colour. This brightly hued apparition, located on the upper terrace, consisted of a pair of garishly striped heliotrope pyjamas and inside the pyjamas was no other than Le Grand Duc, leaning on the balustrade and gazing down towards the forecourt with an expression of what might have been mild interest or benign indifference or, indeed, quite a variety of other things when a large part of what can be seen of the subject's face consists of jaws champing regularly up and down while most of the remainder is concealed by a large red apple. But, clearly, however, he wasn't in the grip of any violent emotion.

Bowman left Le Grand Duc to his munching and resumed his search. The inner end of the parking lot, she had said. But her damned Peugeot wasn't at the inner end. He'd check twice. He turned to the west side and the fourth one along was it. Or he thought it was. A Peugeot, anyway. He climbed inside and the key fitted the ignition. Women, he thought bitterly, but didn't pursue the subject with himself, there were things to be done.

The door he closed as softly as he could: it seemed unlikely that the faint click would have been heard in the forecourt even if the gypsies hadn't been conducting their heated council of war. He released the handbrake, engaged first gear and kept the clutch depressed, reached for and turned on the ignition and headlamp switches simultaneously. Both engine and lamps came on precisely together and the Peugeot, throwing gravel from its rear wheels, jumped forward, Bowman spinning the wheel to the left to head for the archway in the hedge. At once he saw the four gypsies detach themselves from the rear of Czerda's caravan and run to cover what they accurately assumed would be the route he would take between the archway and the exit from the forecourt. Czerda appeared to be shouting and although his voice couldn't be heard above the accelerating roar of the engine his violent gesticulations clearly indicated that he was telling his men to stop the Peugeot although how he proposed to do this Bowman couldn't imagine. As he passed through the archway he could see in the blaze of the headlamps that Ferenc was the only one carrying a firearm and as he was pointing it directly at Bowman he didn't leave Bowman with very much option other than to point the car directly at him. The panic registering suddenly on Ferenc's face showed that he had lost all interest in using the gun and was now primarily concerned with saving himself. He dived frantically to his left and almost got clear but almost wasn't enough. The near side wing of the Peugeot caught him in the thigh and suddenly he wasn't there any more, all Bowman could see was the metallic glint of his gun spinning in the air. On the left, Czerda and the two other gypsies had managed to fling themselves clear. Bowman twisted the wheel again, drove out of the forecourt and down towards the valley road. He wondered what Le Grand Duc had made of all that: probably, he thought, he hadn't missed as much as a munch.

The tyres squealed as the Peugeot rounded the right-angle turn at the foot of the road. Bowman drew up beside Cecile, stopped, got out but left the engine running. She ran to him and thrust out a suitcase.

"Hurry! Quickly!" Angrily, almost, she thrust the case at him. "Can't you hear them coming?"

"I can hear them," Bowman said pacifically. "I think we have time."

They had time. They heard the whine of an engine in low gear, a whine diminishing in intensity as the jeep braked heavily for the corner. Abruptly it came into sight and clearly it was making a very poor job indeed of negotiating the right-hand bend. Czerda was hauling madly on the steering wheel but the front wheels—or tyres, at least—appeared to have a mind of their own. Bowman watched with interest as the jeep carried straight on, careered across the opposite bank of the road, cut down a sapling and landed with a resounding crash.

"Tsk! Tsk!" Bowman said to Cecile. "Did ever you see such careless driving?" He crossed over the road and looked into the field. The jeep, its wheels still spinning, lay on its side while the three gypsies, who had clearly parted company with their vehicle before it had come to rest, lay in a sprawled heap about fifteen feet away. As he watched they disentangled themselves and scrambled painfully to their feet. Ferenc, understandably, was not one of the three. Bowman became aware that he had been joined by Cecile.

"You did this," she said accusingly. "You sabotaged their jeep."

"It was nothing," he said deprecatingly. "I just let a little air out of the tyres."

"But—but you could have killed those men! The jeep could have landed on top of them and crushed them to death."

"It's not always possible to arrange everything as one would wish it," Bowman said regretfully. She gave him the kind of look Dr. Crippen must have got used to after he'd been hauled into court, so Bowman changed his tone. "You don't look like a fool, Cecile, nor do you talk like one. If you think our three friends down there were just out to savour the delights of the nighttime Provençal air, why don't you go and ask them how they are?"

She turned and walked back to the car without a word. He followed and they drove off in a one-sidedly huffy silence. Within a minute he slowed and pulled the car into a small cleared area on the right-hand side of the road. Through the windscreen they could see the vertical limestone bluffs with enormous man-made rectangular openings giving on the impenetrable darkness of the unseen caverns beyond.

"You're not stopping here?" Incredulity in her voice.

He switched the engine off and set the parking brake. "I've stopped."

"But they'll find us here!" She sounded a little desperate. "They're bound to. Any moment now."

"No. If they're capable of thinking at all after that little tumble they had, they'll be thinking that we're halfway to Avignon by this time. Besides, I think it's going to take them some time to recover their first enthusiasm for moonlight driving."

They got out of the car and looked at the entrance to the caverns. Foreboding wasn't the word for it, nor was sinister: something stronger, much stronger. It was, quite literally, an appalling place and Bowman had no difficulty in understanding and sympathizing with the viewpoint of the policeman back at the hotel. But he didn't for a moment believe that you had to be born in Les Baux and grow up hand-in-hand with all the ancient superstitions in order to develop a night phobia about those caves: quite simply it was a place into which no man in his right mind would venture after the sun had gone down. He was, he hoped, in his right mind, and he didn't want to go in. But he had to.

"He took a torch from his suitcase and said to Cecile: "Wait here."

"No! You're not going to leave me alone here." She sounded pretty vehement about it.

"It'll probably be an awful lot worse inside."

"I don't care."

"Suit yourself."

They set off together and passed through the largest of the openings to the left: if you could have put a three-storey house on wheels you could have trundled it through that opening without any trouble. Bowman traversed the walls with his torch, walls covered with the graffiti of countless generations, then opted for an archway to the right that led to an even larger cavern. Cecile, he noticed, even although wearing flat-heeled sandals, stumbled quite a bit, more than the occasional slight undulations in the limestone floor warranted: he was pretty well sure now that her vision was a good deal less than 20/20 which, he reflected, was maybe why she had consented to come with him in the first place.

The next cavern held nothing of interest for Bowman. True, its vaulted heights were lost in darkness, but as only a bat could have got up there anyway that was of no moment. Another archway loomed ahead.

"This is a dreadful place," Cecile whispered.

"Well, I wouldn't like to live here all the time."

Another few paces and she said: "Mr. Bowman."

"Neil."

"May I take your arm?" In these days he didn't think they asked.

"Help yourself," he said agreeably. "You're not the only person in need of reassurance round here."

"It's not that. I'm not scared, really. It's just that you keep flashing that torch everywhere and I can't see and I keep tripping."

"Ah!"

So she took his arm and she didn't trip any more, just shivered violently as if she were coming down with some form of malaria. By and by she said: "What are you looking for?"

"You know damned well what I'm looking for."

"Perhaps—well, they could have hidden him."

"They could have hidden him. They couldn't have buried him, not unless they had brought along some dynamite with them, but they could have hidden him. Under a mound of limestone rock and stones. There's plenty around."

"But we've passed by dozens of piles of limestone rocks. You didn't bother about them."

"When we come to a freshly made mound you'll know the difference," he said matter-of-factly. She shivered again, violently, and he went on: "Why did you have to come in, Cecile? You were telling the truth when you said you weren't scared: you're just plain terrified."

"I'd rather be plain terrified in here with you than plain terrified alone out there." Any moment now and her teeth would start chattering.

"You may have a point there," he admitted. They passed, slightly uphill this time, through another archway, into another immense cavern: after a few steps Bowman stopped abruptly.

"What is it?" she whispered. "What's wrong?"

"I don't know." He paused. "Yes, I do know." For the first time he shivered himself.

"You, too?" Again that whisper.

"Me, too. But it's not that. Some clodhopping character has just walked over my grave."

"Please?"

"This is it. This is the place. When you're old and sinful like me, you can smell it."

"Death?" And now her voice was shaking. "People can't smell death."

"I can."

He switched off the torch.

"Put it on, put it on!" Her voice was high-pitched, close to hysteria. "For God's sake, put it on. *Please*."

He detached her hand, put his arm round her and held her close. With a bit of luck, he thought, they might get some synchronization into their shivering, not as much perhaps as the ballroom champions on TV got in their dancing, but enough to be comfortable. When the vibrations had died down a little he said: "Notice anything different about this cavern?"

"There's light! There's light coming from somewhere."

"There is indeed." They walked slowly forward till they came to a huge pile of rubble on the floor. The jumble of rocks stretched up and up until at the top they could see a large squarish patch of star-dusted sky. Down the centre of this rockfall, all the way from top to bottom, was a narrow patch of disturbed rubble, a pathway that seemed to have been newly made. Bowman switched on his torch and there was no doubt about it: it was newly made. He traversed the base of the rockfall with the beam of the torch and then the beam, almost of its own volition, stopped and locked on a mound of limestone rocks, perhaps eight feet in length by three high.

"With a freshly made mound of limestone," Bowman said, "you can see the difference."

"You can see the difference," she repeated mechanically.

"Please, Walk away a little."

"No. It's funny, but I'm all right now."

He believed her and he didn't think it was funny. Mankind is still close enough to the primeval jungles to find the greatest fear of all in the unknown: but here, now, they knew.

Bowman stooped over the mound and began to throw stones to one side. They hadn't bothered to cover the unfortunate Alexandre to any great depth for inside a moment Bowman came to the slashed remnants of a once white shirt, now saturated in blood. Lying in the encrusted blood and attached to a chain was a silver crucifix. He unclipped the chain and lifted both it and the crucifix away.

*   *   *

Bowman parked the Peugeot at the spot in the valley road where he had picked up Cecile and the cases. He got out.

"Stay here," he said to Cecile. "This time I mean it." She didn't exactly nod her head obediently but she didn't argue either: maybe his training methods were beginning to improve. The jeep, he observed without any surprise, was where he'd last seen it: it was going to require a mobile crane to get it out of there.

The entrance to the forecourt seemed deserted but he'd developed the same sort of affectionate trust for Czerda and his merry band of followers as he would have for a colony of cobras or black widow spiders so he pressed deep into the shadows and advanced slowly into the forecourt. His foot struck something solid and there was a faint metallic clink. He became very still but he'd provoked no reaction that he could see or hear. He stooped and picked up the pistol that he'd inadvertently kicked against the base of a petrol pump. Young Ferenc's pistol, without a doubt. From what last Bowman had seen of Ferenc he didn't think he'd have missed it yet or would be wanting to use it for some time: but Bowman decided to return it to him all the same. He knew he wouldn't be disturbing anyone for lights from inside Czerda's caravan still shone through the windows and the half-open door. Every other caravan in the forecourt was in darkness. He crossed to Czerda's caravan, climbed the steps soundlessly and looked in through the doorway.

Czerda, with a bandaged left hand, bruised cheek and large strip of sticking-plaster on his forehead, wasn't looking quite his old self but he was in mint condition compared to Ferenc to whose injuries he was attending. Ferenc lay on a bunk, moaning and barely half-conscious, exclaiming in pain from time to time as his father removed a blood-soaked bandage from his forehead. When the bandage was at last jerked free to the accompaniment of a final yelp of pain, a pain that had the effect of restoring Ferenc to something pretty close to complete consciousness, Bowman could see that he had a very nasty cut indeed across his forehead, but a cut that faded into insignificance compared to the massive bruising of forehead and face: if he had sustained other bodily bruises of a comparable magnitude Ferenc had to be suffering very considerably and feeling in a very low state indeed. It was not a consideration that moved Bowman: if Ferenc had had his way he, Bowman, would be in a state in which he'd never feel anything again.

Ferenc sat shakily up on the bunk while his father secured a fresh bandage, then sat forward, put his elbows on his knees, his face in his hands and moaned.

"In God's name, what happened? My head———"

"You'll be all right," Czerda said soothingly. "A cut and a bruise. That's all."

"But what *happened?* Why is my head———"

"The car. Remember?"

"The car. Of course. That devil Bowman!" Coming from Ferenc, Bowman thought, that was rather good. "Did he—did he———"

"Damn his soul, yes. He got clear away—and he wrecked our jeep. See this?" Czerda pointed to his hand and forehead. Ferenc looked without interest and looked away. He had other things on his mind.

"My gun, Father! Where's my gun?"

"Here," Bowman said. He pointed his gun at Ferenc and walked into the caravan: the blood-stained chain and crucifix dangled from his left hand. Ferenc stared at him: he looked as a man might look with his head on the block and the executioner starting the back swing on his axe, for executioner Ferenc would have been in Bowman's position. Czerda, whose back had been to the door, swung round and remained as immobile as his son. He didn't seem any more pleased to see Bowman than Ferenc did. Bowman walked forward, two paces, and placed the bloody crucifix on a small table.

"His mother might like to have that," he said. "I should wipe the blood off first, though." He waited for some reaction but there was none, so he went on: "I'm going to kill you, Czerda. I'll have to, won't I, for no one can ever prove you killed young Alexandre? But I don't require proof, all I need is certainty. But not yet. I can't do it yet, can I? I mustn't cause innocent people to die, must I? But later. Later I kill you. Then I kill Gaiuse Strome. Tell him I said so, will you?"

"What do you know of Gaiuse Strome?" he whispered.

"Enough to hang him. And you."

Czerda suddenly smiled but when he spoke it was still in the same whisper.

"You've just said you can't kill me yet." He took a step forward.

Bowman said nothing. He altered the pistol fractionally until it was lined up on a spot between Ferenc's eyes. Czerda made no move to take a second step. Bowman looked at him and pointed to a stool close to the small table.

"Sit down," he said, "and face your son."

Czerda did as he was told. Bowman took one step forward and it was apparent that Ferenc's reactions weren't yet back in working order for his suddenly horrified expression in what little was left of his face that was still capable of registering expressions and his mouth opening to shout a warning came far too late to be of any aid to Czerda who crashed heavily to the floor as the barrel of Bowman's gun caught him behind the ear.

Ferenc bared his teeth and swore viciously at him. At least that was what Bowman assumed he was doing for Ferenc had reverted to his native Romany but he hadn't even started in on his descriptions when Bowman stepped forward wordlessly, his gun swinging again. Ferenc's reactions were even slower than Bowman had imagined: he toppled headlong across his father and lay still.

"What on earth——" The voice came from behind Bowman. He threw himself to one side, dropping to the floor, whirled round and brought the gun up: then, more slowly, he rose. Cecile stood in the doorway, her green eyes wide, her face stilled in shock.

"You fool," Bowman said savagely. "You almost died there. Don't you know that?" She nodded, the shock still in her face.

"Come inside. Shut the door. You *are* a fool. Why the hell didn't you do what I asked and stay where you were?"

Almost as if in a trance she stepped inside and closed the door. She stared down at the two fallen men, then back at Bowman again.

"For God's sake, why did you knock those two men senseless? Two injured men?"

"Because it was inconvenient to kill them at present," Bowman said coldly. He turned his back on her and began to search the place methodically and exhaustively. When one searches any place, be it gypsy caravan or baronial mansion, methodically and exhaustively, one has to wreck it completely in the process. So, in an orderly and systematic fashion, Bowman set about reducing Czerda's caravan to a total ruin. He ripped the beds to pieces, sliced open the mattresses with the aid of a knife he'd borrowed from the recumbent Czerda, scattering the flock stuffing far and wide to ensure that there was nothing hidden inside, and wrenched open cupboards, all locked, again with the aid of Czerda's knife. He moved into the kitchen recess, smashed all the items of crockery that were capable of holding anything, emptied the contents of a dozen food items into the sink, smashed open preserving jars and a variety of wine bottles by the simple expedient of knocking them together two at a time and ended up by spilling the contents of the cutlery drawers on the floor to ensure that there was nothing hidden beneath the lining paper. There wasn't.

Cecile, who had been watching this performance still in the same kind of hypnotic trance, said: "Who's Gaiuse Strome?"

"How long were you listening?"

"All the time. Who's Gaiuse Strome?"

"I don't know," Bowman said frankly. "Never heard of him until to-night."

He turned his attention to the larger clothing drawers. He emptied the contents of each in turn on the floor and kicked them apart. There was nothing there for him, just clothes.

"Other people's property doesn't mean all that much to you, does it?" By this time Cecile's state of trance had altered to the dazed incomprehension of one trying to come to grips with reality.

"He'll have it insured," Bowman said comfortingly. He began an assault on the last piece of furniture still intact, a beautifully carved mahogany bureau worth a small fortune in anybody's money, splintering open the locked drawers with the now invaluable aid of the point of Czerda's knife. He dumped the contents of the first two drawers on the floor and was about to open a third when something caught his eye. He stooped and retrieved a pair of heavy rolled-up woollen socks. Inside them was an elastic-bound package of brand-new crackling bank-notes with consecutive serial numbers. It took him over half a minute to count them.

"Eighty thousand Swiss francs in one-thousand-franc notes," Bowman observed. "I wonder where friend Czerda got eighty thousand Swiss francs in one-thousand-franc notes? Ah, well." He stuffed the notes into a hip pocket and resumed the search.

"But—but that's stealing!" It would be too much, perhaps, to say that Cecile looked horrified but there wasn't much in the way of admiration in those big green eyes: but Bowman was in no mood for moral disapprobation.

"Oh, shut up!" he said.

"But you've *got* money."

"Maybe this is how I get it."

He broke open another drawer, sifted through the contents with the toe of his shoe, then turned as he heard a sound to his left. Ferenc was struggling shakily to his feet, so Bowman took his arm, helped him stand upright, hit him very hard indeed on the side of the jaw and lowered him to the floor again. The shock was back in Cecile's face, a shock mingled with the beginnings of revulsion, she was probably a gently nurtured girl who had been brought up to believe that the opera or the ballet or the theatre constituted the ideal of an evening's entertainment. Bowman started in on the next drawer.

"Don't tell me," he said. "Just an idle layabout laying about. Not funny?"

"No." She had her lips compressed in a very schoolmarmish way.

"I'm pressed for time. Ah!"

"What is it?" In even the most puritanical of females repugnance doesn't stand a chance against curiosity.

"This." He showed her a delicately fashioned rosewood lacquered box inlaid with ebony and mother-of-pearl. It was locked and so exquisitely made that it was quite impossible to insert the point of even Czerda's razor-sharp knife into the microscopic line between lid and box. Cecile seemed to derive a certain malicious satisfaction from this momentary problem for she waved a hand to indicate the indescribable wreckage that now littered almost every square inch of the caravan floor.

"Shall I look for the key?" she asked sweetly.

"No need." He laid the rosewood box on the floor and jumped on it with both heels, reducing it at once to splintered matchwood. He removed a sealed envelope from the ruins, opened it and extracted a sheet of paper.

On it was a typewritten—in capitals—jumble of apparently meaningless letters and figures. There were a few words in plain language but their meaning in the context was completely obscure. Cecile peered over his shoulder. Her eyes were screwed up and he knew she was having difficulty in seeing.

"What is it?" she asked.

"Code, looks like. One or two words straight. There's Monday, a date—May 24th—and a place name—Grau-du-Roi."

"Grau-du-Roi?"

A fishing port and holiday resort down the coast. "Now, why should a gypsy be carrying a message in code?" He thought about this for a bit but it didn't do him any good: he was still awake and on his feet but his mind had turned in for the night. "Stupid question. Up, up and away."

"What? Still two lovely drawers left unsmashed?"

"Leave those for the vandals." He took her arm so that she wouldn't trip too often on the way to the door and she peered questioningly at him.

"Meaning you can break codes?"

Bowman looked around him. "Furniture, yes. Crockery, yes. Codes, no. Come, to our hotel."

They left. Before closing the door Bowman had a last look at the two still unconscious and injured men lying amidst the irretrievably ruined shambles of what had once been a beautifully appointed caravan interior. He felt almost sorry for the caravan.

4

WHEN BOWMAN woke up the birds were singing, the sky was a cloudless translucent blue and the rays of the morning sun were streaming through the window. Not the window of an hotel but the window of the blue Peugeot which he'd pulled off the road in the early hours of the morning into the shelter of a thick clump of trees that had seemed, in the darkness, to offer almost total concealment from the road. Now, in daylight, he could see that it offered nothing of the kind and that they were quite visible to any passer-by who cared to cast a casual sideways glance in their direction and, as there were those not all that far distant whose casual sideways glances he'd much rather not be the object of, he deemed it time to move on.

He was reluctant to wake Cecile. She appeared to have passed a relatively comfortable night—or what had been left of the night—with her dark head on his shoulder, a fact that he dimly resented because he had passed a most uncomfortable night, partly because he'd been loath to move for fear of disturbing her but chiefly because his unaccustomedly violent exercise of the previous night had left him with numerous aches in a wide variety of muscles that hadn't been subjected to such inconsiderate treatment for a long time. He wound down the driver's window, sniffed the fresh cool morning air and lit a cigarette. The rasp of the cigarette lighter was enough to make her stir, straighten and peer rather blearily about her until she realized where she was.

She looked at him and said: "Well, as hotels go, it was cheap enough."

"That's what I like," Bowman said. "The pioneering spirit."

"Do I *look* like a pioneer?"

"Frankly, no."

"I want a bath."

"And that you shall have and very soon. In the best hotel in Arles. Cross my heart."

"You *are* an optimist. Every hotel room will have been taken weeks ago for the gypsy festival."

"Indeed. Including the one *I* took. I booked my room two months ago."

"I see." She moved pointedly across to her own side of the seat which Bowman privately considered pretty ungrateful of her considering that she hadn't disdained the use of his shoulder as a pillow for the most of the night. "You booked your room two months ago. Mr. Bowman——"

"Neil."

"I have been very patient, haven't I, Mr. Bowman? I haven't asked questions?"

"That you haven't." He looked at her admiringly. "What a wife you're going to make. When I come home late from the office——"

"Please. What *is* it all about? Who are you?"

"A layabout on the run."

"On the run? Following the gypsies that——"

"I'm a vengeful layabout."

"I've helped you——"

"Yes, you have."

"I've let you have my car. You've put me in danger——"

"I know. I'm sorry about that and I'd no right to do it. I'll put you in a taxi for Martignane airport and the first plane for England. You'll be safe there. Or take this car. I'll get a lift to Arles.'

"Blackmail!"

"Blackmail? I don't understand. I'm offering you a place of safety. Do you mean that you're prepared to come with me?"

She nodded. He looked at her consideringly.

"Such implicit trust in a man with so much and so very recently spilled blood on his hands?"

She nodded again.

"I still don't understand." He gazed forward through the windscreen. "Could it be that the fair Miss Dubois is in the process of falling in love?"

"Rest easy," she said calmly. "The fair Miss Dubois has no such romantic stirrings in mind."

"Then why come along with me? Who knows, they may be all lying in wait—the mugger up the dark alleyway, the waiter with the poison phial, the smiler with the knife beneath the cloak—any of Czerda's pals, in fact. So why?"

"I honestly don't know."

He started up the Peugeot. "I'm sure I don't know either." But he did know. And she knew. But what she didn't know was that he knew that she knew. It was, Bowman thought, all very confusing at eight o'clock in the morning.

They'd just regained the main road when she said: "Mr. Bowman, you may be cleverer than you look."

"That would be difficult?"

"I asked you a question a minute or two ago. Somehow or other you didn't get around to answering it."

"Question? What question?"

"Never mind," she said resignedly. "I've forgotten what it was myself."

Le Grand Duc, his heliotrope-striped pyjamas largely and mercifully obscured by a napkin, was having breakfast in bed. His breakfast tray was about the same width as the bed and had to be to accommodate the vast meal it held. He had just speared a particularly succulent piece of fish when the door opened and Lila entered without the benefit of knocking. Her blond hair was uncombed. With one hand she held a wrap clutched round her while with the other she waved a piece of paper. Clearly, she was upset.

"Cecile's gone!" She waved the paper some more. "She left this."

"Gone?" Le Grand Duc transferred the forkful of fish to his mouth and savoured the passing moment. "By heavens, this red mullet is superb. Gone where?"

"I don't know. She's taken all her clothes with her."

"Let me see." He stretched out his hand and took the note from Lila. " 'Contact me Poste Restante, Saintes-Maries.' Rather less than informative, one might say. That ruffianly fellow who was with her last night——"

"Bowman? Neil Bowman?"

"That's the ruffianly fellow I meant. Check if he's still here. And your car."

"I hadn't thought of that."

"One has to have the mind for it," Le Grand Duc said kindly. He picked up his knife and fork again, waited until Lila had made her hurried exit from the room, laid down knife and fork, opened a bedside drawer and picked up the notebook which Lila had used the previous night while she was acting as his unpaid secretary when he had been interviewing the gypsies. He compared the handwriting in the notebook with that on the sheet of paper Lila had just handed him: it was indisputably the same handwriting. Le Grand Duc sighed, replaced the notebook, let the scrap of paper fall carelessly to the floor and resumed his attack on the red mullet. He had finished it and was just appreciatively lifting the cover of a dish of kidneys and bacon when Lila returned. She had exchanged her wrap for the blue minidress she had been wearing the previous evening and had combed her hair: but her state of agitation remained unchanged.

"He's gone, too. And the car. Oh, Charles, I *am* worried."

"With Le Grand Duc by your side, worry is a wasted emotion. Saintes-Maries is the place, obviously."

"I suppose so." She was doubtful, hesitant. "But how do I get there. My car—our car——"

"You will accompany me, *chérie*. Le Grand Duc always has some sort of transport or other." He paused and listened briefly to a sudden babble of voices. "Tsk! Tsk! Those gypsies can be a noisy lot. Take my tray, my dear."

Not without some difficulty, Lila removed the tray. Le Grand Duc swung from the bed, enveloped himself in a violently coloured Chinese dressing gown and headed for the door. As it was clear that the source of the disturbance came from the direction of the forecourt the Duke marched across to the terrace balustrade and looked down. A large number of gypsies were gathered round the rear of Czerda's caravan, the one part of the caravan that was visible from where Le Grand Duc was standing. Some of the gypsies were gesticulating, others shouting: all were clearly very angry about something.

"Ah!" Le Grand Duc clapped his hands together. "This is fortunate indeed. It is rare that one is actually on the spot. This is the stuff that folklore is made of. Come."

He turned and walked purposefully towards the steps leading down to the terrace. Lila caught his arm.

"But you can't go down there in your pyjamas!"

"Don't be ridiculous." Le Grand Duc swept on his way, descended the steps to the patio, ignored—or, more probably, was oblivious of—the stares of the early breakfasters on the patio and paused at the head of the forecourt steps to survey the scene. Already, he could see, the parking lot beyond the hedge was empty of caravans and two or three of those that had been in the forecourt had also disappeared while others were obviously making preparations for departure. But at least two dozen gypsies were still gathered round Czerda's caravan.

Like a psychedelic Caligula, with an apprehensive and highly embarrassed Lila following, Le Grand Duc made his imperious way down the steps and through the gypsies crowding round the caravan. He halted and looked at the spectacle in front of him. Battered, bruised, cut and heavily bandaged, Czerda and his son sat on their caravan's steps, both of them with their heads in their hands: both physically and mentally, their condition appeared to be very low. Behind them several gypsy women could be seen embarking on the gargantuan task of cleaning up the interior of the caravan which, in the daytime, looked to be an even more appalling mess than it had been by lamplight. An anarchist with an accurate line in bomb-throwing would have been proud to acknowledge that handiwork as his own.

"Tsk! Tsk! Tsk!" Le Grand Duc shook his head in a mixture of disappointment and disgust. "A family squabble. Very quarrelsome, some of those Romany families, you know. Nothing here for the true folklorist. Come, my dear, I see that most of the gypsies are already on their way. It behoves us to do the same." He led her up the steps and beckoned a passing porter. "My car, and at once."

"Your car's not here?" Lila asked.

"Of course it's not here. Good God, girl, you don't expect my employees to sleep in the same hotel as I do? Be here in ten minutes."

"Ten minutes! I have to bath, breakfast, pack, pay my bill——"

"Ten minutes."

She was ready in ten minutes. So was Le Grand Duc. He was wearing a grey double-breasted flannel suit over a maroon shirt and a panama hat with a maroon band, but for once Lila's attention was centred elsewhere. She was gazing rather dazedly down at the forecourt.

"Le Grand Duc," she repeated mechanically, "always has some sort of transport or other."

The transport in this case was a magnificent and enormous handmade cabriolet Rolls-Royce in lime and dark green. Beside it, holding the rear door open, stood a chauffeuse dressed in a uniform of lime and green, exactly the same shade as that of the car, piped in dark green, again exactly the same shade as the car. She was young, petite, auburn-haired and very pretty. She smiled as she ushered Le Grand Duc and Lila into the back seat, got behind the wheel and drove the car away in what, from inside the car, was a totally hushed silence.

Lila looked at Le Grand Duc who was lighting a large Havana with a lighter taken from a most impressively button-bestrewed console to his right.

"Do you mean to tell me," she demanded, "that you wouldn't let so deliciously pretty a creature stay in the same hotel as yourself?"

"Certainly not. Not that I lack concern for my employees." He selected a button in the console and the dividing window slid silently down into the back of the driver's seat. "And where did you spend the night, Carita, my dear?"

"Well, Monsieur le Duc, the hotels were full and——"

"Where did you spend the night?"

"In the car."

"Tsk! Tsk!" The window slid up and he turned to Lila. "But it is, as you can see, a very comfortable car."

By the time the blue Peugeot arrived in Arles, a coolness had developed between Bowman and Cecile. They had been having a discussion about matters sartorial and weren't quite seeing eye to eye. Bowman pulled up in a relatively quiet side street opposite a large if somewhat dingy clothing emporium, stopped the engine and looked at the girl. She didn't look at him.

"Well?" he said.

"I'm sorry." She was examining some point in the far distance. "It's not on. I think you're quite mad."

"Like enough," he nodded. He kissed her on the cheek, got out, took his case from the rear seat and walked across the pavement, where he stopped to examine some exotic costumes in the drapery window. He could clearly see the reflection of the car and, almost equally clearly, that of Cecile. Her lips were compressed and she was distinctly angry. She appeared to hesitate, then left the car and crossed to where he was standing.

"I could hit you," she announced.

"I wouldn't like that," he said. "You look a big strong girl to me."

"Oh, for heaven's sake, shut up and put that case back in the car."

So he shut up and put the case back in the car, took her arm and led her reluctantly into the faded emporium.

Twenty minutes later he looked at himself in a full-length mirror and shuddered. He was clad now in a black, high-buttoned and very tightly fitting suit which gave him some idea how the overweight and heroically corseted operatic diva must feel when she was reaching for a high C, a floppy white shirt, black string tie and wide-brimmed black hat. It was a relief when Cecile appeared from a dressing room, accompanied by a plump, pleasant, middle-aged woman dressed in black whom Bowman assumed to be the manageress. But he observed her only by courtesy of his peripheral vision, any man who didn't beam his entire ocular voltage directly at Cecile was either a psychiatric case or possessed of the visual acuity of a particularly myopic barnyard owl.

He had never thought of her as an eyesore but now he realized, for the first time but for keeps, that she was a stunningly lovely person. It wasn't because of the exquisite dress she wore, a beautiful, beautifully fitting, exotic and clearly very expensive gypsy costume that hadn't missed out on many of the colours of the rainbow, nor because of her white ruched mantilla headdress affair, complete with voluminous and highly provocative veil, though he had heard tell that the awareness of wearing beautiful things gives women an inner glow that shows through. All he knew was that his heart did a couple of handsprings and it wasn't until he saw her sweet and ever so slightly amused smile that he called his heart to order and resumed what he hoped was his normally inscrutable expression. The manageress put his very thoughts in words.

"Madame," she breathed, "looks beautiful."

"Madame," he said, "*is* beautiful," then reverted to his old self again.

"How much? In Swiss francs. You take Swiss francs?"

"Of course." The manageress summoned an assistant who started adding figures while the manageress packed clothes.

"She's packing up *my* clothes." Cecile sounded dismayed. "I can't go out in the street like this."

"Of course you can." Bowman had meant to be heartily reassuring but the words sounded mechanical, he still couldn't take his eyes off her. "This is fiesta time."

"Monsieur is quite correct," the manageress said. "Hundreds of young Arlésiennes dress like this at this time of year. A pleasant change and very good for them it is, too."

"And it's not bad for business either." Bowman looked at the bill the assistant had just handed him. "Two thousand, four hundred Swiss francs." He peeled three one-thousand-franc notes from Czerda's roll and handed it to the manageress. "Keep the change."

"But monsieur is too kind." From her flabbergasted expression he took it that the citizens of Arles' were not notably openhanded when it came to the question of gratuities.

"Easy come, easy go," he said philosophically and led Cecile from the shop. They got into the Peugeot and he drove for a minute or two before pulling up in an almost deserted car park. Cecile looked at him enquiringly.

"My cosmetic case," he explained. He reached into his case in the back seat and brought out a small black zipped leather bag. "Never travel without it."

She looked at him rather peculiarly. "A man doesn't carry a cosmetic case."

"This one does. You'll see why."

Twenty minutes later, when they stood before the reception desk of the grandest hotel in Arles, she understood why. They were clad as they had been when they had left the clothing emporium but were otherwise barely recognizable as the same people. Cecile's complexion was several shades darker, as was the colour of her neck, hands and wrists, she wore bright scarlet lipstick and far too much rouge, mascara and blue eye shadow: Bowman's face was now the colour of well-seasoned mahogany, his newly acquired moustache dashing to a degree. The receptionist handed him back his passport.

"Your room is ready, Mr. Parker," he said. "This is Mrs. Parker?"

"Don't be silly," Bowman said, took Cecile's suddenly stiff arm and followed the bellboy to the lift. When the bedroom door closed behind them, she looked at Bowman with a noticeable lack of enthusiasm.

"Did you *have* to say that to the receptionist?"

"Look at your hands."

"What's wrong with my hands—apart from the fact that that stuff of yours has made them filthy."

"No rings."

"Oh!"

"Well might you 'Oh!' The experienced receptionist notices those things automatically—that's why he asked. And *he* may be asked questions—any suspicious couples checked in today, that sort of thing. As far as the criminal stakes are concerned a man with his lady love in tow is automatically above suspicion—it is assumed that he has other things in mind."

"There's no need to talk——"

"I'll tell you about the birds and bees later. Meantime, what matters is that the man trusts me. I'm going out for a bit. Have your bath. Don't wash that stuff off your arms, face and neck. There's little enough left."

She looked into a mirror, lifted up her hands and studied both them and her face. "But how in heaven's name am I going to have a bath without——"

"I'll give you a hand, if you like," Bowman volunteered. She walked to the bathroom, closed and locked the door. Bowman went downstairs and paused for a moment outside a telephone kiosk in the lobby, rubbing his chin, a man deep in thought. The telephone had no dialling face which meant that outgoing calls were routed through the hotel switchboard. He walked out into the bright sunshine.

Even at that early hour the Boulevard des Lices was crowded with people. Not sightseers, not tourists, but local tradesmen setting up literally hundreds of stalls on the broad pavements of the boulevard. The street itself was as crowded as the pavements with scores of vehicles ranging from heavy trucks to handcarts unloading a variety of goods that ran the gamut from heavy agricultural machinery, through every type of food, furniture and clothes imaginable, down to the gaudiest of souvenir trinkets and endless bunches of flowers.

Bowman turned into a post office, located an empty telephone booth, raised the exchange and asked for a Whitehall number in London. While he was waiting for the call to come through he fished out the garbled message he had found in Czerda's caravan and smoothed it out before him.

At least a hundred gypsies knelt on the ground in the grassy clearing while the black-robed priest delivered a benediction. When he lowered his arm, turned, and walked towards a small black tent pitched nearby, the gypsies rose and began to disperse, some wandering aimlessly around, others drifting back to their caravans which were parked just off the road a few miles northeast of Arles: behind the caravans loomed the majestic outline of the ancient Abbey de Montmajour.

Among the parked vehicles, three were instantly identifiable: the green-and-white caravan where Alexandre's mother and the three young gypsy girls lived, Czerda's caravan which was now being towed by a garishly yellow-painted breakdown truck and Le Grand Duc's imposing green Rolls. The cabriolet hood of the Rolls was down for the sky was cloudless and the morning already hot. The chauffeuse, her auburn hair uncovered to show that she was temporarily off duty, stood with Lila by the side of the car: Le Grand Duc, reclining in the rear seat, refreshed himself with some indeterminate liquid from the open cocktail cabinet before him and surveyed the scene with interest.

Lila said: "I never associated *this* with gypsies."

"Understandable, understandable," Le Grand Duc conceded graciously. "But then, of course, you do not know your gypsies, my dear, while I am a European authority on them." He paused, considered and corrected himself. "*The* European authority. Which means, of course, the world. The religious element can be very strong, and their sincerity and devotion never more apparent than when they travel to worship the relics of Sara, their patron saint. Every day, in the last period of their travel, a priest accompanies them to bless Sara and their—but enough! I must not bore you with my erudition."

"Boring, Charles? It's all quite fascinating. What on earth is that black tent for?"

"A mobile confessional—little used, I fear. The gypsies have their own codes of right and wrong. Good God! There's Czerda going inside." He glanced at his watch. "Nine-fifteen. He should be out by lunchtime."

"You don't like him?" Lila asked curiously. "You think that he——"

"I know nothing about the fellow," Le Grand Duc said. "I would merely observe that a face such as his has not been fashioned by a lifetime of good works and pious thoughts."

There was certainly little enough indicative of either as Czerda, his bruised face at once apprehensive and grim, closed and secured the tent flap behind him. The tent itself was small and circular, not more than ten feet in diameter. Its sole furnishing consisted of a cloth-screened cubicle which served as a confessional booth.

"You are welcome, my son." The voice from the booth was deep and measured and authoritative.

"Open up, Searl," Czerda said savagely. There was a fumbling motion and a dark linen curtain dropped to reveal a seated priest, with rimless eyeglasses and a thin ascetic face, the epitome of the man of God whose devotion is tinged with fanaticism. He regarded Czerda's battered face briefly, impassively.

"People may hear," the priest said coldly. "I'm 'Monsieur le Curé' or 'Father'."

"You're 'Searl' to me and always will be," Czerda said contemptuously. "Simon Searl, the unfrocked priest. Sounds like a nursery rhyme."

"I'm not here on nursery business," Searl said sombrely. "I come from Gaiuse Strome."

The belligerence slowly drained from Czerda's face: only the apprehension remained, deepening by the moment as he looked at the expressionless face of the priest.

"I think," Searl said quietly, "that an explanation of your unbelievably incompetent bungling is in order. I hope it's a very good explanation."

"I must get out! I must get out!" Tina, the dark crop-haired young gypsy girl stared through the caravan window at the confessional tent, then swung round to face the other three gypsy women. Her eyes were red and swollen, her face very pale. "I must walk! I must breathe the air! I—I can't stand it here any more."

Marie le Hobenaut, her mother and Sara looked at one another. None of them looked very much happier than Tina. Their faces were still as sad and bitter as they had been when Bowman had watched them during the night, defeat and despair still hung as heavily in the air.

"You will be careful, Tina?" Marie's mother said anxiously. "Your father—you must think of your father."

"It's all right, Mother," Marie said. "Tina knows. She knows now." She nodded to the dark girl who hurried through the doorway, and went on softly: "She was so very much in love with Alexandre. You know."

"I know," her mother said heavily. "It's a pity that Alexandre hadn't been more in love with her."

Tina passed through the rear portion of the caravan. Seated on the steps there was a gypsy in his late thirties. Unlike most gypsies, Pierre Lacabro was squat to the point of deformity and extremely broad, and also unlike most gypsies who, in their aquiline fashion, are as aristocratically handsome as any people in Europe, he had a very broad, brutalised face with a thin cruel mouth, porcine eyes and a scar, which obviously had never been stitched, running from right eyebrow to right chin. He was, clearly, an extremely powerful person. He looked up as Tina approached and gave her a broken-toothed grin.

"And where are *you* going, my pretty maid?" He had a deep rasping, gravelly and wholly unpleasant voice.

"For a walk." She made no attempt to keep the revulsion from her face. "I need air."

"We have guards posted—and Maca and Masaine are on the watch. You know that?"

"Do you think I'd run away?"

He grinned again. "You're too frightened to run away."

With a momentary flash of spirit she said: "I'm not frightened of Pierre Lacabro."

"And why on earth should you be?" He lifted his hands, palms upwards. "Beautiful young girls like you—why, I'm like a father to them."

Tina shuddered and walked down the caravan steps. Czerda's explanation to Simon Searl had not gone down well at all. Searl was at no pains to conceal his contempt and displeasure: Czerda had gone very much on the defensive.

"And what about me," he demanded. "*I'm* the person who has suffered, not you, not Gaiuse Strome. I tell you, he destroyed everything in my caravan—and stole my eighty thousand francs."

"Which you hadn't even earned yet. That was Gaiuse Strome's money, Czerda. He'll want it back: if he doesn't get it he'll have your life in place of it."

"In God's name, Bowman's vanished! I don't know——"

"You will find him and then you will use this on him." Searl reached into the folds of his robe and brought out a pistol with a screwed-on silencer. "If you fail, I suggest you save us trouble and just use it on yourself."

Czerda looked at him for a long moment. "Who *is* this Gaiuse Strome?"

"I do not know."

"We were friends once, Simon Searl——"

"Before God, I have never met him. His instructions come either by letter or telephone and even then through an intermediary."

"Then do you know who this man is?" Czerda took Searl's arm and almost dragged him to the flap of the tent, a corner of which he eased back. Plainly in view was Le Grand Duc who had obviously replenished his glass. He was grazing directly at them and the expression of his face was very thoughtful. Czerda hastily lowered the flap. "Well?"

"That man I have seen before," Searl said. "A wealthy nobleman, I believe."

"A wealthy nobleman by the name of Gaiuse Strome?"

"I do not know. I do not wish to know."

"This is the third time I have seen this man on the pilgrimage. It is also the third year I have been working for Gaiuse Strome. He asked questions last night. This morning he was down looking at the damage that had been done to our caravan. And now he's staring straight at us. I think——"

"Keep your thinking for Bowman," Searl advised. "That apart, keep your own counsel. Our patron wishes to remain anonymous. He does not care to have his privacy invaded. You understand?"

Czerda nodded reluctantly, thrust the silenced pistol inside his shirt and left. As he did, Le Grand Duc peered thoughtfully at him over the rim of his glass.

"Good God," he said mildly. "Shriven already."

Lila said politely: "I beg your pardon, Charles."

"Nothing, my dear, nothing." He shifted his gaze and caught sight of Tina who was wandering disconsolately and apparently aimlessly across the grass. "My word, there's a remarkably fine-looking filly. Downcast, perhaps, yes, definitely downcast. But beautiful."

Lila said: "Charles, I'm beginning to think that you're a connoisseur of pretty girls."

"The aristocracy always have been. Carita, my dear, Arles and with all speed. I feel faint."

"Charles!" Lila was instant concern. "Are you unwell? The sun? If we put the hood up———"

"I'm hungry," Le Grand Duc said simply.

Tina watched the whispering departure of the Rolls then looked casually around her. Lacabro had disappeared from the steps of the green-and-white caravan. Of Maca and Masaine there was no sign. Quite fortuitously, as it seemed, she found herself outside the entrance to the black confessional tent. Not daring to look round to make a final check to see whether she was under observation, she pushed the flap to one side and went in. She took a couple of hesitating steps towards the booth.

"Father! Father!" Her voice was a tremulous whisper. "I must talk to you."

Searl's deep grave voice came from inside the booth: "That's what I'm here for, my child."

"No, no!" Still the whisper. "You don't understand. I have terrible things to tell you."

"Nothing is too terrible for a man of God to hear. Your secrets are safe with me, my child."

"But I don't *want* them to be safe with you! I want you to go to the police."

The curtain dropped and Searl appeared. His lean ascetic face was filled with compassion and concern. He put his arm round her shoulders.

"Whatever ails you, daughter, your troubles are over. What is your name, my dear?"

"Tina. Tina Daymel."

"Put your trust in God, Tina, and tell me everything."

In the green-and-white caravan Marie, her mother and Sara sat in gloomy silence. Now and again the mother gave a half-sob and dabbed at her eyes with a handkerchief.

"Where *is* Tina?" she said at length. "Where can she be? She takes so long."

"Don't worry, Madame Zigair," Sara said reassuringly. "Tina's a sensible girl. She'll do nothing silly."

"Sara's right, Mother," Marie said. "After last night———"

"I know. I know I'm being foolish. But Alexandre———"

"Please, Mother."

Madame Zigair nodded and fell silent. Suddenly the caravan door was thrown open and Tina was thrown bodily into the room to fall heavily and face downwards on the caravan floor. Lacabro and Czerda stood framed in the entrance, the former grinning, the latter savage with a barely controlled anger. Tina lay where she had fallen, very still, clearly unconscious. Her clothes had been ripped from her back which was blood-stained and almost entirely covered with a mass of wicked-looking red and purplish weals: she had been viciously, mercilessly whipped.

"Now," Czerda said softly. "Now will you all learn?"

The door closed. The three women stared in horror at the cruelly mutilated girl, then fell to their knees to help her.

5

BOWMAN'S CALL to England came through quickly and he returned to his hotel within fifteen minutes of having left it. The corridor leading to his bedroom was thickly carpeted and his footfalls soundless. He was reaching for the handle of the door when he heard voices coming from inside the room. Not voices, he realized, just one—Cecile's—and it came only intermittently: the tone of her voice was readily recognizable but the muffling effect of the intervening door was too great to allow him to distinguish the words. He was about to lean his ear against the woodwork when a chambermaid carrying an armful of sheets came round a corner of the corridor. Bowman walked unconcernedly on his way and a couple of minutes later walked as unconcernedly back. There was only silence in the room. He knocked and went inside.

Cecile was standing by the window and she turned and smiled at him as he closed the door. Her gleaming dark hair had been combed or brushed or whatever she'd done with it and she looked more fetching than ever.

"Ravishing," he said. "How did you manage without me? My word, if our children only look——"

"Another thing," she interrupted. The smile, he now noticed, lacked warmth. "This Mr. Parker business when you registered. You did show your passport, didn't you—Mr. Bowman?"

"A friend lent it to me."

"Of course. What else? Is your friend very important?"

"How's that?"

"What is your *job,* Mr. Bowman?"

"I've told you——"

"Of course. I'd forgotten. A professional idler." She sighed. "And now—breakfast?"

"First, for me, a shave. It'll spoil my complexion but I can fix that. Then breakfast."

He took the shaving kit from his case, went into the bathroom, closed the door and set about shaving. He looked around him. She'd come in here, divested herself of all her cumbersome finery, had a very careful bath to ensure that she didn't touch the stain, dressed again, reapplied to the palms of her hands some of the stain he'd left her and all this inside fifteen minutes. Not to mention the hair brushing or combing or whatever. He didn't believe it, she had about her the fastidious look of a person who'd have used up most of that fifteen minutes just in brushing her teeth. He looked into the bath and it was indubitably still wet so she had at least turned on the tap. He picked up the crumpled bathtowel and it was as dry as the sands of the Sinai Desert. She'd brushed her hair and that was all. Apart from making a phone call.

He shaved, reapplied some war paint and took Cecile down to a table in a corner of the hotel's rather ornate and statuary-crowded patio. Despite the comparatively early hour it was already well patronized with late breakfasters and early coffee-takers. For the most part the patrons were clearly tourists, but there was a fair sprinkling of the more well-to-do Arlésiens among them, some dressed in the traditional fiesta costumes of that part, some as gypsies.

As they took their seats their attention was caught and held by an enormous lime and dark green Rolls-Royce parked by the kerb: beside it stood the chauffeuse, her uniform matching the colours of the car. Cecile looked at the gleaming car in frank admiration.

"Gorgeous," she said. "Absolutely gorgeous."

"Yes indeed," Bowman agreed. "You'd hardly think she could drive a great big car like that." He ignored Cecile's old-fashioned look and leisurely surveyed the patio. "Three guesses as to the underprivileged owner."

Cecile followed his line of sight. The third table from where they sat was occupied by Le Grand Duc and Lila. A waiter appeared with a very heavy tray which he set before Le Grand Duc who picked up and drained a beaker of orange juice almost before the waiter had time to straighten what must have been his aching back.

"I thought that fellow would never come." Le Grand Duc was loud and testy.

"Charles." Lila shook her head. "You've just *had* an *enormous* breakfast."

"And now I'm having another one. Pass the rolls, *ma chérie*."

"Good God!" At their table, Cecile laid a hand on Bowman's arm. "The Duke—*and* Lila."

"What's all the surprise about." Bowman watched Le Grand Duc industriously ladling marmalade from a large jar while Lila poured him coffee. "Naturally he'd be here—where the gypsies are there the famous gypsy folklorist will be. And, of course, in the best hotel. There's the beginning of a beautiful friendship across there. Can she cook?"

"Can she—funnily enough, she can. A very good one, too. Cordon Bleu."

"Good lord! He'll kidnap her."

"But what is she still doing with him?"

"Easy. You told her about Saintes-Maries. She'll want to go there. And she hasn't a car, not since we borrowed it. He'll definitely want to be going there. And he has a car—a pound to a penny that's his Rolls. And they seem on pretty good terms, though heaven knows what she sees in our large friend. Look at his hands—they work like a conveyor belt. Heaven grant I'm never aboard a lifeboat with him when they're sharing out the last of the rations."

"I think he's good-looking. In his own way."

"So's an orangutan."

"You don't like him, do you?" She seemed amused. "Just because he said you were——"

"I don't trust him. He's a phony. I'll bet he's not a gypsy folklorist, has never written a thing about them and never will. If he's so famous and important a man why has neither of us ever heard of him? And why does he come to this part three years running to study their customs? Once would be enough for even a folklore ignoramus like me."

"Maybe he likes gypsies."

"Maybe. And maybe he likes them for all the wrong reasons."

Cecile looked at him, paused and said in a lowered voice: "You think he's this Gaiuse Strome?"

"I didn't say anything of the kind. And don't mention that name in here—you still want to live, don't you?"

"I don't see——"

"How do you know there's not a real gypsy among all the ones wearing fancy dress on this patio?"

"I'm sorry. That was silly of me."

"Yes." He was looking at Le Grand Duc's table. Lila had risen and was speaking. Le Grand Duc waved a lordly hand and she walked towards the hotel entrance. His face thoughtful, Bowman's gaze followed her as she crossed the patio, mounted the steps, crossed the foyer and disappeared.

"She *is* beautiful, isn't she?" Cecile murmured.

"How's that?" Bowman looked at her. "Yes, yes of course. Unfortunately I can't marry you both—there's a law against it." Still thoughtful, he looked across at Le Grand Duc, then back at Cecile. "Go talk to our well-built friend. Read his palm. Tell his fortune."

"What?"

"The Duke there. Go——"

"I don't think that's funny."

"Neither do I. Never occurred to me when your friend was there—she'd have recognized you. But the Duke won't—he hardly knows you. And certainly wouldn't in that disguise. Not that there's the slightest chance of him lifting his eyes from his plate anyway."

"No!"

"Please, Cecile."

"No!"

"Remember the caverns. I haven't a lead."

"Oh, God, don't!"

"Well, then."

"But *what* can I do?"

"Start off with the old mumbo-jumbo. Then say you see he has very important plans in the near future and if he is successful—then stop there. Refuse to read any more and come away. Give him the impression that he has no future. Observe his reactions."

"Then you really do suspect——"

"I suspect nothing."

Reluctantly she pushed back her chair and rose. "Pray to Sara for me."

"Sara?"

"She's the patron saint of the gypsies, isn't she?"

Bowman watched her as she moved away. She side-stepped politely to avoid bumping into another customer who had just entered, an ascetic and other-worldly looking priest: it was impossible to imagine Simon Searl as anything other than a selfless and dedicated man of God in whose hands one would willingly place one's life. They murmured apologies and Cecile carried on and stopped at the table of Le Grand Duc, who lowered his coffee cup and glanced up in properly ducal irritation.

"Well, what is it?"

"Good morning, sir."

"Yes, yes, yes, good morning." He picked up his coffee cup again. "What is it?"

"Tell your fortune, sir?"

"Can't you see I'm busy? Go away."

"Only ten francs, sir."

"I haven't got ten francs." He lowered his cup again and looked at her closely for the first time. "But by Jove, though, if only you'd blond hair ——"

Cecile smiled, took advantage of the temporary moment of admiration and picked up his left hand.

"You have a long lifeline," she announced.

"I'm as fit as a fiddle."

"And you come of noble blood."

"Any fool can see that."

"You have a very kind disposition——"

"Not when I'm starving." He snatched away his hand, used it to pick up

a roll, then glanced upwards as Lila came back to the table. He pointed his
roll at Cecile. "Remove this young pest. She's upsetting me."

"You don't *look* upset, Charles."

"How can you see what's happening to my digestion?"

Lila turned to Cecile with a smile that was half-friendly, half-apologetic,
a smile that momentarily faded as she realized who it was. Lila put her
smile back in place and said: "Perhaps you would like to read my hand?"
The tone was perfectly done, conciliatory without being patronizing, a gently
implied rebuke to Le Grand Duc's boorishness. Le Grand Duc remained
wholly unaffected.

"At a distance, if you please," he said firmly. "At a distance."

They moved off and Le Grand Duc watched them go with an expression
as thoughtful as possible for one whose jaws are moving with metronomic
regularity. He looked away from the girls and across the table where Lila
had been sitting. Bowman was looking directly at him but almost immediately looked away. Le Grand Duc tried to follow Bowman's altered line of
sight and it seemed to him that Bowman was looking fixedly at a tall thin
priest who sat with a cup of coffee before him, the same priest, Le Grand
Duc realized, as he'd seen blessing the gypsies by the Abbey de Montmajour. And there was no dispute as to where the object of Simon Searl's
interest lay: he was taking an inordinate interest in Le Grand Duc himself.

Bowman watched as Lila and Cecile spoke together some little way off:
at the moment Cecile was holding Lila's hand and appearing to speak
persuasively while Lila smiled in some embarrassment. He saw Lila press
something into Cecile's hand, then abruptly lost interest in both. From the
corner of his eye he had caught sight of something of much more immediate
importance: or he thought he had.

Beyond the patio was the gay and bustling fiesta scene in the Boulevard
des Lices. Tradesmen were still setting up last-minute stalls but by this time
they were far out-numbered by sightseers and shoppers. Together they made
up a colourful and exotic spectacle. The rare person dressed in a sober
business suit was strikingly out of place. Camera-behung tourists were there
in their scores, for the most part dressed with that excruciatingly careless
abandon that appears to afflict most tourists the moment they leave their
own borders, but even they formed a relatively drab backcloth for the three
widely differing types of people who caught and held the eye in the splendid
finery of their clothes—the Arlésienne girls so exquisitely gowned in their
traditional fiesta costumes, the hundreds of gypsies from a dozen different
countries and the *guardians,* the cowboys of the Camargue.

Bowman leaned forward in his seat, his eyes intent. Again he saw what
had attracted his attention in the first place—a flash of titian hair, but
unmistakable. It was Marie le Hobenaut and she was walking very quickly.
Bowman looked away as Cecile rejoined him and sat down.

"Sorry. Up again. A job. Left on the street——"

"But don't you want to hear—and my breakfast——"

"Those can wait. Gypsy girl, titian hair, green and black costume. Follow
her. See where she's going—and she's going some place. She's in a tearing
hurry. Now!"

"Yes, sir." She looked at him quizzically, rose and left. He did not watch
her go. Instead, he looked casually around the patio. Simon Searl, the priest,
was the first to go and he did so almost immediately, leaving some coins by
his coffee cup. Seconds later, Bowman was on his feet and following the
priest out into the street. Le Grand Duc, with his face largely obscured by a
huge coffee cup, watched the departure of both.

Among the colourful crowds, the very drabness of Searl's black robes made him an easy figure to follow. What made him even easier to follow was the fact that, as befitted a man of God, he appeared to have no suspicions of his fellow men for he did not once look back over his shoulder. Bowman closed up till he was within ten feet of him. Now he could clearly see Cecile not much more than the same distance ahead of Searl and, occasionally, there was a brief glimpse of Marie le Hobenaut's titian hair. Bowman closed even more closely on Searl and waited his opportunity.

It came almost at once. Hard by a group of fish stalls half-a-dozen rather unprepossessing gypsies were trying to sell some horses that had seen better days. As Bowman, no more than five feet behind Searl now, approached the horses he bumped into a dark, swarthy young man with a handsome face and hairline moustache: he sported a black sombrero and rather flashy, tight-fitting dark clothes. Both men murmured apologies, side-stepped and passed on. The dark young man took only two steps, turned and looked after Bowman, who was now almost lost to sight, edging his way through the group of horses.

Ahead of him, Searl stopped as a restive horse whinnied, tossed its head and moved to block his progress. The horse reared, Searl stepped prudently backwards and as he did so Bowman kicked him behind the knee. Searl grunted in agony and fell to his sound knee. Bowman, concealed by horses on both sides of him, stooped solicitously over Searl and chopped his knuckles of his right hand into the base of the man's neck. Searl collapsed.

"Watch those damned horses!" Bowman shouted. At once several gypsies quieted the restive horses and pulled them apart to make a clear space round the fallen priest.

"What happened?" one of them demanded. "What happened?"

"Selling that vicious brute?" Bowman asked. "He ought to be destroyed. Kicked him right in the stomach. Don't just stand there. Get a doctor."

One of the gypsies at once hurried away. The others stooped low over the prostrate man and while they did so Bowman made a discreet withdrawal. But it wasn't so discreet as to go unobserved by the same dark young man who had earlier bumped into Bowman: he was busy studying his fingernails.

Bowman was finishing off his breakfast when Cecile returned.

"I'm hot," she announced. She looked it. "*And* I'm hungry."

Bowman crooked a finger at a passing waiter.

"Well?"

"She went into a chemist's shop. She bought bandages—yards and yards—and a whole lot of cream and ointment and then she went back to the caravans—in a square not far from here——"

"The green-and-white caravan?"

"Yes. There were two women waiting for her at the caravan door and then all three went inside."

"Two women?"

"One middle-aged, the other young with auburn hair."

"Marie's mother and Sara. Poor Tina."

"What do you mean?"

"Just rambling." He glanced across the courtyard. "The love birds across there."

Cecile followed his gaze to where Le Grand Duc, who was now sitting back with the relieved air of a man who has narrowly escaped death from starvation, smiled indulgently at Lila as she put her hand on his and talked animatedly.

Bowman said: "Is your girl friend simple-minded or anything like that?"

She gave him a long cool look. "Not any more than I am."

"Um. She knew you, of course. What did you tell her?"

"Nothing—except that you had to run for your life."

"Didn't she wonder why *you* came?"

"Because I wanted to, I said."

"Tell her I was suspicious of the Duke?"

"Well——"

"It doesn't matter. She have anything to tell you?"

"Not much. Just that they stopped by to watch a gypsy service this morning."

"Service?"

"You know—religious."

"Regular priest."

"So Lila said."

"Finish your breakfast." He pushed back his chair. "I won't be long."

"But I thought—I thought you would want to know what the Duke said, his reactions. After all, that's why you sent me."

"Was it?" Bowman seemed abstracted. "Later." He rose and entered the hotel: the girl watched him go with a puzzled expression on her face.

"Tall, you say, El Brocador. Thickset. Very fast." Czerda rubbed his own battered and bandaged face in painfully tender recollection, and looked at the four men seated at the table in his caravan—El Brocador, the swarthy young man Bowman had bumped into in the street, Ferenc, Pierre Lacabro and a still shaken and pale Simon Searl who was trying to rub the back of his neck and the back of his thigh simultaneously.

"His face was darker than you say," El Brocador said. "And a moustache."

"Dark faces and a moustache you can buy in shops. He can't hide his stock in trade—violence."

"I hope I meet this man soon," Pierre Lacabro said. His tone was almost wistful.

"I wouldn't be in too much of a hurry," Czerda said drily. "You didn't see him at all, Searl?"

"I saw nothing. I just felt those two blows in the back—no, I didn't even feel the second blow."

"Why in God's name did you have to go to that hotel patio anyway?"

"I wanted to get a close-up of this Duc de Croytor. It was *you*, Czerda, who made me curious about him. I wanted to hear his voice. Who he spoke to, see if he has any contacts, who——"

"He's with this English girl. He's harmless."

"Clever men do things like that," Searl said.

"Clever men don't do the things you do," Czerda said grimly. "Now Bowman knows who you are. He almost certainly knows now that someone in Madame Zigair's caravan has been badly hurt. If the Duc de Croytor is who you think he is then he must know now that you suspect him of being Gaiuse Strome—and, if he is, he's not going to like any of these three things at all." The expression on Searl's face left no doubt but that he himself was of the same opinion. Czerda went on: "Bowman. He's the only solution. This man must be silenced. Today. But carefully. Quietly. By accident. Who knows what friends this man may not have?"

"I have told you how this can be done," El Brocador said.

"And a good way. We move on this afternoon. Lacabro, you're the only one of us he does not know. Go to his hotel. Keep watch. Follow him. We dare not lose him now.''

"That will be a pleasure."

"No violence," Czerda warned.

"Of course not." He looked suddenly crestfallen. "But I don't know what he looks like. Dark and thickset—there are hundreds of dark and thickset——"

"If he's the man El Brocador described and the man I remember seeing on the hotel patio," Searl said, "he'll be with a girl dressed as a gypsy. Young, dark, pretty, dressed mainly green and gold, four gold bangles on her left wrist."

Cecile looked up from the remains of her breakfast as Bowman joined her at her table.

"You took your time," she observed.

"I have not been idle. I've been out. Shopping."

"I didn't see you go."

"They have a back entrance."

"And now?"

"Now I have urgent business to attend to."

"Like this? Just sitting here?"

"Before I attend to the urgent thing I have to attend to I've something else urgent to attend to first. And that involves sitting here. Do you know they have some very nosy Chinese in the city of Arles?"

"What on earth are you talking about?"

"Couple sitting over by Romeo and Juliet there. Don't look. Man's big for a Chinese, forty, although it's always hard to say with them. Woman with him is younger, Eurasian, very good-looking. Both wearing lightly tinted sunglasses with those built-in reflectors so that you can't see through them from the outside."

Cecile lifted a cup of coffee and looked idly round the patio. She said: "I see them now."

"Never trust people with reflecting sunglasses. He seems to be displaying a very keen interest in Le Grand Duc."

"It's his size."

"Like enough." Bowman looked thoughtfully at the Chinese couple, then at Le Grand Duc and Lila, then back at the Chinese again. Then he said: "We can go now."

She said: "This urgent business—this first urgent business you had to attend to——"

"Attended to. I'll bring the car round to the front."

Le Grand Duc watched his departure and announced to Lila: "In about an hour we mingle with our subjects."

"Subjects, Charles?"

"Gypsies, dear child. But first, I must compose another chapter of my book."

"Shall I bring you pen and paper?"

"No need, my dear."

"You mean—you mean you do it all in your head? It's not possible, Charles."

He patted her hand and smiled indulgently.

"What you can get me is a litre of beer. It's becoming uncommonly warm. Find a waiter, will you?"

Lila moved obediently away and Le Grand Duc looked after her. There was nothing indulgent about the expression on his face when he saw her talk briefly and smilingly to the gypsy girl who had so recently read her fortune: there was nothing indulgent about it when he examined the Chinese couple at an adjacent table: even less so when he saw Cecile join Bowman in a white car in the street: and least of all when he observed another car move off within seconds of Bowman's.

Cecile gazed in perplexity round the interior of the white Simca. She said: "What's all this about, then?"

"Such things as phones," he explained. "Fixed it while you were having breakfast. Fixed two of them, in fact."

"Two what?"

"Two hired cars. Never know when you're going to run short."

"But—but in so short a time."

"Garage is just down the street—they sent a man to check." He took out Czerda's barely depleted wad of Swiss notes, crackled it briefly and returned it. "Depends upon the deposit."

"You really are quite amoral, aren't you?" She sounded almost admiring.

"How's that again?"

"The way you throw other people's money around."

"Life is for the living, money for the spending," Bowman said pontifically. "No pockets in a shroud."

"You're hopeless," she said. "Quite, quite hopeless. And why this car, anyway?"

"Why that get-up you're wearing?"

"Why—oh, I see. Of course the Peugeot's known. I hadn't thought of that." She looked at him curiously as he turned the Simca in the direction of a signpost saying *Nimes*. "Where do you think you're going?"

"I'm not quite sure. I'm looking for a place where I can talk undisturbed."

"To me?"

"Still your apprehensions. I'll have all the rest of my life to talk to you. When we were on the patio a battered-looking gypsy in a battered-looking Renault sat and watched us for ten minutes. Both of them are about a hundred yards behind us now. I want to talk to the battered-looking gypsy."

"Oh!"

"Well might you say 'Oh!' How, one wonders, is it that Gaiuse Strome's henchmen are on to us so soon." He gave her a sidelong glance. "You're looking at me in a very peculiar manner, if I may say so."

"I'm thinking."

"Well?"

"If they're on to you, why did you bother switching cars?"

Bowman said patiently: "When I hired the Simca I didn't know they were on to me."

"And now you're taking me into danger again? Or what might be danger?"

"I hope not. If I am, I'm sorry. But if they're on to me, they're on to the charming gypsy girl who has been sitting by my side—don't forget that it was you that the priest was tailing when he met up with his unfortunate accident. Would you rather I'd left you behind to cope with them alone?"

"You don't offer very much in the way of choices," she complained.

"I've got very little to offer." Bowman looked in the mirror. The battered

Renault was less than a hundred yards behind. Cecile looked over her shoulder.

"Why don't you stop here and talk to him? He'd never dare do anything here. There are far too many people around."

"Far too many," Bowman agreed. "When I talk to him I don't want anyone within half a mile."

She glanced at him, shivered and said nothing. Bowman took the Simca over the Rhône to Trinquetaille, turned left on to the Albaron Road and then left again on to the road that ran south down the right bank of the river. Here he slowed and gently brought the car to a stop. The driver of the Renault, he observed, did the same thing at a discreet distance to the rear. Bowman drove the Simca on its way again: the Renault followed.

A mile farther on into the flat and featureless plains of the Camargue Bowman stopped again. So did the Renault. Bowman got out, went to the rear of the car, glanced briefly at the Renault parked about a hundred yards away, opened the boot, extracted an implement from the toolkit, thrust it inside his jacket, closed the boot and returned to his seat. The implement he laid on the floor beside him.

"What's that?" Cecile looked and sounded apprehensive.

"A wheel brace."

"Something wrong with the wheels?"

"Wheel braces can have other uses."

He drove off. After a few minutes the road began to climb slightly, rounded an unexpectedly sharp left-hand corner and there suddenly, almost directly beneath them and less than twenty feet away lay the murkily gleaming waters of the Grand Rhône. Bowman braked heavily, was out of the car even as it stopped and walked quickly back the way he had come. The Renault rounded the corner and its driver, caught completely unawares, slewed the car to a skidding stop less than ten yards from Bowman.

Bowman, one hand behind his back, approached the Renault and jerked the driver's door open. Pierre Lacabro glared out at him, his broad brutalized face set and savage.

"I'm beginning to think you're following me around," Bowman said mildly.

Lacabro didn't reply. Instead, with one hand on the wheel and the other on the door frame to afford him maximum leverage he launched himself from the car with a speed surprising for a man of his bulk. Bowman had been prepared for nothing else. He stepped quickly to one side and as the diving Lacabro hurtled past him he brought the wheel brace swinging down on Lacabro's left arm. The sound of the blow, the surprisingly loud crack of a breaking bone and Lacabro's shriek of pain were almost instantaneous.

"Who sent you?" Bowman asked.

Lacabro, writhing on the ground and clutching his damaged left forearm, snarled something incomprehensible in Romany.

"Please, please listen," Bowman said. "I'm dealing with murderers. I know I'm dealing with murderers. More important I know how to deal with murderers. I've already broken one bone—I should think it's your forearm. I'm prepared to go right on breaking as many bones as I have to—assuming you stay conscious—until I find out why those four women in that green-and-white-painted caravan are terrified out of their lives. If you do become unconscious, I'll just sit around and smoke and wait till you're conscious again and break a few more bones."

Cecile had left the Simca and was now only feet away. Her face was very pale. She stared at Bowman in horror.

"Mr. Bowman, do you mean———"

"Shut up!" He returned his attention to Lacabro. "Come now, tell me about those ladies."

Lacabro mouthed what was almost certainly another obscenity, rolled over quickly and as he propped himself up on his right elbow Cecile screamed. Lacabro had a gun in his hand but shock or pain or both had slowed his reactions. He screamed and his gun went flying in one direction while the wheel brace went in another. He clutched the middle of his face with both hands: blood seeped through his fingers.

"And now your nose is gone, isn't it?" Bowman said. "That dark girl, Tina, she's been hurt, hasn't she? How badly has she been hurt? Why was she hurt? Who hurt her?"

Lacabro took his hands away from his bleeding face. His nose wasn't broken, but it still wasn't a very pretty sight and wouldn't be for some time to come. He spat blood and a broken tooth, snarled again in Romany and stared at Bowman like a wild animal.

"*You* did it," Bowman said with certainty. "Yes, you did it. One of Czerda's hatchet men, aren't you?" Perhaps *the* hatchet man. I wonder, my friend. I wonder. Was it *you* who killed Alexandre in the caverns?"

Lacabro, his face the face of a madman, pushed himself drunkenly to his feet and stood there, swaying just as drunkenly. He appeared to be on the verge of total collapse, his eyes turning up in his head. Bowman approached and, as he did so Lacabro, showing an incredible immunity to pain, an animal-like cunning and an equally animal-like power of recuperation suddenly stepped forward and brought his right fist up in a tremendous blow which, probably due more to good fortune than calculation, struck Bowman on the side of the chin. Bowman staggered backwards, lost his balance and fell heavily on the short turf only a few feet away from the vertical drop into the Rhône. Lacabro made no move to follow. Dazed with pain and his mind beclouded as it must have been, he made no move to follow. Lacabro had his priorities right. He turned and ran for the gun which had landed only a foot or two from where Cecile was standing, the shock in her face reflected in the immobility in her body.

Bowman pushed himself rather dizzily up on one arm. He could see it all happening in slow motion, the girl with the gun at her feet, Lacabro lurching towards it, the girl standing stock-still. Maybe she couldn't even see the damn thing, he thought despairingly, but her eyes couldn't be all that bad, if she couldn't see a gun two feet away she'd no right to be out without a white stick. But her eyes weren't quite so bad as that. Suddenly she stopped, picked up the gun, threw it into the Rhône, then, with commendable foresight, dropped flat to the ground as Lacabro, his battered bleeding face masked in blood and hate, advanced to strike her down. But even in that moment of what must have been infuriating frustration and where his overriding instinct must have been savagely to maim the girl who had deprived him of his gun, Lacabro still had his priorities right. He ignored the girl, turned and headed for Bowman in a low crouching run.

But Cecile had bought Bowman all the time he needed. By the time Lacabro reached him he was on his feet again, still rather dazed and shaken but a going concern nonetheless. He avoided Lacabro's first bull rush and wickedly swinging boot and caught the gypsy as he passed: it so chanced that he caught him by the left arm. Lacabro shouted in agony, dragged his arm free at whatever unknown cost to himself and came again. This time Bowman made no attempt to avoid him but advanced himself at equal speed. His clubbing right hand had no difficulty in reaching Lacabro's chin, for now Lacabro had no left guard left. He staggered backwards several involuntary paces, tottered briefly on the edge of the bluff, then toppled backwards into the Rhône. The splash caused by his impact on the muddied waters seemed quite extraordinarily loud.

Bowman looked gingerly over the crumbling edge of the bluff: there was no sign of Lacabro. If he'd been unconscious when he'd struck the water he'd have gone to the bottom and that was that: there could be no possibility of locating him in those dark waters. Not that Bowman relished the prospect of trying to rescue the gypsy: if he were not unconscious he would certainly express his gratitude by doing his best to drown his rescuer. Bowman did not feel sufficiently attached to Lacabro to take the risk.

He went to the Renault, searched it briefly, found what he expected to find—nothing—started up the engine, let in first gear, aimed it for the bank of the river and jumped out. The little car trundled to the edge of the bluff, cartwheeled over the edge and fell into the river with a resounding crash that sent water rising to a height of thirty feet.

Much of this water rained down on Lacabro. He was half-sitting, half-lying on a narrow ledge of pebble and sand under the overhang of the bluff. His clothes were soaked, his right hand clutched his left wrist. On his dazed and uncomprehending face was a mixture of pain and bewilderment and disbelief. It was, by any reckoning, the face of a man who has had enough for one day.

Cecile was still sitting on the ground when Bowman approached her. He said: "You're ruining that lovely gypsy costume sitting there."

"Yes, I suppose I am." Her voice was matter-of-fact, remarkably calm. She accepted his hand, got to her feet and looked around her. "He's gone?"

"Let's say I can't find him."

"That wasn't—that wasn't fair fighting."

"That was the whole idea behind it, pet. Ideally, of course, he would have riddled me with bullets."

"But—but can he swim?"

"How the hell should I know?" He led her back to the Simca and after they'd gone a mile in silence he looked at her curiously. Her hands were trembling, her face had gone white and when she spoke her voice was a muted whisper with a shake in it: clearly some sort of delayed shock had set in.

She said: "Who are you?"

"Never mind."

"I—I saved your life today."

"Well, yes, thanks. But you should have used that gun to shoot him or hold him up."

There was a long pause, then she sniffed loudly and said in almost a wail: "I've never fired a gun in my life. I can't *see* to fire a gun."

"I know. I'm sorry about that. I'm sorry about everything, Cecile. But I'm sorriest of all that I ever got you into this damnably ugly mess. God, I should have known better."

"Why blame yourself?" Still the near-sob in her voice. "You had to run someplace last night and my room—" She broke off, peered at him and whispered: "You're thinking of something else, aren't you?"

"Let's get back to Arles," he said. She peered at him some more, looked away and tried to light a cigarette but her hand shook so much he did it for her. Her hand was still shaking when they got back to the hotel.

6

BOWMAN DREW up outside the hotel entrance. Not five yards away Lila sat alone by a table just inside the patio entrance. It was difficult to say whether she looked primarily angry or disconsolate: she certainly did not look happy.

"Boy friend's ditched her," Bowman announced. "Meet me in fifteen minutes. Alleyway at the back entrance of the hotel. Stay out of sight till you see a blue Citroën. I'll be inside. Stay off the patio. You'll be safe in the foyer."

Cecile nodded to Lila. "Can I talk to her?"

"Sure. Inside."

"But if we're seen——"

"It won't matter. Going to tell her what a dreadful person I am?"

"No." A shaky smile.

"Ah: Then you're going to announce our forthcoming nuptials."

"Not that either." Again the smile.

"You want me to make your mind up?"

She put a hand on his arm. "I think you might even be rather a kind person."

"I doubt whether the lad in the Rhône would share your sentiments," Bowman said drily.

The smile vanished. She got out, Bowman drove off, she watched him disappear with a small frown creasing her forehead, then went on to the patio. She looked at Lila, nodded towards the hotel foyer: they went in together, talking.

"You're sure?" Cecile asked. "Charles recognizes Neil Bowman?"

Lila nodded.

"How? Why?"

"I don't know. He's very, very shrewd, you know."

"Something more than a famous wine-grower or folklorist, you would say?"

"I would say."

"And he doesn't trust Bowman?"

"That puts it very mildly indeed."

"Stalemate. You know what Bowman thinks of the Duke. I'm afraid my money's on my man, Lila. He disposed of another of the bad men to-day——"

"He did *what?*"

"Threw him into the Rhône. I saw him do it. He says——"

"So that's why you looked like a ghost when I saw you just now."

"I felt a bit like one, too. He says he's killed two others. I believe him. And I saw him lay out two more. Local colour is local colour but that would be ridiculous, you can't fake a dead man. He's on the side of the angels, Lila. Not, mind you, that I can see the angels liking it very much."

"I'm no angel and I don't like any part of it," Lila said. "I'm out of my depth and I don't know how to cope. What *are* we to do?"

"You're no more lost than I am. Do? Do what we were told to do, I suppose."

"I suppose so." Lila sighed and resumed her earlier woebegone expression. Cecile peered at her.

"Where is Charles?"

"He's gone." Her gloom deepened. "He's just gone off with that little chauffeuse—that's what *he* calls her—and told me to wait here."

"Lila!" Cecile stared at her friend. "It's not possible——"

"Why? Why is it not? What's wrong with Charles?"

"Nothing, of course. Nothing at all." Cecile rose. "Two minutes for an appointment. Our Mr. Bowman does not like to be kept waiting."

"When I think of him with that little minx——"

"She looked a perfectly charming young girl to me."

"That's what I thought, too," Lila admitted. "But that was an hour ago."

Le Grand Duc was not, in fact, with the little minx, nor was he anywhere near her. In the square where the Romanian and Hungarian caravans were pulled up, there was no sign of either Carita or the huge green Rolls and neither could have been said to be normally inconspicuous. Le Grand Duc, on the contrary, was very much in evidence: not far from the green-and-white caravan and, with notebook in hand, he was talking with considerable animation to Simon Searl. Czerda, as befitted the leader of the gypsies and an already established acquaintance of Le Grand Duc, was close by but taking no part in the conversation: Searl, from what few signs of emotion that occasionally registered in his thin ascetic face, looked as if he wished he were taking no part in it either.

"Vastly obliged, Monsieur le Curé, vastly obliged." Le Grand Duc was at his regally gracious best. "I can't tell you how impressed I was by the service you held in the fields by the Abbey this morning. Moving, most moving. By Jove, I'm adding to my store of knowledge every minute." He peered more closely at Searl. "Have you hurt your leg, my dear fellow?"

"A slight strain, no more." The only obvious strain was in his face and voice.

"Ah, but you must look after those slight strains—can develop very serious complications, you know. Yes, indeed, very serious." He removed his monocle, swinging it on the end of its thick black ribbon, the better to observe Searl. "Haven't I seen you somewhere before—I don't mean at the Abbey. Yes, yes, of course—outside the hotel this morning. Odd, I don't recall you limping then. But then, I'm afraid my eyesight——" He replaced his monocle. "My thanks again. And watch that strain. Do exercise the greatest care, Monsieur le Curé. For your own sake."

Le Grand Duc tucked the notebook in an inner pocket and marched majestically away. Czerda looked at Searl, the unbandaged parts of his face registering no expression. Seral, for his part, licked dry lips, said nothing, turned and walked away.

To even a close observer who knew him, the man behind the wheel of the gleamingly blue Citroën parked in the alleyway behind the hotel must have been almost totally unrecognizable as Bowman. He was dressed in a white sombrero, dark glasses, an excruciating blue-and-white polka-dotted shirt, an unbutt oned, embroidered black waistcoat, a pair of moleskin trousers and high boots. The complexion was paler, the moustache larger. Beside him on the seat lay a small purse-stringed bag. The offside front door opened and Cecile peered in, blinking uncertainly.

"I don't bite," Bowman said encouragingly.

"Good God!" She slid into her seat. "What—what's this?"

"I'm a *guardian,* a cowboy in his Sunday best, one of many around. Told you I'd been shopping. Your turn, now."

"What's in that bag?"

"My poncho, of course."

She eyed him with the speculative look that had now become almost habitual with her as he drove her to the clothing emporium they'd visited earlier that morning. After a suitable lapse of time the same manageress fluttered around Cecile, making gushing, admiring remarks, talking with her arms as much as with her voice. Cecile was now attired in the fiesta costume of an Arlésienne, with a long sweeping darkly embroidered dress, a ruched lace white bodice and a wimpled hat of the same material. The hat was perched on a dark red wig.

"Madame looks—fantastic!" the manageress said ecstatically.

"Madame matches the price," Bowman said resignedly. He peeled off some more banknotes and led Cecile to the Citroën where she sat and smoothed the rich material of her dress approvingly.

"Very nice, I must say. You like dressing girls up?"

"Only when I'm being bankrolled by criminals. That's hardly the point. A certain dark gypsy girl has been seen with me. There's not an insurance company in Europe would look at that dark gypsy girl."

"I see." She smiled wanly. "All this solicitude for your future wife?"

"Of course. What else?"

"The fact that, quite frankly, you can't afford to lose your assistant at the moment?"

"Never occurred to me."

He drove the Citroën close to the point where the Hungarian and Romanian caravans were parked in the square. He stopped the Citroën, lifted his purse-stringed bag, got out, straightened and turned. As he did so, he bumped into a large pedestrian who was sauntering slowly by. The pedestrian stopped and glared at him through a black-beribboned monocle: Le Grand Duc was not accustomed to being bumped into by anyone.

"Your pardon, m'sieur," Bowman said.

Le Grand Duc favoured Bowman with a look of considerable distaste. "Granted."

Bowman smiled apologetically, took Cecile's arm and moved off. She said to him, *sotto voce* and accusingly: "You did that on purpose."

"So? If he doesn't recognize us, who will?" He took another couple of steps and halted. "Well, now, what could this be?"

There was a sudden stir of interest as a plain black van turned into the square. The driver got out, made what was evidently an enquiry of the nearest gypsy who pointed across the square, entered the van again and drove it across to the vicinity of Czerda's caravan. Czerda himself was by the steps, talking to Ferenc: neither appeared to have made much progress in the recovery from their injuries.

The driver and an assistant jumped down, went to the rear of the van, opened the doors and, with considerable difficulty and not without willing help, they slid out a stretcher on which, left arm in sling and face heavily bandaged, lay the recumbent form of Pierre Lacabro. The malevolent gleam in the right eye—the left one was completely shut—showed clearly that Lacabro was very much alive. Czerda and Ferenc, consternation in their faces, moved quickly to help the stretcher-bearers. Inevitably, Le Grand Duc was one of the first on the immediate scene. He bent briefly over the battered Lacabro, then straightened.

"Tsk! Tsk! Tsk!" He shook his head sadly. "Nobody's safe on the roads those days." He turned to Czerda. "Isn't this my poor friend Mr. Koscis."

"No." Czerda spoke with considerable restraint.

"Ah! I'm glad to hear it. Sorry for this poor fellow of course. By the way,

I wonder if you'd tell Mr. Koscis that I'd like to have another word with him when he's here? At his convenience, of course."

"I'll see if I can find him." Czerda helped move the stretcher towards the steps of his own caravan and Le Grand Duc turned away, narrowly avoiding coming into collision with the Chinese couple who had earlier been on the patio of the hotel. He doffed his hat in gallant apology to the Eurasian woman.

Bowman had missed none of the by-play. He looked first at Czerda, whose face was registering a marked degree of mixed anger and apprehension, then at Le Grand Duc, then at the Chinese couple: he turned to Cecile.

"There now," he whispered. "I knew he could swim. Let's not show too keen a degree of interest in what's going on." He led her away a few paces. "You know what I want to do—it'll be safe, I promise."

He watched her as she wandered casually past Czerda's caravan and stopped to adjust a shoe in the vicinity of the green-and-white caravan. The window at the side was curtained but the window itself slightly ajar.

Satisfied, Bowman moved off across the square to where a group of horses were tethered by some trees close by several other caravans. He looked aimlessly around to check that he was unobserved, saw Czerda's caravan door close as the stretcher was brought inside, dug into his bag and fetched out a fistful of coiled, brown-paper sheathed objects, each one fitted with an inch of blue touch paper: they were, quite simply, old-fashioned firecrackers . . .

In Czerda's caravan, Czerda himself, Ferenc, Simon Searl and El Brocador were gathered round Pierre Lacabro's still recumbent form. The expression on what little could be seen of Lacabro's face registered a degree of unhappiness that was not entirely attributable to his physical sufferings: he had about him the wounded appearance of one whose injuries are not being accorded their due need of loving care and concerned sympathy.

"You fool, Lacabro!" Czerda's voice was almost a shout. "You crazy idiot! No violence, I told you. *No* violence."

"Maybe you should have told Bowman instead," El Brocador suggested. "Bowman knew. Bowman was watching. Bowman was waiting. Who is going to tell Gaiuse Strome?"

"Who but our unfrocked friend here," Czerda said savagely. "I do not envy you, Searl."

From the look on Searl's face it was clear that he didn't envy himself either. He said unhappily: "That may not be necessary. If Gaiuse Strome is who we now all think he is, then he knows already."

"Knows?" Czerda demanded. "What can he know? He doesn't know that Lacabro is one of my men and so one of his. He doesn't know that Lacabro didn't have a road accident. He doesn't know that Bowman is responsible. He doesn't know that once again we've managed to lose track of Bowman—while at the same time Bowman appears to know all our movements. If you think you have nothing to explain, Searl, you're out of your mind." He turned to Ferenc. "Round the caravans. Now. We leave inside the half-hour. Tell them that tonight we camp by Vaccarès. What was that?"

There had come clearly and sharply the sound of a series of sharp reports. Men shouted, horses whinnied in fear, a policeman's whistle blew and still the series of flat staccato explosions continued. Czerda, followed by the three others, rushed to the door of his caravan and threw it open.

They were not alone in their anxiety and curiosity to discover the source of the disturbance. It would hardly be exaggeration to claim that within thirty seconds every pair of eyes in the square were trained on the north-eastern part of it where a group of gypsies and *guardians,* Bowman prominently active among them, were fighting to restrain a rearing, milling, whinnying and by now thoroughly fear-crazed group of horses.

One pair of eyes only were otherwise engaged and those belonged to Cecile. She was pressed close in to the side of the green-and-white-painted caravan, standing on tiptoe and peering through a gap she had just made in the curtain.

It was dark inside the curtained caravan but the darkness was far from total and even Cecile's eyes quickly became accustomed to the gloom: when they did it was impossible for her to restrain her involuntary shocked gasp of horror. A girl with dark cropped hair was lying face down on a bunk—obviously the only way she could possibly lie. Her bare and savagely mutilated back had not been bandaged but had been liberally covered with salves of some kind. From her continuous restive movements and occasional moans it was clear that she was not sleeping.

Cecile lowered the curtain and moved off. Madame Zigair, Sara and Marie le Hobenaut were on the steps of the cavaran, peering across the square, and Cecile walked by them as unconcernedly as she could, which was not easy when her legs felt shaky and she was sick inside. She crossed the square and rejoined Bowman who had just succeeded in calming down one of the panic-stricken horses. He released the horse, took her arm and led her towards where they'd left the Citroën parked. He looked at her, but didn't have to look closely.

"You didn't like what you saw, did you?" he said.

"Teach me how to use a gun and I'll use it. Even though I can't see. I'll get close enough."

"As bad as that?"

"As bad as that. She's hardly more than a child, a little thin creature, and they've practically flayed the skin from her back. It was horrible. The poor child must be in agony."

"So you don't feel so sorry for the man I threw in the Rhône?"

"I would. If I met him. With a gun in my hand."

"No guns. I don't carry one myself. But I take your point."

"And you seem to take my news very calmly."

"I'm as mad as you are, Cecile, only I've been mad about it for a long time now and I can't keep showing it all the time. As for the beating the girl got, it had to be something like that. Like Alexandre, the poor kid got desperate and tried to pass on a message, some information, so they taught her what they thought would be a permanent lesson to herself and the other women, and it probably will."

"What information?"

"If I knew that I'd have those four women out of that caravan and in safety in ten minutes."

"If you don't want to tell, don't tell."

"Look, Cecile——"

"It's all right. It doesn't matter." She paused. "You know that I wanted to run away this morning? Coming back from the Rhône?"

"I wouldn't have been surprised."

"Not now. Not any more. You're stuck with me now."

"I wouldn't want to be stuck with anyone else."

She looked at him almost in surprise. "You said that without smiling."

"I said it without smiling," he said.

They reached the Citroën, turned and looked back towards the square.

The gypsies were milling around in a state of great activity. Ferenc, they could see, was going from one caravan to the next, speaking urgently to the owners, and as soon as he left them they began making preparations to hitch their towing units onto the caravans.

"Pulling out?" Cecile looked at Bowman in surprise. "Why? Because of a few firecrackers?"

"Because of our friend who's been in the Rhône. And because of me."

"You?"

"They know now, since our friend returned from his bathe, that I'm on to them. They don't know how much I know. They don't know what I look like now but they know that I'll be looking different. They do know that they can't get me here in Arles because they can't have any idea where I am or where I might be staying. They know that to get me they'll have to isolate me and to do that they'll have to draw me out into the open. Tonight they'll camp in the middle of nowhere, somewhere deep in the Camargue. And there they'll hope to get me. For they know now that wherever their caravans are, there I'll be too."

"You are good at making speeches, aren't you?" There was no malice in the green eyes.

"It's just practice."

"And you haven't exactly a low opinion of yourself, have you?"

"No." He regarded her speculatively. "Do you think they have?"

"I'm sorry." She touched the back of his hand in a gesture of contrition. "I talk that way when I'm scared."

"Me too. That's most of the time. We'll leave after you've picked your things up from the hotel and, in the best Pinkerton fashion, tail them from in front. Because if we follow them, they'll string out watchers at regular intervals to check every car that follows. And there won't be all that many cars moving south—tonight's the big fiesta night in Arles and most people won't be moving down to Saintes-Maries for another forty-eight hours."

"They would recognize us? In those rigouts? Surely they can't——"

"They can't recognize us. They can't possibly be on to us yet. Not this time. I'm positive. They don't have to be. They'll be looking for a car with a couple in it. They'll be looking for a car with Arles number plates, because it'll have to be a rented car. They'll be looking for a couple in disguise, because they'll have to be in disguise, and in those parts that means only gypsy or *guardian* fiesta costumes. They'll be looking for a couple with by now certain well-known characteristics such as that you are slender, have high cheekbones and green eyes, while I'm far from slender and have certain scars on my face that only a dye can conceal. How many cars with how many couples going south to Vaccarès this afternoon will match up with all those qualifications?"

"One." She shivered. "You don't miss much, do you?"

"Neither will they. So we go ahead of them. If they don't catch up with us we can always turn back to find out where they've stopped. They won't suspect cars coming from the south. At least, I hope to God they don't. But keep those dark glasses on all the time: those green eyes are a dead give-away."

Bowman drove back to the hotel and stopped about fifty yards from the patio, the nearest parking place he could get. He said to Cecile: "Get packed. Fifteen minutes. I'll join you in the hotel inside ten."

"You, of course, have some little matter to attend to first?"

"I have."

"Care to tell me what it is?"

"No."

"That's funny. I thought you trusted me now."

"Naturally. Any girl who is going to marry me——"

"I don't deserve that."

"You don't. I trust you, Cecile. Implicitly."

"Yes." She nodded as if satisfied. "I can see you mean that. What you don't trust is my ability not to talk under pressure."

Bowman looked at her for several moments, then said: "Did I suggest, sometime during the middle watches of the night, that you weren't—ah—quite as bright as you might be?"

"You called me a fool several times, if that's what you mean."

"You can get around to forgiving me?"

"I'll work on it." She smiled, got out of the car and walked away. Bowman waited till she had turned into the patio, left the car, walked back to the post office, picked up a telegram that was awaiting him in the Poste Restante, took it back to the car and opened it. The message was in English and uncoded. It read:

MEANING UNCLEAR STOP QUOTE IT IS ESSENTIAL THAT CONTENTS BE DELIVERED AIGUES MORTES OR GRAU DU ROI BY MONDAY MAY 28 INTACT AND REPEAT AND INCOGNITO STOP IF ONLY ONE POSSIBLE DO NOT DELIVER CONTENTS STOP IF POSSIBLE RELATIVE EXPENDITURE IMMATERIAL STOP NO SIGNATURE.

Bowman reread the message twice and nodded to himself. The meaning was far from unclear to him: nothing he thought, was unclear any more. He produced matches and burnt the telegram, piece by piece, in the front ashtray, grinding the charred paper into tiny fragments. He glanced around frequently to see if anyone was taking an undue interest in his unusual occupation but no one was. In his rear mirror he could see Le Grand Duc's Rolls stopped at traffic lights some three hundred yards away. Even a Rolls, he reflected, had to stop at a red light: Le Grand Duc must find such annoying trifles a constant source of ducal irritation. He looked through the windscreen and could see the Chinese and his Eurasian lady leisurely sauntering towards the patio, approaching from the west.

Bowman wound down his window, tore his telegram envelope into tiny shreds and dropped them to the gutter: he hoped the citizens of Arles would forgive him his wanton litter-bugging. He left the car and passed into the hotel patio, meeting the Chinese couple on the way. They looked at Bowman impassively from behind their reflector glasses but Bowman did not so much as glance their way.

Le Grand Duc, stalled at the traffic lights, was, surprisingly enough, displaying no signs of irritation at all. He was absorbed in making notes in a book which, curiously, was not the one he habitually used when adding to his increasing store of gypsy folklore. Satisfied, apparently, with what he had written, he put the book away, lit a large Havana and pressed the button which controlled the dividing window. Carita looked at him enquiringly in the rear-view mirror.

"I need hardly ask you, my dear," Le Grand Duc said, "if you have carried out my instructions."

"To the letter, Monsieur le Duc."

"And the reply?"

"Ninety minutes, with luck. Without it, two and a half hours."

"Where?"

"Replies in quadruplicate, Monsieur le Duc. Poste Restante, Arles, Saintes-Maries, Aigues-Mortes and Grau-du-Roi. That is satisfactory, I hope?"

"Eminently." Le Grand Duc smiled in satisfaction. "There are times, my dear Carita, when I hardly know what I'd do without you." The window slid silently up, the Rolls whispered away on the green light and Le Grand Duc, cigar in hand, leaned back and surveyed the world with his customary patriarchal air. Abruptly, after a rather puzzled glance through the windscreen of the car, he bent forward all of two inches, an action which, in Le Grand Duc, indicated an extraordinarily high degree of interest. He pressed the dividing window button.

"There's a parking space behind that blue Citroën. Pull in there."

The Rolls slowed to a stop and the Duke performed the almost unheard-of feat of opening the door and getting out all by himself. He strolled leisurely forward, halted and looked at the pieces of yellow telegram paper lying in the gutter, then at the Chinese who was slowly straightening with some of the pieces in hand.

"You seem to have lost something," Le Grand Duc said courteously. "Can I be of help?"

"You are too kind." The man's English was immaculate, Oxbridge at its most flawless. "It is nothing. My wife has just lost one of her earrings. But it is not here."

"I am sorry to hear it." Le Grand Duc carried on, sauntered through the patio entrance, passed by the seated wife of the Chinese and nodded fractionally in gracious acknowledgment of her presence. She was, Le Grand Duc noted, unmistakably Eurasian and quite beautiful. Not blonde, of course, but beautiful. She was also wearing two earrings. Le Grand Duc paced with measured stride across the patio and joined Lila, who was just seating herself at a table. Le Grand Duc regarded her gravely.

"You are unhappy, my dear."

"No, no."

"Oh, yes, you are. I have an infallible instinct for such things. For some extraordinary reasons you have some reservation about me. Me! Me, if I may say so, the Duc de Croytor!" He took her hand. "Phone your father, my friend the Count Delafont, and phone him now. He will reassure you, you've my word for that. Me! The Duc de Croytor!"

"Please, Charles. Please."

"That's better. Prepare to leave at once. A matter of urgency. The gypsies are leaving—at least the ones we're interested in are leaving—and where they go we must follow." Lila made to rise but he put out a restraining hand. " 'Urgency' is a relative term. In about, say, an hour's time—we must have a quick snack before departing for the inhospitable wastes of the Camargue."

7

To the newcomer the Camargue does indeed appear to be an inhospitable wasteland, an empty wasteland, a desolation of enormous skies and limitless horizons, a flat and arid nothingness, a land long abandoned by life and left to linger and wither and die all summer long under a pitiless sun suspended in the washed-out steel-blue dome above. But if the newcomer remains long enough, he will find that first impressions, as they almost invariably do, give a false and misleading impression. It is, it is true, a harsh land and a bleak land, but one that is neither hostile nor dead, a land that is possessed of none of the uniformly dreadful lifelessness of a tropical desert or a Siberian tundra. There is water here, and no land is dead where water is: there are large lakes and small lakes and lakes that are no lakes at all but marshes sometimes no more than fetlock deep to a horse, others deep enough to drown a house. There are colours here, the ever-changing blues and greys of the wind-rippled waters, the faded yellows of the beds of marshes that line the *étangs,* the near-blackness of smooth-crowned cy-presses, the dark green of windbreak pines, the startlingly bright green of occasional lush grazing pastures, strikingly vivid against the brown and harsh aridity of the tough sparse vegetation and salt flats hard-baked under the sun that occupy so much the larger part of the land area. And, above all, there is life here: birds in great number, very occasional small groups of black cattle and, even more rarely, white horses: there are farms, too, and ranches, but these are set so far back from roads or so well-concealed by windbreaks that the traveller rarely sees them. But one indisputable fact about the Camargue remains, one first impression that never changes, one that wholly justifies its time-and-again description as being an endless plain: the Camargue is as featurelessly smooth and flat as a sun-warmed summer sea.

For Cecile, as the blue Citroën moved south between Arles and Saintes-Maries, the Camargue was nothing but an increasingly featureless desolation: her spirits became correspondingly increasingly depressed. Occasion-ally she glanced at Bowman but found no help there: he seemed relaxed, almost cheerful, and if the consideration of the recently spilled blood he had on his hands bore heavily on him he was concealing his feelings remarkably well. Probably, Cecile thought, he had forgotten all about it: the thought made her feel more depressed than ever. She surveyed the bleak landscape again and turned to Bowman.

"People *live* here?"

"They live here, they love here, they die here. Let's hope we don't today. Die here, I mean."

"Oh, do be quiet. Where are all the cowboys I've heard of—the *guard-ians* as you call them?"

"In the pubs, I should imagine. This is fiesta day, remember—a holiday." He smiled at her. "I wish it was for us too."

"But your life is one long holiday. You said so."

"For us, I said."

"A pretty compliment." She looked at him consideringly. "Can you tell me, offhand, when you last had a holiday?"

"Offhand, no."

Cecile nodded, looked ahead again. Half a mile away, on the left-hand side of the road, was a fairly large group of buildings, some of them quite substantial.

"Life at last," she said. "What's that?"

"A *mas.* A farm, more of a ranch. Also a bit of a dude ranch—living accommodation, restaurant, riding school. Mas de Lavignolle, they call it."

"You've been here before, then?"

"All those holidays," Bowman said apologetically.

"What else?" She turned her attention to the scene ahead again, then suddenly leaned forward. Just beyond the farm was a windbreak of pines and just beyond that again there was coming into view a scene that showed that there could, indeed, be plenty of life in the Camargue. At least a score of caravans and perhaps a hundred cars were parked haphazardly on the hard-packed earth on the right-hand side of the road. On the left, in a field which was more dust than grass, there were lines of what appeared to be brightly coloured tents. Some of the tents were no more than striped awnings with, below them, trestle tables which, dependent on what was piled on them, acted as either bars or snack bars. Other and smaller canvas-topped stalls were selling souvenirs or clothes or candy, while still others had been converted into shooting galleries, roulette stands and other games of chance. There were several hundred people milling around among the stalls, obviously enjoying and making the most of the amenities offered. Cecile turned to Bowman as he slowed to let people cross the road.

"What's all this, then?"

"Obvious, isn't it? A country fair. Arles isn't the only place in the Camargue—some of the people hereabouts don't even consider it as being part of the Camargue and act accordingly. Some communities prefer to provide their own diversions and amusements at fiesta time—the Mas de Lavignolle is one of them."

"My, my, we are well-informed, aren't we?" She looked ahead again and pointed to a large oval-shaped arena with its sides made, apparently, of mud and wattles.

"What's that? A corral?"

"That," Bowman said, "is a genuine old-fashioned bullring where the main attraction of the afternoon will take place."

She made a face. "Drive on."

He drove on. After less than fifteen minutes, at the end of a long straight stretch of dusty road, he pulled the blue Citroën off the road and got out. Cecile looked at him enquiringly.

"Two straight miles of road," he explained. "Gypsy caravans travel at thirty miles an hour. So, four minutes' warning."

"And a panic-stricken Bowman can be on his way in less than fifteen seconds?"

"Less. If I haven't finished off the champagne, longer. But enough. Come. Lunch."

Ten miles to the north, on the same road, a long convoy of gypsy caravans were heading south, raising an immense cloud of dust in their passing. The caravans, normally far from inhibited in the brightness and diversity of their colours, seemed now, in their striking contrast to the bleakness of the landscape around them, more gay and exotic than ever.

The leading vehicle in the convoy, the yellow breakdown truck that had been pressed into the service of hauling Czerda's caravan, was the only one that was completely dust-free. Czerda himself was driving, with Searl and El Brocador seated beside him. Czerda was looking at El Brocador with an expression on his face that came as close to admiration as presently rather battered features were capable of expressing.

He said: "By heavens, El Brocador, I'd rather have you by my side than a dozen incompetent unfrocked priests."

"I am not a man of action," Searl protested. "I never have claimed to be."

"You're supposed to have brains," Czerda said contemptuously. "What happened to them?"

"We mustn't be too hard on Searl," El Brocador said soothingly. "We all know he's under great pressure, he's not, as he says, a man of action and he doesn't know Arles. I was born there, it is the back of my hand to me. I know every shop in Arles that sells gypsy costumes, fiesta costumes and *guardian* clothes. There are not so many as you might think. The men I picked to help me were all natives too. But I was the lucky one. First time, first shop—just the kind of shop Bowman would choose, a seedy old draper's in a side street.''

"I hope, El Brocador, that you didn't have to use too much—ah—persuasion?'' Czerda was almost arch about it and it didn't become him at all.

"If you mean violence, no. Those aren't my methods, you know that, and besides I'm far too well known in Arles to try anything of the sort. Besides, I didn't have to, nobody would have had to. I know Madame Bouvier, everyone knows her, she'd throw her own mother in the Rhône for ten francs. I gave her fifty.'' El Brocador grinned. "She couldn't tell me enough fast enough.''

"A blue and white polka-dotted shirt, white sombrero and black embroidered waistcoat.'' Czerda smiled in anticipation. "It'll be easier than identifying a circus clown at a funeral.''

"True, true. But first we must catch our hare.''

"He'll be there,'' Czerda said confidently. He jerked a thumb in the direction of the following caravans. "As long as they are here, he'll be here. We all know that by this time. You just worry about your part, El Brocador.''

"No worry there.'' El Brocador's confidence matched Czerda's own. "Everyone knows what mad Englishmen are like. Just another crazy idiot who tried to show off before the crowd. And dozens of witnesses will have seen him tear free from us in spite of all we could do to stop him.''

"The bull will have specially sharpened horns? As we arranged?''

"I have seen to it myself.'' El Brocador glanced at his watch. "Can we not make better time? You know I have an appointment in twenty minutes.''

"Never fear,'' Czerda said. "We shall be in Mas de Lavignolle in ten minutes.''

At a discreet distance behind the settling dust the lime-green Rolls swept along in its customary majestic silence. The cabriolet hood was down, with Le Grand Duc sitting regally under the shade of a parasol which Lila held over him.

"You slept well?'' she asked solicitously.

"Sleep? I never sleep in the afternoons. I merely had my eyes closed. I have many things, far too many things, on my mind and I think better that way.''

"Ah! I didn't understand.'' The first quality one required in dealing with Le Grand Duc, she had learned, was diplomacy. She changed the subject rapidly. "Why are we following so few caravans when we've left so many behind in Arles?''

"I told you, those are the ones I am interested in.''

"But why——''

"Hungarian and Romanian gypsies are my special field.'' There was a finality about the way he spoke that effectively sealed off that particular line of discussion.

"And Cecile. I'm worried about——''

"Your friend Miss Dubois has already left and unless I am much mistaken''—his tone left no room to doubt the impiety of any such thought—"she is also on this road and considerably ahead of us. She was, I must concede," he added reflectively, "attired in a very fetching Arlésienne fiesta dress."

"A gypsy dress, Charles."

"Arlésienne fiesta," Le Grand Duc said firmly. "I miss very little, my dear. Gypsy costume when you saw her, perhaps. But Arlésienne when she left."

"But why should she——"

"How should I know?"

"You saw her go?"

"No."

"Then how——"

"Our Carita here also misses very little. She left with, it seems, a shady looking individual in *guardian* clothes. One wonders what happened to that other ruffian—Bowman, wasn't it? Your friend appears to possess a unique talent for picking up undesirables."

"And me?" Lila was suddenly tight-lipped.

"*Touché!* I deserved that. Sorry, I did not intend to slight your friend." He gestured with a hand ahead and to the left where a long narrow line of water gleamed like burnished steel under the early afternoon sun. "And what is that, my dear?"

Lila glanced at it briefly. "I don't know," she said huffily.

"Le Grand Duc never apologizes twice."

"The sea?"

"Journey's end, my dear. Journey's end for all the gypsies who have come hundreds, even thousands of miles from all over Europe. The Étang de Vaccarès."

"Étang?"

"Lake. Lake Vaccarès. The most famous wildlife sanctuary in western Europe."

"You *do* know a lot, Charles."

"Yes, I do," Le Grand Duc conceded.

Bowman packed up the remains of lunch in a wicker basket, disposed of what was left of a bottle of champagne and closed the boot of the car.

"That was delightful," Cecile said. "And how very thoughtful of you."

"Don't thank me, thank Czerda. He paid for it." Bowman looked north along the two-mile straight of road. It was quite empty of traffic. "Well, back to Mas de Lavignolle. The caravans must have stopped at the fair. Heigh-ho for the bull-fight."

"But I hate bull-fights."

"You won't hate this one."

He reversed the Citroën and drove back to Mas de Lavignolle. There seemed to be many fewer people there than there had been when they had passed through although the numbers of cars and caravans had almost doubled, a discrepancy easily and immediately accounted for as soon as the Citroën had stopped by the sound of laughter and shouting and cheering coming from the nearby bull-ring. For the moment Bowman ignored the bull-ring: remaining seated in the car, he looked carefully around him. He did not have to look for long.

"To nobody's surprise," he announced, "Czerda and his missionary pals have turned up in force. At least, their caravans have, so one assumes that Czerda and company have also." He drummed his fingers thoughtfully on the steering wheel. "To nobody's surprise, that is, except mine. Curious. One wonders why?"

"Why what?" Cecile asked.

"Why they're here."

"What do you mean? You expected to find them here. That's why you turned back, wasn't it?"

"I turned back because the time factor, their delay in overtaking us, convinced me that they must have stopped somewhere and this seemed as likely a place as any. The point is that I would not have expected them to stop at all until they reached some of the lonely encampments on one of the *étangs* to the south where they could have the whole wide Camargue all to themselves. But instead they choose to stop here."

He sat in silence and she said: "So?"

"Remember I explained in some detail back in Arles just why I thought the gypsies were pulling out so quickly?"

"I remember some of it. It was a bit confusing."

"Maybe I was confused myself. Somewhere a flaw in the reasoning. My reasoning. But where?"

"I'm sorry. I don't understand."

"I don't think I'm exaggerating my own importance," Bowman said slowly. "Not, at least, as far as they are concerned. I'm convinced they're under pressure, under very heavy pressure, to kill me as quickly as humanly possible. When you're engaged on a job of great urgency you don't stop off and spend a peaceful summer's afternoon watching a bull-fight. You press on and with all speed. You entice Bowman to a lonely campsite at the back of beyond where, because he's the only person who's not a member of your group, he can be detected and isolated with ease and disposed of at leisure. You do not stop at a fair-cum-bull-fight where he would be but one among a thousand people thereby making isolation impossible." Bowman paused. "Not, that is, unless you knew something that he didn't know, and *knew* that you could isolate him even among that thousand. Do I make myself clear?"

"This time I'm not confused." Her voice had dropped almost to a whisper. "You make yourself very clear. You're as certain as can be that they'll get you here. There's only one thing you can do."

"Only one thing," Bowman agreed. He reached for the door handle. "I've got to go and find out for sure."

"Neil." She gripped his right wrist with surprising strength.

"Well, at last. Couldn't keep on calling me Mr. Bowman in front of the kids, could you? Victorian."

"Neil." There was pleading in the green eyes, something close to desperation, and he felt suddenly ashamed of his flippancy. "Don't go. Please, please, don't go. Something dreadful is going to happen here. I know it." She ran the tip of her tongue over dry lips. "Drive away from here. Now. This moment. Please."

"I'm sorry." He forced himself to look away, her beseeching face would have weakened the resolution of an angel and he had no reason to regard himself as such. "I have to stay and it may as well be here. It may as well be here, for a showdown there has to be, it's inevitable, and I still think I stand a better chance here than I would on the shores of some lonely *étang* in the south."

"You said, 'I *have* to stay'?"

"Yes." He continued to look ahead. "There are four good reasons and they're all in that green-and-white caravan." She made no reply and he went on: "Or just Tina alone, Tina and her flayed back. If anyone did that to you I'd kill him. I wouldn't think about it, I'd just naturally kill him. Do you believe that?"

"I think so." Her voice was very low. "No, I know you would."

"It could just as easily have been you." He altered his tone slightly and said: "Tell me, now, would you marry a man who ran away and left Tina?"

"No, I would not." She spoke very matter-of-factly.

"Ha!" He altered his tone some more. "Am I to take it from that if I *don't* run away and leave Tina——" He broke off and looked at her. She was smiling at him but the green eyes were dim, she didn't know whether to laugh or cry and when she spoke it could have been a catch in her voice or the beginning of laughter.

"You're quite, quite hopeless," she said.

"You're repeating yourself." He opened the door. "I won't be long."

She opened her own door. "*We* won't be long," she corrected him.

"You're not——"

"I am. Protecting the little woman is all very nice but not when carried to extremes. What's going to happen in the middle of a thousand people? Besides, you said yourself they can't possibly recognize me."

"If they catch you with me——"

"If they catch you, I won't be there, because if they can't recognize you then their only way of getting you is when you are doing something you shouldn't be doing, like breaking into a caravan."

"In broad daylight? You think I'm insane?"

"I'm not sure." She took his arm firmly. "One thing I *am* sure about. Remember what I said back in Arles? You're stuck with me, mate."

"For life?"

"We'll see about that."

Bowman blinked in surprise and peered at her closely. "You make me a very happy man," he said. "When I was a little boy and I wanted something and my mother said 'We'll see about that' I knew I'd always get it. All feminine minds work the same way, don't they?"

She smiled at him serenely, quite unperturbed. "At the risk of repeating myself again, Neil Bowman, you're a lot cleverer than you look."

"My mother used to say that too."

They paid their admission money, climbed steps to the top of the arena. The terraces were comfortably full, colourfully crowded with hundreds of people, very few of whom could be accused of being drably dressed: *guardians* and gypsies were there in about equal proportions, there was a sprinkling of Arlésiens in their fiesta best but most of the spectators were either tourists or local people.

Between the spectators and the sanded ring itself was an area four feet wide, running the entire circumference of the ring and separated from it by a wooden barrier four feet high: it was into this area, the *callejón,* that the *razateur* leapt for safety when things were going too badly for him.

In the centre of the ring a small but uncommonly vicious-looking black Camargue bull appeared bent upon the imminent destruction of a white-costumed figure who pirouetted and swerved and twisted and turned and closely but easily avoided the rushes of the increasingly maddened bull. The crowd clapped and shouted their approval.

"Well!" Cecile, wide-eyed and fascinated, her fears in temporary abeyance, was almost enjoying herself. "This is more like a bull-fight!"

"You'd rather see the colour of the man's blood than the bull's?"

"Certainly. Well, I don't know. He hasn't even got a sword!"

"Swords are for the Spanish *corridas* where the bull gets killed. This is the Provençal *cours libre* where nobody gets killed although the occasional *razateur*—the bull-fighter—does get bent a bit. See the red button tied between the horns? He's got to pull that off first. Then the two bits of string. Then the two white tassels tied near the tips of the horns."

"Isn't it dangerous?"

"It's not a way of life I'd choose myself," Bowman admitted. He lifted his eyes from the programme note he held in his hand and looked thoughtfully at the ring.

"Anything wrong?" Cecile asked.

Bowman didn't reply immediately. He was still looking at the ring where the white-clad *razateur,* moving in a tight circle with remarkable speed but with all the controlled grace of a ballet dancer, swerved to avoid the charging bull, leaned over at what appeared to be an impossible angle and deftly plucked away the red button secured between the bull's horns, one of which appeared almost to brush the *razateur*'s chest.

"Well, well," Bowman murmured. "So that's El Brocador."

"El who?"

"Brocador. The lad in the ring there."

"You know him?"

"We haven't been introduced. Good, isn't he?"

El Brocador was more than good, he was brilliant. Timing his evasive movements with ice-cold judgment and executing them with an almost contemptuous ease, he continued to avoid the bull's furious rushes with consummate skill: in four consecutive charges he plucked away the two strings that had supported the red button and the two white tassels that had been secured to the tips of the horns. After removing the last tassel and apparently unaware of the bull's existence, he bowed deeply and gravely to the crowd, ran lightly to the barrier and vaulted gracefully into the safety of the *callejón* as the bull, now only scant feet behind, charged full tilt into the barrier, splintering the top plank. The crowd clapped and roared its approval.

But not all of them. There were four men who were not only refraining from enthusiastic applause, they weren't even looking at the bull-ring. Bowman, who had himself spent very little time in watching the spectacle, had picked them out within two minutes of arriving on the terraces—Czerda, Ferenc, Searl and Masaine. They weren't watching the bull-ring because they were too busy watching the crowd. Bowman turned to Cecile.

"Disappointed?"

"What?"

"Very slow bull."

"Don't be horrid. What on earth is this?"

Three clowns, dressed in their traditional baggy and garishly coloured garments, with painted faces, large false noses and ridiculous pillboxes perched on their heads, had appeared in the *callejón*. One carried an accordion which he started to play. His two companions, both managing to trip and fall flat on their faces in the process, climbed over the barrier into the ring and, when they had picked themselves up, proceeded to do a sailor's hornpipe.

As they danced, the *toril* gate opened and a fresh bull appeared. Like its predecessor, it was a small black Camargue bull but what it lacked in inches it more than made up for in sheer bad temper for it had no sooner caught sight of the two dancing clowns than it lowered its head and charged. It went for each clown in turn but they, without in any way breaking step or losing the rhythm of the dance, glided and pirouetted to safety as if unaware of the bull's existence: they were, obviously, *razateurs* of the highest order of experience.

Temporarily, the music stopped, but the bull didn't: it charged one of the clowns who turned and ran for his life, screaming for help. The crowd shouted with laughter. The clown, momentarily incensed, stopped abruptly, shook his fist at them, looked over his shoulder, screamed again, ran, mistimed his leap for the barrier and brought up heavily against it, the bull only feet away. It seemed inevitable that he must be either impaled or crushed. Neither happened, but he did not escape entirely unscathed for when he miraculously broke clear it could be seen that his baggy trousers were hooked on to one of the bull's horns. The clown, clad in white ankle-length underpants, continued his flight, still screaming for help, pursued by a now thoroughly infuriated bull who trailed the trousers along behind him. The crowd was convulsed.

The four gypsies weren't. As before, they ignored the action in the bull-ring. But now they were no longer still. They had begun to move slowly through the crowd, all moving in a clockwise fashion, closely scanning the faces of all whom they passed by. And as closely as they observed others, Bowman observed them.

Down in the *callejón* the accordionist began to play *Tales from the Vienna Woods*. The two clowns came together and waltzed gravely in the centre of the ring. Inevitably, the bull charged the dancing couple. He was almost upon them when they waltzed apart from each other, each completing a single turn before joining up again immediately the bull's headlong rush had carried him beyond them.

The crowd went wild. Cecile laughed to the extent that she had to use a handkerchief to dab tears from her eyes. There was no trace of a smile on Bowman's face: with Czerda not twenty feet away and heading straight for him, he didn't feel like smiling.

"Isn't it marvellous?" Cecile said.

"Marvellous. Wait here."

She was instantly serious, apprehensive. "Where are you——"

"Trust me?"

"Trust you."

"A white wedding. I won't be long."

Bowman moved leisurely away. He had to pass within a few feet of Czerda who was still scrutinizing everyone he went by with a thoroughness that lifted eyebrows and brought frowns. A few feet farther on, close to the exit, he passed behind the politely clapping Chinese couple that he'd seen before in Arles. They were, he thought, a remarkably distinguished-looking couple. As it was extremely unlikely that they had come all the way from China, they obviously must be European residents. He wondered idly what manner of occupation such a man would pursue in Europe, then dismissed the thought from his mind: there were other and more urgent matters to occupy his attention.

He circled the arena at the back, walked about two hundred yards south down the road, crossed it and made his way back north coming up at the back of Czerda's caravans which were parked in two tight rows well back from the side of the road. The caravans appeared to be completely deserted. Certainly there was no apparent guard on Czerda's caravan or on the green-and-white caravan, but on that afternoon he was interested in neither. The caravan he *was* interested in, as he was now certain it would be, did have a guard. On a stool on the top of the steps the gypsy Maca was sitting, beer bottle in hand.

Bowman sauntered leisurely towards the caravan: as he approached Maca

lowered his beer bottle, looked down at him and scowled warningly. Bowman ignored the scowl, approached even more closely, stopped and inspected both Maca and the caravan, taking his time about it. Maca made a
contemptuous jerking movement with his thumb, unmistakably indicating
that Bowman should be on his way. Bowman remained where he was.

"Clear off!" Maca ordered.

"Gypsy swine." Bowman said pleasantly.

Maca, obviously doubting that he had heard aright, stared for a brief
moment of incredulity, then his face contorted in rage as he shifted his grip
to the neck of the bottle, rose and jumped down. But Bowman had moved
even more quickly and he struck Maca very hard indeed even before the
gypsy's feet had reached the ground. The combined effect of the blow and
his own momentum had a devastating effect on Maca: eyes unfocused, he
staggered back dazedly. Bowman struck him again with equal force, caught
the now unconscious man before he could fall, dragged him round to one
side of the caravan, dropped him and pushed him out of sight of any casual
passer-by.

Bowman glanced quickly around him. If anyone had seen the brief fracas
he was taking care not to publicize the fact. Twice Bowman circled the
caravan but there was no lurking watcher in the shadows, no hint of danger
to be seen. He climbed the steps and entered the caravan. The rear, smaller
portion of the caravan was empty. The door leading to the forward compartment was secured by two heavy bolts. Bowman slid back the bolts and
passed inside.

For a moment his eyes were unable to penetrate the gloom. The curtains
were drawn and very heavy curtains they were, too. Bowman drew them
back.

At the front of the caravan was the three-tiered bunk he had observed
when he had peered in late the previous night: as before, three men lay on
the bunks. Previously, that had been a matter of no significance: bunks are
for sleeping in and one would have expected to find them occupied in the
nighttime: one would not have expected to find them occupied in the early
afternoon. But Bowman had known that he would find them occupied.

All three men were awake. They propped themselves up on their elbows,
eyes accustomed to deep gloom blinking in the harsh light of the Camargue.
Bowman advanced, reached over the man in the lowermost bunk and picked
up his right hand. The wrist belonging to that hand was manacled to a ring
bolt let into the front wall of the caravan. Bowman let his wrist fall and
examined the man in the middle bunk: he was similarly secured. Bowman
didn't trouble to look at the wrist of the man on top. He stepped back and
looked at them thoughtfully.

He said: "Count le Hobenaut, husband of Marie le Hobenaut, Mr. Tangevec, husband of Sara Tangevec and the third name I do not know. Who
are you, sir?" This to the man in the bottom bunk, a middle-aged greying
and very distinguished-looking person.

"Daymel."

"You are Tina's father?"

"I am." The expression on his face was that of a man receiving his
executioner and not his saviour. "Who in the name of God are you?"

"Bowman. Neil Bowman. I've come to take you three gentlemen away."

"I don't care who you are." This from the man in the middle bunk who
didn't seem any happier to see Bowman than Daymel had been. "I don't
care who you are. For God's sake go away or you'll be the death of us all."

"You are the Count le Hobenaut?" The man nodded. "You heard about
your brother-in-law? Alexandre?"

Le Hobenaut looked at him with an odd speculative desperation on his face, then said: "What about my brother-in-law?"

"He's dead. Czerda murdered him."

"What crazy talk is this? Alexandre? Dead? How can he be dead? Czerda promised us———"

"You believed him?"

"Of course. Czerda has everything to lose———"

"You two believe him?" Bowman asked. They nodded. "A man who trusts a killer is a fool. You are fools—all three of you. Alexandre *is* dead. I found his body. If you think he's alive why don't you ask Czerda if you can see him? Or you, Daymel. Why don't you ask Czerda if you can see your daughter?"

"She's not—she's———"

"She's not dead. Just half dead. They flayed her back. Why did they flay her back? Why did they kill Alexandre? Because they were both trying to tell someone something. What was it they were trying to tell, gentlemen?"

"I beg you, Bowman." Le Hobenaut's distress was but one step removed from terror. "Leave us!"

"Why are you so terrified for them? Why are they so terrified for you? And don't tell me again to go for I'm not going until I know the answers."

"You'll never know the answers now," Czerda said.

8

BOWMAN TURNED round slowly for there was nothing to be gained by haste now. Of the shock, of the inevitably profound chagrin, there was no sign in his face. But Czerda, standing in the doorway with a silenced gun in his hand, and Masaine, beside him, with a knife in his, made no attempt to disguise their feelings. Both men were smiling and smiling broadly, although their smiles were noticeably lacking in warmth. At a nod from Czerda, Masaine advanced and tested the shackles securing the three men. He said: "They have not been touched."

"He was probably too busy explaining to them just how clever he was." Czerda did not trouble to conceal the immense amount of satisfaction he was deriving from the moment. "It was all too simple, Bowman. You really are a fool. Shopkeepers in Arles who receive a gratuity of six hundred Swiss francs are hardly likely to forget the person who gave it to them. I tell you, I could hardly keep a straight face when I was moving through the crowd there pretending to look for you. But we had to pretend, didn't we, to convince you that we hadn't recognized you or you'd never have come out into the open, would you? You fool, we had you identified before you entered the arena."

"You might have told Maca," Bowman murmured.

"We might, but Maca is no actor I'm afraid," Czerda said regretfully. "He wouldn't have known how to make a fake fight look real. And if we'd left no guard at all you'd have been doubly suspicious." He stretched out his left hand. "Eighty thousand francs, Bowman."

"I don't carry that sort of loose change with me."

"*My* eighty thousand francs."

Bowman looked at him with contempt. "Where would a person like you get eighty thousand francs?"

Czerda smiled, stepped forward unexpectedly and drove the barrel of his silenced gun into Bowman's solar plexus. Bowman doubled up, gasping in agony.

"I would have liked to strike you across the face, as you struck me." He had removed his smile. "But for the moment I prefer that you remain unmarked. The money, Bowman?"

Bowman straightened slowly. When he spoke, his voice came as a harsh croak.

"I lost it?"

"You *lost* it?"

"I had a hole in my pocket."

Czerda's face twisted in anger, he lifted his gun to club Bowman, then smiled. "You'll find it within the minute, you'll see."

The green Rolls-Royce slowed as it approached the Mas de Lavignolle. Le Grand Duc, still with a parasol being held above his head, surveyed the scene thoughtfully.

"Czerda's caravans," he observed. "Surprising. One would not have expected the Mas de Lavignolle to be of any particular interest to our friend Czerda. But a man like that will always have a good reason for what he is doing. However, he will doubtless consider it a privilege to inform me of his reasons . . . What is it, my dear?"

"Look ahead." Lila pointed. "Just there."

Le Grand Duc followed the direction of her arm. Cecile, flanked by El Brocador and Searl, the first all in white, the second all in black, mounted the steps of a caravan and disappeared inside. The door closed behind them.

Le Grand Duc pressed the dividing window button. "Stop the car, if you please." To Lila he said: "You think that's your friend? Same dress, I admit, but all those Arlésienne fiesta dresses look the same to me, especially from the back."

"That's Cecile." Lila was positive.

"A *razateur* and a priest," Le Grand Duc mused. "You really must admit that your friend does have a marked propensity for striking up the most unusual acquaintanceships. You have your notebook?"

"I have what?"

"We must investigate this."

"You're going to investigate——"

"Please. No Greek chorus. Everything is of interest to the true folklorist."

"But you can't just barge in——"

"Nonsense. I am the Duc de Croytor. Besides, I never barge. I always make an entrance."

The ache in his midriff, Bowman guessed, was as nothing compared to some of the aches that he was going to come by very shortly—if, that was, he would then be in a position to feel anything. There was a gleam in Czerda's eye, a barely contained anticipation in the face that bespoke ill, Bowman thought, for the immediate future.

He looked round the caravan. The three shackled men had in their faces the uncomprehending and lackluster despair of those to whom defeat is already an accepted reality. Czerda and Masaine had pleasantly anticipatory smiles on their faces, El Brocador was serious and thoughtful and watchful, Simon Searl had a peculiar look in his eyes which made his unfrocking a readily comprehensible matter, while Cecile just looked slightly dazed, a little frightened, a little angry but as far removed from hysteria as could be.

"You understand now," Czerda said, "why I said you'd find the money within the minute."

"I understand now. You'll find it———"

"What money?" Cecile asked. "What does that—that monster want?"

"His eighty thousand francs back again—minus certain small outlays I've been compelled to make—and who can blame him?"

"Don't tell him anything!"

"And don't you understand the kind of men you're dealing with? Ten seconds from now they'll have your arm twisted up behind your back till it's touching your ear, you'll be screaming in agony and if they happen to break your shoulder or tear a few ligaments, well that's just too bad."

"But—but I'll just faint———"

"Please." Bowman looked at Czerda, carefully avoiding Cecile's gaze. "It's in Arles. Safe-deposit in the station."

"The key?"

"On a ring. In the car. Hidden. I'll show you."

"Excellent," Czerda said. "A disappointment to friend Searl, I'm afraid, but inflicting pain on young ladies gives me no pleasure though I wouldn't hesitate if I had to. As you shall see."

"I don't understand."

"You will. You are a danger, you have been a great danger and you have to go, that's all. You will die this afternoon and within the hour so that no suspicion will ever attach to us."

It was, Bowman thought, as laconic a death sentence as he'd ever heard of. There was something chilling in the man's casual certainty.

Czerda went on: "You will understand now why I didn't injure your face, why I wanted you to go into that bull-ring unmarked."

"Bull-ring?"

"Bull-ring, my friend."

"You're mad. You can't make me go into a bull-ring."

Czerda said nothing and there was no signal. Searl, eagerly assisted by a grinning Masaine, caught hold of Cecile, forced her face downwards onto a bunk and, while Masaine pinned her down, Searl gripped the collar of the Arlésienne costume and ripped it down to the waist. He turned and smiled at Bowman, reached into the folds of his clerical garb and brought out what appeared to be a version of a hunting stock, with a fifteen-inch interwoven leather handle attached to three long thin black thongs. Bowman looked at Czerda and Czerda wasn't watching anything of what was going on: he was watching Bowman and the gun pointing at Bowman was motionless.

Czerda said: "I think perhaps you will go into that bull-ring?"

"Yes." Bowman nodded. "I think perhaps I will."

Searl put his stock away. His face was twisted in the bitter disappointment of a spoilt child who has been deprived of a new toy. Masaine took his hands away from Cecile's shoulders. She pushed herself groggily to a sitting position and looked at Bowman. Her face was very pale but her eyes were mad. It had just occurred to Bowman that she was, as she'd said, quite capable of using a gun if shown how to use one when there came from outside the sound of a solid measured tread, the door opened and Le Grand Duc entered with a plainly apprehensive Lila trailing uncertainly behind him. Le Grand Duc pushed the monocle more firmly into his eye.

"Ah, Czerda, my dear fellow. It's you." He looked at the gun in the gypsy's hand and said sharply: "Don't point that damned thing at me!" He indicated Bowman. "Point it at that fellow there. Don't you know he's your man, you fool?"

Czerda uncertainly trained his gun back on Bowman and just as uncertainly looked at Le Grand Duc.

"What do you want?" Czerda tried to imbue his voice with sharp authority but Le Grand Duc wasn't the properly receptive type and it didn't come off. "Why are you——"

"Be quiet!" Le Grand Duc was at his most intimidating, which was very intimidating indeed. "*I* am speaking. You are a bunch of incompetent and witless nincompoops. You have forced me to destroy the basic rule of my existence—to bring myself into the open. I have seen more intelligence exhibited in a cageful of retarded chimpanzees. You have lost me much time and cost me vast trouble and anxiety. I am seriously tempted to dispose of the services of all of you—permanently. And that means you as well as your services. What are you doing here?"

"What are we doing here?" Czerda stared at him. "But—but—Searl here said that you——"

"I will deal with Searl later." Le Grand Duc's promise was imbued with such menacing overtones that Searl at once looked acutely unhappy. Czerda looked nervous to a degree that was almost unthinkable for him, El Brocador looked puzzled and Masaine had clearly given up thinking of any kind. Lila simply looked stunned. Le Grand Duc went on: "I did not mean, you cretin, what you are doing in Mas de Lavignolle. I meant what are you doing here, as of this present moment, in the caravan."

"Bowman here stole the money you gave me," Czerda said sullenly. "We were——"

"He what?" Le Grand Duc's face was thunderous.

"He stole your money," Czerda said unhappily. "All of it."

"All of it!"

"Eighty thousand francs. That's what we've been doing—finding out where it is. He's about to show me the key to where the money is."

"I trust for your sake that you find it." He paused and turned as Maca came staggering into the caravan, both hands holding what was clearly a very painful face.

"Is this man drunk?" Le Grand Duc demanded. "*Are* you drunk, sir? Stand straight when you talk to me."

"He did it!" Maca spoke to Czerda, he didn't appear to have noticed Le Grand Duc, for his eyes were for Bowman only. "He came along——"

"Silence!" Le Grand Duc's voice would have intimidated a Bengal tiger. "My God, Czerda, you surround yourself with the most useless and ineffectual bunch of lieutenants it's ever been my misfortune to encounter." He looked round the caravan, ignoring the three manacled men, took two steps towards where Cecile was sitting and looked down at her. "Ha! Bowman's accomplice, of course. Why is she here?"

Czerda shrugged. "Bowman wouldn't co-operate——"

"A hostage? Very well. Here's another." He caught Lila by the arm and shoved her roughly across the caravan. She stumbled, almost fell, then sat down heavily on the bunk beside Cecile. Her face, already horror-stricken, now looked stupefied.

"Charles!"

"Be quiet!"

"But Charles! My father—you said——"

"You are a feather-brained young idiot," Le Grand Duc said with contempt. "The real Duc de Croytor, to whom I fortunately bear a strong resemblance, is at present in the upper Amazon, probably being devoured by the savages in the Matto Grosso. I am *not* the Duc de Croytor."

"We know that, Mr. Strome." Simon Searl was at his most obsequious.

Again displaying his quite remarkable speed, Le Grand Duc stepped forward and struck Searl heavily across the face. Searl cried out in pain and staggered heavily, to bring up against the wall of the caravan. There was silence for several seconds.

"I have no name," Le Grand Duc said softly. "There is no such person as you mentioned."

"I'm sorry, sir." Searl fingered his cheek. "I——"

"Silence!" Le Grand Duc turned to Czerda. "Bowman has something to show you? Give you?"

"Yes, sir. And there's another little matter I have to attend to."

"Yes, yes, yes. Be quick about it."

"Yes, sir."

"I shall wait here. We must talk on your return, mustn't we, Czerda?"

Czerda nodded unhappily, told Masaine to watch the girls, put his jacket over his gun and left accompanied by Searl and El Brocador. Masaine, his knife still drawn, seated himself comfortably. Maca, tenderly rubbing his bruised face, muttered something and left, probably to attend to his injuries. Lila, her face woebegone, looked up at Le Grand Duc.

"Oh, Charles, how could you——"

"Ninny!"

She stared at him brokenly. Tears began to roll down her cheeks. Cecile put an arm round her and glared at Le Grand Duc. Le Grand Duc looked through her and remained totally unaffected.

"Stop here," Czerda said.

They stopped, Bowman ahead of Czerda with a silencer prodding his back, El Brocador and Searl on either side of him, the Citroën ten feet away.

"Where's the key?" Czerda demanded.

"I'll get it."

"You will not. You are perfectly capable of switching keys or even finding a hidden gun. Where is it?"

"On a key ring. It's taped under the driver's seat, back, left."

"Searl?" Searl nodded, went to the car. Czerda said sourly: "You don't trust many people, do you?"

"I should, you think?"

"What's the number of this safe-deposit box?"

"Sixty-five."

Searl returned. "These are ignition keys."

"The brass one's not," Bowman said.

Czerda took the keys. "The brass one's not." He removed it from the ring. "Sixty-five. For once, the truth. How's the money wrapped?"

"Oilskin, brown paper, sealing wax. My name's on it."

"Good." He looked round. Maca was sitting on the top of some caravan steps. Czerda beckoned him and he came to where they were, rubbing his chin and looking malevolently at Bowman. Czerda said: "Young José has a motor scooter, hasn't he?"

"You want a message done. I'll get him. He's in the arena."

"No need." Czerda gave him the key. "That's for safe-deposit sixty-five in Arles station. Tell him to open it and bring back the brown paper parcel inside. Tell him to be as careful with it as he would be with his own life. It's a very, very valuable parcel. Tell him to come back here as soon as possible and give it to me and if I'm not here someone will know where I've gone and he's to come after me. Is that clear?''

Maca nodded and left. Czerda said: ''I think it's time we paid a visit to the bull-ring ourselves.''

They crossed the road but went not directly to the arena but to one of several adjacent huts which were evidently used as changing rooms, for the one they entered was behung with *matadors'* and *razateurs'* uniforms and several oufits of clowns' attire. Czerda pointed to one of the last. ''Get into that.''

''That?'' Bowman eyed the garish rigout. ''Why the hell should I?''

''Because my friend here asks you to.'' Czerda waved his gun. ''Don't make my friend angry.''

Bowman did as he was told. When he was finished he was far from surprised to see El Brocador exchange his conspicuous white uniform for his dark suit, to see Searl pull on a long blue smock, then to see all three men put on paper masks and comic hats. They appeared to have a craving for anonymity, a not unusual predilection on the part of would-be murderers. Czerda draped a red flag over his gun and they left for the arena.

When they arrived at the entrance to the *callejón* Bowman was mildly astonished to discover that the comic act that had been in process when he'd left was still not finished: so much seemed to have happened since he'd left the arena that it was difficult to realize that so few minutes had elapsed. They arrived to find that one of the clowns, incredibly, was doing a hand-stand on the back of the bull, which just stood there in baffled fury, its head swinging from side to side. The crowd clapped ecstatically: had the circum-stances been different, Bowman thought, he might even have clapped him-self.

For their final brief act the clowns waltzed towards the side of the arena to the accompaniment of their companion's accordion. They stopped, faced the crowd side by side and bowed deeply, apparently unaware that their backs were towards the charging bull. The crowd screamed a warning: the clowns, still bent, pushed each other apart at the last moment and the bull hurtled wildly over the spot where they had been standing only a second previously and crashed into the barrier with an impact that momentarily stunned it. As the clowns vaulted into the *callejón* the crowd continued to whistle and shout their applause. It occurred to Bowman to wonder whether they would still be in such a happily carefree mood in a few minutes' time: it seemed unlikely.

The ring was empty now and Bowman and his three escorts had moved out into the *callejón*. The crowd stared with interest and in considerable amusement at Bowman's attire and he was, unquestionably, worth a second glance. He was clad in a most outlandish fashion. His right leg was enclosed in red, his left in white and the doublet was composed of red and white squares. The flexible green canvas shoes he wore were so ludicrously long that the toes were tied back to the shins. He wore a white conical Pierrot's hat with a red pom-pom on top: for defence he was armed with a slender three-foot cane with a small tricolor at the end of it.

''I have the gun, I have the girl,'' Czerda said softly. ''You will remem-ber?''

''I'll try.''

''If you try to escape, the girl will not live. You believe me?''

Bowman believed him. He said: ''And if I die, the girl will not live either.''

"No. Without you, the girl is nothing, and Czerda does not make war on women. I know who you are now, or think I do. It is no matter. I have discovered that you never met her until a night or so ago and it is unthinkable that a man like you would tell her anything of importance: professionals never explain more than they have to, do they, Mr. Bowman? And young girls can be made to talk, Mr. Bowman. She can do us no harm. When we've done what we intend to do, and that will be in two days, she is free to go."

"She knows where Alexandre is buried."

"Ah, so. Alexandre? Who is Alexandre?"

"Of course. Free to go?"

"You have my word." Bowman didn't doubt him. "In exchange, you will now put up a convincing struggle." Bowman nodded. The three men grabbed him or tried to grab him and all four staggered about the *callejón*. The colourful crowd were by now in excellent humour, gay, chattering, relaxed: all evidently felt that they were having a splendid afternoon's entertainment and that this mock fight that was taking place in the *callejón*—for mock fight it surely was, there were no upraised arms, no blows being struck in anger—was but the prelude to another hilariously comic turn, it had to be, with the man trying to struggle free dressed in that ridiculous Pierrot's costume. Eventually, to the accompaniment of considerable whistling, laughter and shouts of encouragement, Bowman broke free, ran a little way along the *callejón* and vaulted into the ring. Czerda ran after him, made to clamber over the barrier but was caught and restrained by Searl and El Brocador, who pointed excitedly to the north end of the ring. Czerda followed their direction.

They were not the only ones looking in that direction. The crowd had suddenly fallen silent, their laughter had ceased and the smiles vanished: puzzlement had replaced their humour, a puzzlement that rapidly shaded into anxiety and apprehension. Bowman's eyes followed the direction of those of the crowd: he could not only understand the apprehension of the crowd, he reflected, but shared it to the fullest extent.

The northern *toril* gate had been drawn and a bull stood at the entrance. But this was not the small light black bull of the Camargue that was used in the *cours libre*—the bloodless bull-fight of Provence: this was a huge Spanish fighting bull, one of the Andalusian monsters that fight to the death in the great *corridas* of Spain. It had enormous shoulders, an enormous head and a terrifying spread of horn. Its head was low but not as low as it would be when it launched itself into its charge: it pawed the ground, alternately dragging each front hoof backwards, gouging deep channels in the dark sand.

Members of the crowd were by this time looking at one another in uneasy and rather fearful wonder. For the most part they were *aficionados* of the sport and they knew that what they were seeing was quite unprecedented and that this could be no better than sending a man, no matter how brave and skillful a *razateur* he might be, to his certain death.

The giant bull was now advancing slowly into the ring, at the same time still contriving to make those deep backwards scores in the sand. Its great head was lower than before.

Bowman stood stock-still. His lips were compressed, his eyes narrow and still and watchful. Some twelve hours previously, when inching up the ledge of the cliff face in the ruined battlements of the ancient fortress he had known fear, and now he knew it again and admitted it to himself. It was no bad thing, he thought wryly. Fear it was that sent the adrenalin pumping, and adrenalin was the catalyst that triggered off the capacity for violent action and abnormally swift reaction: as matters stood now he was going to need all the adrenalin he could lay hands on. But he was coldly aware that if he survived at all it could only be for the briefest of periods: all the adrenalin in the world couldn't save him now.

From the safety of the *callejón* Czerda licked his lips, half in unconscious empathy with the man in the ring, half in anticipation of things to come. Suddenly he tensed and the whole crowd tensed with him. An eerie silence as of death enveloped the arena. The great bull was charging.

With unbelievable acceleration for a creature of its size it came at Bowman like an express train. Bowman, unblinking, his racing mind figuring out the correlation between the speed of the bull and the rapidly narrowing distance between them, stood as a man would who is frozen with fear. Trance-like, fearful, the spectators stared in horror, convinced in their minds that this mad Pierrot's destruction was only a couple of heartbeats away. Bowman waited for one of those heartbeats to tick away and then, when the bull was less than twenty feet and a second away, he flung himself to his right. But the bull knew all about such tactics, for with remarkable speed in so massive an animal it veered instantly to its left to intercept: but Bowman had only feinted. He checked violently and threw himself to the left and the bull thundered harmlessly by, the huge right horn missing Bowman by a clear foot. The crowd, unbelieving, heaved a long collective sigh of relief, shook their heads at one another and murmured their relief. But the apprehension, the tension, still lay heavily in the air.

The Andalusian bull could brake as swiftly as it could accelerate. It pulled up in a shower of sand, whirled round and came at Bowman again without pause. Again Bowman judged his moment to a fraction of a second, again he repeated the same manoeuvre, but this time in the reverse order. Again the bull missed, but this time only by inches. There came another murmur of admiration from the crowd, this time to the accompaniment of some sporadic hand-clapping: the tension in the air was beginning to ease, not much, but enough to be perceptible.

Again the bull turned but this time it stood still, less than thirty feet away. Quite without moving, it watched Bowman, just as Bowman, quite without moving, watched him. Bowman stared at the great horns: there could be no doubt about it, their tips had been filed to sharp points. It occurred to Bowman, with a curious sense of detachment, that he had rarely encountered a more superfluous refinement: whether the horn had been sharpened or filed to the diameter of a penny it wouldn't have made a ha'p'orth of difference: a swinging hook of one of those giant horns with all the power of those massive shoulder and neck muscles behind it would go straight through the body irrespective of the condition of the tip. Indeed, being gored by the sharpened horn might prove the easier and less agonising way to die but it was a matter of academic importance anyway, the end result would be inevitable and the same.

The bull's red eyes never wavered. Did it think, Bowman wondered, was it thinking? Was it thinking what he was thinking, that this was but a game of Russian roulette insofar as the terms of probabilities went? Would he expect Bowman to execute the same manoeuvre next time, refuse to be drawn, carry straight on and get him while Bowman had checked to fling himself the other way? Or would he think that Bowman's next evasive action might not be a feint but the real thing, swerve accordingly and still get him? Bluff and double-bluff, Bowman thought, and it was pointless to speculate: the laws of blind chance were at work here and sooner or later, sooner rather than later, for on every occasion he had only a fifty-fifty chance, one of those horns would tear the life out of him.

The thought of that fifty-fifty chance prompted Bowman to risk a quick glance at the barrier. It was only ten feet away. He turned and sprinted for it, three steps, aware that behind him the bull had broken into its charge, aware ahead of him, in the *callejón,* of the figure of Czerda with the red flag over his arm, but the gun beneath clearly hanging downwards. He knew, as Bowman knew he knew, that Bowman had no intention of leaving the ring.

Bowman spun, back to the barrier, to face the bull. Pirouetting like a spinning top, he moved swiftly away along the barrier as the onrushing enraged bull hooked viciously with his right horn, the sharpened point brushing Bowman's sleeve but not even tearing the material. The bull crashed into the barrier with tremendous force, splintered the top two planks, then reared up with his forefeet on top of the planks as he tried furiously to climb over. Some time elapsed before the bull realized that Bowman was still in the same ring though by this time a prudent distance away.

By now the crowd was clapping and shouting its approval. Smiles were reappearing and some were even beginning to enjoy what had originally appeared to be a ludicrously one-sided and suicidal contest.

The bull stood still for a full half-minute, shaking its great head slowly from side to side as if dazed by the power of its head-on collision with the barrier, which it very probably was. When it moved this time, it had changed its tactics. It didn't charge Bowman, it stalked him. It walked forward as Bowman walked backward, slowly gaining on him, and when it abruptly lowered its head and charged it was to close that Bowman had no room left for manoeuvre. He did the only thing open to him and leapt high in the air as the bull tried to toss him. He landed on the bull's shoulders, somersaulted and came to the ground on his feet: although hurt and badly winded he miraculously succeeded in retaining his balance.

The crowd roared and whistled its admiration. Laughing in delight, they clapped one another on the back. Here, below that Pierrot's disguise, must be one of the great *razateurs* of the day. *The* great *razateur* of the day. Some of the spectators looked almost sheepish at having worried about the capacity for survival of so great a master as this.

The three manacled prisoners on their bunks, the two girls and Masaine watched in some trepidation as Le Grand Duc paced restlessly up and down the length of the caravan, glancing in mounting irritation at his watch.

"What in the devil's name is taking Czerda so long?" he demanded. He turned to Masaine. "You, there. Where have they taken Bowman?"

"Why, I thought you knew."

"Answer, you cretin!"

"For the key. For the money. You heard. And then to the bull-ring, of course."

"The bull-ring? Why?"

"Why?" Masaine was genuinely puzzled. "You wanted it done, didn't you?"

"Wanted what done?" Le Grand Duc was exercising massive restraint.

"Bowman. To get him out of the way."

Le Grand Duc laid hands on Masaine's shoulders and shook him in a no-longer-to-be-contained exasperation.

"Why the bull-ring?"

"To fight a bull, of course. A huge black Spanish killer. Bare hands." Masaine nodded at Cecile. "If he doesn't, we're going to kill her. This way, Czerda says, no suspicion can fall on us. Bowman should be dead by now."

Masaine shook his head in admiration. "Czerda's clever."

"He's a raving maniac!" Le Grand Duc shouted. "Kill Bowman? Now? Before we've made him talk? Before I know his contacts, how he broke our ring? Not to mention the eighty thousand francs we haven't got yet. At once, fellow! Stop Czerda! Get Bowman out of there before it's too late."

Masaine shook his head stubbornly. "My orders are to stay here and guard those women."

"I shall attend to you later," Le Grand Duc said chillingly. "I cannot, must not be seen in public with Czerda again. Miss Dubois, run at once——"

Cecile jumped to her feet. Her Arlésienne costume was not the thing of beauty that it had been but Lila had effected running repairs sufficient to preserve the decencies. She made to move forward, but Masaine barred her way.

"She stays here," he declared. "My orders——"

"Great God in heaven," Le Grand Duc thundered. "Are you defying me?"

He advanced ponderously upon a plainly apprehensive Masaine. Before the gypsy could even begin to realize what was about to happen Le Grand Duc smashed down his heel, with all his massive weight behind it, on Masaine's instep. Masaine howled in agony, hobbled on one leg and stooped to clutch his injured foot with both hands. As he did so Le Grand Duc brought down his locked hands on the base of Masaine's neck, who collapsed heavily to the floor, unconscious before he struck it.

"Swiftly, Miss Dubois, swiftly!" Le Grand Duc said urgently. "If not already gone, your friend may well be *in extremis.*"

And *in extremis* Bowman undoubtedly was. He was still on his feet—but it was only an exceptional will-power and instinct, though fast fading, for survival that kept him there. His face was streaked with sand and blood, twisted in pain and drawn in exhaustion. From time to time he held his left ribs which appeared to be the prime source of the pain he was suffering. His earlier Pierrot finery was now bedraggled and dirtied and torn, two long rips on the right-hand side of his tunic were evidence of two extremely narrow escapes from the scything right horn of the bull. He had forgotten how many times now he'd been on the sanded floor of the arena but he hadn't forgotten the three occasions when his visits there had been entirely involuntary: twice the shoulder of the bull had hurled him to the ground, once the back-sweep of the left horn had caught him high on the left arm and sent him somersaulting. And now the bull was coming at him again.

Bowman side-stepped but his reactions had slowed, and slowed badly. Providentially, the bull guessed wrongly and hooked away from Bowman but his left shoulder struck him a glancing blow, though from something weighing about a ton and travelling at thirty miles an hour the word "glancing" is a purely relative term. It sent Bowman tumbling head over heels to the ground. The bull pursued him, viciously trying to gore, but Bowman had still enough awareness and physical resources left to keep rolling over and over, desperately trying to avoid those lethal horns.

The crowd had suddenly become very quiet. This, they knew, was a great *razateur,* a master mime actor, but surely no one would carry the interests of his arts to the suicidal lengths where, every second now as he rolled over the sand, he escaped death by inches and sometimes less, for twice in as many seconds the bull's horn tore through the back of the doublet.

Both times Bowman felt the horn scoring across his back and it was this that galvanized him to what he knew must be his final effort. Half-a-dozen times he rolled away from the bull as quickly as he could, seized what was only half a chance and scrambled upright. He could do no more than just stand there, swaying drunkenly and staggering from side to side. Again, that eerie silence fell across the arena as the bull, infuriated beyond measure and too mad to be cunning any more, came charging in again, but just as it seemed inevitable that the bull must surely this time impale him, an uncontrollable drunken lurch by Bowman took him a bare inch clear of the scything horn: so incensed was the bull that he ran on for another twenty yards before realizing that Bowman was no longer in his way and coming to a halt.

The crowd appeared to go mad. In their relief, in their unbounded admiration for this demigod, they cheered, they clapped, they shouted, they wept tears of laughter. What an actor, what a performer, what a magnificent *razateur!* Such an exhibition, surely, had never been seen before.

Bowman leaned in total exhaustion against the barrier, a smiling Czerda only feet away from where he stood. Bowman was finished and the desperation in his face showed it. He was finished not only physically, he had come to the end of his mental tether. He just wasn't prepared to run any more. The bull lowered its head in preparation for another charge: again, silence fell over the arena. What fresh wonder was this miracle man going to demonstrate now?

But the miracle man was through with demonstrations for the day. Even as the silence fell he heard something that made him spin round and stare at the crowd, incredulity in his face. Standing high at the back of the crowd and waving frantically at him was Cecile, oblivious of the fact that scores of people had turned to stare at her.

"Neil!" Her voice was close to a scream. "Neil Bowman! Come on!"

Bowman came. The bull had started on its charge but the sight of Cecile and the realization that escape was at hand had given Bowman a fresh influx of strength, however brief it might prove to be. He scrambled into the safety of the *callejón* at least two seconds before the bull thundered into the barrier. Bowman removed the Pierrot's hat which had been hanging by its elastic band down the back of his neck, impaled it on one of the sharpened horns, brushed unceremoniously by the flabbergasted Czerda and ran up the terraces as quickly as his leaden legs would permit, waving to the crowd who parted to make way for him: the crowd, nonplussed though it was by this remarkable turn of events, nevertheless gave him a tumultuous reception: so unprecedented had the entire act been that they no doubt considered that this was also part of it. Bowman neither knew nor cared what their reactions were: just so long as they opened up before him and closed again after he had passed it would give him what might prove to be vital extra seconds over the inevitable pursuers. He reached the top, caught Cecile by the arm.

"I just love your sense of timing," he said. His voice, like his breathing, was hoarse and gasping and distressed. He turned and looked behind him. Czerda was ploughing his way up through the crowd and not leaving any newly made friends behind him: El Brocador was moving on a converging course: of Searl he could see no sign. Together they hurried down the broad steps outside the arena, skirting the bull-pens, stables and changing rooms. Bowman slid a hand through one of the many rips in his tunic, located his car keys and brought them out. He tightened his grip on Cecile's arm as they reached the last of the changing rooms and peered cautiously round the corner. A second later he withdrew, his face bitter with chagrin.

"It's not just our day, Cecile. That gypsy I clobbered—Maca—is sitting on the bonnet of the Citroën. Worse, he's cleaning his nails with a knife. One of those knives." He opened a door behind them, thrust Cecile into the changing room where he himself had robed before his performance, and handed her the car keys. "Wait till the crowd comes out. Mingle with them. Take the car, meet me at the southern end—the seaward end—of the church. For God's sake, don't leave the Citroën anywhere nearby—drive it out to the caravan park east of the town and leave it there."

"I see." She was, Bowman thought, remarkably calm. "And meantime you have things to attend to?"

"As always." He peered through a crack in the door: for the moment there was no one in sight. "Four bridesmaids," he said, slipped out and closed the door behind him.

The three manacled men were lying in their bunks, quietly and seemingly uncaring, Lila was sniffing disconsolately and Le Grand Duc scowling thunderously when Searl came running up the steps. The apprehensive look was back on his face again and he was noticeably short of breath.

"I trust," Le Grand Duc said ominously, "that you are not the bearer of ill tidings."

"I saw the girl," Searl gasped. "How did she——"

"By God, Searl, you and your nincompoop friend Czerda will pay for this. If Bowman is dead——" He broke off and stared over Searl's shoulder, then pushed him roughly to one side. "Who in heaven's name is that?"

Searl turned to follow Le Grand Duc's pointing finger. A red-and-white-clad Pierrot was making his way at a lurching stumbling run across the improvised car park: it was evident that he was near total exhaustion.

"That's him," Searl shouted. "That's him." As they watched, three gypsies appeared from behind some huts, Czerda unmistakably one of them, running in pursuit of Bowman and covering the ground a great deal faster than he was. Bowman looked over his shoulder, located his pursuers, swerved to seek cover among several caravans, checked again as he saw his way blocked by El Brocador and two other gypsies, turned at right-angles and headed for a group of horses tethered nearby, white Camargue horses fitted with the heavy-pommelled and high-backed Camargue saddles which look more like ribbed and leather-upholstered armchairs than anything else. He ran for the nearest, unhitched it, got a foot into the peculiarly fenced stirrup and managed, not without considerable effort, to haul himself up.

"Quickly!" Le Grand Duc ordered. "Get Czerda. Tell him if Bowman escapes neither he nor you shall. But I want him alive. If he dies, you die. I want him delivered to me within the hour at the Miramar Hotel in Saintes-Maries. I myself cannot afford to remain here another moment. Don't forget to catch that damned girl and bring her along also. Hurry, man, hurry!"

Searl hurried. As he made to cross the road he had to step quickly and advisedly to one side to avoid being run down by Bowman's horse. Bowman, Le Grand Duc could see, was swaying in the saddle to the extent that even although he had the reins in his hands he had to hold on to the pommel to remain in his seat. Beneath the artificial tan the face was pale, the face drawn in pain and exhaustion. Le Grand Duc became aware that Lila was standing by his side, that she too was watching Bowman.

"I've heard of it," the girl said quietly. No tears now, just a quietness and a sadness and disbelief. "And now I see it. Hounding a man to death."

Le Grand Duc put a hand on her arm. "I assure you, my dear girl——"

She struck his hand from her arm and said nothing. She didn't have to, the contempt and the loathing in her face said it all for her. Le Grand Duc nodded, turned away and watched the diminishing figure of Bowman disappearing round a bend in the road to the south.

Le Grand Duc was not the only one to take so keen an interest in Bowman's departure. Her face pressed against a small square window in the side of the changing room, Cecile watched the galloping white horse and its rider till it was vanished from sight. Sure knowledge of what would happen next kept her there nor did she have long to wait. Within thirty seconds five other horsemen came galloping by—Czerda, Ferenc, El Brocador, Searl and a fifth man whom she did not recognise. Dry-lipped, near tears and sick at heart, she turned away from the window and started searching among the racks of clothes.

Almost at once she found what she wanted—a clown's outfit consisting of the usual very wide trousers, red, with wide yellow braces as support, a red-and-yellow-striped football jersey and a voluminous dark jacket. She pulled on the trousers, stuffing in the long fiesta dress as best she could— the trousers were cut on so generous a scale that the additional bagginess was scarcely noticeable—pulled the red-and-yellow jersey over her head, shrugged into the big jacket, removed her red wig and stuck a flat green cap on her head. There was no mirror in the changing room: that, she thought dolefully, was probably just as well.

She went back to the window. The afternoon show was clearly over and people were streaming down the steps and across the road to their cars. She moved towards the door. Dressed as she was in a dress so shriekingly conspicuous that it conferred a degree of anonymity on the wearer, with the men she most feared in pursuit of Bowman and with plenty of people outside with whom to mingle, this, she realized, would be the best opportunity she would be likely to have to make her way undetected to the Citroën.

And, as far as she could tell, no one remarked her presence as she crossed the road towards the car or, if they did, they made no song and dance about it which, as far as Cecile was then concerned, amounted to the same thing. She opened the car, glanced forwards and back to make sure she was unobserved, slid into the driver's seat, put the key in the ignition and cried out more in fright than in pain as a large and viselike hand closed around her neck.

The grip eased and she turned slowly round. Maca was kneeling on the floor at the back. He was smiling in a not very encouraging fashion and he had a large knife in his right hand.

9

THE HOT afternoon sun beat down mercilessly on the baking plains beneath, on the *étangs,* on the marshes, on the salt flats and the occasional contrasting patches of bright green vegetation. A shimmering haze characteristic of the Camargue rose off the plains and gave a curiously ethereal quality, a strange lack of definition to all the features of the landscape, an illusion enhanced by the fact that none of those features was possessed of any vertical element. All plains are flat, but none as flat as the Camargue.

Half-a-dozen horsemen on steaming horses galloped furiously across the plain. From the air, their method of progress must have seemed peculiar and puzzling in the extreme as the horses seldom galloped more than twenty yards in a straight line and were continuously swerving off course. But seen at ground level the mystery disappeared: the area was so covered with numerous marshes, ranging from tiny little patches to areas larger than a football field that it made continuous progress in a direct line impossible.

Bowman was at a disadvantage and knew it. He was at a disadvantage on three counts: he was, as his strained face showed and the blood stains and dirt streaks could not conceal, as exhausted as ever—this full stretch gallop involving continuous twisting and turning, offered no possibility of recuperating any strength—and his mind was as far below its decision-making best as his body was of executing those decisions: his pursuers knew the terrain intimately whereas he was a complete stranger to it: and, fairly accomplished horseman though he considered himself to be, he knew he could not even begin to compare with the expertise his pursuers had developed and refined almost from the cradle.

Constantly he urged his now flagging horse on but made little or no attempt to guide it as the sure-footed animal, abetted by experience and generations of inborn instinct, knew far better than he did where the ground was firm and where it was not. Occasionally he lost precious seconds in trying to force his horse to go in certain directions when his horse baulked and insisted on choosing his own path.

Bowman looked over his shoulder. It was hopeless, in his heart he knew it was hopeless. When he had left Mas de Lavignolle he had had a lead of several hundred yards over his pursuers: now it was down to just over fifty. The five men behind him were spread out in a shallow fan shape. In the middle was El Brocador who was clearly as superb a horseman as he was a *razateur*. It was equally clear that he had an intimate knowledge of the terrain as from time to time he shouted orders and gestured with an outflung arm to indicate the direction a certain rider should go. On El Brocador's left rode Czerda and Ferenc, still heroically bandaged: on his right rode Simon Searl, an incongruous sight indeed in his clerical garb, and a gypsy whom Bowman could not identify.

Bowman looked ahead again. He could see no sign of succour, no house, no farm, no lonely horseman, nothing: and by this time he had been driven, not, he was grimly aware, without good reason, so far to the west that the cars passing on the main Arles-Saintes-Maries road were no more than little black beetles crawling along the line of the horizon.

He looked over his shoulder again. Thirty yards now, not more. They were no longer riding in a fan shape but were almost in line ahead, bearing down on his left, forcing him now to alter his own line of flight to the right. He was aware that this was being done with some good purpose in mind but, looking ahead, he could see nothing to justify this move. The land ahead appeared as normally variegated as the terrain he had just crossed: there was, directly ahead, an unusually large patch of almost dazzlingly green turf, perhaps a hundred yards long by thirty wide, but, size apart, it was in no way different from scores of others he had passed in the last two or three miles.

His horse, Bowman realized, had run its heart out and was near the end. Sweat-stained, foam-flecked and breathing heavily, it was as exhausted as Bowman himself. Two hundred yards ahead lay that invitingly green stretch of turf and the incongruous thought occurred to Bowman of how pleasant it would be to lie there, shaded, on a peaceful summer's day. He wondered why he didn't give up, the end of this pursuit was as certain as death itself: he would have given up, only he did not know how to set about it.

He looked back again. The five horsemen behind had now adopted a deep crescent shape, the outriders not much more than ten yards behind him. He looked ahead again, saw the greensward not more than twenty yards away, then the thought occurred that Czerda was now within accurate shooting range and Bowman was certain that when the five men returned to the caravans he would not be returning with them. Again he looked backwards and was astonished to see all five men reining in their horses and reining them in strongly at that. He knew something was wrong, terribly wrong, but before he could even start to think about it his own horse stopped abruptly and in an unbelievably short distance, forelegs splayed and sliding on its haunches, at the very edge of the patch of greensward. The horse stopped but Bowman did not. Still looking over his shoulder, he had been taken totally unprepared. He left the saddle, sailed helplessly over the horse's head and landed on the stretch of green grass.

He should have been knocked out, at the worst broken his neck, at the best landed heavily and bruised badly, but none of those things happened because it was at once apparent that the greensward was not what it appeared to be. He did not fall heavily or bounce or roll: instead he landed with a soggy squelching splash on a soft, cushioning and impact-absorbing material. Into this he slowly started to sink.

The five horsemen walked their horses forward, stopped, leaned on their pommels and gazed impassively downwards. Bowman had assumed a vertical position now, although leaning slightly forward. Already, he was hip-deep in the deadly quicksand with the safety of firm land no more than four feet away. Desperately he flailed his arms in an endeavour to reach it but made no progress whatsoever. The watchers remained motionless on their horses: the impassiveness on their faces was frightening in its suggestion of a total implacability.

Bowman sank to the waist. He tried a gentle swimming motion for he realized that frantic struggling was only having the opposite effect to what was intended. It slowed up the sinking but did not stop it: the sucking effect of the quicksand was terrifying in its remorselessness.

He looked at the five men. The total impassivity had disappeared. Czerda was smiling the pleased smile he reserved for occasions like this, Searl was slowly, obscenely licking his lips. All eyes were fixed on Bowman's face, but if he had any thoughts of shouting for help or begging for mercy no signs of it showed in his expressionless face. Nor were there any thoughts of it in his mind. Fear he had known on the battlements of Les Baux and in the bull-ring at Mas de Lavignolle: but here, now, there was no fear. On the other occasions there had been a chance, however slender, of survival, dependent upon his own resourcefulness, his co-ordination of hand and eye: but here all his hard-won knowledge and experience and skill, his exceptional reflexes and physical attributes were useless: from a quicksand there can be no escape. It was the end, it was inevitable and he accepted it.

El Brocador looked at Bowman. The quicksand was now almost up to his armpits, only his shoulders, arms and head were now in view. El Brocador studied the impassive face, nodded to himself, turned and looked at Czerda and Searl in turn, distaste and contempt in his face. He unhooked a rope from his pommel.

"One does not do this to a man like this," he said. "I am ashamed for us all." With a skilful flick of his wrist he sent the rope snaking out: it landed precisely midway between Bowman's outstretched hands.

* * *

Even the most ardent publicist of the attractions of Saintes-Maries—if any exists—would find it difficult to rhapsodize over the beauties of the main street of the town which runs from east to west along a seafront totally invisible behind a high rock wall. It is, like the rest of the town, singularly devoid of scenic, artistic or architectural merit, although on that particular afternoon its drabness was perhaps slightly relieved by the crowds of outlandishly dressed tourists, gypsies, *guardians* and the inevitable fairground booths, shooting galleries, fortunetellers' stands and souvenir shops that had been haphazardly set up for their benefit and edification.

It was not, one would have thought, a spectacle that would have brought a great deal of gratification to Le Grand Duc's aristocratic soul, yet, as he sat in the sidewalk cafe outside the Miramar Hotel, surveying the scene before him, the expression on his face was mellow to the point of benevolence. Even more oddly in light of his notoriously undemocratic principles, Carita, his chauffeuse, was seated beside him. Le Grand Duc picked up a litre carafe of red wine, poured a large amount in a large glass he had before him, a thimbleful into a small glass she had before her and smiled benevolently again, not at the passing scene but at a telegram form that he held in his hand. It was clear that Le Grand Duc's exceptional good humor was not because of Saintes-Maries and its inhabitants, but in spite of them. The source of his satisfaction lay in the paper he held in his hand.

"Excellent, my dear Carita, excellent. Exactly what we wished to know. By Jove, they have moved fast." He contemplated the paper again and sighed. "It's gratifying, most gratifying, when one's guesses turn out to be one hundred per cent accurate."

"Yours always are, Monsieur le Duc."

"Eh? What was that? Yes, yes, of course. Help yourself to some more wine." Le Grand Duc had temporarily lost interest in both the telegram and Carita, and was gazing thoughtfully at a large black Mercedes that had just pulled up a few feet away. The Chinese couple whom Le Grand Duc had last seen on the hotel patio in Arles emerged and made for the hotel entrance. They passed by within a few feet of Le Grand Duc's table. The man nodded, his wife smiled faintly and Le Grand Duc, not to be outdone, bowed gravely. He watched them go as they went inside, then turned to Carita.

"Czerda should be here soon with Bowman. I have decided that this is an inadvisable place for a rendezvous. Too public, too public by far. There's a big lay-by about one mile north of the town. Have Czerda stop there and wait for me while you come back here for me."

She smiled and rose to leave but Le Grand Duc raised a hand.

"One last thing before you go. I have a very urgent phone call to make and I wish it made in complete privacy. Tell the manager I wish to see him. At once."

Le Hobenaut, Tangevec and Daymel were still in their bunks, still manacled to the caravan wall. Bowman, his Pierrot suit now removed and his *guardian* clothes saturated and still dripping, lay on the floor with his hands bound behind his back. Cecile and Lila were seated on a bench under the watchful eyes of Ferenc and Masaine. Czerda, El Brocador and Searl were seated at a table: they weren't talking and they looked very unhappy. Their expression of unhappiness deepened as they listened to the measured tread of footsteps mounting the steps of the caravan. Le Grand Duc made his customary impressive entry. He surveyed the three seated men coldly.

"We have to move quickly." His voice was brusque, authoritative and as cold as his face. "I have received cabled information that the police are becoming suspicious and may well by this time be certain of us—thanks to you, Czerda, and that bungling fool Searl there. Are you mad, Czerda?"

"I do not understand, sir."

"That's precisely it. You understand nothing. You were going to kill Bowman before he'd told us how he broke our ring, who his contacts are, where my eighty thousand francs are. Worst of all, you cretins, you were going to kill him publicly. Can't you see the enormous publicity that would have received? Secrecy, stealth, those are my watchwords."

"We know where the eighty thousand francs are, sir." Czerda tried to salvage something from the wreck.

"Do we? *Do* we? I suspect you have been fooled again, Czerda. But that can wait. Do you know what will happen to you all if the French police get you?" Silence. "Do you know the rigorous penalties French courts impose on kidnappers?" Still silence. "Not one of you here can hope to escape with less than ten years in prison. And if they can trace Alexandre's murder to you . . ."

Le Grand Duc looked at El Brocador and the four gypsies in turn. From the expressions on their faces it was quite clear that they knew what would happen if the murder could be traced to them.

"Very well, then. From this moment on your futures and your lives depend entirely on doing exactly what I order—it is not beyond my powers to rescue you from the consequences of your own folly. Exactly. Is that understood?"

All five men nodded. No one said anything.

"Very well. Unchain those men. Untie Bowman. If the police find them like that—well, it's all over. We use guns and knives to guard them from now on. Bring all their womenfolk in here—I want all our eggs in one basket. Go over our proposed plans, Searl. Go over them briefly and clearly so that even the most incompetent nincompoop, and that includes you, can understand what we have in mind. Bring me some beer, someone."

Searl cleared his throat self-consciously and looked distinctly unhappy. The arrogance, the quietly cold competence with which he'd confronted Czerda in the confessional booth that morning had vanished as if it had never existed.

"Rendezvous any time between last night and Monday night. Fast motor-boat waiting——"

Le Grand Duc sighed in despair and held up a hand.

"Briefly and *clearly*, Searl. Clearly. Rendezvous where, you fool? With whom?"

"Sorry, sir." The Adam's apple in the thin scraggy neck bobbed up and down as Searl swallowed nervously. "Off Palavas in the Gulf of Aigues-Mortes. Freighter *Canton*."

"Bound for?"

"Canton."

"Precisely."

"Recognition signals——"

"Never mind that. The motorboat?"

"At Aigues-Mortes on the Canal du Rhône à Sète. I was going to have it moved down to Le Grau-du-Roi tomorrow—I didn't think—I——"

"You never have done," Le Grand Duc said wearily. "Why aren't those damned women here? And those manacles still fixed? Hurry." For the first time he relaxed and smiled slightly. "I'll wager our friend Bowman still doesn't know who our three other friends are. Eh, Searl?"

"I can tell him?" Searl asked eagerly. The prospect of climbing out of the hot seat and transferring the spotlight elsewhere was clearly an attractive one.

"Suit yourself." Le Grand Duc drank deeply of his beer. "Can it matter now?"

"Of course not." Searl smiled widely. "Let me introduce Count le Hobenaut, Henri Tangevec and Serge Daymel. The three leading rocket fuel experts on the other side of the Iron Curtain. The Chinese wanted them badly, they have been so far unable to develop a vehicle to carry their nuclear warheads. Those men could do it. But there wasn't a single land border between China and Russia that could be used, not a single neutral country that was friendly to both the great powers and wouldn't have looked too closely at any irregular happening. So Czerda brought them out. To the west. No one would ever dream that such men would defect to the west— the west has its own fuel experts. And, at the frontiers, no one ever asks questions of gypsies. Of course, if the three men had clever ideas, their wives would have been killed. If the women got clever ideas, the men would have been killed."

"Or so the women were told," Le Grand Duc said contemptuously. "The last thing that we wanted was that any harm should come to those men. But women—they'll believe anything." He permitted himself a small smile of satisfaction. "The simplicity—if I may say so myself, the staggering simplicity of true genius. Ah, the women. Aigues-Mortes, and with speed. Tell your other caravans, Czerda, that you will rendezvous with them in the morning in Saintes-Maries. Come, Lila, my dear."

"With you?" She stared at him in revulsion. "You must be mad. Go with *you*?"

"Appearances must be maintained, now more than ever. What suspicion is going to attach to a man with so beautiful a young lady by his side? Besides, it's very hot and I require someone to hold my parasol."

Just over an hour later, still fuming and tight-lipped, she lowered the parasol as the green Rolls-Royce drew up outside the frowning walls of Aigues-Mortes, the most perfectly preserved Crusader walled city in Europe. Le Grand Duc descended from the car and waited till Czerda had brought the breakdown truck towing the caravan to a halt.

"Wait here," he ordered. "I shall not be long." He nodded to the Rolls. "Keep a sharp eye on Miss Delafont there. You apart, no others are on any account to show themselves."

He glanced up the road towards Saintes-Maries. Momentarily, it was deserted. He marched quickly away and entered the bleak and forbidding town by the north gate, turned right into the car park and took up position in the concealment of a barrel organ. The operator, a decrepit ancient who, in spite of the heat of the day, was wearing two overcoats and a felt hat, looked up from the stool where he had been drowsing and scowled. Le Grand Duc gave him ten francs. The operator stopped scowling, adjusted a switch and began to crank a handle: the screeching cacophonous result was an atonal travesty of a waltz that no composer alive or dead would ever have acknowledged as his. Le Grand Duc winced, but remained where he was.

Within two minutes a black Mercedes passed in through the archway, turned right and stopped. The Chinese couple got out, looked neither to left nor right, and walked hurriedly down the main street—indeed, Aigues-Mortes' only street—towards the tiny cafe-lined square near the centre of the town. More leisurely and at a discreet distance Le Grand Duc followed.

The Chinese couple reached the square and halted uncertainly on a corner by a souvenir shop, not far from the statue of Saint-Louis. No sooner had they done so than four large men in plain dark clothes emerged from the shop, two from each door, and closed in on them. One of the men showed the Chinese man something cupped in the palm of his hand. The Chinese man gesticulated and appeared to protest violently but the four large men just shook their heads firmly and led the couple away to a pair of waiting black Citroëns.

Le Grand Duc nodded his head in what could not easily have been mistaken for anything other than satisfaction, turned and retraced his steps to the waiting car and caravan.

Less than sixty seconds' drive took them to a small jetty on the Canal du Rhône à Sète, a canal that links the Rhône to the Mediterranean at Grau-du-Roi and runs parallel to the western wall of Aigues-Mortes. At the end of the jetty was moored a thirty-five-foot powerboat with a large glassed-in cabin and an only slightly smaller cockpit aft. From the lines of the broad flaring bows it appeared to be a vessel capable of something unusual in terms of speed.

The Rolls and the caravan pulled clear off the road and halted so that the rear of the caravan was less than six feet from the head of the jetty. The transfer of the prisoners from the caravan to the boat was performed smoothly, expeditiously and in such a fashion that it could have aroused no suspicion in even the most inquisitive of bystanders: in point of fact the nearest person was a rod fisherman a hundred yards away and his entire attention was obviously concentrated on what was happening at the end of his line some feet below the surface of the canal. Ferenc and Searl, each with a barely concealed pistol, stood on the jetty near the top of a short gangway while Le Grand Duc and Czerda, similarly unostentatiously armed, stood on the poop of the boat while first the three scientists, then their womenfolk, then Bowman, Cecile and Lila filed aboard. Under the threat of the guns they took up position on the settees lining the side of the cabin.

Ferenc and Searl entered the cabin, Searl advancing to the helmsman's position. For a moment Le Grand Duc and Masaine remained in the cockpit checking that they were quite unobserved then Le Grand Duc entered the cabin, pocketed his gun and rubbed his hands in satisfaction.

"Excellent, excellent, excellent." He sounded positively cheerful. "Everything, as always, under control. Start the engines, Searl!" He turned and poked his head through the cabin doorway. "Cast off, Masaine!"

Searl pressed buttons and the twin diesels started up with a deep powerful throb of sound, but a sound by no means loud enough to muffle a short sharp exclamation of pain: the sound emanated from Le Grand Duc, who was still looking aft through the doorway.

"Your own gun in your own kidney," Bowman said. "No one to move or you die." He looked at Ferenc and Czerda and Searl and El Brocador. At least three of them, he knew, were armed. He said: "Tell Searl to stop the engines."

Searl stopped the engines without having to have the message relayed through Le Grand Duc.

"Tell Masaine to come here," Bowman said. "Tell him I've got a gun in your kidney." He looked round the cabin: no one had moved. "Tell him to come at once or I'll pull the trigger."

"You wouldn't dare!"

"You'll be all right," Bowman said soothingly. "Most people can get by on one kidney."

He jabbed the gun again and Le Grand Duc gasped in pain. He said hoarsely: "Masaine! Come here at once. Put your gun away. Bowman has his gun on me."

There were a few seconds' silence, then Masaine appeared in the doorway. No profound thinker at the best of times, he was obviously uncertain as to what to do: the sight of Czerda, Ferenc, Searl and El Brocador busy doing nothing convinced him that doing nothing was, for the moment, the wise and prudent course of action. He moved into the cabin.

"Now we come up against the question of the delicate balances of power," Bowman said conversationally. He was still pale and haggard, he felt unutterably tired and stiff and sore all over: but he felt a prince compared to the condition he'd been in two hours previously. "A question of checks and balances. How much influence and authority can I exert on you standing here with this gun in my hand? How much of my will can I impose? So much—but only so much."

He pulled Le Grand Duc back by the shoulder, stepped to one side and watched Le Grand Duc collapse heavily on a settee, a well-made settee which didn't break. Le Grand Duc glared at Bowman, the aristocratic voltage in the blue eyes turned up to maximum power: Bowman remained unshrivelled.

"It's difficult to believe just looking at you," Bowman went on to Le Grand Duc, "but you're almost certainly the most intelligent of your band of ruffians. Not, of course, that that would call for any great intelligence. I have a gun here and it is in my hand. There are four others here who also have guns and although they're not in their hands at the present moment it wouldn't take very long for the guns to get there. If it came to a fight, I think it extremely unlikely that I could get all four before one of you—more probably two—got me. I am not a Wild Bill Hickok. Moreover, there are eight innocent people here—nine, if you count me—and a gunfight in this enclosed space would almost certainly result in some of them being hurt, even killed. I wouldn't like that any more than I would like being shot myself."

"Get to the point," Le Grand Duc growled.

"It's obvious, surely. What demands can I make upon you that wouldn't be too great to precipitate this gunfight that I'm sure we all want to avoid? If I told you to hand over your guns, would you, quietly and tamely, with the knowledge that long prison sentences and probably indictments for murder awaited you all? I doubt it. If I said I'll let you go but take the scientists and their women, would you go along with that? Again, I doubt it, for they would be living evidence of your crimes with the result that if you set foot anywhere in western Europe you'd finish in prison and if you set foot in eastern Europe you'd be lucky to end up in a Siberian prison camp as the Communists aren't too keen on people who kidnap their top scientists. In fact, there'd be no place left for you in any part of Europe. You'd just have to go on the *Canton* and sail all the way home with her and I don't think you'd find life in China all it's cracked up to be—by the Chinese, of course.

"On the other hand, I doubt whether you'd be prepared to fight to the death to prevent the departure of the two young ladies and myself. They're only ciphers, a couple of romantically minded and rather empty-headed young holiday-makers who thought it rather fun to get mixed up in those dark goings on." Bowman carefully avoided looking at the two girls. "I admit that it is possible for me to start trouble, but I don't see I would get very far: it would be only my word against yours, there wouldn't be a shred of evidence I could offer and there's no way I can think of how you could be tied up with the murder in the cave. The only evidence lies in the scientists and their wives and they would be halfway to China before I could do anything. Well?"

"I accept your reasoning," Le Grand Duc said heavily. "Try to make us give ourselves or the scientists up—or their wives—and you'd never leave this boat alive. You and those two young fools there are, as you say, another matter. You can arouse suspicion, but that's all you can do: better that than have two or three of my men die uselessly.''

"It might even be you," Bowman said.

"The possibility had not escaped me."

"You're my number-one choice of hostage and safe-conduct," Bowman said.

"I rather thought I might be." Le Grand Duc rose with obvious reluctance to his feet.

"I don't like this," Czerda said. "What if——"

"You want to be the first to die?" Le Grand Duc asked wearily. "Leave the thinking to me, Czerda."

Czerda, obviously ill at ease, said no more. At a gesture from Bowman the two girls left the cabin and climbed the gangway. Bowman, walking backwards with his gun a few inches from Le Grand Duc's midriff, followed. At the top of the gangway Bowman said to the girls: "Get back and out of sight."

He waited ten seconds then said to Le Grand Duc: "Turn round." Le Grand Duc turned. Bowman gave him a hefty shove that sent him stumbling, almost falling, down the gangway. Bowman threw himself flat: there was always the off-chance of someone or ones down there changing their minds. But no shots were fired, there was no sound of footsteps on the gangway. Bowman raised a cautious head. The engines had started up again.

The powerboat was already twenty yards away and accelerating. Bowman rose quickly and, followed by Cecile and Lila, ran to the Rolls. Carita gazed at him in astonishment.

"Out!" Bowman said.

Carita opened her mouth to protest but Bowman was in no mood for protests. He jerked open the door and practically lifted her onto the road. Immediately afterwards he was behind the wheel himself.

"Wait!" Cecile said. "Wait! We're coming with——"

"Not this time." He leaned down and plucked Cecile's handbag from her. She stared at him, slightly open-mouthed, but said nothing. He went on: "Go into the town. Phone the police in Saintes-Maries, tell them there's a sick girl in a green-and-white caravan in a lay-by a kilometre and a half north of the town and that they're to get her to a hospital at once. Don't tell them who you are, don't tell them a single thing more than that. Just hang up." He nodded at Lila and Carita. "Those two will do for a start."

"Do for what?" She was, understandably, bemused.

"Bridesmaids."

The road between Aigues-Mortes and Grau-du-Roi is only a few kilometres long and, for the most part, it parallels the canal at a distance of a few feet: the only boundary line between them, if such it can be called, is a thin line of tall reeds. It was through those reeds, less than a minute after starting up the Rolls, that Bowman caught his first glimpse of the powerboat, fewer than a hundred yards ahead. It was already travelling at an illegally high speed, its stern dug deep into the water, spray flying high and wide from the deflectors on the bows: the wash set up by the wake of its passing was sending waves high up both sides of the canal banks.

Searl was at the wheel, Masaine, El Brocador and Ferenc were seated but keeping a watchful eye on the passengers, while Le Grand Duc and Czerda were conversing near the after door of the cabin. Czerda still looked most unhappy.

He said: "But how can you be *sure* that he can bring no harm to us?"

"I'm sure." The passage of time had restored Le Grand Duc to his old confident self.

"But he'll go to the police. He's bound to."

"So? You heard what he said himself. His solitary word against all of ours? With all his evidence halfway to China? They'll think he's mad. Even if they don't, there's nothing in the world they can prove."

"I still don't like it," Czerda said stubbornly. "I think——"

"Leave the thinking to me," Le Grand Duc said curtly. "Good God!"

There was a splintering of glass, the sound of a shot and a harsh cry of pain from Searl who abandoned the wheel in favour of clutching his left shoulder. The boat swerved violently and headed straight for the left bank: it would unquestionably have struck it had not Czerda, although elder than any of his companions and the farthest from the wheel, reacted with astonishing speed, hurled himself forward and spun the wheel hard to starboard. He succeeded in preventing the powerboat from burying—and probably crushing—its bows in the bank, but wasn't in time to prevent the wildly slewing boat from crashing its port side heavily against the bank with an impact that threw all who were standing, except Czerda, and quite a few who were seated, to the deck. It was at that instant that Czerda glanced through a side window and saw Bowman, at the wheel of the Rolls-Royce and less than five yards distant on the paralleling road, taking careful aim with Le Grand Duc's pistol through an opened window.

"Down!" shouted Czerda. He was the first down himself. "Flat on the floor."

Again there came the sound of smashing glass, again the simultaneous report from the pistol, but no one was hurt. Czerda rose to a crouch, eased the throttle, handed the wheel over to Masaine, and joined Le Grand Duc and Ferenc who had already edged out, on all fours, to the poopdeck. All three men peered cautiously over the gunwale, then stood upright, thoughtfully holding their guns behind their backs.

The Rolls had dropped thirty yards back. Bowman was being blocked by a farm tractor towing a large four-wheeled trailer, and baulked from overtaking by several cars approaching from the south.

"Faster," Czerda said to Masaine. "Not too fast—keep just ahead of that tractor. That's it. That's it." He watched the last of the northbound cars go by on the other side of the road. "Here he comes now."

The long green nose of the Rolls appeared in sight beyond the tractor. The three men in the cockpit levelled their guns and the tractor driver, seeing them, braked and swerved so violently that he came to a rest with the right front wheel of his tractor overhanging the bank of the canal. Its sudden braking and swerve brought the entire length of the car completely and suddenly in sight. Bowman, gun cocked in hand and ready to use, saw what was about to happen, dropped the gun and threw himself below the level of the door sills. He winced as bullet after bullet thudded into the bodywork of the Rolls. The windscreen suddenly starred and became completely opaque. Bowman thrust his fist through the bottom of the glass, kicked the accelerator down beyond the detente and accelerated swiftly away. It was obvious that, with the element of surprise gone, he stood no chance whatsoever against the three armed men in the poop. He wondered vaguely how Le Grand Duc felt about the sudden drop in the resale market value of his Rolls.

He drove at high speed past the arena on his left into the town of Grau-du-Roi, skidding the car to a halt at the approaches to the swing bridge that crossed the canal and connected the two sides of the town. He opened

Cecile's bag, peeled money from the roll of Swiss francs he had taken from Czerda's caravan, put the roll back in the bag, thrust the bag into a cubby-hole, hoped to heaven the citizens of Grau-du-Roi were honest, left the car and ran down the quayside.

He slowed down to a walk as he approached the craft moored along the left bank, just below the bridge. It was a wide-beamed, high-prowed fishing boat, of wooden and clearly very solid construction, that had seen its best days some years ago. Bowman approached a grey-jerseyed fisherman of middle age who was sitting on a bollard and lethargically mending a net.

"That's a fine boat you've got there," Bowman said in his best admiring tourist fashion. "Is it for rent?"

The fisherman was taken aback by the directness of the approach. Matters involving finance were customarily approached with a great deal more finesse.

"Fourteen knots and built like a tank," the owner said proudly. "The finest wooden-hulled fishing boat in the South of France. Twin Perkins diesels. Like lightning! And so strong. But only for charter, m'sieur. And even then only when the fishing is bad."

"Too bad, too bad." Bowman took out some Swiss francs and fingered them. "Not even for an hour? I have urgent reasons, believe me." He had, too. In the distance he could hear the rising note of Le Grand Duc's powerboat.

The fisherman screwed up his eyes as if in thought: it is not easy to ascertain the denomination of foreign banknotes at a distance of four feet. But sailors' eyes are traditionally keen. He stood and slapped his thigh.

"I will make an exception," he announced, then added cunningly: "But I will have to come with you, of course."

"Of course. I would have expected nothing else." Bowman handed over two one-thousand Swiss franc notes. There was a legerdemain flick of the wrist and the notes disappeared from sight.

"When does m'sieur wish to leave?"

"Now." He could have had the boat anyway, Bowman knew, but he preferred Czerda's banknotes to the waving of a gun as a means of persuasion: that he would eventually have to wave his gun around he did not doubt.

They cast off, went aboard and the fisherman started the engines while Bowman peered casually aft. The sound of the powerboat's engines was very close now. Bowman turned and watched the fisherman push the throttles forward as he gave the wheel a turn to starboard. The fishing boat began to move slowly away from the quayside.

"It doesn't seem too difficult," Bowman observed. "To handle it, I mean."

"To you, no. But it takes a lifetime of knowledge to handle such a vessel."

"Could I try now?"

"No, no. Impossible. Perhaps when we get to the sea——"

"I'm afraid it will have to be now. Please."

"In five minutes——"

"I'm sorry. I really am." Bowman produced his pistol, pointed with it to the starboard for'ard corner of the wheelhouse. "Please sit down there."

The fisherman stared at him, relinquished the wheel and moved across to the corner of the wheelhouse. He said quietly, as Bowman took over the wheel: "I knew I was a fool. I like money too much, I think."

"Don't we all." Bowman glanced over his shoulder. The powerboat was less than a hundred yards from the bridge. He opened the throttles wide and the fishing boat began to surge forward. Bowman dug into his pocket, came up with the last three thousand francs of Czerda's money that he had on him and threw it across to the man. "This will make you even more foolish."

The fisherman stared at the notes, made no attempt to pick them up. He whispered: "When I am dead, you will take it away. Pierre des Jardins is not a fool."

"When you are dead?"

"When you kill me. With that pistol." He smiled sadly. "It is a wonderful thing to have a pistol, no?"

"Yes." Bowman reversed hold on his pistol, caught it by the barrel and threw it gently across to the fisherman. "Do you feel wonderful too, now?"

The man stared at the pistol, picked it up, pointed it experimentally at Bowman, laid it down, picked up and pocketed the money, picked up the pistol a second time, rose, crossed to the wheel and replaced the pistol in Bowman's pocket. He said: "I'm afraid I am not very good at firing those things, m'sieur."

"Neither am I. Look behind you. Do you see a powerboat coming up?"

Pierre looked. The powerboat was no more than a hundred yards behind. He said: "I see it. I know it. My friend Jean——"

"Sorry. Later about your friend." Bowman pointed ahead to where a freighter was riding out in the gulf. "That's the freighter *Canton*. A Communist vessel bound for China. Behind us, in that powerboat are evil men who wish to put aboard that vessel people who do not wish to go there. It is my wish to stop them."

"Why?"

"If you have to ask why I'll take this pistol from my pocket and make you sit down again." Bowman looked quickly behind him: the powerboat was barely more than fifty yards behind.

"You are British, of course?"

"Yes."

"You are an agent of your government?"

"Yes."

"What we call your Secret Service?"

"Yes."

"You are known to our government?"

"I am to your Deuxième Bureau. Their boss is my boss."

"Boss?"

"Chief. *Chef.*"

Pierre sighed. "It has to be true. And you wish to stop this boat coming up?" Bowman nodded. "Then please move over. This is a job for an expert."

Bowman nodded again, took the gun from his pocket, moved to the starboard side of the wheelhouse and wound down the window. The powerboat was less than ten feet astern, not more than twenty feet away on a parallel course and coming up fast. Czerda was at the wheel now, with Le Grand Duc by his side. Bowman raised his pistol, then lowered it again as the fishing boat leaned over sharply and arrowed in on the powerboat. Three seconds later the heavy oaken bows of the fishing boat smashed heavily into the port quarter of the other vessel.

"That was, perhaps, more or less what you had in mind, m'sieur?" Pierre asked.

"More or less," Bowman admitted.

The two boats moved apart on parallel courses. The powerboat, being the faster, pulled ahead. Inside its cabin there was considerable confusion.

"Who was that madman?" Le Grand Duc demanded.

"Bowman!" Czerda spoke with certainty.

"Guns out!" Le Grand Duc shouted. "Guns out! Get him!"

"No."

"No? No? You dare countermand——"

"I smell petrol. In the air. One shot—poof! Ferenc, go and check the port tank." Ferenc departed and returned within ten seconds.

"Well?"

"The tank is ruptured. At the bottom. The fuel is nearly gone." Even as he spoke the port engine faltered, spluttered and stopped. Czerda and Le Grand Duc looked at each other: nothing was said.

Both boats had by now cleared the harbour and were out in the open sea of the Gulf of Aigues-Mortes. The powerboat, on one engine now, had dropped back until it was almost parallel with the fishing boat. Bowman nodded to Pierre, who nodded in turn. He spun the wheel rapidly, their vessel angled in sharply, they made violent contact again in exactly the same place as previously, then sheered off.

"God damn it all!" Aboard the powerboat Le Grand Duc was almost livid with fury and making no attempt to conceal it. "He's holed us! He's holed us! Can't you avoid him?"

"With one engine, it is very difficult to steer." Under the circumstances, Czerda's restraint was commendable. He was in no way exaggerating. The combination of a dead port engine and a holed port quarter made the maintenance of a straight course virtually impossible: Czerda was no seaman and even with his best efforts the powerboat was now pursuing a very erratic course indeed.

"Look!" Le Grand Duc said sharply. "What's that?"

About three miles away, not more than halfway towards Palavas, a large and very old-fashioned freighter, almost stopped in the water, was sending a message by signalling lamp.

"It's the *Canton*!" Searl said excitedly. He so far forgot himself as to stop rubbing the now bandaged flesh wound on top of his shoulder. "The *Canton*! We must send a recognition signal. Three long, three short."

"No!" Le Grand Duc was emphatic. "Are you mad? We mustn't get them involved in this. The international repercussions—look out!"

The fishing boat was veering in again. Le Grand Duc and Ferenc rushed to the cockpit and loosed off several shots. The windows in the wheelhouse of the fishing boat starred and broke, but Bowman and Pierre had already dropped to the deck which Le Grand Duc and Ferenc had to do at almost exactly the same moment as the heavy oaken stern of the fishing boat crashed into the port quarter at precisely the spot where they were standing.

Five times inside the next two minutes the manoeuvre was repeated, five times the powerboat shuddered under the crushing assaults. By now, at Le Grand Duc's orders, all firing had ceased: ammunition was almost exhausted.

"We must keep the last bullets for when and where they will do the most good." Le Grand Duc had become very calm. "Next time——"

"The *Canton* is leaving!" Searl shouted. "Look, she has turned away."

They looked. The *Canton* was indeed turning away, beginning to move with increasing speed through the water.

"What else did you expect?" Le Grand Duc asked. "Never fear, we shall see her again."

"What do you mean?" Czerda demanded.

"Later. As I was saying——"

"We're sinking!" Searl's voice was almost a scream. "We're sinking!" He was in no way exaggerating: the powerboat was now deep in the water, the sea pouring in through gaps torn in the hull by the bows of the fishing boat.

"I am aware of that," Le Grand Duc said. He turned to Czerda. "They're coming again. Hard a starboard—to your right, quickly. Ferenc, Searl, El Brocador, come with me."

"My shoulder," Searl wailed.

"Never mind your shoulder. Come with me."

The four men stood just inside the doorway of the cabin as the fishing boat came at them again. But this time the powerboat, though sluggish and far from responsive because of its depth in the water, had succeeded in turning away enough to reduce the impact to the extent that the two boats merely grazed each other. As the wheelhouse of the fishing boat passed by the cabin of the powerboat, Le Grand Duc and his three men rushed out into the cockpit. Le Grand Duc waited his moment then, with that speed and agility so surprising in a man of his bulk, stood on the gunwale and flung himself on to the poop of the fishing boat. Within two seconds the others had followed.

Ten seconds after that Bowman turned round sharply as the port door of the wheelhouse opened abruptly and Ferenc and Searl stood framed there, both with guns in their hands.

"No." Bowman spun again to locate the voice behind him. He hadn't far to look. The guns of Le Grand Duc and El Brocador were less than a foot from his face. Le Grand Duc said: "Enough is enough?"

Bowman nodded. "Enough is enough."

10

FIFTEEN MINUTES later, with the first shades of evening beginning to fall, the fishing boat, a curiously unperturbed Pierre des Jardins at the wheel, moved placidly up the Canal du Rhône à Sète. The three scientists and their womenfolk, the last of whom had been hauled aboard only seconds before the powerboat had sunk, were seated on the foredeck under the concealed guns of the gypsies, for all the world like vacationing trippers enjoying a leisurely cruise in the warm summer evening. All the glass had been knocked out from the broken windows and the few bullet holes in the woodwork of the wheelhouse were discreetly camouflaged by El Brocador and Masaine, who were leaning negligently against the starboard side of the structure. Pierre apart, the only two other occupants of the wheelhouse were Bowman and Le Grand Duc, the latter with a gun in his hand.

A few kilometres up the canal they passed by the tractor and trailer that had so abruptly left the road when the shooting contest between the Rolls and the powerboat had begun. The tractor was as it had been, a front wheel still overhanging the canal: clearly and understandably, the driver had deemed it wiser to wait for assistance rather than risk a watery grave for his tractor by trying to extricate it under its own power. The driver, oddly enough, was still there, pacing up and down with a legitimately thunderous look on his face.

Czerda joined the three men in the wheelhouse. He said worriedly: "I do not like it at all. It is much too quiet. Perhaps we are going to some kind of trap. Surely some person——"

"Does that make you feel happier?" Le Grand Duc pointed in the direction of Aigues-Mortes: two black police cars, sirens wailing and blue lights flashing were approaching at high speed. "Something tells me that our friend the tractor driver has been complaining to someone."

Le Grand Duc's guess proved to be correct. The police cars swept by and almost at once started slowing as the tractor driver stood in the middle of the road and frantically waved his arms. They stopped and uniformed figures jumped out of the car and surrounded the gesticulating tractor driver who was obviously telling his story with a great deal of verve and gusto.

"Well, if the police are bothering somebody else, they can't very well be bothering us at the same time." Le Grand Duc observed philosophically. "Happier now, Czerda?"

"No," Czerda said and looked as if he meant it. "Two things. Dozens of people, hundreds for all I know, must have seen what was happening out in the gulf. Why did no one stop us on the way in? Why did no one report what was happening to the police?"

"Quite frankly, I don't know," Le Grand Duc said thoughtfully. "I can guess, though. Same thing happens time and again—when large numbers of people see something happening they invariably leave it to someone else to do something about it. Why, there have been cases of pedestrians watching a man being beaten to death in the street and not lifting a hand to help. Mankind is curiously apathetic about that sort of thing. Maybe it's a natural reluctance to step into the limelight. I do not profess to know. All that matters is that we came up the harbour without causing an eyebrow to be lifted. Your other question? You had two?"

"Yes." Czerda was grim. "What in God's name are we going to do now?"

"That is no problem." Le Grand Duc smiled. "Did I not tell you that we would see the good ship *Canton* again?"

"Yes, but how——"

"How long will it take us to drive to Port le Bouc?"

"Port le Bouc?" Czerda furrowed his brow. "With the caravan and truck?"

"How else?"

"Two and a half hours. Not more than three. Why?"

"Because that's where the *Canton* has instructions to await us if any difficulty arose at the Palavas rendezvous. It will remain there until noon tomorrow—and we will be there tonight. Don't you know by now, Czerda, that I always have another string to my bow? Many strings, in fact. And there, tonight, the scientists and their women will be taken aboard. So will Bowman. And so, to eliminate any possibility of risk whatsoever, will the two young ladies and, I'm afraid, this unfortunate fisherman here." Pierre des Jardins glanced at Le Grand Duc, lifted an eyebrow, then concentrated on his task again: it was a minuscule reaction for a man listening to what was virtually a death sentence. "And then, Czerda, you and your men will be as free as the air for when Bowman and his three friends arrive in China they will simply disappear and never be heard of again. The only witnesses against you will be gone forever and no breath of suspicion will ever attach itself to you or your men on either side of the Iron Curtain."

"If I have ever questioned you in the past, I apologize." Czerda spoke slowly, almost reverently. "This is genius." He looked as a man might look after the Forth Bridge had been lifted off his back.

"Elementary, elementary." Le Grand Duc waved a disparaging hand.

"Now, then. We shall be in sight of the jetty shortly and we don't want to give the young ladies any shocks to their delicate nervous systems, the kind of shock, for instance, that might prompt them to drive away at speed with the truck and caravan before we even reach the jetty. Everybody into the fishhold now and to keep out of sight till the word is given. You and I will remain here—seated, of course—while Bowman takes the vessel alongside. Understood?"

"Understood." Czerda looked at him admiringly. "You think of everything!"

"I try," Le Grand Duc said modestly. "I try."

The three girls with a youngster seated on a scooter were at the head of the jetty as Bowman, apparently alone, brought the boat alongside. They ran down, secured the ropes he threw them and jumped aboard. Cecile and Lila were half-smiling half-apprehensive, wondering what news he bore: Carita remained in the background, aloof and rather remote.

"Well?" Cecile demanded. "Well, tell us. What happened?"

"I'm sorry," Bowman said. "Things have gone wrong."

"Not for us," Le Grand Duc said jovially. He stood up, gun in hand, accompanied by Czerda, similarly equipped and beamed at the girls. "Not really, I must say. How nice to see you again, my dear Carita. Had a pleasant time with the two young ladies."

"No," Carita said shortly. "They wouldn't speak to me."

"Prejudice, sheer prejudice. Right, Czerda, everyone on deck and in the caravan inside a minute." He looked towards the head of the jetty. "And who is that youth with the scooter?"

"That's José!" Czerda was as near a mood of excited anticipation as it would ever be possible for him to achieve. "The boy I sent to get the money that Bowman stole from me—from us, I mean." He stepped out on deck and waved an arm. "José! José!"

José swung his leg over the scooter, came down the jetty and jumped aboard. He was a tall thin youth with an enormous shock of black hair, beady eyes and a prematurely knowing expression.

"The money?" Czerda asked. "You have the money?"

"What money?"

"Of course, of course. To you, only a brown paper parcel." Czerda smiled indulgently. "But it was the right key?"

"I don't know." José's mental processes, quite evidently, knew nothing about the intelligent expression on his face.

"What do you mean, you don't know?"

"I don't know whether it was the right key or the wrong key," José explained patiently. "All I know is that there are no safe-deposit boxes in the railway station in Arles."

There was a fairly lengthy silence during which a number of thoughts, none of them particularly pleasant, passed through the minds of several of those present, then Bowman cleared his throat and said apologetically: "I'm afraid this is all rather my fault. That was the key to my suitcase."

There was another silence, more or less of the same length, then Le Grand Duc said with immense restraint: "The key to your suitcase. I would have expected nothing else. Where are the eighty thousand francs, Mr. Bowman?"

"Seventy thousand. I'm afraid I had to deduct a little of it. Current expenses, you know." He nodded to Cecile. "That dress alone cost me——"

"Where are they?" Le Grand Duc shouted. He was through with restraint for the day. "The seventy thousand francs?"

"Ah yes. Well, now." Bowman shook his head. "There's so much happened since last night——"

"Czerda!" Le Grand Duc was back on balance again but it was a close thing. "Put your pistol to Miss Dubois' head. I shall count three."

"Don't bother," Bowman said. "I left it in the Les Baux caves. By Alexandre."

"*By* Alexandre?"

"I'm not an idiot," Bowman said tiredly. "I knew the police might be there this morning. Rather, would be there and might find Alexandre. But it's close by."

Le Grand Duc gave him a long thoughtful stare then turned to Czerda. "This would be only a minor detour on our way to Port le Bouc?"

"Another twenty minutes. No more." He nodded towards Bowman. "The canal here is deep. Do we need him along, sir?"

"Only," Le Grand Duc said ominously, "until we discover whether he's telling the truth or not."

Night had fallen when Czerda pulled up in the lay-by at the head of the Valley of Hell. Le Grand Duc, who, along with El Brocador, had been Czerda's passengers in the front of the towing truck, got out, stretched himself and said: "The ladies we will leave here. Masaine will stay behind to guard them. All of the others will come with us."

Czerda looked his puzzlement. "We require so many?"

"I have my purpose." Le Grand Duc was at his most enigmatic. "Do you question my judgment?"

"Now? Never!"

"Very well, then."

Moments later a large group of people were moving through the terrifying vastness of the tomb-like caverns. There were eleven of them in all—Czerda, Ferenc, Searl, El Brocador, the three scientists, the two girls, Bowman and Le Grand Duc. Several carried torches, their beams reflecting weirdly, whitely, off the great limestone walls. Czerda led the way, briskly, confidently, until he came to a cavern where a broken landfall led up to the vague outline of a starlit sky above. He advanced to the jumbled base of the landfall and stopped.

"This is the place," he said.

Le Grand Duc probed with his torch. "You are sure?"

"I am certain." Czerda directed his torch towards a mound of stones and rubble. "Incredible, is it not?" Those idiots of police haven't even found him yet!"

Le Grand Duc directed his own torch at the mound. "You mean——"

"Alexandre. This is where we buried him."

"Alexandre is of no concern any more." Le Grand Duc turned to Bowman. "The money, if you please."

"Ah, yes. The money." Bowman shrugged and smiled. "This is the end of the road, I'm afraid. There is no money."

"What!" Le Grand Duc advanced and thrust the barrel of his gun into Bowman's ribs. "No money."

"It's there, all right. In a bank. In Arles."

"You fooled us?" Czerda said incredulously. "You brought us all this way——"

"Yes."

"You bought your life for two hours?"

"For a man under sentence of death two hours can be a very long time."

Bowman smiled, looked at Cecile, then turned back to Czerda. "But also a very short time."

"You bought your life for two hours!" Czerda seemed more astonished at this fact than he was concerned by the loss of the money.

"Put it that way."

Czerda brought up his gun. Le Grand Duc stepped forward, seized Czerda's wrist and pressed his gun hand down. He said in a low, harsh, bitter voice: "My privilege."

"Sir."

Le Grand Duc pointed his gun at Bowman, then jerked it to the right. For a moment Bowman seemed to hesitate, then shrugged. They moved away together, Le Grand Duc's gun close to Bowman's back, round a right-angled corner into another cavern. After a few moments the sound of a shot reverberated through the caverns, its echoes followed by the thud of a falling body. The scientists looked stunned, a complete and final despair written in their faces. Czerda and his three companions looked at one another in grim satisfaction. Cecile and Lila clung to each other, both, in the reflected wash of torchlight, ashen-faced and in tears. Then all heard the measured tread of returning footsteps and stared at the right-angled corner where the two men had disappeared.

Le Grand Duc and Bowman came into view at the same instant. Both of them carried guns, rock-steady in their hands.

"Don't," Bowman said.

Le Grand Duc nodded. "As my friend observes, please, please don't."

But after a moment of total disbelief, Ferenc and Searl did. There were two sharp reports, two screams and the sound, sharply metallic, of two guns striking the limestone floor. Ferenc and Searl stood in stupefied agony, clutching shattered shoulders. The second time, Bowman reflected, that Searl had been wounded in that shoulder but he could bring himself to feel no pity for he knew now that it had been Searl who had used the whip to flay the skin from Tina's back.

Bowman said: "Some people take a long time to learn."

"Incorrect, Neil. Some people never learn." Le Grand Duc looked at Czerda, the expression on his face indicating that he would have preferred to be looking elsewhere. "We had nothing against you, from a judicial point of view, that is. Not a shred of proof, not a shred of evidence. Not until you, personally and alone, led us to Alexandre's grave and admitted to the fact that you had buried him. In front of all those witnesses. Now you know why Mr. Bowman bought his life for two hours." He turned to Bowman. "Incidentally, where is the money, Neil?"

"In Cecile's handbag. I just kind of put it there."

The two girls advanced, slowly, uncertainly. There were no longer any signs of tears but they were totally uncomprehending. Bowman pocketed his gun, went to them and put his arms round the shoulders of both.

"It's all right now," he said. "It's all over, it really is." He lifted his hand from Lila's shoulders, pressed her cheek with his fingertips till she turned to look at him in dazed enquiry. He smiled. "The Duc de Croytor is indeed the Duc de Croytor. My boss, these many years."

EPILOGUE

THE MOON shone down on the balcony terrace of the hotel beneath the frowning cliffs of Les Baux. Bowman, sitting on a chair and sipping a drink, lifted an eyebrow as Cecile emerged from a room, tripped and almost fell over an extension cord. She recovered herself and sat beside him.

"Twenty-four hours," she said. "Only twenty-four hours. I just can't believe it."

"You want to get yourself a pair of spectacles," Bowman observed.

"I have a pair of spectacles, thank you."

"Then you want to wear them." Bowman put a kindly hand on hers. "After all, you've got your man now."

"Oh, do be quiet." She made no attempt to remove her hand. "How's that young girl?"

"Tina's in hospital, in Arles. She'll be round in a couple of days. Her father and Madame Zigair are there with her now. The Hobenauts and Tangevecs are having dinner inside. Not a very festive occasion, I should imagine, but I would say they must be experiencing a certain sense of relief, wouldn't you? And Pierre des Jardins, by this time, must be home in Grau-du-Roi."

"I can't believe it." Bowman peered at her, then realized that she had been only half-listening to him and was now on another topic altogether. "He—he's your boss?"

"Charles? He is indeed. Nobody believes anything about Charles. I'm ex-Army Intelligence, ex-Military Attaché in Paris. I've got another job now."

"I'll just bet you have," she said feelingly.

"The only other person who knows anything about this is Pierre, the fishing-boat skipper. That's why he maintained such a marvellous sang-froid. He's sworn to secrecy. So are you."

"I don't know if I like that."

"You'll do what you're told. Charles, I can assure you, is much higher up the pecking order than I am. We've been together for eight years. For the last two years we've known that Iron Curtain gypsies have been smuggling things across the frontier. What, we didn't know. This time, of all people, the Russians tipped us off—but even they didn't know what was really happening."

"But this Gaiuse Strome——"

"Our Chinese pal in Arles and elsewhere. Temporarily held by the French police. He was getting too close to things and Charles had him copped on a technicality. They'll have to let him go. Diplomatic immunity. He arranged it all—he's the Chinese military attaché in Tirana."

"Tirana?"

"Albania."

She reached into her handbag, brought out her glasses, looked at him closely and said: "But we were told——"

"We?"

"Lila and myself, we're secretaries in the Admiralty. To keep an eye on you. We were told that one of you was under suspicion——"

"I'm sorry. Charles and I arranged that. There we were, a goodie and a baddie. We could never be seen together. We had to have a channel of communication. Girl friends chatter. Girls get on the phone to their bosses back home. We had the channel."

"You fixed all this?" She withdrew her hand. "You knew——"

"I'm sorry. We had to do it."

"You mean——"

"Yes."

"Strawberry birthmark——"

"Sorry again." Bowman shook his head admiringly. "But I must say it was the most complete dossier I've ever seen."

"I despise you! I detest you! You're the most utterly contempt-ible——"

"Yes, I know, and I'm not worried. What does worry me is that so far we've only managed to fix up two bridesmaids and I said——"

"Two," she said firmly, "will be quite enough."

Bowman smiled, rose, offered her his hand and together they walked arm in arm to the balustrade and looked down. Almost directly beneath them were the Duc de Croytor and Lila, seated at, inevitably, a loaded table. It was apparent that Le Grand Duc was under a very considerable emotional strain for, despite the fact that he held a paper-sheathed leg of lamb in his hand, he was not eating.

"Good God!" he was saying. "Good God!" He peered at his blond companion's lovely face from a distance of about six inches. "I turn pale at the very thought. I might have lost you forever. I never knew!"

"Charles!"

"You *are* a Cordon Bleu cook?"

"Yes, Charles."

"*Brochettes de queues de langoustines au beurre blanc?*"

"Yes, Charles."

"*Poulet de la ferme au champagne?*"

"Yes, Charles."

"*Filets de sole Retival?*"

"But of course."

"*Pintadeau aux morilles?*"

"My specialty."

"Lila. I love you. Marry me!"

"Oh, Charles!"

They embraced in front of the astonished eyes of the other guests. Sym-bolically, perhaps, Le Grand Duc's leg of lamb fell to the floor.

Still arm in arm, Bowman led Cecile down to the patio. Bowman said: "Don't be fooled by Romeo down there. He doesn't give a damn about the cuisine. Not where your friend is concerned."

"The big bold baron is a little shy boy inside?"

Bowman nodded. "The making of old-fashioned proposals is not exactly his forte."

"Whereas it is yours?"

Bowman ushered her to a table and ordered drinks. "I don't quite under-stand."

"A girl likes to be asked to marry," she said.

"Ah! Cecile Dubois, will you marry me?"

"I may as well, I suppose."

"*Touché!*" He lifted his glass. "To Cecile."

"Thank you, kind sir."

"Not you. Our second-born."

They smiled at each other, then turned to look at the couple at the next table. Le Grand Duc and Lila were still gazing rapturously into each other's eyes, but Le Grand Duc, nevertheless, was back on balance again. Imperi-ously, he clapped his hands together.

"*Encore!*" said Le Grand Duc.

Seawitch

PROLOGUE

NORMALLY THERE are only two types of marine machines concerned with the discovery and recovery of oil from under the ocean floor. The first, mainly engaged in the discovery of oil, is a self-propelled vessel, sometimes of very considerable size. Apart from its towering drilling derrick, it is indistinguishable from any oceangoing cargo vessel; its purpose is to drill boreholes in areas where seismological and geological studies suggest oil may exist. The technical operation of this activity is highly complex, yet these vessels have achieved a remarkable level of success. However, they suffer from two major drawbacks. Although they are equipped with the most advanced and sophisticated navigational equipment, including bow-thrust propellers, for them to maintain position in running seas, strong tides and winds when boring can be extremely difficult, and in really heavy weather operations have to be suspended.

For the actual drilling of oil and its recovery—principally its recovery—the so-called "jack-up system" is in almost universal use. This system has to be towed into position, and consists basically of a platform which carries the drilling rig, cranes, helipads and all essential services, including living accommodations, and is attached to the seabed by firmly anchored legs. In normal conditions it is extremely effective, but like the discovery ships it has drawbacks. It is not mobile. It has to suspend operations in even moderately heavy weather. And it can be used only in comparatively shallow water: the deepest is in the North Sea, where most of those rigs are to be found. This North Sea rig stands in about 450 feet of water, and the cost of increasing the length of those legs would be so prohibitive as to make oil recovery quite uneconomical, even though Americans have plans to construct a rig with 800-foot legs off the California Coast. There is also the unknown safety factor. Two such rigs have already been lost in the North Sea. The cause of those disasters has not been clearly evaluated, although it is suspected, obviously not without basis, that there may have been design, structural or metallic faults in one or more of the legs.

And then there is the third type of oil rig—the TLP—technically, the tension leg drilling/production platform. At the time of this story there was only one of its type in the world. The platform, the working area, was about the size of a football field—if, that is, one can imagine a triangular football field, for the platform was, in fact, an equilateral triangle. The deck was not made of steel but of a uniquely designed ferroconcrete, specially developed

543

by a Dutch shipbuilding company. The supports for this massive platform had been designed and built in England and consisted of three enormous steel legs, each at one corner of the structure, the three being joined together by a variety of horizontal and diagonal hollow cylinders, the total combination offering such tremendous buoyancy that the working platform they supported was out of reach of even the highest waves.

From each of the bases of the three legs, three massive steel cables extended to the base of the ocean floor, where each triple set was attached to large sea-floor anchors. Powerful motors could raise or lower these cables, so that the anchors could be lowered to a depth two or three times that of most modern fixed oil derricks, which meant that this rig could operate at depths far out on the continental shelf.

The TLP had other very considerable advantages.

Its great buoyancy put the anchor tables under constant tension, and this tension practically eliminated the heaving, pitching and rolling of the platform. Thus the rig could continue operating in very severe storms, storms that would automatically stop production on any other type of derrick.

It is was also virtually immune to the effects of an undersea earthquake.

It was also mobile. It had only to up anchors and move to potentially more productive areas.

And compared to standard oil rigs, its cost of establishing position in any given spot was so negligible as to be worth no more than a passing mention.

The name of the TLP was *Seawitch*.

1

IN CERTAIN places and among certain people, the *Seawitch* was a very bad name indeed. But, overwhelmingly, their venom was reserved for a certain Lord Worth, a multi- some said bulti-millionaire, chairman and sole owner of North Hudson Oil Company and, incidentally, owner of the *Seawitch*. When his name was mentioned by any of the ten men present at that shoreside house on Lake Tahoe, it was in tones of less than hushed reverence.

Their meeting was announced in neither the national nor local press. This was due to two factors. The delegates arrived and departed either singly or in couples, and among the heterogeneous summer population of Lake Tahoe such comings and goings went unremarked or were ignored. More importantly, the delegates to the meeting were understandably reluctant that their assembly become common knowledge. The day was Friday the thirteenth, a date that boded no good for someone.

There were nine delegates present, plus their host. Four of them mattered, but only two seriously—Corral, who represented the oil and mineral leases in the Florida area, and Benson, who represented the rigs off Southern California.

Of the other six, only two mattered. One was Patinos of Venezuela; the other, known as Borosoff, of Russia, whose interest in American oil supplies could only be regarded as minimal. It was widely assumed among the others that his only interest in attending the meeting was to stir up as much trouble as possible, an assumption that was probably correct.

All ten were, in various degrees, suppliers of oil to the United States and had one common interest: to see that the price of those supplies did not drop. The last thing they all wanted to see was an oil-value depreciation.

Benson, whose holiday home this was and who was nominally hosting the meeting, opened the discussion.

"Gentlemen, does anyone have any objections if I bring a third party—that is, a man who represents neither ourselves nor Lord Worth—into this meeting?"

Practically everyone had, and there were some moments of bedlamic confusion: they had not only objections but very strong ones at that.

Borosoff, the Russian, said: "No. It is too dangerous." He glanced around the group with calculated suspiciousness. "There are already too many of us privy to these discussions."

Benson, who had not become head of one of Europe's biggest oil companies, a British-based one, just because someone had handed him the job as a birthday present, could be disconcertingly blunt.

"You, Borosoff, are the one with the slenderest claims to be present at this meeting. You might well bear that in mind. Name your suspect." Borosoff remained silent. "Remember, gentlemen, the objective of this meeting—to maintain, at least, the present oil-price levels. The OPEC is now actively considering hiking the oil prices. That doesn't hurt us as much here in the U.S.—we'll just hike our own prices and pass them on to the public."

Patinos said: "You're every bit as unscrupulous and ruthless as you claim us to be."

"Realism is not the same as ruthlessness. Nobody's going to hike anything while North Hudson is around. They are already undercutting us, the majors. A slight pinch, but we feel it. If we raise our prices more and his remain steady, the slight pinch is going to increase. And if he gets some more TLPs into operation, then the pinch will begin to hurt. It will also hurt the OPEC, for the demand for your products will undoubtedly fall off.

"We all subscribe to the gentlemen's agreement among major oil companies that they will not prospect for oil in international waters—that is to say, outside their own legally and internationally recognized territorial limits. Without observance of this agreement, the possibilities of legal, diplomatic, political and international strife, ranging from scenes of political violence to outright armed confrontation, are only too real. Let us suppose that Nation A—as some countries have already done—claims all rights for all waters a hundred miles offshore from its coasts. Let us further suppose that Nation B comes along and starts drilling thirty miles outside those limits. Then let us suppose that Nation A makes a unilateral decision to extend its offshore limits to a hundred and fifty miles—and don't forget that Peru has claimed two hundred miles as its limits: the subsequent possibilities are too awesome to contemplate.

"Alas, not all are gentlemen. The chairman of the North Hudson Oil Company, Lord Worth, and his entire pestiferous board of directors would have been the first to vehemently deny any suggestion that they were gentlemen, a fact held in almost universal acceptance by their competitors in oil. They would also have denied equally vehemently that they were criminals, a fact that may or may not have been true, but it most certainly is not true now.

"He has, in short, committed two of what should be indictable offenses. 'Should,' I say. The first is unprovable; the second, although an offense in moral terms, is not, as yet, strictly illegal.

"The facts of the first—and what I consider much the minor offense—concerns the building of Lord Worth's TLP in Houston. It is no secret in the industry that the plans were stolen—those for the platform from the Mobil Oil Company, those for the legs and anchoring systems from the

Chevron Oilfield Research Company. But, as I say, unprovable. It is commonplace for new inventions and developments to occur at two or more places simultaneously, and he can always claim that his design team, working in secret, beat the others to the punch.''

Benson was perfectly correct. In the design of the *Seawitch* Lord Worth had adopted shortcuts which the narrow-minded could have regarded as unscrupulous, if not illegal. Like all oil companies, North Hudson had its own design team. They were all cronies of Lord Worth, employed solely for tax-deduction purposes; their combined talents would have been incapable of designing a rowboat.

This did not worry Lord Worth. He had no need for a design team. He was a vastly wealthy man, had powerful friends—none of them, needless to say, among the oil companies—and was a master of industrial espionage. With these resources at his disposal, he found little trouble in obtaining those two secret advance plans, which he passed on to a firm of highly competent marine designers, whose exorbitant fees were matched only by their extreme discretion. The designers found little difficulty in marrying the two sets of plans, adding just sufficient modifications and improvements to discourage those with a penchant for patent-rights litigation.

Benson went on: "But what really worries me, and what should worry all you gentlemen here, is Lord Worth's violation of the tacit agreement never to indulge in drilling in international waters." He paused, deliberately for effect, and looked slowly at each of the other nine in turn. "I say in all seriousness, gentlemen, that Lord Worth's foolhardiness and greed may well prove to be the spark that triggers a third world war. Apart from protecting our own interests, I maintain that for the good of mankind—and I speak from no motive of spurious self-justification—if the governments of the world do not intervene, then it is imperative that we should. As the governments show no sign of intervention, then I suggest that the burden lies upon us. This madman must be stopped. I think you gentlemen would agree that only we realize the full implications of all of this and that only we have the technical expertise to stop him."

There were murmurs of approval from around the room. A sincere and disinterested concern for the good of mankind was a much more morally justifiable reason for action than the protection of one's own selfish interest. Patinos, the man from Venezuela, looked at Benson with a smile of mild cynicism on his face. The smile signified nothing. Patinos, a sincere and devout Catholic, wore the same expression when he passed through the doors of his church.

"You seem very sure of this, Mr. Benson?"

"I've given quite some thought to it."

Borosoff said: "And just how do you propose to stop this madman, Mr. Benson?"

"I don't know."

"You don't know?" One of the others at the table lifted his eyebrows a millimeter—for him a sign of complete disapproval. "Then why did you summon us all this distance?"

"I didn't summon you. I asked you. I asked you to approve whatever course of action we might take."

"This course of action being——"

"Again, I don't know."

The eyebrows returned to normal. A twitch of the man's lip showed that he was contemplating smiling.

"This—ah—third party?"

"Yes."

"He has a name?"

"Cronkite. John Cronkite."

A hush descended upon the company. The open objections had turned into pensive hesitation which in turn gave way to a nodding acceptance. Benson apart, no one there had ever met Cronkite, but his name was a household word to all of them. In the oil business that name had long been a legend, although at times a far from savory one. They all knew that any of them might require his incomparable services at any time, while at the same time hoping that that day would never come.

When it came to the capping of blazing gushers, Cronkite was without peer. Wherever in the world a gusher blew fire no one even considered putting it out themselves, they just sent for Cronkite. To wincing observers his *modus operandi* seemed nothing short of Draconian, but Cronkite would blasphemously brook no interference. Despite the extortionate fees he charged, it was more common than not for a four-engined jet to be put at his disposal to get him to the scene of the disaster as quickly as possible. Cronkite always delivered. He also knew all there was to know about the oil business. And he was, hardly surprisingly, extremely tough and utterly ruthless.

Henderson, who represented oil interests in Honduras, said: "Why should a man with his extraordinary qualifications, the world's number one, as we all know, choose to engage himself in—ah—an enterprise of this nature? From his reputation I would hardly have thought that he was one to be concerned about the woes of suffering mankind."

"He isn't. Money. Cronkite comes very high. A fresh challenge—the man's a born adventurer. But, bascially, it's because he hates Lord Worth's guts."

Henderson said: "Not an uncommon sentiment, it seems. Why?"

"Lord Worth sent his own private Boeing for him to come cap a blazing gusher in the Middle East. By the time Cronkite arrived, Lord Worth's own men had capped it. This, alone, Cronkite regarded as a mortal insult. He then made the mistake of demanding the full fee for his services. Lord Worth has a reputation for notorious Scottish meanness, which, while an insult to the Scots, is more than justified in his case. He refused, and said that he would pay him for his time, no more. Cronkite then compounded his error by taking him to court. With the kind of lawyers Lord Worth can afford, Cronkite never had a chance. Not only did he lose but he had to pay the costs."

"Which wouldn't be low?" Henderson said.

"Medium-high to massive. I don't know. All I know is that Cronkite has done quite a bit of brooding about it ever since."

"Such a man would not have to be sworn to secrecy?"

"A man can swear a hundred different oaths and break them all. Besides, because of the exorbitant fees Cronkite charges, his feeling toward Lord Worth and the fact that he might just have to step outside the law, his silence is ensured."

It was the turn of another of those grouped round the table to raise his eyebrows. "Outside the law? We cannot risk being involved——"

" 'Might,' I said. For us, the element of risk does not exist."

"May we see this man?"

Benson nodded, rose, went to a door and admitted Cronkite.

Cronkite was a Texan. In height, build and cragginess of features he bore a remarkable resemblance to John Wayne. Unlike Wayne, he never smiled. His face was of a peculiarly yellow complexion, typical of those who have

had an overdose of antimalarial tablets, which was just what had happened
to Cronkite. Mepacrine does not make for a peaches-and-cream complex
ion—not that Cronkite's had ever remotely resembled that. He was newly
returned from Indonesia, where he had inevitably maintained his 100 per
cent record.

"Mr. Cronkite," Benson said. "Mr. Cronkite, this is——"

Cronkite was brusque. In a gravelly voice he said: "I don't want to know
their names."

In spite of the abruptness of his tone, several of the oilmen round the
table almost beamed. Here was a man of discretion, a man after their own
hearts.

Cronkite went on: "All I understand from Mr. Benson is that I am required to attend to a matter involving Lord Worth and the *Seawitch*. Mr.
Benson has given me a pretty full briefing. I know the background. I would
like, first of all, to hear any suggestions you gentlemen may have to offer."
Cronkite sat down, lit what proved to be a very foul-smelling cigar, and
waited expectantly.

He kept silent during the following half-hour discussion. For ten of the
world's top businessmen, they proved to be an extraordinarily inept, not to
say inane, lot. They talked in an ever-narrowing series of concentric circles.

Henderson said: "First of all, there must be no violence used. Is that
agreed?"

Everybody nodded agreement. Each of them was a pillar of business
respectability who could not afford to have his reputation besmirched in any
way. No one appeared to notice that, except for lifting a hand to his cigar
and puffing out increasingly vile clouds of smoke, Cronkite did not move
throughout the discussion. He also remained totally silent.

After agreeing that there should be no violence, the meeting of ten agreed
on nothing.

Finally Patinos spoke up. "Why don't you—one of you four Americans,
I mean—approach your Congress to pass an emergency law banning offshore drilling in extraterritorial waters?"

Benson looked at him with something akin to pity. "I am afraid, sir, that
you do not quite understand the relations between the American majors and
Congress. On the few occasions we have met with them—something to do
with too much profits and too little tax—I'm afraid we have treated them in
so—ah—cavalier a fashion that nothing would give them greater pleasure
than to refuse any request we might make."

One of the others, known simply as "Mr. A," said: "How about an
approach to that international legal ombudsman, The Hague? After all, this
is an international matter."

Henderson shook his head. "Forget it. The dilatoriness of that august
body is so legendary that all present would be long retired—or worse—
before a decision is made. The decision would just as likely be negative
anyway."

"United Nations?" Mr. A said.

"That talk-shop!" Benson obviously had a low and not uncommon view
of the UN. "They haven't even got the power to order New York to install
a new parking meter outside their front door."

The next revolutionary idea came from one of the Americans.

"Why shouldn't we all agree, for an unspecified time—let's see how it
goes—to *lower* our price below that of North Hudson? In that case no one
would want to buy their oil."

This proposal was met with stunned disbelief.

Corral spoke in a kind voice. "Not only would that lead to vast losses to the major oil companies, but would almost certainly and immediately lead Lord Worth to lower *his* prices fractionally below their new ones. The man has sufficient working capital to keep him going for a hundred years at a loss—in the unlikely event, that is, of his running at a loss at all."

A lengthy silence followed. Cronkite was not quite as immobile as he had been. The granitic expression on his face remained unchanged, but the fingers of his nonsmoking hand had begun to drum gently on the armrest of his chair. For Cronkite, this was equivalent to throwing a fit of hysterics.

It was during this period that all thoughts of maintaining high, gentlemanly and ethical standards against drilling in international waters were forgotten by the ten.

"Why not," Mr. A said, "buy him out?" In fairness it has to be said that Mr. A did not appreciate just how wealthy Lord Worth was and that, immensely wealthy though he, Mr. A, was, Lord Worth could have bought *him* out lock, stock and barrel. "The *Seawitch* rights, I mean. A hundred million dollars. Let's be generous, two hundred million dollars. Why not?"

Coral looked depressed. "The answer to 'Why not?' is easy. By the latest reckoning, Lord Worth is one of the world's five richest men, and even two hundred million dollars would be pennies as far as he was concerned."

Now Mr. A looked depressed.

Benson said: "Sure he'd sell."

Mr. A visibly brightened.

"For two reasons only. In the first place he'd make a quick and splendid profit. In the second place, for less than half the selling price, he could build another *Seawitch,* anchor it a couple of miles away from the present *Seawitch*—there are no leasehold rights in extraterritorial waters—and start sending oil ashore at his same old price."

A temporarily deflated Mr. A slumped back in his armchair.

"A partnership, then," Mr. B said. His tone was that of a man in a state of quiet despair.

"Out of the question." Henderson was very positive. "Like all very rich men, Lord Worth is a born loner. He wouldn't have a combined partnership with the King of Saudi Arabia and the Shah of Iran, even if it were offered him free."

In the gloom of baffled and exhausted silence thoroughly bored and hitherto near-wordless, John Cronkite rose.

He said without preamble: "My personal fee will be one million dollars. I will require ten million dollars for operating expenses. Every cent of this will be accounted for and any unspent balance returned. I demand a completely free hand and no interference from any of you. If I do encounter interference I'll retain the balance of the expenses and abandon the mission. I refuse to disclose what my plans are—or will be when I have made them. Finally, I would prefer to have no further contact with any of you, now or at any time."

The assurance and confidence of the man were astonishing. Agreement among the mightily relieved ten was immediate and total. The ten million dollars—a trifling sum to those accustomed to spending as much in bribes every month or so—would be delivered within twenty-four—at the most, forty-eight—hours to a Cuban numbered account in Miami, the only place in the United States where Swiss-type numbered accounts were permitted. For tax-evasion purposes, the money of course would not come from any of their respective countries: instead, ironically enough, from their bulging offshore funds.

2

LORD WORTH was tall, lean and erect. His complexion was the mahogany hue of the playboy millionaire who spends his life in the sun: Lord Worth seldom worked less than sixteen hours a day. His abundant hair and mustache were snow-white. According to his mood and expression and to the eye of the beholder, he could have been a biblical patriarch, a better-class Roman senator, or a gentlemanly seventeenth-century pirate—except for the fact, of course, that none of those ever, far less habitually, wore lightweight Alpaca suits of the same color as Lord Worth's hair.

He looked and was every inch an aristocrat. Unlike the many Americans who bore the Christian names of Duke or Earl, Lord Worth really was a lord, the fifteenth in succession of a highly distinguished family of Scottish peers of the realm. The fact that their distinction had lain mainly in the fields of assassination, endless clan warfare, the stealing of women and cattle, and the selling of their fellow peers down the river was beside the point: the earlier Scottish peers didn't go in too much for the more cultural activities. The blue blood that had run in their veins ran in Lord Worth's. As ruthless, predatory, acquisitive and courageous as any of his ancestors, Lord Worth simply went about his business with a degree of refinement and sophistication that would have lain several light-years beyond their understanding.

He had reversed the trend of Canadians coming to Britain, making their fortunes and eventually being elevated to the peerage: he had already been a peer, and an extremely wealthy one, before emigrating to Canada. His emigration, which had been discreet and precipitous, had not been entirely voluntary. He had made a fortune in real estate in London before the Internal Revenue had become embarrassingly interested in his activities. Fortunately for him, whatever charges might have been laid at his door were not extraditable.

He had spent several years in Canada, investing his millions in the North Hudson Oil Company and proving himself to be even more able in the oil business than he had been in real estate. His tankers and refineries spanned the globe before he had decided that the climte was too cold for him and moved south to Florida. His splendid mansion was the envy of the many millionaires—of a lesser financial breed, admittedly—who almost literally jostled for elbowroom in the Fort Lauderdale area.

The dining room in that mansion was something to behold. Monks, by the very nature of their calling, are supposed to be devoid of all earthly lusts, but no monk, past or present, could ever have gazed on the gleaming magnificence of that splendid oaken refectory table without turning pale chartreuse with envy. The chairs, inevitably, were Louis XIV. The splendidly embroidered silken carpet, with a pile deep enough for a fair-sized mouse to take cover in, would have been judged by an expert to come from Damascus and to have cost a fortune: the expert would have been right on both counts. The heavy drapes and embroidered silken walls were of the same pale gray, the latter being enhanced by a series of original impressionist paintings, no less than three by Matisse and the same number by Renoir. Lord Worth was no dilettante and was clearly trying to make amends for his ancestors' shortcomings in cultural fields.

It was in those suitably princely surroundings that Lord Worth was at the moment taking his ease, reveling in his second brandy and the two beings whom—after money—he loved most in the world: his two daughters, Marina and Melinda, who had been so named by their now divorced Spanish mother. Both were young, both were beautiful, and could have been mistaken for twins, which they weren't: they were easily distinguishable by the fact that while Marina's hair was black as a raven's, Melinda's was pure titian.

There were two other guests at the table. Many a local millionaire would have given a fair slice of his ill-gotten gains for the privilege and honor of sitting at Lord Worth's table. Few were invited, and then but seldom. Those two young men, comparatively as poor as church mice, had the unique privilege, without invitation, of coming and going as they pleased, which was pretty often.

They were Mitchell and Roomer, two pleasant men in their early thirties for whom Lord Worth had a strong, if concealed, admiration and whom he held in something close to awe—inasmuch as they were the only two completely honest men he had ever met. Not that Lord Worth had ever stepped on the wrong side of the law, although he frequently had a clear view of what happened on the other side: it was simply that he was not in the habit of dealing with honest men. They had both been two highly efficient police sergeants, only they had been too efficient, much given to arresting the wrong people, such as crooked politicians and equally crooked wealthy businessmen who had previously labored under the misapprehension that they were above the law. They were fired, not to put too fine a point on it, for their total incorruptibility.

Of the two, Michael Mitchell was the taller, the broader and the less good-looking. With slightly craggy face, ruffled dark hair and blue chin, he could never have made it as a matinee idol. John Roomer, with his brown hair and trimmed brown mustache, was altogether better-looking. Both were shrewd, intelligent and highly experienced. Roomer was the intuitive one, Mitchell the one long on action. Apart from being charming, both men were astute and highly resourceful. And they were possessed of one other not inconsiderable quality: both were deadly marksmen.

Two years previously they had set up their own private investigative practice, and in that brief space of time had established such a reputation that people in real trouble now made a practice of going to them instead of to the police, a fact that hardly endeared them to the local law. They lived near Lord Worth's estate, where they were frequent and welcome visitors. That they did not come for the exclusive pleasure of his company Lord Worth was well aware. Nor, he knew, were they even in the slightest way interested in his money, a fact that Lord Worth found astonishing, as he had never previously encountered anyone who wasn't thus interested. What they were interested in, and deeply so, were Marina and Melinda.

The door opened and Lord Worth's butler, Jenkins—English, of course, as were the two footmen—made his usual soundless entrance, approached the head of the table and murmured discreetly in Lord Worth's ear. Lord Worth nodded and rose.

"Excuse me, girls, gentlemen. Visitors. I'm sure you can get along together quite well without me." He made his way to his study, entered and closed the door behind him—a very special padded door that, when shut, rendered the room completely soundproof.

The study, in its own way—Lord Worth was no sybarite but he liked his creature comforts as well as the next man—was as sumptuous as the dining room: oak, leather, a wholly unnecessary log fire burning in one corner, all straight from the best English baronial mansions. The walls were lined with thousands of books, many of which Lord Worth had actually read, a fact that must have caused great distress to his illiterate ancestors, who had despised degeneracy above all else.

A tall bronzed man with aquiline features and gray hair rose to his feet. Both men smiled and shook hands warmly.

Lord Worth said: "Corral, my dear chap! How very nice to see you again. It's been quite some time."

"My pleasure, Lord Worth. Nothing recently that would have interested you."

"But now?"

"Now is something else again."

The Corral who stood before Lord Worth was indeed the Corral who, in his capacity as representative of the Florida offshore leases, had been present at the meeting of ten at Lake Tahoe. Some years had passed since he and Lord Worth had arrived at an amicable and mutually satisfactory agreement. Corral, widely regarded as Lord Worth's most avowedly determined enemy and certainly the most vociferous of his critics, reported regularly to Lord Worth on the current activities and, more importantly, the projected plans of the major companies, which didn't hurt Lord Worth at all. Corral, in return, received an annual tax-free retainer of $200,000, which didn't hurt him very much either.

Lord Worth pressed a bell and within seconds Jenkins entered bearing a silver tray with two large brandies. There was no telepathy involved, just years of experience and a long-established foreknowledge of Lord Worth's desires. When he left, both men sat.

Lord Worth said: "Well, what news from the West?"

"The Cherokee, I regret to say, are after you."

Lord Worth sighed and said: "It had to come sometime. Tell me all."

Corral told him all. He had a near-photographic memory and a gift for concise and accurate reportage. Within five minutes Lord Worth knew all that was worth knowing about the Lake Tahoe meeting.

Lord Worth who, because of the unfortunate misunderstanding that had arisen between himself and Cronkite, knew the latter as well as any and better than most, said at the end of Corral's report: "Did Cronkite subscribe to the ten's agreement to abjure any form of violence?"

"No."

"Not that it would have mattered if he had. Man's a total stranger to the truth. And ten million dollars' expenses, you tell me?"

"It did seem a bit excessive."

"Can you see a massive outlay like that being concomitant with anything except violence?"

"No."

"Do you think the others believed that there was no connection between them?"

"Let me put it this way, sir. Any group of people who can convince themselves, or appear to convince themselves, that any proposed action against you is for the betterment of mankind is also prepared to convince themselves, or appear to convince themselves, that the word 'Cronkite' is synonymous with peace on earth."

"So their consciences are clear. If Cronkite goes to any excessive lengths in death and destruction to achieve their ends, they can always throw up their hands in horror and say, 'Good God, we never thought the man would go that far.' Not that any connection between them and Cronkite would ever have to be established. What a bunch of devious, mealy-mouthed hypocrites!"

He paused for a moment.

"I suppose Cronkite refused to divulge his plans?"

"Absolutely. But there is one odd circumstance: just as we were leaving, Cronkite drew two of the ten to one side and spoke to them privately. It would be interesting to know why."

"Any chance of finding out?"

"A fair chance. Nothing guaranteed. But I'm sure Benson could find out—after all, it was Benson who invited us all to Lake Tahoe."

"And you think you could persuade Benson to tell you?"

"A fair chance. Nothing more."

Lord Worth put on his resigned expression. "All right, how much?"

"Nothing. Money won't buy Benson." Corral shook his head in disbelief. "Extraordinary, in this day and age, but Benson is not a mercenary man. But he does owe me some favors, one of them being that, without me, he wouldn't be the president of the oil company that he is now." Corral paused. "I'm surprised you haven't asked me the identities of the two men Cronkite took aside."

"So am I."

"Borosoff of the Soviet Union and Patinos of Venezuela." Lord Worth appeared to lapse into a trance. "That mean anything to you?"

Lord Worth bestirred himself. "Yes. Units of the Russian Navy are making a so-called 'goodwill tour' of the Caribbean. They are, inevitably, based in Cuba. Of the ten, those are the only two that could bring swift—ah—naval intervention to bear against the *Seawitch.*" He shook his head. "Diabolical. Utterly diabolical."

"My way of thinking too, sir. There's no knowing. But I'll check as soon as possible and hope to get results."

"And I shall take immediate precautions." Both men rose. "Corral, we shall have to give serious consideration to the question of increasing this paltry retainer of yours."

"We try to be of service, Lord Worth."

Lord Worth's private radio room bore more than a passing resemblance to the flight deck of his private 707. The variety of knobs, switches, buttons and dials was bewildering. Lord Worth seemed perfectly at home with them all, and proceeded to make a number of calls.

The first were to his four helicopter pilots, instructing them to have his two largest helicopters—never a man to do things by halves, Lord Worth owned no fewer than six of these machines—ready at his own private airfield shortly before dawn. The next four were to people of whose existence his fellow directors were totally unaware. The first of these calls was to Cuba, the second to Venezuela. Lord Worth's worldwide range of contacts—employees, rather—was vast. The instructions to both were simple and explicit. A constant monitoring watch was to be kept on the naval bases in both countries, and any sudden departures of any naval vessels, and their type, was to be reported to him immediately.

The third, to a person who lived not too many miles away, was addressed to a certain Giuseppe Palermo, whose name sounded as if he might be a member of the Mafia, but who definitely wasn't: the Mafia Palermo despised as a mollycoddling organization which had become so ludicrously gentle in its methods of persuasion as to be in imminent danger of becoming respectable. The next call was to Baton Rouge in Louisiana, where lived a person who called himself only "Conde" and whose main claim to fame lay in the fact that he was the highest-ranking naval officer to have been court-martialed and dishonorably discharged since World War II. He, like the others, received very explicit instructions. Not only was Lord Worth a master organizer, but the efficiency he displayed was matched only by his speed in operation.

The noble Lord, who would have stoutly maintained—if anyone had the temerity to accuse him, which no one ever had—that he was no criminal, was about to become just that. Even this he would have strongly denied, and that on three grounds. The Constitution upheld the right of every citizen to bear arms; every man had the right to defend himself and his property against criminal attack by whatever means lay to hand; and the only way to fight fire was with fire.

The final call Lord Worth put through, and this time with total confidence, was to his tried and trusted lieutenant, Commander Larsen.

Commander Larsen was the captain of the *Seawitch*.

Larsen—no one knew why he called himself "Commander," and he wasn't the kind of person you asked—was a rather different breed of man from his employer. Except in a public court or in the presence of a law officer, he would cheerfully admit to anyone that he was both a non-gentleman *and* a criminal. And he certainly bore no resemblance to any aristocrat, alive or dead. But there did exist a genuine rapport and mutual respect between Lord Worth and himself. In all likelihood they were simply brothers under the skin.

As a criminal and non-aristocrat—and casting no aspersions on honest unfortunates who may resemble him—he certainly looked the part. He had the general build and appearance of the more viciously daunting heavyweight wrestler, deep-set black eyes that peered out under the overhanging foliage of hugely bushy eyebrows, an equally bushy black beard, a hooked nose, and a face that looked as if it had been in regular contact with a series of heavy objects. No one, with the possible exception of Lord Worth, knew who he was, what he had been, or from where he had come. His voice, when he spoke, came as a positive shock: beneath that Neanderthalic façade was the voice and the mind of an educated man. It really ought not to have come as such a shock: beneath the façade of many an exquisite fop lies the mind of a retarded fourth-grader.

Larsen was in the radio room at that moment, listening attentively, nodding from time to time; then he flicked a switch that put the incoming call on the loudspeaker.

He said: "All clear, sir. Everything understood. We'll make the preparations. But haven't you overlooked something, sir?"

"Overlooked what?" Lord Worth's voice over the telephone carried the overtones of a man who couldn't possibly have overlooked anything.

"You've suggested that armed surface vessels may be used against us. If they're prepared to go to such lengths, isn't it feasible that they'll go to *any* lengths?"

"Get to the point, man."

"The point is that it's easy enough to keep an eye on a couple of naval bases. But I suggest it's a bit more difficult to keep an eye on a dozen, maybe two dozen, airfields."

"Good God!" There was a long pause during which the rattle of cogs and the meshing of gear wheels in Lord Worth's brain couldn't be heard. "Do you really think——"

"If I were the *Seawitch,* Lord Worth, it would be six and half-a-dozen to me whether I was clobbered by shells or bombs. And planes could get away from the scene of the crime a damn sight faster than ships. They could get clean away, whereas the U. S. Navy or land-based bombers would have a good chance of intercepting surface vessels. And another thing, Lord Worth— a ship could stop at a distance of a hundred miles. No distance at all for the guided missile: I believe they have a range of four thousand miles these days. When the missile was, say, twenty miles from us, they could switch on its heat-source tracking device. God knows, we're the only heat source for a hundred miles around."

Another lengthy pause, then: "Any more encouraging thoughts occur to you, Commander Larsen?"

"Yes, sir. Just one. If I were the enemy—I may call them the enemy——"

"Call the devils what you want."

"If I were the enemy I'd use a submarine. They don't even have to break the surface to loose off a missile. Poof! No *Seawitch.* No signs of any attacker. Could well be put down to a massive explosion aboard the *Seawitch.* Far from impossible, sir."

"You'll be telling me next that they'll be atomic-headed missiles."

"To be picked up by a dozen seismological stations? I should think it hardly likely, sir. But that may just be wishful thinking. I, personally, have no wish to be vaporized."

"I'll see you in the morning." The speaker went dead.

Larsen hung up his phone and smiled widely. One might have expected this action to reveal a set of yellowed fangs: instead, it revealed a perfect set of gleamingly white teeth. He turned to look at Scoffield, his head driller and right-hand man.

Scoffield was a large, rubicund, smiling man, apparently the easygoing essence of good nature. To the fact that this was not precisely the case, any member of his drilling crews would have eagerly and blasphemously testified. Scoffield was a very tough citizen indeed, and one could assume that it was not innate modesty that made him conceal the fact: much more probably it was a permanent stricture of the facial muscles caused by the four long vertical scars on his cheeks, two on either side. Clearly he, like Larsen, was no great advocate of plastic surgery. He looked at Larsen with understandable curiosity.

"What was all that about?"

"The day of reckoning is at hand. Prepare to meet thy doom. More specifically, his lordship is beset by enemies." Larsen outlined Lord Worth's plight. "He's sending what sounds like a battalion of hard men out here in the early morning, accompanied by suitable weaponry. Then in the afternoon we are to expect a boat of some sorts, loaded with even heavier weaponry."

"I wonder where he's getting all those hard men and weaponry from."

"One wonders. One does not ask."

"All this talk—your talk—about bombers and submarines and missiles. Do you believe that?"

"No. It's just that it's hard to pass up the opportunity to ruffle the aristocratic plumage." He paused, then said thoughtfully: "At least I hope I don't believe it. Come on, let us examine our defenses."

"You've got a pistol. I've got a pistol. That's defenses?"

"Well, where we'll mount the defenses when they arrive. Fixed large-bore guns, I should imagine."

"*If* they arrive."

"Give the devil his due. Lord Worth delivers."

"From his own private armory, I suppose."

"It wouldn't surprise me."

"What do you really think, Commander?"

"I don't know. All I know is that if Lord Worth is even halfway right, life aboard may become slightly less monotonous in the next few days."

The two men moved out into the gathering dusk on the platform. The *Seawitch* was moored in a hundred and fifty fathoms of water—nine hundred feet, which was well within the tensioning cables' capacities—safely south of the U.S. mineral leasing blocks and the great east-west fairway, right on top of the biggest oil reservoir yet discovered around the shores of the Gulf of Mexico. The two men paused at the drilling derrick where a drill, at its maximum angled capacity, was trying to determine the extent of the oilfield. The crew looked at them without any particular affection but not with hostility. There was reason for the lack of warmth.

Before any laws were passed making such drilling illegal, Lord Worth wanted to scrape the bottom of this gigantic barrel of oil. Not that he was particularly worried, for government agencies are notoriously slow to act: but there was always the possibility that they might bestir themselves this time and that, horror of horrors, the bonanza might turn out to be vastly larger than estimated.

Hence the present attempt to discover the limits of the strike and hence the lack of warmth. Hence the reason why Larsen and Scoffield, both highly gifted slave drivers, born centuries out of their time, drove their men day and night. The men disliked it, but not to the point of rebellion. They were highly paid, well-housed and well-fed. True, there was little enough in the way of wine, women and song, but then, after an exhausting twelve-hour shift, those frivolities couldn't hope to compete with the attractions of a massive meal, then a long, deep sleep. More importantly and most unusually, the men were paid a bonus on every thousand barrels of oil.

Larsen and Scoffield made their way to the western apex of the platform and gazed out at the massive bulk of the storage tank, its topsides festooned with warning lights. They gazed at this for some time, then turned and walked back toward the accommodation quarters.

Scoffield said: "Decided on your gun emplacements yet, Commander—if there are any guns?"

"There'll be guns." Larsen was confident. "But we won't need any in this quarter."

"Why?"

"Work it out for yourself. As for the rest, I'm not too sure. It'll come to me in my sleep. My turn for an early night. See you at four."

The oil was not stored aboard the rig—it is forbidden by a law based strictly on common sense to store hydrocarbons at or near the working platform of an oil rig. Instead, Lord Worth, on Larsen's instructions—which had prudently come in the form of suggestions—had had built a huge floating tank which was anchored, on a basis precisely similar to that of the *Seawitch* herself, at a distance of about three hundred yards. Cleaned oil was pumped into this after it came up from the ocean floor, or, more precisely, from a massive limestone reef deep down below the ocean floor, a reef caused by tiny marine creatures of a now long-covered shallow sea of some half a billion years ago.

Once, sometimes twice, a day a 50,000-ton-capacity tanker would stop by and empty the huge tank. There were three of those tankers employed on the crisscross run to the southern United States. The North Hudson Oil Company did, in fact, have supertankers, but the use of them in this case did not serve Lord Worth's purpose. Even the entire contents of the *Seawitch's* tank would not have filled a quarter of the supertanker's carrying capacity, and the possibility of a supertanker running at a loss, however small, would have been the source of waking nightmares for the North Hudson: equally importantly, the more isolated ports which Lord Worth favored for the delivery of his oil were unable to offer deep-water berth-side facilities for anything in excess of fifty thousand tons.

It might be explained, in passing, that Lord Worth's choice of those obscure ports was not entirely fortuitous. Among the parties to the gentlemen's agreement against offshore drilling, some of the most vociferous of those who roundly condemned North Hudson's nefarious practices were, regrettably, North Hudson's best customers. They were the smaller companies who operated on marginal profits and lacked the resources to engage in research and exploration, which the larger companies did, investing allegedly vast sums in those projects and then, to the continuous fury of the Internal Revenue Service and the anger of numerous Congressional investigation committees, claiming even vaster tax exemptions.

But to the smaller companies the lure of cheaper oil was irresistible. The *Seawitch,* which probably produced as much oil as all the government official leasing areas combined, seemed a sure and perpetual source of cheap oil—at least until the government stepped in, which might or might not happen in the next decade: the big companies had already demonstrated their capacity to deal with inept Congressional inquiries, and as long as the energy crisis continued nobody was going to worry very much about where oil came from, as long as it came. In addition, the smaller companies felt, if the OPEC—the Organization of Petroleum Exporting Countries—could play ducks and drakes with oil prices whenever they felt like it, why couldn't they?

Less than two miles from Lord Worth's estate were the adjacent homes and combined office of Michael Mitchell and John Roomer. It was Mitchell who answered the doorbell.

The visitor was of medium height, slightly tubby, wore wire-rimmed glasses, and alopecia had hit him hard. He said: "May I come in?" in a clipped but courteous enough voice.

"Sure." Michael Mitchell let him in to their apartment. "We don't usually see people this late."

"Thank you. I come on unusual business. James Bentley." A little sleight of hand and a card appeared. "FBI."

Mitchell didn't even look at it. "You can have those things made at any joke shop. Where you from?"

"Miami."

"Phone number?"

Bently reversed the card, which Mitchell handed to Roomer. "My memory man. Saves me from having to have a memory of my own."

Roomer didn't glance at the card either. "It's okay, Mike. I have him. You're the boss man up there, aren't you?" A nod. "Please sit down, Mr. Bentley."

"One thing clear, first," Mitchell said. "Are *we* under investigation?"

"On the contrary. The State Department has asked us to ask you to help them."

"Status at last," Mitchell said. "We've got it made, John—except for one thing: the State Department doesn't know who the hell we are."

"*I* do." Discussion closed. "I understand you gentlemen are friendly with Lord Worth."

Roomer was careful. "We know him slightly, socially—just as you seem to know a little about us."

"I know a lot about you, including the fact that you are a couple of ex-cops who never learned to look the right way at the right time and the wrong way at the wrong time. Bars the ladder to promotion. I want you to carry out a little investigation of Lord Worth."

"No deal," Mitchell said. "We know him slightly better than slightly."

"Hear him out, Mike." But Roomer's face, too, had lost whatever little friendliness it may have held.

"Lord Worth has been making loud noises—over the phone—to the State Department. He seems to be suffering from a persecution complex. This interests the State Department, because they see him more in the role of the persecutor than persecuted."

"You mean the FBI does," Roomer said. "You've had him in your files for years. Lord Worth always gives the impression of being very capable of looking out for himself."

"That's precisely what intrigues the State Department."

Mitchell said: "What kind of noises?"

"Nonsense noises. You know he has an oil rig out in the Gulf of Mexico?"

"The *Seawitch?* Yes."

"He appears to be under the impression that the *Seawitch* is in mortal danger. He wants protection. Very modest in his demands, as becomes a multimillionaire—a missile frigate or two, some missile fighters standing by, just in case."

"In case of what?"

"That's the question. He refused to say. Just said he had secret information—which, in fact, wouldn't surprise me. The Lord Worths of this world have their secret agents everywhere."

"You'd better level with us," Mitchell said.

"I've told you all I know. The rest is surmise. Calling the State Department means that there are foreign countries involved. There are Soviet naval vessels in the Caribbean at present. The State Department smells an international incident or worse."

"What do you want us to do?"

"Not much. Just to find out Lord Worth's intended movements for the next day or two."

Mitchell said: "And if we refuse? We have our licenses rescinded?"

"I am not a corrupt police chief. If you refuse, you can just forget that you ever saw me. But I thought you might care enough about Lord Worth to help protect him against himself or the consequences of any rash action he might take. I thought you might care even more about the reactions of his two daughters if anything were to happen to their father."

Mitchell stood up, jerked a thumb. "The door. You know too damn much."

"Sit down." A sudden-chill asperity. "Don't be foolish: it's my job to know too damn much. But apart from Lord Worth and his family, I thought you might have some little concern for your country's welfare."

Roomer said: "Isn't that pitching it a little high?"

"Very possibly. But it is the policy of the State Department, the Justice Department and the FBI not to take any chances."

Roomer said: "You're putting us in a damned awkward situation."

"Don't think I don't appreciate that. I know I've put you on a spot and I'm sorry, but I'm afraid you'll have to resolve that particular dilemma yourselves."

Mitchell said: "Thanks for dropping this little problem in our laps. What do you expect us to do? Go to Lord Worth, ask him why he's been hollering to the State Department, ask him what he's up to and what his immediate plans are?"

Bentley smiled. "Nothing so crude. You have a reputation—except, of course, in the police department—of being, in the street phrase, a couple of slick operators. The approach is up to you." He stood. "Keep that card and let me know when you find out anything. How long would that take, do you think?"

Roomer said: "A couple of hours."

"A couple of hours?" Even Bentley seemed momentarily taken aback. "You don't, then, require an invitation to visit the baronial mansion?"

"No."

"Millionaires do."

"We aren't even thousandaires."

"It makes a difference. Well, thank you very much, gentlemen. Good-night."

After Bentley's departure the two men sat for a couple of minutes in silence, then Mitchell said: "We play it both ways?"

"We play it every way." Roomer reached for a phone, dialed a number and asked for Lord Worth. He had to identify himself before he was put through—Lord Worth was a man who respected his privacy.

Roomer said: "Lord Worth? Roomer. Mitchell and I have something to discuss with you, sir, which may or may not be of urgency and importance. We would prefer not to discuss it over the phone." He paused, listened for a few moments, murmured a thank you and hung up.

"He'll see us right away. Says to park the car in the lane. Side door. Study. Says the girls have gone upstairs."

"Think our friend Bentley already has our phone tapped?"

"Not worth his FBI salt if he hasn't."

Five minutes later, car parked in the lane, they were making their way through the trees to the side door. Their progress was observed with interest by Marina, standing by the window in her upstairs bedroom. She looked thoughtful for a moment, then turned and unhurriedly left the room.

Lord Worth welcomed the two men in his study and securely closed the padded door behind them. He swung open the doors of a concealed bar and poured three brandies. There were times when one rang for Jenkins and there were times when one didn't. He lifted his glass.

"Health. An unexpected pleasure."

"It's no pleasure for us," Roomer said gloomily.

"Then you haven't come to ask me for my daughters' hands in marriage?"

"No, sir," Mitchell said. "No such luck. John here is better at explaining these things."

"What things?"

"We've just had a visit from a senior FBI agent." Roomer handed over Bentley's card. "There's a number on the back that we're to ring when we've extracted some information from you."

"How very interesting." There was a long pause, then Lord Worth looked at each man in turn. "What kind of information?"

"In Bentley's words, you have been making 'loud noises' to the State Department. According to them, you seem to think that the *Seawitch* is under threat. They want to know where you got this secret information, and what your proposed movements are."

"Why didn't the FBI come directly to me?"

"Because you wouldn't have told them any more than you told the State Department. If, that is to say, you'd even let them over the threshold of your house. But they know—Bentley told us this—that we come across here now and again, so I suppose they figured you'd be less off your guard with us."

"So Bentley figures that you'd craftily wring some careless talk from me without my being aware that I was talking carelessly."

"Something like that."

"But doesn't this put you in a somewhat invidious position?"

"Not really."

"But you're supposed to uphold the law, no?"

"Yes." Mitchell spoke with some feeling. "But not organized law. Or have you forgotten, Lord Worth, that we're a couple of ex-cops because we wouldn't go along with your so-called organized law? Our only responsibility is to our clients."

"I'm not your client."

"No."

"Would you like me to be your client?"

Roomer said: "What on earth for?"

"It's never something for nothing in this world, John. Services have to be rewarded."

"Failure of a mission." Mitchell was on his feet. "Nice of you to see us, Lord Worth."

"I apologize." Lord Worth sounded genuinely contrite. "I'm afraid I rather stepped out of line there." He paused ruminatively, then smiled. "Just trying to recall when last I apologized to anybody. I seem to have a short memory. Bless my lovely daughters. Information for our friends of the FBI? First, I received my information in context of several anonymous threats— telephone calls—on the lives of my daughters. A double-barreled threat, if you will, against the girls if I didn't stop the flow of oil. As they pointed out, I can't hide them forever and there's nothing one can do against a sniper's bullet—and if I were too difficult they'd have the *Seawitch* blown out of the water. As for my future movements, I'm going out to the *Seawitch* tomorrow afternoon and will remain there for twenty-four hours, perhaps forty-eight."

Roomer said: "Any truth in either of those two statements?"

"Don't be preposterous. Of course not. I *am* going out to the rig—but before dawn. I don't want those beady-eyed bandits watching me from the undergrowth at my heliport as I take off."

"You are referring to the FBI, sir?"

"Who else? Will that do for the moment?"

"Splendidly."

They walked back to the lane in silence. Roomer got in behind the wheel of the car, Mitchell beside him.

Roomer said: "Well, well, well."

"Well, as you say, well, well, well. Crafty old devil."

Marina's voice came from the back. "Crafty he may be, but——"

She broke off in a gasp as Mitchell whirled in his seat and Roomer switched on his interior lights. The barrel of Mitchell's .38 was lined up between her eyes, eyes at the moment wide with shock and fear.

Mitchell said in a soft voice: "Don't ever do that to me again. Next time it may be too late."

She licked her lips. She was normally as high-spirited and independent as she was beautiful, but it is a rather disconcerting thing to look down the muzzle of a pistol for the first time in your life. "I was just going to say that he may be crafty but he's neither old nor a devil. Will you please put that gun away? You don't point guns at people you love."

Mitchell's gun disappeared. He said: "You shouldn't fall in love with crazy young fools."

"Or spies." Roomer was looking at Melinda. "What are you two doing here?"

Melinda was more composed than her sister. After all, she hadn't had to look down the barrel of a pistol. She said: "And you, John Roomer, are a crafty young devil. You're just stalling for time." Which was quite true.

"What's that supposed to mean?"

"It means you're thinking furiously of the answer to the same question we're about to ask you. What are *you* two doing here?"

"That's none of your business." Roomer's normally soft-spoken voice was unaccustomedly and deliberately harsh.

There was a silence from the back seat, both girls realizing that there was more to the men than they had thought, and the gap between their social and professional lives wider than they had thought.

Mitchell signed. "Let's cool it, John. An ungrateful child is sharper than a serpent's tooth."

"Jesus!" Roomer shook his head. "You can say that again." He hadn't the faintest idea what Mitchell was talking about.

Mitchell said: "Why don't you go to your father and ask him? I'm sure he'll tell you—along with the roughest chewing-out you've ever had for interfering in his private business." He got out, opened the rear door, waited until the sisters got out, closed the rear door, said 'Goodnight' and returned to his seat, leaving the girls standing uncertainly at the side of the road.

Roomer drove off. He said: "Very masterful, though I didn't like our doing it. God knows, they meant no harm. In any case, it may stand us in good stead in the future."

"It'll stand us in even better stead if we get to the phone booth right around the corner as soon as you can."

They reached the booth in fifteen seconds, and one minute later Mitchell emerged from it. As he took his seat Roomer said: "What was all that about?"

"Sorry, private matter." Mitchell handed Roomer a piece of paper. Roomer switched on the overhead light. On the paper Mitchell had scrawled: "This car bugged?"

Roomer said: "Okay by me." They drove home in silence. Standing in his carport Roomer said: "What makes you think my car's bugged?"

"Nothing. How far do you trust Bentley?"

"You know how far. But he—or one of his men—wouldn't have had time."

"Five seconds isn't a long time. That's all the time it takes to attach a magnetic clamp."

They searched the car, then Mitchell's. Both were clean. In Mitchell's kitchen Roomer said: "Your phone call?"

"The old boy, of course. I got to him before the girls did. Told him what had happened and that he was to tell them he'd received threats against their lives, that he knew the source, that he didn't trust the local law and so had sent for us to deal with the matter. Caught on at once. Also to give them hell for interfering."

Roomer said: "He'll convince them."

"More importantly, did he convince you?"

"No. He thinks fast on his feet and lies even faster. He wanted to find out how seriously he would be taken in the case of a real emergency. He now has the preliminary evidence that he is being taken seriously. You have to hand it to him—as devious as they come. I suppose we tell Bentley exactly what he told us to tell him?"

"What else?"

"Do you believe what he told us?"

"That he has his own private intelligence corps? I wouldn't question it for a moment. That he's going out to the *Seawitch?* I believe that, too. I'm not so sure about his timing, though. We're to tell Bentley that he's leaving in the afternoon. He told us he's leaving about dawn. If he can lie to Bentley he can lie to us. I don't know why he should think it necessary to lie to us, probably just his second nature. I think he's going to leave much sooner than that."

Roomer said: "Me, too, I'm afraid. If I intended to be up at dawn's early light I'd be in bed by now or heading that way. He showed no sign of going to bed, so I conclude he has no intention of going to bed, because it wouldn't be worth his while." He paused. "So. A double stake-out?"

"I thought so. Up by Lord Worth's house and down by his heliport. You for the heliport, me for the tail job?"

"What else?" Mitchell was possessed of phenomenal night-sight. Except on the very blackest of nights he could drive without any lights at all. "I'll hole up behind the west spinney. You know it?"

"I know it. How about you feeding the story to Bentley while I make a couple of thermoses of coffee and some sandwiches?"

"Fine." Roomer reached for the phone, then paused. "Listen, why are we doing all this? We don't owe the FBI anything. We have no authority from anyone to do anything. You said it yourself: we and organized law walk in different directions. I don't feel I'm under any obligation to save my country from a nonexistent threat. We've got no client, no commission, no prospect of fees. Why should we care if Lord Worth sticks his head into a noose?"

Mitchell paused in slicing bread. "As far as your last question is concerned, why don't you call up Melinda and ask her?"

Roomer gave him a long, quizzical look, sighed and reached for the telephone.

3

Scoffield had been wrong in his guess. Lord Worth was possessed of no private arsenal. But the United States armed services were, and in their dozens, at that.

The two break-ins were accomplished with the professional expertise born of a long and arduous practice that precluded any possibility of mistakes. The targets in both cases were government arsenals, one army and one naval. Both, naturally, were manned by round-the-clock guards, none of whom was killed or even injured if one were to disregard the cranial contusions—and those were few—caused by sandbagging and sapping: Lord Worth had been very explicit on the use of minimal violence.

Giuseppe Palermo, who looked and dressed like a successful Wall Street broker, had the more difficult task of the two, although, as a man who held the Mafia in tolerant contempt, he regarded the exercise as almost childishly easy. Accompanied by nine almost equally respectable men—sartorially respectable, that is—three of whom were dressed as army majors, he arrived at the Florida arms depot at fifteen minutes to midnight. The six young guards, none of whom had even seen or heard a shot fired in anger, were at their drowsiest and expecting nothing but their midnight reliefs. Only two were really fully awake—the other four had dozed away—and those two, responding to a heavy and peremptory hammering on the main entrance door, were disturbed, not to say highly alarmed, by the appearance of three army officers who announced that they were making a snap inspection to test security and alertness. Five minutes later all six were bound and gagged—two of them unconscious and due to wake up with very sore heads because of their misguided attempts to put up a show of resistance—and safely locked up in one of the many so-called secure rooms in the depot.

During this period and the next twenty minutes, one of Palermo's men, an electronics expert called Jamieson, made a thorough search for all the external alarm signals to both the police and nearest military HQ. He either bypassed or disconnected them all.

It was when he was engaged in this that the relief guards, almost as drowsy as those whom they had been expecting to find, made their appearance and were highly disconcerted to find themselves looking at the muzzles of three machine carbines. Within minutes, securely bound but not gagged, they had joined the previous guards, whose gags were now removed. They could now shout until doomsday, as the nearest habitation was more than a mile away: the temporary gagging of the first six guards had been merely for the purpose of preventing their warning off their reliefs.

Palermo now had almost eight hours before the break-in could be discovered.

He sent one of his men, Watkins, to bring round to the front the concealed minibus in which they had arrived. All of them, Watkins excepted, changed from their conservative clothing and military uniforms into rough workclothes, which resulted in rather remarkable changes in their appearance and character. While they were doing this, Watkins went to the depot garage, picked a surprisingly ineffectual lock, selected a two-ton truck, hot-wired the ignition—the keys were, understandably, missing—and drove out to the already open main loading doors of the depot.

Palermo had brought along with him one by the name of Jacobson who, between sojourns in various penitentiaries, had developed to a remarkable degree the fine art of opening any type of lock, combination or otherwise. Fortunately his services were not needed, for nobody, curiously enough, had taken the trouble to conceal some score of keys hanging on the wall in the main office.

In less than half an hour Palermo and his men had loaded aboard the truck—chosen because it was a covered-van type—a staggering variety of weaponry, ranging from bazookas to machine pistols, together with suffi-

cient ammunition for a battalion and a considerable amount of high explosives. Then they relocked the doors and took the keys with them—when the
next relief arrived at eight in the morning it would take them that much
longer to discover what had actually happened. After that, they locked the
loading and main entrance doors.

Watkins drove the minibus, with its load of discarded clothes, back to its
place of concealment, returned to the truck and drove off. The other nine
sat or lay in varying degrees of discomfort among the weaponry in the back.
It was as well for them that it was only twenty minutes' drive to Lord
Worth's private, isolated and deserted heliport—deserted, that is, except for
two helicopters, their pilots and copilots.

The truck, using only its sidelights, came through the gates of the heliport
and drew up alongside one of the helicopters. Discreet portable loading
lights were switched on, casting hardly more than a dull glow, but sufficient
for a man only eighty yards away and equipped with a pair of night glasses
to distinguish clearly what was going on. And Roomer, prone in the spinney
with the binoculars to his eyes, was only eighty yards away. No attempt had
been made to wrap or in any way to disguise the nature of the cargo. It took
only twenty minutes to unload the truck and stow its contents away in the
helicopter under the watchful eye of a pilot with a keen regard for weight
distribution.

Palermo and his men, with the exception of Watkins, boarded the other
helicopter and sat back to await promised reinforcements. The pilot of this
helicopter had already, as was customary, radio-filed his flight plan to the
nearest airport, accurately giving his destination as the *Seawitch*. To have
done otherwise would have been foolish indeed. The radar tracking systems
along the Gulf states are as efficient as any in the world, and any course
deviation from a falsely declared destination would have meant that, in very
short order, two highly suspicious pilots in supersonic jets would be flying
alongside and asking some very unpleasant questions.

Watkins drove the truck back to the garage, dewired the ignition, locked
the door, retrieved the minibus and left. Before dawn, all his friends' clothes
would have been returned to their apartments, and the minibus, which had
of course been stolen, to its parking lot.

Roomer was getting bored and his elbows were becoming sore. Since the
minibus had driven away some half hour ago he had remained in the same
prone position, his night glasses seldom far from his eyes. His sandwiches
were gone, as was all his coffee, and he would have given much for a
cigarette but decided it would be unwise. Clearly those aboard the helicopters were waiting for something, and that something could only be the arrival
of Lord Worth.

He heard the sound of an approaching engine and saw another vehicle,
with only sidelights on, turn through the gateway. It was another minibus.
Whoever was inside was not the man he was waiting for, he knew: Lord
Worth was not much given to traveling in minibuses. The vehicle drew up
alongside the passenger helicopter and its passengers disembarked and climbed
aboard the helicopter. Roomer counted twelve in all.

The last was just disappearing inside the helicopter when another vehicle
arrived. This one didn't pass through the gateway; it swept through it, with
only parking lights on. A Rolls Royce. Lord Worth, for a certainty. As if to
redouble his certainty, there came to his ears the soft swish of tires on the
grass. He twisted round to see a car, both lights and engine off, coasting to
a soundless stop beside his own.

"Over here," Roomer called softly. Mitchell joined him, and together they watched the white-clad figure of Lord Worth leave the Rolls and mount the steps to the helicopter. "I guess that completes the payload for the night."

"The payload being?"

"There are twenty-one other passengers aboard that machine. I can't swear to it, but instinct tells me they are not honest, upright citizens. They say that every multimillionaire had his own private army. I think I've just seen one of Lord Worth's platoons filing by."

"The second chopper's not involved?"

"It sure is. It's the star of the show—loaded to the gunwales with armament."

"That's not a crime in itself. Could be part of Lord Worth's private collection. He's got one of the biggest in the country."

"Private citizens aren't allowed to have bazookas, machine guns and high explosives in their collections."

"He borrowed them, you think?"

"Yeah. Without payment or receipt."

"The nearest government arsenal?"

"I'd say so."

"They're still sitting there. Maybe they're waiting a preset time before takeoff. Might be some time. Let's go to one of the cars and radio the law."

"The nearest army command post is seven miles from here."

"Right."

The two men were on their feet and had taken only two steps toward the cars when, almost simultaneously, the engines of both helicopters started up with their usual clattering roar. Seconds later both machines lifted off.

Mitchell said: "Well, it was a thought."

" 'Was' is right. Look at 'em go: honest God-fearing citizens with all their navigational lights on."

"That's in case someone bumps into them." Mitchell said. "We could call up the nearest air force base and have them forced down."

"On what grounds?"

"Stolen government property."

"No evidence. Just our say-so. They'll find out Lord Worth is aboard. Who's going to take the word of a couple of busted cops against his?"

"No one. A sobering thought. Ever felt like a pariah?"

"Like now. I feel goddamned helpless. Well, let's go and find some evidence. Where's the nearest arsenal from here?"

"About a mile from the command post. I know where."

"Why don't they keep their damned arsenals *inside* the command posts?"

"Because ammunition can and does blow up. How would you like to be sitting in a crowded barracks when an ammo dump blew up next door?"

Roomer straightened from the keyhole of the main door of the arms depot and reluctantly pocketed the very large set of keys which any ill-disposed law officer could have jailed him for carrying.

"I thought I could open any door with this bunch. But not this one. Give you one guess where the keys are now."

"Probably sailing down from a chopper into the Gulf."

"Right. Those loading doors have the same lock. Besides that, nothing but barred windows. You don't have a hacksaw on you, do you, Mike?"

"I will next time." He shone his flashlight through one of the barred windows. All he could see was his own reflection. He took out his pistol and, holding it by the barrel, struck the heavy butt several times against the glass, without any noticeable effect—hardly surprising, considering that the window lay several inches beyond the bars and the force of the blows was minimal.

Roomer said: "What are you trying to do?"

Mitchell was patient. "Break the glass."

"Breaking the glass won't help you get inside."

"It'll help me see and maybe hear. I wonder if that's just plate glass or armored stuff."

"How should I know?"

"Well, we'll find out. If it's armored, the bullet will ricochet. Get down." Both men crouched and Mitchell fired one shot at an upward angle. The bullet did not ricochet. It passed through, leaving a jagged hole with radiating cracks. Mitchell began chipping away round the hole but desisted when Roomer appeared with a heavy car jackhandle: a few powerful blows and Roomer had a hole almost a foot in diameter. Mitchell shone his flash through this: an office lined with filing cabinets and an open door beyond. He put his ear as close to the hole as possible and he heard it at once, the faint but unmistakable sound of metal clanging against metal and the shouting of unmistakably hoarse voices. Mitchell withdrew his head and nodded to Roomer, who leaned forward and listened in turn.

Roomer straightened and said: "There are a lot of frustrated people in there."

About a mile beyond the entrance to the army command post they stopped by a roadside telephone booth. Mitchell telephoned the army post, told them the state of defenses at their arsenal building would bear investigation and that it would be advisable for them to bring along a duplicate set of keys for the main door. When asked who was speaking he hung up and returned to Roomer's car.

"Too late to call in the Air Force now, I suppose?"

"Too late. They'll be well out over extraterritorial waters by now. There's no state of war. Not yet." He sighed. "Why, oh why, didn't I have an infrared movie camera tonight?"

Over in Mississippi Conde's task of breaking into the naval depot there turned out to be ridiculously easy. He had with him only six men, although he had sixteen more waiting in reserve aboard the 120-foot vessel *Roamer,* which was tied up dockside less than thirty feet from the arsenal. Those men had already effectively neutralized the three armed guards who patrolled the dock area at night.

The arsenal was guarded by only two retired naval petty officers, who regarded their job not only as a sinecure but downright nonsense, for who in his right mind would want to steal depth charges and naval guns? It was their invariable custom to prepare themselves for sleep immediately upon arrival, and asleep they soundly were when Conde and his men entered through the door they hadn't even bothered to lock.

They used two forklift trucks to trundle depth charges, light, dual-purpose antiaircraft guns, and a sufficiency of shells down to the dockside, then used one of the scores of cranes that lined the dockside to lower the stolen equipment into the hold of the *Roamer,* which was then battened down. Clearing customs was the merest formality. The customs official had seen the *Roamer* come and go so many times that they had long ago lost count. Besides, no one was going to have the temerity to inspect the oceangoing property of one of the very richest men in the world: the *Roamer* was Lord Worth's seismological survey vessel.

At its base not far from Havana, a small, conventionally powered and Russian-built submarine slipped its moorings and quietly put out to sea. The hastily assembled but nonetheless hand-picked crew was informed that they were on a training cruise designed to test the seagoing readiness of Castro's tiny fleet. Not a man aboard believed a word of this.

Meanwhile Cronkite had not been idle. Unlike the others, he had no need to break into any place to obtain explosives. He had merely to use his own key. As the world's top expert in capping blazing gushers he had access to an unlimited number and great variety of explosives. He made a selection of those and had them trucked down to Galveston from Houston, where he lived; apart from the fact that Houston was the oil-rig center of the South, the nature of Cronkite's business made it essential for him to live within easy reach of an airport with international connections.

As the truck was on its way, another seismological vessel, a converted coast guard cutter, was also closing in on Galveston. Without explaining his reasons for needing the vessel, Cronkite had obtained it through the good offices of Durant, who had represented the Galveston-area companies at the meeting of the ten at Lake Tahoe. The cutter, which went by the name of *Tiburon,* was normally based at Freeport, and Cronkite could quite easily have taken the shipment there, but this would not have suited his purpose. The tanker *Crusader* was unloading at Galveston, and the *Crusader* was one of the three tankers that plied regularly between the *Seawitch* and the Gulf ports.

The *Tiburon* and Cronkite arrived almost simultaneously sometime after midnight. Mulhooney, the *Tiburon's* skipper, eased his ship into a berth conveniently close to the *Crusader.* Mulhooney was not the regular captain of the *Tiburon.* That gentleman had been so overcome by the sight of two thousand dollars in cash that he had fallen ill, and would remain so for a few days. Cronkite had recommended his friend Mulhooney. Cronkite didn't immediately go aboard the *Tiburon.* Instead he chatted with a night-duty dock inspector, who watched with an idle eye as what were obviously explosives were transferred to the *Tiburon.* The two men had known each other for years. Apart from observing that someone out in the Gulf must have been careless with matches again, the port official had no further pertinent comment to make. In response to idle questioning, Cronkite learned that the *Crusader* had finished off-loading its cargo and would be sailing in approximately one hour.

He boarded the *Tiburon,* greeted Mulhooney and went straight to the crew's mess. Seated among the others at this early hour were three divers already fully clad in wetsuits. He gave brief instructions and the three men went on deck. Under cover of the superstructure and on the side of the ship remote from the dock the three men donned scuba gear, went down a rope ladder and slid quietly into the water. Six objects—radio-detonated magnetic mines equipped with metallic clamps—were lowered to them. They were so constructed as to have a very slight negative buoyancy, which made them easy to tow under water.

In the predawn darkness the hulls of the vessels cast so heavy a shadow from the powerful shorelights that the men could have swum unobserved on the surface. But Cronkite was not much given to taking chances. The mines were attached along the stern half of the *Crusader*'s hull, thirty feet apart and at a depth of about ten feet. Five minutes after their departure the scuba divers were back. After a further five minutes the *Tiburon* put out to sea.

Despite his near-legendary reputation for ruthlessness, Cronkite had not quite lost touch with humanity: to say that he was possessed of an innate kindliness would have been a distortion of the truth, for he was above all an uncompromising and single-minded realist, but one with no innate killer instinct. Nonetheless, there were two things that would at that moment have given him considerable satisfaction.

The first of those was that he would have preferred to have the *Crusader* at sea before pressing the sheathed button before him on the bridge. He had no wish that innocent lives should be lost in Galveston, but it was a chance that he had to take. Limpet mines, as the Italian divers had proved at Alexandria in World War II—and this to the great distress of the Royal Navy—could be devastatingly effective against moored vessels. But what might happen to high-buoyancy limpets when a ship got under way and worked up to maximum speed was impossible to forecast, as there was no known case of a vessel under way having been destroyed by limpet mines. It was at least possible that water pressure on a ship under way might well overcome the tenuous magnetic hold of the limpets and tear them free.

The second temptation was to board the helicopter on the *Tiburon*'s after helipad—many such vessels carried helicopters for the purpose of having them drop patterned explosives on the seabed to register on the seismological computer—and have a close look at what would be the ensuing havoc, a temptation he immediately regarded as pure self-indulgence.

He put both thoughts from his mind. Eight miles out from Galveston he unscrewed the covered switch and leaned firmly on the button beneath. The immediate results were wholly unspectacular, and Cronkite feared that they might be out of radio range. But in the port area in Galveston the results were highly spectacular. Six shattering explosions occurred almost simultaneously, and within twenty seconds the *Crusader,* her stern section torn in half, developed a marked list to starboard as thousands of tons of water poured through the ruptured side. Another twenty seconds later the distant rumble of the explosions reached the ears of the listeners on the *Tiburon*. Cronkite and Mulhooney, alone on the bridge—the ship was on automatic pilot—looked at each other with grim satisfaction. Mulhooney, an Irishman with a true Irishman's sense of occasion, produced an opened bottle of champagne and poured two brimming glassfuls. Cronkite, who normally detested the stuff, consumed his drink with considerable relish and set his glass down. It was then that the *Crusader* caught fire.

Its gasoline tanks, true, were empty, but its engine diesel fuel tanks were almost completely topped up. In normal circumstances ignited diesel does not explode but burns with a ferocious intensity. Within seconds the smoke-veined flames had risen to a height of two hundred feet, the height increasing with each moment until the whole city was bathed in a crimson glow, a phenomenon which the citizens of Galveston had never seen before and would almost certainly never see again. Even aboard the *Tiburon* the spectacle had an awe-inspiring and unearthly quality about it. Then, as suddenly as it had begun, the fire stopped as the *Crusader* turned completely over on its side, the harbor waters quenching the flames into hissing extinction. Some patches of floating oil still flickered feebly across the harbor, but that was all that there was to it.

Clearly Lord Worth was going to require a new tanker, a requirement that presented quite a problem. In this area of a gross oversupply of tankers, any one of scores of laid-up supertankers could be had just through exercising enough strength to lift a telephone. But 50,000-ton tankers, though not a dying breed, were a dwindling breed, principally because the main ship-yards throughout the world had stopped producing them. "Had" is the operative word. Keels of that size and even smaller were now being hastily laid down, but would not be in full operation for a year or two to come. The reason was perfectly simple. Supertankers on the Arabian Gulf-Europe run had to make the long and prohibitively expensive circuit around the Cape of Good Hope because the newly reopened Suez Canal could not accommodate their immense draft, a problem that presented no difficulties to smaller tankers. It was said, and probably with more than a grain of truth, that the notoriously wily Greek shipowners had established a corner on this particular market.

The dawn was in the sky.

At that precise moment there were scenes of considerable activity around and aboard the *Seawitch*. The Panamanian-registered tanker *Torbello* was just finishing off-loading the contents of the *Seawitch*'s massive floating conical oil tank. As they were doing so, two helicopters appeared over the northeastern horizon. Both were very large Sikorsky machines which had been bought by the thrifty Lord Worth for the traditional song, not because they were obsolete but because they were two of the scores that had become redundant since the end of the Vietnam War, and the armed forces had been only too anxious to get rid of them: civilian demand for ex-gunships is not high.

The first of those to land on the helipad debarked twenty-two men, led by Lord Worth and Giuseppe Palermo. The other twenty, who from their appearance were not much given to caring for widows and orphans, all carried with them the impeccable credentials of oil experts of one type or another. That they were experts was beyond question; what was equally beyond question was that none of them would have recognized a barrel of oil if he had fallen into it. They were experts in diving, underwater demolition, the handling of high explosives, and the accurate firing of a variety of unpleasant weapons.

The second helicopter arrived immediately after the first had taken off. Except for the pilot and copilot, it carried no other human cargo. What it did carry was the immense and varied quantity of highly offensive weaponry from the Florida arsenal, the loss of which had not yet been reported in the newspapers.

The oil-rig crew watched the arrival of gunmen and weapons with an oddly dispassionate curiosity. They were men to whom the unusual was familiar; the odd, the incongruous, the inexplicable, part and parcel of their daily lives. Oil-rig crews are a race apart, and Lord Worth's men formed a very special subdivision of that race.

Lord Worth called them all together, told of the threat to the *Seawitch* and the defensive measures he was undertaking, measures which were thoroughly approved of by the crew, who had as much regard for their own skins as had the rest of mankind. Lord Worth finished by saying that he knew he had no need to swear them to secrecy.

In this the noble Lord was perfectly correct. Though they were all experienced oilmen, hardly a man aboard had not at one time or another had a

close and painful acquaintanceship with the law. There were ex-convicts
among them. There were escaped convicts among them. There were those
whom the law was very anxious to interview. And there were parolees who
had broken their parole. There could be no safer hideouts for those men than
the *Seawitch* and Lord Worth's privately owned motel where they put up
during their off-duty spells. No law officer in his sane mind was going to
question the towering respectability and integrity of one of the most powerful oil barons in the world, and by inevitable implication this attitude of
mind extended to those in his employ.

In other words, Lord Worth, through the invaluable intermediacy of Commander Larsen, picked his men with extreme care.

Accommodation for the newly arrived men and storage for the weaponry
presented no problem. Like many jack-ups, drill ships and submersibles,
the *Seawitch* had two complete sets of accommodation and messes—one
for Westerners, the other for Orientals: there were at that time no Orientals
aboard.

Lord Worth, Commander Larsen and Palermo held their own private
council of war in the luxuriously equipped sitting room which Lord Worth
kept permanently reserved for himself. They agreed on everything. They
agreed that Cronkite's campaign against them would be distinguished by a
noticeable lack of subtlety: outright violence was the only course open to
him. Once the oil was off-loaded ashore, there was nothing Cronkite could
do about it. He would not attempt to attack and sink a loaded tanker, just as
he would not attempt to destroy their huge floating storage tank. Either
method would cause a massive oil slick, comparable to or probably exceed-
ing the great oil slick caused by the Torrey Canyon disaster off the southwest
coast of England some years previously. The ensuing international uproar
would be bound to uncover something, and if Cronkite were implicated he
would undoubtedly implicate the major oil companies—who wouldn't like
that at all. And that there would be a massive investigation was inevitable:
ecology and pollution were still the watchwords of the day.

Cronkite could attack the flexible oil pipe that connected the rig with the
tank, but the three men agreed that this could be taken care of. After Conde
and the *Roamer* arrived and its cargo had been hoisted aboard, the *Roamer*
would maintain a constant day-and-night patrol between the rig and the
tank. The *Seawitch* was well-equipped with sensory devices, apart from
those which controlled the tensioning anchor cables. A radar scanner was in
constant operation atop the derrick, and sonar devices were attached to each
of the three giant legs some twenty feet under water. The radar could detect
any hostile approach from air or sea, and the dual-purpose antiaircraft guns,
aboard and installed, could take care of those. In the highly unlikely event
of an underwater attack, sonar would locate the source, and a suitably placed
depth charge from the *Roamer* would attend to that.

Lord Worth, of course, was unaware that at that very moment another
craft was moving out at high speed to join Cronkite on the *Tiburon*. It was
a standard and well-established design irreverently known as the "push-
pull," in which water was ducted in through a tube forward under the hull
and forced out under pressure at the rear. It had no propeller and had been
designed primarily for work close inshore or in swamps, where there was
always the danger of the propeller being fouled. The only difference between
this vessel—the *Starlight*—and others was that it was equipped with a bank
of storage batteries and could be electrically powered. Sonar could detect
and accurately pinpoint a ship's engines and propeller vibrations; it was
virtually helpless against an electric push-pull.

Lord Worth and the others considered the possibility of a direct attack on the *Seawitch*. Because of her high degree of compartmentalization and her great positive buoyancy, nothing short of an atom bomb was capable of disposing of something as large as a football field. Certainly no conventional weapon could. The attack, when it came, would be localized. The drilling derrick was an obvious target, but how Cronkite could approach it unseen could not be imagined. But Lord Worth was certain of one thing: when the attack came it would be leveled against the *Seawitch*.

The next half hour was to prove, twice, just how wrong Lord Worth could be.

The first intimations of disaster came as Lord Worth was watching the fully laden *Torbello* just disappearing over the northern horizon; the *Crusader*, he knew, was due alongside the tank late that afternoon. Larsen, his face one huge scowl of fury, silently handed Lord Worth a signal just received in the radio office. Lord Worth read it, and his subsequent language would have disbarred him forever from a seat in the House of Lords. The message told, in cruelly unsparing fashion, of the spectacular end of the *Crusader* in Galveston.

Both men hurried to the radio room. Larsen contacted the *Jupiter*, their third tanker then off-loading at an obscure Louisiana port, told its captain the unhappy fate of the *Crusader* and warned him to have every man on board on constant lookout until they had cleared harbor.

Lord Worth personally called the chief of police in Galveston, identified himself and demanded more details of the sinking of the *Crusader*. These he duly received, and none of them made him any happier. On inspiration, he asked if there had been a man called John Cronkite or a vessel belonging to a man of that name in the vicinity at the time. He was told to hang on while a check was made with Customs. Two minutes later he was told yes, there had been a John Cronkite aboard a vessel called the *Tiburon*, which had been moored directly aft of the *Crusader*. It was not known whether Cronkite was the owner or not. The *Tiburon* had sailed half an hour before the *Crusader* blew up.

Lord Worth peremptorily demanded that the *Tiburon* be apprehended and returned to port and that Cronkite be arrested. The police chief pointed out that international law prohibited the arrest of vessels on the high seas except in time of war and, as for Cronkite, there wasn't a shred of evidence to connect him with the sinking of the *Crusader*. Lord Worth then asked if he would trace the owner of the *Tiburon*. This the police chief promised to do, but warned that there might be a considerable delay. There were many registers to be consulted.

At that moment the Cuban submarine steaming on the surface at full speed was in the vicinity of Key West and heading directly for the *Seawitch*. At almost the same time a missile-armed Russian destroyer slipped its moorings in Havana and set off in apparent pursuit of the Cuban submarine. And very shortly after that, a destroyer departed its home base in Venezuela.

The *Roamer*, Lord Worth's survey vessel under the command of Conde, was now halfway to its destination.

The *Starlight*, under the command of Easton, was just moving away from the *Tiburon,* which was lying stopped in the water. Men on slings had already painted out the ship's name, and with the aid of cardboard stencils were painting in a new name—*Georgia.* Cronkite had no wish that any vessel with whom they might make contact could radio for confirmation of the existence of a cutter called *Tiburon.* From aft there came the unmistakable racket of a helicopter engine starting up, then the machine took off, circled and headed southeast, not on its usual pattern-bombing circuit but to locate and radio back to the *Tiburon* the location and course of the *Torbello,* if and when it found it. Within minutes the *Tiburon* was on its way again, heading in approximately the same direction as the helicopter.

4

LORD WORTH enjoying a very early morning cup of tea, was in his living room with Larsen and Palermo when the radio operator knocked and entered, a message sheet in his hand. He handed it to Lord Worth and said: "For you, sir. But it's in some sort of code. Do you have a code book?"

"No need." Lord Worth smiled with some self-satisfaction, his first smile of any kind for quite some time. "I invented this code myself." He tapped his head. "Here's my code book."

The operator left. The other two watched in mild anticipation as Lord Worth began to decode. The anticipation turned into apprehension as the smile disappeared from Lord Worth's face, and the apprehension gave way in turn to deep concern as reddish-purple spots the size of pennies touched either cheekbone. He laid down the message sheet, took a deep breath, then proceeded to give a repeat performance—though this time more deeply felt, more impassioned—of the unparliamentary language he had used at the news of the loss of the *Crusader.* After some time he desisted, less because he had nothing fresh to say than from sheer loss of breath.

Larsen had more wit than to ask Lord Worth if something were the matter. Instead he said in a quiet voice: "Suppose you tell us, Lord Worth?"

Lord Worth, with no little effort, composed himself and said: "It seems that Cor——" He broke off and corrected himself: it was one of his many axioms that the right hand shouldn't know what the left hand doeth. "I was informed—all too reliably, as it now appears—that a couple of countries hostile to us might well be prepared to use naval force against us. One, it appears, is already prepared to do so. A destroyer has just cleared its Venezuelan home port and is heading in what is approximately our direction."

"They wouldn't dare," Palermo said.

"When people are power- and money-mad they'll stop at nothing." It apparently never occurred to Lord Worth that his description of people applied, *in excelsis,* to himself.

"Who's the other power?" said Larsen.

"The Soviet Union."

"Is it now?" Larsen seemed quite unmoved. "I don't know if I like the sound of that."

"We could do without them." Lord Worth was back on balance again. He flipped out a notebook and consulted it. "I think I'll have a talk with Washington." His hand was just reaching out for the phone when it rang. He lifted the instrument, at the same time turning the switch that cut the incoming call into the bulkhead speaker.

"Worth."

A vaguely disembodied voice came through the speaker. "You know who I am?" Disembodied or not, the voice was known to Worth. Corral.

"Yes."

"I've checked my contact, sir. I'm afraid our guesses were only too accurate. Both X and Y are willing to commit themselves to naval support."

"I know. One of them has just moved out and appears to be heading in our general direction."

"Which one?"

"The one to the south. Any talk of air commitment?"

"None that I've heard, sir. But I don't have to tell you that that doesn't rule out its use."

"Let me know if there is any more good news."

"Naturally. Goodbye, sir."

Lord Worth replaced the instrument, then lifted it again.

"I want a number in Washington."

"Can you hold a moment, sir?"

"Why?"

"There's another code message coming through. Looks like the same code as the last one, sir."

"I shouldn't be surprised." Lord Worth's tone was somber. "Bring it across as soon as possible."

He replaced the phone, pressed a button on the small console before him, lifting the phone again as he did.

"Chambers?" Chambers was his senior pilot.

"Sir?"

"Your chopper refueled?"

"Ready to go when you are, sir."

"May be any second now. Stand by your phone." He replaced the receiver.

Larsen said: "Washington beckons, sir?"

"I have the odd feeling that it's about to. There are things that one can achieve in person that one can't over the phone. Depends upon this next message."

"If you go, anything to be done in your absence?"

"There'll be dual-purpose antiaircraft guns arriving aboard the *Roamer* this afternoon. Secure them to the platform."

"To the north, south, east but not west?"

"As you wish."

"We don't want to start blowing holes in our own oil tank."

"There's that. There'll also be mines. Three piles, each halfway between a pair of legs."

"An underwater explosion from a mine wouldn't damage the legs?"

"I shouldn't think so. We'll just have to find out, won't we? Keep in constant half-hourly touch with both the *Torbello* and the *Jupiter*. Keep the radar and sonar stations constantly manned. Eternal vigilance, if you will. Hell, Commander, I don't have to tell you what to do." He wrote some figures on a piece of paper. "If I do have to go, contact this number in Washington. Tell them that I'm coming. Five hours or so."

"This is the State Department?"

"Yes. Tell them that at least the Under Secretary must be there. Remind him, tactfully, of future campaign contributions. Then contact my aircraft pilot, Dawson. Tell him to be standing by with a filed flight plan for Washington."

The radio operator knocked, entered, handed Lord Worth a message sheet and left. Lord Worth, hands steady and face now untroubled, decoded the message, reached for the phone and told Chambers to get to the helicopter at once.

He said to the two men: "A Russian-built Cuban submarine is on its way from Havana. It's being followed by a Russian guided-missile destroyer. Both are heading this way."

"A visit to the State Department or the Pentagon would appear to be indicated," Larsen said. "There isn't too much we can do about guided missiles. Looks like there might be quite some activity hereabouts. That makes five vessels arrowing in on us—three naval vessels, the *Jupiter* and the *Roamer.*" Larsen might have been even more concerned had he known that the number of vessels was seven, not five: but, then, Larsen was not to know that the *Tiburon* and the *Starlight* were heading that way also.

Lord Worth rose. "Well, keep an eye on the shop. Back this evening sometime. I'll be in frequent radio contact."

Lord Worth was to fly four legs that day: by helicopter to the mainland, by his private Boeing to Washington, the return flight to Florida, and the final leg by helicopter out to the *Seawitch.* On each of those four legs something very unpleasant was going to happen—unpleasant for Lord Worth, that is. Fortunately for Lord Worth, he was not blessed with the alleged Scottish second sight—the ability to look into the future.

The first of those unpleasantnesses happened when Lord Worth was en route to the mainland. A large station wagon swept up to the front door of Lord Worth's mansion, carrying five rather large men who would have been difficult later to identify, for all five wore stocking masks. One of them carried what appeared to be a large coil of clothesline rope, another a roll of adhesive tape. All carried guns.

MacPherson, the elderly head gardener, was taking his customary prework dawn patrol to see what damage the fauna had wreaked on his flora during the night, when the men emerged from the station wagon. Even allowing for the fact that shock had temporarily paralyzed his vocal cords, he never had a chance. In just over a minute, bound hand and foot and with his lips sealed with adhesive tape, he had been dumped unceremoniously into a clump of bushes.

The leader of the group, a man by the name of Durand, pressed the front-door bell. Durand, a man who had a powerful affinity with banks and who was a three-time ex-convict, was by definition a man of dubious reputation, a reputation confirmed by the fact that he was a close and longtime term associate of Cronkite. Half a minute passed, then he rang again. By and by the door opened to reveal a robe-wrapped Jenkins, tousle-haired and blinking the sleep from his eyes—it was still very early in the morning. His eyes stopped blinking and opened wide when he saw the pistol in Durand's hand.

Durand touched the cylinder screwed onto the muzzle of his gun. As hooked a TV addict as the next man, Jenkins recognized a silencer when he saw one.

"You know what this is?"

A fully awake Jenkins nodded silently.

"We don't want to harm anyone in the house. Especially, no harm will come to you if you do what you are told. Doing what you are told includes not telling lies. Understood?"

Jenkins understood.

"How many staff do you have here?"

There was a noticeable quaver in Jenkins's voice. "Well, there's me—I'm the butler——"

Durand was patient. "You we can see."

"Two footmen, a chauffeur, a radio operator, a secretary, a cook and two housemaids. There's a cleaning lady, but she doesn't come until eight."

"Tape him," Durand said. Jenkins's lips were taped. "Sorry about that, but people can be silly at times. Take us to those eight bedrooms."

Jenkins reluctantly led the way. Ten minutes later, all eight of the staff were securely bound and silenced. Durand said: "And now, the two young ladies."

Jenkins led them to a door. Durand picked out three of his men and said softly: "The butler will take you to the other girl. Check what she packs and especially her purse."

Durand, followed by his man, entered the room, his gun in its concealed holster so as not to arouse too much alarm. That the bed was occupied was beyond doubt, although all that could be seen was a mop of black hair on the pillow. Durand said in a conversational voice: "I think you better get up, ma'am." Durand was not normally given to gentleness, but he did not want a case of screaming hysterics on his hands.

A case of hysterics he did not have. Marina turned round in bed and looked at him with drowsy eyes. The drowsiness did not last long. The eyes opened wide, either in fear or shock, then returned to normal. She reached for a robe, arranged it strategically on the bed cover, then sat bolt upright, wrapping the robe round her.

"Who are you and what do you want?" Her voice was not quite as steady as she might have wished.

"Well, would you look at that, now?" Durand said admiringly. "You'd think she was used to being kidnaped every morning of her life."

"This is a kidnap?"

"I'm afraid so." Durand sounded genuinely apologetic.

"Where are you taking me?"

"Vacation. Little island in the sun." Durand smiled. "You won't be needing any swimsuit though. Please get up and get dressed."

"And if I refuse?"

"We'll dress you."

"I'm not going to get dressed with you two watching me."

Durand was soothing. "My friend will stand out in the corridor. I'll go into the bathroom there and leave the door open just a crack—not to watch you, but to watch the window, to make sure that you don't leave by it. Call me when you're ready and be quick about it."

She was quick about it. She called him within three minutes. Blue blouse, blue slacks and her hair combed. Durand nodded his approval.

"Pack a traveling bag. Enough for a few days."

He watched her while she packed. She zipped the bag shut and picked up her purse. "I'm ready."

He took the purse from her, undid the clasp and upended the contents on the bed. From the jumble on the bed he selected a small pearl-handled pistol, which he slipped into his pocket.

"Let's pack the purse again, shall we?"

Marina did so, her face flushed with mortification.

A somewhat similar scene had just taken place in Melinda's bedroom.

Twenty-five minutes had elapsed since the arrival of Durand and his men and their departure with the two girls. No one had been hurt, except in

pride, and the intruders had even been considerate to the extent of seating
Jenkins in a deep armchair in the front hall. Jenkins, as he was now securely
bound hand and foot, did not appreciate this courtesy as much as he might
have done.

About ten minutes after their departure, Lord Worth's helicopter touched
down beside his Boeing in the city airport. There were no customs, no
clearance formalities. Lord Worth had made it plain some years previously
that he did not much care for that sort of thing, and when Lord Worth made
things plain they tended to remain that way.

It was during the second leg of this flight that the second unfortunate
occurrence happened. Again, Lord Worth was happily unaware of what was
taking place.

The *Tiburon*'s (now the *Georgia*'s) helicopter had located the *Torbello*.
The pilot reported that he had sighted the vessel two minutes previously and
gave her latitude and longitude as accurately as he could judge. More importantly, he gave her course as approximately 315 degrees, which was virtually
on a collision course with the *Georgia*. They were approximately forty-five
miles apart. Cronkite gave his congratulations to the pilot and asked him to
return to the *Georgia*.

On the bridge of the *Georgia* Cronkite and Mulhooney looked at each
other with satisfaction. Between planning and execution there often exists
an unbridgeable gap. In this case, however, things appeared to be going
exactly according to plan.

Cronkite said to Mulhooney: "Time, I think, to change into more respectable clothes. And don't forget to powder your nose."

Mulhooney smiled and left the bridge. Cronkite paused only to give a few
instructions to the helmsman, then left the bridge also.

Less than an hour later the *Torbello* stood clear over the horizon. The
Georgia headed straight for it, then at about three miles distance made a
thirty-degree alteration to starboard, judged the timing to a nicety and came
round in a wide sweeping turn to port. Two minutes later the *Georgia* was
on a parallel course to the *Torbello*, alongside its port quarter—the bridge
of a tanker lies very far aft—paralleling its course at the same speed and
not more than thirty yards away. Cronkite moved out onto the wing of the
Georgia's bridge and lifted his loud-hailer.

"Coast Guard. Please stop. This is a request, not an order. We think your
vessel's in great danger. Your permission, please, to bring a trained research
party aboard. For the safety of your men and the ship, don't break radio
silence on any account!"

Captain Thompson, an honest sailor with no criminal propensities whatsoever, used his own loud-hailer.

"What's wrong? Why is this boarding necessary?"

"It's not a boarding. I am making a request for your own good. Believe
me, I'd rather not be within five miles of you. It *is* necessary. I'd rather
come aboard with my lieutenant and explain privately. Don't forget what
happened to your sister ship, the *Crusader*, in Galveston harbor last night."

Captain Thompson, clearly, had not forgotten and was, of course, completely unaware that Cronkite was the man responsible for what had hap-

pened to his sister ship: a ringing of bells from the bridge was indication enough of that. Three minutes later the *Torbello* lay stopped in the calm waters. The *Georgia* edged up alongside the *Torbello* until its midships were just ahead of the bulk of the tanker's superstructure. At this point it was possible to step from the *Georgia*'s deck straight onto the deck of the deep-laden tanker, which was what Cronkite and Mulhooney proceeded to do. They paused there until they had made sure that the *Georgia* was securely moored fore and aft to the tanker, then climbed a series of companion-ways and ladders up to the bridge.

Both men were quite unrecognizable. Cronkite had acquired a splendidly bushy black beard, a neatly trimmed mustache and dark glasses and, with his smartly tailored uniform and slightly rakish peaked cap, looked the epitome of the competent and dashing coast-guard-cutter captain which he was not. Mulhooney was similarly disguised.

There was only Captain Thompson and an idle helmsman on the bridge. Cronkite shook the captain's hand.

"Good morning. Sorry to disturb you when you are proceeding about your lawful business and all that, but you may be glad we stopped you. First, where is your radio room?" Captain Thompson nodded to a door set in back of the bridge. "I'd like my lieutenant to check on the radio silence. This is imperative." Again, Captain Thompson, now feeling distinctly uneasy, nodded. Cronkite looked at Mulhooney. "Go check, Dixon, will you?"

Mulhooney passed through into the radio room, closing the door behind him. The radio operator looked up from his transceiver with an air of mild surprise.

"Sorry to disturb." Mulhooney sounded almost genial, a remarkable feat for a man totally devoid of geniality. "I'm from the Coast Guard cutter alongside. The captain told you to keep radio silence?"

"That's just what I'm doing."

"Made any radio calls since leaving the *Seawitch?*"

"Only the routine half-hourly on-course, on-time calls."

"Do they acknowledge those? I have my reasons for asking." Mulhooney carefully refrained from saying what his reasons were.

"No. Well, just the usual 'roger and out' business."

"What's the call-up frequency?"

The operator pointed to the console. "Preset."

Mulhooney nodded and walked casually behind the operator. Just to make sure that the operator kept on maintaining radio silence, Mulhooney clipped him over the right ear with his pistol. He then returned to the bridge, where he found Captain Thompson in a state of considerable and understandable perturbation.

Captain Thompson, a deep anxiety compounded by a self-defensive disbelief, said: "What you're telling me in effect is that the *Torbello* is a floating time bomb."

"A bomb, certainly. Maybe lots of bombs. Not only possible but almost certain. Our sources of information—sorry, I'm not at liberty to divulge those—are as nearly perfect as can be."

"God's sake, man, no one would be so crazy as to cause a huge oil slick in the Gulf."

Cronkite said: "It's your assumption, not mine, that we're dealing with sane minds. Who but a crazy man would have endangered Galveston by blowing up your sister tanker there?"

The captain fell silent and pondered the question gloomily.

Cronkite went on: "Anyway, it's my intention—with your consent, of course—to search the engine room, living accommodations and every storage space on the ship. With the kind of search crew I have it shouldn't take more than half an hour.''

"What kind of preset time bomb do you think it might be?''

"I don't think it's a time bomb—or bombs—at all. I think that the detonator—or detonators—will be a certain radioactivated device that can be triggered by any nearby craft, plane or helicopter. But I don't think it's fixing to happen till you're close to the U.S. coast.''

"Why?''

"So we'll have maximum pollution along the shores. There'll be a national holler against Lord Worth and the safety standards aboard his—ah—rather superannuated tankers, maybe resulting in closing down of the *Seawitch* or the seizing of any of Worth's tankers that might enter American territorial waters.'' In addition to his many other specialized qualifications, Cronkite was a consummate liar. "Okay if I call my men?'' Captain Thompson nodded without any noticeable enthusiasm.

Cronkite lifted the loud-hailer and ordered the search party aboard. They came immediately, fourteen of them, all of them wearing stocking masks, all of them carrying machine pistols. Captain Thompson stared at them in stupefaction, then turned and stared some more at Cronkite and Mulhooney, both of whom had pistols leveled at him. Cronkite may have been looking satisfied or even triumphant, but such was the abundance of his ersatz facial foliage that it was impossible to tell.

Captain Thompson, in a stupefaction that was slowly turning into a slow burn, said: "What the hell goes?''

"You can see what goes. Hijack. A very popular pastime nowadays. I agree that nobody's ever hijacked a tanker before, but there always has to be a first time. Besides, it's not really something new. Piracy on the high seas. They've been at it for thousands of years. Don't try anything rash, Captain, and please don't try to be a hero. If you all behave, no harm will come to you. Anyway, what could you possibly do with fourteen submachine guns lined up against you?''

Within five minutes all the crew, officers and men, including the recovered radio operator but with one other exception, were herded into the crew's mess under armed guard. Nobody had even as much as contemplated offering resistance. The exception was an unhappy-looking duty engineer in the engine room. There are a few people who don't look slightly unhappy when staring at the muzzle of a Schmeisser from a distance of five feet.

Cronkite was on the bridge giving Mulhooney his final instructions.

"Keep on sending the *Seawitch* its half-hour on-time, on-course reports. Then report a minor breakdown in two or three hours—a fractured fuel line or something of the sort—enough that would keep the *Torbello* immobilized for a few hours. You're due in Galveston tonight and I need time and room to maneuver. Rather, *you* need time and room to maneuver. When it gets dark keep every navigational light extinguished—in fact, *every* light extinguished. Let's don't underestimate Lord Worth.'' Cronkite was speaking with an unaccustomed degree of bitterness, doubtless recalling the day Lord Worth had taken him to the cleaners in court. "He's a very powerful man, and it's quite in the cards that he can have an air-and-sea search mounted for his missing tanker.''

Cronkite rejoined the *Georgia,* cast off and pulled away. Mulhooney, too, got under way, but altered course ninety degrees to port so that he was heading southwest instead of northwest. On the first half hour he sent the reassuring report to the *Seawitch*—"on course, on time.''

Cronkite waited for the *Starlight* to join him, then both vessels proceeded together in a generally southeasterly direction until they were about thirty-five nautical miles from the *Seawitch,* safely over the horizon and out of reach of the *Seawitch*'s radar and sonar. They stopped their engines and settled down to wait.

The big Boeing had almost halved the distance between Florida and Washington. Lord Worth, in his luxurious stateroom immediately abaft the flight deck, was making up for time lost during the previous night and, blissfully unaware of the slings and arrows that were coming at him from all sides, was soundly asleep.

Mitchell had been unusually but perhaps not unexpectedly late in waking that morning. He showered, shaved and dressed while the coffee percolated, all the time conscious of a peculiar and unaccustomed sense of unease. He paced up and down the kitchen, drinking his coffee, then abruptly decided to put his unease at rest. He lifted the phone and dialed Lord Worth's mansion. The other end rang, rang again and kept on ringing. Mitchell replaced the receiver, then tried again with the same result. He finished his coffee, went across to Roomer's house and let himself in with his passkey. He went into the bedroom to find Roomer still asleep. He woke him up. Roomer regarded him with disfavor.

"What do you mean by waking up a man in the middle of the night?"

"It's not the middle of the night." He pulled open the drapes and the bright summer sunlight flooded the room. "It's broad daylight, as you will be able to see when you open your eyes."

"Your house on fire or something, then?"

"I wish it were something as trivial as that. I'm worried, John. I woke up feeling bugged by something, and the feeling got worse and worse. Five minutes ago I called up Lord Worth's house. I tried twice. There was no reply. Must have been at least eight or ten people in that house, but there was no reply."

"What do you think——"

"You're supposed to be the man with the intuition. Get ready. I'll go make some coffee."

Long before the coffee was ready, in fact less than ninety seconds later, Roomer was in the kitchen. He had of course neither showered nor shaved but had had time to run a comb through his hair. He was looking the same way the expressionless Mitchell was feeling."

"Never mind the coffee." Roomer bore an almost savage expression on his face, but Mitchell knew that it wasn't directed at him. "Let's get up to the house."

They took Roomer's car; it was nearer.

Mitchell said: "God, we're really bright! Hit us over the head often enough and maybe—just maybe—we'll begin to see the obvious." He held on to his seat as Roomer, tires screeching, rounded a blind corner. "Easy, boy, easy. Too late to lock the stable now."

With what was a clearly conscious effort of will, Roomer slowed down. He said: "Yeah, we're real clever. Lord Worth used a threat of the girls' abduction as an excuse for his actions. And you told him to offer the threat of the abduction as an excuse for our being there last night. And it never occurred to either of our staggering intellects that their kidnaping would be both logical and inevitable. Worth wasn't exaggerating—he has enemies, and vicious enemies who are out to get him. Two trump cards—and what trumps! He's powerless now. He'll give away half his money to get them back. Just half. He'll use the other half to hunt those people down. Money can buy any co-operation in the world, and the old boy *has* all the money in the world.''

Mitchell now seemed relaxed, comfortable, even calm. He said: "But we'll get to them first, won't we, John?"

Roomer stirred uncomfortably in his seat as they swung into the mansion's driveway. He said: "I'm just as sore as you are. But I don't like it when you start talking that way. You know that."

"I'm expressing an intention—or at least a hope." He smiled. "We'll see."

Roomer stopped his car in a fashion that did little good to Lord Worth's immaculately raked gravel. The first thing that caught Mitchell's eye as he left the car was an odd movement by the side of the driveway in a clump of bushes. He took out his gun and went to investigate, then put his gun away, opened his clasp knife and sliced through MacPherson's bonds. The head gardener, after forty years in Florida, had never lost a trace of a very pronounced Scottish accent, an accent that tended to thicken according to the degree of mental stress he was under-going. On this occasion, with the adhesive removed, his language was wholly indecipherable—which, in view of what he was almost certainly trying to say, was probably just as well.

They went through the front doorway. Jenkins, apparently taking his ease in a comfortable armchair, greeted them with a baleful glare. The glare was in no way intended for them; Jenkins was just in a baleful mood, a mood scarcely bettered by Mitchell's swift and painful yanking away of the adhesive from his lips. Jenkins took a deep breath, preparatory to lodging some form of protest, but Mitchell cut in before he could speak.

"Where does Jim sleep?" Jim was the radio operator.

Jenkins stared at him in astonishment. Was this the way to greet a man who had been through a living hell—snatched, one might almost say, from the jaws of death? Where was the sympathy, the condolence, the anxious questioning? Mitchell put his hands on his shoulders and shook him violently.

"Are you deaf? Jim's room?"

Jenkins looked at the grim face less than a foot from his own and decided against remonstrating. "In back, first floor, first right."

Mitchell left. So, after a second or two, did Roomer. Jenkins called after him in a plaintive voice: "You aren't leaving me too, Mr. Roomer?"

Roomer turned and said patiently: "I'm going to the kitchen to get a nice sharp carver. Mr. Mitchell has taken the only knife we have between us."

Jim Robertson was young, fresh-faced and just out of college, a graduate in electrical engineering in no hurry to proceed with his profession. He sat on the bed massaging his now unbound wrists, wincing slightly as the circulation began to return. As tiers of knots, Durand's henchmen had been nothing if not enthusiastic.

Mitchell said: "How do you feel?"

"Mad."

"I don't blame you. Are you okay to operate your set?"

"I'm okay for anything if it means getting hold of those bastards."

"That's the general idea. Did you get a good look at the kidnapers?"

"I can give you a general description." He broke off and stared at Mitchell. *"Kidnapers?"*

"Looks as though Lord Worth's daughters have been abducted."

"Holy Christ!" The assimilation of this news took some little time. "There'll be all hell to pay for this."

"It should cause a considerable flap. Do you know where Marina's room is?"

"I'll show you."

Her room showed all signs of a hasty and unpremeditated departure. Cupboard doors were open, drawers the same, and some spilled clothing lay on the floor. Mitchell was interested in none of this. He quickly riffled through drawers in the room until he found what he had hoped to find—her States passport. He opened it and it was valid. He made a mental note that she had lied about her age—she was two years older than she claimed to be—returned the passport and hurried down to the radio room with Robertson, who unlocked the door to let them in. Robertson looked questioningly at Mitchell.

"The county police chief. His name is McGarrity. I don't want anyone else. Tell him you're speaking for Lord Worth. That should work wonders. Then let me take over."

Roomer entered while Robertson was trying to make contact. "Seven more of the staff, all suitably immobilized. Makes nine in all. I've left Jenkins to cut them loose. His hands are shaking so bad he'll probably slice an artery or two, but for me freeing elderly cooks and young housemaids is above and beyond the call of duty."

"They must have been carrying a mile of rope," Mitchell said absently. He was figuring out how much not to tell the police chief.

Roomer nodded to the operator. "Who's he trying to contact?"

"McGarrity."

"That hypocritical old brown-noser!"

"Most people would regard that as a charitable description. But he has his uses."

Robertson looked up. "On the line, Mr. Mitchell. That phone." He made discreetly to replace his own, but Roomer took it from him and listened in.

"Chief McGarrity?"

"Speaking."

"Please listen very carefully. This is extremely important and urgent, and the biggest thing that's ever come your way. Are you alone?"

"Yes. I'm all alone." McGarrity's tone held an odd mixture of suspicion and aroused interest.

"Nobody listening in, no recorder?"

"Goddam it, no. Get to the point."

"We're speaking from Lord Worth's house. You know of him?"

"Don't be a damned fool. Who's 'we'?"

"My name is Michael Mitchell. My partner is John Roomer. We're licensed private investigators."

"I've heard of you. You're the guys who give the local law so much trouble."

"I'd put it the other way around, but that's beside the point. What is to the point is that Lord Worth's two daughters have been kidnaped."

"Merciful God in heaven!" There ensued what could fairly have been described as a stunned silence at the other end of the line.

Roomer smiled sardonically and covered the mouthpiece. "Can't you see the old phony grabbing his seat, with his eyes popping and big signs saying 'Promotion' flashing in front of him?"

"Kidnaped, you said?" McGarrity's voice had suddenly developed a certain hoarseness.

"Kidnaped. Abducted. Snatched."

"Sure of this?"

"Sure as can be. The girls' rooms have all the signs of hurried and

unplanned departure. Nine of the staff were bound and gagged. What would
you conclude from that?''

"Kidnap." McGarrity made it sound as if he'd made the discovery all by
himself.

"Can you put a block on all escape routes? They haven't taken the girls'
passports, so that rules out international flights. I hardly think the kidnapers
would have taken any commercial domestic flight. Can you see Lord Worth's
daughters going through any airline terminal without being recognized? I'd
put a stop order and guard at every private airfield and helicopter pad in the
southern part of the state. And likewise at every port, big and small, in the
same area.''

McGarrity sounded bemused, befuddled. "That'd call for hundreds of
policemen.''

The tone of anguished protest was unmistakable. Mitchell sighed, cupped
the mouthpiece, looked at Roomer and said: "Man's out of his depth. Can
I call him lunk-head?'' He removed his hand. "Look, Chief McGarrity, I
don't think you realize what you're sitting on. We're talking about the
daughters of Lord Worth. You could pick up your phone and get a thousand
cops for the asking. You could call out the National Guard if you wanted
to—I'm sure Lord Worth would pick up the tab for every cent of expenses.
Good God, man, there's been nothing like this since the Lindbergh kidnaping!''

"That's so, that's so.'' It wasn't difficult to visualize McGarrity licking
his lips. "Descriptions?''

"Not much help there, I'm afraid. They all wore stocking masks. The
leader wore gloves, which may or may not indicate a criminal record. All
were big, well-built men and all wore dark business suits. I don't have to
give you a description of the girls, I guess.''

"Marina and Melinda?'' McGarrity was a classic snob of awesome proportions, who followed with avid interest the comings and goings of alleged
society, of the internationally famous and infamous. "Hell, no. Of course
not. They're probably the most photographed pair in the state.''

"You'll keep this under wraps, tight as possible, for the moment?''

"I will, I will.'' McGarrity had his baby clutched close to his heart, and
nobody, but nobody was going to take it away from him.

"Lord Worth will have to be informed first of all. I'll refer him to you.''

"You mean you haven't told him yet?'' McGarrity could hardly believe
his good fortune.

"No.''

"Tell him to take it easy—well, as easy as he can, that is. Tell him I'm
taking complete and personal charge of the investigation.''

"I'll do that, Chief.''

Roomer winced and screwed his eyes shut.

McGarrity sounded positively brisk. "Now, about the local law.''

"I suppose I've got to call them in. I'm not too happy about it: they don't
exactly like us. What if they refuse to keep this under wraps . . . ?''

"In which case,'' McGarrity said ominously, "just put the person concerned directly on the line to me. Anyone else know about this yet?''

"Of course not. You're the only man with the power to authorize the
closing of the escape routes. Naturally we contacted you first.''

"And you were perfectly right, Mr. Mitchell.'' McGarrity was warm and
appreciative, as well he might have been, for he had a very shaky re-election
coming up and the massive publicity the kidnaping was bound to generate
would guarantee him a virtual shoo-in. "I'll get the wheels turning at this
end. Keep me posted.''

"Of course, Chief." Mitchell hung up.

Roomer looked at him admiringly. "You are an even bigger and stickier hypocrite than McGarrity."

"Practice. Anyway, we got what we wanted." Mitchell's face was somber. "Has it occurred to you that the birds may have flown?"

Roomer looked equally unhappy. "Yeah. But first things first. Lord Worth next?" Mitchell nodded. "I'll pass this one up. They say that, under provocation, he has a rich command of the English language, not at all aristocratic. I'd be better employed interviewing the staff. I'll ply them with strong drink to help them overcome the rigors of their ordeal and to loosen their tongues—Lord Worth's reserve Dom Perignon for choice—and see what I can get out of them. I don't expect much. All I can do is ask them about descriptions and voices and whether or not they touched anything that might give us fingerprints. Not that that will help if their prints aren't on file."

"The brandy bit sounds the best part of your program. Ask Jenkins to bring a large one"—he looked at Robertson—"*two* large ones."

Roomer was at the door when he turned. "Do you know what happened in ancient times to the bearers of bad news?"

"I know. They got their heads cut off."

"He'll probably blame us for carelessness and lack of foresight—and he'll be right, too, even though he's just as guilty as we are." Roomer left.

"Get me Lord Worth, Jim."

"I would if I knew where he was. He was here last night when I left."

"He's on the *Seawitch*."

Robertson raised an eyebrow, lowered it, said nothing and turned his attention to the switchboard. He raised the *Seawitch* in fifteen seconds. Mitchell took the phone.

"Lord Worth, please."

"Hold on."

Another voice came on, a rasping gravelly voice, not as friendly.

"What d'you want?"

"Lord Worth, please."

"How do you know he's here?"

"How do I—what does that matter? May I speak to him?"

"Look, mister, I'm here to protect Lord Worth's privacy. We get far too many oddball calls from oddball characters. How did you know he was here?"

"Because he told me."

"When?"

"Last night. About midnight."

"What's your name?"

"Mitchell. Michael Mitchell."

"Mitchell." Larsen's tone changed. "Why didn't you say so in the first place?"

"Because I didn't expect a Gestapo third degree, that's why. You must be Commander Larsen."

"That's me."

"Not very civil, are you?"

"I've got a job to do."

"Lord Worth."

"He's not here."

"He wouldn't lie to me." Mitchell thought it impolitic to add that he'd actually seen Lord Worth take off.

"He didn't lie to you. He was here. He left hours ago for Washington."

Mitchell was silent for a few moments while he considered. "Any number where he can be reached?"

"Yes. Why?"

"I didn't ask you why he'd gone to Washington. It's an urgent, private and personal matter. From what I've heard of you from Lord Worth, and that's quite a bit, you'd react in exactly the same way. Give me the number and I'll call back and fill you in just as soon as Lord Worth gives me clearance."

"Your word on that?"

Mitchell gave his promise and Larsen gave him the number.

Mitchell replaced the receiver. He said to Robertson: "Lord Worth has left the *Seawitch* and gone to Washington."

"He does get around. In his Boeing, I presume?"

"I didn't ask. I took that for granted. Do you think you can reach him on the plane?"

Robertson didn't look encouraging. "When did he leave the *Seawitch?*"

"I don't know. Should have asked, I suppose. Hours ago, Larsen said."

Robertson looked even more discouraged. "I wouldn't hold out any hope, Mr. Mitchell. With this set I can reach out a couple of thousand miles. Lord Worth's Boeing can reach any airport not quite as far away, just as the airport can reach him. But the receiving equipment aboard the Boeing hasn't been modified to receive long-range transmissions from this set, which is very specialized. Short-range only. Five hundred miles, if that. The Boeing is bound to be well out of range by now."

"Freak weather conditions?"

"Mighty rare, Mr. Mitchell."

"Try anyway, Jim."

He tried and kept on trying for five minutes, during which it became steadily more apparent that Lord Worth would have at least a bit more time before being set up for his coronary. At the end of five minutes Robertson shrugged his shoulders and looked up at Mitchell.

"Thanks for the try, Jim." He gave Robertson a piece of paper with a number on it. "Washington. Think you can reach that?"

"That I can guarantee."

"Try for it in half an hour. Ask for Lord Worth. Emphasize the urgency. If you don't contact him, try again every twenty minutes. You have a direct line to the study?"

"Yes."

"I'll be there. I have to welcome the law."

Lord Worth, still happily unaware of his disintegrating world, slept soundly. The Boeing, at thirty-three thousand feet, was just beginning its descent to Dulles Airport.

5

LORD WORTH, a glass of scotch in one hand and an illegal Cuban cigar in the other, was comfortably ensconced in a deep armchair in the very plush office of the Assistant Secretary of State. He should have been contented and relaxed: he was, in fact, highly discontented and completely unrelaxed. He was becoming mad, steadily and far from slowly, at the world in general and at the four other people in that room in particular.

The four consisted of Howell, the Assistant Secretary, a tall, thin, keen-faced man with steel-framed glasses who looked like, and in fact was, a Yale professor. The second was his personal assistant, whose name, fittingly enough, Lord Worth had failed to catch, for he had about him the gray anonymity of a top-flight civil servant. The third was Lieutenant-General Zweicker, and all that could be said about him was that he looked every inch a general. The fourth was a middle-aged stenographer who appeared to take notes of the discussion whenever the mood struck her, which didn't appear to be very often: most likely, long experience had taught her that most of what was said at any conference wasn't worth noting anyway.

Lord Worth said: "I'm a very tired man who has just flown up from the Gulf of Mexico. I have spent twenty-five minutes here and appear to have wasted my time. Well, gentlemen, I have no intention of wasting my time. My time is as important as yours. Correction. It's a damn sight more important. 'The big brush-off,' I believe it's called."

"How can you call it a brush-off? You're sitting in my office and General Zweicker is here. How many other citizens rate that kind of treatment?"

"The bigger the façade, the bigger the brush-off. I am not accustomed to dealing with underlings. I am accustomed to dealing with the very top, which I haven't quite reached yet, but will. The cool, diplomatic, deep-freeze treatment will not work. I am no troublemaker, but I'll go any lengths to secure justice. You can't sweep me under your diplomatic carpet, Mr. Howell. I told you recently that there were international threats against the *Seawitch*, and you chose either to disbelieve me or ignore me. I come to you now with additional proof that I am threatened—three naval vessels heading for the *Seawitch*—and still you propose to take no action. And I would point out, incidentally, if you still don't know independently of the movements of those vessels, then it's time you got yourselves a new intelligence service."

General Zweicker said: "We are aware of those movements. But as yet we see no justification for taking any kind of action. You have no proof that what you claim is true. Suspicions, no more. Do you seriously expect us to alert naval units and a squadron of fighter-bombers on the unproven and what may well be the unfounded suspicions of a private citizen?"

"That's it in a nutshell," Howell said. "And I would remind you, Lord Worth, that you're not even an American citizen."

" 'Not even an American citizen.' " He turned to the stenographer. "I trust you made a note of that." He lifted his hand as Howell made to speak. "Too late, Howell. Too late to retrieve your blunder—a blunder, I may say, of classical proportions. Not an American citizen? I would point out that I paid more taxes last year than all your precious oil companies in the States combined—this apart from supplying the cheapest oil to the United States. If the level of competence of the State Department is typical of the way this country is run, then I can only rejoice in the fact that I still retain a British passport. One law for Americans, another for the heathen beyond the pale. Even-handed justice. 'Not an American citizen.' This should make a particularly juicy tidbit for the news conference I intend to hold immediately after I leave."

"A news conference?" Howell betrayed unmistakable signs of agitation.

"Certainly." Lord Worth's tone was as grim as his face. "If you people won't protect me, then, by God, I'll protect myself."

Howell looked at the general, then back to Lord Worth. He strove to inject an official and intimidating note into his voice. "I would remind you that any discussions that take place here are strictly confidential."

Lord worth eyed him coldly. "It's always sad to see a man who has missed his true vocation. You should have been a comedian, Howell, not a senior member of government. Confidential. That's good. How can you remind me of something you never even mentioned before? Confidential. If there wasn't a lady present I'd tell you what I really think of your asinine remark. God, it's rich, a statement like that coming from the number two in a government department with so splendid a record of leaking state secrets to muckraking journalists, doubtless in return for a suitable *quid pro quo*. I cannot abide hypocrisy. And this makes another juicy tidbit for the press conference—the State Department tried to gag me. Classical blunder number two, Howell."

Howell said nothing. He looked as if he were considering the advisability of wringing his hands.

"I shall inform the press conference of the indecision, reluctance, inaction, incompetence and plain running-scared vacillation of a State Department which will be responsible for the loss of a hundred-million-dollar oil rig, the stopping of cheap supplies of fuel to the American people, the biggest oil slick in history, and the possible—no, I would say probable— beginnings of a third major war. In addition to holding this news conference, I shall buy TV and radio time, explain the whole situation, and further explain that I am forced to go to those extraordinary lengths because of the refusal and inability of the State Department to protect me." He paused. "That was rather silly of me. I have my own TV and radio stations. It's going to be such a burning-hot topic that the big three companies will jump at it and it won't cost me a cent. By tonight I'll have the name of the State Department, particularly the names of you and your boss, if not exactly blackened, at least tarnished across the country. I'm a desperate man, gentlemen, and I'm prepared to adopt desperate methods."

He paused for their reactions. Facially they were all he could have wished. Howell, his assistant and the general all too clearly realized that Lord Worth meant every word he said. The implications were too horrendous to contemplate. But no one said anything, so Lord Worth took up the conversational burden again.

"Finally, gentlemen, you base your pusillanimous refusal to act on the fact that I have no proof of evil intent. I do, in fact, possess such proof, and it's cast iron. I will not lay this proof before you because it is apparent that I will achieve nothing here. I require a decision-maker, and the Secretary has the reputation for being just that. I suggest you get him here."

"*Get* the Secretary?" Howell's ears were clearly appalled by this suggested *lèse majesté*. "One doesn't 'get' the Secretary. People make appointments days, even weeks, in advance. Besides, he is in a very important conference."

Lord Worth remained unmoved. "Get him. This conference he'd better have with me will be the most important of his life. If he elects not to come, then he's probably holding the last conference of his political career. I know he's not twenty yards from here. Get him."

"I—I don't really think——"

Lord Worth rose. "I hope your immediate successors—and the operative word is 'immediate'—will, for the country's sake, display more common sense and intestinal fortitude than you have. Tell the man who, through your gross negligence and cowardly refusal to face facts, will be held primarily responsible for the outbreak of the next war, to watch TV tonight. You have had your chance—as your stenographer's notebook will show—and you've thrown it away." Lord Worth shook his head, almost in sadness. "There are none so blind as those who will not see—especially a spluttering fuse leading to a keg of dynamite. I bid you good day, gentlemen."

"No! No!" Howell was in a state of very considerable agitation. "Sit down! Sit down! I'll see what I can do."

He practically ran from the room.

During his rather protracted absence—he was gone for exactly thirteen minutes—conversation in the room was minimal.

Zweicker said: "You really mean what you say, don't you?"

"Do you doubt me, General?"

"Not any more. You really intend to carry out those threats?"

"I think the word you want is 'promises.' "

After this effective conversation-stopper an uncomfortable silence fell on the room. Only Lord Worth appeared in no way discomforted. He was, or appeared to be, calm and relaxed, which was quite a feat, because he knew that the appearance or nonappearance of the Secretary meant whether he had won or lost.

He'd won. The Secretary, John Benton, when Howell nervously ushered him in, didn't look at all like his reputation—which was that of a tough, shrewd-minded, hard-nosed negotiator, ruthless when the situation demanded and not much given to consulting his cabinet colleagues when it came to decision-making. He looked like a prosperous farmer and exuded warmth and geniality—which deceived Lord Worth, a man who specialized in warmth and geniality not a whit. Here, indeed, was a very different kettle of fish from Howell, a man worthy of Lord Worth's mettle. Lord Worth rose.

Benton shook his hand warmly. "Lord Worth! This is a rare privilege— to have, if I may be forgiven the unoriginal turn of speech, to have America's top oil tycoon calling on us."

Lord Worth was courteous but not deferential. "I wish it were under happier circumstances. My pleasure, Mr. Secretary. It's most kind of you to spare a few moments. Well, five minutes, no more. My promise."

"Take as long as you like." Benton smiled. "You have the reputation for not bandying words. I happen to share that sentiment."

"Thank you." He looked at Howell. "Thirteen minutes to cover forty yards." He looked back at the Secretary. "Mr. Howell will have—ah— apprised you of the situation?"

"I have been fairly well briefed. What do you require of us?" Lord Worth refrained from beaming: here was a man after his own heart. John Benton continued: "We can, of course, approach the Soviet and Venezuelan ambassadors, but that's like approaching a pair of powderpuffs. All they can do is report our suspicions and veiled threats to their respective governments. They're powerless, really. Even ten years ago ambassadors carried weight. They could negotiate and make decisions. Not any more. They have become, through no fault of their own, faceless and empty people who are consistently bypassed in state-to-state negotiations. Even their second chauffeurs, who are customarily trained espionage agents, wield vastly more power than the ambassadors themselves.

"Alternatively, we can make a direct approach to the governments concerned. But for that we would have to have proof. Your word doesn't come into question, but it's not enough. We must be able to adduce positive proof of, shall we say, nefarious intent."

Lord Worth replied immediately. "Such proof I can adduce and can give you the outline now. I am extremely reluctant to name names because it will mean the end of a professional career of a friend of mine. But if I have to, that I will do. Whether I release those names to you or to the public will depend entirely upon the department's reaction. If I can't receive a promise of action after I have given you this outline, then I have no recourse other than to approach the public. This is not blackmail. I'm in a corner and the only solution is to fight my way out of it. If you will, as I hope you will, give me a favorable reaction, I shall, of course, give you a list of names, which, I would hope, will not be published by your department. Secrecy, in other words. Not, of course, that this will prevent you from letting loose the FBI the moment I board my helicopter out there."

"The great warm heart of the American public versus the incompetent bumbling of the State Department." Benton smiled. "One begins to understand why you are a millionaire—I do apologize, billionaire."

"Earlier this week a highly secret meeting was held in a lakeside resort out west. Ten people, all of them very senior oilmen, attended this meeting. Four were Americans, representing many of the major oil companies in the States. A fifth was from Honduras. A sixth was from Venezuela, a seventh from Nigeria. Numbers eight and nine were oil sheikhs from the Gulf. The last was from the Soviet Union. As he was the only one there who had no interest whatsoever in the flow of oil into the United States, one can only presume that he was there to stir up as much trouble as possible."

Lord Worth looked around at the five people in the room. That he had their collective ear was beyond dispute. Satisfied, he continued.

"The meeting had one purpose and one only in mind. To stop me and to stop me at all costs. More precisely, they wanted to stop the flow of oil from the *Seawitch*—that is the name of my oil rig—because I was considerably undercutting them in price and thereby raising all sorts of fiscal problems. If there are any rules or ethics in the oil business I have as yet to detect any. I believe your congressional investigative committees would agree one hundred per cent with me on that. Incidentally, North Hudson—that's the official name of my company—has never been investigated.

"The only permanent way to stop the flow of oil is to destroy the *Seawitch*. Halfway through the meeting they called in a professional troubleshooter, a man whom I know well, and a highly dangerous man at that. For reasons I won't explain until I get some sort of guarantee of help, he has a deep and bitter grudge against me. He also happens—just coincidentally, of course—to be one of the world's top experts, if not the very top, on the use of high explosives."

"After the meeting this troubleshooter called aside the Venezuelan and Soviet delegates and asked for naval cooperation. This he was guaranteed." Lord Worth looked at the company with a singular lack of enthusiasm. "Now perhaps you people will believe me."

"I would add that this man so hates me that he would probably do the job for nothing. However, he has asked for—and got—a fee of a million dollars. He also asked for—and got—ten million dollars' 'operating expenses.' What does ten million dollars mean to you—except the unlimited use of violence?"

"Preposterous! Incredible!" The Secretary shook his head. "It has, of course, to be true. You are singularly well-informed, Lord Worth. You would appear to have an intelligence service to rival our own."

"Better. I pay them more. This oil business is a jungle and it's a case of the survival of the most devious."

"Industrial espionage?"

"Most certainly not." It was just possible that Lord Worth actually believed this.

"This friend who may be coming to the end of his——"

"Yes."

"Give me all the details, including a list of the names. Put a cross against the name of your friend. I shall see to it that he is not implicated and that only I will see that list."

"You are very considerate, Mr. Secretary."

"In return I shall consult with Defense and the Pentagon." He paused. "Even that will not be necessary. In return I can personally guarantee you a sufficiency of air and sea cover against any normal or even considerable hazard."

Lord Worth didn't doubt him. Benton had the reputation of being a man of unshakable integrity. More important, he had the justly deserved reputation of being the President's indispensable right-hand man. Benton delivered. Lord Worth decided against showing too much relief.

"I cannot tell you how deeply grateful I am." He looked at the stenographer and then at Howell. "If I could borrow this lady's services——"

"Of course." The stenographer turned to a fresh page in her notebook and waited expectantly.

Lord Worth said: "The place—Lake Tahoe, California. The address——"

The telephone jangled. The stenographer gave Lord Worth an "excuse me" smile and picked up the handset. Howell said to the Secretary: "Dammit, I gave the strictest instructions——"

"It's for Lord Worth." She was looking at Benton. "A Mr. Mitchell from Florida. Extremely urgent." The Secretary nodded and the stenographer rose and handed the phone to Lord Worth.

"Michael? How did you know I was here . . . Yes, I'm listening."

He listened without interruption. As he did so, to the considerable consternation of those watching him, the color drained from his tanned cheeks and left them an unhealthy sallow color. It was Benton himself who rose, poured out a brandy and brought it across to Lord Worth, who took it blindly and drained the not inconsiderable contents at a gulp. Benton took the glass from him and went for a refill. When he came back Lord Worth took the drink but left it untouched. Instead he handed the instrument to Benton and held his left hand over his now screwed-shut eyes.

Benton spoke into the phone. "State Department. Who's speaking?"

Mitchell's voice was faint but clear. "Michael Mitchell, from Lord Worth's home. Is that—is that Dr. Benton?"

"Yes. Lord Worth seems to have received a severe shock."

"Yes, sir. His two daughters have been kidnaped."

"Good God above!" Benton's habitual imperturbability had received a severe dent. No one had ever seen him register shock before. Perhaps it was the bluntness of the announcement. "Are you sure?"

"I wish to hell I wasn't, sir."

"Who are you?"

"We—my partner John Roomer and I—are private investigators. We are not here in an investigative capacity. We are here because we are neighbors and friends of Lord Worth and his daughters."

"Called the police?"

"Yes."

"What's been done?"

"We have arranged for the blocking of all air and sea escape routes."

"You have descriptions?"

"Poor. Five men, heavily armed, wearing stocking masks."

"What's your opinion of the local law?"

"Low."

"I'll call in the FBI."

"Yes, sir. But as the criminals haven't been traced, there's no evidence that they've crossed the state line."

"Hell with state lines and regulations. If I say they're called in, that's it. Hold on. I think Lord Worth would like another word." Lord Worth took the receiver. Some color had returned to his cheeks.

"I'm leaving now. Less than three hours, I should say. I'll radio from the Boeing half an hour out. Meet me at the airport."

"Yes, sir. Commander Larsen would like to know——"

"Tell him." Lord Worth replaced the phone, took another sip of the brandy. "There's no fool like an old fool, and only a blind fool would have overlooked so obvious a move. This is war, even if undeclared war, and in war no holds are barred. To think that it should come to this before you had incontrovertible proof that I am indeed under siege. Unforgivable. To have left my daughters unguarded was wholly unforgivable. Why didn't I have the sense to leave Mitchell and Roomer on guard?" He looked at his now-empty glass and the stenographer took it away.

Benton was faintly skeptical. "But against *five* armed men?"

Lord Worth looked at him morosely. "I had forgotten that you don't know those men. Mitchell, for example, could have taken care of them all by himself. He's lethal."

"So they're your friends, and you respect them. Don't take offense, Lord Worth, but is there any way that they could be implicated in this?"

"You must be out of your mind." Lord Worth, still morose, sipped his third brandy. "Sorry. I'm not myself. Sure, they'd like to kidnap my daughters, almost as much as my daughters would like to be kidnaped by them."

"That the way it is?" Benton seemed mildly astonished. In his experience, billionaires' daughters did not normally associate with the likes of private investigators.

"That's the way. And in answer to your next two questions: yes, I approve and no, they don't give a damn about my money." He shook his head wonderingly. "It is extremely odd. And I shall forecast this, Mr. Secretary. When Marina and Melinda are brought back to me it won't be through the good offices of either the local police or your precious FBI. Mitchell and Roomer will bring them back. One does not wish to sound overly dramatic, but they would, quite literally, give their lives for my daughters."

"And, as a corollary, they would cut down anyone who got in their way?"

For the first time since the phone call Lord Worth smiled, albeit faintly. "I'll take the fifth amendment on that one."

"I must meet those paragons sometime."

"Just as long as it's not over the wrong end of Mitchell's gun." He rose, leaving his drink unfinished, and looked round the room. "I must go. Thank you all for your kindness and consideration, not to say forebearance." He left, with the Secretary by his side.

When the door closed behind him General Zweicker rose and poured himself a brandy. "Well. What may be the kidnaping of the century pales into insignificance compared to the likelihood of the Russkies starting to throw things at us." He took some brandy. "Don't tell me I'm the only person who can see the hellish witches' brew Lord Worth is stirring up for us?"

It was clear that all three listening to him had a very sharp view of the cauldron. Howell said: "Let's give Lord Worth his due. He could even be right when he says he's glad he's got a British passport. The stirrers-up are our own compatriots; the holier-than-thou major American oil companies, who are willing to crucify Lord Worth and put their country at jeopardy because of their blind stupidity."

"I don't care who's responsible." The stenographer's voice was plaintive. "Does anyone know where I can get a bomb shelter cheap?"

Benton led Worth down one flight of stairs and out onto the sunlit lawn, where the helicopter was waiting.

Benton said: "Ever tried to find words to tell someone how damnably sorry you feel?"

"I know from experience. Don't try. But thanks."

"I could have our personal physician accompany you down to Florida."

"Thanks again. But I'm fine now."

"And you haven't had lunch?" Benton, clearly, was finding conversational gambits heavy going.

"As I don't much care for plastic lunches from plastic trays, I have an excellent French chef aboard my plane." Again a faint smile. "And two stewardesses, chosen solely for their good looks. I shall not want."

They reached the steps of the helicopter. Benton said: "You've had neither the time nor opportunity to give me that list of names. For the moment that's of no consequence. I just want you to know that my guarantee of protection remains in force."

Lord Worth shook his hand silently and climbed the steps.

By this time Conde, aboard the *Roamer,* had arrived at the *Seawitch,* and the big derrick crane aboard the platform was unloading the heavy weaponry and mines from the Louisiana arsenal. It was a slow and difficult task, for the tip of the derrick boom was two hundred feet above sea level and, in all, the transfer was to take about three hours. As each dual-purpose antiaircraft gun came aboard Larsen selected its site and supervised Palermo and some of his men in securing it in position: this was done by drilling holes in the concrete platform, then anchoring the gun-carriage base with sledgehammer-driven steel spikes. The guns were supposed to be recoilless, but then neither Larsen nor Palermo was much given to taking chances.

The depth charges, when they came, were stacked together in three groups, each halfway between the three apexes of the triangle. That there was an inherent risk in this Larsen was well aware: a stray bullet or shell—or perhaps not so stray—could well trigger the detonating mechanism of one of the depth charges, which would inevitably send up the other charges in sympathetic detonation. But it was a risk that had to be taken if for no other reason than the fact that there was no other place where they could be stored ready for immediate use. And when and if the time came for their use the need would be immediate.

The drilling crew watched Palermo and his men at work, their expressions ranging from disinterest to approval. Neither group of men spoke to the other. Larsen was no great believer in fraternization.

Things were going well. The defensive system was being steadily installed. The Christmas tree, the peculiar name given to the valve which controlled the flow of oil from the already tapped reservoir, was wide open and oil was being steadily pumped to the huge storage tank while the derrick drill, set at its widest angle, was driving ever deeper into the substratum of the ocean floor, seeking to discover as yet untapped oil deposits. All was going well, there were no overt signs of attack or preparation for attack from air or sea, but Larsen was not as happy as he might have been, even despite the fact that they were still receiving the half-hour regular "on-course, on-time" reports from the *Torbello*.

He was unhappy partly because of the nonexistence of the *Tiburon*. He had recently learned from Galveston that there was no vessel listed in naval or coast guard registries under the name *Tiburon*. He had then asked that they check civilian registrations and had been told that this was a forlorn hope. It would take many hours, perhaps days, to carry out this type of investigation, and private vessels, unless fully insured, would show up neither in official registries nor in those of the major marine-insurance companies. There was no law which said they had to be insured, and the owners of the older and more decrepit craft didn't even bother to insure: there are such things as tax write-offs.

Larsen was not to know that his quest was a hopeless one. When Mulhooney had first taken over the *Tiburon* it had been called the *Hammond,* which he had thoughtfully had painted out and replaced by the name *Tiburon* on the way to Galveston. Since Cronkite had since replaced that by the name *Georgia,* both the *Hammond* and the *Tiburon* had ceased to exist.

But what concerned Larsen even more was his conviction that something was far wrong. He was unable to put a finger on what this might be. He was essentially a pragmatist of the first order, but he was also a man who relied heavily on instinct and intuition. He was a man occasionally given to powerful premonitions, and more often than not those premonitions had turned into reality. And so when the loudspeaker boomed "Commander Larsen to the radio cabin, Commander Larsen to the radio cabin," he was possessed of an immediate certainty that the hour of his premonition had come.

He walked leisurely enough toward the radio cabin, partly because it would never do for Commander Larsen to be seen hurrying anxiously anywhere, partly because he was in no great hurry to hear the bad news he was convinced he was about to hear. He told the radio operator that he would like to take this call privately, waited until the man had left and closed the door behind him, then picked up the telephone.

"Commander Larsen."

"Mitchell. I promised I'd call."

"Thanks. Heard from Lord Worth? He said he'd keep in touch, but no word."

"No wonder. His daughters have been kidnaped."

Larsen said nothing immediately. Judging from the ivoried knuckles, the telephone handpiece seemed in danger of being crushed. Although caring basically only for himself, he had formed an avuncular attachment toward Lord Worth's daughters, but even that was unimportant compared to the implications the kidnaping held for the welfare of the *Seawitch*. When he did speak it was in a steady, controlled voice.

"When did this happen?"

"This morning. And no trace of them. We've blocked every escape route in the southern part of the state. And there is no report from any port or airport of any unusual departure since the time of the kidnaping."

"Vanished into thin air?"

"Vanished, anyway. But not into thin air, we think. Terra firma, more likely. We think they've gone to earth, and are holed up not far away. But it's only a guess."

"No communication, no demands, from the kidnapers?"

"None. That's what makes it all so odd."

"You think this is a ransom kidnap?"

"No."

"The *Seawitch?*"

"Yes."

"Do you know why Lord Worth went to Washington?"

"No. I'd like to."

"To demand naval protection. Early this morning a Russian destroyer and a Cuban submarine left Havana, while another destroyer left Venezuela. They are on converging courses. The point of convergence would appear to be the *Seawitch.*"

There was a silence, then Mitchell said: "This is for sure?"

"Yes. Well, Lord Worth's cup of woes would seem to be fairly full. The only consolation is that nothing much else can happen to him after this. Please keep me informed."

In Lord Worth's radio room both Mitchell and Roomer hung up their phones.

Mitchell briefly indulged in some improper language. "God, I never thought his enemies would go to this length."

Roomer said: "Neither did I. I'm not sure that I even think so now."

"You mean Uncle Sam's not going to let any foreign naval powers play games in our own backyard?"

"Something like that. I don't think the Soviets would go so far as to risk a confrontation. Could be a bluff, a diversionary move. Maybe the real attack is coming from elsewhere."

"Maybe anything. Could be a double bluff. One thing's sure: Larsen's right in saying that Lord Worth's cup of woes is fairly full. In fact, I'd say it was running over."

"Looks that way," Roomer said absently. His thoughts were clearly elsewhere.

Mitchell said: "Don't tell me you're in the throes of intuition again?"

"I'm not sure. When you were talking to Larsen just now you mentioned 'terra firma.' Firm land, dry land. What if it weren't dry land? What if it were *un*firm land?"

Mitchell waited patiently.

Roomer said: "If you wanted to hole up, really get lost in Florida, where would you go?"

Mitchell hardly had to think. "You're right! Unfirm land, infirm land, whatever you want to call it. The Everglades, of course. Where else?"

"Man could hide out for a month there, and a battalion of troops couldn't find him. Which explains why the cops have been unable to find the station wagon." Between them, MacPherson and Jenkins had been able to give a fairly accurate description of the kidnapers' wagon. "They've been checking the highways and byways. I'll bet they never even thought of checking the roads into the swamps."

"Did we?"

"Right. We blew it. There are dozens of those roads into the glades, but most of them are very short and right away you reach a point where a wheeled vehicle can't go any farther. A few dozen police cars could comb the nearest swamps in an hour."

Mitchell said to Robertson: "Get Chief McGarrity."

A knock came on the half-open door and Louise, one of the young housemaids, entered. She held a card in her hand. She said: "I was just making up Miss Marina's bed when I found this between the sheets.''

Mitchell took the card. It was a plain calling card giving Marina's name and address.

Louise said: "Other side."

Mitchell reversed the card, holding it so that Roomer could see. Handwritten with a ballpoint were the words: "Vacation. Little island in the sun. No swimsuit.''

"You know Marina's handwriting, Louise?" Mitchell had suddenly realized that he didn't.

The girl looked at the card. "Yes, sir. I'm sure."

"Thanks, Louise. This could be very useful." Louise smiled and left. Mitchell said to Roomer: "What kind of lousy detective are you? Why didn't *you* think of searching the bedrooms?"

"Hmm. She must have asked them to leave while she dressed."

"You'd have thought she'd have been too scared to think of this."

"The handwriting's steady enough. Besides, she doesn't scare easily. Except, that is, when you point a gun between her eyes."

"I wish, right here and now, that I was pointing a gun between someone else's eyes. Little island in the sun where you can't go bathing. An overconfident kidnaper can talk too much. You thinking what I'm thinking?"

Roomer nodded. "The *Seawitch*."

At thirty-three thousand feet, Lord Worth had just completed a light but delicious lunch accompanied by a splendid Bordeaux wine, specially laid down for him in a Rothschild winery. He had regained his habitual calm. He was almost philosophical. He had, he reckoned, touched his nadir. All that could happen had happened. In common with Larsen, Mitchell and Roomer, he was convinced that the fates could touch him no more. All four were completely and terribly wrong. The worst was yet to come. It was, in fact, happening right then.

Colonel Farquharson, Lieutenant-Colonel Dewings, and Major Breckley were not in fact the people their ID cards claimed they were, for the sufficient reason that there were no officers of that rank with corresponding names in the U.S. Army. But then, it was a very big army, and nobody, not even the officers, could possibly be expected to know the names of more than a tiny fraction of their fellow officers. Nor were their faces their normal faces, although they could hardly be described as being heavily disguised. The man responsible had been a Hollywood make-up artist who preferred subtlety to false beards. All three men were dressed in sober and well-cut business suits.

Farquharson presented his card to the corporal at the outer reception desk. "Colonel Farquharson to see Colonel Pryce."

"I'm afraid he's not here, sir."

"Then the officer in charge, soldier."

"Yes, sir."

A minute later they were seated before a young and apprehensive Captain Martin, who had just finished a rather reluctant and very perfunctory scrutiny of the ID cards.

Farquharson said: "So Colonel Pryce has been called to Washington. I can guess why."

He didn't have to guess. He himself had put through the fake call that had led to Pryce's abrupt departure. "And his second in command?"

"Flu, sir." Martin sounded apologetic.

"At this time of year? How inconvenient. Especially today. You can guess why we're here."

"Yes, sir." Martin looked slightly unhappy. "Security check. I had a phone call telling me of the break-ins into the Florida and Louisiana depots." Dewings had put through that one. I'm sure you'll find everything in order, sir."

"Doubtless. I have already discovered something that is not in order."

"Sir?" There was a definite apprehension now in Martin's voice and appearance.

"Security-consciousness. Do you know that there are literally dozens of shops where I could buy, perfectly legally, a general's uniform. Those are the specialty shops that cater primarily to the film and stage industries. If I walked in dressed in such a uniform, would you accept me for what my uniform proclaimed me to be?"

"I suppose I would, sir."

"Well, don't. Not ever again." He glanced at his identity card lying on the desk. "Forging one of those presents no problems. When a stranger makes an appearance in a top security place like this, always, *always,* check his identity with Area Command. And always talk only to the commanding officer."

"Yes, sir. Do you happen to know his name? I'm new here."

"Major-General Harsworth."

Martin had the corporal at the front desk put him through. On the first ring a voice answered. "Area Command."

The voice did not in fact come from Area Command. It came from a man less than half a mile away, seated at the base of a telephone pole. He had with him a battery-powered transceiver. An insulated copper line from that led up to an alligator clip attached to one of the telephone wires.

Martin said: "Netley Rowan Arsenal. Captain Martin. I'd like to speak to General Harsworth."

"Hold on, please." There was a series of clicks, a pause of some seconds, then the same voice said: "On the line, Captain."

Martin said: "General Harsworth?"

"Speaking." The man by the telephone pole had deepened his voice by an octave. "Problems, Captain Martin?"

"I have Colonel Farquharson with me. He insists that I check out his identity with you."

The voice at the other end was sympathetic. "Been getting a security lecture?"

"I'm afraid I have, sir."

"The colonel's very hot on security. He's with Lieutenant-Colonel Dewings and Major Breckley?"

"Yes, sir."

"Well, it's hardly the end of your professional career. But he's right, you know."

Farquharson himself took the wheel of the car on the three-mile journey, a chastened, compliant Martin sitting up front beside him. A fifteen-foot-high electrical-warning barbed-wire fence surrounded the arsenal, a squat, gray, windowless building covering almost half an acre of land. A sentry with a machine carbine barred the entrance to the compound. He recognized Captain Martin, stepped back and saluted. Farquharson drove up to the one and only door of the building and halted. The four men got out. Farquharson said to Martin: "Major Breckley has never been inside a TNW installation before. A few illuminating comments, perhaps?" It would be illuminating for Farquharson also. He had never been inside an arsenal of any description in his life.

"Yes, sir. TNW—Tactical Nuclear Warfare. Walls thirty-three inches thick, alternating steel and ferroconcrete. Door ten inches tungsten steels. Both walls and door capable of resisting the equivalent of a fourteen-inch armor-piercing naval shell. This glass panel is recording us on TV video-tape. This meshed grill is a two-way speaker which also records our voices." He pressed a button sunk in the concrete.

A voice came through the grill. "Identification, please?"

"Captain Martin with Colonel Farquharson and security inspection."

"Code?"

"Geronimo." The massive door began to slide open and they could hear the hum of a powerful electrical motor. It took all of ten seconds for the door to open to its fullest extent. Martin led them inside.

A corporal saluted their entrance. Martin said: "Security inspection tour."

"Yes, sir." The corporal didn't seem too happy.

Farquharson said: "You worried about something, soldier?"

"No, sir."

"Then you should be."

Martin said: "Something wrong, sir?" He was patently nervous.

"Four things." Martin dipped his head so that Farquharson couldn't see his nervous swallowing. One thing would have been bad enough.

"In the first place, that sentry gate should be kept permanently locked. It should only be opened after a phone call to your HQ and an electronic link for opening the gate installed in your office. What's to prevent a person or persons with a silenced automatic disposing of your sentry and driving straight up here? Second, what would prevent people walking through the open doorway and spraying us all with submachine guns? That door should have been shut the moment we passed through." The corporal started to move but Farquharson stopped him with upraised hand.

"Third, all people who are not base personnel—such as we—should be fingerprinted on arrival. I will arrange to have your guards trained in those techniques. Fourth, and most important, show me the controls for those doors."

"This way, sir." The corporal led the way to a small console. "The red button opens, the green one closes."

Farquharson pressed the green button. The massive door hissed slowly closed. "Unsatisfactory. Totally. Those are the only controls to operate the door?"

"Yes, sir." Martin looked very unhappy indeed.

"We shall have another electronic link established with your HQ, which will render those buttons inoperable until the correct signal is sent." Farquharson was showing signs of irritation. "I would have thought all those things were self-evident."

Martin smiled weakly. "They are now, sir."

"What percentage of explosives, bombs and shells stored here are conventional?"

"Close to ninety-five per cent, sir."

"I'd like to see the nuclear weapons first."

"Of course, sir." A now thoroughly demoralized Martin led the way. The TNW section was compartmented off but not sealed. One side was lined with what appeared to be shells, stowed on racks; the other, with pear-shaped metal canisters about thirty inches high, with buttons, a clockface and a large knurled screw on top. Beyond them were stacked what looked like very odd-shaped fiberglass suitcases, each with two leather handles.

Breckley indicated the pear-shaped canisters. "What are those? Bombs?"

"Both bombs and land mines." Martin seemed glad to talk and take his mind off his troubles. "Those controls on top are relatively simple. Before you get at those two red switches you have to unscrew those two transparent plastic covers. The switches have then to be turned ninety degrees to the right. They are then still in the safe position. They then have to be flipped ninety degrees to the left. This is the ready-to-activate position.

"Before that is done, you have to put the time setting on the clock. That is done by means of this knurled knob here. One complete turn means a one-minute time delay which will show up on this clockface here. It registers in seconds, as you can see. Total time delay is thirty minutes—thirty turns."

"And this black button?"

"The most important of them all. No cover and no turning. You might want to get at it in a hurry. Depressing that stops the clock and, in fact, deactivates the bomb."

"What's the area of damage?"

"Compared to the conventional atom bomb, tiny. The vaporization area would be a quarter-mile radius. Perhaps less. The blast, shock and radiation areas would, of course, be considerably greater."

"You mean they can be used as both bombs and mines?"

"Instead of mines, maybe I should have said an explosive device for use on land. As bombs the setting would probably be only six seconds—in tactical warfare they would be carried by low-flying supersonic planes. They'd be about two miles clear by the time the bomb went off and moving too fast for the shock waves to catch up with them. For land use—well, say you wanted to infiltrate an ammunition dump. You'd check how long it would take you to infiltrate there, calculate how long it would take you to get out and clear of the blast zone, and set the timer accordingly.

"The missiles here——"

"We've seen and heard enough," Farquharson said. "Kindly put your hands up."

Five minutes later, with the furiously reluctant assistance of Martin, they had loaded two of the bombs, safely concealed in their carrying cases, into the trunk of their car. In the process the purpose of the two carrying handles became clear: each bomb must have weighed at least ninety pounds.

Farquharson went back inside, looked indifferently at the two bound men, pressed the button and slipped through the doorway as the door began to close. He waited until the door was completely shut, then climbed into the front seat beside Martin, who was at the wheel this time. Farquharson said: "Remember, one false move and you're a dead man. We will, of course, have to kill the sentry too."

There were no false moves. About a mile from the building the car stopped by a thicket of stunted trees. Martin was marched deep into the thicket, bound, gagged and attached to a tree just in case he might have any ideas about jackknifing his way down to the roadside. Farquharson looked down at him.

"Your security *was* lousy. We'll phone your HQ in an hour or so, let them know where they can find you. I trust there are not too many rattlesnakes around."

6

ROBERTSON LOOKED up from the radio console. "Chief McGarrity."

Mitchell took the phone. "Mitchell? We've found the kidnapers' estate wagon. Down by the Wyanee Swamp." McGarrity sounded positively elated. "I'm going there personally. Tracker dogs. I'll wait for you at the Walnut Tree crossing." Mitchell replaced the receiver and said to Roomer: "McGarrity's got it all wrapped up. He's found the estate wagon. Well . . . *someone* did, but of course it will be made clear eventually that it was McGarrity."

"Empty, of course. Doesn't that old fool know that this makes it more difficult, not easier? At least we knew what transport they were using. Not any more. He didn't mention anything about bringing along a newspaper photographer that he just sort of accidentally bumped into?"

"Tracker dogs were all he mentioned."

"Did he suggest anything for the dogs to sniff at?" Mitchell shook his head, Roomer shook his and called to Jenkins. "Will you get Louise, please?"

Louise appeared very quickly. Roomer said: "We need a piece of clothing that the ladies used to wear a lot."

She looked unceratin. "I don't understand——"

"Some things we can give bloodhounds to sniff so that they pick up their scent."

"Oh." It required only a second's thought. "Their dressing gowns, of course." This with but the slightest hint of disapproval, as if the girls spent most of the day lounging about in those garments.

"Handle as little as possible, please. Put each in a separate plastic bag."

A patrol car and a small closed police van awaited them at the Walnut Tree crossing. McGarrity was standing by the police car. He was a small bouncy man who radiated goodwill and only stopped smiling when he was vehemently denouncing corruption in politics. He was a police chief of incomparable incompetence, but was a consummate and wholly corrupt politician, which was why he was police chief. He shook the hands of Mitchell and Roomer with all the warmth and sincerity of an incumbent coming up for re-election, which was precisely what he was.

"Glad to meet you two gentlemen at last. Heard very good reports about you." He appeared to have conveniently forgotten his allegation that they gave a lot of trouble to the local law. "Appreciate all the co-operation you've given me—and for turning up here now. This is Ron Stewart of the *Herald*." He gestured through an open car window where a man, apparently festooned in cameras, sat in the back seat. "Kind of accidentally bumped into him."

Mitchell choked, turning it into a cough. "Too many cigarettes."

"Same failing myself. Driver's the dog handler. Driver of the van is the other one. Just follow us, please."

Five miles farther on they reached the turnoff—one of many—into the Wyanee Swamp. The foliage of the trees, almost touching overhead, quickly reduced the light to that of a late winter afternoon. The increase in the humidity was almost immediately noticeable, as was the sour, nose-wrinkling miasma as they neared the swamp. A distinctly unhealthy atmosphere, or such was the first impression: but many people with a marked aversion to what passed for civilization lived there all their lives and seemed none the worse for it.

The increasingly rutted, bumpy road had become almost intolerable until they rounded a blind corner and came across the abandoned station wagon.

The first essential was, apparently, that pictures be taken, and the second that McGarrity be well-placed in each one, his hand preferably resting in a proprietorial fashion on the hood. That done, the cameraman fitted a flash attachment and was reaching for the rear door when Roomer clamped his wrist not too gently. "Don't do that!"

"Why not?"

"Never been on a criminal case before? Fingerprints is why not." He looked at McGarrity. "Expecting them soon?"

"Shouldn't be long. Out on a case. Check on them, Don." This to the driver, who immediately got busy on his radio. It was clear that the idea of bringing fingerprint experts along had never occurred to McGarrity.

The dogs were released from the van. Roomer and Mitchell opened up their plastic bags and allowed the dogs to sniff the dressing gowns. McGarrity said: "What you got there?"

"The girls' dressing gowns. To give your hounds a scent. We knew you'd want something."

"Of course. But dressing gowns!" McGarrity was a past master in covering up. Something else, clearly, that had not occurred to him.

The dogs caught the scents at once and strained at their leashes as they nosed their way down a rutted path, for the road had come to an abrupt end. Inside a hundred yards, their path was blocked by water. It wasn't a true part of the swamp but a slow, meandering, mud-brown creek, perhaps twenty feet across, if that. There was a mooring post nearby, with a similar one at the far bank. Also by the far bank was a warped and aged craft which not even the charitable could have called a boat. It was built along the lines of an oversized coffin, with a squared-off end where the bow should have been. The ferry—probably the most kindly name for it—was attached to the two posts by an endless pulley line.

The two dog handlers hauled the boat across, got into it with understandable caution, and were joined by their dogs, who kept on displaying considerable signs of animation, an animation which rapidly diminished, then vanished shortly after they had landed on the far bank. After making a few fruitless circles, they lay down dejectedly on the ground.

"Well, ain't that a shame," a voice said. "Trail gone cold, I guess."

The four men on the near bank turned to look at the source of the voice. He was a bizarre character, wearing a new panama hat with a tartan band, gleaming thigh-length leather boots (presumably as a protection against snakebites), and clothes discarded by a scarecrow. "You folks chasin' someone?"

"We're looking for someone," McGarrity said cautiously.

"Lawmen, yes?"

"Chief of Police McGarrity."

"Honored, I'm sure. Well, Chief, you're wasting your time. Hot trail here, cold on the other side. So the party you're looking for got off halfway across."

"You saw them?" McGarrity asked suspiciously.

"Hah! More than one, eh? No, sir. Just happened by right now. But if I was on the run from the law that's what I'd do, because it's been done hundreds of times. You can get out midway, walk half a mile, even a mile, upstream or downstream. Dozens of little rivulets come into this creek. You could turn up any of those, go a mile into the swamp without setting foot on dry land. Wouldn't find them this side of Christmas, Chief.''

"How deep is the creek?''

"Fifteen inches. If that.''

"Then, why the boat? I mean, with those boots you could walk across without getting your feet wet.''

The stranger looked almost shocked. "No sirree. Takes me an hour every morning to polish up them critters.'' It was assumed that he was referring to his boots. "Besides, there're the water moccasins.'' He seemed to have a rooted aversion to snakes. "The boat? Come the rains, the creek's up to here.'' He touched his chest.

McGarrity called the dog handlers to return. Mitchell said to the stranger: "Anyplace in the swamp where a helicopter could land?''

"Sure. More firm land out there than there is swampland. Never seen any helicopters, though. Yes, lots of clearings.''

The dog handlers and dogs disembarked. Leaving the stranger to flick some invisible dust off his boots, they made their way back to the station wagon. Mitchell said: "Wait a minute. I've got an idea.'' He opened the two plastic bags containing the dressing gowns and presented them to the dogs again. He then walked back up the rutted lane, past the two cars and vans, beckoning the dog handlers to follow him, which they did, almost having to drag the reluctant dogs behind them.

After about twenty yards the reluctance vanished. The dogs yelped and strained at their leashes. For another twenty yards they towed their handlers along behind them, then abruptly stopped and circled a few times before sitting down dispiritedly. Mitchell crouched and examined the surface of the lane. The others caught up with him.

McGarrity said: "What gives, then?''

"This.'' Mitchell pointed to the ground. "There was another vehicle here. You can see where its back wheels spun when it started to reverse. The kidnapers guessed we'd be using dogs—it wasn't all that hard a guess. So they carried the girls twenty yards or so, to break the scent, before setting them down again.''

"Right smart of you, Mr. Mitchell, right smart.'' McGarrity didn't look as pleased as his words suggested. "So the birds have flown, eh? And now we haven't the faintest idea what the getaway vehicle looks like.''

Roomer said: "Somebody's flown, that's for sure. But maybe only one or two. Maybe they've gone to borrow a helicopter.''

"A helicopter?'' The waters didn't have to be very deep for Chief McGarrity to start floundering.

With a trace of weary impatience Mitchell said: "It could be a double bluff. Maybe they reversed the procedure and took the girls back to the station wagon again. Maybe they're still in the swamp, waiting for a helicopter to come and pick them up. You heard the old boy back there—he said there were plenty of places in the swamp where a helicopter could set down.''

McGarrity nodded sagely and appeared to ponder the matter deeply. The time had come, he felt, for him to make a positive contribution. "The swamp's out. Hopeless. So I'll have to concentrate on the helicopter angle.''

Mitchell said: "How do you propose to do that?''

"Just you leave that to me.''

Roomer said: "That's hardly fair, Chief. We've given you our complete confidence. Don't you think we're entitled to some in return?''

"Well, now." McGarrity appeared to ruminate, although he was secretly pleased to be asked the question, as Roomer had known he would be. "If the chopper doesn't get in there, it can't very well lift them out, can it?"

"That's a fact," Roomer said solemnly.

"So I station marksmen round this side of the swamp. It's no big deal to bring down a low-flying chopper."

Mitchell said: "I wouldn't do that if I were you."

"No, indeed." Roomer shook his head. "The law frowns on murder."

"Murder?" McGarrity stared at them. "Who's talking about murder?"

"*We* are," Mitchell said. "Rifle or machine-gun fire could kill someone inside the helicopter. If it brings down the helicopter they'd all probably die. Maybe there are criminals aboard, but they're entitled to a fair trial. And has it occurred to you that the pilot will almost certainly be an innocent party with a pistol pointed at his head?" McGarrity, clearly, had not thought of that. "Not going to make us very popular, is it?"

McGarrity winced. Even the thought of unpopularity and the forthcoming election made him feel weak inside.

"So what the devil do we do?"

Roomer was frank. "I'll be damned if I know. You can post observers. You can even have a grounded helicopter standing by to chase the other one when it takes off. *If* it ever comes in the first place. We're only guessing."

"No more we can do here," Mitchell said. "We've already missed too many appointments today. We'll be in touch."

Back on the highway Roomer said: "How do you think he'd do as a dogcatcher?"

"Place would be overrun by stray dogs in a few months. How much faith have you got in this idea that they might use a helicopter?"

"A lot. If they just wanted to change cars they wouldn't have gone through this elaborate rigmarole. They could have parked their station wagon out of sight almost anyplace. By apparently going into hiding in the swamp they wanted to make it look as though they were preparing to hole up in there for some time. They hadn't figured on our backing—your backtracking—up the lane."

"We're pretty sure their destination is the *Seawitch*. We're pretty sure they'll use a helicopter. Which helicopter and pilot would you use?"

"Lord Worth's. Not only are his pilots almost certainly the only ones who know the exact co-ordinates of the *Seawitch*, but those distinctly marked North Hudson helicopters are the only ones that could approach the *Seawitch* without raising suspicion." Roomer reached for the phone, fiddled with the wave-band control and raised Lord Worth's house. "Jim?"

"Go ahead, Mr. Roomer."

"We're coming back there. Look for Lord Worth's address book. Probably right by you in your radio room. Make us a list of the names and addresses of his helicopter pilots. Is the gatekeeper at the heliport on the radiophone, too?"

"Yes."

"Get that for us too, please."

"Roger."

Roomer said to Mitchell: "Still think we shouldn't warn Larsen about our suspicions?"

"That's for sure." Mitchell was very definite. "The *Seawitch* is Larsen's baby, and the kind of reception he'd prepare for them might be a bit overenthusiastic. How'd you like to explain to Lord Worth how come his daughters got caught in the crossfire?''

"No way!" Roomer spoke with some feeling.

"Or even explain to yourself how Melinda got shot through the lung?" Roomer ignored him. "What if we're wrong about Worth's pilots?"

"Then we turn the whole thing over to that ace detective, McGarrity."

"So we'd better be right."

They were right. They were also too late.

John Campbell was both an avid fisherman and an avid reader. He had long since mastered the techniques of indulging his two pleasures simultaneously. A creek, fairly popular with fish, ran within twenty feet of his back porch. Campbell was sitting on a canvas chair, parasol over his head, alternating every page with a fresh cast of his line, when Durand and one of his men, stocking-masked and holding guns in their hands, came into his line of vision. Campbell rose to his feet, book still in hand.

"Who are you and what do you want?"

"You. You're Campbell, aren't you?"

"What if I am?"

"Like you to do a little job for us."

"What job?"

"Fly a helicopter for us."

"I'll be damned if I will!"

"So you *are* Campbell. Come along."

Following the gesturing of their guns, Campbell moved between the two men. He was within one foot of Durand's gun hand when he chopped the side of his hand on the wrist that held the gun. Durand grunted in pain, the gun fell to the ground and a second later the two men were locked together, wrestling, kicking and punching with a fine disregard for the rules of sport, altering position so frequently that Durand's henchman at first found no opportunity to intervene. But the opportunity came very soon. The unsportsmanlike but effective use of Campbell's right knee doubled Durand over in gasping agony, but enough instinct was left him to seize Campbell's shirt as he fell over backward. This was Campbell's downfall in more ways than one, for the back of his head was now nakedly vulnerable to a swung automatic.

The man who had felled Campbell now pulled him clear, allowing Durand to climb painfully to his feet, although still bent over at an angle of forty-five degrees. He pulled off his stocking mask as if to try to get more air to breathe. Durand was Latin American, with a pale coffee-colored face, thick black curling hair and a pencil-line mustache; he might even qualify as handsome when the twisted lines of agony ceased to contort his face. He straightened inch by inch and finally obtained a modicum of breath—enough, at least, to allow him to announce what he would like to do with Campbell.

"Some other time, Mr. Durand. He can't very well fly a chopper from a hospital bed."

Durand painfully acknowledged the truth of this. "I hope *you* didn't hit him too hard."

"Just a tap."

"Tie him, tape him and blindfold him." Durand was now a scarce twenty degrees off the vertical. His helper left for the car and returned in moments with cord, tape and blindfold. Three minutes later they were on their way, with a rug-covered and still unconscious Campbell on the floor at the back. Resting comfortably on the rug were Durand's feet—he still didn't feel quite up to driving. Both men had their masks off now—even in the free-wheeling state of Florida men driving with stocking masks on were likely to draw more than passing attention.

Mitchell glanced briefly at the list of names and addresses Robertson had given them. "Fine. But what are these checks opposite five of the names?"

Robertson sounded apologetic. "I hope you don't mind—I don't want to butt in—but I took the liberty of phoning those gentlemen to see if they would be at home when you came around. I assumed you'd be seeing them because you asked for the addresses."

Mitchell looked at Roomer. "Why the hell didn't you think of that?"

Roomer bestowed a cold glance on him and said to Robertson: "Maybe I should have you as a partner. What did you find out?"

"One pilot is standing by at the airport. Four of the others are at home. The one whose name I haven't checked—John Campbell—isn't home. I asked one of the other pilots about this and he seemed a bit surprised. Said that Campbell usually spends his afternoons fishing outside the back of his house. He's a bachelor and lives in a pretty isolated place."

"It figures," Roomer said. "A bachelor in isolation. The kidnapers seem to have an excellent intelligence system. The fact that he doesn't answer the phone may mean nothing—he could have gone for a walk, shopping, visiting friends. On the other hand——"

"Yes. Especially on the other hand." Mitchell turned to leave, then said to Robertson: "Does the gatekeeper have a listed phone number as well as the radiophone?"

"I've typed it on that list."

"Maybe we should both have you as a partner."

Mitchell and Roomer stood on Campbell's back lawn and surveyed the scene unemotionally. The canvas chair, on its side, had a broken leg. The parasol was upturned on the grass, over an opened book. The fishing rod was in the water up to its handle and would have floated away had not the reel snagged on a shrub root. Roomer retrieved the rod while Mitchell hurried through the back doorway—the back door was wide open, as was the front. He dialed a phone number, and got an answer on the first ring.

"Lord Worth's heliport. Gorrie here."

"My name's Mitchell. You have a police guard?"

"Mr. Mitchell? You Lord Worth's friend?"

"Yes."

"Sergeant Roper is here."

"That all? Let me speak to him." There was hardly a pause before Roper came on the phone.

"Mike? Nice to hear from you again."

"Listen, Sergeant, this is urgent. I'm speaking from the house of John Campbell, one of Lord Worth's pilots. He has been forcibly abducted, almost certainly by some of the kidnapers of Lord Worth's daughters. I have every reason to believe—no time for explanations now—that they're heading in your direction with the intention of hijacking one of Lord Worth's helicopters and forcing Campbell to fly it. There'll be two of them at least, maybe three, armed and dangerous. I suggest you call up reinforcements immediately. If we get them we'll break them—at least Roomer and I will; you can't, you're a law officer and your hands are tied—and we'll find where the girls are and get them back."

"Reinforcements coming up. Then I'll look the other way."

Mitchell hung up. Roomer was by his side. Roomer said: "You prepared to go as far as back-room persuasion to get the information we want?"

Mitchell looked at him bleakly. "I look forward to it. Don't you?"

"No. But I'll go along with you."

Once again Mitchell and Roomer had guessed correctly. And once again they were too late.

Mitchell had driven to Lord Worth's heliport with a minimum regard for traffic and speed regulations, and now, having arrived there, he realized bitterly that his haste had been wholly unnecessary.

Five men greeted their arrival, although it was hardly a cheerful meeting: Gorrie, the gateman, and four policemen. Gorrie and Sergeant Roper were tenderly massaging their wrists. Mitchell looked at Roper.

"Don't tell me." Mitchell sounded weary. "They jumped you before the reinforcements were to hand."

"Yeah." Roper's face was dark with anger. "I know it sounds like the old lame excuse, but we never had a chance. This car comes along and stops outside the gatehouse, right here. The driver—he was alone in the car—seemed to be having a sneezing fit and was holding a big wad of Kleenex to his face."

Roomer said: "So you wouldn't recognize him again?"

"Exactly. Well, we were watching this dude when a voice from the back—the back window was open—told us to freeze. I didn't even have my hand on my gun. We froze. Then he told me to drop my gun. Well, this guy was no more than five feet away . . . I dropped my gun. Dead heroes are no good to anyone. Then he told us to turn around. He was wearing a stocking mask. Then the driver came and tied our wrists behind our backs. When we turned around he was wearing a stocking mask too."

"Then they tied your feet and tied you together so that you wouldn't have any funny ideas about using a telephone?"

"That's how it was. But they weren't worried about the phones. They cut the lines before they took off."

"They took off immediately?"

Gorrie said: "No. Five minutes later. The pilots always radio-file a flight plan before takeoff. I suppose these guys forced Campbell to do the same. To make it look kosher."

Mitchell shrugged his indifference. "Means nothing. You can file a flight plan to anyplace. Doesn't mean you have to keep it. How about fuel—for the helicopters, I mean?"

"Fuel's always kept topped up. My job. Lord Worth's orders."

"What direction did they go?"

"Thataway." Gorrie indicated with an outstretched arm.

"Well, the birds have flown. Might as well be on our way."

"Just like that?" Roper registered surprise.

"What do you expect me to do that the police can't?"

"Well, for starters, we could call in the Air Force."

"Why?"

"They could force it down."

Mitchell sighed. "There's a great deal of crap being talked about forcing planes down. What if they refuse to be forced down?"

"Then shoot it down."

"With Lord Worth's daughters aboard? Lord Worth wouldn't be very pleased. Neither would you. Think of all the cops that would be out of a job."

"Lord Worth's daughters!"

"It's all this routine police work," Roomer said. "Atrophies the brain. Who the hell do you think that helicopter has gone to pick up?"

Once clear of the heliport, Roomer extended an arm. " 'Thataway,' the man said. 'Thataway' is northwest. The Wyanee Swamp."

"Even if they'd taken off to the southeast they'd still have finished up in Wyanee." Mitchell pulled up by a public booth. "How are you with Mc-Garrity's voice?" Roomer was an accomplished mimic.

"It's not the voice that's hard. It's the thought processes. I'll give it a try." He didn't say what he was going to try because he didn't have to. He left for the booth and was back inside two minutes.

"Campbell filed a flight plan for the *Seawitch*."

"Any questions asked?"

"Not really. Told them that some fool had made a mistake. Anyone who knows McGarrity would know who the fool was that made the mistake."

Mitchell started the engine, then switched off as the phone rang. Mitchell lifted the receiver.

"Jim here. Tried to ring you a couple of times, fifteen minutes ago, five minutes ago."

"Figures. Out of the car both times. More bad news?"

"Not unless you consider Lord Worth bad news. Touchdown in fifteen minutes."

"We got time."

"Says he's coming up to the house."

"Sent for the Rolls?"

"No. Probably wants to talk private. And it looks as if he's planning to stay away some time. Ordered a bag packed for a week."

"Seven white suits." Mitchell hung up.

Roomer said: "Looks as if we're going to have to do some bag-packing ourselves." Mitchell nodded and started up again.

Lord Worth was looking his old self when he settled in the back seat of their car. Not quite radiating his old bonhomie, to be sure, but calm and lucid and, to all appearances, relaxed. He told of his success in Washington, for which he was duly and politely congratulated. Roomer then told him in detail what had happened in his absence: this time the absence of congratulations was marked.

"You've notified Commander Larsen of your suspicions, of course?"

"Not suspicions," Mitchell said. "Certainties. And there's no 'of course' and no, we didn't notify him. I'm primarily responsible for that."

"Taking the law into your own hands, eh? Mind telling me why?"

"You're the person who knows Larsen best. You know how possessive he is about the *Seawitch*. You yourself have told us about his anger and violence. Do you think a man like that, duly forewarned, wouldn't have a very warm reception waiting for the kidnapers? Stray bullets, ricocheting bullets, are no respecter of persons, Lord Worth. You want a daughter crippled for life? We prefer that the kidnapers establish a bloodless beach-head."

"Well, all right." The words came grudgingly. "But from now on keep me fully informed of your intentions and decisions." Lord Worth, Roomer noted with sardonic amusement, had no intention of dispensing with their unpaid services. "But no more taking the law into your own hands, do you hear?"

Mitchell stopped car and engine. Roomer's amusement changed to apprehension. Mitchell twisted in his seat and looked at Lord Worth in cool speculation.

"You're a fine one to talk."

"What do you mean, sir?" There were fifteen generations of highland aristocracy in the glacial voice.

Mitchell remained unmoved. "For taking the law into your own hands by breaking into and robbing that arsenal last night. If Roomer and I were decent citizens and law-abiding detectives, we'd have had you behind bars last night. Not even a billionaire can get away with that sort of thing, especially when it involves the assault and locking up of the arsenal guards. John and I were there." Mitchell was not above a little prevarication when the need arose.

"*You* were there." Most rarely for him, Lord Worth was at a loss for words. He recovered quickly. "But *I* wasn't there."

"We know that. We also know you sanctioned the break-in. Ordered it, rather."

"Balderdash. And if you actually witnessed this, why did you not stop it?"

"John and I take our chances. But not against nine men armed with machine guns."

This gave Lord Worth pause. They had their figures and facts right. Clearly they had been there. He said: "Supposing any of this rigmarole were true, how in God's name do you tie me up with it?"

"Now you're being a fool. We were also at your heliport. We saw the truck arrive. We saw nine men unload a fairly massive quantity of more than fairly lethal weaponry into one helicopter. Then a man drove the truck away—an army truck, of course—back to the arsenal from where it had been stolen. The other eight men boarded another helicopter. Then a minibus arrived, carrying twelve heavily armed thugs who joined the other eight. John and I recognized no fewer than five of them—two of them we've personally put behind bars." Roomer looked at him admiringly, but Mitchell wasn't looking at Roomer, he was looking at Lord Worth, and both voice and tone were devoid of any form of encouragement. "It came as a shock to both of us to find that Lord Worth was consorting with common criminals. You're sweating a little, Lord Worth. Why are you sweating?"

Lord Worth didn't enlighten them as to why he was sweating.

"And then, of course, you came along in the Rolls. One of the very best sequences we got on our infrared movie camera last night." Roomer blinked, but that Lord Worth believed Mitchell Roomer did not for a moment doubt: everything that Mitchell had said, even the slight embellishments, Lord Worth knew or believed to be true, so he had no reason to doubt the truth of the camera fiction.

"We actually considered phoning the nearest army HQ and having them send along some armored cars and a trailered tank. Even your thugs wouldn't have stood a chance. We thought of going down the road, blocking the Rolls and holding you until the army arrived—it was perfectly obvious that the helicopters had no intention of leaving until you turned up. Once captured, God knows how many of them—especially those who had already served prison terms—would have jumped at the chance of turning state's evidence and incriminating you. It's quite true, you know—there *is* no honor among thieves." If Lord Worth had any objections to being categorized as a thief, it didn't register in his face. "But after the standard bit of soul-searching we decided against it."

"Why, in God's name?"

"So you admit it." Mitchell sighed. "Why couldn't you do that at the beginning and save me all this trouble?"

"Why?" Lord Worth repeated his question.

It was Roomer who answered. "Partly because even though you're a confessed lawbreaker, we still have a regard for you. But mainly because we didn't want to see your daughters confronted with seeing their father behind bars. In hindsight, of course, we're glad we didn't. In comparison with the kidnaping of your daughters, your own capers outside the law fade into a peccadillo."

Mitchell started the motor again and said: "It is understood that there will be no more peccadilloes. It is also understood that there will be no more talk about our taking the law into our own hands."

Lord worth lay back in his study armchair. His second brandy tasted just as good as his first—it seemed to be his day for brandies. He hadn't spoken a word for the rest of the trip—which, fortunately, had been mercifully short, for Lord Worth had felt urgently in need of restoratives. Not for the first time, he found himself silently blessing his kidnaped daughters.

He cleared his throat and said: "I assume you are still willing to come out to the rig with me?"

Mitchell contemplated his glass. "We never expressed our intentions one way or another about that. But I suppose someone has to look after you and your daughters."

Lord Worth frowned. There had, he felt, been more than a subtle change in their relationship. Perhaps the establishment of an employer-employee status would help redress the balance. He said: "I feel it's time we put your co-operation on a businesslike footing. I propose to retain you in your professional capacities as investigators—in other words, become your client. I shall not quibble at your demanded fees." He had no sooner finished than he realized that he had made a mistake.

Roomer's voice was coldly unenthusiastic. "Money doesn't buy everything, Lord Worth. Particularly, it doesn't buy us. We have no intention of being shackled, of having our freedom of action curtailed. And as far as the fees and your sky's-the-limit implication are concerned, the hell with it. How often do we have to tell you we don't trade money for your daughters' lives?"

Lord Worth didn't even bother frowning. The change in relationship, he reflected sadly, had been even greater than he had realized. "As you will. One assumes that you will be suitably disguised?"

Mitchell said: "Why?"

Lord Worth was impatient. "You said you saw some ex-convicts boarding the helicopter. People you recognized. They'll surely recognize you?"

"We never saw 'em before in our lives."

Lord Worth was properly shocked. "But you told me——"

"You told us big black lies. What's a little white lie? We'll go aboard as—say—your technological advisers. Geologists, seismologists—it's all the same to us, we know nothing about geology or seismology. All we need are business suits, horn-rimmed glasses—for the studious look—and briefcases." He paused. "And we'll also need a doctor, with full medical kit and a large supply of bandages."

"A doctor?"

"For extracting bullets, sewing up gunshot wounds. Or are you naive enough to believe that no shot will be fired in anger aboard the *Seawitch?*"

"I abhor violence."

"Sure. That's why you sent twenty heavily armed thugs out to the *Seawitch* during the night? Fine, so you abhor violence. Others welcome it. Can you find us a doctor?"

"Dozens of them. The average doctor hereabouts rates his scanning of X-rays a very poor second to the scanning of his bank balances. I know the man. Greenshaw. After seven years in Vietnam, he should fill your bill."

Roomer said: "And ask him to bring along two spare white hospital coats."

"Why?" Mitchell said.

"Want to look scientific, don't you?"

Lord Worth picked up the phone, made the arrangements, replaced the instrument and said: "You must excuse me. I have some private calls to make from the radio room." Lord Worth's sole reason for returning to his house was to contact his inside man, Corral, and have him, without incriminating himself, inform Benson, who had hosted the Lake Tahoe meeting, that the government intended to blast out of the water any foreign naval ships that approached the *Seawitch.* An exaggeration but, Lord Worth thought, a pardonable one. Despite the secretary's promise, Lord Worth placed more faith in his direct approach.

Mitchell said: "Which one of us do you want to go with you?"

"What do you mean? 'Private,' I said." His face darkened in anger. "Am I to be ordered around in my own house, supervised as if I'm an irresponsible child?"

"You behaved responsibly last night? Look, Lord Worth, if you don't want either of us around, then it's obvious you want to say something that you don't want us to hear." Mitchell gave him a speculative look. "I don't like that. You're either up to something we wouldn't like, something shady maybe, or it's a vote of no confidence in us."

"It's a personal and highly important business call. I don't see why you should be privy to my business affairs."

Roomer said: "I agree. But it so happens that we don't think that it is a business call, that business would be the last thing in your mind right now." Both Mitchell and Roomer stood up. "Give our regards to the girls—if you ever find them."

"Blackmail! Damned blackmail!" Lord Worth rapidly weighed the importance of his call to Corral compared to the importance of having Mitchell and Roomer around. It took all of two seconds to make up his mind, and Corral was clear out of sight at the wire. He was sure that the two men were bluffing, but there was no way he could call their bluff, for that was the one sure way of provoking a genuine walkout.

Lord Worth put on his stony face. "I suppose I have no option other than to accede to your threats. I suggest you go and pack your bags and I'll pick you up in the Rolls."

Mitchell said: "Packing will take some time. I think it would be more polite if we wait here until you're ready."

Lord Worth mentally gnashed his teeth. "You think I'd head for a telephone the moment your backs are turned?"

Mitchell smiled. "Funny the same thought should occur to the three of us at the same instant, isn't it?"

7

COMMANDER LARSEN and Scoffield observed the approach of the North Hudson helicopter with surprise but without undue concern. Lord Worth customarily gave advance warning of his arrival but could occasionally be forgetful on this point. In any event it was his helicopter and just about his expected time of arrival. They sauntered across the platform and arrived at the northeast helipad just as the helicopter touched down.

Surprisingly, no one emerged immediately from the machine. Larsen and Scoffield looked at each other in some perplexity, a perplexity that was considerably deepened when the disembarkation door slid back and Durand appeared in the doorway with a machine pistol cradled in his hands. Just behind him stood a similarly equipped henchman. From their shadowed position it was impossible for them to be observed by any of the rig duty crew.

Durand said: "Larsen and Scoffield? If you are carrying weapons, please don't be so foolish as to try to use them." The boarding steps swung down. "Come and join us."

The two men had no option. Once aboard, without taking his eyes off them, Durand said: "Kowenski, Rindler—see if they're armed."

Both Larsen and Scoffield carried automatics but seemed quite indifferent to being deprived of them: their attention was directed exclusively to the presence of Lord Worth's daughters.

Marina smiled; albeit a trifle wanly. "We could have met under happier circumstances, Commander."

Larsen nodded. "Your kidnapers. This can carry a death sentence." He looked at Campbell. "Why did you fly those criminals out here?"

"Because I get very cowardly when I have a pistol barrel stuck in the back of my neck all the way from takeoff to touchdown." Campbell spoke with a certain justifiable bitterness.

Larsen looked at Melinda. "Have you been mistreated in any way?"

"No."

"And they won't be," Durand said. "Unless, of course, you refuse to do as we tell you."

"What does that mean?"

"You close down the Christmas tree." This meant closing off all the oil supplies from the ocean floor.

"I'll be damned if I do." Larsen's dark piratical face was suffused with fury. Here, Durand realized, was a man who, even without arms, could be highly dangerous. He glanced briefly at Rindler, who struck Larsen on the back of the neck with his machine pistol, a blow calculated to daze but not knock out. When Larsen's head had cleared he found that he had handcuffs and shackles around wrists and ankles. His attention then focused on a pair of gleaming stainless-steel medical cutters of the type favored by the surgical fraternity for snipping through ribs. The handles were in Durand's firm grip: the unpleasant operating end was closed lightly round the little finger of Melinda's right hand.

Durand said: "Lord Worth isn't going to like you too much for this, Larsen."

Larsen, apparently, was of the same opinion. "All right, take those damned pliers away and get these bracelets off. I'll close down your damned Christmas tree."

"And I'll come with you just to see that you really do turn it off. Not that

I would recognize one if I saw it, but I do know that there are such things as flow gauges. I'll be carrying a walkie-talkie with me. Rindler here has another. I'll keep in constant contact with him. If anything should happen to me——'' Durand looked consideringly at the medical cutters, then handed them to Heffer, the fifth man in his team. He told Campbell to put his arms behind his seat back and handcuffed his wrists.

"Don't miss much, do you?'' Larsen's voice was sour.

"You know how it is. So many villains around these days. Come on.''

The two men walked across the platform in the direction of the drilling rig. After only a few paces Durand stopped and looked around him admiringly.

"Well, well, now. Dual-purpose antiaircraft guns. Piles of depth charges. You'd almost think you're prepared to withstand a siege. Dear me, dear me. Federal offense you know. Lord Worth, even with the millions he can pay for lawyers, can get at least ten years in the pen for this.''

"What're you talking about?''

"Hardly standard equipment aboard an oil rig. I'll bet it wasn't here twenty-four hours ago. I'll bet it was inside the Mississippi naval arsenal that was broken into last night. The Government takes a dim view of people who steal military equipment. And, of course, you got to have specialists aboard who're skilled at handling stuff like that, and that's hardly part of the basic training of oil-rig crews. I wonder if those crews are also carrying special equipment—like, for instance, what was stolen from a Florida arsenal last night. I mean, two unrelated arsenal break-ins in the same night is too much coincidence. Twenty years in prison, with no chance for parole for you too, for aiding and abetting. And people call us criminals.''

Larsen had a few choice observations to make in return, none of which would have received the approval of even the most tolerant board of censors.

The Christmas tree was duly neutralized. The pressure gauges registered zero. Durand turned his attention to the *Roamer,* carrying out its short and wearisome patrol between the rig and the huge floating oil tank. "What's our friend up to?''

"Even a landlubber like you ought to be able to guess. He's patrolling the pipeline.''

"What the hell for? You could replace a cut line in a day. What would that get anybody? It's crazy.''

"You have to use crazy methods to deal with crazy people. From all accounts, Lord Worth's enemies should be locked up for their own good. For everybody's good.''

"Worth's band of cutthroats aboard this rig—who's their leader?''

"Giuseppe Palermo.''

"That mobster! So the noble Lord, along with his grand larceny, is an associate of convicted felons.''

"You know him, then?''

"Yeah.'' Durand saw no point in elaborating upon the fact that he and Palermo had spent two prison terms together. "I want to talk to him.''

The talk was brief and one-sided. Durand said: "We've got Lord Worth's daughters prisoner. We're going to bring them toward the living quarters here, but we don't want you taking our two aces away from us. You'll stay inside in your quarters. If you don't you're gonna hear a lot of screaming and see pieces of fingers or ears dropped through your windows. I hope you believe me.''

Palermo believed him. Palermo had a reputation for ruthlessness that matched Durand's, but it couldn't begin to match Durand's unholy joy in sadism. Durand was perfectly capable of not only doing what he threatened but of deriving immense satisfaction in so doing.

Palermo returned to his oriental quarters. Durand called up Rindler on the walkie-talkie and told them all to come across, including Campbell, the pilot. Campbell was tough and resourceful and it was just possible that, by standing up, he could slip his manacled arms over the back of his seat, step through them and take off. Whether he would have enough fuel for the return flight would be a problem for him, even though he would almost certainly head not for Florida but for the nearest spot on the mainland, which would be due south of New Orleans.

As the prisoners and guards disembarked from the helicopter Durand said: "Accommodations?"

"Plenty. There are spare rooms in the oriental quarters. There's Lord Worth's private suite."

"Lockups?"

"What do you mean? This isn't a prison."

"Storerooms? Ones that can be locked from the outside?"

"Yes."

Durand looked at Larsen consideringly. "You're being very co-operative, Larsen. Your reputation says otherwise."

"Two minutes' walk around and you could confirm all I'm saying for yourself."

"You'd like to kill me, wouldn't you, Larsen?"

"When the time is ripe, yes. But it's not yet ripe."

"Even so." Durand produced a pistol. "Stay about ten feet away. You might be tempted to grab me and try to make the men let the girls go. A tempting thought, no?"

Larsen looked at him yearningly and said nothing.

The girls, the pilots and their four escorts arrived. Durand said: "Well, now, we gotta find some suitable overnight accommodation for you." He led the way to the first of several storehouses and opened the door to reveal a room packed roof-high with canned goods. He shoved Campbell inside, locked the door and pocketed the key. The next storehouse contained coils of rope, a powerful smell of crude oil and an active, scuttling population of those indestructible creatures, cockroaches. Durand said to the two girls: "Inside."

The girls took one shuddering look, then turned away. Marina said: "We will not go inside that disgusting place."

Kowenski said in a gently chiding voice which accorded ill with the Colt he held in his hand: "Do you know what this is?" Rindler had a similar weapon trained on Melinda.

Both girls glanced briefly at each other and then, in what was obviously a prepared and rehearsed movement, walked toward the men with the guns, seized the barrels with their right hands and hooked their right thumbs behind their trigger forefingers, pulling the guns hard against themselves.

"Jesus Christ!" Durand was badly shaken; he had run up against many situations in his life, but this one lay far beyond his most remote conception. "You trying to commit suicide?"

Melinda said: "Precisely." Her eyes never left Rindler's. "You're lower than those horrible cockroaches in there. You are vermin who are trying to destroy our father. With us dead, you won't have a single card left to play."

"You're crazy! Simple plain crazy!"

"Maybe," Marina said. "But for crazy people our logic is pretty good. With nothing to tie his hands you can imagine how our father will react—

especially since he and everyone else will believe that you murdered us. He won't have to go to the law, of course—you simply have no idea what power a few billion dollars can bring to bear. He'll destroy you and all your people to the last man.'' She looked at Kowenski with contempt. "Why don't you press the trigger? No? Then let go your gun.'' Kowenski released his gun and Rindler did the same, and the girls dropped them to the deck.

Melinda said: "My sister and I are taking a walk. We will return when you have quarters prepared fitting for Lord Worth's daughters.''

Durand's face had definitely lost color and his voice was hoarse and not quite steady as he tried to regain a measure of authority. "So take your walk. Heffer, go with them. Any trouble, shoot them in the legs.''

Marina stooped, picked up Kowenski's Colt, walked up to Heffer and rammed the muzzle into his left eye. Heffer recoiled, howling in agony. Marina said: "Fair deal. You shoot me through the leg—now, I mean—and I'll blow your brains out.''

"God's sake!'' Durand's voice was almost imploring. Hee was one step removed from wringing his hands. "Somebody's got to go with you. If you're out there on your own and in no danger, Palermo's men will cut us to pieces.''

"What a perfectly splendid idea.'' Marina lowered the pistol and looked in distaste at Heffer, a rodent-faced creature of indeterminate age and nationality. "We see your point. But this—this animal is not to approach within ten yards of us at any time. That is understood?''

"Yes, yes, of course.'' If they asked him for the moon, Durand would have somehow levitated himself and got it for them. Having overwhelmingly displayed what it was to have seventeen generations of highland aristocratic ancestry behind them, the two girls walked away toward one of the triangular perimeters. It was fully twenty yards before they both began, at the same instant, to tremble violently. Once started, they could not control the trembling and they prayed that the following Heffer could not notice it.

Marina whispered shakily: "Would you do that again?''

"Never, never, never. I'd die.''

"I think we came pretty close to it. Do you think that Michael and John would be shaking like us after an experience like that?''

"No. If there's any truth in what Daddy hints, they'd already be planning what to do next. And Durand and his obnoxious friends wouldn't be shaking either. Dead men don't shake very much.''

Marina's trembling turned into a genuine shiver. "I only wish to God they were here right now.''

They stopped ten feet short of the platform perimeter. Neither girl had a head for heights. They turned and looked northeastward as the distant and muted roar of an aircraft engine came to their ears.

Durand and Larsen heard it at the same time. They could see nothing because dusk had already fallen, but neither man had any doubt as to the identity of the approaching helicopter and its occupants. With some satisfaction Durand said: "Company. This has to be Lord Worth. Where will they land?''

"The southeast helipad.''

Durand glanced across the platform to where the two girls were standing with Heffer, gun carried loosely in his right hand, less than the regulation ten yards away. Satisfied, Durand picked up his machine pistol and said: "Let's go and welcome his lordship aboard. Aaron, come with us.''

Larsen said: "You'd better hope Lord Worth proves more tractable than his daughters.''

"What do you mean?"

Larsen smiled in sardonic satisfaction. "You caught a couple of tigresses by the tails, didn't you?"

Durand scowled and walked away, followed by Larsen and Aaron, the latter armed similarly to Durand. They reached the southeast helipad just as the North Hudson helicopter touched down. Lord Worth himself was the first out. He stood at the foot of the steps and stared in disbelief at the armed men. He said to Larsen: "What in God's name goes on here?"

Durand said: "Welcome aboard the *Seawitch,* Lord Worth. You can regard me as your host and yourself as a guest—an honored guest, of course. There has been a slight change of ownership."

"I'm afraid that this man here—his name is Durand and I assume that he is one of Cronkite's lieutenants——"

"Cronkite!" Durand was jarred. "What do you know about Cronkite?"

"I can hardly congratulate him on his choice of lieutenants." When Lord Worth poured on his icy contempt he used a king-sized trowel. "Do you think we are such fools as not to know who your employer is? Not that Cronkite has long to live. Nor you, either, for that matter." Durand stirred uneasily—Lord Worth sounded far too much like his daughters for his peace of mind. Lord Worth directed his attention to Larsen. "One assumes that this ruffian arrived with accomplices. How many?"

"Four."

"Four! But with Palermo and his men you have over twenty! How is it possible——"

Durand was back on balance. When he spoke it was with a slight, if logical, smugness. "We have something that Larsen hasn't. We have your daughters."

What was apparently pure shock rendered Lord Worth temporarily speechless; then in a hoarse voice he said: "Great God almighty! My daughters!" Lord Worth could have had his Oscar just for the asking. "You—*you* are the kidnaper?"

"Fortunes of war, sir." It said much for Lord Worth's aristocratic magnetism that even the most villainous eventually addressed him in respectful tones. "Now, if we could see the rest of the passengers."

Mitchell and Roomer descended. In tan alpaca suits and horn-rimmed glasses they were innocuousness personified. Lord Worth said: "Mitchell and Roomer. Scientists—geologists and seismologists." He turned to Mitchell and Roomer and said dully: "They're holding my daughters captive aboard the *Seawitch.*"

"God God!" Mitchell was properly shocked. "But surely this is the last place——"

"Of course. The unexpected, keeping a couple of steps ahead of the opposition. What'd you come here for?"

"To find new sources of oil. We have a perfectly equipped laboratory here——"

"You could have saved your time. Can we search your bag and your friend's?"

"Have I any choice?"

"No."

"Go ahead."

"Aaron."

Aaron carried out a quick examination of Mitchell's bag. "Clothes. Some scientific books and scientific instruments. Is all."

Dr. Greenshaw clambered down the ladder, reached up and relieved the pilot of various bags and boxes. Durand looked at the door and said: "Who the hell is he?"

"Dr. Greenshaw," Lord Worth said. "A highly respected doctor and surgeon. We did expect a certain amount of violence aboard the *Seawitch*. We came prepared. We do have a dispensary and small sick bay here."

"Another wasted trip. We hold all the cards, and violence is the last thing we expect. We'll examine your equipment too, Doctor."

"If you wish. As a doctor, I deal in life and not in death. I have no concealed weapons. The medical code forbids it." Greenshaw sighed. "Please search but do not destroy."

Durand pulled out his walkie-talkie. "Send one of Palermo's men across here with an electric truck—there's quite a bit of equipment to pick up." He replaced his walkie-talkie and looked at Mitchell. "Your hands are shaking. Why?"

"I'm a man of peace." Mitchell said. He crossed his hands behind his back to conceal the tremor.

Roomer, the only man to recognize the signals, licked his lips and looked at Mitchell in exaggerated nervous apprehension. Durand said: "Another hero. I hate cowards."

Mitchell brought his hands in front of him. The tremor was still there. Durand stepped forward, his right hand swinging back as if to strike Mitchell open-handed, then let his hand fall in disgust, which was, unwittingly, the wisest thing he could have done. Durand's mind was incapable of picking up any psychic signals: had it been so attuned, he could not have failed to hear the black wings of the bird of death flapping above his head.

The only person who derived any satisfaction, carefully concealed, from this vignette, was Larsen. Although he had talked to Mitchell on the telephone he had never met him—but he had heard a great deal about him from Lord Worth, more than enough to make him realize that Mitchell would have reduced Durand to mincemeat sooner than back down before him. Mitchell had taken only seconds to establish the role he wished to establish—that of the cowardly nonentity who could be safely and contemptuously ignored. Larsen, who was no mean hand at taking care of people himself, felt strangely comforted.

Lord Worth said: "May I see my daughters?"

Durand considered, then nodded. "Search him, Aaron."

Aaron, carefully avoiding Lord Worth's basilisk glare of icy outrage, duly searched. "He's clean, Mr. Durand."

"Across there." Durand pointed through the gathering gloom. "By the side of the platform."

Lord Worth walked off without a word. The others made their way toward the accommodation quarters. As Lord Worth approached his daughters, Heffer barred his way.

"Where do you think you're going, mister?"

"Lord Worth to you, peasant."

Heffer pulled out his walkie-talkie. "Mr. Durand? There's a guy here——"

Durand's voice crackled over the receiver. "That's Lord Worth. He's been searched and he's got my permission to speak to his daughters."

Lord Worth plucked the walkie-talkie from Heffer. "And would you please instruct this individual to remain outside listening range?"

"You heard, Heffer." The walkie-talkie went dead.

The reunion between father and daughters was a tearful and impassioned one, at least on the daughters' side. Lord Worth was all that a doting parent reunited with his kidnaped children should have been, but his effusiveness was kept well under control. Marina was the first to notice this.

"Aren't you *glad* to see us again, Daddy?"

Lord Worth hugged them both and said simply: "You two are my whole life. If you don't know that by this time, you will never know it."

"You've never said that before." Even in the deepening dusk it was possible to see the sheen of tears in Melinda's eyes.

"I did not think it necessary. I thought you always knew. Perhaps I'm a remiss parent, perhaps still too much the reserved highlander. But all my billions aren't worth a lock of your black hair, Marina, or a lock of your red hair, Melinda."

"Titian, Daddy, titian. How often must I tell you?" Melinda was openly crying now.

It was Marina, always the more shrewd and perceptive of the two, who put her finger on it. "You aren't surprised to see us, Daddy, are you? You *knew* we were here."

"Of course I knew."

"How?"

"My agents," Lord Worth said loftily, "lie thick upon the ground."

"And what is going to happen now?"

Lord Worth was frank. "I'm damned if I know."

"We saw three other men come off the helicopter. Didn't recognize them—getting too dark."

"One was a Dr. Greenshaw. Excellent surgeon."

Melinda said: "What do you want a surgeon for?"

"Don't be silly. What does anyone want a surgeon for? You think we're going to hand over the *Seawitch* on a platter?"

"And the other two?"

"You don't know them. You've never heard of them. And if you do meet them you will give no indication that you recognize them or have ever seen them before."

Marina said: "Michael and John."

"Yes. Remember—you've never seen them before."

"We'll remember," the girls said almost in chorus. Their faces were transformed. Marina said: "But they'll be in great danger. Why are they here?"

"Something to do, I understand, with their stated intent of taking you back home."

"How are they going to do that?"

Again Lord Worth was frank. "I don't know. If they know, they wouldn't tell me. They've become bossy, very bossy. Watch me like a hawk. Won't even let me near my own blasted phone." The girls refrained from smiling, principally because Lord Worth didn't seem particularly perturbed. "Mitchell, especially, seems in a very tetchy mood." Lord Worth spoke with some relish. "Near as a whisker killed Durand inside the first minute. Would have, too, if you weren't being held hostage. Well, let's go to my suite. I've been to Washington and back. Long tiring day. I need refreshment."

Durand went into the radio room, told the regular operator that his services would not be required until further notice and that he was to return to his quarters and remain there. The operator left. Durand, himself an expert radio operator, raised the *Georgia* within a minute and was speaking to Cronkite thirty seconds later.

"Everything under control on the *Seawitch*. We have the two girls here and Lord Worth himself."

"Excellent." Cronkite was pleased. Everything was going his way, but, then, he had expected nothing else. "Lord Worth bring anyone with him?"

"The pilot and three other people. A doctor—surgeon, he says, and he seems on the level. Worth seems to have expected some blood to be spilled. I'll check his credentials in Florida in a few minutes. Also, two technicians—seismologists, or something like them. Genuine and harmless—the sight of a machine pistol gives them St. Vitus's Dance. They're unarmed."

"So no worries?"

"Well, three. Worth has a squad of about twenty men aboard. They look like trained killers and I'm pretty sure they're all ex-military. They have to be because of my second worry—Worth has eight dual-purpose antiaircraft guns bolted to the platform."

"The hell he has!"

"Yeah—also piles of mines on the sides of the platform. Now we know who heisted the Mississippi naval arsenal last night. And the third problem is that we're far too thin on the ground. There's only me and four others to watch everybody. Some of us have to sleep sometime. I need reinforcements and I need 'em fast."

"You'll have over twenty arriving at dawn tomorrow morning. The relief rig crew are due in then. A man named Gregson—you'll recognize him by the biggest red beard you ever saw—will be in charge."

"I can't wait that long. I need reinforcements now. You have your chopper on the *Georgia*."

"What do you think I carry on the *Georgia,* an army of reinforcements?" Cronkite paused, then went on reluctantly: "I can spare eight men, no more."

"They have radar aboard."

"So they have radar. What difference does it make? You're in command."

"Yeah, Mr. Cronkite. But your own golden rule—never take a chance."

"When you hear our helicopter has taken off, neutralize it."

"Destroy the radar cabin?"

"No. We're going to want to use it when we've completely taken over. The scanner will be on top of the drilling derrick. Right?"

"Right."

"It's a simple mechanical job to stop it from turning. All you need is someone with a wrench and a head for heights. Now tell me exactly where Worth's men are quartered. Gregson will need this information."

Durand told him what he wanted to know and hung up.

The dispensary-sick bay and the laboratory were next to each other. Mitchell and Roomer were helping Dr. Greenshaw unpack his very considerable amount of medical equipment. They were, understandably, not unguarded, but Aaron and his Schmeisser were on watch on the two outside doors, and Aaron was hardly in an alert or trigger-ready state of mind. In fact, he regarded his vigil as being close to pointless. He had been present when the three men disembarked from the helicopter and had formed the same opinion of them as Durand.

In the sick bay Dr. Greenshaw upended and removed the false bottom of one of his medical supply boxes. With a gingerly and patently nervous apprehension, he took out two belt holsters, two Smith & Wesson .38s, two silencers and two spare magazines. Wordlessly, Mitchell and Roomer buckled on the weaponry. Dr. Greenshaw, a man, as they were discovering, of a genuinely devout turn of mind, said: "I only hope no one discovers you wearing those pistols."

Roomer said: "We appreciate your concern, Doctor. But don't worry about us."

"I wasn't worrying about you." Dr. Greenshaw assumed his most somber expression. "A good Christian can also pray for the souls of the ungodly."

A long distance away the meeting of ten was again assembled at Lake Tahoe. At the former meeting the atmosphere had been hopeful, forceful and determined, the participants confident that things would go their way, spuriously motivated by their expressed intent to avert a third world war. On this evening the spirit—if that was the word—of the meeting had changed about by 180 degrees. They were depressed, vacillating, uncertain and wholly lacking in confidence, especially in view of the fact that their allegedly humanitarian attempts to prevent the outbreak of war seemed to be having precisely the opposite effect.

Again, as it was his holiday home, Benson was hosting the meeting. But this time Benson was also undoubtedly the man in charge. Opening the discussion, he said: "Gentlemen, we are in trouble. Not just simple, plain trouble, but enormous trouble that could bring us all down. It stems from two facts—we underestimated Lord Worth's extraordinary power and we overestimated Cronkite's ability to handle the situation with a suitable degree of discretion and tact. I admit I was responsible for introducing Cronkite to you, but on the other hand, you were unanimous in your belief that Cronkite was the only man to handle the job. And we were not aware that Cronkite's detestation of Lord Worth ran to the extent of a virulent and irresponsible hatred.

"I have friends in the Pentagon, not important ones but ones that matter. The Pentagon, normally, like any other department of government, leaks secrets like a broken sieve. This time I had to pay twenty thousand dollars to a stenographer and the same to a cipher clerk which, for a pair of comparatively lowly paid government employees, represents a pretty fair return for a few hours' work.

"First, everything is known about our previous meeting here, every word and sentiment that was expressed and the identities of all of us." Benson paused and looked round the room, partly to allow time for the damning enormity of this information to sink in, partly to make it clear that he expected to be recompensed for his very considerable outlay.

Mr. A, one of the vastly powerful Arabian Gulf potentates, said: "I thought our security here was one hundred per cent. How could anyone have known of our presence?"

"No external agency was involved. I have good friends in California intelligence. Their interest in us is zero. Nor was the FBI involved. For that to have happened we'd have had to commit some crime and then cross state lines. Neither of those have we done. And before we met last time I had an electronics expert in to check not only this room but the entire house for bugs. There were none."

Mr. A said: "Perhaps *he* planted a bug?"

"Impossible. Apart from the fact that he's an old friend of immaculate reputation, I was with him all the time, a fact that did not prevent me from calling in a second expert.''

Patinos, the Venezuelan, said: ''We give you full marks for security. That leaves only one possibility. One of us here is a traitor.''

''Yes.''

''Who?''

''I have no idea. We shall probably never know.''

Mr. A stroked his beard. ''Mr. Corral here lives very close to Lord Worth, no?''

Corral said: ''Thank you very much.''

Benson said: ''Intelligent men don't make so obvious a link.''

''As you said at our previous meeting, I'm the only person who had no declared interest in being here.'' Borosoff seemed quietly relaxed. ''I could be your man.''

''It's a point, but one which I don't accept. Whether you are here to stir up trouble between the United States and the Soviet Union may or may not be the case. Again it comes down to the factor of intelligence.'' Benson was being disarmingly frank. ''You could be, and probably are, a Soviet agent. But top agents are never caught in the role of *agent provocateur.* I am not complimenting you on your unquestioned intelligence. I prefer to rely on simple common sense.'' Benson, who appeared to have developed a new maturity and authority, looked around the company. ''Every word spoken here will doubtless be relayed to either Lord Worth or the State Department. It no longer matters. We are here to set right any wrongs for which we may have been—however unwittingly, I may say—responsible.

''We know that a Russian missile naval craft and a Russian-built Cuban submarine are closing in on the *Seawitch.* We also know that a Venezuelan destroyer is doing the same. What you don't know is that countermeasures are being taken. My information—and the source is impeccable—is that Lord Worth was today closeted with Benton, the Secretary of State, in Washington. My further information is that Benton was only partially convinced by Lord Worth's suspicions. He was, unfortunately, wholly convinced when the news came through of Cronkite's irresponsible folly in kidnaping Lord Worth's two daughters. As a result, a United States cruiser and destroyer, both armed with the most sophisticated weaponry, have moved out into the Gulf of Mexico. An American nuclear submarine is already patrolling those waters. Another American vessel is already shadowing your destroyer, Mr. Patinos: your destroyer, with its vastly inferior detecting equipment, is wholly unaware of this. Additionally, at a Louisiana air base, a squadron of supersonic fighter-bombers is on instant alert.

''The Americans are no longer in any mood to play around. My information is that they are prepared for a showdown and are prepared for the eyeball-to-eyeball confrontation which John Kennedy had with Khrushchev over Cuba. The Russians, clearly, would never risk a local nuclear confrontation where the home-territory advantages are so overwhelmingly American. Neither side would dream of mounting a pre-emptive strike over the issue of a few pennies on a barrel of oil. But if the hot line between Washington and Moscow begins to burn, national prestige will make it difficult for either side to back down until they arrive at a face-saving formula, which could take quite some time and would, much worse, generate overwhelming worldwide publicity. This would inevitably involve us. So I would advise you, Mr. Borosoff and Mr. Patinos, to call off your dogs of war before that hot line starts burning. That way, and only in that way, can we survive with our good names left unbesmirched. I blame neither of you gentlemen. You may have given the nod to Cronkite, but you did not reckon on the possibility that Cronkite would carry matters to such ridiculous lengths. Please, please believe me that the Americans will not hesitate to blast your ships out of the water.''

Oil ministers do not become oil ministers because they are mentally retarded. Patinos smiled a smile of wry resignation. ''I do not relish the thought of personal ruin. Nor do I relish the thought of becoming a scapegoat for my government.'' He looked across at Borosoff. ''We call off the dogs of war?''

Borosoff nodded. ''Back to their kennels and no alas. I wish to return to my Russia and this will give me great face, for they will not have to lose face in the world.''

Mr. A leaned back in his chair. His relief was manifest. ''Well, that would seem to cover that.''

''It covers most of it,'' Benson said. ''But not all. Another very unpleasant and potentially terrifying crime occurred this afternoon. I heard of it only an hour ago and it will be the hottest topic in the nation tonight. I only hope to God that, although we were in no way responsible for it, we won't be implicated in it. A place called the Netley Rowan Arsenal was broken into this afternoon. It's supposed to be just another arms depot insofar as the public is concerned—and so, mainly, it is. But it's also a TNW arsenal. TNW means 'tactical nuclear weapons.' Two of them were stolen in the break-in and appear to have vanished without trace.''

''God above!'' The expression and tone of the man from Honduras accurately reflected the shocked feelings of all around the table. ''Cronkite?''

''I'd bet on it. No proof, naturally, but who the hell else?''

Henderson said: ''No disrespect to Mr. Borosoff here, but couldn't the Russians, say, have been seeking a prototype?''

Benson looked as weary as his voice sounded. ''The Russians already have God knows how many of those things. It's public knowledge that they have thousands of them deployed along the border between the Warsaw pact and NATO countries—many of them, it is suspected, more sophisticated than ours. The Russians need our TNWs the way they need bows and arrows.'' Borosoff, despite the anxiety he shared with the others, permitted himself the ghost of a smile of complacency. ''Cronkite. The man's running wild.''

Mr. A said: ''You think he's so totally crazy as to use a nuclear device against the *Seawitch?*''

''I do not profess to understand the workings of an obviously diseased mind,'' Benson said. ''He's capable of anything.''

Patinos said: ''What's this weapon like?''

''I don't know. I phoned the Pentagon, a very senior official there, but although he's an old friend of mine, he refused to release highly classified information. All I know is that it can be used as a land-based time bomb— I suppose that includes the sea as well—or as an aircraft bomb. We can forget the second use. It can only be used in a limited number of supersonic fighter-bombers, which will already, I suppose, be under the heaviest security guard ever, which would strike me as a superfluous precaution as there is no chance that Cronkite, even with his obviously wide range of contacts, could know anyone who could fly one of those planes.''

''So what happens?''

''I think we'd better consult an astrologer on that one. All I know is that Cronkite has gone stark raving mad.''

Cronkite, aboard the *Georgia,* would have thought the same of them. He had a job to do and he was doing it to the best of his ability. Had he known of the possible withdrawal of the warships that had sailed from Cuba and Venezuela, he would not have been unduly concerned. He had had some vague idea that they might have been useful to him in some way, but he had primarily wished to have them as a cover and a smokescreen. Cronkite's vendetta against Lord Worth was a highly personal and extremely vindictive one and he wanted no other than himself to administer the *coup de grâce*. Retribution exacted through the medium of other hands would not do at all.

Meantime, he was well content. He was convinced that the *Seawitch* was in his hands. Come the dawn it would be doubly in his hands. He knew of their defenses and radar. The *Starlight*, under Easton, was waiting until full darkness before it moved in for the initial attack, and as rain had been falling steadily for some time now and the lowering sky blotted out the quarter-moon, it promised to be as nearly dark as it ever becomes at sea.

A message was brought to him from the radio office. Cronkite glanced at it briefly, picked up the phone to the helipad and reached the pilot in his shelter. "Ready to go, Wilson?"

"Whenever you say, Mr. Cronkite."

"Then, now." Cronkite closed a rheostat switch and a dull glow of light outlined the helipad, just enough to let Wilson make a clean takeoff. The helicopter made a half-circle, switched on its landing light and made a smooth landing on the calm waters less than a hundred yards from the stationary *Georgia*.

Cronkite called the radar room. "You have him on the screen?"

"Yes, sir. He's making an instrument approach on our radar."

"Let me know when he's about three miles out."

Less than a minute later the operator gave him the word. Cronkite turned the rheostat to full and the helipad became brilliantly illuminated.

A minute later a helicopter, landing lights on, appeared from the north through the driving rain. Just over another minute later it touched down as delicately as a moth, an understandable precaution by the pilot, in view of the cargo he was carrying. The fueling hoses were connected immediately. The door opened and three men descended—the alleged Colonel Farquharson, Lieutenant Colonel Dewings and Major Breckley, who had been responsible for the Netley Rowan Arsenal break-in. They helped unload two large, double-handed and obviously very heavy suitcases. Cronkite, with suitable admonitions as to delicacy in handling, showed crew members where to stow the cases in shelter.

Within ten minutes the helicopter was on its way back to the mainland. Five minutes after that, the *Georgia*'s own helicopter had returned and all the helipad lights were switched off.

8

IT WAS due only to cruel ill luck and the extremely jittery state of Durand's nerves that John Roomer and Melinda Worth found themselves the first patients in Dr. Greenshaw's sick bay.

Durand was in a highly apprehensive state of mind, a mood that transferred itself all too easily to his four subordinates. Although he held control of the *Seawitch*, he knew that his hold was a tenuous one: he had not bargained on finding Palermo and his cutthroats on board, and even though he held the master keys to both the occidental and oriental quarters in his pocket—the drilling crew was in the former quarters, Palermo and his men in the latter—he was acutely aware that there were far too many windows in both quarters and he didn't have the men to cover every possible exit. He had broadcast a message over the external loud-hailer that anyone found on the platform would be shot on sight and had two men on constant patrol round the oriental quarters—he had no fear of the unarmed drilling-rig crew—and another two constantly patrolling the platform. He had no fear of Lord Worth, his seismologists and the girls—as sources of danger he held them in contempt. Besides, they were unarmed. Even so, the two men patrolling the platform had been instructed to do so in such a fashion as to make sure that at least one had an eye on the doors to the suite of Lord Worth, the laboratory and the sick bay, all three of which had intercommunicating doors.

No one inside those three places had heard the warning broadcast—and this, ironically, because Lord Worth was not above indulging in what he regarded as the bare minimum of basic creature comforts. Oil rigs can be uncommonly noisy places, and those quarters he had heavily insulated.

Mitchell had been in his tiny cubicle of the laboratory at the time, reading the complete plan of the layout of the *Seawitch* over and over again until he was certain that he could have found his way around the rig blindfolded. This had taken him about twenty minutes. It was in the fifth minute of his studying that the shots had been fired, but again, because of the soundproofing, the sound had not reached him. He had just put the plans away in a drawer when his door opened and Marina entered. She was white-faced and shaking and her face was streaked with tears. He put his arms round her and she grabbed him tightly.

"Why weren't you there?" she sobbed. "Why weren't you there? You could have stopped them. You could have saved them!"

Mitchell took no time out to dwell upon the injustices of life. He said gently: "Stopped what? Saved who?"

"Melinda and John. They've been terribly hurt."

"How?"

"Shot."

"Shot? I didn't hear anything."

"Of course you didn't. This area is all soundproofed. That's why Melinda and John didn't hear the broadcast warning."

"Broadcast warning? Tell it to me slowly."

So she told him as slowly and coherently as she could. There had been such a warning but it had gone unheard in Lord Worth's suite. The rain had stopped, at least temporarily, and when Mitchell had retired to study the plans, Melinda and Roomer had elected to go for a stroll. They had been wandering around the foot of the drilling rig, where most of the lights had been turned off since Durand had ordered the abandonment of drilling, and it was there that they had been gunned down without warning.

"Terribly hurt, you said. How bad?"

"I'm not sure. Dr. Greenshaw is operating in the sick bay. I'm not a coward, you know that, but there was so much blood that I didn't want to look."

Arrived in the sick bay, Mitchell could hardly blame her. Melinda and Roomer lay in adjacent cots and both were saturated with blood. Melinda already had her left shoulder heavily bandaged. Roomer had bandages swathing his neck and Dr. Greenshaw was working on his chest.

Lord Worth, his face a mask of bitter fury, was sitting in a chair. Durand, his face a mask of nothingness, was standing by the doorway. Mitchell looked speculatively at both, then spoke to Dr. Greenshaw. "What can you tell so far, Doctor?"

"Would you listen to him?" Roomer's voice was a hoarse whisper and his face creased with near-agony. "Never think of asking us how *we* feel."

"In a minute. Doctor?"

"Melinda's left shoulder is bad. I've extracted the bullet but she needs immediate surgery. I'm a surgeon, but I'm not an orthopedic surgeon, and that's what she must have. Roomer hasn't been quite so lucky. He got hit twice. The one through the neck missed his carotid artery by a whisker, but the bullet passed straight through and there's no worry there. The chest wound is serious. Not fatal but very serious. The bullet struck the left lung, no doubt about that, but the internal bleeding isn't that much, so I think it's a nick, no more. The trouble is, I think the bullet is lodged against the spine."

"Can he wiggle his toes?"

Roomer moaned. "My God, what sympathy."

"He can. But the bullet should be removed as soon as possible. I could do it but I have no X-ray equipment here. I'll give them both blood transfusions in a moment."

"Shouldn't they be flown to a hospital as soon as possible?"

"Of course."

Mitchell looked at Durand. "Well?"

"No."

"But it wasn't their fault. They didn't hear the warning."

"Tough. There's no way I'll fly them ashore. Think I want a batallion of U. S. Marines out here in a few hours?"

"If they die it'll be your fault."

"Everybody's got to die sometime." Durand left, slamming the door behind him.

"Dear, dear." Roomer tried to shake his head, then winced at the pain in his neck. "He shouldn't have said that."

Mitchell turned to Lord Worth. "You can be of great help, sir. Your suite is in direct contact with the radio room; can you hear what is being said in the radio room?"

"That's no problem. Two switches and I can hear both sides of any conversation, either on the telephone, earphones or wall receivers."

"All right—go, and don't stop listening for a second." He looked at the two patients on the cots. "We'll have them airborne for the hospital within a half hour."

"How can that be possible?"

"I don't know." Mitchell sounded vague. "But we'll think of something."

Lord Worth left. Mitchell pulled out a slender pencil flashlight and started to flick it on and off in apparent aimlessness. His complexion had gone pale and the hands that held the pencil light trembled slightly. Marina looked at him first uncomprehendingly, then in dismay, finally in something approaching contempt. Incredulously, she said: "You're frightened."

"Your gun?" Mitchell said to Roomer.

"When they went off for help I managed to drag myself a bit nearer the edge. I unclipped the belt and threw the whole thing over the side."

"Good. We're still in the clear." He seemed to become aware of the tremor in his hands, put away his flash and thrust his hands into his pockets. He said to Melinda: "Who shot you?"

"A pair of very unpleasant characters named Kowenski and Rindler. We had trouble with them before."

"Kowenski and Rindler," Mitchell repeated. He left the sick bay.

Marina said, half in sadness, half in bitterness: "My idol with the feet of clay."

Roomer said huskily: "Put out the light and then put out the light."

"What did you say?"

"*I* didn't say it. Man named Othello. That's the trouble with you million-aires' daughters. Illiterate. First Mitchell puts out the lights. He's got cat's eyes. He can see in almost total darkness where an ordinary man is blind. Did you know that?"

"No."

"Gives him a tremendous advantage. And then he puts out other lights."

"I know what you mean and I don't believe you. I saw him shaking."

"Ahh . . . you don't deserve him."

She stared at him in disbelief. "What did you say?"

"You heard me." Roomer sounded tired and the doctor was looking at him in disapproval. He went on in a somber voice: "Kowenski and Rindler are dead men. They have just minutes to live. He loves Melinda almost as much as he does you, and I've been his closest friend and partner since we were kids. Mitchell looks after his own." He smiled faintly. "I'm afraid he takes care of things in a sort of final way."

"But he was shaking . . ." Her voice was now lacking in conviction.

"He isn't afraid of anything that lives. As for the shaking—he's a throw-back to the old Scandinavian berserkers: he's just trying to hold in his rage. He usually smiles." He smiled. "You're shaking now."

She said nothing.

Roomer said: "There's a cupboard in the vestibule. If there's anything in it, bring it to me."

She looked at him uncertainly, left and returned in a few minutes, carry-ing a pair of shoes. She held them at arm's length and from the look of horror on her face might have been holding a cobra.

Roomer said: "Mitchell's?"

"Yes."

"Okay. Better return them. He'll be needing them pretty soon."

When she came back, Melinda said to her: "Do you really think you could marry a man who kills people?"

Marina shivered and said nothing. Roomer said sardonically: "Better than marrying a coward, I'd say."

In the generator room, Mitchell found what he wanted right away—a circuit breaker marked "Deck Lights." He pulled the lever and stepped out onto the now darkened platform. He waited a half minute until his eyes adjusted themselves to the darkness, then moved in the direction of the derrick crane where he could hear two men cursing in far from muted voices. He approached on soundless stockinged feet until he was less than two yards away. Still soundlessly, he held his pencil flash on top of the barrel of the Smith & Wesson and slid forward the flash switch.

The two men swung round in remarkably swift unison, hands reaching for their guns.

Mitchell said: "You know what this is, don't you?"

They knew. The deep-bluish sheen of a silencer-equipped .38 is not readily mistakable for a popgun. Their hands stopped reaching for their guns. It was, to say the least, rather unnerving to see an illuminated silenced gun and nothing but blackness beyond it.

"Clasp your hands behind your necks, turn round and start walking."

They walked until they could walk no more, for the good reason that they had reached the end of the platform. Beyond that lay nothing but the 200-foot drop to the Gulf of Mexico.

Mitchell said: "Keep your hands clasped and turned round."

They did so. "You're Kowenski and Rindler?"

There was no reply.

"You're the two who gunned down Melinda and Mr. Roomer?"

Again there was no reply. Vocal cords can become paralyzed when the mind is possessed of the irrevocable certainty that one is but one step, one second, removed from eternity. Mitchell squeezed the trigger twice and was walking away before the dead men had hit the waters of the Gulf. He had taken only four steps when a flashlight beam struck him in the face.

"Well, well, if it isn't smart-ass Mitchell, the scared scientist." Mitchell couldn't see the man—and the gun undoubtedly behind the flashlight—but he had no difficulty in recognizing the voice of Heffer, the one with the sharp nose and ratlike teeth. "*And* carrying a silenced gun. Whatcha up to, Mr. Mitchell?"

Heffer had made the classic blunder of all incompetent would-be assassins. He should have shot Mitchell on sight and then asked the questions. Mitchell flicked on his pencil torch and spun it upward, where it spiraled around like a demented firefly. Heffer would have been less than human not to have had the instinctive reaction of glancing upward as his subconscious mind speculated as to what the hell Mitchell was up to: a speculation of very brief duration indeed, because Heffer was dead before the flash fell back onto the platform.

Mitchell picked up the flash, still surprisingly working, pocketed it, then dragged Heffer by the heels and rolled him off to join his friends at the bottom of the Gulf. He returned to the sick-bay vestibule, donned his shoes and entered the sick bay itself. Dr. Greenshaw had both his patients on blood transfusion.

Roomer looked at his watch. "Six minutes. What took you so long?"

A plainly unnerved Marina looked at Roomer, half in disbelief, half in stupefaction.

"Well, I'm sorry." Mitchell actually managed to sound apologetic. "I had the misfortune to run into Heffer on the way back."

"You mean he had the misfortune to run into you. And where are our friends?"

"I'm not rightly sure."

"I understand." Roomer sounded sympathetic. "It's hard to estimate the depth of the water out here."

"I could find out. But it hardly seems to matter. Dr. Greenshaw, you have stretchers? Complete with straps and so forth?" Greenshaw nodded. "Get them ready. Let them stay where they are meantime. Can you carry on the blood transfusions in flight?"

"That's no problem. I assume you want me to accompany them?"

"Yes, please. I know it's asking an awful lot, but after you've handed them over to the competent medical authorities, I'd like you to return."

"It will be a pleasure. I am now in my seventieth year and I thought there was nothing fresh left in life for me to experience. I was wrong."

Marina stared at them in disbelief. All three men seemed calm and relaxed. Melinda appeared to have dropped off into a coma-like stupor, but she was merely, in fact, under heavy sedation. Marina said with conviction: "You're all mad."

Mitchell said: "That's what a lunatic asylum inmate says about the outside world—and he may well be right. However, that's hardly the point at issue. You, Marina, will be accompanying the others on the trip back to Florida. You will be perfectly safe there—your father will see that the most massive security guard ever mounted will be there."

"How splendid. I love being made a fuss over, being the center of attraction. However, mastermind, there's just one small flaw in your reasoning. I'm not going. I'm staying with my father."

"That's exactly the point I'm going to discuss with him now."

"You mean you're going out to kill someone else?"

Mitchell held out his hands, fingers splayed. They could have been carved from marble.

"Later," Roomer said. "He appears to have some other things on his mind at the moment."

Mitchell left. Marina turned furiously on Roomer. "You're just as bad as he is."

"I'm a sick man. You mustn't upset me."

"You and his berserker moods. He's just a killer."

Roomer's face went very still. "You know, I don't look forward to the prospect of having a mentally retarded person as a sister-in-law."

She was shocked and the shock showed. Her voice was a whisper. "I don't really know you, do I?"

"No. We're the men who walk down the dark side of the streets. Somebody has to look after the people on the dark side. *We* do it. Do you know how much your father offered us to take you home?" Roomer smiled. "I'm afraid I'm not much good in that department at the moment, but Mike will take care of it."

"How much did he offer you?"

"Whatever we wanted in the world. A million dollars to take you home? A hundred million if we'd ask for it? Sure."

"How much did you ask for?" Her face wasn't registering much in the way of expression.

Roomer sighed, "Poor Mike. To think that he regards you as the pot of gold at the foot of the rainbow. Poor me, too. I'm going to have to live with you too, even at second hand. Let's be corny. Your father loves you. We love you. To pile cliché on cliché, there are some things that can't be bought. Pearls beyond price. Don't make yourself an artificial pearl, Marina. And don't ever insult us again that way. But we have to live on something, so we'll send him a bill."

"For what?"

"Ammunition expended."

She crossed to his cotside, knelt and kissed him. Roomer seemed too weak to resist. Dr. Greenshaw was severe. "Marina, he's not only having a blood transfusion, there's also the factor of blood pressure."

Roomer said: "My blood pressure is registering no complaints."

She kissed him again. "Is that apology enough?" Roomer smiled and said nothing. " 'Berserker' you said. Can anyone stop him when he's like that? Can I?"

"No. Someday, yes."

"The one person is you. Yes?"

"Yes."

"You didn't."

"No."

"Why?"

"They carried guns."

"You carry guns."

"Yes. But we're not evil people who carry evil guns to do evil things."

"That's all?"

"No." He looked across at Melinda. "You see?"

"Please."

"If Kowenski and Rindler hadn't been such damned lousy shots, she'd be dead."

"So you let Michael loose?"

"Yes."

"You're going to marry her?"

"Yes."

"Have you asked her?"

"No."

"You don't have to. Sisters talk."

"Mike?"

"I don't know, John. I'm a running coward, running scared."

"Well?"

"He kills."

"I've killed."

"He'll kill again?"

"I don't know."

"John."

He reached out, took a lock of her gleaming black hair, picked out a single thread. "That."

"You mean?"

"Yes."

"I have to see." She kicked off her high-heeled shoes.

"So much to learn. Sit."

She sat on his bed. Dr. Greenshaw rolled his eyes heavenward. She was wearing blue jeans and a white blouse. Roomer reached up and undid the top button of her blouse. She looked at him and said nothing. Roomer said: "You do the rest. Navy or black jumper."

She was back in thirty seconds, wearing a navy polo. She looked inquiringly at Roomer, who nodded. She left the sick bay.

In Lord Worth's living room, he and Mitchell were seated in adjacent armchairs. The wallspeakers were on. When Marina came in, Mitchell waved her to urgent silence.

Over the speakers Durand's unmistakable voice sounded testy. "All I know is that the deck lights went out some minutes ago and then came back on." Marina glanced at Mitchell, who nodded. "All the light you need to land."

"Have you neutralized the radar scanner yet?"

Marina had never heard the voice before, but the tightening of Lord Worth's lip showed that Cronkite's voice was no stranger to him.

"We don't need to now."

"It was your idea. Do it. We'll leave in ten minutes, then about fifteen minutes' flying time."

" 'We'll leave'? That mean you're coming too?"

"No. I've more important things to do." There was a click: Cronkite had ceased to transmit.

Lord Worth said uneasily: "I wonder what that devious devil means by that?"

"We'll just have to find out the hard way." Mitchell looked at Marina. "Where are your shoes?"

She smiled sweetly. "I'm a quick study. Shoes make too much noise out on the platform."

"You're not going out on any platform."

"I am. There are gaps in my education. I want to see how killers operate."

Mitchell said in irritation: "I'm not going to kill anyone. Go get your bag packed. You'll be leaving soon."

"I'm not leaving."

"Why?"

"Because I want to stay with Daddy—and with you. Don't you think that's natural?"

"You're leaving if I have to tie you up."

"You can't tie my tongue up. Wouldn't the law just love to know where the guns stolen from the Mississippi arsenal are?"

Lord Worth looked slightly stunned. "You'd do that to me? Your own father?"

"You'd tie me up and force me aboard that helicopter? Your own daughter?"

"Talk about logic." Mitchell shook his head. "Lord Worth seems to have fathered a nutcase. If you think——"

The wallspeakers crackled again. "Well, don't just hang around. Stop that radar."

"How?" It was Aaron and he sounded grieved. "Do you expect me to climb that damned drilling rig——"

"Don't be stupid. Go to the radar room. There's a red lever switch just above the console. Pull it down."

"That I can do." Aaron sounded relieved. They heard the sound of a door closing. Mitchell kicked off his shoes, turned off the lights in the living room and eased the door open a crack. Aaron, his back already to them, was heading for the radar room. He reached it, opened the door and passed inside. Mitchell moved after him, pulling out his silenced gun and holding it in his left hand. A soft voice behind him said: "I thought you were right-handed."

Mitchell didn't even bother to curse. He said in a resigned whisper: "I am."

Aaron was just pulling the red lever when Mitchell made his soundless entrance. He said: "Don't turn round."

Aaron didn't turn round.

"Clasp your hands behind your neck, then turn and come over here."

Aaron turned. "Mitchell!"

"Don't try anything clever. I've already had to kill three of your friends. A fourth isn't going to give me a sleepless night. Stop right there and turn round again."

Aaron did as he was told. Mitchell withdrew his right hand from his coat pocket. The braided leather sap attached to his wrist by a thong was no more than five inches long, but when it struck Aaron with considerable force and accuracy above and behind the right ear it was apparent that five inches was quite long enough. Mitchell caught him as he fell and eased him to the deck.

"Did you have to do that——" Marina choked and stopped speaking involuntarily as Mitchell's hand clamped itself none too gently over her mouth. She flinched as he shook the sap before her eyes.

"Keep your voice down." The whisper was intentionally savage. He knelt over Aaron, removed and pocketed his gun.

"Did you have to do that?" she said in a low voice. "You could have tied him up and gagged him."

"When I require advice from amateurs I'll come right to you. I haven't time for games. He'll just have a half-hour peaceful rest, and then all he'll need is an aspirin."

"And now?"

"Durand."

"Why?"

"Fool."

"I'm getting tired of people calling me fool. John just called me that. He also said I was mentally retarded and an artificial pearl."

"No shrewder judge of character than old John," Mitchell said approvingly. "If Aaron doesn't return, Durand will come looking for him. Then he'll get on the radio-phone and stop the helicopter flight."

"Well, that's what you want, isn't it?"

"No."

He switched off the light and walked away, Marina following. Mitchell stopped outside the entrance to Lord Worth's sitting room.

"Get inside. You're both an irritation and a liability. I can't function properly with you around. Heroines I can do without."

"I promise you I won't say a word. I promise——"

He caught her by the arm and thrust her forcibly inside. Lord Worth looked up in mild surprise. Mitchell said: "I will hold you personally responsible, Lord Worth, if you let this pesky daughter of yours outside that door again. Also, I'm dimming the deck lights. Anybody moving around the platform will be shot. That's my promise and you'd better believe it. This is no place for children who want to play games." The door closed behind him.

"Well!" Marina sat down and gripped her hands together. "What kind of husband do you think *he* would make?"

"A perfectly splendid one, I should imagine. Look, my dear, one of Mitchell's outstanding assets is a hair-trigger reaction. You blunt it. And you know damn well how he feels about you—your presence just constitutes an additional worry at a time when he can least afford either. A wife doesn't accompany her husband down a coal mine or on a wartime bombing mission. And Mitchell is much more of a loner than such people are."

She attempted something between a glower and a scowl, but her beautiful face really wasn't made for it, so she settled for a rueful smile, rose and replenished his glass of malt whisky.

Mitchell removed the gun and two large keys from the pockets of an unconscious Durand, made his way to the main entrance to the oriental quarters, opened the door and switched on the corridor lights.

"Commander Larsen," he called out. "Palermo."

Doors opened and the two men were with him in a few seconds. Larsen said: "Mitchell! What the hell are you doing here?"

"Just a harmless seismologist taking a stroll."

"But didn't you hear the broadcast warning—anyone on the platform will be shot on sight?"

"That's past. One piece of bad news, two of good. Bad news first. Roomer and Miss Melinda didn't hear the warning—those quarters are sound-insulated. So they took a walk. Both were hurt badly. Melinda has a shattered left shoulder. Roomer was shot through the neck and chest. The doctor thinks the bullet is lodged against his spine. We've got to get them to the hospital and quick. Who's Lord Worth's personal pilot?''

"Chambers," Larsen said.

"Get one of your men to have him refuel his machine. Now the good news. Durand is in the radio room; his number two, guy named Aaron, is in the radar room. Both are unconscious." He looked at Palermo. "When they come to—it'll be some time yet—can you have them looked after with loving care and attention?''

"Our pleasure.''

Larsen said: "Durand had three other men.''

"They're dead.''

"You?''

"Yes.''

"We didn't hear any shooting.''

Mitchell gave them a brief sight of his silenced .38. Larsen looked thoughtful. "Lord Worth has talked about you: I used to think he was exaggerating.''

"The other bit of good news. Cronkite is sending some reinforcements by helicopter—not many, I believe, eight or nine—and they should be taking off about now. A fifteen-minute flight, I gather, so I think Cronkite's boat is somewhere just below the horizon, below our radar sweep.''

Palermo brightened. "We blast this chopper out of the sky?''

"My first thought, I must admit. But let's try to play it smart and put him off his guard. Let's let them land, then take them. We'll make their leader report to Cronkite that everything's okay.''

"What if he won't? Or tries to warn him?''

"We'll write out his script. If he changes one word I'll shoot him. Silencer. Cronkite won't hear it.''

"He might hear the guy scream.''

"When a .38 slug enters the base of your skull and travels upward at forty-five degrees, you don't scream very much.''

"You mean you'd kill him?'' While not exactly incredulous, Larsen was obviously taken aback.

"Yes. Then we'd line up number two. We shouldn't have too much trouble with him.''

Larsen said with some feeling: "When Lord Worth talked about you he didn't tell me the half of it.''

"Another thing. I want that helicopter. We'll fake a story that the engine failed above the pad and it crash-landed, and will take several hours to repair. It's always handy to have another helicopter around but, more important, I want to deprive Cronkite of the use of his." He looked at Palermo. "I take it that the reception committee can be safely left in your hands?''

"It sure can. Any suggestions?''

"Well, I doubt that I need to lecture an expert like you.''

"You know me?''

"I used to be a cop. In any case, the rig is loaded with portable searchlights. They'll head for the administration buildings. I'd stay in hiding, switch off the deck lights and then turn on the searchlights when they're, say, thirty yards away. They'll be blinded and won't be able to see you.''

"You can't count on what nutcases like that'll do.''

"I'll bet *you* can." Mitchell smiled briefly at him, cop to crook. He said to Larsen: "I have a feeling that Lord Worth would like to confer with his rig boss.''

"Yes." They walked away as Palermo was already giving rapid instructions to his men. "Lord Worth know what you're up to?"

"I haven't had time. Anyway, I wouldn't tell Lord Worth how to make a billion out of oil."

"Good point." They stopped briefly by the radio room. Larsen gazed at the crumpled form of Durand, half in appreciation, half in regret. "What a beautiful sight. Wish it had been me, though."

"I'll bet Durand—when he wakes up—doesn't. Plastic surgeons come high."

They made their next brief stop at the sick bay. Larsen looked at a still comatose Melinda and a wide-awake Roomer and his massive fists clenched. Roomer smiled. "I know. But you're too late. How deep's the water here?"

"Nine hundred feet."

"Then you'd need a diving bell to get your hands round the throats of those responsible. And how are things with you, Commander Larsen? You can see how things are with us."

"I've been resting. Mitchell has been more active. Besides the three men at the bottom of the Gulf, he's also deprived me of the pleasure of beating the hell out of Durand. Aaron isn't feeling too well either."

Roomer said apologetically: "He doesn't go in much for diplomacy. So the *Seawitch* is in our hands?"

"For the moment."

"For the moment?"

"Do you expect a man like Cronkite to give up? So he's lost five men and is probably about to lose another eight or nine. What's that for a man with ten million to play around with? And he's got his personal vendetta against Lord Worth. If he has to cripple or even destroy the *Seawitch,* including everybody aboard—well, it isn't going to bother Cronkite's conscience for long." He turned to Dr. Greenshaw. "I think it's time you got busy with the stretchers. Can you spare four of your drilling crew, Commander, to help transfer them to the stretchers and then across to the helicopter? I'm afraid, John, you're going to have some unpleasant company on the trip. Durand and Aaron. Tied up like chickens, of course."

"Well, thank you very much."

"I can—occasionally—be as leery as you. I wouldn't put it past Cronkite to get aboard the *Seawitch.* How, I haven't the faintest idea, but with a highly devious mind a driven man can accomplish most anything. If he succeeded I don't want Durand and Aaron blowing the whistle on me. I want to stay an inconspicuous and harmless seismologist."

Larsen gave a few orders on the phone, then he and Mitchell went through to Lord Worth's room. Lord Worth was on the phone, listening and scowling. Marina looked at Mitchell with an expression as forbidding as her father's.

"I suppose you've been littering the platform with a few more dead men?"

"You do me a grave injustice. There's no one left to kill." She gave what might have been a tiny shudder and looked away.

Larsen said: "The ship is in our hands, Miss Marina. We're expecting a little more trouble in about ten minutes, but we can take care of that."

Lord Worth replaced his receiver. "What's that?"

"Cronkite is sending some reinforcements by helicopter. Not many— eight or nine. They won't have a chance. He's under the impression that Durand is still in charge here."

"I take it he's not."

"He's unconscious and tied up. So is Aaron."

A yearning look came over Lord Worth's face. "Is Cronkite coming with them?"

"No."

"How very unfortunate. And I've just had some more bad news. The *Torbello* has broken down."

"Sabotage?"

"No. The main fuel-supply line to its engine has fractured. Just a temporary stop, though it may take some hours to repair. But there's no cause for worry, and half-hourly reports on the state of repairs should be forthcoming."

Another disturbing point had arisen: Lord Worth disclosed that no major marine-insurance companies or Lloyd's of London had ever heard of the existence of the *Tiburon*. The fact was less than surprising if one knew of Mulhooney's renaming exploits—*Hammond* to *Tiburon* to *Georgia*. The vessel had virtually ceased to exist. Even more disturbing, however, was the fact that the Marine Gulf Corporation had reported the disappearance of its seismological survey vessel from Freeport. It was called the *Hammond*.

The U. S. Navy had two points of cold comfort to offer. What the United States did with its obsolete submarines was to scrap them or sell them to foreign governments: none had ever fallen into the hands of commercial companies or private individuals. Nor were there any Cousteau-type submersibles along the Gulf Coast.

The telephone bell jangled. Lord Worth switched on the wall receivers. The radio officer was succinct.

"Helicopter, flying low, due northwest, five miles out."

"Well, now," Larsen said, "this should provide a diversion. Coming, Mitchell?"

"In a minute. I have a little note to write. Remember?"

"The note, of course." Larsen left. Mitchell penned a brief note in neat printed script that left no room for misinterpretation, folded it in his pocket and went to the door. Lord Worth said: "Mind if I come along?"

"Well, there won't be any danger, but I think you'd do better to listen for messages from radar, radio, sonar and so forth."

"Agreed. And I'll call up the Secretary to see what luck he's had in hauling those damned warships off my back."

Marina said sweetly: "If there's no danger I'm coming with you."

"No."

"You have a very limited vocabularly, Mr. Mitchell."

"Instead of trying to be a heroine you might try the Florence Nightingale bit—there are two very sick people through there who need their hands held."

"You're much too bossy, Michael."

"As they say, a male chauvinist pig."

"Could you imagine me marrying a person like you?"

"Your imagination is your own business. Besides, I've never asked you to." He left.

"Well!" She looked suspiciously at her father, but Lord Worth had his risibility under complete control. He picked up a phone and asked that the Christmas tree be opened and the exploratory drilling restarted.

The helicopter was making its landing approach as Mitchell joined Larsen and Palermo and his men in the deep shadows of the accommodation area. The platform light had been dimmed but the helipad was brightly illuminated. Palermo had six portable searchlights in position. He nodded to Mitchell, then made his unhurried way to the pad. He was carrying an envelope in his hand.

The helicopter touched down, the door opened and men with a discouraging assortment of automatic weapons started to disembark. Palermo said: "I'm Marino. Who's in charge here?"

"Me. Mortensen." He was a bulky young man in battle fatigues, looking more like a bright young lieutenant than the thug he undoubtedly was. "I thought Durand was in charge here."

"He is. Right now he's having a talk with Lord Worth. He's waiting for you in Worth's quarters."

"Why are the deck lights so dim?"

"Voltage drop. Being fixed. The landing pads have their own generators." He pointed. "Over there."

Mortensen nodded and led his eight men away. Palermo said: "Be with you in a minute. I've got a private message for the pilot from Cronkite."

Palermo climbed up into the helicopter. He greeted the pilot and said: "I got a message here for you from Cronkite."

The pilot registered a degree of surprise. "I was told to fly straight back."

"Won't be long. Seems Cronkite is anxious to see Worth and his daughters."

The pilot grinned and took the envelope from Palermo. He opened it, examined both sides of a blank sheet of paper and said: "What gives?"

"This." Palermo showed him a gun about the size of a small cannon. "Don't be a dead hero."

The platform lights went out and six searchlights came on. Larsen's stentorian voice carried clearly. "Throw down your guns. You haven't got a chance."

One of Mortensen's men suicidally thought different. He flung himself to the platform deck, loosed off a burst of submachine fire and successfully killed one of the searchlights. If he felt any sense of gratification it must have been the shortest on record, for he was dead before the shattered glass stopped tinkling down on the platform. The other eight men threw down their guns.

Palermo sighed. He said to the pilot: "See? Dead heroes are no good to anyone. Come on."

Eight of the nine men, including the pilot, were shepherded into a windowless storeroom and locked inside. The ninth, Mortensen, was taken to the radio room where he was shortly joined by Mitchell. For the occasion, Mitchell had changed into a boiler suit and makeshift hood, which not only effectively masked his face but also muffled his voice. He had no wish to be identified.

He produced the paper on which he had made notes, screwed the muzzle of his .38 into the base of Mortensen's neck, told him to contact Cronkite and read out the message and that the slightest deviation from the script would mean a shattered brain. Mortensen was no fool and in his peculiar line of trade he had looked into the face of death more than once. He made the contact, said all was well, that he and Durand were in complete control of the *Seawitch*, but that it might be several hours before the helicopter could return, as last-minute engine failure had damaged the undercarriage. Cronkite seemed reasonably satisfied and hung up.

When Larsen and Mitchell returned to Lord Worth's cabin the latter seemed in a more cheerful frame of mind. The Pentagon had reported that the two naval vessels from Cuba and the one from Venezuela were stopped in the water and appeared to be waiting instructions. The *Torbello* was on its way again and was expected to arrive in Galveston in ninety minutes. Lord Worth might have felt less satisfied if he'd known that the *Torbello*, shaking in every rivet, seam and plate, was several hundred miles from Galveston, traveling southwest in calm seas. Mulhooney was in no mood to hang around.

Marina said accusingly: "I heard shots being fired out there."

"Just warning shots in the air," Mitchell said. "Scares the hell out of people."

"You made them all prisoner."

Lord Worth said irritably: "Don't talk nonsense. Now do be quiet. The commander and I have important matters to discuss."

"We'll leave," Mitchell said. He looked at Marina. "Come on—let's see the patients off."

They followed the two stretchers out to the helicopter. They were accompanied by Durand and Aaron—both with their hands tied behind their backs and on a nine-inch hobble—Dr. Greenshaw and one of Palermo's men, a menacing individual with a sawed-off shotgun who was to ride guard on the captives until they reached the mainland.

Mitchell said to Marina: "Last chance."

"No."

"We're going to make a great couple," Mitchell said gloomily. "Monosyllabic, yet."

They said their goodbyes, watched the helicopter lift off and made their way back to Lord Worth's quarters. Both Worth and Larsen were on separate lines, and from the expressions on their faces it was clear that they were less happy with life than they might have been. Both men were trying, with zero effect, to obtain some additional tankerage. There were, in fact, some half-dozen idle tankers on the south and east coasts in the 50,000-ton range, but all belonged to the major oil companies, who would have gone to the stake before chartering any of their vessels to the North Hudson Oil Company. The nearest tankers of the required tonnage were either in Britain, Norway or the Mediterranean, and to have brought them across would have involved an intolerable loss of time, not to say money—this last matter lying very close to Lord Worth's heart. He and Larsen had even considered bringing one of their supertankers into service, but had decided against it. Because of the tankers' huge carrying capacity, the loss in revenue would have been unbearably high—and what had happened to the *Crusader* might happen to a supertanker. True, they were insured at Lloyd's, but that august firm's marine-accident investigators were notoriously, if justifiably, cagey, prudent and cautious men; and although they invariably settled any genuine claim, they tended to deliberate at length before making any final decision.

Another call came through from the *Torbello*. On course, its estimated time of arrival in Galveston was one hour. Lord Worth said gloomily that they had at least two tankers in operation: they would just have to step up their already crowded schedules.

One half hour later another message came through from the tanker. One half hour to Galveston. Lord Worth might have felt less assured had he known that now that dark had fallen, the *Starlight*, leaving the *Georgia* where it was, had already moved away in the direction of the *Seawitch*, its engines running on its electrical batteries. Its chances of sonar detection by the *Seawitch* were regarded as extremely small. It carried with it highly skilled divers and an unpleasant assortment of mines, limpet mines and amatol beehives, all of which could be activated by remote radioactive control.

Yet another half hour passed before the welcome news came through that the tanker *Torbello* was safely berthed in Galveston. Lord Worth informed Larsen he intended to make an immediate voice-link call to the port authorities in Galveston to ensure the fastest turnaround ever, money no object.

He got his voice link in just one minute—the Lord Worths of this world are never kept waiting. When he made his customary peremptory demands the harbor-master expressed a considerable degree of surprise.

"I really don't know what you're talking about, sir."

"Goddam it, I always know what I'm talking about."

"Not in this case, Lord Worth. I'm afraid you've been misinformed or hoaxed. The *Torbello* has not arrived."

"But dammit, I've just heard——"

"One moment, please."

The moment passed into about thirty during which Mitchell thoughtfully brought Lord Worth a glass of scotch, which he half-consumed at one gulp. Then the voice came through again.

"Bad news. There's not only no sign of your tanker, but our radar scanners show no signs of any vessel of that size within a radius of forty miles."

"Then, what the devil can have happened to her? I was speaking to her only two or three minutes ago."

"On her own call sign?"

"Yes, dammit."

"Then obviously she's in no trouble."

Lord Worth hung up without as much as a courtesy thank you. He glowered at Larsen and Mitchell as if what had happened had been their fault. He said at length: "I can only conclude that the captain of the *Torbello* has gone off his rocker."

Mitchell said: "And I conclude that he's under lock and key aboard his own ship."

Lord Worth was heavily ironic. "In addition to your many other accomplishments you've now become psychic."

"Your *Torbello* has been hijacked."

"Hijacked! Hijacked? Now *you've* gone off your rocker. Who ever heard of a tanker being hijacked?"

"Who ever heard of a jumbo jet being hijacked until the first one was? After what happened to the *Crusader* in Galveston, the captain of the *Torbello* would have been extremely leery of being approached, much less boarded, by any other vessel unless it were a craft with respectability beyond question. The only two such types of craft are naval or coast guard. We've heard that the Marine Gulf Corporation's survey vessel has been stolen. A lot of those survey vessels are ex-coast guard with landing space for a helicopter to carry out seismological pattern bombing. That ship was called the *Hammond*. With your connections you could find out about it in minutes."

Lord Worth did find out in minutes. He said: "So you're right." He was too dumbfounded even to apologize. "And this of course was the *Tiburon* that Cronkite sailed from Galveston. God only knows what name it goes under now. What next, I wonder?"

Mitchell said: "A call from Cronkite, I'd guess."

"What would he call me for?"

"Some tough demands, I'd say. I don't know."

Lord Worth was nothing if not resilient. He had powerful and influential friends. He called an admiral in naval headquarters in Washington and demanded that an air-sea search unit be dispatched immediately to the scene. The Navy apologetically said that they would have to obtain the permission of the Commander-in-Chief—that is, the President. The President, he knew, would profess a profound if polite degree of disinterest. Neither he nor Congress had any reason to love the oil companies who had so frequently flouted them—which was less than fair to Lord Worth, who had never flouted anyone in Washington in his life. More, the search almost certainly lay outside their jurisdictional waters. Besides, it was raining in the Gulf and black as the pit, and though their radar might well pick up a hundred ships in the area, visual identification would be impossible.

He tried the CIA. Their disinterest was even more profound. In the several years past they had had their fingers badly burned in public and all their spare time was devoted to licking their wounds.

The FBI curtly reminded him that their activities were purely internal and that anyway they got seasick whenever they ventured on water.

Lord Worth considered making an appeal to the UN, but was dissuaded by Larsen and Mitchell. Not only would the Arab states, Venezuela, Nigeria, every Communist country, and what now went by the name of the Third World—and they held the vast majority of votes in the UN—veto any such suggestion: the UN had no legal power to initiate any such action. Apart from that, by that time the entire UN complex were probably in bed anyway.

For once in his life, Lord Worth appeared to be at a loss. Life, it appeared, could hold no more for him. Lord Worth was discovering that, upon occasion, he could be as fallible as the next man.

A voice-over call came through. It was, as Mitchell had predicted it would be, Cronkite. He was glad to inform Lord Worth that there was no cause for concern over the *Torbello*, as she was in safe and sound hands.

"Where?" Had his daughter not been present, Lord Worth would undoubtedly have qualified his question with a few choice adjectives.

"I prefer not to specify exactly. Enough to say that she is securely anchored in the territorial waters of a Central American country. It is my intention to dispose of this oil to this very poor and oil-deficient country"— he did not mention that it was his intention to sell it at half price, which would bring in a few acceptable hundred thousands of dollars—"then take the tanker out to sea and sink it. Unless, of course——"

"Unless what?" Lord Worth asked. His voice had assumed a peculiar hoarseness.

"Unless you close down the Christmas tree on the *Seawitch* and immediately stop all pumping and drilling."

"Fool."

"How's that?"

"Your thugs have already attended to that. Haven't they told you?"

"I want proof. I want Mortensen."

Lord Worth said wearily: "Hold on. We'll get him."

Mitchell went to fetch him. By the time he returned, overalled and masked, Mortensen had been thoroughly briefed. He confirmed to Cronkite that all pumping and drilling had stopped. Cronkite expressed his satisfaction and the radio link went dead. Mitchell removed the .38 from below Mortensen's ear and two of Palermo's men took him from the room. Mitchell took off his hood and Marina looked at him with a mixture of horror and incredulity.

She whispered: "You were ready to kill him."

"Not at all. I was going to pat him on the head and tell him what a good boy he was. I asked you to get off this rig."

9

LORD WORTH had barely begun to wipe his brow when two men hurried into the room. One was Palermo and the other was one of the rig crew, Simpson, whose duty it was to monitor the sensory instruments attached to the platform's legs and the tensioning anchor cables. He was obviously in a state of considerable agitation.

Lord Worth said: "What fresh horror does fate hold in store for us now?"

"Somebody below the rig, sir. My instruments have gone a bit haywire. Some object, almost certainly metallic, is in intermittent contact with the western leg."

"There can be no doubt about this?" Simpson shook his head. "Seems damnably odd that Cronkite would try to bring down the *Seawitch* with his own men on board."

Mitchell said: "Maybe he doesn't want to bring it down, just damage the leg enough to destroy the buoyancy in the leg and the adjacent members and tilt the *Seawitch* so the drill and pumping mechanisms don't work. Maybe anything. Or maybe he would be prepared to sacrifice his own men to get you." He turned to Palermo. "I know you've got scuba equipment aboard. Show me." They left.

Marina said: "I suppose he's off to murder someone else. He's not really human, is he?"

Lord Worth looked at her without enthusiasm. "If you call being inhuman wanting to see that you don't die, then he's inhuman. There's only one person aboard this rig he really cares for, and you damned well know it. I never thought I'd be ashamed of a daughter of mine."

Palermo had, in fact, two trained scuba divers with him, but Mitchell chose only one to accompany him. Palermo was not a man to be easily impressed, but he had seen enough of Mitchell not to question his judgment. In remarkably quick time Mitchell and the other man, who went by the name of Sawyers, were dressed in scuba outfits and were equipped with reloadable compressed-air harpoon guns and sheath knives. They were lowered to the water by the only available means on such a giant TLP—a wire-mesh cage attached to the boom of the derrick crane. At water level they opened the hinged door, dived and swam to the giant western leg.

Simpson had made no mistake. They were indeed at work down there, two of them, attached by airlines and cables to the shadowy outline of a vessel some twenty feet above them. Both wore powerful headlamps. They were energetically engaged in attaching limpet mines, conventional magnetic mines and wraparound rolls of beehive amatol to the enormous leg. They had enough explosives there, Mitchell figured, to bring down the Eiffel Tower. Maybe Cronkite did intend to destroy the leg. That Cronkite was unhinged seemed more probable than not.

The two saboteurs were not only energetically engaged in their task, they were so exclusively preoccupied with it that they failed to notice the stealthy approach of Mitchell and Sawyers. The two scuba divers pressed their masks together, looked into each other's eyes—there was sufficient reflected light from the other divers to allow them to do this—and nodded simultaneously. Not much given to squeamishness where potential killers were concerned, they harpooned the two saboteurs through their backs. In both cases, death was instantaneous. Mitchell and Sawyers reloaded their compressed-air harpoons then, for good measure, sliced their two victims' breathing tubes, which also contained the communication wires.

On the *Starlight*, Easton and his crew were instantly aware that something had gone drastically wrong. The dead men were pulled up, the harpoons still imbedded in their backs, and as the corpses were being hauled over the gunwales two of the crew cried out in agony: Mitchell and Sawyers had surfaced and picked off two more targets. Whether either had been mortally or grievously injured was impossible to say, but far more than enough had happened for Easton to take off at speed, this time on his much faster diesels: the engines were admittedly noisy, but the darkness was so intense that it was impossible for the alerted gunners on the platform to obtain an accurate fix on them.

The two scuba divers, their own headlights now switched on, swam down to the spot where the mines and explosives had been attached to the legs. There were time fuses attached to both mines and explosives. Those they detached and let fall to the bottom of the ocean. For good measure they also removed the detonators. The explosives, now harmless, they unwound and let them follow the time fuses. The mines they prudently left where they were. Both men were explosives experts but not deep-water explosives experts. Mines, as many ghosts can attest, can be very tricky and unpredictable. They consist of TNT, amatol, or some such conventional explosive as the main charge. In their central tube they have a primer, which may consist of one of a variety of slow-burning explosives, and fitted to the top of the primer is a traveling detonator, activated by sea pressure, which usually consists of seventy-seven grains of fulminate of mercury. Even with this detonator removed, the primer can still detonate under immense pressure. Neither diver had any wish to blow up the pile-driven anchors or the tensioning cables attached to the anchors. Via the derrick crane they made their way back to the platform and reported to the radio room. They had to wait for some time before making their report, for Lord Worth was in a far from amicable telephone conversation with Cronkite. Marina sat apart, her hands clenched and her normally tanned face a grayish color. She looked at Mitchell, then averted her eyes as if she never wished to set eyes on him again, which, at the moment, she probably didn't.

Cronkite was furious. "You murderous bastard, Worth." He was clearly unaware that he was talking in the presence of ladies. "Three of my men dead, harpooned through the back." Involuntarily, Marina looked at Mitchell again. Mitchell had the impression that he was either a monster from outer space or from the nethermost depths: at any rate, a monster.

Lord Worth was no less furious. "It would be a pleasure to repeat the process—with you as the central figure this time."

Cronkite choked, then said with what might have been truth: "My intention was just temporarily to incapacitate the *Seawitch* without harming anyone aboard. But if you want to play it rough you'll have to find a new *Seawitch* in twenty-four hours. That's if you're fortunate enough to survive: I'm going to blast you out of the water."

Lord Worth was calmer now. "It would be interesting to know how you're going to achieve that. My information is that your warships have been ordered back to base."

"There's more than one way of blasting you out of the water." Cronkite sounded very sure of himself. "In the meantime I'm going to offload the *Torbello*'s oil, then sink it." In point of fact, Cronkite had no intention of sinking the tanker: the *Torbello* was a Panamanian registered tanker, and Cronkite was not lacking in Panamanian friends. A tanker could be easily disposed of for a very considerable sum. The conversation, if such an acrimonious exchange could be so called, ended abruptly.

Mitchell said: "One thing's for sure. Cronkite is a fluent liar. He's nowhere near Central America. Not with that kind of reception. And we heard him talking to his friend Durand. He elected not to come on that helicopter flight—which lasted only fifteen minutes. He's lying out there somewhere just over the horizon."

Lord Worth said: "How did things go down there?"

"You heard what Cronkite said. There was no trouble on our part."

"Do you expect more?"

"Yeah. Cronkite sounds too damn confident for me."

"How do you think it'll come?"

"Your guess is as good as mine. He might even try the same thing again."

Lord Worth was incredulous. "After what happened to him?"

"He may be counting on the unexpected. One thing I'm sure of. If he does try the same again he'll use different tactics. I'm sure he won't try an air or submarine approach, if for no other reason than that he doesn't—he can't—have skilled men. So I don't think you'll need your radar or sonar watchers tonight. In any case, your radio operator may need a rest—after all, he's got an alarm call-up in his cabin. I'd keep Simpson on duty, though. Just in case our friends try for one of the legs again."

Palermo said: "But they'd be waiting this time. They'd be operating close to the surface. They'd have armed guards waiting to protect the divers, maybe even infrared searchlights that we couldn't see from the platform. You and Sawyers were lucky the first time, and luck depends on surprise: but there wouldn't be any surprise this time."

"We don't need luck. Lord Worth wouldn't have had all those depth charges stolen and brought aboard unless one of your men is an expert in depth charges. You've got such a man?"

"Yeah." Palermo eyed him speculatively. "Cronin. Ex-petty officer. Why?"

"He could arrange the detonator setting so that the depth charge would explode immediately or soon after hitting the water?"

"I guess so. Again, why?"

"We roll three depth charges along the platform to within, say, twenty-five yards of each of the legs. Your friend Cronin could advise us on this. My distance could be wrong. If Simpson detects anything on his sensors we just push one of the depth charges over the side. The blast effect should have no effect on the leg. I doubt if the boat with the divers would get anything more than a hard shaking. But for divers in the water the concussive shock effects could hardly miss being fatal."

Palermo looked at him with cold appraising eyes. "For a man supposed to be on the side of the law, Mitchell, you're the most cold-blooded bastard I've ever met."

"If you want to die just say so. You'd find it a bit uncomfortable nine hundred feet down in the Gulf. I suggest you get Cronin and a couple of your men and get going on the depth charges."

Mitchell followed to watch Palermo, Cronin and two of their men at work. Cronin agreed with Mitchell's estimate of placing the depth charges twenty-five yards from the legs. As he stood there Marina came up to him.

She said: "More men are going to die, aren't they, Michael?"

"I hope not."

"But you are getting ready to kill, aren't you?"

"I'm getting ready to survive. I'm getting ready for all of us to survive." She took his arm. "Do you like killing?"

"No."

"Then how come you're so good at it?"

"Somebody has to be."

"For the good of mankind, I suppose?"

"Look, you don't have to talk to me." He paused and went on slowly. "Cops kill. Soldiers kill. Airmen kill. They don't have to like it. In the First World War a guy named Marshal Foch got to be the most decorated soldier of the war for being responsible for the deaths of a million men. The fact that most of them were his own men would seem to be beside the point. I don't hunt, I don't shoot game, I don't even fish. I mean, I like lamb as much as the next man, but I wouldn't put a hook in one's throat and drag it around a field for half an hour before it dies from agony and exhaustion. All I do is exterminate vermin. To me, all crooks, armed or not, are vermin."

"Is that why you and John got fired from the police?"

"Do I have to tell you that?"

"Have you ever killed what you, what I, would call a good person?"

"No. But unless you shut up———"

"In spite of everything, I think I might still marry you."

"I've never asked you."

"Well, what are you waiting for?"

Mitchell sighed, then smiled. "Marina Worth, would you do me the honor———"

Behind them, Lord Worth coughed. Marina swung round. "Daddy," she said, "you have a genius for turning up at the wrong moment."

Lord Worth was mild. "The right moment I would have said. My unreserved congratulations." He looked at Mitchell. "Well, you certainly took your time about it. Everything shipshape and secured for the night?"

"As far as I can guess at what goes on in Cronkite's mind."

"My confidence in you, my boy, is total. Well, it's bed for me—I feel, perhaps not unaccountably, extremely tired."

Marina said: "Me, too. Well, goodnight, fiancé." She kissed him lightly and left with her father.

For once, Lord Worth's confidence in Mitchell was slightly misplaced. The latter had made a mistake, though a completely unwitting one, in sending the radio officer off duty. For had that officer remained on duty he would undoubtedly have picked up the news flash about the theft of the nuclear weapons from the Netley Rowan Arsenal: Mitchell could not have failed to put two and two together.

During the third hour of Lord Worth's conscience-untroubled sleep Mulhooney had been extremely active. He had discharged his fifty thousand tons of oil and taken the *Torbello* well out to sea, far over the horizon. He returned later with two companions in the ship's only motorized lifeboat with the sad news that, in the sinking of the tanker, a shattering explosion had occurred which had decimated his crew. They three were the only survivors. The decimated crew were, at that moment, taking the *Torbello* south to Panama. The official condolences were widespread, apparently

sincere and wholly hypocritical: when a tanker blows up its motorized lifeboat does not survive intact. The republic had no diplomatic relations with
the United States, and the only things they would cheerfully have extradited
to that country were cholera and the bubonic plague. A private jet awaited
the three at the tiny airport. Passports duly stamped, Mulhooney and his
friends filed a flight plan for Guatemala.

Some hours later they arrived at the Houston International Airport. With
much of the ten million dollars still remaining at his disposal, Cronkite was
not the man to worry about incidental expenses. Mulhooney and his friends
immediately hired a long-range helicopter and set out for the Gulf.

In the fourth hour of his sleep, which had remained undisturbed by the
sound of a considerable underwater explosion, Lord Worth was unpleasantly
awakened by a call from a seethingly mad Cronkite, who accused him of
killing two more of his men and warned that he was going to extract a
fearful vengeance. Lord Worth hung up without bothering to reply, sent for
Mitchell and learned that Cronkite had indeed made another attempt to
sabotage the western leg. The depth charge had apparently done everything
expected of it, for their searchlights had picked up the bodies of two divers
floating on the surface. The craft that had been carrying them could not have
been seriously damaged for they had heard the sound of its diesels starting
up. Instead of making a straight escape, it had disappeared under the rig,
and by the time they had crossed to the other side of the *Seawitch* it was
long gone into the darkness and rain. Lord Worth smiled happily and went
back to sleep.

In the fifth hour of his sleep he would not have been smiling quite so
happily if he had been aware of certain strange activities that were taking
place in a remote Louisiana motel, one exclusively owned by Lord Worth
himself. Here it was that the *Seawitch*'s relief crews spent their time off in
the strictest seclusion. In addition to abundant food, drink, films, TV and a
high-class bordello, it offered every amenity off-duty oil-rig men could ever
have wished for. Not that any of them would have wanted to leave the
compound gates anyway: nine out of ten of them were wanted by the law,
and total privacy was a paramount requirement.

The intruders, some twenty in all, arrived in the middle of the night. They
were led by a man named Gregson: of all Cronkite's associates, he was by
far the most dangerous and lethal and was possessed of the morality and
instincts of a fer-de-lance with a toothache. The motel staff were all asleep
and were chloroformed before they had any opportunity of regaining consciousness.

The rig relief crew, also, were all asleep but in a somewhat different
fashion and for different reasons. Liquor is forbidden on oil rigs, and the
relief crews on the night before returning to duty generally made the best of
their last chance. Their dormant states ranged from the merely befuddled to
the paralytic. The rounding up of them, most of whom remained still asleep
on their feet, took no more than five minutes. The only two relatively sober
members of the relief crew tried to offer resistance. Gregson, with a silenced
Biretta, gunned them down as if they had been wild dogs.

The captives were transported in a completely standard, albeit temporarily
purloined, moving van and transported to an abandoned and very isolated

warehouse on the outskirts of town. Somewhat less than salubrious, it was perfectly fitted for Gregson's purpose. The prisoners were neither bound nor gagged, which would have been pointless in the presence of two armed guards who carried the customary intimidating machine carbines. In point of fact, the carbines too were superfluous: the besotted captives had already drifted off into a dreamless slumber.

It was in the sixth hour of Lord Worth's equally dreamless slumber that Gregson and his men lifted off in one of Lord Worth's helicopters. The two pilots had been reluctant to accept them as passengers, but Schmeissers are powerfully persuasive agents.

It was in the seventh hour of Lord Worth's slumber that Mulhooney and his two colleagues touched down on the empty helipad of the *Georgia*. As Cronkite's own helicopter was temporarily marooned on the *Seawitch*, he had no compunction in impounding both the helicopter and its hapless pilot.

At almost exactly the same moment another helicopter touched down on the *Seawitch* and a solitary passenger and pilot emerged. The passenger was Dr. Greenshaw, and he looked, and was, a very tired elderly man. He went straight to the sick bay and, without even trying to remove his clothes, lay down on one of the cots and composed himself for sleep. He should, he supposed, have reported to Lord Worth that his daughter Melinda and John Roomer were in good hands and good shape, but good news could wait.

On the eighth hour, with the dawn in the sky, Lord Worth, a man who enjoyed his sleep, awoke, stretched himself luxuriously, pulled on his splendidly embroidered dressing gown and strolled out onto the platform. The rain had stopped, the sun was tipping the horizon and there was every promise of a beautiful day to come. Privately congratulating himself on his prescience that no trouble would occur during the night, he retired to his quarters to perform his customary and leisurely morning ablutions.

Lord Worth's self-congratulations on his prescience were entirely premature. Fifteen minutes earlier the radio operator, newly returned to duty, had picked up a news broadcast that he didn't like at all and gone straight to Mitchell's room. Like every man on board, even including Larsen and Palermo, he knew that the man to contact in an emergency was Mitchell: the thought of alerting Lord Worth never entered his head.

He found Mitchell shaving. Mitchell looked tired—less than surprising, as he had spent most of the night awake. Mitchell said: "No more trouble, I hope?"

"I don't know." He handed Mitchell a strip of teletype. It read: "Two tactical nuclear weapons stolen from the Netley Rowan Arsenal yesterday afternoon. Intelligence suspects they are being flown or helicoptered south over Gulf of Mexico to an unknown destination. A worldwide alert has been issued. Anyone able to provide information should——"

"Jesus! Get hold of this arsenal any way you can. Use Lord Worth's name. Be with you in a minute."

Mitchell was with him in half a minute. The operator said: "I'm through already. Not much co-operation, though."

"Give me that phone. My name's Mitchell. Who's speaking, please?"

"Colonel Pryce." The tone wasn't exactly distant, just a senior officer talking to a civilian.

"I work for Lord Worth. You can check that with the Fort Lauderdale Police, the Pentagon or the Secretary of State." He said to the operator but loudly enough that Pryce could hear: "Get Lord Worth here. I don't care if he's in his damned bath, just get him here now." Back on the phone, he said: "Colonel Pryce, an officer of your grade should know that Lord Worth's daughters have been kidnaped. I was hired to recover them and I did so. More important, this oil rig, the *Seawitch,* is now under threat of destruction. Two attempts have already been made. They were unsuccessful. The Pentagon will confirm that they've stopped three foreign warships headed here for the purpose of destroying the *Seawitch.* I believe those nukes weapons are heading this way. I want full information about them and I'll warn you that Worth will interpret any failure to provide this information as a gross dereliction of duty. And you know the clout that Lord Worth has."

There was a far from subtle change in Colonel Pryce's tone. "It's quite unnecessary to threaten me."

"Just a minute. Lord Worth's just arrived." Mitchell gave a brief resume of his phone conversation, making sure that Pryce could hear every word.

"Nuclear bloody bombs! That's why Cronkite said he could blast us out of the water!" Lord Worth snatched the phone from Mitchell. "Worth here. I have a hotline to the Secretary of State, Dr. Benton. I could patch him in in fifteen seconds. Do you want me to do that?"

"That will not be necessary, Lord Worth."

"Then give us a detailed description of those damned things and tell us how they work."

Pryce, almost eagerly, gave the description. It was almost precisely similar to the one that Captain Martin had given to the bogus Colonel Farquharson. "But Martin was a new officer and shaky on his details. The nuclear devices—you can hardly call them bombs—are probably twice as effective as he said. They took the wrong type—those devices have no black button to shut off in emergency. And they have a ninety-minute setting, not sixty. *And* they can be radioactivated."

"Something complicated? I mean, a VHF number or something of the kind?"

"Something very uncomplicated. You can't expect a soldier in the heat of battle to remember abstruse numbers. It's simply a pear-shaped device with a plastic seal. Strip that off and turn a black switch through three hundred and sixty degrees. It's important to remember that turning this switch off will deactivate the detonating mechanism in the device. It can be turned on again at any time."

"If it should be used against us . . . we have a huge oil-storage tank nearby. Wouldn't this cause a massive oil slick?"

"Sir—oil is by nature combustible and much more easily vaporized than steel."

"Thank you."

"Seems to me you need a squadron of supersonic fighter-bombers out there. I'll relay the request, but they'll have to get Pentagon permission first."

"Thank you again."

Lord Worth and Mitchell left for the former's quarters. Lord Worth said: "Two things. We're only assuming, although it would be dangerous not to assume, that those damned things are meant for us. Besides, if we keep our radar, sonar and sensory posts manned I don't see how Cronkite could approach and deliver them.''

"It's hard to see how. But then, it's harder to figure out that bastard's turn of mind.''

From Lord Worth's helicopter Gregson made contact with the *Georgia*. "We're fifteen miles out.''

Cronkite himself replied, "We'll be airborne in ten.''

A wall radio crackled in Lord Worth's room. "Helicopter approaching from the northeast.''

"No sweat. Relief crew.''

Lord Worth had gone back to his shower when the relief helicopter touched down. Mitchell was in his laboratory, looking very professional in his white coat and glasses. Dr. Greenshaw was still asleep.

Apart from gagging and manacling the pilots, the helicopter passengers had offered them no violence. They disembarked in quiet and orderly fashion. The drill duty crew observed their arrival without any particular interest. They had been well-trained to mind their own business and had highly personal reasons for not fraternizing with unknowns. And the new arrivals were unknowns. Off the coast Lord Worth owned no fewer than nine oil rigs—all legally leased and paid for—and for reasons best known to his devious self he was in the habit of regularly rotating his drill crews. The new arrivals carried the standard shoulder-slung clothesbags. Those bags did indeed contain a minimal amount of clothes, but not clothing designed to be worn: the clothes were there merely to conceal and muffle the shape of the machine pistols and other more deadly weapons in the bags.

Thanks to the instructions he had received from Cronkite via Durand, Gregson knew exactly where to go. He noted the presence of two idly patrolling guards and marked them down for death.

He led his men to the oriental quarters, where they laid their bags on the platform and unzipped them. Windows were smashed and what followed was sheer savage massacre. Within half a dozen seconds of machine-gun fire, bazooka fire and incinerating flamethrowers, all of which had been preceded by a flurry of tear-gas bombs, all screaming inside had ceased. The two advancing guards were mown down even as they drew their guns. The only survivor was Larsen, who had been in his own private room in the back: Palermo and all his men were dead.

Figures appeared almost at the same instant from the quarters at the end of the block. Soundproofed though those quarters were, the noise outside had been too penetrating not to be heard. There were four of them—two men in white coats, a man in a Japanese kimono and a black-haired guard in a wrap. One of Gregson's men fired twice at the nearest white-coated figure, and Mitchell staggered and fell backward to the deck. Gregson brutally smashed the wrist of the man who had fired, who screamed in agony as the gun fell from his shattered hand.

"You bastard idiot!'' Gregson's voice was as vicious as his appearance. "The hard men only, Mr. Cronkite said.''

Gregson was nothing if not organized. He detailed five groups of two men. One group herded the drilling-rig crew into the occidental quarters. The second, third and fourth went respectively to the sensory room, the sonar room and the radar room. There they tied up but did not otherwise harm the operators, before they riddled all the equipment with a burst of machine-gun bullets. For all practical purposes, the *Seawitch* was now blind, deaf and benumbed. The fifth group went to the radio room, where the operator was tied up but his equipment left intact.

Dr. Greenshaw approached Gregson. "You are the leader?"

"Yes."

"I'm a doctor." He nodded to Mitchell, whose white coat accentuated the stains of his blood and was rolling about in a convincing manner, Marina bending over him with bitter tears rolling down her cheeks. "He's hurt bad. I must take him into the sick bay and patch him up."

"We got no quarrel with you," Gregson said, which was, unwittingly, the most foolish remark he'd ever made.

Dr. Greenshaw helped the weak and staggering Mitchell into the sick bay, where, the door closed behind him, he made an immediate and remarkable recovery. Marina stared at him in astonishment, then in something approaching relieved ire.

"Why, you deceiving . . ."

"That's no way to talk to a wounded man." He was pulling off his white coat, coat and shirt. "I've never seen you cry before. Makes you look even more beautiful. And that's real blood." He turned to Dr. Greenshaw. "Superficial wound on the left shoulder, a scratch on the right forearm. Deadeye Dick himself. Now do a real good job on me, Doc. Right arm bandaged from elbow to wrist. Left arm bandaged from shoulder to above the elbow with a great big sling. Marina, even ravishing beauties like you carry face powder. I hope you're no exception."

Not yet mollified, she said stiffly: "I have some. Baby powder," she added nastily.

"Get it, please."

Five minutes later, Mitchell had been rendered into the epitome of the walking wounded. His right arm was heavily bandaged and his left arm was swathed in white from shoulder to wrist. The sling was voluminous. His face was very pale. He left for his room and returned a few seconds later.

"Where have you been?" she asked suspiciously.

He reached inside the depths of the sling and pulled out his silenced .38. "Fully loaded." He returned it to its hiding place, where it was quite invisible.

"Never give up, do you?" Her voice held a curious mixture of awe and bitterness.

"Not when I'm about to be vaporized."

Dr. Greenshaw stared at him. "What do you mean?"

"Our friend Cronkite has heisted a couple of tactical nuclear weapons. He plans to finish off the *Seawitch* in Fourth of July style. He should be here about now. Now, Doc, I want you to do something for me. Take the biggest medical bag you have and tell Gregson that it is your humanitarian duty to go into the occidental quarters to help any of the dying or, if necessary, put them out of their agony. I know they've got a fair supply of hand grenades in there. I want some."

"No sooner said than done. God, you look awful! Destroys my faith in myself as a doctor."

They went outside. Cronkite's helicopter was indeed just touching down. Cronkite himself was the first out, followed by Mulhooney, the three bogus officers who had stolen the nuclear weapons, the commandeered pilot and, lastly, Easton. Easton was the unknown quantity. Mitchell did not appreciate it at the time but Easton's *Starlight* had been so badly damaged by the depth charge that it was no longer serviceable. Less than four miles away what appeared to be a coast guard cutter was heading straight for the *Seawitch*. It required no guessing to realize that this was the missing *Hammond,* the infamous *Tiburon,* the present *Georgia*.

Dr. Greenshaw approached Gregson. "I'd like to have a look at what you've left of those quarters. Maybe there's someone still alive in there . . ."

Gregson pointed to an iron door. "I'm more interested in who's in there. Spicer"—this to one of his men—"a bazooka shot at that lock."

"That's hardly necessary," Greenshaw said mildly. "A knock from me is all that's needed. That's Commander Larsen, the boss of the oil rig. He's no enemy of yours. He just sleeps here because he likes his privacy." Dr. Greenshaw knocked. "Commander Larsen, it's okay. It's me, Greenshaw. Come on out. If you don't, there're some people who're going to blast your door down and you with it. Come on, man."

There was the turning of a heavy key and Larsen emerged. He looked dazed, almost shell-shocked, as well he might. He said: "What the hell goes on?"

"You've been taken over, friend," Gregson said. Larsen was dressed, Greenshaw was pleased to note, in a voluminous lumberjacket cinched at the waist. "Search him." They searched and found nothing.

"Where's Scoffield?" Larsen said.

Greenshaw said: "In the other quarters. He should be okay."

"Palermo?"

"Dead. And all his men. At least I think so. I'm just going to have a look." Stooping his shoulders to look more nearly eighty than seventy, Dr. Greenshaw shambled along the shattered corridor, but he could have saved himself the trouble of acting. Gregson had just met Cronkite outside the doorway and the two men were talking in animated and clearly self-congratulatory terms.

After the first few steps, Greenshaw realized that there could be nobody left alive in that charnel house. Those who were dead were very dead indeed, most of them destroyed beyond recognition, either cut up by machinegun fire, shattered by bazookas or shriveled by the flamethrowers. But he did find the primary reason of his visit—a box of hand grenades in prime condition and a couple of Schmeisser subautomatics, fully loaded. A few of the grenades he stuffed into the bottom of his medical bag. He peered out of one of the shattered windows at the back and found the area below in deep shadow. He carefully lowered some grenades to the platform and the two Schmeissers beside them. Then he made his way outside again.

It was apparent that Cronkite and Lord Worth had already met, although the meeting could not have been a normal one. Lord Worth was lying apparently senseless on his back, blood flowing from smashed lips and apparently broken nose, while both cheeks were badly bruised. Marina was bending over him, daubing at his wounds with a flimsy handkerchief. Cronkite, his face unmarked but his knuckles bleeding, had apparently, for the moment at least, lost interest in Lord Worth, no doubt waiting until Lord Worth had regained full consciousness before starting in on him again.

Lord Worth whispered between smashed lips: "Sorry, my darling; sorry, my beloved. My fault and all my fault. The end of the road."

"Yes." Her voice was as low as his own, but strangely there were no tears in her eyes. "But not for us. Not while Michael is alive."

Lord Worth looked at Michael through rapidly closing eyes. "What can a cripple like that do?"

She said quietly but with utter conviction: "He'll kill Cronkite and his whole mob."

He tried to smile through his smashed lips. "I thought you hated killing."

"Not vermin. Not people who do things like this to you."

Mitchell spoke quietly to Dr. Greenshaw, then both men approached Cronkite and Gregson, who broke off what appeared to be either a discussion or an argument. Dr. Greenshaw said: "You've done your damn murderous work all too well, Gregson. There's hardly a soul in there even recognizable as a human being."

Cronkite said: "Who's he?"

"A doctor."

Cronkite looked at Mitchell, who was looking worse by the minute. "And this?"

"A scientist. Shot by mistake."

"He's in great pain," Greenshaw said. "I've no X-ray equipment, but I suspect the arm's broken just below the shoulder."

Cronkite was almost jovial, the joviality of a man now almost detached from reality. "An hour from now he won't be feeling a thing."

Greenshaw said wearily: "I don't know what you mean. I want to take him back to the sick bay and give him a pain-killing injection."

"Why, sure: I want everyone to be fully prepared for what's about to happen."

"And what's that?"

"Later, later."

Greenshaw and the unsteady Mitchell moved off. They reached the sick bay, passed inside, went through the opposite side and made their unobserved way to the radio room. Greenshaw stood guard just inside the door while Mitchell, ignoring the bound operator, went straight to the transceiver. He raised the *Roamer* inside twenty seconds.

"Give me Captain Conde."

"Speaking."

"On your next circuit out to the oil tank get around behind it, then head south at full speed. The *Seawitch* has been taken over, but I'm sure there's nobody here who can operate the antiaircraft guns. Stop at twenty miles and issue a general warning to all ships and aircraft not to approach within twenty miles of the *Seawitch*. You have its co-ordinates."

"Yes. But why——"

"Because there's going to be a mighty big bang. Christ's sake, don't argue."

"Don't argue about what?" a voice behind Mitchell said.

Mitchell turned round slowly. The man behind the pistol was smiling a smile that somehow lacked a genuine warmth. Greenshaw had been pushed to one side and the gun moved in a slow arc covering them both. "I got a hunch Gregson would like to see you both."

Mitchell rose, turned, half-staggered and clutched his right forearm inside the sling. Greenshaw said sharply: "God's sake, man, can't you see he's ill?"

The man glanced at Greenshaw for just a second, but a second was all that Mitchell required. The bullet from the silenced .38 took the gunman through the heart. Mitchell peered through the doorway. There was a fair degree of shadow there, no one in sight and the edge of the platform not more than twenty feet away. A few seconds later the dead man vanished over the edge. Mitchell and Greenshaw returned to the main body of the company via the sick bay. Cronkite and Gregson were still in deep discussion. Larsen stood some distance apart, apparently in a state of profound dejection. Greenshaw approached him and said quietly: "How do you feel?"

"How would you feel if you knew they intended to kill us all?"

"You'll feel better soon. Round the back of the building, when you get the chance, you'll find some hand grenades which should rest comfortably inside that lumberjacket of yours. You'll also find two loaded Schmeissers. I have a few grenades in my bag here. And Mitchell has his .38 inside his sling."

Larsen took care not to show his feelings. He looked as morose as ever. All he said was: "Boy, oh boy, oh boy."

Lord Worth was on his feet now, supported by his daughter. Mitchell joined them. "How do you feel?"

Lord Worth mouthed his words with understandable bitterness. "I'm in great shape."

"You'll feel better soon." He lowered his voice and spoke to Marina. "When I give the word, say you want to go to the ladies' room. But don't go there. Go to the generator room. You'll see a red lever there marked 'Deck Lights.' Pull it down. After you count twenty, throw it back on again."

Cronkite and Gregson appeared to have finished their discussion. From Cronkite's smile it appeared that his view had prevailed. Lord Worth, Marina, Larsen, Greenshaw and Mitchell stood together, a forlorn and huddled group. Facing them were the ranks of Cronkite, Mulhooney, Easton, and the bogus Colonel Farquharson, Lieutenant-Colonel Dewings, Major Breckley, Gregson and his killers, a formidable group and armed to the teeth.

Cronkite spoke to a man by his side. "Check."

The man lifted a walkie-talkie, spoke into it and nodded. He said to Cronkite: "Charges secured in position."

"Excellent. Tell them to go due north for twenty miles and stay there." This was done. Unfortunately for Cronkite, his view to the west was blocked by the shattered building behind him and he could not see that the *Roamer* was already proceeding steadily to the south.

Cronkite smiled. "Well, Worth, it's the end of the road for both you and the *Seawitch*." He dug into a pocket and produced a black pear-shaped metal container. "This is a radioactive detonating device. Note this small switch here. It's supposed to be good for sixty minutes, but I have already run off ten minutes of it. Fifty more minutes and poof: the *Seawitch*, you, Worth, and everyone aboard will be vaporized. Nobody's going to feel a thing, I assure you."

"You mean you intend to kill all my innocent employees aboard the rig? Cronkite, you are stark raving mad."

"Never saner. Can't have any witnesses left to identify us. Then we destroy two of the helicopters, cripple your derrick crane, smash your radio room and take off in the other two helicopters. You could, of course, figure on jumping into the Gulf, but your chances of survival would be about the same as suicide jumping off the Golden Gate Bridge."

Mitchell nudged Marina. She said in a faint voice: "May I go to the ladies' room?"

Cronkite was joviality itself. " 'Course. But make it snappy."

Fifteen seconds later the deck lights went out.

In the end it was Mitchell, with his extraordinary capacity to see in the dark, who ran round the corner of the shattered building, retrieved the two Schmeissers—he didn't bother about the grenades—returned and thrust one into Larsen's hands. In eight seconds two men with submachine guns can achieve an extraordinary amount of carnage. Larsen was firing blind but Mitchell could see and pick out his targets. They were helped in a most haphazard fashion by Dr. Greenshaw, who flung grenades at random, inflicting even more damage on the already shattered building but not actually injuring anyone.

The lights came on again.

There were still seven people left alive—Cronkite, Mulhooney, Easton, Gregson and three of his men. To those seven Mitchell said: "All right, drop your guns." Shattered and stunned though the survivors were, they still had enough wits left to comply at once.

Marina arrived back and was promptly sick in a very unladylike fashion.

Mitchell put down his Schmeisser and advanced on Cronkite. "Give me that detonating device."

Cronkite removed it slowly from his pocket and lifted his arm preparatory to throwing it over the side. Whatever else, it would have meant the destruction of the *Seawitch*. Cronkite screamed in agony as the bullet from Mitchell's .38 shattered his right elbow. Mitchell caught the detonating device even before it could reach the deck.

He said to Larsen: "Are there two absolutely secure places, with no windows and iron doors, which can be locked without any possibility of opening them from the inside?"

"Just two. Safe as Fort Knox vaults. Along here."

"Search these guys and search them thoroughly. Make sure they haven't even got a penknife."

Larsen searched. "Not even a penknife." He led them to a steel-reinforced cell-like structure and he and Mitchell ushered them inside.

In spite of his agony, Cronkite said: "You're not going to leave us in here, for God's sake!"

"Same as you were going to leave us." Mitchell paused, then added soothingly: "As you said, you won't feel a thing." He closed the door, double-locked it and put the key in his pocket. He said to Larsen: "The other cell?"

"Along here."

"This is madness!" Lord Worth's voice was almost a shout. "The *Seawitch* is safe now. Why in God's name destroy it?"

Mitchell ignored him. He glanced at the timing device on the detonator. "Twenty-nine minutes to go. We'd better move." He placed the device on the floor of the cell, locked the door and sent the key spinning far out over the Gulf. "Get the men out of the occidental buildings, and out of the sensory, radar, sonar and radio rooms and make sure that all the helicopter pilots are safe." He glanced at his watch. "Twenty-five minutes."

Everyone moved with alacrity except for Lord Worth, who merely stood with a stunned look on his face. Larsen said: "Do we need this mad rush?"

Mitchell said mildly: "How do we know that the settings on that detonator are accurate?"

The mad rush redoubled itself. Thirteen minutes before the deadline the last of the helicopters took off and headed south. The first to land on the *Roamer*'s helipad held Mitchell, Larsen, Lord Worth and his daughter, in addition to the doctor and several rig men, while the other helicopters still hovered overhead. They were still only about fourteen miles south of the *Seawitch*, which was as far as the *Roamer* had succeeded in getting. But

Mitchell reckoned the margin of safety more than sufficient. He spoke to Conde, who assured him that every vessel and aircraft had been warned to keep as far away as possible from the danger area.

When the *Seawitch* blew up, dead on schedule, it did so with a spectacular effect that would have satisfied even the most ghoulish. There was even a miniature mushroom cloud such as the public had become accustomed to in the photographs of detonating atom bombs. Seventeen seconds later, those on the *Roamer* heard the thunderclap of sound, and shortly afterward a series of miniature but harmless tidal waves rocked but did not unduly disturb the *Roamer*. After Mitchell had told Conde to broadcast the news to all aircraft and shipping, he turned to find a stony-faced Marina confronting him.

"Well, you've lost Daddy his *Seawitch*. I do hope you're satisfied with yourself."

"My, my, how bitter we are. Yes, it's a satisfactory job, even if I have to say it myself: obviously nobody else is going to."

"Why? Why? Why?"

"Every man who died there was a murderer, some of them mass murderers. They might have got away to countries with no extradition treaties with us. Even if they were caught, their cases might have dragged on for years. It would have been very difficult to get proof. And, of course, parole after a few years. This way, we know they'll never kill again."

"And it was worth it to destroy Daddy's pride and joy?"

"Listen, stupid. My father-in-law-to-be is——"

"That he'll never be." She was glaring at him.

"So okay. The old pirate is almost as big a crook as any of them. He associated with and hired for lethal purposes known criminals. He broke into two federal arsenals and mounted the equipment on the *Seawitch*. If the *Seawitch* had survived, federal investigators would have been aboard in an hour or so. He'd have got at least fifteen to twenty years in prison, and he'd probably have died in prison." Now her eyes were wide, with fear and understanding. "But now every last bit of evidence is at the bottom of the Gulf. Nothing can ever be traced against him."

"That's really why you vaporized the *Seawitch?*"

He eyed her affectionately. "Why should I admit anything to an ex-fiancée?"

"Mrs. Michael Mitchell." She mused. "I suppose I could go through life with a worse name."

Goodbye California

Gisela

FOREWORD

IT WAS at twenty seconds to six o'clock on the morning of February 9, 1972, that the earth shook. As such tremors go, it could hardly even be called noteworthy; it was certainly no more remarkable than those that afflict the citizens of Tokyo and its surrounding countryside scores of times a year. Pendant lamps oscillated briefly, some precariously balanced objects fell from their shelves, but those were the only discernible effects of the passing of the earth ripple. The aftershock, considerably weaker, came twenty seconds later. It was learned afterward that there had been four more aftershocks but those were of so low a magnitude that they registered only on the seismographs. Altogether a rather inconsequential affair but memorable for me, at least, inasmuch as it was the first tremor I had experienced: having the ground move beneath your feet provides a distinctly disquieting sensation.

The area where the maximum damage had occurred lay only a few miles to the north and I drove out to see it the following day. The township of Sylmar, which had borne the brunt of the earthquake, lies in the San Fernando Valley in California, some miles north of Los Angeles. Damage to buildings was widespread but not severe, except in one very localized area: the Veterans Administration Hospital. Before the earthquake it had consisted of three parallel blocks of buildings. The two outer blocks had remained virtually intact; the central one had collapsed like a house of cards. Destruction was total: no part of it was left standing. More than sixty patients died.

It had been destroyed by an earthquake the epicenter of which had been some eight miles distant to the northeast. But what was important—and significant—about the earthquake that had caused this considerable damage was the factor of its power—or lack of it. The magnitude of an earthquake is registered on an arbitrarily chosen Richter scale which ranges from 0 to 12. And what is important to bear in mind is that the Richter scale progresses not arithmetically but logarithmically. Thus, a 6 on the Richter scale is ten times as powerful as a 5 or a hundred times as powerful as a 4. The earthquake that leveled this hospital in Sylmar registered 6.3 on the Richter scale; the one that wreaked havoc on San Francisco in 1906 registered 8.3 in the former estimate (7.9 according to the recent modifications of the Richter scale). Thus, the earthquake that caused this damage in Sylmar was possessed of only 1 per cent of the effective power of the San Francisco one. It is a sobering thought and, to those burdened with an overactive imagination, a fearful one.

653

What is even more sobering and frightening is the fact that, to the best of our knowledge, no great earthquake—"great" is arbitrarily taken to be anything 8 and above on the Richter scale—has ever occurred beneath or in the immediate vicinity of any major city, except apparently for that awesome North Chinese earthquake of July 1976 when two thirds of a million people in and around Taugshan are reported to have died, although the Chinese have not officially confirmed any statistics. But the law of averages would indicate strongly that major earthquakes will occur in places not conveniently uninhabited or, at least, sparsely populated. There is reason to imagine, unless one chooses to take refuge behind I-don't-want-to-know mental blinders, that this possibility may even today be a probability.

The word "probability" is used because the law of averages is strengthened by the fact that earthquakes largely tend to take place in coastal areas, whether those coastal areas be of land masses or islands; and it is in these coastal areas, for the purposes of trade and because they are the points of ingress to the hinterland, that many of the world's great cities have been built. Tokyo, Los Angeles and San Francisco are three such examples.

That earthquakes should be largely confined to those areas is in no way fortuitous: their cause, as well as that of volcanoes, is now a matter of almost universal agreement among geologists. The theory is simply that in the unimaginably distant past when land first appeared, it was in the form of one gigantic supercontinent surrounded by—inevitably—one massive ocean. With the passage of time and for reasons not yet definitely ascertained this supercontinent broke up into several different continental masses which, borne on what are called their tectonic plates—which float on the still molten magma layer of the earth—drifted apart. Those tectonic plates occasionally bang or rub against one another; the effects of the collisions are transmitted either to the land above or the ocean floor and appear in the form of earthquakes or volcanoes.

Most of California lies on the North American plate, which, while tending to move westward, is not the real villain of the piece. That unhappy distinction belongs to that same North Pacific plate which deals so hardly with China, Japan and the Philippines and on which that section of California lying to the west of the San Andreas fault so unhappily lies. Although the North Pacific plate appears to be rotating slightly, its movement in California is still roughly to the northwest and, now and then, when the pressure between the two plates becomes too much, the North Pacific plate eases this pressure by jerking northwest along the San Andreas fault and so producing one of those earthquakes that Californians don't care so much about.

The extent of the dislocation along this right-slip fault—so-called because if you stand on either side of the fault after an earthquake the other side appears to have moved to the right—is crucial in relation to the magnitude of the shock. Occasionally, there may be no lateral slip at all. Sometimes, it may be only a foot or two. But, even though its consequences are not to be contemplated lightly, a lateral slip of forty feet is eminently possible.

In fact, and in this context, all things are possible. The active earthquake and volcanic belt that circumgirdles the Pacific is commonly—and appropriately—known as the ring of fire. The San Andreas fault is an integral part of this and it is on this ring of fire that the two greatest monster earthquakes (in Japan and South America) ever recorded have occurred. They were on the order of 8.9 on the old Richter scale. California can lay no more claim to divine protection than any other part of the ring of fire and there is no compelling reason why the next monster, about six times as powerful as the great San Francisco one, shouldn't occur, say, in San Bernardino, thus effectively dumping Los Angeles into the Pacific. And the Richter scale goes up to 12!

Earthquakes on the ring of fire can show another disadvantageous aspect—they can occur offshore as well as under land. When this occurs, huge tidal waves result. In 1976 Mindanao in the southern Philippines was inundated and all but destroyed and thousands of lives were lost when an undersea earthquake at the mouth of the crescent-shaped Moro Gulf caused a fifteen-foot tidal wave that engulfed the shores of the bay. Such an ocean earthquake off San Francisco would devastate the Bay area and, in all probability, wouldn't do any good to the Sacramento and San Joaquin valleys.

As it is said, it is the wandering nature of those tectonic plates that is the prime cause of earthquakes. But there are two other imponderable possibilities that could well act as triggering factors which could conceivably cause earthquakes.

The first of those is emissions from the sun. It is known that the strength and content of solar winds alter considerably and wholly unpredictably. It is also known that they can produce considerable alterations in the chemical structure of our atmosphere which in turn can have the effect of either accelerating or braking the rotation of the earth; an effect which, because it would be measurable in terms of only hundredths of a second, would be wholly undetected by many but could have (and may have had in the past) an influence ranging from the considerable to the profound on the unanchored tectonic plates.

There is a respectable body of scientific opinion that holds that the gravitational influences of the planets act on the Sun to modulate the strength of these solar winds. This is of immediate concern since a rare alignment of all the planets of the Solar System is due in 1982. If this theory, known as *The Jupiter Effect* from the title of a book by Drs. John Gribbin and Stephen Plagemann, is correct that alignment will be the trigger for unprecedented solar activity, with repercussions on the stability of planet Earth. So scientists are waiting for 1982 with considerable interest, and not a little trepidation.

The second potential trigger is man. He has gratuitously and haphazardly interfered with due natural processes since the dawn of recorded time and there appears no logical reason why he shouldn't extend his unwanted tinkering to the realm of earthquakes. A species that is capable of prying into and eventually exploiting the ultimate secrets of nature and coming up with the hydrogen bomb is capable of anything. That man should consider the regulation of earthquakes, either by staged triggering or inhibition, is not a new idea. Experiments along those lines have already been carried out for peaceful purposes. Unfortunately (if inevitably), the idea has also occurred that the triggering of earthquakes might be an interesting innovation in the next nuclear war and, indeed, has occurred to such a marked extent that there already exists a multinational agreement, duly signed and solemnly sworn to, prohibiting the use of nuclear weapons that could endanger the environment by causing such things as atmospheric pollution and the creation of tidal waves.

The existence of this sacred treaty will, of course, only serve to incite the signatories, especially the nuclear powers, to intensify their frenzied research into exploiting the capacities of this hitherto unthought of weapon to its fullest possible extent. One has only to think of the similarly sacred SALT treaties—the Strategic Arms Limitation Talks—signed by America and Russia in Helsinki which resulted in the immediate redoubling of activities of the scientists on both sides in their quest for the golden grail, the speedy development of new and more dreadful means for annihilating large sections of mankind. The signing of worthless pieces of paper does not remove the spots from the coat of the leopard.

And, apart from war, this concept can be employed for a variety of other interesting purposes, which is what this book is about.

1

RYDER OPENED his tired eyelids and reached for the telephone without enthusiasm. "Yes?"

"Lieutenant Mahler. Get down here right away. And bring your son."

"What's wrong?" The lieutenant customarily made a point of having his subordinates call him "sir," but in Sergeant Ryder's case he'd given up years ago. Ryder reserved that term for those he held in respect; no friends or acquaintances, to the best of their knowledge, had ever heard him use it.

"Not over the phone." The receiver clicked and Ryder rose reluctantly to his feet, pulled on his sports coat and fastened the central button, effectively concealing the .38 Smith & Wesson strapped to the left-hand side of what had once been his waist. Still reluctantly, as became a man who had just finished a twelve-hour nonstop duty stint, he glanced around the room, all chintzy curtains and chair covers, ornaments and vasefuls of flowers: Sergeant Ryder, clearly, was no bachelor. He went into the kitchen, sniffed sorrowfully at the aroma coming from the contents of a simmering casserole, turned off the oven and wrote "Gone downtown" at the foot of a note instructing him when and to what temperature he should turn a certain switch, which was as near to cooking as Ryder had ever come in his twenty-seven years of marriage.

His car was parked in the driveway. It was a car that no self-respecting police officer would care to have been found shot in. That Ryder was just such a policeman was beyond doubt, but he was attached to the Detective Division and had little use for gleaming sedans equipped with illuminated "Police" signs, flashing lights and sirens. The car, for want of a better word, was an elderly and battered Peugeot of the type much favored by Parisians of a sadistic bent of mind whose great pleasure it was to observe the drivers of shining limousines slow down and pull into the curb whenever they caught sight of those vintage chariots in their rearview mirrors.

Four blocks from his own home Ryder parked his car, walked up a flagged pathway and rang the front doorbell. A young man opened the door.

Ryder said: "Dress uniform, Jeff. We're wanted downtown."

"Both of us? Why?"

"Your guess. Mahler wouldn't say."

"It's all those TV cop series he keeps watching. You've got to be mysterious or you're nothing." Jeff Ryder left and returned in twenty seconds, tie in position and buttoning up his uniform. Together they walked down the flagged path.

They made an odd contrast, father and son. Sergeant Ryder was built along the general lines of a Mack truck that had seen better days. His crumpled coat and creaseless trousers looked as if they had been slept in for a week: Ryder could buy a new suit in the morning and by evenfall a second-hand clothes dealer would have crossed the street to avoid meeting him. He had thick dark hair, a dark mustache and a worn, lined, lived-in face that held a pair of eyes, dark as the rest of him, that had looked at too many things in the course of a lifetime and had liked little of what they had seen. It was also a face that didn't go in for much in the way of expressions. Jeff Ryder was two inches taller and thirty-five pounds lighter than his father. His immaculately pressed California Highway Patrolman's uniform looked like a custom-built job by Saks. He had fair hair, blue eyes—both inherited from his mother—and a lively, mobile, intelligent face. Only a clairvoyant could have deduced that he was Sergeant Ryder's son.

On the way, they spoke only once. Jeff said: "Mother's late on the road tonight—something to do with our summons to the presence?"

"Your guess again."

Central Office was a forbidding brownstone edifice overdue for demolition. It looked as if it had been specifically designed to further depress the spirits of the many miscreants who passed or were hauled through its doorway. The desk officer, Sergeant Dickson, looked at them gravely but that was of no significance: the very nature of his calling inhibits any desk sergeant's latent tendency toward levity. He waved a discouraged arm and said: "His Eminence awaits."

Lieutenant Mahler looked no less forbidding than the building he inhabited. He was a tall thin man with grizzled hair at the temples, thin unsmiling lips, a thin beaky nose and unsentimental eyes. No one liked him, for his reputation as a martinet had not been easily come by: on the other hand, no one actively disliked him for he was a fair cop and a fairly competent one. "Fairly" was the operative and accurate word. Although no fool, he was not overburdened with intelligence and had reached his present position partly because he was the very model of the strict upholder of justice, partly because his transparent honesty offered no threat to his superiors.

For once, and rarely for him, he looked ill at ease. Ryder produced a crumpled packet of his favored Gauloises, lit a forbidden cigarette—Mahler's aversion to wine, women, song and tobacco was almost pathological—and helped him out.

"Something wrong at San Ruffino?"

Mahler looked at him in sharp suspicion. "How do you know? Who told you?"

"So it's true. Nobody told me. We haven't committed any violations of the law recently. At least, my son hasn't. Me, I don't remember."

Mahler allowed acidity to overcome his unease. "You surprise me."

"First time the two of us have ever been called in here together. We have a couple of things in common. First, we're father and son, which is no concern of the police department. Second, my wife—Jeff's mother—is employed at the nuclear reactor plant in San Ruffino. There hasn't been an accident there or the whole town would have known in minutes. An armed break-in, perhaps?"

"Yes." Mahler's tone was almost grudging. He hadn't relished the role of being the bearer of bad news but a man doesn't like having his lines taken from him.

"Who's surprised?" Ryder was very matter-of-fact. For any sign of reaction he showed Mahler could well have remarked that it looked as if it might rain soon. "Security up there is lousy. I filed a report on it. Remember?"

"Which was duly turned over to the proper authorities. Powerplant security is not police business. That's IAEA's responsibility." He was referring to the International Atomic Energy Agency, one of the responsibilities of which was to supervise the safeguard system for the protection of power plants, specifically against the theft of nuclear fuels.

"For God's sake!" Not only had Jeff failed to inherit his father's physical characteristics, he was also noticeably lacking in his parent's massive calm. "Let's get our priorities right, Lieutenant Mahler. My mother. Is she all right?"

"I think so. Let's say I have no reason to think otherwise."

"What the hell is that supposed to mean?"

Mahler's features tightened into the preliminary for a reprimand but Sergeant Ryder got in first. "Abduction?"

"I'm afraid so."

"Kidnap?" Jeff stared his disbelief. "Kidnap? Mother is the director's secretary. She doesn't know a damn thing about what goes on there. She's not even security classified."

"True. But remember she was picked for the job; she didn't apply. Cops' wives are supposed to be like Caesar's wife—beyond suspicion."

"But why pick on her?"

"They didn't just pick on her. They took about six others, or so I gather—the deputy director, deputy security chief, a secretary and a control-room operator. More importantly—although not, of course, from your point of view—they took two visiting university professors. Both are highly qualified specialists in nuclear physics."

Ryder said: "That makes five nuclear scientists to have disappeared in the past two months."

"Five it is." Mahler looked acutely unhappy.

Ryder said: "Where did those scientists come from?"

"San Diego and U.C.L.A., I believe. Does it matter?"

"I don't know. It may be too late already."

"What's that supposed to mean, Sergeant?"

"It means that if those two men have families they should be under immediate police guard." Mahler, Ryder could see, wasn't quite with him so he went on: "If those two men have been kidnaped then it's with a special purpose in mind. Their co-operation will be required. Wouldn't you co-operate a damn sight faster if you saw someone with a pair of pliers removing your wife's fingernails one by one?"

Possibly because he didn't have a wife the thought had clearly not occurred to Lieutenant Mahler, but then thinking was not his forte. To his credit, once the thought had been implanted he wasted no time. He spent the next two minutes on the telephone.

Jeff was grim-faced, edgy, his voice soft but urgent. "Let's get out there fast."

"Easy. Don't go off half-cocked. The time for hurry is past. It may come again but right now it's not going to help any."

They waited in silence until Mahler replaced his phone. Ryder said: "Who reported the break-in?"

"Ferguson. Security chief. Day off, but his house is wired into the San Ruffino alarm system. He came straight down."

"He did what? Ferguson lives thirty miles out in the hills in the back of nowhere. Why didn't he use his phone?"

"His phone had been cut, that's why."

"But he has a police band car radio——"

"That had been attended to also. So had the only phones on the way in. One was at a garage—owner and his mechanic had been locked up."

"But there's an alarm tie-in to this office."

"There was."

"An inside job?"

"Look, Ferguson called only two minutes after he got there."

"Anybody hurt?"

"No violence. All the staff locked up in the same room."

'The sixty-four dollar question . . .'

"Theft of nuclear fuel? That'll take time to establish, according to Ferguson."

"You going out there?"

"I'm expecting company." Mahler looked unhappy.

"I'll bet you are. Who's out there now?"

"Parker and Davidson."

'We'd like to go out and join them."

Mahler hesitated, still unhappy. He said, defensively: "What do you expect to find that they won't? They're good detectives. You've said so yourself."

"Four pairs of eyes are better than two. And because she's my wife and Jeff's mother and we know how she might have behaved and reacted we might be able to pick up something that Parker and Davidson might miss."

Mahler, his chin in the heels of his hands, gazed morosely at his desk. Whatever decision he took the chances were high that his superiors would say it was the wrong one. He compromised by saying nothing. With a nod from Ryder both men left the room.

The evening was fine and clear and windless and a setting sun was laying a path of burnished gold across the Pacific as Ryder and his son drove through the main gates of San Ruffino. The nuclear station was built on the very edge of the San Ruffino cove—like all such stations it required an immense amount of water, some 1,800,000 gallons of sea water a minute, to cool the reactor cores down to their optimum operating temperatures: no domestic utility supply could hope to cope with the tiniest fraction of this amount.

The two massive, gleamingly white and domed containment structures that housed the reactor cores were at once beautiful—in the pure simplicity of their external design—and also sinister and threatening, if one chose to view them that way. They were certainly awe-inspiring. Each was about the height of a twenty-five-story building with a diameter of about 150 feet. The three-and-a-half-feet-thick concrete walls were hugely reinforced by the largest steel bars in the United States. Between those containment structures—which also held the four steam generators that produced the actual electricity—was a squat and undeniably ugly building of absolutely no architectural merit. This was the Turbine Generator Building, which, apart from its two turbogenerators, also housed two condensers and two sea-water evaporators.

On the seaward side of those buildings was the rather inaptly named auxiliary building, a six-story structure, some 240 feet in length, which held the control centers for both reactor units, the monitoring and instrumentation centers and the vastly complicated control system, which ensured the plant's safe operation and public protection.

Extending from each end of the auxiliary building were the two wings, each about half the size of the main building. These in their own ways were areas as delicate and sensitive as the reactor units themselves for it was in these that all the nuclear fuels were handled and stored. In all, the building of the complex had called for something like a third of a million cubic yards of concrete and some fifty thousand tons of steel. What was equally remarkable was that it required only eight people, including a good proportion of security staff, to run this massive complex twenty-four hours a day.

Twenty yards beyond the gate Ryder was stopped by a security guard wearing an irregular uniform and a machine carbine that was far from menacing inasmuch as the guard had made no move to unsling it from his shoulder. Ryder leaned out.

"What's this, open-house day? Public free to come and go?"

"Sergeant Ryder." The little man with the strong Irish accent tried to smile and succeeded only in looking morose. "Fine time now to lock the stable door. Besides, we're expecting lawmen. Droves of them."

"And all of them asking the same stupid questions over and over again just as I'm going to do. Cheer up, John. I'll see they don't get you for high treason. Were you on duty at the time?"

"For my sins. Sorry about your wife, Sergeant. This'll be your son?" Ryder nodded. "My sympathies. For what they're worth. But don't waste any sympathy on me. I broke regulations. If it's the old cottonwood tree for me, I've got it coming. I shouldn't have left my box."

Jeff said: "Why?"

"See that glass there? Not even the Bank of America has armored plate like that. Maybe a Magnum .44 could get through. I doubt it. There's a two-way speaker system. There's an alarm buzzer by my hand and a foot switch to trigger off a ten-pound charge of gelignite that would discourage anything short of a tank. It's buried under the asphalt just where the vehicles pull up. But no, old smarty-pants McCafferty had to unlock the door and go outside."

"Why?"

"No fool like an old fool. The van was expected at just that time—I had the note on my desk. Standard fuel pickup from San Diego. Same color, same lettering, driver and guard with the same uniforms, even the same license plates."

"Same van, in other words. Hijack. If they could hijack it when it was empty why not on the return journey when it was full?"

"They came for more than the fuel."

"That's so. Recognize the driver?"

"No. But the pass was in order, so was the photograph."

"Well, would you recognize that driver again?"

McCafferty scowled in bitter recollection. "I'd recognize that damned great black beard and mustache again. Probably lying in some ditch by this time."

"The guard?"

"Didn't have time even to see the old shotgun, just the one glance and then the van gate—they're side loaders—fell down. The only uniform the guys inside were wearing were stocking masks. God knows how many of them there were, I was too busy looking at what they were carrying—pistols, sawed-off twelve gauges, even one guy with a bazooka."

"For blasting open any electronically locked steel doors, I suppose."

"I suppose. Fact of the matter is, there wasn't one shot fired from beginning to end. Professionals, if ever I saw any. They knew exactly what they were doing, where to go, where to look. Anyway, I was grabbed into that van and had hand and leg cuffs on before I had time to close my mouth."

Ryder was sympathetic. "I can see it must have been a bit of a shock. Then?"

"One of them jumped down and went into the box. Bastard had an Irish accent, I could have been listening to myself talking. He picked up the phone, got through to Carlton—he's the number two man in security, if you recollect, Ferguson was off today—told him the transport van was here and asked for permission to open the gate. He pressed the button, the gates opened, he waited until the van had passed through, closed the door, came out through the other door and climbed into the van that had stopped for him."

"And that's all?"

"All I know. I stayed in there—I didn't have much option, did I?—until the raid was over, then they locked me up with the others."

"Where's Ferguson?"

"In the north wing."

"Checking on missing articles, no doubt? Tell him I'm here."

McCafferty went to his guard box, spoke briefly on the phone and returned. "It's O.K."

"No comments?"

"Funny you should ask that. He said: 'Dear God, as if we haven't got enough trouble here.' "

Ryder half-smiled a very rare half-smile and drove off.

Ferguson, the security chief, greeted them in his office with civility but a marked lack of enthusiasm. Although it was some months since he had read Ryder's acerbic report on the state of security at San Ruffino, Ferguson had a long memory. The fact that Ryder had been all too accurate in his report and that Ferguson had neither the authority nor the available funds to carry out all the report's recommendations hadn't helped matters any. He was a short stocky man with wary eyes and a habitually worried expression. He replaced a telephone and made no attempt to rise from behind his desk.

"Come to write another report, Sergeant?" He tried to sound acid but all he did was sound defensive. "Create a little more trouble for me?"

Ryder was mild. "Neither. If you don't get support from your blinkered superiors with their rose-colored glasses then the fault is theirs, not yours."

"Ah." The tone was surprised but the face still wary.

Jeff said: "We have a personal interest in this, Mr. Ferguson."

"You the sergeant's son?" Jeff nodded. "Sorry about your mother. I guess saying that doesn't help very much."

"You were thirty miles away at the time," Ryder said reasonably. Jeff looked at his father in some apprehension; he knew that a mild-mannered Ryder was potentially the most dangerous Ryder of all, but in this case there seemed no undue cause for alarm. Ryder went on: "I'd expect to find you down in the vaults assessing the amount of loot our friends have made off with."

"Not my job at all. Never go near their damned storage facilities except to check the alarm systems. I wouldn't even begin to know what to look for. The director himself is down there with a couple of assistants finding what the score is."

"Could we see him?"

"Why? Two of your men, I forget their names——"

"Parker and Davidson."

"Whatever. They've already talked to him."

"My point. He was still making his count then."

Ferguson reached a grudging hand for the telephone, spoke to someone in tones of quiet respect, then said to Ryder: "He's just finishing. Here in a moment, he says."

"Thanks. Any way this could have been an inside job?"

"An inside job. You mean, one of my men involved?" Ferguson looked at him suspiciously. He himself had been thirty miles away at the time, which should have put himself, personally, beyond suspicion: but equally well, if he had been involved he'd have made good and certain that he was thirty miles away on the day that the break-in had occurred. "I don't follow. Ten heavily armed men don't need assistance from inside."

"How could they have walked through your electronically controlled doors and crisscross of electric eyes undetected?"

Ferguson sighed. He was on safer ground here. "The pickup was expected and on schedule. When Carlton heard from the gate guard about its arrival he would automatically have turned them off."

"Accepting that, how did they find their way to wherever they wanted to go? This place is a rabbits' warren, a maze."

Ferguson was on even surer ground now. "Nothing simpler. I thought you would know about that."

"A man never stops learning. Tell me."

"You don't have to bribe an employee to find out the precise layout of any atomic plant. No need to infiltrate or wear false uniforms, get hold of copies of badges or use any violence whatsoever. You don't have to come within a thousand miles of any damned atomic plant to know all about it, what the layout is, the precise location of where uranium and plutonium are stored, even when nuclear fuel shipments might be expected to arrive or depart as the case may be. All you have to do is to go to a public reading room run by the Atomic Energy Commission at 1717 H Street in Washington, D.C. You'd find it most instructive, Sergeant Ryder—especially if you were bent on breaking into a nuclear plant."

"This some kind of a sick joke?"

"Very sick. Especially if, like me, you happen to be the head of security in a nuclear plant. There are card indexes there containing dockets on all nuclear facilities in the country in private hands. There's always a very friendly clerk at hand—I've been there—who on request will give you a stack of more papers than you can handle giving you what I and many others would regard as being top-secret and classified information on any nuclear facility you want—except governmental ones, of course. Sure it's a joke, but it doesn't make me and lots of others laugh out loud."

"They must be out of their tiny minds." It would be an exaggeration to say that Sergeant Ryder was stunned; though facial and verbal over-reactions were alien to him, he was unquestionably taken aback.

Ferguson assumed the expression of one who was buttoning his hair shirt really tight. "They even provide a Xerox machine for copying any documents you choose."

"Jesus! And the government permits all this?"

"Permits? It authorized it. Atomic Energy Act, amended 1954, states that citizen John Doe—undiscovered nut case or not—has the right to know about the private use of nuclear materials. I think you'll have to revise your insider theory, Sergeant."

"It wasn't a theory, just a question. In either case, consider it revised."

Dr. Jablonsky, the director of the reactor plant, came into the room. He was a burly, sun-tanned and white-haired man in his mid-sixties but looking about ten years younger, a man who normally radiated bonhomie and good cheer. At the moment he was radiating nothing of the kind.

"Damnable, damnable, damnable," he said to no one in particular. "Evening, Sergeant. It would have been nice to meet again in happier circumstances for both of us." He looked at Jeff interrogatively. "Since when did they call C.H.P.s on an——"

"Jeff Ryder, Dr. Jablonsky. My son." Ryder smiled slightly. "I hope you don't subscribe to the general belief that highway patrolmen only arrest on highways. They can arrest anyone, anywhere, in the state of California."

"My goodness, I hope he's not going to arrest me." He peered at Jeff over the top of rimless glasses. "You must be worried about your mother, young man, but I can't see any reason why she should come to any harm."

"And I can't see any reason why she shouldn't," Ryder interrupted. "Ever heard of any kidnapee who was not threatened with actual bodily harm? I haven't."

"Threats? Already?"

"Give them time. Wherever they're going they probably haven't got there yet. How is it with the inventory of stolen goods?"

"Bad. We have three types of nuclear fuel in storage here—uranium-238, uranium-235 and plutonium. U-238 is the prime source of all nuclear fuel and they didn't bother taking any of that. Understandably."

"Why understandably?"

"Harmless stuff." Absently, almost, Dr. Jablonsky fished in the pocket of his white coat and produced several small pellets, each no more than the size of a .38-caliber bullet. "That's U-238. Well, almost. Contains about three percent U-235. Slightly enriched, as we call it. You have to get an awful lot of this stuff together before it starts to fission, giving off the heat that converts water to steam that spins the turbine blades that makes our electricity. Here in San Ruffino we crowd six and three quarter million of these, two hundred and forty into each of twenty-eight thousand twelve-foot rods, into the nuclear reactor core. This we figure to be the optimum critical mass for fissioning, a process controlled by huge supplies of cooling water and one that can be stopped altogether by dropping boron rods between the uranium tubes."

Jeff said: "What would happen if the water supply stopped and you couldn't activate the boron rods or whatever? Bang?"

"No. The results would be bad enough, clouds of radioactive gas that might cause some thousands of deaths and poison tens, perhaps thousands of square miles of soil, but it's never happened yet and the chances of it happening have been calculated at five billion to one so we don't worry too much about it. But a bang? A nuclear explosion? Impossible. For that you require U-235 over ninety per cent pure, the stuff we dropped on Hiroshima. Now that is nasty stuff. There were one hundred and thirty-two pounds of it in that bomb, but it was so crudely designed—it really belonged to the nuclear horse-and-buggy age—that only about twenty-five ounces of it fissioned, but was still enough to wipe out the city. We have progressed, if that's the word I want, since then. Now the Atomic Energy Commission reckons that a total of five kilograms—eleven pounds—is the so-called trigger quantity, enough for the detonation of a nuclear bomb. It's common knowledge among scientists that the AEC is most conservative in its estimate—it could be done with less."

Ryder said: "No U-238 was stolen. You used the word 'unfortunately.' Couldn't they have stolen it and converted it into U-235?"

"No. Natural uranium contains one hundred and forty atoms of U-238 to each atom of U-235. The task of leaching out the U-235 from the U-238 is probably the most difficult scientific task that man has ever overcome. We use a process called gaseous diffusion and the process is prohibitively expensive, enormously complicated and impossible to conceal. The going cost for a gaseous diffusion plant, at today's inflated rates, is in the region of three billion dollars. Even today only a very limited number of men know how the process works—I don't. All I know is that it involves thousands of incredibly fine membranes, thousands of miles of tubes, pipes and conduits and enough electric power to run a fair-sized city. Then those plants are so enormous that they couldn't possibly be built in secret. They cover so many hundreds of acres that you require a car or electric cart to get around one. No private group, however wealthy or criminally-minded, could ever hope to build one.

"We have three in this country, none located in this state. The British and French have one apiece. The Russians aren't saying. China is reported to have one in Langchow in Kansu Province.

"It can be done by high-speed centrifuges, spinning at such a speed that the marginally heavier U-238 is flung to the outside. But this process would use hundreds of thousands of centrifuges and the cost would be mind-boggling. I don't know whether it's ever been done. The South Africans claim to have discovered an entirely new process but they aren't saying what and U.S. scientists are skeptical. The Australians say they've discovered a method by using laser beams. Again, we don't know—but if it were possible a small group—and they'd all have to be top-flight nuclear physicists—could make U-235 undetected. But why bother going to such impossible lengths when you can just go to the right place and steal the ready-made damned stuff just as they did here this afternoon?"

Ryder said: "How is this stuff stored?"

"In ten-liter steel bottles each containing seven kilograms of U-235, in the form of either an oxide or metal, the oxide in the form of a very fine brown powder, the metal in little lumps known as broken buttons. The bottles are placed in a cylinder five inches wide that's braced with welded struts in the center of a perfectly ordinary fifty-five gallon steel drum. I needn't tell you why the bottles are held in suspension in the air space of the drum—stack them all together in a drum or box and you'd soon reach the critical mass where fissioning starts."

Jeff said: "This time it goes bang?"

"Not yet. Just a violent irradiation which would have a very nasty effect for miles around, especially on human beings. Drum plus bottle weighs about a hundred pounds so is easily movable. Those drums are called bird cages, Lord knows why, they don't look like any bird cage I've ever seen."

Ryder said: "How is this transported?"

"Long distance by plane. Shorter hauls by common carrier."

"Common carrier?"

"Any old truck you can lay hands on." Ferguson sounded bitter.

"How many of those cages go in the average truck shipment?"

"That hijacked San Diego truck carries twenty."

"One hundred and forty pounds of the stuff. Right?"

"Right."

"A man could make himself a fair collection of nuclear bombs from that. How many drums were actually taken?"

"Twenty."

"A full load for the van?"

"Yes."

"So they didn't touch your plutonium?"

"More bad news, I'm afraid. When they were being held at gunpoint but before they were locked up some of the staff heard the sound of another engine. A diesel. Heavy. Could have been big—no one saw it." The telephone on his desk rang. He reached for it and listened in silence except for the occasional "Who?" "Where?" and "When?" He hung up.

"Still more bad news?" Jablonsky asked.

"Don't see it makes any difference one way or another. The hijacked van's been found. Empty, of course, except for the driver and guard trussed up like turkeys in the back. They say they were following a furniture van around a blind corner when it braked so sharply that they almost ran into it. Back doors of the van opened and the driver and the guard decided to stay just where they were. They say they didn't feel like doing much else with two leveled machine guns and a bazooka six feet from their windshield."

"An understandable point of view," Jablonsky said. "Where were they found?"

"In a quarry, up an unused side road. By a couple of young kids."

"And the furniture van is still there?"

"As you say, Sergeant. How did you know?"

"Do you think they'd have transferred their cargo into an identifiable van and drive off with it? They'd have a second plain van." Ryder turned to Dr. Jablonsky. "As you were about to say about this plutonium——"

"Interesting stuff and if you're a nuclear bomb-making enthusiast it's far more suitable for making an atom bomb than uranium although it would call for greater expertise. Probably call for the services of a nuclear physicist."

"A captive physicist would do as well?"

"What do you mean?"

"They—the kidnapers—took a couple of visiting physicists with them this afternoon. From San Diego and Los Angeles, I believe they were."

"Professor Burnett and Schmidt? That's a ludicrous suggestion. I know both men well, intimately, you might say. They are men of probity, men of honor. They'd never co-operate with the criminals who stole this stuff."

Ryder sighed. "My regard for you is high, Doctor, so I'll only say that you lead a very sheltered life. Men of principle? Decent men?"

"Our regard is mutual so I'll just content myself with saying that I don't have to repeat myself."

"Men of compassion, no doubt?"

"Of course they are."

"They took my wife, and a stenographer——"

"Julie Johnson."

"Julie Johnson. When our hijacking thieves start feeding those ladies through a meat grinder, what do you think is going to win our—your friends' high principles or their compassion?"

Jablonsky said nothing. He just lost a little color.

Ferguson coughed in a skeptical fashion, which is a difficult thing to do, but in his line of business he'd had a lot of practice. "And I'd always thought you were devoid of imagination, Sergeant. That's stretching things a bit, surely."

"Is it? As security chief it's your job to vet everybody applying for a job here. This stenographer, Julie. What's her background?"

"Ordinary. Typist making a living. Shares a small flat, nothing fancy, with two other girls. Drives a beat-up Volkswagen. Parents dead."

"Not a millionairess doing the job for kicks?"

"Millionairess! Her old man was a gardener."

Ryder looked at Jablonsky. "So. A stenographer's paycheck. A sergeant's paycheck. A patrolman's paycheck. Maybe you think they're going to hold those ladies for ransom of a million dollars each? Maybe just to rest their eyes on after a long day at the nuclear bench?" Jablonsky said nothing. "The meat grinder. You were talking about this plutonium."

"God, man, haven't you got any feelings?"

"Time and a place for everything. Right now, a little thinking, a little knowledge might help more."

"I suppose." Jablonsky spoke with the restrained effort of a man whose head is trying to make his heart see sense. "Plutonium—plutonium 239, to be precise. Stuff that destroyed Nagasaki. Synthetic—doesn't exist in nature. Man-made—we Californians had the privilege of creating it. Unbelievably toxic—a cobra's bite is a thing of joy compared to it. If you had it in an aerosol in liquid form with Freon under pressure—no one has as yet got around to figuring out how to do this but they will, they will—you'd have an indescribably lethal weapon on your hands. A couple of squirts of this into a crowded auditorium, say, with a couple of thousand people, and all you'd require would be a couple of thousand coffins.

"It's the inevitable by-product of the fissioning of uranium in a nuclear reactor. The plutonium, you understand, is still inside the uranium fuel rods. The rods are removed from the reactor and chopped up——"

"Who does the chopping? Not a job I'd want."

"I don't know whether you would or not. First chop and you'd be dead. Done by remote-controlled guillotines in a place we call the 'canyon.' Nice little place with five-foot walls and five-foot-thick windows. You wouldn't want to go inside. The cuttings are dissolved in nitric acid then washed with various reactive chemicals to separate the plutonium from the uranium and other unwanted radioactive fission products."

"How's this plutonium stored?"

"Plutonium nitrate, actually. About ten liters of it goes into a stainless-steel flask, about fifty inches high by five in diameter. That works out about two and a half kilograms of pure plutonium. Those flasks are even more easily handled than the uranium drums and quite safe if you're careful."

"How much of this stuff do you require to make a bomb?"

"No one knows for sure. It is believed that it is theoretically possible although at the moment practically impossible to make a nuclear device no bigger than a cigarette. The AEC puts the trigger quantity at two kilograms. It's probably an overestimate. But you could for sure carry enough plutonium in a lady's purse to make a nuclear bomb."

"I'll never look at a lady's purse with the same eyes again. So that's a bomb flask?"

"Easily."

"Is there much of this plutonium around?"

"Too much. Private companies have stock-piled more plutonium than there is in all the nuclear bombs in the world."

Ryder lit a Gauloise while he assimilated this. "You did say what I thought you said?"

"Yes."

"What are they going to do with the stuff?"

"That's what the private companies would like to know. The half-life of this plutonium is about twenty-six thousand years. Radioactively, it'll still be lethal in a hundred thousand years. Quite a legacy we're leaving to the unborn. If mankind is still around in a hundred thousand years, which no scientist, economist, environmentalist or philosopher seriously believes, can't you just see them cursing their ancestors some three thousand generations removed?''

"They'll have to handle that problem without me. It's this generation I'm concerned with. Is this the first time nuclear fuel has been stolen from a plant?"

"God, no. The first forced entry I know of, but others may have been hushed up. We're touchy about those things, much more touchy than the Europeans, who admit to several terrorist attacks on their reactor stations.''

"Tell the man straight out.'' Ferguson sounded weary. "Theft of plutonium goes on all the time. I know it, Dr. Jablonsky knows it. The Office of Nuclear Safeguards—that's the watchdog of the AEC—knows about it best of all, but gets very coy when questioned, even though their director did admit to a congressional energy subcommittee that perhaps one half of one percent of fuel was unaccounted for. He didn't seem very worried about it. After all, what's one half of one per cent, especially when you say it quickly. Just enough to make enough bombs to wipe out the United States, that's all. The great trusting American public knows nothing about it—what they don't know can't frighten them. Do I sound rather bitter to you, Sergeant?''

"You do a bit. You have reason to?''

"I have. One of the reasons I resented your security report. There's not a security chief in the country that doesn't feel bitter about it. We spend billions every year preventing nuclear war, hundreds of millions for preventing accidents at the reactor plants but only about eight million on security. The probability of those occurrences are in the reverse order. The AEC says they have up to ten thousand people keeping track of material. I would laugh if I didn't feel like crying. The fact of the matter is they know where it is only about once a year. They come around, balance books, count cans, take samples and feed the figures into some luckless computer that usually comes up with the wrong answers. Not the computer's fault—not the inspector's. There're far too few of them and the system is ungovernable anyway.

"The AEC, for instance, says that theft by employees, because of the elaborate built-in protection and detection systems, is impossible. They say this in a loud voice for public consumption. It's rubbish. Sample pipes lead off from the plutonium runoff spigot from the canyon—for testing strength, purity and so forth. Nothing easier than to run off a little plutonium into a small flask. If you're not greedy and take only a small amount occasionally the chances are that you can get away with it almost indefinitely. If you can bribe two of the security guards—the one who monitors the TV screens of the cameras in the sensitive areas and the person who controls the metal-detector beam you pass through on leaving—you can get away with it forever.''

"Has it ever been done?''

"The government doesn't believe in paying high salaries for what is basically an unskilled job. Why do you think there are so many corrupt and crooked cops? If you don't mind me saying so.''

"I don't mind. This is the only way? Stealing the stuff in dribs and drabs. Hasn't been done on a large scale?''

"Sure it has. Again, nobody's talking. As far back as 1964, when the Chinese exploded their first nuclear bomb, it was taken for granted in this country that the Chinese just didn't have the scientific know-how to separate out U-235 from natural uranium. Ergo, they must have pinched it somewhere. They wouldn't have stolen it from Russia because Chinese, to say the least, are not welcome there. But they're welcome here, especially in

California. In San Francisco you have the biggest Chinese community outside China. Their students are received with open arms in California's
universities. It's no secret that that's how the Chinese came to have the
secrets of making an atom bomb. Their students came over here, took a
post-graduate course in physics, including nuclear physics, then hightailed
it back to the mother country with the necessary information.''

"You're digressing.''

"That's what bitterness does for you. Shortly after they exploded their
bomb it came to light, perhaps accidentally, that sixty kilos of U-235 had
disappeared from a nuclear fuel fabricating plant in Appolo, Pennsylvania.
Coincidence? Nobody's accusing anybody of anything. The stuff's showing
up missing right and left. A security chief in the East once told me that a
hundred and ten kilos of U-235 somehow got lost from his plant.'' He broke
off and shook his head dejectedly. "The whole thing is so damned stupid
anyway.''

"What's stupid?''

"Pilfering a few grams at a time from a plant or breaking into one to steal
it on a grand scale. That's being stupid. It's stupid because it's unnecessary.
If you'd wanted a king-size haul of U-235 or plutonium today what would
you have done?''

"That's obvious. I'd have let the regular crew of that truck load up and
hijack it on the way back.''

"Exactly. One or two plants send out their enriched nuclear fuel in such
massive steel and concrete drums—transported in big fifteen–twenty-ton
trucks—that the necessity for a crane effectively rules out hijacking. Most
don't. We don't. A strong man on his own would have no difficulty in
handling our drums. More than one nuclear scientist has publicly suggested
that we approach the Kremlin and contract the Red Army for the job. That's
the way the Russians do it—a heavily armored truck with an escort armored
vehicle in front and behind.''

"Why don't we do that?''

"Not to be thought of. Same reason again—mustn't scare the pants off
the public. Bad for the nuclear image. Atoms for peace, not war. In the
whole fuel cycle, transportation is by so far the weakest link in security that
it doesn't deserve to be called a link at all. The major road shippers—like
Pacific Intermountain Express or Tri-state or MacCormack—are painfully
aware of this—and are worried sick about it. But there's nothing they can
do about it and, more importantly, there's nothing their drivers can do about
it. In the trucking business—many would prefer the word 'racket'—theft
and shortages are frequently the name of the game.

"Every day two per cent of goods being transported by road in this
country just turn up missing—the figure may even be higher. The wise don't
complain; in the minority cases where people do complain the insurers pay
up quietly because their premiums are loaded against what they regard as an
occupational hazard. 'Occupational' is the key word. Eighty-five per cent of
hijackings involve collusion—which has to involve truck drivers.''

"Has there ever been a case of nuclear hijack on the open road?''

"Hijacks don't happen on the open road. Well, hardly ever. They occur
at transfer points and drivers' stopovers. Driver Jones visits the local lock-
smith and has a fresh set of keys for ignition and cab doors cut and hands it
over to Smith. Next day he stops at a drivers' pull-over, carefully locks the
door and goes—either himself or with his buddy—for his hamburger and
french fries or whatever. When he comes out, he goes through the well-
rehearsed routine of double-take, calling to heaven for vengeance and hot-

footing it to the nearest phone box to call the cops, who know perfectly well what is going on but are completely incapable of proving anything. Those hijackings are rarely reported and pass virtually unnoticed because there are very rarely any crimes of violence involved.''

Ryder was patient. "I've been a cop all my life. I know that. Nuclear hijack, I said.''

"I don't know.''

"You don't know or you aren't telling?''

"That's up to you to decide, Sergeant.''

"Yes. Thank you.'' It was possible for anyone to say whether Ryder had decided anything or not. He turned to Jablonsky.

"Okay, Doc, if we go and have a look at Susan's office?''

Jablonsky's voice was dry. "Unusual of you, Sergeant, to ask anybody's permission for anything.''

"That's downright unkind. Fact is, we haven't been officially assigned to this investigation.''

"I know that.'' He looked at Jeff. "This is hardly the stamping ground for a highway patrolman. Have you been expressly forbidden to come here?''

"No.''

"Makes no difference. Heavens, man, in your place I'd be worried to death. Search the whole damned building if you want.'' He paused briefly. "I suggest I come with you.''

" 'The whole damned building,' as you call it, can be left to Parker and Davidson, who are already here, and the lawmen in their droves who will be here in any moment. Why do you want to come with us to my wife's office? I've never tampered with evidence in my life.''

"Who says you did?'' He looked at Jeff. "You know your father has a long-standing and well-justified reputation for taking the law into his own hands?''

"I've heard rumors, I have to admit. So you'd guarantee on the witness stand the good behavior of someone in need of care and protection?'' It was the first time that Jeff had smiled since he'd heard of his mother's kidnaping.

Jablonsky said: "First time I ever heard anyone mention care and protection and Sergeant Ryder in the same breath.''

"Jeff could be right.'' Ryder was unruffled. "I am getting on.''

Jablonsky smiled his total disbelief.

2

THE OFFICE door, slightly ajar, had four splintered holes tightly grouped around the lock and handle. Ryder looked at them with no reaction, pushed open the door and walked inside. Sergeant Parker stopped what he was doing, which was pushing scraps of paper around a desk top with the rubber tip of a pencil, and turned around. He was a burly, pleasant-faced man in his late thirties who didn't look a bit like a cop, which was why his arrest record ranked second only to Ryder's.

"Been expecting you,'' he said. "A damnable business, just incredible.'' He smiled as if to alleviate the tension which Ryder didn't seem to be feeling at all. "Did you come to take over, to show the incompetents how a professional goes about it?''

"Just looking. I'm not on this and I'm sure old Fatso will take great pleasure in keeping me off it." "Fatso" referred to their far from revered police chief.

"The sadistic blubber of lard would love to do just that." He ignored the slight frown of Dr. Jablonsky, who had never had the privilege of making the police chief's acquaintance. "Why don't you and I break his neck someday?"

"Assuming he's got a neck inside that twenty-inch collar." Ryder looked at the bullet-ridden door. "McCafferty—the gate guard—told me there was no shooting. Termites?"

"Silencer."

"Why the gun at all?"

"Susan is why." Parker was a family friend of long standing. "They'd rounded up the staff and put them in the room across the hallway there. Susan just happened to look out of the door and saw them coming so she closed the door and locked it."

"So they blasted it open. Maybe they thought she was making a dive for the nearest telephone."

"You made the security report."

"That's so. I remember. Only Dr. Jablonsky here and Mr. Ferguson were permitted direct lines to the outside. All other calls have to be cleared through the switchboard. They'd have taken care of the girl there first. Maybe they thought she was leaving through a window."

"Not a chance. From all I've heard—I haven't had time to take statements yet—those guys would have been perfectly at home here with blindfolds on. They'd have known there was no fire escape outside. They'd have known that every room is air conditioned and that you can't very well jump through plate-glass windows sealed like those are."

"Then why?"

"Maybe in a hurry. Maybe just the impatient type. At least he gave warning. His words were: 'Stand well to one side, Mrs. Ryder, I'm going to blast open that door.' "

"Well, that seems to prove two things. The first is that they're not wanton killers. But I said 'seem.' A dead hostage isn't much good for bargaining purposes or as a lever to make reluctant physicists bend to their task. Second, they knew enough to be able to identify individual members of the staff."

"That they did."

"They seem to have been very well informed." Jeff tried to speak calmly, to emulate the monolithic calm of his father, but a rapidly beating pulse in his neck gave him away.

Ryder indicated the tabletop strewn with scraps of torn paper. "Man of your age should be beyond jigsaws."

"You know me, thorough, painstaking, the conscientious detective who leaves no stone unturned."

"You've got all the pieces the right way up, I'll say that for you. Make anything of it?"

"No. You?"

"No. Contents of Susan's wastepaper basket, I take it."

"Yes." Parker looked at the tiny scraps in irritation. "I know secretaries, typists, frequently tear up bits of papers destined for the wastepaper basket. But did she have to be so damned thorough about it?"

"You know Susan. Never does things by halves. Or quarters. Or eighths." He pushed some of the scraps around—remnants of letters, carbons, some pieces of shorthand. "Sixteenths, yes. Not halves." He turned away. "Any other clues you haven't come up with?"

"Nothing on her desk, nothing in her desk. She took her handbag and umbrella with her."

"How do you know she had an umbrella?"

"I asked," Parker said patiently. "Nothing but this left." He picked up a framed and unflattering picture of Ryder, replaced it on the desk and said apropos of nothing: "Some people can function efficiently under any circumstances. And that's it, I'm afraid."

Dr. Jablonsky escorted them to the battered Peugeot. "If there's anything I can do, Sergeant——"

"Two things, as a matter of fact. Without letting Ferguson know, can you get hold of the dossier on Carlton? You know, the details of his past career, references, that sort of thing."

"Jesus, man, he's number two in security."

"I know."

"Any reason to suspect him?"

"None. I'm just curious why they took him as a hostage. A senior security man is supposed to be tough and resourceful. Not the kind of man I'd have around. His record may show some reason why. Second thing, I'm still a pilgrim lost in this nuclear desert. If I need any more information, can I contact you?"

"You know where my office is."

"I may have to ask you to come to my place. Head office can put a stop order against my coming here."

"A cop?"

"A cop, no. An ex-cop, yes."

Jablonsky looked at him consideringly. "Expecting to be fired? God knows it's been threatened often enough."

"It's an unjust world."

On the way back to the station Jeff said: "Three questions. Why Carlton?"

"Bad choice of hostage, like I said. Secondly, if the bastards could identify your mother they could probably identify anyone in the plant. No reason why they should be especially interested in our family. The best source of names and working locations of the staff is in the security files. Only Ferguson and Carlton—and, of course, Dr. Jablonsky—have access to them."

"Why kidnap him?"

"To make it look good? I don't know. Maybe he wasn't kidnaped. You heard what Ferguson said about the government not paying highly for unskilled jobs. Maybe greener fields were beckoning."

"Sergeant Ryder, you have an unpleasantly suspicious imagination. What's more, you're no better than a common thief." Ryder drew placidly on his cigarette and remained unmoved. "You told Jablonsky you never tampered with evidence. I saw you palm pieces of paper from the table where Sergeant Parker was trying to sort them out."

"Suspicious minds would seem to run in this family," Ryder said mildly. "I didn't tamper with evidence. I took it. If it is evidence, that is."

"Why did you take it if you don't know?"

"You saw what I took?"

"Didn't look much to me. Squiggles, doodles."

"Shorthand, you clown. Notice anything about the cut of Jablonsky's coat?"

"First thing any cop would notice. He should have his coat cut looser to conceal the bulge of his gun."

"It's not a gun. It's a cassette recorder. Jablonsky dictates all his letters and memos into that, wherever he is in the plant, as often as not when he's walking around.''

"So?'' Jeff thought for a bit, then looked properly chagrined. "Guess I'll just stick to my trusty bike and handing out tickets to traffic violators. That way my lack of intelligence doesn't show up so much. No shorthand required, is that it?''

"I would have thought so.''

"But why tear it up into little bits?''

"Just goes to show that you can't believe half the experts who say that intelligence is hereditary.'' Ryder puffed on his cigarette with just a hint of complacency. "Think I would have married someone who panicked and lacked resource?''

"Like she runs from a room when she sees a spider? A message?''

"I would think. Know anyone who knows shorthand?''

"Sure. Marge.''

"Who's Marge?''

"Goddamnit, Dad, your goddaughter. Ted's wife.''

"Ah. Your fellow easy rider on the lonely trails of the freeways? Marjory, you mean? Ask them around for a drink when we get home.''

"What did you mean back there by saying to Jablonsky that you expected to be fired?''

"He said it, not me. Let's say I sense premature retirement coming up. I have a feeling that Chief Donahure and I aren't going to be seeing very much eye to eye in a few minutes' time.'' Even the newest rookie in the police force knew of the police chief's enmity toward Ryder, a feeling exceeded only by the massive contempt in which Ryder held his superior.

Jeff said: "He doesn't much like me either.''

"That's a fact.'' Ryder smiled reminiscently. Some time before her divorce from the chief of police, Mrs. Donahure had gotten a speeding ticket from Jeff although he had known perfectly well who she was. Donahure had first of all asked Jeff and then demanded that he tear up the citation. Jeff had refused, as Donahure must have known in advance he would. The California Highway Patrol had the reputation, of which it was justifiably proud, of being perhaps the only police force in the country that was wholly above corruption. Not too long ago a patrolman had handed out a speeding ticket to the governor. The governor had written a letter of commendation to police headquarters—but he still had to pay up.

Sergeant Dickson was still behind his desk. He was: "Where have you two been?''

"Detecting,'' Ryder said. "Why?''

"The brass have been trying to reach you at San Ruffino.'' He lifted a phone. "Sergeant Ryder, Patrolman Ryder, Lieutenant. They've just come in.'' He listened briefly and hung up. "The pleasure of your company, gentlemen.''

"Who's with him?''

"Major Dunne.'' Dunne was the area head of the FBI. "A Dr. Durrer from Erda or something.''

"Capitals,'' Ryder said. "E-R-D-A. Energy Research and Development Administration. I know him.''

"And, of course, your soul mate, the chief.''

Four men were seated in Mahler's office. Mahler, behind the desk, was wearing his official face to conceal his unhappiness. Two men sat in chairs:

Dr. Durrer, an owlish-looking individual with a bottle-glass pince-nez that gave his eyes the appearance of those of a startled fawn, and Major Dunne, lean, graying, intelligent with the smiling eyes of one who didn't find too much in life to smile about. The standing figure was Donahure, chief of police. Although he wasn't very tall, his massively pear-shaped body took up a disproportionate amount of space. The layered fat above and below his eyes left very little space for them to peer out: he had a fleshy nose, fleshy lips and a formidable array of chins. He was eying Ryder with distaste.

"Case all sewn up, I suppose, Sergeant?"

Ryder ignored him. He said to Mahler: "You sent for us?"

Donahure's face had turned an instant purple; one had only to rile him enough and he'd be his own executioner. "I was speaking to you, Ryder. I sent for you. Where the hell have you been?"

"You just used the word 'case.' And you've been phoning San Ruffino. If we must have questions do they have to be stupid ones?"

"By God, Ryder, no man talks to me——"

"Please." Dunne's voice was calm, quiet but incisive. "I'd be glad if your gentlemen would leave your bickering for another time. Sergeant Ryder, Patrolman, I've heard about Mrs. Ryder and I'm damned sorry. Find anything interesting up there?"

"No," Ryder said. Jeff kept his eyes carefully averted. "And I don't think anyone will. Too clean a job, too professional. No violence offered. The only established fact is that the bandits made off with enough weapons-grade material to blow up half the state."

"How much?" Dr. Durrer said.

"Twenty drums of U-235 and plutonium; I don't know how much. A truckload, I should think. A second truck arrived after they had taken over the building."

"Dear, dear." Durrer looked and sounded depressed.

"Inevitably, the threats come next."

Ryder said: "You get many threats?"

"I wouldn't bother answering that," Donahure said. "Ryder has no official standing in this case."

"Dear, dear," Durrer said again. He removed his pince-nez and regarded Donahure with eyes that weren't owlish at all. "Are you curtailing my freedom of speech?" Donahure was clearly taken aback and looked at Dunne but found no support in the coldly smiling eyes. Durrer returned his attention to Ryder. "We get threats. It is the policy of the state of California not to disclose how many, which is really a rather stupid policy as it is known— the figures have been published and are in the public domain—that some two hundred and twenty threats have been made against federal and commercial facilities since 1969." He paused, as if expectantly, and Ryder accommodated him.

"That's a lot of threats." He appeared oblivious of the fact that the most immediate threat was an apopletic one: Donahure was clenching and unclenching his big ham fists and his purpled complexion was shading into an odd tinge of puce.

"It is indeed. All of them, so far, have proved to be hoaxes. But someday the threat may prove to be real—that is, either the government or private industry may have to pay up or suffer the effects of a nuclear detonation or nuclear radiation. We list six types of threat—two as highly improbable, four reasonably credible. The highly improbable are the detonation of a home-made bomb made from stolen weapons-grade materials or the detonation of a ready-made nuclear bomb stolen from a military ordnance depot—the credible are the dispersion of radioactive material other than plutonium, the release of hijacked radioactive materials from a spent fuel shipment, the detonation of a conventional high explosive salted with strontium-90, krypton-85, cesium-137 or even plutonium itself or simply by the release of plutonium for contamination purposes.''

"From the businesslike way those criminals behaved in San Ruffino it might be that they mean business.''

"The time has to come. We know that. This may be the time we receive a threat that really is a threat. We have made preparations, formulated in 1975. 'Nuclear Blackmail Emergency Response Plan for the State of California' it's called. The FBI has the over-all control of the investigation. They can call on as many federal, state and local agencies as they wish, including, of course, the police. They can call on nuclear experts from such places as Donner Lab in Berkeley and Lawrence at Livermore. Search and decontamination teams and medical teams, headed by doctors who specialize in radiology, are immediately available, as is the Air Force, to carry those teams anywhere in the state. We, at ERDA, have the responsibility of assessing the validity of the threat.''

"How's that done?''

"Primarily by checking with the government's computerized system that determines very quickly if unexpected amounts of fissionable material are missing.''

"Well, Dr. Durrer, in this case we know already how much is missing so we don't have to ask the computers. Just as well. I believe the computers are useless anyway.''

For the second time Durrer removed his pince-nez. "Who told you this?''

Ryder looked vague. "I don't remember. It was some time ago.'' Jeff kept his sardonic smile under cover. Sure, it was some time ago: must have been almost half an hour since Ferguson had told him. Durrer looked at him thoughtfully, then clearly decided there was no point in pursuing the subject. Ryder went on, addressing himself to Mahler. "I'd like to be assigned to this investigation. I'd look forward to working under Major Dunne.''

Donahure smiled, not exactly an evil smile, just that of a man savoring the passing moment. His complexion had reverted to its customary mottled red. He said: "No way.''

Ryder looked at him. His expression wasn't encouraging. "I have a very personal interest in this. Forgotten?''

"There'll be no discussion, Sergeant. As a policeman, you take orders from only one person in this county and that's me.''

"As a policeman.'' Donahure looked at him in sudden uncertainty.

Dunne said: "I'd appreciate having Sergeant Ryder working with me. Your most experienced man and your best in the Detective Division—and with the best arrest record in the county—any county, come to that.''

"That's his trouble. Arrest-happy. Trigger-happy. Violent. Unstable if he was emotionally involved as he would be in a case like this.'' Donahure tried to assume the expression of pious respectability but he was attempting the impossible. "Can't have the good name of my force brought into disrepute.''

"Jesus!'' It was Ryder's only comment.

Dunne was mildly persistent. "I'd still like to have him.''

"No. And with all due respect, I needn't remind you that the authority of the FBI stops on the other side of that door. It's for your own sake, Major Dunne. He's a dangerous man to have around in a delicate situation like this.''

"Kidnaping innocent women is delicate?" Durrer's dry voice made it apparent that he regarded Donahure as something less than a towering intelligence. "You might tell us how you arrive at that conclusion?"

"Yes. How about that, Chief?" Jeff could restrain himself no longer; he was visibly trembling with anger. Ryder observed him in mild surprise but said nothing. "My mother, Chief. And my father. Dangerous? Arrest-happy? Both of those things—but only to you, Chief, only to you. My father's trouble is that he goes around arresting all the wrong people—pimps, drug pushers, crooked politicians, honest, public-spirited members of the Mafia, respected businessmen who are no better than scofflaws, even—isn't it sad?—corrupt cops. Consult his records, Chief. The only time his arrests have failed to secure either a conviction or a probation order was when he came up against Judge Kendrick. You remember Judge Kendrick, don't you, Chief? Your frequent house guest who pocketed twenty-five thousand dollars from your buddies in City Hall and finished up in the penitentiary. Five years. There were quite a lot of people who were lucky not to join him behind bars, weren't there, Chief?"

Donahure made an indeterminate sound as if he were suffering from some constriction of the vocal chords. His hands were clenching and unclenching and his complexion was changing color with the speed and unpredictability of a chameleon crawling over tartan.

Dunne said: "You put him there, Sergeant?"

"Somebody had to. Old Fatso here had all the evidence but wouldn't use it. Can't blame a man for not incriminating himself." Donahure made the same strangled noise. Ryder took something from his coat pocket and held it hidden, glancing quizzically at his son.

Jeff was calm now. He said to Donahure: "You've also slandered my father in front of witnesses." He looked at Ryder. "Going to sue? Or just leave him alone with his conscience?"

"His what?"

"You'll never make a cop." Jeff sounded almost sad. "There are all those finer points that you've never mastered, like bribery, corruption, kickbacks and having a couple of bank accounts under false names." He looked at Donahure. "It's true, isn't it, Chief? Some people have lots of accounts under false names?"

"You insolent young bastard." Donahure had his vocal chords working again, but only just. He tried to smile. "Kinda forgotten who you're talking to, haven't you?"

"Sorry to deprive you of the pleasure, Chief." Jeff laid gun and badge on Mahler's table. "Forward those to the Highway Patrol," he said, and looked at his father in no surprise as Ryder placed a second badge on the table.

Donahure said hoarsely: "Your gun."

"It's mine, not police property. Anyway, I've got others at home. All the licenses you want."

"I can have those revoked tomorrow, copper." The viciousness of his tone matched the expression on his porcine face.

"I'm not a copper." Ryder lit a Gauloise and drew on it with obvious satisfaction.

"Put that damned cigarette out!"

"You heard. I'm not a copper. Not anymore. I'm just a member of the public. The police are servants of the public. I don't care to have my servants talk to me that way. Revoke my licenses? You do just that and you'll have a photostat of a private dossier I have, complete with photostats of signed affidavits. Then you'll revoke the order revoking my licenses."

"What the devil's that mean?"

"Just that the original of the dossier should make very interesting reading up in Sacramento."

"You're bluffing." The contempt and certainty in Donahure's voice would have carried more conviction if he hadn't licked his lips immediately afterward.

"Could be." Ryder contemplated a smoke ring with a mildly surprised interest.

"I'm warning you, Ryder." Donahure's voice was shaking and it could have been with something else other than anger. "Get in the way of this investigation and I'll have you locked up for obstruction of justice."

"It's just as well you know me, Donahure. I don't have to threaten you. Besides, it gives me no pleasure to see fat blobs of lard shaking with fear."

Donahure dropped his hand to his gun. Ryder slowly unbuttoned his jacket and pushed it back to put a hand on each hip. His .38 was in full view but his hands were clear of it.

Donahure said to Lieutenant Mahler: "Arrest this man."

Dunne spoke in cold contempt. "Don't be more of a fool than you can help, Donahure, and don't put your lieutenant in an impossible position. Arrest him on what grounds, for heaven's sake?"

Ryder buttoned his jacket, turned and left the office, Jeff close behind him. They were about to climb into the Peugeot when Dunne caught up with them.

"Was that wise?"

Ryder shrugged. "Inevitable."

"He's a dangerous man, Ryder. Not face to face, we all know that. Different when your back's turned. He has powerful friends."

"I know his friends. A contemptible bunch, like himself. Half of them should be behind bars."

"Still doesn't make them any less dangerous on a moonless night. You're going ahead with this, of course?"

"My wife, in case you have forgotten. Think we're going to leave her to that big fat slob's tender care?"

"What happens if he comes up against you?"

Jeff said: "Don't tempt my father with such pleasant thoughts."

"Suppose I shouldn't. I said I'd like you to work with me, Ryder. You, too, if you wish, young man. The offer stands. Always room for enterprising and ambitious young in the FBI."

"Thanks. We'll think it over. If we need help, advice, can we contact you?"

Dunne looked at them consideringly, then nodded. "Sure. You have my number. Well, you have an option. I don't. Like it or not I've got to work with that big fat slob, as you so accurately call him. Carries a lot of political clout in the valley." He shook hands with the two men. "Don't turn your backs on him."

In the car, Jeff said: "Going to consider his offer?"

"Hell, no. That would be out of the frying pan into the fire. Not that Sassoon—he's the California head of the FBI—isn't honest. He is. But he's too strict, goes by the book all the time and frowns on free enterprise."

Marjory Hohner, a brown-haired girl who looked too young to be married, sat beside her uniformed C.H.P. husband and studied the scraps of paper she had arranged on the table in front of her. Ryder said: "Come on, goddaughter. A bright young girl like you——"

She lifted her head and smiled. "Easy. I suppose it will make sense to you. It says: 'Look at back of your photograph.'"

"Thank you, Marjory." Ryder reached for the phone and made two calls.

Ryder and his son had just finished the reheated contents of the casserole Susan had left in the oven when Dr. Jablonsky arrived an hour after the departure of the Hohners, brief case in hand. Without expression or inflection of voice, he said: "You must be psychic. The word's out that you've been fired. You and Jeff here."

"Not at all." Ryder assumed an aloof dignity. "We retired. Voluntarily. But only temporarily, of course."

"You did say 'temporarily'?"

"That's what I said. For the moment it doesn't suit me to be a cop. Restricts my spheres of activities."

Jeff said: "You *did* say temporarily?"

"Sure. Back to work when this blows over. I've got a wife to support."

"But Donahure——"

"Don't worry about Donahure. Let Donahure worry about himself. Drink, Doctor?"

"Scotch, if you have it." Ryder went behind the small wet bar and pulled back a sliding door to reveal an impressive array of different bottles. Jablonsky said: "You have it."

"Beer for me. That's for my friends. Lasts a long time," he added inconsequentially.

Jablonsky took a folder from his brief case. "This is the file you wanted. Wasn't easy, Ferguson's like a cat on a hot tin roof. Jumpy."

"Ferguson's straight."

"I know he is. This is a photostat. I didn't want Ferguson or the FBI to find out that the original dossier is missing."

"Why's Ferguson so jumpy?"

"Hard to say. But he's being evasive, uncommunicative. Maybe he feels his job is in danger since his security defenses were so easily breached. Running scared, a little. I think we all are in the past few hours. Even goes for me." He looked gloomy. "I'm even worried that my presence here——" he smiled to rob his words of offense—"consorting with an ex-cop might be noted."

Jablonsky stopped smiling. "What?"

"There's a closed van about fifty yards down the road on the other side. No driver in the cab—he's inside the van looking through a one-way window."

Jeff rose quickly and moved to a window. He said: "How long has he been there?"

"A few minutes. He arrived just as Dr. Jablonsky did. Too late for me to do anything about it then." He thought briefly, then said: "I don't much care to have those snoopers around my house. Go to my gun cupboard and take what you want. You'll find a few old police badges there, too."

"He'll know I'm no longer a cop."

"Sure he will. But d'you think he'd dare say so and put the finger on Donahure?"

"Hardly. What do you want me to do? Shoot him?"

"It's a tempting thought, but no. Smash his window open with the butt of your gun and tell him to open up. His name is Raminoff and he looks a bit like a weasel, which he is. He carries a gun. Donahure reckons he's his top undercover man. I've kept tabs on him for years. He's not a cop—he's a criminal with several sentences behind him. You'll find a police band radio transmitter. Ask him for his license. He won't have one. Ask him for his police identification. He won't have that either. Make the usual threatening noises and tell him to push off."

Jeff smiled widely. "Retirement has its compensations."

Jablonsky looked after him doubtfully. "You sure got a lot of faith in that boy, Sergeant."

"Jeff can look after himself," Ryder said comfortably. "Now Doctor, I hope you're not going to be evasive about telling me why Ferguson was being evasive."

"Why should I?" He looked glum. "Seeing that I'm a marked man anyway."

"He *was* evasive with me?"

"Yes. I feel more upset about your wife than you realize. I think you have the right to know anything that can help you."

"And I think that deserves another drink." It was a measure of Jablonsky's preoccupation that he'd emptied his glass without being aware of it. Ryder went to the bar and returned. "What didn't he tell me?"

"You asked him if any nuclear material had been hijacked. He said he didn't know. Fact is, he knows far too much about it to be willing to talk about it. Take the recent Hematite Hangover business, so-called, I imagine, because it's given a headache to everybody in nuclear security. Hematite is in Missouri and is run by Gulf United Nuclear. They may have anything up to a thousand kilograms of U-235 on the premises at any given time. This comes to them, bottled, in the form of UF6, from Portsmouth, Ohio. This is converted into U-235 oxide. Much of this stuff, fully enriched and top weapons-grade material, goes from Hematite to Kansas City by truck, thence to Los Angeles as air cargo, then is again trucked a hundred and twenty miles down the freeways to General Atomic in San Diego. Three wide-open transits. Do you want the horrifying details?"

"I can imagine them. Why Ferguson's secretiveness?"

"No reason really. All security men are professional clams. There's literally tons of the damned stuff missing. That's no secret. The knowledge is in public domain."

"According to Dr. Durrer of ERDA—I spoke to him this evening—the government's computer system can tell you in nothing flat if any significant amount of weapons-grade material is missing."

Jablonsky scowled, a scowl which he removed by fortifying himself with some more scotch. "I wonder what he calls significant. Ten tons? Just enough to make a few hundred atom bombs, that's all. Dr. Durrer is either talking through his hat, which, knowing him as I do, is extremely unlikely, or he was just being coy. ERDA has been suffering from very sensitive feelings since the GAO gave them a black eye in, let me see, I think it was in July of '76."

"GAO?"

"General Accounting Office." Jablonsky broke off as Jeff entered and deposited some material on a table. He looked very pleased with himself.

"He's gone. Heading for the nearest swamp I'd guess." He indicated his haul. "One police radio—no license for it so I couldn't let him keep that, could I? One gun—clearly a criminal type so I couldn't let him keep that either, could I? One driver's license—identification in lieu of police author-ization, which he didn't seem to have. And one pair of Zeiss binoculars stamped L.A.P.D.—he couldn't recall where he got that from and swore blind that he didn't know that the initials stood for Los Angeles Police Department.''

"I've always wanted one of those," Ryder said. Jablonsky frowned in heavy disapproval but removed the frown in the same way he had removed his scowl.

"I also wrote down his license plate number, opened the hood and took down the engine and chassis numbers. I told him that all the numbers and confiscated articles would be delivered to the station tonight.''

Ryder said: "You know what you've done, don't you? You've gone and upset Chief Donahure. Or he's going to be upset any minute now." He looked wistful. "I wish we had a tap on his private line. He's going to have to replace the equipment, which will hurt him enough but not half as much as replacing that van is going to hurt him.''

Jablonsky said: "Why should he have to replace the van?''

"It's hot. If Raminoff were caught with that van he'd get laryngitis singing at the top of his voice to implicate Donahure. He's the kind of trusty henchman that Donahure surrounds himself with.''

"Donahure could block the inquiry.''

"No chance. John Aaron, the editor of the *Examiner*, has been campaign-ing for years against police corruption in general and Chief Donahure in particular. A letter to the editor asking why Donahure failed to act on information received would be transferred from the letters page to page one. The swamp, you say, Jeff? Me, I'd go for Cypress Bluff. Two hundred feet sheer into the Pacific, then sixty feet of water. Ocean bed's littered with cars past their best. Anyway, I want you to take your own car and go up there and drop all this confiscated stuff and the rest of those old police badges to join the rest of the hardware down there.''

Jeff pursed his lips. "You don't think that old goat would have the nerve to come around here with a search warrant?''

"Sure I do. Trump up any old reason—he's done it often enough before.''

Jeff said, wooden-faced: "He might even invent some charge about tampering with evidence at the reactor plant?''

"Man's capable of anything.''

"There's some people you just can't faze." Jeff left to get his car.

Jablonsky said: "What was that supposed to mean?''

"Today's generation? Who can tell? You mentioned the GAO. What about the GAO?''

"Ah, yes. They produced a report on the loss of nuclear material for a government department with the memorable name of the House Small Busi-ness Subcommittee on Energy and Environment. The report was and is classified. The subcommittee made a summary of the report and declassified it. The GAO would appear to have a low opinion of ERDA. Says it doesn't know its job. Claims that there are literally tons of nuclear material—number of tons unspecified—missing from the thirty-four uranium and plu-tonium processing plants in the country. GAO says they seriously question ERDA's accountability procedures and that they haven't really a clue as to whether stuff is missing or not.''

"Dr. Durrer wouldn't have liked that?''

"ERDA was hopping. They said there was—and I know it's true—up to sixty miles of piping in the processing system of any given plant and if you multiply that by thirty-four you have a couple of thousand miles of piping and there could be a great deal of nuclear material stuck in those pipes. GAO completely agreed but rather spoiled things by pointing out that there was no way in which the contents of those two thousand miles could be checked.''

Jablonsky peered gloomily at the base of his empty glass. Ryder rose obligingly and when he returned Jablonsky said accusingly but without heat: "Trying to loosen my tongue?''

"What else? What did ERDA say?''

"Practically nothing. They'd even less to say shortly afterward when the Nuclear Regulatory Commission compounded that attack on them. They said in effect two things—that practically any plant in the country could be taken by a handful of armed and determined men and that the theft-detection systems were defective.''

"You believe that?''

"No silly questions, please—especially not after what happened today.''

"So there could be tens of tons of the stuff cached around the country?''

"I could be quoted on my answer?''

"Now it's your turn for silly questions.''

Jablonsky sighed. "What the hell. It's eminently possible and more than probable. Why are you asking these questions, Sergeant?''

"One more and I'll tell you. Could *you* make an atom bomb?''

"Sure. Any competent scientist—he doesn't have to be a nuclear physicist—could. Thousands of them. There's a school of thought that says no one could make an atomic bomb without retracing the Manhattan Project— that extremely long, enormously complicated and billion dollar program that led to the invention of the atom bomb in World War II. Rubbish. The information is freely available. Write to the Atomic Energy Commission, enclose three dollars and they'll be glad to let you have a copy of *The Los Alamos Primer,* which details the mathematical fundamentals of fission bombs. A bit more expensive is the book called *Manhattan District History, Project Y, the Los Alamos Project.* For this you have to approach the Office of Technical Services of the U.S. Department of Commerce, who will be delighted to let you have a copy by return mail. Tells you all about it. Most importantly, it tells you of all the problems that arose in the building of the first atomic bomb and how they were overcome. Stirring stuff. There's any amount of works in public print—just consult your local library—that consist of what used to be the supersecret information. All else failing, the Encyclopedia Americana will probably tell any intelligent person as much as he needs to know.''

"We have a very helpful government.''

"Very. Once the Russians had started exploding atom bombs they reckoned the need for secrecy was past. What they didn't reckon on was that some patriotic citizen or citizens would up and use this knowledge against them.'' He sighed. "It would be easy to call the government of the day a bunch of clowns but they lacked the gift of Nostradamus: 'Hindsight makes us all wise.' ''

"Hydrogen bombs?''

"A nuclear physicist for that.'' He paused, then went on with some bitterness: "Provided, that is, he's fourteen years of age or over.''

"Explain.''

"Back in 1970 there was an attempted nuclear blackmail of a city in Florida. Police tried to hush it up but it came out all the same. Give me a million dollars and a safe-conduct out of America or I'll blast your city out of existence, the blackmailer said. Next day came the same threat, this time accompanied by a diagram of a hydrogen bomb—a cylinder filled with lithium hydride wrapped in cobalt, with an implosion system at one end.''

"That how they make a hydrogen bomb?"

"I wouldn't know."

"Isn't that sad? And you a nuclear physicist. They nail the blackmailer?"

"Yes. A fourteen-year-old boy."

"It's an advance on fireworks." For almost a minute Ryder gazed into the far distance, which appeared to be located in the region of his toe caps, through a drifting cloud of blue-gray smoke, then said:

"It's a come-on. A con job. A gambit. A phony. Don't you agree?"

Jablonsky was guarded. "I might. If, that is to say, I had the faintest idea what you are talking about."

"Will this theft of the uranium and plutonium be made public?"

Jablonsky gave an exaggerated shrug. "No, sir. Not if we can help it. Mustn't give the shivers to the great American public."

"Not if you can help it. I'll take long odds that the bandits won't be so bashful and that the story will have banner headlines in every paper in the state tomorrow. Not to mention the rest of the country. It smells, Doc. The people responsible are obviously experts and must have known that the easiest way to get weapons-grade material is to hijack a shipment. With all that stuff already missing, it's long odds that they've got more than enough than they need already. And you know as well as I do that three nuclear physicists in the state have just vanished in the past couple of months. Would you care to guess who their captors were?"

"I don't think so. I mean, I don't think I have to."

"I didn't think so. You could have saved me all this thinking—I prefer to avoid it where possible. Let's assume they already had the fuel. Let's assume they already had the physicists to make the nuclear devices, quite possibly even hydrogen explosives. Let's even assume that they have already got one of those devices—and why stop at one?—manufactured and tucked away at some safe place."

Jablonsky looked unhappy. "It's not an assumption I care to assume."

"I can understand that. But if something's there, wishing it wasn't won't make it go away. Some time back you described something as being eminently possible and more than probable. Would you describe this assumption in the same words?"

Jablonsky thought for some moments then said: "Yes."

"So. A smoke screen. They didn't really need the fuel or the physicists or the hostages. Why did they take something they didn't need? Because they needed them."

"That makes a lot of sense."

Ryder was patient. "They didn't need them to make bombs. I would think they needed them for three other reasons. The first would be to obtain maximum publicity, to convince people that they had means to make bombs and meant business. The second is to lull us into the belief that we have time to deal with the threat. I mean, you can't make a nuclear bomb in a day or a week, can you?"

"No."

"So. We have breathing space. But we haven't."

"Getting the hang of your double-talk takes time. If our assumption is correct, we haven't."

"And the third thing is to create the proper climate of terror. People don't behave rationally when they're scared out of their wits, do they? Behavior becomes no longer predictable. You don't think, you just react."

"And where does all this lead us?"

"That's as far as my thinking goes. How the hell should I know?"

Jablonsky peered into his scotch and found no inspiration there. He sighed again and said: "The only thing that makes sense out of all of this is that it accounts for your behavior."

"Something odd about my behavior?"

"That's the point. There should be. Or there should have been. Worried stiff about Susan. But if you're right in your thinking—well, I understand."

"I'm afraid you don't. If I'm right in what you so kindly call my thinking she's in greater danger than she would have been if we'd accepted the facts at their face value. If the bandits are the kind of people that I think they are then they're not to be judged by ordinary standards. They're mavericks. They're power-mad, megalomaniacs if you like, people who will stop at nothing, people who will go all the way in ruthlessness, especially when thwarted or shoved into a corner."

Jablonsky digested this for some time, then said: "Then you ought to look worried."

"That would help a lot." The doorbell rang. Ryder rose and went to the hall. Sergeant Parker, a bachelor who looked on Ryder's house as a second home, had already let himself in. He, like Jablonsky, was carrying a brief case: unlike Jablonsky, he looked cheerful.

"Evening. Shouldn't be associating with a fired cop but in the sacred name of friendship——"

"I resigned."

"Comes to the same thing. Leaves the way clear for me to assume the mantle of the most detested and feared cop in town. Look on the bright side. After thirty years of terrifying the local populace, you deserve a break." He followed Ryder into the living room. "Ah! Dr. Jablonsky. I didn't expect to find you here."

"I didn't expect to be here."

"Lift up your spirits, Doc. Consorting with disgraced cops is not a statutory crime." He looked accusingly at Ryder. "Speaking of lifting—or lifting up spirits—this man's glass is almost empty. Imported London gin for me." A year on an exchange visit to Scotland Yard had left Parker with the profound conviction that American gin hadn't advanced since Prohibition days and was still made in bathtubs.

"Thanks for reminding me." Ryder looked at Jablonsky. "He's only consumed about a couple of hundred crates of the stuff here in the past fourteen years. Give or take a crate."

Parker smiled, delved into his brief case and came up with Ryder's photograph. "Sorry to be so late with this. Had to go back and report to our fat friend. Seemed to be recovering from some sort of heart attack. He was less interested in my report than in discussing you freely and at some length. Poor man was very upset so I congratulated him on his character analysis. This picture has some importance?"

"I hope so. What makes you think so?"

"You asked for it. And it seems Susan was going to take it with her then changed her mind. Seems she took it with her into the room where they were all locked up. She told the guard she felt sick. Guard checked the washroom for windows and telephone, I guess, then let her in. She came out in a few minutes looking, so I'm told, deathly pale."

"Morning Dawn," Ryder said.

"What's that?"

"Face powder she uses."

"Ah! Then—peace to the libbers—she exercised a woman's privilege of changing her mind and changed her mind about taking the picture with her."

"Have you opened it up?"

"I'm a virtuous honest cop and I wouldn't dream——"

"Stop dreaming."

Parker eased off the six spring-loaded clips at the back, removed the rectangle of white cardboard and peered with interest at the back of Ryder's photograph. "A clue, by heavens, a clue! I see the word 'Morro.' The rest, I'm afraid, is in shorthand.

"Figures. She'd be in a hurry." He crossed to the phone, dialed, then hung up in about thirty seconds. "Damn! She's not there."

"Who?"

"My shorthand translator. Marjory. She and Ted have gone to eat, drink, dance, go to a show or whatever. I've no idea what they do at night or where the young hang out these days. Jeff will know. We'll just have to wait till he returns."

"Where is your fellow ex-cop?"

"Up on Cypress Bluff throwing some of Chief Donahure's most treasured possessions into the Pacific."

"Not Chief Donahure himself? Too bad. I'm listening."

3

AMERICA, LIKE England, has much more than its fair share of those people in the world who choose not to conform to the status quo. They are the individualists who pursue their own paths, their own beliefs, their own foibles and what are commonly regarded as their own irrational peculiarities with a splendid disregard, leavened only with a modicum of kindly pity and sorrow and benign resignation, for those unfortunates who are not as they are, the hordes of faceless conformists among whom they are forced to move and have their being. Some few of those individualists, confined principally to those who pursue the more esoteric forms of religions of their own inventions, try sporadically to lead the more gullible of the unenlightened along the road that leads to ultimate revelation: basically, however, they regard the unfortunate conformists as being sadly beyond redemption and are resigned to leaving them to wallow in the troughs of their ignorance while they follow the meandering highways and byways of their own chosen life-style, oblivious of the paralleling motorways that carry the vast majority of blinkered mankind. They are commonly known as eccentrics.

America, as said, has its fair share of such eccentrics—and more. But California, as both the inhabitants of that state and the rest of the union would agree, has vastly more than its fair share of American eccentrics: they are extremely thick upon the ground. They differ from your true English eccentric, who is almost invariably a loner. California eccentrics tend to polarize, and could equally well be categorized as cultists, whose beliefs range from the beatific to the cataclysmic, from the unassailable—because incapable of disproof—pontifications of the self-appointed gurus to the courageous resignation of those who have the day, hour and minute of the world's end or those who crouch on the summit of a high peak in the Sierras awaiting the next flood which will surely lap their ankles—but no higher—

before sunset. In a less free, less open, less inhibited and less tolerant society than California's, they would be tidied away in those institutions reserved for imbalanced mavericks of the human race: the Golden State does not exactly cherish them but does regard them with an affectionate, if occasionally exasperated, amusement.

But they cannot be regarded as the true eccentrics. In England, on the eastern seaboard of the States, one can be poor and avoid all contact with like-minded deviants and still be recognized as an outstanding example of what the rest of mankind is glad it isn't. In the group-minded togetherness of California, such solitary peaks of eccentric achievement are almost impossible to reach, although there have been one or two notable examples, outstandingly the self-proclaimed Emperor of San Francisco and Defender of Mexico. Emperor Norton the First became so famous and cherished a figure that even the burial ceremony of his dog attracted such a vast concourse of tough and hard-headed nineteenth-century Franciscans that the entire business life of the city, saloons and bordellos apart, ground to a complete halt. But it was rare indeed for a penniless eccentric to scale the topmost heights.

To hope to be a successful eccentric in California one has to be a millionaire: being a millionaire brings with it a cast-iron guarantee. Von Streicher had been one of the latter, one of the favored few. Unlike the bloodless and desiccated calculating machines of the oil, manufacturing and marketing billionaires of today, Von Streicher had been one of the giants of the era of steamships, railways and steel. Both his vast fortune and his reputation as an eccentric had been made and consolidated by the early twentieth century and his status in both fields was unassailable. But every status requires its symbol: a symbol for your billionaire cannot be intangible: it has to be seen and the bigger the better: and all self-respecting eccentrics with the proper monetary qualifications invariably settled on the same symbol: a home that would properly reflect the uniqueness of the owner. Kubla Khan had built his own Xanadu and, as he had been incomparably wealthier than any run-of-the-mill billionaire, what was good enough for him was good enough for them.

Von Streicher's choice of location had been governed by two very powerful phobias: one of tidal waves, the other of heights. The fear of tidal waves stemmed from his youth, when he had read of the volcanic eruption and destruction of the island of Thera, north of Crete, when a tidal wave, estimated at some 165 feet in height, destroyed much of the early Minoan, Grecian and Turkish civilizations. Since then he had lived with the conviction that he would be similarly engulfed someday. There was no known basis for his fear of heights but an eccentric of good standing does not require any reason for his whimsical beliefs and behavior. He had taken this fearful dilemma with him on his one and only return to his German birthplace, where he had spent two months examining the architectural monuments, almost exclusively castles, left behind by the mad Ludwig of Bavaria, and on his return had settled for what he regarded as the lesser of two evils—height.

He didn't, however, go too high. He selected a plateau some fifteen hundred feet high on a mountain range some fifty miles from the ocean and there proceeded to build his own Xanadu, which he later christened Adlerheim—the home of the eagle. The poet speaks of Kubla Kahn's pied-à-terre as being a stately pleasure dome. Adlerheim wasn't like that at all. It was a castellated neo-Gothic horror, a Baroque monstrosity that came close to being awe-inspiring in its totally unredeemed vulgarity. Massively built of northern Italian marble, it was an incredible hodgepodge of turrets, onion towers, crenelated battlements and slit windows for the use of archers. All it lacked was a moat and drawbridge but Von Streicher had been more than satisfied with it as it was. For others, living in more modern and hopefully more enlightened times, the sole redeeming feature was to be seen from the battlements, looking west: the view across the broad valley to the distant coastal range, Von Streicher's first breakwater against the inevitable tidal wave, was quite splendid.

Fortunately for the seven captives in the rear of the second two vans grinding around the hairpins up to the castle, they were doubly unable to see what lay in store for them. Doubly, because in addition to the van body being wholly enclosed, they wore blindfolds as well as handcuffs. But they were to know the inside of Adlerheim more intimately than even the most besotted and aesthetically retarded admirer of all that was worst in nineteenth-century design would have cared to.

The prisoners' van jolted to a stop. Rear doors were opened, bandages removed and the eight still handcuffed passengers were helped to jump down onto the authentically cobbled surface of what proved to be a wholly enclosed courtyard. Two guards were closing two massive, iron-bound oak doors to seal off the archway through which they had just enetered. There were two peculiarities about those guards. They were carrying Ingram submachine guns fitted with silencers, a favorite weapon of Britain's elite Special Air Service—despite its name, an Army regiment—which had two rare privileges: the first was that they had access to their own private armory, almost certainly the most comprehensively stocked in the world, the second being that any member of the unit had complete freedom to pick the weapon of his own particular choice. The popularity of the Ingram was testimony to its deadly effectiveness.

The second idiosyncrasy about the two guards was that, from top of burnous to sandal-brushing skirts of robe, they were dressed as Arabs, not the type of gleamingly white garb that one would normally look to find in the state of California but, nonetheless, eminently suitable for both the very warm weather and the instantaneous concealment of Ingrams in voluminous folds. Two other men, bent over colorful flower borders that paralleled all four walls of the courtyard, and two others carrying slung rifles were all dressed similarly. All six had the sun-tanned swarthiness of an Eastern desert dweller but some of their facial bone structures were wrong.

The man who was obviously the leader of the abductors, and had been in the leading van, approached the captives and let them see his face for the first time—he had removed his stocking mask on leaving San Ruffino. He was a tall man, lean but broad-shouldered and, unlike the pudgy Van Streicher, who had habitually worn lederhosen and a Tyrolean hat with a pheasant's feather when in residence, he looked as if he belonged in an eagle's home. He had a lean, sun-tanned face, a hooked nose and a piercing light blue eye. One eye. His right eye was covered by a black patch.

He said: "My name is Morro. I am the leader of this community here." He waved at the white-robed figures. "Those are my followers, acolytes, you might almost call them, all faithful servants of Allah."

"That's what *you* would call them. I'd call them refugees from a chain gang." The tall thin man in the black alpaca suit had a pronounced stoop and bifocal glasses and looked the prototype of the absent-minded academic, which was half true. Professor Burnett of San Diego was anything but absent-minded: in his professional circle, he was justly famous for his extraordinarily acute intelligence and justly notorious for his extraordinarily short temper.

Morro smiled. "Chains can be literal or figurative, Professor. One way or another we are all slaves to something or other." He gestured to the two men with rifles. "Remove their handcuffs. Ladies and gentlemen, I have to apologize for a rather upsetting interruption of the even tenor of your ways. I trust none of you suffered discomfort on our journey here." His speech had the fluently correct precision of an educated man to whom English is not a native language. "I do not wish to sound alarming or threatening"— there is no way of sounding more alarming and threatening than to say you don't intend to—"but, before I take you inside, I would like you to have a look at the walls of this courtyard."

They had a look. The walls were about twenty feet high and topped with a three-stranded barbed-wire fence. The wires were supported by but not attached to the L-shaped steel posts imbedded in the marble, but passed instead through insulated apertures.

Morro said: "Those walls and the gates are the only way to leave here. I do not advise that you try to use either. Especially the wall. The fence above is electrified."

"Has been for sixty years." Burnett sounded sour.

"You know this place, then?" Morro didn't seem surprised. "You've been here?"

"Thousands have. Von Streicher's Folly. Open to the public for about twenty years when the state ran it."

"Still open to the public, believe it or not. Tuesdays and Fridays. Who am I to deprive Californians of part of their cultural heritage. Von Streicher put fifty volts through it as a deterrent. It would only kill a person with a bad heart—and a person with a bad heart wouldn't try to scale that wall in the first place. I have increased the current to two thousand volts. Follow me, please."

He led the way through an archway directly opposite the entrance. Beyond lay a huge hall, some sixty feet by sixty. Three open fireplaces, of stone, not granite, were let into each of three walls, each fireplace large enough for a man to stand upright: the three crackling log fires were not for decorative purposes because even in the month of June the thick granite walls effectively insulated the interior from the heat outside. There were no windows, illumination being provided by four massive chandeliers that had come all the way from Prague. The gleaming floor was of inlaid redwood. Of the floor space, only half of the area was occupied, this by a row of refectory tables and benches: the other was empty except for a hand-carved oaken rostrum and, close by, a pile of very undistinguished mats.

"Von Streicher's banqueting hall," Morro said. He looked at the battered tables and benches. "I doubt whether he would have approved of the change."

Burnett said: "The Louis XIV chairs, the Empire period tables. All gone? They would have made excellent firewood."

"You must not equate non-Christian with being barbaric, Professor. The original furniture is intact. The Adlerheim has massive cellars. The castle, I'm afraid, its splendid isolation apart, is not as ideal as we would have wished for our religious purposes. The refectory half of this hall is profane. The other half"—he indicated the bare expanse—"is consecrated. We have to make do with what we have. Someday we hope to build a mosque adjoining here—for the present this has to serve. The rostrum is for the readings of the Koran—the mats, of course, are for prayers. For calling the faithful to prayer we have again been forced to make a most reluctant compromise. For Mohammedans, those onion towers, the grotesque architectural symbol of the Greek Orthodox Church, are anathema, but we have again consecrated one of them and it now serves as our minaret from which the muezzin summons the acolytes to prayer."

Dr. Schmidt, like Burnett an outstanding nuclear physicist and, like Burnett, renowned for his inability to suffer fools gladly, looked at Morro from under bushy white eyebrows that splendidly complemented his impossible mane of white hair—which had to be a wig but wasn't. His ruddy face held an expression of almost comical disbelief.

"This is what you tell your Tuesday and Friday visitors?"

"But of course."

"My God!"

"Allah, if you please."

"And I suppose you conduct those personal tours yourself? I mean, you must derive enormous pleasure from feeding this pack of lies to my gullible fellow citizens."

"May Allah send that you someday see the light." Morro was not patronizing, just kindly. "And this is a chore—what am I saying?—a sacred duty that is performed for me by my deputy Abraham."

"Abraham?" Burnett permitted himself a professional sneer. "A fitting name for a follower of Allah."

"You have not been in Palestine lately, have you, Professor?"

"Israel."

"Palestine. There are many Arabs there who profess the Jewish faith. Why take exception to a Jew practicing the Muslim faith? Come. I shall introduce you to him. I daresay you will find the surroundings more congenial there."

The very large study—for that it unquestionably was—into which he led them was not only more congenial, it was unashamedly sybaritic. Von Streicher had left the internal design and furnishings of the Adlerheim to his architects and interior designers and, for once, they had got something right. The study was clearly modeled on an English ducal library: book-lined walls on three sides of the room, each book expensively covered in the finest leather, deep-piled russet carpet, silk damask drapes, also russet, comfortable and enveloping leather armchairs, oak side tables and a leather-topped desk with a padded leather swivel chair behind it. A slightly incongruous note was struck by the three men already present in the room. All dressed in Arab clothes. Two were diminutive with unremarkable features not worth a second glance: but the third man was worth all the attention that the other two were spared. He looked as if he had started out to grow into a basketball player then changed his mind to become an American football player. He was immensely tall and had shoulders like a draft horse: he could have weighed anything up to three hundred pounds.

Morro said: "Abraham, our guests from San Ruffino. Ladies and gentlemen, Mr. Abraham Dubois, my deputy."

The giant bowed. "My pleasure, I assure you. Welcome to the Adlerheim. We hope your stay here will be a pleasant one." Both the voice and the tone of the voice came as a surprise. Like Morro, he spoke with the easy fluency of an educated man and, coming from that bleak impassive face, one would have expected any words to have either sinister or threatening overtones. But he sounded courteous and genuinely friendly. His speech did not betray his nationality but his features did. Here was no Arab, no Jew, no Levantine and, despite his surname, no Frenchman. He was unmistakably American. Not your clean-cut All-American campus hero, but a native American aristocrat whose unbroken lineage was shrouded in the mists of time: Dubois was a full-blooded red Indian.

Morro said: "A pleasant stay and, we hope, a short one." He nodded to Dubois, who nodded to his two diminutive companions, who left. Morro moved behind the desk. "If you would be seated, please. This will not take long. Then you'll be shown to your quarters—after I have introduced you to some other guests.'' He pulled up his swivel chair, sat, and took some papers from a desk drawer. He uncapped a pen and looked up as the two small white-robed men, each bearing a silver tray filled with glasses, entered. "As you see, we are civilized. Refreshments?''

Professor Burnett was the first to be offered a tray. He glowered at it, looked at Morro and made no move. Morro smiled, rose from his seat and came toward him.

"If we had intended to dispose of you—and can you think of any earthly reason why we should—would I have brought you all the way here to do so? Hemlock we leave to Socrates, cyanide to professional assassins. We prefer our refreshments undiluted. Which one, my dear professor, would you care to have me select at random?''

Burnett, whose thirst was legendary, hesitated only briefly before pointing. Morro lifted the glass, lowered the amber level by almost a quarter and smiled appreciatively. "Glenfiddich. An excellent Scottish malt. I recommend it.''

The professor did not hesitate. Malt was malt no matter what the moral standards of one's host. He drank, smacked his lips and sneered ungratefully. "Muslims don't drink.''

"Breakaway Muslims do.'' Morro registered no offense. "We are a breakaway group. As for those who call themselves true Muslims, it's a rule honored in the breach. Ask the manager of any five-star hotel in London which, as the pilgrimage center of the upper echelons of Arabian society, is now taking over from Mecca. There was a time when the oil sheiks used to send out their servants daily to bring back large crates of suitably disguised refreshments until the managements discreetly pointed out that this was wholly unnecessary and all that was required was that they charge such expenses up to laundry, phones or stamps. I understand that various governments in the Gulf remained unmoved at stamp bills for a thousand pounds sterling.''

"Breakaway Muslims.'' Burnett wasn't through with sneering yet. "Why the front?''

"Front?'' Morro smilingly refused to take umbrage. "This is no front, Professor. You would be surprised how many Muslims there are in your state, Professor. You'd be surprised how highly placed a large number of them are. You'd be surprised how many of them come here to worship and to meditate—Adlerheim, and not slowly, is becoming a place of pilgrimage in the West. Above all, you'd be surprised how many influential citizens, citizens who cannot afford to have their good names impugned, would vouch for our unassailable good name, dedication and honesty of purpose.''

Dr. Schmidt said: "If they knew what your real purpose was I wouldn't be surprised, I'd be utterly incredulous.''

Morro turned his hands palms upward and looked at his deputy. Dubois shrugged, then said: "We are respected, trusted and—I have to say this—even admired by the local authorities. And why not? Because Californians not only tolerate and even cherish their eccentrics, regarding them as a protected species? Certainly not. We are registered as a charitable organization and, unlike the vast majority of charities, we do not solicit money, we give it away. In the eight months we have been established, we have given over two million dollars to the poor, the crippled, the retarded and to deserving pension funds, regardless of race or creed.''

"Including police pension funds?'' Burnett wasn't through with being nasty for the evening.

"Including just that. There is no question of bribery and corruption." Dubois was so open and convincing that disbelief came hard. "A *quid pro quo* you may say for the security and protection that they offer us. Mr. Curragh, county chief of police, a man widely respected for his integrity, has the whole-hearted support of the governor of the state in ensuring that we can carry out our good works, peaceful projects and selfless aims without let or hindrance. We even have a permanent police guard at the entrance to our private road down in the valley to ensure that we are not molested." Dubois shook his massive head and his face was grave. "You would not believe, gentlemen, the number of evilly intentioned people in this world who derive pleasure from harassing those who would do good."

"Sweet Jesus!" Burnett was clearly trying to fight against speechlessness. "Of all the cant and hypocrisy I've encountered in my life . . . You know, Morro, I believe you. I can quite believe that you have—not bribed, not subverted—you have conned or persuaded honest citizens, an honest chief of police and an honest police force into believing that you are what you claim to be. I can't see any reason why they shouldn't believe you— after all, they have two million good reasons, all green, to substantiate your claims. People don't throw around a fortune like that for amusement, do they?"

Morro smiled. "I'm glad you're coming around to our point of view."

"They don't throw it around like that unless they are playing for extremely high stakes. Speculate to accumulate. Isn't that it, Morro?" He shook his head in slow disbelief, remembered the glass in his hand and took further steps to fortify himself against unreality. "Out of context, one would be hard put not to believe you. In context, it is impossible."

"In context?"

"The theft of weapons-grade materials and mass kidnaping. Rather difficult to equate that with your alleged humanitarian purposes. Although I have no doubt you can equate anything with anything. All you have to have is a sick enough mind."

Morro returned to his seat and propped his chin on his fists. For some reason, he had not seen fit to remove the black leather gloves that he had worn throughout. "We are not sick. We are not zealots. We are not fanatics. We have but one purpose in mind—the betterment of the human lot."

"Which human lot? Yours?"

Morro sighed. "I waste my time. Perhaps you think you are here for ransom? You are not. Perhaps you think it is our purpose to compel you and Dr. Schmidt to make some kind of crude atomic weapon for us? Ludicrous— no one can compel men of your stature and integrity to do what they do not wish to do. You might think—the world might think—that we might compel you to work by the threat of torturing the other hostages, particularly the ladies? Preposterous. I would remind you again that we are no barbarians. Professor Burnett, if I pointed a six-gun between your eyes and told you not to move, would you move?"

"I suppose not."

"Would you or wouldn't you?"

"Of course not."

"So, you see, the gun doesn't have to be loaded. You take my point?" Burnett remained silent.

"I will not give you my word that no harm will come to any of you for clearly my word will carry no weight with any of you. We shall just have to wait and see, will we not?" He smoothed the sheet in front of him. "Professor Burnett and Dr. Schmidt I know. Mrs. Ryder I recognize." He looked at a bespectacled young girl with auburn hair and a rather scared expression. "You must, of course, be Miss Julie Johnson, stenographer."

He looked at the three remaining men. "Which of you is Mr. Haverford, deputy director?"

"I am." Haverford was a portly young man with sandy hair and a choleric expression who added as an afterthought: "Damn you anyway."

"Dear me. And Mr. Carlton? Security deputy?"

"Me." Carlton was in his mid-thirties, with black hair, permanently compressed lips and, at that moment, a disgusted expression.

"You mustn't reproach yourself." Morro was almost kindly. "There never has been a security system that couldn't be breached." He looked at the eighth hostage, a thin pale young man with thin pale hair whose bobbing Adam's apple and twitching left eye were competing in sending distress signals. "And you are Mr. Rollins, from the control room." Rollins didn't say whether he was or not.

Morro folded the sheet. "I suggest that when you get to your rooms each of you should write a letter. Writing materials you will find in your quarters. To your nearest and dearest, just to let them know that you are alive and well, that—apart from the temporary curtailment of your liberty—you have no complaints of ill treatment and have not been and will not be threatened in any way. You will not, of course, mention anything about Adlerheim or Muslims or anything that could give an indication as to your whereabouts. Leave your envelopes unsealed—we shall do that."

"Censorship, eh?" Burnett's second scotch still had had no mellowing effect.

"Don't be naïve."

"And if we—or I—refuse to write?"

"If you'd rather not reassure your families that's your decision entirely." He looked at Dubois. "I think we could have Drs. Healey and Bramwell in now."

Dr. Schmidt said: "Two of the missing nuclear physicists!"

"I promised to introduce you to some guests."

"Where is Professor Aachen?"

"Professor Aachen?" Morro looked at Dubois, who pursed his lips and shook his head. "We know no one of that name."

"Professor Aachen was the most prestigious of the three nuclear physicists who disappeared some weeks ago." Schmidt could be very precise, even pedantic, in his speech.

"Well, he didn't disappear in our direction. I have never heard of him. I'm afraid that we cannot accept responsibility for every scientist who chooses to vanish. Or defect."

"Defect? Never. Impossible."

"I'm afraid that's been exactly the reaction of American and British colleagues of scientists who have found the attractions of state-subsidized flats in Moscow irresistible. Ah! Your nondefecting colleagues, gentlemen."

Apart from a six-inch difference in height, Healey and Bramwell were curiously alike. Dark, with thin intelligent faces and identical horn-rimmed glasses and wearing neat conservatively cut clothes, they would not have looked out of place in a Wall Street board room. Morro didn't have to make any introductions: top-ranking nuclear physicists form a very close community. Characteristically, it occurred to neither Burnett nor Schmidt to introduce their companions in distress.

After the customary hand shaking, gripping of upper arms and not-so-customary regrets that their acquaintance should be renewed in such deplorable circumstances, Healey said: "We were expecting you. Well, colleagues." Healey favored Morro with a look that lacked cordiality.

Burnett said: "Which was more than we did for you." By "we" he clearly referred only to Schmidt and himself. "But if you're here we expected Willi Aachen to be with you."

"I'd expected the same myself. But no Willi. Morro here is under the crackpot delusion that he may have defected. Man had never even heard of him, far less met him."

" 'Crackpot' is right," Schmidt said, then added grudgingly: "You two look pretty fit, I must say."

"No reason why not." It was Bramwell. "An enforced and unwanted holiday, but the seven most peaceful weeks I've had in years. Ever, I suppose. Walking, eating, sleeping, drinking and, best, no telephone. Splendid library, as you can see, and, in every suite, color TV for the weak-minded."

"Suite?"

"You'll see. Those old-time billionaires didn't begrudge themselves anything. Any idea why you are here?"

"None," Schmidt said. "We were looking to you to tell us——"

"Seven weeks and we haven't a clue."

"He hasn't tried to make you work for him?"

"Like building a nuclear device? Frankly, that's what we thought would be demanded of us. But nothing." Healey permitted himself a humorless smile. "Almost disappointing, isn't it?"

Burnett looked at Morro. "The gun with the empty magazine, is that it?" Morro smiled politely.

"How's that?" Bramwell said.

"Psychological warfare. Against whomsoever the inevitable threat will ultimately be directed. Why kidnap a nuclear physicist if not to have him manufacture atom bombs under duress? That's what the world will think."

"That's what the world will think. The world does not know that you don't require a nuclear physicist for that. But the people who really matter are those who know that for a hydrogen bomb you do require a nuclear physicist. We figured that out our first evening here."

Morro was courteous as ever. "If I could interrupt your conversation, gentlemen. Plenty of time to discuss the past—and the present and future—later. A late supper will be available here in an hour. Meantime, I'm sure our new guests would like to see their quarters and attend to some—ah—optional correspondence."

Susan Ryder was forty-five and looked ten years younger. She had dark blond hair, laughing cornflower-blue eyes and a smile that could be bewitching or coolly disconcerting according to the company. Intelligent and blessed with a sense of humor, she was not, however, feeling particularly humorous at that moment. She had no reason to. She was sitting on her bed in the quarters that had been allocated to her. Julie Johnson, the stenographer, was standing in the middle of the room.

"They certainly know how to put up their guests," said Julie. "Or old Von Streicher did. Living and bedroom from the Beverly Wilshire. Bathroom with gold-plated taps—it's got everything."

"I might even try out some of these luxuries," said Susan in a loud voice. She rose, putting a warning finger to her lips. "In fact I'm going to try a quick shower. Won't be long."

She passed through the bedroom into the bathroom, waited some prudent seconds, turned the shower on, returned to the living room and beckoned Julie, who followed her back to the bathroom. Susan smiled at the young girl's raised eyebrows and said in a soft voice: "I don't know whether these rooms are bugged or not."

"Of course they are."

"What makes you so sure?"

"I wouldn't put anything past that creep."

"Mr. Morro. I thought him quite charming, myself. But I agree. Running a shower gets a hidden mike all confused. Or so John told me once." Apart from herself and Parker, no one called Sergeant Ryder by his given name, probably because very few people knew it: Jeff invariably called her Susan but never got beyond "Dad" where his father was concerned. "I wish to heaven he was here now—though mind you, I've already written a note to him."

Julie looked at her blankly.

"Remember when I was overcome back in San Ruffino and had to retire to the powder room? I took John's picture with me, removed the backing, scribbled a few odds and ends on the back of the picture, replaced the backing and left the picture behind."

"Isn't it a pretty remote chance that it would ever occur to him to open up the picture?"

"Yes. So I scribbled a tiny note in shorthand, tore it up and dropped it in my wastepaper basket."

"Again, isn't it unlikely that that would occur to him? To check your basket? And even if he did, to guess that a scrap of shorthand would mean anything?"

"It's a slender chance. Well, a little better than slender. You can't know him as I do. Women have the traditional right of being unpredictable, and that's one of the things about him that does annoy me—ninety-nine point something per cent of the time he can predict precisely what I will do."

"Even if he does find what you left—well, you couldn't have been able to tell him much."

"Very little. A description—what little I could give of anybody with a stocking mask—his stupid remark about taking us to some place where we wouldn't get our feet wet and his name."

"Funny he didn't warn his thugs against calling him by name. Unless, of course, it wasn't his name."

"Sure it's not his name. Probably a twisted sense of humor. He broke into a power station, so it probably tickled him to call himself after another station, the one in Morro Bay. Though I don't know if that will help us much."

Julie smiled doubtfully and left. When the door closed behind her Susan turned around to locate the draft that had suddenly made her shoulders feel cold, but there was no place a draft could have come from.

Showers were in demand that evening. A little way along the hallway Professor Burnett had his running for precisely the same reason as Susan had. In this case the person he wanted to talk to was, inevitably, Dr. Schmidt. Bramwell, when listing the amenities of Adlerheim, had omitted to include what both Burnett and Schmidt regarded as by far the most important amenity of all: every suite was provided with its own wet bar. The two men silently toasted each other, Burnett with his scotch, Schmidt with his gin and tonic: unlike Sergeant Parker, Schmidt had no esoteric preferences as to the source of his gin. A gin was a gin was a gin.

Burnett said: "Do you make of all this what I make of all of this?"

"Yes." Like Burnett, Schmidt had no idea whatsoever what to make of it.

"Is the man mad, a crackpot or just a cunning devil?"

"A cunning devil, that's quite obvious." Schmidt pondered. "Of course, there's nothing to prevent him from being all three at the same time."

"What do you reckon our chances are of getting out of here?"

"Zero."

"What do you reckon our chances are of getting out of here alive?"

"The same. He can't afford to let us live. We could identify them afterward."

"You honestly think he'd be prepared to kill all nine of us in cold blood?"

"He'd have to." Schmidt hesitated. "Can't be sure. Seems civilized enough in his own oddball way. Could be a veneer, of course—but he just possibly could be a man with a mission." Schmidt helped his meditation along by emptying his glass, left and returned with a refill. "Could even be prepared to bargain our lives against freedom from prosecution. Speaking no ill of the others, of course"—he clearly was—"but with four top-ranking nuclear physicists in his hands he holds pretty strong cards to deal with either state or government as the case may be."

"Government. No question. Dr. Durrer of ERDA would have called in the FBI hours ago. And while we may be important enough we mustn't overlook the tremendous emotional factor of having two innocent women as hostages. The nation will clamor for the release of all of us, irrespective of whether it means stopping the wheels of justice."

"It's a hope." Schmidt was glum. "We could be whistling in the dark. If only we knew what Morro was up to. All right, we suspect it's some form of nuclear blackmail because we can't see what else it could be but *what* form we can't even begin to guess."

"Healey and Bramwell could tell us. After all, we haven't had a chance to talk to them. They're mad, sure, but they seemed fairly relaxed and not running scared. Before we start jumping to conclusions perhaps we should talk to them. Odds are that they know something we don't."

"Too relaxed." Schmidt pondered some time. "I hesitate to suggest this, I'm no expert in the field, but could they have been brainwashed, subverted in some way?"

"No." Burnett was positive. "The thought occurred to me while we were talking to them. Very long odds against it. I know them too well."

Burnett and Schmidt found the other two physicists in Healey's room. Soft music was playing. Burnett put a finger to his lips. Healey smiled and turned up the cassette volume.

"That's just to put your minds at rest. We haven't been here for seven weeks without knowing the rooms aren't bugged. But something's bugging you?"

"Yes. Bluntly, you're too casual by far. How do you know Morro isn't going to feed us to the lions when he gets whatever he wants?"

"We don't. Maybe we're stir-happy. He's repeatedly told us that we will come to no harm and that he has no doubt about the outcome of his negotiations with the authorities when he's carried out whatever mad scheme he has in mind."

"That's roughly what *we* had in mind. It doesn't seem like much of a guarantee to us."

"It's all we have. Besides, we've had time to figure it out. He doesn't want us for any practical purposes. Therefore we're for psychological purposes, like the theft of uranium and plutonium—as you said, the pointed gun without bullets. If we were wanted for only psychological purposes then the very fact of our disappearance would have achieved all he wanted and he could have disposed of us on the spot. Why keep us around for seven weeks before disposing of us? For the pleasure of our company?''

"Well, there's no harm in looking on the bright side. Maybe Dr. Schmidt and I will come around to your way of thinking. I only hope it doesn't take another seven weeks." Healey pointed toward the bar and lifted an interrogative eyebrow, but Burnett shook his head, clear indication of how perturbed he was. "Something else still bugs me. Willi Aachen. Where has he disappeared to? Reason tells me that if four physicists have fallen into Morro's hands so would the fifth. Why should he be so favored? Or, depending on your point of view, so blessed?''

"Lord only knows. One thing for sure, he's no defector.''

Schmidt said: "He could be an involuntary defector?''

Burnett said: "Such things have happened. But it's one thing to take a horse to water.''

"I've never met him," Schmidt said. "He's the best, isn't he? From all I hear and all I read, that is.''

Burnett smiled at Healey and Bramwell, then said to Schmidt: "We physicists are a jealous and self-opinionated lot who yield second place to no one. But well, yes, he's the best.''

"I assume because I've been naturalized only six months and that he works in a supersensitive area is why I've been kept away from him. What's he like? I don't mean his work. His fame is international.''

"Last seen at that symposium in Washington ten weeks ago. The three of us were there. Cheerful, happy-go-lucky type. Frizzled head of black hair. Tall as I am, and heavily built—about two hundred and ten pounds, I'd say. And stubborn as they come—the idea of the Russians or anybody making him work for them just isn't conceivable.

Unknown to Professor Burnett, unknown to any other person who had ever known Willi Aachen in his prime, Burnett was wrong on every count. Professor Aachen's face was drawn, haggard and etched with a hundred lines, none of which had existed three months previously. The mane of frizzled hair he still had but it had turned the color of snow. He was no longer tall because he had developed a severe stoop akin to that of an advanced sufferer from kyphoscoliosis. His clothes hung on a shrunken frame of 150 pounds. And Aachen would work for anybody, especially Lopez. If Lopez had asked him to step off the Golden Gate Bridge, Aachen would have done it unhesitatingly.

Lopez was the man who had worked this change on the seemingly indestructible, seemingly impregnable Aachen. Lopez—nobody knew his surname and his given name was probably fictitious anyway—had been a lieutenant in the Argentinian Army, where he had worked as an interrogator in the security forces. Iranians and Chileans are widely championed as being the most efficient torturers in the world, but the army of the Argentine, who are reluctant to talk about such matters, make all others specializing in the field of extracting information appear to be fumbling adolescents. It said a great deal for Lopez's unholy expertise that he had sickened his ruthless commanders to the extent that they had felt compelled to get rid of him.

Lopez was vastly amused at stories of World War heroes gallantly defying torture for weeks, even months, on end. It was Lopez's claim—no boast, for his claim had been substantiated a hundred times over—that he could have the toughest and most fanatical of terrorists screaming in unspeakable agony within five minutes and, within twenty minutes, have the name of every member of his cell.

It had taken him forty minutes to break Aachen and he had to repeat the process several times in the following three weeks. For the past month, Aachen had given no trouble. It was a tribute and testimony to Lopez's evil skill that, although Aachen was a physically shattered man with the last vestiges of pride, will and independence gone forever, his mind and memory remained unimpaired.

Aachen gripped the bars of his cell and gazed through them with lack-luster eyes veined with blood, at the immaculate laboratory-cum-workshop that had been his home and his hell for the previous seven weeks. He stared unblinkingly, interminably, as if in a hypnotic trance, at the rack against the opposite wall. It held twelve cylinders. Each had a lifting ring welded to the top. Eleven of those were about twelve feet high and, in diameter, no more than the barrel of a 4.5-inch naval gun, to which they bore a strong resemblance. The twelfth was of the same diameter but less than half the height.

The workshop, hewn out of solid rock, lay forty feet beneath the banqueting hall of the Adlerheim.

4

RYDER, DR. JABLONSKY, Sergeant Parker and Jeff waited with varying degrees of patience as Marjory transcribed Susan's shorthand, a task that took her less than two minutes. She handed her notepad to Ryder.

"Thank you. This is what she says: 'The leader is called Morro. Odd.' "

Jablonsky said: "What's odd about that? Lot of unusual names around."

"Not the name. The fact that he should permit one—or more—of his men to identify him by his name."

"Bogus," Jeff said.

"Sure. 'Six foot, lean, broad-shouldered, educated voice. American? Wears black gloves. Only one with gloves. Think I see black patch over his right eye. Stocking mask makes it difficult to be certain. Other men nondescript. Says no harm will come to us. Just regard the next few days as a holiday. Bracing vacation resort. Not the sea. Can't have anyone getting their feet wet. Meaningless chatter? Don't know. Turn the oven off.' That's all."

"It's not much." Jeff's disappointment showed.

"What did you expect? Addresses and telephone numbers? Susan wouldn't have missed anything so that was all she had to go on. Two things. This Morro may have something wrong with both hands—disfigurement, scarring, amputation of fingers—and with one eye—could be a result of an accident, car crash, explosion, even a shoot-out. Then, like all criminals, he may occasionally be so sure of himself that he talks too much. Not the sea, but bracing. Could have been telling lies to mislead but why mention it at all? Bracing. Hills. Mountains."

"Lots of hills and mountains in California." Parker sounded less than encouraging. "Maybe two thirds. Just leaves an area about the size of Britain to search. And for what?"

There was a brief silence, then Ryder said: "Maybe it's not what. Maybe it's not where. Maybe we should be asking ourselves why."

The front doorbell rang for an unnecessary length of time. Jeff left and returned with the chief of police, who appeared to be in his customary foul mood, and an unhappy young detective called Kramer. Donahure looked around him with the thunderously proprietorial air of a house owner whose premises have been invaded by a hippie commune. His glare settled on Jablonsky.

"What are you doing here?"

"Funny you should ask that." Jablonsky spoke in a cold voice and removed his glasses so that Donahure could see that those were cold too. "I was about to ask you the same."

Donahure let him have some more of the glare, then switched it to Parker. "And what the hell are you doing here?"

Parker took a slow sip of his gin, an action that had a predictable effect on Donahure's complexion. "An old friend visiting an old friend. Maybe for the thousandth time. Talking over old times." Parker took another leisurely sip. "Not that it's any of your goddamned business."

"Report to me first thing in the morning." Donahure's larynx was giving him trouble again. "I know what you're talking about—the break-in. Ryder is not only not on the case, he's not a cop anymore. You don't discuss police business with the public. Now, get out. I want to talk to Ryder privately."

Ryder was on his feet with surprising ease for a man of his bulk. "You'll be getting me a reputation for downright lack of hospitality. I can't have that."

"Out!" A difficult word to snarl but Donahure made a creditable attempt. Parker ignored him. Donahure swung around, crossed the room, lifted a telephone and yelped in agony as Ryder's left hand closed over his arm. The ulnar nerve in the elbow is the most exposed and sensitive of all peripheral nerves and Ryder had powerful fingers. Donahure dropped the telephone on the table to free his right hand for the purpose of massaging his left elbow: Ryder replaced the phone on its rest.

"What the hell was that for?" Donahure rubbed his elbow industriously. "Right. Kramer. Book Ryder for assault and obstruction of justice."

"What?" Ryder looked around. "Anyone here see me assault Fatso?" Nobody, apparently, had seen anything. "A Californian's home is his castle. Nobody touches anything without my say-so."

"Is that so?" Triumph overcame the throbbing nerve. He dug into a pocket and produced a piece of paper which he flourished at Ryder. "I'll touch anything I like in this house. Know what that is?"

"Sure. A search warrant with LeWinter's name on it."

"It's a warrant, mister."

Ryder took the warrant. "Law says I've the right to read it. Or didn't you know?" Ryder glanced at it for all of a second. "Judge LeWinter it is. Your poker-playing pal at City Hall. Next to only yourself the most corrupt official in town, the only judge in town who would issue you with a warrant on a trumped-up charge." He looked at the four seated people. "Now please watch the reactions of this upholder of public morality, especially his complexion. Jeff, would you have any idea what this trumped-up charge might be?"

"Well, now," Jeff thought. "A theft trumped-up charge, I'd think. A stolen driver's license? A missing police radio? Or something really ridiculous, like harboring a set of binoculars with an L.A.P.D. stamp."

"Observe the complexion," Ryder said. "An interesting clinical study. Violet with overtones of purple. I'll bet a good psychologist could make something of that. A guilt complex, perhaps?"

"I've got it," Jeff said happily. "He's come to search the place for evidence stolen from the scene of the crime."

Ryder studied the warrant. "I don't know how you do it."

Donahure snatched the warrant back. "Too damn right. And when I do find it——"

"Find what? That's why it's a put-up job—you've no idea what you're looking for. You haven't even been out to San Ruffino."

"*I* know what I'm looking for." He marched off to an adjacent bedroom, then halted as he became aware that Ryder was following him. He turned. "I don't need you, Ryder."

"I know. But my wife does."

"What do you mean?"

"She's got some pretty nice jewelry in there."

Donahure balled his fists, looked at Ryder's eyes, changed his mind and stalked—if a hippopotamus could ever be said to stalk—into the bedroom, Ryder at his heels.

He started with a dressing-table drawer, riffled through a pile of blouses, left them in an untidy heap, slammed the drawer shut, moved to the next drawer and repeated his cry of pain as Ryder found the ulnar nerve again. In the living room, Parker rolled up his eyes, rose, picked up his own glass and that of Jablonsky and headed purposefully for the bar.

Ryder said: "I don't like untidy people. Especially, I don't want filthy fingers touching my wife's clothing. *I'll* go through her clothing and you can watch. As I've no idea what the hell you're looking for I can't very well hide it, can I?" Ryder made a meticulous search of his wife's clothing, then allowed Donahure to take over.

Jeff brought a drink into the kitchen. Kramer, leaning against the sink with his arms folded, looked glum and unhappy. Jeff said: "You look like a man who could do with a morale booster. Gin. Donahure is loaded up with Bourbon. He'll never smell it." Kramer took the drink gratefully. "What are you supposed to be doing?"

"Thanks. You can see what I'm doing. I'm searching the kitchen."

"Found anything yet?"

"I will when I start looking. Pots and pans, plates and saucers, knives and forks—all sorts of things." He gulped some of his drink. "Don't know what the hell I'm supposed to be looking for. I'm damned sorry about this, Jeff. What can I do?"

"Just what you're doing. Nothing. Inactivity becomes you. Any idea what our fat friend is looking for?"

"No. You?"

"No."

"Your father?"

"It's possible. If he knows, he hasn't told me. Not that he's had a chance to."

"Must be something important. Something that makes Donahure pretty close to desperate."

"How come?"

"Sergeant Ryder is how come. Or maybe you don't know the reputation of the bogeyman?"

"Ah."

"Yes. Takes a desperate man to provoke your old man."

"Like a man playing for high stakes. Well, now. You interest me."

"I interest myself."

"Looking for incriminating evidence, perhaps."

"Incriminating whom, I wonder?"

"I wonder."

Footsteps and voices approached. Jeff plucked the glass from Kramer, who had a drawer open before Donahure entered. Ryder was close behind him. Donahure gave Jeff the benefit of his customary glare.

"What are you doing here?"

Jeff lowered the glass from his lips. "Keeping an eye on the cutlery."

Donahure jerked a thumb. "Out." Jeff glanced at his father.

"Stay," Ryder said. "Fatso's the one who leaves."

Donahure breathed heavily. "By God, Ryder, push me any more and I'll——"

"You'll do what? Give yourself a heart attack by picking up your teeth?"

Donahure took it out on Kramer. "What did you find? Nothing?"

"Nothing that shouldn't be here."

"Sure you searched properly?"

"Never mind," Ryder said. "If there was an elephant in this house Donahure would miss it. He never tapped a wall, lifted a rug, tried to find a loose tile, didn't even look under a mattress. They couldn't have had police schools in his days." He ignored Donahure's apoplectic splutterings and led the way back to the living room. He said to no one in particular: "Whoever made this jerk a chief of police was either mentally deficient or a victim of blackmail. Fatso, I'm now looking at you with what is known as undisguised contempt. You better go make a fast report to your boss. Tell him you've made a classic blunder. Two blunders. One psychological, one tactical. I'll bet for once you acted on your own—no one with an IQ above fifty would have tipped his hand in that stupid way."

"Boss? Boss? What the hell do you mean boss?"

"You'd make as good an actor as you are a police chief. You know, I do believe I'm right. Bluster—your only stock in trade, of course, but beneath the blunder you're running scared. Boss I said, boss I meant. Every puppet needs his puppet master. Next time you're thinking of making any independent move I suggest you first consult someone with intelligence. One assumes your boss must have a little intelligence."

Donahure tried out his basilisk stare, realized it was the wrong fit, turned on his heel and left. Ryder followed him to the front door. "It's not your day, Donahure. But then it wasn't quite Raminoff's day either, was it? But I hope his had a better ending. I mean, I hope he managed to jump clear before he dumped your van in the Pacific." He clapped Kramer on the shoulder. "Don't look so perplexed, young man. I'm sure the chief will tell you all about it on the way back to the station."

He went back into the living room. Parker said: "What was all that about?"

"I'm not quite sure. I talked about his blunders and I'm sure I was right. He'd never play the lead in *The Great Stone Face*. I blundered myself, but in a different way. I blundered into what seemed to be a sensitive area. I wonder what that area could be."

"You said it yourself. He's taking orders from someone."

"That crook's been taking orders all his life. Don't look so shocked, Dr. Jablonsky. He's a crook and has been for as long as I've known him, which is far too long. Sure, the California police forces are no better than the other states in the country as far as the three P's are concerned—power, politics and promotion. But it is remarkably free from genuine corruption—Donahure is the exception that proves the rule."

"You have proof?" Jablonsky said.

"Just look at him. He's living proof. But you mean documented proof. That I have. What I'm going to say you can't quote me on, because I didn't say it."

Jablonsky smiled. "You can't faze me anymore. As I said, I've got the hang of your double-talk now."

"Not for repetition. Ah! Something else." He picked up the picture with the shorthand. "Not for repetition either."

"I can tell Ted?" Marjory said.

"I'd rather not."

"Wait till I tell Susan you keep secrets from her."

"Okay. But a secret shared is no longer a secret." He caught her interrogative glance at Jablonsky and Parker. "My dear child, the first thing nuclear physicists and intelligence cops learn is how to hold their tongues."

"I won't talk. Ted won't talk. We just want to help."

"I don't want your help."

She made a *moue*. "You're a rotten old godparent."

"Sorry." He took her hand in apology. "That wasn't nice. If I need you, I'll ask. I just don't want to involve you in what may be a messy business."

She smiled. "Thank you." Both of them knew that he would never ask.

"Chief of Police Donahure. He has a rather special house, Spanish-Moroccan, swimming pool, wet bars everywhere, expensive furniture in awful taste, no mortgage. Mexican couple. Late-model Lincoln, full payment on delivery. Twenty thousand dollars on bank deposit. Living high off the hog, you might say, but then Donahure doesn't have a wife to spend all his money for him—understandably, he's a bachelor. An acceptable lifestyle—he doesn't get paid in pennies. What's not so acceptable is that in seven different banks under seven different names he has just over half a million dollars salted away. He might have some difficulty in accounting for that."

"Nothing that goes on or is said in this house is going to surprise me anymore." Jablonsky nevertheless managed to look surprised. "Proof?"

"Sure he's got proof," Jeff said. As Ryder didn't seem disposed to deny this, he carried on: "I didn't know until this evening. My father has a dossier on him, complete with signed affidavits, which would make very interesting reading in Sacramento."

Jablosky said: "This true?"

"You don't have to believe it," Ryder said.

"I'm sorry. But why don't you lower the boom on him? Repercussions wouldn't matter a damn to you."

"They wouldn't. But they'd matter to others. Nearly half of our friend's ill-gotten gains come from blackmail. Three prominent citizens of this town, basically as clean and innocent as most of us are, which doesn't say a very great deal, have been badly compromised. They could also be badly hurt. I'll use this document if my hand is forced, of course."

"And what would it take to force your hand?"

"State secrets, Doc." Parker smiled as he said it and rose to his feet.

"So state secrets." Jablonsky rose also, nodded toward the file he'd brought. "Hope that's of some use to you."

"Thank you. Thank you both very much."

Jablonsky and Parker walked together to their cars. Jablonsky said: "You know him better than I do, Sergeant. Ryder really cares about his family? He doesn't seem terribly upset to me."

"He cares. He's just not much for the emotional scene; he'll probably be just as relaxed when he kills the man who took Susan."

"He would do that?" Jablonsky seemed unhappy.

"Sure. Wouldn't be the first time. Not in cold blood, of course—he'd have to have a reason. And if he has no reason, he'll just leave a nice challenging case for the plastic surgeon. And either of those two things could happen to anyone who gets in his way when he's trying to get next to Morro or whatever his name is. I'm afraid the kidnapers made a big mistake—they kidnaped the wrong person."

"What do you think he's going to do?"

"Don't know. I'm just guessing when I say I know what I'm going to do, something I never thought I would. I'm going right home and say a prayer for the health of our chief of police."

Jeff nodded toward the file Jablonsky had brought. "How about your homework? I always had to do it first thing when I came home."

"I need uninterrupted thought for that one."

"I suppose he thinks that's a gentle hint. Come on, Marge, take you home. See you when I see you."

"Half an hour."

"Ha!" Jeff looked pleased. "So you're not going to sit there all night and do nothing?"

"No, I'm not going to sit here all night and do nothing."

For some time after they had left it seemed as if he intended to do just that. After some minutes he put his photograph back in the frame, rose and placed it between two others on the upright piano. The one to the left was that of his wife: the other, that of Peggy, his daughter, a sophomore in arts at San Diego. She was a laughing girl with dancing eyes who had inherited her father's coloring in eyes and hair but, fortunately, neither his features nor build, both of which belonged strictly to her mother. It was common knowledge that she was the only person who could wrap the formidable Sergeant Ryder around her little finger, a state of affairs of which Ryder was well aware and by which he appeared completely untroubled. He looked at the three photographs for some seconds, shook his head, sighed, removed his own and placed it in a drawer. He made a call to San Diego, listened for a full half minute and hung up. The next call he made was to Major Dunne of the FBI. After the first ring Ryder suddenly replaced the receiver. Some thought had evidently occurred to make him change his mind. Instead, he poured himself an unaccustomed scotch, picked up the file on Carlton, sat and began to leaf through it, making neat, precise notes as he reached the foot of each page. He had just gone through a second time when Jeff returned. Ryder rose.

"Let's go take a little ride in your car."

"Sure. Where?"

"Anywhere."

"Anywhere? I can manage that," Jeff thought. "Donahure might be more persistent than one would give him credit for?"

"Yes."

They drove off in Jeff's Ford. After half a mile Jeff said: "I don't know how you do it. There was a stake-out. We're being followed."

"Make sure."

Jeff made sure. Another half mile and he said: "I'm sure."

"You know what to do."

Jeff nodded. He turned left at the first intersection, turned right up a poorly lit lane, passed the entrance of a builder's yard and came to a stop opposite a second entrance, turning his lights off. Both men got out and walked unhurriedly into the yard.

The car following drew up about fifty yards behind. A lean man of medium height, his face shadowed by a fedora that had become passé in the thirties, emerged and walked quickly toward the Ford. He had just passed the first entrance when something told him that all was not well. He swung around, reached inside his coat, then lost all interest in what he was doing when a heavy toe cap caught him just below the knee: in any event it is difficult to reach for a gun when hopping around on one leg and clutching the other with both hands.

"Stop that noise," Ryder said. He reached inside the man's coat, pulled out an automatic, transferred his grip to the barrel and struck the man squarely in the face with the butt. This time the man screamed. Jeff flashed a torch in his face and said in a voice that could have been steadier: "His nose is gone. Some of his top teeth, too."

"So's your mother." The tone of the voice made Jeff flinch and he looked at a man that he'd never seen before. "You rode your luck too far, Raminoff. If I catch you within a mile of my house again you'll be a month in Belvedere." Belvedere was the city hospital. "Then after that I'll go and attend to your boss. Tell him that. Who is your boss, Raminoff?" He lifted the gun. "You have two seconds."

"Donahure." It was a peculiar gurgling sound and one for which Raminoff could hardly be blamed. Blood was pumping steadily from mouth and nose. Ryder watched him for a couple of dispassionate seconds, then turned on his heel.

Back in the Ford, Ryder said: "Stop at the first phone booth." Jeff glanced at him questioningly but Ryder wasn't looking at him.

Ryder spent three minutes in the booth and made two calls. He returned to the car, lit a Gauloise and said: "Drive home."

"We've got a phone there. Tapped?"

"Would you put anything past Donahure? Two things. I've just made a call to John Aaron. Editor of the *Examiner*. No word yet from the kidnapers. He'll let me know as soon as anything comes through. I've also made a call to Major Dunne of the FBI. I'll be seeing him shortly. After you've dropped me off home I want you to come inside, pick up a gun and something that will serve as a mask and go out to Donahure's place and find out whether he's at home or not. Discreetly, of course."

"He's having visitors tonight?"

"Two. You and me. If he's there, call me at this number." He switched on a map light and wrote on a notepad, tearing the page off. "The Redox in Bay Street. Know it?"

"By reputation." Jeff sounded severe. "A singles, full of gays and drug pushers, not to mention addicts. Hardly your scene, I would have thought."

"That's why I'm going there. Must say Dunne didn't sound too happy about it either."

Jeff hesitated. "Going to give Donahure the Raminoff treatment?"

"It's a tempting thought, but no. He'd have nothing to tell us. Anyone smart enough to pull off this raid would be smart enough not to establish any direct contact with a clown like Donahure. He would certainly use an intermediary, maybe even two. I would."

"Then what would you be looking for?"

"I wouldn't know until I have looked."

Ryder was in disguise—he was wearing a freshly pressed business suit which only his family knew he possessed. Dunne, too, was in disguise: he wore a beret, dark glasses and a pencil mustache, none of which suited him and made him, as he was uncomfortably aware, look slightly ridiculous. But the gray eyes were as intelligent and watchful as ever. He looked in distaste at the oddly attired clientele, mainly teen-agers and those in their early twenties, and sniffed the air in nose-wrinkling disgust.

"Place smells like a damn bordello."

"You frequent those places?"

"Only in the line of duty." Dunne smiled. "Okay, so no one would look for us here. Certainly I wouldn't." He broke off as a creature dressed in pink pantaloons deposited two drinks on their booth table and left. Ryder poured both into a convenient potted plant.

"Can't do it any harm. Teaspoonful of blend topped with water." He produced a flask from an inside pocket and poured generous measures. "Scotch. Always prepared. Your health."

"Excellent. And now?"

"Four things. One, our chief of police. For your information only. Donahure and I are not seeing eye to eye."

"You surprise me."

"Probably not half as surprised as Donahure is right now. I've been upsetting him. I've been the cause of his losing a van of his this evening— it fell off a cliff into the Pacific. I've confiscated some of his personal goods and interviewed a tail he set on me."

"The tail in the hospital?"

"He'll need medical care. Right now I'd guess he's reporting to Donahure on the failure of a mission."

"How did you link him to Donahure?"

"He told me."

"Naturally. Well, can't say I'm sorry. But I did warn you—he's dangerous. Rather, his friends are. And you know how cornered rats behave. You have a tie-in between him and San Ruffino?"

"Things point that way. I'll look through his house later on tonight, see what I can find."

"He might be at home."

"What difference does that make? Then I think I'll go have a word with Judge LeWinter."

"You will? He's a different kettle of fish from Donahure. Spoken of as the next chief justice of the state supreme court."

"He's still tarred with the same brush. What do you know of him?"

"We have a file on him." Dunne peered at his glass.

"That means he's poison?"

"I'm being noncommittal."

"Yes. Well, something else for your file. Donahure called tonight with a search warrant on such an obviously trumped-up charge that only a crooked judge would have signed it."

"Any prizes for guessing?"

"No. Number two. I'd appreciate your help in this and the next couple of matters." He drew Carlton's file and the notes he had made on it from a large envelope. "Security deputy. One of the seven snatched this afternoon. His curriculum vitae or whatever you call it. Seems aboveboard."

"All the best villains are."

"Yes. Army, intelligence, two security jobs before coming to San Ruffino. As he's always worked for the Army or the AEC his past should be an open book. However, I'd like an answer to those few questions I've noted, especially his past contacts. The contacts, no matter how unimportant, are the important things."

"You have reason to suspect this man Carlton?"

"I've no reason not to, which is the same thing to me."

"Routine. Number three?"

Ryder produced another paper, Marjory's transcription of Susan's short-hand, and explained how he had come by it. Dunne read through it several times. Ryder said: "You seem to find this interesting?"

"Odd. This bit about not getting feet wet. About once a year since the turn of the century some people in this state have been confidently expecting the second flood. Cranks, of course."

"Cranks and highly organized criminals like this Morro or whoever don't go together?"

"They're not mutually exclusive either."

"Does the FBI have their names?"

"Of course. Thousands of them."

"Forget it. If you were to lock up all the nonconformists in this state you'd have half the population behind bars."

"And maybe the wrong half at that." Dunne was pensive. "You mentioned the word 'organized.' We do have groups of what you might call organized and successful cranks."

"Subversives?"

"Weirdos. But weirdos who have managed to put it together in an acceptable and comprehensible fashion. Acceptable and comprehensible to them, that is."

"Are there many of those so-called organized groups?"

"Haven't seen the list lately. Couple of hundred perhaps."

"Just a handful. No stone unturned, is that it?"

"And no avenue unexplored. I'll get a list. But that's not what you're interested in. This Morro character. Fictitious name, of course. *May* have disfigurement or damage to hands and right eye. That's easy. Number four?"

"Bit more personal, Major." Ryder slid a photograph and piece of paper across the table. "I want this person taken care of."

Dunne looked at the photograph with appreciation. "Lovely young lady. Obviously no relation of yours so what's the connection?"

"Peggy. My daughter."

"Ah!" Dunne was not an easy man to knock off stride. "Mrs. Ryder must be a beautiful person."

"Well, thank you very much." Ryder smiled and was quickly his old impassive self. "She's a sophomore at San Diego. The address is the flat she shares with three other girls. Tried to phone her—that's her number there—but no reply. I'm sure one of your men could find out where she is in no time. I'd like her to know what's happened before she finds out on the radio or TV in some crowded discotheque."

"No problem. But that's not all, is it. You said 'taken care of.' "

"They already have my wife. If Donahure is tied into this—and I'll know within an hour—Morro and his friends might not like me."

"The request is unusual."

"So are the circumstances." Dunne was hesitating. "You have children, Major."

"Damn it, yes. I mean, damn you, yes. How old is your Peggy?"

"Eighteen."

"So's my Jane. Blackmail, Sergeant, downright blackmail. All right, all right. But you know I'm supposed to be co-operating closely with Donahure. Putting me in a difficult position."

"What kind of position do you think I'm in?" He looked up as pink pantaloons approached their table and looked at Ryder.

"You Mr. Green?"

"Yes. How did you know?"

"Caller said a wide man in a dark suit. You're the only wide man in a dark suit here. Phone's this way."

Ryder followed and picked up the phone. "Well-built, son, not 'wide.' What's new?"

"Raminoff's been and left. Houseboy drove him. Still bleeding. Gone to some unlicensed quack, probably."

"Donahure there?"

"Well I don't think Raminoff spent five minutes talking to the houseboy."

"Meet you at the corner of Fourth and Hawthorne. Ten minutes, maybe fifteen."

Ryder had arrived back at his table but had not yet sat down when pink pantaloons appeared again. "Another call, Mr. Green."

Ryder was back inside a minute. He sat and brought out his flask again.

"Two calls. The tail did, in fact, report back to Donahure. Going out there in a minute." Under Dunne's puzzled gaze Ryder gulped the contents of his refilled glass. "Second call was from John Aaron. You know him?"

"The *Examiner?* I know him."

"AP and Reuters are burning up the wires. Gentleman called them. You'd never guess the name he gave."

"Morro."

"Morro it was. Said he's engineered the San Ruffino break-in, which he was sure they knew nothing about. Gave in specific detail the amount of uranium-235 and plutonium that had been taken and asked any interested party to check with the power station. Also gave names and addresses of hostages and asked all interested parties to contact their relatives to check."

Dunne was calm. "No more than what you expected. Your phone must be ringing constantly at the moment. Any threats?"

"None. Just thought he'd let us know and give us time to consider the implications."

"Aaron say when the news is being released?"

"Be an hour at least. TV and radio stations are jittery as hell. They don't know whether it's a hoax or not and they don't want to appear the biggest fools in the West. Also, even if it were true, they're not sure whether they'd be contravening national security regulations. Personally, I've never heard of any such regulations. They're apparently waiting confirmation and clearance from the AEC. If they get it, there'll be a simultaneous statewide release at eleven."

"I see. Well, it gives me plenty of time to get a man around to your Peggy."

"I'd much appreciate that. In the circumstances, most people would have forgotten all about a mere teen-ager."

"I told you. I have one. She doesn't think she's mere at all. You have your car?" Ryder nodded. "If you drop me off at my place I'll get hold of San Diego and have a couple of men on the job in ten minutes. No sweat." Dunne became thoughtful. "You won't be able to say that about the citizens of this state tomorrow. They'll be sweating buckets. Clever lad, this Morro. Mustn't underestimate him. He's craftily reversed the old maxim of better the devil you know than the devil you don't. Now it's a case of worse the devil you don't know than the devil you do. He'll have everyone in fits."

"Yes. The citizens of San Diego, Los Angeles, San Francisco, Sacramento wondering who's going to be the first for vaporization and each hoping to hell it's going to be one of the other three."

"You seriously think that, Sergeant?"

"I haven't really had time to think about anything. I'm just trying to imagine how other people would think. No, I don't seriously think so. Clever men like our friend Morro have an objective in mind and indiscriminate annihilation wouldn't be any way to achieve that. Threats would be enough."

"That's what I would think. But, then, it will take the public some time to realize—if they ever do—that we're up against a cunning and crafty person."

"And for such a person the mental climate is just right. For him, it couldn't be better." Ryder ticked off his fingers. "We've had the bubonic plague bugaboo. Didn't come to much, granted, but it scared half the people out of their wits. Then the swine flu—you could say exactly the same about that. Now practically everybody in the state, especially those on the coast, has this obsessive and—what's the word—?"

"Paranoid?"

"I didn't get to college. Paranoid. This paranoid fear about when the next, the biggest and perhaps the last earthquake is going to come. And now this. The nuclear holocaust—you know, at least we think we know there isn't going to be any such thing. But try convincing people of that." Ryder laid money on the table. "At least it should take their minds off earthquakes for the time being."

Ryder met Jeff as arranged. They left their cars at the intersection and made their way on foot up Hawthorne Drive, a steep, narrow and winding lane lined with palms.

"The houseboy's back," Jeff said. "He came back alone so I should imagine Raminoff's either having his nose set or is being kept for the night in the emergency room. The houseboy and his wife don't sleep in the house—there's a little bungalow at the foot of the garden. They're both inside there, for the night, I guess. Up this bank here."

They scramble up a grassy bank, pulled themselves over a wall and parted some rose bushes. Donahure's house was built around three sides of an oblong swimming pool, with the center section, a long, low living room, brightly illuminated. The night had turned cool and steam over the pool hung motionless in the still night air, but not so opaque as to prevent the watchers seeing Donahure, glass in hand, pacing heavily up and down. The sliding glass doors were opened wide.

"Go down to the corner there," Ryder said. "Hide in the bushes. I'll get as close as I can to that living room. When I wave my arm, attract his attention."

They took up position, Jeff among the rose bushes, Ryder, on the other side of the pool, in the dark shadow between two yew trees—the Californians, unlike Europeans, do not relegate their yews and cypresses to graveyards. Jeff made a loud moaning sound. Donahure stopped his pacing, listened, went to the opening between the sliding glass doors and listened again. Jeff repeated the sound. Donahure slipped off his shoes and padded silently across the tiles, a gun in his hand. He had taken only five steps when the butt of a Smith & Wesson caught him behind the right ear.

They used a pair of Donahure's own handcuffs to secure him to the standpipe of a radiator, Scotch tape from his desk to gag him and a table runner to blindfold him.

Ryder said: "The main entrance will be at the back. Go down to the bungalow and check that the houseboy and his wife are still there. When you come back, lock it and if anyone rings, don't answer. Lock every door and window in the house. Pull the curtains here, then start on that desk. I'll be in his bedroom. If there's anything to be found it will be in one of those two rooms."

"Still don't know what we're looking for?"

"No. Something that would make you lift an eyebrow if you saw it in your house or mine." He looked around the room. "No sign of a safe—and you can't have secret wall safes in a wooden house."

"If I had as much on my conscience as you say he has I wouldn't have anything in the house. I'd have it in a bank safe-deposit. Well, at least you've got the satisfaction of knowing that he'll have a headache when he wakes," Jeff thought. "He could have a study or office or den—lots of these houses do."

Ryder nodded and left. There was no such study. The first bedroom he came to was plainly unoccupied. The second bedroom was Donahure's. Ryder used a pencil flashlight, established that the curtains of both windows were open, closed them and switched on overhead and bedside lights.

The immaculate room clearly reflected the efficient tidiness of the house-boy's wife, a tidiness that made Ryder's task all that easier. Ryder was painstaking, methodical, took all of fifteen minutes for his search and found nothing for there was nothing to find. For all that, he made an interesting discovery. One wall cupboard was given over to a positive armory of weap-ons—revolvers, automatics, shotguns and rifles with a copious supply of ammunition to match. There was nothing sinister in this, many American gun buffs had their own private armories, frequently setting aside an entire gun room to display them. But two particular weapons caught his atten-tion—peculiarly-shaped lightweight rifles of a type not to be found in any gun store in America. Ryder took them both and a box of matching ammu-nition, then, for good measure, pocketed three of the splendid collection of handcuffs that Donahure had hanging from hooks on the side. All those items he laid on the bed while he went to examine the bathroom. There was nothing there that shouldn't have been. He picked up his newly acquired possessions from the bed and rejoined Jeff.

Donahure, chin slumped on his chest, appeared to be asleep. With the rifle barrel Ryder prodded him far from gently in the region of his expansive solar plexus. He was asleep. Jeff was sitting by the desk looking down into an opened drawer. Ryder said: "Anything?"

"Yes." Jeff looked pleased with himself. "I'm a slow starter but when I get going——"

"What do you mean, a slow starter?"

"Desk was locked. Took me some time to find the key—it was in the bottom of Fatso's holster." Jeff deposited a bundle of currency notes on the table. They were in eight separate lots, each secured with an elastic band.

"Hundreds of bills, all small denominations, looks like. What's Dona-hure doing with hundreds of bills?"

"What indeed? Got any gloves?"

"Now he asks me. Do I have any gloves? Masks—hoods, rather—be-cause you told me. Now that I—and I suppose you—have smeared finger-prints all over the shop you ask for gloves."

"Our fingerprints don't matter. You think Donahure is going to report this matter and complain about the disappearance of all this money that we are about to take with us? I just want you to count the stuff and not smear up fingerprints. Old notes are no good, they could carry a hundred smears. Maybe some new notes. Count from the bottom left—most people and most tellers count from the top right."

"Where did you get those toys?"

"From Donahure's toy shop." Ryder looked at the two rifles. "Always wanted one of those. Thought you might want one too."

"You've got rifles."

"Not these. I've never seen one. I've seen a diagram."

"What are they?"

"You'll be surprised. Unobtainable in this country. We think we make the best rifles in the world. The British think they do and the Belgians think the same of their own NATO rifles. Well, we don't think, we say. But they all know that this is the best. Light, deadly accurate, can be stripped down in seconds and hidden in the pockets of your topcoat. Splendid weapon for terrorists—as the British soldiers in Northern Ireland have found out to their cost."

"The IRA have those?"

"Yes. It's called the Kalashnikov. If a person's hunting you at night with one of those fitted with infrared telescopic sights you might as well shoot yourself. Or so they say."

"Russian?"

"Yes."

"Catholics and Communists make strange bedfellows."

"The people who use those in Northern Ireland are Protestants. An extremist splinter group officially disowned by the IRA. Not that the Communists care very much who they associate with as long as they can stir up trouble."

Jeff took one of the rifles, examined it, looked at the unconscious Donahure and then at Ryder.

Ryder said: "Don't ask me. All I know about our friend's early background is that he's a first-generation American."

"From Northern Ireland?"

"From Northern Ireland. Fits in neatly. Probably fits in too neatly."

"Donahure—a Communist?"

"We mustn't look for a Red under every bush. No law against it—well, not since McCarthy departed this scene. I don't think so, anyway. He's too stupid and too selfish to be interested in any ideology. That's not to say, of course, that he wouldn't accept their money. Count those notes and then check the rest of the desk. I'll go over the rest of the room."

Ryder looked while Jeff counted. After some minutes Jeff looked up, his face alight. "Boy, this is interesting. Eight packets of notes, each containing one thousand two hundred and fifty dollars. Ten thousand."

"So I was wrong. He's now got an eighth unofficial bank account. Very interesting I agree. But nothing to get excited about."

"No? There are several new notes in each packet. I've only made a quick check but as far as I can see they're in series. *And* they're the bicentennial two dollar notes."

"Ah, this *is* interesting. The one the ungrateful American public turned their thumbs down on. The Treasury had carloads of the stuff printed but there's only a small percentage of it in circulation. If they really are in series, the FBI should be able to trace it without trouble."

Nothing more came to light and they left five minutes later after freeing a now stirring Donahure of his handcuffs, Scotch tape and blindfold.

Major Dunne was still in his office, handling two phones at the same time. When he'd hung up, Ryder said: "Not yet abed?"

"No. And I don't expect to be—not this night, anyway. I'll have plenty of company in my misery. Statewide alert, twenty-four-hour basis, for every agent who could walk. Description of Morro has been telexed, or is being telexed, throughout the country. I've arranged for this list of the organized weirdos but I won't have that until tomorrow. Your Peggy has been taken care of."

Jeff said to Ryder: "*Our* Peggy?"

"Forgot to tell you. The kidnapers have made a statement to AP and Reuters. No threats, just details what materials they've stolen and the names of the people they kidnaped. It will be released at eleven tonight." He looked at his watch. "Half an hour. I didn't want your sister to have the shock of hearing of the kidnaping of her mother over the TV or radio. Major Dunne has kindly taken care of that."

Jeff looked from one man to another, then said: "It's just a thought. But has it occurred to you that Peggy might just possibly be in danger?"

"It is a thought and it has occurred." Dunne could be very precise and clipped in his speech. "It has also been taken care of." He peered at the rifles in Ryder's hand. "Late hour to go shopping."

"We borrowed them from your friend Donahure."

"Ah! How is he?"

"Unconscious. Not that there's much difference between that and his walking state. He knocked his head against the butt of an automatic."

Dunn brightened. "Disgraceful. You had reason for taking those? Something special?"

"I'm pretty sure. These are Kalashnikovs. Russian. Can you check with Washington, import controls, to see if any licenses have been issued to bring those in? I very much doubt it. The Russians just love to unload their arms on anyone with the cash to pay, but it's a fair guess they wouldn't part with the most advanced rifle in the business, which this is."

"Illegal possession? That would make him an ex-chief of police."

"Unimportant. He'll be that soon anyway."

"Communist?"

"Unlikely. Of course, he's capable of being an empty convert to anything if the money's good enough."

"I'd like to have those, if I may."

"Sorry. Finders keepers. You want to admit in court that you abetted breaking and entering? Don't be upset. Jeff's got a little present for you." Jeff placed the wad of bank notes on the table. "Ten thousand dollars exactly. All yours. How many consecutively listed brand-new two dollar notes are there, Jeff."

"Forty."

"Manna," Dunne said reverently. "I'll have the names of the bank, teller and drawer by noon tomorrow. Pity you weren't able to find out the name of the drawer."

"I told you. Donahure was asleep. I'll go back and ask him later on."

"Like that? May be pushing your luck, Sergeant."

"No. I've had the great misfortune to know Chief Donahure longer than you have. He's a bully—I know it's commonplace to say that all bullies are cowards, which is not at all true—but in his case it is. Take his face. A disaster, but the only one he has and he probably cherishes it. He saw what happened to his stake-out's face tonight."

"Mm." Dunne's momentarily beatific expression had been replaced by a frown and it wasn't because of anything that Ryder had said. He tapped the bundle of notes. "This. How am I to account for this, to explain it away? I mean, where did it come from?"

"Yes." It was Jeff's turn to frown. "I didn't think of that either."

"Easy. Donahure gave it to you."

"He what?"

"Despite the fact that he has about half a million in ill-gotten gains salted away under seven or eight forged names, we all know that he's basically a decent, upright, honorable man, deeply committed to the welfare of his fellow man, to upholding the rule of justice and ruthlessly crushing bribery and corruption wherever it raises its ugly head. He was approached by the syndicate responsible for the San Ruffino break-in and given this money in return for a blow-by-blow account of the steps being taken by the state and federal authorities in investigating this case. You and he worked out a plan to feed false and misleading information to the crooks. Naturally, he handed you this tainted money for safekeeping. You have to admire the man's unshakable integrity."

"Ingenious, but you've overlooked the obvious. All Donahure has to do is to deny it."

"With his fingerprints all over those notes—especially those new ones? He's either got to go with the story or admit that he had the notes cached away in the house, which would leave him the rather awkward task of explaining where he got them from. Which option do you think he'll elect?"

Dunne said admiringly, "You have a very devious mind."

"Set a thief to catch a thief?" Ryder smiled. "Maybe. Two things, Major. When you or whoever handle those notes don't touch the top right. Fingerprints, especially on the two dollar bills."

Dunne looked at the notes. He said: "I'd estimate there's about two thousand bills there. You expect me to try them *all* for fingerprints?"

"I said you or whoever."

"Well, thanks. And the second thing?"

"Have you got a fingerprinting set here?"

"Lots. Why?"

"Oh, I don't know." Ryder was vague. "You never know when those things come in handy."

Judge LeWinter lived in a rather splendidly impressive house as befitted one who was widely touted to become the next chief justice of the state supreme court. Within a few miles of the California coast is to be found a greater variety of home architecture than anywhere, but, even by such standards, LeWinter's home was unusual, a faithful replica of an Alabama antebellum house, gleaming white, with its two-story colonnaded porch, balconies, a profusion of surrounding magnolias and a plethora of white oak and long-bearded Spanish moss, neither of which seemed to find the climate very congenial. Within so imposing a residence—one couldn't call it a home—could only dwell, one would have thought, a pillar of legal rectitude. One could be wrong.

How wrong Ryder and his son found out when the opened the bedroom door without the courtesy of a prior knock and found the legal luminary in bed, but not alone—nor was he "not alone" with his wife either. The judge, bronzed, white-haired and white-mustached, the absence of a white winged collar and black string tie an almost jarring note, looked perfectly at home in the gilded Victorian iron bedstead, which was more than could be said for his companion, a sadly overpainted and sadly youthful demimondaine who looked as if she would have been much more at home in what could delicately be termed as the outermost fringes of society. Both wore startled and wide-eyed expressions as people tend to wear when confronted with two hooded men bearing guns, the girl's expression shading gradually into a guilty fear, the judge's, predictably, into outrage. His speech was equally predictable.

"What the devil! Who the devil are you?"

"We're no friends, you can be sure of that," Ryder said. "We know who you are. Who's the young lady?" He didn't bother to wait for the inevitable silence but turned to Jeff. "Bring your camera, Perkins?"

"Sorry."

"Pity." He looked at LeWinter. "I'm sure you would have loved us to send a snapshot to your wife to show that you're not pining too much in her absence." The judge's outrage subsided. "Right, Perkins, the prints."

Jeff was no expert but he was not long enough out of police school to have forgotten how to make clean prints. A deflated LeWinter, who clearly found the situation beyond him, offered neither objection nor resistance. When Jeff had finished he glanced at the girl and then at Ryder, who hesitated and nodded. Ryder said to her: "Nobody's going to hurt you, miss. What's your name?"

She compressed her lips and looked away. Ryder sighed, picked up a purse which could only be hers, opened it and emptied the contents on a dressing table. He riffled through those, picked up an envelope and said: "Bettina Ivanhoe, 888 South Maple." He looked at the girl, frightened, flaxen-haired, with high and rather wide Slavonic cheekbones: but for her efforts to improve on nature she would have been strikingly good-looking. "Ivanhoe? Ivanov would be nearer it. Russian?"

"No. I was born here."

"I'll bet your parents weren't." She made no reply to this. He looked through the scattered contents of the purse and picked up two photographs, one each of the girl and LeWinter. That made her more than a one-time visitor. There had to be a forty-year gap in their ages. "Darby and Joan," Ryder said. The contempt in his voice was matched by his gesture of flicking the cards to the floor.

"Blackmail?" LeWinter tried to inject some contempt of his own but he wasn't up to it. "Extortion, eh?"

Ryder said indifferently: "I'd blackmail you to death if you were what I think you might be. In fact, I'd put you to death without any blackmail." The words hung chillingly in the air. "I'm after something else. Where's your safe and where's the key to it?"

LeWinter sneered, but there was—it could have been imagined—a hint of relief behind the sneer. "A petty heistman."

"Unbecoming language from the bench." Ryder produced and opened a penknife, then approached the girl, "Well, LeWinter?"

LeWinter folded his arms and looked resolute.

"The flower of southern chivalry." Ryder tossed the knife to Jeff, who placed the tip against LeWinter's second chin and pressed.

"It's red," Jeff said. "Just the same as the rest of us. Should I have sterilized this?"

"Down and to the right," Ryder said. "That's where the external jugular is."

Jeff removed the knife and examined it. The blade was narrow and only the top half inch had blood on it. To LeWinter, who had stopped looking resolute, it must have seemed that the arterial floodgates had burst. His voice was husky. "The safe's in my study downstairs. The key's in the bathroom."

Ryder said: "Where?"

"In a jar of shaving soap."

"Odd place for an honest man to keep a key. The contents of this safe should be interesting." He went into the bathroom and returned in a few seconds, key in hand. "Any servants on the premises?"

"No."

"Probably not. Think of the stirring tales they could tell your wife. Believe him, Perkins?"

"On principle, no."

"Me neither." Ryder produced three sets of handcuffs, all, until very recently, the property of the police chief. One set secured the girl's right wrist to a bedpost, the second LeWinter's left to the other bedpost, the third, passing behind a central headrail, secured their other two wrists together. For gags they used a couple of pillow slips. Before securing LeWinter's gag, Ryder said: "A hypocrite like you, who makes all those stirring speeches against the Washington gun lobby, is bound to have some lying around. Where are they?"

"Study."

Jeff began a meticulous search of the room. Ryder went below, located the study, located the gun cupboard and opened it. No Kalashnikovs. But one particular handgun, of a make unknown to him, took his attention. He wrapped it in a handkerchief and dropped it into one of his capacious coat pockets.

The safe was massive, six feet by three, weighing well over a quarter of a ton and built at some time in the remote past before safebreakers had developed the highly sophisticated techniques of today. The locking mechanism and key were woefully inadequate. Had the safe been free-standing Ryder would have opened it without hesitation. But it was set into a brick wall for a depth of several inches, a most unusual feature for that type of safe. Ryder returned upstairs, removed LeWinter's gag and produced his knife.

"Where's the cutoff switch for the safe?"

"What damned switch?"

"You were too quick in telling me where the key was. You wanted me to open that safe." For the second time that night LeWinter winced, more in apprehension than pain, as the knife tip punctured the skin of his neck. "The switch that cuts the alarm relay to the local sheriff's office."

LeWinter was more obdurate this time, but not markedly so. Ryder returned downstairs and slid back a panel above the study door to expose a simple switch. Half of it was designed as a filing cabinet; the files, in the customary fashion, were suspended by metal lugs from parallel rails. Nearly all of those were given over to personal notes on court cases that had come before him. Two files were marked "Private Correspondence" but apparently weren't all that private, as some of them had been signed on his behalf by his secretary, a (Miss) B. Ivanhoe: clearly the young lady upstairs carried secretarial devotion to her boss to lengths above and beyond the call of duty. In the shelves above, only three things caught his attention and were removed. One was a list of names and telephone numbers. The second was a leather-bound copy of Sir Walter Scott's *Ivanhoe*. The third was a green and also leather-bound notebook.

As notebooks go, it was large—about eight inches by five—and secured by a locked brass clasp, a sufficient deterrent against the young or merely curious but of no avail against the ill-intentioned armed with a knife. Ryder sliced open the spine and riffled through the exposed pages, which told him nothing inasmuch as they were covered with neatly typed figures, not letters. He wasted no time on the notebook. He knew nothing of cryptography, which didn't worry him: the FBI had its own highly specialized department of code breakers who could decipher anything except the most highly sophisticated military codes and even that they could do if given enough time. Time. Ryder looked at his watch. It was one minute to eleven.

He found Jeff methodically going through the pockets of LeWinter's very considerable number of custom-made suits. LeWinter and the girl were still resting comfortably. Ryder ignored them and switched on a TV set. He didn't bother to select any particular station: the same program would be on every station. Ryder didn't bother to look at the screen. He didn't appear to be watching anything at all but, in fact, he didn't allow the couple on the bed to move out of peripheral vision.

The announcer, who might just coincidentally have been dressed in a dark suit and tie, used his state funeral voice. He confined himself to the facts. The San Ruffino nuclear power reactor station had been broken into that late afternoon and the criminals had made good their escape, taking with them weapons-grade material and hostages. The precise amount of material taken was specified as were the names, addresses and occupations of the hostages. Neither the person giving this information nor the source from which it had come had been identified but the genuineness of the information was beyond dispute as it had been confirmed in detail by the authorities. The same authorities were carrying out an intensive investigation. The usual meaningless poppycock, Ryder thought; they had no leads to investigate. He switched off the set and looked at Jeff.

"Notice anything, Perkins?"

"The same thing you were noticing. What you can see of Casanova's face here didn't show much change in expression. Didn't show anything, in fact. Guilty as hell, I'd say."

"Good as a signed confession. That news was no news to him." He looked at LeWinter and appeared momentarily lost in thought before saying: "I've got it. Your rescuers, I mean. I'll send along a reporter and a photographer from the *Globe*."

"Isn't that interesting," Jeff said. "I do believe Don Juan has registered a slight change in expression."

LeWinter had, in fact, registered a marked change in expression. The bronzed skin had assumed a grayish hue and the suddenly protuberant eyes seemed bent on parting company with their sockets. One could enjoy the *Globe* without being able to read too well. It specialized in artistic portraits of unclad feminine illiterates who spent their evenings reading Sophocles in the original, in candid shots of newsworthy caught in apparently compromising or undignified situations and, for the intelligentsia among their readers, extensive muckraking couched in terms of holy crusades against shocked morality and, perforce, in the very simplest of prose: such was the intolerable pressure brought to bear through the demands imposed by the clamorous urgency, the evangelistic immediacy and the socially important content of those journalist imperatives that the overworked editorial staff were frequently and reluctantly compelled to encapsulate, hold over or, most commonly, altogether forget, such trivia as the international news or, indeed, any but the most salaciously elevating items of the local news. One did not require telepathic aid to guess that the judge's mind was touching on such matters in general and, in particular, on page one, where the unretouched and considerably enlarged picture of himself and his handcuffed amorita would leave room only for the appalled caption.

Downstairs in the study Ryder said: "Glance through those court cases in the files. You may find something of interest, although I doubt it. I have a call to make." He dialed a number and, while waiting for his call to come through, glanced at the list of names and telephone numbers he had taken from the safe. His number answered and he asked for Mr. Jamieson. Jamieson was the night manager at the telephone exchange. He was on the line almost at once.

"Sergeant Ryder here. Important and confidential, Mr. Jamieson." Jamieson had delusions about his self-importance and liked to have those kept well stoked. "I have a number here and would be glad if you made a note of it." He gave the number, had it read back to him and said: "I think it's Sheriff Hartman's home number. Would you check and give me the address—it's not in the book."

"Important, huh?" Jamieson sounded eager. "Hush-hush?"

"You don't know how important. Heard the news?"

"San Ruffino? My God, yes. Just now. Bad, eh?"

"You better believe it." He waited patiently until Jamieson came back to him. "Well?"

"You got the right name, right number. Classified, God knows why—118 Rowena."

Ryder thanked him and hung up. Jeff said: "Who's Hartman?"

"Local sheriff. That safe is wired to his office. Missed something up there, didn't you?"

"I know."

"How?"

"If I hadn't missed it, you wouldn't mention it."

"You noticed how readily LeWinter parted with the key to that safe. What does that tell you about Sheriff Hartman?"

"Nothing much. Correction, nothing good."

"Yes. LeWinter would willingly be found in such a scandalous and compromising situation by very, very few people. But he knows that Sheriff Hartman wouldn't talk. So there's a bond between them."

"LeWinter *could* have a friend in this world."

"We're talking about the probabilities, not the near impossible. Blackmail? Unlikely. If the judge were blackmailing Hartman this would be a once in a lifetime chance for the sheriff to make sure that the blackmail ended here and now. LeWinter could be the victim but I can't see it that way. What I do see is that they are in some very profitable business together. Criminal business. An honest judge would never compromise himself by going into business with a lawman. Anyway, I know LeWinter is bent. I know nothing about this Hartman but he's probably the same."

"As honest—if unemployed—cops it's our duty to find out what Hartman's bent about. In what now appears to be the usual fashion?" Ryder nodded. "Donahure can wait?"

"He'll keep. Turned up anything?"

"Hell, no. All these 'whereases' and 'whereofs' and 'hereintofores' are too much for me."

"You can forget it. Even LeWinter wouldn't express his deepest thoughts—or criminal intentions—in legalese." Ryder again dialed a number, waited, then said: "Mr. Aaron? Sergeant Ryder here. Now, don't get me wrong but how would you like one of your photographers to take a picture of a prominent citizen caught in a compromising situation?"

Aaron's tone was uncomprehending. Not cold, just not understanding. "I am surprised, Sergeant. You know that the *Examiner* is not a yellow tabloid."

"Pity. I thought you were and would be interested in Judge LeWinter's peccadilloes."

"Ah!" LeWinter ranked with Chief Donahure at the top of the list of

Aaron's targets for critical editorials. "What's that crooked old goat up to now?"

"He's not up to anything. He's lying down. He's with his secretary, who is young enough to be his granddaughter. When I say 'with' I mean 'with.' He's handcuffed to her and they're both handcuffed to the bed."

"Good God!" Aaron made a coughing sound, probably trying to stifle laughter. "That intrigues me vastly, Sergeant. But I'm still afraid we couldn't publish——"

"No one asked you to publish anything. Just take a photograph."

"I see." There was a brief silence. "All you want is for him to know that such a picture has been taken?"

"That's it. I'd be glad if your boys would maintain the fiction I've told him—that I was sending people from the *Globe*."

This time Aaron positively cackled. "That would make him happy."

"He's having fits. Many thanks. I'm leaving the handcuff keys on the study table."

Dunne, as he'd promised, was still in his office when they returned. Ryder said: "Progress?"

"None—almost impossible to make an outgoing call. Switchboard's been jammed since the news announcement. At least a hundred people have seen the criminals—in, as usual, a hundred different places. You?"

"Don't know. You'll have to help us if you will. First off here's Judge LeWinter's fingerprints."

Dunne looked at him in disbelief. "He *gave* you his fingerprints?"

"Sort of."

"I warned you, Ryder. Tangle with that old bird and you step out of your class. Donahure has powerful friends locally but LeWinter has them where it counts—in Sacramento. Don't tell me you used violence again."

"Certainly not. We left him peacefully in bed and unharmed."

"Did he recognize you?"

"No. We wore hoods."

"Well, thank you very much. As if I haven't got enough on my hands. Do you know what kind of hornet's nest you'll have stirred up? And where will it all end up? In my lap." He closed his eyes. "I know who'll be the next caller on those damned phones."

"Not LeWinter. He's a bit restricted right now. Matter of fact we left him handcuffed to a bedpost and his secretary. They were there when we arrived. She's Russian."

Dunne closed his eyes again. When he'd assimilated this and steeled himself for whatever was to come, he said carefully: "And?"

"This is interesting." Ryder unwrapped the handgun he had taken. "I wonder what an upright judge is doing with a silenced automatic. Can you have it tested for fingerprints? Incidentally, the girl's fingerprints are already there. This is a notebook, coded. I imagine the key is in this copy of *Ivanhoe*. Perhaps the FBI can find out. Finally, this is his private list of telephone numbers. Some may or may not be significant and I've neither the time nor the facilities to find out."

Dunne was heavily sarcastic. "Anything else you'd like me to do for you?"

"Yes. A copy of the file you have on LeWinter."

Dunne shook his head. "FBI personnel only."

"Would you listen to him," Jeff said. "After all the legwork we do for him, after all the valuable clues we put in his hands——"

"Okay, okay. But I'm promising nothing. Where to now?"

"To see another lawman."

"He has my advance sympathies. Do I know him?"

"No. And I don't. Hartman. Must be new. Anyway, he's in Redbank. County division."

"What has this unfortunate done to incur your displeasure?"

"He's a pal of LeWinter's."

"That, of course, explains everything."

Hartman lived in a small and unpretentious bungalow on the outskirts of town. For a California house it was virtually a slum: it had no swimming pool. Ryder said: "His association with LeWinter must be pretty recent."

"Yes. He lets the side down, doesn't he? Door's open. Do we knock?"

"Hell, no."

They found Hartman seated at his desk in a small study. He was a large, heavily built man and must have stood several inches over six feet when he stood up: but Sheriff Hartman would never stand up again. Somebody had carefully cross-filed a soft-nosed bullet, which had entered by the left cheek-bone: the dum-dum effect had taken off the back of his head.

It was pointless to search the house: whoever had been there before them would have made certain that nothing incriminating a third party—or parties—had been left behind.

They took the dead man's fingerprints and left.

5

THAT WAS the night the earth shook. Not all of the earth, of course, but for a goodly portion of the residents of Southern California it might have been just that. The shock came at twenty-five minutes past midnight and the tremors were felt as far north as Merced in the San Joaquin Valley, as far south as Oceanside, between Los Angeles and San Diego, as far west as San Luis Obispo, close by the Pacific, to the southeast clear across the Mojave Desert and to the east as far as Death Valley. In Los Angeles, though no structural damage was done, the shake was felt by all who were awake and it was pronounced enough to wake many of those who were sleeping. In the other main centers of population—Oakland-San Francisco, Sacramento and San Diego—no tremors were felt but the earthquake, a very minor one at 4.2 on the Richter scale, was duly recorded on the delicate seismographs.

Ryder and Jeff, seated in the former's living room, both felt it and saw it—a ceiling lamp, traveling through an arc of not more than two inches at maximum, oscillated for about twenty seconds before coming to rest. Dunne, still in his office, felt it and paid no attention to it—he had been through many such tremors before and he had more important things on his mind. LeWinter, dressed now, as was his secretary, felt it through the open door of his safe, the remaining contents of which he was examining with some anxiety. Even Donahure, despite an aching occiput and a mind somewhat beclouded by his fourth consecutive large scotch, was dimly aware of it. And, although its foundations were firmly imbedded on the very solid rock of the Sierra Nevada, the Adlerheim felt it most acutely of all, for the excellent reason that the epicenter of the earthquake was no more than a dozen miles distant: even more importantly, the quake registered strongly in the seismographical office installed in one of the caves—wine cellars—

which Von Streicher had excavated out of the rock and on two other seismographs which Morro had foresightedly had installed in two private resi-
dences he owned, each about fifteen miles distant and in diametrically
different directions.

And the shocks were registered, too, in institutes which, one would have
thought, had considerably more legitimate interest in such matters than
Morro. Those were the offices of the Seismology Field Survey, those of the
California Department of Water Resources, in the California Institute of
Technology and the U.S. Geological Survey's National Center for Earthquake Research. The last two, and probably most important of the four,
were conveniently located where they would be the first to be demolished
should a massive earthquake affect either Los Angeles or San Francisco, for
the Institute of Technology was located in Pasadena and the Earthquake
Research Center in Menlo Park. The nerve centers of all four institutes were
in direct and permanent contact with each other and it had taken them only
minutes to pin-point, with complete precision, the exact epicenter of the
earthquake.

Alec Benson was a large calm man in his early sixties. Except on ceremonial occasions, which he avoided wherever and whenever possible, he
invariably wore a gray flannel suit and a gray polo jersey, which went well
enough with the gray hair that topped the tubby, placid and usually smiling
face. Director of the seismology department, he held two professorships and
so many doctorates and scientific degrees that, for simplicity's sake, his
numerous scientific colleagues referred to him just as "Alec." In Pasadena,
at least, he was regarded as the world's leading seismologist: while the
Russians and Chinese may have disputed this it was noteworthy that those
two countries were always among the first to nominate him as chairman of
the not infrequent international seismological conferences. This esteem
stemmed primarily from the fact that Benson never made any distinction
between himself and his world-wide colleagues and sought advice as frequently as he gave it.

His chief assistant was Professor Hardwick, a quiet, retiring, almost self-
effacing scientist with a track record that almost matched Benson's. Hardwick said: "Well, about a third of the people in the state must have felt the
shock. It's already been on TV and radio and will be in all the late editions
of the morning's papers. At the least, there must be a couple of million
amateur seismologists in California. What do we tell them? The truth?"

For once, Alec Benson wasn't smiling. He looked thoughtfully around
the half-dozen scientists in the room, the vastly experienced nucleus of his
research team, and studied their expressions, which were neither helpful nor
unhelpful: clearly, they were all waiting for him to give a lead. Benson
sighed. He said: "No one admires George Washington more than I do—but,
no, we don't tell them the truth. A little white lie and it won't even rest
uneasily on my conscience. What's to be gained if we tell the truth, other
than scaring our fellow Californians even further out of their wits than they
are now? If anything major is going to happen then it's just going to happen
and there's nothing we can do about it. In any event, we have no evidence
that this is a prelude to a major shake."

Hardwick looked doubtful. "No intimation, no warning, nothing?"

"What point would it serve?"

"Well, there's never been a quake in that spot in recorded history."

"No matter. Even a major quake there wouldn't be of great importance.
Devastation of property and loss of life would be insignificant, because the
area is so sparsely populated. Owens Valley, 1872, the largest recorded
earthquake in California's history—how many people died there? Maybe

sixty. The Arvin-Tehachapi quake of 1952, at 7.7 the largest in Southern California—how many died there? Perhaps a dozen.'' Benson permitted himself his customary smile. ''Now, if this latest jolt had happened along the Inglewood-Newport fault, I'd take a different view entirely.'' The Inglewood-Newport fault, which had been responsible for the Long Beach earthquake of 1933, actually ran under the city of Los Angeles itself. ''As it is, I'm in favor of letting sleeping dogs lie.''

Hardwick nodded. Reluctantly, but he nodded. ''So we blame it on the poor old blameless White Wolf fault?''

''Yes. A calmly reassuring release to the media. Tell them again, briefly, about our EPSP, that we are cautiously pleased that it seems to be going according to plan and that the intensity of this shake corresponds pretty closely to our expected estimate of fault slippage.''

''Release to the TV and radio stations?''

''No. General. Wire service. We don't want to lend anything that smacks of undue urgency or importance to our—ah—findings.''

Preston, another senior assistant, said: ''We don't let ethics creep into this, huh?''

Benson was quite cheerful. ''Scientifically indefensible. But from the humanitarian point of view—well, call it justifiable.''

It said much for the immense weight of Benson's prestige that the consensus was heavily on his side.

In the refectory hall in the Adlerheim, Morro was being equally cheerful and reassuring to the anxious hostages who had gathered there. ''I can assure you, ladies and gentlemen, that there is no cause for alarm. I grant you, it was quite a nasty shake, the worst we have experienced here, but a shake of a thousand times that magnitude would leave us completely unharmed. Apart from the fact that you may probably have already learned from your TVs that there has been no damage throughout the state, you must all be intelligent enough and widely read enough to know that earthquakes spell danger only for those who live in dwellings on made-up filled land, marshy land whether drained or not and on alluvial soil. Damage rarely occurs to dwellings that have their foundations on rock—and we have our foundations on thousands of feet of rock. The Sierra Nevada has been here for millions of years—it is not likely to disappear overnight. It is unlikely that you could find any safer or more desirable—from the earthquake point of view— residence in the state of California.'' Morro glanced smilingly around his audience, nodding his approval when he saw that his words seemed to have had the desired calming effect. ''I don't know about you people, but I have no intention of allowing this passing trifle to interfere with my night's sleep. I bid you all good night.''

When Morro entered his private office the smile was markedly absent. Abraham Dubois was seated behind his, Morro's, desk, a phone in one hand, a pencil in the other, his huge shoulders hunched over a large-scale map of California. Morro said: ''Well?''

''It is not well.'' Dubois replaced the phone and delicately pricked a pencil dot on the map. ''Here. Exactly here.'' He used a rule, then set it against a mileage scale. ''The epicenter, to be precise, is exactly eleven and a half miles from the Adlerheim. This is not so good, Mr. Morro.''

''It's not so good,'' Morro lowered himself into an armchair. ''Does it not strike you as rather ironic, Abraham, that we should pick the one spot in the state where an earthquake takes place outside our back door, so to speak?''

"Indeed. It could be an ill omen. I wish I could fault the triangulation, but I can't. It's been checked and rechecked." Dubois smiled. "At least we didn't pick an extinct volcano that has suddenly turned out not to be so extinct after all. What option do we have? There is no time, there is no alternative. This is our operating base. This is our perfectly secure cover. This is our weaponry. This is the only multiband radio transmitting station we have. All our eggs are in one basket but if we pick up that basket and try to walk away with it the chances are that we will fall and be left with only the ruined ingredients for an omelet."

"I'll go sleep on it, although I don't think I'll wake up feeling any differently from the way you do now." Morro pushed himself heavily to his feet. "We mustn't let what could be only a once in a lifetime coincidence affect our thinking and planning too much. Who knows, there may not be another quake centered in this area for a hundred years. After all, there hasn't been one for hundreds, not at least that we know of or that has been recorded. Sleep well."

But Dubois did not sleep well for the excellent reason that he did not go to bed. Morro did sleep, but it was for only an hour or so. He awoke to find his light on and Dubois shaking his shoulder.

"My apologies." Dubois looked rather more cheerful than when last he had been seen. "But I've just made a videotape of a TV newscast and I think you ought to see it as soon as possible."

"The earthquake, I take it?" Dubois nodded. "Good or bad?"

"One could not call it bad. I think you might well turn it to your advantage."

The replay of the videotape lasted no more than five minutes. The newscaster, a bright and knowledgeable youngster who clearly knew enough about what he was talking about not to have recourse to a teleprompter, was remarkably brisk and fresh for one who was up and around at the unchristian hour of 3 A.M. He had a large relief map of California hanging on the wall behind him and wielded a slender cane with all the fluent dexterity of a budding Toscanini.

He began by giving concise details of what was known of the earthquake, the area over which it had been felt, the degree of apprehension felt in various areas and the amount of damage which it had caused, which was zero. He then went on to say: "From the latest authoritative statement, it would appear that this earthquake is to be regarded as a plus and not a minus, as a matter for some self-congratulation and not as a pointer toward some further calamity. In short, according to the state's top seismological sources, this may well be the first earthquake ever knowingly and deliberately brought about by man.

"If this is correct, then it must be regarded as a landmark in earthquake control, the first success of the implementation of the EPSP. For Californians, this can only be good news. To remind you: EPSP stands for Earthquake Preventative Slip Program, which must be one of the clumsiest and most misleading titles thought up by the scientific fraternity in recent years. By 'slip' is meant simply the rubbing, sliding, jarring, earthquake-producing process which occurs when one of the eight, maybe ten, no one seems very sure, of the earth's tectonic plates, on which the continents float, push into, above, under or alongside each other. The title is misleading because it gives the impression that earthquakes may be brought under control by preventing this slip from taking place. In fact, it means precisely the opposite—the prevention of earthquakes, or at least major earthquakes, by permitting, indeed encouraging, this slipping factor to take place—but to take place in a gradual and controlled process in which there is a continuing and progressive easing of the strain between the plates by allowing them to slide comparatively smoothly past one another producing a series of minor and harmless quakes at frequent intervals instead of massive ones at long intervals. The secret, not surprisingly, is lubrication.

"It was purely a chance discovery that led to this possibility—which would now appear a strong possibility—of modifying earthquakes by increasing their frequency. Somebody, for reasons best known to themselves, injected waste water into a particularly deep well near Denver and discovered, to their surprise, that this triggered off a series of earthquakes, tiny, but unquestionably earthquakes. Since then there have been many experiments, both in the laboratory and under actual field conditions, that have clearly demonstrated that frictional resistance in a fault zone is lessened by decreasing the stress along the fault.

"In other words, increasing the amount of fluid in the fault lessens the resistance in the fault while withdrawing the fluid increases the resistance— if an existing stress is present between the faces of two tectonic plates it can be eased by injecting fluid and causing a small earthquake, the size of which can be fairly accurately controlled by the amount of fluid injected. This was proved some years ago when Geological Survey scientists, experimenting in the Rangeley oil fields in Colorado, found that by alternately forcing in and then withdrawing fluids they could turn earthquakes off and on at will.

"To what may be to their eternal credit, seismologists in our state were the first to put those theories to practical use." The newscaster, who seemed to relish his role as lecturer, was now tapping the map on the wall. "From here to here"—he indicated a line that stretched from the Mexican border to the San Francisco Bay area—"massive drills, specifically designed for this task, have bored holes to an incredible depth of up to forty thousand feet in ten selected areas along this roughly southeast-northwest line. All of those boreholes are in known earthquake faults and all in areas where some of the most severe of recorded earthquakes have taken place."

Starting from the south, he tapped out a number of spots on the map. "Ten boreholes in all. The scientists are experimenting with various mixtures of water and oil for lubricating purposes. Well, not quite mixtures, for oil and water don't readily mix. First oil, then stuff they call mud, the whole pushed farther down and through cracks in the rocks by water under high pressure."

He stopped, looked at the camera for a dramatic five seconds, turned, placed the tip of the cane against a spot at the southern tip of the San Joaquin Valley, then, holding the cane in position, turned to face the camera again.

"And here—if I may coin a phrase—we seem to have struck oil at 1:25 A.M. today. Twenty, thirty miles southeast of Bakersfield. Exactly where a massive earthquake struck a quarter of a century ago. And exactly where the sixth borehole from the south is located. Ladies and gentlemen, I give you the villain of the piece—the White Wolf fault." The newscaster relaxed and smiled boyishly. "And now, folks, you know as much about it as I do, which I'm afraid isn't very much. But have no fear—I'm sure the real seismological experts will be busy lecturing you on this for days to come."

Wordlessly, Dubois and Morro rose from their seats, looked at each other, then went to the map still spread on Morro's table. Morro said: "You are quite certain that the triangulation is correct?"

"Our three seismologists will swear to it."

"And our three bright boys place the epicenter in the Garlock fault not the White Wolf fault?"

"They should know. Not only are they highly experienced but we're practically sitting on top of the Garlock fault."

"The Seismology Field Survey, Cal Tech, the Geological Survey and God knows how many other scientific bodies—how could they all possibly—especially when they were all certainly working in collaboration—come up with the same mistake?"

"They didn't." Dubois was positive. "For earthquakes, this is the best monitored area in the world and those are among the world's top experts."

"They lied?"

"Yes."

"Why should they lie?"

Dubois was almost apologetic. "I've had a little time to think about this. I think there are two reasons. California is today obsessed with the fear, the almost certainty, that someday, maybe quite soon according to a few eminent earthquake researchers, the big one is going to strike, one that will make the San Francisco 1906 look like a firecracker; it's more than possible that state officials are trying to allay this fear by stating that this quake was man-made. Secondly, all those clever seismologists may be living with a brand-new fear which particularly affects themselves—that they may have been dabbling in murky waters, that they may not really have known what they were doing, that by messing around with those various faults they may have inadvertently triggered off something they didn't expect—a movement in the Garlock fault where they *don't* have a borehole. But they do have a drilling rig sitting fair and square in the middle of the Tejon Pass on the San Andreas fault—and at Frazier Park, near Fort Tejon, the San Andreas and the Garlock faults intersect."

"I suppose it *is* a possibility. And if that were correct it might happen again, perhaps even on a major scale, and I don't think we'd like that at all." Morro compressed his lips then slowly smiled. "You *have* had more time to think about this than I have. I seem to recall your saying that we might just possibly turn this to our advantage." Dubois smiled in return and nodded. "Ten past three in the morning and what better time for a glass of that splendid Glenfiddich. Don't you agree?"

"For inspirational purposes."

"Indeed. You think perhaps we should relieve those prestigious seismological institutes of the fear that the public may come to associate unexpected earthquakes—quakes in the wrong place, that is—with their indiscriminate tampering with seismic faults? If the public were to know the truth, that is?"

"Something like that."

Morro smiled again. "I look forward to writing this communiqué."

Ryder wasn't smiling when he woke up. He cursed, quietly but with considered feeling, as he reached out for his bedside phone. It was Dunne.

"Sorry to wake you, Ryder."

"No sweat. I've had almost three hours' sleep."

"I've had none. Did you see that newcast shortly before three this morning?"

"The one about the White Wolf fault? Yes."

"There'll be another and even more interesting newscast in less than five minutes. Any channel should do."

"What's it this time?"

"I think the impact will be greater if you watch for yourself. I'll call you afterward."

Ryder replaced the receiver, lifted it again, told a querulous Jeff that there was something worth watching on TV, cursed again and went through to his living room. The newscaster—the same cheerful youngster whom he'd seen just over three hours previously—came to the point without preamble.

He said: "We have received a further communication from the same Mr. Morro who claimed last night to have been responsible for the break-in at the San Ruffino nuclear power station and theft of nuclear fuel. We had no reason to doubt that claim as the amounts claimed as stolen corresponded precisely to the amounts that were stolen. This station cannot guarantee the authenticity of this communication, that is to say, that it is from the same man. It may be a hoax. But as the various communications media received this message in exactly the same way as the previous one we regard this as prima facie evidence that the message is genuine. Whether the information it contains is also genuine is not, of course, for us to say. The message reads:

" 'The people of California have been subjected to a hoax in that they have been deliberately lied to by the state's leading seismological authorities. The earthquake which took place at 1:25 this morning did not, as so falsely alleged, take place in the White Wolf fault and I am sure this can easily be verified by consulting the owners of scores of privately owned seismographs throughout the state. None of them would alone dare challenge the authority of the state's official institute but their combined testimony would make it clear that those state institutes are lying. I expect this statement to bring in massive confirmation of what I am saying.

" 'The reason why the institutes put out this untrue statement lies in their hope of allaying the people's increasing fear of imminent earthquake activity on an unprecedented scale and their own fear that the citizens of this state might come to associate fresh earthquakes, in areas other than those in which they are operating their EPSP plan, with their controversial attempts to tamper with the earth's crust.

" 'I can allay their latter fear. They were not responsible for this seismic shock. I was. The epicenter lay not in the White Wolf fault but in the Garlock fault, which, next to the San Andreas, is the largest in the state and is parallel and so close to the White Wolf fault that seismologists may easily have been deceived into believing that they had misread their instruments or that their instruments were in error.

" 'To be honest, I did not expect to trigger off this minor shock as there has been no earthquake in recorded history that would help explain the existence of this huge fracture. The small atomic device I exploded at 1:25 this morning was for purely experimental purposes, to see, in effect, whether it worked or not. The results were gratifying.

" 'It is possible that there will be many in the state who will disbelieve my claim. There will be none in the state, or in the nation, who will have any doubts remaining when I explode a second nuclear device tomorrow at a place and time to be announced later. This device is already in position and is in the kiloton range of that which destroyed Hiroshima.'

"That's it, then." This time there was no trace of the boyish grin he'd permitted himself in the earlier newcast. "It *could* be a hoax. If not, the prospect is at best sobering, at worst chilling. It would be interesting to speculate on the effects and intentions of——"

Ryder switched off. He was quite capable of doing his own speculating. He made and drank several cups of coffee while he showered, shaved and dressed for what promised to be a very long day ahead.

He was into his fourth cup of coffee when Dunne rang and apologized for the delay in calling him back.

Ryder said: "The impact was guaranteed. There's only one question I can see—has the state, in the persons of our seismologists, been lying to us?"

"I have no idea."

"I have."

"Maybe so. Fact is, we have no closed line to Pasadena. But we have to our Los Angeles office. Sassoon is very unhappy, not least about you, and wants to see us. Nine o'clock. Bring your son. As soon as possible."

"Now? It's only 6:40."

"I have things to tell you. Not over an open line."

"Tapping phones here, tapping phones there," Ryder complained. "Man's got no privacy left in this state."

Ryder and his son arrived at Dunne's office a few minutes after seven. Dunne, his alert, precise and efficient self, showed no trace of his sleepless night. He was alone.

Ryder said: "This room isn't bugged?"

"When I leave two suspects alone in it, yes. Otherwise, no."

"Where's the big white chief?"

"Sassoon's still in L.A. He's staying there. He is, as I said, unhappy. First, because this is happening in his own back yard. Second, the director of the FBI is winging his merry way from Washington. Third, the CIA has got wind of this and want into the act. As everybody must be very well aware, the FBI and the CIA are barely speaking to each other these days and even when they do speak you can hear the ice crackling."

"How did they get into the act?"

"I'll come to that in a moment. We're going on a short trip by helicopter soon. Pasadena. Nine A.M. the boss says, and we meet him exactly at that time."

Ryder was mild. "The FBI has no jurisdiction over a retired cop."

"I wouldn't even bother saying 'please.' Wild horses wouldn't stop you." Dunne shuffled some papers into a neat pile. "While you and Jeff have been resting lightly we, as usual, have been toiling all through the night. Want to make some notes?"

"No need. Jeff's my memory bank. He can identify over a thousand license plates within thirty miles of here."

"I wish it were only license plates we were dealing with. Well, now, our friend Carlton, the security deputy taken along with the nuclear fuel. A dossier of sorts. Captain, Army Intelligence, NATO, Germany. Nothing fancy. No cloak-and-dagger espionage or counterespionage stuff. Seems he infiltrated a Communist cell among Germans working in the base camp. Unsubstantiated suspicion of having become too intimate with them. Offered transfer to regular tank battalion and refused. Resigned. He wasn't cashiered, he wasn't pressured to resign; let's say the Army didn't stand in his way. At least that's what they say. Probably correct. No matter how unjustified the suspicions that hang over a man, the Army understandably doesn't take chances. End of that line. When the Pentagon decides to clam up, that's it."

"Just a hint of a Communist tie-up?"

"That would be enough for the CIA. You can't move around the Pentagon without stepping on one of their agents. A whiff of a Red under the bed and they're reaching for their cyanide guns or whatever before you know it."

"His security references. Worked for an AEC plant in Illinois. Good record. Security chief checking on contacts. Then a reference from TVA's twin Brown's Ferry nuclear plants in Decatur, Alabama. But the man's never been there. Certainly not under that name, certainly not in security. Maybe some other capacity, some other name, but unlikely. Disastrous fire during the time, incidentally, but not caused by him. Technician looking for a leak with a lighted candle—he found it.''

"How come the reference?''

"Forged.''

Jeff said: "Wouldn't Ferguson, the security chief, have checked out the reference?''

Briefly, Dunne sounded weary. "He admits he didn't. Ferguson himself had been there and said that Carlton knew so many details about the place, including the details of the fire, that he thought a check-out pointless.''

"How would he have known about the fire?''

"Unclassified. It's in the public domain.''

Ryder said, "How long was he supposed to have been there?''

"Fifteen months.''

"So he may just have dropped out of the scene for that time?''

"Sergeant Ryder, a man with the knowhow can go underground for fifteen years in this nation and never surface once.''

"He may not have been in the country. He could have a passport at home.''

Dunne looked at him, nodded and made a note. "Washington checked out with the AEC at 1717 H Street. They keep records there of those seeking information, those consulting card indexes and dockets on nuclear facilities. No one had ever checked information on San Ruffino—there were none to check. I got Jablonsky out of bed over this one. He was reluctant to talk. Usual threatening noises from the FBI. Then he admitted they have advanced plans for building a fast breeder reactor there. This comes under AEC control. Top secret. No records.''

"So Carlton's our man?''

"Yes. Not that that's going to help much now that he's holed up with Morro.'' Dunne consulted another paper. "You wanted a list of all the organized and—'successful,' I think you said—cranks, weirdos, eccentrics or whatever in the state. This is it. I think I said two hundred. Actually, it's a hundred and thirty-five. Even so, I'm told it would take forever to investigate them all. Besides, if they're as clever and organized as they seem to be, they'll have an unbreakable cover.''

"We can narrow it down. To start with, it'll have to be a large group. Also, a comparatively new group, formed just for this purpose. Say within the past year.''

"Numbers and dates.'' Resignedly, Dunne made another note. "Don't mind how hard we have to work, do you? Next comes our friend Morro. Not surprisingly, nothing is known about him, as a man, a criminal with an eye patch and damaged hands, to us or to the police authorities.''

Jeff looked at his father. "Susan's note. Remember she wrote 'American?' American, question mark?''

"And so she did. Well, Major, another little note if you please. Contact Interpol in Paris.''

"So Interpol it is. Now the notes you took from Donahure. Easy—just meant waking up half the bank managers and tellers in the county. Local Bank of America. Drawn four days ago by a young woman with pebbled tinted glasses and long blond hair.''

"You mean twenty-twenty vision and a long blond wig.''

"Like enough. A Mrs. Jean Hart, 800 Cromwell Ridge. There is a Mrs. Jean Hart at that address. In her seventies, no account with the bank. Bank teller didn't count notes—just handed over ten banded thousands.''

"Which Donahure split up eight ways for eight banks. We'll have to get his prints."

"We got them. One of my boys with the help of a friend of yours, a Sergeant Parker—who, like you, doesn't seem to care very much for Donahure—got them from his office about three this morning."

"You *have* been busy."

"Not me. I just sit here running up phone bills. But I've had fourteen good men and true working for me during the night—had to scrape the Southern Californian barrel to get them. Anyway, we've got some lovely clear specimens of Donahure's prints on those notes. More interestingly, we have some lovely clear specimens of LeWinter's, too."

"The paymaster. And how about the paymaster's automatic?"

"Nothing there. Not registered. Nothing suspicious in that—judges get threats all the time. Not used recently—film of dust in that barrel. Silencer probably a pointer to the type of man he is but you can't hang a man for that."

"The FBI file on him. Still reluctant to tell me about it?"

"Not now I'm not. Nothing positive. Nothing very good either. Not known to associate with criminals. His open list of telephone numbers would appear to confirm that. From that list he would appear to know every politician and city hall boss in the state."

"And you say he's not known to associate with criminals . . .! What else?"

"Both we and the police are dissatisfied with some—more than some—of the sentences he has been handing out over the past years." Dunne consulted a sheet before him. "Enemies of known cronies getting unduly stiff sentences; criminal associates of cronies—repeat, he himself has no direct criminal associates—getting light, sometimes ludicrously light, sentences."

"Pay-off?"

"No proof, but what would you think? Anyway, he's not as naïve as his minion Donahure. No local accounts under false names—none that we know of, anyway. But we monitor—without opening—his correspondence from time to time."

"You're as bad as the KGB."

Dunne ignored this. "He gets occasional letters from Zurich. Never sends any, though. Keeps his tracks pretty well covered."

"Intermediaries feeding pay-offs into a numbered account?"

"What else? No hope there. Swiss banks will open up only in the case of a convicted criminal."

"This copy of *Ivanhoe* that LeWinter had in his safe? And the coded notebook?"

"Seems to be a mishmash of telephone numbers, mainly in this state and Texas and what are beginning to look like meteorological reports. We're making progress. At least Washington is. There are no specialized Russian cryptographers in California."

"Russian?"

"Apparently. A simple variation—well, simple to them, I suppose—of a well-known Russian code. Reds lurking in the undergrowth again? Could mean anything, could mean nothing. Another reason, I suppose, for the keen interest being shown by the CIA. I imagine, without actually knowing, that the bulk of Washington cryptographers are on the CIA's payroll, one way or another."

"And LeWinter's secretary is Russian. Russian descent, anyway. A cypher clerk?"

"If this were any of a dozen countries in the world I'd have the fair Bettina in here and have the truth out of her in ten minutes. Unfortunately, this is not one of those dozen different countries." He paused. "And Donahure has—had—Russian rifles."

"Ah! The Kalashnikovs. Import permits——"

"None. So, officially, there are none of those rifles in the country. The Pentagon does have some but they're not saying where they got them. The British, I imagine—some captured IRA arms cache in Northern Ireland."

"And Donahure is, of course, a second-generation Irishman."

"God, as if I haven't got enough headaches." To illustrate just how many he had Dunne laid his forehead briefly on the palms of his hands then looked up. "Incidentally, what was Donahure looking for in your house?"

"I've figured that out." Ryder didn't seem to derive much satisfaction from the thought. "Just give me a lifetime and by the end of it I'll add up two and two and come pretty close to the right answer. He didn't come because Jeff and I hadn't been too nice to his stake-out and deprived him of a lot of his personal property, including his spy van—he'd never have dared connect himself with that. He didn't come for the evidence I'd taken from San Ruffino because he didn't know I'd taken any and, in the first place, he hadn't even had time to go to San Ruffino. By the same token he didn't have time to go to LeWinter's for a search warrant either. He wouldn't have dared to, anyway, for if he'd told LeWinter the real reason why he wanted the search warrant LeWinter might have considered him such a menace that he'd not only refuse a warrant but might have had him eliminated altogether."

Dunne wasn't looking quite so brisk and alert as when they had arrived. He said in complaint: "I told you I've got a headache."

"My guess is that a proper search of Donahure's home or office would turn up a stack of warrants already signed and officially stamped by Le-Winter. All Donahure had to do was to fill them in himself. I'd told him about the dossier I had on him. He'd come for that. So obvious that I missed it at the time. And I'd told him he was so bone-headed that he just had to be acting on his own. So he was, because it was something that concerned only himself personally."

"Of course it has to be that. The two of them might run for cover."

"Don't think so. They don't know the evidence is in *our* hands. Dona hure, being a crook at heart, will automatically assume that only crooks would have stolen the money and the guns and they wouldn't be likely to advertise the fact. And I don't think that LeWinter will run either. He'll have been worried sick at first, especially at the thought of the stolen code book and the fact that his fingerprints had been taken. But when he finds out—if he hasn't already found out—that the picture of himself and his accommodating secretary has *not* appeared in the *Globe,* he'll have discreet inquiries made and find out that the two men who came to photograph him were *not* employed on the *Globe* and will come to the inevitable conclusion that they were blackmailers, perhaps out to block his appointment as chief justice of the state supreme court. You said yourself he had powerful friends— by the same token such a man must also have powerful enemies. Whatever their reason, he wouldn't be scared of blackmailers. Blackmailers wouldn't know a Russian code. True, fingerprints had been taken, but cops don't wear hoods and take your prints in bed. They arrest you first. And he could take care of blackmailers. California law is ruthless toward that breed—and LeWinter is the law."

Jeff said in injured reproach: "You might have told me all this."

"I thought you understood."

"You had all this figured in advance? Before you moved in on them?" Dunne said. Ryder nodded. "You're smarter than the average cop. Might even make the FBI. Any suggestions?"

"A tap on LeWinter's phone."

"Illegal. Congress is very uptight about tapping these days—chiefly, one supposes, because they're terrified of having their own phones tapped. It'll take an hour or two."

"You appreciate, of course, that this will be the second tap on his line."

"Second?"

"Why do you think Sheriff Hartman's dead?"

"Because he'd talk? A new recruit, still not deeply involved, wanting to get out from under before it was too late?"

"That, too. But how come he's dead? Because Morro had LeWinter's line tapped. I called the night telephone manager from LeWinter's house to get Hartman's address—he was unlisted but that's probably because he was fairly new to the area. Someone intercepted the call and got to Hartman before Jeff and I did. By the way, there's no point in recovering the bullet that killed him. It was a dum-dum and would have been distorted out of recognition and further mangled on imbedding itself in the brick wall. Ballistic experts are not wizards—you couldn't hope to match up what's left of that bullet with any gun barrel."

" 'Someone,' you said?"

"Perhaps Donahure—he was showing signs of coming to when we left him—or, just possibly, one of Donahure's underworld connections. Raminoff wasn't the only one."

"You gave your name over the phone?"

"Had to—to get the information I wanted."

"So now Donahure knows you were in LeWinter's house. So now LeWinter knows."

"No chance. To tell LeWinter that he'd have to tell him that he either had LeWinter's phone tapped or knew that it was tapped. By the same token, if my call to Aaron of the *Examiner* was tapped Donahure or whoever would still be unable to tell LeWinter. But unlikely that that second call was tapped—our eavesdropping friend would have taken off like a bat after he'd heard mention of Hartman's name and address."

Dunne looked at him curiously, it might almost have been with respect. "To coin a phrase, you got all the angles figured."

"I wish I had. But I haven't."

One of the desk phones rang. Dunne listened in silence and his lips compressed as all trace of expression left his face. He nodded several times in silence, said "Yes, I'll do that," and replaced the receiver. He looked at Ryder in silence.

Without any particular inflection in tone, Ryder said: "I told you I didn't have all the angles figured. They've got Peggy?"

"Yes."

Jeff's chair crashed over backward. He was on his feet, face almost instantly drained of color, clenched fists ivory-knuckled on Dunne's desk. "Peggy! What's happened to Peggy?"

"They've taken her. As hostage."

"Hostage! But you promised us last night—so much for your damned FBI!"

Dunne's voice was quiet. "Two of the damned FBI, as you call them, were gunned down and are in the hospital. One is on the critical list. Peggy, at least, is unharmed."

"Sit down, Jeff." Still no inflection in the voice. He looked at Dunne. "I've been told to lay off."

"Yes. Would you recognize the amethyst she wears on the little finger of her left hand?" Dunne's eyes were bitter. "Especially, they say, if it's still attached to her little finger?"

Jeff had just straightened his chair. He was still standing, both hands holding the back bar as if he intended to crush it. His voice was husky. "Good God, Dad! Don't just sit there. It's not—it's not human. It's Peggy! Peggy! We can't stay here. Let's leave now! We can be there in no time!"

"Easy, Jeff, easy. *Where* in no time?"

"San Diego!"

Ryder allowed an edge of coolness to creep into his voice. Deliberately, he allowed it. "You'll never make a cop until you learn to think like one. Peggy, San Diego, they're just tangled up on the outside strand of the spider's web. We've got to find the spider at the heart of the web. Find it and kill it. And it's not in San Diego."

"I'll go myself, then! You can't stop me. If you want to sit around——"

"Shut up!" Dunne's voice was as deliberately harsh as Ryder's had been cool, but at once he spoke more gently. "Look, Jeff, we know she's your sister. Your only sister, your kid sister. But San Diego's no village lying out in the sticks—it's the second biggest city in the state. Hundreds of cops, scores of trained detectives, FBI—all experts in this sort of manhunt. You're not an expert, you don't even know the town. There're probably upward of a hundred men trying to find her right now. What could you hope to do that they can't?" Dunne's tone became even more reasonable, more persuasive. "Your father's right. Wouldn't you rather go kill the spider at the heart of the web?"

"I suppose so." Jeff sat in his chair but the slight shaking of the hand showed that blind rage and fear for his sister still had him in their grip. "I suppose so. But why you, Dad? Why get at you through Peggy?"

Dunne answered. "Because they're afraid of him. Because they know his reputation, his resolution, the fact that he never gives up. Most of all they're afraid of the fact that he's operating outside the law. LeWinter, Donahure, Hartman—three cogs in their machine, four if you count Raminoff—and he gets to them all in a matter of hours. A man operating inside the law would never have got to any of them."

"Yes, but how did they——"

"Simply with hindsight," Ryder said. "I said that Donahure would never dare tell I—we—were in LeWinter's place. But he told whoever ordered him to fix the tap. Now that it's too late I can see that Donahure is far too dumb to think of fixing a tap himself."

"Who's the whoever?"

"Just a voice on the phone, most likely. A link man. A link man to Morro. And I call Donahure dumb. What does that make me?" He lit a Gauloise and gazed at the drifting smoke. "Good old Sergeant Ryder. All the angles figured."

6

GOLDEN MORNINGS are far from rare in the Golden State and this was one of them, still and clear and calm and beautiful, the sun already hot in a deep blue sky bereft of cloud, the view from the Sierras across the mist-streaked San Joaquin Valley to the sunlit peaks and valleys of the Coastal Range quite breathtakingly lovely, a vista to delight, to warm the hearts of all but the very sick, the very near-sighted, the irredeemably misanthropical and, in this particular instance, those who were held prisoner behind the grim walls of the Adlerheim. In the last case, additionally, it had to be admitted that the view from the western battlement, high above the courtyard, was rather marred, psychologically if not actually, by the triple-stranded barbed-wire fence with its further unseen deterrent of two thousand volts.

Susan Ryder felt no uplift of the heart whatsoever. Nothing could ever make her anything less than beautiful but she was pale and tired and the dusky blueness under her lower lids had not come from any bottle of eye shadow. She had not slept except for a brief fifteen-minute period during the night from which she had awakened with the profound conviction that something was far wrong, something more terrible than even their incarceration in that dreadful place. A heaviness of heart is as much a physical as mental sensation and she was at a loss to account for it. So much, she thought morosely, for her reputation as the cheerful, smiling extrovert, the sun who lit up any company in which she happened to find herself. She would have given the world to have a hand touch her arm and find herself looking into the infinitely reassuring face of her husband, to feel his rocklike presence by her side.

A hand did touch her arm, then took it. It was Julie Johnson. Her eyes were dulled and tinged with red as if she had spent a goodly part of the night ensconced behind the wet bar so thoughtfully provided by Morro. Susan put an arm around the girl's slender shoulders and held her. Neither said anything. There didn't seem to be anything to say.

They were the only two on the battlements. Five of the other hostages were wandering, apparently aimlessly around the courtyard, none speaking to any of the others. It could have been that each wished to be alone with his or her personal thoughts or that they were only now beginning to appreciate the predicament in which they found themselves: on the other hand the inhibitory and intimidatory efforts of those bleak walls were sufficient to stifle the normal morning courtesies of even the most gregarious.

The ringing of the bell from the door of the great hall came almost as a relief. Susan and Julie made their careful way down the stone steps—there was no guard rail—and joined the others at one of the long tables where breakfast was being served. It was a first-class meal that would have done justice to any hotel of good standing, but apart from Dr. Healey and Dr. Bramwell, who ate with a gusto becoming guests of long standing, the others did no more than sip some coffee and push pieces of toast around. In atmosphere, it was the early morning equivalent of the Last Supper.

They had just finished what most of them hadn't even started when Morro and Dubois entered, smiling, affable, courteous, freely bestowing good mornings and hopes that they had spent the night in peaceful and relaxing slumber. This over, Morro lifted a quizzical eyebrow. "I observe that two of our new guests, Professor Burnett and Dr. Schmidt, are absent. Achmed"— this to one of the white-robed acolytes—"ask them if they would be good enough to join us."

Which, after five minutes, the two nuclear scientists did. Their clothes were crumpled as if they had slept in them, which, in fact, was what they had done. They had unshaven faces and what was known to the trade as tartan eyes for which Morro had only himself to blame in having left refreshments so freely available in their suites; in fairness, he was probably not to know that the awesome scientific reputations of the two physicists from San Diego and U.C.L.A. were matched only by their awesome reputations in the field of bacchanalian conviviality.

Morro allowed a decent interval to elapse, then said: "Just one small matter. I would like you all to sign your names. If you would be so good. Abraham?"

Dubois nodded amiably, picked up a sheaf of papers and went around the table, laying a typed letter, typed envelope and pen before each of the ten hostages.

"What the devil is the meaning of this, you witless bastard?" The speaker was, inevitably, Professor Burnett, his legendary ill temper understandably exacerbated by a monumental hangover. "This is a copy of the letter I wrote my wife last night."

"Word for word, I assure you. Just sign it."

"I'll be damned if I will."

"It's a matter of utter indifference to me," Morro said. "Asking you to write those letters was purely a courtesy gesture to enable you to assure your loved ones that you are safe and well. Starting from the top of the table you will all sign your letters in rotation, handing your pens to Abraham. Thank you. You look distraught, Mrs. Ryder?"

"Distraught, Mr. Morro?" She gave him a smile but it wasn't one of her best. "Why should I?"

"Because of this." He laid an envelope on the table before her, address upward. "You wrote this?"

"Of course. That's my writing."

"Thank you." He turned the envelope face down and she saw, with a sudden dryness in her mouth, that both edges had been slit. Morro opened the edges, smoothed the envelope flat and indicated a small grayish squidge in the middle of the back of the envelope. "Paper was completely blank, of course, but there are chemical substances that bring out even the most invisible of writing. Now, even the most dedicated policeman's wife wouldn't carry invisible ink around with her. This little squiggle here has an acetic acid base, most commonly used in the making of aspirin but also, in some cases, nail polish. You, I observe, use colorless nail polish. Your husband is a highly experienced, perhaps even brilliant, detective and he would expect similar signs of intelligence from his wife. Within a few minutes of receiving this letter he would have had it in a police laboratory. Shorthand, of course. What does it say, Mrs. Ryder?"

Her voice was dull. "Adlerheim."

"Very, very naughty, Mrs. Ryder. Enterprising, of course, clever, spirited, call it what you like, but naughty."

She stared down at the table. "What are you going to do with me?"

"Do with you? Fourteen days' bread and water? I think not. We do not wage war on women. Your chagrin will be punishment enough." He looked around. "Professor Burnett, Dr. Schmidt, Dr. Healey, Dr. Bramwell, I would be glad if you would accompany me."

Morro led the way to a large room next to his own study. It was notable for the fact that it lacked any window and was covered on three sides by metal filing cabinets. The remaining wall—a side wall—was, incongruously enough, given over to rather repulsively Baroque paintings framed in heavy gilt—one presumed they had formed the prized nucleus of Von Streicher's art collection—and a similarly gilt-edged mirror. There was a large table in the center, with half a dozen chairs around it and, on it, a pile of large sheets of paper, about four feet by two, the top one of which was clearly a diagram of some sort. At one end of the table there was a splendidly equipped drink trolley.

Morro said: "Well, now, gentlemen, I'll be glad if you do me a favor. Nothing, I assure you, that will involve you in any effort. Be so kind as to have a look at them and tell me what you think of them."

"I'll be damned if we do," Burnett said. He spoke in his normal tone, that of defiant truculence. "I speak for myself, of course."

Morro smiled. "Oh, yes, you will."

"Yes? Force? Torture?"

"Now we are being childish. You will examine them and for two reasons. You will be overcome by your natural scientific curiosity—and surely, gentlemen, you want to know why you are here?"

He left and closed the door behind him. There was no sound of a key being turned in a lock, which was reassuring in itself. But, then, a push-button, hydraulically operated bolt is completely silent in any event.

Morro moved into his study, now lit by only two red lamps. Dubois was seated before a large glass screen, which was completely transparent. Half an inch from that was the back of the one-way mirror of the room where the four scientists were. From this gap the maximum of air had been extracted, not with any insulation purposes in mind but to eliminate the possibility of the scientists hearing anything that was said in the study. Those in the study, however had no difficulty whatsoever in hearing what the scientists had to say, owing to the positioning of four suitably spaced and cunningly concealed microphones in the scientists' room. Those were wired into a speaker above Dubois' head and a tape recorder by his side.

"Not all of it," Morro said. "Most of it will probably be unprintable—unrepeatable, rather—anyway. Just the meat on the bones."

"I understand. Just to be sure, I'll err on the cautious side. We can edit it afterward."

They watched the four men in the room look around uncertainly. Then Burnett and Schmidt looked at each other and this time there was no uncertainty in their expressions. They strode purposefully toward the drink trolley, Burnett selecting the inevitable Glenfiddich, Schmidt homing in on the Gordon's gin. A brief silence ensued while the two men helped themselves in generous fashion and set about restoring a measure of tranquility to the disturbances plaguing their nervous systems.

Healey watched them sourly then made a few far from oblique references to Morro, which was one of the passages that Morro and Dubois would have to edit out of the final transcript. Having said that, Healey went on: "He's right, damn him. I've just had a quick glance at that top blueprint and I must say it interests me strangely—and not in a way that I like at all; and I do want to know what the hell we are doing here."

Burnett silently scrutinized the top diagram for all thirty seconds and even the aching head of a top physicist can absorb a great deal of information in that time. He looked around at the other three, noted in vague surprise that his glass was empty, returned to the drink trolley and rejoined the others armed with another glass of the whiskey, which he raised to the level of his speculative eyes. "This, gentlemen, is not for my hangover, which is still unfortunately with me—it's to brace myself for whatever we find out or, more precisely, for what I fear we may find out. Shall we have a look at it then, gentlemen?"

In the study next door Morro clapped Dubois on the shoulder and left.

*   *   *

Barrow, with his plump, genial, rubicund face, ingenuous expression and baby-blue eyes, looked like a pastor—to be fair, a bishop—in mufti. He was the head of the FBI, a man feared by his own agents almost as much as he was by the criminals who were the object of his lifelong passion to put behind bars for as long a period as the law allowed and, if possible, longer. Sassoon, head of the California FBI, was a tall, ascetic, absent-minded looking man who looked as if he would have been far more at home on a university campus, a convincing impression that a large number of convicted California felons deeply regretted having taken at its face value. Crichton was the only man who looked his part: big, bulky, tight-lipped, with an aquiline nose and cold gray eyes, he was the deputy head of the CIA. Neither he nor Barrow liked each other very much, which pretty well symbolized the relationship between the two organizations they represented.

Alec Benson, Professor Hardwick by his side, bent his untroubled and, indeed, his unimpressed gaze on the three men, then let it rest on Dunne and the two Ryders in turn. He said to Hardwick: "Well, well, Arthur, we are honored today—three senior gentlemen from the FBI and one senior gentleman from the CIA. A red-letter day for the faculty. Well, their presence here I can understand—not too well, but I understand." He looked at Ryder. "No offense, but you would appear to be out of place in this distinguished company. You are, if the expression be pardoned, just ordinary policemen. If, of course, there are any such."

"Professor," Ryder said. "There are ordinary policemen, a great many of them far too ordinary. And we aren't even ordinary policemen—we're ex-ordinary policemen."

Benson lifted his brows. Dunne looked at Barrow, who nodded. "Sergeant Ryder and his son, Patrolman Ryder, resigned from the force yesterday. They had urgent and private reasons for doing so. They know more about the peculiar circumstances surrounding this affair than any of us. They have achieved considerably more than any of us, who have, in fact, achieved nothing so far, hardly surprising in view of the fact that the affair began only last evening. For good measure, Sergeant Ryder's wife and his daughter have both been kidnaped and are being held hostage by this man Morro."

"Jesus!" Benson no longer looked untroubled. "My apologies, certainly—and my sympathies, certainly. It may be we who haven't the right to be here." He singled out Barrow, the most senior of the investigative officers present. "You are here to ascertain whether or not Cal Tech, as spokesmen for the various other state institutes, and especially whether I, as spokesman for the spokesmen, so to speak, have been guilty of misleading the public—or, more bluntly, have I been caught lying in my teeth?"

Even Barrow hesitated. Formidable man though he was, he recognized another formidable man when he met one and he was aware of Benson's formidable reputation. He said: "Could this tremor have been triggered off by an atomic device?"

"It's possible, of course, but it's equally impossible to tell. A seismograph is incapable of deciding the nature of the source of shock waves. Generally, almost invariably, we are in no doubt as to the source. We ourselves, the British and the French, announce our nuclear tests—the other two members of the so-called nuclear club are not so forthcoming. But there are still ways of telling. When the Chinese detonated a nuclear device in the megaton range—a megaton, as you are probably aware, is the equivalent of a million tons of TNT—clouds of radiation gas drifted eventually across the United States. The cloud was thin, high and caused no damage, but was easily detected—this was in November 1976. Again, earthquakes, almost invariably, give off aftershocks.

"There was one classical exception—again, oddly enough, in November of 1976. Seismology stations in both Sweden and Finland detected an earthquake—not major, on the 4-something Richter scale—off the coast of Estonia. Other scientists disputed this, figuring that the Soviets had been responsible, accidentally or otherwise, for a nuclear detonation on the floor of the Baltic. They have been disputing the matter ever since—the Soviets, naturally, have not seen fit to give any enlightenment on the matter."

Barrow said: "But earthquakes do not occur in that region of the world."

"I would not seek, Mr. Barrow, to advise you in the matter of law enforcement. It's a minor area, but it's there."

Barrow's smile was at its most genial. "The FBI stands corrected."

"So whether this man Morro detonated a small nuclear device there or not I can't tell you." He looked at Hardwick. "You think any reputable seismologist in the state would venture a definite opinion one way or another on this, Arthur?"

"No."

"Well, that's the answer to one question, unsatisfactory though it may be. But that, of course, is not the question you really want to ask. You wanted to know whether we—I, if you like—were entirely accurate in locating the epicenter of the shock in the White Wolf fault instead of, as Morro claims, in the Garlock fault. Gentlemen, I was lying in my teeth."

There was a predictable silence.

"Why?" Crichton was a man not noted for his loquacity.

"Because, in the circumstances, it seemed the best thing to do. In retrospect, it still seems the best thing." Benson shook his head in regret. "Pity this fellow Morro had to come along and spoil things."

"Why?" Crichton was also noted for his persistency.

"I'll try to explain. Mr. Sassoon, Major Dunne and the two policemen here—sorry, ex-policemen—will understand. For you and Mr. Barrow, it may not be so easy."

"Why?"

It seemed to Alec Benson that Crichton was a man of remarkably limited vocabulary, but he refrained from comment. "Because those four are Californians. You two are not."

Barrow smiled. "A state apart. I always knew it. Secession next, is that it?"

"It is a state apart, but not in that sense. It's apart because it's the only state in the union where, in the back—and maybe not so far back—of the mind of any reasonably intelligent person lies the thought of tomorrow. Not *when* tomorrow comes, gentlemen—*if* tomorrow comes.

"Californians live in a state of fear or fearful resignation or just pure resignation. There has always been the vague thought, the entertainment of the vague possibility, that one day the big one is going to hit us."

Barrow said: "The big one. Earthquake?"

"Of devastating proportions. This fear never really crystallized until as late as 1976—third time I've mentioned that year this morning, isn't it? 1976 was the bad year, the year that made the minds of people in this state turn to thoughts they'd rather not think about." Benson lifted a sheet of paper. "February 4, Guatemala—7.5 on the Richter scale. Tens of thousands died. May 6, northern Italy—6.5. Hundreds dead, widespread devastation, and later on in the same year another quake came back to wipe out the few buildings that were still left standing after the first one. May 16,

Soviet Central Asia—7.2. Death rate and damage unknown—the Soviets are reluctant to discuss those things. July 27, Tangshan—8.2. Two thirds of a million died and three quarters of a million were injured—as this occurred in a densely populated area, large cities like Peking and Teintsin were involved. Then in the following month, the far south of the Philippines— 8.0. Widespread devastation, exact deaths unknown but running into tens of thousands—this partly due to the earthquake, partly due to the giant *tsunami*—tidal wave—that followed because the earthquake had occurred under the sea. They had a lesser earthquake in the Philippines some way farther north on November 9—6.8. No precise figures released. In fact, November of that year was quite a month, with yet another earthquake in the Philippines, one in Iran, one in northern Greece, five in China and two in Japan. Worst of all Turkey—five thousand dead.

"And all those earthquakes, with the exception of the ones in Greece and Italy, were related to the movement of what they call the Pacific plate, which causes the so-called ring of fire around the Pacific. The section that mainly concerns us, as everyone knows, is the San Andreas fault, where the north-east-moving Pacific plate rubs against the westward-pressing American plate. In fact, gentlemen, where we are now is, geologically speaking, not really part of America at all but part of the Pacific plate and it hardly requires an educated guess to know that in the not too distant future we won't physically be part of America either. Someday the Pacific plate is going to carry the western seaboard of California into the oceanic equivalent of the wild blue yonder, for where we're sitting at the moment lies to the *west* of the San Andreas fault—only a few miles, mind you; it passes under San Bernardino, just a hop, skip and jump to the east. For good measure, we're only about the same distance from the Newport-Inglewood fault to the west—that's what caused the Long Beach quake of 1933—and not all that much farther from the San Fernando fault to the north, which caused, as you may recall, that very nasty business back in February '72. Seismologically speaking, only a lunatic would choose to live in the county of Los Angeles. A comforting thought, isn't it, gentlemen?"

Benson looked around him. No one seemed to find it a comforting thought at all.

"Little wonder, then, that people's thoughts started turning inward. Little wonder that they increasingly wondered, 'When's our time going to come?' We're sitting fair and square astride the ring of fire and our turn might be any time now. It is not a happy thought to live with. And they're not thinking in terms of earthquakes in the past. We've only had four major earthquakes in our known past, two of them really big ones on the order of 8.3 on the Richter scale, Owens Valley in 1872 and San Francisco in 1906. But, I say, it's not those they're thinking of. Not in the terms of major earthquakes but of monster earthquakes, of which there have been only two recorded in history, both of the Richter order of 8.9, or about six times the destructive force of the San Francisco one." Benson shook his head. "An earthquake up to 10 on the Richter scale is theoretically possible but not even the scientific mind cares to contemplate the awfulness of it.

"Those two monster quakes occurred also, perhaps not coincidentally, in 1906 and 1933, the first in Ecuador, the second in Japan. I won't describe the effects to you two gentlemen from Washington or you'd be taking the plane back East. Both Ecuador and Japan sit astride the Pacific ring of fire. So does California. Why shouldn't it be our turn next?"

Barrow said: "That idea about a plane is beginning to sound good to me. What *would* happen if one of those struck?"

"Assuming a properly somber tone of voice, I must admit I've given a great deal of thought to this. Say it struck where we're sitting now. You'd wake up in the morning—only of course the dead don't wake—and find the Pacific where Los Angeles is and Los Angeles buried in what used to be Santa Monica Bay and the San Pedro Channel. The San Gabriel Mountains might well have fallen down smack on top of where we are now. If it happened at sea——''

"How could it happen at sea?'' Barrow was a degree less jovial than he had been. "The fault runs through California.''

"Easterner. It runs out into the Pacific south of San Francisco, by-passes the Golden Gate, then rejoins the mainland to the north. A monster quake off the Golden Gate would be of interest. For starters, San Francisco would be a goner. Probably the whole of the San Francisco peninsula. Marin County would go the same way. But the real damage——''

"The *real* damage?'' Crichton said.

"Yes. The real damage would come from the immense ocean of water that would sweep into the San Francisco Bay. When I say immense, I mean just that. Up in Alaska—we have proof—earthquakes have generated water levels three and four hundred feet above normal. Richmond, Berkeley, Oakland, all the way down through Palo Alto to San Jose would be drowned. The Santa Cruz Mountains would become an island. And even worse—to anticipate, Mr. Crichton, there is worse—the agricultural heart of California, the two great valleys of San Joaquin and Sacramento—would be flooded, and the vast part of those valleys lie under an altitude of three hundred feet.'' Benson became thoughtful. "I hadn't really thought of it before but, come to that, I don't think I'd much care to be living in the capital either at that time for it would be dead in line of the first great wall of water rushing up the Sacramento River Valley. Perhaps you are beginning to understand why I and my colleagues prefer to keep people's minds off such things?''

"I think I'm beginning to.'' Barrow looked at Dunne. "How do you—as a Californian, of course—feel about this?''

"Unhappy.''

"You go along with this way of thinking?''

"Go along with it? If anything, I'm even ahead of it, I have the unpleasant feeling that Professor Benson is not only catching me up in my thinking but passing me by.''

Benson said: "There are, I must admit, another couple of factors. In the past year or so people have begun delving into records and then wishing they hadn't delved. Take the northern part of the San Andreas fault. It is known that a great earthquake struck there in 1833 although, at the time, there was no way of calibrating its strength. The great San Francisco quake of 1906 struck there sixty-eight years later. There was one in Daly City in 1957 but at a magnitude of 5.3 it was geologically insignificant. There hasn't been, if I may use the term, a proper earthquake up north for seventy-one years. It may well be overdue.

"In the southern San Andreas there has been no major quake since 1857, one hundred and twenty years ago. Now, triangulation surveys have shown that the Pacific plate, in relation to the American plate, is moving northeast at two inches a year. When an earthquake occurs one plate jerks forward in relation to the other—this is called a lateral slip. Slips in 1906 of between fifteen and eighteen feet have been measured. On the two-inch-a-year basis, one hundred and twenty years could mean an accumulated pressure potential amounting to twenty feet. If we accept this basis—not everyone does—a major earthquake in the Los Angeles area is considerably overdue.

"As for the central area of the San Andreas, no major quake has ever been recorded. Lord only knows how long that one may be overdue. And, of course, the big one may occur in any of the other faults, such as the Garlock, the next biggest in the state, which has been quiet for centuries.'' Benson smiled. ''Now, that would be something, gentlemen. A monster lurking in the Garlock fault.

''The third thing that rather tends to preoccupy people's minds is that reputable scientists have begun to talk out loud—in print, radio and television—about the prospects that lie ahead of us. Whether they should talk out loud or not is a matter for their own principles and consciences—I prefer not to, but I'm not necessarily correct.

''A physicist, and a highly regarded one, Peter Franken, expects the next earthquake to be of a giant size, and he has openly predicted death-toll figures between twenty thousand and a million. He has also predicted that if it happens in the long quiescent central section of the San Andreas the severity of the shock waves would rock both Los Angeles and San Francisco and, in his own words, 'quite possibly wipe them out'; it is perhaps not surprising that, per head of population, California consumes more tranquilizers and sleeping tablets than any place on earth.

''Or take the San Francisco emergency plan. It is known that no fewer than sixteen hospitals in 'kit' form are stored in various places around the city ready to be set up when disaster strikes. A leading scientist commented somewhat gloomily that most of those, should a major earthquake occur, would probably be destroyed anyway, and if the city was inundated or the peninsula cut off the whole lot would be useless. San Franciscans must find this kind of statement vastly heartening.

''Other scientists posit a maximum of five years' existence for both Los Angeles and San Francisco. Some say two. One seismologist gives Los Angeles less than a year to live. A crackpot? A Cassandra? No. The one person they should listen to. A James H. Whitcomb of Cal Tech, the best earthquake forecaster in the business. He has predicted before with an almost uncanny degree of accuracy. It won't necessarily be located in the San Andreas fault but it's coming very soon.''

Barrow said: ''Do you believe him?''

''Let me put it this way. If the roof fell in on us while we're sitting here I wouldn't raise an eyebrow—provided, that is, I had time to raise an eyebrow. I, personally, do not doubt that, sooner rather than later, Los Angeles will be razed to the ground.''

''What were the reactions to this forecast?''

''Well, he terrified a lot of people. Some scientists just shrugged their shoulders and walked away—earthquake prediction is still in its infancy or, at best, an inexact science. Most significantly, he was immediately threatened with a lawsuit by a Los Angeles city official on the grounds that such reports undermined property values. This is on record.'' Benson sighed. ''All part of the 'Jaws Syndrome,' as it has come to be called. Greed, I'd call it. Recall the film—no one who had commercial interests at stake wanted to believe in the killer shark. Or take a dozen years ago in Japan in a place called Matsushiro. Local scientists predicted an earthquake there, of such and such a magnitude at such and such a time. Local hoteliers were furious, threatened them with God knows what. But, at the predicted place, magnitude and time, along came the earthquake.''

''What happened?''

''The hotels fell down. Commercial interests, commercial interests. Say Dr. Whitcomb predicted a quake on the Newport-Inglewood fault. One certain result would be the temporary closing of the Hollywood Park Race Track—it's almost smack on the fault and you can't have tens of thousands of people jammed into a potential death trap. A week goes by, two weeks, and nothing happens. Loss of profits might run into millions. Can you imagine how much Dr. Whitcomb would be sued for?

"And the Jaws Syndrome is just first cousin to the 'Ostrich Syndrome.' Put your head in the sand, pretend it's not there and it'll go away. But fewer and fewer people are indulging in that with the result that fear, in many areas, is reaching a state dangerously close to hysteria. Let me tell you a story, not my story, but a very prophetic short story written some five years ago by a writer called R. L. Stevens.

"If I recall correctly, it was called 'The Forbidden Word.' There was a California Enabling Act which prohibited all reference to earthquakes in print or public. Penalty of five years. The state, apparently, had lost, by death or flight, fifty per cent of its population because of earthquakes. Roadblocks at state lines and people forbidden to leave. A man and girl were arrested for mentioning the word 'earthquake' in a public place. I wonder when we're going to have a real-life enabling act, when a mounting hysteria will drive us into a 1984 Orwellian situation?"

"What happened?" Barrow said. "In the story?"

"It's not relevant, but they got to New York, which was crowded by the millions of Californians who'd fled East and were arrested by the Population Control Board for mentioning the word 'love' in public. You can't win. The same as we can't win in this situation. To warn, to cry doom, the end of the world is nigh? Or not to warn, not to frighten them into a state of near panic? For me, there is one crucial factor. How can you evacuate three million people, as in Los Angeles, on a mere prediction? This is a free society. How in God's name can you close down coastal California, ten million, maybe more, and hang around for an indeterminate time while you wait for your predictions to come true? How can you *make* them leave when they know there is no place to go? This is where their homes are, their jobs are, their friends are. There are no homes anywhere else, no jobs anywhere else, no friends anywhere else. This is where they live, this is where they'll have to live, and, even though it's sooner rather than later, this is where they're going to have to die.

"And while they're waiting to die, I think they should be allowed to live with as much peace of mind, relative though that may be, as is possible. You're a Christian in the dungeons in Rome and you know it's only a matter of time before you're driven into the arena where the lions are waiting. It doesn't help a great deal if you are reminded of the prospect every minute. Hope, however irrational, springs eternal.

"Well, that's my attitude and that's my answer. I have lied in my teeth and I intend to go on doing so. Any suggestions that we were wrong will be vehemently denied. I am not, gentlemen, committed to a lie—I am committed to a belief. I have, I think, made my position very clear. Do you accept it?"

Barrow and Crichton looked briefly at each other, then turned to Benson and nodded in unison.

"Thank you, gentlemen. As for this maniac Morro, I can be of no help there. He's all yours, I'm afraid." He paused. "Threatening to explode an atomic bomb, or suchlike. I must say that, as a concerned citizen, I'd dearly love to know what he's up to. Do you believe him?"

Crichton said: "We have no idea."

"No inkling what he's up to?"

"None."

"Suspense, war of nerves, tension. Creating fear, hoping to panic you into precipitate and misguided action?"

"Very likely," Barrow said. "Only, we haven't got anything to act against yet."

"Well, just as long as he doesn't let if off under my seat or in any other inhabited area. If you learn the time and place of this proposed—ah—demonstration, may I request a grandstand seat?"

"Your request has already been granted," Barrow said. "We were going to ask you anyway. Would there be anything else, gentlemen?"

"Yes," Ryder said. "Would it be possible to borrow some reading material on earthquakes, especially recent ones?"

Everyone looked at him in perplexity. Everyone, that is, except Benson. "My pleasure, Sergeant. Just give this card to the librarian."

Dunne said: "A question, Professor. This Earthquake Preventative Slip Program of yours. Shouldn't that delay or minimize the great quake that everyone seems to think is coming?"

"Had it been started five years ago, perhaps. But we're only just beginning. Three, maybe four years before we get results. I know in my bones that the monster will strike first. It's out there, crouched on the doorstep, waiting."

7

AT HALF-PAST ten that morning Morro re-entered his study. Dubois was no longer at the observation window but was sitting at Morro's desk, two revolving tape recorders in front of him. He switched them off and looked up.

Morro said: "Deliberations over?"

"Twenty minutes ago. They're deliberating something else now."

"How to stop us, no doubt."

"What else? I gave up listening some time ago, they couldn't stop a retarded five-year-old. Besides, they can't even speak coherently, far less think rationally."

Morro crossed to the observation window and switched on the speaker above his head. All four scientists were sitting—more accurately sprawling—around the table, bottles in front of them to save them the labor of having to rise and walk to the drink trolley. Burnett was speaking, his face suffused with alcohol or anger or both and every other word was slurred.

"Damn it to hell. All the way to hell. Back again, too. There's the four of us. Look at us. Best brains in the country, that's what we are suposed to be. Best *nuclear* brains. Is it beyond our capacity, gentlemen, beyond our intelligence, to devise a means whereby to circument—I mean circumvent—the devilish machinations of this monster Morro? What I maintain is——"

Bramwell said: "Oh, shut up. That makes the fourth time we've heard this speech." He poured himself some vodka, leaned back and closed his eyes. Healey had his elbows on the table and his hands covering his eyes. Schmidt was gazing into infinity, riding high on a cloud of gin. Morro switched off the speaker and turned away.

"I don't know either Burnett or Schmidt but I should imagine they are about par for their own particular courses. I'm surprised at Healey and Bramwell, though. They're relatively sober but you can tell they're not their usual selves. In the seven weeks we've been here—well, they've been very moderate."

"In their seven weeks here they haven't had such a shock to their nervous systems. They've probably never had a shock like this."

"They know? A superfluous question, perhaps."

"They suspected right away. They knew for certain in fifteen minutes. The rest of the time they've been trying to find a fault, any fault, in the designs. They can't. And all four of them know *how* to make a hydrogen bomb."

"You're editing, I take it. How much longer?"

"Say twenty minutes."

"If I give a hand?"

"Ten."

"Then in fifteen minutes we'll give them another shock, and one that should have the effect of sobering them up considerably if not completely."

And in fifteen minutes the four men were escorted into the study. Morro showed them personally to their deep armchairs, a glass on a table beside each armchair. There were two other berobed acolytes in the room. Morro wasn't sure precisely what kind of reaction the physicists might provoke. The acolytes could have their Ingram submachine guns out from under their robes before any of the scientists could get halfway out of their chairs.

Morro said: "Well, now. Glenfiddich for Professor Burnett, gin for Dr. Schmidt, vodka for Dr. Bramwell, Bourbon for Dr. Healey." Morro was a great believer in the undermining of confidence. When they had entered, Burnett and Schmidt had had expressions of scowling anger, Bramwell of thoughtfulness, Healey of something approaching apprehension. Now they all wore looks of suspicion compounded by surprise.

Burnett was predictably truculent. "How the hell did you know what we were drinking?"

"We're observant. We try to please. We're also thoughtful. We thought your favorite restorative might help you over what may come as a shock to you. To business. What did you make of those blueprints?"

"How would you like to go to hell?" Burnett said.

"We may all meet there someday. I repeat the question."

"And I repeat the answer."

"You will tell me, you know."

"And how do you propose to set about making us talk. Torture?" Burnett's truculence had given way to contempt. "We can't tell you anything we don't know."

"Torture. Oh, dear me, no. I might—in fact, I shall be needing you later on. But torture? Hmm. Hadn't occurred to me. You, Abraham?"

"No, Mr. Morro." Dubois considered. "It is a thought." He came to Morro and whispered something in his ear.

Morro looked shocked. "Abraham, you know me, you know I don't wage war on innocents."

"You damned hypocrite!" Burnett's voice was a hoarse shout. "Of course that's why you brought the women here."

"My dear fellow——"

Bramwell said in a weary voice: "It's a bomb of some sort. That's obvious. It might well be a blueprint for a nuclear bomb, a thought that immediately occurred to us because of your propensity for stealing nuclear fuel. Whether it's viable, whether it will work, we have just no idea. There are hundreds of nuclear scientists in this country. But the number of those who can make, actually *make,* a nuclear bomb is severely restricted. We are not among the chosen few. As for those who can actually *design* a hydrogen bomb—well I, personally, have never met one. Our science is devoted to exclusively peaceful nuclear pursuits. Healey and I were kidnaped while working in a laboratory where they produced nothing but electricity. Burnett and Schmidt, as we are well aware, were taken in the San Ruffino nuclear reactor station. For God's sake, man, you don't build hydrogen bombs in reactor stations.''

"Very clever.'' Morro was almost approving. "You do think fast on your feet. In your armchair, rather. Enough. Abraham, that particular excerpt we selected. How long will it take?''

"Thirty seconds.''

Dubois put a tape recorder on a fast rewind, his eye on the counter, slowed and finally stopped it. He pressed a switch, saying: "Healy first.''

Healy's voice: "So we are in no doubt then?''

Schmidt's voice: "None. I haven't been since the first time I clapped eyes on those hellish blueprints.''

Bramwell's voice: "Circuitry, materials, sheathing, triggering, design. All there. Your final confirmation, Burnett?''

There was a pause here, then came Burnett's voice, strangely flat and dead. "Sorry, gentlemen, I need that drink. It's the Aunt Sally, all right. Estimated three and a half megatons—about four hundred times the power of the bombs that destroyed Hiroshima and Nagasaki. God, to think that Willi Aachen and I had a champagne party the night we completed the design!''

Dubois switched off. Morro said: "I'm sure you could even reproduce those plans from your head, Professor Burnett, if the need arose. A useful man to have around.''

The four physicists sat like men in a dream. They didn't look stunned, they just weren't registering anything. Morro said: "Come here, gentlemen.''

He led the way to the window, pressed an overhead switch and illuminated the room in which the scientists had examined the blueprints. He looked at the scientists, but without satisfaction, gratification or triumph. Morro did not seem to specialize very much in the way of feelings.

"The expressions on your faces were more than enough to tell us all we wanted to know.'' If the four men had not been overcome by the enormity of the situation in which they found themselves, the ludicrous ease with which they had been tricked, they would have appreciated that Morro, who clearly had further use for them, was doing no more than establishing a moral ascendancy, inducing in them a feeling of helplessness and hopelessness. "But the recordings helped. That's the first thing I would have expected. Alas, outside your own arcane specialities, men with abnormally gifted minds are no better than little children. Abraham, how long does the entire edited version take?''

"Seven and a half minutes, Mr. Morro.''

"Let them savor it to the full. I'll see about the helicopter. Back shortly.''

He was back in ten minutes. Three of the scientists were sitting in their chairs, bitter, dejected and defeated. Burnett, not unexpectedly, was helping himself to some more of the endless supply of Glenfiddich.

"One further small task, gentlemen. I want each of you to make a brief recording stating that I have in my possession the complete blueprints for the making of a hydrogen bomb in the megaton range. You will make no mention whatsoever of the dimensions, no mention of its code name 'Aunt Sally'—what puerile names you scientists give those toys, just another sign of how limited your imagination is outside your own field—and above all, you will make no reference to the fact that Professor Burnett was the co-designer, along with Professor Aachen, of this bomb.''

Schmidt said: "Why should those damn things be kept so secret when you'll let the world know everything else?''

"You will understand well enough inside the next two days or so.''

"You've trapped us, fooled us, humiliated us and above all used us as pawns.'' Burnett said all this with his teeth clenched, no mean feat in itself. "But you can push a man too far, Morro. We're still men.''

Morro sighed, made a small gesture of weariness, opened the door and beckoned. Susan and Julie came in and looked curiously around them. There was no apprehension or fear on their faces, just puzzlement.

"Give me that damned microphone.'' Without permission Burnett snatched it from the table and glared at Dubois. "Ready?''

"Ready.''

Burnett's voice, though charged with emotion—pure, black rage—was remarkably clear and steady, without a trace of the fact that he had, since his nonexistent breakfast, consumed the better part of a bottle of Glenfiddich, which said a great deal either for Professor Burnett or Glenfiddich.

"This is Professor Andrew Burnett of San Diego. It's not someone trying to imitate me—my voiceprints are in security in the university. This black-hearted bastard Morro has in his possession a complete set of plans for the construction of a hydrogen bomb in the megaton range. You had better believe me. Also you had better believe Dr. Schmidt and Drs. Healey and Bramwell—Drs. Healey and Bramwell have been held captive in this damned place for seven weeks. I repeat, for God's sake believe me. This is a step-by-step, fully composited, fully integrated plan ready to build now.'' There was a pause. "For all I know, the bastard may already have built one.''

Morro nodded to Dubois, who switched off. Dubois said: "The third and last sentences, Mr. Morro——''

"Leave them in.'' Mooro smiled. "Leave them. Eliminates the need for checking voiceprints. They carry with them the normal characteristic flavor of the professor's colorful speech. You can cope, Abraham? Ridiculous question. Come, ladies.''

He ushered them out and closed the door. Susan said: "Do you mind enlightening us? I mean, what *is* going on?''

"Certainly not, my dears. Our learned nuclear physicists have been doing a chore for me this morning. Not that they were aware of that fact—unknown to them I had their conversation recorded.

"I showed them a set of plans. I proved to them that I am indeed in possession of the secrets of the manufacture of hydrogen bombs. Now they are proving that to the world. Simple.''

"Is that why you brought the scientists here?''

"I still have a further important use for them but, primarily, yes.''

"Why did you bring us into that room, your study?''

"See? You are an inquisitive person. I was just satisfying your curiosity.''

"Julie here is not an inquisitive person.''

Julie nodded vigorously. For some reason she seemed close to tears. "I just want out of here.''

Susan shook her arm. "What is it?''

"You know very well what it is. You know why he brought us in there. The men were turning balky. That's why *we* were brought up here.''

"The thought hadn't escaped me,'' Susan said. "Would you—or that dreadful giant—have twisted our arms until we screamed? Or do you have dungeons—castles always have dungeons, don't they? You know, thumb-screws and racks and iron maidens? Do you break people on the wheel, Mr. Morro?''

"A dreadful giant! Abraham would be hurt. A kind and gentle giant. As for the rest? Dear me, dear me, dear me. Direct intimidation, Mrs. Ryder, is less effective than indirect. If people can bring themselves to believe something it's always more effective than having to prove it to them."

"Would you have proved it?" Morro was silent. "Would you have had us tortured?"

"I wouldn't even contemplate it."

"Don't believe him, don't believe him!" Julie's voice shook. "He's a monster and a liar."

"He's a monster all right." Susan was very calm, even thoughtful. "He may even be a liar. But in this case I believe him. Odd."

In a kind of despair, Julie said: "You don't know what you're saying!"

"I think I do. I think Mr. Morro will have no further use for us."

"How can you *say* that?"

Morro looked at Julie. "Someday you will be as wise and understanding as Mrs. Ryder. But first you will have to meet a great number of people and read a great number of characters. You see, Mrs. Ryder *knows* that the person who laid a finger on either of you would have to answer to me. She knows that I never would. She will, of course, convince those disbelieving gentlemen we've just left and they will know I couldn't use this threat again. I do not have to. You are of no more use to me." Morro smiled. "Oh dear, that does sound vaguely threatening. Let me rather say that no harm will come to you."

Julie looked at him briefly, the fear and suspicion in her eyes undimmed, then looked abruptly away.

"Well, I tried, young lady. I cannot blame you. You cannot have heard what I said at the breakfast table this morning. 'We do not wage war on women.' Even monsters have to live with their monstrous selves." He turned and walked away.

Susan watched him go and murmured: "And therein lie the seeds of his own destruction."

Julie looked at her. "I—I didn't catch that. What did you say?"

"Nothing, Julie, nothing. I'm just rambling. I think this place is getting to me also." But she knew it wasn't.

"A complete waste of time." Jeff was in a black mood and didn't care who knew it. He had almost to raise his voice to a shout to make himself heard above the clamorous racket of the helicopter engine. "Nothing, just nothing. A lot of academic waffle about earthquakes and a useless hour in Sassoon's office. Nothing, just nothing. We didn't learn a thing."

Ryder looked up from the sheaf of notes he was studying. He said, as mildly as one could in a necessarily loud voice: "Oh, I don't know. We discovered that even learned academics can tamper with the truth when they see fit. We learned—at least I did—about earthquakes and this earthquake syndrome. As for Sassoon, nobody expected to learn anything from him. How could we? He knew nothing—how could he? He was learning things from us." He returned his attention to his notes.

"Well, my God! They've got Susan, they've got Peggy and all you can do is to sit there and read that load of old rubbish just as if——"

Dunne leaned across. No longer as alert and brisk as he had been some hours ago, he was beginning to show the effects of a sleepless night. He said: "Jeff. Do me a favor."

"Yes?"

"Shut up."

There was a pile of papers lying on Major Dunne's desk. He looked at them without enthusiasm, placed his brief case beside them, opened a cupboard, brought out a bottle of Jack Daniels and looked interrogatively at Ryder and his son. Ryder smiled but Jeff shook his head: he was still smarting from the effects of Dunne's particular brand of curtness.

Glass in hand, Dunne opened a side door. In the tiny cubicle beyond was an already made-up camp bed. Dunne said: "I'm not one of your superhuman FBI agents who can go five nights and days without sleep. I'll have Delage"—Delage was one of his juniors—"man the phones here. I can be reached any time but the excuse had better be a good one."

"Would an earthquake do?"

Dunne smiled, sat and went through the papers on his desk. He pushed them all to one side and lifted a thick envelope which he slit open. He peered at the contents inside and said: "Guess what?"

"Carlton's passport."

"Damn you. Anyway, nice to see someone's been busy around here." He extracted the passport, flipped through the pages and passed it to Ryder. "And damn you again."

"Intuition. The hallmark of the better-class detective." Ryder went through the pages, more slowly than Dunne. "Intriguing. Covers fourteen out of the fifteen months when he seemed to have vanished. A bad case of wander-bug infection. Did get around in that time, didn't he? Los Angeles, London, New Delhi, Singapore, Manila, Hong Kong, Manila again, Singapore, Manila yet again, Tokyo, Los Angeles." He passed the passport to Jeff. "Fallen in love with the mysterious East, it would seem. Especially the Philippines."

Dunne said: "Make anything of it?"

"Not a thing. Maybe I did have some sleep but it wasn't much. Mind seems to have gone to sleep. That's what we need, my mind and myself—sleep. Maybe when I wake up I'll have a flash of inspiration. Wouldn't bet on it, though."

He dropped Jeff outside the latter's house. "Sleep?"

"Straight to bed."

"First one awake calls the other. Okay?"

Jeff nodded and went inside. But he didn't go straight to bed. He went to the bay-fronted window of his living room and looked up the street. From there he had an excellent view of the short driveway by his father's house.

Ryder didn't head for bed either. He dialed the station house and asked for Sergeant Parker. He got through at once.

"Dave? No ifs, no buts. Meet me at Delmino's in ten minutes."

He went to the gas fire grate, tilted it forward, lifted out a polythene-covered green folder, went to the garage, pushed the folder under the Peugeot back seat, climbed in behind the wheel and backed the car down the driveway and into the road. Jeff moved as soon as he saw the rear of the car appearing, ran to his garage, started the engine and waited until Ryder's car had passed by. He followed.

Ryder appeared to be in a tearing hurry. Halfway toward the first intersection he was doing close to seventy, a speed normally unacceptable in a thirty-five m.p.h. limit, but there wasn't a policeman in town who didn't know that battered machine and its occupant and who would ever have been so incredibly foolish as to detain Sergeant Ryder when he was going about his lawful operations. Ryder got through the lights on the green but Jeff caught the red. He was still there when he saw the Peugeot go through the next set of lights. By the time Jeff got to the next set they too had turned to red. When he did cross the intersection the Peugeot had vanished from sight. Jeff cursed, pulled over, parked and pondered.

Parker was in his usual booth in Delmino's when Ryder arrived. He was drinking a scotch and had one ready for Ryder, who remembered that he'd had nothing to eat so far that day. It didn't however, affect the taste of the scotch.

Ryder said without preamble: "Where's Fatso?"

"Suffering from the vapors, I'm glad to say. At home with a bad head-ache."

"Shouldn't be surprised. Very hard thing, the butt of a .38. Maybe I hit him harder than I thought. Enjoyed it at the time, though. Twenty minutes from now he's going to feel a hell of a sight more fragile. Thanks. I'm off."

"Wait a minute, wait a minute. *You* clobbered Donahure. Tell me."

Briefly and impatiently, Ryder told him. Parker was suitably impressed.

"Ten thousand bucks. Two Russian rifles. *And* this dossier you have on him. You have the goods on him all right—our ex-chief of police. But look, John, there's a limit as to how far you can go in taking the law into your own hands."

"There's no limit." Ryder put his hand on Parker's. "Dave, they've got Peggy."

There was a momentary incomprehension, then Parker's eyes went very cold. Peggy had first sat on his knees at the age of four and had sat there at regular intervals ever since, always with the mischievously disconcerting habit of putting her elbow on his shoulder, her chin on her palm and peering at him from a distance of six inches. Fourteen years later, dark, lovely and mischievous as ever, it was a habit she had still not abandoned, especially on those occasions when she wanted to wheedle something from Ryder, laboring under the misapprehension that this made her father jealous. Parker said nothing. His eyes said it for him.

Ryder said: "San Diego. During the night. They gunned down the two FBI men who were looking after her."

Parker stood up. "I'm coming with you."

"No. You're still an officer of the law. You'll see what I'm going to do with Fatso and you'll have to arrest me."

"I've just turned blind."

"Please, Dave. I may be breaking the law but I'm still on the side of the law and I need at least one person inside the law I can trust. There's only you."

"Okay. But if any harm comes to her or Susan, I'm out of a job."

"You'll be welcome in the ranks of the unemployed."

They left. As the door swung to behind them, a lean Mexican youth with a straggling mustache that reached his chin rose from the next booth, in-serted his dime and dialed. For a full minute the phone rang at the other end without reply. The youth tried again with the same result. He fumbled in his pockets, went to the counter, changed a bill for loose change, returned and tried another number. Twice he tried, twice he failed, and his mounting frustration, as he kept glancing at his watch, was obvious: on the third time he was lucky. He started to speak in low, hurried, urgent Spanish.

There was a certain lack of aesthetic appeal about the way in which Chief of Police Donahure had arranged his sleeping form. Fully clothed, he lay face down on a couch, his left hand on the floor clutching a half-full glass of Bourbon, his hair in disarray and his cheeks glistening with what could have been perspiration but was, in fact, water steadily dripping down from the now melting ice bag that Donahure had strategically placed on the back of his head. It was to be assumed that the loud snoring was caused not by the large lump that undoubtedly lay concealed beneath the ice bag but from the Bourbon, for a man does not recover consciousness from a blow, inform the office that he's sorry but he won't be in today and then relapse into unconsciousness. Ryder laid down the polythene folder he was carrying, removed Donahure's Colt and prodded him far from gently with its muzzle.

Donahure groaned, stirred, displaced the ice bag in turning his head and managed to open one eye. His original reaction must have been that he was gazing down a long dark tunnel. When the realization gradually dawned upon his befuddled brain that it was not a tunnel but the barrel of his own .45, his Cyclopean gaze traveled above and beyond the barrel until Ryder's face swam into focus. Two things happened: both eyes opened wide and his complexion changed from its normal revolting puce to an even more unpleasant shade of dirty gray.

Ryder said: "Sit up."

Donahure remained where he was. His jowls were actually quivering. Then he screamed in agony as Ryder grabbed his hair and jerked him into the vertical. Clearly, no small amount of that hair had been attached to the bruised bump on his head. A sudden scalp pain predictably produces an effect on the corneal ducts and Donahure was no exception: his eyes were swimming like bloodshot goldfish in peculiarly murky water.

Ryder said: "You know how to conduct a cross-examination, Fatso?"

"Yes." He sounded as if he was being garroted.

"No you don't. I'm going to show you. It's not in any textbook and I'm afraid you'll never have an opportunity to use it. But, by comparison, the cross-examination you'll get on the witness stand in court will seem almost pleasant. Who's paying you off, Donahure?"

"What in God's name——" He broke off with a shout of pain and clapped his hands to his face. He reached finger and thumb inside his mouth, removed a displaced tooth and dropped it on the floor. His left cheek was cut both inside and out and blood was trickling down his chin: Ryder had laid the barrel of Donahure's Colt against his face with a heavy hand. Ryder transferred the Colt to his left hand.

"Who's paying you, Donahure?"

"What in the hell——" Another shout and another hiatus in the conversation while Donahure attended to the right-hand side of his face. The blood was now flowing freely from his mouth and dripping onto his shirt front. Ryder transferred the revolver back to his right hand.

"Who's paying you, Donahure?"

"LeWinter." A strangely gurgling sound; he must have been swallowing blood. Ryder regarded him without compassion.

"What for?"

Donahure gurgled again. The ensuing croak was unintelligible.

"For looking the other way?"

A nod. There was no hate in Donahure's face, just plain naked fear.

"For destroying evidence against guilty parties, faking evidence against innocent parties?" Another nod. "How much did you make, Donahure? Over the years, I mean. Blackmail on the side of course."

"I don't know."

Ryder lifted his gun again.

"Twenty thousand, maybe thirty." Once more he screamed. His nose had gone the same way as Raminoff's.

Ryder said: "I won't say I'm not enjoying this any more than you are, because I am. I'm more than prepared to keep this up for hours yet. Not that you'll last more than twenty minutes and we don't want your face smashed into such a bloody pulp that you can't talk. Before it comes to that

I'll start breaking your fingers one by one." Ryder meant it and the abject terror on what was left of Donahure's face showed that he knew Ryder meant it. "How much?"

"I don't know." He cowered behind raised hands. "I don't know how much. Hundreds."

"Of thousands?" A nod. Ryder picked up the polythene folder and extracted papers which he showed to Donahure. "Total of just over five hundred and fifty thousand dollars in seven banks under seven different names. That would be about right." Another nod. Ryder returned the papers to the polythene folder. If this represented only Donahure's rake-off, how much did LeWinter have safe and sound in Zurich?

"The last pay-off. Ten thousand dollars. What was that for?" Donahure was now so befuddled with pain and fright that it never occurred to him to ask how Ryder knew about it.

"Cops."

"Bribes to do what?"

"Cut all the public phones between here and Ferguson's house. Cut Ferguson's phone. Wreck his police band radio. Clear the roads."

"Clear the roads? No patrols on the hijack van's escape route?"

Donahure nodded. He obviously felt this easier than talking.

"Jesus. You are a sweet bunch. I'll have their names later. Who gave you those Russian rifles?"

"Rifles?" A frown appeared in the negligible clearance between Donahure's hairline and eyebrows, sure indication that at least part of his mind was working again. "*You* took them. And the money. You——" He touched the back of his head.

"I asked a question. Who gave you the rifles?"

"I don't know." Donahure raised defensive hands just as Ryder lifted his gun. "Smash my face to pieces and I still don't know. Found them in the house when I came back one night. Voice over the phone said I was to keep them." Ryder believed him.

"This voice have a name?"

"No." Ryder believed that also. No intelligent man would be crazy enough to give his name to a man like Donahure.

"This the voice that told you to tap LeWinter's phone?"

"How in God's name——" Donahure broke off not because of another blow or impending blow but because, swallowing blood from both mouth and nose, he was beginning to have some difficulty with his breathing. Finally he coughed and spoke in a gasp. "Yes."

"Name Morro mean anything to you?"

"Morro? Morro who?"

"Never mind." If Donahure didn't know the name of Morro's intermediary he most certainly didn't know Morro's.

Jeff had first tried the Redox in Bay Street, the unsavory bar-restaurant where his father had had his rendezvous with Dunne. No one answering to either of their descriptions had been there, or, if they had, no one was saying.

From there he went to the FBI office. He'd expected to find Delage there, and did. He also found Dunne, who clearly hadn't been to bed. He looked at Jeff in surprise. "So soon. What's up?"

"My father been here?"

"No. Why?"

"When we got home he said he was going to bed. He didn't. He left after two or three minutes. I followed him, don't know why; I had the feeling he was going to meet someone, that he was stepping into danger. Lost him at the lights."

"Worry about the other guy," Dunne advised. "Some news for you and your father, not all that good. Both shot FBI men were under heavy sedation during the night, but one's clear now. He says that the first person shot last night was neither him nor his partner but Peggy. She got it through the left shoulder."

"No!"

"I'm afraid so, boy. I know this agent well. He doesn't make mistakes."

"But—but—if's she's wounded, I mean medical attention, hospital, she must have——"

"Sorry, Jeff. That's all we know. The kidnapers took her away, remember."

Jeff made to speak, turned and left the office. He went to Delmino's, the station officer's favorite hang-out. Yes, Sergeants Ryder and Parker had been there. No, the barman didn't know where they had gone.

Jeff drove the short distance to the station house. Parker was there along with Sergeant Dickson. Jeff said: "Seen my father?"

"Yes, why?"

"You know where he is?"

"Yes. Again why?"

"Just *tell* me!"

"I'm not rightly sure I should." He looked at Jeff, saw the urgency and intensity. He said reluctantly: "He's at Chief Donahure's. But I'm not sure——" He stopped. Jeff had already gone. Parker looked at Dickson and shrugged.

Ryder said, almost conversationally: "Heard that my daughter has been kidnaped?"

"No. I swear to God——"

"All right. Any idea how anyone might have got hold of her address in San Diego."

Donahure shook his head—but his eyes had flickered, just once. Ryder broke open the revolver: the hammer was lined up against an empty cylinder, one of two. He closed the gun, shoved the stubby finger of Donahure's right hand through the trigger guard, held the Colt by barrel and butt and said: "On the count of three I twist both hands. One——"

"I did, I did."

"How did you get it?"

"Week or two ago. You were out for lunch and——"

Ryder was contemplating Donahure speculatively.

"And I'd left my address book in my drawer so you kind of naturally wrote down a few names and addresses. I really should break your finger for this. But you can't sign a statement if I break your writing forefinger, can you?"

"A statement?"

"I'm not a law officer anymore. It's a citizen's arrest. Just as legal. I arrest you, Donahure, for larceny, corruption, bribery, the acceptance of bribes—and for murder in the first degree."

Donahure said nothing. His face, grayer than ever, had slumped between his sagging shoulders. Ryder sniffed the muzzle. "Fired recently." He broke open the gun. "Two bullets gone. We only carry five in a cylinder, so one's been fired recently." He eased out one cartridge and scraped the tip with a nail. "And soft-nosed, just like the one that took off Sheriff Hartman's head. A perfect match for this barrel I'll bet." He knew that a match-up was impossible, but Donahure either didn't know or was too far gone to think. "And you left your fingerprints on the door handle, which was a very careless thing to do."

Donahure said dully: "It was the man on the phone——"

"Save it for the judge."

"Freeze," a high-pitched voice behind Ryder said. Ryder had survived to his present age by knowing exactly the right thing to do at the right time and at the moment the right thing appeared to be to do what he was told. He froze.

"Drop that gun."

Ryder obediently dropped the gun, a decision which was made all the easier for him by the fact that he was holding the gun by the barrel anyway and the cylinder was hinged out.

"Now turn around nice and slow." He must have been brought up on a strict diet of B movies, Ryder reflected, but that didn't make him any less dangerous. He turned around nice and slow. The visitor had a black handkerchief tied below his eyes, wore a dark suit, dark shirt, white tie and, of all things, a black fedora. B movies, late 1930s.

"Donahure ain't going to meet no judge." He had the dialogue right, too. "But you're going to meet your maker. No time for prayers, mister."

"You drop that gun," said a voice from the doorway.

Obviously the masked man was considerably younger than Ryder for he didn't know the right thing to do. He whipped around loosed off a snap shot at the figure in the doorway. In the circumstances it was a pretty good effort, ripping the cloth on the upper right sleeve of Jeff's coat. Jeff's reply was considerably more effective. The man in the mask folded in the middle like a collapsing hinge and crumpled to the floor. Ryder dropped to one knee beside him.

"I tried for his gun hand," Jeff said uncertainly. "Reckon I missed."

"You did. Didn't miss his heart, though." Ryder plucked off the handkerchief mask. "Well. What a shame. Lennie the Linnet has gone riding off across the great divide."

"Lennie the Linnet?" Jeff was visibly shaken.

"Yes. Linnet. A song bird. Well, wherever Lennie's singing now you can take long odds that it won't be to the accompaniment of a harp." Ryder glanced sideways, straightened, took the gun from Jeff's lax hand and fired, all in seemingly slow motion. For the fifth time that night Donahure cried out in pain. The Colt he'd picked up from the floor spun across the room along with parts of his little and fourth fingers. Ryder said: "Do be quiet. You can still sign the statement. And to the charge of murder we'll now add one of attempted murder."

Jeff said: "One easy lesson, right?"

Ryder touched his shoulder. "Well, thanks, anyway."

"I didn't mean to kill him."

"Shed no sad tears for Lennie. A heroin pusher. You followed me?"

"Tried to. Sergeant Parker told me where you were. How did *he* get here?"

"Ah, now. If you want the detective sergeant at his brilliant best, ask him after the event. I thought our line was tapped so I phoned Parker to meet me at Delmino's. Never occurred to me they'd put a stake-out there."

Jeff looked at Donahure. "So that's why you didn't want me along. He ran into a truck?"

"Self-inflicted injuries. From now on, you're welcome along anytime. Get a couple of towels from the bathroom. Don't want him to bleed to death before his trial."

Jeff hesitated: he had to tell his father and actively feared for Donahure's life. "Some bad news, Dad. Peggy was shot last night."

"Shot?" The lips compressed whitely. Ryder's eyes switched to Donahure, the grip on Jeff's gun tightened, but he was still under his iron control. He looked back at Jeff. "Bad?"

"Don't know. Bad enough, I should think. Left shoulder."

"Get the towels." Ryder lifted the phone, got through to Sergeant Parker. "Come out here, will you, Dave? Bring an ambulance, Doc Hinkley"— Hinkley was the police surgeon—"and young Kramer to take a statement. Ask Major Dunne to come. And Dave—Peggy was shot last night. Through the shoulder." He hung up.

Parker passed on the requests to Kramer then went up to see Mahler. Mahler viewed him as he was viewing life at the moment, with a harassed and jaundiced eye.

Parker said: "I'm going out to Chief Donahure's place. Some trouble out there."

"What trouble?"

"Something that calls for an ambulance."

"Who said so?"

"Ryder."

"Ryder." Mahler pushed back his chair and rose. "What the hell is Ryder doing out there?"

"Didn't say. I think he wanted a talk with him."

"I'll have him behind bars for this. I'll take charge of this personally."

"I'd like to come, Lieutenant."

"You stay here. That's an order, Sergeant Parker."

"Nothing personal, Lieutenant." Parker put his badge on the desk. "I'm not taking orders anymore."

They all arrived together—the two ambulance men, Kramer, Major Dunne, Mahler and Dr. Hinkley. As befitted the occasion, Dr. Hinkley was in the lead. A small wiry man with darting eyes, he was, if not exactly soured by life, at least possessed of a profoundly cynical resignation. He looked at the recumbent figure on the floor.

"Good lord! Lennie the Linnet. A black day for America." He peered more closely at the white tie with the red-rimmed hole through it. "Heart damage of some kind. Gets them younger every day. And Chief of Police Donahure!" He crossed to where a moaning Donahure was sitting on his couch, his left hand tenderly cradling the blood-soaked towel around his right hand. None too gently, Hinkley unwrapped the towel. "Dear me. Where's the rest of these two fingers?"

Ryder said: "He tried to shoot me. Through the back, of course."

"Ryder." Lieutenant Mahler had a pair of handcuffs ready. "I'm placing you under arrest."

"Put those things away and don't make more a fool of yourself than you can help if *you* don't want to be charged with obstructing justice. I am making, I have made, a perfectly legal citizen's arrest. The charges are larceny, corruption, bribery, the acceptance of bribes, attempted murder and murder in the first degree. Donahure will admit to all of them and I can prove all of them. Also he's an accessory to the wounding of my daughter.''

''Your daughter shot?'' Oddly, this seemed to affect Mahler more than the murder accusation. He had put his handcuffs away. A disciplinary martinet, he was nonetheless a fair man.

Ryder looked at Kramer. ''He has a statement to make but as he's suffering from a minor speech impairment right now I'll make it for him and he'll sign it. Give the usual warnings, of course, about legal rights, that his statement can be used in evidence, you know the form.'' It took Ryder only four minutes to make the statement on Donahure's behalf and by the time he had finished the damning indictment there wasn't a man in that room, Mahler included, who wouldn't have testified that the statement had been voluntary.

Major Dunne took Ryder aside. ''So fine, so you've cooked Donahure's goose. You're doubtless aware that you've also cooked your own goose. You can't imprison a man without preferring charges and the law says those charges must be made public.''

''There are times when I admire the Russian legal system.''

''Yeah. So Morro will know in a couple of hours. And he's got Susan and Peggy.''

''I don't seem to have many options open. Somebody has to do something. I haven't noticed that the police or the FBI or the CIA have been particularly active.''

''Miracles take a little time.'' Dunne was impatient. ''Meantime, they still have your family.''

''Yes. I'm beginning to wonder about that. If they are in danger, I mean.''

''Jesus! Danger? Course they are. God's sake man, look at what happened to Peggy.''

''An accident. They could have killed her if they came that close. A dead hostage is no good to anyone.''

''I suppose I could call you a cold-blooded bastard but I don't believe you are. You know something I don't?''

''No. You have all the facts that I have. Only I have this feeling that we're being conned, that we're following a line that they want us to follow. I told Jablonsky last night that I didn't think the scientists had been taken in order to force them to make a bomb of some kind. They've been taken for some other purpose. And if I don't think that then I no longer think that the women were taken to force them to build a bomb. And not for a lever on me either—why should they worry about me in advance?''

''What's bugging you, Ryder?''

''I'd like to know why Donahure has—had—those Kalashnikovs in his possession. He doesn't seem to know either.''

''I don't follow you.''

''Unfortunately, I don't follow myself.''

Dunne remained in silent thought for some time. Then he looked at Donahure, winced at the sight of the battered face and said: ''Who's next in line for your kindly ministrations? LeWinter?''

''Not yet. We've got enough to pull him in for questioning but not enough to hold him on the uncorroborated word of an unconvicted man. And unlike Donahure, he's a wily bird who'll give away nothing. I think I'll call on his secretary after an hour or two's sleep.''

The phone rang. Jeff answered and held it out to Dunne, who listened briefly, hung up and said to Ryder: ''I think you'll have to postpone your sleep for a little. Another message from our friends.''

8

DELAGE WAS with a man the Ryders hadn't seen before, a young man, fair-haired, broad, wearing a gray flannel suit cut loose to conceal whatever weaponry he was carrying and a pair of dark glasses of the type much favored by Secret Service men who guard presidents and heads of state.

"Leroy," Dunne said. "San Diego. He's liaising with Washington on LeWinter's codes. He's also in touch with the AEC plant in Illinois, checking on Carlton's past contacts, and has a team working on the lists of the weirdos. Anything yet, Leroy?"

Leroy shook his head. "Late afternoon, hopefully."

Dunne turned to Delage. "So what didn't you want to tell me over the phone? What's so hush-hush?"

"Won't be hush-hush much longer. The wire services have it but Barrow told them to sit on it. When the director tells people to sit on something, it's sat on." He nodded to a tape recorder. "We recorded this over the direct line from Los Angeles. Seems that Durrer of ERDA was sent a separate recording."

He pressed a switch and a smooth educated voice began to speak, in English, but not American English. "My name is Morro and I am, as many of you will know by this time, the person responsible for the San Ruffino reactor break-in. I have messages to you from some eminent scientists and I suggest you all listen very carefully. For your own sakes, please listen carefully." The tape stopped as Dunne raised a hand.

He said: "Anyone recognize that voice?" Clearly no one did.

"Anyone identify that accent? Would it give you any idea where Morro comes from?"

Delage said: "Europe? Asia? Could be any place. Could be an American with a phony accent."

"Why don't you ask the experts?" Ryder said. "University of California. On one campus or another, anywhere between San Diego and Davis, you'll find some professor or lecturer who'll recognize it. Don't they claim to teach every major and most of the important minor languages in the world somewhere in this state?"

"A point. Barrow and Sassoon may already have thought of it. We'll mention it." He nodded to Delage, who flipped the switch again.

A rasping and indignant voice said: "This is Professor Andrew Burnett of San Diego. It's not someone trying to imitate me—my voiceprints are in security in the university. This black-hearted bastard Morro——" And so Burnett continued until he had finished his wrathful tirade. Dr. Schmidt, who followed him on the tape, sounded just as furious as Burnett. Healey and Bramwell were considerably more moderate, but all four men had one thing in common—they were utterly convincing.

Dunne said to no one in particular: "We believe them?"

"*I* believe them." Delage's certainty was absolute. "That's the fourth time I've heard that played and I believe it more every time. You could tell they weren't being coerced, under the influence of drugs, physical intimidation, anything like that. Especially not with Professor Burnett. You can't fake that kind of anger. Provided, of course, that those four men are who they claim to be and they have to be—they'll be on TV and radio any time and there must be hundreds of colleagues, friends, students who can confirm their genuineness. A megaton? That's the equivalent of a million tons of TNT, isn't it? Downright nasty."

Ryder said to Dunne: "Well, that's part of the answer to what we were talking about back in Donahure's house. To confirm the existence of those plans and scare the living daylights out of us. Us and everybody in California. They're going to succeed, don't you think?"

Leroy said: "What gets me is that they haven't given the faintest indication as to what they're up to."

That's what's going to get everyone," Ryder said. "That's part of his psychological gambit. Scare hell out of everyone."

"And speaking of scaring, I'm afraid there is more to come." Delage flicked the "on" switch again and Morro's voice came through once more.

"A postscript, if you please. The authorities claim that the earthquake felt in the southern part of the state this morning came from White Wolf fault and, as I have already said, this is a lie. As already said, I was responsible. To prove that the state authorities are lying, I will detonate another nuclear device at exactly 10 A.M. tomorrow morning. The device is already in place in a site specially chosen so that I can have it under permanent surveillance—any attempt to locate or approach this device will leave me no alternative other than to detonate it by radio control.

"People are advised not to approach within five miles of the site. If they do, I shall not be responsible for their lives. If they don't, but are still foolish enough not to wear specially darkened lenses, I shall not be responsible for their sight.

"The chosen site is in Nevada, about twelve miles northwest of Skull Peak, where Yucca Flat adjoins Frenchman's Flat.

"This device is in the kiloton range, of the approximate destructive power of those which destroyed Hiroshima and Nagasaki."

Delage switched off. After about thirty seconds' silence, Dunne said thoughtfully: "Well, that's a nice touch, I must say. Going to use the United States official testing ground for his purposes. As you ask, what the devil is the man up to? Does anyone here believe what we've just heard?"

"I do," Ryder said. "I believe it absolutely. I believe it's in position, I believe it will be detonated at the time he says it will, and I believe there is nothing we can do to stop him. I believe all you can do is to prevent as many rubber-neckers as possible from going there and having themselves incinerated or radiated or whatever. A traffic problem of sorts."

Jeff said: "For a traffic problem you require roads. No major roads there. Dirt tracks, that's all."

"Not a job for us," Dunne said. "Army, National Guard, tanks, armored cars, jeeps, a couple of Phantoms to discourage air-borne snoopers—there should be no problem in cordoning the area off. For all I know everybody might be more interested in running in the other direction. All that concerns me is why, why, why. Blackmail and threats, of course, but again, what, what, what. A man feels so damned helpless. Nothing you can do, nothing you can go on."

"I know what I'm going to do," Ryder said. "I'm going to bed."

The Sikorsky cargo helicopter landed in the courtyard of the Adlerheim but none of those seated in the refectory paid it any attention: the helicopter, which ferried in nearly all the supplies for the Adlerheim, was constantly coming and going and one just learned to live with its deafening clatter. That apart, the few guards, the hostages, Morro and Dubois were considerably more interested in what was taking place on the big TV screen before them. The announcer, arms folded in a form of noble resignation and his features arranged in a solemn gravity appropriate to the occasion, had just finished the playing of the tape recordings of the four physicists and had embarked upon Morro's postscript. The pilot of the helicopter, clad in a red plaid mackinaw, entered and approached Morro but was waved to a seat: Morro was not concerned with listening to his own voice but appeared to derive interest and amusement from listening to the comments and watching the expressions of the others.

When Morro had finished his postscript, Burnett turned to Schmidt and said loudly: "Well, what did I tell you, Schmidt? The man's a raving lunatic."

The remark seemed to cause Morro no offense; nothing ever seemed to. "If you are referring to me, Professor Burnett, and I assume you are, that's a most uncharitable conclusion. How do you arrive at it?"

"In the first place you don't have an atom bomb——"

"And, even worse, that's a stupid conclusion. I never claimed it was an atom bomb. It's an atomic device. Same effect, though. And eighteen kilotons is not to be regarded lightly."

Bramwell said: "There is just your word——"

"At one minute past ten tomorrow morning you and Burnett will doubtless have the courtesy to apologize to me."

Bramwell was no longer so certain. "Even if such a thing did exist what would be the point in detonating it out in the desert?"

"Simple, surely. Just to prove to people that I have nuclear explosive power available. And if I can prove that, what is to prevent them from believing that I have unlimited nuclear armament power available? One creates a climate first of uncertainty, then of apprehension, then of pure fear, finally of outright terror."

"You have more of those devices available?"

"I shall satisfy the scientific curiosity of you and your three physicist colleagues this evening."

Schmidt said: "What in God's name are you trying to play at, Morro?"

"I am not trying, and I am not playing, as the citizens of this state and indeed of the whole world will soon know."

"Aha! And therein lies the psychological nub of the matter, is that it? Let them imagine what they like. Let them brood on the possibilities. Let them imagine the worst. And then tell them that the worst is worse than they ever dreamed of. Is that it?"

"Excellent, Schmidt, quite splendid. I shall include that in my next broadcast. 'Imagine what you like. Brood on the possibilities. Imagine the worst. But can you imagine that the worst is worse than you ever dreamed of?' Yes. Thank you, Schmidt. I shall take all the credit for myself, of course." Morro rose, went to the helicopter pilot, bent to listen to a few whispered words, nodded, straightened and approached Susan. "Come with me, please, Mrs. Ryder."

He led her along a passage. She said, curiously: "What is it, Mr. Morro? Or do you want to keep it as a surprise for me? A shock, perhaps? You seem to delight in shocking people. First you shock us all by bringing us here, then you shock the four physicists with your hydrogen weapon plan, now you shock millions of people in the state. Does it give you pleasure to shock people?"

Morro considered. "No, not really. The shocks I have administered so far have been either inevitable or calculated to further my own designs. But a warped and sadistic pleasure, no. I've just been wondering how to tell you. You *are* in for a shock, but not a serious one, for there's nothing serious to be worried about. I have your daughter here, Mrs. Ryder, and she's been hurt. Not badly. She'll be all right."

"My daughter! Peggy? Here? What in God's name is she doing here? And how hurt?"

For an answer, Morro opened a door in one side of the passageway. Inside was what looked like—and was—a small private hospital ward. There were three beds but only one was in use. The occupant was a pale-faced girl with long dark hair, in which point lay the only difference from her remarkable resemblance to her mother. Her lips parted and brown eyes opened wide in astonishment as she stretched out her right arm: the bandages around her left shoulder were clearly visible. Mother and daughter exchanged the exclamations, endearments, murmurs and sympathies which mothers and daughters might be expected to exchange in such circumstances while Morro considerately maintained a discreet distance, using his right hand mutely to bar the further progress of a man who had just entered: the newcomer wore a white coat, wore a stethoscope around his neck and carried a black bag. Even without the trappings, he had, indefinably, the word "doctor" written large upon him.

Susan said: "Your shoulder, Peggy. Does it hurt?"

"Not now. Well, a little."

"How did it happen?"

"I was shot. When I was kidnaped."

"I see. You were shot when you were kidnaped." Susan squeezed her eyes shut, shook her head and looked at Morro. "You, of course."

"Mommy." The girl's face showed a complete lack of understanding. "What is all this? Where am I? What hospital——"

"You're not in the hospital. This is the private residence of Mr. Morro here. The man who broke into the San Ruffino reactor plant. The man who kidnaped you. The man who kidnaped me."

"You!"

Susan said bitterly, "Mr. Morro is not a piker. He doesn't do things on a small scale. He's holding eight others hostage too."

Peggy slumped back on her pillows. "I just don't understand."

The doctor touched Morro's arm. "The young lady is overtired, sir."

"I agree. Come, Mrs. Ryder. Your daughter's shoulder requires attention. Dr. Hitushi here is a highly qualified physician." He paused and looked at Peggy. "I am genuinely sorry about this. Tell me, did you notice anything peculiar about either of your attackers?"

"Yes." Peggy gave a little shiver. "One of them—a little man—didn't have a left hand."

"Did he have anything at all?"

"Yes. Like two curved fingers, only they were made of metal, with rubber tips."

"I'll be back soon," Susan said and permitted Morro to guide her by the elbow out into the passageway where she angrily shook her arm free. "Did you have to do that to the poor child?"

"I regret it extremely. A beautiful child."

"You don't wage war on women." Morro should have shriveled on the spot but didn't. "Why bring her here?"

"I don't hurt women or permit them to be hurt. This was an accident. I brought her here because I thought she'd be better with her mother with her."

"So you shock people, you tell lies and now you're a hypocrite." Again Morro remained unshriveled.

"Your contempt is understandable, your spirit commendable, but you're wrong on all three counts. I also brought her here for proper medical treatment."

"What was wrong with San Diego?"

"I have friends there, but no medical friends."

"I would point out, Mr. Morro, that they have fine hospitals there."

"And I would point out that hospitals would have meant the law. How many small Mexicans do you think there are in San Diego with a prosthetic appliance in place of a left hand? He'd have been picked up in hours and led them to me. I'm afraid I couldn't have that, Mrs. Ryder. But I couldn't leave her with my friends either because there she would be lonely with no one capable of looking after her wound, and that would have been psychologically and physically very bad for her. Here she has you and skilled medical attention. As soon as the doctor has finished treating her I'm sure he'll permit her to be wheeled to your suite to stay there with you."

Susan said: "You're a strange man, Mr. Morro." He looked at her without expression, turned and left.

Ryder awoke at 5:30 P.M., feeling less refreshed than he should have, because he had slept only fitfully, less because of worry about his family—he was becoming increasingly if irrationally of the opinion, it was no certainty, that they weren't in as grave danger as he had at once thought—but because there were several wandering wisps of thought tugging at the corners of his mind which he couldn't identify for what they were. He rose, made sandwiches and coffee, consumed them while he plowed through the earthquake literature he had borrowed from Pasadena. Neither the coffee nor the literature helped him any. He went out and called up the FBI office. Delage answered.

Ryder said: "Is Major Dunne around?"

"Sound asleep. Is it urgent?"

"No. Let him be. Got anything that might interest me?"

"Leroy has, I think."

"Anything from 888 South Maple?"

"Nothing of interest. Local nosy neighbor, a rheumy-eyed old goat—I'm quoting, you understand—who would clearly like to know your Bettina Ivanhoe, if that's her name, better than he does, says that she hasn't been to work today, that she hasn't been out all morning."

"He's sure?"

"Foster—that's our stake-out man, spends most of his time around the back—says he believes him."

"Eternal vigilance, you'd say?"

"Probably with a pair of high-powered binoculars. She went out this afternoon, but walking—there's a supermarket on the corner and she came back with a couple of shopping bags. Foster got a good look at her. Says he hardly blames the old goat. While she was out Foster let himself in and put a bug on her phone."

"Anything?"

"She hasn't used the phone since. More interesting, our legal friend was on the phone twice today. Well, only the second conversation was interesting. The first was made by the judge himself to his chambers. Said he's been stricken by a case of severe lumbago and could they get a deputy to stand in for him in court. The second was made *to* him. Very enigmatic. Told him to let his lumbago attack last for another couple of days and everything should be all right. That was all."

"Where did the call come from?"

"Bakersfield."

"Odd."

"What?"

"Close to the White Wolf fault where the earthquake was supposed to originate."

"How do you know that?"

"Education." Courtesy of the Cal Tech library, he'd learned the fact only ten minutes previously. "Coincidence. Pay phone, of course?"

"Yes."

"Thanks. Be down soon."

He returned to the house, called Jeff—he'd nothing to say to his son that a phone tapper would find of any interest—woke him and told him to call around but to wear different clothes from those he had been wearing the previous night. While he was waiting, he himself went to change.

Jeff arrived, looked at his father's usual crumpled clothes, looked at his own well-pressed blue suit and said: "Well, no one could accuse you of entering the sartorial stakes. Are we supposed to be in disguise?"

"Sort of. For the same reason I'm going to call up Sergeant Parker on the way in and have him meet us at the FBI office. Delage says they may have something for us, by the way. No, we're going to have the pleasure of interviewing a lady tonight, although I doubt whether she'll regard it as such. Bettina Ivanhoe or Ivanov or whatever. She'll recognize the clothes we were wearing last night, which is more than we can say about her. She won't recognize our faces, but she would our voices, which is why I'm having Sergeant Parker briefed and having him do the talking for us."

"What happens if something occurs to you—even me—and we want Sergeant Parker to ask a particular question?"

"That's why we are going along—just in case that possibility arises. We'll arrange a signal, then she'll be told that we have to go out and check something with the station by the car radiophone. Never fails to panic the conscience-stricken. Might even panic her into making a distress call to someone. Her phone's bugged."

"Cops are a lousy bunch."

Ryder glanced at him briefly and said nothing. He didn't have to.

"Let's start with Carlton," Leroy said. "The security chief at the reactor plant in Illinois never got to know him well. Neither did any of the staff there—the ones that are left, that is. That was two years or so ago and a good number have moved on elsewhere. Secretive kind of lad, it would appear."

"Nothing wrong with that," Ryder said. "Nothing I like better than minding my own business—in off-duty hours, that is. But in his case? Who knows? Any leads?"

"One, but it sounds more than fair. The security chief—name of Daimler—has traced his old landlady. She says Carlton and her son used to be very close, used to go away weekends quite a bit. Says she doesn't know where they went. Daimler says it's more likely that she didn't care where they went. She's well off—or was—her husband left her a good annuity but she takes in boarders because most of her money goes for gin and cards. Most of her time and interest too, it would appear."

"Sensible husband."

"Probably died in self-defense. Daimler offered—he wasn't too enthusiastic about the offer—to go and see her. I said thanks, we'd send one of

our boys—an NFI card carries more weight. He's going there this evening—
boy still lives at home.

"That's all. Except for his mother's comment about him—says he's a
religious nut and should be put away somewhere."

"It's the maternal instinct. What else?"

"LeWinter's fancy codes. We've traced nearly all the telephone numbers—I think you've been told they were mainly California or Texas. Seem
a respectable enough bunch—at least, preliminary inquiries haven't turned
up anything about the ones investigated so far—but, on the face of it they
would seem an odd group for a senior judge like LeWinter to be associated
with."

"I've got a lot of friends—well, friends and acquaintances—who aren't
cops," Jeff said. "But none of them, as far as I know, has ever seen the
inside of a courtroom, much less a prison."

"Yes. But here's an eminent lawyer—or what a cock-eyed world regards
as an eminent lawyer—with a list of people who are primarily engineers,
and not only that, but specialists in the engineering field. Specializing in
petrochemicals and not only chemists, metallurgists, geologists, what you
would expect to find, but also oil-rig owners, drillers and explosives experts."

Ryder said: "A strange crew, agreed. Maybe LeWinter is figuring on
moving into the oil exploration field—the old crook has probably accumulated enough in the way of pay-offs to finance a stake in something of that
nature. But I think that's too far-fetched. Much more likely that those names
have something to do with cases that have come up before him. They could
be people that have been called as expert witnesses."

Leroy smiled. "You wouldn't believe it, but we thought of that all by
ourselves. We turned up a list of his civil, as distinct from criminal, court
cases over the years and he has been involved in quite a number of lawsuits
primarily involved with oil—exploration, leases, environmental pollution,
marine trusts, lord knows what. Before he became a judge he was a defend-
ing counsel, and a highly successful one, as you would expect from such a
devious character——"

"Assumption, assumption," Ryder said.

"So? You just called him an old crook. As I was saying, he made quite a
reputation for himself for protecting the legal interests of various oil companies that had quite clearly transgressed the law until LeWinter proved
otherwise. In fact, the amount of oil litigation that goes on in this fair state
of ours is quite staggering. But it would seem that that's all irrelevant. To
me, anyway. You, I don't know. But, one way or another, he's been swimming around in this oil business for close to twenty years, so I can't see
how it bears on this present business."

"Neither do I," Ryder said. "On the other hand he could have been
preparing for this day for all those years and is only now putting his knowledge to use. But, again, I think this is far-fetched. If there's any connection
between oil prospecting or oil recovery I've never heard of it. How about
this code-book-Ivanhoe thing? I was given to understand that the Washington Russian code breakers were making progress on that."

"They may well be. Unfortunately, they've gotten very coy. The center
of their inquiries appears to have shifted to Geneva."

Ryder was patient. "Could you enlighten me, or did they choose to
enlighten you, on just what the hell Geneva has to do with a nuclear theft in
this state?"

"No, I can't enlighten you, because they clammed up. It's this damned
interservice jealousy, if you ask me. 'Internecine' would be a better word."

Ryder was sympathetic. "You'll be telling me next that the damned CIA is shoving its oar in again."

"Has shoved, apparently. Bad enough to have them operating in friendly countries—allies, if you like—such as Britain and France, which they freely do without the permission of their hosts, but to start poking around in a strictly neutral Switzerland——"

"They don't operate there?"

"Of course not. Those agents you see lurking around the UNO, WHO and Lord knows how many international agencies in Geneva, are only figments of your imagination. Heady alpine air, or something like that. The Swiss are so sorry for them they offer them chairs in the shade, or under cover, depending on the weather."

"You sound bitter. Let's hope you'll resolve your differences in this particular case, and quickly. How has Interpol been doing with Morro?"

"They haven't. You have to remember that a good bit more than half the world has never even heard of the word 'Interpol.' It might help if we had the faintest clue as to where this pest comes from."

"The copies of the tapes of his voice? The ones that were to be sent out to our learned scholars?"

"There hasn't been time yet for any significant amount of comments to come in. We have had only four replies yet. One is positive that he has the voice of a Middle Easterner. In fact, he's positive enough to state categorically that the guy comes from Beirut. As Beirut is a hodgepodge of most of the nationalities in Europe, the Middle East, the Far East and a fair sprinkling of Africans, by which I mean people in African nations, it's hard to see what he's basing his conviction on. Another says, although not prepared to swear, that he's Indian. A third says he's definitely from the southeast of Asia. The last says that, as he's spent twenty years in Japan, he'd recognize Japanese-learned English anywhere."

Ryder said: "My wife described Morro as being a broad-shouldered six-footer."

"And Japanese answering to that description are not thick on the ground. I'm beginning to lose faith in the University of California." Leroy sighed. "Well, with the possible—and I'm now beginning to regard it as only faintly possible—exception of Carlton, we don't appear to have been making much headway. However, we may have something more encouraging for you in the way of those odd-ball organizations you wanted us to inquire about. You specified a year in existence and a large group. We're not saying you're wrong, but it did occur to us that it could conceivably be a smaller group, or one that has been in existence for a considerably longer period than a year and that may have been infiltrated or taken over by Morro and his friends. Here's the list. It's probably not a complete list; there's no state law that says you have to register yourself, or yourself and your like-minded friends, as a nut or nuts. But I'd guess it's as complete as we can get, certainly within the limited time available."

Ryder glanced at the list, handed it to Jeff, turned to say a few words to Sergeant Parker, who had just entered, then returned his attention to Leroy.

"List's fine as far as it goes, dates and existence, approximate numbers, but it doesn't tell me what they're nutty about."

"Could that be important?"

"How should I know?" Ryder was, understandably, a mite irritable. "Might give me an idea, even an inkling, just the shadow of a clue, just by looking at such a list. God knows I can't come up with one by myself."

With the air of a conjurer producing a rabbit from a hat, Leroy produced another sheet of paper. "And here we have what you want." He looked at the paper with some disfavor. "They're so damned long-winded about their reasons, their motivations for existence as groups, that it was impossible to get it all on one sheet. They tend to be a forthright, not to say garrulous, bunch about their ideals."

"Any religious nuts among them?"

"Why?"

"Carlton is said to be associated, or have associated, with one. Okay, so it's a far-out connection, but any straw for a drowning man."

"I think you're mixing your metaphors," Leroy said kindly. "But I see what you mean." He eyed the sheet. "Well, *most* of them are religious organizations. I think you'd expect that. But quite a number have been established too long—long enough to achieve a measure of respectability—to be classified as nuts. The followers of Zen Buddhism, the Hindu Guru groups, the Zoroastrians and some home-grown California groups—at least eight of those—you can't go around calling them nuts without having a lawsuit slapped on you."

"Call them what you want." Ryder took the sheet and examined it more in hope than expectation. He said in complaint: "Can't pronounce half of them, far less understand them."

"This is a very cosmopolitan state, Sergeant Ryder." Ryder looked at him in suspicion but Leroy's face was perfectly straight.

"Borundians," Ryder went on. "Corinthians. The Judges. The Knights of Calvary. The Blue Cross. The Blue Cross?"

"Not the hospital insurance people, Sergeant."

"The Seekers?"

"Not the singing group."

"1999?"

"That's the day the world ends."

"Ararat?"

"Splinter group of 1999. Where Noah's ark ended up. Working with a group called the Revelations, high up in the Sierras. Building a boat for the next flood."

"They could be right. According to Professor Benson of Cal Tech a large chunk of California is going to disappear into the Pacific. They may have to wait a bit though—million years, give or take. Ah, now. This is more like it. Group over a hundred strong. Established only eight months. The Temple of Allah."

"Muslims. Also operating out of Sierra Nevada but not quite so high up. Forget them. They've been checked out too."

"Still. Carlton's a religious nut——"

"You call a Muslim a nut, you have to call a Christian one too."

"Carlton's landlady's phrase. She probably thinks anyone who crosses a church door a nut. Morro *could* come from Beirut. Muslims there."

"And Christians. Spent 1976 wiping each other out. I've been up that blind alley, Sergeant. Morro could be Indian. Carlton's been in New Delhi. Hindu, not Muslim. Or Morro could be southeast Asian. So Carlton's been to Singapore, Hong Kong and Manila. First two—if anything—are Buddhist, third is Catholic. Or Japan—Carlton's been there, Morro may have been. Shintoism. You can't just pick the religion that fits your theory—and there's no record of Carlton ever having been in Beirut. I told you, this place has been checked out. Chief of police swears by them——"

"That's enough for an immediate arrest warrant."

"Not every police chief is a Donahure. This man—Curragh—is widely respected. The governor of California is their patron. They've given two million—I repeat, two million—to charity. Open to the public——''

Ryder held up a hand. ''All right, all right. You made your point. Where does this bunch of paragons hang out?''

''Some kind of castle. Adlerheim, it's called.''

''I know it. Been there, in fact. Brainchild of some wealthy crank called Von Streicher.'' He paused. ''Muslim or not, anybody who lives there has to be a nut.'' He paused again, longer this time, made as if to speak, then clearly changed his mind.

Leroy said: ''Sorry I can't help you more.''

''Thanks. I'll take those lists if I may. Along with my earthquake studies, they're bound to lead me to point zero.''

Parker led the way to the car. In a quiet voice, Jeff said to Ryder: ''Come on, out with it. What were you about to say in there that you didn't?''

''When you consider the size of this state, the Adlerheim is only a stone's throw from Bakersfield. That's where LeWinter's mysterious phone call came from.''

''Could mean something?''

''Could mean that I'm still in a far-fetched mood tonight. Be interesting to find out whether there's a direct line from the castle to Bakersfield.''

On the way out to the suburbs Ryder briefed Parker as exhaustively as he could.

South Maple was short, straight, tree-lined, pleasant and quiet, all the houses of the pseudo-Spanish-Moroccan architectural design so popular in the south. Two hundred yards short of his destination Ryder pulled up behind a black unmarked car, got out and walked forward. The man sitting behind the wheel glanced interrogatively at Ryder.

Ryder said: ''You must be George Green.''

''And you must be Sergeant Ryder. Office called me.''

''Listen in to her phone all the time?''

''Don't have to. Very educated little bug.'' He tapped the square base of his telephone. ''When she lifts her phone this little box goes tinkle-tinkle. Automatic recorder, too.''

''We're going to have a word with her and going to find an excuse to leave her for a minute. She may put a panic call through in our absence.''

''I'll have it for you.''

Bettina Ivanhoe lived in a surprisingly nice house, small, not on the scale of Donahure's or LeWinter's homes, but large enough to provoke the thought that for a twenty-one-year-old secretary she was doing surprisingly well for herself or someone was doing surprisingly well for her. She answered the doorbell and looked a little apprehensively at the three men.

''Police officers,'' Parker said. ''Could we have a word with you?''

''Police officers? Yes, I suppose so. I mean, of course.''

She led the way to a small sitting room and tucked her legs under her while the three men took an armchair apiece. She looked sweet and demure and proper, but that wasn't anything much to go by: she'd looked sweet and demure—if hardly proper—when she'd been lying chained to LeWinter in his bed.

''Am I—am I in any kind of trouble?''

''We hope not.'' Parker had a deep booming voice, one of those rare voices that could sound hearty, reassuring and ominous all at the same time. ''We're just looking for any information that will help us. We're investigating allegations—they're more than that, I'm afraid—of widespread and illegal bribery involving foreigners and several high-placed individuals in public services in this state. A year or two back the South Koreans were giving away millions, seemingly out of the goodness of their hearts.'' He sighed. ''And now the Russians are at it. You will understand that I can't be more specific.''

''Yes. Yes, I understand.'' Clearly she didn't understand at all.

''How long have you lived here?'' The hearty reassurance in his voice had gone all diminuendo.

''Five months.'' The apprehension was still there but it had been joined by a certain wariness. ''Why?''

''Asking questions is my job.'' Parker looked around leisurely. ''Very nice place you have here. What's your job, Miss Ivanhoe?''

''I'm a secretary.''

''How long?''

''Two years.''

''Before that?''

''School. San Diego.''

''University of California?'' A nod. ''You left?'' Another nod.

''Why did you leave?'' She hesitated. ''Don't forget, we can check all this out. Failed grades?''

''No. I couldn't afford to——''

''You couldn't afford to?'' Parker looked around again. ''Yet in two years, a secretary, a beginner, really, you can afford to live here. Your average secretary has to make do with a single room in the beginning. Or live with her parents.'' He tapped his forehead lightly. ''Of course. Your parents. Must be very understanding folk. Not to say generous.''

''My parents are dead.''

''I am sorry.'' He didn't sound sorry. ''Then somebody must have been very generous.''

''I haven't been charged with anything.'' She compressed her lips and swung her feet to the floor. ''I won't answer another question until I've talked to my lawyer.''

''Judge LeWinter is not answering the phone today. He's got lumbago.'' This got to her. She sank back against the cushions, looking oddly vulnerable and defenseless. She could have been acting but probably was not. If Parker felt a twinge of pity he didn't show it. ''You're Russian, aren't you?''

''No. No. No.''

''Yes, yes, yes. Where were you born?''

''San Diego.''

''You'll have to do better than that. Your name is not in any birth register.'' Parker had no idea whether it was or not but it seemed a reasonable assumption. ''Where were you born?''

''Vladivostok.'' She'd given up.

''Where are your parents buried?''

''They're alive. They went back to Moscow.''

''When?''

''Four years ago.''

''Why?''

''I think they were called back.''

''They were naturalized?''

''Yes. A long time.''

''Where did your father work?''

''Burbank.''

''Lockheed, I suppose?''

"Yes."

"How did you get your job?"

"Classified ad. For an American secretary who could speak Russian and Chinese."

"There wouldn't be many of those around?"

"Only me."

"Judge LeWinter has private clients then?"

"Yes."

"Including Russian and Chinese."

"Yes. Sometimes they need a translator in court."

"Does he require any translation done for him out of court?" She hesitated. "Sometimes."

"Military stuff. Russian, of course. In code."

Her voice was low now, barely above a whisper. "Yes."

"Anything about weather at any time?"

Her eyes were wide. "How do you know?"

"Don't you know it's wrong? Don't you know it's treason? Don't you know the penalty for treason?"

She put her forearm on the side of the couch and laid her blond head on it. She made no reply.

Ryder said: "You like LeWinter?" His voice didn't seem to register with her as the one she'd heard the previous night.

"I hate him! I hate him! I hate him!" The voice was shaking but the vehemence left no room for disbelief.

Ryder stood and jerked his head to the door. Parker said: "We're going to the car to call the station. Back in a minute or two." The three men went outside.

Ryder said: "She hates LeWinter and I, Dave, hate you."

"That makes two of us."

"Jeff, go see if the FBI man is intercepting a phone call. But I know I'm just wasting your time." Jeff left.

"Poor kid." Parker shook his head. "Imagine if that were Peggy."

"Just what I mean. Old man a spy, probably an industrial one. Called back to Russia to report and now being held over her head—along with her mother, probably. Being blackmailed to hell and back. One thing, we can probably tell our superspies in Geneva what they can do with themselves. She's intelligent. I'll bet she has total recall about this Russian weather report or whatever."

"Hasn't she had enough, John? And what will happen to her parents?"

"Nothing, I'd guess. Not if the report leaks out that she has been arrested or disappeared or held incommunicado. That's the way they'd act themselves."

"Not the way we act in our great American democracy."

"They don't believe in our great American democracy."

They waited until Jeff returned. He looked at them and shook his head.

"It figures," Ryder said. "Our poor little Bettina has no place left to go."

They went back inside. She was sitting straight again, looking at them without expectation. Her brown eyes were dulled and there were tear stains on her cheeks. The men didn't bother to sit down. She looked at Ryder.

"I know who you are."

"You have the advantage over me. I've never seen you before in my life. We are going to take you into protective custody, that's all."

"I know what that means. Protective custody. Spying, treason, a morals charge. Protective custody!"

Ryder caught her wrist, pulled her to her feet, and held her by the shoulders. "You're in California, not Siberia. Protective custody means that we're going to take you in and keep you safe and unharmed until this blows over. There will be no charges preferred against you because there are none to prefer. We promise that no harm will come to you, not now, nor later." He led her toward the door and opened it. "If you want to, you can go. Pack some things, take them to your car and drive off. But it's cold out there and dark and you'll be alone. You're too young to be alone."

She looked through the doorway, turned back, made a movement of the shoulders that could have been a shrug or a shiver and looked at Ryder uncertainly. He said: "We know a safe place. We'll send a policewoman with you, not a battle-ax to guard you but a young and pretty girl like yourself to keep you company." He nodded to Jeff. "I know my son here will take the greatest care, not to say pleasure, in picking out just the girl for you." Jeff grinned and it was probably his smile more than anything else that convinced her. "You will, of course, have an armed guard outside. Two or three days, no more. Just pack enough for that. All we want to do is to look after you."

She smiled for the first time, nodded and left the room. Jeff grinned again. "I've often wondered how you managed to trap Susan but now I'm beginning to——"

Ryder gave him a cold look. "Green's all through here. Go and explain to him why."

Jeff left, still smiling.

Healey, Bramwell and Schmidt had forgathered in Burnett's sitting room after dinner, excellent as was all the food in the Adlerheim. It had been a somber meal, as most meals were, and the atmosphere had not been lightened by the absence of Susan, who had been eating with her injured daughter. Carlton had not been there either, but this had hardly been remarked upon, because the deputy chief of security had become a highly unsociable creature, gloomy, withdrawn, almost secretive: it was widely assumed that he was brooding over his own defects and failures in the field of security. After a meal eaten quickly and in funereal silence all had left as soon as they decently could. And now Burnett was dispensing his post-prandial hospitality—in this case an excellent Martell—with his customary heavy hand.

"Woman's not normal." Burnett was speaking and, as usual, he wasn't saying something, but was announcing it.

Bramwell said cautiously: "Which one?"

"Which woman is?" Burnett would have gone over big with women's lib. "But I was referring to Mrs. Ryder, of course."

Healey steepled judicious fingers. "Charming, I thought."

"Charming? To be sure, to be sure. Charming. Quite beautiful. But deranged." He waved a vague arm around. "All this, I suppose, did it. Women can't take it. Went along to see her after dinner, pay respects, commiserate with injured daughter, you know. Damn pretty young girl. Lying there all shot up." To listen to Burnett, one would have assumed that the patient had been riddled with machine gun fire. "Well, I'm a pretty even-tempered fellow"—he seemed to be genuinely unaware of his own reputation—"but I must say I rather lost my temper. I said that Morro was at worst a cold-blooded monster that should be destroyed, at best a raving lunatic that should be locked up. Would you believe it, she didn't agree at all." He briefly contemplated the enormity of her error in character assessment, then shook his head at its being beyond normal comprehension. "Admitted that he should be brought to justice, but said he was kind, considerate and even thoughtful of others at times. An intelligent, I had thought highly intelligent, woman." Burnett shook his head again, whether in self-reproach at his own character assessment or because he was sadly figuring out what the rest of womankind might be like it was hard to say. He drank his brandy, clearly not savoring it at all. "I ask you, gentlemen. I simply ask you."

"He's a maniac, all right. That I grant you." Bramwell was being cautious again. "But not amoral as a madman should be. If he really wanted an impressive debut for this atom bomb of his—assuming he has one, and none of us here doubt it—he'd detonate it without warning on Wilshire Boulevard instead of with warning out in the desert."

"Balderdash. The extreme cunning of extreme madness. Wants to convince people that they're dealing with a rational human being." Burnett examined his empty glass, rose and made for the bar. "Well, he'll never convince me of that. I detest clichés but, gentlemen—mark my words."

They marked his words in silence and were still sitting in silence when Morro and Dubois entered. He was either oblivious of or ignored the thunder on Burnett's face, the gloom on that of the others.

"I am sorry to disturb you, gentlemen, but the evenings are a bit dull here and I thought you might care to see something to titillate your scientific curiosity. I do not want to sound like a showman in a circus, but I'm sure you will be astonished—dumb-founded, I might almost say—by what Abraham and I are about to show you. Would you care to accompany me, gentlemen?"

Burnett wasn't going to pass up the opportunity to exercise his truculence. "And if we refuse?"

"Your privilege. And I mean yours, Professor. I somehow think your colleagues might be quite interested, and would take great pleasure in telling you afterward. Of course, you may all choose to refuse. I will bring no pressure to bear."

Healey rose. "I was born nosy. Your food is excellent but the entertainment factor is zero. Nothing on the TV—not that there ever is much—except the precautions being taken to keep people away from the Yucca Flat tomorrow and the rather fearful speculation as to what the next threat is going to be and what is the motivation behind it all. What *is* the motivation, Morro?"

"Later. Meantime, those of you who care——"

They all cared, even Burnett. Two white-robed acolytes were waiting in the passage. This didn't worry the four psysicists, there was nothing new in this, nor in the certain knowledge that they would be carrying their Ingrams in the folds of their robes. What was unusual was that one of them was carrying a tape recorder. Burnett, as ever, was the first and principal objector.

"What's your devious mind planning on now, Morro? What's the damned recorder for?"

Morro was patient. "To make a recording. I thought you might like to be the first to inform your fellow citizens of what I have here and, by implication, what's in store for them. We will bring to an end what you, Dr. Healey, call their fearful speculations and let them know the dreadful reality. Their fears, almost certainly will be replaced by a mindless panic such as a people have never known before. But it is justifiable. It is justifiable because it will enable me to achieve what I wish—and, more importantly from your point of view, to achieve it without the loss of the lives of perhaps millions of people. That loss is just conceivable—if you refuse to co-operate.''

The quiet voice carried a total conviction but when a mind is confronted by the unconceivable it takes refuge in disbelief and nonacceptance.

''You are quite, quite mad.'' For once Burnett was neither furious nor truculent but he carried as much conviction as Morro had done. ''If we refuse to, as you say, co-operate? Torture? The threat of the women?''

''Mrs. Ryder will have told you that they are safe from me. You really can be tedious at times, Professor. No torture, except that of your own consciences, the thought that will haunt you as long as you may live—you could have saved countless lives but have chosen not to.''

Healey said: ''What you are saying in effect is that while people might not believe you and take a chance that you are bluffing they would believe us and take no such chance.''

Morro smiled. ''It wounds what passes for my *amour-propre* but, yes, precisely.''

''Let's go and see just how mad he is.''

The lift was of a quite extraordinary construction. Its floor measured about four feet by six but, in height, it must have been at least fourteen feet. The faces of the four physicists reflected their puzzlement. As the lift whined down Morro smiled again. ''It is peculiar, I admit. You will understand the reason for its unique design in a very few moments.''

The lift stopped, the door opened and the eight men moved out into a large chamber about twenty feet square. The walls and roof were as they had been when cut from the solid rock, the floor of smooth concrete. On one side were vertically stacked sheets of steel, whether hardened or stainless it was impossible to judge; on the other were unmistakable sheets of aluminum. For the rest, it was no more or less than a comprehensively equipped machine shop, with lathes, machine presses, drills, power cutters, oxyacetylene equipment and racks of gleaming tools. Morro waved a hand.

''In an automobile plant, what you would call the body shop. Here we make the casings. I need say no more.''

Running lengthwise along the roof of the chamber was a heavy metal rail from which were suspended traveling chain blocks. This extended into the next compartment. Morro led the way in. There was a long table running the length of the chamber, a table fitted with circular metal clamps. On either side were racked storage compartments, wire-net fronted, both containing metal drums well separated at clearly calculated intervals.

Morro didn't even break stride. ''Plutonium to the left, Uranium-235 to the right.'' He carried straight on to a smaller room. ''The electrical shop, gentlemen. But that wouldn't interest you.'' He kept on walking. ''But this next room should fascinate you. Again in auto manufacturing parlance, this is what you would call the assembly shop.''

Morro had made no mistake. The four physicists were, beyond any question, fascinated as they had never been in their lives. But not in the details of the assembly shop. What caught and held fast their disbelieving and horrified attention was the rack bolted to the right-hand wall. More precisely, what the rack held. Clamped vertically, side by side, were ten twelve-feet-high cylinders, each four and a half inches in diameter. They were painted matte black with the exception of two red bands, each an inch thick, that circled the cylinders one third and two thirds the way up their height. At the farther end of the row were two more sets of clamps which held nothing. Morro looked at each of the four physicists in turn. Each face held the same expression, a profound dismay coupled with a sick and shocked certainty. Morro's face registered nothing, no humor, no triumph, no satisfaction, nothing. The silence dragged on for a seemingly interminable time but, then, in circumstances sufficiently appalling, a few seconds cannot be measured in the normally accepted unit of time. In the accepted units of seconds, twenty had passed before Healey broke the silence. His face was gray his voice husky as he broke from his thrall and turned to look at Morro.

"This is a nightmare."

"This is no nightmare. From a nightmare you wake up. Not from this, for this is the dreadful reality. A walking nightmare, if you will."

Burnett was as hoarse as Healey had been. "The Aunt Sally!"

Morro corrected him. "The Aunt Sallies. Ten of them. You, Professor, are an excellent designer of hydrogen weapons. Your brainchild in its final physical form. One could wish that you could have seen it under happier circumstances."

There was something very close to hate in Burnett's eyes. "You, Morro, are an evil and vindictive bastard."

"You can save your breath, Professor, and for two reasons. Your statement is untrue for I derive no gloating pleasure from this; and, as you should know by now, I am impervious to insults."

With what must have been, for him, a Herculean effort, Burnett brought his temper and outrage under control and regarded Morro with an expression of suspicious thoughtfulness. He said slowly: "I have to admit they *look* like Aunt Sallies."

"You are suggesting something, Professor Burnett?"

"Yes. I'm suggesting this is a hoax, a gigantic bluff. I'm suggesting that all this fancy machinery you have down here, the steel and aluminum sheets, the nuclear fuel, the electrical shop, this so-called assembly shop, is just window dressing on an unprecedented scale. I suggest you are trying to trick my colleagues and myself into convincing the world at large that you really are in possession of those nuclear weapons whereas, in fact, they are only dummies. You could have those cylinders made in a hundred places in this state alone without arousing any suspicion. But you couldn't have the components, the very intricate and sophisticated components made without providing the very complex and highly sophisticated plans, and that *would* have aroused suspicion. I'm afraid, Morro, that you are no engineer. To make those components here you would have required highly skilled pattern cutters, template makers, turners and machinists. Such men are very hard to come by and are highly paid professionals who most certainly would not jeopardize their careers by working for a criminal."

Morro said: "Well spoken. Interesting but, if I may say so, merely amusing observations. You have quite finished?"

When Burnett made no reply Morro crossed to a large steel plate let into one wall and pressed a button by its side. The steel plate slid sideways with a mute whine to reveal a square wire-meshed door. Behind the mesh were seated six men, two watching TV, two reading and two playing cards. All six men looked toward the mesh door. Their faces were pale and gaunt and held expressions of what could be called neither hatred nor fear but were compounded of both.

"Those may be the men you are looking for, Professor?" Again there was neither satisfaction nor triumph in Morro's voice. "One template maker, one pattern cutter, two lathe specialists, one machinist and one electrician or, should I say, a specialist in electronics." He looked at the six men and said: "Perhaps you would confirm that you are indeed the skilled practitioners of the arts that I have claimed you to be?"

The six men looked at him and said nothing, but their tightened lips and the loathing in their faces said it for them.

Morro shrugged. "Well, well. They do get like this occasionally—an irritating, if momentary, lack of co-operation. Or, to put it another way, they simply never learn." He crossed the chamber, entered a boothlike office and lifted a phone. His voice was inaudible to the watchers. He remained inside till a newcomer, a stranger to the physicists, entered the chamber. Morro met him and together they approached the waiting group.

"This is Lopez," Morro said. Lopez was a short tubby man with an appropriately chubby face, a low hairline, dark mustache and what appeared to be a permanently good-humored smile. He nodded and kept on smiling as Morro made introductions but said nothing.

"Lopez, I am just a little disappointed in you." Morro spoke severely but his smile matched Lopez's own. "And to think I pay you such a handsome salary."

"I am desolate, señor." If he was, he didn't look it; the smile remained firmly in place. "If you would let me know in what way I have fallen short——"

Morro nodded at the six men behind the mesh. Fear, not hatred, was now the dominant expression in their faces. Morro said: "They refuse to talk to me."

Lopez sighed. "I do try to teach them manners, Señor Morro—but even Lopez is no magician." He pressed another button and the mesh gate slid open. He smiled with even greater good humor and beckoned. "Come, Peters. We'll go to my room and have a little talk, will we?"

The man addressed as Peters said: "My name is John Peters and I am a lathe operator." There was no mistaking the abject terror in his face and his voice shook. The four physicists looked at one another with a dimly comprehending shock on their faces.

A second man said: "I am Conrad Bronowski. I am an electrician." And, in a precisely similar fashion, each of the other four in turn gave his name and occupation.

"Thank you, gentlemen." Morro touched both buttons in succession and looked inquiringly at the four scientists as both gate and door closed. But they weren't looking at him, they were staring at Lopez.

Schmidt said: "Who is this man?"

"Lopez? Their guide and mentor. You could see how well they responded to his friendliness, his kindly good humor. Thank you, Lopez."

"My pleasure, Señor Morro."

With considerable difficulty Burnett removed his eyes from Lopez and looked at Morro. "Those men in there. They—they look like men I have seen in a concentration camp. Forced labor. And this man—he is their guard, their torturer. I have never seen such fear in men's faces."

"You are both unkind and unjust. Lopez has a deep concern for his fellow man. Those six men, I have to confess, are here under restraint but they will be——"

"Kidnaped, you mean?"

"As you will. But, as I was about to say, they will very shortly be returned unharmed to their families."

"You see?" Burnett turned to his three colleagues. "Just as Mrs. Ryder said. Kind, considerate and thoughtful of others. You're a goddamned evil hypocrite."

"Sticks and stones, Professor Burnett, sticks and stones. Now, perhaps, we can get on with this recording?"

"One minute." An expression of puzzlement had replaced the revulsion in Healey's face. "Accepting that those men in there are what they claim they are or what this monster made them claim to be"—Lopez continued to smile his genial smile, he was clearly as impervious to insults as Morro himself—"it's still impossible that they could have assembled this mechanism without the guidance of a first-class nuclear physicist. Which leads me to believe that those men in there have simply been brainwashed into saying what they have just said."

"Astute," Morro said, "but only superficially so. If I just wanted six men to say what those six just have then I would surely have rehearsed six of my own men who would have required neither persuasion or incarceration to play the parts. Not so, Dr. Healey?" Healey's crestfallen expression showed that it was indeed so. Morro sighed resignedly. "Lopez, if you would be so kind as to remain in the office?" Lopez smiled, this time as if in anticipation, and walked across to the booth from which Morro had telephoned. Morro led the others to a second steel door, pressed a button to open it, then another to open the cage gate behind.

The cell was dimly lit but bright enough to show clearly an old man slumped in a tattered armchair, the only item of furniture there with the slightest suggestion of comfort. He had frizzy white hair, a haggard and unbelievably lined face and wore shabby clothes that hung loosely on a frame as emaciated as the face. His eyes were closed and he appeared to be asleep. Were it not for the occasional twitching of thin blue-veined hands he could equally well have been dead.

Morro gestured toward the sleeping man. "Recognize him?"

The four men studied him without recognition, then Burnett said contemptuously: "This your trump card? This your mastermind behind the alleged nuclear weapons? You forget, Morro, that I know every top-ranking nuclear physicist in the country. I've never seen this man before."

"People can change," Morro said mildly. He shook the old man by the shoulder until he started and opened his eyelids to reveal clouded and bloodshot eyes. With a hand under a thin arm, Morro persuaded him to his feet and urged him out into the brighter light of the assembly room. "Perhaps you recognize him now?"

"What kind of put-on is this?" Burnett peered closely and shook his head. "I repeat, I have never seen this man."

Morro said: "It's sad how one can forget old friends. You know him very well, Professor. Imagine if he were, say, seventy pounds heavier. Imagine if the lines had gone from his face and his hair was as black as it now is white. Think, Professor, think."

Burnett thought. Suddenly his searching gaze changed to a stare, his face drained of expression just as his complexion drained of blood. He seized the old man by the shoulders.

"Jesus Christ Almighty! Willi Aachen! Willi Aachen! What in God's name have they done to you?"

"My old friend Andy!" The voice matched the appearance, a voice old and faint and quavering. "How good to see you again."

"What have they done to you?"

"Well. You can see. Kidnaped." He shivered and tried to smile at the same time. "They persuaded me to work for them."

Burnett flung himself toward Morro but didn't get halfway. Dubois' great hands closed on his upper arms from behind. Burnett was a powerful man and his fury gave him a momentarily berserker strength but he had no more chance of freeing himself from that monstrous grip than the wasted and shrunken Aachen would have had.

"It's no use, Andy." Aachen sounded sad. "No use. We are powerless."

Burnett stopped his futile struggling. Breathing heavily, he said for the third time: "What have they done to you? How? Who did it?"

Lopez, certainly in answer to some unseen signal from Morro, appeared at Aachen's elbow. Aachen saw him and took an involuntary step backward, flipping up an arm as if to protect a face suddenly contorted with fear. Morro, still holding him by the arm, smiled at Burnett.

"How naïve, how childlike and unthinking even the highest intelligences can be. There are, Professor Burnett, only two copies of plans for the Aunt Sally, drawn up by yourself and Professor Aachen, in existence and those are in the vaults of the Atomic Energy Commission. You must know that they are still there, so I could have obtained those plans from only two men in America. They are both with me now. Do you understand?"

Burnett was still having difficulty with his breathing. "I know Professor Aachen. I know him better than anyone. No one could have made him work for you. No one! No one!"

Lopez broadened his ever-genial smile. "Perhaps, Señor Morro, if I had a friendly little chat in my room with Professor Burnett here. Ten minutes would suffice, I think."

"I agree. That should be sufficient to convince him that anyone on earth would work for me."

"Don't, don't, don't!" Aachen was close to hysteria. "For God's sake, Andy you've got to believe Morro." He looked in fearful loathing at Lopez. "This inhuman monster knows more awful, more unspeakable, more fiendish tortures than any sane man can conceive of, can imagine. In the name of heaven, Andy, don't be mad—this creature will break you as he broke me."

"I'm convinced." Healey had stepped forward and taken Burnett by the arm just as Dubois released his grip. He looked at Schmidt and Bramwell, then turned back to Burnett. "The three of us are convinced. Absolutely. What's the point of being broken on the modern equivalent of the rack if it's going to prove nothing? We *have* the proof. God's sake, you couldn't recognize an old friend you last saw ten weeks ago. Isn't that proof? And those six zombie technicians. Isn't that proof?" He looked at Morro. "There could, of course, be a final proof. If those Aunt Sallies are for real you must have some way of triggering them and the only way can be either by a time device or radio. It wouldn't be the former, because then you would have committed yourself to an irrevocable decision and I can't see a man like you committing yourself to the irrevocable—so I assume you have elected for a controllable radio impulse."

"Well, well." Morro smiled. "This time you have not been just superficially obtuse. You are correct, of course. Follow me, gentlemen."

He led the way to the small booth from which he had telephoned. Its inner wall held yet another steel door. There was no press button to open this. Instead, alongside the door, was a small brass panel, highly polished, measuring about ten inches by six. Morro placed his flat palm and fingers against it; the door slid smoothly open.

Inside was a tiny room, not more than six by six feet. On the wall opposite the door was a metal table which supported a simple radio transmitter, smaller than an attaché case, with calibrated dials and tuning knobs. On top of the case was a plastic-covered red button. Clamped to one side of the table was an eight-inch cylinder with a diameter about half that. At one end of the cylinder was a cranking handle; at the other end an insulated lead to a terminal in one side of the transmitter. There were two other terminals close by that one. From one, a lead reached down to a storage battery on the floor. The third terminal connected to a wall socket.

"An almost childishly simple device, gentlemen," Morro said. "A perfectly ordinary radio transmitter but one serving a most extraordinary purpose. It is programed with a specific code on a preset wave length. The chances of anyone duplicating both the wave length and the code are so astronomically remote they can be said to be nonexistent. We have, as you see, guarded against any chance of a power failure—we have main current, battery and this hand-cranked generator." He touched the plastic-covered red button on top. "To operate, one simply unscrews the plastic dome, turns the button through ninety degrees and presses." He ushered them out, laid his hand against the brass panel and watched the door slide close. "One cannot very well have buttons for this purpose. Some careless person might accidentally lean against them."

Healey said: "Only your handprint can open that door?"

"You didn't imagine that plate was simply an elaborate press button? Well, gentlemen, the recording."

"One last thing," Burnett said. He nodded toward the row of Aunt Sallies. "There are two empty sets of clamps there. Why?"

"Well, now." Morro smiled his empty smile. "I thought you'd never ask."

The four physicists sat around the table in Burnett's room, contemplating both their brandies and the future with an understandably profound gloom.

"Well, I said it, didn't I?" Burnett said heavily. " 'Mark my words,' I said. Didn't I say that?"

No one said whether he'd said it or not. There didn't seem to be anything to say.

"Even that control room could have been part of a massive hoax." Schmidt was grasping at nonexistent straws.

No one said anything to that either and for the same reason.

"And to think that I said he wasn't amoral as a madman should be," Burnett said. "That if he were really mad he'd set off his atomic bomb on Wilshire Boulevard?"

No one had anything to say to that either. Burnett rose and said: "Back shortly, gentlemen."

Peggy was still in bed but looked considerably better than she had on her arrival at the Adlerheim. Her mother sat in an armchair to one side. Burnett had a brandy glass in his hand. He hadn't brought his own with him; he'd gone straight behind Susan's bar the moment he had arrived. He was still behind it, his elbows on the counter, bending an apocalyptic gaze upon his audience and addressing them in apocalyptic tones. Armageddon, it was clear, was at hand, and the dark angel was there to announce the fact.

"You will not, ladies, doubt our unanimous conclusion that we are sitting atop enough nuclear explosive power to blast the biggest man-made crater of all time, enough to send us all into orbit—in a vaporized state, that is? The equivalent of thirty-five million tons of conventional explosive. It should cause quite a bang, don't you think?"

It was a night for silences, for unanswered questions. Burnett's doom-laden gaze homed in on Susan.

"Kind, gentle, humane, considerate—that's what you said Morro was. He may very well go down in history as the most cold-blooded, calculating monster ever. Seven broken men down in the vaults there whom he has

tortured—or has had tortured—beyond the breaking point of screaming
agony. Humane, considerate.

"And this kindly gentleman—where has he put the missing hydrogen
bomb? It's a rather scaled-down version of the Aunt Sally—a trifling one
and a half megatons, about seventy-five times as powerful as the ones that
destroyed Hiroshima and Nagasaki. Released at a height of between ten and
twenty thousand feet it could destroy half the population of Southern California. Those whom the blast didn't get, radiation and fire storms would.
But as this bomb is already in position, it must be on or below ground level.
The results will still be unimaginably dreadful. So, tell me, where do you
think this gentle Christ-like figure placed this hydrogen device so that no
harm will come to any of God's children?"

He was still looking fixedly at Susan but she wasn't looking at him. She
wasn't avoiding his gaze; her mind, like those of the others, was numbed
with shock and incomprehension: she just wasn't seeing anything.

"So must I tell you?"

It was still a night for silences.

"Los Angeles."

9

ON THE following morning the absenteeism rate at work was the highest in
the history of the state. The same almost certainly applied to the other states
in the union and, to a somewhat lesser degree, through many of the civilized
countries throughout the world, for the TV coverage of the projected—or
threatened—atomic explosion in the Yucca Flat was begin transmitted by
satellite. Europe was hardly affected—though none the less concerned—for
there the day's work was all over and most Europeans were home for the
evening.

But in California the absenteeism was almost total. Even the corporations
running the public and utilities services, the transport systems and police
forces, had to operate with skeleton staffs. It could have been a great day
for the criminals, particularly the robbers and burglars of California, were
it not for the fact that they, too, had also stayed at home.

For reasons whether of prudence, sloth, the knowledge of the inaccessi-
bility of Yucca Flat or the handy convenience of their TV sets, not one
Californian in ten thousand made their way to the explosion site that morning. Those who did go—and there couldn't have been over two thousand of
them—were outnumbered by members of the military, the National Guard
and police, who found their task of keeping civilians at the mandatory five-
mile distance almost ridiculously easy.

Among the spectators present were most of the ranking scientists in the
state, especially and understandably those who specialized in the nuclear
and earthquake fields. Why, precisely, they *were* there was difficult to see,
for the blast, shock and radiation effects of an eighteen-kiloton atomic
device had been known with sufficient precision for over thirty years. Most
of them, admittedly, had never seen an atomic explosion before, but the
reason lay elsewhere. Blessed or cursed by that insatiable and rubber-necking curiosity that had been the driving force or bane of scientists since
recorded history, they just wanted to see where the bomb would go off.
They, too, could, of course, have stayed at home, but your true scientist is
in the field or he is nothing.

Among those who stayed at home were Major Dunne in his office and Sergeant Ryder at his house. Even by helicopter the round trip was over five hundred miles, and that, for Dunne, represented a waste of valuable investigative time. For Ryder it represented a waste of thinking time, which he no longer regarded as being necessarily valuable but was better than not thinking at all. Jeff Ryder had originally wanted to go, but when coldly asked by his father how he hoped to help his family by spending what could be irreplaceable hours rubber-necking, he had readily agreed not to go, especially when Ryder had said that he wanted Jeff to help him. His father, Jeff thought, had a peculiar idea of what helping meant or, as far as he could see, his parent was doing absolutely nothing. He, Jeff, had been asked to type out every detail, however apparently insignificant, of the investigations that had been carried out till then, including, as far as possible, verbatim recollections of all conversations, and to this end he was employing his rather remarkable memory as best he could. From time to time he glanced rather resentfully at Ryder, who appeared to be doing nothing other than leafing idly through the pile of earthquake literature he'd picked up from Professor Benson.

About ten minutes before ten Jeff switched on the TV. The screen showed a bluish-tinged stretch of extremely unprepossessing desert, so unattractive a spectacle that the commentator was trying, and making extremely heavy weather of it, to compensate by an intense and breathless account of what was taking place, a gallant and foredoomed effort, as nothing whatsoever was taking place. He informed the watchers that the camera was stationed in Frenchman's Flat at a distance of five miles southwest from the estimated point of explosion, as if anyone cared from what direction his camera was pointing. He said that as the device was almost certainly buried to a considerable depth, there wasn't expected to be much in the way of a fireball, which everyone had been reminded of for hours past. They were, he said, using a color filter, which everyone who wasn't color-blind could readily see. Finally, he told them that the time was nine minutes to ten, as if he were the only person in California who owned a watch. He had, of course, to say something, but it was an extremely mundane build-up to something that might prove to be of historic significance. Jeff looked at his father in some exasperation: Ryder was certainly not looking and very probably not listening to anything that was going on. He was no longer leafing through the pages but was gazing, apparently unseeing, at one particular page. He laid down the literature and headed for the telephone.

Jeff said: "Dad, do you mind? There's just thirty seconds to go."

"Ah!" Ryder returned to his seat and gazed placidly at the screen.

The commentator was now speaking in that tense, breathless, near hysterical voice which commonly afflicts race-track commentators when they are endeavoring to generate some spurious excitement toward the end of a race. In this particular instance the tone was quite misplaced; a calm relaxed voice would have been much more appropriate: the imminent event carried in itself all the excitement that could be generated. The commentator had now started a countdown, starting at thirty, the numbers decreasing as the dramatic impact of his voice increased. The effect was rather spoiled because either his watch was wrong or Morro's was. The device exploded fourteen seconds ahead of time.

To a people who had long become accustomed to seeing atomic explosions on the screen, whether at home or in the cinema, to a people who had become blasé about and bored with the spectacle of moon rockets blasting off from Cape Canaveral, the effect, visually speaking, of this latest demonstration of science's resolute retrograde march was curiously—or perhaps

not so curiously—anticlimactic. True, the fireball was considerably greater
than predicted—the searing blue-white flash was of an intensity that caused
many viewers to wince or even momentarily screw shut their eyes—but the
column of smoke, fire and desert dust that streaked up into the blue Nevada
sky, a blueness dramatically intensified by the camera filters, culminating in
the mushrooming of the deadly radioactive cloud, faithfully followed the
accustomed scenario. To the inhabitants of the central Amazon basin such a
titanic convulsion would presumably have heralded the end of the world; to
the most sophisticated peoples of the world it was passé, old hat, and had it
occurred on some remote Pacific atoll the great majority of people wouldn't
even have bothered to watch it.

But it hadn't happened on any remote Pacific atoll nor had it been Morro's
purpose to provide the Californians with a diversionary spectacle to relieve
the ennui of their daily lives. It had been intended, instead, to provide them
with a chilling warning, an ominous threat, all the more frightening because
unspecified, of impending evil, of some unimagined disaster that would
surely strike at the whim of whoever had planted and triggered the atomic
device. On a more mundane level it was intended to show that here was a
man who meant what he said, who was not just there to play around and
who had both the desire and ability to carry out whatever he had threatened.
Had that been Morro's intention, and there obviously had been none other,
then he had succeeded to a degree which perhaps even he had not realized
was possible. He had struck fear into the hearts of the great majority of
rational Californians and from that time on there was practically only one
topic of conversation in the state: when and where would this unpredictable
madman strike again and what in the name of all that was holy—it wasn't
expressed in quite that way—were his motivations. This topic, to be precise,
was to last for only ninety minutes: then they were to be given something
really definite and concrete to worry about or, more accurately, to reduce
that part of California most directly concerned to a state of not unreasoning
terror that was swiftly to shade off into panic.

Ryder rose."Well, we never doubted that he was a man of his word.
Aren't you glad you didn't waste your time going up to see that side show?
For that's all it was. Well, it should at least keep people's minds off taxes
and the latest shenanigans in Washington for a little.''

Jeff didn't answer. It was doubtful if he'd even heard. He was still looking
at the ever-expanding mushroom over the Nevada desert, still listening to
the suitably awe-stricken voice of the commentator describing in great and
wholly unnecessary detail what anyone with half an eye could see perfectly
well for himself. Ryder shook his head and picked up the telephone. Dunne
answered.

Ryder said: "Anything? You know this line is bugged."
"Some things coming in."
"Interpol?"
"Some things coming in."
"How long?"
"Half an hour."

He hung up, called Parker, arranged to have them meet in Dunne's office
in half an hour, hung up, sat, briefly ruminated on the fact that both Dunne
and Parker had taken the reality of Morro's threat so much for granted that
neither of them had thought fit to comment on it, then resumed his reading.
Fully five minutes passed before Jeff switched off the TV, glanced with
some irritation at his father, sat down at his table, typed a few words and
said acidly: "I hope I'm not disturbing you."

"Not at all. How many pages have you got down?"

"Six."

Ryder stretched out his hand and took them. "We're leaving in fifteen minutes to see Dunne. Something's come up—or is coming up."

"What?"

"You have forgotten, perhaps, that one of Morro's henchmen is wearing a headset tied into our phone?"

A chagrined Jeff resumed his typing while Ryder began a placid reading of Jeff's notes.

A much refreshed Dunne, who had obviously a good night's rest behind him, was waiting with Delage and Leroy when Ryder, Jeff and Parker arrived. Delage and Leroy were looking a good deal less rested: the assumption was that they did not have a good night's rest behind them. Dunne confirmed this, nodding at Delage and Leroy.

"A couple of devoted agents who think their boss is past it. Quite right too." He tapped a sheaf of papers in front of him. "Up all night—the devoted agents, I mean—collecting snippets of this and that. Some possibly useful information, some dead ends. What did you think of friend Morro's demonstration?"

"Impressive. What do you have?"

Dunne sighed. "The niceties of salon conversation, Sergeant Ryder, are not for all. Report from Daimler, remember him?"

"Security chief in the AEC reactor plant in Illinois?"

"Yes. Nothing wrong with your memory."

"Even less with Jeff's. I've just been reading some notes he typed out. Well?"

"He says that Carlton did associate with some far-out group. As I said, we preferred to have one of our boys do the direct legwork. Interviewed Carlton's landlady's son. He wasn't very forthcoming—he'd only attended two or three meetings then gave it up. Couldn't stand the mumbojumbo, he said."

"What were they called?"

"The Damascene Disciples. Nothing known of them. Never registered as a church or religious organization. Disbanded after six months."

"They had a religion? I mean, they preached, they had a message?"

"They didn't preach. They had a message, all right. They advocated the eternal damnation of all Christians, Jews, Buddhists, Shintoists—in fact, as far as I can make out, everybody who wasn't a Damascene."

"Nothing original about that. Were the Muslims on their list, do you know?"

Dunne looked at a list. "Oddly enough, no. Why?"

"Curiosity. Could this landlady's son recognize any of them?"

"That would have been difficult. The Damascenes wore cloaks, masks and those pixie witches' hats affected by the Ku Klux Klan. Only this gang were dressed in black."

"Something in common, all the same—as I recall it the Ku Klux Klan aren't all that devoted to Jews, Catholics and Negroes. Anyway, no possible means of identification?"

"None. Except that this kid told our agent that one of them was the biggest man he had ever seen, a giant, maybe six-eight, and shoulders like a cart horse."

"This person didn't note anything peculiar about any of their voices?"

"This person, according to our agent, just escaped being classified as a moron."

"But Carlton was no moron. Interesting, isn't it? What word about Morro?"

"Well, his accent. We've now had reports from—what shall we call them?—linguistic experts throughout the state. Thirty-eight so far, and more coming in every minute. All of them willing to stake their reputations, etc., etc. Point is, no less than twenty-eight plump for a southeast Asian origin."

"Do they indeed? Any attempt to pin-point the exact source?"

"That's as far as they will go."

"Again, still interesting. Interpol?"

"Nothing."

"You have a list of all the places they've contacted?" Dunne looked at Leroy, who nodded. "The Philippines, for instance?"

Leroy consulted a list. "No."

"Try Manila. Ask them to try around the Cotabato area in Mindanao."

"The what in what?"

"Mindanao is the large southern island in the Philippines. Cotabato is a seaside town. Manila may not be too interested in what goes on in Cotabato—it's at least five hundred and fifty miles away as the crow flies, maybe a thousand by road and ferry. Try, anyway."

"I see." Dunne paused. "You know something that we don't know?"

"No. Chances are I'm making a complete fool of myself, just a wild guess based upon ludicrous improbability. LeWinter?"

"Two things. The first one is extraordinarily odd. You will recall that in his telephone notebook he'd listed the numbers of all kinds of people with whom—outside his court cases, of course—LeWinter would not be expected to be on either social or professional terms. Engineers, drillers, oil-rig men. There were forty-four of those in all. Barrow, for reasons best known to himself, he's almost as close-mouthed as you, assigned a federal agent to interview each and every one of them."

"Forty-four. That's a lot of FBI agents."

Dunne was patient. "There are approximately eight thousand FBI men in the country. If Barrow cares to allocate one half of one per cent of his men to a particular case, that's his privilege. He could allocate four hundred and forty if he wanted. Point is, twenty-six of those agents came up with the same puzzling—I'd call it astonishing—discovery—twenty-six of the men being investigated are missing. Wives, children, relatives, friends—none of them have any idea where they might be, none were given the slightest indication of their intention to depart. What do you make of that?"

"Well, that's interesting too."

"Interesting, interesting, interesting. Is that all you can say?"

"Well, as you say, it's damned odd."

"Look, Ryder, if you have any idea, if you're holding anything back ____."

"Obstructing justice, you mean?"

"Just that."

"I thought I might be a complete fool, Dunne. Now I know you are." There was a silence, not long but extremely uncomfortable. "Sure I'm obstructing the course of justice. How many of *your* family is Morro holding hostage?" Another silence. "I'm going to talk to our friend LeWinter. Rather, he's going to talk to me. It's as plain as the hand in front of your face that he's supplied Morro with that list and that Morro has either had them bought or taken by force. Your twenty-six agents might be profitably engaged on checking on the criminal backgrounds, if any, of those twenty-six men. LeWinter will talk; I'll see to that—and not if I die in the attempt. He'll talk if *he* dies in *my* attempt."

The quietly spoken, cold ferocity in Ryder's voice had a chilling effect on everyone in the room. Jeff licked his lips and looked at a man he'd never seen before. Parker regarded the ceiling. Delage and Leroy looked at Dunne. Dunne looked at the hand before his face and used the back of it to smooth his brow.

Dunne said: "Maybe I'm not myself. Maybe we're not any of us ourselves. The apologies go without saying. Next you'll be accusing us of being a bunch of lily-livered incompetents. But, hell, Sergeant, there's a limit to how far you can step outside the law. Sure he has a list which included the twenty-six men who have disappeared. A dozen others may have similar lists and all for innocuous purposes. You're proceeding on the basis of assumptions. There isn't a shred of evidence, direct or otherwise, to link LeWinter and Morro."

"I don't need evidence."

Once again Dunne used the back of his hand. "You have just said, in the presence of three government officers, that you're prepared to use torture to obtain your information."

"Who said anything about torture? It'll look like a heart attack. You said you had two things to tell me about LeWinter. Well, that's one."

"Jesus!" Dunne wasn't smoothing his brow now, he was mopping it. "Delage, you have the information. Me, I need time to think."

"Yes. Well." Delage didn't look any happier than his superior. "Miss Ivanhoe, if that's her name, well, LeWinter's secretary, has talked. There's a Geneva connection all right. It all sounds very much like something out of science fiction, but if it's even halfway true, then it's damn frightening. It must be if most of the nations of the world—major ones, that is, thirty to be precise—sit down at a disarmament conference in Geneva and talk about it."

"I have all morning," Ryder said.

"Sorry. Well, the lady talked and it didn't seem to make much sense so we contacted ERDA with the result that one of Dr. Durrer's senior assistants was called in, shown what Miss Ivanhoe said and had no trouble at all in making sense of it. He's an expert on the subject."

"I haven't got the afternoon too."

"Give me a break, will you? He wrote a condensed report. This is what he has to say."

"Classified?"

"Declassified. It's a bit formal, but here it is. He says: It has long been accepted that any nuclear war, even on a limited scale, would cause megadeaths. He puts in brackets, millions of deaths. The U. S. Arms Control and Disarmament Agency came to the conclusion a couple of years ago that megadeaths could arise from another agency which did not directly involve nuclear war. A large number of nuclear explosions, almost certainly in the megaton range, could damage the layer of ozone that shields the earth from the sun's lethal ultraviolet radiation.

"Most people are under the impression that ozone is what they sniff at the seaside. Ozone is an allotropic condition of oxygen, having three atoms instead of the normal two, and *can* be smelled at the seaside by the electrolysis of water and also after the discharge of electricity through the air, as occurs in a thunderstorm. But ozone in its natural state occurs almost solely in the lower stratosphere at an altitude between ten and thirty miles.

"The intense heat given off by a nuclear explosion causes the oxygen and nitrogen molecules in the atmosphere to combine. Those form oxides of nitrogen which would be borne upward in the atomic cloud. Those would react with the ozone layer and by a well-understood chemical reaction convert the three atoms of ozone into two, that is, normal oxygen, which offers zero protection against ultraviolet radiation. This would effectively blow a hole in the ozone layer and would expose the earth underneath the hole to the direct effects of the sun.

"Two effects remain unclear. The first of those——"

Delage broke off as a telephone rang. Leroy picked it up, listened in silence, thanked the caller and hung up. He said: "I don't know why I thanked him for that call. From the local TV station. It seems that Morro wants to strike while the iron is hot. He has another statement to make. At eleven o'clock. That's in eight minutes' time. It will be carried on every TV and radio station in the state. For the rest of the states, too, I'd guess."

"Isn't that wonderful?" Dunne said. "A morning to remember. I wonder why it wasn't cleared with the FBI first—we would have heard, wouldn't we?"

Ryder said: "You blame them? After what the FBI did to stop the atomic blast in Nevada this morning? This is a matter for national concern now, not just for the FBI. Since when have you had the power to impose martial law? Their attitude, and probably the attitude of every citizen in the country, is that the FBI can go take a jump." He looked at Delage. "The first unclear effect?"

"You're a cold-blooded bastard, Ryder." Dunne undoubtedly meant what he said.

Delage looked unhappily at Dunne, but Dunne had his head in his hands. Delage returned to his notes.

"We just don't know what will happen. The consequences might be small, they might be catastrophic. We might just all end up becoming very heavily sun-tanned; or the ultraviolet could conceivably destroy all human, animal and plant life. Subterranean and aquatic life might survive any conditions. We have no means of knowing." Delage looked up. "He *is* a cheery one, isn't he?"

"Let's take that up later," Ryder said. "Let's have the second unclear effect."

"Well. He says it is not known whether this hole in the stratosphere would remain localized and keep pace with the rotation of the earth. Worse, it is not known whether or not this hole can spread through the rest of the ozone layer. Chemical reactions at that level in the stratosphere are unknown and wholly unpredictable—there might well exist a form of breeder reaction, in which case large areas of the earth might well be devastated.

"The possibility must be taken into account that some nation may already have experimented in some remote and uninhabited region——"

Parker said: "Siberia?"

"He doesn't say. He goes on: It may have been established that such a hole can be blown through the ozone layer and has been found to be stable as to both location and extent. This, however, is pure conjecture.

"This introduces the Geneva connection. As long ago as September 3 of 1976, the thirty-nation disarmament conference there sent a draft treaty banning modification of the environment for military purposes to the United Nations General Assembly. The matter, not unexpectedly, is still under UNO's consideration.

"The treaty is designed, in the words of the communiqué, to prevent artificial induction by the military of such phenomena as earthquakes——"

"Earthquakes!" Ryder seemed jolted.

"Yes, earthquakes. He goes on: Tidal waves——"

"Tidal waves?" It was almost as if Ryder was beginning to comprehend something.

"That's what it says here. There's some more: ecological imbalance, alteration of weather and climate and changes in ocean currents, in the state of the ozone layer and the ionosphere, that is, the Appleton and Kennelly-Heaviside layers. Then he goes on to say that the United States delegate at Geneva, one Mr. Joseph Martin, believed that it would be a treaty amounting to a very strong practical inhibition against the hostile use of environmental modification techniques. He further comments that Mr. Martin appears to have forgotten or ignored the fact that the only effect of the Strategic Arms Limitation Talks was to encourage the Russians, in the sacred name of détente, to embark on a new and massive program of building a bigger and better generation of intercontinental ballistic missiles." Delage appeared to run his eye down the page. "He runs on a bit more but I'm afraid his scientific detachment gives way to a certain irony and bitterness. I would say that's about all—Miss Ivanhoe's rather vague ramblings in a coherent form."

"Switch on that TV," Dunne said. "A minute or so. Your sixty seconds' worth of observations, Sergeant Ryder?"

"Poppycock. Or if you want it in plain language——"

"That's plain enough. No Reds under the bed?" Dunne had a very disbelieving right eyebrow.

"I didn't say that. Neither do I say I disbelieve this story—theory, if you like—about blowing a hole through the ozone layer. I'm no scientist. All I'm saying is that I don't believe in its relevance in those circumstances. Russian secret codes." On the rare occasions that Ryder expressed contempt he came across very strongly. "You think the Russians—anyone—would use a young innocent, a marshmallow guaranteed to crack under the pressure of a fingertip, to decode a message or supposed secret that's been in the public domain for two years? The idea's preposterous."

"Laying a false scent, you would think?"

"Yes. No."

"You've forgotten 'perhaps.' "

" 'Perhaps' is what I mean. Morro's intention may lie elsewhere. On the other hand, it may not. Maybe he thinks the idea's so ridiculous that we'll dismiss it out of hand and so he'll go ahead and use that idea. Or not. Maybe the Russians *are* involved. Again, or not. It's the old story. Three ranchers are chasing a rustler who's disappeared up a canyon. Halfway up this canyon there's a branch canyon. Rancher A figures the rustler has gone hell for leather for the end of the canyon. Rancher B thinks he's smarter than A and that the rustler, figuring that's the way his pursuers will think, has taken the branch. C reckons that he's smarter than both A and B, that the rustler will figure what B has figured and go to the end. No end to how long we could keep on outsmarting ourselves."

He paused. "There could, of course, be a second branch canyon that we know nothing about. Just as we know nothing about the first."

"It's a rare privilege," Dunne said, "to see a detective's mind at work."

Ryder might not have heard him. "*Another* interesting thing. This expert from ERDA. A nuclear physicist, I assume. About blasting a hole through the ozone layer. If the Russians—or whoever—had carried out any such experiments with God knows how many hydrogen bombs we or one of our allies would have been bound to know of it. It would have made headlines—big, big headlines—throughout the world. But there haven't been any. Have there?"

No one said whether there had or hadn't.

"Well, so no experiments. Maybe the Russians—or again, whoever—are as scared of the outcome as we are. Maybe there never will be a nuclear war fought on land. Some people say it will be in space. Our friend in ERDA suggests—what did he say—subterranean or aquatic use of nuclear devices. How do we fancy getting our feet wet?"

"A rush on the stores for fishermen's waders?" Dunne turned toward the TV. "I'm sure our friend Morro is about to enlighten us on that one."

The newscaster, this time, was a much older man, which boded ill in itself. What boded worse was that he was dressed for a funeral in a suit of somber hue, a color in which the normal Californian newscaster would not normally have been found dead. What boded still worse was the doomsday expression customarily reserved for those occasions when the local gridiron heroes had been crushingly defeated by some out-of-state upstarts. The tone of voice accorded well with both clothes and expression.

"We have received another communication from this criminal Morro." The newscaster clearly held in contempt the fundamental tenet of Anglo-Saxon law that a man is presumed innocent until found guilty.

"It contains a dire warning, an unprecedentedly grave threat to the citizens of California and one that cannot be taken lightly in view of what occurred this morning in Yucca Flat. I have with me in the studio a panel of experts who will later explain the implications of this threat. But first, Morro."

"Good evening. This is a prerecorded message." As before, the voice was calm and relaxed, he could have been discussing some minor change in the Dow Jones Index. "It is prerecorded because I am completely confident of the outcome of my little experiment in Yucca Flat. By the time you hear those words you will know that my confidence has not been misplaced.

"This little demonstration of my nuclear resources inconvenienced nobody and hurt nobody. The next demonstration will be on a vastly larger scale, may well inconvenience millions and may well prove disastrous for an untold number of people if they are so stupid as to fail to appreciate the gravity of this warning. However, I am sure you would first like scientific confirmation, on the highest level, that I do have the means at hand. Professor Burnett?"

"He's got the means, all right, the black-hearted bastard." For a man of unquestionably brilliant intellect, Burnett was singularly lacking in resource when it came to the selection of suitable epithets. "I hate to use the word 'beg' in the presence of a monstrous lunatic but I do beg you to believe me that he has the resources he claims. Of that my fellow physicists and I are in no doubt. He has no fewer than eleven hydrogen nuclear devices here, any one of which could, say, turn Southern California into a desert as lifeless as Death Valley. They are in the three and a half megaton range—that is, each has the explosive potential of three and a half million tons of TNT. You will appreciate the significance of what I mean when I say this bomb is about two hundred times as powerful as the one that destroyed Hiroshima. And he has eleven of those monsters.

"Correction. He has only ten here. The other is already in position. Where this crazy bastard intends to put it——"

Morro interrupted. "Revealing the location of the weapon is a privilege I reserve for myself. Dr. Schmidt, Dr. Healey, Dr. Bramwell, perhaps you would be so kind as to confirm your colleague's statement." With varying degrees of forcefulness, gravity and outrage, all three left listeners in no doubt as to the chilling genuineness of the threat. When Bramwell had finished, Morro said: "And now, the most telling confirmation of all, that of Professor Aachen, probably the country's leading nuclear weaponry physicist, who personally supervised every step in the building of the bombs. Professor Aachen, you may recall, vanished some seven weeks ago. He has been working with me ever since.''

"Working with you? Working with you?" Aachen's voice held the high quavering note of senility. "You monster! You—you—I would never work with you——" He broke into a weak sobbing and there was a brief silence.

"He's been tortured!" Burnett's voice was a shout. "Tortured, I tell you. He and six kidnaped technicians have been subjected to the most unspeakable——" His voice broke off in a peculiar gasp which sounded as if he was being strangled, which he probably was.

"How you do run on, Professor Burnett." Morro's tone was resigned. "Well, Professor Aachen. About the viability of those bombs?"

"They will work." The voice was low and still shaking.

"How do you know?"

"I built them." Aachen sounded desperately weary. "There are half a dozen nuclear physicists—if I were to give the design characteristics——"

"That will not be necessary." There was a brief silence, then Morro went on: "Well, that's it. All the confirmation that any but the most mentally retarded should ever require. One small correction. Although the ten bombs remaining here are all of the three and a half megaton range, the one already placed in position is only of the one and a half megaton range because, frankly, I am uncertain of the effect of a three and a half megaton bomb which may unleash forces I do not wish unleashed—not, that is, as yet." Here he paused.

Dunne said with conviction: "He's quite crazy."

"Maybe," Ryder said. "One thing, he'd have made one hell of an actor. Pause for effect. Timing."

Morro said: "This bomb, a mere twenty inches by forty inches—it would fit into a car trunk—lies on the floor of the Pacific, off Los Angeles, roughly on the outskirts of Santa Monica Bay. When it is detonated, the resultant *tsunami*—tidal wave—will, it is calculated, be between fifteen and twenty feet high, although it may well reach twice this height when being funneled through the east-west streets of Los Angeles. The effects will be felt at least as far north as Point Arguello and as far south as San Diego. Residents in the Channel Islands—particularly, I should mention, Santa Catalina—should seek high ground. One unknown, I am afraid, is that it might trigger off the Newport-Inglewood fault, but then I would expect that area of the city to be evacuated anyway.

"I need hardly warn against any foolish attempt to locate this device. The device can be detonated at any time and will be if any attempt is made to interfere with it and if this should occur before any attempt is made to evacuate the area the results could not fail to be catastrophic. What I am saying is that any person or persons responsible for sending any aircraft or ships to investigate the area roughly between Santa Cruz Island and Santa Catalina will be directly responsible for the deaths of countless thousands.

"I have certain demands to make which will be announced at 1 P.M. If they are not met by midnight I will trigger the hydrogen bomb at 10 A.M. tomorrow morning. If, after that, the demands are still not met, the next bombs—not bomb but all the remaining bombs—will go off at some time between dusk and dawn on Saturday night."

On this cheerful note Morro ended his message. The newscaster started to introduce his panel of experts but Dunne switched off the set with the observation that if Morro was uncertain as to the effects of the explosion then it was unlikely that the so-called experts had a clue. "Well, Ryder, consider yourself a prophet with honor. Inspired. We get our feet wet. Believe him?''

"Sure. Don't you?"

"Yes. What to do?"

"That's a matter for the authorities, whoever they might be. Me, I take to the hills.''

Delage said: "I simply don't believe it."

"Bully for you," Dunne said. "The spirit that won the West. Tell you what. Leave me the details of your next of kin and stroll along the sea front at Long Beach tomorrow. Better still, take a deck chair on the Catalina ferry.'' He bent a cold glance on the unfortunate Delage, then turned to Ryder. "You would say that Los Angelinos are going to be rather preoccupied for the rest of the day?''

"Look on the bright side. The biggest break ever for the most neurotic city ever. The perfect excuse for giving full and public rein to all those hidden phobias and neuroses. Th drug counters should be doing a roaring trade for the rest of the day.''

Parker said: "He clearly doesn't expect this second warning to be sufficient or he wouldn't have all those back-up bmbs. Jesus, his demands must be sky-high.''

"*And* we don't know what those demands are yet." Dunne sighed. "Two hours yet. Evil bastard. He certainly knows how to turn the screw on psychological tension.'' He thought briefly. "I wonder why he didn't erase those references to torture. Rather spoils his image, no?''

"Did you believe it?" Ryder said. Dunne nodded. "That's it then. That was no act, that was for real. Conviction. Authenticity. What interests me more is that Morro *may* be growing careless or that he *may* be so sure of himself that he's talking too much. Why did he forbid Aachen to give any specifications about the bombs and then gratuitously inform us that it was about twenty by forty inches or something of the kind? It was not in character. He's an economical speaker and that was unnecessary. If Aachen had given us details they would have been accurate. Granted, Morro didn't give us any specifications but I have a faint suspicion that the measurements given were inaccurate. If they were, why should he want to mislead us?''

"I don't follow," Dunne said. "What are you getting at?''

"I wish I knew. It would be instructive to find out what kind of bombs Aachen was in the habit of designing. I mean, if he didn't know about the design how could he supervise the construction? I wonder if you could find out.''

"I'll phone the director and try. I wouldn't have much hope. That would be top secret and there are some people with whom the FBI has very limited powers of investigation. The Atomic Energy Commission is one of those.''

"Even in a national emergency?"

"I said I'll try."

"And can you find out anything about Sheriff Hartman's background? Not police records. We can be sure that either LeWinter or Donahure or both had a hand in his installation in which case his records are bound to be faked. His *true* background.''

"We're ahead of you, Sergeant. It's in hand.''

"Well, thanks. In view of what we've just heard what do you feel now about my intentions of going to trample all over LeWinter's civic rights?''

"LeWinter? Who's LeWinter?"

"Indeed," Ryder said and left followed by Parker and Jeff.

* * *

They stopped off at the *Examiner* building. Ryder went inside, spoke briefly to Aaron, the editor, and emerged within two minutes, a buff envelope in his hand. Inside the car, he extracted a photograph and showed it to Parker and Jeff. Parker studied it with interest.

"Beauty and the Beast? April and December? How much do you think the *Globe* would give us for this masterpiece?"

LeWinter was at home and had the look of a man who didn't intend to leave it. If he was informed by the spirit of *joie de vivre* and good will toward his fellow man, he was concealing it well. In fact, he made no attempt to conceal his displeasure as the three policemen bustled him into his own luxurious living room. Parker did the talking.

"Police. We'd like to ask you a few questions."

"I'm a judge." The cold dignity came off in neither tone nor expression. "Where's your warrant?"

"You were a judge. 'Were' or 'are,' you're stupid. For questions, no warrant. Which leads me rather neatly into the first question. Why did you provide Donahure with signed blank search warrants? Don't you know that's illegal? You, a judge? Or do you deny it?"

"Most certainly I deny it."

"That was a foolish thing for a supposedly learned judge to say. Do you think we would make such an accusation unless we could substantiate it? We have them. You can see them down at the station. Well that's for starters. We've established you're a liar. Henceforth, every statement you make will automatically be disbelieved unless we have independent corroboration. Still deny it?"

LeWinter said nothing. Parker had an excellent line in intimidation and demoralization.

Parker went on: "Found in his safe. We searched his house."

"On what grounds?"

"You're no longer a judge. He's under arrest."

LeWinter forgot he was no longer a judge. "On what grounds?"

"Bribery and corruption. You know, blackmail, taking dirty money and dishing it out to dishonest cops. Kept most of it for himself, though." He looked reproachfully at LeWinter. "You should have taught him the basic tricks of the trade."

"What the devil do you mean?"

"How to stash away illegal money. Did you know he had half a million in eight accounts? He should have been sophisticated, shouldn't he? The clown stashed it away in local accounts. Switzerland's the place. Your numbered account in Zurich. We have it. Bank's been co-operative."

LeWinter's attempted look at outrage fell just short of the pathetic. "If you're insinuating that I, a senior judge of the state of California, have been involved in any illegal financial transactions——"

"Shut up and save it for a real judge. We're not insinuating. We know. And perhaps you would care to explain how come that ten thousand dollars found in Donahure's possession had your prints all over them?"

LeWinter didn't care to explain. His eyes were moving restlessly from side to side but it couldn't have been because of any thought of escape in his mind: he could not bear to meet the three pairs of coldly accusing eyes.

Parker had LeWinter on the hook and had no intention of letting him get off it. "Not that that's the only thing that Donahure's been charged with. Oh, no. Unfortunately for you, oh, no. He also faces a rap and certain conviction for attempted murder *and* murder, witnesses and confession respectively. On the murder rap, you will be charged as an accessory.''

"Murder? Murder!" In the course of his legal practice LeWinter must have heard the word a thousand times but it was long odds that it had ever affected him as it did now.

"You're a friend of Sheriff Hartman, aren't you?"

"Hartman?" LeWinter was caring less and less for the line the conversation was taking.

"So he says. After all, you do have an alarm connected from your safe to his office.''

"Ah! Hartman.''

"Ah, as you say, Hartman. Seen him recently?"

LeWinter had actually started wetting his lips, that indication of corrosive anxiety to which he had succeeded in reducing hundreds of suspects over the years. "I can't remember.''

"But you can remember what he looked like, I hope. You'd never recognize him now. Honestly. Back of his head blown off. It was downright uncivil of you to have your friend's head blown off.''

"You're mad. You're crazy.'' Even the most newly qualified intern would have disapproved of LeWinter's peculiar complexion, which had acquired all the healthy vitality of that of a corpse. "You've no proof.''

"Don't be so original. No proof. That's what they all say when they're guilty. Where's your secretary?"

"What secretary?" The latest switch in attack seemed to have a momentarily paralyzing effect on his thought processes.

"God help us.'' Parker lifted his eyes upward in temporary supplication. "Rather, God help you. Bettina Ivanhoe. Where is she?"

"Excuse me.'' LeWinter went to a cupboard, poured himself some Bourbon and drank it in one gulp. It didn't seem to do him any good.

Parker said: "You may have needed that but that wasn't why you took it. Time to think, isn't that it? Where is she?"

"I gave her the day off.''

"Whiskey didn't help. Wrong answer. When did you speak to her?"

"This morning.''

"Another lie. She's been in custody since last night, assisting police with their inquiries. So you didn't give her a day off.'' Parker was quite without pity. "But it seems you gave yourself a day off. Why aren't you down in the court dispensing justice in your usual even-handed fashion?"

"I'm not well.'' His appearance bore him out. Jeff looked at his father to see if he would stop the ruthless interrogation but Ryder was regarding LeWinter with what appeared to be an expression of profound indifference.

"Not well? Compared to the way you're going to feel very soon—when you're in your court being tried for murder—you're in blooming health. You're at home because one of your criminal accomplices, masters, more like, called you from Bakersfield and told you to lie low. Tell me, how well do you know Miss Ivanhoe? You know, of course, that her proper name is Ivanov?''

LeWinter had further recourse to his liquor cupboard. He said wearily, almost despairingly: "How long is this—this inquisition to go on?"

"Not long. If you tell the truth, that is. I asked a question.''

"How well—she's my secretary. That's enough.''

"No more than that?"

"Of course not.''

Ryder stepped foward and showed LeWinter the photograph he'd collected from the *Examiner's* office. LeWinter stared at it as if hypnotized, then got back to his lip licking.

"A nice kid." Ryder was being conversational. "Blackmail, of course. She's told us. Not with this end in view—this is just a spin-off. Principally, as we know, she came in handy for the translation of phony Russian documents."

"Phony?"

"Ah! So the documents do exist. I wonder why Morro wanted you to provide him with the names of engineers, drillers, oil-rig men. Even more, I wonder why twenty-six of them are missing."

"God knows what you're talking about."

"And you. Watched TV this morning?" LeWinter shook his head in a dazed and uncomprehending manner. "So perhaps you don't know he's detonating a hydrogen bomb in Santa Monica Bay or thereabouts at ten o'clock tomorrow morning." LeWinter made no reply and registered no expression, no doubt because he'd no expressions left to register. "For an eminent judge you do keep odd company, LeWinter."

It was a measure of LeWinter's mental distress that comprehension came so slowly. He said in a dull voice: "You were the man who was here last night?"

"Yes." Ryder nodded to Jeff. "And this is Perkins. Remember Perkins? Patrolman Ryder. My son. Unless you're blind and deaf you must know that your friend Morro holds two of our family captive. One of them, my daughter—my son's sister—has been wounded. We feel kindly disposed to you. Well, LeWinter, apart from being as corrupt as all hell, a lecherous old goat, a traitor and accessory to murder, you're also a patsy, a sucker, a fall guy, scapegoat—call it what you will. You were conned, LeWinter, just as you thought you were conning Donahure and Miss Ivanov and Hartman. Used as a red herring to set up a nonexistent Russian connection.

"Only two things I want to know: who gave you something and to whom did you give something? Who gave you the money, the code book, the instructions to hire Miss Ivanov and to obtain the names and addresses of the now missing twenty-six men—and to whom did *you* give the names and addresses?"

LeWinter eventually registered an expression: he clamped his lips shut. Jeff winced as his father stepped forward, his expression, or lack of it, not changing, a gun swinging in his hand. LeWinter shut his eyes, flung up a protective forearm, stepped quickly back, caught his heel in a throw rug and fell heavily, striking the back of his head against a chair. He lay on the floor for ten seconds, perhaps longer, then slowly sat up. He looked dazed, as if having difficulty in relating himself to the circumstances in which he found himself and he was clearly not acting.

He said in a croaking voice: "I've got a bad heart." Looking at and listening to him it was impossible to doubt it.

"I'll cry tomorrow. Meantime, you think your heart will last out long enough to let you get to your feet?" Slowly, shaking, using both a chair and a table, LeWinter got to his unsteady feet. He still had to hang on to the table for support. Ryder remaind unmoved. He said. "The man who gave you all those things. The man to whom you gave the names. Was it the same man?"

"Call my doctor." LeWinter was clutching his chest. "God's sake, I've already *had* two heart attacks." His face was registering an expression now. It was contorted in fear and pain; he clearly felt, and was probably right, that his life was in mortal danger and was begging to have it saved. Ryder regarded him with the dispassionate eye of a medieval headsman.

"I'm glad to hear it." Jeff looked at him in something close to horror but Ryder had eyes only for LeWinter. "Then I'll have nothing on my conscience if you die and there won't be a mark on you when the mortuary wagon comes to collect you. Was it the same man?"

"Yes." A barely audible whisper.

"The same man as called from Bakersfield?"

"Yes."

"What's his name?"

"I don't know." Ryder half lifted his gun. LeWinter looked at him in defeat and despair and repeated: "I don't know. I don't know."

Jeff spoke for the first time and his voice was urgent. "He *doesn't* know."

"I believe him." Ryder hadn't looked away from LeWinter. "Describe this man."

"I can't."

"Or won't."

"He wore a hood. Before God, he wore a hood."

"If Donahure got ten thousand dollars, then you got a lot more. Probably a great deal more. Give him a receipt?"

"No." LeWinter shuddered. "Just said if I would break my word he would break my back. He could have it done too. Biggest man I ever saw."

"Hal!" Ryder paused, seemed to relax, smiled briefly and went on far from encouragingly: "He could still come and do it. Look at all the trouble it would save the law and the prison hospital." He produced a pair of handcuffs and snapped them on LeWinter's wrists.

The judge's voice was weak and lacked conviction. "You have no arrest warrant."

"Don't be simple-minded and don't make me laugh. I don't want any vertebrae snapping. I don't want you getting on the wrong phone. I don't want any escape attempt. And I don't want any suicide." He looked at the photograph he still held. "I'll be a long time forgetting. I want to see you rot in San Quentin." He led him toward the door, stopped and looked at Parker and Jeff. "Observe, if you will. I never laid a finger on him."

Jeff said: "Major Dunne will never believe it. Neither do I."

10

"You used us!" Burnett's face was white and bitter and he was shaking with such uncontrollable anger that his Glenfiddich was slopping over onto the floor of Morro's study, a shocking waste of which he was uncharacteristically oblivious. "You double-crossed us! You evil wicked bastard! A beautiful job, wasn't it, the way you spliced together our recordings and your own recording?"

Morro raised an admonitory finger. "Come, now, Professor. This helps no one. You really must learn to control yourself."

"Why the hell should he?" Schmidt's fury was as great as Burnett's but he had it under better control. All five physicists were there, together with Morro, Dubois and two guards. "We're not thinking just about our good names, our reputations. We're thinking about lives, maybe thousands of them, and if those lives are lost we're going to be held responsible. Morally at least. Every viewer, every listener, every reader in the state is going to be convinced that the hydrogen device you left off the coast is in the one and a half range. We know damn well it's in the three and a half. But because people will believe—they can't help believing—that it was all part of the same recording they're going to imagine that what you said was said with our tactic approval. You—you monster! Why did you do it?"

"Effect." Morro was unruffled. "Very elementary psychology. The detonation of this three and a half megaton device is going to have rather spectacular consequences and I want people to say to themselves: If this is the effect of a mere one and half megaton what in the name of heaven will the cataclysmic effects of thirty-five megatons be like? It will lend persuasive weights to my demands, don't you think? In the climate of terror all things are possible."

"I can believe anything of you," Burnett said. He looked at the shattered wreck of what had once been Willi Aachen. "Anything. Even that you are prepared to put thousands of lives at risk in order to achieve a psychological effect. You can have no idea what this *tsunami* will be like, what height it will reach, whether or not the Newport-Inglewood fault will trigger an earthquake. And you don't care. The effect is all."

"I think you exaggerate, Professor. I think that, where height is concerned, people will leave a very considerable margin of safety between the water levels I suggested and the worst they can fear. As for the Newport-Inglewood fault, only a madman would remain in the area at ten o'clock tomorrow morning. I do not visualize throngs of people heading for the Hollywood Park race track—if they head at that time of the morning, which I don't know. I think your fears are mainly groundless."

"Mainly! Mainly! You mean only a few thousand may drown?"

"I have no cause to love American people." Morro still maintained his monolithic calm. "They have not exactly been kind to mine."

There was a brief silence, then Healey said in a low voice: "This is even worse than I feared. Race, religion, politics, I don't know. The man's a zealot, a fanatic."

"He's nuts." Burnett reached for the bottle.

"Judge LeWinter wishes to make a voluntary statement," Ryder said.

"Does he now?" Dunne peered at the trembling fearful figure, a pale and almost unimaginable shadow of the imposing figure who had so long dominated the courts. "Is that the case, Judge?"

Ryder was impatient. "Sure it is."

"Look, Sergeant, I was asking the judge."

"We were there," Parker said. "Jeff and I. There was no coercion, no force, the only time Sergeant Ryder touched him was to put on handcuffs. We wouldn't perjure ourselves, Major Dunne."

"You wouldn't." He turned to Delage. "Next door. I'll take his statement in a minute."

"One moment before he goes," Ryder said. "Any word about Hartman?"

Dunne permitted himself his first smile. "For once, some luck. Just came in. Hartman, it seems, has been living out there for some years. With his widowed sister, which accounts for the fact that his name was not in the phone book. Didn't spend much time there until a year or so ago. Traveled a lot. You'd never guess what his business is—well, was, till last year."

"Oil rigs."

Dunne said without heat: "Damn you, Ryder, you spoil a man's simplest pleasures. Yes. Boss roustabout. First-class record. How did you know?"

"I didn't. Who were his sponsors—you know, character endorsers?"

"Two prominent local businessmen and—well?"

"Donahure and LeWinter."

"Indeed."

Ryder looked at LeWiner. "You and Hartman made up that list of drillers and engineers together, you from your court cases and extensive briefs from the oil companies, Hartman from his field experience?"

LeWinter said nothing.

"Well, at least he doesn't deny it. Tell me, LeWinter, was it his job to recruit those men?"

"I don't know."

"To kidnap them?"

"I don't know."

"Well, then, to contact them, one way or another?"

"Yes."

"And deliver them?"

"I suppose so."

"Yes or no."

LeWinter gathered together the shreds of his dignity and turned to Dunne. "I am being subjected to harassment."

"If that's what you choose to call it," Dunne said unsympathetically. "Proceed, Sergeant."

"Yes or no?"

"Yes, damn you, yes."

"So, to be obvious, he must have known where to deliver those men after recruitment, voluntary or not. So, assuming it *was* Morro who was responsible for their disappearance, Hartman had a direct line to Morro or knew how to contact him. You must agree with that."

LeWinter sat down in a chair. He looked more like a cadaver than ever. "If you say so."

"And, of course, you and Donahure had the same line."

"No!" The denial was immediate and almost vehement.

"Well." Ryder was approving. "That's more like it."

Dunne said: "You believe him? That he had no line on Morro?"

"Sure. If he had, he'd be dead by now. A sweet lad, this Morro. Even playing the cards close to the chest he never lets his left hand know what the right is doing. Only Hartman knew. Morro thought that Hartman was totally in the clear. How was he to know, how was anyone to guess, that I'd trace him because of the alarm linking LeWinter's safe and Hartman's office? Morro certainly knew nothing about that. If he did, he'd never have exposed LeWinter and Donahure by planting misleading evidence on them. But Morro had taken no chances. He'd given strict orders to both LeWinter and Donahure that if anyone got a line on Hartman, the only man who had a line to him, then Hartman was to be eliminated. It's really all so simple, isn't it?" He looked consideringly at LeWinter, then back at Dunne. "Remove that pillar of justice, will you? He makes me sick."

When he'd gone, Dunne said: "A fair morning's work. I underestimated you, Sergeant Ryder. Not breaking his neck, I mean. I'm beginning to wonder if I could have done the same."

"You're either born with a heart of gold or you aren't. Any word from the boss man—Barrow, isn't it?—about what kind of bombs this Professor Aachen was designing when Morro snatched him?"

"I phoned him. He said he'd contact the AEC and call back. He's not a man to waste time. No reply from him yet. He was curious why we wanted to find out."

"Don't rightly know myself. I said I thought Morro was trying to mislead us, that's all. What you call an outside chance of nothing. And speaking of Morro—there wouldn't be any word from Manila?"

Dunne looked at his watch, then in a quietly exasperated patience at Ryder. "You've been gone exactly one hour and five minutes. Manila, I would remind you, is not just a couple of blocks down the road. Would there be anything else?"

"Well, since you're offering." Dunne momentarily closed his eyes. "Carlton's friend back in Illinois mentioned a very big man in the group of weirdos Carlton was flirting with. LeWinter has just mentioned, in a very very scared voice, a similar person who's threatened to break his back. Could be one and the same man. There can't be many eighty inchers around."

"Eighty inchers?"

"Six foot eight. That's what Carlton's pal said. Shouldn't be difficult to check whether anyone of that size has been charged or convicted at some time in this state. Nor should it be very difficult to find if such a character is a member of any of the oddball organizations in California. You can't *hide* a man that size and apparently this person doesn't go to much trouble to keep hidden. And then there's the question of helicopters."

"Ah."

"Not just any helicopter. A special helicopter. It would be nice if you could trace it."

"A trifle." Dunne was being heavily sarcastic. "First, there are more helicopters in this state than there are in any comparable region on earth. Second, the FBI is stretched to its limits——"

"Stretched to its limits! Look, Major, I'm in no mood for light humor this morning. Eight thousand agents stretched to their limits and what have they achieved? Zero. I could even ask what they are doing and the answer could be the same. When I said a special helicopter, I meant a very very special helicopter. The one that delivered this atom bomb to Yucca Flat. Or have your eight thousand agents already got that little matter in hand?"

"Explain."

Ryder turned to his son. "Jeff, you've said you know that area. Yucca and Frenchman's Flats."

"I've been there."

"Would a vehicle leave tracks up there?"

"Sure. Not everywhere. There's a lot of rock. But there's also shingle and rubble and sand. Chances are good, yes."

"Now then, Major. Would any of the eight thousand have been checking on tracks—trucks, cars, dune buggies—in the area of the crater—those, that is, that they didn't obliterate in their mad dash to the scene of the crime?"

"I wasn't there myself. Delage?" Delage picked up a phone. "Helicopters? An interesting speculation?"

"I think so. And I also think that if I were Morro that is the way I'd have dumped that hydrogen bomb in the Pacific. Cuts out all this tricky—and maybe attention-catching business—of trucking the bomb to the coast and then transferring it to a boat."

Dunne was doubtful. "There's still an awful lot of helicopters in the state."

"Let's limit it to the communes, the oddballs, the disenchanted."

"With a road transport system like we've got, who would want——?"

"Let's limit it to the mountains. Remember, we'd more or less decided that Morro and his friends have sought out high ground."

"Well, the more extreme the group, the higher they tend to go. I suppose some would require a chopper to get any place. But helicopters come expensive. They'd be hired on an hourly basis and you could hardly persuade a hired pilot to carry a hydrogen bomb—"

"Maybe the pilot isn't hired. Nor the helicopter. Then there's the matter of a truck. Trucks. For the transport of weapons-grade material—the stuff taken from San Ruffino."

Dunne said: "You have that, Leroy?" Leroy nodded and, like Delage, reached for a telephone.

"Thanks." Ryder pondered briefly. "That's all. See you around—some time this afternoon."

Jeff looked at his watch. "Don't forget. Forty-five minutes. Morro will be on the air with his terms or demands or blackmail or whatever."

"Probably not worth listening to. Anyway, you can tell me all about it."

"Where are you going?"

"Public library. The study of contemporary history. I've fallen way behind in my reading."

"I see." Jeff watched the door swing to behind Ryder, then looked at Dunne. "I don't see. He's all right?"

Dunne was thoughtful. "If *he* isn't, what about us?"

Ryder arrived home some ninety minutes later to find Jeff and Parker drinking beer in front of the television. Ryder seemed in remarkably good spirits. He wasn't smiling broadly, far less laughing, nor was he cracking any jokes, for that was not his way. But for a man with two of his family held hostage and the threat of being drowned and vaporized far from being an impossibility, he was bafflingly composed and relaxed. He looked at the TV screen where literally hundreds of small craft, some with sails raised, were milling about in hopeless confusion, traveling at apparent random and ramming each other with a frequency that was matched only by blind determination. It was an enclosed harbor with half a dozen piers thrusting out toward a central channel: the room to maneuver was minimal, the chaos absolute.

"Wow," Ryder said. "This is something. Like Trafalgar or Jutland. Those were very confused sea battles too."

"Dad." Jeff was heroically patient. "That's Marina del Rey in Los Angeles. The yachtsmen are trying to leave."

"I know the place. The boys of the California Yacht Club and the Del Rey Yacht Club displaying their unusal nautical composure, not to say stoicism. At this rate they'll take a week to sort themselves out. What's the great rush? Incidentally, this will pose a problem for Morro. This must be happening at every harbor in Los Angeles. He said any vessel moving into the area between Santa Cruz Island and Santa Catalina would result in the detonation of the bomb. A couple of hours and there will be a couple of thousand craft in those waters. Careless of Morro. Anybody could have foreseen this."

Parker said: "According to the announcer, nobody intends to go anywhere near there. They're going to use the Santa Barbara and San Pedro channels and go as far north and south on the coast as possible."

"Lemmings. Even a small boat can ride out a tidal wave at sea. Not much more than a fast-traveling ripple, really. It's only when it reaches shallow water or estuaries that it starts to pile up into what people regard as a tidal wave. Why all this confusion, anyway?"

"Panic," Parker said. "The owners of smaller crafts are trying to lift them out of the water onto trailers and get them away but there are facilities available for only a few per cent at a time and those are so overloaded they keep breaking down. Diesel and gasoline supplies are almost exhausted and those that have been fueled are so hemmed in by boats looking for fuel that they can't get out. And then, of course, there are craft taking off under full power with their mooring lines still attached." Parker shook his head sadly. "I don't think urban Californians are really a sea-going race."

"That's nothing," Jeff said. "We're supposed to be *the* automobile race. You'd never know it. They've just been showing us street scenes in Santa Monica and Venice. Just a land-based version of what we're seeing here. Biggest traffic jams ever. Cars being used like tanks to batter a way through. Drivers jumping from their cars and knocking each other silly. Incredible."

"It would be the same the world over," Ryder said. "I'll bet Morro's glued to his screen in ecstasy. And everybody heading east, of course. City fathers issued any instructions yet?"

"Not that we've heard of."

"They will. Give them time. They're like all politicians. They'll wait to see what the majority of the people are doing then go ahead and tell them to do what they're already doing. Any food in this house?"

"What?" Jeff, understandably, was momentarily off balance. "Yes. Sandwiches in the kitchen."

"Thanks." Ryder turned to go then stopped abruptly as something on the screen caught his eye. "What an extraordinary coincidence. We can only hope that if it is a good omen then it's for us and not for Morro."

Jeff said: "We can wait forever."

"See that dock at the lower right of your screen? It's to the Southeast. The broad one. Unless I'm totally wrong, that's the source of all our troubles."

"*That* dock?" Jeff stared his incredulity.

"The name of it. Mindanao."

A minute later Ryer was taking his ease in an armchair, sandwich in one hand, beer in the other, half an eye on the screen. He focused both eyes on the screen and said: "That's interesting."

The picture was not without its interest. Three private planes, all twin-engined, had clearly been engaged in a multiple collision. The broken wing tip of one rested on the ground. The undercarriage of a second had crumpled while a lazy plume of smoke arose from the third.

"Land, sea and air." Ryder shook his head. "I know that place. Clover Field in Santa Monica. Apparently the air traffic controller has hightailed it for the Sierras."

"Honest to God, Dad!" Jeff was trying to contain himself. "You're the most infuriating, exasperating character that's ever walked. Haven't you got anything to say about Morro's ultimatum?"

"Well, no."

"Jesus!"

"Be reasonable. I've seen, heard and read nothing about it."

"Jesus!" Jeff repeated and fell into silence. Ryder looked inquiringly at Parker, who clearly steeled himself for the task.

"Morro was on time. As always. This time he really was economical with his words. I'll make it even more economical. His ultimatum was simply this. Give me the locations and all the operating wave bands of all your radar stations on both the East and West coasts, your cruising radar bombers both here and in NATO and in all your spy satellites or I'll pull the plug."

"He said that, did he?"

"Well, quite a bit more, but that was the gist of it."

"Bull. Poppycock. I told you he wouldn't be worth listening to. I'd

thought better of Morro than that. Babies along the Potomac and the Pentagon spinning around like a high-speed centrifuge.''

"You don't believe it.''

"If that's what you gather from my reactions, you're right.''

"But look, Dad——''

"Look nothing. Rubbish. Maybe I'd better revise that snap judgment on
Morro. Maybe he was well aware that he was making an impossible demand.
Maybe he was well aware that it wouldn't be met. Maybe he didn't want it
to be met. But just try convincing the American public—especially that
section of it represented by this state—of that. It will take a long, long time
and a long, long time is the one thing we don't have.''

"Impossible demand?'' Jeff said carefully.

"Let me think.'' Ryder chewed some more and drank some more while
he thought. "Three things occur and none of them make sense and wouldn't
to the Pentagon, which can't possibly be as retarded as the New York and
Washington columnists say it is. First off, what's to prevent the Pentagon
feeding him a long and highly convincing rigmarole of completely misleading information? What would lead him to suspect that it was misleading?
And even if he did, how on earth could he possibly set about checking on
the accuracy of the information? It's impossible. Second, the Pentagon
would probably and quite cheerfully see California being wiped out rather
than give away our first defense against nuclear attack. Third, if he's in a
position to wipe out Los Angeles and San Francisco—and we must assume
that he is—what's to prevent him repeating the dose to New York, Chicago
and Washington itself and so on until he achieved by direct means what he
would achieve by indirect means by blinding our radar? It makes no kind of
sense at all. But it all fits in.''

Jeff digested this in silence. Parker said slowly: "It's all very well for you
to sit there in—what kind of judgment do you call it?''

"Olympian?'' Ryder said helpfully.

"That's it. It's all very well for you to sit there in Olympian judgment
but you'd made up that crafty mind in advance that you weren't going to
believe a word Morro said and you were also certain that he wouldn't say
what you were convinced he couldn't say.''

"Very shrewd, Sergeant Parker. Confusing, mind you, but shrewd.''

"And you've just said it all fits in.''

"I did say that.''

"You know something we don't know?''

"I don't know any facts that you don't know, except for those I get from
reading about earthquakes and contemporary history, a practice for which
Jeff here thinks I need the services of a head shrinker.''

"I never said——''

"You don't have to speak to say something.''

"I have it,'' Parker said. "All good detectives come up with a theory. You
have a theory?''

"Well, in all due modesty——''

"Modesty? So now the sun sets in the east. I don't even have to take time
out for a reflective pause. Mindanao?''

"Mindanao.''

When Ryder had finished, Parker said to Jeff: "Well, what do you make
of that?''

"I'm still trying to assimilate it all.'' Jeff spoke in a kind of dazed protest. "I mean, I've just heard it. You've got to give me time to think."

"Come, come, boy. First impressions."

"Well, I don't see any holes in it. And the more I think—and if you would give me more time I could think more—the fewer holes I can see. I think it *could* be right."

"Look at your old man," Parker said. "Can you see any sign of 'could' in his face?"

"That's just smirking. Well, I can't see any way in which it must be wrong." Jeff thought some more then took the plunge. "It makes sense to me."

"There you are now, John." Parker sounded positively jovial. "As near a compliment as you'll ever be likely to extract from your son. It makes a lot of sense to me. Come, gentlemen, let's try it out for size on Major Dunne."

Dunne didn't even bother saying it made sense. He turned to Leroy and said: "Get me Mr. Barrow. And have the helicopter stand by." He rubbed his hands briskly. "Well, well. Looks as if you're going to ruffle a few feathers in Los Angeles, Sergeant."

"You go and ruffle them. Top brass rub me the wrong way. Your boss seems almost human but that's more than I can say for Mitchell. You know as much about it now as I do and I'm only guessing anyway. The person I would like to see is Professor Benson. If you could fix that, I'd be grateful."

"Delighted. If you fly north."

"Blackmail." Ryder didn't sound too heated.

"Of course." Dunne regarded him over steepled fingers. "Seriously. Several things. First off, we could kill two birds with one stone—Pasadena is only ten minutes' helicopter hop from our offices up there. Again, if you don't turn up, both Barrow and Mitchell will automatically assume that you lack the courage of your own convictions. *You* can talk to them in a way that would get me fired on the spot. They can probe more deeply than I've done and ask questions that I couldn't answer—I know you've told me all that you regard as the essentials but there must be details that you consider irrelevant at the moment. What's the point in staying here—there's nothing more you can accomplish here and you know it—to convince the mandarins of your belief would be a major accomplishment." Dunne smiled. "Would you be so heartless as to deprive me of the pleasure of this—ah—encounter?"

"He's just scared of the big bad wolves," Jeff said.

Ryder smiled.

Like all such rooms designed to give its occupants a proper sense of their own importance, the conference room was suitably impressive. It had the only mahogany-paneled walls in the building, behung with pictures of individuals who looked like the Ten Most Wanted but were, in fact, past and present directors and senior administrators of the FBI. It held the only mahogany oval table in the building, one that gleamed with that refulgent splendor rarely found among tables that have seen an honest day's work. Around it were grouped the only twelve leather and brass-studded chairs in the building. Before each chair was a leather-cornered blotter, indispensable for doodling but otherwise wholly superfluous, a brass tray for pens and pencils, a water jug and glass; the comprehensively stocked bar lay behind a sliding wooden panel. The over-all effect was slightly dimmed by the two stenographer's chairs that faced a battery of red, white and black telephones; those were covered in plastic leather. There were no stenographers there that afternoon; this was a top-secret meeting of the gravest national importance and the faces of most of the twelve seated men accurately reflected their awareness of this.

Nobody occupied the rounded head of the table: Barrow and Mitchell each sat an equidistant foot from the center line so that there could be no claimant for the chairman's position. The heavens might be falling but that would have to wait until protocol had been served. Each had three senior aides at the table—none of the six had been introduced—and all of them had brief cases and important-looking papers on the blotters before them. The fact that it had been deemed necessary to call the meeting clearly indicated that the contents of those papers were worthless, but at the conference table one has to have papers to shuffle or one is nothing. Mitchell opened the meeting; a toss of a coin had decided that.

He said: "To begin with I must request, in the politest possible way, that Sergeant Parker and Patrolman Ryder withdraw."

Ryder said: "Why?"

Nobody queried Mitchell's orders. He bent a cold eye on Ryder. "Given the opportunity, Sergeant, I was about to explain. This meeting is on the highest level of national security and those are not sworn men. Moreover, they are junior police officers both of whom have resigned their positions and therefore have no official capacity—they have not even been assigned to this investigation. That, I think, is a reasonable attitude."

Ryder considered Mitchell for a few moments, then looked across at Dunne, who sat opposite him. He said, in a tone of exaggerated disbelief: "You brought me all the way up here just to listen to this pompous and arrogant rubbish?"

Dunne looked at his fingernails. Jeff looked at the ceiling. Barrow looked at the ceiling. Mitchell looked mad. His tone would have frozen mercury.

"I don't think I can be hearing properly, Sergeant."

"Then why don't you vacate your position to someone who can? I spoke clearly enough. I didn't want to come here. I know your reputation. I don't give a damn about it. If you throw Mr. Parker and my son out then, by the same token, you have to throw me out. You say they have no official capacity—neither have you. You just muscled your way in. They have as much right to order you out as you have to order them out. You have no official jurisdiction inside the United States. If you can't understand that and stop antagonizing people who are doing an honest job of work, then it's time you yielded your chair to someone who can."

Ryder looked leisurely around the table. No one appeared disposed to make any comment. Mitchell's face was frozen. Barrow's was set in an expression of calmly judicial impartiality, a remarkable tribute to the man's self-control. Had he been eavesdropping and alone he would unquestionably have been rolling around holding his sides.

"So, having established the fact that there are no fewer than seven of us here in an unofficial capacity, let's look at the investigation. Mr. Parker and my son have already achieved a very considerable amount, as Major Dunne will confirm. They have helped solve the murder of a county sheriff, put a corrupt police chief behind bars on a charge of murder and also put behind bars, on a charge of accessory to murder, a judge widely regarded as the likely Chief Justice of the state supreme court. All three, including the murdered man, were deeply involved in the business at hand—this has provided us with extremely valuable information.''

Mitchell had the grace to part his lips about half an inch. Barrow remained without expression. Clearly he'd been briefed by Dunne; equally clear was the fact that he hadn't bothered to pass on his information.

"And what has the CIA achieved? I'll tell you. It has succeeded in making a laughingstock of itself in general and its director in particular, not to mention uselessly wasting the taxpayer's money by sending its agents to pussyfoot around Geneva in search of so-called secret information that has been in the public domain for two years. Apart from that, what? An educated guess would say zero.''

Barrow coughed. "Aren't you being needlessly intransigent?'' He could have put more reproof into his voice if he'd tried, even a little.

"Needless intransigence is the only language some people seem to understand.''

Mitchell's voice surfaced through layers of cracked ice. "Your point is taken, Sergeant. You have come to teach us how to do our jobs.''

Ryder wasn't quite through with being intransigent or letting Mitchell off the hook. "I am not a sergeant. I'm a private citizen and as such beholden to no one. I can't teach the CIA anything—I wouldn't know how to go about subverting foreign governments or assassinating their presidents. I can't teach the FBI anything. All I want is a fair hearing but it's really a matter of indifference whether I get it or not.'' His eyes were looking at Mitchell's. "You can shut up and let me say what I've been brought here to say, against my better judgment, or not. I'd as soon leave. I find the atmosphere here uncomfortable, not to say hostile, and Major Dunne has all the essentials.''

Mitchell said in a toneless voice: "We will hear you out.''

"I don't like that expression either.'' Barrow winced. Despite his antipathy toward Mitchell, it was not hard to guess that, even although momentarily, he was putting himself in the other's position. "It's the term used by the chairman of the board when he's giving a carpeted executive the chance to justify himself before being fired.''

"Please.'' Barrow turned the palms of his hands upward. "We get the point that you're a plain speaker. Please take our point that you haven't been brought here for nothing. We will listen carefully.''

"Thank you.'' Ryder wasted no time on preamble. "You've all seen the streets around this block. As we came into your pad on the roof we saw a hundred streets like it. Blocked. Choked. The people are running scared. I don't blame them. If I lived here, I'd be running scared too. They believe that Morro is going to trigger off this bomb at ten tomorrow morning. So do I. I also believe that he will set off or is prepared to set off the other ten nuclear devices he claims to have. What I don't for a moment believe in is his demand. It's utter foolishness; he must know it is and we should recognize it for what it is—an empty threat, a meaningless demand that can't be met.''

"Perhaps you should know,'' Barrow said. "Just before you arrived word came through that protests have been lodged by the Kremlin and Peking, and by their embassies in Washington, crying to high heaven that they are as innocent as the driven snow of this monstrous accusation against them— no one has accused them of anything but one gets their point—and that it's all part of a warmongering capitalist plot. First time in living memory that they've totally agreed with each other on anything.''

"Not just the usual standard denial?''

"No. They're hopping mad.''

"Don't blame them. The suggestion is ludicrous."

"You're sure the fact that you already seem to have discounted evidence pointing to some Communist connection has not influenced your thinking in this?"

"I'm sure. So are you."

Mitchell said: "I'm not so sure."

"You wouldn't be. Last thing you do every night is look under your bed."

Mitchell just stopped short of grinding his teeth. "If not that, what?" The words were innocuous enough but their tone left no doubt that he was prepared to fight to the death for his disbelief of every word Ryder was about to say.

"Bear with me. It all seems to start with the Philippines. I'm sure you all know how it is out there and I'm sure the last thing I am is a specialist in foreign affairs but I've been reading all about it in the library just a couple of hours ago. I'll briefly recap what I read, as much for my own sake as anybody else's.

"The Philippines are in a financial mess. Hugely ambitious development plans, mounting internal and external debts, heavy military expenditures—they're strapped. But like a good many other countries they know what to do when the kitty's empty—put the arm on Uncle Sam. And they're in an excellent position to apply pressure.

"The Philippines are the keystone of America's Pacific military strategy and the huge Seventh Fleet anchorage at Subic Bay and the strategically crucial Air Force base are regarded by the Pentagon as being indispensable and well worth the rent—many people regard it as a cross between ransom and extortion money—that they demand.

"The south of the Philippines—the island of Mindanao—is inhabited by Muslims. You all know that. Unlike Christianity, the Muslim religion has no moral laws against the killing of mankind in general—just against the killing of Muslims, period. The concept of a holy war is an integral part of their lives and this is what they're doing right now—carrying out a holy crusade against President Marcos and his predominantly Catholic government. They regard it as a religious war being waged by an oppressed people. Whether it's a justifiable war or not is—well, it's none of my business. In any event, it is an intensely bitter war. I think all this is well known.

"What is, perhaps, not quite so well known is that they feel almost equally bitter toward the United States. It's not hard to understand. Although Congress raises its hand in holier-than-thou horror at Marcos' long-term track record on civil liberties, they still cheerfully, as I said, ante up the rent for our bases to the tune of several hundred million dollars a year in military aid, no small amount of which is put to what the Philippine Government regards as being perfectly good use in crushing the Muslims.

"Even less known is the fact that the Muslims aren't all that much fonder of Russia, China and Vietnam. Not, as far as is known, that those countries have caused them any harm—it's just that the Philippine Government has established cordial—and diplomatic—relations with those three countries and countries that reciprocate the Philippine Government's overtures are automatically classified by the Mindanaon Muslims as belonging to the enemy camp.

"What the Muslims desperately lack is arms. Provided that they were armed to the same standards as the government's well-equipped eighty field battalions—well-equipped, mainly, by the courtesy of Uncle Sam—they could give a good account of themselves. Until last year what little supplies they received came from Libya—until Imelda Marcos went there and sweet-talked Colonel Gadhafi and his foreign minister, Ali Tureiki, into cutting off the Mindanaon Muslims' last lifeline.

"So what were they to do? They couldn't obtain or manufacture their own arms in the Philippines. Even if they didn't hate America there was no way the Americans would supply arms to insurgents against the Philippine Government. They weren't even speaking to the Communists. And their own fellow Muslims had turned against them. So the Muslim rebels came up with the only answer. Any big armament firm in the world will supply arms to anyone—if the money is right and on the barrelhead, irrespective of race, creed and politics. Why shouldn't they? Governments do it all the time—America, Britain and France are the worst offenders. All they had to do was to find the cash to put on the barrelhead.

"The solution was simple. Let the enemy provide. In this case the unfortunate provider was to be Uncle Sam. All the better if you can wound him in the process. Rob him blind, hurt him and—to kill two birds with one stone—discredit the U.S.S.R. and China by using them as a smoke screen. That's what I believe is happening in California here and now. And the frightening thing about it is that we have to remember that the Koran gives a Muslim a conscience-free hand to knock off anyone who isn't a Muslim. And if your conscience is free, what's the difference between one and one million? If all's free in love and war, what's it like in a holy war?"

"It's an interesting hypothesis," Mitchell said. His tone implied that he was a courteous man tolerently listening to another theorizing about how the moon is made of green cheese. "You have evidence to back this up, of course?"

"Nothing that you would regard as positive evidence. Elimination, circumstantial evidence, all perhaps better than nothing. In the first place it's the only theory that explains the situation in which we find ourselves now."

"But you said they're after cash. If that's so, why didn't they blackmail the government *for* cash?"

"I don't know. I have the glimmerings of an idea but I know what you would do with a glimmering. Second, speech experts place Morro's area of origin as southeast Asia—which includes the Philippines. Third, it is certain—there is no question about this—that he is in criminal association with Carlton, the supposedly kidnaped San Ruffino deputy of security, and there is also no question that Carlton has been in Manila several times. Fourth, if Morro has a weakness, it seems to be that it tickles his ironic fancy to give himself an alias associated with the operation he is conducting. The first stage of his operation here was concerned with nuclear fuel so he may well have purposely chosen to call himself after the nuclear station at Morro Bay. Fifth, that's not the only name pronounced that way—there's another in the Philippines, called Moro Gulf. Sixth, this is in Mindanao and is the focus of the Muslim insurgent movement. Seventh, last year, Moro Gulf was the scene of the greatest natural disaster in Philippine history. An earthquake at the mouth of the gulf—the interior bay is crescent-shaped—caused a gigantic tidal wave that took over five thousand lives and left seventy thousand homeless, all along the shores. A tidal wave we're promised for tomorrow. I'll take long odds that we'll be promised an earthquake on Saturday. I think that this may be Morro's Achilles' heel. I think it would mightily tickle his fancy to have his name associated with nuclear weapons, tidal waves and earthquakes."

"You call this evidence?" Mitchell's tone was nasty, but it could have been nastier.

"No proof, I agree. Indicators, that's all. But they're all important. In police work you can't look anywhere until you have *some* indication of where to look. You start hunting where the hound dog points. Put it another way. I'm looking for a lodestone and I set down a compass. The needle swings and steadies. That *might* indicate the direction of the lodestone. I put down a second compass and it points in the same direction. That could be coincidence, although a remarkable one. I put five more and they *all* point the same way. I stop thinking about coincidences. I have seven needles here and they all point toward Mindanao." Ryder paused. "I'm convinced. I understand, of course, that you gentlemen would require some sort of proof."

Barrow said: "I think I'm convinced if only for the reason that I can't see any needle pointing any other damned way. But some proof would be nice. What would you call proof, Mr. Ryder?"

"For me, any one answer to any one of, oddly, seven questions." He took a sheet of paper from his pocket. "What is Morro's place of origin? Where can we locate a six-foot-eight giant who must be a senior lieutenant of Morro's? What kind of bomb did this Professor Aachen design? I think Morro lied about its dimensions for the simple reason that he didn't have to mention it at all." He looked reproachfully at Barrow and Mitchell. "I understand the AEC has put up the shutters on this one. If you two gentlemen can't make them open up, who can? Then I want to know if there are any private organizations up in the mountains using their own helicopters. Any using their own private vans. Major Dunne is working on those two. After that, I'd like to know if Morro is going to threaten us with an earthquake on Saturday. I've said I'm sure he is. Lastly, I'd like to know if the post office can discover whether there's a radiophone link between Bakersfield and a place called the Adlerheim."

"Adlerheim?" Mitchell had lost some of his intransigence: it was reasonable to assume that he hadn't become director because his aunt's cousin knew some stenographer in a CIA typing pool. "What's that?"

"I know it," Barrow said. "Up in the Sierra Nevada. Von Streicher's Folly, they call it, isn't it?"

"Yes. I think that's where we'll find Morro. Anyone mind if I smoke?"

Not only did nobody object, nobody even seemed to have heard his request. They were busy. They were busy studying the insides of their closed eyelids, or the papers before them, or infinity. Ryder was almost an inch down on his Gauloise before Barrow spoke.

"That's quite a thought, Mr. Ryder. Having heard what you've had to say so far I don't think anyone is going to dismiss it out of hand." He made a point of not looking at Mitchell. "Wouldn't you agree, Sassoon?"

Sassoon spoke for the first time. "I've heard enough not to make a fool of myself. You will, of course, have your pointers, Mr. Ryder." He smiled as he said it.

"None that you don't all have. In that rather cryptic note my wife left when she was kidnaped, she said that Morro referred to their destination as having bracing air and a place where they wouldn't get their feet wet. Mountains. It's been taken over by a group of Muslims, quite openly—this would be typical of Morro's effrontery—and his overconfidence. It's called the Temple of Allah or some such now. It's got official police protection to ensure its privacy—a fact which would again appeal to Morro's ironic—if warped—sense of humor. It's virtually impregnable to outside assault. It's close to Bakersfield, where LeWinter had a telephone contact. I should think the chances are high that they have a helicopter—we'll soon know. A guess, you might say, and too damned obvious. The clever investigator overlooks the obvious. Me, I'm stupid—I'd go for the obvious, which is the last thing that Morro would expect us to do.''

Barrow said: "You don't actually *know* this Morro?"

"Unfortunately, no."

"You seem to have got inside his mind pretty well. I only hope you haven't taken any wrong turnings."

Parker said in a mild tone: "He's quite good at getting inside minds, actually. No pun intended, but ask anyone inside. Ryder's put away more felons than any detective in this state."

"Let's hope his luck doesn't run out. That all, Mr. Ryder?"

"Yes. Two thoughts. When this is all over you might make out a citation to my wife. If she hadn't thought she'd seen a black eye patch and *suspected* there was something wrong with his hands we'd still be back in square one. We still don't know for certain if she was right. The second thought is just amusing and irrelevant except that it probably again has a bearing on Morro's twisted sense of humor. Anyone know why Von Streicher built the Adlerheim where he did?"

Nobody knew.

"I'll bet Morro did. Von Streicher had a phobia about tidal waves."

Nobody said anything because, for the moment, they had nothing to say. After some time, Barrow stirred and pressed a bell twice. The door opened, two girls entered and Barrow said: "We're thirsty." The girls moved to one wall and slid back a wooden panel.

A few minutes later Barrow laid down his glass. "I wasn't really thirsty. I just wanted time to think. Neither the time nor the scotch has helped any."

"We go for the Adlerheim?" Mitchell's aggression was in abeyance: this was just a doubtful suggestion put up for discussion.

"No." Ryder gave a negative shake of the head in a very positive way. "I think I'm right; I could be wrong. Either way I wouldn't give a damn about proof and legality and I don't think anyone else here would either. But it's both the hostages and the physical factor. You can't storm the place. I told you it's impregnable. If Morro's there he'll have it guarded like Fort Knox. If we did attack the place and there was armed resistance then we'd know for sure he's there. What then? You can't use tanks and artillery up a mountainside. Planes with rockets, missiles, bombs? What a lovely idea with thirty-five megatons of hydrogen bombs in there."

"It would be a bang," Mitchell said. He seemed almost human. "And what a bang. How many dead? Tens of thousands? Hundreds? Millions? With the radioactive fallout all over the western states? Yes, millions."

Ryder said: "Not to mention blasting a hole through the ozone layer."

"What?"

"Nothing."

"It's out of the question, anyway," Barrow said. "Only the Commander-in-Chief could authorize such an attack and whether he's motivated by political cynicism or humanity no President is going to let himself go down in history as the man directly responsible for the deaths of millions of his fellow citizens."

"That apart," Ryder said, "I'm afraid we're all missing the point, which is that those bombs will be triggered by radio wave and Morro will be sitting up there all the time with his thumb on the button. If he has the bombs sited—which he could well have by now—he has only to press that button.

They could be in transit—and he has still only to press that button. Even if he's sitting on top of the damn things he'd still do the same. It would be a splendid way to pay the Americans back for the billion or more dollars and military aid they've given Marcos' government to use to crush the Muslims. American lives are nothing to them and, in a holy war, neither are theirs. They can't lose—the gates of Paradise are standing wide.''

There was a long pause, then Sassoon said: ''It's getting a bit chilly in here. Anyone join me in a scotch or Bourbon or something?''

Everyone, it seemed, was conscious of a drop in the temperature. There was another, and equally long pause, then Mitchell said, almost plaintively: ''How do we get at those damn bombs?''

''You can't,'' Ryder said. ''I've had more time than you to think this out. Those bombs will be under constant surveillance all the time. Go anywhere near any of them and it'll blow up in your face. I wouldn't fancy having a three and a half megaton bomb blow up in my face.'' He lit another cigarette. ''Well, I don't know. No worry, really. In my vaporized state I wouldn't be likely to know much about it. Forget the bombs. We want to get to that button before Morro presses it.''

Barrow said: ''Infiltration?''

''How else?''

''How?''

''Using his overconfidence and colossal arrogance against him.''

''How?''

''How?'' Ryder showed his first irritaion. ''You forget that I'm just an unofficial interferer.''

''As far as I'm concerned—and, in these United States of ours, I'm the only one who *is* concerned—you're now a fully accredited, paid-up and charter member of the FBI.''

''Well, thanks very much.''

''How?''

''I wish to God I knew.''

The silence was profound. By and by Barrow turned to Mitchell. ''Well, what are we going to do?''

''That's the FBI all over.'' Mitchell was scowling heavily but not at anyone in particular. ''Always trying to beat us to it. I was about to ask you the same question.''

''I know what I'm going to do.'' Ryder pushed back his chair. ''Major Dunne, you will recall that you promised me a lift out to Pasadena.''

A knock came at the door and a girl entered, an envelope in her hand. She said: ''Major Dunne?'' Dunne stretched out an arm, took the envelope, withdrew a sheet of paper and read it. He looked across at Ryder.

''Cotabato,'' he said.

Ryder pulled his chair back in. Dunne rose, walked to the head of the table and handed the letter to Barrow, who read it, handed it across to Mitchell, waited until he had finished, took it back and began to read aloud.

''Manila. Chief of police, also countersigned by a General Huelva, whom I know. It says: 'Description referring to person called Morro exactly tallies with that of a wanted criminal well known to us. Confirm he has two badly damaged hands and the sight of only one eye. Injuries sustained when one of group of three participating in aborted attempt to blow up presidential holiday retreat. One accomplice—a man of enormous stature and known as Dubois—unscathed. The third, a small man, lost left hand. Shot way out.' '' He paused and looked at Ryder.

''A small world. Our large friend again. The other is probably the lad with the prosthetic appliance who put the arm on my daughter in San Diego.''

" 'Morro's real name is Amarak. Inquiry confirms our belief that he is in your country. Enforced exile. There is one million U.S. dollars on his head. Native of Cotabato, focal point for Muslim insurgents in Mindanao.

" 'Amarak is the head of the MNLF—Moro National Liberation Front.' ''

11

"ONE SOMETIMES despairs of mankind," Professor Alec Benson said sadly. "Here we are, twenty miles from the ocean, and still they go marching steadily east—if cars moving at an average of a mile per hour can be said to be marching. They're as safe from a tidal wave here as they would be if they lived in Colorado but don't suppose any of them intend stopping until they pitch camp atop the San Gabriel Mountains." He turned away from the window, picked up a cane and pressed a switch to illuminate a nine-by-eight wall chart of the state of California.

"Well, gentlemen, to our Earthquake Preventative Slip Program—EPSP. Where we have selected certain locations for drilling and why. The where and the why are really one and the same thing. As I explained last time, the theory, in essence, is that by injecting lubricating fluid along certain fault lines we will ease the frictional resistance between tectonic plates and so— hopefully—cause them to slide past each other with a minimum of fuss and bother—a series of tiny earthquakes at frequent intervals instead of major earthquakes at long intervals. If the frictional coefficient is allowed to build up until the lateral stress becomes intolerable then something has to go and one plate jerks forward, perhaps anything up to twenty feet, in relation to the other. That's when we have a big one. Our sole purpose—perhaps I should say our hope—is to release this frictional coefficient gradually." He tapped the chart with the cane. "I'll start from the bottom—the south.

"This is actually the first borehole we started digging, the first of what we call our trigger spots. It's in the Imperial Valley, between Imperial and El Centro. We had an earthquake here in 1915, 6.3 on the Richter scale; another in 1940, a fairly big one of 7.6; and a small one in 1966. This is the only known section of the San Andreas fault near the U.S.–Mexican border." He moved his cane.

"We've drilled this one here near Hemet. There was a heavy earthquake here in 1899—no seismological recordings of it—in the area of the Cajon Pass, another of 6.8 in 1918 in the same fracture—this is the San Jacinto fault.

"This third drill hole is the nearest to where we are now—in the San Bernardino area. Latest earthquake there was seventy years ago and that was only 6 on the scale. We have a strong feeling here that this may be a sleeper with a slip overdue—but that may be because we are living so close to the damn thing."

Barrow said: "What effects would such earthquakes have if they did occur? Big ones, I mean."

"Any one of the three would certainly make the citizens of San Diego unhappy, and the second and third would offer a direct threat to Los Angeles." He moved the pointer again. "The next borehole lies in a fault which *was* a sleeper until 1971—6.6 in the San Fernando Valley. We hope that easing the pressure here might take some of the strain off the Newport–Inglewood fault, which, as you know, lies directly under the city of Los Angeles and had its own earthquake of 6.3 in 1933. I say 'hope.' We don't know. We don't know how the two faults are connected. We don't even know *if* they're connected. There's an awful lot we don't know and is guesswork, hopefully inspired, probably not. But it's no guess that a big one there could hurt Los Angeles badly—after all, the community of Sylmar, the worst-hit area in the shock, actually lies inside the Los Angeles city boundaries.'' The point of the cane moved again.

"Tejon Pass. This one has us worried. Long overdue activity here and the last one—a hundred and twenty years ago—was a beauty, the strongest in Southern California history. Well, it wasn't as great as the massive earthquake that hit Owens Valley in 1873—that was the biggest in recorded California history—but we're a parochial lot hereabouts and don't regard Owens Valley as being in Southern California. A big slip here would very definitely give the Los Angelinos something to think about—if I knew about it in advance I, personally, would get out of town. Tejon Pass is on the San Andreas fault, and it's close by here, at Frazier Park by Fort Tejon, that the San Andreas and Garlock faults intersect. There's been no major earthquake in the Garlock that is known of—whether that recent small shake was caused by our friend Morro or not we have no means of telling—and none is expected—but then, no one expected the 1971 business in San Fernando.'' The cane moved on.

"Here we have our—let me see—sixth drilling hole. It's on the White Wolf fault. It was the scene——''

He broke off as the phone rang. One of his assistants answered, looked around the seated men. "Which one of you is Major Dunne, please?''

Dunne took the phone, listened briefly, thanked the caller and hung up. He said: "The Adlerheim has quite a transport fleet. Not one but two helicopters, two unmarked plain vans and a jeep.'' He smiled at Ryder. "Two more pointers you can tick off, Sergeant.'' Ryder nodded; if he experienced any satisfaction he didn't show it; more probably, he had been so convinced in advance of what Dunne had just said that the confirmation of his conviction hardly called for comment.

Benson said: "What's all this about pointers.''

"Routine investigative checks, Professor.''

"Ah. Ah, well, I suppose it's none of my business. I was saying—yes, the White Wolf—7.7, 1952, the biggest in Southern California since 1857. The epicenter was somewhere between Arvin and Tehachapi here.'' He paused and looked at Ryder. "You frown, Sergeant? Quite heavily, if I may say so.''

"Nothing, really, Professor. Passing thoughts. Please carry on.''

"Well. This is a very tricky area. It's all conjecture, really. Anything happening in the White Wolf could affect both the Garlock fault and the San Andreas at Tejon. We don't know. There could be a link with the Santa Ynez, Mesa and Channel Islands faults. Very attractive earthquake area, reports going back to the beginning of the nineteenth century, last big one at Lompoc in 1927. It's all so uncertain. Any major disturbance in the Santa Ynez area would certainly cause a major disturbance in Los Angeles.'' He shook his head. "Poor old Los Angeles.'' Benson wasn't smiling. "It's ringed by earthquake centers—apart from having its own private and personal one at Long Beach. Last time I saw you I talked about the monster earthquake. If it were to hit San Jacinto, San Bernardino, San Fernando, the White Wolf, Tejon Pass, Santa Ynez—or, of course, Long Beach itself—the Western Hemisphere would be one major city less. If our civilization vanishes and another arises, then that new one will be talking about Los Angeles as we today talk about the lost city of Atlantis.''

Barrow said: "You are in a jovial mood today, Professor."

"Alas, events happening around me and people asking me the questions do tend to make me less than my optimistic sunny self. Forgive me. Next, up here in the central San Andreas, we are digging an interesting hole between Cholame and Parkfield. We know we're smack on the San Andreas there. Very active area, lots of shaking and banging going on most of the time but, again ominously, no great earthquake has ever been recorded in this area. There was a pretty big one some way to the west, back in the eighties, at San Luis Obispo, which could have been caused by the San Andreas or the Nacimiento fault paralleling the coast west of the San Andreas.'' He smiled without any particular mirth. "A monster striking in either fault would almost certainly dump the Morro Bay nuclear reactor station into the sea.

"Farther north, we've drilled deep down between Hollister and San Juan Bautista, a few miles to the west, partly because this is another dormant area—again there have only been comparatively minor shakes in this area—and because it's just south of Hollister that the Hayward fault branches off to the right to go to the east of San Francisco Bay, cutting up through or close by Hayward, Oakland, Berkeley and Richmond then out under the San Pablo Bay. In Berkeley, the fault actually runs under the university football stadium, which can't be a very nice thought for the crowds of people who attend there regularly. There have been two very big earthquakes along this fault, in 1836 and 1868—until 1906 San Franciscans always referred to the latter as 'the great earthquake'—and it's there that we've drilled our ninth hole by Lake Temescal.

"The tenth one we put down at Walnut Creek in the Calaveras fault, which parallels the Hayward. Our suspicions about this fault are in the inverse proportion to what we know about it, which is almost zero."

Barrow said: "That makes ten and that, I take it, is all. You spoke a few minutes ago about poor old Los Angeles. How about poor old San Francisco?"

"To be thrown to the wolves, it would seem, the orphan left out in the snow. San Francisco is, geologically and seismologically, a city that waits to die. Frankly, we are terrified to tamper with anything up there. The Los Angeles area has had seven what you might call historic quakes that we know of; the Bay area has had sixteen and we have no idea in the world where the next, the monster, may hit. There was a suggestion—frankly, it was mine—that we sink a borehole near Searsville Lake. This is close by Stanford University, which had a bad time of it during the 1906 earthquake, and, more importantly, just where the Pilarcitos fault branches off from the San Andreas. The Pilarcitos, which runs into the Pacific some six miles south of the San Andreas, may, for all we know, be the true line of the San Andreas and certainly was some millions of years ago. Anyway, the 1906 shake ran through many miles of unpopulated hill regions. Since then, unscrupulous property developers have built virtual cities along both fault lines and the consequences of another 8-plus earthquake are too awful to contemplate. I suggested a possible easement there but certain vested interests in nearby Menlo Park were appalled at the very idea."

Barrow said: "Vested interests?"

"Indeed." Benson sighed. "It was in 1966 that the U.S. Geological Survey's National Center for Earthquake Research was established there. Very touchy about earthquakes, I'm afraid."

"Those boreholes," Ryder said. "What diameter drills do you use?"

Benson looked at him for a long moment then sighed again. "That had to be the next question. That's why you're all here, isn't it?"

"Well?"

"You can use any size within reason. Down in Antarctica they use a twelve-inch drill to bore through the Ross Ice Shelf, but here we get by with a good deal less, five, perhaps six inches, I don't know. Find out very easy enough. So you think the EPSP drillings are a double-edged weapon that's going to turn in our hands? There's a limit to what you can achieve by tidal waves, isn't there? But this is earthquake country, so why not harness the latent powers of nature and trigger off immense earthquakes, and where better to pull the triggers than in the very EPSP sites we've chosen?"

Barrow said: "Is it feasible?"

"Eminently."

"And if——" He broke off. "Ten bombs, ten sites. Matches up a damn sight too well. If this were to happen?"

"Let's think about something else, shall we?"

"If it *were?*"

"There are so many unknown factors——"

"An educated guess, Professor."

"Goodbye California! That's what I would guess. Or a sizable part of it—bound to affect more than half of the population. Maybe it will fall into the Pacific. Maybe just shattered by a series of monster earthquakes—and if you set off hydrogen bombs in the faults monster earthquakes are what you are going to have. And radiation, of course, would get those the sea and the earthquake didn't. An immediate trip back east—and I mean immediate—suddenly seems a very attractive prospect."

"You'd have to walk," Sassoon said. "The roads are jammed and the airport is besieged. The airlines are sending in every plane they can lay hands on but it's hardly helping—they're stacked heaven knows how many deep just waiting for a chance to land. And, of course, when a plane does land there's a hundred passengers for every seat available."

"Things will be better tomorrow. It's not in human nature to stay permanently panic-stricken."

"And it's not in an aircraft's nature to take off in twenty feet of water, which is what the airport might be under tomorrow." He broke off as the phone rang again. This time Sassoon took it. He listened briefly, thanked the caller and hung up.

"Two things," he said. "The Adlerheim does have a radiotelephone. All quite legal. The post office doesn't know the name or the address of the person who answers it. They assume that we wouldn't want to make inquiries. Secondly, there *is* a very big man up in the Adlerheim." He looked at Ryder. "It seems you were not only right but right about their arrogant self-confidence. He hasn't even bothered to change his name. Dubois."

"Well, that's it, then," Ryder said. If he was surprised or gratified, no trace of those feelings showed. "Morro has kidnaped twenty-six drillers, engineers—anyway, oil men. Six are being used as forced labor in the Adlerheim. Then he'll have a couple of men at each of the drilling rigs—they'll have guns on them but he has to have experienced men to lower those damn things. I don't think we need bother the AEC any more to find out about Professor Aachen's design—whatever nuclear device he's constructed it's not going to be more than five inches in diameter." He turned to Benson. "Do the crews on those rigs work on weekends?"

"I don't know."

"I'll bet Morro does."

Benson turned to one of his assistants. "You heard. Find out, please."

Barrow said: "Well, we know for sure now that Morro lied about the dimensions of the bomb. You can't stick something twenty inches in diameter down a five- or six-inch borehole. I think I have to agree that this man is very dangerously over-confident."

Mitchell was glum. "He's got plenty to be confident about. All right, we know he's up in his fancy castle and we know, or are as certain as can be, that he has those nuclear devices up there. And a lot of good that knowledge does us. How do we get at him or them?"

An assistant spoke to Benson. "The drilling crew, sir. They don't work weekends. A guard at nights. Just one. Gentlemen says no one's likely to wheel away a derrick on a wheelbarrow."

The profound silence that followed was sufficient comment. Mitchell, whose splendid self-confidence had vanished off the bottom of the chart, said in a plaintive voice: "Well, what in the hell are we going to do?"

Barrow broke the next silence. "I don't think that there's anything else that we can do. By that, I mean the people in this room. Apart from the fact that our function is primarily investigative, we don't have the authority to make any decisions on a national level."

"International, you mean," Mitchell said. "If they can do it to us they can also do it to London or Paris or Rome." He almost brightened. "They might even do it to Moscow. But I agree. It's a matter for the White House, Congress, the Pentagon. Personally, I prefer the Pentagon. I'm convinced that the threat of force—and if this isn't a threat of force I've never known of one—can be met only by force. I'm further convinced that we should choose the lesser of two evils, that we should consider the greatest good for the greatest number. I think an attack should be launched on the Adlerheim. At least the damage, though catastrophic, would be localized. I mean, we wouldn't have a half of the damn state being devastated." He paused, then a thought struck him.

"By God, I believe I have it! We're not thinking. What we require is a nuclear physicist here, an expert on hydrogen bombs and missiles. We're laymen. What do we know about the triggering mechanisms of those devices? For all we know they may be immune to—what's it called—sympathetic detonation. If that were the case, a fighter-bomber or two with tactical nuclear missiles—and poof!—all life would be immediately extinct. Instant annihilation for everyone in the Adlerheim." Archimedes in his bath or Newton with his apple couldn't have shown more revelationary enthusiasm.

Ryder said: "Well, thank you very much."

"What do you mean?"

Dunne answered him. "Mr. Ryder's lack of enthusiasm is understandable, sir. Or have you forgotten that his wife and daughter are being held hostage there, not to mention nine others, including five of the country's outstanding nuclear physicists?"

"Ah! Oh!" Much of the missionary zeal vanished. "I'm sorry, no, I'm afraid I'd forgotten that. Nevertheless——"

"Nevertheless, you were going to say, the greatest good for the greatest number. Your proposal would almost certainly achieve the opposite—the greatest destruction of the greatest number."

"Justify that, Mr. Ryder." Mitchell cherished his brain children and no one was going to take his baby away if he could help it.

"Easily. You are going to use atomic missiles. The southern end of the San Joaquin Valley is quite heavily populated. It is your intention to wipe those people out?"

"Of course not. We evacuate them."

"Heaven send me strength," Ryder said wearily. "Didn't it occur to you that from the Adlerheim Morro has an excellent view of the valley and you can bet he has more than a scattering of spies and informants down there? What do *you* think *he* is going to think when he sees the citizens of the plain disappearing *en masse* over the northern and southern horizons? He's going to say to himself: 'Ha! I've been rumbled'—and apart from anything else that's the last thing we want him to know—'I must teach those people a lesson for they're clearly preparing to make an atomic attack on me.' So he sends one of his helicopters down south to the Los Angeles area and another up north to the Bay area. Six million dead. I should think that's a conservative estimate. Is that your idea of military tactics, of reducing casualties to a minimum?"

From the crestfallen expression on his face it didn't seem to be. Clearly, it wasn't anybody else's either.

Ryder went on: "A personal opinion, gentlemen, and offered for what it's worth, but this is what I think. I don't think there *are* going to be any nuclear casualties—not unless we're stupid enough to provoke them ourselves." He looked at Barrow. "Back in your office some little time ago I said that I believed Morro is going to trigger off this bomb in the Bay tomorrow. I still do. I also said I believed he would set off or would be prepared to set off the other ten devices on Saturday night. I've modified that thinking a bit. I still think that if he's given sufficient provocation he'd still be prepared to trigger his device, but I now don't believe that he'll do it on Saturday night. In fact, I would take odds that he won't."

"It's odd." Barrow was thoughtful. "I could almost believe that myself. Because of his kidnaping of nuclear physicists, his theft of weapons-grade material, our knowledge that he does have those damned nuclear devices, his constant nuclear threats, his display in Yucca Flat and our conviction that he is going to explode his device in the Bay tomorrow morning, we have been hypnotized, mesmerized, conditioned into the certainty of the inevitability of further nuclear blasts. God knows we have every reason to believe what this monster says. And yet——"

"It's a brainwash job. A top-flight propagandist can make you believe anything. Our friend should have met Goebbels in his heyday—they would have been bloodbrothers."

"Any idea what he *doesn't* want us to believe?"

"I think so. I told Mr. Mitchell an hour ago that I had a glimmering but that I knew what he would do with a glimmering. It's a pretty bright beacon now. Here's what I think Morro will be doing—or what I would do if I were in Morro's shoes.

"First, I'd bring my submarine through the——"

"Submarine!" Mitchell had obviously—and instantly—reverted to his earlier opinion of Ryder.

"Please. I'd bring it through the Golden Gate and park it alongside one of the piers in San Francisco."

"San Francisco?" Mitchell again.

"It has better and more piers, better loading facilities and calmer waters than, say, Los Angeles."

"Why a submarine?"

"To take me back home." Ryder was being extremely patient. "Me and my faithful followers and my cargo."

"Cargo?"

"For God's sake, shut up and listen. We'll be able to move with complete safety and impunity in the deserted streets of San Franciso. No single soul will be there because no hour was specified as to when the hydrogen bombs will be detonated during the night and there'll be nobody within fifty miles. A gallant pilot six miles up will be able to see nothing because it's night and even if it's a completely suicidal low-flying pilot he'll still be able to see nothing because we know where every breaker for every transformer and power station in the city is.

"Then our moving vans will roll. I'll have three and will lead them down California Street and stop outside the Bank of America, which, as you know, is the largest single bank in the world containing loot as great as that of the federal vaults. Other vans will go to the Transamerica Pyramid, Wells Fargo, the Federal Reserve Bank, Crockers and other interesting places. There will be ten hours of darkness that night. We estimate we will require six at the outset. Some big robberies, such as the famous break-in to a Nice bank a year or two ago, took a whole leisurely weekend, but gangs like those are severely handicapped because they have to operate in silence. We shall use as much high explosive as need be and for difficult cases will use a self-propelled 120-mm. tank gun firing armor-piercing shells. We may even blow some buildings up but this won't worry us. We can make all the noise in the world and not care—there'll be nobody there to hear us. Then we load up the vans, drive down to the piers, load the submarine and take off." Ryder paused. "As I said earlier, they've come for cash to buy their arms and there's more cash lying in the vaults of San Francisco than all the kings of Saudi Arabia and maharajas of India have ever seen. As I said before it takes a simple and unimaginative mind to see the obvious and in this case, for me at least, it's so obvious that I can't see any flaws in it. What do you think of my scenario?"

"I think it's damned awful," Barrow said. "That's to say, damned awful because it's so inevitable. That has to be it, first, because it's so right, and second, because it just can't be anything else." He looked around at the company. "You agree?"

Everyone, with exception, nodded. The exception, inevitably, was Mitchell. "And what if you're wrong?"

"Must you be so damnably pigheaded and cantankerous?" Barrow was irritated to the point of exasperation.

Ryder didn't react, just lifted his shoulders and said: "So I'm wrong."

"You must be mad! You would take the burden of the deaths of countless fellow Californians on your hands?"

"You're beginning to bore me, Mitchell. In fact, not to put it too politely, you do bore me and have done so for some time. I think you should question your own sanity. Do you think I would breathe a word of our conclusions—with you being excepted from our conclusions—outside this room? Do you think I would try to persuade anybody to remain in their homes on Saturday night? When Morro knew that people had ignored the threat and had heard, as he inevitably would, the reason why—namely, that his scheme was known—the chances are very high that in his rage and frustration he'd just go ahead and press the button anyway."

The singularly ill-named Café Cleopatra was a watering hole of unmatched dinginess but on that hectic, frenetic and stifling evening it possessed the singular charm of being the only such establishment open in the blocks around Sassoon's office. There were dozens of others but their doors were rigorously barred by proprietors who, when the opportunity was open to them, were lugging their dearest possessions to higher levels or who, when such opportunity was denied them, had already joined the panic-stricken rush to the hills.

Fear most certainly was abroad that evening but the rush was purely in the mind and heart: it was most certainly not physical for the cars and people who jammed the street were almost entirely static. It was an evening for selfishness, ill temper, envy, argument, and antisocial behavior ranging from the curmudgeonly to the downright bellicose. Phlegmatic the citizens of the Queen of the Coast were not.

It was an evening for those who ranged the nether scale from the ill-intentioned to the criminally inclined as they displayed in various measure that sweet concern, Christian charity and brotherly love for their fellow man in the hour of crisis by indulging in red-faced altercation, splendidly unin-hibited swearing, bouts of fisticuffs, purse snatching, wallet removal, mug-ging and kicking in the plate-glass windows of the more prosperous-looking emporiums. They were free to indulge their peccadilloes unhindered: the police were powerless as they, too, were immobilized. It was a night for pyromaniacs, as many small fires had broken out throughout the city al-though, in fairness, many of those were caused by the unseemly speed of the departure of householders who left on unconsidered cookers, ovens and heating appliances. Again, the fire brigades were powerless, their only consolation being the faint hope that significant numbers of the smaller conflagrations would be abruptly extinguished at ten o'clock the following morning. It was not a night for the sick and the infirm: elderly ladies, widows and orphans were crushed against walls or, more commonly, depos-ited in unbecoming positions in the gutter as their fitter brethren pressed on eagerly for the high land. Unfortunates in wheel chairs knew what it was to share the emotions of the charioteer who observes his inner wheel coming adrift as he rounds the first bend of the Circus Maximus. Especially distress-ing was the case of thoughtless pedestrians knocked down by cars, driven by owners concerned only with the welfare of their families, which mounted the pavement in order to overtake the less enterprising who elected to remain on the highway; where they fell, there they remained, for doctors and am-bulances were as helpless as any. It was hardly an edifying spectacle.

Ryder surveyed the scene with a jaundiced and justifiably misanthropic eye although, in truth, he had been in a particularly ill humor even before arriving to sample the sybaritic pleasures of the Café Cleopatra. On their return from Cal Tech he had listened to, without participating in, the endless wrangling as to how best they should counter and hopefully terminate the evil machinations of Morro and his Muslims. Finally, in frustration and disgust, he had announced that he would return wthin the hour and had left with Jeff and Parker. There had been no attempt to dissuade him: there was something about Ryder, as Barrow, Mitchell and their associates had come to appreciate in a very brief period of time, that precluded the very idea of dissuasion and, besides, he owed neither allegiance nor obedience to any man.

"Cattle," Luigi said with a splendid contempt. He had just brought fresh beers to the three men and was now surveying the pandemoniac scenes being enacted beyond his unwashed windows. Luigi, the proprietor, re-garded himself as a cosmopolitan par excellence in a city of cosmopolitans. Neapolitan by birth, he claimed to be a Greek and did his undistinguished best to run what he regarded as an Egyptian establishment. From his slurred speech and unsteady gait it was clear that he had been his own best customer for the day. *"Canaille!"* His few words of French served, as he fondly imagined, to enhance his cosmopolitan aura. "All for one and one for all. The spirit that won the West! How true. The California gold rush, the Klondike. Every man for himself and the devil take the rest. Alas, I fear they lack the Athenian spirit." He swung a dramatic arm around him and almost fell over in the process. "Today, this beautiful establishment—tomorrow, the deluge. And Luigi? Luigi laughs at the gods for they are but mannequins that masquerade as gods else they would not permit this catastrophe to overtake those mindless infants." He paused and reflected. "My ancestors fought at Thermopylae." Overcome by his own eloquence and the alcohol-accentuated effects of gravity, Luigi collapsed in the nearest chair.

Ryder looked around at the incredible dilapidation which was the outstanding characteristic of Luigi's beautiful establishment, at the vanished patterns on the cracked linoleum, the stained formica table tops, the aged infirmity of the bentwood chairs, the unwashed stuccoed walls behung with sepia daguerreotypes of pharaonic-profiled bas-reliefs, each with two eyes on the same side of the face, portraits of so unbelievable an awfulness that the only charitable thing that could be said about them was that they tended to restore to a state of almost pristine purity the unlovely walls which they desecrated. He said: "Your sentiments do you great credit, Luigi. This country could do with more men like you. Now, please, would you leave us alone? We have important matters to discuss."

They had, indeed, important matters to discuss and their discussion led to a large and uncompromising zero. The problems of what to do with the apparently unassailable inhabitants of the Adlerheim seemed insuperable. In point of fact, the discussion was a dialogue between Ryder and Parker, for Jeff took no part in it. He just leaned back, his beer untouched, his eyes closed as if he were fast asleep or had lost all interest in solving the unsolvable. He appeared to subscribe to the dictum laid down by the astronomer J. Allen Hynek: "In science it's against the rules to ask questions when we have no way of approaching the answers." The problem on hand was not a scientific one: but the principle appeared to be the same.

Unexpectedly, Jeff stirred and said: "Good old Luigi."

"What?" Parker stared at him. "What's that?"

"And Hollywood only a five-minute hop from here."

Ryder said carefully: "Look, Jeff, I know you've been through a hard time. We've all been through——"

"Dad?"

"What?"

"I have it. Mannequins masquerading as gods."

Five minutes later Ryder was on his third beer, but this time back in Sassoon's office. The other nine men were still there and had indeed not stirred since Ryder, Jeff and Parker had left. The air was full of tobacco smoke, the powerful aroma of scotch and, most disquietingly, an almost palpable aura of defeat.

Ryder said: "The scheme we have to propose is a highly dangerous one. It possibly verges on the desperate but there are degrees of desperation and it's by no means as desperate as the circumstances in which we find ourselves. Success or failure depends entirely on the degree of co-operation we receive from every person in this nation whose duty is in any way concerned with the enforcement of the law, those not concerned directly with the law, even those, if need be, outside the law." He looked in turn at Barrow and Mitchell. "It's of no consequence, gentlemen, but your jobs are on the line."

Barrow said: "Let's have it."

"My son will explain it to you. It is entirely his brainchild." Ryder smiled faintly. "To save you gentlemen any cerebral stress, he even has all the details worked out."

Jeff explained. It took him no more than three minutes. When he had finished the expressions around the table ranged from the stunned, through incredulity, then intense consideration and, finally, in Barrow's case, the tentative dawning of hope where all hope had been abandoned.

Barrow whispered: "My God! I believe it could be done."

"It has to be done," Ryder said. "It means the instant and total co-operation of every police officer, every FBI officer, every CIA officer in the country. It means the scouring of every prison in the country and even if the man we require is a multiple murderer awaiting execution in death row he gets a free pardon. How long would it take?"

Barrow looked at Mitchell. "The hell with the hatchets. Bury them. Agreed?" There was a fierce urgency in his voice. Mitchell didn't answer, but he did nod. Barrow went on: "Organization is the name of the game. This is what we were born for."

"How long?" Ryder repeated.

"A day?"

"Six hours. Meantime, we can get the preliminaries under way."

"Six hours?" Barrow smiled faintly. "It used to be the wartime motto of the Seabees that the impossible takes a little longer. Here, it would appear, it has to take a little shorter. You know, of course, that Muldoon has just had his third heart attack and is in Bethesda hospital?"

"I don't care if you have to raise him from the dead. Without Muldoon we are nothing."

At eight o'clock that evening it was announced over every TV and radio station in the country that at ten o'clock Western standard time—the times for the other zones were given—the President would be addressing the nation on a matter of the utmost national gravity which concerned an emergency unprecedented in the history of the republic. As instructed, the announcement gave no further details. The brief and cryptic message was guaranteed to ensure the obsessive interest and compulsory viewing of every citizen in the republic who was neither blind nor deaf nor both.

In the Adlerheim, Morro and Dubois looked at each other and smiled. Morro reached out a hand for his bottle of Glenfiddich.

In Los Angeles, Ryder showed no reaction whatsoever, which was hardly surprising in view of the fact that he had helped draft the message himself. He asked Major Dunne for permission to borrow his helicopter and dispatched Jeff to pick up some specified articles from his, Ryder's home. Then he gave Sassoon a short list of other specified articles he required. Sassoon looked at him and said nothing. He just lifted a phone.

Exactly at ten, the President appeared on TV screens throughout the country. Not even the first landing on the moon had attracted so vast a viewing—and listening—audience.

He had four men with him in the studio and those he introduced as his Chief of Staff and the Secretaries of State, Defense and the Treasury, which seemed largely superfluous as all of them were nationally and indeed internationally known figures. Muldoon, the Secretary of the Treasury, was the one who caught the attention of everyone. Color TV showed him for what he was, a very sick man indeed. His face was ashen and, surprisingly, almost haggard. Surprisingly because, although not particularly tall, he was a man of enormous girth and, as he sat, his great pot belly seemed almost to touch his knees. He was said to weigh 330 pounds but his precise weight was irrelevant. What was truly remarkable about him was not the unsurprising fact that he had had three heart attacks but the fact that he had managed to survive any of them.

"Citizens of America." The President's deep, resonant voice was trembling, not with fear but with an outraged fury that he made no attempt to suppress. "You all know the great misfortune that has befallen, or is about to befall, our beloved state of California. Although the government of these United States will never yield to coercion, threats or blackmail, it is clear that we must employ every means in our power—and in this, the greatest country in the world, our resources are almost infinite—to avert the impending doom, the threatened holocaust that looms over the West." Even in the moments of the greatest stress, he was incapable of talking in other than presidential language.

"I hope the villainous architect of this monstrous scheme is listening to me, for, despite the best efforts—and those have been immense and indefatigable—of hundreds of our best law enforcement officers, his whereabouts remain a complete secret and I know of no other means whereby I can contact him. I trust, Morro, you are either watching or listening. I know I am in no position to bargain or treat with you"—here the President's voice broke off on an oddly strangled note and he was forced to have recourse to several gulps of water—"because you would appear to be an utterly ruthless criminal wholly devoid of even the slightest trace of humanitarian scruples.

"But I suggest that it might be to our mutual advantage and that we might arrive at some mutually satisfactory arrangement if I, and my four senior governmental colleagues with me here, were to parley with you and try to arrive at some solution to this unparalleled problem. Although it goes violently against the grain, against every principle dear to me and every citizen of this great nation, I suggest we meet at a time and a place, under whatever conditions you care to impose, at the earliest possible moment." The President had quite a bit more to say, most of it couched in ringingly patriotic terms which could have deceived only those mentally retarded beyond any hope of recovery. But he had, in fact, said all that he had needed to.

In the Adlerheim, the normally impassive and unemotional Dubois wiped tears from his eyes.

"Never yield to coercion, threats or blackmail! No condition to bargain or treat with us. Mutually satisfactory arrangement! Five billion dollars to begin with, perhaps? And then, of course, we proceed with our original plan?" He poured out two more glasses of Glenfiddich, handed one to Morro.

Morro sipped some of the whiskey. He, too, was smiling but his voice, when he spoke, held an almost reverent tone.

"We must have the helicopter camouflaged. Think of it, Abraham, my dear friend. The dream of a lifetime come true. America on its knees." He sipped some more of his drink then, with his free hand, reached out for a microphone and began to dictate a message.

Barrow said to no one in particular: "I've always maintained that to be a successful politician you have to be a good actor. But to be a president, you must be a superlative one. We must find some way to bend the rules of the world of the cinema. The man must have an Oscar.''

Sassoon said: ''With a bar and crossed leaves.''

At eleven o'clock it was announced over TV and radio that a further message from Morro would be broadcast in an hour's time.

At midnight, Morro was on the air again. He tried to speak in his customary calm and authoritative voice, but beneath it were the overtones of a man aware that the world lay at his feet. The message was singularly brief.

''I address this to the President of the United States. We''—the ''we'' had more of the royal than the editorial about it—''accede to your request. The conditions of the meeting, which will be imposed entirely by us, will be announced tomorrow morning. We shall see what can be accomplished when two reasonable men meet and talk together.'' He sounded genuinely aware of his incredibly mendacious effrontery.

He went on in a portentous voice: ''This proposed meeting in no way affects my intention to detonate the hydrogen device in the ocean tomorrow morning. Everybody, and that includes you, Mr. President, must be convinced beyond all doubt that I have the indisputable power to carry out my promises.

''With reference to my promises, I have to tell you that the devices I still intend to detonate on Saturday night will produce a series of enormous earthquakes that will have a cataclysmic effect beyond any natural disaster ever recorded in history. That is all.''

Barrow said: ''Well, damn you, Ryder, you were right again. About the earthquakes, I mean.''

Ryder said mildly: ''That hardly seems to matter now.''

At 12:15 A.M. word came through from the AEC that the hydrogen bomb, code-named Aunt Sally, designed by professors Burnett and Aachen, had a diameter of 4.73 inches.

That didn't seem to matter at all.

12

AT EIGHT o'clock the next morning Morro made his next contact with the anxiously and—such is mankind's morbidly avid love of vicarious doom and disaster—vastly intrigued world. His message he delivered with his now accustomed terseness.

He said: ''My meeting with the President and his senior advisers will take place at eleven o'clock tonight. However, I insist that the presidential party arrive in Los Angeles—if the airport is functioning, if not, San Francisco— by six o'clock this evening. The meeting place I cannot and will not specify. The travel arrangements will be announced late this afternoon.

"I trust the low-lying regions of Los Angeles, the coastal regions north to Point Arguello and south to the Mexican border, in addition to the Channel Islands, have been evacuated. If not, I will accept no responsibility. As promised, I shall detonate this nuclear device in two hours' time."

Sassoon was closeted in his office with Brigadier General Culver of the U.S. Air Force. Far below, a deathly hush lay over the totally deserted streets. The low-lying regions of the city had indeed been evacuated, thanks in large part to Culver and over two thousand soldiers and national guardsmen under his command who had been called in to help the hopelessly overworked police restore order. Culver was a ruthlessly efficient man and had not hesitated to call in tanks in number close to battalion strength, which had a marvelously chastening effect on citizens who, prior to their arrival, had seemed hell-bent not on self-preservation but on self-destruction. The deployment of the tanks had been co-ordinated by a fleet of police, coast guard and army helicopters, which had pin-pointed the major traffic bottlenecks. The empty streets were littered with abandoned cars, many of which bore the appearance of having been involved in major crashes, a state of affairs for which the tanks had been in no way responsible: the citizens had done it all by themselves.

The evacuation had been completed by midnight, but long before that the fire brigades, ambulances and police cars had moved in. The fires, none of them major, had been extinguished, the injured had been removed to far-away hospitals and the police had made a record number of arrests and forced evacuation of hoodlums whose greed in taking advantage of this unprecedented opportunity had quite overcome their sense of self-preservation and were still looting away with gay abandon when policemen with drawn guns had taken a rather less than a paternal interest in their activities.

Sassoon switched off the TV set and said to Culver: "What do you make of that?"

"One has to admire the man's colossal arrogance."

"Overconfidence."

"If you like. Understandably, he wants to conduct his meeting with the President under cover of darkness. Obviously the travel arrangements, as he calls them, are linked with the deadline for the plane arrival. He wants to make good and sure that the President has arrived before he gives instructions."

"Which means that he'll have an observer stationed at both San Francisco and Los Angeles airports. Well, he has three separate phones with three separate numbers in the Adlerheim and we have them all tapped."

"They could use short-wave radio communication."

"We've thought of that and discounted the possibility. Morro is convinced that we have no idea where he is. In which case, why bother with unnecessary refinements? Ryder has been right all along—Morro's divine belief in himself is going to bring him down." Sassoon paused. "We hope."

"This fellow Ryder. What's he like?"

"You'll see for yourself. I expect him within the hour. At the moment he's out at the police shooting range practicing with some fancy Russian toys he took away from the opposition. Quite a character. Don't expect him to call you 'sir.' "

At eight-thirty that morning a special news broadcast announced that James Muldoon, Secretary of the Treasury, had had a relapse in the early hours of the morning and had had to have emergency treatment for cardiac arrest. Had he not been in the hospital and with the cardiac arrest unit standing by his bedside, it was unlikely that he would have survived. As it was, he was off the critical list and swearing that he could make the journey out to the West Coast even though he had to be carried aboard *Air Force One* on a stretcher.

Culver said: "Sounds bad."

"Doesn't it though? Fact is, he slept soundly the whole night through. We just want to convince Morro that he's dealing with a man in a near critical condition, a man who clearly must be treated with every gentle consideration. It also, of course, gives a perfect excuse for two additional people to accompany the presidential delegation—a doctor and a Treasury undersecretary to deputize for Muldoon in the event of his expiring as soon as he sets foot in the Adlerheim."

At nine o'clock an Air Force jet lifted off from Los Angeles airport. It carried only nine passengers, all from Hollywood and all specialists in their own arcane crafts. Each carried a suitcase. In addition, a small wooden box had been loaded aboard. Exactly half an hour later the jet touched down in Las Vegas.

A few minutes before ten Morro invited his hostages along to his special screening room. All the hostages had TV sets of their own but Morro's was something special. By a comparatively simple magnification and back-projection method he was able to have a screened picture some six feet by four and a half, about four times the width and height of a normal twenty-one-inch set. Why he had invited them was unclear. When not torturing people—or, more, precisely, having them tortured—Morro was capable of many small courtesies. Perhaps he just wanted to watch their faces. Perhaps he wanted to revel in the magnitude of his achievement and the sense of his invincible power and the presence of an audience always heightened the enjoyment of such an experience, but that last was unlikely as gloating did not appear to be a built-in factor in Morro's mental make-up. Whatever the reason, none of the hostages refused the invitation. In the presence of catastrophe, even though such catastrophe be at second hand, company makes for comfort.

It was probably true to say that every citizen in America, except those engaged in running absolutely essential services, was watching the same event on their screens: the number watching throughout the rest of the world must have run into hundreds of millions.

The various TV companies filming the incident were, all too understandably, taking no chances. Normally all outdoor events on a significantly large scale, ranging from *grand prix* racing to erupting volcanoes, are filmed from helicopters, but here they were dealing with the unknown. No one had even an approximate idea of what the extent of the blast and radiation would be and the companies had elected against the use of helicopters—which was prudent of them in more ways than one as the camera crews would have refused to fly in them anyway. All the companies had elected the same type of site for their cameras—on the tops of high buildings at a prudent distance from the ocean front: the viewers in the Adlerheim could see the blurred outline of the city abutting the Pacific in the lower segment of their screens. If the nuclear device was anywhere near where Morro had said it was— between the islands of Santa Cruz and Santa Catalina—then the scene of action had to be at least thirty miles distant, but the telescopic zoom lenses of the cameras would take care of that with ease. And at that moment the zoom lenses were fully extended, which accounted for the out-of-focus blurring of the city front.

The day was fine and bright and clear with cloudless skies, which, in the circumstances, formed an impossibly macabre setting for the convulsion the watchers were about to witness, a circumstance that must have pleased Morro greatly for it could not but increase the emotional impact of the spectacle. A storm-wracked sky, lowering clouds, driving rain, fog, any face of nature that showed itself in a somber and minor key would have been far more in keeping with the occasion—and would have lessened the impact of the spectacle of the explosion. There was only one favorable aspect about the weather. Normally, at that time of the day and at that time of year the wind would have been westerly and onshore. Today, because of a heavy front pressing down from the northwest, the wind was slightly west of southerly and in that direction the nearest land mass of any size lay as far distant as the Antarctic.

"Pay attention to the sweep-second hand on the wall clock," Morro said. "It is perfectly synchronized with the detonating mechanism. There are, as you can see, twenty seconds to go."

A pure measure of time is only relative. To a person in ecstasy it can be less than the flicker of an eyelid; for a person on the rack it can be an eternity. The watchers were on no physical rack but they were on an emotional one and those twenty seconds seemed interminable. All of them behaved in precisely the same way, their eyes constantly flickering between the clock and the screen and back again at least once in every second.

The sweep second reached sixty and nothing happened. One second passed, two, three and still nothing. Almost as if by command the watchers glanced at Morro, who sat relaxed and apparently unworried. He smiled at them.

"Be of good faith. The bomb lies deep and you forget the factor of the earth's curvature."

Their eyes swiveled back to the screen and then they saw it. At first it was no more than a tiny protuberance on the curve of the distant horizon, but a protuberance that rose and swelled with frightening rapidity with the passage of every second. There was no blinding white glare of light; there was no light whatsoever of any color, just that monstrous eruption of water and vaporized water that rose and spread, rose and spread until it filled the screen. It bore no resemblance whatsoever to the mushroom cloud of an atomic bomb but was perfectly fan-shaped in appearance, much thicker in the center than at the edges, the lowermost sides of which were streaking outward just above and almost parallel with the sea. The cloud, had it been possible to see it from above, must have looked exactly like an inverted umbrella, but from the side it still looked like a gigantic fan opened to its full 180 degrees, much more dense in the center presumably because there the blast had had the shortest distance to cover before reaching the surface of the sea. Suddenly the giant fan, which had run completely off the screen, shrank until it occupied no more than half of it.

A woman's voice, awed and shaky, said: "What's happened to it? What's happened to it?"

"Nothing's happened to it." Morro looked and sounded very comfortable. "It's the camera. The operator has pulled in his zoom to get the picture inside the frame."

The commentator, who had been babbling on almost incoherently, telling the world what they could see perfectly well for themselves, was still babbling on.

"It must be eight thousand feet high, now. No, more. Ten thousand would be nearer it. Think of it, just think of it! Two miles high and four miles across the base. Good God, is the thing never going to stop growing?"

"I think congratulations are in order, Professor Aachen," Morro said. "Your little contraption seems to have worked quite well."

Aachen gave him a look which meant to be a glare, but wasn't. A broken spirit can take a long time to heal.

For about the next thirty seconds the commentator stopped commentating. It was no instance of a gross dereliction of duty, he was probably so awestruck that he could find no words to describe his emotions. It was not often that a commentator had the opportunity to witness the terrifying spectacle unfolding before his eyes: more precisely, no commentator had ever had the opportunity before. By and by he bestirred himself. "Could we have full zoom, please?"

All but the base of the center of the fan disappeared. A tiny ripple could be seen advancing lazily across the ocean. The commentator said: "That, I suppose, must be the tidal wave." He sounded disappointed; clearly he regarded it as an altogether insignificant product of the titanic explosion he'd just seen. "Doesn't look much like a tidal wave to me."

"Ignorant youth," Morro said sadly. "That wave is probably traveling something about four hundred miles an hour at the moment. It will slow down very quickly as it reaches shallower water but its height will increase in direct proportion to its deceleration. I think the poor boy is in for a shock."

About two and a half minutes after the detonation a thunderous roar, which seemed as if it might shake the TV to pieces, filled the room. It lasted about two seconds before it was suddenly reduced to a tolerable level. A new voice cut in.

"Sorry about that. We couldn't reach the volume control in time. Whew! We never expected a deafening racket like that. In fact, to be quite honest, we didn't expect any sound at all from an explosion so deep under the water."

"Fool." Liberal as ever, Morro had supplied refreshment for the entertainment and he now took a delicate sip of his Glenfiddich. Burnett took a large gulp of his.

"My word, that was a bang." The original commentator was back on the air. He was silent for some time while the camera, still on full zoom, remained fixed on the incoming tidal wave. "I don't think I like this too much. That wave might not be so big but I've never seen anything moving so fast. I wonder——"

The viewers were not to find out what he was wondering about. He gave an inarticulate cry, there was an accompanying crashing sound and suddenly the tidal wave on the screen was replaced by an empty expanse of blue sky.

"He's been hit by the blast shock wave. I should have warned them about that, I suppose." If Morro was covered with remorse, he was hiding it well. "Couldn't have been all that bad or the camera wouldn't still be functioning."

As usual, Morro was right. Within seconds the commentator was on the air again but was clearly so dazed that he had forgotten the fact.

"Jesus Christ! My head!" There was a pause, punctuated by a fair amount of wheezing and groaning. "Sorry about that, viewers. Mitigating circumstances. Now I know what it's like to be hit by an express train. If I may be spared a feeble joke, I know the occupation I'd like to have tomorrow. A glazier. That blast must have broken a million windows in the city. Let's see if this camera is still functioning."

It was functioning. As the camera was lifted back to the upright the blue sky was gradually replaced by the ocean. The operator had obviously advanced the zoom for the fan was once again in the picture. It had grown no larger and appeared to be in the first beginnings of disintegration because it had become ragged and was gradually losing its shape. A faint grayish cloud, perhaps two miles high, could be seen faintly drifting away.

"I think it's falling back into the ocean. Can you see that cloud drifting away to the left—to the south? That can't be water, surely. I wonder if it's a radioactive cloud."

"It's radioactive, all right," Morro said. "But that grayness is not radioactivity, it's water vapor held in suspension."

Burnett said: "I suppose you're aware, you lousy bastard, that cloud is lethal?"

"An unfortunate by-product. It will disperse. Besides, no land mass lies in its way. One assumes that the competent authorities, if there are any in this country, will warn shipping."

The center of interest had now clearly changed from the now dispersing giant fan to the incoming tidal wave because the camera had now locked on that.

"Well, there she comes." There was just a hint of a tremor in the commentator's voice. "It's slowed down but it's still going faster than any express train I've ever seen. And it's getting bigger. And bigger." He paused for a few seconds. "Apart from hoping that the police and army are a hundred per cent right in saying that the entire lower area of the city has been evacuated, I think I'll shut up for a minute. I don't have the words for this. Nobody could. Let the camera do the talking."

He fell silent and it was a reasonable assumption that hundreds of millions of peoples throughout the world did the same. Words could never convey to the mind the frightening immensity of that massive onrushing wall of water—but the eyes could.

When the tidal wave was a mile away it had slowed down to not much more than fifty miles an hour, but was at least twenty feet in height. It was not a wave in the true sense, just an enormously smooth and unbroken swell, completely silent in its approach, a silence that served only to intensify the impression that here was an alien monster, evil, malevolent, bent upon a mindless destruction. Half a mile away it seemed to rear its evil head and white showed along the top, like a giant surf about to break, and it was at this point that the level of the still untroubled waters between the tidal wave and the shore perceptibly began to fall as if being sucked into the ravenous jaw of the monster, as indeed they were.

And now they could hear the sound of it, a deep and rumbling roar which intensified with the passing of every moment, rising to such a pitch that the volume controller had to turn down the sound. When it was fifty yards away, just as it was breaking, the waters by the foreshore drained away completely, leaving the ocean bed showing. And then, with the explosive sound of a giant thunderclap directly overhead, the monster struck.

Momentarily, that was all there was to it as all visual definition was lost in a sheet of water that rose a hundred vertical feet and spray that rose five times that height as the wave smashed with irresistible power into the buildings that lined the waterfront. The sheet of water was just beginning to fall, although the spray was still high enough to obliterate the view of the dispersing fan of the hydrogen explosion, when the tidal wave burst through the concealing curtain and laid its ravenous claws on the numbly waiting city.

Great torrents of water, perhaps thirty to forty feet high, seething, bubbling, white like giant maelstroms, bearing along on their tortured surfaces an infinity of indescribable—in that they were wholly unidentifiable—debris, rushed along the east–west canyons of the area, sweeping along in their paths the hundreds of abandoned cars that lay in their paths. It seemed as if the city was to be inundated, drowned and remain no more than a memory, but, surprisingly, this was not to be so, largely, perhaps, because of the rigid building controls that had been imposed after the Long Beach earthquake of 1933. Every building lining the front had been destroyed: the city itself remained intact.

Gradually, with the rising lift of the land and the spending of their strength, the torrents slowed, their levels fell away and, finally exhausted, began with an almost obscenely sucking sound and its appetite slaked, to return to the ocean whence they had come. As always with a tidal wave there was to be a secondary one, but, although this, too, reached into the city it was on such a comparatively minor scale that it was hardly worth the remarking.

Morro, for once, bordered almost on the complacent. "Well, I think that possibly might give them something to think about."

Burnett began to swear, with a fervor and singular lack of repetition that showed clearly that a considerable part of his education must have been spent in fields other than the purely academic, remembered belatedly that he was in the presence of ladies, reached for the Glenfiddich and fell silent.

Ryder stood in stoical silence as a doctor removed splinters of glass from his face: like many others, he had been looking out through the windows when the blast had struck. Barrow, who had just suffered the attentions of the same doctor, was mopping blood from his face. He accepted a glass of some stimulant from an aide and said to Ryder: "Well, what did you think of that little operation?"

"Something will have to be done about it and that's a fact. There's only one thing to do with a mad dog and that is to do away with it."

"The chances?"

"Better than even."

Barrow looked at him curiously. "It's hard to tell. Do you look forward to gunning him down?"

"Certainly not. You know what they call us—peace officers. However, if he even starts to bat an eye——"

"I'm still unhappy about this." Brigadier General Culver's expression bore out his words. "I think this is most inadvisable, most. Not that I doubt your capabilities, Sergeant. God knows you're a proven man. But you have to be emotionally involved. That is not a good thing. And your fiftieth birthday is behind you. I'm being honest, you see. I have young, fit, highly trained—well, killers if you want. I think——"

"General." Culver turned as Major Dunne touched his arm. Dunne said gently: "I'll give you my personal affidavit that Sergeant Ryder is probably the most emotionally stable character in the state of California. As for those superfit young assassins in your employ—why don't you bring one of them in here and watch Ryder take him apart?''

"Well. No. I still——''

"General.'' It was Ryder and still showing no emotion. "Speaking with my accustomed modesty, *I* tracked Morro down. Jeff, here, devised the plan for tonight. My wife is up there, as is my daughter. Jeff and I have the motivation. None of your boys has. But much more importantly, we have the right. Would you deny a man his rights?''

Culver looked at him for a long moment, then smiled and nodded acceptance. "It is perhaps a pity, I think, that you're about a quarter century beyond the age for enlistment.''

As they were leaving the viewing room, Susan Ryder said to Morro: "I understand that you are having visitors tonight?''

Morro smiled. As far as it was possible for him to form an attachment for anyone, he had formed one for Susan. "We are being honored.''

"Would it—would it be possible to just see the President?''

Morro raised an eyebrow. "I would not have thought, Mrs. Ryder——''

"Me? If I were a man instead of the lady I pretend to be, I would tell you what to do with the President. Any president. It's for my daughter—she'll talk about it forever.''

"Sorry. It's out of the question.''

"What *harm* would it do?''

"None. One does not mix business with pleasure.'' He looked curiously at her. "After you've seen what I've just done—you still talk to me?''

She said calmly: "I don't believe you intend to kill anyone.''

He looked at her in near astonishment. "Then I'm a failure. The rest of the world does.''

"The rest of the world hasn't met you. Anyway, the President might ask to see us.''

"Why should he?'' He smiled again. "I cannot believe that you and the President are in league.''

"I wouldn't like to be either. Remember what he said about you last night—an utterly ruthless criminal wholly devoid of even the slightest trace of humanitarian scruples. I don't for a moment believe that you intend any harm to any of us but the President might well ask to view the bodies as a preliminary to negotiations.''

"You are a clever woman, Mrs. Ryder.'' He touched her once on the shoulder, very gently. "We shall see.''

At eleven o'clock a Lear jet touched down at Las Vegas. Two men emerged and were escorted to one of five waiting police cars. Within fifteen minutes four other planes arrived and eight men were transferred to the four other police cars. The police convoy moved off. The route to their destination was sealed off to all traffic.

At four o'clock in the afternoon three gentlemen arrived at Sassoon's office from Culver City. They were warned upon arrival that they would not be allowed to leave until midnight. They accepted the news with equanimity.

*   *   *

At four forty-five *Air Force One,* the presidential jet, touched down at Las Vegas.

At five-thirty Culver, Barrow, Mitchell and Sassoon entered the small anteroom off Sassoon's office. The three gentlemen from Culver City were smoking, drinking and had about them an air of justifiable pride. Culver said: "I've just learned about this. Nobody ever tells me anything."

Ryder now had brown hair, brown mustache, brown eyebrows and even brown eyelashes. The well-filled cheeks now had pouches in them and there were slight traces of a long-healed double scar on the right cheek. His nose was not the one he'd had that morning. Susan would have brushed by him in the street without a second glance. Nor would her son or Parker have merited a second glance either.

At five-fifty *Air Force One* touched down at Los Angeles International airport. Even a tidal wave has no effect on the massively reinforced concrete of a runway.

At six o'clock Morro and Dubois were seated before a microphone. Morro said: "There can be no mistake?" It was a question but there was no question in his voice.

"Presidential seal, sir. They were met by two unmarked police cars and an ambulance. Seven men disembarked. Five of them were the men we saw on TV last night. Bet my life on that. Mr. Muldoon seems to be in very poor shape. He was helped down the steps by two men who took him to the ambulance. One was carrying what I took to be a doctor's bag."

"Describe them."

The observer, obviously a very highly trained one, described them. Down to the last detail his description tallied exactly with the way both Jeff and Parker looked at that moment.

Morro said: "Thank you. Return." He switched off, smiled and looked at Dubois. "Mumain is the best in the business."

"He has no equal."

Morro picked up another microphone and began to dictate.

At seven-thirty the next and last message came through from Morro. He said: "It is to be hoped that there was no loss of life this morning. As I have said, if there was, the fault was not mine. One regrets the considerable physical damage inevitable in the circumstances. I trust that the display was sufficiently impressive to convince everyone that I have in my power the means to implement my promises.

"It will come as a surprise to no one to know that I am aware that the presidential party landed at ten minutes to six this evening. They will be picked up by helicopter at exactly nine o'clock. The helicopter will land in the precise center of Los Angeles airport, which will be fully illuminated by searchlights or whatever means you care to employ. No attempt will be made to trace or follow the helicopter after take-off. We will have the President of the United States aboard. That is all."

At nine o'clock the presidential party duly boarded the helicopter. Considerable difficulty was experienced in hoisting Muldoon aboard but it was finally achieved without precipitating another heart seizure. For air hostesses they had two guards, each equipped with an Ingram submachine gun. One of them went around and fitted each of the seven men with a black hood which was secured at the neck by drawstrings. The President protested furiously and was ignored.

The "President" was actually Vincent Hillary, widely regarded as the best character actor Hollywood had ever produced. Even to begin with, he had borne a remarkable resemblance to the President. By the time the make-up artist had finished with him in Las Vegas the President himself would have stood in front of a plate of transparent glass and sworn that he was looking into a mirror. He had a remarkable capacity for modulating his voice so as to imitate a remarkably wide range of people. Hillary was expendable and was cheerfully prepared to acknowledge the fact.

The Chief of Staff was a certain Colonel Greenshaw, lately retired from the Green Berets. Nobody knew the number of deaths that lay at his door and he had never cared to enumerate. It was widely said that the only thing he really cared about was killing people and he was unquestionably very good at this.

The Defense Secretary was one called Harlinson, a man tapped to be one of the choices to succeed Barrow as head of the FBI. He looked almost more like the Defense Secretary than the Defense Secretary did. He was said to be very good at looking after himself.

The Secretary of State was, of all things, a remarkably successful attorney at law who had once been an Ivy League professor. Johannsen had nothing in particular to recommend him—he wouldn't even have known how to load a gun—except the intense patriotism of a first-generation American and his uncanny resemblance to the real Secretary. But his own private make-up men had improved even on that.

The Assistant Treasury Secretary, one Myron Bonn, also had some pretensions toward being a scholar and uncannily bore out a statement earlier made by Ryder. He was at present in the throes of writing a thesis for his Ph.D., and remarkably erudite it was, but then the thesis was about prison conditions and the suggested ameliorations thereof, upon which he was an undoubted expert as the thesis was being written in a cell in death row, where he was awaiting execution. He had three things going for him. Being a criminal does not necessarily make a man less a patriot. His original resemblance, now perfected, to the Assistant Secretary, had been astonishing. And he was widely regarded by the police as being the most lethal man in the United States, behind bars or outside them. He was a multiple murderer. Oddly, he was an honest man.

Muldoon, the Treasury Secretary, was unquestionably the *pièce de résistance*. Like Hillary, he was an actor—both of them were to give performances that night worth platinum Oscars. It had taken the unremitting efforts of no less than three of the best special-effects make-up men in Hollywood six hours of work to transform him into what he was. Ludwig Johnson had suffered in the process and was still suffering, for even a man weighing two hundred pounds to begin with does not care to carry another unnecessary sixty pounds around with him. On the other hand, the make-up men had made that sixty pounds look like one hundred and thirty, and for that he was reasonably grateful.

So, purely by chance and not from necessity, three of them were men of unquestionable action while three would not have said boo to the proverbial goose. Ryder would not have cared if all six were in the latter category. But so the cards had fallen.

13

THE HELICOPTER hedge-hopped its way due east, no doubt to fly under the radar which the pilot may have mistakenly imagined was following him. After a certain distance he turned sharply to the northwest and set his craft down near the town of Gorman. At this point they were transferred to a minibus which stopped just south of Greenfield. Here they were transferred to another helicopter. Throughout, Muldoon's sufferings were heart-wrenching to behold. At eleven o'clock precisely, the helicopter set them down in the courtyard of the Adlerheim. Not that anyone was to know that. Their blindfolds were not removed until they were inside the refectory-cum-prayer-hall of the castle.

Morro and Dubois greeted them. There were others in the unofficial welcoming committee but they hardly counted as all they did was to stand around watchfully with Ingram submachine guns in their hands. They were in civilian clothes. To have worn their customary robes would have been to wear too much.

Morro was unexpectedly deferential. "You are welcome, Mr. President."

"Renegade!"

"Come, come." Morro smiled. "We have met together to negotiate, not recriminate. And as a non-American, how can I be a renegade?"

"Worse! A man who is capable of doing today what you did to the Los Angeles area is capable of anything. Capable, perhaps, of kidnaping the President of the United States and holding him to ransom?" Hillary laughed contemptuously and it was more than possible that he was even enjoying himself. "I have put my life at risk, sir."

"If you care, you may leave now. Call me what you wish—renegade, rogue, criminal, murderer, a man, as you say, totally without any humanitarian scruples. But my personal integrity, even though it may be that of what you would term an international bandit, my word of honor, is not in question. You could not be safer, sir, in the Oval Room."

"Ha!" Hillary went slowly red in the face with anger, an achievement which the world would have regarded as a remarkable Thespian feat and for which he was widely renowned: in fact, many people can do just that by holding their breath and expanding the stomach muscles to the maximum extent. Slowly, imperceptibly, Hillary relaxed his muscles and began, again unobtrusively, to breathe again. His color returned to normal. "Damned if I couldn't even begin to believe you."

Morro bowed. It wasn't much of a bow, an inch at the most, but it was nevertheless a token of appreciation. "You do me an honor. The photographs, Abraham."

Dubois handed across several blown-up pictures of the presidential party. Morro went from man to man, carefully scrutinizing both man and picture in turn. When he was finished he returned to Hillary. "A word apart, if you please?"

Whatever emotion Hillary felt, his thirty-five years acting experience concealed it perfectly. He had not been briefed for this. Morro said: "Your Assistant Treasury Secretary. Why is he here? I recognize him, of course, but why?"

Hillary's face slowly congealed until both it and his eyes were positively glacial. "Look at Muldoon."

"I take your point. You have come, perhaps, to discuss, shall we say, financial matters?"

"Among other things."

"That man with the brown hair and mustache. He looks like a police-man."

"Damn it to hell, he *is* a policeman. A Secret Service guard. Don't you know that the President always has a Secret Service guard?"

"He didn't accompany you on the plane today."

"Of course he didn't. He's the head of my West Coast Secret Service. I thought you'd be better informed than that. Don't you know that in flight I never——" He broke off. "How did you know——"

Morro smiled. "Perhaps my intelligence is almost as good as yours. Come, let us rejoin the others." They walked back and Morro said to one of the guards: "Bring the doctor."

It was a bad moment. Morro could have sent for the doctor, Ryder thought, to check on Muldoon. No one had thought of this possibility.

Morro said: "I am afraid, gentlemen, that it will be necessary to search you."

"Search *me?* Search the President?" Hillary did his turkey-cock act again, then unbuttoned his overcoat and coat and flung them wide. "I have never been subjected to such damnable humiliation in my life. Do it yourself."

"My apologies. On second thought it will not be necessary. Not for the other gentlemen. Except one. Ah, Doctor." The physician had appeared on the scene. He pointed to Jeff. "This young man is alleged to be a physician. Would you examine his case?"

Ryder breathed freely again and was quite unmoved when Morro pointed a finger at him. "This, Abraham, is the President's Secret Service agent. He might, perhaps, be a walking armory."

The giant approached. Unbidden, Ryder removed his coat and dropped it to the floor. Dubois searched him with an embarrassing thoroughness, smil-ing at the sight of Ryder's tightly clenched fist, even going to the lengths of poking inside his socks and examining his shoes for false heels. He looked at Morro and said: "So far, so good."

He then picked up Ryder's coat and examined it with excruciating thor-oughness, paying particular attention to the linings and the hem. Finally, he returned it to Ryder, keeping only the two ballpoints he had taken from the coat's breast pocket.

During the time of this examination, Morro's physician was examining Jeff's case with a thoroughness that matched Dubois' examination of Ryder.

Dubois crossed to Morro, took a photograph, pulled a particularly un-pleasant gun from his waist, reversed the photograph, handed one of the pens to Ryder and said: "The point is retracted. I do not care to press the button. People can do all sorts of things with ballpoints these days. I mean no offense, of course. Perhaps you would care to write something. My gun is on your heart."

"Jesus!" Ryder took photograph and pen, pressed the button, wrote, retracted the point and handed both back to Dubois. Dubois glanced at it and said to Morro: "This is not a very friendly message. It says: 'The hell with you all.' " He handed the other pen to Ryder. "My gun is still on your heart."

Ryder wrote and handed the photograph back to Dubois, who turned to Morro and smiled. " 'In triplicate,' he says." He handed both pens back.

Morro's physician returned and handed the case back to Jeff. He looked at Morro and smiled gently. "Someday, sir, you will supply me with a medical case as superb as this one."

"We can't all be the President of the United States."

The doctor smiled, bowed and left.

Hillary said: "Now that all this needless tomfoolery is over may I ask you if you know something about the late evening habits of the President? I know we haven't all night, but surely there is time——"

"I am aware that I have been most remiss in my hospitality. But I had to observe certain precautions. You must know that. Gentlemen."

Settled in Morro's private office suite, the company might have been sampling the sybaritic comforts of some exclusive country club. Two of Morro's staff, incongruously—for them—in black-tie evening suits, moved around with drinks. Morro kept his usually impassive, but occasionally smiling, calm. It could have been the greatest moment of his life but he wasn't letting it show. He was sitting beside Hillary.

Hillary said: "I *am* the President of the United States."

"I am aware of that."

"I am also a politician and, above all, I hope, a statesman. I have learned to accept the inevitable. You will appreciate that I am in a dreadfully embarrassing position."

"I am aware of that also."

"I have come to bargain." There was a long pause. "A famous British Foreign Secretary once demanded: 'Would you send me naked to the conference table?' "

Morro said nothing.

"One request. Before I commit myself publicly, even to my cabinet, may I talk to you privately?"

Morro hesitated.

"I bear no arms. Bring that giant with you if you will. Or do I ask too much?"

"No."

"You agree?"

"In the circumstances, I can do no less."

"Thank you." An irritable note crept into Hillary's voice. "Is it necessary that we have *three* armed guards to watch eight defenseless men?"

"Habit, Mr. President."

Muldoon was slumped forward in his chair—his massive back was almost to them—and Jeff, a stethoscope hanging from his neck, was holding a glass of water and some tablets in his hand. Hillary raised his voice and said: "The usual, Doctor?"

Jeff nodded.

"Digitalis," Hillary said.

"Ah! A heart stimulant, is it not?"

"Yes." Hillary sipped his drink, then said abruptly: "You have hostages here, of course."

"We have. They have come to no harm, I assure you."

"I can't understand you, Morro. Highly civilized, highly intelligent, reasonable—yet you behave as you do. What drives you?"

"There are some matters I prefer not to discuss."

"Bring me those hostages."

"Why?"

"Bring them or, as sure as God's in heaven, I will not deal with you. I may be making the mistake of taking you at your face value. You may—I only say *may*—be the inhuman monster you're said to be. If they are dead, which God forbid, you may take the life of the President before he will deal with you."

Some time passed, then Morro said: "Do you know Mrs. Ryder?"

"Who is she?"

"One of our hostages. It sounds as if you were in telepathic communication with her."

Hillary said: "I have China to worry about. I have Russia to worry about. I have the European Common Market. The economy. The recession. A man's mind can accommodate only so many things. Who is this—her name?"

"Mrs. Ryder."

"*If* she is alive, bring her. If she's all that telepathic I could replace my Vice-President. And the others."

"I knew beforehand—and the lady knew—that you would make such a request. Very well. Ten minutes." Morro snapped his fingers at a guard.

The ten minutes passed swiftly enough, much too swiftly for the hostages, but it was time and to spare for Ryder. Morro, with his customary hospitality, had offered each hostage a drink and warned them that their stay would be brief. The center of attraction was inevitably Hillary, who, wearily but charmingly, out-presidented any President who had ever lived. Morro did not leave his side. Even an inhuman monster had his human side: it is not given to every man to present a President to his people.

Ryder, glass in hand, wandered around, spending an inconsequential word with those whom he met. He approached one of the hostages, who was perhaps the fifth or sixth person he'd chatted to, and said: "You're Dr. Healey."

"Yes. How did you know?"

Ryder didn't tell him how he knew. He'd studied too many photographs too long. "Can you maintain a deadpan face?"

Healey looked at him and maintained a deadpan face.

"Yes."

"My name is Ryder."

"Oh yes?" Healey smiled at the waiter who refilled his glass.

"Where's the button? The switch?"

"To the right. Elevator. Four rooms, fourth along."

Ryder wandered away, spoke to one or two others, then accidentally ran into Healey again.

"Tell no one. Not even Susan." This, he knew, would establish his credibility beyond any doubt. "In the fourth room?"

"Small booth. Steel door inside. He has the key. The button's inside."

"Guards?"

"Four. Six. Courtyard."

Ryder wandered away and sat down. Healey happened by. "There are steps beyond the elevator." Ryder didn't even look up.

Ryder observed, without observing, that his son was doing magnificently. The dedicated physician, he did not once leave Muldoon's side, didn't once glance at his mother or his sister. He was due, Ryder reflected, for promotion to sergeant, at least. It never occurred to him to think about his own future.

Two minutes later Morro courteously called a halt to the proceedings. Obediently, the hostages filed out. Neither Susan nor Peggy had as much as given a second glance to either Ryder or his son.

Morro rose. "You will excuse me, gentlemen. I am going to have a brief and private talk with the President. A few minutes only, I assure you." He looked around the room. Three armed guards, each with an Ingram, two waiters, each with a concealed pistol. Carrying security to ridiculous lengths— but that was how he survived, had survived all those long and hazardous years. "Come, Abraham."

The three men left and moved along the corridor to the second door on the right. It was a small room, bare to the point of bleakness, with only a table and a few chairs. Morro said: "We have come to discuss high finance, Mr. President."

Hillary sighed. "You are refreshingly—if disconcertingly—blunt. Do you mean to tell me you have no more of that splendid scotch left?"

"Heaven send—or should I say Allah send—that we should show any discourtesy to the leader of—well, never mind. You mentioned the inevitable. It takes a great mind to accept the inevitable." He sat in silence while Dubois brought a glass and a bottle of what appeared to be the inevitable Glenfiddich to the small desk before Morro. He watched in silence while Dubois poured, then raised his glass. It was not to be in a toast. He said: "The negotiating point?"

"You will understand why I wished to talk in private. I, the President of the United States, feel that I am selling out the United States. Ten billion dollars."

"We shall drink to that."

Ryder, glass in hand, wandered slowly, aimlessly, around the room. In his coat pocket he had, as instructed, pressed the button of his ballpoint six times and, as promised, the writing tip had fallen off at the sixth time. Harlinson was standing close to one of the waiters. Greenshaw had just ordered another drink.

Muldoon—Ludwig Johnson—had his back to the company. He shuddered and made a peculiar moaning noise. Instantly, Jeff bent over him, hand on his pulse and stethoscope to his heart. Jeff's face could be seen to tighten. Jeff pulled back his coat, undid the massive waistcoat and proceeded to do something that none of the guards could see.

One of them said: "What is wrong?"

"Shut up!" Jeff was very curt indeed. "He is very ill. Heart massage." He looked at Bonn. "Lift his back up."

Bonn bent to do so and as he did there came a faint zipping noise. Ryder cursed inwardly. Plastic zips were meant to be noiseless. The guard who had spoken took a step forward. His face was a blend of suspicion and uncertainty. "What was that?"

The nearest guard was only three feet from Ryder. Even with a pen, it was impossible to miss at that range. The guard made a weird sighing noise, crumpled and fell sideways to the floor. The two other guards turned and stared in disbelief. They stared for almost three seconds, which was a ludicrously ample time for Myron Bonn, the legal luminary from Donnemara, to shoot them both through the heart with a silenced Smith & Wesson. At the same instant Greenshaw chopped the man bending over him with a drink and Harlinson did the same for the other waiter standing in front of him.

Johnson had worn a double-thickness zipped bodice under his shirt. Below that he had worn a cover of foam rubber, almost a foot thick where the lower part of his stomach ought to have been. Next to his skin he had worn another sheet of foam rubber almost but not quite as thick, which was why it had taken three special make-up men six man hours to fit him out to Muldoon's physical specifications. Between the two layers of rubber lay three rubber-wrapped pistols and the disassembled parts of two Kalashnikov machine rifles. It took Ryder and his son less than a minute to reassemble the Kalashnikovs.

Ryder said: "Bonn, you're the marksman. Stay outside the door. Anybody comes along the corridor, either side, you know what to do.''

"I get to finish my thesis? A doctorate, no less?"

"I'll come to your graduation ceremony. Jeff, Colonel Greenshaw, Harlinson—there are armed guards out in the courtyard. I don't care how much noise you make. Kill them.''

"Dad!" Jeff's face was white and shocked and beseeching.

"Give that Kalashnikov to Bonn. Those people would have killed a million, millions, of your fellow Californians.''

"But God! Dad!"

"Your mother——"

Jeff left. Greenshaw and Harlinson followed. Bonn and Ryder moved out after them into the corridor and it was then that Ryder made his first mistake since his grouchy lieutenant had called him at home to inform him of the San Ruffino break-in. It wasn't a mistake, really, he had no idea where Morro and Dubois had taken Hillary. It was just that he was very very tired. He normally would have taken into account the possibility that Morro had gone to a room between where he stood and the elevator to the caverns below. But he was very very tired. To all the world he looked like a man of indestructible iron. But no man is indestructible. No man is made of iron.

He listened to the stuttering bark of the Kalashnikovs and wondered whether Jeff would ever forgive him. Probably not, he thought, probably not, and it was a little consolation to know that millions of Californians would. If. Not yet. The time was not yet.

Fifteen feet down the corridor to his right Dubois, gun in hand, came out, followed by Morro dragging Hillary with him. Ryder lifted his Kalashnikov and Dubois died. It was impossible to see where the bullet had struck and Ryder had not pressed the trigger. The future doctor of philosophy was still earning his degree.

Morro was moving away, dragging his human shield with him. The elevator gate was less than fifteen feet away.

"Stay here," Ryder said. His voice was strangely quiet. "Watch out to the left." He switched the Kalashnikov to single-shot and squeezed the trigger. He didn't want to do it, he hated to do it, Hillary had cheerfully admitted that he was expendable, but he still remained, as he had proved that night, a strangely likable human being. Brave, cheerful, courageous and human—but so were millions of Californians.

The bullet hit Morro's left shoulder. He didn't shriek or cry, he just grunted and kept on dragging Hillary to the elevator. The gate was open. He thrust Hillary in and was disappearing himself when the second bullet struck him in the thigh, and this time he did cry out. Any ordinary man with a smashed femur either passes into unconsciousness or just waits for an ambulance to come, for, after the initial impact of a serious wound there is no great pain, just a numbed shock: the pain comes later. But Morro, as the world now knew, was no ordinary man. The elevator gate closed and the sound of its whining descent was proof enough that Morro still had the awareness to find the descent button.

Ryder reached the blanked face of the shaft and stopped. For a second, two, three, all he could think of was Morro making his way toward the apocalyptic button. Then he remembered what Healey had said. Stairs.

They were only ten feet away and unlit. There had to be a light but he did not know where the switch was. He stumbled down the first flight in total darkness and fell heavily as he struck a wall. There were flights of stairs. He turned right, found the next flight and this time was careful enough to anticipate the end of them. Automatically, as many people do, he had counted the number of steps to a flight. Thirteen. The third flight he negotiated with all the careful speed at his command. The fourth was easy, for it was awash with light.

The lift was there, its door open, a dazed Hillary sitting against one side and massaging the back of his head. He didn't see Ryder and Ryder didn't see him. Ahead were a series of what appeared to be caverns. The fourth, Healey had said, the fourth. Ryder reached the fourth and then he saw Morro inside the little plywood booth hauling himself to his feet. He must have been dragging himself along the floor like a wounded animal, for his leg was useless and the agonizing progress he had made was clearly limned by the track of blood.

Morro fumbled with the brass panel and had the door open. He lurched inside, an insane dreamer in an insane dreamer's world. Ryder lifted his Kalashnikov. There was no dramatic urgency. There was time.

Ryder said: "Stop, Morro, stop! Please stop."

Morro was dreadfully injured. By that time, his mind must have been in the same way. But, even if he had been well both in body and mind he would probably have acted in the same way for, sick or in health, for the mercifully few of the Morros in the world, fanaticism is the sole sustaining power, the wellspring of their being.

Morro had incredibly reached a calibrated, dialed metallic box and was beginning to unscrew a transparent plastic cover that housed a red knob. Ryder was still ten feet away, too far away to stop him.

He switched the Kalashnikov's slide from single-shot to automatic.

Susan said: "How can you bear to drink that dreadful man's whiskey?"

"Any port in a storm." Susan was both crying and shaking, a combination Ryder had never seen before. He tightened his arm around his daughter, who was sitting on the other arm of his chair, and nodded across Morro's office where Burnett was conducting a seminar. "What's good enough for a professor——"

"Do be quiet. You know, I rather like the way you look. Maybe you should stay that way."

Ryder sipped some more Glenfiddich in silence.

She said: "I'm sorry in a way. Okay, he was a fiend. But he was a kindly fiend."

Ryder knew how to treat the one person in his world. He kept silent.

"End of nightmare," Susan said. "Happy ever after."

"Yes. The first chopper should be here in ten minutes. Bed for you ladies. Happy ever after? Maybe. Perhaps we'll be as lucky as Myron Bonn there and have a stay of execution. Perhaps not. I don't know. Somewhere out there in the darkness the monster is still crouched on the doorstep, waiting."

"What on earth do you mean, John? You never talk like that."

"True. Something a professor at Cal Tech said. I think maybe we should go and live in New Orleans."

"What on earth for?"

"They've never had an earthquake there."

EPIDOURAL ANESTHESIA   EPIDOURAL CATHETER
    + MORPHINE - POST OPERATIVELY

FM - 2 - S   PPT?
        RUBY

LASIX